The Great Book of

Amber

The Complete Amber Chronicles, 1-10

D0875129

Also by Roger Zelazny

A NIGHT IN THE LONESOME OCTOBER

Also by Roger Zelazny and Jane Lindskold

DONNERJACK
LORD DEMON

ROGER ZELAZNY

The Great Book of
Amber

The Complete Amber Chronicles, 1–10

AVON · EOS

AVON BOOKS, INC.
1350 Avenue of the Americas
New York, New York 10019

Compilation copyright © 1999 by Avon Books, Inc.
Nine Princes in Amber copyright © 1970 by Roger Zelazny
    First Avon Books Mass Market Printing: June 1972
The Guns of Avalon copyright © 1972 by Roger Zelazny
    First Avon Books Mass Market Printing: August 1974
Sign of the Unicorn copyright © 1975 by Roger Zelazny
    A serialized version of this book appeared in January, February, and March 1975 issues of *Galaxy* magazine, copyright © 1974, 1975 by Universal Publishing and Distributing Corporation.
    First Avon Books Mass Market Printing: November 1976
The Hand of Oberon copyright © 1976 by Roger Zelazny
    First Avon Books Mass Market Printing: June 1977
The Courts of Chaos copyright © 1978 by Roger Zelazny
    A serialized version of this book appeared in *Galaxy* magazine, November 1977 to February 1978.
    First Avon Books Mass Market Printing: September 1979
Trumps of Doom copyright © 1985 by The Amber Corporation
    First Avon Books Mass Market Printing: February 1986
Blood of Amber © 1986 by The Amber Corporation
    First Avon Books Mass Market Printing: July 1987
Sign of Chaos © 1987 by The Amber Corporation
    First Avon Books Mass Market Printing: July 1988
Knight of Shadows © 1989 by The Amber Corporation
    First Avon Books Mass Market Printing: September 1990
Prince of Chaos © 1991 by The Amber Corporation
    First Avon Books Mass Market Printing: November 1992

Cover illustration by Tim White
Interior design by Elizabeth M. Glover
ISBN: 0-380-80906-0
www.avonbooks.com/eos

Library of Congress Cataloging in Publication Data:

Zelazny, Roger.
    The great book of Amber : the complete Amber chronicles, 1–10 / Roger Zelazny.
        p.   cm.
    Contents: Nine princes in amber—The guns of Avalon—Sign of the unicorn—The hand of Oberon—The courts of chaos—Trumps of doom—Blood of Amber—Sign of chaos—Knight of shadows—Prince of chaos.
    1. Amber (Imaginary place) Fiction.   2. Fantasy fiction, American.   3. Science fiction, American.
I. Title.
PS3576.E43G7   1999   99-36983
813'.54—dc21   CIP

First Avon Eos Printing: December 1999

AVON EOS TRADEMARK REG. U.S. PAT. OFF. AND IN OTHER COUNTRIES, MARCA REGISTRADA, HECHO EN U.S.A.

Printed in the U.S.A.

LSC   40 39

The Great Book of

Amber

The Complete Amber Chronicles, 1-10

BOOK ONE
NINE PRINCES IN AMBER

ONE

It was starting to end, after what seemed most of eternity to me.

I attempted to wriggle my toes, succeeded. I was sprawled there in a hospital bed and my legs were done up in plaster casts, but they were still mine.

I squeezed my eyes shut, and opened them, three times.

The room grew steady.

Where the hell was I?

Then the fogs were slowly broken, and some of that which is called memory returned to me. I recalled nights and nurses and needles. Every time things would begin to clear a bit, someone would come in and jab me with something. That's how it had been. Yes. Now, though, I was feeling halfway decent. They'd have to stop.

Wouldn't they?

The thought came to assail me: *Maybe not.*

Some natural skepticism as to the purity of all human motives came and sat upon my chest. I'd been over-narcotized, I suddenly knew. No real reason for it, from the way I felt, and no reason for them to stop now, if they'd been paid to keep it up. So play it cool and stay dopey, said a voice which was my worst, if wiser, self.

So I did.

1

A nurse poked her head in the door about ten minutes later, and I was, of course, still sacking Z's. She went away.

By then, I'd reconstructed a bit of what had occurred.

I had been in some sort of accident, I remembered vaguely. What had happened after that was still a blur; and as to what had happened before, I had no inkling whatsoever. But I had first been in a hospital and then brought to this place, I remembered. Why? I didn't know.

However, my legs felt pretty good. Good enough to hold me up, though I didn't know how much time had lapsed since their breaking—and I knew they'd been broken.

So I sat up. It took me a real effort, as my muscles were very tired. It was dark outside and a handful of stars were standing naked beyond the window. I winked back at them and threw my legs over the edge of the bed.

I was dizzy, but after a while it subsided and I got up, gripping the rail at the head of the bed, and I took my first step.

Okay. My legs held me.

So, theoretically, I was in good enough shape to walk out.

I made it back to the bed, stretched out and thought. I was sweating and shaking. Visions of sugar plums, etc.

In the State of Denmark there was the odor of decay. . . .

It had been an accident involving an auto, I recalled. One helluva one. . . .

Then the door opened, letting in light, and through slits beneath my eyelashes I saw a nurse with a hypo in her hand.

She approached my bedside, a hippy broad with dark hair and big arms. Just as she neared, I sat up.

"Good evening," I said.

"Why—good evening," she replied.

"When do I check out?" I asked.

"I'll have to ask Doctor."

"Do so," I said.

"Please roll up your sleeve."

"No thanks."

"I have to give you an injection."

"No you don't. I don't need it."

"I'm afraid that's for Doctor to say."

"Then send him around and let him say it. But in the meantime, I will not permit it."

"I'm afraid I have my orders."

"So did Eichmann, and look what happened to him," and I shook my head slowly.

"Very well," she said. "I'll have to report this. . . ."

"Please do," I said, "and while you're at it, tell him I've decided to check out in the morning."

"That's impossible. You can't even walk—and there were internal injuries. . . ."

"We'll see," said I. "Good night."

She swished out of sight without answering.

So I lay there and mulled. It seemed I was in some sort of private place—so somebody was footing the bill. Whom did I know? No visions of relatives appeared behind my eyes. Friends either. What did that leave? Enemies?

I thought a while.

Nothing.

Nobody to benefact me thus.

I'd gone over a cliff in my car, and into a lake, I suddenly remembered. And that was all I remembered.

I was . . .

I strained and began to sweat again.

I didn't know *who* I was.

But to occupy myself, I sat up and stripped away all my bandages. I seemed all right underneath them, and it seemed the right thing to do. I broke the cast on my right leg, using a metal strut I'd removed from the head of the bed. I had a sudden feeling that I had to get out in a hurry, that there was something I had to do.

I tested my right leg. It was okay.

I shattered the cast on my left leg, got up, went to the closet.

No clothes there.

Then I heard the footsteps. I returned to my bed and covered over the broken casts and the discarded bandages.

The door swung inward once again.

Then there was light all around me, and there was a beefy guy in a white jacket standing with his hand on the wall switch.

"What's this I hear about you giving the nurse a hard time?" he asked, and there was no more feigning sleep.

"I don't know," I said. "What is it?"

That troubled him for a second or two, said the frown, then, "It's time for your shot."

"Are you an M.D.?" I asked.

"No, but I'm authorized to give you a shot."

"And I refuse it," I said, "as I've a legal right to do. What's it to you?"

"You'll have your shot," he said, and he moved around to the left side of the bed. He had a hypo in one hand, which had been out of sight till then.

It was a very foul blow, about four inches below the belt buckle, I'd say, and it left him on his knees.

"—— ——!" he said, after a time.

"Come within spitting distance again," I said, "and see what happens."

"We've got ways to deal with patients like you," he gasped.

So I knew the time had come to act.

"Where are my clothes?" I said.

"—— ——!" he repeated.

"Then I guess I'll have to take yours. Give them to me."

It became boring with the third repetition, so I threw the bedclothes over his head and clobbered him with the metal strut.

Within two minutes, I'd say, I was garbed all in white, the color of Moby Dick and vanilla ice cream. Ugly.

I shoved him into the closet and looked out the latticed window. I saw the Old Moon with the New Moon in her arms, hovering above a row of poplars. The grass was silvery and sparkled. The night was bargaining weakly with the sun. Nothing to show, for me, where this place was located. I seemed to be on the third floor of the building though, and there was a cast square of light off to my left and low, seeming to indicate a first floor window with someone awake behind it.

So I left the room and considered the hallway. Off to the left, it ended against a wall with a latticed window, and there were four more doors, two on either side. Probably they let upon more doors like my own. I went and looked out the window and saw more grounds, more trees, more night, nothing new. Turning, I headed in the other direction.

Doors, doors, doors, no lights from under any of them, the only sounds my footsteps from the too big borrowed shoes.

Laughing Boy's wristwatch told me it was five forty-four. The metal strut was inside my belt, under the white orderly jacket, and it rubbed against my hip bone as I walked. There was a ceiling fixture about every twenty feet, casting about forty watts of light.

I came to a stairway, off to the right, leading down. I took it. It was carpeted and quiet.

The second floor looked like my own, rows of rooms, so I continued on.

When I reached the first floor I turned right, looking for the door with light leaking out from beneath it.

I found it, way up near the end of the corridor, and I didn't bother to knock.

The guy was sitting there in a garish bathrobe, at a big shiny desk, going over some sort of ledger. This was no ward room. He looked up at me with burning eyes all wide and lips swelling toward a yell they didn't reach, perhaps because of my determined expression. He stood, quickly.

I shut the door behind me, advanced, and said:

"Good morning. You're in trouble."

People must always be curious as to trouble, because after the three seconds it took me to cross the room, his words were:

"What do you mean?"

"I mean," I said, "that you're about to suffer a lawsuit for holding me incommunicado, and another one for malpractice, for your indiscriminate use of narcotics. I'm already suffering withdrawal symptoms and might do something violent. . . ."

He stood up.

"Get out of here," he said.

I saw a pack of cigarettes on his desk. I helped myself and said, "Sit down and shut up. We've got things to talk about."

He sat down, but he didn't shut up:

"You're breaking several regulations," he said.

"So we'll let a court decide who's liable," I replied. "I want my clothes and my personal effects. I'm checking out."

"You're in no condition—"

"Nobody asked you. Pony up this minute, or answer to the law."

He reached toward a button on his desk, but I slapped his hand away.

"Now!" I repeated. "You should have pressed that when I came in. It's too late now."

"Mr. Corey, you're being most difficult. . . ."

Corey?

"I didn't check me in here," I said, "but I damn well have a right to check me out. And now's the time. So let's get about it."

"Obviously, you're in no condition to leave this institution," he replied. "I cannot permit it. I am going to call for someone to escort you back to your room and put you to bed."

"Don't try it," I said, "or you'll find out what condition I'm in. Now, I've several questions. The first one's Who checked me in, and who's footing my bill at this place?"

"Very well," he sighed, and his tiny, sandy mustaches sagged as low as they could.

He opened the drawer, put his hand inside, and I was wary.

I knocked it down before he had the safety catch off: a .32 automatic, very neat; Colt. I snapped the catch myself when I retrieved it from the desk top; and I pointed it and said: "You will answer my questions. Obviously you consider me dangerous. You may be right."

He smiled weakly, lit a cigarette himself, which was a mistake, if he intended to indicate aplomb. His hands shook.

"All right, Corey—if it will make you happy," he said, "your sister checked you in."

"?" thought I.

"Which sister?" I asked.

"Evelyn," he said.

No bells. So, "That's ridiculous. I haven't seen Evelyn in years," I said. "She didn't even know I was in this part of the country."

He shrugged.

"Nevertheless . . ."

"Where's she staying now? I want to call her," I said.

"I don't have her address handy."

"Get it."

He rose, crossed to a filing cabinet, opened it, riffled, withdrew a card.

I studied it. *Mrs. Evelyn Flaumel.* . . . The New York address was not familiar either, but I committed it to memory. As the card said, my first name was Carl. Good. More data.

I stuck the gun in my belt beside the strut then, safety back on, of course.

"Okay," I told him. "Where are my clothes, and what're you going to pay me?"

"Your clothes were destroyed in the accident," he said, "and I must tell you that your legs were definitely broken—the left one in two places. Frankly, I can't see how you're managing to stay on your feet. It's only been two weeks—"

"I always heal fast," I said. "Now, about the money. . . ."

"What money?"

"The out-of-court settlement for my malpractice complaint, and the other one."

"Don't be ridiculous!"

"Who's being ridiculous? I'll settle for a thousand, cash, right now."

"I won't even discuss such a thing."

"Well, you'd better consider it—and win or lose, think about the name it will give this place if I manage enough pretrial publicity. I'll certainly get in touch with the AMA, the newspapers, the—"

"Blackmail," he said, "and I'll have nothing to do with it."

"Pay now, or pay later, after a court order," I said. "I don't care. But it'll be cheaper this way."

If he came across, I'd know my guesses were right and there was something crooked involved.

He glared at me, I don't know how long.

Finally, "I haven't got a thousand here," he said.

"Name a compromise figure," I said.

After another pause, "It's larceny."

"Not if it's cash-and-carry, Charlie. So, call it."

"I might have five hundred in my safe."

"Get it."

He told me, after inspecting the contents of a small wall safe, there was four-thirty, and I didn't want to leave fingerprints on the safe, just to check him out. So I accepted and stuffed the bills into my side pocket.

"Now what's the nearest cab company that serves this place?"

He named it, and I checked in the phone book, which told me I was upstate.

I made him dial it and call me a cab, because I didn't know the name of the place and didn't want him to know the condition of my memory. One of the bandages I had removed *had* been around my head.

While he was making the arrangement I heard him name the place: it was called Greenwood Private Hospital.

I snubbed out my cigarette, picked up another, and removed perhaps two hundred pounds from my feet by resting in a brown upholstered chair beside his bookcase.

"We wait here and you'll see me to the door," I said.

I never heard another word out of him.

TWO

It was about eight o'clock when the cab deposited me on a random corner in the nearest town. I paid off the driver and walked for around twenty minutes. Then I stopped in a diner, found a booth and had juice, a couple of eggs, toast, bacon and three cups of coffee. The bacon was too greasy.

After giving breakfast a good hour, I started walking, found a clothing store, and waited till its nine-thirty opening.

I bought a pair of slacks, three sport shirts, a belt, some underwear, and a pair of shoes that fit. I also picked up a handkerchief, a wallet, and pocket comb.

Then I found a Greyhound station and boarded a bus for New York. No one tried to stop me. No one seemed to be looking for me.

Sitting there, watching the countryside all autumn-colored and tickled by brisk winds beneath a bright, cold sky, I reviewed everything I knew about myself and my circumstances.

I had been registered at Greenwood as Carl Corey by my sister Evelyn Flaumel. This had been subsequent to an auto accident some fifteen or so days past, in which I had suffered broken bones which no longer troubled me. I didn't remember Sister Evelyn. The Greenwood people had been instructed to keep me passive, were afraid of the law when I got loose and threatened them with it. Okay. Someone was afraid of me, for some reason. I'd play it for all it was worth.

I forced my mind back to the accident, dwelled upon it till my head hurt. It was no accident. I had that impression, though I didn't know why. I would find out, and someone would pay. Very, very much would they pay. An anger, a terrible one, flared within the middle of my body. Anyone who tried to hurt me, to use me, did so at his own peril and now he would receive his due, whoever he was, this one. I felt a strong desire to kill, to destroy whoever had been responsible, and I knew that it was not the first time in my life that I had felt this thing, and I knew, too, that I had followed through on it in the past. More than once.

I stared out the window, watching the dead leaves fall.

When I hit the Big City, the first thing I did was to get a shave and haircut in the nearest clip joint, and the second was to change my shirt and undershirt in the men's room, because I can't stand hair down my back. The

7

.32 automatic, belonging to the nameless individual at Greenwood, was in my right-hand jacket pocket. I suppose that if Greenwood or my sister wanted me picked up in a hurry, a Sullivan violation would come in handy. But I decided to hang onto it. They'd have to find me first, and I wanted a reason. I ate a quick lunch, rode subways and buses for an hour, then got a cab to take me out to the Westchester address of Evelyn, my nominal sister and hopeful jogger of memories.

Before I arrived, I'd already decided on the tack I'd take.

So, when the door to the huge old place opened in response to my knock, after about a thirty-second wait, I knew what I was going to say. I had thought about it as I'd walked up the long, winding, white gravel driveway, between the dark oaks and the bright maples, leaves crunching beneath my feet, and the wind cold on my fresh-scraped neck within the raised collar of my jacket. The smell of my hair tonic mingled with a musty odor from the ropes of ivy that crowded all over the walls of that old, brick place. There was no sense of familiarity. I didn't think I had ever been here before.

I had knocked, and there had come an echo.

Then I'd jammed my hands into my pockets and waited.

When the door opened, I had smiled and nodded toward the mole-flecked maid with a swarthy complexion and a Puerto Rican accent.

"Yes?" she said.

"I'd like to see Mrs. Evelyn Flaumel, please."

"Who shall I say is calling?"

"Her brother Carl."

"Oh come in please," she told me.

I entered a hallway, the floor a mosaic of tiny salmon and turquoise tiles, the wall mahogany, a trough of big-leafed green things occupying a room divider to my left. From overhead, a cube of glass and enamel threw down a yellow light.

The gal departed, and I sought around me for something familiar.

Nothing.

So I waited.

Presently, the maid returned, smiled, nodded, and said, "Please follow me. She will see you in the library."

I followed, up three stairs and down a corridor past two closed doors. The third one to my left was open, and the maid indicated I should enter it. I did so, then paused on the threshold.

Like all libraries, it was full of books. It also held three paintings, two indicating quiet landscapes and one a peaceful seascape. The floor was heavily carpeted in green. There was a big globe beside the big desk with Africa facing me and a wall-to-wall window behind it, eight stepladders of glass. But none of these was the reason I'd paused.

The woman behind the desk wore a wide-collared, V-necked dress of blue-green, had long hair and low bangs, all of a cross between sunset clouds and the outer edge of a candle flame in an otherwise dark room, and natural,

I somehow knew, and her eyes behind glasses I didn't think she needed were as blue as Lake Erie at three o'clock on a cloudless summer afternoon; and the color of her compressed smile matched her hair. But none of these was the reason I'd paused.

I knew her, from somewhere, though I couldn't say where.

I advanced, holding my own smile.

"Hello," I said.

"Sit down," said she, "please," indicating a high-backed, big-armed chair that bulged and was orange, of the kind just tilted at the angle in which I loved to loaf.

I did so, and she studied me.

"Glad to see you're up and around again."

"Me, too. How've you been?"

"Fine, thank you. I must say I didn't expect to see you here."

"I know," I fibbed, "but here I am, to thank you for your sisterly kindness and care." I let a slight note of irony sound within the sentence just to observe her response.

At that point an enormous dog entered the room—an Irish wolfhound—and it curled up in front of the desk. Another followed and circled the globe twice before lying down.

"Well," said she, returning the irony, "it was the least I could do for you. You should drive more carefully."

"In the future," I said, "I'll take greater precautions, I promise." I didn't know what sort of game I was playing, but since she didn't know that I didn't know, I'd decided to take her for all the information I could. "I figured you would be curious as to the shape I was in, so I came to let you see."

"I was, am," she replied. "Have you eaten?"

"A light lunch, several hours ago," I said.

So she rang up the maid and ordered food. Then, "I thought you might take it upon yourself to leave Greenwood," she said, "when you were able. I didn't think it would be so soon, though, and I didn't think you'd come here."

"I know," I said, "that's why I did."

She offered me a cigarette and I took it, lit hers, lit mine.

"You always were unpredictable," she finally told me. "While this has helped you often in the past, however, I wouldn't count on it now."

"What do you mean?" I said.

"The stakes are far too high for a bluff, and I think that's what you're trying, walking in here like this. I've always admired your courage, Corwin, but don't be a fool. You know the score."

Corwin? File it away, under "Corey."

"Maybe I don't," I said. "I've been asleep for a while, remember?"

"You mean you haven't been in touch?"

"Haven't had a chance, since I woke up."

She leaned her head to one side and narrowed her wonderful eyes.

"Rash," she said, "but possible. Just possible. You might mean it. *You* might. I'll pretend that you do, for now. In that case, you may have done a smart safe thing. Let me think about it."

I drew on my cigarette, hoping she'd say something more. But she didn't, so I decided to seize what seemed the advantage I'd obtained in this game I didn't understand with players I didn't know for stakes I had no inkling of.

"The fact that I'm here indicates something," I said.

"Yes," she replied, "I know. But you're smart, so it could indicate more than one thing. We'll wait and see."

Wait for what? See what? Thing?

Steaks then arrived and a pitcher of beer, so I was temporarily freed from the necessity of making cryptic and general statements for her to ponder as subtle or cagey. Mine was a good steak, pink inside and full of juice, and I tore at the fresh tough-crested bread with my teeth and gulped the beer with a great hunger and thirst. She laughed as she watched me, while cutting off tiny pieces of her own.

"I love the gusto with which you assail life, Corwin. It's one of the reasons I'd hate to see you part company with it."

"Me, too," I muttered.

And while I ate, I pondered her. I saw her in a low-cut gown, green as the green of the sea, with full skirts. There was music, dancing, voices behind us. I wore black and silver and . . . The vision faded. But it was a true piece of my memory, I knew; and inwardly I cursed that I lacked it in its entirety. What had she been saying, in her green, to me in my black and silver, that night, behind the music, the dancing and the voices?

I poured us more beer from the pitcher and decided to test the vision.

"I remember one night," I said, "when you were all in green and I in my colors. How lovely things seemed—and the music . . ."

Her face grew slightly wistful, the cheeks smoothing.

"Yes," she said. "Were not those the days? . . . You really have not been in touch?"

"Word of honor," I said, for whatever that was worth.

"Things have grown far worse," she said, "and the Shadows contain more horrors than any had thought. . . ."

"And . . . ?" I inquired.

"He still has his troubles," she finished.

"Oh."

"Yes," she went on, "and he'll want to know where you stand."

"Right here," I said.

"You mean . . . ?"

"For now," I told her, perhaps too quickly, for her eyes had widened too much, "since I still don't know the full state of affairs," whatever that meant.

"Oh."

And we finished our steaks and the beer, giving the two bones to the dogs. We sipped some coffee afterward, and I came to feel a bit brotherly but suppressed it. I asked, "What of the others?" which could mean anything, but sounded safe.

I was afraid for a moment that she was going to ask me what I meant. Instead, though, she leaned back in her chair, stared at the ceiling, and said, "As always, no one new has been heard from. Perhaps yours was the wisest way. I'm enjoying it myself. But how can one forget—the glory?" I lowered my eyes, because I wasn't sure what they should contain. "One can't," I said. "One never can."

There followed a long, uncomfortable silence, after which she said: "Do you hate me?"

"Of course not," I replied. "How could I—all things considered?"

This seemed to please her, and she showed her teeth, which were very white.

"Good, and thank you," she said. "Whatever else, you're a gentleman."

I bowed and smirked.

"You'll turn my head."

"Hardly," she said, "all things considered."

And I felt uncomfortable.

My anger was there, and I wondered whether she knew who it was that I needed to stay it. I felt that she did. I fought with the desire to ask it outright, suppressed it.

"Well, what do you propose doing?" she finally asked, and being on the spot I replied, "Of course, you don't trust me. . . ."

"How could we?"

I determined to remember that we.

"Well, then. For the time being, I'm willing to place myself under your surveillance. I'll be glad to stay right here, where you can keep an eye on me."

"And afterward?"

"Afterward? We'll see."

"Clever," she said, "very clever. And you place me in an awkward position." (I had said it because I didn't have any place else to go, and my blackmail money wouldn't last me too long). "Yes, of course you may stay. But let me warn you"—and here she fingered what I had thought to be some sort of pendant on a chain about her neck—"this is an ultrasonic dog whistle. Donner and Blitzen here have four brothers, and they're all trained to take care of nasty people and they all respond to my whistle. So don't start to walk toward any place where you won't be desired. A toot or two and even you will go down before them. Their kind is the reason there are no wolves left in Ireland, you know."

"I know," I said, realizing that I did.

"Yes," she continued, "Eric will like it that you are my guest. It should cause him to leave you alone, which is what you want, n'est-ce-pas?"

"Oui," I said.

Eric! It meant something! I had known an Eric, and it had been very important, somehow, that I did. Not recently. But the Eric I had known was still around, and that was important.

Why?

I hated him, that was one reason. Hated him enough to have contemplated killing him. Perhaps I'd even tried.

Also, there was some bond between us, I knew.

Kinship?

Yes, that was it. Neither of us liked it being—brothers. . . . I remembered, I remembered. . . .

Big, powerful Eric, with his wet curly beard, and his eyes—just like Evelyn's!

I was racked with a new surge of memory, as my temples began to throb and the back of my neck was suddenly warm.

I didn't let any of it show on my face, but forced myself to take another drag on my cigarette, another sip of beer, as I realized that Evelyn was indeed my sister! Only Evelyn wasn't her name. I couldn't think of what it was, but it wasn't Evelyn. I'd be careful, I resolved. I'd not use any name at all when addressing her, until I remembered.

And what of me? And what was it that was going on around me?

Eric, I suddenly felt, had had some connection with my accident. It should have been a fatal one, only I'd pulled through. *He* was the one, wasn't he? Yes, my feelings replied. It had to be Eric. And Evelyn was working with him, paying Greenwood to keep me in a coma. Better than being dead, but . . .

I realized that I had just somehow delivered myself into Eric's hands by coming to Evelyn, and I would be his prisoner, would be open to new attack, if I stayed.

But she had suggested that my being her guest would cause him to leave me alone. I wondered. I couldn't take anything at face value. I'd have to be constantly on my guard. Perhaps it would be better if I just went away, let my memories return gradually.

But there was this terrible sense of urgency. I had to find out the full story as soon as possible and act as soon as I knew it. It lay like a compulsion upon me. If danger was the price of memory and risk the cost of opportunity, then so be it. I'd stay.

"And I remember," Evelyn said, and I realized that she had been talking for a while and I hadn't even been listening. Perhaps it was because of the reflective quality of her words, not really requiring any sort of responses—and because of the urgency of my thoughts.

"And I remember the day you beat Julian at his favorite game and he threw a glass of wine at you and cursed you. But you took the prize. And he was suddenly afraid he had gone too far. But you laughed then, though, and drank a glass with him. I think he felt badly over that show of temper, normally being so cool, and I think he was envious of you that day. Do you recall? I think he has, to a certain extent, imitated many of your ways since then. But I still hate him and hope that he goes down shortly. I feel he will. . . ."

Julian, Julian, Julian. Yes and no. Something about a game and my baiting a man and shattering an almost legendary self-control. Yes, there was a feeling of familiarity; and no, I couldn't really say for certain what all had been involved.

"And Caine, how you gulled *him!* He hates you yet, you know. . . ."

I gathered I wasn't very well liked. Somehow, the feeling pleased me.

And Caine, too, sounded familiar. Very.

Eric, Julian, Caine, Corwin. The names swam around in my head, and in a way, it was too much to hold within me.

"It's been so long. . . ." I said, almost involuntarily, and it seemed to be true.

"Corwin," she said, "let's not fence. You want more than security, I know that. And you're still strong enough to get something out of this, if you play your hand just right. I can't guess what you have in mind, but maybe we can make a deal with Eric." The *we* had obviously shifted. She had come to some sort of conclusion as to my worth in whatever was going on. She saw a chance to gain something for herself, I could tell. I smiled, just a little. "Is that why you came here?" she continued. "Do you have a proposal for Eric, something which might require a go-between?"

"I may," I replied, "after I've thought about it some more. I've still so recently recovered that I have much pondering to do. I wanted to be in the best place, though, where I could act quickly, if I decided my best interests lay with Eric."

"Take care," she said. "You know I'll report every word."

"Of course," I said, not knowing that at all and groping for a quick hedge, "unless your best interests were conjoined with my own."

Her eyebrows moved closer together, and tiny wrinkles appeared between them.

"I'm not sure what you're proposing."

"I'm not proposing anything, yet," I said. "I'm just being completely open and honest with you and telling you I don't know. I'm not positive I want to make a deal with Eric. After all . . ." I let the words trail off on purpose, for I had nothing to follow them with, though I felt I should.

"You've been offered an alternative?" She stood up suddenly, seizing her whistle. "Bleys! Of course!"

"Sit down," I said, "and don't be ridiculous. Would I place myself in your hands this calmly, this readily, just to be dog meat because you happen to think of Bleys?"

She relaxed, maybe even sagged a little, then reseated herself.

"Possibly not," she finally said, "but I know you're a gambler, and I know you're treacherous. If you came here to dispose of a partisan, don't even bother trying. I'm not that important. You should know that by now. Besides, I always thought you rather liked me."

"I did, and I do," I said, "and you have nothing to worry about, so don't. It's interesting, though, that you should mention Bleys."

Bait, bait, bait! There was so much I wanted to know!

"Why? *Has* he approached you?"

"I'd rather not say," I replied, hoping it would give me an edge of some kind, and now that I knew Bleys' gender: "If he had, I'd have answered him the same as I would Eric—'I'll think about it.'"

"Bleys," she repeated, and *Bleys*, I said to myself inside my head, *Bleys. I like you. I forget why, and I know there are reasons why I shouldn't—but I like you. I know it.*

We sat awhile, and I felt fatigue but didn't want to show it. I should be strong. I knew I had to be strong.

I sat there and smiled and said, "Nice library you've got here," and she said, "Thank you."

"Bleys," she repeated after a time. "Do you really think he has a chance?"

I shrugged.

"Who knows? Not I, for certain. Maybe he does. Maybe not, too."

Then she stared at me, her eyes slightly wide, and her mouth opening.

"Not you?" she said. "You're not proposing to try yourself, are you?"

I laughed then, solely for purposes of countering her emotion.

"Don't be silly," I said when I'd finished. "Me?"

But as she said it, I knew she'd struck some chord, some deep-buried thing which replied with a powerful "Why not?"

I was suddenly afraid.

She seemed relieved, though, at my disavowal of whatever it was I was disavowing. She smiled then, and indicated a built-in bar off to my left.

"I'd like a little Irish Mist," she said.

"So would I, for that matter," I replied, and I rose and fetched two.

"You know," I said, after I'd reseated myself, "it's pleasant to be together with you this way, even if it is only for a shot time. It brings back memories."

And she smiled and was lovely.

"You're right," she said, sipping her drink. "I almost feel in Amber with you around," and I almost dropped my drink.

Amber! The word had sent a bolt of lightning down my spine!

Then she began to cry, and I rose and put my arm around her shoulders to comfort her.

"Don't cry, little girl. Please don't. It makes me unhappy, too." *Amber! There was something there, something electrical and potent!* "There will be good days once again," I said, softly.

"Do you really believe that?" she asked.

"Yes," I said loudly. "Yes, I do!"

"You're crazy," she said. "Maybe that's why you were always my favorite brother too. I can almost believe anything you say, even though I know you're crazy."

Then she cried a little more and stopped.

"Corwin," she said, "if you do make it—if by some wild and freakish chance out of Shadow you should make it—will you remember your little sister Florimel?"

"Yes," I said, knowing it to be her name. "Yes, I will remember you."

"Thank you. I will tell Eric only the essentials, and mention Bleys not at all, nor my latest suspicions."

"Thank you, Flora."

"But I don't trust you worth a damn," she added. "Remember that, too."

"That goes without saying."

Then she summoned her maid to show me to a room, and I managed to undress, collapsed into the bed, and slept for eleven hours.

THREE

In the morning she was gone, and there was no message. Her maid served me breakfast in the kitchen and went away to do maid-things. I'd disregarded the notion of trying to pump information out of the woman, as she either wouldn't know or wouldn't tell me the things I wanted to know and would no doubt also report my attempt to Flora. So, since it seemed I had the run of the house, I decided I'd return to the library and see what I could learn there. Besides, I like libraries. It makes me feel comfortable and secure to have walls of words, beautiful and wise, all around me. I always feel better when I can see that there is something to hold back the shadows.

Donner or Blitzen, or one of their relatives, appeared from somewhere and followed me up the hallway, walking stiff-legged and sniffing after my spoor. I tried to make friends with him, but it was like exchanging pleasantries with the state trooper who signaled you to pull off the road. I looked into some of the other rooms as I went along, and they were just places, innocuous-looking ones.

So I entered the library, and Africa still faced me. I closed the door behind me to keep the dogs out, and I strolled around the room, reading the titles on the shelves.

There were lots of history books. In fact, they seemed to dominate her collection. There were also many art books, of the big and expensive variety, and I leafed through a few of these. I usually do my best real thinking when I'm thinking about something else.

I wondered at the sources of Flora's obvious wealth. If we were related, did that mean that perhaps I enjoyed somewhat of opulence, also? I thought about my economic and social status, my profession, my origins. I had the feeling that I'd never worried much about money, and that there'd always been enough or ways of getting it, to keep me satisfied. Did I own a big house like this? I couldn't remember.

What did I do?

I sat behind her desk and examined my mind for any special caches of knowledge I might possess. It is difficult to examine yourself this way, as a stranger. Maybe that's why I couldn't come up with anything. What's yours is yours and a part of you and it just seems to belong there, inside. That's all.

A doctor? That came to mind as I was viewing some of Da Vinci's anatomical drawings. Almost by reflex, in my mind, I had begun going through the steps of various surgical operations. I realized then that I had operated on people in the past.

But that wasn't it. While I realized that I had a medical background, I knew that it was a part of something else. I knew, somehow, that I was not a practicing surgeon. What then? What else was involved?

Something caught my eye.

Seated there at the desk, I commanded a view of the far wall, on which, among other things, hung an antique cavalry saber, which I had overlooked the first time around the room. I rose and crossed over to it, took it down from its pegs.

In my mind, I *tsked* at the shape it was in. I wanted an oily rag and a whetstone, to make it the way it should be once again. I knew something about antique arms, edged weapons in particular.

The saber felt light and useful in my hand, and I felt capable with it. I struck an *en garde*. I parried and cut a few times. Yes, I could use the thing.

So what sort of background was that? I looked around for new memory joggers.

Nothing else occurred to me, so I replaced the blade and returned to the desk. Sitting there, I decided to go through the thing.

I started with the middle one and worked my way up the left side and down the right, drawer by drawer.

Stationery, envelopes, postage stamps, paper clips, pencil stubs, rubber bands—all the usual items.

I had pulled each drawer all the way out though, and held it in my lap as I'd inspected its contents. It wasn't just an idea. It was part of some sort of training I'd once received, which told me I should inspect the sides and bottoms as well.

One thing almost slipped by me, but caught my attention at the last instant: the back of the lower right-hand drawer did not rise as high as the backs of the other drawers.

This indicated something, and when I knelt and looked inside the drawer space I saw a little box-like affair fixed to the upper side.

It was a small drawer itself, way in the back, and it was locked.

It took me about a minute of fooling around with paper clips, safety pins, and finally a metal shoehorn I'd seen in another drawer. The shoehorn did the trick.

The drawer contained a packet of playing cards.

And the packet bore a device which caused me to stiffen where I knelt, perspiration suddenly wetting my brow and my breath coming rapidly.

It bore a white unicorn on a grass field, rampant, facing to the dexter.

And I knew that device and it hurt me that I could not name it.

I opened the packet and extracted the cards. They were on the order of tarots, with their wands, pentacles, cups, and swords, but the Greater Trumps were quite different.

I replaced both drawers, being careful not to lock the smaller one, before I continued my inspection.

They were almost lifelike in appearance, the Greater Trumps ready to step right out through those glistening surfaces. The cards seemed quite cold to my touch, and it gave me a distinct pleasure to handle them. I had once had a packet like this myself, I suddenly knew.

I began spreading them on the blotter before me.

The one bore a wily-looking little man, with a sharp nose and a laughing mouth and a shock of straw-colored hair. He was dressed in something like a Renaissance costume of orange, red, and brown. He wore long hose and a tight-fitting embroidered doublet. And I knew him. His name was Random.

Next, there was the passive countenance of Julian, dark hair hanging long, blue eyes containing neither passion nor compassion. He was dressed completely in scaled white armor, not silver or metallic-colored, but looking as if it had been enameled. I knew, though, that it was terribly tough and shock-resistant, despite its decorative and festive appearance. He was the man I had beaten at his favorite game, for which he had thrown a glass of wine at me. I knew him and I hated him.

Then came the swarthy, dark-eyed countenance of Caine, dressed all in satin that was black and green, wearing a dark three-cornered hat set at a rakish angle, a green plume of feathers trailing down the back. He was standing in profile, one arm akimbo, and the toes of his boots curled upwards, and he wore an emerald-studded dagger at his belt. There was ambivalence in my heart.

Then there was Eric. Handsome by anyone's standards, his hair was so dark as to be almost blue. His beard curled around the mouth that always smiled, and he was dressed simply in a leather jacket and leggings, a plain cloak, high black boots, and he wore a red sword belt bearing a long silvery saber and clasped with a ruby, and his high cloak collar round his head was lined with red and the trimmings of his sleeves matched it. His hands, thumbs hooked behind his belt, were terribly strong and prominent. A pair of black gloves jutted from the belt near his right hip. He it was, I was certain, that had tried to kill me on that day I had almost died. I studied him and I feared him somewhat.

Then there was Benedict, tall and dour, thin; thin of body, thin of face, wide of mind. He wore orange and yellow and brown and reminded me of haysticks and pumpkins and scarecrows and the *Legend of Sleepy Hollow*. He had a long strong jaw and hazel eyes and brown hair that never curled. He stood beside a tan horse and leaned upon a lance about which was twined a rope of flowers. He seldom laughed. I liked him.

I paused when I uncovered the next card, and my heart leaped forward and banged against my sternum and asked to be let out.

It was me.

I knew the me I shaved and this was the guy behind the mirror. Green eyes, black hair, dressed in black and silver, yes. I had on a cloak and it was slightly furled as by a wind. I had on black boots, like Eric's, and I too wore a blade, only mine was heavier, though not quite as long as his. I had my gloves on and they were silver and scaled. The clasp at my neck was cast in the form of a silver rose.

Me, Corwin.

And a big, powerful man regarded me from the next card. He resembled me quite strongly, save that his jaw was heavier, and I knew he was bigger than I, though slower. His strength was a thing out of legend. He wore a dressing gown of blue and gray clasped about the middle with a wide, black belt, and he stood laughing. About his neck, on a heavy cord, there hung a silver hunting horn. He wore a fringe beard and a light mustache. In his right hand he held a goblet of wine. I felt a sudden affection for him. His name then occurred to me. He was Gérard.

Then came a fiery bearded, flame-crowned man, dressed all in red and orange, mainly of silk stuff, and he held a sword in his right hand and a glass of wine in his left, and the devil himself danced behind his eyes, as blue as Flora's, or Eric's. His chin was slight, but the beard covered it. His sword was inlaid with an elaborate filigree of a golden color. He wore two huge rings on his right hand and one on his left: an emerald, a ruby, and a sapphire, respectively. This, I knew, was Bleys.

Then there was a figure both like Bleys and myself. My features, though smaller, my eyes, Bleys' hair, beardless. He wore a riding suit of green and sat atop a white horse, heading toward the dexter side of the card. There was a quality of both strength and weakness, questing and abandonment about him. I both approved and disapproved, liked and was repelled by, this one. His name was Brand, I knew. As soon as I laid eyes upon him, I knew.

In fact, I realized that I knew them all well, remembered them all, with their strengths, their weaknesses, their victories, their defeats.

For they were my brothers.

I lit a cigarette I'd filched from Flora's desk box, and I leaned back and considered the things I had recalled.

They were my brothers, those eight strange men garbed in their strange costumes. And I knew that it was right and fitting that they should dress in whatever manner they chose, just as it was right for me to wear the black and the silver. Then I chuckled, as I realized what I was wearing; what I had purchased in the little clothing store of that little town I had stopped in after my departure from Greenwood.

I had on black slacks, and all three of the shirts I had purchased had been of a grayish, silvery color. And my jacket, too, was black.

I returned to the cards, and there was Flora in a gown green as the sea, just as I'd remembered her the previous evening; and then there was a black-haired girl with the same blue eyes, and her hair hung long and she was dressed all in black, with a girdle of silver about her waist. My eyes filled with tears, why I don't know. Her name was Deirdre. Then there was Fiona, with hair like Bleys or Brand, my eyes, and a complexion like mother of pearl. I hated her the second I turned over the card. Next was Llewella, whose hair matched her jade-colored eyes, dressed in shimmering gray and green with a lavender belt, and looking moist and sad. For some reason, I knew she was not like the rest of us. But she, too, was my sister.

I felt a terrible sense of distance and removal from all these people. Yet somehow they seemed physically close.

The cards were so very cold on my fingertips that I put them down again, though with a certain sense of reluctance at having to relinquish their touch.

There were no more, though. All the rest were minor cards. And I knew, somehow, that *somehow*, again—ah, somehow!—that several were missing.

For the life of me, however, I did not know what the missing Trumps represented.

I was strangely saddened by this, and I picked up my cigarette and mused.

Why did all these things rush back so easily when I viewed the cards— rush back without dragging their contexts along with them? I knew more now than I'd known before, in the way of names and faces. But that was about all.

I couldn't figure the significance of the fact that we were all done up in cards this way. I had a terribly strong desire to own a pack of them, however. If I picked up Flora's, though, I knew she'd spot in a hurry that they were missing, and I'd be in trouble. Therefore, I put them back in the little drawer behind the big drawer and locked them in again. Then, God, how I racked my brains! But to little avail.

Until I recalled a magical word.

Amber.

I had been greatly upset by the word on the previous evening. I had been sufficiently upset so that I had avoided thinking of it since then. But now I courted it. Now I rolled it around my mind and examined all the associations that sprang up when it struck.

The word was charged with a mighty longing and a massive nostalgia. It had, wrapped up inside it, a sense of forsaken beauty, grand achievement, and a feeling of power that was terrible and almost ultimate. Somehow, the word belonged in my vocabulary. Somehow, I was part of it and it was a part of me. It was a place name, I knew then. It was the name of a place I once had known. There came no pictures, though, only emotions.

How long I sat so, I do not know. Time had somehow divorced itself from my reveries.

I realized then, from the center of my thoughts, that there had come a gentle rapping upon the door. Then the handle slowly turned and the maid, whose name was Carmella, entered and asked me if I was interested in lunch.

It seemed like a good idea, so I followed her back to the kitchen and ate half a chicken and drank a quart of milk.

I took a pot of coffee back to the library with me, avoiding the dogs as I went. I was into the second cup when the telephone rang.

I longed to pick it up, but I figured there must be extensions all over the house and Carmella would probably get it from somewhere.

I was wrong. It kept ringing.

Finally, I couldn't resist it any longer.

"Hello," I said, "this is the Flaumel residence."

"May I speak with Mrs. Flaumel please?"

It was a man's voice, rapid and slightly nervous. He sounded out of breath and his words were masked and surrounded by the faint ringing and the ghost voices that indicate long distance.

"I'm sorry," I told him. "She's not here right now. May I take a message or have her call you back?"

"Who am I talking to?" he demanded.

I hesitated, then, "Corwin's the name," I told him.

"My God!" he said, and a long silence followed.

I was beginning to think he'd hung up. I said, "Hello?" again, just as he started talking.

"Is she still alive?" he asked.

"Of course she's still alive! Who the hell am I talking to?"

"Don't you recognize the voice, Corwin? This is Random. Listen, I'm in California and I'm in trouble. I was calling to ask Flora for sanctuary. Are you with her?"

"Temporarily," I said.

"I see. Will you give me your protection, Corwin?" Pause, then, "Please?"

"As much as I can," I said, "but I can't commit Flora to anything without consulting her."

"Will you protect me against her?"

"Yes."

"Then you're good enough for me, man. I'm going to try to make it to New York now. I'll be coming by a rather circuitous route, so I don't know how long it will take me. If I can avoid the wrong shadows, I'll be seeing you whenever. Wish me luck."

"Luck," I said.

Then there was a click and I was listening to a distant ringing and the voices of the ghosts.

So cocky little Random was in trouble! I had a feeling it shouldn't have bothered me especially. But now, he was one of the keys to my past, and quite possibly my future also. So I would try to help him, in any way I could, until I'd learned all I wanted from him. I knew that there wasn't much brotherly love lost between the two of us. But I knew that on the one hand he was nobody's fool; he was resourceful, shrewd, strangely sentimental over the damnedest things; and on the other hand, his word wasn't worth the spit behind it, and he'd probably sell my corpse to the medical school of his choice if he could get much for it. I remembered the little fink all right, with only a touch of affection, perhaps for a few pleasant times it seemed we had spent together. But trust him? Never. I decided I wouldn't tell Flora he was coming until the last possible moment. He might be made to serve as an ace, or at least a knave, in the hole.

So I added some hot coffee to what remained in my cup and sipped it slowly.

Who was he running from?

Not Eric, certainly, or he wouldn't have been calling here. I wondered then concerning his question as to whether Flora was dead, just because I happened to be present here. Was she really that strongly allied with the brother I knew I hated that it was common knowledge in the family that I'd do her in, too, given the chance? It seemed strange, but then he'd asked the question.

And what was it in which they were allied? What was the source of this tension, this opposition? Why was it that Random was running?

Amber.

That was the answer.

Amber. Somehow, the key to everything lay in Amber, I knew. The secret of the entire mess was in Amber, in some event that had transpired in that place, and fairly recently, I'd judge. I'd have to be on my toes. I'd have to pretend to the knowledge I didn't possess, while piece by piece I mined it from those who had it. I felt confident that I could do it. There was enough distrust circulating for everyone to be cagey. I'd play on that. I'd get what I needed and take what I wanted, and I'd remember those who helped me and step on the rest. For this, I knew, was the law by which our family lived, and I was a true son of my father. . . .

My headache came on again suddenly, throbbing to crack my skull.

Something about my father I thought, guessed, felt—was what had served to set it off. But I wasn't sure why or how.

After a time, it subsided and I slept, there in the chair. After a much longer time, the door opened and Flora entered. It was night outside, once more.

She was dressed in a green silk blouse and a long woolen skirt that was gray. She had on walking shoes and heavy stockings. Her hair was pulled back behind her head and she looked slightly pale. She still wore her hound whistle.

"Good evening," I said, rising.

But she did not reply. Instead, she walked across the room to the bar, poured herself a shot of Jack Daniels, and tossed it off like a man. Then she poured another and took it with her to the big chair.

I lit a cigarette and handed it to her.

She nodded, then said, "The Road to Amber—is difficult."

"Why?"

She gave me a very puzzled look.

"When is the last time you tried it?"

I shrugged.

"I don't remember."

"Be that way then," she said. "I just wondered how much of it was your doing."

I didn't reply because I didn't know what she was talking about. But then I recalled that there was an easier way than the Road to get to the place called Amber. Obviously, she lacked it.

"You're missing some Trumps," I said then suddenly, in a voice which was almost mine.

She sprang to her feet, half her drink spilling over the back of her hand. "Give them back!" she cried, reaching for the whistle.

I moved forward and seized her shoulders.

"I don't have them," I said. "I was just making an observation."

She relaxed a bit, then began to cry, and I pushed her back down, gently, into the chair.

"I thought you meant you'd taken the ones I had left," she said. "Rather than just making a nasty and obvious comment."

I didn't apologize. It didn't seem right that I should have to.

"How far did you get?"

"Not far at all." Then she laughed and regarded me with a new light in her eyes.

"I see what you've done now, Corwin," she said, and I lit a cigarette in order to cover any sort of need for a reply.

"Some of those things were yours, weren't they? You blocked my way to Amber before you came here, didn't you? You knew I'd go to Eric. But I can't now. I'll have to wait till he comes to me. Clever. You want to draw him here, don't you? He'll send a messenger, though. He won't come himself."

There was a strange tone of admiration in the voice of this woman who was admitting she'd just tried to sell me out to my enemy, and still would— given half a chance—as she talked about something she thought I'd done which had thrown a monkey wrench into her plans. How could anyone be so admittedly Machiavellian in the presence of a proposed victim? The answer rang back immediately from the depths of my mind: it is the way of our kind. We don't have to be subtle with each other. Though I thought she lacked somewhat the finesse of a true professional.

"Do you think I'm stupid, Flora?" I asked. "Do you think I came here just for purposes of waiting around for you to hand me over to Eric? Whatever you ran into, it served you right."

"All right, I don't play in your league! But you're in exile, too! That shows you weren't so smart!"

Somehow her words burned and I knew they were wrong.

"Like hell I am!" I said.

She laughed again.

"I knew that would get a rise out of you," she said. "All right, you walk in the Shadows on purpose then. You're crazy."

I shrugged.

She said, "What do you want? Why did you really come here?"

"I was curious what you were up to," I said. "That's all. You can't keep me here if I don't want to stay. Even Eric couldn't do that. Maybe I really did just want to visit with you. Maybe I'm getting sentimental in my old age. Whatever, I'm going to stay a little longer now, and then probably go away for good. If you hadn't been so quick to see what you could get for me, you might have profited a lot more, lady. You asked me to remember you one day, if a certain thing occurred. . . ."

It took several seconds for what I thought I was implying to sink in.

Then she said, "You're going to try! You're really going to try!"

"You're goddamn right I'm going to try," I said, knowing that I would, whatever it was, "and you can tell that to Eric if you want, but remember that I might make it. Bear in mind that if I do, it might be nice to be my friend."

I sure wished I knew what the hell I was talking about, but I'd picked up enough terms and felt the importance attached to them, so that I could use them properly without knowing what they meant. But they *felt* right, so very right. . . .

Suddenly, she was kissing me.

"I won't tell him. Really, I won't, Corwin! I think you can do it. Bleys will be difficult, but Gérard would probably help you, and maybe Benedict. Then Caine would swing over, when he saw what was happening—"

"I can do my own planning," I said.

Then she drew away. She poured two glasses of wine and handed one to me.

"To the future," she said.

"I'll always drink to that."

And we did.

Then she refilled mine and studied me.

"It had to be Eric, Bleys, or you," she said. "You're the only ones with any guts or brains. But you'd removed yourself from the picture for so long that I'd counted you out of the running."

"It just goes to show: you never can tell."

I sipped my drink and hoped she'd shut up for just a minute. It seemed to me she was being a bit too obvious in trying to play on every side available. There was something bothering me, and I wanted to think about it.

How old was I?

That question, I knew, was a part of the answer to the terrible sense of distance and removal that I felt from all the persons depicted on the playing cards. I was older than I appeared to be. (Thirtyish, I'd seemed when I looked at me in the mirror—but now I knew that it was because the Shadows would lie for me.) I was far, far older, and it had been a very long time since I had seen my brothers and my sisters, all together and friendly, existing side by side as they did on the cards, with no tension, no friction among them.

We heard the sound of the bell, and Carmella moving to answer the door.

"That would be brother Random," I said, knowing I was right. "He's under my protection."

Her eyes widened, then she smiled, as though she appreciated some clever thing I had done.

I hadn't, of course, but I was glad to let her think so.

It made me feel safer.

FOUR

I felt safe for perhaps all of three minutes.

I beat Carmella to the door and flung it open.

He staggered in and immediately pushed the door shut behind himself and shot the bolt. There were lines under those light eyes and he wasn't wearing a bright doublet and long hose. He needed a shave and he had on a brown wool suit. He carried a gabardine overcoat over one arm and wore dark suede shoes. But he was Random, all right—the Random I had seen on the card—only the laughing mouth looked tired and there was dirt beneath his fingernails.

"Corwin!" he said, and embraced me.

I squeezed his shoulder. "You look as if you could use a drink," I said.

"Yes. Yes. Yes. . . ." he agreed, and I steered him toward the library.

About three minutes later, after he had seated himself, with a drink in one hand and a cigarette in the other, he said to me, "They're after me. They'll be here soon."

Flora let out a little shriek, which we both ignored.

"Who?" I asked.

"People out of the Shadows," he said. "I don't know who they are, or who sent them. There are four or five though, maybe even six. They were on the plane with me. I took a jet. They occurred around Denver. I moved the plane several times to subtract them, but it didn't work—and I didn't want to get too far off the track. I shook them in Manhattan, but it's only a matter of time. I think they'll be here soon."

"And you've no idea at all who sent them?"

He smiled for an instant.

"Well, I guess we'd be safe in limiting it to the family. Maybe Bleys, maybe Julian, maybe Caine. Maybe even you, to get me here. Hope not, though. You didn't, did you?"

" 'Fraid not," I said. "How tough do they look?"

He shrugged. "If it were only two or three, I'd have tried to pull an ambush. But not with that whole crowd."

He was a little guy, maybe five-six in height, weighing perhaps one thirty-five. But he sounded as if he meant it when he said he'd take on two or three bruisers, single-handed. I wondered suddenly about my own physical strength, being his brother. I felt comfortably strong. I knew I'd be willing to take on any one man in a fair fight without any special fears. How strong was I?

Suddenly, I knew I would have a chance to find out.

There came a knocking at the front door.

"What shall we do?" asked Flora.

Random laughed, undid his necktie, tossed it atop his coat on the desk. He stripped off his suit jacket then and looked about the room. His eyes fell upon the saber and he was across the room in an instant and had it in his hand. I felt the weight of the .32 within my jacket pocket and thumbed off the safety catch.

"Do?" Random asked. "There exists a probability that they will gain entrance," he said. "Therefore, they will enter. When is the last time you stood to battle, sister?"

"It has been too long," she replied.

"Then you had better start remembering fast," he told her, "because it is only a matter of small time. They are guided, I can tell you. But there are three of us and at most only twice as many of them. Why worry?"

"We don't know what they are," she said.

The knocking came again.

"What does it matter?"

"Nothing," I said. "Shall I go and let them in?"

They both blanched slightly.

"We might as well wait. . . ."

"I might call the cops," I said.

They both laughed, almost hysterically.

"Or Eric," I said, suddenly looking at her.

But she shook her head.

"We just don't have the time. We have the Trump, but by the time he could respond—if he chose it—it would be too late."

"And this might even be his doing, eh?" said Random.

"I doubt it," she replied, "very much. It's not his style."

"True," I replied, just for the hell of it, and to let them know I was with things.

The sound of knocking came once again, and much more loudly.

"What about Carmella?" I asked, upon a sudden thought.

Flora shook her head.

"I have decided that it is improbable that she will answer the door."

"But you don't know what you're up against," Random cried, and he was suddenly gone from the room.

I followed him, along the hallway and into the foyer, in time to stop Carmella from opening the door.

We sent her back to her own quarters with instructions to lock herself in, and Random observed, "That shows the strength of the opposition. Where are we, Corwin?"

I shrugged.

"If I knew, I'd tell you. For the moment at least, we're in this together. Step back!"

And I opened the door.

The first man tried to push me aside, and I stiff-armed him back.

There were six, I could see that.

"What do you want?" I asked them.

But never a word was spoken, and I saw guns.

I kicked out and slammed the door again and shot the bolt.

"Okay, they're really there," I said. "But how do I know you're not pulling something?"

"You don't," he said, "but I really wish I were. They look wild."

I had to agree. The guys on the porch were heavily built and had hats pulled down to cover their eyes. Their faces had all been covered with shadows.

"I wish I knew where we are," said Random.

I felt a hackle-raising vibration, in the vicinity of my eardrums. I knew, in that moment, that Flora had blown her whistle.

When I heard a window break, somewhere off to my right, I was not surprised to hear a growled rumbling and some baying, somewhere off to my left.

"She's called her dogs," I said, "six mean and vicious brutes, which could under other circumstances be after us."

Random nodded, and we both headed off in the direction of the shattering.

When we reached the living room, two men were already inside and both had guns.

I dropped the first and hit the floor, firing at the second. Random leaped above me, brandishing his blade, and I saw the second man's head depart his shoulders.

By then, two more were through the window. I emptied the automatic at them, and I heard the snarling of Flora's hounds mixed with gunfire that was not my own.

I saw three of the men upon the floor and the same number of Flora's dogs. It made me feel good to think we had gotten half of them, and as the rest came through the window I killed another in a manner which surprised me.

Suddenly, and without thinking, I picked up a huge overstuffed chair and hurled it perhaps thirty feet across the room. It broke the back of the man it struck.

I leaped toward the remaining two, but before I crossed the room, Random had pierced one of them with the saber, leaving him for the dogs to finish off, and was turning toward the other.

The other was pulled down before he could act, however. He killed another of the dogs before we could stop him, but he never killed anything again after that. Random strangled him.

It turned out that two of the dogs were dead and one was badly hurt.

Random killed the injured one with a quick thrust, and we turned our attention to the men.

There was something unusual about their appearance.

Flora entered and helped us to decide what.

For one thing, all six had uniformly bloodshot eyes. Very, very bloodshot eyes. With them, though, the condition seemed normal.

For another, all had an extra joint to each finger and thumb, and sharp, forward-curving spurs on the backs of their hands.

All of them had prominent jaws, and when I forced one open, I counted forty-four teeth, most of them longer than human teeth, and several looking to be much sharper. Their flesh was grayish and hard and shiny.

There were undoubtedly other differences also, but those were sufficient to prove a point of some sort.

We took their weapons, and I hung onto three small, flat pistols.

"They crawled out of the Shadows, all right," said Random, and I nodded. "And I was lucky, too. It doesn't seem they suspected I'd turn up with the reinforcements I did—a militant brother and around half a ton of dogs." He went and peered out the broken window, and I decided to let him do it himself. "Nothing," he said, after a time. "I'm sure we got them all," and he drew the heavy orange drapes closed and pushed a lot of high-backed furniture in front of them. While he was doing that, I went through all their pockets.

I wasn't really surprised that I turned up nothing in the way of identification.

"Let's go back to the library," he said, "so I can finish my drink."

He cleaned off the blade, carefully, before he seated himself, however, and he replaced it on the pegs. I fetched Flora a drink while he did this.

"So it would seem I'm temporarily safe," he said, "now that there are three of us sharing the picture."

"So it would seem," Flora agreed.

"God, I haven't eaten since yesterday!" he announced.

So Flora went to tell Carmella it was safe to come out now, so long as she stayed clear of the living room, and to bring a lot of food to the library.

As soon as she left the room, Random turned to me and asked, "Like, what's it between you?"

"Don't turn your back on her."

"She's still Eric's?"

"So far as I can tell."

"Then what are you doing here?"

"I was trying to sucker Eric into coming around after me himself. He knows it's the only way he'll really get me, and I wanted to see how badly he wanted to."

Random shook his head.

"I don't think he'll do it. No percentage. So long as you're here and he's there, why bother sticking his neck out? He's still got the stronger position. If you want him, you'll have to go after him."

"I've just about come to the same conclusion."

His eyes gleamed then, and his old smile appeared. He ran one hand through his straw-colored hair and wouldn't let go of my eyes.

"Are you going to do it?" he asked.

"Maybe," I said.

"Don't 'maybe' me, baby. It's written all over you. I'd almost be willing to go along, you know. Of all my relations, I like sex the best and Eric the least."

I lit a cigarette, while I considered.

"You're thinking," he said while I thought, " 'How far can I trust Random this time? He is sneaky and mean and just like his name, and he will doubtless sell me out if someone offers him a better deal.' True?"

I nodded.

"However, brother Corwin, remember that while I've never done you much good, I've never done you any especial harm either. Oh, a few pranks, I'll admit. But, all in all, you might say we've gotten along best of all in the family—that is, we've stayed out of each other's way. Think it over. I believe I hear Flora or her woman coming now, so let's change the subject. . . . But quick! I don't suppose you have a deck of the family's favorite playing cards around, do you?"

I shook my head.

Flora entered the room and said, "Carmella will bring some food shortly."

We drank to that, and he winked at me behind her back.

The following morning, the bodies were gone from the living room, there were no stains upon the carpet, the window appeared to have been repaired, and Random explained that he had "taken care of things." I did not see fit to question him further.

We borrowed Flora's Mercedes and went for a drive. The countryside seemed strangely altered. I couldn't quite put my finger on what it was that was missing or new, but somehow things felt different. This, too, gave me a headache when I attempted to consider it, so I decided to suspend such thinking for the nonce.

I was at the wheel, Random at my side. I observed that I would like to be back in Amber again—just to see what sort of response I would obtain.

"I have been wondering," he replied, "whether you were out for vengeance, pure and simple, or something more," thereby shifting the ball back to me, to answer or not to answer, as I saw fit.

I saw fit. I used the stock phrase:

"I've been thinking about that, too," I said, "trying to figure my chances. You know, I just might 'try.' "

He turned toward me then (he had been staring out of the side window) and said:

"I suppose we've all had that ambition, or at least that thought—I know I have, though I dismissed me early in the game—and the way I feel about it, it's worth the attempt. You're asking me, I know, whether I'll help you. The answer is 'yes.' I'll do it just to screw up the others." Then, "What do you think of Flora? Would she be of any help?"

"I doubt it very much," I said. "She'd throw in if things were certain. But, then, what's certain at this point?"

"Or any," he added.

"Or any," I repeated, so he'd think I knew what sort of response I would obtain.

I was afraid to confide in him as to the condition of my memory. I was also afraid to trust him, so I didn't. There were so very many things I wanted to know, but I had no one to turn to. I thought about it a bit as we drove along.

"Well, when do you want to start?" I asked.

"Whenever you're ready."

And there it was, right in my lap, and I didn't know what to do with it. "What about now?" I said.

He was silent. He lit a cigarette, I think to buy time.

I did the same.

"Okay," he finally said. "When's the last time you've been back?"

"It's been so damn long," I told him, "that I'm not even sure I remember the way."

"All right," he said, "then we're going to have to go away before we can come back. How much gas have you got?"

"Three-quarters of a tank."

"Then turn left at the next corner, and we'll see what happens."

I did this thing, and as we drove along all the sidewalks began to sparkle.

"Damn!" he said. "It's been around twenty years since I've taken the walk. I'm remembering the right things too soon."

We kept driving, and I kept wondering what the hell was happening. The sky had grown a bit greenish, then shaded over into pink.

I bit my lip against the asking of questions.

We passed beneath a bridge and when we emerged on the other side the sky was a normal color again, but there were windmills all over the place, big yellow ones.

"Don't worry," he said quickly, "it could be worse."

I noticed that the people we passed were dressed rather strangely, and the roadway was of brick.

"Turn right."

I did.

Purple clouds covered over the sun, and it began to rain. Lightning stalked the heavens and the skies grumbled above us. I had the windshield wipers going full speed, but they weren't doing a whole lot of good. I turned on the headlights and slowed even more.

I would have sworn I'd passed a horseman, racing in the other direction, dressed all in gray, collar turned high and head lowered against the rain.

Then the clouds broke themselves apart and we were riding along a seashore. The waves splashed high and enormous gulls swept low above them. The rain had stopped and I killed the lights and the wipers. Now the road was of macadam, but I didn't recognize the place at all. In the rear-view mirror there was no sign of the town we had just departed. My grip tightened upon the wheel as we passed by a sudden gallows where a skeleton was suspended by the neck, pushed from side to side by the wind.

Random just kept smoking and staring out of the window as our road turned away from the shore and curved round a hill. A grassy treeless plain swept away to our right and a row of hills climbed higher on our left. The sky by now was a dark but brilliant blue, like a deep, clear pool, sheltered and shaded. I did not recall having ever seen a sky like that before.

Random opened his window to throw away the butt, and an icy breeze came in and swirled around inside the car until he closed the window again. The breeze had a sea scent to it, salty and sharp.

"All roads lead to Amber," he said, as though it were an axiom.

Then I recalled what Flora had said the day before. I didn't want to sound like a dunce or a withholder of crucial information, but I had to tell him, for my sake as well as his own, when I realized what her statement implied.

"You know," I began, "when you called the other day and I answered the phone because Flora was out, I've a strong feeling she was trying to make it to Amber, and that she found the way blocked."

At this, he laughed.

"The woman has very little imagination," he replied. "Of course it would be blocked at a time like this. Ultimately, we'll be reduced to walking, I'm sure, and it will doubtless take all of our strength and ingenuity to make it, if we make it at all. Did she think she could walk back like a princess in state, treading on flowers the whole way? She's a dumb bitch. She doesn't really deserve to live, but that's not for me to say, yet.

"Turn right at the crossroads," he decided.

What was happening? I knew he was in some way responsible for the exotic changes going on about us, but I couldn't determine how he was doing it, where he was getting us to. I knew I had to learn his secret, but I couldn't just ask him or he'd know I didn't know. Then I'd be at his mercy. He seemed to do nothing but smoke and stare, but coming up out of a dip in the road we entered a blue desert and the sun was now pink above our heads within the shimmering sky. In the rear-view mirror, miles and miles of desert stretched out behind us, for as far as I could see. Neat trick, that.

Then the engine coughed, sputtered, steadied itself, repeated the performance.

The steering wheel changed shape beneath my hands.

It became a crescent; and the seat seemed further back, the car seemed closer to the road, and the windshield had more of a slant to it.

I said nothing, though, not even when the lavender sandstorm struck us.

But when it cleared away, I gasped.

There was a godawful line of cars all jammed up, about half a mile before us. They were all standing still and I could hear their horns.

"Slow down," he said. "It's the first obstacle."

I did, and another gust of sand swept over us.

Before I could switch on the lights, it was gone, and I blinked my eyes several times.

All the cars were gone and silent their horns. But the roadway sparkled now as the sidewalks had for a time, and I heard Random damning someone or something under his breath.

"I'm sure I shifted just the way he wanted us to, whoever set up that block," he said, "and it pisses me off that I did what he expected—the obvious."

"Eric?" I asked.

"Probably. What do you think we should do? Stop and try it the hard way for a while, or go on and see if there are more blocks?"

"Let's go on a bit. After all, that was only the first."

"Okay," he said, but added, "who knows what the second will be?"

The second was a thing—I don't know how else to describe it.

It was a thing that looked like a smelter with arms, squatting in the middle of the road, reaching down and picking up cars, eating them.

I hit the brakes.

"What's the matter?" Random asked. "Keep going. How else can we get past them?"

"It shook me a bit," I said, and he gave me a strange, sidelong look as another dust storm came up.

It had been the wrong thing to say, I knew.

When the dust cleared away, we were racing along an empty road once more. And there were towers in the distance.

"I think I've screwed him up," said Random. "I combined several into one, and I think it may be one he hasn't anticipated. After all, no one can cover all roads to Amber."

"True," I said, hoping to redeem myself from whatever faux pas had drawn that strange look.

I considered Random. A little, weak-looking guy who could have died as easily as I on the previous evening. What was his power? And what was all this talk of Shadows? Something told me that whatever Shadows were, we moved among them even now. How? It was something Random was doing, and since he seemed at rest physically, his hands in plain sight, I decided it was something he did with his mind. Again, how?

Well, I'd heard him speak of "adding" and "subtracting," as though the universe in which he moved were a big equation.

I decided—with a sudden certainty—that he was somehow adding and subtracting items to and from the world that was visible about us to bring us into closer and closer alignment with that strange place, Amber, for which he was solving.

It was something I'd once known how to do. And the key to it, I knew in a flash, was remembering Amber.

But I couldn't.

The road curved abruptly, the desert ended, to give way to fields of tall, blue, sharp-looking grass. After a while, the terrain became a bit hilly, and at the foot of the third hill the pavement ended and we entered upon a narrow dirt road. It was hard-packed, and it wound its way among greater hills upon which small shrubs and bayonet-like thistle bushes now began to appear.

After about half an hour of this, the hills went away, and we entered a forest of squat, big-boled trees with diamond-shaped leaves of autumn orange and purple.

A light rain began to fall, and there were many shadows. Pale mists arose from mats of soggy leaves. Off to the right somewhere, I heard a howl.

The steering wheel changed shape three more times, its latest version being an octagonal wooden affair. The car was quite tall now, and we had somewhere acquired a hood ornament in the shape of a flamingo. I refrained from commenting on these things, but accommodated myself to whatever positions the seat assumed and new operating requirements the vehicle obtained. Random, however, glanced at the steering wheel just as another howl occurred, shook his head, and suddenly the trees were much higher, though festooned with hanging vines and something like a blue veiling of Spanish Moss, and the car was almost normal again. I glanced at the fuel gauge and saw that we had half a tank.

"We're making headway," my brother remarked, and I nodded.

The road widened abruptly and acquired a concrete surface. There were canals on both sides, full of muddy water. Leaves, small branches, and colored feathers glided along their surfaces.

I suddenly became lightheaded and a bit dizzy, but "Breathe slowly and deeply," said Random, before I could remark on it. "We're taking a short cut, and the atmosphere and the gravitation will be a bit different for a time. I think we've been pretty lucky so far, and I want to push it for all it's worth—get as close as we can, as quickly as we can."

"Good idea," I said.

"Maybe, maybe not," he replied, "but I think it's worth the gam—Look out!"

We were climbing a hill and a truck topped it and came barreling down toward us. It was on the wrong side of the road. I swerved to avoid it, but it swerved, too. At the very last instant, I had to go off the road, onto the soft shoulder to my left, and head close to the edge of the canal in order to avoid a collision.

To my right, the truck screeched to a halt. I tried to pull off the shoulder and back onto the road, but we were stuck in the soft soil.

Then I heard a door slam, and saw that the driver had climbed down from the right side of the cab—which meant that he probably was driving on the proper side of the road after all, and we were in the wrong. I was sure that nowhere in the States did traffic flow in a British manner, but I was certain by this time that we had long ago left the Earth that I knew.

The truck was a tanker. It said ZUÑOCO on the side in big, blood-red letters, and beneath this was the motto "Wee covir the werld." The driver covered me with abuse, as I stepped out, rounded the car, and began apologizing. He was as big as I was, and built like a beer barrel, and he carried a jack handle in one hand.

"Look, I said I'm sorry," I told him. "What do you want me to do? Nobody got hurt and there was no damage."

"They shouldn't turn goddamn drivers like you loose on the road!" he yelled. "You're a friggin' menace!"

Random got out of the car then and said, "Mister, you'd better move along!" and he had a gun in his hand.

"Put that away," I told him, but he flipped the safety catch off and pointed.

The guy turned around and started to run, a look of fear widening his eyes and loosening his jaw.

Random raised the pistol and took careful aim at the man's back, and I managed to knock his arm to the side just as he pulled the trigger.

It scored the pavement and ricocheted away.

Random turned toward me and his face was almost white.

"You bloody fool!" he said. "That shot could have hit the tank!"

"It could also have hit the guy you were aiming at."

"So who the hell cares? We'll never pass this way again, in this generation. That bastard dared to insult a Prince of Amber! It was *your* honor I was thinking about."

"I can take care of my own honor," I told him, and something cold and powerful suddenly gripped me and answered, "for he was mine to kill, not yours, had I chosen," and a sense of outrage filled me.

He bowed his head then, as the cab door slammed and the truck took off down the road.

"I'm sorry, brother," he said. "I did not mean to presume. But it offended me to hear one of them speak to you in such a manner. I know I should have waited to let you dispose of him as you saw fit, or at least have consulted with you."

"Well, whatever," I told him, "let's get back onto the road and get moving, if we can."

The rear wheels were sunken up to their hubcaps, and as I stared at them, trying to decide the best way to go about things, Random called out, "Okay, I've got the front bumper. You take the rear and we'll carry it back to the road—and we'd better deposit it in the left lane."

He wasn't kidding.

He'd said something about lesser gravitation, but I didn't feel that light. I knew I was strong, but I had my doubts about being able to raise the rear end of a Mercedes.

But on the other hand, I had to try, since he seemed to expect it of me, and I couldn't tip him off as to any gaps in my memory.

So I stooped, squatted, grasped, and started to straighten my legs. With a sucking sound, the rear wheels freed themselves from the moist earth. I was holding my end of the car about two feet above the ground! It was heavy—damn! it was heavy!—but I could do it!

With each step that I took, I sank about six inches into the ground. But I was carrying it. And Random was doing the same with his end.

We set it down on the roadway, with a slight jouncing of springs. Then I took off my shoes and emptied them, cleaned them with swatches of grass, wrung out my socks, brushed off the cuffs of my trousers, threw my footgear into the rear seat and climbed back into the front, bare-footed.

Random jumped in, on the passenger's side, and said, "Look, I want to apologize again—"

"Forget it," I said. "It's over and done with."

"Yes, but I don't want you to hold it against me."

"I won't," I told him. "Just curb your impetuosity in the future, when it involves life-taking in my presence."

"I will," he promised.

"Then let's get rolling," and we did.

We moved through a canyon of rocks, then passed through a city which seemed to be made entirely of glass, or glass-like substance, of tall buildings, thin and fragile-appearing, and of people through whom the pink sun shone, revealing their internal organs and the remains of their last meals. They stared at us as we drove by. They mobbed the corners of their streets, but no one attempted to halt us or pass in front of us.

"The Charles Forts of this place will doubtless quote this happening for many years," said my brother.

I nodded.

Then there was no roadway whatsoever, and we were driving across what seemed an eternal sheet of silicon. After a while it narrowed and became our road, and after another while there were marshes to our left and our right, low, brown, and stinking. And I saw what I'd swear to be a Diplodocus raise its head and stare down upon us. Then, overhead, an enormous bat-winged shape passed by. The sky was now a royal blue, and the sun was of fallow gold.

"We've now got less than a quarter tank of gas," I commented.

"Okay," said Random, "stop the car."

I did this and waited.

For a long time—like maybe six minutes—he was silent, then, "Drive on," he said.

After about three miles we came to a barricade of logs and I began driving around it. A gate occurred on one side, and Random told me, "Stop and blow your horn."

I did so, and after a time the wooden gate creaked upon its huge iron hinges and swung inward.

"Go on in," he said. "It's safe."

I drove in, and off to my left were three bubble-headed Esso pumps, the small building behind them being one of the kind I had seen countless times before, under more ordinary circumstances. I pulled up before one of the pumps and waited.

The guy who emerged from the building was about five feet tall, of enormous girth, with a strawberry-like nose, and his shoulders maybe a yard across.

"What'll it be?" he asked. "Fill 'er up?"

I nodded. "With regular," I said.

"Pull it up a bit," he directed.

I did, and asked Random, "Is my money any good here?"

"Look at it," he told me, and I did.

My wallet was stuffed with orange and yellow bills, Roman numerals in their corners, followed by the letters "D.R."

He grinned at me as I examined the sheaf.

"See, I've taken care of everything," he said.

"Great. By the way, I'm getting hungry."

We looked around us, and we saw a picture of a gent who sells Kentucky Fried Chicken in another place, staring down at us from a big sign.

Strawberry Nose sloshed a little on the ground to make it come out even, hung up the hose, approached, and said, "Eight Drachae Regums."

I found an orange note with a "V D.R." on it and three more with "I D.R." and passed them to him.

"Thanks," he said, and stuffed them in his pocket. "Check your oil and water?"

"Yeah."

He added a little water, told me the oil level was okay, and smeared the windshield a bit with a dirty rag. Then he waved and walked back into the shack.

We drove over to Kenni Roi's and got us a bucket full of Kentucki Fried Lizzard Partes and another bucket of weak, salty-tasting beer.

Then we washed up in the outbuilding, beeped the horn at the gate, and waited till a man with a halberd hanging over his right shoulder came and opened it for us.

Then we hit the road again.

A tyrannosaurus leaped before us, hesitated for a moment, then went on his way, off to the left. Three more pterodactyls passed overhead.

"I am loath to relinquish Amber's sky," said Random, whatever that meant, and I grunted back at him.

"I'm afraid to try it all at once, though," he continued. "We might be torn to bits."

"Agreed," I agreed.

"But on the other hand, I don't like this place."

I nodded, so we drove on, till the silicon plain ended and bare rock lay all about us.

"What are you doing now?" I ventured.

"Now that I've got the sky, I'm going to try for the terrain," he said.

And the rock sheet became rocks, as we drove along. There was bare, black earth between. After a while, there was more earth and fewer rocks. Finally, I saw splotches of green. First a bit of grass here and there. But it was a very, very bright green, of a kind like yet unlike that common on Earth as I knew it.

Soon there was much of it.

After a time there were trees, spotted occasionally along our way.

Then there was a forest.

And what a forest!

I had never seen trees such as this—mighty and majestic, of a deep, rich green, slightly tinged with gold. They towered, they soared. They were enormous pines, oaks, maples, and many others which I could not distinguish. Through them crept a breeze of fantastic and lovely fragrance, when I cracked the window a bit. I decided to open it all the way and leave it like that after I'd had a few whiffs.

"The Forest of Arden," said the man who was my brother, and I knew he was right, and somehow I both loved and envied him for his wisdom, his knowledge.

"Brother," said I, "you're doing all right. Better than I'd expected. Thank you."

This seemed to take him somewhat aback. It was as if he'd never received a good word from a relative before.

"I'm doing my best," he said, "and I'll do it all the way, I promise. Look at it! We've got the sky, and we've got the forest! It's almost too good to be true! We've passed the halfway point, and nothing's bugged us especially. I think we're very fortunate. Will you give me a Regency?"

"Yes," I said, not knowing what it meant, but willing to grant it, if it lay within my powers.

He nodded then and said, "You're okay."

He was a homicidal little fink, who I recalled had always been sort of a rebel. Our parents had tried to discipline him in the past, I knew, never very successfully. And I realized, with that, that we had shared common parents, which I suddenly knew was not the case with me and Eric, me and Flora, me and Caine and Bleys and Fiona. And probably others, but these I'd recalled, I knew for sure.

We were driving on a hard, dirt roadway through a cathedral of enormous trees. It seemed to go on forever and ever. I felt safe in the place. Occasionally, we startled a deer, surprised a fox crossing or standing near the road. In places, the way was marked with hoofprints. The sunlight was sometimes filtered through leaves, angling like tight golden strings on some Hindu musical instrument. The breeze was moist and spoke of living things. It came to me that I knew this place, that I had ridden this road often in the past. I had ridden through the Forest of Arden on horseback, walked through it, hunted in it, lay on my back beneath some of those great boughs, my arms beneath my head, staring upward. I had climbed among the branches of some of those giants and looked down upon a green world, constantly shifting.

"I love this place," I said, only half realizing I had said it aloud, and Random replied, "You always did," and there might have been a trace of amusement in his voice. I couldn't be sure.

Then off in the distance I heard a note which I knew to be the voice of a hunting horn.

"Drive faster," said Random suddenly. "That sounds to be Julian's horn." I obeyed.

The horn sounded again, nearer.

"Those damn hounds of his will tear this car to pieces, and his birds will feed on our eyes!" he said. "I'd hate to meet him when he's this well prepared. Whatever he hunts, I know he'd willingly relinquish it for quarry such as two of his brothers."

" 'Live and let live' is my philosophy these days," I remarked.

Random chuckled.

"What a quaint notion. I'll bet it will last all of five minutes."

Then the horn sounded again, even nearer, and he remarked, "Damn!"

The speedometer said seventy-five, in quaint, runic numerals, and I was afraid to go any faster on that road.

And the horn sounded again, much nearer now, three long notes, and I could hear the baying of hounds, off to the left.

"We are now very near to the real Earth, though still far from Amber," said my brother. "It will be futile to run through adjacent Shadows, for if it is truly us that he follows, he will pursue us. Or his shadow will."

"What shall we do!"

"Speed, and hope it is not us that he follows."

And the horn sounded once again, almost next to us this time.

"What the hell is he riding, a locomotive?" I asked.

"I'd say he is riding the mighty Morgenstern, the fastest horse he has ever created."

I let that last word roll around in my head for a while, wondering at it and wondering at it. Yes, it was true, some inner voice told me. He did create Morgenstern, out of Shadows, fusing into the beast the strength and speed of a hurricane and a pile driver.

I remembered that I had call to fear that animal, and then I saw him.

Morgenstern was six hands higher than any other horse I'd ever seen, and his eyes were the dead color of a Weimaraner dog's and his coat was all gray and his hooves looked like polished steel. He raced along like the wind, pacing the car, and Julian was crouched in his saddle—the Julian of the playing card, long black hair and bright blue eyes, and he had on his scaled white armor.

Julian smiled at us and waved, and Morgenstern tossed his head and his magnificent mane rippled in the wind, like a flag. His legs were a blur.

I recalled that Julian had once had a man wear my castoff garments and torment the beast. This was why it had tried to trample me on the day of a hunt, when I'd dismounted to skin a buck before it.

I'd rolled the window shut once more, so I didn't think it could tell by scent that I was inside the car. But Julian had spotted me, and I thought I knew what that meant. All about him ran the Storm Hounds, with their tough, tough bodies and their teeth like steel. They too had come out of Shadow, for no normal dog could run like that. But I knew, for a certainty, that the word "normal" did not really apply to anything in this place.

Julian signaled us to stop then, and I glanced at Random and he nodded. "If we don't, he'll just run us down," he said. So I hit the brakes, slowed, stopped.

Morgenstern reared, pawed the air, struck the earth with all four hooves and cantered over. The dogs milled about, their tongues hanging out, their sides heaving. The horse was covered with a glistening sheen that I knew to be perspiration.

"What a surprise!" said Julian, in his slow, almost impeded way of speaking; and a great hawk that was black and green circled and settled upon his left shoulder.

"Yes, isn't it," I replied. "How have you been?"

"Oh, capital," he decided, "as always. What of yourself and brother Random?"

"I'm in good shape," I said, and Random nodded and remarked, "I thought you'd be indulging in other sports at a time like this."

Julian tipped his head and regarded him crookedly, through the windshield.

"I enjoy slaughtering beasts," he said, "and I think of my relatives constantly."

A slight coldness worked its way down my back.

"I was distracted from my hunt by the sound of your motor vehicle," he said. "At the time, I did not expect it to contain two such as you. I'd assume you are not simply riding for pleasure, but have a destination in mind, such as Amber. True?"

"True," I agreed. "May I inquire why you are here, rather than there?"

"Eric set me to watching this road," he replied, and my hand came to rest upon one of the pistols in my belt as he spoke. I had a feeling a bullet couldn't breach that armor, though. I considered shooting Morgenstern.

"Well, brothers," he said, smiling, "I welcome you back and I wish you a good journey. I'll doubtless see you shortly in Amber. Good afternoon," and with that he turned and rode toward the woods.

"Let's get the hell out of here," said Random. "He's probably planning an ambush or a chase," and with this he drew a pistol from his belt and held it in his lap.

I drove on at a decent speed.

After about five minutes, when I was just beginning to breathe a bit easily, I heard the horn. I pushed down on the gas pedal, knowing that he'd catch us anyhow, but trying to buy as much time and gain as much distance as I could. We skidded around corners and roared up hills and through dales. I almost hit a deer at one point, but we made it around the beast without cracking up or slowing.

The horn sounded nearer now, and Random was muttering obscenities.

I had the feeling that we still had quite a distance to go within the forest, and this didn't hearten me a bit.

We hit one long straight stretch, where I was able to floor it for almost a minute. Julian's horn notes grew more distant at that time. But we then entered a section where the road wound and twisted and I had to slow down. He began to gain on us at once again.

After about six minutes, he appeared in the rear-view mirror, thundering along the road, his pack all around him, baying and slavering.

Random rolled down his window, and after a minute he leaned out and began to fire.

"Damn that armor!" he said. "I'm sure I hit him twice and nothing's happened."

"I hate the thought of killing that beast," I said, "but try for the horse."

"I already have, several times," he said, tossing his empty pistol to the floor and drawing the other, "and either I'm a lousier shot than I thought, or it's true what they say: that it will take a silver bullet to kill Morgenstern."

He picked off six of the dogs with his remaining rounds, but there were still about two dozen left.

I passed him one of my pistols, and he accounted for five more of the beasts.

"I'll save the last round," he said, "for Julian's head, if he gets close enough!"

They were perhaps fifty feet behind me at that point, and gaining, so I slammed on the brakes. Some of the dogs couldn't halt in time, but Julian was suddenly gone and a dark shadow passed overhead.

Morgenstern had leaped over the car. He wheeled then, and as horse and rider turned to face us I gunned the engine and the car sped forward.

With a magnificent leap, Morgenstern got them out of the way. In the rear-view mirror, I saw two dogs drop a fender they'd torn loose and renew the pursuit. Some were lying in the road, and there were about fifteen or sixteen giving chase.

"Good show," said Random, "but you're lucky they didn't go for the tires. They've probably never hunted a car before."

I passed him my remaining pistol, and "Get more dogs," I said.

He fired deliberately and with perfect accuracy, accounting for six.

And Julian was beside the car now, a sword in his right hand.

I blew the horn, hoping to spook Morgenstern, but it didn't work. I swerved toward them, but the horse danced away. Random crouched low in his seat and aimed past me, his right hand holding the pistol and resting upon his left forearm.

"Don't fire yet," I said. "I'm going to try to take him."

"You're crazy," he told me, as I hit the brakes again.

He lowered his weapon, though.

As soon as we came to a halt, I flung open my door and leaped out—barefooted yet! Damn it!

I ducked beneath his blade, seized his arm, and hurled him from the saddle. He struck me once on the head with his mailed left fist, and there were Roman candles going off all around me and a terrible pain.

He lay where he had fallen, being groggy, and there were dogs all around me, biting me, and Random kicking them. I snatched up Julian's blade from where it lay and touched his throat with its point.

"Call them off!" I cried. "Or I'll nail you to the ground!"

He screamed orders at the dogs and they drew back. Random was holding Morgenstern's bridle and struggling with the horse.

"Now, dear brother, what do you have to say for yourself?" I asked.

There was a cold blue fire within his eyes, and his face was without expression.

"If you're going to kill me, be about it," he said.

"In my own good time," I told him, somehow enjoying the sight of dirt on his impeccable armor. "In the meantime, what is your life worth to you?"

"Anything I've got, of course."

I stepped back.

"Get up and get into the back seat of the car," I told him.

He did this thing, and I took away his dagger before he got in. Random resumed his own seat, and kept his pistol with the single remaining round aimed at Julian's head.

"Why not just kill him?" he asked.

"I think he'll be useful," I said. "There is much that I wish to know. And there is still a long way to travel."

I began to drive. I could see the dogs milling around. Morgenstern began cantering along after the car.

"I'm afraid I won't be worth much to you as a prisoner," Julian observed. "Although you will torture me, I can only tell you what I know, and that isn't much."

"Start with that then," I said.

"Eric looks to have the strongest position," he told us, "having been right there in Amber when the whole thing broke loose. At least this is the way I saw it, so I offered him my support. Had it been one of you, I'd probably have done the same thing. Eric charged me with keeping guard in Arden, since it's one of the main routes. Gérard controls the southern seaways, and Caine is off in the northern waters."

"What of Benedict?" Random asked.

"I don't know. I haven't heard anything. He might be with Bleys. He might be off somewhere else in Shadow and not even have heard of this thing yet. He might even be dead. It's been years since we've heard from him."

"How many men have you got in Arden?" asked Random.

"Over a thousand," he said. "Some are probably watching you right now."

"And if they want you to go on living, that's all they'll do," said Random.

"You are doubtless correct," he replied. "I have to admit, Corwin did a shrewd thing in taking me prisoner rather than killing me. You just might make it through the forest this way."

"You're just saying that because you want to live," said Random.

"Of course I want to live. May I?"

"Why?"

"In payment for the information I've given you."

Random laughed.

"You've given us very little, and I'm sure more can be torn from you. We'll see, as soon as we get a chance to stop. Eh, Corwin?"

"We'll see," I said. "Where's Fiona?"

"Somewhere to the south, I think," Julian replied.

"How about Deirdre?"

"I don't know."

"Llewella?"

"In Rebma."

"Okay," I said, "I think you've told me everything you know."

"I have."

We drove on in silence, and finally the forest began to thin. I'd lost sight of Morgenstern long ago, though I sometimes saw Julian's falcon pacing us. The road took a turn upward, and we were heading toward a pass between two purple mountains. The gas tank was a little better than a quarter full. Within an hour, we were passing between high shoulders of stone.

"This would be a good place to set up a road block," said Random.

"That sounds likely," I said. "What about it, Julian?"

He sighed.

"Yes," he agreed, "you should be coming upon one very soon. You know how to get by it."

We did. When we came to the gate, and the guard in green and brown leather, sword unsheathed, advanced upon us, I jerked my thumb toward the back seat and said, "Get the picture?"

He did, and he recognized us, also.

He hastened to raise the gate, and he saluted us as we passed by.

There were two more gates before we made it through the pass—and somewhere along the way it appeared we had lost the hawk. We had gained several thousand feet in elevation now, and I braked the car on a road that crawled along the face of a cliff. To our right hand, there was nothing other than a long way down.

"Get out," I said. "You're going to take a walk."

Julian paled.

"I won't grovel," he said. "I won't beg you for my life." And he got out.

"Hell," I said, "I haven't had a good grovel in weeks! Well . . . go stand by the edge there. A little closer please." And Random kept his pistol aimed at his head. "A while back," I told him, "you said that you would probably have supported anyone who occupied Eric's position."

"That's right."

"Look down."

He did. It was a long way.

"Okay," I said, "remember that, should things undergo a sudden change. And remember who it was who gave you your life where another would have taken it.

"Come on, Random. Let's get moving."

We left him standing there, breathing heavily, his brows woven together.

We reached the top and were almost out of gas. I put it in neutral, killed the engine, and began the long roll down.

"I've been thinking," said Random; "you've lost none of your old guile. I'd probably have killed him, myself, for what he tried. But I think you did the right thing. I think he will throw us his support, if we can get an edge on Eric. In the meantime, of course, he'll report what happened *to* Eric."

"Of course," I said.

"And you have more reason to want him dead than any of us."

I smiled.

"Personal feelings don't make for good politics, legal decisions, or business deals."

Random lit two cigarettes and handed me one.

Staring downward through the smoke, I caught my first glimpse of that sea. Beneath the deep blue, almost nighttime sky, with that golden sun hanging up there in it, the sea was so rich—thick as paint, textured like a piece of cloth, of royal blue, almost purple—that it troubled me to look upon it. I found myself speaking in a language that I hadn't realized I knew. I was reciting "The Ballad of the Water-Crossers," and Random listened until I had finished and asked me, "It has often been said that you composed that. Is that true?"

"It's been so long," I told him, "that I don't really remember any more."

And as the cliff curved further and further to the left, and as we swung downward across its face, heading toward a wooded valley, more and more of the sea came within our range of vision.

"The Lighthouse of Carba," said Random, gesturing toward an enormous gray tower that rose from the waters, miles out to sea. "I had all but forgotten it."

"And I," I replied. "It is a very strange feeling—coming back," and I realized then that we were no longer speaking English, but the language called Thari.

After almost half an hour, we reached the bottom. I kept coasting for as far as I could, then turned on the engine. At its sound, a flock of dark birds beat its way into the air from the shrubbery off to the left. Something gray and wolfish-looking broke from cover and dashed toward a nearby thicket; the deer it had been stalking, invisible till then, bounded away. We were in a lush valley, though not so thickly or massively wooded as the Forest of Arden, which sloped gently but steadily toward the distant sea.

High, and climbing higher on the left, the mountains reared. The further we advanced into the valley, the better came our view of the nature and full extent of that massive height of rock down one of whose lesser slopes we had coasted. The mountains continued their march to the sea, growing larger as they did so, and taking upon their shoulders a shifting mantle tinged with green, mauve, purple, gold, and indigo. The face they turned to the sea was invisible to us from the valley, but about the back of that final, highest peak swirled the faintest veil of ghost clouds, and occasionally the golden sun touched it with fire. I judged we were about thirty-five miles from the place of light, and the fuel gauge read near empty. I knew that the final peak was out destination, and an eagerness began to grow up within me. Random was staring in the same direction.

"It's still there," I remarked.

"I'd almost forgotten. . . ." he said.

And as I shifted gears, I noticed that my trousers had taken on a certain sheen which they had not possessed before. Also, they were tapered considerably as they reached toward my ankles, and I noted that my cuffs had vanished. Then I noticed my shirt.

It was more like a jacket, and it was black and trimmed with silver; and my belt had widened considerably.

On closer inspection, I saw that there was a silver line down the outer seams of my pants legs.

"I find myself garbed effectively," I observed, to see what that wrought.

Random chuckled, and I saw then that he had somewhere acquired brown trousers streaked with red and a shirt of orange and brown. A brown cap with a yellow border rested on the seat beside him.

"I was wondering when you'd notice," he said. "How do you feel?"

"Quite good," I told him, "and by the way, we're almost out of gas."

"Too late to do much about that," he said. "We are now in the real world, and it would be a horrible effort to play with Shadows. Also, it would not go unnoticed. I'm afraid we'll have to hoof it when this gives out."

It gave out two and a half miles later. I coasted off to the side of the road and stopped. The sun by now was westering farewell, and the shadows had grown long indeed.

I reached into the back seat, where my shoes had become black boots, and something rattled as my hand groped after them.

I drew forth a moderately heavy silver sword and scabbard. The scabbard fit my belt perfectly. There was also a black cloak, with a clasp like a silver rose.

"Had you thought them lost forever?" asked Random.

"Damn near," said I.

We climbed out of the car and began walking. The evening was cool and briskly fragrant. There were stars in the east already, and the sun was diving toward its bed.

We trudged along the road, and Random said:

"I don't feel right about this."

"What do you mean?"

"Things have gone too easily, thus far," he told me. "I don't like it. We made it all the way through to the Forest of Arden with barely a hitch. True, Julian tried to take care of us there—but I don't know. . . . We've made it so very far so readily that I'd almost suspect we were permitted to do it."

"This thought has also crossed my mind," I lied. "What do you think it portends?"

"I fear," said he, "that we are walking into a trap."

We walked on for several minutes in silence.

Then "Ambush?" said I. "These woods seem strangely still."

"I don't know."

We made maybe two miles, and then the sun was gone. The night was black and studded with brilliant stars.

"This is no way for two such as we to move," Random said.

"True."

"Yet I fear to fetch us steeds."

"And I, also."

"What is your assessment of the situation?" Random asked.

"Death and *dreck*," said I. "I feel they may be upon us soon."

"Do you think we should abandon the roadway?"

"I've been thinking about it," I lied again, "and I don't see that it would hurt any of us to walk off to the side a bit."

So we did.

We passed among trees, we moved past the dark shapes of rocks and bushes. And the moon slowly rose, big, of silver, and lighting up the night.

"I am taken by this feeling that we cannot do it," Random told me.

"And what reliance can we give this feeling?" I asked.

"Much."

"Why?"

"Too far and too fast," he responded. "I don't like it at all. Now we're in the real world, it is too late to turn back. We cannot play with Shadows, but must rely on our blades." (He wore a short, burnished one himself.) "I feel, therefore, that it is perhaps Eric's will that we have advanced to this point. There is nothing much to do about it now, but now we're here, I wish we'd had to battle for every inch of the way."

We continued for another mile and paused for cigarettes, which we held cupped in our hands.

"It's a lovely night," I said, to Random and the cool breeze.

"I suppose. . . . What was that?"

There was a soft rustling of shrubbery a bit of a way behind us.

"Some animal, maybe."

His blade was in his hand.

We waited, several minutes, but nothing more was heard.

So he sheathed it and we started walking again.

There were no more sounds from behind us, but after a time I heard something from up ahead.

He nodded when I glanced at him, and we began to move more cautiously.

There was a soft glow, as from a campfire, away, far, in the distance.

We heard no more sounds, but his shrug showed acquiescence to my gesture as I headed toward it, into the woods, to the right.

It was the better part of an hour before we struck the camp. There were four men seated about the fire and two sleeping off in the shadows. The girl who was bound to a stake had her head turned away from us, but I felt my heart quicken as I looked upon her form.

"Could that be . . . ?" I whispered.

"Yes," he replied, "I think it may."

Then she turned her head and I knew it was.

"Deirdre!"

"I wonder what the bitch has been up to?" Random said. "From those guys' colors, I'd venture they're taking her back to Amber."

I saw that they wore black, red, and silver, which I remembered from the Trumps and from somewhere else to be the colors of Eric.

"Since Eric wants her, he can't have her," I said.

"I never much cared for Deirdre," Random said, "but I know you do, so . . ." and he unsheathed his blade.

I did the same.

"Get ready," I told him, rising into a crouch.

And we rushed them.

Maybe two minutes, that's about what it took.

She was watching us by then, the firelight making her face into a twisted mask. She cried and laughed and said our names, in a loud and frightened voice, and I slashed her bonds and helped her to her feet.

"Greetings, sister. Will you join us on the Road to Amber?"

"No," she said. "Thanks for my life, but I want to keep it. Why do you walk to Amber, as if I didn't know."

"There is a throne to be won," said Random, which was news to me, "and we are interested parties."

"If you're smart, you'll stay away and live longer," she said, and God! she was lovely, though a bit tired-looking and dirty.

I took her into my arms because I wanted to, and squeezed her. Random found a skin of wine and we all had a drink.

"Eric is the only prince of Amber," she said, "and the troops are loyal to him."

"I'm not afraid of Eric," I replied, and I knew I wasn't certain about that statement.

"He'll never let you into Amber," she said. "I was a prisoner myself, till I made it out one of the secret ways two days ago. I thought I could walk in Shadows till all things were done, but it is not easy to begin this close to the real place. So his troops found me this morning. They were taking me back. I think he might have killed me, had I been returned—though I'm not sure. At any rate, I'd have remained a puppet in the city. I think Eric may be mad—but again, I'm not sure."

"What of Bleys?" Random inquired.

"He sends things out of the Shadows, and Eric is greatly disturbed. But he has never attacked with his real force, and so Eric is troubled, and the disposition of the Crown and Scepter remains uncertain, though Eric holds the one in his right hand."

"I see. Has he ever spoken of us?"

"Not of you, Random. But of Corwin, yes. He still fears the return of Corwin to Amber. There is relative safety for perhaps five more miles—but beyond that, every step of the way is studded with peril. Every tree and rock is a booby trap and an ambush. Because of Bleys and because of Corwin. He wanted you to get at least this far, so that you could not work with Shadows nor easily escape his power. It is absolutely impossible for either of you to enter into Amber without falling into one of his traps."

"Yet you escaped. . . ."

"That was different. I was trying to get out, not in. Perhaps he did not guard me so carefully as he would one of you, because of my sex and my lack of ambition. And nevertheless, as you can, I did not succeed."

"You have now, sister," I said, "so long as my blade is free to swing on your behalf," and she kissed my brow and squeezed my hand. I was always a sucker for that.

"I'm sure we're being followed," said Random, and with a gesture the three of us faded into the darkness.

We lay still beneath a bush, keeping watch on our trail.

After a time, our whispers indicated that there was a decision for me to make. The question was really quite simple: What next?

The question was too basic, and I couldn't stall any more. I knew I couldn't trust them, even dear Deirdre, but if I had to level with anybody, Random was at least in this thing with me, up to his neck, and Deirdre was my favorite.

"Beloved relatives," I told them, "I've a confession to make," and Random's hand was already on the hilt of his blade. That's how far we could trust one another. I could already hear his mind clicking: *Corwin brought me here to betray me,* he was saying to himself.

"If you brought me here to betray me," he said, "you won't take me back alive."

"Are you kidding?" I asked. "I want your help, not your head. What I have to say is just this: I don't know what the hell's going on. I've made some guesses, but I don't really know where the devil we are, what Amber is, or why we're crouched here in the bushes hiding from his troops," I told him, "or for that matter, who I am, really."

There was an awfully long silence, and then Random whispered, "What do you mean?"

"Yes," said Deirdre.

"I mean," I said, "that I managed to fool you, Random. Didn't you think it strange that all I did on this trip was drive the car?"

"You were the boss," he told me, "and I figured you were planning. You did some pretty shrewd things along the way. I know that you're Corwin."

"Which is a thing I only found out a couple of days ago, myself," I said. "I know that I am the one you call Corwin, but I was in an accident a while back. I had head injuries—I'll show you the scars when we've got more light—and I am suffering from amnesia. I don't dig all this talk about Shadows. I don't even remember much about Amber. All I remember is my relatives, and the fact that I can't trust them much. That's my story. What's to be done about it?"

"Christ!" said Random. "Yes, I can see it now! I understand all the little things that puzzled me along the way. . . . How did you take Flora in so completely?"

"Luck," I said, "and subconscious sneakiness, I guess. No! That's not it! She was stupid. Now I really need you, though."

"Do you think we can make it into the Shadows?" said Deirdre, and she was not speaking to me.

"Yes," said Random, "but I'm not for it. I'd like to see Corwin in Amber, and I'd like to see Eric's head on a pole. I'm willing to take a few chances to see these things, so I'm not turning back to the Shadows. You can if you want. You all think I'm a weakling and a bluff. Now you're going to find out. I'm going to see this through."

"Thanks, brother," I said.

"Ill-met by moonlight," said Deirdre.

"You could still be tied to a stake," said Random, and she did not reply.

We lay there a while longer and three men entered the campsite and looked about. Then two of them bent down and sniffed at the ground.

Then they looked in our direction.

"*Weir*," whispered Random, as they moved in our direction.

I saw it happen, though only in shadow. They dropped to all fours and the moonlight played tricks with their gray garments. Then there were the six blazing eyes of our stalkers.

I impaled the first wolf on my silver blade and there was a human howl. Random beheaded one with a single blow, and to my amazement, I saw Deirdre raise one in the air and break its back across her knee with a brittle, snapping sound.

"Quick, your blade!" said Random, and I ran his victim through, and hers, and there were more cries.

"We'd better move fast," said Random. "This way!" and we followed.

"Where are we going?" asked Deirdre, after perhaps an hour of furtive movement through the undergrowth.

"To the sea," he replied.

"Why?"

"It holds Corwin's memory."

"Where? How?"

"Rebma, of course."

"They'd kill you there and feed your brains to the fishes."

"I'm not going the full distance. You'll have to take over at the shore and talk with your sister's sister."

"You mean for him to take the Pattern again?"

"Yes."

"It's risky."

"I know. . . . Listen, Corwin," he said, "you've been decent enough with me recently. If by some chance you're not really Corwin, you're dead. You've got to be, though. You can't be someone else. Not from the way you've operated, without memory even. No, I'll bet your life on it. Take a chance and try the thing called the Pattern. Odds are, it'll restore your memory. Are you game?"

"Probably," I said, "but what is the Pattern?"

"Rebma is a ghost city," he told me. "It is the reflection of Amber within the sea. In it, everything in Amber is duplicated, as in a mirror. Llewella's people live there, and dwell as though in Amber. They hate me for a few past peccadilloes, so I cannot venture there with you, but if you would speak them fair and perhaps hint at your mission, I feel they will let you walk the Pattern of Rebma, which, while it is the reverse of that in Amber, should have the same effect. That is, it gives to a son of our father the power to walk among Shadows."

"How will this power help me?"

"It should make you know what you are."

"Then I'm game," I said.

"Good man. In that case, we'll keep heading south. It will take several days to reach the stairway . . . You will go with him, Deirdre?"

"I will go with my brother Corwin."

I knew she would say that, and I was glad. I was afraid, but I was glad.

We walked all that night. We avoided three parties of armed troops, and in the morning we slept in a cave.

FIVE

We spent two evenings making our way to the pink and sable sands of the great sea. It was on the morning of the third day that we arrived at the beach, having successfully avoided a small party the sundown before. We were loath to step out into the open until we had located the precise spot, Faiella-bionin, the Stairway to Rebma, and could cross quickly to it.

The rising sun cast billions of bright shards into the foaming swell of the waters, and our eyes were dazzled by their dance so that we could not see beneath the surface. We had lived on fruit and water for two days and I was ravenously hungry, but I forgot this as I regarded the wide, sloping tiger beach with its sudden twists and rises of coral, orange, pink, and red, and its abrupt caches of shells, driftwood, and small polished stones; and the sea beyond: rising and falling, splashing softly, all gold and blue and royal purple, and casting forth its life-song breezes like benedictions beneath dawn's violet skies.

The mountain that faces the dawn, Kolvir, which has held Amber like a mother her child for all of time, stood perhaps twenty miles to our left, the north, and the sun covered her with gold and made rainbow the veil above the city. Random looked upon it and gnashed his teeth, then looked away. Maybe I did, too.

Deirdre touched my hand, gestured with her head, and began to walk toward the north, parallel to the shore. Random and I followed. She had apparently spotted some landmark.

We'd advanced perhaps a quarter of a mile, when it seemed that the earth shook lightly.

"Hoofbeats!" hissed Random.

"Look!" said Deirdre, and her head was tilted back and she was pointing upward.

My eyes followed the gesture.

Overhead a hawk circled.

"How much farther is it?" I asked.

"That cairn of stones," she said, and I saw it perhaps a hundred yards away, about eight feet in height, built of head-sized, gray stones, worn by the wind, the sand, the water, standing in the shape of a truncated pyramid.

The hoofbeats came louder, and then there were the notes of a horn, not Julian's call, though.

"Run!" said Random, and we did.

After perhaps twenty-five paces, the hawk descended. It swooped at Random, but he had his blade out and took a cut at it. Then it turned its attention to Deirdre.

I snatched my own blade from its sheath and tried a cut. Feathers flew. It rose and dropped again, and this time my blade hit something hard—and I think it fell, but I couldn't tell for sure, because I wasn't about to stop and look back. The sound of hoofbeats was quite steady now, and loud, and the horn notes were near at hand.

We reached the cairn and Deirdre turned at right angles to it and headed straight toward the sea.

I was not about to argue with someone who seemed to know what she was doing. I followed, and from the corner of my eye I saw the horsemen.

They were still off in the distance, but they were thundering along the beach, dogs barking and horns blowing, and Random and I ran like hell and waded out into the surf after our sister.

We were up to our waists when Random said, "It's death if I stay and death if I go on."

"One is imminent," I said, "and the other may be open to negotiation. Let's move!"

We did. We were on some sort of rocky surface which descended into the sea. I didn't know how we would breathe while we walked it, but Deirdre didn't seem worried about it, so I tried not to be.

But I was.

When the water swirled and swished about our heads, I was very worried. Deirdre walked straight ahead, though, descending, and I followed, and Random followed.

Each few feet there was a drop. We were descending an enormous staircase, and it was named Faiella-bionin, I knew.

One more step would bring the water above my head, but Deirdre had already dropped below the water line.

So I drew a deep breath and took the plunge.

There were more steps and I kept following them. I wondered why my body was not naturally buoyed above them, for I continued to remain erect and each step bore me downward as though on a natural staircase, though my movements were somewhat slowed. I began wondering what I'd do when I could hold my breath no longer.

There were bubbles about Random's head, and Deirdre's. I tried to observe what they were doing, but I couldn't figure it. Their breasts seemed to be rising and falling in a normal manner.

When we were about ten feet beneath the surface, Random glanced at me from where he moved at my left side, and I heard his voice. It was as though I had my ear pressed against the bottom of a bathtub and each of his words came as the sound of someone kicking upon the side.

They were clear, though:

"I don't think they'll persuade the dogs to follow, even if the horses do," he said.

"How are you managing to breathe?" I tried saying, and I heard my own words distantly.

"Relax," he said quickly. "If you're holding your breath, let it out and don't worry. You'll be able to breathe so long as you don't venture off the stairway."

"How can that be?" I asked.

"If we make it, you'll know," he said, and his voice had a ringing quality to it, through the cold and passing green.

We were about twenty feet beneath the surface by then, and I exhaled a small amount of air and tried inhaling for perhaps a second.

There was nothing disturbing about the sensation, so I protracted it. There were more bubbles, but beyond that I felt nothing uncomfortable in the transition.

There was no sense of increasing pressure during the next ten feet or so, and I could see the staircase on which we moved as though through a greenish fog. Down, down, down it led. Straight. Direct. And there was some kind of light coming from below us.

"If we can make it through the archway, we'll be safe," said my sister.

"*You'll* be safe," Random corrected, and I wondered what he had done to be despised in the place called Rebma.

"If they ride horses which have never made the journey before, then they'll have to follow on foot," said Random. "In that case, we'll make it."

"So they might not follow—if that is the case," said Deirdre.

We hurried.

By the time we were perhaps fifty feet below the surface, the waters grew quite dark and chill, but the glow before us and below us increased, and after another ten steps, I could make out the source:

There was a pillar rising to the right. At its top was something globe-like and glowing. Perhaps fifteen steps lower, another such formation occurred to the left. Beyond that, it seemed there was another one on the right, and so on.

When we entered the vicinity of the thing, the waters grew warmer and the stairway itself became clear: it was white, shot through with pink and green, and resembled marble but was not slippery despite the water. It was perhaps fifty feet in width, and there was a wide banister of the same substance on either side.

Fishes swam past us as we walked it. When I looked back over my shoulder, there seemed to be no sign of pursuit.

It became brighter. We entered the vicinity of the first light, and it wasn't a globe on the top of a pillar. My mind must have added that touch to the phenomenon, to try to rationalize it at least a bit. It appeared to be a flame, about two feet in height, dancing there, as atop a huge torch. I decided to ask about it later, and saved my—if you'll excuse the expression—breath, for the rapid descent we were making.

After we had entered the alley of light and had passed six more of the torches, Random said, "They're after us," and I looked back again and saw distant figures descending, four of them on horseback.

It is a strange feeling to laugh under water and hear yourself.

"Let them," I said, and I touched the hilt of my blade, "for now we have made it this far, I feel a power upon me!"

We hurried though, and off to our left and to our right the water grew black as ink. Only the stairway was illuminated, in our mad flight down it, and distantly I saw what appeared to be a mighty arch.

Deirdre was leaping down the stairs two at a time, and there came a vibration now, from the staccato beat of the horses' hooves behind us.

The band of armed men—filling the way from banister to banister—was far behind and above. But the four horsemen had gained on us. We followed Deirdre as she rushed downward, and my hand stayed upon my blade.

Three, four, five. We passed that many lights before I looked back again and saw that the horsemen were perhaps fifty feet above us. The footmen were now almost out of sight. The archway loomed ahead, perhaps two hundred feet distant. Big, shining like alabaster, and carved with Tritons, sea nymphs, mermaids, and dolphins, it was. And there seemed to be people on the other side of it.

"They must wonder why we have come here," said Random.

"It will be an academic point if we don't make it," I replied, hurrying, as another glance revealed that the horsemen had gained ten feet on us.

I drew my blade then, and it flashed in the torchlight. Random followed suit.

After another twenty steps or so, the vibrations were terrible within the green and we turned, so as not to be cut down as we ran.

They were almost upon us. The gates lay a hundred feet to our back, and it might have been a hundred miles, unless we could take the four horsemen.

I crouched, as the man who was headed toward me swung his blade. There was another rider to his right and slightly to his rear, so naturally I moved to his left, near to the rail. This required that he strike cross-body, as he held his blade in his right hand.

When he struck, I parried in *quarte* and riposted.

He was leaning far forward in the saddle, and the point of my blade entered his neck on the right side.

A great billow of blood, like crimson smoke, arose and swirled within the greenish light. Crazily, I wished Van Gogh were there to see it.

The horse continued past, and I leaped at the second rider from the rear.

He turned to parry the stroke, succeeded. But the force of his speed through the water and the strength of my blow removed him from the saddle. As he fell, I kicked, and he drifted. I struck at him, hovering there above me, and he parried again, but this carried him beyond the rail. I heard him scream as the pressure of the waters came upon him. Then he was silent.

I turned my attention then to Random, who had slain both a horse and a man and was dueling with a second man on foot. By the time I reached them, he had slain the man and was laughing. The blood billowed above them, and I suddenly realized that I *had* known mad, sad, bad Vincent Von Gogh, and it was really too bad that he couldn't have painted this.

The footmen were perhaps a hundred feet behind us, and we turned and headed toward the arches. Deirdre had already passed through them.

We ran and we made it. There were many swords at our sides, and the footmen turned back. Then we sheathed our blades, and Random said, "I've had it," and we moved to join with the band of people who had stood to defend us.

Random was immediately ordered to surrender his blade, and he shrugged and handed it over. Then two men came and stood on either side of him and a third at his back, and we continued on down the stair.

I lost all sense of time in that watery place, but I feel that we walked for somewhere between a quarter of an hour and half an hour before we reached our destination.

The golden gates of Rebma stood before us. We passed through them. We entered the city.

Everything was to be seen through a green haze. There were buildings, all of them fragile and most of them high, grouped in patterns and standing in colors that entered my eyes and tore through my mind, seeking after remembrance. They failed, the sole result of their digging being the now familiar ache that accompanies the half recalled, the unrecalled. I had walked these streets before, however, that I knew, or ones very much like them.

Random had not said a single word since he had been taken into custody. Deirdre's only conversation had been to inquire after our sister Llewella. She had been informed that Llewella was in Rebma.

I examined our escort. They were men with green hair, purple hair, and black hair, and all of them had eyes of green, save for one fellow whose were of a hazel color. All wore only scaled trunks and cloaks, cross-braces on their breasts, and short swords depending from sea-shell belts. All were pretty much lacking in body hair. None of them spoke to me, though some stared and some glared. I was allowed to keep my weapon.

Inside the city, we were conducted up a wide avenue, lighted by pillar flames set at even closer intervals than on Faiella-bionin, and people stared out at us from behind octagonal, tinted windows, and bright-bellied fishes swam by. There came a cool current, like a breeze, as we turned a corner; and after a few steps, a warm one, like a wind.

We were taken to the palace in the center of the city, and I knew it as my hand knew the glove in my belt. It was an image of the palace of Amber, obscured only by the green and confused by the many strangely placed mirrors which had been set within its walls, inside and out. A woman sat upon the throne in the glassite room I almost recalled, and her hair was green, though streaked with silver, and her eyes were round as moons of jade and her brows rose like the wings of olive gulls. Her mouth was small, her chin was small; her cheeks were high and wide and rounded. A circlet of white gold crossed her brow and there was a crystal necklace about her neck. At its tips there flashed a sapphire between her sweet bare breasts, whose nipples were also a pale green. She wore scaled trunks of blue and a silver belt, and she held a scepter of pink coral in her right hand and had a ring upon every finger, and each ring had a stone of a different blue within it. She did not smile as she spoke:

"What seek you here, outcasts of Amber?" she asked, and her voice was a lisping, soft, flowing thing.

Deirdre spoke in reply, saying: "We flee the wrath of the prince who sits in the true city—Eric! To be frank, we wish to work his downfall. If he is loved here, we are lost, and we have delivered ourselves into the hands of our enemies. But I feel he is not loved here. So we come asking aid, gentle Moire—"

"I will not give you troops to assault Amber," she replied. "As you know, the chaos would be reflected within my own realm."

"That is not what we would have of you, dear Moire," Deirdre continued, "but only a small thing, to be achieved at no pain or cost to yourself or your subjects."

"Name it! For as you know, Eric is almost as disliked here as this recreant who stands at your left hand," and with this she gestured at my brother, who stared at her in frank and insolent appraisal, a small smile playing about the corners of his lips.

If he was going to pay—whatever the price—for whatever he had done, I could see that he would pay it like a true prince of Amber—as our three dead brothers had done ages ago, I suddenly recalled. He would pay it, mocking them the while, laughing though his mouth was filled with the blood of his body, and as he died he would pronounce an irrevocable curse which would come to pass. I too, had this power, I suddenly knew, and I would use it if circumstances required its use.

"The thing I would ask," she said, "is for my brother Corwin, who is also brother to the Lady Llewella, who dwells here with you. I believe that he has never given you offense. . . ."

"That is true. But why does he not speak for himself?"

"That is a part of the problem, Lady. He cannot, for he does not know what to ask. Much of his memory has departed, from an accident which occurred when he dwelled among Shadows. It is to restore his remembrance that we have come here, to bring back his recollection of the old days, that he might oppose Eric in Amber."

"Continue," said the woman on the throne, regarding me through the shadows of her lashes on her eyes.

"In a place in this building," she said, "there is a room where few would go. In that room," she continued, "upon the floor, traced in fiery outline, there lies a duplicate of the thing we call the Pattern. Only a son or daughter of Amber's late liege may walk this Pattern and live; and it gives to such a person a power over Shadow." Here Moire blinked several times, and I speculated as to the number of her subjects she had sent upon that path, to gain some control of this power for Rebma. Of course, she had failed. "To walk the Pattern," Deirdre went on, "should, we feel, restore to Corwin his memory of himself as a prince of Amber. He cannot go to Amber to do it, and this is the only place I know where it is duplicated, other than Tir-na Nog'th, where of course we may not go at this time."

Moire turned her gaze upon my sister, swept it over Random, returned it to me.

"Is Corwin willing to essay this thing?" she asked.

I bowed.

"Willing, m'lady," I said, and she smiled then.

"Very well, you have my permission. I can guarantee you no guarantees of safety beyond my realm, however."

"As to that, your majesty," said Deirdre, "we expect no boons, but will take care of it ourselves upon our departure."

"Save for Random," she said, "who will be quite safe."

"What mean you?" asked Deirdre, for Random would not, of course, speak for himself under the circumstances.

"Surely you recall," she said, "that one time Prince Random came into my realm as a friend, and did thereafter depart in haste with my daughter Morganthe."

"I have heard this said, Lady Moire, but I am not aware of the truth or the baseness of the tale."

"It is true," said Moire, "and a month thereafter was she returned to me. Her suicide came some months after the birth of her son Martin. What have you to say to that, Prince Random?"

"Nothing," said Random.

"When Martin came of age," said Moire, "because he was of the blood of Amber, he determined to walk the Pattern. He is the only of my people to have succeeded. Thereafter, he walked in Shadow and I have not seen him since. What have you to say to that, Lord Random?"

"Nothing," Random replied.

"Therefore, I will punish thee," Moire continued. "You shall marry the woman of my choice and remain with her in my realm for a year's time, or you will forfeit your life. What say you to that, Random?"

Random said nothing, but he nodded abruptly.

She stuck her scepter upon the arm of her turquoise throne.

"Very well," she said. "So be it."

And so it was.

We repaired to the chambers she had granted us, there to refresh ourselves. Subsequently she appeared at the door of my own.

"Hail, Moire," I said.

"Lord Corwin of Amber," she told me, "often have I wished to meet thee."

"And I thee," I lied.

"Your exploits are legend."

"Thank you, but I barely recall the high points."

"May I enter here?"

"Certainly," and I stepped aside.

She moved into the well-appointed suite she had granted me. She seated herself upon the edge of the orange couch.

"When would you like to essay the Pattern?"

"As soon as possible," I told her.

She considered this, then said, "Where have you been, among Shadows?"

"Very far from here," I said, "in a place that I learned to love."

"It is strange that a lord of Amber should possess this capacity."

"What capacity?"

"To love," she replied.

"Perhaps I chose the wrong word."

"I doubt it," she said, "for the ballads of Corwin do touch upon the strings of the heart."

"The lady is kind."

"But not wrong," she replied.

"I'll give you a ballad one day."

"What did you do when you dwelled in Shadow?"

"It occurs to me that I was a professional soldier, madam. I fought for whoever would pay me. Also, I composed the words and music to many popular songs."

"Both these things occur to me as logical and natural."

"Pray tell me, what of my brother Random?"

"He will marry with a girl among my subjects who is named Vialle. She is blind and has no wooers among our kind."

"Are you certain," said I, "that you do the best thing for her?"

"She will obtain good status in this manner," said Moire, "though he depart after a year and never return. For whatever else may be said of him, he *is* a prince of Amber."

"What if she comes to love him?"

"Could anyone really do this thing?"

"In my way, I love him, as a brother."

"Then this is the first time a son of Amber has ever said such a thing, and I attribute it to your poetic temperament."

"Whatever," said I, "be very sure that it is the best thing for the girl."

"I have considered it," she told me, "and I am certain. She will recover from whatever pain he inflicts, and after his departure she will be a great lady of my court."

"So may it be," I said, and looked away, feeling a sadness come over me—for the girl, of course.

"What may I say to you?" I said. "Perhaps you do a good thing. I hope so." And I took her hand and kissed it.

"You, Lord Corwin, are the only prince of Amber I might support," she told me, "save possibly for Benedict. He is gone these twelve years and ten, however, and Lir knows where his bones may lie. Pity."

"I did not know this," I said. "My memory is so screwed up. Please bear with me. I shall miss Benedict, an' he be dead. He was my Master of Arms and taught me of all weapons. But he was gentle."

"As are you, Corwin," she told me, taking my hand and drawing me toward her.

"No, not really," I replied, as I seated myself on the couch at her side. Then she said, "We've much time till we dine." Then she leaned against me with the front of her shoulder which was soft.

"When do we eat?" I asked.

"Whenever I declare it," she said, and she faced me more fully.

So I drew her upon me and found the catch to the buckle which covered the softness of her belly. There was more softness beneath, and her hair was green.

Upon the couch, I gave her her ballad. Her lips replied without words.

After we had eaten—and I had learned the trick of eating under water, which I might detail later on if circumstances really warrant—we rose from our places within the marble high hall, decorated with nets and ropes of red and brown, and we made our way back along a narrow corridor, and down, down, beneath the floor of the sea itself, first by means of a spiral staircase that screwed its way through absolute darkness and glowed. After about twenty paces, my brother said, "Screw!" and stepped off the staircase and began swimming downward alongside it.

"It *is* faster that way," said Moire.

"And it is a long way down," said Deirdre, knowing the distance of the one in Amber.

So we all stepped off and swam downward through darkness, beside the glowing, twisting thing.

It took perhaps ten minutes to reach the bottom, but when our feet touched the floor, we stood, with no tendency to drift. There was light about us then, from a few feeble flames set within niches in the wall.

"Why is this part of the ocean, within the double of Amber, so different from waters elsewhere?" I asked.

"Because that is the way it is," said Deirdre, which irritated me.

We were in an enormous cavern, and tunnels shot off from it in all directions. We moved toward one.

After walking along it for an awfully long while, we began to encounter side passages, some of which had doors or grilles before them and some of which did not.

At the seventh of these we stopped. It was a huge gray door of some slate-like substance, bound in metal, towering to twice my height. I remembered something about the size of Tritons as I regarded the doorway. Then Moire smiled, just at me, and produced a large key from a ring upon her belt and set it within the lock.

She couldn't turn it, though. Perhaps the thing had been unused for too long.

Random growled and his hand shot forward, knocking hers aside.

He seized the key in his right hand and twisted.

There came a click.

Then he pushed the door open with his foot and we stared within.

In a room the size of a ballroom the Pattern was laid. The floor was black and looked smooth as glass. And on the floor was the Pattern.

It shimmered like the cold fire that it was, quivered, made the whole room seem somehow unsubstantial. It was an elaborate tracery of bright power, composed mainly of curves, though there were a few straight lines near its middle. It reminded me of a fantastically intricate, life-scale version of one of those maze things you do with a pencil (or ballpoint, as the case may be), to get you into or out of something. Like, I could almost see the words "Start Here," somewhere way to the back. It was perhaps a hundred yards across at its narrow middle, and maybe a hundred and fifty long.

It made bells ring within my head, and then came the throbbing. My mind recoiled from the touch of it. But if I were a prince of Amber, then somewhere within my blood, my nervous system, my genes, this pattern was recorded somehow, so that I would respond properly, so that I could walk the bloody thing.

"Sure wish I could have a cigarette," I said, and the girls giggled, though rather a little too rapidly and perhaps with a bit of a twist of the treble control.

Random took my arm and said, "It's an ordeal, but it's not impossible or we wouldn't be here. Take it very slowly and don't let yourself be distracted. Don't be alarmed by the shower of sparks that will arise with each step. They can't hurt you. You'll feel a mild current passing through you the whole time, and after a while you'll start feeling high. But keep concentrating, and don't forget—keep walking! Don't stop, whatever you do, and don't stray from the path, or it'll probably kill you," and as he spoke, we walked. We walked close to the right-hand wall and rounded the Pattern, heading toward its far end. The girls trailed behind us.

I whispered to him.

"I tried to talk her out of this thing she's planned for you. No luck."

"I figured you would," he said. "Don't worry about it. I can do a year standing on my head, and they might even let me go sooner—if I'm obnoxious enough."

"The girl she has lined up for you is named Vialle. She's blind."

"Great," he said. "Great joke."

"Remember that regency we spoke of?"

"Yeah."

"Be kind to her then, stay the full year, and I will be generous."

Nothing.

Then he squeezed my arm.

"Friend of yours, huh?" he chuckled. "What's she like?"

"Is it a deal?" I said, slowly.

"It's a deal."

Then we stood at the place where the Pattern began, near to the corner of the room.

I moved forward and regarded the line of inlaid fires that started near to the spot where I had placed my right foot. The Pattern constituted the only illumination within the room. The waters were chill about me.

I strode forward, setting my left foot upon the path. It was outlined by blue-white sparks. Then I set my right foot upon it, and I felt the current Random had mentioned. I took another step.

There was a crackle and I felt my hair beginning to rise. I took another step.

Then the thing began to curve, abruptly, back upon itself. I took ten more paces, and a certain resistance seemed to arise. It was as if a black barrier had grown up before me, of some substance which pushed back upon me with each effort that I made to pass forward.

I fought it. It was the First Veil, I suddenly knew.

To get beyond it would be an Achievement, a good sign, showing that I was indeed part of the Pattern. Each raising and lowering of my foot suddenly required a terrible effort, and sparks shot forth from my hair.

I concentrated on the fiery line. I walked it breathing heavily.

Suddenly the pressure was eased. The Veil had parted before me, as abruptly as it had occurred. I had passed beyond it and acquired something.

I had gained a piece of myself.

I saw the paper skins and the knobby, stick-like bones of the dead of Auschwitz. I had been present at Nuremberg, I knew. I heard the voice of Stephen Spender reciting "Vienna," and I saw Mother Courage cross the stage on the night of a Brecht premiere. I saw the rockets leap up from the stained hard places, Peenemunde, Vanderberg, Kennedy, Kyzyl Kum in Kazakhstan, and I touched with my hands the Wall of China. We were drinking beer and wine, and Shaxpur said he was drunk and went off to puke. I entered the green forests of the Western Reserve and took three scalps one day. I hummed a tune as we marched along and it caught on. It became "Auprés de ma Blonde." I remembered, I remembered . . . my life within the Shadow place its inhabitants had called the Earth. Three more steps, and I held a bloody blade and saw three dead men and my horse, on which I had fled the revolution in France. And more, so much more, back to—

I took another step.

Back to—

The dead. They were all about me. There was a horrible stink—the smell of decaying flesh—and I heard the howls of a dog who was being beaten to death. Billows of black smoke filled the sky, and an icy wind swept around me bearing a few small drops of rain. My throat was parched and my hands shook and my head was on fire. I staggered alone, seeing everything through the haze of the fever that burned me. The gutters were filled with garbage and dead cats and the emptyings of chamber pots. With a rattle and the ringing of a bell, the death wagon thundered by, splashing me with mud and cold water.

How long I wandered, I do not know, before a woman seized my arm and I saw a Death's Head ring upon her finger. She led me to her rooms, but discovered there that I had no money and was incoherent. A look of fear crossed her painted face, erasing the smile on her bright lips, and she fled and I collapsed upon her bed.

Later—again, how much later I do not know—a big man, the girl's Black Davy, came and slapped me across the face and dragged me to my feet. I seized his right biceps and hung on. He half carried, half pulled me toward the door.

When I realized that he was going to cast me out into the cold, I tightened my grip to protest it. I squeezed with all my remaining strength, mumbling half-coherent pleas.

Then through sweat and tear-filled eyes, I saw his face break open and heard a scream come forth from between his stained teeth.

The bone in his arm had broken where I'd squeezed it.

He pushed me away with his left hand and fell to his knees, weeping. I sat upon the floor, and my head cleared for a moment.

"I . . . am . . . staying here," I said, "until I feel better. Get out. If you come back—I'll kill you."

"You've got the plague!" he cried. "They'll come for your bones tomorrow!" and he spat then, got to his feet, and staggered out.

I made it to the door and barred it. Then I crawled back to the bed and slept.

If they came for my bones the next day, they were disappointed. For, perhaps ten hours later, in the middle of the night, I awoke in a cold sweat and realized my fever had broken. I was weak, but rational once more.

I realized I had lived through the plague.

I took a man's cloak I found in the wardrobe and took some money I found in a drawer.

Then I went forth into London and the Night, in a year of the plague, looking for something. . . .

I had no recollection of who I was or what I was doing there.

That was how it had started.

I was well into the Pattern now, and the sparks flashed continually about my feet, reaching to the height of my knees. I no longer knew which direction I faced, or where Random and Deirdre and Moire stood. The currents swept through me, and it seemed my eyeballs were vibrating. Then came a pins-and-needle feeling in my cheeks and a coldness on the back of my neck. I clenched my teeth to keep them from chattering.

The auto accident had not given me my amnesia. I had been without full memory since the reign of Elizabeth I. Flora must have concluded that the recent accident had restored me. She had known of my condition. I was suddenly struck by the thought that she was on that Shadow Earth mainly to keep tabs on me.

Since the sixteenth century, then?

That I couldn't say. I'd find out, though.

I took six more rapid steps, reaching the end of an arc and coming to the beginning place of a straight line.

I set my foot upon it, and with each step that I took, another barrier began to rise against me. It was the Second Veil.

There was a right-angle turn, then another, then another.

I was a prince of Amber. It was true. There had been fifteen brothers and six were dead. There had been eight sisters, and two were dead, possibly four. We had spent much of our time in wandering in Shadow, or in our own universes. It is an academic, though valid philosophical question, as to whether one with power over Shadow could create his own universe. Whatever the ultimate answer, from a practical point we could.

Another curve began, and it was as though I were walking in glue as I moved slowly along it.

One, two, three, four . . . I raised my fiery boots and let them down again.

My head throbbed and my heart felt as though it were fibrillating to pieces.

Amber!

The going was suddenly easy once more, as I remembered Amber.

Amber was the greatest city which had ever existed or ever would exist. Amber had always been and always would be, and every other city, everywhere, every other city that existed was but a reflection of a shadow of some phase of Amber. Amber, Amber, Amber . . . I remember thee. I shall never forget thee again. I guess, deep inside me, I never really did, through all those centuries I wandered the Shadow Earth, for often at night my dreams were troubled by images of thy green and golden spires and thy sweeping terraces. I remember thy wide promenades and the decks of flowers, golden and red. I recall the sweetness of thy airs, and the temples, palaces, and pleasances thou containest, contained, will always contain. Amber, immortal city from which every other city has taken its shape, I cannot forget thee, even now, nor forget that day on the Pattern of Rebma when I remembered thee within thy reflected walls, fresh from a meal after starvation and the loving of Moire, but nothing could compare with the pleasure and the love of remembering thee; and even now, as I stand contemplating the Courts of Chaos, telling this story to the only one present to hear, that perhaps he may repeat it, that it will not die after I have died within; even now, I remember thee with love, city that I was born to rule. . . .

Ten paces, then a swirling filigree of fire confronted me. I essayed it, my sweat vanishing into the waters as fast as it sprang forth.

It was tricky, so devilishly tricky, and it seemed that the waters of the room suddenly moved in great currents which threatened to sweep me from the Pattern. I struggled on, resisting them. Instinctively, I knew that to leave the Pattern before I'd completed it would mean my death. I dared not raise my eyes from the places of light that lay before me, to see how far I had come, how far I had yet to go.

The currents subsided and more of my memories returned, memories of my life as a prince of Amber. . . . No, they are not yours for the asking; they are mine, some vicious and cruel, other perhaps noble—memories going back to my childhood in the great palace of Amber, with the green banner of my father Oberon flaring above it, white unicorn rampant, facing to the dexter.

Random had made it through the Pattern. Even Deirdre had made it. Therefore, I, Corwin, would make it, no matter what the resistance.

I emerged from the filigree and marched along the Grand Curve. The forces that shape the universe fell upon me and beat me into their image.

I had an advantage over any other person who attempted the walk, however. I knew that I had done it before, so I knew that I could do it. This helped me against the unnatural fears which rose like black clouds and were gone again, only to return, their strength redoubled. I walked the Pattern and I remembered all, I remembered all the days before my centuries on the Shadow Earth and I remembered other places of Shadow, many of them special and dear to me, and one which I loved above all, save for Amber.

I walked three more curves, a straight line, and a series of sharp arcs, and I held within me once again a consciousness of the things which I had never really lost: mine was the power over Shadows.

Ten turns which left me dizzy, another short arc, a straight line, and the Final Veil.

It was agony to move. Everything tried to beat me aside. The waters were cold, then boiling. It seemed that they constantly pushed against me. I struggled, putting one foot before the other. The sparks reached as high as my waist at this point, then my breast, my shoulders. They were into my eyes. They were all about me. I could barely see the Pattern itself.

Then a short arc, ending in blackness.

One, two. . . . And to take the last step was like trying to push through a concrete wall.

I did it.

Then I turned slowly and looked back over the course I had come. I would not permit myself the luxury of sagging to my knees. I was a prince of Amber, and by God! nothing could humble me in the presence of my peers. Not even the Pattern!

I waved jauntily in what I thought to be the right direction. Whether or not I could be made out very clearly was another matter.

Then I stood there a moment and thought.

I knew the power of the Pattern now. Going back along it would be no trick at all.

But why bother?

I lacked my deck of cards, but the power of the Pattern could serve me just as well. . . .

They were waiting for me, my brother and sister and Moire with her thighs like marble pillars.

Deirdre could take care of herself from here on out—after all, we'd saved her life. I didn't feel obligated to go on protecting her on a day-to-day basis. Random was stuck in Rebma for a year, unless he had guts enough to leap forward and take the Pattern to this still center of power and perhaps escape. And as for Moire, it had been nice knowing her, and maybe I'd see her again some day, and like that. I closed my eyes and bowed my head.

Before I did so, though, I saw a fleeting shadow.

Random? Trying it? Whatever, he wouldn't know where I was headed. No one would.

I opened my eyes and I stood in the middle of the same Pattern, in reverse.

I was cold, and I was damn tired, but I was in Amber—in the real room, of which the one I had departed was but an image. From the Pattern, I could transfer myself to any point I wished within Amber.

Getting back would be a problem, however.

So I stood there and dripped and considered.

If Eric had taken the royal suite, then I might find him there. Or perhaps in the throne room. But then, I'd have to make my own way back to the place of power. I'd have to walk the Pattern again, in order to reach the escape point.

I transferred myself to a hiding place I knew of within the palace. It was a windowless cubicle into which some light trickled from observation slits high overhead. I bolted its one sliding panel from the inside, dusted off a wooden bench set beside the wall, spread my cloak upon it and stretched out for a nap. If anyone came groping his way down from above, I'd hear him long before he reached me.

I slept.

After a while, I awakened. So I arose, dusted off my cloak and donned it once more. Then I began to negotiate the series of pegs which laddered their way up into the palace.

I knew where it was, the third floor, by the markings on the walls.

I swung myself over to a small landing and searched for the peephole. I found it and gazed through. Nothing. The library was empty. So I slid back the panel and entered.

Within, I was stricken by the multitudes of books. They always do that to me. I considered everything, including the display cases, and finally moved toward the place where a crystal case contained everything that led up to a family banquet—private joke. It held four decks of the family cards, and I sought about for a means of obtaining one without setting off an alarm which might keep me from using it.

After maybe ten minutes, I succeeded in gimmicking the proper case. It was tricky. Then, pack in hands, I found a comfortable seat for the consideration thereof.

The cards were just like Flora's and they held us all under glass and were cold to the touch. Now, too, I knew why.

So I shuffled and spread them all out before me in the proper manner. Then I read them, and I saw that bad things were in store for the entire family; and I gathered them all together then.

Save for one.

It was the card depicting my brother Bleys.

I replaced the others in their case and tucked it into my belt. Then I considered Bleys.

At about that time there came a scratching in the lock of the great door to the library. What could I do? I loosened my blade in its scabbard and waited. I ducked low behind the deck, though.

Peering out, I saw that it was a guy named Dik, who had obviously come to clean the place, as he set out emptying the ashtrays and wastebaskets and dusting the shelves.

Since it would be demeaning to be discovered, I exposed myself.

I rose and said, "Hello, Dik, Remember me?"

He turned three kinds of pale, half bolted, and said:

"Of course, Lord. How could I forget?"

"I suppose it would be possible, after all this time."

"Never, Lord Corwin," he replied.

"I suppose I'm here without official sanction, and engaged in a bit of illicit research," I said "but if Eric doesn't like it when you tell him that you saw me, please explain that I was simply exercising my rights, and he will be seeing me personally—soon."

"I'll do that, m'lord," he said, bowing.

"Come sit with me a moment, friend Dik, and I'll tell you more."

And he did, so I did.

"There was a time," I said, addressing this ancient visage, "when I was considered gone for good and abandoned forever. Since I still live, however, and since I maintain all my faculties, I fear that I must dispute Eric's claim to the throne of Amber. Though it's not a thing to be settled simply, as he is not the first-born, nor do I feel he would enjoy popular support if another were in sight. For these, among other reasons—most of them personal—I am about to oppose him. I have not yet decided how, nor upon what grounds, but by God! he deserves opposition! Tell him that. If he wishes to seek me, tell him that I dwell among Shadows, but different ones than before. He may know what I mean by that. I will not be easily destroyed, for I will guard myself at least as well as he does here. I will oppose him from hell to eternity, and I will not cease until one of us is dead. What say you to this, old retainer?"

And he took my hand and kissed it.

"Hail to thee, Corwin, Lord of Amber," he said, and there was a tear in his eye.

Then the door cracked a crack behind him and swung open.

Eric entered.

"Hello," said I, rising and putting a most obnoxious twang to my voice. "I didn't expect to meet with you this early in the game. How go things in Amber?"

And his eyes were wide with amaze and his voice heavy with that which men call sarcasm, and I can't think of a better word, as he replied:

"Well, when it comes to things, Corwin. Poorly, on other counts, however."

"Pity," said I, "and how shall we put things aright?"

"I know a way," he said, and then he glared at Dik, who promptly departed and closed the door behind him. I heard it *snick* shut.

Eric loosened his blade in its scabbard.

"You want the throne," he said.

"Don't we all?" I told him.

"I guess so," he said, with a sigh. "It's true, that uneasy-lies-the-head bit. I don't know why we are driven to strive so for this ridiculous position. But you must recall that I've defeated you twice, mercifully granting you your life on a Shadow world the last occasion."

"It wasn't that merciful," I said. "You know where you left me, to die of the plague. The first time, as I remember, it was pretty much a draw."

"Then it is between the two of us now, Corwin," he said. "I am your elder and your better. If you wish to try me at arms, I find myself suitably attired. Slay me, and the throne will probably be yours. Try it. I don't think you can succeed, however. And I'd like to quit your claim right now. So come at me. Let's see what you learned on the Shadow Earth."

And his blade was in his hand and mine in mine.

I moved around the desk.

"What an enormous *chutzpah* you possess," I told him. "What makes you better than the rest of us, and more fit to rule?"

"The fact that I was able to occupy the throne," he replied. "Try and take it."

And I did.

I tried a head-cut, which he parried; and I parried his riposte to my heart and cut at his wrist.

He parried this and kicked a small stool between us. I set it aside, hopefully in the direction of his face, with my right toe, but it missed and he had at me again.

I parried his attack, and he mine. Then I lunged, was parried, was attacked, and parried again myself.

I tried a very fancy attack I'd learned in France, which involved a beat, a feint in *quarte,* a feint in *sixte,* and a lunge veering off into an attack on his wrist.

I nicked him and the blood flowed.

"Oh, damnable brother!" he said, retreating. "Report has it Random accompanies thee."

"This is true," said I. "More than one of us are assembled against you."

And he lunged then and beat me back, and I felt suddenly that for all my work he was still my master. He was perhaps one of the greatest swordsmen I had ever faced. I suddenly had the feeling that I couldn't take him, and I parried like mad and retreated in the same fashion as he beat me back, step by step. We'd both had centuries under the greatest masters of the blade in business. The greatest alive, I knew, was brother Benedict, and he wasn't around to help, one way or the other. So I snatched things off the desk with my left hand and threw them at Eric. But he dodged everything and came on strong, and I circled to his left and all like that, but I couldn't draw the point of his blade from my left eye. And I was afraid. The man was magnificent. If I didn't hate him so, I would have applauded his performance.

I kept backing away, and the fear and the knowledge came upon me: I knew I still couldn't take him. He was a better man than I was, when it came to the blade. I cursed this, but I couldn't get around it. I tried three more elaborate attacks and was defeated on each occasion. He parried me and made me retreat before his own attacks.

Now don't get the wrong idea. I'm damn good. It's just that he seemed better.

Then there were some alarms and excursions in the hall outside. Eric's retainers were coming, and if he didn't kill me before they arrived, then I was confident that they'd do the job—probably with a bolt from a crossbow.

There was blood dripping from his right wrist. His hand was still steady but I had the feeling then that under other circumstances, by fighting a defensive fight, I just might be able to wear him down with that wrist injury going against him, and perhaps I could get through his guard at the proper moment when he began to slow.

I cursed softly and he laughed.

"You're a fool to have come here," he said.

He didn't realize what I was doing until it was too late. (I'd been retreating until the door was at my back. It was risky, leaving myself with no room for retreat, but it was better than sure death.)

With my left hand, I managed to drop the bar. It was a big, heavy door and they'd have to knock it down now to get in. That gave me a few more minutes. It also gave me a shoulder wound, from an attack I could only partly parry as I dropped the bar. But it was my left shoulder. My sword arm remained intact.

I smiled, to put up a good front.

"Perhaps *you* were a fool, to enter *here,*" I said. "You're slowing, you know," and I tried a hard, fast, vicious attack.

He parried it, but he fell back two paces in doing so.

"That wound's getting to you," I added. "Your arm's weakening. You can feel the strength leaving it—"

"Shut up!" he said, and I realized I'd gotten through to him. This increased my chances by several percent, I decided, and I pressed him as hard as I could, realizing I couldn't keep that pace up very long.

But Eric didn't realize it.

I'd planted the seeds of fear, and he fell back before my sudden onslaught.

There was a banging on the door but I didn't have to worry about that for a while anyway.

"I'm going to take you, Eric," I said. "I'm tougher than I used to be, and you've had it, brother."

I saw the fear begin in his eyes, and it spread over his face, and his style shifted to follow suit. He began fighting a completely defensive battle, backing away from my attack. I'm sure he wasn't faking either. I felt I had bluffed him, for he had always been better than I. But what if it had been partly psychological on my part too? What if I had almost beaten myself with this attitude, which Eric had helped to foster? What if I had bluffed myself all along? Maybe I was as good. With a strange sense of confidence, I tried the same attack I had used before and I scored, leaving another trail of red on his forearm.

"That was rather stupid, Eric," I said, "to fall for the same trick twice," and he backed around a wide chair. We fought across it for a time.

The banging on the door stopped, and the voices which had been shouting inquiries through it fell silent.

"They've gone for axes," Eric panted. "They'll be in here in no time."

I wouldn't drop my smile. I held it and said: "It'll take a few minutes—which is more time than I'll need to finish this. You can hardly keep your guard now, and the blood keeps running—look at it!"

"Shut up!"

"By the time they get through, there will be only one prince of Amber, and it won't be you!"

Then, with his left arm, he swept a row of books from a shelf and they struck me and fell about me.

He didn't seize the opportunity to attack, however. He dashed across the room, picking up a small chair, which he held in his left hand.

He wedged himself into a corner and held the chair and his blade before him.

There were rapid footsteps in the hall outside, and then axes began to ring upon the door.

"Come on!" he said. "Try and take me now!"

"You're scared," I said.

He laughed.

"Academic," he replied. "You can't take me before that door falls, and then it will be all over for you."

I had to agree. He could hold off my blade with that setup, at least for quite a few minutes.

I crossed the room quickly, to the opposite wall.

With my left hand, I opened the panel through which I had entered.

"Okay," I said, "it looks like you're going to live—for a time. You're lucky. Next time we meet, there won't be anyone to help you."

He spat and called me a few traditional vile names, even putting down the chair to add an obscene gesture, as I ducked through the panel and closed it behind me.

There came a *thunk*, and eight inches of steel gleamed on my side of the panel as I was fastening it. He had thrown his blade. Risky, if I chose to return. But he knew I wouldn't, for the door sounded about ready to fall.

I descended the pegs as rapidly as I could, to the place where I had slept earlier. As I did, I considered my increased skill with the blade. At first, in the battle, I had been awed by the man who had beaten me before. Now, though, I wondered. Perhaps those centuries on the Shadow Earth were not a waste. Maybe I had actually gotten better during that time. Now I felt that I might be Eric's equal with the weapon. This made me feel good. If we met again, as I was sure we would, and there was no outside interference—who knew? I would court the chance, however. Today's encounter had scared him. I was certain. That might serve to slow his hand, to cause the necessary hesitation on the next occasion.

I let go and dropped the final fifteen feet, bending my knees as I landed. I was the proverbial five minutes ahead of the posse, but I was sure I could take advantage of it and escape.

For I had the cards in my belt.

I drew the card that was Bleys and stared at it. My shoulder hurt, but I forgot it, as the coldness came upon me.

There were two ways to depart directly from Amber into Shadow. . . .

One was the Pattern, seldom used for this purpose.

Another was the Trumps, if you could trust a brother.

I considered Bleys. I could almost trust him. He *was* my brother, but he was in trouble and could use my help.

I stared at him, flame-crowned, dressed all in red and orange, with a sword in his right hand and a glass of wine in his left. The devil danced in his blue eyes, his beard blazed, and the tracery on his blade, I suddenly realized, flared with a portion of the Pattern. His rings flashed. He seemed to move.

The contact came like an icy wind.

The figure on the card seemed life-sized now and changed position into whatever stance he presently held. His eyes did not quite focus upon me, and his lips moved.

"Who is it?" they said, and I heard the words.

"Corwin," said I, and he held forth his left hand, which no longer bore the goblet.

"Then come to me, if you would."

I reached forth and our fingers met. I took a step.

I was still holding the card in my left hand, but Bleys and I stood together on a cliff and there was a chasm to our side and a high fortress to our other side. The sky above us was the color of flame.

"Hello, Bleys," I said, tucking the card into my belt with the others. "Thanks for the assistance."

I suddenly felt weak and realized the blood was still flowing from my left shoulder.

"You're wounded!" he said, throwing an arm about my shoulders, and I started to nod but fainted instead.

Later that night, I sprawled in a big chair within the fortress and drank whisky. We smoked and passed the bottle and talked.

"So you were actually in Amber?"

"Yes, that's right."

"And you wounded Eric in your duel?"

"Yes."

"Damn! I wish you'd killed him!" Then he reflected. "Well, maybe not. Then you'd have held the throne. I might have a better chance against Eric than I'd have had against you. I don't know. What are your plans?"

I decided upon complete honesty.

"We all want the throne," I said, "so there's no reason to lie to one another. I'm not about to try killing you for it—that would be foolish—but on the other hand, I'm not about to renounce my claim because I'm enjoying your hospitality. Random would like it, but he's pretty much out of the picture. No one has heard from Benedict for some time now. Gérard and Caine seem to be supporting Eric, rather than promoting their own claims. The same goes for Julian. That leaves Brand and our sisters. I don't know what the hell Brand is up to these days, but I do know that Deirdre is without power, unless she and Llewella can raise something in Rebma, and Flora is Eric's creature. I don't know what Fiona is up to."

"And so that leaves us," said Bleys, pouring us each another drink. "Yes, you're right. I don't know what's going on in everyone's head right now, but I can assess our relative strengths and I think I'm in the best position. You made a wise choice in coming to me. Support me, and I'll give you a regency."

"Bless your heart," I said. "We'll see."

We sipped our whiskies.

"What else is there to do?" he asked, and I realized that the question was important.

"I might raise an army of my own, to lay siege to Amber," I told him.

"Where among Shadows lies your army?" he inquired.

"That, of course, is my affair," I said. "I don't think I'd oppose you. When it comes to monarchs, I'd like to see either you, me, Gérard, or Benedict—if he still lives—upon the throne."

"Preferably you, of course."

"Of course."

"Then we understand one another. So I think we can work together, for the time being."

"And I," I agreed, "else I would not have delivered myself into your hands."

He smiled within his beard.

"You needed someone," he said, "and I was the lesser evil."

"True," I agreed.

"I wish Benedict were here. I wish Gérard had not sold out."

"Wishes, wishes," I told him. "Wish in one hand and do something else in the other, and squeeze them both and see which comes true."

"Well taken," he said.

We smoked a while in silence.

"How far can I trust you?" he asked.

"As far can I trust you."

"Then let's make a deal. Frankly, I had thought you dead for many years. I hadn't foreseen your showing up at a crucial time and pressing your own claim. But you're here, and that's that. Let's form an alliance—combine our forces and lay siege to Amber. Whichever of us lives through it winds up on top. If we both do, well—hell!—we can always fight a duel!"

I thought about it. It sounded like the best deal I'd get anywhere.

So I said, "I'd like to sleep on it. Tell you in the morning, okay?"

"Okay."

We finished our drinks then and fell to reminiscing. My shoulder throbbed a bit, but the whisky helped, and the salve which Bleys had supplied. After a time, we were almost maudlin.

It is strange, I guess, to have kin and to be without kinship, for as long as our lives had led us along our separate paths. Lord! We talked the moon out of the heavens before either of us grew tired. Then he clapped me upon my good shoulder and told me that he was beginning to feel his load and that a servant would be by in the morning to bring my breakfast. I nodded, we embraced, and he retired.

Then I moved to the window, and from that vantage I could see down far into the chasm.

The campfires below burned like stars. There were thousands of them. I could tell that Bleys had assembled a mighty force, and I was envious. But, on the other hand, it was a good thing. If anyone could take Eric, it was probably Bleys. He wouldn't be a bad thing in Amber; it was just that I preferred me.

Then I watched a while longer, and I saw that strange shapes moved among the lights. I wondered then as to the nature of his army.

Whatever, it was more than I possessed.

I made my way back to the table and poured me a final drink.

Before I quaffed it, however, I lighted a taper. In its light, I withdrew the pack of cards I had stolen.

I spread them before me and I came across the one depicting Eric. I laid it in the center of the table and put the rest away.

After a time, it came to life; and I saw Eric in his sleeping garments and I heard the words, "Who is it?" His arm was bound.

"Me," I said, "Corwin. How are you?"

He cursed then, and I laughed. This was a dangerous game and maybe the whisky had contributed to it, but I continued: "I just felt like telling you that all goes well with me. I also wanted to advise you that you were right when you spoke of the uneasy head. You won't be wearing it long, though. So cheerio! Brother! The day I come again to Amber is the day you die! Just thought I'd tell you—since that day is not too far off."

"Come ahead," he told me, "and I'll not want for grace in the matter of your passing."

His eyes focused on me then and we were close.

I thumbed my nose at him and passed my palm over the card.

It was like hanging up a telephone, and I shuffled Eric in with all the rest.

I wondered though, as I approached sleep, concerning those troops of Bleys which occupied the defile below, and I thought upon Eric's defenses.

It would not be easy.

SIX

The land was known as Avernus, and the assembled troops were not quite men. I reviewed them the following morning, walking behind Bleys. They were all of them around seven feet in height, had very red skins and little hair, cat-like eyes, and six-digited hands and feet. They wore garments that looked as light as silk, but were woven of something else and were mainly gray or blue in color. Each bore two short blades, hooked at the end. Their ears were pointed and their many fingers clawed.

The climate was warm and the colors bewildering, and everyone thought we were gods.

Bleys had found a place where the religion involved brother-gods who looked like us and had their troubles. Invariably, in the terms of this *mythos*, an evil brother would seize power and seek to oppress the good brothers. And of course there was the legend of an Apocalypse where they themselves would be called upon to stand on the side of the surviving good brothers.

I wore my left arm in a black sling and considered those who were about to die.

I stood before a trooper and looked up at him. I asked him, "Do you know who Eric is?"

"The Lord of Evil," he replied.

I nodded and said, "Very good," and passed on.

Bleys had custom-made cannon fodder.

"How large is your army?" I asked him.

"Around fifty thousand," he replied.

"I salute those who are about to Give Their All," I told him. "You can't take Amber with fifty thousand men, even providing you can get them all to the foot of Kolvir intact—and you can't. It's silly even to consider using these poor bastards against the immortal city, with their toy swords and all."

"I know," he said, "but they're not all I've got."

"You'll need a lot more."

"Then how do three navies sound—half again the size of Caine's and Gérard's fleets put together?

"I've a way."

"Not yet enough," said I, "and barely a beginning."

"I know. I'm still building," he said.

"Well, we'd better build a lot more. Eric will sit in Amber and kill us as we march through Shadows. When the remaining forces finally reach the foot of Kolvir, he'll decimate them there. Then there will be the climb to Amber. How many hundred do you think will remain when we reach the city? Enough to be dispatched in five minutes, at almost no cost to Eric. If this is the best you've got, brother Bleys, I have misgivings concerning this expedition."

"Eric has announced his coronation in three months' time," he said. "I can triple my forces by then—at least. Perhaps I can even have a quarter of a million Shadow troops to lead against Amber. There are other worlds like this one, and I will penetrate them. I will raise me such a force of holy crusaders as has never been sent against Amber before."

"And Eric will have had the same time to intensify his defenses. I don't know, Bleys . . . it's almost a suicide run. I didn't know the full situation when I came here—"

"And what have you brought with you?" he asked. "Nothing! It is rumored that you once commanded troops. Where are they?"

I turned away from him.

"They are no more," I said. "I am certain."

"Could you not find a Shadow of your Shadow?"

"I don't want to try," I said. "I'm sorry."

"Then what real good are you to me?"

"I'll go," I told him, "if that's all you had in mind, if that's all you really wanted me around for—more bodies."

"Wait!" he cried out. "I spoke hastily. I don't want to lose your counsel, if nothing else. Stay with me, please. I will even apologize."

"That is not necessary," I said, knowing what this thing means to a prince of Amber. "I'll stay. I think I can help you."

"Good!" and he clapped me upon my good shoulder.

"And I'll get your more troops," I added. "Never fear."

And I did.

I walked among Shadows, and found a race of furry creatures, dark and clawed and fanged, reasonably man-like, and about as intelligent as a freshman in the high school of your choice—sorry, kids, but what I mean is they were loyal, devoted, honest, and too easily screwed by bastards like me and my brother. I felt like the dee-jay of your choice.

Around a hundred thousand worshiped us to the extent of taking up arms.

Bleys was impressed and shut up. After a week my shoulder was healed. After two months we had our quarter million and more.

"Corwin, Corwin! You're still Corwin!" he said, and we took another drink.

But I was feeling kind of funny. Most of these troops were destined to die. I was the agent responsible for much of this. I felt some remorse, though I knew the difference between Shadow and Substance. Each death would be a real death; however, I knew that also.

And some nights I dwelled upon the playing cards. The missing Trumps had been restored to the pack I held. One of them was a portrait of Amber itself, and I knew it could bear me back into the city. The others were those of our dead or missing relatives. And one was Dad's, and I skipped it over quickly. He was gone.

I stared at each face for a long while to consider what might be gained from each. I cast the cards several times, and the same thing came up on each occasion.

His name was Caine.

He wore satin that was green and black, and a dark three-cornered hat with a green plume of feathers trailing down behind. At his belt there was an emerald-studded dagger. He was dark.

"Caine," I said.

After a time, there came a reply.

"Who?" he asked.

"Corwin," said I.

"Corwin! Is this a joke?"

"No."

"What do you want?"

"What've you got?"

"You know that," and his eyes shifted and lay upon me, but I watched his hand, which was near to his dagger.

"Where are you?"

"With Bleys."

"There was a rumor you'd shown up in Amber recently—and I wondered at the bandages on Eric's arm."

"You're looking at the reason," I said. "What's your price?"

"What do you mean?"

"Let us be frank and to the point. Do you think Bleys and I can take Eric?"

"No, that's why I'm with Eric. And I won't sell out my armada either, if that's what you're after—and I'd imagine you are."

I smiled.

"Perceptive brother," I replied. "Well, it's been nice talking to you. See you in Amber—maybe."

I moved my hand, and he cried out.

"Wait!"

"Why?"

"I don't even know your offer."

"Yes, you do," I said. "You've guessed it, and you're not interested."

"I didn't say that. It's just that I know where the equities lie."

"You mean the power."

"Okay, the power. What've you got to offer?"

We talked for maybe an hour, after which time the northern seaways were open to the three phantom fleets of Bleys, which might enter expecting reinforcements.

"If you fail, there'll be three beheadings in Amber," said he.

"But you don't really expect that, do you?" I asked.

"No, I think either you or Bleys will sit upon the throne before too very long. I'll be satisfied to serve the winner. That regency would be nice. I'd still like Random's head as part of the price, though."

"No deal," I said. "Take it as you've heard it or forget it."

"I'll take it."

I smiled and placed my palm upon the card and he was gone.

Gérard was a matter I'd leave for the morrow. Caine had exhausted me. I rolled into bed and slept.

Gérard, when he learned the score, agreed to lay off us. Mainly because it was I who was asking, as he had considered Eric a lesser of potent evils.

I concluded the deal quickly, promising him everything he asked, as no heads were involved.

Then I reviewed the troops again and told them more of Amber. Strangely, they got along like brothers, the big red guys and the little hairy ones.

It was sad and it was true.

We were their gods, and that was that.

I saw the fleet, sailing on a great ocean the color of blood. I wondered. In the Shadow worlds through which they sailed, many of them would be lost.

I considered the troops of Avernus, and my recruits from the place called Ri'ik. Theirs was the task of marching to Earth and Amber.

I shuffled my cards and cast them. I picked up the one called Benedict. For a long while I searched it, but there was nothing but the cold.

Then I seized upon Brand's. For another long while there was nothing but the cold.

Then there came a scream. It was a horrible, tormented thing.

"Help me!" came the cry.

"How can I?" I asked.

"Who is that?" he asked, and I saw his body writhe.

"Corwin."

"Deliver me from this place, brother Corwin! Anything you name shall be yours in return!"

"Where are you?"

"I—"

And there came a swirling of things my mind refused to conceive of, and another scream, torn forth as though in agony and ending in silence.

Then the coldness came in again.

I found that I was shaking. From what, I did not know.

I lit a cigarette and moved to the window to consider the night, leaving the cards where they had fallen upon the table-top of my room within the garrison.

The stars were tiny and misted over. There were no constellations that I could recognize. A small blue moon dropped quickly through the darkness. The night had come on with a sudden, icy chill and I wrapped my cloak close about me. I thought back to the winter of our disastrous campaign in Russia. Gods! I'd almost frozen to death! And where did it all lead?

To the throne of Amber, of course.

For that was sufficient justification for anything.

But what of Brand? Where was he? What was happening about him, and who had done this thing to him?

Answers? None.

I wondered, though, as I stared up and out, tracing the path of that blue disk in its descent. Was there something I was missing in the whole picture, some factor I didn't quite dig?

No answer.

I seated myself at the table once more, a small drink at my hand.

I fingered my way through the pack and found Dad's card.

Oberon, Lord of Amber, stood before me in his green and his gold. High, wide, and thick, his beard black and shot with silver, his hair the same. Green rings in gold settings and a blade of golden color. It had once seemed to me that nothing could ever displace the immortal liege of Amber from his throne. What had happened? I still didn't know. But he was gone. How had my father met with his end?

I stared and concentrated.

Nothing, nothing—

Something?

Something.

There came a responding movement, though ever so weak, and the figure on the card turned in upon itself and shriveled to a shadow of the man he had been.

"Father?" I asked.

Nothing.

"Father?"

"Yes . . ." Very faint and distant, as though through a seashell, immersed in its monotone humming.

"Where are you? What has happened?"

"I . . ." Long pause.

"Yes? This is Corwin, your son. What came to pass in Amber, that you are gone?"

"My time," he said, sounding even further away.

"Do you mean that you abdicated? None of my brothers has given me the tale, and I do not trust them sufficiently to ask them. Eric now holds the city and Julian guards the Forest of Arden. Caine and Gérard maintain the seas. Bleys would oppose all and I am allied with him. What are your wishes in this matter?"

"You are the only one—who—has asked," he gasped. "Yes . . ."

" 'Yes,' what?"

"Yes, oppose—them. . . ."

"What of you? How can I help you?"

"I am—beyond help. Take the throne. . . ."

"I? Or Bleys and I?"

"You!" he said.

"Yes?"

"You have my blessing. . . . Take the throne—and be quick—about it!"

"Why, Father?"

"I lack the breath—Take it!"

Then he, too, was gone.

So Dad lived. That was interesting. What to do now?

I sipped my drink and thought about it.

He still lived, somewhere, and he was king in Amber. Why had he left? Where had he gone? What kind of, which, and how many? Like that.

Who knew? Not I. So there was no more to say, for now.

However . . .

I couldn't put the thing down. I want you to know that Dad and I never got along very well. I didn't hate him, like Random or some of the others. But I, sure as hell, had no reason to be especially fond of him. He had been big, he had been powerful, and he had been there. That was about it. He was also most of the history of Amber, as we knew it, and the history of Amber stretches back for so many millennia that you may as well stop counting. So what do you do.

As for me, I finished my drink and went to bed.

The following morning I attended a meeting of Bley's general staff. He had four admirals, each in charge of roughly a quarter of his fleet, and a whole mess of army officers. Altogether there were about thirty of the high-ranking brass at the meeting, big and red or small and hairy, as the case might be.

The meeting lasted perhaps four hours, and then we all broke for lunch. It was decided that we would move three days hence. Since it would require one of the blood to open the way to Amber, I was to lead the fleet aboard the flagship, and Bleys would take his infantry through lands of Shadow.

I was troubled by this, and I asked him what would have happened had I not shown up to give this assistance. I was told two things in reply: one, if he had had to go it alone, he would have led the fleet through and left them at a great distance from shore, returned in a single vessel to Avernus and led his foot soldiers forward to rendezvous at a given time; and two, he had purposely sought for a Shadow in which a brother would appear to give him aid.

I had some misgivings when I heard about the latter, though I knew I was really me. The former smacked of being a bit unworkable, since the fleet would be too far out to sea to receive any signals from the shore, and the chance of missing the date—allowing the mishaps when it came to a body that large—was too great, as I saw it, to encourage a whole big lot of faith in his general plan.

But as a tactician, I had always thought him brilliant; and when he laid out the maps of Amber and the outlying country which he himself had drawn, and when he had explained the tactics to be employed therein, I knew that he was a prince of Amber, almost matchless in his guile.

The only thing was, we were up against another prince of Amber, one who occupied what was definitely a stronger position. I was worried, but with the impending coronation, it seemed about the only course available to us, and I decided to go along for the whole ride. If we lost, we were creamed, but he held the biggest threat available and had a workable time schedule, which I didn't.

So I walked the land called Avernus and considered its foggy valleys and chasms, its smoking craters, its bright, bright sun against its crazy sky, its icy nights and too hot days, its many rocks and carloads of dark sand, its tiny, though vicious and poisonous beasts, and its big purple plants, like spineless cacti; and on the afternoon of the second day, as I stood on a cliff overlooking the sea, beneath a tower of massed vermilion clouds, I decided that I rather liked the place for all that, and if its sons would perish in the wars of the gods, I would immortalize them one day in song if I were able.

This mild balm in mind for what I feared, I joined the fleet and took command. If we made it, they would be feted forever in the halls of the immortals.

I was guide and opener of the way. I rejoiced.

So we set sail the following day, and I directed things from the lead ship. I led us into a storm, and we emerged that much nearer our destination. I led us past an enormous whirlpool, and we were so much to the good. I led us through a shallow rocky place, and the shade of the waters deepened afterward. Their colors began to approximate those of Amber. So I still knew how to do it. I could influence our fate in time and place. I could take us home. Home for me, that is.

I led us past strange islands where green birds cawed and green apes hung like fruit in the trees, swung, sometimes gibbered, and threw rocks into the sea, aimed, doubtless, at us.

I took us far out to sea, and then nosed the fleet around back in the direction of shore.

Bleys by now was marching across the plains of the worlds. Somehow, I knew he would make it, past whatever defenses Eric had set up. I kept in touch with him by means of the cards, and I learned of his encounters along the way. Like, ten thousand men dead in a plains battle with centaurs, five thousand lost in an earthquake of frightening proportions, fifteen hundred dead of a whirlwind plague that swept the camps, nineteen thousand dead or missing in action as they passed through the jungles of a place I didn't recognize, when the napalm fell upon them from the strange buzzing things that passed overhead, six thousand deserting in a place that looked like the heaven they had been promised, five hundred unaccounted for as they crossed a sand flat where a mushroom cloud burned and towered beside them, eighty-six hundred gone as they moved through a valley of suddenly militant machines that rolled forward on treads and fired fires, eight hundred sick and abandoned, two hundred dead from flash floods, fifty-four dying of duels among themselves, three hundred dead from eating poisonous native fruits, a thousand slain in a massive stampede of buffalo-like creatures, seventy-three gone when their tents caught fire, fifteen hundred carried away by the floods, two thousand slain by the winds that came down from the blue hills.

I was pleased that I'd lost only a hundred and eighty-six ships in that time.

To sleep, perchance to dream. . . . Yeah, there's a thing that rubs. Eric was killing us by inches and hours. His proposed coronation was only a few weeks away, and he obviously knew we were coming against him, because we died and we died.

Now, it is written that only a prince of Amber may walk among Shadows, though of course he may lead or direct as many as he chooses along such courses. We led our troops and saw them die, but of Shadow I have this to say: there is Shadow and there is Substance, and this is the root of all things. Of Substance, there is only Amber, the real city, upon the real Earth, which contains everything. Of Shadow, there is an infinitude of things. Every possibility exists somewhere as a Shadow of the real. Amber, by its very existence, has cast such in all directions. And what may one say of it beyond? Shadow extends from Amber to Chaos, and all things are possible within it. There are only three ways of traversing it, and each of them is difficult.

If one is a prince or princess of the blood, then one may walk, crossing through Shadows, forcing one's environment to change as one passes, until it is finally in precisely the shape one desires it, and there stop. The Shadow world is then one's own, save for family intrusions, to do with as one would. In such a place had I dwelled for centuries.

The second means is the cards, cast by Dworkin, Master of the Line, who had created them in our image, to facilitate communications between members of the royal family. He was the ancient artist to whom space and perspective meant nothing. He had made up the family Trumps, which permitted the willer to touch his brethren wherever they might be. I had a feeling that these had not been used in full accord with their author's intention.

The third was the Pattern, also drawn by Dworkin, which could only be walked by a member of our family. It initiated the walker into the system of the cards, as it were, and at its ending gave its walker the power to stride across Shadows.

The cards and the Pattern made for instant transport from Substance through Shadow. The other way, walking, was harder.

I knew what Random had done in delivering me into the true world. As we had driven, he kept adding, from memory, that which he recalled of Amber, and subtracting that which did not agree. When everything corresponded, he knew we had arrived. It was no real trick, for had he the knowledge, any man could reach his own Amber. Even now, Bleys and I could find Shadow Ambers where each of us ruled, and spend all the time and eternity ruling there. But this would not be the same, for us. For none would be the true Amber, the city into which we were born, the city from which all others take their shapes.

So we were taking the hardest route, the walk through Shadow, for our invasion of Amber itself. Anyone knowing this and possessing the power could interpose obstacles. Eric had done so, and now we faced them as we died. What would come of this? No one knew.

But if Eric were crowned king, it would be reflected and shadowed everywhere.

All the surviving brothers, we princes of Amber, I am sure, felt it much better, each in his own simple way, personally to achieve this status and thereafter let the Shadows fall where they might.

We passed ghost fleets, the ships of Gérard, as we sailed—the Flying Dutchmen of this world—that world, and we knew we were coming near. I used them as reference points.

On the eighth day of our voyaging we were near to Amber. That is when the storm broke.

The sea turned dark, the clouds collected overhead, and the sails grew slack within the still that followed. The sun hid its face—an enormous blue one—and I felt that Eric had found us at last.

Then the winds arose, and—if you'll excuse the expression—broke—upon the vessel I rode.

We were tempest-tossed and storm-torn, as the poets say, or said. My guts felt loose and watery as the first billows hit us. We were hurled from side to side like dice in a giant's hand. We were swept over the waters of the sea and the waters from the sky. The sky turned black, and there was sleet mixed in with the glassy bell ropes that pulled the thunder. Everyone, I'm sure, cried out. I know I did. I pulled my way along the shifting deck to seize the abandoned wheel. I strapped myself in place and held it. Eric had cut loose in Amber, that was for damn sure.

One, two, three, four, and there was no letup. Five hours, then. How many men had we lost? I dunno.

Then I felt and heard a tingling and a tinkling, and I saw Bleys as through a long gray tunnel.

"What's the matter?" he asked. "I've been trying to reach you."

"Life is full of vicissitudes," I replied. "We're riding out one of them."

"Storm?" he said.

"You bet your sweet ass. It's the granddaddy of them all. I think I see a monster off to port. If he has any brains, he'll aim for the bottom. . . . He just did."

"We just had one ourselves," Bleys told me.

"Monster or storm?"

"Storm," he replied. "Two hundred dead."

"Keep the faith," I said, "hold the fort, and talk to me later. Okay?"

He nodded, and there were lightnings at his back.

"Eric's got our number," he added, before he cut off.

I had to agree.

It was three more hours before things let up, and many more later I learned that we had lost half of the fleet (and on my vessel—the flagship—we had lost forty of the crew of one hundred and twenty). It was a hard rain that fell.

Somehow, to the sea over Rebma, we made it.

I drew forth my cards and held Random's before me.

When he realized who was talking, the first thing he said was "Turn back," and I asked him why.

" 'Cause, according to Llewella, Eric can cream you now. She says wait a while, till he relaxes, and hit him then—like a year from now, maybe."

I shook my head.

"Sorry," said I. "Can't. Too many losses involved in getting us this far. It's a now-or-never situation."

He shrugged, wearing a "Like, I warned you" expression.

"Why, though?" I asked him.

"Mainly because I just learned he can control the weather around here," he said.

"We'll still have to chance it."

He shrugged again.

"Don't say I didn't tell you."

"He definitely knows we're coming?"

"What do you think? Is he a cretin?"

"No."

"Then he knows. If I could guess it in Rebma, then he knows in Amber—and I *did* guess, from a wavering of Shadow."

"Unfortunately," I said, "I have some misgivings about this expedition, but it's Bleys' show."

"You cop out and let him get axed."

"Sorry, but I can't take the chance. He might win. I'm bringing in the fleet."

"You've spoken with Caine, with Gérard?"

"Yes."

"Then you must think you have a chance upon the waters. But listen, Eric has figured a way to control the Jewel of Judgment, I gather, from court gossip about its double. He *can* use it to control the weather here. That's definite. God knows what else he might be able to do with it."

"Pity," I said. "We'll have to suffer it. Can't let a few storms demoralize us."

"Corwin, I'll confess. I spoke with Eric himself three days ago."

"Why?"

"He asked me. I spoke with him out of boredom. He went into great detail concerning his defenses."

"That's because he learned from Julian that we came in together. He's sure it'll get back to me."

"Probably," he said. "But that doesn't change what he said."

"No." I agreed.

"Then let Bleys fight his own war," he told me. "You can hit Eric later."

"He's about to be crowned in Amber."

"I know, I know. It's as easy to attack a king, though, as a prince, isn't it? What difference does it make what he calls himself at the time, so long as you take him? It'll still be Eric."

"True," I said, "but I've committed myself."

"Then uncommit yourself," he said.

" 'Fraid I can't do that."

"Then you're crazy, Charlie."

"Probably."

"Well, good luck, anyhow."

"Thanks."

"See you around."

And that was that, and it troubled me.

Was I heading into a trap?

Eric was no fool. Perhaps he had a real death-gig lined up. Finally, I shrugged and leaned out over the rail, the cards once again behind my belt.

It is a proud and lonely thing to be a prince of Amber, incapable of trust. I wasn't real fond of it just then, but there I was.

Eric, of course, had controlled the storm we'd just passed through, and it seemed in line with his being weather master in Amber, as Random had told me.

So I tried something myself.

I headed us toward an Amber lousy with snow. It was the most horrible blizzard I could conjure up.

The big flakes began to fall, out there on the ocean.

Let him stop them a normal enough Shadow offering, if he could.

And he did.

Within a half hour's time the blizzard had died. Amber was virtually impervious—and it was really the only city. I didn't want to go off course, so I let things be. Eric *was* master of the weather in Amber.

What to do?

We sailed on, of course. Into the jaws of death.

What can one say?

The second storm was worse than the first, but I held the wheel. It was electrified, and focused only on the fleet. It drove us apart. It cost us forty vessels more.

I was afraid to call Bleys to see what had been done to him.

"Around two hundred thousand troops are left," he said. "Flash flood," and I told him what Random had told me.

"I'll buy it," he said. "But let's not dwell on it. Weather or no, we'll beat him."

"I hope so."

I lit a cigarette and leaned across the bow.

Amber should be coming into sight soon. I knew the ways of Shadow now, and I knew how to get there by walking.

But everyone had misgivings.

There would never be a perfect day, though. . . .

So we sailed on, and the darkness came upon us like a sudden wave, and the worst storm of them all struck.

We managed to ride out its black lashings, but I was scared. It was all true, and we were in northern waters. If Caine had kept his word, all well and good. If he was getting us out, he was in an excellent position.

So I assumed he had sold us out. Why not? I prepared the fleet— seventy-three vessels remaining—for battle, when I saw him approach. The cards had lied—or else been very correct—when they'd pointed to him as the key figure.

The lead vessel headed toward my own, and I moved forward to meet it. We hove to, and side by side regarded one another. We could have communicated via the Trumps, but Caine didn't choose to; and he was in the stronger position. Therefore, family etiquette required that he choose his own means. He obviously wanted to be on record as he called out, through an amplifier:

"Corwin! Kindly surrender command of your fleet! I've got you outnumbered! You can't make it through!"

I regarded him across the waves and raised my own amplifier to my lips.

"What of our arrangement?" I asked.

"Null and void," he said. "Your force is far too weak to hurt Amber, so save lives and surrender it now."

I looked over my left shoulder and regarded the sun.

"Pray hear me, brother Caine," said I, "and grant me this then: give me your leave to confer with my captains till the sun stands in high heaven."

"Very well," he replied, without hesitation. "They appreciate their positions, I'm sure."

I turned away then and ordered that the ship be turned about and headed back in the direction of the main body of vessels.

If I tried to flee, Caine would pursue me through the Shadows and destroy the ships, one by one. Gunpowder did not ignite on the real Earth, but if we moved very far away, it too would be employed to our undoing. Caine would find some, for it was probable, were I to depart, the fleet could not sail the Shadow seas without me, and would be left as sitting ducks upon the real waters here. So the crews were either dead or prisoners, whatever I did.

Random had been right.

I drew forth Bleys' Trump and concentrated till it moved.

"Yes?" he said, and his voice was agitated. I could almost hear the sounds of battle about him.

"We're in trouble," I said. "Seventy-three ships made it through, and Caine has called on us to surrender by noon."

"Damn his eyes!" said Bleys. "I haven't made it as far as you. We're in the middle of a fight now. An enormous cavalry force is cutting us to pieces. So I can't counsel you fairly. I've got my own problems. Do as you see fit. They're coming again!" And the contact was broken.

I drew forth Gérard's, and sought contact.

When we spoke it seemed I could see a shore line behind him. I seemed to recognize it. If my guess was correct, he was in southern waters. I don't like to remember our conversation. I asked him if he could help me against Caine, and if he would.

"I only agreed to let you by," he said. "That is why I withdrew to the south. I couldn't reach you in time if I wanted to. I did not agree to help you kill our brother."

And before I could reply, he was gone. He was right, of course. He'd agreed to give me an opportunity, not to fight my battle for me.

What then did that leave me?

I lit a cigarette. I paced the deck. It was no longer morning. The mists had long vanished and the sun warmed my shoulders. Soon it would be noon. Perhaps two hours. . . .

I fingered my cards, weighed the deck in my hand. I could try a contest of wills through them, with either Eric or Caine. There was that power present, and perhaps even others of which I knew nothing. They had been so designed, at the command of Oberon, by the hand of the mad artist Dworkin Barimen, that wild-eyed hunchback who had been a sorcerer, priest, or psychiatrist—the stories conflicted on this point—from some distant Shadow where Dad had saved him from a disastrous fate he had brought upon himself. The details were unknown, but he had always been a bit off his rocker since that time. Still, he was a great artist, and it was undeniable that he possessed some strange power. He had vanished ages ago, after creating the cards and tracing the Pattern in Amber. We had often speculated about him, but no one seemed to know his whereabouts. Perhaps Dad had done him in, to keep his secrets secret.

Caine would be ready for such an attack, and I probably couldn't break him, though I might be able to hold him. Even then, though, his captains had doubtless been given the order to attack.

Eric would surely be ready for anything, but if there was nothing else left to do, I might as well try it. I had nothing to lose but my soul.

Then there was the card for Amber itself. I could take myself there with it and try an assassination, but I figured the odds were about a million to one against my living to effect it.

I was willing to die fighting, but it was senseless for all these men to go down with me. Perhaps my blood was tainted, despite my power over the Pattern. A true prince of Amber should have had no such qualms. I decided then that my centuries on the Shadow Earth had changed me, softened me perhaps, had done something to me which made me unlike my brothers.

I decided to surrender the fleet and then transport myself to Amber and challenge Eric to a final dual. He'd be foolish to accept. But what the hell— I had nothing else left to do.

I turned to make my wishes known to my officers, and the power fell upon me, and I was stricken speechless.

I felt the contact and I finally managed to mutter "Who?" through clenched teeth. There was no reply, but a twisting thing bored slowly within my mind and I wrestled with it there.

After a time when he saw that I could not be broken without a long struggle, I heard Eric's voice upon the wind:

"How goes the world with thee, brother?" he inquired.

"Poorly," I said or thought, and he chuckled, though his voice seemed strained by the efforts of our striving.

"Too bad," he told me. "Had you come back and supported me, I would have done well by you. Now, of course, it is too late. Now, I will only rejoice when I have broken both you and Bleys."

I did not reply at once, but fought him with all the power I possessed. He withdrew slightly before it, but he succeeded in holding me where I stood.

If either of us dared divert his attention for an instant, we could come into physical contact or one of us get the upper hand on the mental plane. I could see him now, clearly, in his chamber in the palace. Whichever of us made such a move, though, he would fall beneath the other's control.

So we glared at each other and struggled internally. Well, he had solved one of my problems, by attacking me first. He held my Trump in his left hand and his brows were furrowed. I sought for an edge, but couldn't find one. People were talking to me but I couldn't hear their words as I stood there back against the rail.

What time was it?

All sense of time had departed since the beginning of the struggle. Could two hours have passed? Was that it? I couldn't be sure.

"I feel your troubled thought," said Eric. "Yes, I am coordinated with Caine. He contacted me after your parley. I can hold you thus while your fleet is demolished around you and sent down to Rebma to rot. The fishes will eat your men."

"Wait," I said. "They are guiltless. Bleys and I have misled them, and they think we are in the right. Their deaths would serve no purpose. I was preparing to surrender the fleet."

"Then you should not have taken so long," he replied, "for now it is too late. I cannot call Caine to countermand my orders, without releasing you, and the moment I release you I will fall beneath your mental domination or suffer physical assault. Our minds are too proximate."

"Supposing I give you my word that I won't do this thing?"

"Any man would be forsworn to gain a kingdom," said Eric.

"Can't you read the thought? Can't you feel it within my mind? I'll keep my word!"

"I feel there is a strange compassion for these men you have duped, and

I know not what may have caused such a bond, but no. You know it yourself. Even if you are sincere at this moment—as you well may be—the temptation will be too great the instant the opportunity occurs. You know it yourself. I can't risk it."

And I knew it. Amber burned too strongly in the blood of us.

"Your swordsmanship has increased remarkably," he commented. "I see that your exile has done you some good in that respect. You are closer to being my equal now than anyone save Benedict, who may well be dead."

"Don't flatter yourself," I said. "I know I can take you now. In fact—"

"Don't bother. I won't duel with you at this late date," and he smiled, reading my thought, which burned all too clearly.

"I more than half wish you had stood by me," he said. "I could have used you more than any of the others. Julian I spit upon. Caine is a coward. Gérard is strong, but stupid."

I decided to put in the only good word I might.

"Listen," I said. "I conned Random into coming here with me. He wasn't hot on the idea. I think he would have supported you, had you asked him."

"That bastard!" he said. "I wouldn't trust him to empty chamber pots. One day I'd find a piranha in mine. No thanks. I might have pardoned him, save for your present recommendation. You'd like me to clasp him to my bosom and call him brother now, wouldn't you? Oh no! You leap too quickly to his defense. It reveals his true attitude, of which he has doubtless made you aware. Let us forget Random in the courts of clemency."

I smelled smoke then and heard the sounds of metal on metal. That would mean that Caine had come upon us and was doing his job.

"Good," said Eric, catching it from my mind.

"Stop them! Please! My men don't have a chance against that many!"

"Not even were you to yield—" and he bit it off and cursed. I caught the thought, then. He could have asked me to yield in return for their lives, and then let Caine continue with the slaughter. He would have liked to have done that, but he'd let those first words slip out in the heat of his passion.

I chuckled at his irritation.

"I'll have you soon, anyhow," he said. "As soon as they take the flagship."

"Until then," I said, "try this!" And I hit him with everything I had, boring into his mind, hurting him with my hatred. I felt his pain and it drove me harder. For all the years of exile I'd spent, I lashed at him, seeking at least this payment. For his putting me through the plague, I beat at the barriers of his sanity, seeking this vengeance. For the auto accident, for which I knew he had been responsible, I struck at him, seeking some measure of anguish in return for my hurt.

His control began to slip and my frenzy increased. I bore down upon him and his hold upon me began to slacken.

Finally, "You devil!" he cried, and moved his hand to cover the card that he held.

The contact was broken, and I stood there shaking.

I had done it. I had bested him in a contest of wills. No longer would I fear my tyrant brother in any form of single combat. I was stronger than he.

I sucked in several deep breaths and stood erect, ready for the moment the coldness of a new mental attack occurred. I knew that it wouldn't, though, not from Eric. I sense that he feared my fury.

I looked about me and there was fighting. There was already blood on the decks. A ship had come alongside us and we were being boarded. Another vessel was attempting the same maneuver on the opposite side. A bolt whistled by my head.

I drew my blade and leaped into the fray.

I don't know how many I slew that day. I lost count somewhere after number twelve or thirteen. It was more than twice that, on that engagement alone, though. The strength with which a prince of Amber is naturally endowed, which had allowed me to lift a Mercedes, served me that day, so that I could raise a man with one hand and hurl him over the rail.

We slew everyone aboard both boarding ships and opened their hatches and sent them down to Rebma where Random would be amused by the carnage. My crew had been cut in half in the battle, and I had suffered innumerable nicks and scratches, but nothing serious. We went to the aid of a sister vessel and knocked off another of Caine's raiders.

The survivors of the rescued vessel came aboard the flagship and I had a full crew once more.

"Blood!" I called out. "Give me blood and vengeance this day, my warriors, and you will be remembered in Amber forever!"

And as a man, they raised their weapons and cried out, "Blood!" And gallons—no, rivers—of it were let that day. We destroyed two more of Caine's raiders, replenishing our numbers from those of the survivors of our own fleet. As we headed toward a sixth, I climbed the mainmast and tried to take a quick count.

We looked to be outnumbered three to one. There seemed to be between forty-five and fifty-five remaining of my fleet.

We took the sixth, and we didn't have to look for the seventh and the eighth. They came to us. We took them too, but I received several wounds in the fighting that again left me with half a crew. My left shoulder and my right thigh had been cut deeply, and a slash along my right hip was hurting.

As we sent those ships to the bottom, two more moved toward us.

We fled and gained an ally in one of my own ships which had been victorious in its own recent battle. We combined crews once more, this time transferring the standard to the other vessel, which had been less damaged than my own, which had begun shipping water badly and was beginning to list to starboard.

We were allowed no breathing space, as another vessel neared and the men attempted to board.

My men were tired, and I was getting that way. Fortunately the other crew wasn't in such great shape either. Before the second of Caine's vessels came to its aid, we had overwhelmed it, boarded, and transferred the standard again. That ship had been in even better shape.

We took the next and I was left with a good ship, forty men, and gasping.

There was no one in sight to come to our aid now. All of my surviving ships were engaged by at least one of Caine's. A raider was heading toward us and we fled.

We gained perhaps twenty minutes this way. I tried to sail into Shadow, but it's a hard, slow thing that near to Amber. It's much easier to get this close than it is to depart, because Amber is the center, the nexus. If I'd had another ten minutes, I could have made it.

I didn't, though.

As the vessel hove nearer, I saw another one off in the distance turning in our direction. It bore the black and green standard beneath Eric's colors and the white unicorn. It was Caine's ship. He wanted to be there for the kill.

We took the first one and didn't even have time to open its hatches before Caine was upon us. I was left standing on the bloody deck, with a dozen men about me, and Caine moved to the bow of his ship and called upon me to surrender.

"Will you grant my men their lives if I do this thing?" I asked him.

"Yes," he said. "I'd lose a few crewmen myself if I didn't, and there's no need for that."

"On your word as a prince?" I asked.

He thought about it a moment, then nodded.

"Very well," he said. "Have your men lay down their arms and board my vessel when I come alongside."

I sheathed my blade and nodded about me.

"You have fought the good fight, and I love you for it," I said. "But we have lost in this place." I dried my hands on my cloak as I spoke and wiped them carefully, as I'd hate to smudge a work of art. "Lay down your arms and know that your exploits of this day will never be forgotten. One day I will praise you before the court of Amber."

The men, the nine big red ones and the three remaining hairy ones, wept as they put down their arms.

"Do not fear that all is lost in the struggle for the city," I said. "We have lost only one engagement and the battle still continues elsewhere. My brother Bleys hacks his way toward Amber at this moment. Caine will keep his word to spare your lives when he sees that I have gone to join with Bleys upon the land, for he would not have knowledge that he was forsworn come into Amber. I am sorry that I cannot take you with me."

And with this, I drew Bleys' Trump from the pack and held it low and before me, out of sight of the other vessel.

Just as Caine came alongside, there was movement beneath that cold, cold surface.

"Who?" Bleys asked.

"Corwin," I said. "How fare you?"

"We won the battle, but lost many troops. We're resting now before we renew the march. How go things with you?"

"I think we've destroyed nearly half of Caine's fleet, but he's won the day. He's about to board me now. Give me escape."

He held forth his hand and I touched it and collapsed into his arms.

"This is getting to be a habit," I muttered, and then I saw that he was wounded too, about the head, and there was a bandage around his left hand. "Had to grab the wrong end of a saber," he remarked, as he saw my eyes fall upon it. "It smarts."

I caught my breath and then we walked to his tent, where he opened a bottle of wine and gave me bread, cheese, and some dried meat. He still had plenty of cigarettes and I smoked one as a medical officer dressed my wounds.

He still had around a hundred and eighty thousand men behind him. As I stood on a hilltop and the evening began around me, it seemed as if I looked out over every camp I had ever stood within, stretching on and on over the miles and the centuries without end. I suddenly felt tears come into my eyes, for the men who are not like the lords of Amber, living but a brief span and passing into dust, that so many of them must meet their ends upon the battlefields of the world.

I returned to Bleys' tent and we finished the bottle of wine.

SEVEN

That night there was a bad storm. It hadn't let up when dawn struggled to cross the world's palm with silver, and it continued on through the day's march.

It is a very demoralizing thing to tramp along and be rained on, a cold rain at that. How I've always hated the mud, through which it seems I've spent centuries marching!

We sought after a Shadow way that was free of rain, but nothing we did seemed to matter.

We could march to Amber, but we would do it with our clothing sticking to us, to the drumbeat of the thunder, with the flashing of the lightning at our backs.

The next night the temperature plummeted, and in the morning I stared past the stiff flags and regarded a world gone white beneath a gray sky, filled with flurries. My breath went back in plumes behind me.

The troops were ill-equipped for this, save for the hairy ones, and we got them all moving quickly, to prevent frostbite. The big red guys suffered. Theirs had been a very warm world.

We were attacked by tiger, polar bear, and wolf that day. The tiger Bleys killed measured over fourteen feet from tail tip to nose.

We marched on well into the night, and the thaw began. Bleys pushed the troops to get them out of the cold Shadows. The Trump of Amber indicated that a warm, dry autumn prevailed there, and we were nearing the real Earth.

By midnight on that second night we'd marched through slush and sleet, cold rains, warm rains, and on into a dry world.

The orders were given to make camp then, with triple security cordons. Considering the tired condition of the men we were ripe for an attack. But the troops were staggering and couldn't be pushed much further.

The attack came several hours later, and Julian led it, I learned later from the description given by survivors.

He headed commando raids against our most vulnerable campsites on the periphery of the main body. Had I known it to be Julian, I would have used his Trump to try to hold him, but I only knew it after the fact.

We'd lost perhaps two thousand men in the abrupt winter, and I didn't yet know how many Julian had accounted for.

It seemed the troops were beginning to get demoralized, but they followed when we ordered them ahead.

The next day was one continuous ambush. A body of men the size of ours could not be allowed to deviate sufficiently to try to deal with the harassing raids Julian led against our flanks. We got some of his men, but not enough—one for every ten of ours, perhaps.

By high noon we were crossing the valley that paralleled the seacoast. The Forest of Arden was to the north and our left. Amber lay directly ahead. The breezes were cool and filled with the odors of earth and its sweet growing things. A few leaves fell. Amber lay eighty miles distant and was but a shimmer above the horizon.

That afternoon, with a gathering of clouds and but the lightest of rains, the bolts began to fall from the heavens. Then the storm ceased and the sun came forth to dry things off.

After a time, we smelled the smoke.

After another time, we saw it, flapping skyward all about us.

Then the sheets of flame began to rise and fall. They moved toward us, with their crunching, constant footsteps; and as they came nearer, we began to feel the heat, and somewhere, way back along the lines, a panic arose. There were cries, and the columns swelled and welled forward.

We began to run.

Flakes of ash were falling about us now, and the smoke grew thicker. We sprinted ahead and the flames rushed even closer. The sheets of light and heat flapped a steady, welling thunder as we ran, and the waves of warmth beat upon us, washed over us. Soon they were right there alongside us, and the trees blackened and the leaves flaked down, and some of the smaller trees began to sway. For as far ahead as we could see, our way was an alley of fires.

We ran faster, for soon things would be worse.

And we were not mistaken.

Big trees began to topple across our path. We leaped over them, we circled around them. At least, we were on a trail. . . .

The heat became stifling and the breath came heavy in our lungs. Deer and wolves and foxes and rabbits darted past us, fleeing with us, ignoring our presence and that of their natural enemies. The air above the smoke seemed filled with crying birds. Their droppings fell among us, went unnoticed.

To burn this ancient wood, as venerable as the Forest of Arden, seemed almost an act of sacrilege to me. But Eric was prince in Amber, and soon to be king. I suppose I might have, too. . . .

My eyebrows and hair were singed. My throat felt like a chimney. How many would this assault cost us? I wondered.

Seventy miles of wooded valley lay between us and Amber, and over thirty behind us, going back to the forest's end.

"Bleys!" I gasped. "Two or three miles ahead of us the trail forks! The right branch comes more quickly to the river Oisen, which goes down to the sea! I think it's our one chance! The whole Valley of Garnath is going to be burned! Our only hope lies in reaching the water!"

He nodded.

We raced on, but the fires outpaced us.

We made it to the fork, though, beating out flames on our smoldering clothing, wiping ashes from our eyes, spitting such from our mouths, running hands through our hair when the flamelets nested there.

"Only about a quarter mile more," I said.

I had been struck several times by falling boughs. All the exposed areas of my skin pulsed with a more than feverish pain, and many of the covered areas as well. We ran through burning grasses, heading down a long slope, and when we reached the bottom we saw the water, and our speed increased, though we didn't think it possible. We plunged in and let the cold wetness embrace us.

Bleys and I contrived to float as near together as possible as the currents took us and we were swept along the twisting course of the Oisen. The interlocked branches of the trees overhead had become as the beams in a cathedral of fire. As they broke apart and collapsed in places, we had to turn onto our bellies and swim or dive for the deepest places, depending on how near we were. The waters about us were filled with hissing and blackened debris, and at our backs our surviving troops' heads in the river seemed as a strip of floating coconuts.

The waters were dark and cold and our wounds began to ache, and we shivered and our teeth chattered.

It was several miles before we left the burning wood and reached the low, flat, treeless place that led on to the sea. It would be a perfect place for Julian to be waiting, with archers, I decided. I mentioned this to Bleys and he agreed, but he didn't reckon there was much we could do about it. I was forced to agree.

The woods burned all around us, and we swam and we drifted.

It seemed like hours, but must have been less, before my fears began to materialize and the first volley of arrows descended.

I dove, and I swam underwater for a long distance. Since I was going with the current, I made it quite a way along the river before I had to surface once more.

As I did, more arrows fell about me.

The gods knew how long this gauntlet of death might be drawn, but I didn't want to stick around and find out.

I gulped air and dove once more.

I touched bottom, I felt my way among rocks.

I moved along for as far as I could, then headed toward the right bank, exhaling as I rose.

I burst through the surface, gasped, took a deep breath and went down again, without sticking around to get the lay of the land.

I swam on till my lungs were bursting, and surfaced then.

This time I wasn't quite so lucky. I took an arrow through my biceps. I managed to dive and break off the shaft when I struck bottom. Then I pulled out the head and continued on by means of the frog kick and underbody sculling with my right hand. The next time up I'd be a sitting duck, I knew.

So I forced myself on, till the red flashes crossed my eyeballs and the blackness crept into my head. I must have stayed down for three minutes.

When I surfaced this time, though, nothing happened, and I trod water and gasped.

I made my way to the left bank and grabbed hold of the trailing undergrowth.

I looked all around me. We were running short on trees at this point, and the fires hadn't gotten this far. Both banks seemed empty, but so did the river. Could I have been the only survivor? It didn't seem possible. After all, there had been so many of us when the last march began.

I was half dead with fatigue and my entire body was laced with aches and pains. Every inch of my skin seemed to have been burned, but the waters were so cold that I was shaking and probably blue. I'd have to leave the river soon, if I wanted to live. I felt that I could manage a few more underwater expeditions, and I decided to chance them before departing from the sheltering depths.

Somehow I managed four more laps, and I felt then that I might not come up again if I tried a fifth. So I hung onto a rock and caught my breath, then crawled ashore.

I rolled onto my back and looked all around. I didn't recognize the locale. The fires hadn't reached it yet, though. There was a thick clump of bushes off to my right and I crawled toward it, crawled into it, fell flat on my face and went to sleep.

When I awoke, I wished I hadn't. Every inch of me ached, and I was sick. I lay there for hours, half delirious, and finally managed to stagger back to the river for a long drink of water. Then I headed back for the thicket, made it, and slept again.

I was still sore when consciousness came once more, but a little bit stronger. I walked to the river and back, and by means of my icy Trump found that Bleys was still alive.

"Where are you?" he asked, when I had made the contact.

"Damned if I know," I replied. "Lucky to be anywhere at all. Near the sea, though. I can hear the waves and I know the smell."

"You're near the river?"

"Yes."

"Which bank?"

"Left, as you'd face the sea. North."

"Then stay put," he told me, "and I'll send someone after you. I'm assembling our forces now. I've already got over two thousand together, and Julian won't come near us. More keep straggling in every minute."

"Okay," I said, and that was it.

I stayed put. I slept as I did so.

I heard them bashing about in the bushes and was alert. I pushed some fronds aside and peered forth.

It was three of the big red guys.

So I straightened my gear and brushed all my garments, ran a hand through my hair, stood erect and swayed, took several deep breaths, and stepped forth.

"I am here," I announced.

Two of them did double-takes, blades in their hands, as I said it.

But they recovered, smiled, paid me deference, and conducted me back to the camp. It was perhaps two miles distant. I made it without leaning.

Bleys appeared and said, "We've got over three thousand now." Then he called for a medical officer to take care of me again.

We were undisturbed all through the night, and the rest of our troops straggled in that night and the following day.

We had perhaps five thousand by then. We could see Amber in the distance.

We slept another night and on the following morning we set forth.

By afternoon we had made maybe fifteen miles. We marched along the beach, and there was no sign of Julian anywhere.

The feeling of pain from my burns began to subside. My thigh was healthy, but my shoulder and arm still hurt from here to hell and back again.

We marched on, and soon we were within forty miles of Amber. The weather stayed clement, and all of the wood to our left was a desolate, blackened ruin. The fire had destroyed most of the timber in the valley, so for once there was a thing in our favor. Julian nor anybody else could ambush us. We'd see them coming a mile off. We made another ten miles ere the sun fell and we bivouacked on the beach.

The next day, I remembered that Eric's coronation was near at hand and I reminded Bleys. We had almost lost count of the days, but realized we still had a few remaining.

We led a speed-march till noon, then rested. By then, we were twenty-five miles away from the foot of Kolvir. By twilight, the distance was ten.

And we kept on. We marched till midnight and we bivouacked once again. By that time, I was beginning to feel fairly alive once more. I practiced a few cuts with my blade and could almost manage them. The next day, I felt even better.

We marched until we came to the foot of Kolvir, where we were met by all of Julian's forces, combined with many from Caine's fleet who now stood as foot soldiers.

Bleys stood there and called things, like Robert E. Lee at Chancellorsville, and we took them.

We had maybe three thousand men when we had finished off everything Julian had to throw against us. Julian, of course, escaped.

But we had won. There was celebration that night. We had won.

I was very afraid by then, and I made my fears known to Bleys. Three thousand men against Kolvir.

I had lost the fleet, and Bleys had lost over ninety-eight percent of his foot soldiers. I did not look upon these as rejoiceable items.

I didn't like it.

But the next day we began the ascent. There was a stairway, allowing for the men to go two abreast along it. This would narrow soon, however, forcing us to go single file.

We made it a hundred yards up Kolvir, then two, then three.

Then the storm blew in from the sea, and we held tight and were lashed by it.

Afterward, a couple of hundred men were missing.

We struggled on and the rains came down. The way grew steeper, more slippery. A quarter of the way up Kolvir we met with a column of armed men descending. The first of these traded blows with the leaders of our vanguard, and two men fell. Two steps were gained, and another man fell.

This went on for over an hour, and by then we were about a third of the way up and our line was wearing back toward Bleys and myself. It was good that our big red warriors were stronger than Eric's troops. There would come a clash of arms, a cry, and a man would be brought by. Sometimes he would be red, occasionally furry, but more often he wore Eric's colors.

We made it to the halfway point, fighting for every step. Once we reached the top, there would be the broad stair of which the one to Rebma had been but an image. It would lead up to the Great Arch, which was the eastern entranceway to Amber.

Perhaps fifty of our vanguard remained. Then forty, thirty, twenty, a dozen. . . .

We were about two-thirds of the way up by then, and the stair zigged and zagged its way back and forth across the face of Kolvir. The eastern stair is seldom used. It is almost a decoration. Our original plans had been to cut through the now blackened valley and then circle, climbing, and to take the western way over the mountains and enter Amber from behind. The fire and

Julian had changed all this. We'd never have made it up and around. It was now a frontal assault or nothing. And it wasn't going to be nothing.

Three more of Eric's warriors fell and we gained four steps. Then our front man made the long descent and we lost one.

The breeze was sharp and cool from off the sea, and birds were collecting at the foot of the mountain. The sun broke through the clouds, as Eric apparently put aside his weather-making now that we were engaged with his force.

We gained six steps and lost another man.

It was strange and sad and wild. . . .

Bleys stood before me, and soon his turn would come. Then mine, should he perish.

Six of the vanguard remained.

Ten steps . . .

Then five remained.

We pushed on, slowly, and there was blood on every step for as far back as I could see. There's a moral there, somewhere.

The fifth man slew four before he fell himself, so bringing us another zig, or zag, as the case may be.

Onward and upward, our third man fighting with a blade in either hand. It was good that he fought in a holy war, for there was real zeal behind each blow. He took three before he died.

The next wasn't as zealous, or as good with his blades. He fell immediately, and then there were two.

Bleys drew his long, filigreed blade, and its edge sparkled in the sun.

"Soon, brother," he said, "we will see what they can do against a prince."

"Only one, I hope," I replied, and he chuckled.

I'd say we were three-quarters of the way there when Bleys' turn finally came.

He leaped forward, immediately dislodging the first man to face him. The point of his blade found the throat of the second, and the flat of it fell alongside the head of the third, dislodging him also. He dueled a moment with the fourth and dispatched him.

My own blade was in my hand, ready, as I watched and advanced.

He was good, even better than I remembered him to be. He advanced like a whirlwind, and his blade was alive with light. They fell before it—how they fell, my friend! Whatever else you might say of Bleys, on that day he acquitted himself as became his rank. I wondered how long he could keep going.

He'd a dagger in his left hand, which he used with brutal efficiency whenever he could manage a corps à corps. He left it in the throat of his eleventh victim.

I could see no end to the column which opposed us. I decided that it must stretch all the way to the landing at the top. I hoped my turn wouldn't come. I almost believed it.

Three more men plummeted past me and we came to a small landing and a turn. He cleared the landing and began the ascent. For half an hour I watched him, and they died and they died. I could hear the murmurs of awe from the men behind me. I almost thought he could make it to the top.

He used every trick available. He baffled blades and eyes with his cloak. He tripped the warriors. He seized wrists and twisted, with his full strength.

We made it to another landing. There was some blood on his sleeve by then, but he smiled constantly, and the warriors behind the warriors he killed were ashen. This helped him, too. And perhaps the fact that I stood ready to fill the gap also contributed to their fears and so slowed them, worked on their nerves. They'd heard of the naval engagement, I later learned.

Bleys worked his way to the next landing, cleared it, turned again, began to ascend. I hadn't thought he could make it that far, then. I didn't think I could make it as far as he had. It was the most phenomenal display of swordsmanship and endurance I'd seen since Benedict had held the pass above Arden against the Moonriders out of Ghenesh.

He was tiring, though, I could see that, too. If only there were some way for me to relieve him, to spell him for a time. . . .

But there wasn't. So I followed, fearing every stroke might be his last.

I knew that he was weakening. We were within a hundred feet of the top at that point.

I suddenly felt for him. He was my brother and he'd done well by me. I don't think he thought he'd make it then, yet he was fighting on . . . in effect, giving me my chance for the throne.

He killed three more men, and his blade moved more slowly each time. He fought with the fourth for perhaps five minutes before he took him. I was certain the next would be his last.

He wasn't, though.

As he slew that man, I transferred my blade from my right hand to my left, drew my dagger with my right and threw it.

It went in up to the hilt, in the throat of the next man.

Bleys sprang over two steps and hamstrung the man before him, casting him downward.

Then he cup upward, ripping open the belly of the one behind that one.

I rushed to fill the gap, to be right behind him and ready. He didn't need me yet, though.

He took the next two, with a new burst of energy. I called for another dagger and one was passed to me from somewhere along the line.

I kept it ready till he slowed once more, and I used it on the man he fought.

The man was lunging as it spun in, so the hilt rather than the blade caught him. It struck against his head, though, and Bleys pushed against his shoulder and he fell. But the next man leaped forward, and though he impaled himself, he struck Bleys upon the shoulder and they went over the edge together.

By reflex, almost without knowing what I was doing, yet knowing fully in one of those microsecond decisions you justify after the fact, my left hand leaped to my belt, whipped out my pack of the Trumps and cast them toward Bleys as he seemed to hang there for an instant—so rapidly did my muscles and perceptions respond—and I cried out, "Catch them, you fool!"

And he did.

I didn't have time to see what happened next, as I parried and thrust.

Then began the final lap of our journey up Kolvir.

Let's just say I made it and was gasping, as my troops came over the edge to support me there on the landing.

We consolidated our forces and pressed ahead.

It took us an hour to reach the Great Arch.

We passed through. We entered Amber.

Wherever Eric was, I'm sure he'd never guessed we'd make it this far.

And I wondered where Bleys was. Had he gotten a chance to grab a Trump and use it, before he reached the bottom? I guessed that I'd never know.

We had underestimated, all the way around. We were outnumbered now, and the only thing left to do was to fight on for as long as we could hold out. Why had I done such a foolish thing as throw Bleys my Trumps? I knew he had none of his own and that's what had dictated my response, conditioned perhaps by my years on the Shadow Earth. But I might have used them to escape, if things went badly.

Things went badly.

We fought on until twilight, and by then there was only a small band of us remaining.

We were surrounded at a point a thousand yards within Amber, and still far from the palace. We were fighting a defensive fight, and one by one we died. We were overwhelmed.

Llewella or Deirdre would have given me sanctuary. Why had I done it?

I killed another man and put the question out of my mind.

The sun went down and darkness filled the sky. We were down to a few hundred by then, and not much closer to the palace.

Then I saw Eric and heard him shouting orders. If only I could reach him!

But I couldn't.

I'd probably have surrendered, to save my remaining troops, who had served me far too well.

But there was no one to surrender to, no one asking for a surrender. Eric couldn't even hear me if I cried out. He was out of the way, directing.

So we fought on, and I was down to a hundred men.

Let's be brief.

They killed everyone but me.

At me they threw nets and unleashed blunted arrows.

Finally, I fell and was clubbed and hog-tied, and then everything went away but a nightmare which attached itself and wouldn't let go, no matter what.

We had lost.

I awoke in a dungeon far below Amber, sorry that I had made it that far.

The fact that I still lived meant Eric had plans for me. I visualized racks and braces, flames and tongs. I foresaw my coming degradation as I lay there on the damp straw.

How long had I been unconscious? I did not know.

I searched my cell for a means of committing suicide. I found nothing that would serve this purpose.

All my wounds blazed like suns, and I was so very tired.

I lay me down and slept once more.

I awakened, and still no one came to me. There was none to buy, none to torture.

Also, there was nothing for me to eat.

I lay there, wrapping in my cloak, and I reviewed everything that had happened since I'd awakened in Greenwood and refused my hypo. Better, perhaps, if I hadn't.

I knew despair.

Soon Eric would be crowned king in Amber. This thing might already have occurred.

But sleep was so lovely a thing, and I so tired.

It was the first real chance I'd had to rest and forget my wounds.

The cell was so dark and smelly and damp.

EIGHT

How many times I awakened and returned to sleep, I do not know. Twice I found bread and meat and water on a trap by the door. Both times, I emptied the tray. My cell was almost pitch dark and very chilly. I waited there, and I waited.

Then they came for me.

The door swung open and a feeble light entered. I blinked at it as I was called forth.

The corridor without was filled to overflowing with armed men, so I wasn't about to try anything.

I rubbed at the stubble on my chin and went where they took me.

After a long walk, we came to the hall of the spiral stair and began to ascend. I asked no questions as we moved, and no one offered me any information.

When we reached the top, I was conducted further into the palace proper. They took me to a warm, clean room and ordered me to strip, which I did. Then I entered a steaming tub of water, and a servant came forth and scrubbed me and shaved me and trimmed my hair.

When I was dry again, I was given fresh garments, of black and of silver.

I donned them, and a black cloak was hung about my shoulders, its clasp a silver rose.

"You are ready," said the sergeant of the guard. "Come this way."

I followed him, and the guard followed me.

I was taken far to the back of the palace where a smith placed manacles about my wrists, fetters on my ankles, with chains upon them too heavy for me to break. Had I resisted, I knew I would have been beaten unconscious and the result would have been the same. I had no desire to be beaten unconscious again, so I complied.

Then the chains were taken up by several of the guards, and I was led back toward the front of the palace. I had no eyes for the magnificence that lay all about me. I was a prisoner. I would probably soon be dead or on the rack. There was nothing I could do right now. A glance out of the window showed me that it was early evening, and there was no place for nostalgia as I passed through the rooms where we had played as children.

I was led up a long corridor and into the great dining room.

There were tables all over the place, and people seated all about them, many of whom I knew.

All the fine gowns and suits of Amber burned about me on the bodies of the nobles, and there was music beneath the torchlight and food already upon the tables, though no one was eating yet.

I saw faces that I recognized, like Flora's, and some strange faces. There was the minstrel, Lord Rein—yes, he had been knighted, by me—whom I had not seen in centuries. He turned his eyes away when my gaze fell upon him.

I was taken to the foot of the huge center table and seated there.

The guards stayed and stood behind me. They fastened the ends of my chains to rings fresh-set in the floor. The seat at the head of my table was as yet unoccupied.

I did not recognize the woman to my right, but the man to my left was Julian. I ignored him and stared at the lady, a little wisp of a blonde.

"Good evening," I said. "I don't believe we've been introduced. My name is Corwin."

She looked at the man at her right for support, a heavy, redheaded guy with lots of freckles. He looked away and suddenly became engaged in an animated conversation with the woman to his right.

"It's all right to talk with me, honest," I said. "It's not contagious."

She managed a weak smile and said, "I'm Carmel. How are you, Prince Corwin?"

"That's a sweet name," I replied, "and I'm just fine. What's a nice girl like you doing in a place like this?"

She took a quick drink of water.

"Corwin," said Julian, louder than necessary. "I think the lady finds you offensive and obnoxious."

"What's she said to you so far this evening?" and he didn't blush. He whitened.

"That will be enough from you."

I stretched then, and rattled my chains on purpose. Outside of the effect it produced, it also showed me how much slack I had. Not enough, of course. Eric had been careful.

"Come closer and whisper me your objections, brother," I said.

But he didn't.

I had been the last to be seated, so I knew the time was near at hand. And it was.

There came five trumpet notes from six trumpets and Eric entered the hall.

Everybody stood.

Except for me.

The guards had to drag me to my feet by means of the chains and hold me there.

Eric smiled and descended the stair to my right. I could barely see his own colors beneath the ermine robe that he wore.

He moved to the head of the table and stood before his chair. A servant came and stood behind him, and the wine stewards made their rounds, pouring.

When all the glasses were filled, he raised his.

"May you dwell forever in Amber," he said, "which endureth forever," and everyone raised his glass.

Except for me.

"Pick it up!" said Julian.

"Shove it up," said I.

He didn't, only glared. But I leaned forward quickly then and raised my glass.

There were a couple hundred people between us, but my voice carried. And Eric's eyes were upon me all the while, as I said, "To Eric, who sits at the foot of the table!"

No one moved to touch me as Julian emptied his glass upon the floor. All the others did the same, but I managed to quaff most of mine, before it was struck from my hand.

Eric seated himself then and the nobles followed suit, and I was released to fall into my chair.

The serving began, and since I was hungry I ate as well as the rest of them, and better than most.

There was constant music and the meal lasted for over two hours. No one said a word to me during the whole time, and I said nothing more myself. But my presence was felt, and our table was quieter than the others.

Caine sat farther up along the table. At Eric's right hand. I gathered that Julian was out of favor. Neither Random or Deirdre was present. There were many other nobles whom I recognized, some of whom I had once counted as friends, but none of these would return my glances.

I gathered then that it only required a small formality for Eric to be king in Amber.

And this followed shortly.

After dinner, there were no speeches. Eric simply stood.

There came another flash of trumpets and a raucous sound upon the air.

Then there was a procession, leading all the way to the throne room of Amber.

I knew what was coming next.

Eric stood before the throne and everybody bowed.

Except for me, that is, and I was forced to my knees anyway.

Today was the day of his coronation.

There was silence. Then Caine bore in the cushion which held the crown, the crown of Amber. He knelt and froze in that position, offering it.

Then I was jerked to my feet and dragged forward. I knew what was about to happen. It came upon me in a flash, and I fought. But I was beaten down and brought to my knees at the foot of the stair before the throne.

The music rose up softly—it was "Greensleeves"—and somewhere at my back Julian said, "Behold the crowning of a new king in Amber!" Then to me, in a whisper, "Take up the crown and hand it to Eric. He will crown himself."

I stared at the crown of Amber upon the crimson cushion Caine held.

It was wrought of silver and had seven high points, each topped by a gem stone. It was studded with emeralds, and there were two huge rubies at either temple.

I didn't move, thinking of the times I had seen the face of our father beneath it.

"No," I said simply, and I felt a blow upon my left cheek.

"Take it and give it to Eric," he repeated.

I tried to strike at him, but my chains were drawn tight. I was struck again.

I stared at the high sharp peaks.

"Very well," I finally said, and reached for it.

I held it in both hands for a moment then quickly placed it on my own head and declared, "I crown me, Corwin, king of Amber!"

It was removed immediately and replaced upon the cushion. Several blows fell upon my back. There came a murmuring throughout the hall.

"Now pick it up and try it again," said Julian. "Take it and hand it to Eric."

Another blow fell.

"Okay," I told him, feeling my shirt grow wet.

This time I hurled it, hoping it put out one of Eric's eyes.

He caught it in his right hand and smiled down at me as I was beaten.

"Thank you," he said. "Now hear me, all you present, and those of you who listen in Shadow. I assume the crown and throne this day. I take into my hand the scepter of the kingdom of Amber. I have won the throne fairly, and I take it and hold it by the right of my blood."

"Liar!" I cried, and a hand was clapped over my mouth.

"I crown myself Eric the First, King of Amber."

"Long live the king!" cried the nobles, three times.

Then he leaned forward and whispered to me, "Your eyes have looked upon the fairest sight they will ever behold. . . . Guards! Take Corwin away to the stithy, and let his eyes be burnt from out his head! Let him remember the sights of this day as the last he might ever see! Then cast him into the darkness of the deepest dungeon beneath Amber, and let his name be forgotten!"

I spat and was beaten.

I fought every step of the way, but was taken forth from the hall. No one would look upon me as I went, and the last thing I remember was the sight of Eric seated upon his throne, pronouncing his blessing upon the nobles of Amber, and smiling.

That which he said was done to me, and mercifully I fainted before it was finished.

I have no idea how much later it was that I awakened within absolute blackness and felt the terrible pains within my head. Perhaps it was then that I pronounced the curse, or perhaps it had been at the time that the white-hot irons had descended. I don't remember. But I knew that Eric would never rest easy upon the throne, for the curse of a prince of Amber, pronounced in a fullness of fury, is always potent.

I clawed at the straw, in the absolute blackness of my cell, and no tears came. That was the horror of it. After a time—only you and I, gods, know how long—sleep came again.

When I awakened, there was still the pain. I rose to my feet. I measured off the dimensions of my cell. Four paces in width, five in length. There was a lavatory hole in the floor and a straw-tick mattress in a corner. The door contained a small slot at the bottom, and behind it there was a tray which held a stale piece of bread and a bottle of water. I ate and I drank, but I was not refreshed.

My head ached so, and there was nothing of peace within me.

I slept as much as I could, and no one came to see me. I awakened and crossed my cell and felt for food and ate it when I found it. I slept as much as I could.

After seven sleeps, the pain was gone from out my eye sockets. I hated my brother who was king in Amber. Better he had killed me.

I wondered at the popular reaction, but could not guess.

When the darkness reached as far as Amber, however, I knew that Eric would have his regrets. This much I knew, and this comforted me.

Thus began my days of darkness, and I had no way of measuring their passage. Even if I had had eyes, I could not have distinguished day from night in that place.

Time went on its way, ignoring me. There were occasions when I broke into a sweat over this and shivered. Had I been there months? Only hours? Or weeks? Or had it been years?

I forgot all about time. I slept, I paced (I knew exactly where to place my feet and when to turn), and I reflected upon things I had done and hadn't done. Sometimes I would sit cross-legged and breathe slowly and deeply, and empty my mind and keep it that way for as long as I could. This helped—thinking of nothing.

Eric had been clever. Although the power lived within me, now it was useless. A blind man cannot walk among Shadows.

My beard had grown down to my chest and my hair was long. I was always hungry at first, but after a time my appetite waned. Sometimes I grew dizzy when I stood up too rapidly.

I could still see, in my nightmares, but this hurt me even more when I awakened.

Later, though, I felt somewhat distant from the events which had led up to this. It was almost as though they had happened to a different person. And this, too, was true.

I had lost a lot of weight. I could visualize myself, pallid and thin. I couldn't even cry, though I felt like it a couple of times. There was something wrong with my tear ducts. It was a dreadful thing that any man should be brought to this.

Then one day there came a light scratching upon the door. I ignored it.

It came again, and still I did not respond.

Then I heard my name whispered, in the interrogative.

I crossed the cell.

"Yes?" I replied.

"It's me, Rein," he said. "How are you?"

I laughed at that.

"Fine! Oh just fine!" I said. "Steak and champagne every night, and dancing girls. God! You should make the scene sometime!"

"I'm sorry," he said, "that there is nothing I can do for you," and I could feel the pain in his voice.

"I know," I said.

"I would if I could," he told me.

"I know that, too."

"I brought you something. Here."

The little gate at the bottom of the cell door creaked slightly as it swung inward several times.

"What is it?" I asked.

"Some clean clothes," he said, "and three loaves of fresh bread, a head of cheese, some beef, two bottles of wine, a carton of cigarettes, and a lot of matches."

My voice caught in my throat.

"Thanks, Rein. You're all right. How did you arrange this?"

"I know the guard who's standing duty this shift. He won't talk. He owes me too much."

"He might try to cancel his debts by squealing," I said. "So don't do it again—much as I appreciate it. Needless to say, I'll dispose of the evidence."

"I wish it had turned out different, Corwin."

"You and me both. Thanks for thinking of me when you were ordered not to."

"That part was easy," he said.

"How long have I been in this place?"

"Four months and ten days," he said.

"So what's new in Amber?"

"Eric reigns. That's all."

"Where's Julian?"

"Back in the Forest of Arden with his guard."

"Why?"

"Some strange things made it through Shadow recently."

"I see. How about Caine?"

"He's still in Amber, enjoying himself. Wenching and drinking, mostly."

"And Gérard?"

"He's admiral of the entire fleet."

I sighed with a bit of relief. I was afraid his withdrawal during the naval engagement might have cost him something with Eric.

"And what of Random?"

"He's up the hall aways."

"What? He was taken?"

"Yes. He walked the Pattern in Rebma and showed up here, with a crossbow. He wounded Eric before he was taken."

"Really? Why wasn't he slain?"

"Well, rumor has it he's married a noblewoman of Rebma. Eric didn't want to court an incident with Rebma at this point. Moire has quite a kingdom, and there is talk that Eric is even considering asking her to be his queen. All gossip, of course. But interesting."

"Yes," I said.

"She liked you, didn't she?"

"Somewhat. How did you hear?"

"I was present when Random was sentenced. I got to speak with him for a moment. The Lady Vialle, who claims to be his wife, has asked to join him in prison. Eric is not yet certain how to reply."

I thought upon the blind girl, who I had never met, and I wondered at this.

"How long ago did all this happen?" I asked.

"Mm. Thirty-four days," he replied. "That was when Random showed up. A week later, Vialle made her request."

"She must be a strange woman, if she really loves Random."

"Those were my sentiments," he replied. "I can't think of a more unusual combination."

"If you should get to see him again, give him my regards and my regrets."

"Yes."

"How fare my sisters?"

"Dierdre and Llewella remain in Rebma. The Lady Florimel has been enjoying Eric's favors and stands high in the present court. I do not know where Fiona is presently."

"Has anything more been heard of Bleys? I am sure that he died."

"He must have died," said Rein. "His body was never recovered, though."

"What of Benedict?"

"As absent as ever."

"How about Brand?"

"No word."

"Then I guess that covers the whole family tree, as it stands at present. Have you written any new ballads?"

"No," he said. "I'm still working on 'The Siege of Amber,' but it will be an underground hit, if at all."

I reached my hand out through the tiny gate at the bottom of the door.

"I would clasp hands with thee," I said, and I felt his hand touch mine.

"It was good of thee to do this thing for me. Don't do it again, though. It would be foolish to risk Eric's wrath."

He squeezed my hand, muttered something, and was gone.

I found his CARE package and stuffed myself with the meat, which was the most perishable item. I ate a lot of the bread, to accompany it, and I realized that I had almost forgotten how good food can taste. Then I grew drowsy and slept. I don't think I slept very long, and when I awoke I opened one of the bottles of wine.

It didn't take as much as usual, in my weakened condition, to get me kind of high. I had a cigarette, sat down on my mattress, leaned back against the wall, and mused.

I remembered Rein as a child. I was already full grown by then and he was a candidate for court jester. A thin, wise kid. People had kidded him too much. Me included. But I wrote music, composed ballads, and he'd picked up a lute somewhere and had taught himself how to use it. Soon we were singing with voices together raised and all like that, and before long I took a liking to him and we worked together, practicing the martial arts. He was lousy at them, but I felt kind of sorry for the way I had treated him earlier, what with the way he had dug my stuff, so I forced the fake graces upon him and also made him a passable saber man. I'd never regretted it, and I guess he didn't either. Before long, he became minstrel to the court of Amber. I had called him my page all that while, and when the wars beckoned, against the dark things out of Shadow called Weirmonken, I made him my squire, and we had ridden off to the wars together. I knighted him upon the battlefield, at Jones Falls, and he had deserved it. After that, he had gone on to become my better when it came to the ways of words and music. His colors were crimson and his words were golden. I loved him, as one of my two or three friends in Amber. I didn't think he'd take the risk he had to bring me a decent meal, though. I didn't think anyone would. I had another drink and smoked another cigarette, in his name, to celebrate him. He was a good man. I wondered how long he would survive.

I threw all the butts in the head and also—eventually—the empty bottle.

I didn't want anything around to show that I had been "enjoying" myself, should a sudden inspection be held. I ate all the good food he had brought me, and I felt surfeited for the first time since I had been in durance. I saved the last bottle for one massive spell of drunkenness and forgetfulness.

And after that time had passed, I returned to my cycle of recriminations.

I hoped, mainly, that Eric had no measure of our complete powers. He was king in Amber, granted, but he didn't know everything. Not yet. Not the way Dad had known. There was a million-in-one shot that might still work in my favor. So much so, and so different that at least it served to grant me my small purchase upon sanity, there in the grip of despair.

But maybe I did go mad for a time, I don't know. There are days that are great blanks to me now, as I stand here on the brink of Chaos. God knows what they held, and I'll never see a shrink to find out.

There are none of you, good doctors, could cope with my family, anyway.

I lay there and I paced there, within the numbing darkness. I grew quite sensitive to sounds. I listened to the scurry of rats' feet through straw, the distant moaning of other prisoners, the echoes of a guard's footsteps as he approached with a tray of food. I began estimating distances and direction from things like this.

I suppose I became more sensitive to odors also, but I tried not to think about them too much. Aside from the imaginable nauseating ones there was, for a long while, what I would swear to be the odor of decaying flesh. I wondered. If I were to die, how long would it be before someone took notice? How many chunks of bread and bowls of slop would go uneaten before the guard thought to check within after my continued existence?

The answer to that one could be very important.

The death odor was around for a long while. I tried to think in terms of time again, and it seemed that it persisted for over a week.

Though I rationed myself carefully, resisting the compulsion, the handy temptation, for as long as I could, I finally found myself down to my final pack of cigarettes.

I tore it open and lit one. I had had a carton of Salems and I had smoked eleven packs. That was two hundred and twenty cigarettes. I had once timed myself with one, and it had taken me seven minutes to smoke it. That made for a total of one thousand five hundred and forty minutes spent smoking, or twenty-five hours and forty minutes. I was sure I had spent at least an hour between cigarettes, more like an hour and a half. Say an hour and a half. Now figure that I was sleeping six to eight hours per day. That left sixteen to eighteen waking hours. I guessed I was smoking ten or twelve per day. So that meant maybe three weeks had passed since Rein's visit. He had told me it was four months and ten days since the coronation, which meant that it was now around five months.

I nursed my last pack, enjoying each one like a love affair. When they were all gone, I felt depressed.

Then a lot more time must have passed.

I got to wondering about Eric. How was he making out as leige? What problems was he encountering? What was he up to right now? Why hadn't he been around to torment me? Could I ever truly be forgotten in Amber, even by imperial decree? Never, I decided.

And what of my brothers? Why had none of them contacted me? It would be so easy to draw forth my Trump and break Eric's decree.

No one did, though.

I thought for a long while upon Moire, the last woman I had loved. What was she doing? Did she think of me ever? Probably not. Maybe she was Eric's mistress by now, or his queen. Did she ever speak to him of me? Again, probably not.

And what of my sisters? Forget it. Bitches all, they.

I had been blinded once before, by a cannon flashback in the eighteenth century on the Shadow Earth. But it had only lasted for around a month and my sight had returned. Eric had had a permanent thing in mind, however, when he had given his order. I still perspired and shuddered, and sometimes woke up screaming, whenever memory of the white-hot irons returned to me—hung there before my eyes—and then the contact!

I moaned softly and continued to pace.

There was absolutely nothing I could do. That was the most horrible part of the whole thing. I was as helpless as an embryo. To be born again into sight and fury was a thing for which I would give my soul. Even for an hour, with a blade in my hand, to duel once again with my brother.

I lay back on my mat and slept. When I awakened, there was food, and I ate once again and paced. My fingernails and my toenails had grown long. My beard was very long and my hair fell across my eyes, constantly. I felt filthy, and I itched all the time. I wondered whether I had fleas.

That a prince of Amber could be brought to this state drew a terrible emotion from the center of my being, wherever that may be. I had been reared to think of us as invincible entities, clean and cool and diamond-hard, like our pictures on the Trumps. Obviously, we were not.

At least, we were enough like other men to have our resources.

I played mental games, I told myself stories, I reviewed pleasant memories—there were many of these. I recalled the elements: wind, rain, snow, the summer's warmth, and the spring's cool breezes. I had had a small airplane on the Shadow Earth, and when I flew it I had enjoyed the sensation. I recalled the glistening panoramas of color and distance, the miniaturization of cities, the broad blue sweep of sky, the herds of clouds (where were they now?) and the clean expanse of the ocean beneath my wings. I remembered women I had loved, parties, military engagements. And when all was done, and I could help it no longer, I thought of Amber.

One time, when I did so, my tear glands began to function again. I wept.

After an interminable time, a time filled with blackness and many sleeps, I heard footsteps which paused before the door to my cell, and I heard the sound of a key within the lock.

It was a time so long after Rein's visit that I had forgotten the taste of the wine and the cigarettes. I could not really estimate its span, but it had been long.

There were two men in the corridor. I could tell this from their footsteps even before I heard the sounds of their voices.

One of the voices I recognized.

The door swung open and Julian said my name.

I didn't answer right away, and he repeated it.

"Corwin? Come here."

Since I didn't have much choice in the matter, I drew myself erect and advanced. I stopped when I knew I was near him.

"What do you want?" I asked.

"Come with me." And he took my arm.

We walked along the corridor, and he said nothing and I'd be damned if I'd ask him any questions.

From the echoes, I could tell when we entered the big hall. Soon after, he guided me up the stair.

Up, and into the palace proper we went.

I was taken to a room and seated in a chair. A barber set to work cutting my hair and my beard. I didn't recognize his voice when he asked me if I wanted the beard trimmed or removed.

"Cut it off," I said, and a manicurist set to work on my nails, all twenty of them.

Then I was bathed, and someone helped me to dress in clean garments. They hung loose on me. I was deloused also, but forget that.

Then I was led into another black place filled with music and the odors of good food and the sounds of many voices and some laughter. I recognized it to be the dining room.

The voices subsided a bit as Julian led me in and seated me.

I sat there until the trumpet notes, to which I was forced to rise.

I heard the toast called out:

"To Eric the First, King of Amber! Long live the king!"

I didn't drink to that, but no one seemed to notice. It was Caine's voice that had called out the toast, from far up along the table.

I ate as much as I could, because it was the best meal I had been offered since the coronation. I gathered from conversation overheard that today was the anniversary of Eric's coronation, which meant I had spent an entire year in the dungeons.

No one spoke to me, and I didn't make any overtures. I was present as a ghost only. To humiliate me, and to serve as a reminder to my brothers, no doubt, as to the price of defying our liege. And everyone had been ordered to forget me.

It went on well into the night. Someone kept me well provided with wine, which was something, and I sat there and listened to the music of all the dances.

The tables had been removed by this time, and I was seated off somewhere in a corner.

I got stinking drunk and was half dragged, half carried back to my cell in the morning, when the whole thing was over save for the cleaning up. My only regret was that I hadn't gotten sick enough to dirty the floor or someone's pretty garments.

Thus ended the first year of darkness.

NINE

I shall not bore you with repetition. My second year was pretty much like my first, with the same finale. Ditto for the third. Rein came twice that second year, with a basket of goodies and a mouthful of gossip. Both times I forbade him ever to come again. The third year he came down six times, every other month, and each time I forbade him anew and ate his food and heard what he had to say.

Something was wrong in Amber. Strange *things* walked through Shadow and presented themselves, with violence, to all and sundry. They were destroyed, of course. Eric was still trying to figure out how they had occurred. I did not mention my curse, though I later rejoiced in the fact that it had come to pass.

Random, like myself, was still a prisoner. His wife *had* joined him. The positions of my other brothers and sisters remained unchanged. This bolstered me through the third anniversary of the coronation, and it made me feel almost alive again.

It . . .

It! One day it was there, and it made me feel so good that I immediately broke out the final bottle of wine Rein had brought me and opened the last pack of cigarettes, which I had been saving.

I smoked them and sipped and enjoyed the feeling that I had somehow beaten Eric. If he found this out, I felt it might be fatal. But I knew he didn't know.

So I rejoiced, smoking, drinking and reveling in the light of that which had occurred.

Yes, the *light*.

I'd discovered a tiny patch of brightness, off somewhere to my right.

Well, let's take it like this: I had awakened in a hospital bed and learned that I had recovered all too soon. Dig?

I heal faster than others who had been broken. All the lords and ladies of Amber have something of this capacity.

I'd lived through the Plague, I'd lived through the march on Moscow. . . .

I regenerate faster and better than anybody I've ever known.

Napoleon had once made a remark about it. So had General MacArthur. With nerve tissue it takes me a bit longer, that's all.

My sight was returning to me, that's what it meant—that lovely patch of brightness, off somewhere to my right.

After a time, I knew that it was the little barren area in the door to my cell.

I had grown new eyes, my fingers told me. It had taken me over three years, but I had done it. It was the million-in-one thing I spoke of earlier, the thing which even Eric could not properly assess, because of the variances of powers among the individual members of the family. I had beaten him to this extent: I had learned that I could grow new eyeballs. I had always known that I could regenerate nerve tissues, given sufficient time. I had been left paraplegic from a spine injury received during the Franco-Prussian wars. After two years, it had gone away. I had had my hope—a wild one, I'll admit— that I could do what I had done then, with my burned-out orbs. And I had been right. They felt intact, and the sight was returning, slowly.

How long till the next anniversary of Eric's coronation? I stopped pacing and my heart beat faster. As soon as someone saw that I'd recovered my eyes, I'd lose them again.

Therefore, I'd have to escape before the four years had passed.

How?

I hadn't thought about it much up to this time, because even if I could figure a way to get out of my cell, I'd never make it out of Amber—or out of the palace, for that matter—without eyes or aid, and neither were available to me.

Now, though . . .

The door of my cell was a big, heavy, brass-bound thing, with only a tiny grille at a height of about five feet for purposes of looking in to see whether I was still alive, if anyone cared. Even if I succeeded in removing it, I could tell that I couldn't reach out far enough to touch the lock. There was a little swinging gate at the bottom of the door, large enough to push my food through and that's about all. The hinges were either on the outside or in between the door and the jamb, I couldn't tell for sure. Either way, I couldn't get at them. There were no windows and no other doors.

It was still almost like being blind, save for that feeble reassuring light through the grille. I knew my sight hadn't returned fully. That was still a long way off. But even if it had, it was nearly pitch dark in there. I knew this because I knew the dungeons under Amber.

I lit a cigarette, paced some more, and assessed my possessions, seeking anything that might be of aid. There was my clothing, my sleeping mat, and all the damp straw I wanted. I also had matches, but I quickly rejected the notion of setting fire to the straw. I doubted anyone would come and open the door if I did. Most likely the guard would come and laugh, if he came at all. I had a spoon I'd picked up at the last banquet. I'd wanted a knife, really, but Julian had caught me trying to lift one and snatched it away. What he didn't know, though, was that that was my second attempt. I already had the spoon tucked inside my boot.

So what good was it?

I'd heard these stories of guys digging their way out of cells with the damnedest things—belt buckles (which I didn't have)—etc. But I didn't have time to try the Count of Monte Cristo bit. I needed out in a matter of months, or my new eyes wouldn't mean anything.

The door was mainly wood. Oak. It was bound with four metal strips. One went around it near the top, one near the bottom, right above the gate, and there were two which ran from top to bottom, passing along either side of the foot-wide grille. The door opened outward, I knew, and the lock was to my left. My memories told me the door was about two inches thick, and I recalled the approximate position of the lock, which I verified by leaning against the door and feeling the tension at that point. I knew that the door was also barred, but I could worry about that later. I might be able to raise it by sliding the handle of the spoon upward between the door's edge and the jamb.

I knelt on my sleeping mat and with the spoon I traced a box about that area which contained the lock. I worked until my hand was quite sore—maybe a couple of hours. Then I ran my fingernail over the surface of the wood. I hadn't scarred it much, but it was a beginning. I switched the spoon to my left hand and continued until it began to ache.

I kept hoping that Rein would show up. I was sure I could talk him into giving me his dagger if I really pressed the matter. He didn't put in an appearance, though, so I just kept grinding away.

Day after day I worked, until I was perhaps half an inch into the wood. Each time I'd hear a guard's footsteps I'd move the pallet back to the far wall and lie down on it with my back to the door. When he had passed, I'd resume work. Then I had to stop for a while, as much as I hated to. Even though I had wrapped them in cloth torn from my garments, my hands had blistered and the blisters had broken, and after a time the raw flesh underneath began to bleed. So I took a break to let them heal. I decided to devote the time to planning what I'd do after I got out.

When I'd worked my way far enough through the door, I'd raise the bar. The sound of it falling would probably bring a guard. By then, though, I'd be out. A couple of good kicks would break out the piece I was working on and the lock could stay right where it was if it wanted to. The door would swing open then and I would face the guard. He would be armed and I wouldn't. I'd have to take him.

He might be overconfident, thinking I couldn't see. On the other hand, he might be a bit afraid, if he recalled how I had entered into Amber. Either way he would die and I would then be armed. I gripped my right biceps with my left hand and my fingertips touched. Gods! I was emaciated! Whatever, I was of the blood of Amber, and I felt that even in that condition I could take any ordinary man. Maybe I was kidding myself, but I'd have to try it.

Then if I succeeded, with a blade in my hand, nothing could keep me from reaching the Pattern. I'd walk it, and when I made it to the center, I could transport myself to any Shadow world I chose. There I would recuperate, and this time I would not rush things. If it took me a century, I'd have everything letter-perfect before I moved against Amber again. After all, I was technically its liege. Hadn't I crowned myself in the presence of all, before Eric had done the same? I'd make good my claim to the throne!

If only it weren't impossible to walk into Shadow from Amber itself! Then I wouldn't have to fool around with the Pattern. But my Amber is the center of all, and you just don't depart it that easily.

After, say, a month my hands had healed and I was developing large callouses from my scraping activities. I heard a guard's footsteps and removed myself to the far side of the cell. There was a brief creak and my meal was slipped beneath the door. Then there were footsteps again, this time diminishing in the distance.

I returned to the door. Without looking, I knew what was on the tray: a chunk of stale bread, a crock of water, and a piece of cheese if I was lucky. I positioned the mat, knelt on it and felt at the groove. I was about halfway through.

Then I heard the chuckle.

It came from behind me.

I turned, not needing my eyes to tell me that someone else was present. There was a man standing near the left wall, giggling.

"Who is it?" I asked, and my voice sounded strange. I realized then that these were the first words I had spoken in a long while.

"Escape," he said. "Trying to escape." And he chuckled again.

"How did you get in here?"

"Walked," he replied.

"From where? How?"

I struck a match and it hurt my eyes, but I held it.

He was a small man. Tiny, might be an even better word. He was around five feet tall and a hunchback. His hair and beard were as heavy as my own. The only distinguishing features in that great mass of fur were his long, hook nose and his almost black eyes, now squinted against the light.

"Dworkin!" I said.

He chuckled again.

"That's my name. What's yours?"

"Don't you know me, Dworkin?" I struck another match and held it near my face. "Look hard. Forget the beard and the hair. Add a hundred pounds to my frame. You drew me, in exquisite detail, on several packs of playing cards."

"Corwin," he said at last. "I remember you. Yes."

"I had thought you were dead."

"I'm not, though. See?" and he pirouetted before me. "How is your father? Have you seen him recently? Did he put you here?"

"Oberon is no more," I replied. "My brother Eric reigns in Amber, and I am his prisoner."

"Then I have seniority," he told me, "for I am Oberon's prisoner."

"Oh? None of us knew that Dad had locked you up."

I heard him weeping.

"Yes," he said after a time. "He didn't trust me."

"Why not?"

"I told him I'd thought of a way to destroy Amber. I described it to him, and he locked me in."

"That wasn't very nice," I said.

"I know," he agreed, "but he did give me a pretty apartment and lots of things to do research with. Only he stopped coming to visit me after a time. He used to bring men who showed me splotches of ink and made me tell stories about them. That was fun, until I told a story I didn't like and turned the man into a frog. The king was angry when I wouldn't turn him back, and it's been so long since I've seen anybody that I'd even turn him back now, if he still wanted me to. Once—"

"How did you get here, into my cell?" I asked again.

"I told you. I walked."

"Through the wall?"

"Of course not. Through the Shadow wall."

"No man can walk through Shadows in Amber. There are no Shadows in Amber."

"Well, I cheated," he admitted.

"How?"

"I designed a new Trump and stepped through it, to see what was on this side of the wall. Oh my!—I just remembered. . . . I can't get back without it. I'll have to make another. Have you got anything to eat? And something to draw with? And something to draw on?"

"Have a piece of bread," I said, and handed it to him, "and here's a piece of cheese to go along with it."

"Thank you, Corwin," and he wolfed them down and drank all my water afterward. "Now, if you'll give me a pen and a piece of parchment, I'll be returning to my own rooms. I want to finish a book I was reading. It's been nice talking to you. Too bad about Eric. I'll stop back again some time and we'll talk some more. If you see your father, please tell him not to be angry with me because I'll—"

"I don't have a pen, or parchment," I observed.

"Goodness," he said, "that's hardly civilized."

"I know. But then, Eric isn't very."

"Well, what have you got? I prefer my own apartment to this place. At least, it's better lighted."

"You have dined with me," I said, "and now I am going to ask you a favor. If you will grant me this request, I promise that I will do everything I can to make things right between you and Dad."

"What is it that you want?" he asked.

"Long have I admired your work," I said, "and there is something I have always desired as a work of your hand. Do you recall the Lighthouse of Cabra?"

"Of course. I've been there many times. I know the keeper, Jopin. I used to play chess with him."

"More than anything else I can think of," I told him, "for most of my adult life, I have longed to see one of your magical sketches of that great gray tower."

"A very simple subject," he said, "and rather an appealing one, at that. I did some preliminary sketches in the past, but I never got beyond that point. Other work kept getting in the way. I'll fetch you one, if you'd like."

"No," I said. "I'd like something more enduring, to keep me company here in my cell—to comfort me, and any others who may later occupy this place."

"Commendable," he said. "What have you in mind as the medium."

"I have a stylus here," I told him (the spoon was fairly sharp by then), "and I'd like to see it traced upon the far wall, so that I might look at it as I take my rest."

He was silent a moment, then, "The illumination is quite poor," he remarked.

"I have several books of matches," I replied. "I'll light them and hold them for you. We might even burn some of this straw if we run low."

"Those are hardly ideal working conditions. . . ."

"I know," I said, "and I apologize for them, great Dworkin, but they are the best I have to offer. A work of art by your hand would brighten my humble existence beyond measure."

He chuckled again.

"Very well. But you must promise me that you will provide light afterwards, so that I may sketch myself a way back to my own chambers."

"Agreed," I said, and I felt in my pocket.

I had three full packages of matches and part of a fourth.

I pressed the spoon into his hand and led him to the wall.

"Do you have the feel of the instrument?" I asked him.

"Yes, it's a sharpened spoon, isn't it?"

"Yes. I'll make a light as soon as you say you are ready. You'll have to sketch rapidly, because my supply of matches is limited. I'll allot half for the lighthouse and the other half for your own business."

"All right," he said, and I struck a match and he began to trace lines upon the moist gray wall.

First he did an upright rectangle to frame and contain the thing. Then with several deft strokes, the lighthouse began to appear. It was amazing, daft as he was, his skill was intact. I held each match at its barest base, spat on my left thumb and forefinger, and when I could hold it no longer in my right I took hold of the blackened end and inverted it, letting the match burn away completely before I struck another.

When the first book of matches was gone, he had finished the tower and was working on the sea and the sky. I encouraged him, I murmured appreciation at every stroke.

"Great, really great," I said, when it appeared to be almost finished. Then he made me waste another match while he signed it. I was almost through the second book by then.

"Now let's admire it," he said.

"If you want to get back to your own apartments, you'll have to leave the admiring to me," I told him. "We're too low on matches to be art critics at this point."

He pouted a bit, but moved to the other wall and began sketching as soon as I struck a light.

He sketched a tiny study, a skull on the desk, a globe beside it, walls full of books all around.

"Now that's good," he said, when I had finished the third pack and was starting on the remaining partial pack.

It took him six more to finish up and one to sign it.

He gazed at it while the eighth match burned—there were only two remaining—then he took a step forward and was gone.

The match was burning my fingertips by then and I dropped it and it sizzled when it hit the straw and went out.

I stood there shaking, full of mixed feelings, and then I heard his voice and felt his presence at my side. He was back again.

"I just thought of something," he said. "How can you see the picture when it's so dark in here?"

"Oh. I can see in the dark," I told him. "I've lived with it so long that it has become my friend."

"I see. I just wondered. Give me a light so I can go back now."

"Very well," I agreed, considering my second to last match. "But you'd better bring your own illumination next time you stop around. I'll be out of matches after this."

"All right." And I struck a light and he considered his drawing, walked toward it, and vanished once more.

I turned quickly and considered the Lighthouse of Cabra before the match failed. Yes, the power was there. I could feel it.

Would my final match serve me, though?

No, I didn't think it would. A longer period of concentration than that was required for me to use a Trump as a gateway.

What could I burn? The straw was too damp and might not take fire. It would be horrible to have the gateway—my road to freedom—right there with me and not be able to use it.

I needed a flame that would last awhile.

My sleeping roll! It was a cloth liner stuffed with straw. That straw would be drier, and the cloth would burn, too.

I cleared half the floor, down to the bare stone. Then I sought the sharpened spoon, to use to cut the liner. I cursed then. Dworkin had carried it off with him.

I twisted and tore at the thing.

Finally, it came open and I pulled out the dry straw from the middle. I made a little heap of it and I set the liner nearby, to use as extra fuel if I needed it. The less smoke the better, though. It would attract attention if a guard passed this way. This wasn't too likely, though, since I had just recently been fed, and I got one meal a day.

I struck my last match, then used it to set fire to the cardboard book that had continued it. When this got going, I used it on the straw.

It almost didn't take. The straw was damper than I'd thought, even though it came from the center of my mat. But finally there was a glow, and then a flame. It took two of the other empty matchbooks to achieve this, so I was glad I hadn't thrown them down the john.

I tossed on the third, held the liner in my left hand, and stood and faced the drawing.

The glow spread up the wall as the flames danced higher, and I concentrated on the tower and recalled it. I thought I heard the cry of a gull. I sniffed something like a salt breeze, and the place became more real as I stared.

I tossed the liner onto the fire, and the flames subsided for a moment, then sprang higher. I didn't remove my eyes from the drawing as I did this.

The magic was still there, in Dworkin's hand, for soon the lighthouse seemed as real to me as my cell. Then it seemed the only reality, and the cell but a Shadow at my back. I heard the splashing of the waves and felt something like the afternoon sun upon me.

I stepped forward, but my foot did not descend into the fire.

I stood upon the sandy, rock-stewn edge of the small island Cabra, which held the great gray lighthouse that lit a path for the ships of Amber by night. A flock of frightened gulls wheeled and screamed about me, and my laughter was one with the booming of the surf and the free song of the wind. Amber lay forty-three miles behind my left shoulder.

I had escaped.

TEN

I made my way to the lighthouse and climbed the stone stair that led to the door on its western face. It was high, wide, heavy, and watertight. Also, it was locked. There was a small quay about three hundred yards behind me. Two boats were moored at it. One was a rowboat and the other was a sailboat with a cabin. They swayed gently, and beneath the sun and water was mica behind them. I paused for a moment to regard them. It had been so long since I had seen anything that for an instant they seemed more than real, and I caught a sob within my throat and swallowed it.

I turned and knocked on the door.

After what seemed too long a wait, I knocked again.

Finally, I heard a noise within and the door swung open, creaking on its three dark hinges.

Jopin, the keeper, regarded me through bloodshot eyes and I smelled whisky upon his breath. He was about five and a half feet tall and so stooped that he reminded me somewhat of Dworkin. His beard was as long as mine, so of course it seemed longer, and it was the color of smoke, save for a few yellow stains near his dry-looking lips. His skin was as porous as an orange rind and the elements had darkened it to resemble a fine old piece of furniture. His dark eyes squinted, focused. As with many people who are hard of hearing, he spoke rather loudly.

"Who are you? What do you want?" he asked.

If I was that unrecognizable in my emaciated, hairy condition, I decided that I might as well maintain my anonymity.

"I am a traveler from the south and I was shipwrecked recently," I said. "I clung to a piece of wood for many days and was finally washed ashore here. I slept on the beach all morning. It was only recently that I recovered sufficient strength to walk to your lighthouse."

He moved forward and took my arm. He threw his other arm around my shoulders.

"Come in, come in then," he said. "Lean on me. Take it easy. Come this way."

He led me to his quarters, which were extraordinarily messy, being strewn with many old books, charts, maps, and pieces of nautical equipment. He wasn't any too steady himself, so I didn't lean too hard, just enough to maintain the impression of weakness I had tried to convey as I'd leaned against his doorframe.

He led me to a daybed, suggested I lie down, and left to secure the door and fetch me something to eat.

I removed my boots, but my feet were so filthy that I put them back on again. If I'd been drifting about very long, I wouldn't be dirty. I didn't want to give away my story, so I drew a blanket that was there over me and leaned back, really resting.

Jopin returned shortly with a pitcher of water, a pitcher of beer, a great slice of beef, and half a loaf of bread upon a square wooden tray. He swept clear the top of a small table, which he then kicked into a position beside the couch. Then he set the tray down on it and bade me eat and drink.

I did. I stuffed myself. I glutted myself. I ate everything in sight. I emptied both pitchers.

Then I felt tremendously tired. Jopin nodded when he saw it come over me, and he told me to go to sleep. Before I knew it, I had.

When I awakened, it was night time and I felt considerably better than I had in many weeks. I got to my feet and retraced my earlier route and departed the building. It was chilly out there, but the sky was crystal clear and there seemed to be a million stars. The lens at the top of the tower blazed at my back, then went dark, blazed, then went dark. The water was cold, but I just had to cleanse myself. I bathed and washed my clothing and wrung it out. I must have spent an hour doing that. Then I went back to the lighthouse, hung my clothing over the back of an old chair to dry out, crawled beneath the blanket, slept again.

In the morning, when I awoke, Jopin was already up. He prepared me a hearty breakfast, and I treated it the same way as I had the dinner of the previous evening. Then I borrowed a razor, a mirror, and a pair of scissors and gave myself a shave and a sort of haircut. I bathed again afterward, and when I donned my salty, stiff, clean garments I felt almost human again.

Jopin stared at me when I returned from the sea and said, "You look kinda familiar, fella," and I shrugged.

"Now tell me about your wreck."

So I did. Out of whole cloth. What a disaster I detailed! Down to the snapping of the mainmast, yet.

He patted me on the shoulder and poured me a drink. He lit the cigar he had given me.

"You just rest easy here," he told me. "I'll take you ashore any time you like, or I'll signal you a passing ship if you see one you recognize."

I took him up on his offered hospitality. It was too much of a lifesaver not to. I ate his food and drank his drinks and let him give me a clean shirt which was too big for him. It had belonged to a friend of his who'd drowned at sea.

I stayed with him for three months, as I recovered my strength. I helped him around the place—tending the light on nights when he felt like getting smashed, and cleaning up all the rooms in the house—even to the extent of painting two of them and replacing five cracked windowpanes—and watching the sea with him on stormy nights.

He was apolitical, I learned. He didn't care who reigned in Amber. So far as he was concerned, the whole bloody crew of us were rotten. So long as he could tend his lighthouse and eat and drink of good food and brew, and consider his nautical charts in peace, he didn't give half a damn what happened ashore. I came to be rather fond of him, and since I knew something of old charts and maps also, we spent many a good evening correcting a few. I had sailed far into the north many years ago, and I gave him a new chart based on my recollections of the voyage. This seemed to please him immensely, as did my description of those waters.

"Corey" (that was how I'd named myself), "I'd like to sail with you one day," he said. "I hadn't realized you were skipper of your own vessel one time."

"Who knows?" I told him. "You were once a captain yourself, weren't you?"

"How'd you know?" he asked.

Actually, I'd remembered, but I gestured about me in reply.

"All these things you've collected," I said, "and your fondness for the charts. Also, you bear yourself like a man who once held a command."

He smiled.

"Yes," he told me, "that's true. I had a command for over a hundred years. That seems long ago. . . . Let's have another drink."

I sipped mine and sort of put it aside. I must have gained over forty pounds in the months I had spent with him. Any day now, I was expecting him to recognize me as a member of the family. Maybe he would turn me in to Eric if he did—and maybe not. Now that we'd established this much of camaraderie, I had a feeling that he might not do it. I didn't want to take the chance and find out.

Sometimes as I sat tending the light I wondered, "How long should I stay here?"

Not too much longer, I decided, adding a drop of grease to a swivel bearing. Not much longer at all. The time was drawing near when I should take to the road and walk among Shadows once again.

Then one day I felt the pressure, gentle and questing at first. I couldn't tell for sure who it was.

I immediately stood stock still, closed my eyes and made my mind go blank. It was about five minutes before the questing presence withdrew.

I paced then and wondered, and I smiled when I realized the shortness of my course. Unconsciously, I had been pacing out the dimensions of my cell back in Amber.

Someone had just tried to reach me, via my Trump. Was it Eric? Had he finally become aware of my absence and decided to try locating me in this manner? I wasn't sure. I felt that he might fear mental contact with me again. Julian, then? Or Gérard? Caine? Whoever it had been, I had closed him out completely, I knew that. And I would refuse such contact with any of my family. I might be missing some important news or a helpful call, but I couldn't afford to take the chance. The attempted contact and my blocking efforts left me with a chill. I shuddered. I thought about the thing all the rest of the day and decided that the time had come for me to move on. It wouldn't do for me to remain this close to Amber while I was so vulnerable. I had recovered sufficiently to make my way among Shadows, to seek for the place where I had to go if Amber were ever to be mine. I had been lulled into something close to peace by old Jopin's ministrations. It would be a pain to leave him, for in the months of our association I had come to like the old guy. So that evening, after we'd finished a game of chess, I told him of my plans to depart.

He poured us two drinks then raised his and said, "Good luck to you, Corwin. I hope to see you again one day."

I didn't question the fact that he had called me by my proper name, and he smiled as he realized that I hadn't let it slip by.

"You've been all right, Jopin," I told him. "If I should succeed in what I'm about to try, I won't forget what you did for me."

He shook his head.

"I don't want anything," he said. "I'm happy right where I am, doing exactly what I'm doing. I enjoy running this damned tower. It's my whole life. If you should succeed in whatever you're about—no, don't tell me about it, please! I don't want to know!—I'll be hoping you'll stop around for a game of chess sometime."

"I will," I promised.

"You can take the *Butterfly* in the morning, if you'd like."

"Thanks."

The *Butterfly* was his sailboat.

"Before you go," he said, "I suggest you take my spyglass, climb the tower, and look back on the Vale of Garnath."

"What's there to see?"

He shrugged.

"You'll have to make up your own mind about that."

I nodded.

"Okay, I will."

We then proceeded to get pleasantly high and turned in for the night. I'd miss old Jopin. With the exception of Rein, he was the only friend I'd found since my return. I wondered vaguely about the valley which had been a sheet of flame the last time I had crossed it. What could it be that was so unusual about it now, these four years later?

Troubled by dreams of werewolves and Sabbats, I slept, and the full moon rose above the world.

At the crack of dawn I did the same. Jopin was still sleeping, which was good, because I don't really like to say good-bye, and I had a funny feeling that I would never see him again.

I climbed the tower to the room that housed the big light, spyglass at my side. I moved to the window facing the shore and focused on the valley.

There was a mist hanging above the wood. It was a cold, gray, wet-looking thing that clung to the tops of the small, gnarly trees. The trees were dark, and their branches twisted together like the fingers of wrestling hands. Dark things darted among them, and from the patterns of their flight I knew they were not birds. Bats, probably. There was something evil present in that great wood, I knew, and then I recognized it. It was myself.

I had done this thing with my curse. I had transformed the peaceful Valley of Garnath into what it now represented: it was a symbol of my hate for Eric and for all those others who had stood by and let him get away with his power grab, let him blind me. I didn't like the looks of that forest, and as I stared at it I realized how my hate had objectified itself. I knew it because it was a part of me.

I had created a new entranceway into the real world. Garnath was now a pathway through Shadows. Shadows dark and grim. Only the dangerous, the malicious might walk that pathway. This was the source of the *things* Rein had mentioned, the things that troubled Eric. Good—in a way—if they kept him occupied. But as I swung the glass, I couldn't escape the feeling that I had done a very bad thing indeed. At the time, I'd had no idea that I'd ever see the light of day's bright skies again. Now that I did, I realized that I'd unleashed a thing that would take an awful lot of undoing. Even now, strange shapes seemed to move within that place. I had done a thing which had never been done before, not during the whole of Oberon's reign: I had opened a new way to Amber. And I had opened it only to the worst. A day would come when the liege of Amber—whoever he might be—would be faced with the problem of closing that dreadful way. I knew this as I stared, realizing the thing to be a product of my own pain, anger, and hate. If I won out in Amber one day, I might have to cope with my own handiwork, which is always a devilish thing to attempt. I lowered the glass and sighed.

So be it, I decided. In the meantime, it would give Eric something to have insomnia over.

I grabbed a quick bite to eat, outfitted the *Butterfly* as rapidly as I could, hoisted some canvas, cast off, and set sail. Jopin was usually up by that hour, but maybe he didn't like good-bys either.

I headed her out to sea, knowing where I was going but not real certain how to get there. I'd be sailing through Shadow and strange waters, but it would be better than the overland route, what with my handiwork abroad in the realm.

I had set sail for a land near as sparkling as Amber itself, an almost immortal place, a place that did not really exist, not any longer. It was a place which had vanished into Chaos ages ago, but of which a Shadow must somewhere survive. All I had to do was find it, recognize it, and make it mine once again, as it had been in days long gone by. Then, with my own forces to back me up, I would do another thing Amber had never known. I didn't know how yet, but I promised myself that guns would blaze within the immortal city on the day of my return.

As I sailed into Shadow, a white bird of my desire came and sat upon my right shoulder, and I wrote a note and tied it to its leg and sent it on its way. The note said, "I am coming," and it was signed by me.

I would never rest until I held vengeance and the throne within my hand, and good night sweet prince to anybody who stood between me and these things.

The sun hung low on my left and the winds bellied the sails and propelled me onward. I cursed once and then laughed.

I was free and I was running, but I had made it this far. I now had the chance I'd wanted all along.

A black bird of my desire came and sat on my left shoulder, and I wrote a note and tied it to its leg and sent it off into the west.

It said, "Eric—I'll be back," and it was signed: "Corwin, Lord of Amber."

A demon wind propelled me east of the sun.

BOOK TWO
THE GUNS OF AVALON

To Bob and Phyllis Rozman

ONE

I stood there on the beach and said, "Good-by, *Butterfly*," and the ship slowly turned, then headed out toward deep water. It would make it back into port at the Lighthouse of Cabra, I knew, for that place lay near to Shadow.

Turning away, I regarded the black line of trees near at hand, knowing that a long walk lay ahead of me. I moved in that direction, making the necessary adjustments as I advanced. A pre-dawn chill lay upon the silent forest, and this was good.

I was perhaps fifty pounds underweight and still occasionally experienced double vision, but I was improving. I had escaped the dungeons of Amber and recuperated somewhat, with the assistance of mad Dworkin and drunken Jopin, in that order. Now I had to find me a place, a place resembling another place—one which no longer existed. I located the path. I took it.

After a time, I stopped at a hollow tree that had to be there. I reached inside and drew forth my silvered blade and strapped it to my waist. It mattered not that it had been somewhere in Amber. It was here now, for the wood that I walked was in Shadow.

I continued for several hours, the unseen sun somewhere behind my left shoulder. Then I rested awhile, then moved on. It was good to see the leaves and the rocks and the dead tree trunks, the live ones, the grass, the dark earth. It was good to smell all the little smells of life, and to hear its buzzing/humming/chirping sounds. God! How I treasured my eyes! Having them back again after nearly four years of blackness was a thing for which I lacked words. And to be walking free . . .

I went on, my tattered cloak flapping in the morning breeze. I must have looked over fifty years old, my face creased, my form sparse, lean. Who would have known me for what I was?

As I walked, walked in Shadow, moved toward a place, I did not reach that place. It must be that I had grown somewhat soft. Here is what happened—

I came upon seven men by the side of the road, and six of them were dead, lying in various stages of red dismemberment. The seventh was in a semi-reclined position, his back against the mossy bole of an ancient oak. He held his blade across his lap and there was a large wet wound in his right side, from which the blood still flowed. He wore no armor, though some of the others did. His gray eyes were open, though glassy. His knuckles were skinned and his breathing was slow. From beneath shaggy brows, he watched the crows eat out the eyes of the dead. He did not seem to see me.

I raised my cowl and lowered my head to hide my face. I moved nearer.

I knew him, or someone very like him, once.

His blade twitched and the point rose as I advanced.

"I'm a friend," I said. "Would you like a drink of water?"

He hesitated a moment, then nodded.

"Yes."

I opened my canteen and passed it to him.

He drank and coughed, drank some more.

"Sir, I thank you," he said as he passed it back. "I only regret it were not stronger. Damn this cut!"

"I've some of that, too. If you're sure you can handle it."

He held out his hand and I unstoppered a small flask and gave it to him. He must have coughed for twenty seconds after a slug of that stuff Jopin drinks.

Then the left side of his mouth smiled and he winked lightly.

"Much better," he said. "Mind if I pour a drop of this onto my side? I hate to waste good whisky, but—"

"Use it all, if you have to. On second thought, though, your hand looks shaky. Maybe I'd better do the pouring."

He nodded, and I opened his leather jacket and with my dagger cut away at his shirt until I had exposed the wound. It was nasty-looking, deep, running from front to back a couple inches above the top of his hip. He had other, less serious gashes on his arms, chest, and shoulders.

The blood kept oozing from the big one, and I blotted it a bit and wiped it clean with my kerchief.

"Okay," I said, "clench your teeth and look away," and I poured.

His entire body jerked, one great spasm, and then he settled down to shivering. But he did not cry out. I had not thought he would. I folded the kerchief and pressed it in place on the wound. I tied it there, with a long strip I had torn from the bottom of my cloak.

"Want another drink?" I asked him.

"Of water," he said. "Then I fear I must sleep."

He drank, then his head leaned forward until his chin was resting upon his breast. He slept, and I made him a pillow and covered him over with dead men's cloaks.

Then I sat there at his side and watched the pretty black birds.

He had not recognized me. But then, who would? Had I revealed myself to him, he might possibly have known me. We had never really met, I guess, this wounded man and I. But in a peculiar sense, we were acquainted.

I was walking in Shadow, seeking a place, a very special place. It had been destroyed once, but I had the power to re-create it, for Amber casts an infinity of shadows. A child of Amber may walk among them, and such was my heritage. You may call them parallel worlds if you wish, alternate universes if you would, the products of a deranged mind if you care to. I call them shadows, as do all who possess the power to walk among them. We select a possibility and we walk until we reach it. So, in a sense, we create it. Let's leave it at that for now.

I had sailed, had begun this walk toward Avalon.

Centuries before, I had lived there. It is a long, complicated, proud and painful story, and I may go into it later on, if I live to finish much more of this telling.

I was drawing nearer to my Avalon when I came upon the wounded knight and the six dead men. Had I chosen to walk on by, I could have reached a place where the six men lay dead and the knight stood un- wounded—or a place where he lay dead and they stood laughing. Some would say it did not really matter, since all these things are possibilities, and therefore all of them exist somewhere in Shadow.

Any of my brothers and sisters—with the possible exceptions of Gérard and Benedict—would not even have given a second glance. I have become somewhat chickenhearted, however. I was not always that way, but perhaps the shadow Earth, where I spent so many years, mellowed me a bit, and maybe my hitch in the dungeons of Amber reminded me somewhat of the quality of human suffering. I do not know. I only know that I could not pass by the hurt I saw on the form of someone much like someone who had once been a friend. If I were to speak my name in this man's ear, I might hear myself reviled, I would certainly hear a tale of woe.

So, all right. I would pay this much of the price: I would get him back on his feet, then I would cut out. No harm done, and perhaps some small good within this Other.

I sat there, watching him, and after several hours, he awakened.

"Hello," I said, unstoppering my canteen. "Have another drink?"

"Thank you." He extended a hand.

I watched him drink, and when he handed it back he said, "Excuse me for not introducing myself. I was not in good manner . . ."

"I know you," I said. "Call me Corey."

He looked as if he were about to say, "Corey of What?" but thought better of it and nodded.

"Very well, Sir Corey," he demoted me. "I wish to thank you."

"I am thanked by the fact that you are looking better," I told him. "Want something to eat?"

"Yes, please."

"I have some dried meat here and some bread that could be fresher," I said. "Also a big hunk of cheese. Eat all you want."

I passed it to him and he did.

"What of yourself, Sir Corey?" he inquired.

"I've already eaten, while you were asleep."

I looked about me, significantly. He smiled.

". . . And you knocked off all six of them by yourself?" I said.

He nodded.

"Good show. What am I going to do with you now?"

He tried to see my face, failed.

"I do not understand," he said.

"Where are you headed?"

"I have friends," he said, "some five leagues to the north. I was going in that direction when this thing happened. And I doubt very much that any man, or the Devil himself, could bear me on his back for one league. And I could stand, Sir Corey, you'd a better idea as to my size."

I rose, drew my blade, and felled a sapling—about two inches in diameter—with one cut. Then I stripped it and hacked it to the proper length.

I did it again, and with the belts and cloaks of dead men I rigged a stretcher.

He watched until I was finished, then commented:

"You swing a deadly blade, Sir Corey—and a silver one, it would seem . . ."

"Are you up to some traveling?" I asked him.

Five leagues is roughly fifteen miles.

"What of the dead?" he inquired.

"You want to maybe give them a decent Christian burial?" I said. "Screw them! Nature takes care of its own. Let's get out of here. They stink already."

"I'd like at least to see them covered over. They fought well."

I sighed.

"All right, if it will help you to sleep nights. I haven't a spade, so I'll build them a cairn. It's going to be a common burial, though."

"Good enough," he said.

I laid the six bodies out, side by side. I heard him mumbling something, which I guessed to be a prayer for the dead.

I ringed them around with stones. There were plenty of stones in the vicinity, so I worked quickly, choosing the largest so that things would go faster. That is where I made a mistake. One of them must have weighed around four hundred pounds, and I did not roll it. I hefted it and set it in place.

I heard a sharp intake of breath from his direction, and I realized that he had noted this.

I cursed then:

"Damn near ruptured myself on that one!" I said, and I selected smaller stones after that.

When I had finished, I said, "All right. Are you ready to move?"

"Yes."

I raised him in my arms and set him on the stretcher. He clenched his teeth as I did so.

"Where do we go?" I asked.

He gestured.

"Head back to the trail. Follow it to the left until it forks. Then go right at that place. How do you propose to . . . ?"

I scooped the stretcher up in my arms, holding him as you would a baby, cradle and all. Then I turned and walked back to the trail, carrying him.

"Corey?" he said.

"Yes?"

"You are one of the strongest men I have ever met—and it seems I should know you."

I did not answer him immediately. Then I said, "I try to keep in good condition. Clean living and all."

". . . And your voice sounds rather familiar."

He was staring upward, still trying to see my face.

I decided to get off the subject fast.

"Who are these friends of yours I am taking you to?"

"We are headed for the Keep of Ganelon."

"That ratfink!" I said, almost dropping him.

"While I do not understand the word you have used, I take it to be a term of opprobrium," he said, "from the tone of your voice. If such is the case, I must be his defender in—"

"Hold on," I said. "I've a feeling we're talking about two different guys with the same name. Sorry."

Through the stretcher, I felt a certain tension go out of him.

"That is doubtless the case," he said.

So I carried him until we reached the trail, and there I turned to the left.

He dropped off to sleep again, and I made better time after that, taking the fork he had told me about and sprinting while he snored. I began wondering about the six fellows who had tried to do him in and almost succeeded. I hoped that they did not have any friends beating about the bushes.

I slowed my pace back to a walk when his breathing changed.

"I was asleep," he said.

". . . And snoring," I added.

"How far have you borne me?"

"Around two leagues, I'd say."

"And you are not tired?"

"Some," I said, "but not enough to need rest just yet."

"*Mon Dieu!*" he said. "I am pleased never to have had you for an enemy. Are you certain you are not the Devil?"

"Yeah, sure," I said. "Don't you smell the brimstone? And my right hoof is killing me."

He actually sniffed a couple times before he chuckled, which hurt my feelings a bit.

Actually, we had traveled over four leagues, as I reckoned it. I was hoping he would sleep again and not be too concerned about distances. My arms were beginning to ache.

"Who were those six men you slew?" I asked him.

"Wardens of the Circle," he replied, "and they were no longer men, but men possessed. Now pray to God, Sir Corey, that their souls be at peace."

"Wardens of the Circle?" I asked. "What Circle?"

"The dark Circle—the place of iniquity and loathsome beasts . . ." He took a deep breath. "The source of the illness that lies upon the land."

"This land doesn't look especially ill to me," I said.

"We are far from that place, and the realm of Ganelon is still too strong for the invaders. But the Circle widens. I feel that the last battle will be fought here."

"You have aroused my curiosity as to this thing."

"Sir Corey, if you know not of it 'twere better you forgot it, skirted the Circle, and went your way. Though I should dearly love to fight by your side, this is not your fight—and who can tell the outcome?"

The trail began winding upward. Then, through a break in the trees, I saw a distant thing that made me pause and caused me to recall another, similar place.

"What . . . ?" asked my charge, turning. Then, "Why, you moved much more quickly than I had guessed. That is our destination, the Keep of Ganelon."

I thought then about *a* Ganelon. I did not want to, but I did. He had been a traitorous assassin and I had exiled him from Avalon centuries before. I had actually cast him through Shadow into another time and place, as my brother Eric had later done to me. I hoped it was not to this place that I had sent him. While not very likely, it was possible. Though he was a mortal man with his allotted span, and I had exiled him from that place perhaps six hundred years ago, it was possible that it was only a few years past in terms of this world. Time, too, is a function of Shadow, and even Dworkin did not know all of its ins and outs. Or perhaps he did. Maybe that is what drove him mad. The most difficult thing about Time, I have learned, is doing it. In any case, I felt that this could not be my old enemy and former trusted aide, for *he* would certainly not be resisting any wave of iniquity that was sweeping across the land. He would be right in there pitching for the loathsome beasts, I felt sure.

A thing that caused me difficulty was the man that I carried. His counterpart had been alive in Avalon at the time of the exiling, meaning that the time lag could be just about right.

I did not care to encounter the Ganelon I had known and be recognized by him. He knew nothing of Shadow. He would only know that I had worked some dark magic on him, as an alternative to killing him, and while he had survived that alternative it might have been the rougher of the two.

But the man in my arms needed a place of rest and shelter, so I trudged forward.

I wondered, though . . .

There did seem to be something about me that lent itself to recognition by this man. If there were some memories of a shadow of myself in this place that was like yet not like Avalon, what form did they take? How would they condition a reception of the actual me should I be discovered?

The sun was beginning to sink. A cool breeze began, hinting of a chilly night to come. My ward was snoring once more, so I decided to sprint most of the remaining distance. I did not like the feeling that this forest after dark might become a place crawling with unclean denizens of some damned Circle that I knew nothing about, but who seemed to be on the make when it came to this particular piece of real estate.

So I ran through lengthening shadows, dismissing rising notions of pursuit, ambush, surveillance, until I could do so no longer. They had achieved the strength of a premonition, and then I heard the noises at my back: a soft *pat-pat-pat*, as of footfalls.

I set the stretcher down, and I drew my blade as I turned.

There were two of them, cats.

Their markings were precisely those of Siamese cats, only these were the size of tigers. Their eyes were of a solid, sun-bright yellow, pupilless. They seated themselves on their haunches as I turned, and they stared at me and did not blink.

They were about thirty paces away. I stood sideways between them and the stretcher, my blade raised.

Then the one to the left opened its mouth. I did not know whether to expect a purr or a roar.

Instead, it spoke. It said, "Man, most mortal."

The voice was not human-sounding. It was too high-pitched.

"Yet still it lives," said the second, sounding much like the first.

"Slay it here," said the first.

"What of the one who guards it with the blade I like not at all?"

"Mortal man?"

"Come find out," I said, softly.

"It is thin, and perhaps it is old."

"Yet it bore the other from the cairn to this place, rapidly and without rest. Let us flank it."

I sprang forward as they moved, and the one to my right leaped toward me.

My blade split its skull and continued on into the shoulder. As I turned, yanking it free, the other swept past me, heading toward the stretcher. I swung wildly.

My blade fell upon its back and passed completely through its body. It emitted a shriek that grated like chalk on a blackboard as it fell in two pieces and began to burn. The other was burning also.

But the one I had halved was not yet dead. Its head turned toward me and those blazing eyes met my own and held them.

"I die the final death," it said, "and so I know you, Opener. Why do you slay us?"

And then the flames consumed its head.

I turned, cleaned my blade and sheathed it, picked up the stretcher, ignored all questions, and continued on.

A small knowledge had begun within me, as to what the thing was, what it had meant.

And I still sometimes see that burning cat head in dreams, and then I awaken, wet and shivering, and the night seems darker, and filled with shapes I cannot define.

The Keep of Ganelon had a moat about it, and a drawbridge, which was raised. There was a tower at each of the four corners where its high walls met. From within those walls many other towers reached even higher, tickling the bellies of low, dark clouds, occluding the early stars, casting shadows of jet down the high hill the place occupied. Several of the towers were already lighted, and the wind bore me the faint sound of voices.

I stood before the drawbridge, lowered my charge to the ground, cupped my hands about my mouth, and called out:

"Hola! Ganelon! Two travelers are stranded in the night!"

I heard the clink of metal on stone. I felt that I was being studied from somewhere above. I squinted upward, but my eyes were still far from normal.

"Who is there?" the voice came down, big and booming.

"Lance, who is wounded, and I, Corey of Cabra, who bore him here."

I waited as he called this information to another sentry, and I heard more voices raised as the message was passed along the line.

After a pause of several minutes, a reply came back in the same manner. Then the guard called down:

"Stay clear! We're going to lower the drawbridge! You may enter!"

The creaking began as he spoke, and in a brief time the thing banged to earth on our side of the moat. I raised my charge once more and walked across it.

Thus did I bear Sir Lancelot du Lac to the Keep of Ganclon, whom I trusted like a brother. That is to say, not at all.

There was a rush of people about me, and I found myself ringed by armed men. There was no hostility present, however, only concern. I had entered a large, cobbled courtyard, lit by torches and filled with bedrolls. I could smell sweat, smoke, horses, and the odors of cooking. A small army was bivouacked there.

Many had approached me and stood staring and murmuring, but then there came up two who were fully arrayed, as for battle, and one of them touched my shoulder.

"Come this way," he said.

I followed and they flanked me. The ring of people parted as we passed. The drawbridge was already creaking back into place. We moved toward the main complex of dark stone.

Inside, we walked along a hallway and passed what appeared to be a reception chamber. Then we came upon a stairway. The man to my right indicated that I should mount it. On the second floor, we stopped before a heavy wooden door and the guard knocked upon it.

"Come in," called out a voice which unfortunately seemed very familiar. We entered.

He sat at a heavy wooden table near a wide window overlooking the courtyard. He wore a brown leather jacket over a black shirt, and his trousers were also black. They were bloused over the tops of his dark boots. He had about his waist a wide belt which held a hoof-hilted dagger. A short sword lay on the table before him. His hair and beard were red, with a sprinkling of white. His eyes were dark as ebony.

He looked at me, then turned his attention to a pair of guards who entered with the stretcher.

"Put him on my bed," he said. Then, "Roderick, tend to him."

His physician, Roderick, was an old guy who didn't look as if he would do much harm, which relieved me somewhat. I had not fetched Lance all that distance to have him bled.

Then Ganelon turned to me once more.

"Where did you find him?" he asked.

"Five leagues to the south of here."

"Who are you?"

"They call me Corey," I said.

He studied me too closely, and his worm-like lips twitched toward a smile beneath his mustache.

"What is your part in this thing?" he asked.

"I don't know what you mean," I said.

I had let my shoulders sag a bit. I spoke slowly, softly, and with a slight falter. My beard was longer than his, and lightened by dust. I imagined I looked like an older man. His attitude on appraisal tended to indicate that he thought I was.

"I am asking you why you helped him," he said.

"Brotherhood of man, and all that," I replied.

"You are a foreigner?"

I nodded.

"Well, you are welcome here for so long as you wish to stay."

"Thanks. I will probably move on tomorrow."

"Now join me in a glass of wine and tell me of the circumstances under which you found him."

So I did.

Ganelon let me speak without interrupting, and those piercing eyes of his were on me all the while. While I had always felt laceration by means of the eyeballs to be a trite expression, it did not feel so that night. He stabbed at me with them. I wondered what he knew and what he was guessing concerning me.

Then fatigue sprang and seized me by the scruff of the neck. The exertion, the wine, the warm room—all of these worked together, and suddenly it was as if I were standing off in the corner somewhere and listening to myself, watching myself, feeling dissociated. While I was capable of great exertion in short bursts, I realized that I was still very low when it came to stamina. I also noticed that my hand was trembling.

"I'm sorry," I heard myself saying. "The day's labors are beginning to get to me . . ."

"Of course," said Ganelon. "I will talk with you more on the morrow. Sleep now. Sleep well."

Then he called in one of the guards and ordered him to conduct me to a chamber. I must have staggered on the way, because I remember the guard's hand on my elbow, steering me.

That night I slept the sleep of the dead. It was a big, black thing, about fourteen hours long.

In the morning, I ached all over.

I bathed myself. There was a basin on the high dresser, and soap and a washcloth someone had thoughtfully set beside it. My throat felt packed with sawdust and my eyes were full of fuzz.

I sat down and assessed myself.

There had been a day when I could have carried Lance the entire distance without going to pieces afterward. There had been a day when I had fought my way up the face of Kolvir and into the heart of Amber itself.

Those days were gone. I suddenly felt like the wreck I must have looked.

Something would have to be done.

I had been putting on weight and picking up strength slowly. The process would have to be accelerated.

A week or two of clean living and violent exercise could help a lot, I decided. Ganelon had not given any real indication of having recognized me. All right. I would take advantage of the hospitality he had offered.

With that resolve, I sought out the kitchen and conned a hearty breakfast. Well, it was really around lunchtime, but let's call things by their proper names. I had a strong desire for a smoke and felt a certain perverse joy in the fact that I was out of tobacco. The Fates were conspiring to keep me true to myself.

I strolled out into the courtyard and a brisk, bright day. For a long while, I watched the men who were quartered there as they went through their training regime.

There were bowmen off at the far end, thwanging away at targets fastened to bales of hay. I noted that they employed thumb rings and an oriental grip on the bowstring, rather than the three-fingered technique with which I was more comfortable. It made me wonder a bit about this Shadow. The swordsmen used both the edges and points of their weapons, and there was a variety of blades and fencing techniques in evidence. I tried to estimate, and guessed there were perhaps eight hundred of them about—and I had no idea as to how many of them there might be out of sight. Their complexions, their hair, their eyes, varied from pale to quite dark. I heard many strange accents above the thwanging and the clanging, though most spoke the language of Avalon, which is of the tongue of Amber.

As I stood watching, one swordsman raised his hand, lowered his blade, mopped his brow, and stepped back. His opponent did not seem especially winded. This was my chance for some of the exercise I was seeking.

I moved forward, smiled, and said, "I'm Corey of Cabra. I was watching you."

I turned my attention to the big, dark man who was grinning at his resting buddy.

"Mind if I practice with you while your friend rests?" I asked him.

He kept grinning and pointed at his mouth and his ear. I tried several other languages, but none of them worked. So I pointed at the blade and at him and back to myself until he got the idea. His opponent seemed to think it was a good one, as the smaller fellow offered me his blade.

I took it into my hands. It was shorter and a lot heavier than Grayswandir. (That is the name of my blade, which I know I have not mentioned up until now. It is a story in itself, and I may or may not go into it before you learn what brought me to this final pass. But should you hear me refer to it by name again, you will know what I am talking about.)

I swung my blade a few times to test it, removed my cloak, tossed it off to the side, and struck an *en garde*.

The big fellow attacked. I parried and attacked. He parried and riposted. I parried the riposte, feinted, and attacked. Et cetera. After five minutes, I knew that he was good. And I knew that I was better. He stopped me twice so that I could teach him a maneuver I had used. He learned both very quickly. After fifteen minutes, though, his grin widened. I guess that was around the point where he broke down most opponents by virtue of sheer staying power, if they were good enough to resist his attacks up until then. He had stamina, I'll say that. After twenty minutes, a puzzled look came onto his face. I just didn't look as if I could stand up that long. But then, what can any man really know of that which lies within a scion of Amber?

After twenty-five minutes, he was sheathed in sweat, but he continued on. My brother Random looks and acts, on occasion, like an asthmatic, teenage hood—but once we had fenced together for over twenty-six hours, to see who would call it quits. (If you're curious, it was me. I had had a date lined up for the next day and had wanted to arrive in reasonably good condition.) We could have gone on. While I was not up to a performance like that just then, I knew that I could outlast the man I faced. After all, he was only human.

After about half an hour, when he was breathing heavily and slowing down on his counterstrokes and I knew that in a few minutes he might guess that I was pulling mine, I raised my hand and lowered my blade as I had seen his previous opponent do. He ground to a halt also, then rushed forward and embraced me. I did not understand what he said, but I gathered that he was pleased with the workout. So was I.

The horrible thing was, I felt it. I found myself slightly heady.

But I needed more. I promised me I would kill myself and exercise that day, glut myself with food that night, sleep deeply, wake, and do it again.

So I went over to where the archers stood. After a time, I borrowed a bow, and in my three-fingered style unleashed perhaps a hundred arrows. I did not do too badly. Then, for a time, I watched the men on horseback, with their lances, shields, maces. I moved on. I watched some practice in hand-to-hand combat.

Finally, I wrestled three men in succession. Then I did feel beat. Absolutely. Entirely.

I sat down on a bench in the shade, sweating, breathing heavily. I wondered about Lance, about Ganelon, about supper. After perhaps ten minutes, I made my way back to the room I had been given and I bathed again.

By then I was ravenously hungry, so I set forth to find me dinner and information.

Before I had gone very far from the door, one of the guards whom I recognized from the previous evening—the one who had guided me to my chamber—approached and said, "Lord Ganelon bids you dine with him in his quarters, at the ringing of the dinner bell."

I thanked him, said I would be there, returned to my chamber, and rested on my bed until it was time. Then I made my way forth once again.

I was beginning to ache deeply and I had a few additional bruises. I decided this was a good thing, would help me to seem older. I banged on Ganelon's door and a boy admitted me, then dashed off to join another youth who was spreading a table near to the fireplace.

Ganelon wore a green shirt and trousers, green boots and belt, sat in a high-backed chair. He rose as I entered, walked forward to greet me.

"Sir Corey, I've heard report of your doings this day," he said, clasping my hand. "It makes your carrying Lance seem more believable. I must say you're more a man than you look—meaning no offense by that."

I chuckled.

"No offense."

He led me to a chair, handed me a glass of pale wine that was a bit too sweet for my taste, then said, "Looking at you, I'd say I could push you over with one hand—but you carried Lance five leagues and killed two of those bastard cats on the way. And he told me about the cairn you built, of big stones—"

"How is Lance feeling today?" I interrupted.

"I had to place a guard in his chamber to be sure he rested. The muscle-bound clod wanted to get up and walk around. He'll stay there all week, though, by God!"

"Then he must be feeling better."

He nodded.

"Here's to his health."

"I'll drink to that."

We drank. Then: "Had I an army of men like you and Lance," he said, "the story might have been different."

"What story?"

"The Circle and its Wardens," he said. "You've not heard of it?"

"Lance mentioned it. That's all."

One boy tended an enormous chunk of beef on a spit above a low fire. Occasionally, he sloshed some wine over it as he turned the shaft. Whenever the odor drifted my way, my stomach would rumble and Ganelon would chuckle. The other boy left the room to fetch bread from the kitchen.

Ganelon was silent a long while. He finished his wine and poured himself another glass. I sipped slowly at my first.

"Have you ever heard of Avalon?" he finally asked.

"Yes," I replied. "There is a verse I heard long ago from a passing bard: 'Beyond the River of the Blessed, there we sat down, yea, we wept, when we remembered Avalon. Our swords were shattered in our hands and we hung our shields on the oak tree. The silver towers were fallen, into a sea of blood. How many miles to Avalon? None, I say, and all. The silver towers are fallen.' "

"Avalon fallen . . . ?" he said.

"I think the man was mad. I know of no Avalon. His verse stayed in my mind, though."

Ganelon averted his face and did not speak again for several minutes. When he did, his voice was altered.

"There was," he said. "There was such a place. I lived there, years ago. I did not know it was fallen."

"How came you here from that place?" I asked him.

"I was exiled by its sorcerer Lord, Corwin of Amber. He sent me through darkness and madness to this place, that I might suffer and die here—and I *have* suffered and come near to the final lay many a time. I've tried to find the way back, but nobody knows it. I've spoken with sorcerers, and even a captured creature of the Circle before we slew the thing. But none knew the road to Avalon. It is as the bard said, 'No miles, and all,' " he misquoted my lyric. "Do you recall the bard's name?"

"I am sorry, but I do not."

"Where is this Cabra place you hie from?"

"Far to the east, across the waters," I said. "Very far. It is an island kingdom."

"Any chance they could furnish us with some troops? I can afford to pay quite a bit."

I shook my head.

"It is a small place with a small militia, and it would be several months' travel both ways—sea and land. They have never fought as mercenaries, and for that matter they are not very warlike."

"Then you seem to differ a great deal from your countrymen," he said, looking at me once more.

I sipped my wine.

"I was an arms instructor," I said, "to the Royal Guard."

"Then you might be inclined to hire out, to help train my troops?"

"I'll stay a few weeks and do that," I said.

He nodded a tight-lipped microsecond of a smile, then, "It saddens me to hear this indication that fair Avalon is gone," he said. "But if it is so, it means that my exiler is also likely dead." He drained his wineglass. "So even the demon came to a time when he could not defend his own," he mused. "That's a heartening thought. It means we might have a chance here, against these demons."

"Begging your pardon," I said, sticking my neck out for what I thought good reason, "if you were referring to that Corwin of Amber, he did not die when whatever happened happened."

The glass snapped in his hand.

"*You know Corwin?*" he said.

"No, but I know of him," I replied. "Several years ago, I met one of his brothers—a fellow named Brand. He told me of the place called Amber, and of the battle in which Corwin and a brother of his named Bleys led a horde against their brother Eric, who held the city. Bleys fell from the mountain Kolvir and Corwin was taken prisoner. Corwin's eyes were put out after Eric's coronation, and he was cast into the dungeons beneath Amber, where he may yet remain if he has not since died."

Ganelon's face was drained of color as I spoke.

"All those names you mentioned—Brand, Bleys, Eric," he said. "I heard him mention them in days long gone by. How long ago did you hear of this thing?"

"It was about four years back."

"He deserved better."

"After what he did to you?"

"Well," said the man, "I've had a lot of time to think about it, and it is not as if I gave him no cause for what he did. He was strong—stronger than you or Lance, even—and clever. Also, he could be merry on occasion. Eric should have killed him quickly, not the way that he did. I've no love for him, but my hate's died down a bit. The demon deserved better than he got, that's all."

The second boy returned with a basket of bread. The one who had prepared the meat removed it from the spit and set it on a platter in the center of the table.

Ganelon nodded toward it.

"Let's eat," he said.

He rose and moved to the table.

I followed. We did not talk much during the meal.

After stuffing myself until my stomach would hold no more and soaking down its contents with another glass of too-sweet wine, I began to yawn. Ganelon cursed after the third one.

"Damn it, Corey! Stop that! It's contagious!"

He stifled a yawn of his own.

"Let's take some air," he said, rising.

So we walked out along the walls, passing the sentries in their rounds. They would come to attention and salute Ganelon as soon as they saw who it was approaching, and he would give them a word of greeting and we would move on. We came to a battlement, where we paused to rest, seating ourselves on the stone, sucking in the evening air, cool and damp and full of the forest, and noting the appearance of the stars, one by one, in the darkening sky. The stone was cold beneath me. Far off in the distance, I thought I could detect the shimmer of the sea. I heard a night bird, from somewhere below us. Ganelon produced a pipe and tobacco from a pouch he wore at his belt. He filled it, tamped it, and struck a flame. His face would have been satanic in the spark light, save for whatever turned his mouth downward and drew the muscles in his cheeks up into that angle formed by the inner corners of his eyes and the sharp bridge of his nose. A devil is supposed to have an evil grin, and this one looked too morose.

I smelled the smoke. After a time, he began to speak, softly and very slowly at first:

"I remember Avalon," he began. "My birth there was not ignoble, but virtue was never one of my strong points. I went through my inheritance quickly and I took to the roads where I waylaid travelers. Later, I joined with a band of other men such as myself. When I discovered I was the strongest and most fit to lead, I became the leader. There were prices on all our heads. Mine was the highest."

He spoke more rapidly now, and his voice grew more refined and his choice of words came as an echo from out of his past.

"Yes, I remember Avalon," he said, "a place of silver and shade and cool waters, where the stars shone like bonfires at night and the green of day was always the green of spring. Youth, love, beauty—I knew them in Avalon. Proud steeds, bright metal, soft lips, dark ale. Honor . . ."

He shook his head.

"One later day," he said, "when war commenced within the realm, the ruler offered full pardon to any outlaws who would follow him in battle against the insurgents. This was Corwin. I threw in with him and rode off to the wars. I became an officer, and then—later—a member of his staff. We won the battles, put down the uprising. Then Corwin ruled peacefully once more, and I remained at his court. Those were the good years. There later came some border skirmishes, but these we always won. He trusted me to handle such things for him. Then he granted a Dukedom to dignify the House of a minor noble whose daughter he desired in marriage. I had wanted that Dukedom, and he had long hinted it might one day be mine. I was furious, and I betrayed my command the next time I was dispatched to settle a dispute along the southern border, where something was always stirring. Many of my men died, and the invaders entered into the realm. Before they could be routed, Lord Corwin himself had to take up arms once more. The invaders had come through in great strength, and I thought they would conquer the realm. I hoped they would. But Corwin, again, with his foxy tactics, prevailed. I fled, but was captured and taken to him for sentencing. I cursed him and spat at him. I would not bow. I hated the ground he trod, and a condemned man has no reason not to put up the best front he can, to go out like a man. Corwin said he would show me a measure of mercy for favors past. I told him to shove his mercy, and then I realized that he was mocking me. He ordered me released and he approached me. I knew he could kill me with his hands. I tried to fight with him, but to no avail. He struck me once and I fell. When I awakened, I was strapped across his horse's rump. He rode along, jibing at me the while. I would not reply to anything he said, but we rode through wondrous lands and lands out of nightmare, which is one way I learned of his sorcerous power—for no traveler I have ever met has passed through the places I saw that day. Then he pronounced my exile, released me in this place, turned, and rode away."

He paused to relight his pipe, which had gone out, puffed upon it for a time, went on: "Many a bruising, cudgeling, biting, and beating did I take in this place, at the hands of man and beast, only barely preserving my life. He had left me in the wickedest portion of the realm. But then one day my fortunes took a turn. An armored knight bade me depart the roadway that he might pass. At that point, I cared not whether I lived or died, so I called him a pock-marked whoreson and bade him go to the Devil. He charged me and I seized his lance and pushed its point into the ground, so unhorsing him. I drew him a smile beneath his chin with his own dagger, and thus obtained me mounting and weapons. Then did I set about paying back those who had used me poorly. I took up my old trade on the highways once again and I gained me another band of followers. We grew. When there were hundreds of us our needs were considerable. We would ride into a small town and make it ours. The local militia would fear us. This, too, was a good life, though not so splendid as the Avalon I never shall know again. All the roadside inns came to fear the thunder of our mounts, and travelers would soil their britches when they heard us coming. Ha! This lasted for several years. Large parties of armed men were sent to track us and destroy us, but always we evaded them or ambushed them. Then one day there was the dark Circle, and no one really knows why."

He puffed more vigorously on his pipe, stared off into the distance.

"I am told it began as a tiny ring of toadstools, far to the west. A child was found dead in its center, and the man who found her—her father—died of convulsions several days later. The spot was immediately said to be accursed. It grew quickly in the months that followed, until it was half a league across. The grasses darkened and shone like metal within it, but did not die. The trees twisted and their leaves blackened. They swayed when there was no wind, and bats danced and darted among them. In the twilight, strange shapes could be seen moving—always *within* the Circle, mind you—and there were lights, as of small fires, throughout the night. The Circle continued to grow, and those who lived near it fled—mostly. A few remained. It was said that those who remained had struck some bargain with the dark things. And the Circle continued to widen, spreading like the ripple from a rock cast into a pond. More and more people remained, living, within it. I have spoken with these people, fought with them, slain them. It is as if there is something dead inside them all. Their voices lack the thrust and dip of men chewing over their words and tasting them. They seldom do much with their faces, but wear them like death masks. They began to leave the Circle in bands, marauding. They slew wantonly. They committed many atrocities and defiled places of worship. They put things to the torch when they left them. They never stole objects of silver. Then, after many months, other creatures than men began to come forth—strangely formed, like the hellcats you slew. Then the Circle slowed in its growth, almost halting, as though it were nearing some sort of limit. But now all manner of raiders emerged from it—some even faring forth during the day—laying waste to the countryside about its borders. When they had devastated the land about its entire circumference, the Circle moved to encompass those areas, also. And so its growth began again, in this fashion. The old king, Uther, who had long hunted me, forgot all about me and set his forces to patrolling that damned Circle. It was beginning to worry me, also, as I did not relish the notion of being seized by some hell-spawned bloodsucker as I slept. So I got together fifty-five of my men—that was all who would volunteer, and I wanted no cowards—and we rode into that place one afternoon. We came upon a pack of those dead-faced men burning a live goat on a stone altar and we lit into the lot of them. We took one prisoner and tied him to his own altar and questioned him there. He told us that the Circle would grow until it covered the entire land, from ocean to ocean. One day it would close with itself on the other side of the world. We had best join with them, if we wished to save our hides. Then one of my men stabbed him and he died. He really died, for I know a dead man when I see one. I've made it happen often enough. But as his blood fell upon the stone, his mouth opened and out came the loudest laugh I ever heard in my life. It was like thunder all about us. Then he sat up, unbreathing, and began to burn. As he burned, his form changed, until it was like that of the burning goat—only larger—there upon the altar. Then a voice came from the thing. It said, 'Flee, mortal man! But you shall never leave this Circle!' And believe me, we fled! The sky grew black with bats and other—things. We heard the sound of hoofbeats. We rode with our blades in our hands, killing everything that came near us. There were cats such as you slew, and snakes and hopping things, and God knows what all else. As we neared the edge the Circle, one of King Uther's patrols saw us and came to our aid. Sixteen of the fifty-five who had ridden in with me rode back out. And the patrol lost perhaps thirty men itself. When they saw who I was, they hustled me off to court. Here. This used to be Uther's palace. I told him what I had done, what I had seen and heard. He did with me as Corwin had. He offered full pardon to me and to my men if we would join with him against the Wardens of the Circle. Having gone through what I had gone through, I realized that the thing had to be stopped. So I agreed. Then I fell ill, I am told that I was delirious for three days. I was as weak as a child after my recovery, and I learned that everyone who had entered the Circle had been likewise taken. Three had died. I visited the rest of my men, told them the story, and they were enlisted. The patrols about the Circle were strengthened. But it would not be contained. In the years that followed, the Circle grew. We fought many skirmishes. I was promoted until I stood at Uther's right hand, as once I had at Corwin's. Then the skirmishes became more than skirmishes. Larger and larger parties emerged from that hellhole. We lost a few battles. They took some of our outposts. Then one night an army emerged, an army—a horde— of both men and the other things that dwelled there. That night we met the largest force we had ever engaged. King Uther himself rode to battle, against my advice—for he was advanced in years—and he fell that night and the land was without a ruler. I wanted my captain, Lancelot, to sit in stewardship, for I knew him to be a far more honorable man than myself. . . . And it is strange here. I had known a Lancelot, just like him, in Avalon—but this man knew me not when first we met. It is strange. . . . At any rate, he declined, and the position was thrust upon me. I hate it, but here I am. I have held them back for over three years now. All my instincts tell me to flee. What do I owe these damned people? What do I care if the bloody Circle widens? I could cross over the sea to some land it would never reach during my lifetime, and then forget the whole thing. Damn it! I didn't want this responsibility! Now it is mine, though!"

"Why?" I asked him, and the sound of my own voice was strange to me.

There was silence.

He emptied his pipe. He refilled it. He relit it. He puffed it.

There was more silence.

Then, "I don't know," he said. "I'd stab a man in the back for a pair of shoes, if he had them and I needed them to keep my feet from freezing. I once did, that's how I know. But . . . this is different. This is a thing hurting everybody, and I'm the only one who can do the job. God damn it! I know they're going to bury me here one day, along with all the rest of them. But I can't pull out. I've got to hold that thing back as long as I can."

My head was cleared by the cold night air, which gave my consciousness a second wind, so to speak, though my body felt mildly anesthetized about me.

"Couldn't Lance lead them?" I asked.

"I'd say so. He's a good man. But there is another reason. I think that goat-thing, whatever it was, on the altar, is a bit afraid of me. I had gone in there and it had told me I'd never make it back out again, but I did. I lived through the sickness that followed after. It knows it's me that has been fighting it all along. We won that great bloody engagement on the night Uther died, and I met the thing again in a different form and it knew me. Maybe this is a part of what is holding it back now."

"What form?"

"A thing with a manlike shape, but with goat horns and red eyes. It was mounted on a piebald stallion. We fought for a time, but the tide of the battle swept us apart. Which was a good thing, too, for it was winning. It spoke again, as we swaggered swords, and I knew that head-filling voice. It called me a fool and told me I could never hope to win. But when morning came, the field was ours and we drove them back to the Circle, slaying them as they fled. The rider of the piebald escaped. There have been other sallyings forth since then, but none such as that night's. If I were to leave this land, another such army—one that is readying even now—would come forth. That thing would somehow know of my departure—just as it knew that Lance was bringing me another report on the disposition of troops within the Circle, sending those Wardens to destroy him as he returned. It knows of you by now, and surely it must wonder over this development. It must wonder who you are, for all your strength. I will stay here and fight it till I fall. I must. Do not ask me why. I only hope that before that day comes, I at least learn how this thing came to pass—*why* that Circle is out there."

Then there came a fluttering near to my head. I ducked quickly to avoid whatever it was. It was not necessary, though. It was only a bird. A white bird. It landed on my left shoulder and stood there, making small noises. I held up my wrist and it hopped over onto it. There was a note tied to its leg. I unfastened it, read it, crumpled it in my hand. Then I studied invisible things distant.

"What is the matter, Sir Corey?" cried Ganelon.

The note, which I had sent on ahead to my destination, written in my own hand, transmitted by a bird of my desire, could only reach the place that had to be my next stop. This was not precisely the place that I had in mind. However, I could read my own omens.

"What is it?" he asked. "What is it that you hold? A message?"

I nodded. I handed it to him. I could not very well throw it away, since he had seen me take it.

It read, "I am coming," and it bore my signature.

Ganelon puffed his pipe and read it in the glow.

"*He* lives? And he would come *here*?" he said.

"So it would seem."

"This is very strange," he said. "I do not understand it at all . . ."

"It sounds like a promise of assistance," I said, dismissing the bird, which cooed twice, then circled my head and departed.

Ganelon shook his head.

"I do not understand."

"Why number the teeth of a horse you may receive for nothing?" I said. "You have only succeeded in containing that thing."

"True," he said. "Perhaps he could destroy it."

"And perhaps it's just a joke," I told him. "A cruel one."

He shook his head again.

"No. That is not his style. I wonder what he is after?"

"Sleep on it," I suggested.

"There is little else that I can do, just now," he said, stifling a yawn.

We rose then and walked the wall. We said our good nights, and I staggered off toward the pit of sleep and fell headlong into it.

TWO

Day. More aches. More pains.

Someone had left me a new cloak, a brown one, which I decided was a good thing. Especially if I put on more weight and Ganelon recalled my colors. I did not shave my beard, because he had known me in a slightly less hairy condition. I took pains to disguise my voice whenever he was about. I hid Grayswandir beneath my bed.

For all of the following week I drove myself ruthlessly. I worked and sweated and strove until the aches subsided and my muscles grew firm once more. I think I put on fifteen pounds that week. Slowly, very slowly, I began feeling like my old self.

The country was called Lorraine, and so was she. If I happened to be in the mood to hand you a line, I would tell you we met in a meadow behind the castle, she gathering flowers and me walking there for exercise and fresh air. Crap.

I guess a polite term would be camp follower. I met her at the end of a hard day's work, spent mainly with the saber and the mace. She was standing off on the side lines waiting for her date when I first caught sight of her. She smiled and I smiled back, nodded, winked, and passed her by. The next day I saw her again, and I said "Hello" as I passed her. That's all.

Well, I kept running into her. By the end of my second week, when my aches were gone and I was over a hundred-eighty pounds and feeling that way again, I arranged to be with her one evening. By then, I was aware of her status and it was fine, so far as I was concerned. But we did not do the usual thing that night. No.

Instead, we talked, and then something else happened.

Her hair was rust-colored with a few strands of gray in it. I guessed she was under thirty, though. Eyes, very blue. Slightly pointed chin. Clean, even teeth inside a mouth that smiled at me a lot. Her voice was somewhat nasal, her hair was too long, her make-up laid on too heavily over too much tiredness, her complexion too freckled, her choice in clothing too bright and tight. But I liked her. I did not think I'd actually feel that way when I asked her out that night because, as I said, liking her was not what I had in mind.

There was no place to go but my chamber, so we had gone there. I had become a captain, and I took advantage of my rank by having dinner brought to us, and an extra bottle of wine.

"The men are afraid of you," she said. "They say you never grow tired."

"I do," I said, "believe me."

"Of course," she said, shaking her too-long locks and smiling. "Don't we all?"

"I daresay," I replied.

"How old are you?"

"How old are *you?*"

"A gentleman would not ask that question."

"Neither would a lady?"

"When you first came here, they thought you were over fifty."

"And . . . ?"

"And now they have no idea. Forty-five? Forty?"

"No," I said.

"I didn't think so. But your beard fooled everyone."

"Beards often do that."

"You look better every day. Bigger . . ."

"Thanks. I feel better than I did when I arrived."

"Sir Corey of Cabra," she said. "Where's Cabra? What's Cabra? Will you take me there with you, if I ask you nicely?"

"I'd tell you so," I said, "but I'd be lying."

"I know. But it would be nice to hear."

"Okay. I'll take you there with me. It's a lousy place."

"Are you really as good as the men say?"

"I'm afraid not. Are you?"

"Not really. Do you want to go to bed now?"

"No. I'd rather talk. Have a glass of wine."

"Thank you. . . . Your health."

"Yours."

"Why is it you are such a good swordsman?"

"Aptitude and good teachers."

". . . And you carried Lance all that distance and slew those beasts . . ."

"Stories grow with the telling."

"But I have watched you. You *are* better than the others. That is why Ganelon made you whatever deal he did. He knows a good thing when he sees it. I've had many friends who were swordsmen, and I've watched them at practice. You could cut them to pieces. The men say you are a good teacher. They like you, even if you do scare them."

"Why do I frighten them? Because I am strong? There are many strong men in the world. Because I can stand up and swing a blade for a long while?"

"They think there is something supernatural involved."

I laughed.

"No, I'm just the second-best swordsman around. Pardon me—maybe the third. But I try harder."

"Who's better?"

"Eric of Amber, possibly."

"Who is he?"

"A supernatural creature."

"He's the best?"

"No."

"Who is?"

"Benedict of Amber."

"Is he one, too?"

"If he is still alive, he is."

"Strange, that's what you are," she said. "And why? Tell me. *Are* you a supernatural creature?"

"Let's have another glass of wine."

"It'll go to my head."

"Good."

I poured them.

"We are all going to die," she said.

"Eventually."

"I mean here, soon, fighting this thing."

"Why do you say that?"

"It's too strong."

"Then why stick around?"

"I've no place else to go. That's why I ask you about Cabra."

"And why you came here tonight?"

"No. I came to see what you were like."

"I am an athlete who is breaking training. Were you born around here?"

"Yes. In the wood."

"Why'd you pick up with these guys?"

"Why not? It's better than getting pig shit on my heels every day."

"Never have a man of your own? Steady, I mean?"

"Yes. He's dead. He's the one who found . . . the Fairy Ring."

"I'm sorry."

"I'm not. He used to get drunk whenever he could borrow or steal enough to afford it and then come home and beat me. I was glad when I met Ganelon."

"So you think that the thing is too strong, that we are going to lose to it?"

"Yes."

"You may be right. But I think you're wrong."

She shrugged.

"You'll be fighting with us?"

"I'm afraid so."

"Nobody knew for sure, or would say if they did. That might prove interesting. I'd like to see you fight with the goat-man."

"Why?"

"Because he seems to be their leader. If you killed him, we'd have more of a chance. You might be able to do it."

"I have to," I said.

"Special reason?"

"Yes."

"Private one?"

"Yes."

"Good luck."

"Thanks."

She finished her wine, so I poured her another.

"I know *he* is a supernatural creature," she said.

"Let's get off the subject."

"All right. But will you do me a thing?"

"Name it."

"Put on armor tomorrow, pick up a lance, get hold of a horse, and trounce that big cavalry officer Harald."

"Why?"

"He beat me last week, just like Jarl used to. Can you do it?"

"Yes."

"Will you?"

"Why not? Consider him trounced."

She came over and leaned against me.

"I love you," she said.

"Crap."

"All right. How about, 'I like you'?"

"Good enough. I—"

Then a chill and numbing wind blew along my spine. I stiffened and resisted what was to come by blanking my mind completely.

Someone was looking for me. It was someone of the House of Amber, doubtless, and he was using my Trump or something very like it. There was no mistaking the sensation. If it was Eric, then he had more guts than I gave him credit for, since I had almost napalmed his brain the last time we had been in contact. It could not be Random, unless he was out of prison, which I doubted. If it was Julian or Caine, they could go to hell. Bleys was probably dead. Possibly Benedict, too. That left Gérard, Brand, and our sisters. Of these, only Gérard might mean me well. So I resisted discovery, successfully. It took me perhaps five minutes, and when it was finished I was shaking and sweating and Lorraine was staring at me strangely.

"What happened?" she asked. "You aren't drunk yet, and neither am I."

"Just a spell I sometimes get," I said. "It's a disease I picked up in the islands."

"I saw a face," she said. "Perhaps it was on the floor, maybe it was in my head. It was an old man. The collar of his garment was green and he looked a lot like you, except that his beard was gray."

I slapped her then.

"You're lying! You couldn't have . . ."

"I'm just telling you what I saw! Don't hit me! I don't know what it meant! Who was he?"

"I think it was my father. God, it's strange . . ."

"What happened?" she repeated.

"A spell," I said. "I sometimes get them, and people think they see my father on the castle wall or floor. Don't worry about it. It's not contagious."

"Crap," she said. "You're lying to me."

"I know. But please forget the whole thing."

"Why should I?"

"Because you like me," I told her. "Remember? And because I'm going to trounce Harald for you tomorrow."

"That's true," she said, and I started shaking again and she fetched a blanket from the bed and put it about my shoulders.

She handed me my wine and I drank it. She sat beside me and rested her head on my shoulder, so I put my arm about her. A devil wind began to scream and I heard the rapid rattle of the rainfall that came with it. For a second, it seemed that something beat against the shutters. Lorraine whimpered slightly.

"I do not like what is happening tonight," she said.

"Neither do I. Go bar the door. It's only bolted right now."

As she did this, I moved our seat so that it faced my single window. I fetched Grayswandir out from beneath the bed and unsheathed it. Then I extinguished every light in the room, save for a single candle on the table to my right.

I reseated myself, my blade across my knees.

"What are we doing?" Lorraine asked, as she came and sat down at my left.

"Waiting," I said.

"For what?"

"I am not positive, but this is certainly the night for it."

She shuddered and drew near.

"You know, perhaps you had better leave," I said.

"I know," she said, "but I'm afraid to go out. You'll be able to protect me if I stay here, won't you?"

I shook my head.

"I don't even know if I'll be able to protect myself."

She touched Grayswandir.

"What a beautiful blade! I've never seen one like it."

"There isn't another," I said, and each time that I shifted a little, the light fell differently upon it, so that one moment it seemed filmed over with unhuman blood of an orange tint and the next it lay there cold and white as snow or a woman's breast, quivering in my hand each time a little chill took me.

I wondered how it was that Lorraine had seen something I had not during the attempted contact. She could not simply have imagined anything that close to home.

"There is something strange about *you*," I said.

She was silent for four or five flickerings of the candle, then said, "I've a touch of the second sight. My mother had more of it. People say my grandmother was a sorceress. I don't know any of that business, though. Well, not much of it. I haven't done it for years. I always wind up losing more than I gain."

Then she was silent again, and I asked her, "What do you mean?"

"I used a spell to get my first man," she said, "and look what he turned out to be. If I hadn't, I'd have been a lot better off. I wanted a pretty daughter, and I made that happen—"

She stopped abruptly and I realized she was crying.

"What's the matter? I don't understand . . ."

"I thought you knew," she said.

"No, I'm afraid not."

"She was the little girl in the Fairy Circle. I thought you knew . . ."

"I'm sorry."

"I wish I didn't have the touch. I never use it any more. But it won't let me alone. It still brings me dreams and signs, and they are never over things I can do anything about. I wish it would go away and devil somebody else!"

"That's the one thing it will not do, Lorraine. I'm afraid you are stuck with it."

"How do you know?"

"I've known people like you in the past, that's all."

"You've a touch of it yourself, haven't you?"

"Yes."

"Then you feel that there is something out there now, don't you?"

"Yes."

"So do I. Do you know what it is doing?"

"It's looking for me."

"Yes, I feel that, too. Why?"

"Perhaps to test my strength. It knows that I am here. If I am a new ally come to Ganelon, it must wonder what I represent, who I am . . ."

"Is it the horned one himself?"

"I don't know. I think not, though."

"Why not?"

"If I am really he who would destroy it, it would be foolish to seek me out here in the keep of its enemy when I am surrounded by strength. I would say one of its minions is looking for me. Perhaps, somehow, that is what my father's ghost . . . I do not know. If its servant finds me and names me, it will know what preparations to make. If it finds me and destroys me, it will have solved the problem. If I destroy the servant, it will know that much more about my strength. Whichever way it works out, the horned one will be something ahead. So why should it risk its own pronged dome at this stage in the game?"

We waited, there in the shadow-clad chamber, as the taper burned away the minutes.

She asked me, "What did you mean when you said, if it finds you and names you . . . ? Names you what?"

"The one who almost did not come here," I said.

"You think that it might know you from somewhere, somehow?" she asked.

"I think it might," I said.

She drew away from me then.

"Don't be afraid," I said. "I won't hurt you."

"I am afraid, and you will hurt me!" she said. "I know it! But I want you! Why do I want you?"

"I don't know," I said.

"There is something out there now!" she said, sounding slightly hysterical. "It's near! It's very near! Listen! Listen!"

"Shut up!" I said, as a cold, prickly feeling came to rest on the back of my neck and coiled about my throat. "Get over on the far side of the room, behind the bed!"

"I'm afraid of the dark," she said.

"Do it, or I'll have to knock you out and carry you. You'll be in my way here."

I could hear a heavy flapping above the storm, and there came a scratching on the stone of the wall as she moved to obey me.

Then I was looking into two hot, red eyes which were looking back into my own. I dropped mine quickly. The thing stood there on the ledge outside the window and regarded me.

It was well over six feet in height, with great branches of antlers growing out of its forehead. Nude, its flesh was a uniform ash-gray in color. It appeared to be sexless, and it had gray, leathery wings extending far out behind it and joining with the night. It held a short, heavy sword of dark metal in its right hand, and there were runes carved all along the blade. With its left hand, it clutched at the lattice.

"Enter at your peril," I said loudly, and I raised the point of Grayswandir to indicate its breast.

It chuckled. It just stood there and chuckled and giggled at me. It tried to meet my eyes once more, but I would not let it. If it looked into my eyes for long, it would know me, as the hellcat had known me.

When it spoke, it sounded like a bassoon blowing words.

"You are not the one," it said, "for you are smaller and older. Yet . . . That blade . . . It could be his. Who are you?"

"Who are you?" I asked.

"Strygalldwir is my name. Conjure with it and I will eat your heart and liver."

"Conjure with it? I can't even pronounce it," I said, "and my cirrhosis would give you indigestion. Go away."

"Who are you?" it repeated.

"*Misli, gammi gra'dil, Strygalldwir*," I said, and it jumped as if given a hotfoot.

"You seek to drive me forth with such a simple spell?" it asked when it settled again. "I am not one of the lesser ones."

"It seemed to make you a bit uncomfortable."

"Who are you?" it said again.

"None of your business, Charlie. Ladybird, Ladybird, fly away home—"

"Four times must I ask you and four times be refused before I may enter and slay you. Who are you?"

"No," I said, standing. "Come on in and burn!"

Then it tore away the latticework, and the wind that accompanied it into the chamber extinguished the candle.

I lunged forward, and there were sparks between us when Grayswandir met the dark rune-sword. We clashed, then I sprang back. My eyes had adjusted to the half dark, so the loss of the light did not blind me. The creature saw well enough, also. It was stronger than a man, but then so am I. We circled the room. An icy wind moved about us, and when we passed the window again, cold droplets lashed my face. The first time that I cut the creature—a long slash across the breast—it remained silent, though tiny flames danced about the edges of the wound. The second time that I cut it—high upon the arm—it cried out, cursing me.

"Tonight I will suck the marrow from your bones!" it said. "I will dry them and work them most cunningly into instruments of music! Whenever I play upon them, your spirit will writhe in bodiless agony!"

"You burn prettily," I said.

It slowed for a fraction of a second, and my opportunity was there.

I beat that dark blade aside and my lunge was perfect. The center of its breast was my target. I ran it through.

It howled then, but did not fall. Grayswandir was torn from my grasp and flames bloomed about the wound. It stood there wearing them. It advanced a step toward me and I picked up a small chair and held it between us.

"I do not keep my heart where men do," it said.

Then it lunged, but I blocked the blow with the chair and caught it in the right eye with one of the legs. I threw the chair to the side then, and stepping forward, seized its right wrist and turned it over. I struck the elbow with the edge of my hand, as hard as I could. There came a sharp crack and the rune-sword clattered to the floor. Then its left hand struck my head and I fell.

It leaped for the blade, and I seized its ankle and jerked.

It sprawled, and I threw myself atop it and found its throat. I turned my head into the hollow of my shoulder, chin against my breast, as it clawed for my face with its left hand.

As my death grip tightened, its eyes sought mine, and this time I did not avoid them. There came a tiny shock at the base of my brain, as we both knew that we knew.

"You!" it managed to gasp, before I twisted my hands hard and the life went out of those red red eyes.

I stood, put my foot upon its carcass, and withdrew Grayswandir.

The thing burst into flames when my blade came free, and kept burning until there was nothing remaining but a charred spot upon the floor.

Then Lorraine came over and I put my arm about her and she asked me to take her back to her quarters and to bed. So I did, but we didn't do anything but lie there together until she had cried herself to sleep. That is how I met Lorraine.

Lance and Ganelon and I sat atop our mounts on a high hill, the late morning sun hitting us in the back, and we looked down into the place. Its appearance confirmed things for me.

It was akin to that twisted wood that filled the valley to the south of Amber.

Oh my father! What have I wrought? I said within my heart, but there was no answer other than the dark Circle that lay beneath me and spread for as far as the eye could see.

Through the bars of my visor, I looked down upon it—charred-seeming, desolate, and smelling of decay. I lived inside my visor these days. The men looked upon it as an affectation, but my rank gave me the right to be eccentric. I had worn it for over two weeks, since my battle with Strygalldwir. I had put it on the following morning before I trounced Harald to keep my promise to Lorraine, and I had decided that as my girth increased I had better keep my face concealed.

I weighed perhaps fourteen stone now, and felt like my old self again. If I could help clean up this mess in the land called Lorraine, I knew that I would have a chance at least to try what I most wanted, and perhaps succeed.

"So that's it," I said. "I don't see any troops mustering."

"I believe we will have to ride north," said Lance, "and we will doubtless only see them after dark."

"How far north?"

"Three or four leagues. They move about a bit."

We had ridden for two days to reach the Circle. We had met a patrol earlier that morning and learned that the troops inside the thing continued to muster every night. They went through various drills and then were gone— to someplace deeper inside—with the coming of morning. A perpetual thunderhead, I learned, rode above the Circle, though the storm never broke.

"Shall we breakfast here and then ride north?" I asked.

"Why not?" said Ganelon. "I'm starved and we've time."

So we dismounted and ate dried meat and drank from our canteens.

"I still do not understand that note," said Ganelon, after belching, patting his stomach, and lighting his pipe. "Will he stand beside us in the final battle, or will he not? Where is he, if he intends to help? The day of conflict draws nearer and nearer."

"Forget him," I said. "It was probably a joke."

"I can't, damn it!" he said. "There is something passing strange about the whole business!"

"What is it?" asked Lance, and for the first time I realized that Ganelon had not told him.

"My old liege, Lord Corwin, sends an odd message by carrier bird, saying he is coming. I had thought him dead, but he sent this message," Ganelon told him. "I still do not know what to make of it."

"Corwin?" said Lance, and I held my breath. "Corwin of Amber?"

"Yes, Amber and Avalon."

"Forget his message."

"Why?"

"He is a man without honor, and his promise means nothing."

"You know him?"

"I know of him. Long ago, he ruled in this land. Do you not recall the stories of the demon lordling? They are the same. That was Corwin, in days before my days. The best thing he did was abdicate and flee when the resistance grew too strong against him."

That was not true!

Or was it?

Amber casts an infinity of shadows, and my Avalon had cast many of its own, because of my presence there. I might be known on many earths that I had never trod, for shadows of myself had walked them, mimicking imperfectly my deeds and my thoughts.

"No," said Ganelon, "I never paid heed to the old stories. I wonder if it *could* have been the same man, ruling here. That is interesting."

"Very," I agreed, to keep my hand in things. "But if he ruled so long ago, surely he must be dead or decrepit by now."

"He was a sorcerer," said Lance.

"The one I knew certainly was," said Ganelon, "for he banished me from a land neither art nor artifice can discover now."

"You never spoke of this before," said Lance. "How did it occur?"

"None of your business," said Ganelon, and Lance was silent once again.

I hauled out my own pipe—I had obtained one two days earlier—and Lance did the same. It was a clay job and drew hot and hard. We lit up, and the three of us sat there smoking.

"Well, he did the smart thing," said Ganelon. "Let's forget it now."

We did not, of course. But we stayed away from the subject after that.

If it had not been for the dark thing behind us, it would have been quite pleasant, just sitting there, relaxing. Suddenly, I felt close to the two of them. I wanted to say something, but I could not think what.

Ganelon solved that by bringing up current business once more.

"So you want to hit them before they hit us?" he said.

"That's right," I replied. "Take the fight to their home territory."

"The trouble is that it *is* their home territory," he said. "They know it better than we do now, and who knows what powers they might be able to call on there?"

"Kill the horned one and they will crumble," I said.

"Perhaps. Perhaps not. Maybe you could do it," said Ganelon. "Unless I got lucky, though, I don't know whether I could. He's too mean to die easily. While I think I'll still as good a man as I was some years ago, I may be fooling myself. Perhaps I've grown soft. I never wanted this damn stay-at-home job!"

"I know," I said.

"I know," said Lance.

"Lance," said Ganelon, "should we do as our friend here says? Should we attack?"

He could have shrugged and equivocated. He did not.

"Yes," he said. "They almost had us last time. It was very close the night King Uther died. If we do not attack them now, I feel they may defeat us next time. Oh, it would not be easy, and we would hurt them badly. But I think they could do it. Let us see what we can see now, then make our plans for an attack."

"All right," said Ganelon. "I am sick of waiting too. Tell me that again after we return and I'll go along with it."

So we did that thing.

We rode north that afternoon, and we hid ourselves in the hills and looked down upon the Circle. Within it, they worshiped, after their fashion, and they drilled. I estimated around four thousand troops. We had about twenty-five hundred. They also had weird flying, hopping, crawling things that made noises in the night. We had stout hearts. Yeah.

All that I needed was a few minutes alone with their leader, and it would be decided, one way or another. The whole thing. I could not tell my companions that, but it was true.

You see, I was the party responsible for the whole thing down there. I had done it, and it was up to me to undo it, if I could.

I was afraid that I could not.

In a fit of passion, compounded of rage, horror, and pain, I had unleashed this thing, and it was reflected somewhere in every earth in existence. Such is the blood curse of a Prince of Amber.

We watched them all that night, the Wardens of the Circle, and in the morning we departed.

The verdict was, attack!

So we rode all the way back and nothing followed us. When we reached the Keep of Ganelon, we fell to planning. Our troops were ready—over-ready, perhaps—and we decided to strike within a fortnight.

As I lay with Lorraine, I told her of these things. For I felt that she should know. I possessed the power to spirit her away into Shadow—that very night, if she would agree. She did not.

"I'll stay with you," she said.

"Okay."

I did not tell her that I felt everything lay within my hands, but I have a feeling she knew and that for some reason she trusted me. I would not have, but that was her affair.

"You know how things might be," I said.

"I know," she said, and I knew that she knew and that was it.

We turned our attention to other subjects, and later we slept.

She'd had a dream.

In the morning, she said to me, "I had a dream."

"What about?" I asked.

"The coming battle," she told me. "I see you and the horned one locked in combat."

"Who wins?"

"I don't know. But as you slept, I did a thing that might help you."

"I wish you had not," I said. "I can take care of myself."

"Then I dreamed of my own death, in this time."

"Let me take you away to a place I know."

"No, my place is here," she told me.

"I don't pretend to own you," I said, "but I can save you from whatever you've dreamed. That much lies within my power, believe me."

"I do believe you, but I will not go."

"You're a damned fool."

"Let me stay."

"As you wish. . . . Listen, I'll even send you to Cabra . . ."

"No."

"You're a damned fool."

"I know. I love you."

". . . And a stupid one. The word is 'like.' Remember?"

"You'll do it," she said.

"Go to hell," I said.

Then she wept, softly, until I comforted her once again.

That was Lorraine.

THREE

I thought back, one morning, upon all that had gone before. I thought of my brothers and sisters as though they were playing cards, which I knew was wrong. I thought back to the rest home where I had awakened, back to the battle for Amber, back to my walking the Pattern in Rebma, and back to that time with Moire, who just might be Eric's by now. I thought of Bleys and of Random, Deirdre, Caine, Gérard, and Eric, that morning. It was the morning of the battle, of course, and we were camped in the hills near the Circle. We had been attacked several times along the way, but they had been brief, guerrilla affairs. We had dispatched our assailants and continued. When we reached the area we had decided upon, we made our camp, posted guards, and retired. We slept undisturbed. I awoke wondering whether my brothers and sisters thought of me as I thought of them. It was a very sad thought.

In the privacy of a small grove, my helmet filled with soapy water, I shaved my beard. Then I dressed, slowly, in my private and tattered colors. I was as hard as stone, dark as soil, and mean as hell once more. Today would be the day. I donned my visor, put on chain mail, buckled my belt, and hung Grayswandir at my side. Then I fastened my cloak at my neck with a silver rose and was discovered by a messenger who had been looking for me to tell me that things were about ready.

I kissed Lorraine, who had insisted on coming along. Then I mounted my horse, a roan named Star, and rode off toward the front.

There I met with Ganelon and with Lance. They said, "We are ready."

I called for my officers and briefed them. They saluted, turned and rode away.

"Soon," said Lance, lighting his pipe.

"How is your arm?"

"Fine, now," he replied, "after that workout you gave it yesterday. Perfect."

I opened my visor and lit my own pipe.

"You've shaved your beard," said Lance. "I cannot picture you without it."

"The helm fits better this way," I said.

"Good fortune to us all," said Ganelon. "I know no gods, but if any care to be with us, I welcome them."

"There is but one God," said Lance. "I pray that He be with us."

"Amen," said Ganelon, lighting his pipe. "For today."

"It will be ours," said Lance.

"Yes," said I, as the sun stirred the east and the birds of morning the air, "it has that feel to it."

We emptied our pipes when we had finished and tucked them away at our belts. Then we secured ourselves with final tightenings and claspings of our armor and Ganelon said, "Let us be about it."

My officers reported back to me. My sections were ready.

We filed down the hillside, and we assembled outside the Circle. Nothing stirred within it, and no troops were visible.

"I wonder about Corwin," Ganelon said to me.

"He is with us," I told him, and he looked at me strangely, seemed to notice the rose for the first time, then nodded brusquely.

"Lance," he said, when we had assembled. "Give the order."

And Lance drew his blade. His cried "Charge!" echoed about us.

We were half a mile inside the Circle before anything happened. There were five hundred of us in the lead, all mounted. A dark cavalry appeared, and we met them. After five minutes, they broke and we rode on.

Then we heard the thunder.

There was lightning, and the rain began to fall.

The thunderhead had finally broken.

A thin line of foot soldiers, pikemen mainly, barred our way, waiting stoically. Maybe we all smelled the trap, but we bore down upon them.

Then the cavalry hit our flanks.

We wheeled, and the fighting began in earnest.

It was perhaps twenty minutes later . . .

We held out, waiting for the main body to arrive.

Then the two hundred or so of us rode on . . .

Men. It was men that we slew, that slew us—gray-faced, dour-countenanced men. I wanted more. One more . . .

Theirs must have been a semi-metaphysical problem in logistics. How much could be diverted through this Gateway? I was not sure. Soon . . .

We topped a rise, and far ahead and below us lay a dark citadel.

I raised my blade.

As we descended, they attacked.

They hissed and they croaked and they flapped. They meant, to me, that he was running low on people. Grayswandir became a flame in my hand, a thunderbolt, a portable electric chair. I slew them as fast as they approached, and they burned as they died. To my right, I saw Lance draw a similar line of chaos, and he was muttering beneath his breath. Prayers for the dead, no doubt. To my left, Ganelon laid about him, and a wake of fires followed behind his horse's tail. Through the flashing lightning, the citadel loomed larger.

The hundred or so of us stormed ahead, and the abominations fell by the wayside.

When we reached the gate, we were faced by an infantry of men and beasts. We charged.

They outnumbered us, but we had little choice. Perhaps we had pre-ceeded our own infantry by too much. But I thought not. Time, as I saw it, was all important now.

"I've got to get through!" I cried. "He's inside!"

"He's mine!" said Lance.

"You're both welcome to him!" said Ganelon, laying about him. "Cross when you can! I'm with you!"

We slew and we slew and we slew, and then the tide turned in their favor. They pressed us, all the ugly things that were more or less than human, mixed in with human troops. We were drawn up into a tight knot, defending ourselves on all sides, when our bedraggled infantry arrived and began hacking. We pressed for the gate once more and made it this time, all forty or fifty of us.

We won through, and then there were troops in the courtyard to be slain.

The dozen or so of us who made it to the foot of the dark tower were faced by a final guard contingent.

"Go it!" cried Ganelon, as we leaped from our horses and waded into them.

"Go it!" cried Lance, and I guess they both meant me, or each other.

I took it to mean me, and I broke away from the fray and raced up the stairs.

He would be there, in the highest tower, I knew; and I would have to face him, and face him down. I did not know whether I could, but I had to try, because I was the only one who knew where he really came from—and I was the one who put him there.

I came to a heavy wooden door at the top of the stairs. I tried it, but it was secured from the other side. So I kicked it as hard as I could.

It fell inward with a crash.

I saw him there by the window, a man-formed body dressed in light armor, goat head upon those massive shoulders.

I crossed the threshold and stopped.

He had turned to stare as the door had fallen, and now he sought my eyes through steel.

"Mortal man, you have come too far," he said. "Or *are* you mortal man?" and there was a blade in his hand.

"Ask Strygalldwir," I said.

"You are the one who slew him," he stated. "Did he name you?"

"Maybe."

There were footsteps on the stairs behind me. I stepped to the left of the doorway.

Ganelon burst into the chamber and I called "Halt!" and he did.

He turned to me.

"This is the thing," he said. "What is it?"

"My sin against a thing I loved," I said. "Stay away from it. It's mine."

"You're welcome to it."

He stood stock still.

"Did you really mean that?" asked the creature.

"Find out," I said, and leaped forward.

But it did not fence with me. Instead, it did what any mortal fencer would consider foolish.

It hurled its blade at me, point forward, like a thunderbolt. And the sound of its passage came like a clap of thunder. The elements outside the tower echoed it, a deafening response.

With Grayswandir, I parried that blade as though it were an ordinary thrust. It embedded itself in the floor and burst into flames. Without, the lightning responded.

For an instant, the light was as blinding as a magnesium flare, and in that moment the creature was upon me.

It pinned my arms to my sides, and its horns struck against my visor, once, twice . . .

Then I threw my strength against those arms, and their grip began to weaken.

I dropped Grayswandir, and with a final heave broke the hold it had upon me.

In that moment, however, our eyes met.

Then we both struck, and we both reeled back.

"Lord of Amber," it said then, "why do you strive with me? It was you who gave us this passage, this way . . ."

"I regret a rash act and seek to undo it."

"Too late—and this a strange place to begin."

It struck again, so quickly that it got through my guard. I was slammed back against the wall. Its speed was deadly.

And then it raised its hand and made a sign, and I had a vision of the

Courts of Chaos come upon me—a vision that made my hackles rise, made a chill wind blow across my soul, to know what I had done.

". . . You see?" it was saying. "You gave us this Gateway. Help us now, and we will restore to you that which is yours."

For a moment I was swayed. It was possible that it could do just what it had offered, if I would help.

But it would be a threat forever after. Allies briefly, we would be at each other's throats after we got what we wanted—and those dark forces would be much stronger by then. Still, if I held the city . . .

"Do we have a bargain?" came the sharp, near-bleat of the question.

I thought upon the shadows, and of the places beyond Shadow . . .

Slowly, I reached up and unbuckled my helm . . .

Then I hurled it, just as the creature seemed to relax. I think Ganelon was moving forward by then.

I leaped across the chamber and drove it back against the wall.

"No!" I cried.

Its manlike hands found my throat at about the same instant mine wrapped about its own.

I squeezed, with all my strength, and twisted. I guess it did the same.

I heard something snap like a dry stick. I wondered whose neck had broken. Mine sure hurt.

I opened my eyes and there was the sky. I was lying on my back on a blanket on the ground.

"I'm afraid he's going to live," said Ganelon, and I turned my head, slowly, in the direction of his voice.

He was seated on the edge of the blanket, sword across his knees. Lorraine was with him.

"How goes it?" I said.

"We've won," he told me. "You've kept your promise. When you killed that thing, it was all over. The men fell senseless, the creatures burned."

"Good."

"I have been sitting here wondering why I no longer hate you."

"Have you reached any conclusions?"

"No, not really. Maybe it's because we're a lot alike. I don't know."

I smiled at Lorraine.

"I'm glad you're very poor when it comes to prophecy. The battle is over and you're still alive."

"The death has already begun," she said, not returning my smile.

"What do you mean?"

"They still tell stories of how the Lord Corwin had my grandfather executed—drawn and quartered publicly—for leading one of the early uprisings against him."

"That wasn't me," I said. "It was one of my shadows."

But she shook her head and said, "Corwin of Amber, I am what I am," and she rose and left me then.

"What was it?" asked Ganelon, ignoring her departure. "What was the thing in the tower?"

"Mine," I said; "one of those things which was released when I laid my curse upon Amber. I opened the way then for that which lies beyond Shadow to enter the real world. The paths of least resistance are followed in these things, through the shadows to Amber. Here, the path was the Circle. Elsewhere, it might be some different thing. I have closed their way through this place now. You may rest easy here."

"That is why you came here?"

"No," I said. "Not really. I was but passing on the road to Avalon when I came upon Lance. I could not let him lie there, and after I took him to you I became involved in this piece of my handiwork."

"Avalon? Then you lied when you said it was destroyed?"

I shook my head.

"Not so. Our Avalon fell, but in Shadow I may find its like once more."

"Take me with you."

"Are you mad?"

"No, I would look once again on the land of my birth, no matter what the peril."

"I do not go to dwell there," I said, "but to arm for battle. In Avalon there is a pink powder the jewelers use. I ignited a sample of it one time in Amber. I go there only to obtain it and to build guns that I may lay siege to Amber and gain the throne that is mine."

"What of those things from beyond Shadow you spoke of."

"I will deal with them afterwards. Should I lose this time, then they are Eric's problem."

"You said that he had blinded you and cast you into the dungeons."

"That is true. I grew new eyes. I escaped."

"You *are* a demon."

"This has often been said. I no longer deny it."

"You will take me with you?"

"If you really wish to come. It will differ from the Avalon you knew, however."

"To Amber!"

"You *are* mad!"

"No. Long have I wished to look upon that fabled city. After I have seen Avalon once again I will want to turn my hand to something new. Was I not a good general?"

"Yes."

"Then you will teach me of these things you call guns, and I will help you in the greatest battle. I've not too many good years remaining before me, I know. Take me with you."

"Your bones may bleach at the foot of Kolvir, beside my own."

"What battle is certain? I will chance it."

"As you would. You may come."

"Thank you, Lord."

We camped there that night, rode back to the keep in the morning. Then I sought after Lorraine. I learned that she had run off with one of her former lovers, an officer named Melkin. Although she had been upset, I resented the fact that she had not given me the opportunity to explain something of which she only knew rumors. I decided to follow them.

I mounted Star, turned my stiff neck in the direction they had supposedly taken, and rode on after. In a way, I could not blame her. I had not been received back at the keep as the slayer of the horned one might have been were he anyone else. The stories of their Corwin lingered on, and the demon tag was on all of them. The men I had worked with, fought beside, now looked at me with glances holding something more than fear—glances only, for they quickly dropped their eyes or turned them to another thing. Perhaps they feared that I wished to stay and reign over them. They might have been relieved, all save Ganelon, when I took to the trail. Ganelon, I think, feared that I would not return for him as I had promised. This, I feel, is the reason that he offered to ride with me. But it was a thing that I had to do by myself.

Lorraine had come to mean something to me, I was surprised to discover, and I found myself quite hurt by her action. I felt that she owed me a hearing before she went her way. Then if she still chose her mortal captain, they could have my blessing. If not, I realized that I wanted to keep her with me. Fair Avalon would be postponed for so long as it took me to resolve this to ending or continuance.

I rode along the trail and the birds sang in the trees about me. The day was bright with a sky-blue, tree-green peace, for the scourge had been lifted from the land. In my heart, there was something like a bit of joy that I had undone at least a small portion of the rottenness I had wrought. Evil? Hell, I've done more of it than most men, but I had picked up a conscience too, somewhere along the way, and I let it enjoy one of its rare moments of satisfaction. Once I held Amber, I could allow it a little more leeway, I felt. Ha!

I was heading north, and the terrain was foreign to me. I followed a clearly marked trail, which bore the signs of two riders' recent passage. I followed all that day, through dusk and into evening, dismounting periodically to inspect the way. Finally, my eyes played too many tricks on me, so I located a small glen—several hundred yards to the left of the trail—and there I camped for the night. It was the pains in my neck, doubtless, that made me dream of the horned one and relive that battle. "Help us now, and we will restore to you that which is yours," it said. I awoke suddenly at that point, with a curse on my lips.

When morning paled the sky, I mounted and continued on. It had been a cold night, and the day still held me in hands out of the north. The grasses sparkled with a light frost and my cloak was damp from having been used as a bedroll.

By noon, something of warmth had returned to the world and the trail was fresher. I was gaining on them.

When I found her, I leaped down from my mount and ran to where she lay, beneath a wild rosebush without flowers, the thorns of which had scratched her cheek and shoulder. Dead, she had not been so for long, for the blood was still damp upon her breast where the blade had entered, and her flesh yet warm.

There were no rocks with which to build her a cairn, so I cut away the sod with Grayswandir and laid her there to rest. He had removed her bracelets, her rings, and her jeweled combs, which had held all she possessed of fortune. I had to close her eyes before I covered her over with my cloak, and here my hand faltered and my own eyes grew dim. It took me a long while.

I rode on, and it was not long before I overtook him, riding as though he were pursued by the Devil, which he was. I spoke not a word when I unhorsed him, nor afterward, and I did not use my blade, though he drew his own. I hurled his broken body into a high oak tree, and when I looked back it was dark with birds.

I replaced her rings, her bracelets, her combs, before I closed the grave, and that was Lorraine. All that she had ever been or wanted to be had come to this, and that is the whole story of how we met and how we parted, Lorraine and I, in the land called Lorraine, and it is like onto my life, I guess, for a Prince of Amber is part and party to all the rottenness that is in the world, which is why whenever I do speak of my conscience, something else within me must answer, "Ha!" In the mirrors of the many judgments, my hands are the color of blood. I am a part of the evil that exists in the world and in Shadow. I sometime fancy myself an evil which exists to oppose other evils. I destroy Melkins when I find them, and on that Great Day of which prophets speak but in which they do not truly believe, on that day when the world is completely cleansed of evil, then I, too, will go down into darkness, swallowing curses. Perhaps even sooner than that, I now judge. But whatever . . . Until that time, I shall not wash my hands nor let them hang useless.

Turning, I rode back to the Keep of Ganelon, who knew but would never understand.

FOUR

Riding, riding, through the wild, weird ways that led to Avalon, we went, Ganelon and I, down alleys of dream and of nightmare, beneath the brass bark of the sun and the hot, white isles of night, till these were gold and diamond chips and the moon swam like a swan. Day belled forth the green of spring, we crossed a mighty river and the mountains before us were frosted by night. I unleashed an arrow of my desire into the midnight and it took fire overhead, burned its way like a meteor into the north. The only dragon we encountered was lame and limped away quickly to hide, singeing daisies as it panted and wheezed. Migrations of bright birds arrowed our destination, and crystalline voices from lakes echoed our words as we passed. I sang as we rode, and after a time, Ganelon joined me. We had been traveling for over a week, and the land and the sky and the breezes told me we were near to Avalon now.

We camped in a wood near a lake as the sun slid behind stone and the day died down and ceased. I went off to the lake to bathe while Ganelon unpacked our gear. The water was cold and bracing. I splashed about in it for a long while.

I thought I heard several cries as I bathed, but I could not be certain. It was a weird wood and I was not overly concerned. However, I dressed quickly and hurried back to the camp.

As I walked, I heard it again: a whine, a plea. Drawing nearer, I realized that a conversation was in progress.

Then I entered the small clearing we had chosen. Our gear was spread about and the beginnings of a campfire had been laid.

Ganelon squatted on his haunches beneath an oak tree. The man hung from it.

He was young and fair of hair and complexion. Beyond that, it was hard to say at a glance. It is difficult, I discovered, to obtain a clear initial impression as to a man's features and size when he is hanging upside down several feet above the ground.

His hands had been tied behind his back and he hung from a low bough by a rope that had been knotted about his right ankle.

He was talking—brief, rapid phrases in response to Ganelon's questions— and his face was moist with spittle and sweat. He did not hang limply, but swung back and forth. There was an abrasion on his cheek and several spots of blood on his shirt front.

Halting, I restrained myself from interrupting for a moment and watched. Ganelon would not have put him where he was without a reason, so I was not immediately overwhelmed with sympathy for the fellow. Whatever it was that had prompted Ganelon to question him thus, I knew that I, too, would be interested in the information. I was also interested in whatever the session would show me concerning Ganelon, who was now something of an ally. And a few more minutes upside down could not do that much additional damage . . .

As his body slowed, Ganelon prodded him in the sternum with the tip of his blade and set him to swinging violently once again. This broke the skin lightly and another red spot appeared. At this, the boy cried out. From his complexion, I could see now that he was a youth. Ganelon extended his blade and held its point several inches beyond the place the boy's throat would come to on the backswing. At the last moment, he snatched it back and chuckled as the boy writhed and cried out, "Please!"

"The rest," said Ganelon. "Tell me everything."

"That's all!" said the other. "I know no more!"

"Why not?"

"They swept on by me then! I could not see!"

"Why did you not follow?"

"They were mounted. I was on foot."

"Why did you not follow on foot then?"

"I was dazed."

"Dazed? You were afraid! You deserted!"

"No!"

Ganelon held his blade forth, snapped it away again at the final moment.

"No!" cried the youth.

Ganelon moved the blade again.

"Yes!" the boy screamed. "I was afraid!"

"And you fled then?"

"Yes! I kept running! I've been fleeing ever since . . ."

"And you know nothing of how things went after that?"

"No."

"You lie!"

He moved the blade again.

"No!" said the boy. "Please . . ."

I stepped forward then.

"Ganelon," I said.

He glanced at me and grinned, lowering the blade. The boy sought my eyes.

"What have we here?" I asked.

"Ha!" he said, slapping the inside of the youth's thigh so that he cried out. "A thief, a deserter—with an interesting tale to tell."

"Then cut him down and let me hear it," I said.

Ganelon turned and cut through the cord with one swipe of his blade. The boy fell to the ground and began sobbing.

"I caught him trying to steal our supplies and thought to question him about the area," Ganelon said. "He's come from Avalon—quickly."

"What do you mean?"

"He was a foot soldier in a battle that took place there two nights ago. He turned coward during the fighting and deserted."

The youth began to mouth a denial and Ganelon kicked him.

"Silence!" he said. "I'm telling it now—as you told me!"

The boy moved sideways like a crab and looked at me with wide, pleading eyes.

"Battle? Who was fighting?" I asked.

Ganelon smiled grimly.

"It sounds somewhat familiar," he said. "The forces of Avalon were engaged in what seems to have been the largest—and perhaps final—of a long series of confrontations with beings not quite natural."

"Oh?"

I studied the boy and his eyes dropped, but I saw the fear that was there before they fell.

". . . Women," Ganelon said. "Pale furies out of some hell, lovely and cold. Armed and armored. Long, light hair. Eyes like ice. Mounted on white, fire-breathing steeds that fed on human flesh, they came forth by night from a warren of caves in the mountains an earthquake opened several years ago.

They raided, taking young men back with them as captives, killing all others. Many appeared later as a soulless infantry, following their van. This sounds very like the men of the Circle we knew."

"But many of those lived when they were freed," I said. "They did not seem soulless then, only somewhat as I once did—amnesiac. It seems strange," I went on, "that they did not block off these caves during the day, since the riders only came forth by night . . ."

"The deserter tells me this was tried," said Ganelon, "and they always burst forth after a time, stronger than before."

The boy was ashen, but he nodded when I looked toward him inquiringly.

"Their General, whom he calls the Protector, routed them many times," Ganelon continued. "He even spent part of a night with their leader, a pale bitch named Lintra—whether in dalliance or parlay, I'm not certain. But nothing came of this. The raids continued and her forces grew stronger. The Protector finally decided to mass an all-out attack, in hopes of destroying them utterly. It was during that battle that this one fled," he said, indicating the youth with a gesture of his blade, "which is why we do not know the ending of the story."

"Is that the way it was?" I asked him.

The boy looked away from the weapon's point, met my eyes for a moment, then nodded slowly.

"Interesting," I said to Ganelon. "Very. I've a feeling their problem is linked to the one we just solved. I wish I knew how their fight turned out."

Ganelon nodded, shifted his grip on his weapon.

"Well, if we're finished with him now . . ." he said.

"Hold. I presume he was trying to steal something to eat?"

"Yes."

"Free his hands. We'll feed him."

"But he tried to steal from us."

"Did you not say that you had once killed a man for a pair of shoes?"

"Yes, but that was different."

"How so?"

"I got away with it."

I laughed. It broke me up completely, and I could not stop laughing. He looked irritated, then puzzled. Then he began laughing himself.

The youth regarded us as if we were a pair of maniacs.

"All right," said Ganelon finally, "all right," and he stooped, turned the boy with a single push, and severed the cord that bound his wrists.

"Come, lad," he said. "I'll fetch you something to eat," and he moved to our gear and opened several food parcels.

The boy rose and limped slowly after him. He seized the food that was offered and began eating quickly and noisily, not taking his eyes off Ganelon. His information, if true, presented me with several complications, the foremost being that it would probably be more difficult to obtain what I wanted in a war-ravaged land. It also lent weight to my fears as to the nature and extent of the disruption pattern.

I helped Ganelon build a small fire.

"How does this affect our plans?" he asked.

I saw no real choice. All of the shadows near to what I desired would be similarly involved. I could lay my course for one which did not possess such involvement, but in reaching it I would have achieved the wrong place. That which I desired would not be available there. If the forays of chaos kept occurring on my desire-walk through Shadow, then they were bound up with the nature of the desire and would have to be dealt with, one way or another, sooner or later. They could not be avoided. Such was the nature of the game, and I could not complain because I had laid down the rules.

"We go on," I said. "It is the place of my desire."

The youth let out a brief cry, and then—perhaps from some feeling of indebtedness for my having prevented Ganelon from poking holes in him— warned, "Do not go to Avalon, sir! There is nothing there that you could desire! You will be slain!"

I smiled to him and thanked him. Ganelon chuckled then and said, "Let us take him back with us to stand a deserter's trial."

At this, the youth scrambled to his feet and began running.

Still laughing, Ganelon drew his dagger and cocked his arm to throw it. I struck his arm and his cast went wide of its mark. The youth vanished within the wood and Ganelon continued to laugh.

He retrieved the dagger from where it had fallen and said, "You should have let me kill him, you know."

"I decided against it."

He shrugged.

"If he returns and cuts our throats tonight you may find yourself feeling somewhat different."

"I should imagine. But he will not, you know that."

He shrugged again, skewering a piece of meat and warming it over the flames.

"Well, war has taught him to show a good pair of heels," he acknowledged. "Perhaps we *will* awaken in the morning."

He took a bite and began to chew. It seemed like a good idea and I fetched some for myself.

Much later, I was awakened from a troubled sleep to stare at stars through a screen of leaves. Some omen-making portion of my mind had seized upon the youth and used us both badly. It was a long while before I could get back to sleep.

In the morning we kicked dirt over the ashes and rode on. We made it into the mountains that afternoon and passed through them the following day. There were occasional signs of recent passage on the trail we followed, but we encountered no one.

The following day we passed several farmhouses and cottages, not pausing at any of them. I had opted against the wild, demonic route I had followed when I had exiled Ganelon. While quite brief, I knew that he would have found it massively disconcerting. I had wanted this time to think, so much a journeying was not called for. Now, however, the long route was nearing its end. We achieved Amber's sky that afternoon, and I admired it in silence. It might almost be the Forest of Arden through which we rode. There were no horn notes, however, no Julian, no Morgenstern, no stormhounds to harry us, as there had been in Arden when last I passed that way. There were only the bird notes in the great-boled trees, the complaint of a squirrel, the bark of a fox, the splash of a waterfall, the whites and blues and pinks of flowers in the shade.

The breezes of the afternoon were gentle and cool; they lulled me so that I was unprepared for the row of fresh graves beside the trail that came into sight when we rounded a bend. Near by, there was a torn and trampled glen. We tarried there briefly but learned nothing more than had been immediately apparent.

We passed another such place farther along, and several fire-charred groves. The trail was well worn by then and the side brush trampled and broken, as by the passage of many men and beasts. The smell of ashes was occasionally upon the air, and we hurried past the partly eaten carcass of a horse now well ripened where it lay.

The sky of Amber no longer heartened me, though the way was clear for a long while after that.

The day was running to evening and the forest had thinned considerably when Ganelon noted the smoke trails to the southeast. We took the first side path that seemed to lead in that direction, although it was tangent to Avalon proper. It was difficult to estimate the distance, but we could tell that we would not reach the place until after nightfall.

"Their army—still encamped?" Ganelon wondered.

"Or that of their conqueror."

He shook his head and loosened his blade in its scabbard.

Toward twilight, I left the trail to follow a sound of running water to its source. It was a clear, clean stream that had made its way down from the mountains and still bore something of their chill within it. I bathed there, trimming my new bearding and cleaning the dust of travel from my garments as well. As we were nearing this end of our journeying, it was my wish to arrive with what small splendor I could muster. Appreciating this, Ganelon even splashed water over his face and blew his nose loudly.

Standing on the bank, blinking my rinsed eyes at the heavens, I saw the moon resolve itself sharp and clear, the fuzziness fading from its edges. This was the first time it had happened. My breathing jerked to a halt and I kept staring. Then I scanned the sky for early stars, traced the edges of clouds, the distant mountains, the farthest trees. I looked back at the moon, and it still held clear and steady. My eyesight was normal once again.

Ganelon drew back at the sound of my laughter, and he never inquired as to its cause.

Suppressing an impulse to sing, I remounted and headed back toward the trail once again. The shadows deepened as we rode, and clusters of stars bloomed among the branches overhead. I inhaled a big piece of the night, held it a moment, released it. I was myself once again and the feeling was good.

Ganelon drew up beside me and said in a low voice, "There will doubtless be sentries."

"Yes," I said.

"Then hadn't we better leave the trail?"

"No. I would rather not seem furtive. It matters not to me whether we arrive with an escort. We are simply two travelers."

"They may require the reason for our travels."

"Then let us be mercenaries who have heard of strife in the realm and come seeking employment."

"Yes. We look the part. Let us hope they pause long enough to notice."

"If they cannot see us that well, then we are poor targets."

"True, but I am not fully comforted by the thought."

I listened to the sounds of the horses' hoofs on the trail. The way was not straight. It twisted, curved, and wandered for a time, then took an upward turn. As we mounted the rise it followed, the trees thinned even more.

We came to the top of a hill then, and into a fairly open area. Advancing, we achieved a sudden view that covered several miles. We drew rein at an abrupt drop that curved its way into a gradual slope after ten or fifteen precipitous meters, sweeping downward to a large plain perhaps a mile distant, then continuing on through a hilly, sporadically wooded area. The plain was dotted with campfires and there were a few tents toward the center of things. A large number of horses grazed near by, and I guessed there were several hundred men sitting beside the fires or moving about the compound.

Ganelon sighed.

"At least they seem to be normal men," he said.

"Yes."

". . . And if they are normal military men, we are probably being watched right now. This is too good a vantage to leave unposted."

"Yes."

There came a noise from behind us. We began to turn, just as a near by voice said, "Don't move!"

I continued to turn my head, and I saw four men. Two of them held crossbows trained on us and the other two had blades in their hands. One of these advanced two paces.

"Dismount!" he ordered. "On this side! Slowly!"

We climbed down from our mounts and faced him, keeping our hands away from our weapons.

"Who are you? Where are you from?" he asked.

"We are mercenaries," I replied, "from Lorraine. We heard there was fighting here, and we are seeking employment. We were headed for that camp below. It is yours, I hope?"

". . . And if I said no, that we are a patrol for a force about to invade that camp?"

I shrugged. "In that case, is your side interested in hiring a couple of men?"

He spat. "The Protector has no need for your sort," he said. Then, "From what direction do you ride?"

"East," I said.

"Did you meet with any—difficulty—recently?"

"No," I said. "Should we have?"

"Hard to say," he decided. "Remove your weapons. I'm going to send you down to the camp. They will want to question you about anything you may have seen in the east—anything unusual."

"We've seen nothing unusual," I said.

"Whatever, they will probably feed you. Though I doubt you will be hired. You have come a bit late for the fighting. Remove your weapons now."

He called two more men from within the trees while we unbuckled our sword belts. He instructed them to escort us below, on foot. We were to lead our horses. The men took our weapons, and as we turned to go our interrogator cried out, "Wait!"

I turned back toward him.

"You. What is your name?" he asked me.

"Corey," I said.

"Stand still."

He approached, drawing very near. He stared at me for perhaps ten seconds.

"What is the matter?" I asked.

Instead of replying, he fumbled with a pouch at his belt. He withdrew a handful of coins and held them close to his eyes.

"Damn! It's too dark," he said, "and we can't make a light."

"For what?" I said.

"Oh, it is not of any great importance," he told me. "You struck me as familiar, though, and I was trying to think why. You look like the head stamped on some of our old coins. A few of them are still about.

"Doesn't he?" he addressed the nearest bowman.

The man lowered his crossbow and advanced. He squinted at me from a few paces' distance.

"Yes," he said then, "he does."

"What was it—the one we're thinking of?"

"One of those old men. Before my time. I don't remember."

"Me neither. Well . . ." He shrugged. "No importance. Go ahead, Corey. Answer their questions honestly and you'll not be harmed."

I turned away and left him there in the moonlight, gazing after me and scratching the top of his head.

The men who guarded us were not the talkative sort. Which was just as well.

All the way down the hill I wondered about the boy's story and the resolution of the conflict he had described, for I had achieved the physical analogue of the world of my desire and would now have to operate within the prevailing situations.

The camp had the pleasant smell of man and beast, wood smoke, roasting meat, leather and oil, all intermingled in the firelight where men talked, honed weapons, repaired gear, ate, gamed, slept, drank, and watched us as we led our mounts through their midst, escorted in the direction of a nearly central trio of tattered tents. A sphere of silence expanded about us as we went.

We were halted before the second-largest tent and one of our guards spoke with a man who was pacing the area. The man shook his head several times and gestured in the direction of the largest tent. The exchange lasted for several minutes, then our guard returned and spoke with the other guard who waited at our left. Finally, our man nodded and approached me while the other summoned a man from the nearest campfire.

"The officers are all at a meeting in the Protector's tent," he said. "We are going to hobble your horses and put them to graze. Unstrap your things and set them here. You will have to wait to see the captain."

I nodded, and we set about unstowing our belongings and rubbing the horses down. I patted Star on the neck and watched a small man with a limp lead him and Ganelon's mount Firedrake off toward the other horses. We sat on our packs then and waited. One of the guards brought us some hot tea and accepted a pipeful of my tobacco. They moved then to a spot somewhat to our rear.

I watched the big tent, sipped my tea, and thought of Amber and a small night club in the Rue de Char et Pain in Brussels, on the shadow Earth I had so long inhabited. Once I obtained the jewelers rouge I needed from here, I would be heading for Brussels to deal with the arms merchants of the Gun Bourse once again. My order would be complicated and expensive, I realized, because some ammunition manufacturer would have to be persuaded to set up a special production line. I knew dealers on that Earth other than Interarmco, thanks to my itinerant military background in that place, and I estimated that it would only take me a few months to get outfitted there. I began considering the details and time passed quickly and pleasantly.

After what was probably an hour and a half, the shadows stirred within the large tent. It was several minutes after that before the entrance flap was thrown aside and men began to emerge, slowly, talking among themselves, glancing back within. The last two tarried at the threshold, still talking with someone who remained inside. The rest of them passed into the other tents.

The two at the entrance edged their way outside, still facing the interior. I could hear the sounds of their voices, although I could not make out what was being said. As they drifted farther outside, the man with whom they were speaking moved also and I caught a glimpse of him. The light was at his back and the two officers blocked most of my view, but I could see that he was thin and very tall.

Our guards had not yet stirred, indicating to me that one of the two officers was the captain mentioned earlier. I continued to stare, willing them to move farther and grant me a better look at their superior.

After a time they did, and a few moments later he took a step forward.

At first, I could not tell whether it was just a play of light and shadow . . . But no! He moved again and I had a clear view for a moment. He was missing his right arm, from a point just below the elbow. It was so heavily bandaged that I guessed the loss to have been quite recent.

Then his large left hand made a downward, sweeping gesture and hovered a good distance out from his body. The stump twitched at the same moment, and so did something at the back of my mind. His hair was long and straight and brown, and I saw the way that his jaw jutted . . .

He stepped outside then, and a breeze caught the cloak he wore and caused it to flare to his right. I saw that his shirt was yellow, his trousers brown. The cloak itself was a flame-like orange, and he caught its edge with an unnaturally rapid movement of his left hand and drew it back to cover his stump.

I stood quickly, and his head snapped in my direction.

Our gazes met, and neither of us moved for several heartbeats after that.

The two officers turned and stared, and then he pushed them aside and was striding toward me. I heard Ganelon grunt and climb quickly to his feet. Our guards were taken by surprise, also.

He halted several paces before me and his hazel eyes swept over me. He seldom smiled, but he managed a faint one this time.

"Come with me," he said, and he turned back toward his tent.

We followed him, leaving our gear where it lay.

He dismissed the two officers with a glance, halted beside the tent's entrance and motioned us in. He followed and let the flap fall behind him. My eyes took in his bedroll, a small table, benches, weapons, a campaign chest. There was an oil lamp on the table, as well as books, maps, a bottle, and some cups. Another lamp flickered atop the chest.

He clasped my hand and smiled again.

"Corwin," he said, "and still alive."

"Benedict," I said, smiling myself, "and breathing yet. It has been devilish long."

"Indeed. Who is your friend?"

"His name is Ganelon."

"Ganelon," he said, nodding toward him but not offering to clasp hands.

He moved to the table then and poured three cups of wine. He passed one to me, another to Ganelon, raised the third himself.

"To your health, brother," he said.

"To yours."

We drank.

Then, "Be seated," he said, gesturing toward the nearest bench and seating himself at the table, "and welcome to Avalon."

"Thank you—Protector."

He grimaced.

"The sobriquet is not unearned," he said flatly, continuing to study my face. "I wonder whether their earlier protector could say the same?"

"It was not really this place," I said, "and I believe that he could."

He shrugged.

"Of course," he said. "Enough of that! Where have you been? What have you been doing? Why have you come here? Tell me of yourself. It has been too long."

I nodded. It was unfortunate, but family etiquette as well as the balance of power required that I answer his questions before asking any of my own. He was my elder, and I had—albeit unknowing—intruded in his sphere of influence. It was not that I begrudged him the courtesy. He was one of the few among my many relatives whom I respected and even liked. It was that I was itching to question him. It had been, as he had said, too long.

And how much should I tell him now? I had no notion where his sympathies might lie. I did not desire to discover the reasons for his self-imposed exile from Amber by mentioning the wrong things. I would have to begin with something fairly neutral and sound him out as I went along.

"There must be a beginning," he said then. "I care not what face you put upon it."

"There are many beginnings," I said. "It is difficult . . . I suppose I should go all the way back and take it from there."

I took another sip of the wine.

"Yes," I decided. "That seems simplest—though it was only comparatively recently that I recalled much of what had occurred.

"It was several years after the defeat of the Moonriders out of Ghenesh and your departure that Eric and I had a major falling out," I began. "Yes, it was a quarrel over the succession. Dad had been making abdication noises again, and he still refused to name a successor. Naturally, the old arguments were resumed as to who was more legitimate. Of course, you and Eric are both my elders, but while Faiella, mother to Eric and myself, was his wife after the death of Clymnea, they—"

"Enough!" cried Benedict, slapping the table so hard that it cracked.

The lamp danced and sputtered, but by some small miracle was not upset. The tent's entrance flap was immediately pushed aside and a concerned guard peered in. Benedict glanced at him and he withdrew.

"I do not wish to sit in on our respective bastardy proceedings," Benedict said softly. "That obscene past-time was one of the reasons I initially absented myself from felicity. Please continue your story without the benefit of footnotes."

"Well—yes," I said, coughing lightly. "As I was saying, we had some rather bitter arguments concerning the whole matter. Then one evening it went beyond mere words. We fought."

"A duel?"

"Nothing that formal. A simultaneous decision to murder one another is more like it. At any rate, we fought for a long while and Eric finally got the upper hand and proceeded to pulverize me. At the risk of getting ahead of my story, I have to add that all of this was only recalled to me about five years ago."

Benedict nodded, as though he understood.

"I can only conjecture as to what occurred immediately after I lost consciousness," I went on. "But Eric stopped short of killing me himself. When I awakened, I was on a shadow Earth in a place called London. The plague was rampant at the time, and I had contracted it. I recovered with no memory of anything prior to London. I dwelled on that shadow world for centuries, seeking some clue as to my identity. I traveled all over it, often as part of some military campaign. I attended their universities, I spoke with some of their wisest men, I consulted famous physicians. But nowhere could I find the key to my past. It was obvious to me that I was not like other men and I took great pains to conceal this fact. I was furious because I could have anything that I wanted except what I wanted most—my own identity, my memories.

"The years passed, but this anger and this longing did not. It took an accident that fractured my skull to set off the changes that led to the return of my first recollections. This was approximately five years ago, and the irony of it is that I have good reason to believe Eric was responsible for the accident. Flora had apparently been resident on that shadow Earth all along, keeping watch over me.

"To return to conjecture, Eric must have stayed his hand at the last moment, desiring my death, but not wanting it traceable to him. So he transported me through Shadow to a place of sudden, almost certain death—doubtless to return and say that we had argued and I had ridden off in a huff, muttering something about going away again. We had been hunting in the Forest of Arden that day—just the two of us, together."

"I find it strange," Benedict interrupted, "that two rivals such as yourselves should elect to hunt together under such circumstances."

I took a sip of wine and smiled.

"Perhaps it was a trifle more contrived than I made it sound," I said. "Perhaps we both welcomed the opportunity to hunt together—just the two of us."

"I see," he said. "So it is possible that your situations could have been reversed?"

"Well," I said, "that is difficult to say. I do not believe I would have gone that far. I am talking as of now, of course. People do change, you know. Back then . . . ? Yes, I might have done the same thing to him. I cannot say for certain, but it is possible."

He nodded again, and I felt a flash of anger which passed quickly into amusement.

"Fortunately, I am not out to justify my own motives for anything," I continued. "To go on with my guesswork, I believe that Eric kept tabs on me after that, doubtless disappointed at first that I had survived, but satisfied as to my harmlessness. So he arranged to have Flora keep an eye on me, and the world turned peacefully for a long while. Then, presumably, Dad abdicated and disappeared without the question of the succession having been settled—"

"The hell he did!" said Benedict. "There was no abdication. He just vanished. One morning he simply was not in his chambers. His bed had not even been slept in. There were no messages. He had been seen entering the suite the evening before, but no one saw him depart. And even this was not considered strange for a long while. At first it was simply thought that he was sojourning in Shadow once again, perhaps to seek another bride. It was a long while before anyone dared suspect foul play or chose to construe this as a novel form of abdication."

"I was not aware of this," I said. "Your sources of information seem to have been closer to the heart of things than mine were."

He only nodded, giving rise to uneasy speculations on my part as to his contact in Amber. For all I knew, he could be pro-Eric these days.

"When was the last time you were back there yourself?" I ventured.

"A little over twenty years ago," he replied, "but I keep in touch."

Not with anyone who had cared to mention it to me! He must have known that as he said it, so did he mean me to take it as a caution—or a threat? My mind raced. Of course he possessed a set of the Major Trumps. I fanned them mentally and went through them like mad. Random had professed ignorance as to his whereabouts. Brand had been missing a long while. I had had indication that he was still alive, imprisoned in some unpleasant place or other and in no position to report on the happenings in Amber. Flora could not have been his contact, as she had been in virtual exile in Shadow herself until recently. Llewella was in Rebma. Deirdre was in Rebma also, and had been out of favor in Amber when last I saw her. Fiona? Julian had told me she was "somewhere to the south." He was uncertain as to precisely where. Who did that leave?

Eric himself, Julian, Gérard, or Caine, as I saw it. Scratch Eric. He would not have passed along the details of Dad's non-abdication in a manner that would allow things to be taken as Benedict had taken them. Julian supported Eric, but was not without personal ambitions of the highest order. He would pass along information if it might benefit him to do so. Ditto for Caine. Gérard, on the other hand, had always struck me as more interested in the welfare of Amber itself than in the question of who sat on its throne. He was not over-fond of Eric, though, and had once been willing to support either Bleys or myself over him. I believed he would have considered Benedict's awareness of events to be something in the nature of an insurance policy for the realm. Yes, it was almost certainly one of these three. Julian hated me. Caine neither liked nor disliked me especially, and Gérard and I shared fond memories that went all the way back to my childhood. I would have to find out who it was, quickly—and he was not yet ready to tell me, of course, knowing nothing of my present motives. A liaison with Amber could be used to hurt me or benefit me in short order, depending upon his desire and the person on the other end. It was therefore both sword and shield to him, and I was somewhat hurt that he had chosen to display these accoutrements so quickly. I chose to take it that his recent injury had served to make him abnormally wary, for I had certainly never given him cause for distress. Still, this caused me to feel abnormally wary also, a sad thing to know when meeting one's brother again for the first time in many years.

"It is interesting," I said, swirling the wine within my cup. "In this light, then, it appears that everyone may have acted prematurely."

"Not everyone," he said.

I felt my face redden.

"Your pardon," I said.

He nodded curtly.

"Please continue your telling."

"Well, to continue my chain of assumptions," I said, "when Eric decided that the throne had been vacant long enough and the time had come to make his move, he must also have decided that my amnesia was not sufficient and that it would be better to see my claim quitted entirely. At this time, he arranged for me to have an accident off on that shadow Earth, an accident which should have proven fatal but did not."

"How do you know this? How much of it is guesswork?"

"Flora as much as admitted it to me—including her own complicity in the thing—when I questioned her later."

"Very interesting. Go on."

"The bash on my head provided what even Sigmund Freud had been unable to obtain for me earlier," I said. "There returned to me small recollections that grew stronger and stronger—especially after I encountered Flora and was exposed to all manner of things that stimulated my memory. I was able to convince her that it had fully returned, so her speech was open as to people and things. Then Random showed up, fleeing from something—"

"Fleeing? From what? Why?"

"From some strange creatures out of Shadow. I never found out why."

"Interesting," he said, and I had to agree. I had thought of it often, back in my cell, wondering just why Random had entered, stage left, pursued by Furies, in the first place. From the moment we met until the moment we parted, we had been in some sort of peril; I had been preoccupied with my own troubles and he had volunteered nothing concerning his abrupt appearance. It had crossed my mind, of course, at the time of his arrival, but I was uncertain as to whether it was something of which I might be expected to have knowledge, and I let it go at that. Events then submerged it until later in my cell and again the present moment. Interesting? Indeed. Also, troubling.

"I managed to take in Random as to my condition," I continued. "He believed I was seeking the throne, when all that I was consciously seeking was my memory. He agreed to help me return to Amber, and he succeeded in getting me back. Well, almost," I corrected. "We wound up in Rebma. By then, I had told Random my true condition, and he proposed my walking the Pattern again as a means of restoring it fully. The opportunity was there, and I took it. It proved effective, and I used the power of the Pattern to transport myself into Amber."

He smiled.

"At this point, Random must have been a very unhappy man," he said.

"He was not exactly singing with glee," I said. "He had accepted Moire's judgment, that he wed a woman of her choosing—a blind girl named Vialle— and remain there with her for at least a year. I left him behind, and I later learned that he had done this thing. Deirdre was also there. We had encountered her along the way, in flight from Amber, and the three of us had entered Rebma together. She remained behind, also."

I finished my wine and Benedict nodded toward the bottle. It was almost empty, though, so he fetched a fresh bottle from his chest and we filled our cups. I took a long swallow. It was better wine than the previous. Must have been his private stock.

"In the palace," I went on, "I made my way to the library, where I obtained a pack of the Tarots. This was my main reason for venturing there. I was surprised by Eric before I could do much else and we fought, there in the library. I succeeded in wounding him and believe I could have finished him, save that reinforcements arrived and I was forced to flee. I contacted Bleys then, who gave me passage to him in Shadow. You may have heard the rest from your own sources. How Bleys and I threw in together, assaulted Amber, lost. He fell from the face of Kolvir. I tossed him my Tarots and he caught them. I understand that his body was never found. But it was a long way down—though I believe the tide was high by then. I do not know whether he died that day or not."

"Neither do I," said Benedict.

"So I was imprisoned and Eric was crowned. I was prevailed upon to assist in the coronation, despite a small demurrer on my part. I did succeed in crowning myself before that bastard—genealogically speaking—had it back and placed it on his own head. Then he had me blinded and sent to the dungeons."

He leaned forward and studied my face.

"Yes," he said, "I had heard that. How was it done?"

"Hot irons," I said, wincing involuntarily and repressing an impulse to clutch at my eyes. "I passed out partway through the ordeal."

"Was there actual contact with the eyeballs?"

"Yes," I said. "I think so."

"And how long did the regeneration take?"

"It was close to four years before I could see again," I said, "and my vision is just getting back to normal now. So—about five years altogether, I would say."

He leaned back, sighed, and smiled faintly.

"Good," he said. "You give me some small hope. Others of us have lost portions of their anatomy and experienced regeneration also, of course, but I never lost anything significant—until now."

"Oh yes," I said. "It is a most impressive record. I reviewed it regularly for years. A collection of bits and pieces, many of them forgotten I daresay, but by the principals and myself: fingertips, toes, ear lobes. I would say that there is hope for your arm. Not for a long while, of course.

"It is a good thing that you are ambidextrous," I added.

His smile went on and off and he took a drink of wine. No, he was not ready to tell me what had happened to him.

I took another sip of my own. I did not want to tell him about Dworkin. I had wanted to save Dworkin as something of an ace in the hole. None of us understood the man's full power, and he was obviously mad. But he could be manipulated. Even Dad had apparently come to fear him after a time, and had had him locked away. What was it that he had told me back in my cell? That Dad had had him confined after he had announced his discovery of a means for destroying all of Amber. If this was not just the rambling of a psychotic and was the real reason for his being where he was, then Dad had been far more generous that I would have been. The man was too dangerous to let live. On the other hand, though, Dad had been trying to cure him of his condition. Dworkin had spoken of doctors, men he had frightened away or destroyed when he had turned his powers against them. Most of my memories of him were of a wise, kindly old man, quite devoted to Dad and the rest of the family. It would be difficult readily to destroy someone like that if there was some hope. He had been confined to what should have been inescapable quarters. Yet when he had grown bored one day, he had simply walked out. No man can walk through Shadow in Amber, the very absence of Shadow, so he had done something I did not understand, something involving the principle behind the Trumps, and had left his quarters. Before he returned to them, I managed to persuade him to provide me with a similar exit from my own cell, one that transported me to the Lighthouse of Cabra, where I recovered somewhat, then set out upon the voyage that took me to Lorraine. Most likely he was still undetected. As I understood it, our family had always possessed special powers, but it was he who analyzed them and formalized their functions by means of the Pattern and the Tarots. He had often tried to discuss the matter, but it had seemed awfully abstract and boring to most of us. We are a very pragmatic family, damn it! Brand was the only one who seemed to have had any interest in the subject. And Fiona. I had almost forgotten. Sometimes Fiona would listen. And Dad. Dad knew an awful lot of things that he never discussed. He never had much time for us, and there were so many things about him that we did not know. But he was probably as well versed as Dworkin in whatever principles were involved. Their main difference was one of application. Dworkin was an artist. I do not really know what Dad was. He never encouraged intimacy, though he was not an unkind father. Whenever he took note of us, he was quite lavish with gifts and diversions. But he left our upbringing to various members of his court. He tolerated us, I feel, as occasionally inevitable consequences of passion. Actually, I am quite surprised that the family is not much larger. The thirteen of us, plus two brothers and a sister I knew who were now dead, represent close to fifteen hundred years of parental production. There had been a few others also, of whom I had heard, long before us, who had not survived. Not a tremendous batting average for so lusty a liege, but then none of us had proved excessively fertile either. As soon as we were able to fend for ourselves and walk in Shadow, Dad had encouraged us to do so, find places where we would be happy and settle there. This was my connection with the Avalon which is no more. So far as I knew, Dad's own origins were known only to himself. I had never encountered anyone whose memory stretched back to a time when there had been no Oberon. Strange? Not to know where one's own father comes from, when one has had centuries in which to exercise one's curiosity? Yes. But he was secretive, powerful, shrewd—traits we all possess to some degree. He wanted us well situated and satisfied, I feel—but never so endowed as to present a threat to his own reign. There was in him, I guessed, an element of uneasiness, a not unjustifiable sense of caution with respect to our learning too much concerning himself and times long gone by. I do not believe that he had ever truly envisioned a time when he would not rule in Amber. He occasionally spoke, jokingly or grumblingly, of abdication. But I always felt this to be a calculated thing, to see what responses it would provoke. He must have realized the state of affairs his passing would produce, but refused to believe that the situation would ever occur. And no one of us really knew all of his duties and responsibilities, his secret commitments. As distasteful as I found the admission, I was coming to feel that none of us was really fit to take the throne. I would have liked to blame Dad for this inadequacy, but unfortunately I had known Freud too long not to feel self-conscious about it. Also, I was now beginning to wonder about the validity of any of our claims. If there had been no abdication and he did indeed still live, then the best any of us could really hope to do was sit in regency. I would not look forward—especially from the throne—to his returning and finding things otherwise. Let's face it, I was afraid of him, and not without cause. Only a fool does not fear a genuine power that he does not understand. But whether the title be king or regent, my claim on it was stronger than Eric's and I was still determined to have it. If a power out of Dad's dark past, which none of us really understood, could serve to secure it, and if Dworkin did represent such a power, then he must remain hidden until he could be employed on my behalf.

Even, I asked myself, if the power he represented was the power to destroy Amber itself, and with it to shatter the shadow worlds and capsize all of existence as I understood it?

Especially then, I answered myself. For who else could be trusted with such power?

We are indeed a very pragmatic family.

More wine, and then I fumbled with my pipe, cleaning it, repacking it.

"That, basically, is my story to date," I said, regarding my handiwork, rising and taking a light from the lamp. "After I recovered my sight, I managed to escape, fled Amber, tarried for a time in a place called Lorraine, where I encountered Ganelon, then came here."

"Why?"

I reseated myself and looked at him again.

"Because it is near to the Avalon I once knew," I said.

I had purposely refrained from mentioning any earlier acquaintanceship with Ganelon, and hoped that he would take a cue from it. This shadow was near enough to our Avalon so that Ganelon should be familiar with its topography and most of its customs. For whatever it was worth, it seemed politic to keep this information from Benedict.

He passed over it as I thought he might, buried there where it was beside more interesting digging.

"And of your escape?" he asked. "How did you manage that?"

"I had help, of course," I admitted, "in getting out of the cell. Once out— Well, there are still a few passages of which Eric is unaware."

"I see," he said, nodding—hoping, naturally, that I would go on to mention my partisans' names, but knowing better than to ask.

I puffed my pipe and leaned back, smiling.

"It is good to have friends," he said, as if in agreement with some unvoiced thought I might be entertaining.

"I guess that we all have a few of them in Amber."

"I like to think so," he said. Then, "I understand you left the partly whittled cell door locked behind you, had set fire to your bedding, and had drawn pictures on the wall."

"Yes," I said. "Prolonged confinement does something to a man's mind. At least, it did to mine. There are long periods during which I know I was irrational."

"I do not envy you the experience, brother," he said. "Not at all. What are your plans now?"

"They are still uncertain."

"Do you feel that you might wish to remain here?"

"I do not know," I said. "What is the state of affairs here?"

"I am in charge," he said—a simple statement of fact, not a boast. "I believe I have just succeeded in destroying the only major threat to the realm. If I am correct, then a reasonably tranquil period should be at hand. The price was high"—he glanced at what remained of his arm—"but will have been worth it—as shall be seen before very long, when things have returned to normal."

He then proceeded to relate what was basically the same situation the youth had described, going on to tell how they had won the battle. The leader of the hellmaids slain, her riders had bolted and fled. Most of them were also slain then, and the caverns had been sealed once more. Benedict had decided to maintain a small force in the field for mopping-up purposes, his scouts the while combing the area for survivors.

He made no mention of the meeting between himself and their leader, Lintra.

"Who slew their leader?" I asked him.

"I managed it," he said, making a sudden movement with his stump, "though I hesitated a moment too long on my first blow."

I glanced away and so did Ganelon. When I looked back, his face had returned to normal and he had lowered his arm.

"We looked for you. Did you know that, Corwin?" he asked. "Brand searched for you in many shadows, as did Gérard. You guessed correctly as to what Eric said after your disappearance that day. We were inclined to look farther than his word, however. We tried your Trump repeatedly, but there was no response. It must be that brain damage can block it. That is interesting. Your failure to respond to the Trump led us to believe you had died. Then Julian, Caine, and Random joined the search."

"All that? Really? I am astonished."

He smiled.

"Oh," I said then, and smiled myself.

Their joining the hunt at that point meant that it was not my welfare that concerned them, but the possibility of obtaining evidence of fratricide against Eric, so as to displace him or blackmail him.

"I sought for you in the vicinity of Avalon," he continued, "and I found this place and was taken by it. It was in a pitiful condition in those days, and for generations I worked to restore it to its former glory. While I began this in memory of you, I developed a fondness for this land and its people. They came to consider me their protector, and so did I."

I was troubled as well as touched by this. Was he implying that I had fouled things up terribly and that he had tarried here to put them in order— so as to clean up after his kid brother this one last time? Or did he mean that he realized I had loved this place—or a place very much like it—and that he had worked to set it in good order as something I might have wished done? Perhaps I was becoming oversensitive.

"It is good to know that I was sought," I said, "and it is very good to know that you are the defender of this land. I would like to see this place, for it does remind me of the Avalon that I knew. Would you have any objections to my visiting here?"

"That is all that you wish to do? Visit?"

"That is all that I had in mind."

"Know then that what is remembered of the shadow of yourself that once reigned here is not good. Children are not named Corwin in this place, nor am I brother to any Corwin here."

"I understand," I said. "My name is Corey. Can we be old friends?"

He nodded.

"Old friends of mine are always welcome to visit here," he said.

I smiled and nodded. I felt insulted that he would entertain the notion that I had designs upon this shadow of a shadow: I, who had—albeit but for an instant—felt the cold fire of Amber's crown upon my brow.

I wondered what his attitude would have been had he known of my responsibility, when it came down to basics, for the raids. For that matter, I suppose, I was also responsible for the loss of his arm. I preferred to push things one step farther back, however, and hold Eric responsible. After all, it was his action that had prompted my curse.

Still, I hoped that Benedict would never find out.

I wanted very badly to know where he stood with respect to Eric. Would he support him, throw his weight behind me, or just stay out of the way when I made my move? Conversely, I was certain that he wondered whether my ambitions were dead or still smoldering—and if the latter, what my plans were for stoking them. So . . .

Who was going to raise the matter?

I took several good puffs on my pipe, finished my wine, poured some more, puffed again. I listened to the sounds of the camp, the wind, my stomach . . .

Benedict took a sip of wine.

Then, "What are your long-range plans?" he asked me, almost casually.

I could say that I had not made up my mind yet, that I was simply happy to be free, alive, seeing. . . . I could tell him that that was enough for me, for now, that I had no special plans. . . .

. . . And he would know that I lied in my teeth. For he knew me better than that.

So, "You know what my plans are," I said.

"If you were to ask for my support," he said, "I would deny it. Amber is in bad enough shape without another power grab."

"Eric is a usurper."

"I choose to look upon him as regent only. At this time, any of us who claims the throne is guilty of usurpation."

"Then you believe Dad still lives?"

"Yes. Alive and distressed. He has made several attempts to communicate."

I succeeded in keeping my face from showing anything. So I was not the only one, then. To reveal my experiences at this point would sound hypocritical, opportunistic, or a flat lie—since in our seeming contact of five years ago he had given me the go-ahead to take the throne. Of course, he could have been referring to a regency then. . . .

"You did not lend support to Eric when he took the throne," I said. "Would you give it to him now that he holds it, if an attempt were made to unseat him?"

"It is as I said," he told me. "I look upon him as regent. I do not say that I approve of this, but I desire no further strife in Amber."

"Then you *would* support him?"

"I have said all that I have to say on the matter. You are welcome to visit my Avalon, but not to use it as a staging area for an invasion of Amber. Does that clarify matters with respect to anything you may have in mind?"

"It clarifies matters," I said.

"This being the case, do you still wish to visit here?"

"I do not know," I said. "Does your desire to avoid strife in Amber work both ways?"

"What do you mean?"

"I mean that if I were returned to Amber against my will, I would damn well create as much strife as I could to prevent a recurrence of my previous situation."

The lines went out of his face and he slowly lowered his eyes.

"I did not mean to imply that I would betray you. Do you think that I am without feelings, Corwin? I would not see you imprisoned again, blinded—or worse. You are always welcome to visit here, and you may leave your fears along with your ambitions at the border."

"Then I would still like to visit," I said. "I have no army, nor did I come here to recruit one."

"Then you know that you are most welcome."

"Thank you, Benedict. While I did not expect to find you here, I am glad that I did."

He reddened faintly and nodded.

"It pleases me, also," he said. "Am I the first of us you have seen—since your escape?"

I nodded.

"Yes, and I am curious as to how everyone is faring. Any major reports?"

"No new deaths," he said.

We both chuckled, and I knew that I would have to turn up the family gossip on my own. It had been worth the attempt, though.

"I am planning on remaining in the field for a time," he said, "and continuing my patrols until I am satisfied that none of the invaders remain. It could be another week before we withdraw."

"Oh? Then it was not a total victory?"

"I believe that it was, but I never take unnecessary chances. It is worth a little more time to be certain."

"Prudent," I said, nodding.

". . . So unless you have a strong desire to remain here in camp, I see no reason why you should not proceed on toward town and get near the center of things. I maintain several residences about Avalon. I have in mind for your use a small manor house that I have found pleasant. It is not far from town."

"I look forward to seeing it."

"I will provide you with a map and a letter to my steward in the morning."

"Thank you, Benedict."

"I will join you there as soon as I have finished here," he said, "and in the meantime, I have messengers passing that way daily. I will keep in touch with you through them."

"Very good."

"Then find yourselves a comfortable piece of ground," he said. "You'll not miss the breakfast call, I'm sure."

"I seldom do," I said. "Is it all right if we sleep at that spot where we left our gear?"

"Certainly," he said, and we finished the wine.

As we left his tent, I seized the flap up high when I opened it and was able to squeeze it several inches to the side when I cast it before me. Benedict bade us good night and turned away as he let it fall, not noticing the gap of several inches that I had created along its one side.

I made my bed up a good distance to the right of our equipment, facing in the direction of Benedict's tent, and I moved the gear itself as I rummaged through it. Ganelon shot me a quizzical look, but I simply nodded and made a movement with my eyes toward the tent. He glanced that way, returned the nod, and proceeded to spread his own blankets farther to the right.

I measured it with my eyes, walked over, and said, "You know, I'd much rather sleep here. Would you mind switching with me?" I added a wink for emphasis.

"Makes no difference to me," he said, shrugging.

The campfires had died or were dying, and most of the company had turned in. The guard only paid us heed a couple of times around. The camp was very quiet and there were no clouds to obscure the brilliance of the stars. I was tired, and the smells of the smoke and the damp earth came pleasantly to my nostrils, reminding me of other times and places such as this and the rest at the day's end.

Instead of closing my eyes, however, I fetched my pack and propped my back against it, filled my pipe again, and struck it to life.

I adjusted my position twice as he paced within the tent. Once, he vanished from my field of vision and remained hidden for several moments. But the far light moved then, and I knew that he had opened the chest. Then he came into sight once more and cleared the table, dropped back for an instant, returned and reseated himself in his earlier position. I moved so that I could keep sight of his left arm.

He was paging through a book, or sorting something of about that size.

Cards, maybe?

Naturally.

I would have given a lot for one glimpse of the Trump that he finally settled upon and held before him. I would have given a lot to have Grayswandir beneath my hand, in case another person suddenly came into the tent by means other than the entrance through which I spied. My palms and the soles of my feet tingled, in anticipation of flight or combat.

But he remained alone.

He sat there unmoving for perhaps a quarter of an hour, and when he finally stirred it was only to replace the cards somewhere in his chest and to extinguish the lamps.

The guard continued on his monotonous rounds and Ganelon began to snore.

I emptied my pipe and rolled over onto my side.

Tomorrow, I told myself. If I wake up here tomorrow, everything will be all right . . .

FIVE

I sucked on a blade of grass and watched the mill wheel turn. I was lying on my stomach on the stream's opposite bank, my head propped in my hands. There was a tiny rainbow in the mist above the froth and boil at the foot of the waterfall, and an occasional droplet found its way to me. The steady splashing and the sound of the wheel drowned out all other noises in the wood. The mill was deserted today, and I contemplated it because I had not seen its like in ages. Watching the wheel and listening to the water were more than just relaxing. It was somewhat hypnotic.

It was our third day at Benedict's place, and Ganelon was off in town seeking amusement. I had accompanied him on the previous day and learned what I wanted to know at that time. Now I had no time for sight-seeing. I had to think and act quickly. There had been no difficulty at the camp. Benedict had seen us fed and had furnished us with the map and the letter he had promised. We had departed at sunrise and arrived at the manor around midday. We were well received, and after settling into the quarters we were shown, we had made our way into town, where we had spent the balance of the day.

Benedict was planning to remain in the field for several more days. I would have to be done with the task I had set myself before he came home. So a hellride was in order. There was no time for leisurely journeying, I had to remember the proper shadows and be under way soon.

It would have been refreshing, being in this place that was so like my Avalon, except that my thwarted purposes were reaching the point of obsession. Realizing this was not tantamount to controlling it, however. Familiar sights and sounds had diverted me only briefly, then I had turned once more to my planning.

It should work out neatly, as I saw it. This one journey should solve two of my problems, if I could manage it without arousing suspicion. It meant that I would definitely be gone overnight, but I had anticipated this and had already instructed Ganelon to cover for me.

My head nodding with each creak of the wheel, I forced everything else from my mind and set about remembering the necessary texture of the sand, its coloration, the temperature, the winds, the touch of salt in the air, the clouds . . .

I slept then and I dreamed, but not of the place that I sought.

I regarded a big roulette wheel, and we were all of us on it—my brothers, my sisters, myself, and others whom I knew or had known—rising and falling, each with his allotted section. We were all shouting for it to stop for us and wailing as we passed the top and headed down once more. The wheel had begun to slow and I was on the rise. A fair-haired youth hung upside down before me, shouting pleas and warnings that were drowned in the cacophony of voices. His face darkened, writhed, became a horrible thing to behold, and I slashed at the cord that bound his ankle and he fell from sight. The wheel slowed even more as I neared the top, and I saw Lorraine then. She was gesturing, beckoning frantically, and calling my name. I leaned toward her, seeing her clearly, wanting her, wanting to help her. But as the wheel continued its turning she passed from my sight.

"Corwin!"

I tried to ignore her cry, for I was almost to the top. It came again, but I tensed myself and prepared to spring upward. If it did not stop for me, I was going to try gimmicking the damned thing, even though falling off would mean my total ruin. I readied myself for the leap. Another click . . .

"Corwin!"

It receded, returned, faded, and I was looking toward the water wheel again with my name echoing in my ears and mingling, merging, fading into the sound of the stream.

I blinked my eyes and ran my fingers through my hair. A number of dandelions fell about my shoulders as I did so, and I heard a giggle from somewhere behind me.

I turned quickly and stared.

She stood about a dozen paces from me, a tall, slender girl with dark eyes and close-cropped brown hair. She wore a fencing jacket and held a rapier in her right hand, a mask in her left. She was looking at me and laughing. Her teeth were white, even and a trifle long; a band of freckles crossed her small nose and the upper portions of her well-tanned cheeks. There was that air of vitality about her which is attractive in ways different from mere comeliness. Especially, perhaps, when viewed from the vantage of many years.

She saluted me with her blade.

"*En garde*, Corwin!" she said.

"Who the Devil are you?" I asked, just then noticing a jacket, mask, and rapier beside me in the grass.

"No questions, no answers," she said. "Not till we've fenced."

She fitted her mask over her head then and waited.

I rose and picked up the jacket. I could see that it would be easier to fence than argue with her. The fact that she knew my name disturbed me, and the more that I thought of it the more she seemed somehow familiar. It was best to humor her, I decided, shrugging into the jacket and buckling it.

I picked up the blade, pulled on the mask.

"All right," I said, sketching a brief salute and advancing. "All right."

She moved forward then and we met. I let her carry the attack.

She came on very fast with a beat-feint-feint-thrust. My riposte was twice as fast, but she was able to parry it and come back with equal speed. I began a slow retreat then, drawing her out. She laughed and came on, pressing me hard. She was good and she knew it. She wanted to show off. She almost got through twice, too, in the same way—low-line—which I did not like at all. I caught her with a stop-thrust as soon as I could after that. She cursed softly, good-naturedly, as she acknowledged it and came right back at me. I do not ordinarily like to fence with women, no matter how good they are, but this time I discovered that I was enjoying myself. The skill and grace with which she carried the attacks and bore them gave me pleasure to behold and respond to, and I found myself contemplating the mind that lay behind that style. At first, I had wanted to tire her quickly, to conclude the match and question her. Now I found myself desiring to prolong the encounter.

She did not tire readily. There was small cause for concern on that count.

I lost track of time as we stamped back and forth along the bank of the stream, our blades clicking steadily.

A long while must have passed, though, before she stamped her heel and threw up her blade in a final salute. She tore off her mask then and gave me another smile.

"Thank you!" she said, breathing heavily.

I returned the salute and drew off the bird cage. I turned and fumbled with the jacket buckles, and before I realized it she had approached and kissed me on the cheek. She had not had to stand tiptoe to do it either. I felt momentarily confused, but I smiled. Before I could say anything, she had taken my arm and turned me back in the direction from which we had come.

"I've brought us a picnic basket," she said.

"Very good. I am hungry. I am also curious . . ."

"I will tell you anything that you want to hear," she said merrily.

"How about telling me your name?" I said.

"Dara," she replied. "My name is Dara, after my grandmother."

She glanced at me as she said it, as though hoping for a reaction. I almost hated to disappoint her, but I nodded and repeated it, then, "Why did you call me Corwin?" I asked.

"Because that is your name," she said. "I recognized you."

"From where?"

She released my arm.

"Here it is," she said, reaching behind a tree and raising a basket that had been resting upon the ridges of exposed roots.

"I hope the ants didn't get to it," she said, moving to a shaded area beside the stream and spreading a cloth upon the ground.

I hung the fencing gear on a nearby shrub.

"You seem to carry quite a few things around with you," I observed.

"My horse is back that way," she said, gesturing downstream with her head.

She returned her attention to weighing down the cloth and unpacking the basket.

"Why way back there?" I asked.

"So that I could sneak up on you, of course. If you'd heard a horse clomping around you'd have been awake sure as hell."

"You're probably right," I said.

She paused as though pondering deeply, then spoiled it with a giggle.

"But you didn't the first time, though. Still . . ."

"The first time?" I said, seeing she wanted me to ask it.

"Yes, I almost rode over you awhile back," she said. "You were sound asleep. When I saw who it was, I went back for a picnic basket and the fencing gear."

"Oh. I see."

"Come and sit down now," she said. "And open the bottle, will you?"

She put a bottle beside my place and carefully unwrapped two crystal goblets, which she then set in the center of the cloth.

I moved to my place and sat down.

"That is Benedict's best crystal," I noted, as I opened the bottle.

"Yes," she said. "Do be careful not to upset them when you pour—and I don't think we should clink them together."

"No, I don't think we should," I said, and I poured.

She raised her glass.

"To the reunion," she said.

"What reunion?"

"Ours."

"I have never met you before."

"Don't be so prosaic," she said, and took a drink.

I shrugged.

"To the reunion."

She began to eat then, so I did too. She was so enjoying the air of mystery she had created that I wanted to cooperate, just to keep her happy.

"Now where could I have met you?" I ventured. "Was it some great court? A harem, perhaps . . . ?"

"Perhaps it was in Amber," she said. "There you were . . ."

"Amber?" I said, remembering that I was holding Benedict's crystal and confining my emotions to my voice. "Just who are you, anyway?"

". . . There you were—handsome, conceited, admired by all the ladies," she continued, "and there I was—a mousy little thing, admiring you from afar. Gray, or pastel—not vivid—little Dara—a late bloomer, I hasten to add— eating her heart out for you—"

I muttered a mild obscenity and she laughed again.

"That wasn't it?" she asked.

"No," I said, taking another bite of beef and bread. "More likely it was that brothel where I sprained my back. I was drunk that night—"

"You remember!" she cried. "It was a part-time job. I used to break horses during the day."

"I give up," I said, and I poured more wine.

The really irritating thing was that there *was* something damnably familiar about her. But from her appearance and her behavior, I guessed her age at about seventeen. This pretty much precluded our paths ever having crossed.

"Did Benedict teach you your fencing?" I asked.

"Yes."

"What is he to you?"

"My lover, of course," she replied. "He keeps me in jewels and furs— and he fences with me."

She laughed again.

I continued to study her face.

Yes, it was possible. . . .

"I am hurt," I said, finally.

"Why?" she asked.

"Benedict didn't give me a cigar."

"Cigar?"

"You are his daughter, aren't you?"

She reddened, but she shook her head.

"No," she said. "But you are getting close."

"Granddaughter?" I said.

"Well . . . sort of."

"I am afraid that I do not understand."

"Grandfather is what he likes me to call him. Actually, though, he was my grandmother's father."

"I see. Are there any others at home like you?"

"No, I am the only one."

"What of your mother—and your grandmother?"

"Dead, both of them."

"How did they die?"

"Violently. Both times it happened while he was back in Amber. I believe that is why he has not returned there for a long while now. He does not like to leave me unprotected—even though he knows that I can take care of myself. You know that I can, too, don't you?"

I nodded. It explained several things, one of them being why he was Protector here. He had to keep her somewhere, and he certainly would not want to take her back to Amber. He would not even want her existence known to the rest of us. She could be made into an easy armlock. And it would be out of keeping to make me aware of her so readily.

So, "I do not believe that you are supposed to be here," I said, "and I feel that Benedict would be quite angry if he knew that you were."

"You are just the same as he is! I am an adult, damn it!"

"Have you heard me deny it? You *are* supposed to be someplace else, though, aren't you?"

She filled her mouth instead of answering. So I did, too. After several uncomfortable minutes of chewing, I decided to start on a fresh subject.

"How did you recognize me?" I asked.

She swallowed, took a drink of wine, grinned.

"From your picture, of course," she said.

"What picture?"

"On the card," she said. "We used to play with them when I was very small. I learned all my relatives that way. You and Eric are the other good swordsmen, I knew that. That is why I—"

"You have a set of the Trumps?" I interrupted.

"No," she said, pouting. "He wouldn't give me a set—and I know he has several, too."

"Really? Where does he keep them?"

She narrowed her eyes, focusing them on my own. Damn! I hadn't meant to sound that eager.

But, "He has a set with him most of the time," she said, "and I have no idea where he keeps the others. Why? Won't he let you see them?"

"I haven't asked him," I told her. "Do you understand their significance?"

"There were certain things I was not allowed to do when I was near them. I gather that they have a special use, but he never told me what it is. They are quite important, aren't they?"

"Yes."

"I thought so. He is always so careful with them. Do you have a set?"

"Yes, but it's out on loan just now."

"I see. And you would like to use them for something complicated and sinister."

I shrugged.

"I would like to use them, but for very dull, uncomplicated purposes."

"Such as?"

I shook my head.

"If Benedict does not want you to know their function yet, I am not about to tell you."

She made a small growling noise.

"You're afraid of him," she said.

"I have considerable respect for Benedict, not to mention some affection."

She laughed.

"Is he a better fighter than you, a better swordsman?"

I looked away. She must have just gotten back from someplace fairly removed from things. The townspeople I'd met had all known about Benedict's arm. It was not the sort of news that traveled slowly. I certainly was not going to be the first to tell her.

"Have it as you would," I said. "Where have you been?"

"The village," she said, "in the mountains. Grandpa took me there to stay with some friends of his called Tecys. Do you know the Tecys?"

"No, I don't."

"I've been there before," she said. "He always takes me to stay with them in the village when there is any sort of trouble here. The place has no name. I just call it the village. It is quite strange—the people, as well as the village. They seem to—sort of—worship us. They treat me as if I were something holy, and they never tell me anything I want to know. It is not a long ride, but the mountains are different, the sky is different—everything!—and it is as if there were no way back, once I am there. I had tried coming back on my own before, but I just got lost. Grandpa always had to come for me, and then the way was easy. The Tecys follow all of his instructions concerning me. They treat him as if he were some sort of god."

"He is," I said, "to them."

"You said that you do not know them."

"I don't have to. I know Benedict."

"How does he do it? Tell me."

I shook my head.

"How did you do it?" I asked her. "How did you get back here this time?"

She finished her wine and held out the glass. When I looked up from refilling it, her head was cocked toward her right shoulder, her brows were furrowed, and her eyes were focused on something far away.

"I do not really know," she said, raising the glass and sipping from it automatically. "I am not quite certain how I went about it. . . ."

With her left hand, she began to toy with her knife, finally picking it up.

"I was mad, mad as hell for having been packed off again," she said. "I told him that I wanted to stay here and fight, but he took me riding with him and after a time we arrived at the village. I do not know how. It was not a long ride, and suddenly we were there. I know this area. I was born here, I grew up here. I've ridden all over, hundreds of leagues in all directions. I was never able to find it when I went looking. But it seemed only a brief while that we rode, and suddenly we were at the Tecys' again. But it had been several years, and I can be more determined about things now that I am grown. I resolved to return by myself."

With the knife, she began scraping and digging at the ground beside her, not seeming to notice what she was doing.

"I waited till nightfall," she went on, "and studied the stars to take my direction. It was an unreal feeling. The stars were all different. I didn't recognize any of the constellations. I went back inside and thought about it. I was a little bit afraid and did not know what to do. I spent the next day trying to get more information out of the Tecys and the other people in the village. But it was like a bad dream. Either they were stupid or they were purposely trying to confuse me. Not only was there no way to get from there to here, they had no idea where 'here' was and were none too certain about 'there.' That night I checked the stars again, to be sure about what I had seen, and I was about ready to begin believing them."

She moved the knife back and forth as if honing it now, smoothing the soil and packing it flat. Then she began to trace designs.

"For the next several days, I tried to find my way back," she continued. "I thought I could locate our trail and backtrack along it, but it just sort of vanished. Then I did the only other thing I could think of. Each morning I struck out in a different direction, rode until noon, then headed back. I came across nothing that was familiar. It was totally bewildering. Each night I went to sleep more angry and upset over the way things were turning out—and more determined to find my own way back to Avalon. I had to show Grandpa that he could no longer dump me like a child and expect me to stay put.

"Then, after about a week, I began having dreams. Nightmares, sort of. Did you ever dream that you were running and running and not going anyplace? That is sort of what it was like—with the burning spider web. Only it wasn't really a spider web, there was no spider and it wasn't burning. But I was caught in this thing, going around it and through it. But I wasn't really moving. That is not completely right, but I do not know how else to put it. And I had to keep trying—actually, I wanted to—to move about it. When I woke up I was tired, as if I had actually been exerting myself all night long. This went on for many nights, and each night it seemed stronger and longer and more real.

"Then this morning I got up, the dream still dancing in my head, and I knew that I could ride home. I set out, still half dreaming, it seemed. I rode the entire distance without stopping once, and this time I paid no special heed to my surroundings, but kept thinking of Avalon—and as I rode, things kept getting more and more familiar until I was here again. Only then did it seem as if I were fully awake. Now the village and the Tecys, that sky, those stars, the woods, the mountains, they all seem like a dream to me. I am not at all certain that I could find my way back there. Is that not strange? Can you tell me what happened?"

I rose and circled the remains of our lunch. I sat down beside her.

"Do you remember the looks of the burning spider web that really wasn't a spider web, or burning?" I asked her.

"Yes—sort of," she said.

"Give me that knife," I said.

She passed it to me.

With its point, I began adding to her doodling in the dirt, extending lines, rubbing some out, adding others. She did not say a word the entire time, but she watched every move that I made. When I had finished, I put the knife aside and waited for a long, silent while.

Then, finally, she spoke very softly.

"Yes, that is it," she said, turning away from the design to stare at me. "How did you know? How did you know what I had dreamed?"

"Because," I said, "you dreamed a thing that is inscribed in your very genes. Why, how, I do not know. It demonstrates, however, that you are indeed a daughter of Amber. What you did was walk in Shadow. What you dreamed was the Great Pattern of Amber. By its power do those of the blood royal hold dominion over shadows. Do you understand what I am talking about?"

"I am not certain," she said. "I do not think so. I have heard Grandpa cursing shadows, but I never understood what he meant."

"Then you do not know where Amber truly lies."

"No. He was always evasive. He told me of Amber and of the family. But I do not even know the direction in which Amber lies. I only know that it is far."

"It lies in all directions," I said, "or any direction one chooses. One need but—"

"Yes!" she interrupted. "I had forgotten, or thought he was just being mysterious or humoring me, but Brand said exactly the same thing a long while ago. What does it mean, though?"

"Brand! When was Brand here?"

"Years ago," she said, "when I was just a little girl. He used to visit here often. I was very much in love with him and I pestered him mercilessly. He used to tell me stories, teach me games . . ."

"When was the last time you saw him?"

"Oh, eight or nine years ago, I'd say."

"Have you met any of the others?"

"Yes," she said. "Julian and Gérard were here not too long ago. Just a few months back."

I suddenly felt very insecure. Benedict had certainly been quiet about a lot of things. I would rather have been ill advised than kept totally ignorant of affairs. It makes it easier for you to be angry when you find out. The trouble with Benedict was that he was too honest, though. He would rather tell me nothing than lie to me. I felt something unpleasant coming my way, however, and knew that there could be no dawdling now, that I would have to move as quickly as possible. Yes, it had to be a hard hellride for the stones. Still, there was more to be learned here before I essayed it. Time . . . Damn!

"Was that the first time you met them?" I asked.

"Yes," she said, "and my feelings were very hurt." She paused, sighed. "Grandpa would not let me speak of our being related. He introduced me as his ward. And he refused to tell me why. Damn it!"

"I'm sure he had some very good reasons."

"Oh, I am too. But it does not make you feel any better, when you have been waiting all your life to meet your relatives. Do you know why he treated me like that?"

"These are trying times in Amber," I said, "and things will get worse before they get better. The fewer people who know of your existence, the less chance there is of your getting involved and coming to harm. He did it only to protect you."

She made a spitting noise.

"I do not need protecting," she said. "I can take care of myself."

"You are a fine fencer," I said. "Unfortunately, life is more complicated than a fair dueling situation."

"I know that. I'm not a child. But—"

" 'But' nothing! He did the same thing I'd do if you were mine. He's protecting himself as well as you. I'm surprised he let Brand know about you. He's going to be damned mad that I found out."

Her head jerked and she stared at me, eyes wide.

"But you wouldn't do anything to hurt us," she said. "We—we're related . . ."

"How the hell do you know why I'm here or what I'm thinking?" I said. "You might have just stuck both your necks in nooses!"

"You are joking, aren't you?" she said, slowly raising her left hand between us.

"I don't know," I said. "I need not be—and I wouldn't be talking about it if I did have something rotten in mind, would I?"

"No . . . I guess not," she said.

"I am going to tell you something Benedict should have told you long ago," I said. "Never trust a relative. It is far worse than trusting strangers. With a stranger there is a possibility that you might be safe."

"You really mean that, don't you?"

"Yes."

"Yourself included?"

I smiled.

"Of course it does not apply to me. I am the soul of honor, kindness, mercy, and goodness. Trust me in all things."

"I will," she said, and I laughed.

"I will," she insisted. "You would not hurt us. I know that."

"Tell me about Gérard and Julian," I said, feeling uncomfortable, as always, in the presence of unsolicited trust. "What was the reason for their visit?"

She was silent for a moment, still studying me, then, "I have been telling you quite a few things," she said, "haven't I? You are right. One can never be too careful. I believe that it is your turn to talk again."

"Good. You are learning how to deal with us. What do you want to know?"

"Where is the village, really? And Amber? They are somehow alike, aren't they? What did you mean when you said that Amber lies in all directions, or any? What are shadows?"

I got to my feet and looked down at her. I held out my hand. She looked very young and more than a little frightened then, but she took it.

"Where . . . ?" she asked, rising.

"This way," I said, and I took her to stand at the place where I had slept and regarded the falls and the water wheel.

She began to say something, but I stopped her.

"Look. Just look," I said.

So we stood there looking at the rushing, the splashing, the turning while I ordered my mind. Then, "Come," I said, turning her by the elbow and walking her toward the wood.

As we moved among the trees, a cloud obscured the sun and the shadows deepened. The voices of the birds grew more shrill and a dampness came up out of the ground. As we passed from tree to tree, their leaves became longer and broader. When the sun appeared again, its light came more yellow, and beyond a turning of the way we encountered hanging vines. The bird cries grew hoarser, more numerous. Our trail took an upward turn, and I led her past an outcropping of flint and onto higher ground. A distant, barely perceptible rumble seemed to come from behind us. The sky was a different blue as we moved through an open place, and we frightened a large, brown lizard that had been sunning itself on a rock. As we took a turn about another mass of stone, she said, "I did not know this was here. I have never been this way before." But I did not answer her, for I was busy shifting the stuff of Shadow.

Then we faced the wood once more, but now the way led uphill through it. Now the trees were tropical giants, interspersed with ferns, and new noises—barks, hisses, and buzzes—were to be heard. Moving up this trail, the rumble grew louder about us, the very ground beginning to vibrate with it. Dara held tightly to my arm, saying nothing now, but searching everything with her eyes. There were big, flat, pale flowers and puddles where the moisture dripped from overhead. The temperature had risen considerably and we were perspiring quite a bit. Now the rumble grew to a mighty roar, and when at length we emerged from the wood again, it was a sound like steady thunder that fell against us. I guided her to the edge of the precipice and gestured outward and down.

It plunged for over a thousand feet: a mighty cataract that smote the gray river like an anvil. The currents were rapid and strong, bearing bubbles and flecks of foam a great distance before they finally dissolved. Across from us, perhaps half a mile distant, partly screened by rainbow and mist, like an island slapped by a Titan, a gigantic wheel slowly rotated, ponderous and gleaming. High overhead, enormous birds rode like drifting crucifixes the currents of the air.

We stood there for a fairly long while. Conversation was impossible, which was just as well. After a time, when she turned from it to look at me, narrow-eyed, speculative, I nodded and gestured with my eyes toward the wood. Turning then, we made our way back in the direction from which we had come.

Our return was the same process in reverse, and I managed it with greater ease. When conversation became possible once more, Dara still kept her silence, apparently realizing by then that I was a part of the process of change going on around us.

It was not until we stood beside our own stream once more, watching the small mill wheel in its turning, that she spoke.

"Was that place like the village?"

"Yes. A shadow."

"And like Amber?"

"No. Amber casts Shadow. It can be sliced to any shape, if you know how. That place was a shadow, your village was a shadow—and *this* place is a shadow. Any place that you can imagine exists somewhere in Shadow."

". . . And you and Grandpa and the others can go about in these shadows, picking and choosing what you desire?"

"Yes."

"That is what I did, then, coming back from the village?"

"Yes."

Her face became a study in realization. Her almost-black eyebrows dropped half an inch and her nostrils flared with a quick inhalation.

"I can do it, too . . ." she said. "Go anywhere, do anything I want!"

"The ability lies within you," I said.

She kissed me then, a sudden, impulsive thing, then rotated away, her hair bobbing on her slim neck as she tried to look at everything at once.

"Then I can do anything," she said, coming to a standstill.

"There are limitations, dangers . . ."

"That is life," she said. "How do I learn to control it?"

"The Great Pattern of Amber is the key. You must walk it in order to gain the ability. It is inscribed on the floor in a chamber beneath the palace in Amber. It is quite large. You must begin on the outside and walk it to its center without stopping. There is considerable resistance and the feat is quite an ordeal. If you stop, if you attempt to depart the Pattern before completing it, it will destroy you. Complete it, though, and your power over Shadow will be subject to your conscious control."

She raced to our picnic site and studied the pattern we had drawn on the ground there.

I followed more slowly. As I drew near, she said, "I must go to Amber and walk it!"

"I am certain that Benedict plans for you to do so, eventually," I said.

"Eventually?" she said. "Now! I must walk it now! Why did he never tell me of these things?"

"Because you cannot do it yet. Conditions in Amber are such that it would be dangerous to both of you to allow your existence to become known there. Amber is barred to you, temporarily."

"It is not fair!" she said, turning to glare at me.

"Of course not," I said. "But that is the way things stand just now. Don't blame me."

The words came somewhat stickily to my lips. Part of the blame, of course, was mine.

"It would almost be better if you had not told me of these things," she said, "if I cannot have them."

"It is not as bad as all that," I said. "The situation in Amber will become stable again—before too very long."

"How will I learn of it?"

"Benedict will know. He will tell you then."

"He has not seen fit to tell me much of anything!"

"To what end? Just to make you feel bad? You know that he has been good to you, that he cares for you. When the time is ready, he will move on your behalf."

"And if he does not? Will you help me then?"

"I will do what I can."

"How will I be able to find you? To let you know?"

I smiled. It had gotten to this point without my half trying. No need to tell her the really important part. Just enough to be possibly useful to me later. . . .

"The cards," I said, "the family Trumps. They are more than a mere sentimental affectation. They are a means of communication. Get hold of mine, stare at it, concentrate on it, try to keep all other thoughts out of your mind, pretend that it is really me and begin talking to me then. You will find that it really is, and that I am answering you."

"Those are all the things Grandpa told me not to do when I handle the cards!"

"Of course."

"How does it work?"

"Another time," I said. "A thing for a thing. Remember? I have told you now of Amber and of Shadow. Tell me of the visit here by Gérard and Julian."

"Yes," she said. "There is not really much to tell, though. One morning, five or six months ago, Grandpa simply stopped what he was doing. He was pruning some trees back in the orchard—he likes to do that himself—and I was helping him. He was up on a ladder, snipping away, and suddenly he just stopped, lowered the clippers, and did not move for several minutes. I thought that he was just resting, and I kept on with my raking. Then I heard him talking—not just muttering—but talking as though he were carrying on a conversation. At first, I thought he was talking to me, and I asked him what he had said. He ignored me, though. Now that I know about the Trumps, I realize that he must have been talking to one of them just then. Probably Julian. Anyway, he climbed down from the ladder quite quickly after that, told me he had to go away for a day or so, and started back toward the manor. He stopped before he had gone very far, though, and returned. That was when he told me that if Julian and Gérard were to visit here that I was to be introduced as his ward, the orphaned daughter of a faithful servant. He rode away a short while later, leading two spare horses. He was wearing his blade.

"He returned in the middle of the night, bringing both of them with him. Gérard was barely conscious. His left leg was broken, and the entire left side of his body was badly bruised. Julian was quite battered also, but he had no broken bones. They remained with us for the better part of a month, and they healed quickly. Then they borrowed two horses and departed. I have not seen them since."

"What did they say as to how they had been injured?"

"Only that they had been in an accident. They would not discuss it with me."

"Where? Where did it happen?"

"On the black road. I overheard them talking about it several times."

"Where is this black road?"

"I do not know."

"What did they say about it?"

"They cursed it a lot. That was all."

Looking down, I saw that there was some wine left in the bottle. I stooped and poured two final drinks, passed her one.

"To the reunion," I said, and smiled.

". . . The reunion," she agreed, and we drank.

She began cleaning the area and I assisted her, my earlier sense of urgency upon me once again.

"How long should I wait before I try to reach you?" she asked.

"Three months. Give me three months."

"Where will you be then?"

"In Amber, I hope."

"How long will you be staying here?"

"Not very. In fact, I have to take a little trip right now. I should be back tomorrow, though. I will probably only be staying for a few days after that."

"I wish you would stay longer."

"I wish that I could. I would like to, now that I have met you."

She reddened and turned what seemed all of her attention to repacking the basket. I gathered up the fencing gear.

"Are you going back to the manor now?" she said.

"To the stables. I'll be leaving immediately."

She picked up the basket.

"We will go together then. My horse is this way."

I nodded and followed her toward a footpath to our right.

"I suppose," she said, "that it would be best for me not to mention any of this to anybody, Grandpa in particular?"

"That would be prudent."

The splash and gurgle of the stream, as it flowed to the river, on its way to the sea, faded, faded, was gone, and only the creak of the land-locked wheel that cut it as it went, remained for a time in the air.

SIX

Steady movement is more important than speed, much of the time. So long as there is a regular progression of stimuli to get your mental hooks into, there is room for lateral movement. Once this begins, its rate is a matter of discretion.

So I moved slowly, but steadily, using my discretion. No sense in tiring Star unnecessarily. Rapid shifts are hard enough on people. Animals, who are not so good at lying to themselves, have a rougher time of it, sometimes going completely berserk.

I crossed the stream at a small wooden bridge and moved parallel to it for a time. My intention was to skirt the town itself, but to follow the general direction of the watercourse until I reached the vicinity of the coast. It was midafternoon. My way was shaded, cool. Grayswandir hung at my side.

I bore west, coming at length to the hills that rose there. I refrained from beginning the shift until after I had reached a point that looked down upon the city that represented the largest concentration of population in this realm that was like my Avalon. The city bore the same name, and several thousand people lived there, worked there. Several of the silver towers were missing, and the stream cut the city at a somewhat different angle farther south, having widened or been widened eight-fold by then. There was some smoke from the stithies and the public houses, stirred lightly by breezes from the south; people, mounted, afoot, driving wagons, driving coaches, moved through the narrow streets, entered and departed shops, hostels, residences; flocks of birds wheeled, descended, rose about the places where horses were tethered; a few bright pennons and banners stirred listlessly; the water sparkled and there was a haze in the air. I was too far away to hear the sounds of voices, and of clanking, hammering, sawing, rattling, and creaking as anything other than a generalized hum. While I could distinguish no individual odors, had I still been blind I would have known by sniffing the air that a city was near.

Seeing it from up there, a certain nostalgia came over me, a wistful ragtail of a dream accompanied by a faint longing for the place that was this place's namesake to me in a vanished shadowland of long ago, where life had been just as simple and I happier than I was at that moment.

But one does not live as long as I have lived without achieving that quality of consciousness which strips naïve feelings as they occur and is generally loath to participate in the creation of sentimentality.

Those days were passed, that thing done with, and it was Amber now that held me completely. I turned and continued southward, confirmed in my desire to succeed. Amber, I do not forget . . .

The sun became a dazzling, bright blister above my head and the winds began to scream about me. The sky grew more and more yellow and glaring as I rode, until it was as if a desert stretched from horizon to horizon overhead. The hills grew rockier as I descended toward the lowlands, exhibiting wind-sculpted forms of grotesque shape and somber coloration. A dust storm struck me as I emerged from the foothills, so that I had to muffle my face with my cloak and narrow my eyes to slits. Star whinnied, snuffled repeatedly, plodded on. Sand, stone, winds, and the sky more orange then, a slate-like crop of clouds toward which the sun was heading . . .

Then long shadows, the dying of the wind, stillness . . . Only the click of hoof on rock and the sounds of breathing . . . Dimness, as they rushed together and the sun is foiled by clouds . . . The walls of the day shaken by thunder . . . An unnatural clarity of distant objects . . . A cool, blue, and electric feeling in the air . . . Thunder again . . .

Now, a rippling, glassy curtain to my right as the rain advances . . . Blue fracture lines within the clouds . . . The temperature plummeting, our pace steady, the world a monochromatic backdrop now . . .

Gonging thunder, flashing white, the curtain flaring toward us now . . . Two hundred meters . . . One-fifty . . . Enough!

Its bottommost edge plowing, furrowing, frothing . . . The moist smell of the earth . . . Star's whinny . . . A burst of speed . . .

Small rivulets of water creeping outward, sinking, staining the ground . . . Now bubbling muddily, now trickling . . . Now a steady flow . . . Streamlets all about us, splashing . . .

High ground ahead, and Star's muscles bunching and relaxing, bunching and relaxing beneath me, as he leaps the rills and freshets, plunges through a racing, roiling sheet, and strikes the slope, hoofs sparkling against stones as we mount higher, the voice of the gurgling, eddying flow beneath us deepening to a steady roar . . .

Higher, then, and dry, pausing to wring out the corners of my cloak. . . . Below, behind, and to the right a gray, storm-tossed sea laps at the foot of the cliff we hold . . .

Inland now, toward clover fields and evening, the boom of the surf at my back . . .

Pursuing falling stars into the darkening east and eventual silence and night . . .

Clear the sky and bright the stars, but a few small wisps of cloud . . .

A howling pack of red-eyed things, twisting along our trail . . . Shadow . . .
Green-eyed . . . Shadow . . . Yellow . . . Shadow . . . Gone . . .

But dark peaks with skirts of snow, jostling one another about me . . . Frozen
snow, as dry as dust, lifted in waves by the icy blasts of the heights . . . Powdery
snow, flour-like . . . Memory here, of the Italian Alps, of skiing . . . Waves
of snow drifting across stone faces . . . A white fire within the night air . . .
My feet rapidly numbing within my wet boots . . . Star bewildered and
snorting, testing each step and shaking his head as if in disbelief . . .

So shadows beyond the rock, a gentler slope, a drying wind, less snow . . .

A twisting trail, a corkscrew trail, an adit into warmth . . . Down, down,
down the night, beneath the changing stars . . .

Far the snows of an hour ago, now scrubby plants and level plain . . .
Far, and the night birds stagger into the air, wheeling above the carrion feast,
shedding hoarse notes of protest as we pass . . .

Slow again, to the place where the grasses wave, stirred by the less cold
breeze . . . The cough of a hunting cat . . . The shadowy flight of a bounding,
deer-like beast . . . Stars sliding into place and feelings in my feet once
more . . .

Star rearing, neighing, racing ahead from some unseen thing . . . A long
time in the soothing then, and longer still till the shivers go . . .

Now icicles of a partial moon falling on distant treetops . . . Moist earth
exhaling a luminescent mist . . . Moths dancing in the night light . . .

The ground momentarily buckling and swaying, as if mountains were
shifting their feet . . . To every star its double . . . A halo round the dumbbell
moon . . . The plain, the air above it, filled with fleeting shapes . . .

The earth, a wound-down clock, ticks and grows still   Stability . . .
Inertia . . . The stars and the moon reunited with their spirits . . .

Skirting the growing fringe of trees, west . . . Impressions of a sleeping
jungle: delirium of serpents under oil cloth . . .

West, west . . . Somewhere a river with broad, clean banks to ease my
passage to the sea . . .

Thud of hoofs, shuttling of shadows . . . The night air upon my face . . .
A glimpse of bright beings on high, dark walls, shining towers . . . The air is
sweetened . . . Vision swims . . . Shadows . . .

We are merged, centaur-like, Star and I, under a single skin of sweat . . .
We take the air and give it back in mutual explosions of exertion . . . Neck
clothed in thunder, terrible the glory of the nostrils . . . Swallowing the
ground . . .

Laughing, the smell of the waters upon us, the trees very near to our
left . . .

Then among them . . . Sleek bark, hanging vines, broad leaves, droplets
of moisture . . . Spider web in the moonlight, struggling shapes within . . .
Spongy turf . . . Phosphorent fungus on fallen trees . . .

A clear space . . . Long grasses rustling . . .

More trees . . .

Again, the riversmell . . .

Sounds, later . . . Sounds . . . The grassy chuckling of water . . .

Closer, louder, beside it at last . . . The heavens buckling and bending in its belly, and the trees . . . Clean, with a cold, damp tang . . . Leftward beside it, pacing it now . . . Easy and flowing, we follow . . .

To drink . . . Splashing in its shallows, then hock-high with head depressed, Star, in it, drinking like a pump, blasting spray from his nostrils . . . Upriver, it laps at my boots . . . Dripping from my hair, running down my arms . . . Star's head turning, at the laughter . . .

Then downriver again, clean, slow, winding . . . Then straight, widening, slowing . . .

Trees thickening, then thinning . . .

Long, steady, slow . . .

A faint light in the east . . .

Sloping downward now, and fewer trees . . . Rockier, and the darkness made whole once again . . .

The first, dim hint of the sea, lost an odor later . . . Clicking on, on, in the nightsend chill . . . Again, an instant's salt . . .

Rock, and an absence of trees . . . Hard, steep, bleak, down . . . Ever-increasing precipitousness . . .

Flashing between walls of stone . . . Dislodged pebbles vanishing in the now racing current, their splashes drowned in the roar's echoes . . . Deeper the defile, widening . . .

Down, down . . .

Farther still . . .

Now pale once more the east, gentler the slope . . . Again, the touch of salt, stronger . . .

Shale and grit . . . Around a corner, down, and brighter still . . .

Steady, soft and loose the footing . . .

The breeze and the light, the breeze and the light . . . Beyond a crop of rock . . .

Draw rein.

Below me lay the stark seaboard, where rank upon rank of rolling dunes, harassed by the winds out of the southwest, tossed spumes of sand that partly obliterated the distant outlines of the bleak morning sea.

I watched the pink film spread across the water from the east. Here and there, the shifting sands revealed dark patches of gravel. Rugged masses of rock reared above the swell of the waves. Between the massive dunes—hundreds of feet in height—and myself, there high above that evil coast, lay a smashed and pitted plain of angular rocks and gravel, just now emerging from hell or night into dawn's first glow, and alive with shadows.

Yes, it was right.

I dismounted and watched the sun force a bleak and glaring day upon the prospect. It was the hard, white light I had sought. Here, *sans* humans, was the necessary place, just as I had seen it decades earlier on the shadow Earth of my exile. No bulldozers, sifters, broom-wielding blacks; no maximum-security city of Oranjemund. No X-ray machines, barbed wire, or armed guards. None of these things here. No. For this shadow had never known a Sir Ernest Oppenheimer, and there had never been a Consolidated Diamond Mines of South West Africa, nor a government to approve their amalgamation of coastal mining interests. Here was the desert called Namib in that place some four hundred miles to the northwest of Cape Town, a strip of dunes and rocks ranging from a couple to a dozen miles in width and running along that forsaken coast line for perhaps three hundred miles on the seaward side of the Richtersveld Mountains, within whose shadow I now stood. Here, unlike any conventional mine, the diamonds were scattered as casually as bird droppings across the sand. I, of course, had brought along a rake and a sieve.

I broke out the rations and prepared breakfast. It was going to be a hot, dusty day.

As I worked the dunes, I thought of Doyle, the little wispy-haired jeweler with the brick-red complexion and wens on his cheeks, back in Avalon. Jewelers rouge? Why did I want all that jewelers rouge—enough to supply an army of jewelers for a dozen lifetimes? I had shrugged. What was it to him what I wanted it for, so long as I was able to pay for it? Well, if there was some new use for the stuff and good money to be made, a man would be a fool . . . In other words, he would be unable to furnish me with such a quantity within a week? Small, square chuckles had escaped through the gaps in his smile. A week? Oh, no! Of course not! That was ridiculous, out of the question. . . . I saw. Well, a quick thanks and perhaps his competitor up the way might be able to produce the stuff, and might also be interested in a few uncut diamonds I was expecting in a matter of days. . . . Diamonds, did I say? Wait. He was always interested in diamonds himself. . . . Yes, but he was sadly deficient in the jewelers rouge department. A raised hand. It might be that he had spoken hastily with respect to his ability to produce the polishing material. It was the quantity that had disturbed him. But the ingredients were plentiful and the formula fairly simple. Yes, that was no real reason why something could not be worked out. Within a week, at that. Now, about the diamonds . . .

Before I left his shop, something had been worked out.

I have met many persons who thought that gunpowder explodes, which of course is incorrect. It burns rapidly, building up gas pressure which ejects a bullet from the mouth of a shell and drives it through the barrel of a weapon, after having been ignited by the primer, which does the actual exploding when the firing pin is driven into it. Now, with typical family foresight, I had experimented with a variety of combustibles over the years. My disappointment at the discovery that gunpowder would not ignite in Amber, and that all of the primers I tested were equally inert there, was a thing mitigated only by the knowledge that none of my relatives could bring firearms into Amber either. It was much later, during a visit to Amber, after polishing a bracelet I had brought for Deirdre, that I discovered this wonderful property of jewelers rouge from Avalon when I disposed of the polishing cloth in a fireplace. Fortunately, the quantity involved was small, and I was alone at the time.

It made an excellent primer, straight from the container. When cut with a sufficient quantity of inert material, it could also be made to burn properly.

I kept this bit of information to myself, feeling that one day it would be used to decide certain basic issues in Amber. Unfortunately, Eric and I had our run-in before that day arrived and it went into storage along with all my other memories. When things finally did clear for me, my fortunes were quickly cast with those of Bleys, who was preparing an assault on Amber. He had not really needed me then, but had taken me in on the enterprise, I feel, so that he could keep an eye on me. Had I furnished him with guns, he would have been invincible and I would have been unnecessary. More important, had we succeeded in seizing Amber in accordance with his plans, the situation would have become strained indeed, with the bulk of the occupying forces, as well as the officers' loyalty, his. Then I would have required something to adjust the balance of power more equitably. A few bombs and automatic weapons, say.

Had I been my whole self even a month earlier, things would have been quite different. I could have been sitting in Amber, rather than being scorched, abraded, and desiccated, with another hellride before me and a knot of troubles to be worked out after that.

I spat sand so that I would not choke when I laughed. Hell, we make our own ifs. I had better things to think about than what could have happened. Like Eric . . .

I remember that day, Eric. I was in chains and I had been forced to my knees before the throne. I had already crowned myself, to mock you, and been beaten for it. The second time I had the crown in my hands, I threw it at you. But you caught it and smiled. I was glad that it was not damaged when it failed to damage you. Such a beautiful thing. . . . All of silver, with its seven high points, and studded with emeralds to beat all diamonds. Two large rubies at either temple. . . . You crowned yourself that day, all arrogance and hasty pomp. The first words that you spoke then were whispered to me, before the echoes of "Long live the king!" had died within the hall. I remember every one of them. "Your eyes have looked upon the fairest sight they ever will behold," you said. Then, "Guards!" you ordered. "Take Corwin away to the stithy, and let his eyes be burnt from out his head! Let him remember the sights of this day as the last he might ever see! Then cast him into the darkness of the deepest dungeon beneath Amber, and let his name be forgotten!"

"Now you reign in Amber," I said aloud. "But I have my eyes, and I have neither forgotten nor been forgotten."

No, I thought. Wrap yourself in the kingship, Eric. The walls of Amber are high and thick. Stay behind them. Ring yourself with the futile steel of blades. Ant-like, you armor your house in dust. You know now that you will never be secure so long as I live, and I have told you that I will be back. I am coming, Eric. I will bring me up guns out of Avalon, and I will break down your doors and smite your defenders. Then it will be as it was, briefly, another time, before your men came to you and saved you. That day I had only a few drops of your blood. This time, I will have it all.

I uncovered another rough diamond, the sixteenth or so, and flipped it into the sack at my waist.

As I faced the setting sun, I wondered about Benedict, Julian, and Gérard. What was the connection? Whatever, I did not like any combination of interests which involved Julian. Gérard was all right. I had been able to sleep back at the camp when I had thought that it was he whom Benedict was contacting. If he was now allied with Julian, though, it was cause for increased uneasiness. If anyone hated me even more than Eric, it was Julian. If he knew where I was, then my danger was great. I was not yet ready for a confrontation.

I supposed Benedict could find a moral justification for selling me out at this point. After all, he knew that whatever I did—and he knew that I was going to do something—would result in strife in Amber. I could understand, even sympathize with, his feelings. He was dedicated to the preservation of the realm. Unlike Julian, he was a man of principle, and I regretted having to be at odds with him. My hope was that my coup would be as quick and painless as a tooth extraction under gas, and that we would be back on the same side again soon afterward. Having met Dara now, I also wanted it this way for her sake.

He had told me too little for comfort. I had no way of knowing whether he really intended to remain in the field the entire week, or whether he was even now cooperating with the forces of Amber in the laying of my trap, the walling of my prison, the digging of my grave. I had to hurry, though I longed to linger in Avalon.

I envied Ganelon, in whatever tavern or brothel he drank, whored, or fought, on whatever hillside he hunted. He had come home. Should I leave him to his pleasures, despite his offer to accompany me to Amber? But no, he would be questioned on my departure—used badly, if Julian had anything to do with it—and then become an outcast in what must seem his own land to him, if they let him go at all. Then he would doubtless become an outlaw again, and the third time would probably prove his undoing. No, I would keep my promise. He would come with me, if that was what he still wanted. If he had changed his mind, well—I even envied him the prospect of outlawry in Avalon. I would have liked to remain longer, to ride with Dara in the hills, tramp about the countryside, sail upon the rivers. . . .

I thought about the girl. The knowledge of her existence changed things somewhat. I was not certain how. Despite our major hatreds and petty animosities, we Amberites are a very family-conscious bunch, always eager for news of one another, desirous to know everyone's position in the changing picture. A pause for gossip has doubtless stayed a few death blows among us. I sometimes think of us as a gang of mean little old ladies in a combination rest home and obstacle course.

I could not fit Dara into things yet because she did not know where she fit herself. Oh, she would learn eventually. She would receive superb tutelage once her existence became known. Now that I had brought her awareness of her uniqueness it would only be a matter of time before this occurred and she joined in the games. I had felt somewhat serpent-like at points during our conversation in the grove—but hell, she had a right to know. She was bound to find out sooner or later, and the sooner she did the sooner she could start shoring up her defenses. It was for her own benefit.

Of course, it was possible—even likely—that her mother and grandmother had lived their lives in ignorance of their heritage . . .

And where had it gotten them? They died violently, she had said.

Was it possible, I wondered, that the long arm of Amber had reached for them out of Shadow? And that it might strike again?

Benedict could be as tough and mean and nasty as any of us when he wanted to be. Tougher, even. He would fight to protect his own, doubtless even kill one of us if he thought it necessary. He must have assumed that keeping her existence a secret and keeping her ignorant would protect her. He would be angry with me when he found out what I had done, which was another reason for clearing out in a hurry. But I had not told her what I had out of sheer perverseness. I wanted her to survive, and I did not feel he was handling things properly. When I returned, she would have had time to think things over. She would have many questions and I would seize the opportunity to caution her at length and to give specifics.

I gnashed my teeth.

None of this should be necessary. When I ruled in Amber, things would be different. They had to be . . .

Why had no one ever come up with a way to change the basic nature of man? Even the erasure of all my memories and a new life in a new world had resulted in the same old Corwin. If I were not happy with what I was it could be a proposition worthy of despair.

In a quiet part of the river, I washed away the dust, the sweat, wondering the while about the black road which had so injured my brothers. There were many things that I needed to know.

As I bathed, Grayswandir was never far from my hand. One of us is capable of tracking another through Shadow, when the trail is still warm. As it was, my bath was undisturbed, though I used Grayswandir three times on the way back, on less mundane things than brothers.

But this was to be expected, as I had accelerated the pace considerably. . . .

It was still dark, though dawn was not too far away, when I entered the stables at my brother's manor. I tended Star, who had grown somewhat wild, talking to him and soothing him as I rubbed him down, then putting out a good supply of food and water. Ganelon's Firedrake greeted me from the opposite stall. I cleaned up at the pump to the rear of the stable, trying to decide where I was going to catch a little sleep.

I needed some rest. A few hours' worth would hold me for a time, but I refused to take them beneath Benedict's roof. I would not be taken that easily, and while I had often said that I wanted to die in bed, what I really meant was that in my old age I wanted to be stepped on by an elephant while making love.

I was not averse to drinking his booze, though, and I wanted a belt of something strong. The manor was dark; I entered quietly and I found the sideboard.

I poured a stiff one, tossed it off, poured another, and carried it to the window. I could see for a great distance. The manor stood on a hillside and Benedict had landscaped the place well.

" 'White in the moon the long road lies,' " I recited, surprised at the sound of my own voice. " 'The moon stands blank above . . .' "

"So it does. So it does, Corwin my lad," I heard Ganelon say.

"I didn't see you sitting there," I said softly, not turning from the window.

"That's because I'm sitting so still," he said.

"Oh," I said. "How drunk are you?"

"Hardly at all," he said, "now. But if you would care to be a good fellow and fetch me a drink . . ."

I turned.

"Why can't you get your own?"

"It hurts to move."

"All right."

I went and poured him one, carried it to him. He raised it slowly, nodded his thanks, took a sip.

"Ah, that's good!" he sighed. "May it numb things a bit."

"You were in a fight," I decided.

"Aye," he said. "Several."

"Then bear your wounds like a good trooper and let me save my sympathy."

"But I won!"

"God! Where did you leave the bodies?"

"Oh, they are not that bad off. 'Twas a girl did this to me."

"Then I'd say you got your money's worth."

" 'Twas not that sort of thing at all. I believe I've embarrassed us."

"Us? How?"

"I did not know she was the lady of the house. I came in feeling jolly, and I thought her some serving wench . . ."

"Dara?" I said, tensing.

"Aye, the same. I slapped her on the rump and went for a kiss or two—" He groaned. "Then she picked me up. She raised me off the ground and held me up over her head. Then she told me she was the lady of the house. Then she let me fall. . . . I'm eighteen stone if I'm a pebble, man, and it was a long way down."

He took another drink, and I chuckled.

"She laughed, too," he said ruefully. "She helped me up then and was not unkind, and of course I apologized—That brother of yours must be quite a man. I never met a girl that strong. The things she could do to a man . . ."

There was awe in his voice. He shook his head slowly and tossed back the rest of his drink. "It was frightening—not to mention embarrassing," he concluded.

"She accepted your apology?"

"Oh, yes. She was quite gracious about the whole thing. She told me to forget all about it, and said that she would, too."

"Then why are you not in bed sleeping it off?"

"I was waiting up, in case you came in at an odd hour. I wanted to catch you right away."

"Well, you have."

He rose slowly and picked up his glass.

"Let's go outside," he said.

"Good idea."

He picked up the brandy decanter on the way out, which I also thought was a good idea, and we followed a path through the garden behind the house. Finally, he heaved himself onto an old stone bench at the foot of a large oak tree, where he refilled both our glasses and took a drink from his own.

"Ah! He has good taste in liquor, too, your brother," he said.

I seated myself beside him and filled my pipe.

"After I told her I was sorry and introduced myself, we got to talking for a time," he said. "As soon as she learned I was with you, she wanted to know all sorts of things about Amber and shadows and you and the rest of your family."

"Did you tell her anything?" I said, striking a light.

"Couldn't have if I wanted to," he said. "I had none of the answers."

"Good."

"It got me to thinking, though. I do not believe Benedicts tells her too much, and I can see why. I would be careful what I say around her, Corwin. She seems over-curious."

I nodded, puffing.

"There is a reason for it," I said. "A very good reason. I am glad to know, though, that you keep your wits about you even when you have been drinking. Thanks for telling me."

He shrugged and took a drink.

"A good bashing is a sobering thing. Also, your welcome is my welfare."

"True. Does this version of Avalon meet with your approval?"

"Version? It *is* my Avalon," he said. "A new generation of people is in the land, but it is the same place. I visited the Field of Thorns today, where I put down Jack Hailey's bunch in your service. It was the same place."

"The Field of Thorns . . ." I said, remembering.

"Yes, this is my Avalon," he continued, "and I'll be coming back here for my old age, if we live through Amber."

"You still want to come along?"

"All my life I've wanted to see Amber—well, since I first heard of it. That was from you, in happier times."

"I do not really remember what I said. It must have been a good telling."

"We were both wonderfully drunk that night, and it seemed but a brief while that you talked—weeping some of the time—telling me of the mighty mountain Kolvir and the green and golden spires of the city, of the promenades, the decks, the terraces, the flowers, the fountains. . . . It seemed but a brief while, but it was most of the night—for before we staggered off to bed, the morning had begun. God! I could almost draw you a map of the place! I must see it before I die."

"I do not remember that night," I said slowly. "I must have been very, very drunk."

He chuckled.

"We had some good times here in the old days," he said. "And they do remember us here. But as people who lived very long ago—and they have many of the stories wrong. But hell! How many people get their stories right from day to day?"

I said nothing, smoking, thinking back.

". . . All of which leads me to a question or two," he said.

"Shoot."

"Will your attack on Amber put you at great odds with your brother Benedict?"

"I really wish that I knew the answer to that one," I said. "I think that it will, initially. But my move should be completed before he can reach Amber from here, in response to any distress call that goes out. That is, reach Amber with reinforcements. He could get there in no time at all, personally, if someone on the other end were helping. But that would serve little purpose. No. Rather than tear Amber apart, he will support whoever can hold it together, I am certain. Once I have ousted Eric, he will want the strife to stop right there and he will go along with my holding the throne, just to put an end to it. He will not really approve of the seizure in the first place, of course."

"That is what I am getting at. Will there be bad blood between you afterward as a result of that?"

"I do not believe so. This is purely a matter of politics, and we have known one another most of our lives, he and I, and have always been on better terms with each other than either of us with Eric."

"I see. Since you and I are in this together and Avalon seems to be Benedict's now, I was wondering what his feelings would be about my returning here one day. Would he hate me for having helped you?"

"I doubt that very much. He has never been that sort of person."

"Then let me carry things a step further. God knows I am an experienced military man, and if we succeed in taking Amber he will have ample evidence of the fact. With his right arm injured the way that it is and all, do you think he might consider taking me on as a field commander for his militia? I know this area so well. I could take him to the Field of Thorns and describe that battle. Hell! I would serve him well—as well as I served you."

He laughed then.

"Pardon me. Better than I served you."

I chuckled, sipped my drink.

"It would be tricky," I said. "Of course I like the idea. But I am not too certain that you could ever enjoy his trust. It would seem too obvious a ploy on my part."

"Damn politics! That is not what I meant! Soldiering is all that I know, and I love Avalon!"

"I believe you. But would he?"

"With only one arm he will be needing a good man about. He could—"

I began to laugh and restrained myself quickly, for the sound of laughter seems to carry for a good distance. Also, Ganelon's feelings were involved.

"I am sorry," I said. "Excuse me, please. You do not understand. You do not really understand who it was we talked with in the tent that night. He may have seemed an ordinary man to you—a handicapped one, at that. But this is not so. I fear Benedict. He is unlike any other being in Shadow or reality. He is the Master of Arms for Amber. Can you conceive of a millennium? A thousand years? Several of them? Can you understand a man who, for almost every day of a lifetime like that, has spent some time dwelling with weapons, tactics, strategies? Because you see him in a tiny kingdom, commanding a small militia, with a well-pruned orchard in his back yard, do not be deceived. All that there is of military science thunders in his head. He has often journeyed from shadow to shadow, witnessing variation after variation on the same battle, with but slightly altered circumstances, in order to test his theories of warfare. He has commanded armies so vast that you could watch them march by day after day and see no end to the columns. Although he is inconvenienced by the loss of his arm, I would not wish to fight with him either with weapons or barehanded. It is fortunate that he has no designs upon the throne, or he would be occupying it right now. If he were, I believe that I would give up at this moment and pay him homage. I fear Benedict."

Ganelon was silent for a long while, and I took another drink, for my throat had become dry.

"I did not realize this, of course," he said then. "I will be happy if he just lets me come back to Avalon."

"That much he will do. I know."

"Dara told me she had a message from him today. He has decided to cut short his stay in the field. He will probably be returning tomorrow."

"Damn!" I said, standing. "We will have to move soon, then. I hope Doyle has that stuff ready. We must go to him in the morning and expedite matters. I want to be away from here before Benedict gets back!"

"You have the pretties then?"

"Yes."

"May I see them?"

I undid the sack at my belt and passed it to him. He opened it and withdrew several stones, holding them in the palm of his left hand and turning them slowly with his fingertips.

"They do not look like much," he said, "from what I can see of them in this light. Wait! There's a glimmer! No . . ."

"They are in the rough, of course. You are holding a fortune in your hands."

"Amazing," he said, dropping them back in the sack and refastening it. "It was so easy for you."

"It was not all that easy."

"Still, to gather a fortune so quickly seems somehow unfair."

He passed it back.

"I will see that you are provided with a fortune when our labors are done," I said. "That should prove some compensation, should Benedict not offer you a position."

"Now that I know who he is, I am more determined than ever to work for him one day."

"We will see what can be done."

"Yes. Thank you, Corwin. How shall we work our departure?"

"I want you to go and get some rest, for I will roust you out of bed early. Star and Firedrake will take unkindly to the notion of draft duty, I fear, but we will then borrow one of Benedict's wagons and head into town. Before this, I will try to arrange a good smoke screen here for our orderly withdrawal. We will then hurry Doyle the jeweler about his task, obtain our cargo, and depart into Shadow as quickly as possible. The greater our head start, the more difficult it will be for Benedict to track us. If I can get half a day's lead into Shadow, it will be practically impossible for him."

"Why should he be so eager to come after us in the first place?"

"He does not trust me worth a damn—and justly so. He is waiting for me to make my move. He knows there is something I need here, but he does not know what. He wants to find out, so that he can seal off another threat to Amber. As soon as he realizes we have gone for good, he will know that we have it and he will come looking."

Ganelon yawned, stretched, finished his drink.

"Yes," he said then. "We'd best rest now, to be in condition for the hurrying. Now that you have told me more about Benedict, I am less surprised by the other thing I meant to tell you—though no less discomfited."

"That being . . . ?"

He rose to his feet, picked up the decanter carefully, then pointed down the path.

"If you continue on in that direction," he said, "passing the hedge that marks the end of this bower and entering the woods that lie below—and then go on for another two hundred paces or so—you will come to a place where there is a little grove of saplings off to the left, standing in a sudden declivity perhaps four feet lower than the level of the trail itself. Down in it, stamped down and strewn over with leaves and twigs, there is a fresh grave. I found it while taking the air earlier, when I paused to relieve myself down there."

"How do you know it is a grave?"

He chuckled.

"When holes have bodies in them that is how they are generally called.

It was quite shallow, and I poked around a bit with a stick. There are four bodies in there—three men and a woman."

"How recently dead?"

"Very. A few days, I'd judge."

"You left it as you found it?"

"I'm not a fool, Corwin."

"Sorry. But this troubles me considerably, because I don't understand it at all."

"Obviously they gave Benedict some trouble and he returned the favor."

"Perhaps. What were they like? How did they die?"

"Nothing special about them. They were in their middle years, and their throats had been cut—save for one fellow who got it in the guts."

"Strange. Yes, it is good that we are leaving soon. We have enough problems of our own without getting involved in the local ones."

"Agreed. So let us be off to bed."

"You go ahead. I am not quite ready yet."

"Take your own advice and get some rest," he said, turning back toward the manor. "Don't sit up and worry."

"I won't."

"Good night, then."

"See you in the morning."

I watched him return along the path. He was right, of course, but I was not yet ready to surrender my consciousness. I went over my plans again, to be certain there was nothing I was overlooking, finished my drink and set the glass on the bench. I rose then and strolled, trailing wisps of tobacco smoke about me. There was a bit of moonlight from over my shoulder and dawn was still a few hours' distant, as I reckoned it. I was firm in my resolve to spend the rest of the night out of doors, and I thought to find me a good place to sack out.

Of course, I eventually wandered down the path and into the grove of saplings. A little poking around showed me that there had been some recent digging, but I was in no mood to exhume bodies by moonlight and was perfectly willing to take Ganelon's word as to what he had found there. I am not even certain why I went there. Morbid streak, I guess. I did decide against sleeping in the vicinity, though.

I made my way into the northwest corner of the garden, finding an area that was out of line of sight from the manor. There were high hedgerows and the grass was long, soft, and sweet-smelling. I spread my cloak, sat down upon it, and pulled off my boots. I put my feet down into the cool grass and sighed.

Not too much longer, I decided. Shadows to diamonds to guns to Amber. I was on my way. A year ago I had been rotting in a cell, crossing and recrossing the line between sanity and madness so many times that I had all but rubbed it out. Now I was free, strong, sighted, and had a plan. Now I was a threat seeking fulfillment once again, a deadlier threat than I had been previously. This time I did not have my fortunes tied up with the plans of another. Now I was responsible for my own success or failure.

The feeling was good, as was the grass, as was the alcohol which had now seeped through my system and warmed me with a pleasant flame. I cleaned my pipe, put it away, stretched, yawned, and was about to recline.

I detected a distant movement, propped myself on my elbows and watched for it again. I did not have long to wait. A figure was passing slowly along the path, pausing frequently, moving quietly. It vanished beneath the tree where Ganelon and I had been sitting, and did not emerge again for a long while. Then it continued on for several dozen paces, stopped and seemed to be staring in my direction. Then it advanced toward me.

Passing about a clump of shrubbery and emerging from the shadows, her face was suddenly touched by the moonlight. Apparently aware of this, she smiled in my direction, slowing as she came near, stopping when she stood before me.

She said, "I take it your quarters are not to your liking, Lord Corwin."

"Not at all," I said. "It is such a beautiful night that it appealed to the outdoorsman in me."

"Something must have appealed to you last night, also," she said, "despite the rain," and she seated herself beside me on my cloak. "Did you sleep indoors or out?"

"I spent it out," I said. "But I did not sleep. In fact, I have not slept since I saw you last."

"Where have you been?"

"Down by the seaside, sifting sand."

"Sounds depressing."

"It was."

"I have been doing a lot of thinking, since we walked in Shadow."

"I would imagine."

"I have not done too much sleeping either. That was why I heard you come in, heard you talking with Ganelon, knew you were out here somewhere when he came back alone."

"You were right."

"I must get to Amber, you know. And walk the Pattern."

"I know. You will."

"Soon, Corwin. Soon!"

"You are young, Dara. There is plenty of time."

"Damn it! I have been waiting all my life—without even knowing about it! Is there no way I can go now?"

"No."

"Why not? You could take me on a quick journey through shadows, take me to Amber, let me walk the Pattern . . ."

"If we are not slain immediately, we might be fortunate enough to be given adjoining cells for a time—or racks—before we are executed."

"Whatever for? You are a Prince of the City. You have a right to do as you please."

I laughed.

"I am an outlaw, dear. If I return to Amber I will be executed, if I am lucky. Or something much worse if I am not. But seeing as how things turned out last time, I should think they would kill me quickly. This courtesy would doubtless also be extended to my companions."

"Oberon would not do such a thing."

"Given sufficient provocation, I believe that he would. But the question does not really arise. Oberon is no more, and my brother Eric sits on the throne and calls himself liege."

"When did this occur?"

"Several years ago, as time is measured in Amber."

"Why would he want to kill you?"

"To keep me from killing him, of course."

"Would you?"

"Yes, and I will. Soon, too, I think."

She turned to face me then.

"Why?"

"So that I can occupy the throne myself. It is rightly mine, you see. Eric has usurped it. I am just recently escaped from torture and several years' imprisonment at his hands. He made the mistake, however, of allowing himself the luxury of keeping me alive so that he could contemplate my wretchedness. He never thought that I would get free and return to challenge him again. Neither did I, for that matter. But since I have been fortunate enough to obtain a second chance, I shall be careful not to make the same mistake he did."

"But he is your brother."

"Few are more aware of that fact than he and I, I assure you."

"How soon do you expect to accomplish—your objectives?"

"As I said the other day, if you can get hold of the Trumps, contact me in about three months. If you cannot, and things come about according to my plans, I will get in touch with you fairly early in my reign. You should have your chance to take the Pattern before another year passes."

"And if you fail?"

"Then you will have a longer wait ahead of you. Until Eric has assured the permanency of his own reign, and until Benedict has acknowledged him king. You see, Benedict is not willing to do this. He has remained away from Amber for a long while, and for all Eric knows, he is no longer among the living. Should he put in an appearance now, he is going to have to take a position either for or against Eric. Should he come out for him, then the continuance of Eric's reign will be assured—and Benedict does not want to be responsible for that. Should he come out against him, there will be strife— and he does not want to be responsible for that either. He has no desire for the crown himself. Only by remaining out of the picture entirely can he assure the measure of tranquility that does prevail. Were he to appear and refuse to take either position, *he* could possibly get away with it, but it would be tantamount to denying Eric's kingship and would still lead to trouble. Were he to appear with you, he would be surrendering his will, for Eric would put pressure on him through you."

"Then if you lose I might never get to Amber!"

"I am only describing the situation as I see it. There are doubtless many factors of which I am unaware. I have been out of circulation for a long while."

"You *must* win!" she said. Then, suddenly, "Would Grandpa support you?"

"I doubt it. But the situation would be quite different. I am aware of his existence, and of yours. I will not ask his support. So long as he does not oppose me, I will be satisfied. And if I am quick, efficient, and successful, he will not oppose me. He will not like my having found out about you, but when he sees that I mean you no harm all will be well on that count."

"Why would you not use me? It seems the logical thing to do."

"It is. But I've discovered I like you," I said, "so that's out of the question."

She laughed.

"I've charmed you!" she said.

I chuckled.

"In your own delicate way, at sword's point, yes."

Abruptly, she sobered.

"Grandpa is coming back tomorrow," she said. "Did your man Ganelon tell you?"

"Yes."

"How does that affect whatever you are about?"

"I intend to be hell and gone out of here before he returns."

"What will he do?"

"The first thing that he will do will be to get very angry with you for being here. Then he will want to know how you managed your return and how much you have told me about yourself."

"What should I tell him?"

"Tell him the truth about how you got back. That will give him something to think about. As to your status, your woman's intuition cautioned you concerning my trustworthiness, and you took the same line with me as you did with Julian and Gérard. As to my whereabouts, Ganelon and I borrowed a wagon and headed into town, saying that we would not be back until quite late."

"Where will you really be going?"

"Into town, briefly. But we will not be coming back. I want as much of a head start as possible because he can track me through Shadow, up to a point."

"I will delay him as best I can for you. Were you not going to see me before you left?"

"I was going to have this talk with you in the morning. You got it ahead of time by being restless."

"Then I am glad that I was—restless. How are you going to conquer Amber?"

I shook my head. "No, dear Dara. All scheming princes must keep a few small secrets. That's one of mine."

"I am surprised to learn there is so much distrust and plotting in Amber."

"Why? The same conflicts exist everywhere, in various forms. They are all about you, always, for all places take their form from Amber."

"It is difficult to understand . . ."

"One day you will. Leave it at that for now."

"Then tell me another thing. Since I am able to negotiate shadows somewhat, even without having taken the Pattern, tell me more precisely how you go about it. I want to get better at it."

"No!" I said. "I will not have you fooling with Shadow until you are ready. It is dangerous even after you have taken the Pattern. To do it before is foolhardy. You were lucky, but do not try it again. I'll even help, by not telling you anything more about it."

"All right!" she said. "Sorry. I guess I can wait."

"I guess you can. No hard feelings?"

"No. Well—" She laughed. "They wouldn't do me any good, I guess. You must know what you are talking about. I am glad that you care what happens to me."

I grunted, and she reached out and touched my cheek. At this, I turned my head again and her face was moving slowly toward my own, smile gone and lips parting, eyes almost closed. As we kissed, I felt her arms slide about my neck and shoulders and mine found their way into a similar position around her. My surprise was lost in the sweetness, gave way to warmth and a certain excitement.

If Benedict ever found out, he was going to be more than just irritated with me. . . .

SEVEN

The wagon creaked, monotonously, and the sun was already well into the west, though it still poured hot streams of daylight upon us. Back among the cases, Ganelon snored, and I envied him his noisy occupation. He had been sleeping for several hours, and this was my third day without rest.

We were perhaps fifteen miles out of the city, and heading into the northeast. Doyle had not had my order completely ready, but Ganelon and I had persuaded him to close up his shop and accelerate its production. This involved several additional hours' curse-worthy delay. I had been too keyed-up to sleep then and was unable to do so now, as I was edging my way through shadows.

I forced back the fatigue and the evening and found some clouds to shade me. We moved along a dry, deeply rutted, clay road. It was an ugly shade of yellow, and it cracked and crumbled as we went. Brown grasses hung limply on either side of the way, and the trees were short, twisted things, their barks thick and shaggy. We passed numerous outcrops of shale.

I had paid Doyle well for his compounds, and had also purchased a handsome bracelet to be delivered to Dara the following day. My diamonds were at my belt, Grayswandir near to my hand. Star and Firedrake walked steadily, strongly. I was on my way to having it made.

I wondered whether Benedict had returned home yet. I wondered how long he would remain deceived as to my whereabouts. I was by no means out of danger from him. He could follow a trail for a great distance through Shadow, and I was leaving him a good one. I had little choice in the matter, though. I needed the wagon, I was stuck with our present speed, and I was in no condition to manage another hellride. I handled the shifts slowly and carefully, very conscious of my dulled senses and growing weariness, counting on the gradual accumulation of change and distance to build up a barrier between Benedict and myself, hoping that it would soon become an impenetrable one.

I found my way from late afternoon back to noontide within the next two miles, but kept it a cloudy noon, for it was only its light that I desired, not its heat. Then I managed to locate a small breeze. It increased the probability of rain, but it was worth it. You can't have everything.

I was fighting back drowsiness by then, and the temptation was great to awaken Ganelon and simply add more miles to our distance by letting him drive while I slept. But I was afraid to try it this early in the journey. There were still too many things to do.

I wanted more daylight, but I also wanted a better road, and I was sick of that goddamned yellow clay, and I had to do something about those clouds, and I had to keep in mind where we were headed. . . .

I rubbed my eyes, I took several deep breaths. Things were starting to jump around inside my head, and the steady clop-clop of the horses' hoofs and the creaking of the wagon were starting to have a soporific effect. I was already numb to the jolting and the swaying. The reins hung loosely in my hands, and I had already nodded and let them slip once. Fortunately, the horses seemed to have a good idea as to what was expected of them.

After a time, we mounted a long, easy slope that led down into midmorning. By then, the sky was quite dark, and it took several miles and half a dozen twistings of the road to dissipate the cloud cover somewhat. A storm could turn our way into a river of mud quite quickly. I winced at the thought, let the sky alone and concentrated on the road once more.

We came to a dilapidated bridge leading across a dry stream bed. On its other side, the road was smoother, less yellow. As we proceeded, it grew darker, flatter, harder, and the grass came green beside it.

By then, though, it had begun raining.

I fought with this for a time, determined not to surrender my grass and the dark, easy road. My head ached, but the shower ended within a quarter of a mile and the sun came out once more.

The sun . . . oh yes, the sun.

We rattled on, finally coming to a dip in the road that kept twisting its way down among brighter trees. We descended into a cool valley, where we eventually crossed another small bridge, this one with a narrow band of water drifting along the middle of the bed beneath it. I had wrapped the reins about my wrist by then, because I kept nodding. As from a great distance, I focused my concentration, straightening, sorting . . .

Birds queried the day, tentatively, from within the woods to my right. Glistening droplets of dew clung to the grass, the leaves. A chill came into the air, and the rays of the morning sun slanted down through the trees . . .

But my body was not fooled by the awakening within this shadow, and I was relieved finally to hear Ganelon stir and curse. If he had not come around before much longer I would have had to awaken him.

Good enough. I tugged gently on the reins and the horses got the idea and halted. I put on the brake, as we were still on an incline, and located a water bottle.

"Here!" said Ganelon, as I drank. "Leave a drop for me!"

I passed the bottle back to him.

"You are taking over now," I told him. "I have to get some sleep."

He drank for half a minute, then let out an explosive exhalation.

"Right," he said, swinging himself over the edge of the wagon and down. "But bide a moment. Nature summons."

He stepped off the road, and I crawled back onto the bed of the wagon and stretched out where he had lain, folding my cloak into a pillow.

Moments later, I heard him climb onto the driver's seat, and there was a jolt as he released the brake. I heard him cluck his tongue and snap the reins lightly.

"Is it morning?" he called back to me.

"Yes."

"God! I've slept all day and all night!"

I chuckled.

"No. I did a little shadow-shifting," I said. "You only slept six or seven hours."

"I don't understand. But never mind, I believe you. Where are we now?"

"Still heading northeast," I said, "around twenty miles out of the city and maybe a dozen or so from Benedict's place. We have moved through Shadow, also."

"What am I to do now?"

"Just keep following the road. We need the distance."

"Could Benedict still reach us?"

"I think so. That's why we can't give the horses their rest yet."

"All right. Is there anything special I should be alert for?"

"No."

"When should I rouse you?"

"Never."

He was silent then, and as I waited for my consciousness to be consumed, I thought of Dara, of course. I had been thinking of her on and off all day.

The thing had been quite unpremeditated on my part. I had not even thought of her as a woman until she came into my arms and revised my thinking on the subject. A moment later, and my spinal nerves took over, reducing much of what passes for cerebration down to its basics, as Freud had once said to me. I could not blame it on the alcohol, as I had not had that much and it had not affected me especially. Why did I want to blame it on anything? Because I felt somewhat guilty, that was why. She was too distant a relation for me to really think of her as one. That was not it. I did not feel I had taken unfair advantage of her, for she had known what she was doing when she came looking for me. It was the circumstances that made me question my own motives, even in the midst of things. I had wanted to do more than simply win her confidence and a measure of friendship when I had first spoken with her and taken her on that walk into Shadow. I was trying to alienate some of her loyalty, trust, and affection from Benedict and transfer it to myself. I had wanted her on my side, as a possible ally in what might become an enemy camp. I had hoped to be able to use her, should the need arise when the going got rough. All this was true. But I did not want to believe that I had had her as I did just to further this end. I suspected there was some truth to it, though, and it made me feel uncomfortable and more than a little ignoble. Why? I had done plenty of things in my time that many would consider much worse, and I was not especially troubled by these. I wrestled with it, not liking to admit it but already knowing the answer. I cared for the girl. It was as simple as that. It was different from the friendship I had felt for Lorraine, with its element of world-weary understanding between two veterans about it, or the air of casual sensuality that had existed briefly between Moire and myself back before I had taken the Pattern for the second time. It was quite different. I had known her so briefly that it was most illogical. I was a man with centuries behind me. Yet . . . I had not felt this way in centuries. I had forgotten the feeling, until now. I did not want to be in love with her. Not now. Later, perhaps. Better yet, not at all. She was all wrong for me. She was a child. Everything that she would want to do, everything that she would find new and fascinating, I had already done. No, it was all wrong. I had no business falling in love with her. I should not let myself . . .

Ganelon hummed some bawdy tune, badly. The wagon jounced and creaked, took a turn uphill. The sun fell upon my face, and I covered my eyes with my forearm. Somewhere thereabout, oblivion fixed its grip and squeezed.

When I awoke, it was past noon and I was feeling grimy. I took a long drink of water, poured some in the palm of my hand, and rubbed it in my eyes. I combed my hair with my fingers. I took a look at our surroundings.

There was greenery about us, small stands of trees and open spaces where tall grasses grew. It was still a dirt road that we traveled, hard-packed and fairly smooth. The sky was clear, but for a few small clouds, and shade alternated with sunlight fairly regularly. There was a light breeze.

"Back among the living. Good!" said Ganelon, as I climbed over the front wall and took a seat beside him.

"The horses are getting tired, Corwin, and I'd like to stretch my legs a bit," he said. "I'm also getting very hungry. Aren't you?"

"Yes. Pull off into that shady place to the left and we'll stop awhile."

"I would like to go on a bit farther than that," he said.

"For any special reason?"

"Yes. I want to show you something."

"Go ahead."

We clopped along for perhaps a half a mile, then came to a bend in the road that took us in a more northerly direction. Before very long we came to a hill, and when we had mounted it there was another hill, leading even higher.

"How much farther do you want to go?" I said.

"Let's take this next hill," he replied. "We might be able to see it from up there."

"All right."

The horses strained against the steepness of that second hill, and I got out and pushed from behind. When we finally reached the top, I felt even grimier from the mixture of sweat and dust, but I was fully awake once more. Ganelon reined in the horses and put on the brake. He climbed back in the wagon and up onto a crate then. He stood, facing to the left, and shaded his eyes.

"Come up here, Corwin," he called.

I climbed over the tailgate and he squatted and extended a hand. I took it, and he helped me up onto the crate, where I stood beside him. He pointed, and I followed the gesture.

Perhaps three-quarters of a mile distant, running from left to right for as far as I could see, was a wide, black band. We were several hundred yards higher than the thing and had a decent view of, I would say, half a mile of its length. It was several hundred feet across, and though it curved and turned twice that I could see, its width appeared to remain constant. There were trees within it, and they were totally black. There seemed to be some movement. I could not say what it was. Perhaps it was only the wind rippling the black grasses near its edge. But there was also a definite sensation of flowing within it, like currents in a flat, dark river.

"What is it?" I said.

"I thought perhaps you could tell me," Ganelon replied. "I had thought it a part of your shadow-sorceries."

I shook my head slowly.

"I was quite drowsy, but I would remember if I had arranged for anything that strange to occur. How did you know it was there?"

"We skirted it several times as you slept, then edged away again. I did not like the feeling at all. It was a very familiar one. Does it not remind you of something?"

"Yes. Yes, it does. Unfortunately."

He nodded.

"It's like that damned Circle back in Lorraine. That's what it's like."

"The black road . . ." I said.

"What?"

"The black road," I repeated. "I did not know what she was referring to when she mentioned it, but now I begin to understand. This is not good at all."

"Another ill omen?"

"I am afraid so."

He cursed, then, "Will it cause us any immediate trouble?" he asked.

"I don't believe so, but I am not certain."

He climbed down from the crate and I followed.

"Let's find some forage for the horses then," he said, "and tend to our own bellies as well."

"Yes."

We moved forward and he took the reins. We found a good spot at the foot of the hill.

We tarried there for the better part of an hour, talking mainly of Avalon. We did not speak again of the black road, though I thought of it quite a bit. I had to get a closer look at the thing, of course.

When we were ready to move on, I took the reins again. The horses, somewhat refreshed, moved out at a good pace.

Ganelon sat beside me on the left, still in a talkative mood. I was only just then beginning to realize how much this strange homecoming had meant to him. He had revisited many of his old haunts from the days of his outlawry, as well as four battlefields where he had distinguished himself greatly after he had achieved respectability. I was in many ways moved by his reminiscences. An unusual mixture of gold and clay, this man. He should have been an Amberite.

The miles slid by quickly and we were drawing near to the black road again when I felt a familiar mental jab. I passed the reins to Ganelon.

"Take them!" I said. "Drive!"

"What is it?"

"Later! Just drive!"

"Should I hurry?"

"No. Keep it normal. Don't say anything for a while."

I closed my eyes and rested my head in my hands, emptying my mind and building a wall around the emptiness. No one home. Out to lunch. No solicitors. This property is vacant. Do not disturb. Trespassers will be prosecuted. Beware of dog. Falling rock. Slippery when wet. To be razed for urban renewal . . .

It eased, then came on again, hard, and I blocked it again. There followed a third wave. I stopped that one, too.

Then it was gone.

I sighed, massaged by eyeballs.

"It's all right now," I said.

"What happened?"

"Someone tried to reach me by a very special means. It was almost certainly Benedict. He must just now have found out any of a number of things that could make him want to stop us. I'll take the reins again now. I fear he will be on our trail soon."

Ganelon handed them over.

"What are our chances of escaping him?"

"Pretty fair now, I'd say, that we've got more distance behind us. I am going to shuffle some more shadows as soon as my head stops spinning."

I guided us on, and our way twisted and wound, paralleling that black road for a time, then heading in closer to it. Finally, we were only a few hundred yards away from it.

Ganelon studied it in silence for a long while, then said, "It reminds me too much of that other place. The little tongues of mist that lick about things, the feeling that something is always moving just at the corner of your eye . . ."

I bit my lip. I began to perspire heavily. I was trying to shift away from the thing now and there was some sort of resistance. It was not the same feeling of monolithic immovability as occurs when you try to move through Shadow in Amber. It was altogether different. It was a feeling of— inescapability.

We moved through Shadow all right. The sun drifted higher in the heavens, heading back toward noonday—for I did not relish the thought of nightfall beside that black strip—and the sky lost something of its blue and the trees shot higher about us and mountains appeared in the distance.

Was it that the road cut through Shadow itself?

It must. Why else would Julian and Gérard have located it and been sufficiently intrigued to explore the thing?

It was unfortunate, but I feared we had much in common, that road and I. Damn it!

We moved beside it for a long while, gradually moving closer together, also. Soon, only about a hundred feet separated us. Fifty . . .

. . . And, as I had felt they eventually must, our paths finally intersected.

I drew rein. I packed my pipe and lit it, smoked as I studied the thing. Star and Firedrake obviously did not approve of the black area that cut across our way. They had whinnied and tried to pull off to the side.

It was a long, diagonal cut across the black place if we wanted to keep to the road. Also, part of the terrain was hidden from our sight by a series of low, stone hills. There were heavy grasses at the edge of the black and patches of it, here and there, about the foot of the hills. Bits of mist scudded among them and faint, vaporous clouds hovered in all the hollows. The sky, seen through the atmosphere that hung about the place, was several shades darker, with a smeared, sooty tone to it. A silence that was not the same as stillness lay upon it, almost as though some unseen entity were poised, holding its breath.

Then we heard a scream. It was a girl's voice. The old lady in distress trick?

It came from somewhere to the right, beyond those hills. It smelled fishy. But hell! It could be real.

I tossed the reins to Ganelon and jumped to the ground, taking Grayswandir into my hand.

"I'm going to investigate," I said, moving off to the right and leaping the gulley that ran beside the road.

"Hurry back."

I plowed through some brush and scrambled up a rocky slope. I pushed my way through more shrubbery on its down side and mounted another, higher slope. The scream came again as I was climbing it, and this time I heard other sounds as well.

Then I reached the top and was able to see for a good distance.

The back area began about forty feet below me, and the scene I sought was laid about a hundred-fifty feet within it.

It was a monochromatic sight, save for the flames. A woman, all in white, black hair hanging loose, down to her waist, was bound to one of those dark trees, smoldering branches heaped around her feet. Half a dozen hairy, albino men, almost completely naked and continuing the process of undressing as they moved, shuffled about, muttering and chuckling, poking at the woman and the fire with sticks that they carried and clutching at their loins repeatedly. The flames were high enough now to singe the woman's garments, causing them to smolder. Her long dress was sufficiently torn and disarrayed so that I could see she possessed a lovely, voluptuous form, though the smoke wrapped her in such a manner that I was unable to see her face.

I rushed forward, entering the area of the black road, leaping over the long, twining grasses, and charged into the group, beheading the nearest man and running another through before they knew I was upon them. The others turned and flailed at me with their sticks, shouting as they swung them.

Grayswandir ate off big chunks of them, until they fell apart and were silent. Their juices were black.

I turned, holding my breath, and kicked away the front of the fire. Then I moved in close to the lady and cut her bonds. She fell into my arms, sobbing.

It was only then that I noticed her face—or, rather, her lack of one. She wore a full, ivory mask, oval and curving, featureless, save for two tiny rectangular grilles for her eyes.

I drew her away from the smoke and the gore. She clung to me, breathing heavily, thrusting her entire body against me. After what seemed an appropriate period of time, I attempted to disentangle myself. But she would not release me, and she was surprisingly strong.

"It is all right now," I said, or something equally trite and apt, but she did not reply.

She kept shifting her grip upon my body, with rough caressing movements and a rather disconcerting effect. Her desirability was enhanced, from instant to instant. I found myself stroking her hair, and the rest of her as well.

"It is all right now," I repeated. "Who are you? Why were they burning you? Who were they?"

But she did not reply. She had stopped sobbing, but her breathing was still heavy, although in a different way.

"Why do you wear this mask?"

I reached for it and she jerked her head back.

This did not seem especially important, though. While some cold, logical part of me knew that the passion was irrational, I was as powerless as the gods of the Epicureans. I wanted her and I was ready to have her.

Then I heard Ganelon cry out my name and I tried to turn in that direction. But she restrained me. I was amazed at her strength.

"Child of Amber," came her half-familiar voice. "We owe you this for what you have given us, and we will have all of you now."

Ganelon's voice came to me again, a steady stream of profanities.

I exerted all my strength against that grip and it weakened. My hand shot forward and I tore away the mask.

There came a brief cry of anger as I freed myself, and four final, fading words as the mask came away:

"Amber must be destroyed!"

There was no face behind the mask. There was nothing there at all.

Her garment collapsed and hung limply over my arm. She—or it—had vanished.

Turning quickly, I saw that Ganelon was sprawled at the edge of the black, his legs twisted unnaturally. His blade rose and fell slowly, but I could not see at what he was striking. I ran toward him.

The black grasses, over which I had leaped, were twined about his ankles and legs. Even as he hacked at them, others lashed about as though seeking to capture his sword arm. He had succeeded in partly freeing his right leg, and I leaned far forward and managed to finish the job.

I moved to a position behind him, out of reach of the grasses, and tossed away the mask, which I just then realized I was still clutching. It fell to earth beyond the edge of the black and immediately began to smolder.

Catching him under the arms, I strove to drag Ganelon back. The stuff resisted fiercely, but at last I tore him free. I carried him then, leaping over the remaining dark grasses that separated us from the more docile, green variety beyond the road.

He regained his footing and continued to lean heavily against me, bending forward and slapping at his leggings.

"They're numb," he said. "My legs are asleep."

I helped him back to the wagon. He transferred his grip to its side and began stamping his feet.

"They're tingling," he announced. "It's starting to come back. . . . Oow!"

Finally, he limped to the front of the wagon. I helped him climb onto the seat and followed him up.

He sighed.

"That's better," he said. "They're coming along now. That stuff just sucked the strength out of them. Out of the rest of me, too. What happened?"

"Our bad omen made good on its promise."

"What now?"

I picked up the reins and released the brake.

"We go across," I said. "I have to find out more about this thing. Keep your blade handy."

He grunted and laid the weapon across his knees. The horses did not like the idea of going on, but I flicked their flanks lightly with the whip and they began to move.

We entered the black area, and it was like riding into a World War II newsreel. Remote though near at hand, stark, depressing, grim. Even the creaking and the hoof falls were somehow muffled, made to seem more distant. A faint, persistent ringing began in my ears. The grasses beside the road stirred as we passed, though I kept well away from them. We passed through several patches of mist. They were odorless, but our breathing grew labored on each occasion. As we neared the first hill, I began the shift that would take us through Shadow.

We rounded the hill.

Nothing.

The dark, miasmal prospect was unaltered.

I grew angry then. I drew the Pattern from memory and held it blazing before my mind's eye. I essayed the shift once more.

Immediately, my head began to ache. A pain shot from my forehead to the back of my skull and hung there like a hot wire. But this only fanned my anger and caused me to try even harder to shift the black road into nothingness.

Things wavered. The mists thickened, rolled across the road in billows. Outlines grew indistinct. I shook the reins. The horses moved faster. My head began to throb, felt as if it were about to come apart.

Instead, momentarily, everything else did. . . .

The ground shook, cracking in places, but it was more than just that. Everything seemed to undergo a spasmodic shudder, and the cracking was more than mere fracture lines in the ground.

It was as though someone had suddenly kicked the leg of a table on which a loosely assembled jigsaw puzzle lay. Gaps appeared in the entire prospect: here, a green bough; there, a sparkle of water, a glimpse of blue sky, absolute blackness, white nothingness, the front of a brick building, faces behind a window, fire, a piece of star-filled sky . . .

The horses were galloping by then, and I had all I could do to keep from screaming for the pain.

A babble of mixed noises—animal, human, mechanical—washed over us. It seemed that I could hear Ganelon cursing, but I could not be certain.

I thought that I would pass out from the pain, but I determined, out of sheer stubbornness and anger, to persist until I did. I concentrated on the Pattern as a dying man might cry out to his God, and I threw my entire will against the existence of the black road.

Then the pressure was off and the horses were plunging wildly, dragging us into a green field. Ganelon snatched at the reins, but I drew on them myself and shouted to the horses until they halted.

We had crossed the black road.

I turned immediately and looked back. The scene had the wavering quality of something seen through troubled waters. Our path through it stood clean and steady, however, like a bridge or a dam, and the grasses at its edge were green.

"That was worse," Ganelon said, "than the ride you took me on when you exiled me."

"I think so, too," I said, and I spoke to the horses, gently, finally persuading them to return to the dirt road and continue on along it.

The world was brighter here, and the trees that we soon moved among were great pines. The air was fresh with their fragrance. Squirrels and birds moved within them. The soil was darker, richer. We seemed to be at a higher altitude than we had been before the crossing. It pleased me that we had indeed shifted—and in the direction I had desired.

Our way curved, ran back a bit, straightened. Every now and then we caught a glimpse of the black road. It was not too far off to our right. We were still running roughly parallel to it. The thing definitely cut through Shadow. From what we saw of it, it appeared to have settled back down to being its normal, sinister self once more.

My headache faded and my heart grew somewhat lighter. We achieved higher ground and a pleasant view over a large area of hills and forest, reminding me of parts of Pennsylvania I had enjoyed driving through years earlier.

I stretched; then, "How are your legs now?" I asked.

"All right," Ganelon said, looking back along our trail. "I can see for a great distance, Corwin . . ."

"Yes?"

"I see a horseman, coming very fast."

I stood and turned. I think I might have groaned as I dropped back into the seat and shook the reins.

He was still too far off to tell for certain—on the other side of the black road. But who else could it be, pushing along at that speed on our trail?

I cursed then.

We were nearing the crest of the rise. I turned to Ganelon and said, "Get ready for another hellride."

"It's Benedict?"

"I think so. We lost too much time back there. He can move awfully fast—especially through Shadow—all alone like that."

"Do you think you can still lose him?"

"We'll find out," I said. "Real soon now."

I clucked to the horses and shook the reins again. We reached the top and a blast of icy air struck us. We leveled off and the shadow of a boulder to our left darkened the sky. When we had passed it, the darkness remained and crystals of fine-textured snow stung our faces and hands.

Within a few moments, we were heading downward once more and the snowfall became a blinding blizzard. The wind screamed in our ears and the wagon rattled and skidded. I leveled us quickly. There were drifts all about by then and the road was white. Our breath fumed and ice glistened on trees and rocks.

Motion and temporary bafflement of the senses. That was what it took. . . .

We raced on, and the wind slammed and bit and cried out. Drifts began to cover the road.

We rounded a bend and emerged from the storm. The world was still a glacéed-over thing and an occasional flake flitted by, but the sun pulled free of the clouds, pouring light upon the land, and we headed downward once more. . . .

. . . Passing through a fog and emerging in a barren, though snowless waste of rock and pitted land. . . .

. . . We bore to the right, regained the sun, followed a twisted course on a level plain, winding among tall, featureless strands of blue-gray stone. . . .

. . . Where far off to our right the black road paced us.

Waves of heat washed over us and the land steamed. Bubbles popped in boiling stews that filled the craters, adding their fumes to the dank air. Shallow puddles lay like a handful of old, bronze coins.

The horses raced, half-maddened now, as geysers began to erupt along the trail. Scalding waters spewed across the roadway, narrowly missing us, running in steaming, slick sheets. The sky was brass and the sun was a mushy apple. The wind was a panting dog with bad breath.

The ground trembled, and far off to our left a mountain blew its top toward the heavens and hurled fires after it. An ear-splitting crash temporarily deafened us and concussion waves kept beating against our bodies. The wagon swayed and shimmied.

The ground continued to shake and the winds slammed us with near-hurricane force as we rushed toward a row of black-topped hills. We left what there was of a roadway when it turned in the wrong direction and headed, bumping and shuddering, across the plain itself. The hills continued to grow, dancing in the troubled air.

I turned when I felt Ganelon's hand on my arm. He was shouting something, but I could not hear him. Then he pointed back and I followed his gesture. I saw nothing that I had not expected to see. The air was turbulent, filled with dust, debris, ashes. I shrugged and returned my attention to the hills.

A greater darkness occurred at the base of the nearest hill. I made for it.

It grew before me as the ground slanted downward once more, an enormous cavern mouth, curtained by a steady fall of dust and gravel.

I cracked the whip in the air and we raced across the final five or six hundred yards and plunged into it.

I began slowing the horses immediately, letting them relax into a walk.

We continued to move downward, turned a corner, and came into a wide, high grotto. Light leaked down from holes high above, dappling stalactites and falling upon quivering green pools. The ground continued to shake, and my hearing took a turn for the better as I saw a massive stalagmite crumble and heard the faint tinkle of its fall.

We crossed a black-bottomed chasm on a bridge that might have been limestone, which shattered behind us and vanished.

Bits of rock rained down from overhead and sometimes large stones fell. Patches of green and red fungus glowed in corners and cracks, streaks of minerals sparkled and bent, large crystals and flat flowers of pale stone added to the moist, eerie beauty of the place. We wheeled through caverns like chains of bubbles and coursed a white-chested torrent until it vanished into a black hole.

A long, corkscrew gallery took us upward once more, and I heard Ganelon's voice, faint and echoing, "I thought that I glimpsed movement—that might be a rider—at the crest of the mountain—just for an instant—back there."

We moved into a slightly brighter chamber.

"If it was Benedict, he's got a hard act to follow," I shouted, and there came the tremors and muffled crashings as more things collapsed behind us.

We proceeded onward and upward, until finally openings began to occur overhead, giving upon patches of clear blue sky. The hoof clicks and the sounds of the wagon gradually assumed a normal volume and their echoes came to us also. The tremors ceased, small birds darted above us, and the light increased in intensity.

Then another twisting of the way, and our exit lay before us, a wide, low opening onto day. We had to duck our heads as we passed beneath the jagged lintel.

We bounced up and over a jutting lip of moss-covered stone, then looked upon a bed of gravel that lay like a scythed track upon the hillside, passing among gigantic trees, vanishing within them, below. I made a clicking noise with my tongue, encouraging the horses on their way.

"They are very tired now," Ganelon remarked.

"I know. Soon they will get to rest, one way or another."

The gravel crunched beneath our wheels. The smell of the trees was good.

"Have you noticed it? Down there, off to the right?"

"What . . . ?" I began, turning my head. Then, "Oh," I finished.

The infernal black road was with us still, perhaps a mile distant.

"How many shadows does it cut across?" I mused.

"All of them, it would seem," Ganelon suggested.

I shook my head slowly.

"I hope not," I said.

We proceeded downward, beneath a blue sky and a golden sun westering in a normal way.

"I was almost afraid to come out of that cave," Ganelon said after a time. "No telling what would be on this side."

"The horses couldn't take much more. I had to let up. If that was Benedict we saw, his horse had better be in very good condition. He was pushing it hard. Then to have it face all that. . . . I think he would fall back."

"Maybe it's used to it," Ganelon said, as we crunched around a bend to the right, losing sight of the cave mouth.

"There is always that possibility," I said, and I thought of Dara again, wondering what she was doing at that moment.

We wove our way steadily downward, shifting slowly and imperceptibly. Our trail kept drifting to the right, and I cursed when I realized we were nearing the black road.

"Damn! It's as persistent as an insurance salesman!" I said, feeling my anger turn to something like hatred. "When the time is right, I am going to destroy that thing!"

Ganelon did not reply. He was taking a long drink of water. He passed me the bottle and I did, too.

At length, we achieved level terrain, and the trail continued to twist and curve at the least excuse. It allowed the horses to take it easy and it would slow a mounted pursuer.

About an hour later, I began to feel comfortable and we stopped to eat. We had just about finished our meal when Ganelon—who had not removed his gaze from the hillside—stood and shaded his eyes.

"No," I said, leaping to my feet. "I don't believe it."

A lone rider had emerged from the mouth of the cave. I watched as he halted for a moment, then continued on down the trail.

"What do we do now?" Ganelon asked.

"Let's pick up our stuff and get moving again. We can at least delay the inevitable a little longer. I want more time to think."

We rolled once more, still moving at a moderate pace, though my mind was racing at full speed. There had to be a way to stop him. Preferably, without killing him.

But I couldn't think of any.

Except for the black road, which was edging nearer once more, we had come into a lovely afternoon in a beautiful place. It was a shame to dampen it with blood, particularly if it might be my blood. Even with his blade in his left hand, I was afraid to face him. Ganelon would be of no use to me. Benedict would barely notice him.

I shifted as we took another turning. Moments later, a faint smell of smoke came to my nostrils. I shifted slightly again.

"He's coming fast!" Ganelon announced. "I just saw—There's smoke! Flames! The woods are on fire!"

I laughed and looked back. Half the hillside swam under smoke and an orange thing raced through the green, its crackling just then reaching my ears. Of their own accord, the horses increased their pace.

"Corwin! Did you—?"

"Yes! If it were steeper and there were no trees, I'd have tried an avalanche."

The air was momentarily filled with birds. We drew nearer the black way. Firedrake tossed his head and whinnied. There were flecks of foam on his muzzle. He tried to bolt, then reared and pawed the air. Star made a frightened noise and pulled to the right. I fought a moment, regained control, decided to let them run a bit.

"He's still coming!" cried Ganelon.

I cursed and we ran. Eventually, our path brought us alongside the black road. We were on a long straightaway, and a glance back showed me that the whole hillside was ablaze, the trail running like a nasty scar down its middle. It was then that I saw the rider. He was almost halfway down and moving like something in the Kentucky Derby. God! What a horse that had to be! I wondered what shadow had borne him.

I drew on the reins, gently at first, then harder, until finally we began to slow. We were only a few hundred feet from the black road by then, and I had seen to it that there was a place not too far ahead where the gap narrowed to thirty or forty. I managed to rein in the horses when we reached it, and they stood there quivering. I handed the reins to Ganelon, drew Grayswandir, and stepped down to the road.

Why not? It was a good, clear, level area, and perhaps that black, blasted slice of land, contrasting with the colors of life and growth immediately beside it, appealed to some morbid instinct in me.

"What now?" Ganelon asked.

"We cannot shake him," I said, "and if he makes it through the fire he will be here in a few minutes. There is no sense to running any farther. I'll meet him here."

Ganelon twisted the reins around a side bar and reached for his blade.

"No," I said. "You cannot affect the outcome one way or the other. Here is what I want you to do: Take the wagon on up the road and wait there with it. If things are resolved to my satisfaction, we will be continuing on. If they are not, surrender immediately to Benedict. It is me that he wants, and he will be the only one left who can take you back to Avalon. He will do it, too. You will at least retire to your homeland that way."

He hesitated.

"Go on," I told him. "Do as I said."

He looked down at the ground. He unwound the reins. He looked at me.

"Good luck," he said, and he shook the horses forward.

I backed off the trail, moved to a position before a small stand of saplings, and waited. I kept Grayswandir in my hand, glanced once at the black road, then fixed my eyes on the trail.

Before long, he appeared up near the flame line, smoke and fire all about him, burning branches falling. It was Benedict all right, his face partly muffled, the stump of his right arm upraised to shield his eyes, coming like some ghastly escapee from hell. Bursting through a shower of sparks and cinders, he came into the clear and plunged on down the trail.

Soon, I could hear the hoofbeats. A gentlemanly thing to do would be to sheathe my blade while I waited. If I did that, though, I might not have a chance to draw it again.

I found myself wondering how Benedict would be wearing his blade and what sort it would be. Straight? Curved? Long? Short? He could use them all with equal facility. He had taught me how to fence. . . .

It might be smart as well as gentlemanly to sheathe Grayswandir. He might be willing to talk first—and this way I was asking for trouble. As the hoofbeats grew louder, though, I realized I was afraid to put it away.

I wiped my palm only once before he came into view. He had slowed for the turn, and he must have seen me at the same instant I saw him.

He rode straight toward me, slowing. But halting did not appear to be his immediate aim.

It was almost a mystical experience. I do not know how else to put it. My mind outran time as he neared, and it was as though I had an eternity to ponder the approach of this man who was my brother. His garments were filthy, his face blackened, the stump of his right arm raised, gesturing anywhere. The great beast that he rode was striped, black and red, with a wild red mane and tail. But it really was a horse, and its eyes rolled and there was foam at its mouth and its breathing was painful to hear. I saw then that he wore his blade slung across his back, for its haft protruded high above his right shoulder. Still slowing, eyes fixed upon me, he departed the road, bearing slightly toward my left, jerked the reins once and released them, keeping control of the horse with his knees. His left hand went up in a salute-like movement that passed above his head and seized the hilt of his weapon. It came free without a sound, describing a beautiful arc above him and coming to rest in a lethal position out from his left shoulder and slanting back, like a single wing of dull steel with a minuscule line of edge that gleamed like a filament of mirror. The picture he presented was burned into my mind with a kind of magnificence, a certain splendor that was strangely moving. The blade was a long, scythe-like affair that I had seen him use before. Only then we had stood as allies against a mutual foe I had begun to believe unbeatable. Benedict had proved otherwise that night. Now that I saw it raised against me I was overwhelmed with a sense of my own mortality, which I had never experienced before in this fashion. It was as though a layer had been stripped from the world and I had a sudden, full understanding of death itself.

The moment was gone. I backed into the grove. I had stood there so that I could take advantage of the trees. I dropped back about twelve feet among them and took two steps to my left. The horse reared at the last possible moment and snorted and whinnied, moist nostrils flaring. It turned aside, tearing up turf. Benedict's arm moved with near-invisible speed, like the tongue of a toad, and his blade passed through a sapling I'd guess at three inches in diameter. The tree continued to stand upright for a moment, then slowly toppled.

His boots struck the earth and he strode toward me. I had wanted the grove for this reason, also, to make him come to me in a place where a long blade would be hampered by branches and boles.

But as he advanced, he swung the weapon, almost casually, back and forth, and the trees fell about him as he passed. If only he were not so infernally competent. If only he were not Benedict. . . .

"Benedict," I said, in a normal voice, "she is an adult now, and she is capable of making up her own mind about things."

But he gave no sign of having heard me. He just kept coming, swinging that great blade from side to side. It made an almost ringing sound as it passed through the air, followed by a soft *thukk!* as it bit through another tree, slowing only slightly.

I raised Grayswandir to point at his breast.

"Come no farther, Benedict," I said. "I do not wish to fight with you."

He moved his blade into an attack position and said one word:

"Murderer!"

His hand twitched then and my blade was almost simultaneously beaten aside. I parried the ensuing thrust and he brushed my riposte aside and was at me again.

This time I did not even bother to riposte. I simply parried, retreated, and stepped behind a tree.

"I don't understand," I said, beating down his blade as it slid by the trunk and nearly skewered me. "I have not murdered anyone recently. Certainly not in Avalon."

Another *thukk!* and the tree was falling toward me. I got out of its way and retreated, parrying.

"Murderer," he said again.

"I don't know what you are talking about, Benedict."

"Liar!"

I stood my ground then and held it. Damn it! It was senseless to die for the wrong reason! I riposted as fast as I could, seeking openings everywhere. There were none.

"At least tell me!" I shouted. "Please!"

But he seemed to be finished with talking. He pressed forward and I had to fall back once more. It was like trying to fence with a glacier. I became convinced then that he was out of his mind, not that that helped me any. With anybody else, an insane madness would cause the loss of some control in a fight. But Benedict had hammered out his reflexes over the centuries, and I seriously believed that the removal of his cerebral cortex would not have altered his movements from their state of perfection.

He drove me steadily back, and I dodged among trees and he cut them down and kept coming. I made the mistake of attacking and barely stopped his counterthrusts inches from my breast. I fought down the first wave of panic that came to me when I saw that he was driving me back toward the edge of the grove. Soon he would have me in the open, with no trees to slow him.

My attention was focused on him so completely that I did not realize what was then to occur until it did.

With a mightly cry, Ganelon sprang from somewhere, wrapping his arms about Benedict and pinning his sword arm to his side.

Even had I really wanted to, though, I did not have the opportunity to kill him then. He was too fast, and Ganelon was not aware of the man's strength.

Benedict twisted to his right, interposing Ganelon between us, and at the same time brought the stump of his arm around like a club, striking Ganelon in the left temple. Then he pulled his left arm free, seized Ganelon by his belt, swept him off his feet, and threw him at me. As I stepped aside, he retrieved his blade from where it had fallen near his feet and came at me again. I barely had time to glance and see that Ganelon had landed in a heap some ten paces to my rear.

I parried and resumed my retreat. I only had one trick remaining, and it saddened me that if it failed Amber would be deprived of its rightful liege.

It is somewhat more difficult to fence with a good left-hander than a good right-hander, and this worked against me also. But I had to experiment a bit. There was something I had to learn, even if it meant taking a chance.

I took a long step back, moving momentarily out of range, then leaned forward and attacked. It was a very calculated thing, and very fast.

One unexpected result, which I am certain was at least partly luck, was that I got through, even though I missed my target. For an instant, Grayswandir rode high off one of his parries and nicked his left ear. This slowed him slightly for a few moments, but not enough to matter. If anything, it served to strengthen his defense. I continued to press my attack, but there was simply no getting through then. It was only a small cut, but the blood ran down to his ear lobe and spattered off, a few drops at a time. It could even be distracting, if I permitted myself to do more than take note of it.

Then I did what I feared, but had to try. I left him a small opening, just for a moment, knowing that he would come right through it toward my heart.

He did, and I parried it at the last instant. I do not like to think about how close he came that time.

Then I began to yield once more, giving ground, backing out of the grove. Parrying and retreating, I moved past the spot where Ganelon lay. I fell back another fifteen feet or so, fighting defensively, conservatively.

Then I gave Benedict another opening.

He drove in, as he had before, and I managed to stop him again. He pressed the attack even harder after that, pushing me back to the edge of the black road.

There, I stopped and held my ground, shifting my position to the spot I had chosen. I would have to hold him just a few moments longer, to set him up. . . .

They were very rough moments, but I fought furiously and readied myself.

Then I gave him the same opening again.

I knew he would come in the same as before, and my right leg was across and back behind my left, then straightening, as he did. I gave his blade but the barest beat to the side as I sprang backward onto the black road, immediately extending my arm full length to discourage a balaestra.

Then he did what I had hoped. He beat at my blade and advanced normally when I dropped it into quarte . . .

. . . causing him to step into the patch of black grasses over which I had leaped.

I dared not look down at first. I simply stood my ground and gave the flora a chance.

It only took a few moments. Benedict became aware of it the next time that he tried to move. I saw the puzzled expression flash across his face, then the strain. It had him, I knew.

I doubted, though, that it could hold him very long, so I moved immediately.

I danced to the right, out of range of his blade, rushed forward and sprang across the grasses, off the black road once again. He tried to turn, but they had twined themselves about his legs all the way up to his knees. He swayed for a moment, but retained his balance.

I passed behind him and to his right. One easy thrust and he was a dead man, but of course there was no reason to do it now.

He swung his arm back behind his neck and turned his head, pointing the blade at me. He began pulling his left leg free.

But I feinted toward his right, and when he moved to parry it I slapped him across the back of the neck with the flat of Grayswandir.

It stunned him, and I was able to move in and punch him in the kidney with my left hand. He bent slightly and I blocked his sword arm and struck him in the back of the neck again, this time with my fist, hard. He fell, unconscious, and I removed his blade from his hand and cast it aside. The blood from his left ear lobe trailed down his neck like some exotic earring.

I put Grayswandir aside, seized Benedict under the armpits, and dragged him back from the black road. The grasses resisted mightily, but I strained against them and finally had him free.

Ganelon had gotten to his feet by then. He limped up and stood beside me, looking down at Benedict.

"What a fellow he is," he said. "What a fellow he is. . . . What are we going to do with him?"

I picked him up in a fireman's carry and stood.

"Take him back toward the wagon right now," I said. "Will you bring the blades?"

"All right."

I headed up the road and Benedict remained unconscious—which was good, because I did not want to have to hit him again if I could help it. I deposited him at the base of a sturdy tree beside the road near the wagon.

I resheathed our blades when Ganelon came up, and set him to stripping ropes from several of the cases. While he did this, I searched Benedict and found what I was looking for.

I bound him to the tree then, while Ganelon fetched his horse. We tethered it to a nearby bush, upon which I also hung his blade.

Then I mounted to the driver's seat of the wagon and Ganelon came up alongside.

"Are you just going to leave him there?" he asked.

"For now," I said.

We moved on up the road. I did not look back, but Ganelon did.

"He hasn't moved yet," he reported. Then, "Nobody ever just took me and threw me like that. With one hand yet."

"That's why I told you to wait with the wagon, and not to fight with him if I lost."

"What is to become of him now?"

"I will see that he is taken care of, soon."

"He will be all right, though?"

I nodded.

"Good."

We continued on for perhaps two miles and I halted the horses. I climbed down.

"Don't be upset by anything that happens," I said. "I am going to make arrangements for Benedict now."

I moved off the road and stood in the shade, taking out the deck of Trumps Benedict had been carrying. I riffled through them, located Gérard, and removed him from the pack. The rest I returned to the silk-lined, wooden case, inlaid with bone, in which Benedict had carried them.

I held Gérard's Trump before me and regarded it.

After a time, it grew warm, real, seemed to stir. I felt Gérard's actual presence. He was in Amber. He was walking down a street that I recognized. He looks a lot like me, only larger, heavier. I saw that he still wore his beard.

He halted and stared.

"Corwin!"

"Yes, Gérard. You are looking well."

"Your eyes! You can see?"

"Yes, I can see again."

"Where are you?"

"Come to me now and I will show you."

His gaze tightened.

"I am not certain that I can do that, Corwin. I am very involved just now."

"It is Benedict," I said. "You are the only one I can trust to help him."

"Benedict? He is in trouble?"

"Yes."

"Then why does he not summon me himself?"

"He is unable to. He is restrained."

"Why? How?"

"It is too long and involved to go into now. Believe me, he needs your help, right away."

He raked his beard with his upper teeth.

"And you cannot handle it yourself?"

"Absolutely not."

"And you think I can?"

"I know you can."

He loosened his blade in its scabbard.

"I would not like to think this is some sort of trick, Corwin."

"I assure you it is not. With all the time I have had to think, I would have come up with something a little more subtle."

He sighed. Then he nodded.

"All right. I'm coming to you."

"Come ahead."

He stood for a moment, then took a step forward.

He stood beside me. He reached out and clasped my shoulder. He smiled.

"Corwin," he said. "I'm glad you've your eyes back."

I looked away.

"So am I. So am I."

"Who is that in the wagon?"

"A friend. His name is Ganelon."

"Where is Benedict? What is the problem?"

I gestured.

"Back there," I said. "About two miles down the road. He is bound to a tree. His horse is tethered near by."

"Then why are you here?"

"I am fleeing."

"From what?"

"Benedict. I'm the one who bound him."

He wrinkled his brow.

"I do not understand . . ."

I shook my head.

"There is a misunderstanding between us. I could not reason with him and we fought. I knocked him unconscious and I tied him up. I cannot free him, or he would attack me again. Neither can I leave him as he is. He may come to some harm before he can free himself. So I summoned you. Please go to him, release him, and see him home."

"What will you be doing the while?"

"Getting the hell out of here, losing myself in Shadow. You will be doing both of us a favor to keep him from trying to follow me again. I do not want to have to fight him a second time."

"I see. Now will you tell me what happened?"

"I am not certain. He called me a murderer. I give you my word I slew no one the whole time I was in Avalon. Please tell him I said that. I have no reason to lie to you, and I swear that it is true. There is another matter which may have disturbed him somewhat. If he mentions it, tell him that he will have to rely on Dara's explanation."

"And what is it?"

I shrugged.

"You will know if he mentions it. If he does not, forget it."

"Dara, you say?"

"Yes."

"Very well, I shall do as you have asked. . . . Now, will you tell me how you managed your escape from Amber?"

I smiled.

"Academic interest? Or do you feel you might have need of the route yourself one day?"

He chuckled.

"It strikes me as a handy piece of information to have."

"I regret, dear brother, that the world is not yet ready for this knowledge. If I had to tell anyone, I would tell you—but there is no way it could benefit you, whereas its secrecy may serve me in the future."

"In other words, you have a private way into and out of Amber. What are you planning, Corwin?"

"What do you think?"

"The answer is obvious. But my feelings on the matter are mixed."

"Care to tell me about them?"

He gestured toward a section of the black road that was visible from where we stood.

"That thing," he said. "It runs to the foot of Kolvir now. A variety of menaces travel it to attack Amber. We defend, we are always victorious. But the attacks grow stronger and they come more frequently. Now would not be a good time for you to move, Corwin."

"Or it might be the perfect time," I said.

"For you then, but not necessarily for Amber."

"How has Eric been handling the situation?"

"Adequately. As I said, we are always victorious."

"I do not mean the attacks. I mean the entire problem—its cause."

"I have traveled the black road myself, going a great distance along it."

"And?"

"I was unable to go the entire distance. You know how the shadows grow wilder and stranger the farther you get from Amber?"

"Yes."

". . . Until the mind itself is twisted and turned toward madness?"

"Yes."

". . . And somewhere beyond this lie the Courts of Chaos. The road goes on, Corwin. I am convinced that it runs the entire distance."

"Then it is as I feared," I said.

"That is why, whether I sympathize with you or not, I do not recommend the present time for your efforts. The security of Amber must come before all else."

"I see. Then there is nothing more to be said just now."

"And your plans?"

"Since you do not know what they are, it is meaningless to tell you that they are unchanged. But they are unchanged."

"I do not know whether to wish you luck, but I wish you well. I am glad that you have your sight back." He clasped my hand. "I had best get on to Benedict now. I take it he is not badly hurt?"

"Not by me. I only hit him a few times. Do not forget to give him my message."

"I won't."

"And take him back to Avalon."

"I will try."

"Then good-by for now, Gérard."

"Good-by, Corwin."

He turned then and walked on down the road. I watched until he was out of sight before I returned to the wagon. Then I replaced his Trump in the deck and continued on my way to Antwerp.

EIGHT

I stood on the hilltop and looked down at the house. There was shrubbery all about me, so I was not especially obtrusive.

I do not really know what I expected to see. A burned-out shell? A car in the driveway? A family scattered about the redwood patio furniture? Armed guards?

I saw that the roof could use some new slate, that the lawn had long ago returned to a natural condition. I was surprised that I could see only one broken window there in the rear.

So the place was supposed to look deserted. I wondered.

I spread my jacket on the ground and seated myself on it. I lit a cigarette. There were no other houses for quite a distance.

I had gotten close to seven hundred thousand dollars for the diamonds. It had taken me a week and a half to make the deal. From Antwerp we had traveled to Brussels, spending several evenings at a club on the Rue de Char et Pain before the man I wanted found me.

Arthur was quite puzzled by the arrangement. A slight, white-haired man with a neat mustache, ex-RAF officer, Oxonian, he had begun shaking his head after the first two minutes and kept interrupting me with questions about delivery. While he was no Sir Basil Zaharoff, he became genuinely concerned when a client's ideas sounded too half-baked. It troubled him if something went sour too soon after delivery. He seemed to think it reflected back on him in some way. For this reason, he was often more helpful than the others when it came to shipment. He was concerned about my plans for transportation because I did not seem to have any.

What one generally requires in an arrangement of this sort is an end-use certificate. What it is, basically, is a document affirming that country X has ordered the weapons in question. You need the thing in order to get an export permit from the manufacturer's country. This keeps them looking honest, even if the shipment should be reconsigned to country Y once it has crossed their border. The customary thing to do is to buy the assistance of an ambassadorial representative of country X—preferably one with relatives or friends connected with the Defense Department back home—in order to get the papers. They come high, and I believe Arthur had a list of all the going rates in his head.

"But how are you going to ship them?" he had kept asking. "How will you get them where you want them?"

"That," I said, "will be my problem. Let me worry about it."

But he kept shaking his head.

"It is no good trying to cut corners that way, Colonel," he said. (I had been a colonel to him since we had first met, some dozen years before. Why, I am not certain.) "No good at all. Try to save a few dollars that way and you might lose the whole shipment and wind up in real trouble. Now I can fix you up through one of these young African nations quite reasonably—"

"No. Just fix me up with the weapons."

During our talk, Ganelon just sat there drinking beer, as red-bearded and sinister-looking as ever, and nodding to everything that I said. As he spoke no English, he had no idea as to the state of negotiations. Nor, for that matter, did he really care. He followed my instructions, though, and spoke to me periodically in Thari and we would chat briefly in that language about nothing in particular. Sheer perversity. Poor old Arthur was a good linguist and he wanted to know the destination of the pieces. I could feel him straining to identify the language each time that we spoke. Finally, he began nodding as though he had.

After some more discussion, he stuck his neck out and said, "I read the newspapers. I am certain his crowd can afford the insurance."

That was almost worth the price of admission to me.

But, "No," I said. "Believe me, when I take possession of those automatic rifles, they are going to vanish off the face of the Earth."

"Neat trick, that," he said, "considering I don't even know where we will be picking them up yet."

"It does not matter."

"Confidence is a fine thing. Then there is foolhardiness. . . ." He shrugged. "Have it as you say then—your problem."

Then I told him about the ammo and he must have been convinced as to my mental deterioration. He just stared at me for a long while, not even shaking his head this time. It was a good ten minutes before I could even get him to look at the specifications. It was then that he began shaking his head and mumbling about silver bullets and inert primers.

The ultimate arbiter, cash, convinced him we would do it my way, however. There was no trouble on the rifles or the trucks, but persuading an arms factory to produce my ammo was going to be expensive, he told me. He was not even certain he could find one that would be willing. When I told him that the cost was no object, it seemed to upset him even more. If I could afford to indulge in weird, experimental ammo, an end-use certificate would not come to that much—

No. I told him no. My way, I reminded him.

He sighed and tugged at the fringe of his mustache. Then he nodded. Very well, we would do it my way.

He overcharged me, of course. Since I was rational in all other matters, the alternative to psychosis would be that I was party to an expensive boondoggle. While the ramifications must have intrigued him, he apparently decided not to look too far into such a sticky-seeming enterprise. He was willing to seize every opportunity I extended for dissociating himself from the project. Once he found the ammo people—a Swiss outfit as it turned out—he was quite willing to put me into contact with them and wash his hands of everything but the money.

Ganelon and I went to Switzerland on fake papers. He was a German and I was Portuguese. I did not especially care what my papers showed, so long as the forgery was of good quality, but I had settled on German as the best language for Ganelon to learn, since he had to learn one and German tourists have always seemed to be all over the place. He picked it up quite rapidly. I had told him to tell any real Germans and any Swiss who asked that he had been raised in Finland.

We spent three weeks in Switzerland before I was satisfied with the quality controls on my ammo. As I had suspected, the stuff was totally inert in this shadow. I had worked out the formula, though, which was all that really mattered at that point. The silver came high, of course. Perhaps I was being over-cautious. Still, there are some things about Amber that are best dispatched with that metal, and I could afford it. For that matter, what better bullet— short of gold—for a king? Should I wind up shooting Eric, there would be no *lèse-majesté* involved. Indulge me, brothers.

Then I left Ganelon to shift for himself for a time, since he had thrown himself into his tourist role in a true Stanislavskian fashion. I saw him off to Italy, camera about his neck and a faraway look in his eyes, and I flew back to the States.

Back? Yes. That run-down place on the hillside below me had been my home for the better part of a decade. I had been heading toward it when I was forced off the road and into the accident which led to everything which has since occurred.

I drew on my cigarette and regarded the place. It had not been run-down then. I had always kept it in good shape. The place had been completely paid for. Six rooms and an attached two-car garage. Around seven acres. The whole hillside, actually. I had lived there alone most of the time. I had liked it. I had spent much of my time in the den and in my workshop. I wondered whether the Mori woodcut still hung in my study. *Face to Face* it was called, and it depicted two warriors in mortal combat. It would be nice to have it back. It would be gone, though, I felt. Probably everything that had not been stolen had been sold for back taxes. I imagined that was what the State of New York would do. I was surprised that the house itself seemed not to have acquired new occupants. I kept watching, to make certain. Hell, I was in no hurry. There was no place else I had to be.

I had contacted Gérard shortly after my arrival in Belgium. I had decided against trying to talk with Benedict for the time being. I was afraid that he would simply try to attack me, one way or the other, if I did.

Gérard had studied me quite carefully. He was out somewhere in open country and he seemed to be alone.

"Corwin?" he had said, then, "Yes . . ."

"Right. What happened with Benedict?"

"I found him as you said he would be and I released him. He was set to pursue you once again, but I was able to persuade him that a considerable time had passed since I had seen you. Since you said you had left him unconscious, I figured that was the best line to take. Also, his horse was very tired. We went back to Avalon together. I remained with him through the funerals, then borrowed a horse. I am on my way back to Amber now."

"Funerals? What funerals?"

Again, that calculating look.

"You really do not know?" he said.

"If I knew, damn it, I would not ask!"

"His servants. They were murdered. He says you did it."

"No," I said. "No. That is ridiculous. Why should I want to murder his servants? I do not understand . . ."

"It was not long after his return that he went looking for them, as they were not on hand to welcome him. He found them murdered and you and your companion gone."

"Now I see how it looked," I said. "Where were the bodies?"

"Buried, but not too deeply, in the little wood behind the garden to the rear of the house."

Just so, just so. . . . Better not to mention I had known about the grave.

"But what possible reason does he think I could have for doing such a thing?" I protested.

"He is puzzled, Corwin. Very puzzled, now. He could not understand why you did not kill him when you had the chance, and why you sent for me when you could have just left him there."

"I see now why he kept calling me a murderer as we fought, but— Did you tell him what I said about not having slain anyone?"

"Yes. At first he shrugged it off as a self-serving statement. I told him you sounded sincere, and very puzzled yourself. I believe it bothered him a bit that you should be so insistent. He asked me several times whether I believed you."

"Do you?"

He dropped his eyes.

"Damn it, Corwin! What am I supposed to believe? I came into the middle of this. We have been apart for so long . . ."

He met my gaze.

"There is more to it," he said.

"What is that?"

"Why did you call me to help him? That was a complete deck you took. You could have called any of us."

"You must be joking," I said.

"No, I want an answer."

"Very well. You are the only other one I trust."

"Is that all?"

"No. Benedict does not want his whereabouts known back in Amber. You and Julian are the only two I know for certain to be aware of his location. I don't like Julian, I don't trust him. So I called you."

"How did you know that Julian and I knew about him?"

"He helped you both out when you ran into trouble on the black road awhile back, and he put you up while you recuperated. Dara told me about it."

"Dara? Who is this Dara anyway?"

"The orphaned daughter of a couple who once worked for Benedict," I said. "She was around when you and Julian were there."

"And you sent her a bracelet. You also mentioned her to me by the road, back when you summoned me."

"Correct. What is the matter?"

"Nothing. I do not really remember her, though. Tell me, why did you leave so suddenly? You have to admit, it seemed the act of a guilty man."

"Yes," I said, "I was guilty—but not of murder. I went to Avalon to obtain something that I wanted, I got it, and I cleared out. You saw that wagon, and you saw that I had a cargo in it. I got out before he returned to keep from answering questions Benedict might ask me about it. Hell! If I just wanted to run, I wouldn't go dragging a wagon along behind me! I'd have traveled on horseback, fast and light."

"What was in the wagon?"

"No," I said. "I did not want to tell Benedict and I do not want to tell you. Oh, he can find out, I suppose. But let him do it the hard way, if he must. It is immaterial, though. The fact I went there for something and really obtained it should be sufficient. It is not especially valuable there, but is in another place. Fair enough?"

"Yes," he said. "It does make a kind of sense."

"Then answer my question. Do you think I murdered them?"

"No," he said. "I believe you."

"What about Benedict, now? What does he think?"

"He would not attack you again without talking first. There is doubt in his mind, I know that."

"Good. That's something, anyway. Thank you, Gérard. I am going away now."

I moved to break the contact.

"Wait, Corwin! Wait!"

"What is it?"

"How did you cut the black road? You destroyed a section of it at the place you crossed over. How did you do it?"

"The Pattern," I said. "If you ever get in trouble with that thing, hit it with the Pattern. You know how you have to sometimes hold it in your mind if shadows begin to run away from you and things start going wild?"

"Yes. I tried that and it didn't work. All I got was a headache. It is not of Shadow."

"Yes and no," I said. "I know what it is. You did not try hard enough. I used the Pattern until my head felt as if it were being torn apart, until I was half blind from the pain and about ready to pass out. Then the road came apart about me instead. It was no fun, but it did work."

"I will remember," he said. "Are you going to talk to Benedict now?"

"No," I said. "He already has everything we've gone over. Now that he is cooling off, he will begin pushing the facts around some more. I would just as soon he do it on his own—and I do not want to risk another fight. When I close this time I will be silent for a long while. I will resist all efforts to communicate with me, also."

"What of Amber, Corwin? What of Amber?"

I dropped my eyes.

"Don't get in my way when I come back, Gérard. Believe me, it will be no contest."

"Corwin . . . Wait. I'd like to ask you to reconsider. Do not hit Amber now. She is weak in all the wrong ways."

"I am sorry, Gérard. But I am certain I have given the matter more thought during the past five years than all the rest of you put together."

"I am sorry, too, then."

"I guess I had better be going now."

He nodded.

"Good-by, Corwin."

"Good-by, Gérard."

After waiting several hours for the sun to disappear behind the hill, leaving the house in a premature twilight, I mashed a final cigarette, shook out my jacket and donned it, rose to my feet. There had been no signs of life about the place, no movement behind the dirty windows, the broken window. Slowly, I descended the hill.

Flora's place out in Westchester had been sold some years before, which came as no surprise to me. I had checked merely as a matter of curiosity, since I was back in town. Had even driven past the place once. There was no reason for her to remain on this shadow Earth. Her long wardenship having ended successfully, she was being rewarded in Amber the last time I had seen her. To have been so near for as long as I had without even realizing her presence was a thing I found somewhat galling.

I had debated contacting Random, decided against it. The only way he could possibly benefit me would be with information as to current affairs in Amber. While this would be nice to have, it was not absolutely essential. I was fairly certain that I could trust him. After all, he had been of some assistance to me in the past. Admitted, it was hardly altruism—but still, he had gone a bit further than he had had to. It was five years ago, though, and a lot had happened since. He was being tolerated around Amber again, and he had a wife now. He might be eager to gain a little standing. I just did not know. But weighing the possible benefits against the possible losses, I thought it better to wait and see him personally the next time I was in town.

I had kept my word and resisted all attempts to make contact with me. They had come almost daily during my first two weeks back on the shadow Earth. Several weeks had passed, though, and I had not been troubled since. Why should I give anyone a free shot at my thinking machinery? No thanks, brothers.

I advanced upon the rear of the house, sidled up to a window, wiped it with my elbow. I had been watching the place for three days, and it struck me as very unlikely that anyone was inside. Still . . .

I peered in.

It was a mess, of course, and a lot of my stuff was missing. But some of it was still there. I moved to my right and tried the door. Locked. I chuckled.

I walked around to the patio. Ninth brick in, fourth brick up. The key was still beneath it. I wiped it on my jacket as I walked back. I let myself in.

There was dust on everything, but it had been disturbed in some places. There were coffee containers, sandwich wrappers, and the remains of a petrified hamburger in the fireplace. A lot of weather had found its way down that chimney in my absence. I crossed over and closed the damper.

I saw that the front door had been broken about the lock. I tried it. It seemed to be nailed shut. There was an obscenity scrawled on the wall in the foyer. I walked on into the kitchen. It was a total mess. Anything that had survived plunder was on the floor. The stove and the refrigerator were gone, the floor scarred where they had been pushed along.

I backed away, went and checked my workshop. Yes, it had been stripped. Completely. Passing on, I was surprised to find my bed, still unmade, and two expensive chairs all intact in my bedroom.

My study was a more pleasant surprise. The big desk was covered with the litter and muss, but then it always had been. Lighting a cigarette, I went and sat behind it. I guess it was just too heavy and bulky for anyone to make off with. My books were all on their shelves. Nobody steals books but your friends. And there—

I could not believe it. I got to my feet again and crossed the room to stare at close range.

Yoshitoshi Mori's beautiful woodcut hung right where it had always been, clean, stark, elegant, violent. To think that no one had made off with one of my most prized possessions. . . .

Clean?

I scrutinized it. I ran my finger along the frame.

Too clean. It bore none of the dust and grit which covered everything else in the house.

I checked it for trip wires, found none, removed it from its hook, lowered it.

No, the wall was no lighter behind it. It matched the rest of the wall perfectly.

I put Mori's work on the window seat and returned to my desk. I was troubled, as someone doubtless intended me to be. Someone had obviously removed it and taken good care of it—a thing for which I was not ungrateful— and then only just recently restored it. It was as if my return had been anticipated.

Which should be adequate reason for immediate flight, I suppose. But that was silly. If it was part of some trap, it had already been sprung. I jerked the automatic from my jacket pocket and tucked it behind my belt. I had not even known that I would be coming back myself. It was just something I had decided to do since I had had some time on my hands. I was not even certain as to why I had wanted to see the place again.

So this was some sort of contingency arrangement. If I should come by the old homestead, it might be to obtain the only thing in the place worth having. So preserve it and display it so that I will have to take notice. All right, I had. I had not been attacked yet, so it did not seem a trap. What then?

A message. Some sort of a message.

What? How? And who?

The safest place in the house, had it remained unravaged, should still be the safe. It was not beyond any of my siblings' skill. I moved to the rear wall, pressed the panel loose, and swung it out. I spun the dial through its combination, stepped back, opened the door with my old swagger stick.

No explosion. Good. Not that I had expected any.

There had been nothing of any great value inside—a few hundred dollars in cash, some bonds, receipts, correspondence.

An envelope. A fresh, white envelope lay in plain sight. I did not remember it.

My name upon it, written in an elegant hand. Not with ballpoint either.

It contained a letter and a card.

Brother Corwin, the letter said, *If you are reading this, then we still think enough alike for me to be able to anticipate you somewhat. I thank you for the loan of the woodcut—one of two possible reasons, as I see it, for your returning to this squalid shadow. I am loathe to relinquish it, as our tastes are also somewhat akin and it has graced my chambers for several years now. There is something to the subject that strikes a familiar chord. Its return is to be taken as evidence of my good will and a bid for your attention. In that I must be honest with you if I am to stand a chance of convincing you of anything, I will not apologize for what has been done. My only regret, actually, is that I did not kill you when I should have. Vanity it was, that played me for a fool. While time may have healed your eyes, I doubt it will ever significantly alter our feelings for one another. Your letter—"I'll be back"—lies upon my writing table at this moment. Had I written it, I know that I would be back. Some things being equal between us, I anticipate your return, and not without somewhat of apprehension. Knowing you for no fool, I contemplate your arriving in force. And here is where past vanity is paid of present pride. I would have peace between us, Corwin, for the sake of the realm, not my own. Strong forces out of Shadow have come to beset Amber regularly, and I do not fully understand their nature. Against these forces, the most formidable in my memory ever to assail Amber, the family has united behind me. I would like to have your support in this struggle. Failing that, I request that you forbear invading me for a time. If you elect to assist, I will require no homage of you, simply acknowledgment of my leadership for the duration of the crisis. You will be accorded your normal honors. It is important that you contact me to see the truth of what I say. As I have failed to reach you by means of your Trump, I enclose my own for your use. While the possibility that I am lying to you is foremost in your mind, I give you my word that I am not. — Eric, Lord of Amber.*

I reread it and chuckled. What did he think curses were for, anyway?

No good, my brother. It was kind of you to think of me in your moment of need—and I believe you, never doubt it, for we are all of us honorable men—but our meeting will come according to my schedule, not yours. As for Amber, I am not unmindful of her needs, and I will deal with them in my own time and fashion. You make the mistake, Eric, of considering yourself necessary. The graveyards are filled with men who thought they could not be replaced. I will wait though, to tell you this, face to face.

I tucked his letter and the Trump in my jacket pocket. I killed my cigarette in the dirty ashtray on my desk. Then I fetched some linen from the bedroom to wrap my combatants. They would wait for me in a safer place, this time.

As I passed through the house once again, I wondered why I had come back, really. I thought of some of the people I had known when I had lived there, and wondered whether they ever thought of me, whether they wondered what had become of me. I would never know, of course.

Night had begun and the sky was clear and its first stars bright as I stepped outside and locked the door behind me. I went around to the side and returned the key to its place beneath the patio. Then I mounted the hill.

When I looked back from the top, the house seemed to have shrunken there in the darkness, to have become a piece of the desolation, like an empty beer can tossed beside the road. I crossed over and down, heading across a field toward the place where I had parked, wishing I had not looked back.

NINE

Ganelon and I departed Switzerland in a pair of trucks. We had driven them there from Belgium, and I had taken the rifles in mine. Figuring ten pounds per piece, the three hundred had come to around a ton and a half, which was not bad. After we took on the ammo, we still had plenty of room for fuel and other supplies. We had taken a short cut through Shadow, of course, to avoid the people who wait around borders to delay traffic. We departed in the same fashion, with me in the lead to open the way, so to speak.

I led us through a land of dark hills and narrow villages, where the only vehicles we passed were horsedrawn. When the sky grew bright lemon, the beasts of burden were striped and feathered. We drove for hours, finally encountering the black road, parallelling it for a time, then heading off in another direction. The skies went through a dozen shiftings, and the contours of the land melted and merged from hill to plain and back again. We crept along poor roads and skidded on flats as smooth and hard as glass. We edged our way across a mountain's face and skirted a wine-dark sea. We passed through storms and fogs.

It took me half a day to find them once again, or a shadow so close that it made no difference. Yes, those whom I had exploited once before. They were short fellows, very hairy, very dark, with long incisors and retractable claws. But they had trigger fingers, and they worshiped me. They were overjoyed at my return. It little mattered that five years earlier I had sent the cream of their manhood off to die in a strange land. The gods are not to be questioned, but loved, honored, and obeyed. They were quite disappointed that I only wanted a few hundred. I had to turn away thousands of volunteers. The morality of it did not especially trouble me this time. One way of looking at it might be that by employing this group I was seeing to it that the others had not died in vain. Of course I did not look at it that way, but I enjoy exercises in sophistry. I suppose I might also consider them mercenaries being paid in spiritual coin. What difference did it make whether they fought for money or for a belief? I was capable of supplying either one when I needed troops.

Actually, though, these would be pretty safe, being the only ones in the place with fire power. My ammo was still inert in their homeland, however, and it took several days of marching through Shadow to reach a land sufficiently like Amber for it to become functional. The only catch was that shadows follow a law of congruency of correspondences, so that the place actually was close to Amber. This kept me somewhat on edge throughout their training. It was unlikely that a brother would blunder through that shadow. Still, worse coincidences have occurred.

We drilled for close to three weeks before I decided we were ready. Then, on a bright, crisp morning, we broke camp and moved on into Shadow, the columns of troops following behind the trucks. The trucks would cease to function when we neared Amber—they were already giving us some trouble— but they might as well be used to haul the equipment as far along as possible.

This time, I intended to go over the top of Kolvir from the north, rather than essay its seaward face again. All of the men had an understanding of the layout, and the disposition of the rifle squads had already been determined and run through in practice.

We halted for lunch, ate well, and continued on, the shadows slowly slipping away about us. The sky became a dark but brilliant blue, the sky of Amber. The earth was black among rocks and the bright green of the grass. The trees and the shrubs had a moist lucency to their foliage. The air was sweet and clean.

By nightfall, we were passing among the massive trees at the fringes of Arden. We bivouacked there, posting a very heavy guard. Ganelon, now wearing khakis and a beret, sat with me long into the night, going over the maps I had drawn. We still had about forty miles to go before we hit the mountains.

The trucks gave out the following afternoon. They went through several transformations, stalled repeatedly, and finally refused to start at all. We pushed them into a ravine and cut branches to cover them over. We distributed the ammo and the rest of the rations and continued on.

We departed the hard, dirt roadway after that and worked our way through the woods themselves. As I still knew them well, it was less of a problem than it might have been. It slowed us, naturally, but lessened chances of surprise by one of Julian's patrols. The trees were quite large, as we were well into Arden proper, and the topography sprang back into mind as we moved.

We encountered nothing more menacing than foxes, deer, rabbits, and squirrels that day. The smells of the place and its green, gold, and brown brought back thoughts of happier times. Near sunset, I scaled a forest giant and was able to make out the range that held Kolvir. A storm was playing about its peaks just then and its clouds hid their highest portions.

The following noon we ran into one of Julian's patrols. I do not really know who surprised whom, or who was more surprised. The firing broke out almost immediately. I shouted myself hoarse stopping it, as everyone seemed anxious to try out his weapon on a live target. It was a small group—a dozen and a half men—and we got all of them. We suffered only one minor casualty, from one of our men wounding another—or perhaps the man had wounded himself. I never got the story straight. We moved on quickly then, because we had made a hell of a racket and I had no idea as to the disposition of other forces in the vicinity.

We gained considerable distance and altitude by nightfall, and the mountains were in sight whenever there was a clear line of vision. The storm clouds still clung to their peaks. My troops were excited over the day's slaughter and took a long while getting to sleep that night.

The next day we reached the foothills, successfully avoiding two patrols. I pushed us on and up well after nightfall, to reach a place of cover I had had in mind. We bedded down at an altitude perhaps half a mile higher than we had the previous night. We were under the cloud cover, but there was no rainfall, despite a constant atmospheric tension of the sort that precedes a storm. I did not sleep well that night. I dreamed of the burning cat head, and of Lorraine.

In the morning, we moved out under gray skies, and I pushed the troops remorselessly, heading steadily upward. We heard the sounds of distant thunder, and the air was alive and electric.

About mid-morning, as I led our file up a twisted, rocky route, I heard a shout from behind me, followed by several bursts of gunfire. I headed back immediately.

A small knot of men, Ganelon among them, stood staring down at something, talking in low voices. I pushed my way through.

I could not believe it. Never in my memory had one been seen this near to Amber. Perhaps twelve feet in length, bearing that terrible parody of a human face on the shoulders of a lion, eagle-like wings folded above its now bloody sides, a still-twitching tail like that of a scorpion, I had glimpsed the manticora once in isles far to the south, a frightful beast that had always held a spot near the top on my unclean list.

"It tore Rall in half, it tore Rall in half," one of the men kept repeating.

About twenty paces away, I saw what was left of Rall. We covered him over with a tarp and weighted it down with rocks. That was really about all that we could do. If nothing else, it served to restore a quality of wariness that had seemed to vanish after the previous day's easy victory. The men were silent and cautious as we continued on our way.

"Quite a thing, that," Ganelon said. "Has it the intelligence of a man?"

"I do not really know."

"I've a funny, nervous feeling, Corwin. As though something terrible is about to happen. I don't know how else to put it."

"I know."

"You feel it, too?"

"Yes."

He nodded.

"Maybe it's the weather," I said.

He nodded again, more slowly.

The sky continued to darken as we climbed, and the thunder never ceased. Flashes of heat lightning occurred in the west, and the winds grew stronger. Looking up, I could see great masses of clouds about the higher peaks. Black, bird-like shapes were constantly outlined against them.

We encountered another manticora later, but we dispatched it with no damage to ourselves. About an hour later, we were attacked by a flock of large, razor-beaked birds, the like of which I had never seen before. We succeeded in driving them off, but this, too, disturbed me.

We kept climbing, wondering when the storm was going to begin. The winds increased in velocity.

It grew quite dark, though I knew the sun had not yet set. The air took on a misty, hazy quality as we neared the cloud clusters. A feeling of dampness worked its way into everything. The rocks were more slippery. I was tempted to call a halt, but we were still a good distance from Kolvir and I did not want to strain the rations situation, which I had calculated quite carefully.

We achieved perhaps another four miles and several thousand feet in elevation before we were forced to stop. It was pitch black by then, the only illumination at all coming from the intermittent flashes of lightning. We camped in a large circle on a hard, bare slope, sentries all about the perimeter. The thunder came like long flourishes of martial music. The temperature plummeted. Even had I permitted fires, there was nothing burnable about. We settled down for a cold, clammy, dark time.

The manticoras attacked several hours later, sudden and silent. Seven men died and we killed sixteen of the beasts. I have no idea how many others fled. I cursed Eric as I bound my wounds and wondered from what shadow he had drawn the things.

During what passed for morning, we advanced perhaps five miles toward Kolvir before bearing off to the west. It was one of three possible routes we could follow, and I had always considered it the best for a possible attack. The birds came to plague us again, several times, with greater numbers and persistency. Shooting a few of them, though, was all it took to route the entire flock.

Finally, we rounded the base of a huge escarpment, our way taking us outward and upward through thunder and mist, until we were afforded a sudden vista, sweeping down and out for dozens of miles across the Valley of Garnath that lay to our right.

I called a halt and moved forward to observe.

When last I had seen that once lovely valley, it had been a twisted wilderness. Now, things were even worse. The black road cut through it, running to the base of Kolvir itself, where it halted. A battle was raging within the valley. Mounted forces swirled together, engaged, wheeled away. Lines of foot soldiers advanced, met, fell back. The lightning kept flashing and striking among them. The dark birds swept about them like ashes on the wind.

The dampness lay like a cold blanket. The echoes of the thunder bounced about the peaks. I stared, puzzling, at the conflict far below.

The distance was too great for me to determine the combatants. At first it occurred to me that someone else might be about the same thing I was—that perhaps Bleys had survived and returned with a new army.

But no. These were coming in from the west, along the black road. And I saw now that the birds accompanied them, and bounding forms that were neither horses nor men. The manticoras, perhaps.

The lightnings fell upon them as they came, scattering, burning, blasting. As I realized that they never struck near the defenders, I recalled that Eric had apparently gained some measure of control over that device known as the Jewel of Judgment, with which Dad had exercised his will upon the weather about Amber. Eric had employed it against us with considerable effect five years earlier.

So the forces from Shadow about which I had been hearing reports, were even stronger than I had thought. I had envisioned harassment, but not a pitched battle at the foot of Kolvir. I looked down at the movements within the blackness. The road seemed almost to writhe from the activity about it.

Ganelon came and stood beside me. He was silent for a long while.

I did not want him to ask me, but I felt powerless to say it except as answer to a question.

"What now, Corwin?"

"We must increase the pace," I said. "I want to be in Amber tonight."

We moved again. The going was better for a time, and that helped. The storm without rain continued, its lightnings and thunders increasing in brilliance and volume. We moved through a constant twilight.

When we came to a safe-seeming place later that afternoon—a place within five miles of the northern skirts of Amber—I halted us again, for rest and a final meal. We had to scream at one another in order to be heard, so I could not address the men. I simply passed the word along concerning our proximity and the need for readiness.

I took my rations with me and scouted on ahead while the others rested. About a mile farther along, I mounted a steep upturn, pausing when I achieved its crest. There was a battle of some sort in progress on the slopes ahead.

I kept out of sight and observed. A force out of Amber was engaged with a larger body of attackers which must have either preceded us up the slope or arrived by different means. I suspected the latter, inasmuch as we had seen no signs of recent passage. The engagement explained our own good fortune in not encountering defensive patrols on the way up.

I moved nearer. While the attackers could have come up by one of the two other routes, I saw additional evidence that this need not have been the case. They were still arriving, and it was a most fearsome sight, for they were airborne.

They swept in from the west like great gusts of windblown leaves. The aerial movement I had witnessed from the distance had been of greater variety than the belligerent bird life. The attackers came in on winged, two-legged, dragon-like creatures, the closest parallel with which I was familiar being a heraldic beast, the wyvern. I had never seen a non-decorative wyvern before, but then I had never felt any great desire to go looking for one.

Among the defenders were numerous archers, who took a deadly toll of these in flight. Sheets of pure hell erupted among them also, as the lightnings flashed and flared, sending them like cinders toward the ground. But still they came on, landing, so that both man and beast could attack those entrenched. I looked for and located the pulsating glow given off by the Jewel of Judgment when it has been tuned to operate. It came from the midst of the largest body of defenders, dug in near the base of a high cliff.

I stared and studied, focusing on the wearer of the gem. Yes, there could be no doubt. It was Eric.

On my belly now, I crawled even farther. I saw the leader of the nearest party of defenders behead a landing wyvern with a single sword stroke. With his left hand, he seized the harness of its rider and hurled him over thirty feet, out beyond the lip-like brink of the place. As he turned then to shout an order, I saw that it was Gérard. He appeared to be leading a flanking assault on a mass of the attackers who were assailing the forces at the foot of the cliff. On its far side, a similar body of troops was doing likewise. Another of my brothers?

I wondered how long the battle had been in progress, both in the valley and here above. Quite a while, I guessed, considering the duration of the unnatural storm.

I moved to the right, turning my attention to the west. The battle in the valley continued unabated. From this distance, it was impossible to tell who was who, let alone who was winning. I could see, though, that no new forces were arriving from out of the west to supplement the attackers.

I was perplexed as to my own best course of action. Clearly, I could not attack Eric when he was engaged in anything this crucial to the defense of Amber herself. Waiting to pick up the pieces afterward might be wisest. However, I could already feel the rat teeth of doubt at work on that idea.

Even without reinforcements for the attackers, the outcome of the encounter was by no means clear-cut. The invaders were strong, numerous. I had no idea as to what Eric might have in reserve. At that moment, it was impossible for me to gauge whether war bonds for Amber would be a good investment.

If Eric lost, it would then be necessary for me to take on the invaders myself, after much of Amber's manpower had been wasted.

If I were to move in now with automatic weapons, there was little doubt in my mind that we would crush the wyvern-riders quickly. For that matter, one or more of my brothers had to be down in the valley. A gateway for some of my troops could be set up by means of the Trumps. It would surprise whatever was down there for Amber suddenly to come up with riflemen.

I returned my attention to the conflict nearer at hand. No, it was not going well. I speculated as to the results of my intervening. Eric would certainly be in no position to turn on me. Besides any sympathy that might be mine for what he had put me through, I would be responsible for pulling his nuts out of the fire. While he would be grateful for the relief, he would not be too happy over the general sentiment this would arouse. No, indeed. I would be back in Amber with a very deadly personal bodyguard and a lot of good will going for me. An intriguing thought. It would provide a far smoother route to my objective than the brutal frontal assault culminating in regicide that I had had in mind.

Yes.

I felt myself smiling. I was about to become a hero.

I must grant myself a small measure of grace, however. Given the choice only between Amber with Eric on the throne and Amber fallen, there is no question but that my decision would have been the same, to attack. Things were not going well enough to be certain, and while it would work to my advantage to save the day, my own advantage was not, ultimately, essential. I could not hate thee, Eric, so much, loved I not Amber more.

I withdrew and hurried back down the slope, flashes of lightning hurling my shadow in every which direction.

I halted at the periphery of my encampment. At its farther edge, Ganelon stood in shouting converse with a lone horseman, and I recognized the horse.

I advanced, and at a sign from its rider the horse moved forward, winding its way among the troops, heading in my direction. Ganelon shook his head and followed.

The rider was Dara. As soon as she was within earshot, I shouted at her.

"What the hell are you doing here?"

She dismounted, smiling, and stood before me.

"I wanted to come to Amber," she said. "So I did."

"How did you get here?"

"I followed Grandpa," she said. "It is easier to follow someone through Shadow, I discovered, than to do it yourself."

"Benedict is here?"

She nodded.

"Down below. He is directing the forces in the valley. Julian is there, too."

Ganelon came up and stood near.

"She said that she followed us up here," he shouted. "She has been behind us for a couple days."

"Is that true?" I asked.

She nodded again, still smiling.

"It was not hard to do."

"But why did you do it?"

"To get into Amber, of course! I want to walk the Pattern! That is where you are going, isn't it?"

"Of course it is. But there happens to be a war in the way!"

"What are you going to do about it?"

"Win it, of course!"

"Good. I'll wait."

I cursed for a few moments to give myself time to think, then, "Where were you when Benedict returned?" I asked.

The smile went away.

"I do not know," she said. "I was out riding after you left, and I stayed away the entire day. I wanted to be alone to think. When I returned in the evening, he was not there. I rode again the following day. I traveled quite a distance, and when it grew dark I decided to camp out. I do that often. The next afternoon, as I was returning home, I came to the top of a hill and saw him passing below, heading to the east. I decided to follow him. The way led through Shadow, I understand that now—and you were right about it being easier to follow. I do not know how long it took. Time got all mixed up. He came here, and I recognized it from the picture on one of the cards. He met with Julian in a wood to the north, and they returned together to that battle below." She gestured toward the valley. "I remained in the forest for several days, not knowing what to do. I was afraid of getting lost if I tried to backtrack. Then I saw your force climbing the mountains. I saw you and I saw Ganelon at their head. I knew that Amber lay that way, and I followed. I waited until now to approach, because I wanted you to be too near to Amber to send me back when I did."

"I don't believe you are telling me the whole truth," I said, "but I haven't the time to care. We are going ahead now, and there will be fighting. The safest thing for you will be to remain here. I will assign you a couple of bodyguards."

"I do not want them!"

"I don't care what you want. You are going to have them. When the fighting is over I will send for you."

I turned then and selected two men at random, ordering them to remain behind and guard her. They did not seem overjoyed at the prospect.

"What are those weapons your men bear?" Dara asked.

"Later," I said. "I'm busy."

I relayed a sketchy briefing and ordered my squads.

"You seem to have a very small number of men," she said.

"They are sufficient," I replied. "I will see you later."

I left her there with her guards.

We moved back along the route I had taken. The thunder ceased as we advanced, and the silence became less a thing of relief than of suspense to me. The twilight resettled about us, and I perspired within the damp blanket of the air.

I called a halt before we reached the first point from which I had observed the action. I returned to it then, accompanied by Ganelon.

The wyvern-riders were all over the place and their beasts fought along with them. They were pressing the defenders back against the cliff face. I sought for but could not locate Eric or the glow of his jewel.

"Which ones are the enemy?" Ganelon asked me.

"The beast-riders."

They were all of them landing now that heaven's artillery had let up. As soon as they struck the solid surface, they charged forward. I searched among the defenders, but Gérard was no longer in sight.

"Bring up the troops," I said, raising my rifle. "Tell them to get the beasts and the riders both."

Ganelon withdrew, and I took aim at a descending wyvern, fired, and watched its swoop turn into a sudden flurry of pinions. It struck against the slope and began to flop about. I fired again.

The beast began to burn as it died. Soon I had three bonfires going. I crawled up to my second previous position. Secure, I took aim and fired once more.

I got another, but by then some of them were turning in my direction. I fired the rest of my ammo and hastened to reload. Several of them had begun moving toward me by then. They were quite fast.

I managed to stop them and was reloading again when the first rifle squad arrived. We put down a heavier fire, and began to advance as the others came up.

It was all over within ten minutes. Within the first five they had apparently realized that they hadn't a chance, and they began to flee back toward the ledge, launching themselves into space, becoming airborne again. We shot them down as they ran, and burning flesh and smoldering bones lay everywhere about us.

The moist rock rose sheer to our left, its summit lost in the clouds, so that it seemed as if it might tower endlessly above us. The winds still whipped the smoke and the mists, and the rocks were smeared and splotched with blood. As we had advanced, firing, the forces of Amber quickly realized that we represented assistance and began to push forward from their position at the base of the cliff. I saw that they were being led by my brother Caine. For a moment our eyes locked together across the distance, then he plunged ahead into the fray.

Scattered groups of Amberites united into a second force as the attackers fell back. Actually, they limited our field of fire when they attacked the far flank of the wizened beast-men and their wyverns, but I had no way of getting word of this to them. We drew closer, and our firing was accurate.

A small knot of men remained at the base of the cliff. I had a feeling they were guarding Eric, and that he had possibly been wounded, since the storm effects had ceased abruptly. I worked my own way off in that direction.

The firing was already beginning to die down as I drew near the group, and I was hardly aware of what happened next until it was too late.

Something big came rushing up from behind and was by me in an instant. I hit the ground and rolled, bringing my rifle to bear automatically. My finger did not tighten on the trigger, however. It was Dara, who had just plunged past me on horseback. She turned and laughed as I screamed at her.

"Get back down there! Damn you! You'll be killed!"

"I'll see you in Amber!" she cried, and she shot on across the grisly rock and made it up the trail that lay beyond.

I was furious. But there was nothing I could do about it just then. Snarling, I got back to my feet and continued on.

As I advanced upon the group, I heard my name spoken several times. Heads turned in my direction. People moved aside to let me pass. I recognized many of them, but I paid them no heed.

I think that I saw Gérard at about the same time that he saw me. He had been kneeling in their midst, and he rose to his feet and waited. His face was expressionless.

As I drew nearer, I saw that it was as I had suspected. He had been kneeling to tend an injured man who rested upon the ground. It was Eric.

I nodded to Gérard as I came up beside him, and I looked down at Eric. My feelings were quite mixed. The blood from his several chest wounds was very bright and there was a lot of it. The Jewel of Judgment, which still hung on a chain about his neck, was covered with it. Eerily, it continued its faint, glowing pulsation, heart-like beneath the gore. Eric's eyes were closed, his head resting upon a rolled-up cloak. His breathing was labored.

I knelt, unable to take my eyes off that ashen face. I tried to push my hate aside just a little, since he was obviously dying, so that I might have a better chance to understand this man who was my brother for the moments that remained to him. I found that I could muster up something of sympathy by considering all that he was losing along with his life and wondering whether it would have been me lying there if I had come out on top five years earlier. I tried to think of something in his favor, and all I could come up with were the epitaph-like words, *He died fighting for Amber*. That was something, though. The phrase kept running through my mind.

His eyes tightened, flickered, opened. His face remained without expression as his eyes focused on mine. I wondered whether he even recognized me.

But he said my name, and then, "I knew that it would be you." He paused for a couple of breaths and went on, "They saved you some trouble, didn't they?"

I did not reply. He already knew the answer.

"Your turn will come one day," he continued. "Then we will be peers." He chuckled and realized too late that he should not have. He went into an unpleasant spasm of moist coughing. When it passed, he glared at me.

"I could feel your curse," he said. "All around me. The whole time. You didn't even have to die to make it stick."

Then, as if reading my thoughts, he smiled faintly and said, "No, I'm not going to give you my death curse. I've reserved that for the enemies of Amber—out there." He gestured with his eyes. He pronounced it then, in a whisper, and I shuddered to overhear it.

He returned his gaze to my face and stared for a moment. Then he plucked at the chain about his neck.

"The Jewel . . ." he said. "You take it with you to the center of the Pattern. Hold it up. Very close—to an eye. Stare into it—and consider it a place. Try to project yourself—inside. You don't go.. But there is— experience. . . . Afterward, you know how to use it. . . ."

"How—?" I began, but stopped. He had already told me how to attune to it. Why ask him to waste his breath on how he had figured it out?

But he caught it and managed, "Dworkin's notes . . . under fireplace . . . my—"

Then he was taken with another coughing spell and the blood came out of his nose and his mouth. He sucked in a deep breath and heaved himself into a sitting position, eyes rolling wildly.

"Acquit yourself as well as I have—bastard!" he said, then fell into my arms and heaved out his final, bloody breath.

I held him for several moments, then lowered him into his former position. His eyes were still open, and I reached out and closed them. Almost automatically, I put his hands together atop the now lifeless gem. I had no stomach to take it from him at that moment. I stood then, removed my cloak, and covered him with it.

Turning, I saw that all of them were staring at me. Familiar faces, many of them. Some strange ones mixed in. So many who had been there that night when I had come to dinner in chains. . . .

No. It was not the time to think of that. I pushed it from my mind. The shooting had stopped, and Ganelon was calling the troops back and ordering some sort of formation.

I walked forward.

I passed among the Amberites. I passed among the dead. I walked by my own troops and moved to the edge of the cliff.

In the valley below me, the fighting continued, the cavalry flowing like turbulent waters, merging, eddying, receding, the infantry still swarming like insects.

I drew forth the cards I had taken from Benedict. I removed his own from the deck. It shimmered before me, and after a time there was contact.

He was mounted on the same red and black horse on which he had pursued me. He was in motion and there was fighting all about him. Seeing that he confronted another horseman, I remained still. He spoke but a single word.

"Bide," he said.

He dispatched his opponent with two quick movements of his blade. Then he wheeled his mount and began to withdraw from the fray. I saw that his horse's reins had been lengthened and were looped and tied loosely about the remainder of his right arm. It took him over ten minutes to remove himself to a place of relative calm. When he had, he regarded me, and I could tell that he was also studying the prospect that lay at my back.

"Yes, I am on the heights," I told him. "We have won. Eric died in the battle."

He continued to stare, waiting for me to go on. His face betrayed no emotion.

"We won because I brought riflemen," I said. "I finally found an explosive agent that functions here."

His eyes narrowed and he nodded. I felt that he realized immediately what the stuff was and where it had come from.

"While there are many things I want to discuss with you," I continued, "I want to take care of the enemy first. If you will hold the contact, I will sent you several hundred riflemen."

He smiled.

"Hurry," he said.

I shouted for Ganelon, and he answered me from only a few paces away. I told him to line the troops up, single file. He nodded and went off, shouting orders.

As we waited, I said, "Benedict, Dara is here. She was able to follow you through Shadow when you rode in from Avalon. I want—"

He bared his teeth and shouted: "Who the hell is this Dara you keep talking about? I never heard of her till you came along! Please tell me! I would really like to know!"

I smiled faintly.

"It's no good," I said, shaking my head. "I know all about her, though I have told no one else that you've a great granddaughter."

His lips parted involuntarily and his eyes were suddenly wide.

"Corwin," he said, "you are either mad or deceived. I've no such descendant that I know of. As for anyone following me here through Shadow, I came in on Julian's Trump."

Of course. My only excuse for not tripping her up immediately was my preoccupation with the conflict. Benedict would have been notified of the battle by means of the Trumps. Why should he waste time traveling when an instant means of transport was at hand?

"Damn!" I said. "She is in Amber by now! Listen, Benedict! I am going to get Gérard or Caine over here to handle the transfer of the troops to you. Ganelon will come through, also. Give them their orders through him."

I looked around, saw Gérard talking with several of the nobles. I shouted for him with a desperate urgency. His head turned quickly. Then he began running in my direction.

"Corwin! What is it?" Benedict was shouting.

"I don't know! But something is very wrong!"

I thrust the Trump at Gérard as he came up.

"See that the troops get through to Benedict!" I said. "Is Random in the palace?"

"Yes."

"Free or confined?"

"Free—more or less. There will be some guards about. Eric still doesn't—didn't trust him."

I turned.

"Ganelon," I called out. "Do what Gérard here tells you. He is going to send you to Benedict—down there." I gestured. "See that the men follow Benedict's orders. I have to get into Amber now."

"All right," he called back.

Gérard headed in his direction, and I fanned the Trumps once more. I located Random's and began to concentrate. At that moment, it finally began to rain.

I made contact almost immediately.

"Hello, Random," I said, as soon as his image came to life. "Remember me?"

"Where are you?" he asked.

"In the mountains," I told him. "We just won this part of the battle, and I am sending Benedict the help he needs to clean up in the valley. Now, though, I need your help. Bring me across."

"I don't know, Corwin. Eric—"

"Eric is dead."

"Then who is in charge?"

"Who do you think? Bring me across!"

He nodded quickly and extended his hand. I reached out and clasped it. I stepped forward. I stood beside him on a balcony overlooking one of the courtyards. The railing was of white marble, and not much was blooming down below. We were two stories up.

I swayed and he seized my arm.

"You're hurt!" he said.

I shook my head, only just then realizing how tired I was. I had not slept very much the past few nights. That, and everything else . . .

"No," I said, glancing down at the gory mess that was my shirt front. "Just tired. The blood is Eric's."

He ran a hand through his straw-colored hair and pursed his lips.

"So you *did* finally nail him . . ." he said softly.

I shook my head again.

"No. He was already dying when I got to him. Come with me now! Hurry! It is important!"

"Where to? What is the matter?"

"To the Pattern," I said. "Why? I am not certain, but I know that it is important. Come on!"

We entered the palace, moving toward the nearest stairwell. There were two guards at its head, but they came to attention as we approached and did not attempt to interfere with our passage.

"I'm glad it's true about your eyes," Random said as we headed down. "Do you see all right?"

"Yes. I hear that you are still married."

"Yes. I am."

When we reached the ground floor, we hurried to the right. There had been another pair of guards at the foot of the stair, but they did not move to stop us.

"Yes," he repeated, as we headed toward the center of the palace. "You are surprised, aren't you?"

"Yes. I thought you were going to get the year over with and be done with it."

"So did I," he said. "But I fell in love with her. I really did."

"Stranger things have happened."

We crossed the marble dining hall and entered the long, narrow corridor that led far back through shadows and dust. I suppressed a shudder as I thought of my condition the last time I had come this way.

"She really cares for me," he said. "Like nobody else ever has before."

"I'm glad for you," I said.

We reached the door that opened onto the platform hiding the long, spiral stairway down. It was open. We passed through and began the descent.

"I'm not," he said, as we hurried around and around. "I didn't want to fall in love. Not then. We've been prisoners the whole time, you know. How can she be proud of that?"

"That is over now," I said. "You became a prisoner because you followed me and tried to kill Eric, didn't you?"

"Yes. Then she joined me here."

"I will not forget," I said.

We rushed on. It was a great distance down, and there were only lanterns every forty feet or so. It was a huge, natural cavern. I wondered whether anyone knew how many tunnels and corridors it contained. I suddenly felt myself overwhelmed with pity for any poor wretches rotting in its dungeons, for whatever reasons. I resolved to release them all or find something better to do with them.

Long minutes passed. I could see the flickering of the torches and the lanterns below.

"There is a girl," I said, "and her name is Dara. She told me she was Benedict's great-granddaughter and gave me reason to believe it. I told her somewhat concerning Shadow, reality, and the Pattern. She does possess some power over Shadow, and she was anxious to walk the Pattern. When last I saw her, she was headed this way. Now Benedict swears she is not his. Suddenly I am fearful. I want to keep her from the Pattern. I want to question her."

"Strange," he said. "Very. I agree with you. Do you think she might be there now?"

"If she is not, then I feel she will be along soon."

We finally reached the floor, and I began to race through the shadows toward the proper tunnel.

"Wait!" Random cried.

I halted and turned. It took me a moment to locate him, as he was back behind the stairs. I returned.

My question did not reach my lips. I saw that he knelt beside a large, bearded man.

"Dead," he said. "A very thin blade. Good thrust. Just recently."

"Come on!"

We both ran to the tunnel and turned up it. Its seventh side passage was the one we wanted. I drew Grayswandir as we neared it, for that great, dark, metal-bound door was standing ajar.

I sprang through. Random was right behind me. The floor of that enormous room is black and looks to be smooth as glass, although it is not slippery. The Pattern burns upon it, within it, an intricate, shimmering maze of curved lines, perhaps a hundred and fifty yards long. We halted at its edge, staring.

Something was out there, walking it. I felt that old, tingling chill the thing always gives me as I watched. Was it Dara? It was difficult for me to make out the figure within the fountains of sparks that spewed constantly about it. Whoever it was had to be of the blood royal, for it was common knowledge that anyone ele would be destroyed by the Pattern, and this individual had already made it past the Grand Curve and was negotiating the complicated series of arcs that led toward the Final Veil.

The firefly form seemed to change shape as it moved. For a time, my senses kept rejecting the tiny subliminal glimpses that I knew must be coming through to me. I heard Random gasp beside me, and it seemed to breach my subconscious dam. A horde of impressions flooded my mind.

It seemed to tower hugely in that always unsubstantial-seeming chamber. Then shrink, die down, almost to nothing. It seemed a slim woman for a moment—possibly Dara, her hair lightened by the glow, streaming, crackling with static electricity. Then it was not hair, but great, curved horns from some wide, uncertain brow, whose crook-legged owner struggled to shuffle hoofs along the blazing way. Then something else . . . An enormous cat . . . A faceless woman . . . A bright-winged thing of indescribable beauty . . . A tower of ashes . . .

"Dara!" I cried out. "Is that you?"

My voice echoed back, and that was all. Whoever/whatever it was struggled now with the Final Veil. My muscles strained forward in unwilling sympathy with the effort.

Finally, it burst through.

Yes, it was Dara! Tall and magnificent now. Both beautiful and somehow horrible at the same time. The sight of her tore at the fabric of my mind. Her arms were upraised in exultation and an inhuman laughter flowed from her lips. I wanted to look away, yet I could not move. Had I truely held, caressed, made love to—that? I was mightily repelled and simultaneously attracted as I had never been before. I could not understand this overwhelming ambivalence.

Then she looked at me.

The laughter ceased. Her altered voice rang out.

"Lord Corwin, are you liege of Amber now?"

From somewhere, I managed a reply.

"For all practical purposes," I said.

"Good! Then behold your nemesis!"

"Who are you? *What* are you?"

"You will never know," she said. "It is just exactly too late now."

"I do not understand. What do you mean?"

"Amber," she said, "will be destroyed."

And she vanished.

"What the hell," said Random then, "was that?"

I shook my head.

"I do not know. I really do not know. And I feel that it is the most important thing in the world that we find out."

He gripped my arm.

"Corwin," he said. "She—it—meant it. And it may be possible, you know."

I nodded.

"I know."

"What are we going to do now?"

I resheathed Grayswandir and turned back toward the door.

"Pick up the pieces," I said. "I have what I thought I always wanted within my grasp now, and I must secure it. And I cannot wait for what is to come. I must seek it out and stop it before it ever reaches Amber."

"Do you know where to seek it?" he asked.

We turned up the tunnel.

"I believe it lies at the other end of the black road," I said.

We moved on through the cavern to the stairs where the dead man lay and went round and round above him in the dark.

BOOK THREE

SIGN OF THE UNICORN

*For Jadawin and his Demiurge,
not to forget Kickaha.*

ONE

I ignored the questions in the eyes of the groom as I lowered the grisly parcel and turned the horse in for care and maintenance. My cloak could not really conceal the nature of its contents as I slung the guts over my shoulder and stamped off toward the rear entrance to the palace. Hell would soon be demanding its paycheck.

I skirted the exercise area and made my way to the trail that led toward the southern end of the palace gardens. Fewer eyes along that route. I would still be spotted, but it would be a lot less awkward than going in the front way, where things are always busy. Damn.

And again, damn. Of troubles I considered myself amply possessed. But those who have do seem to get. Some spiritual form of compound interest, I suppose.

There were a few idlers beside the fountain at the far end of the garden. Also, a couple of guards were passing among the bushes near the trail. The guards saw me coming, held a brief discussion, and looked the other way. Prudent.

Me, back less than a week. Most things, still unresolved. The court of Amber, full of suspicion and unrest. This, now: a death to further jeopardize the brief, unhappy prereign of Corwin I: me.

Time now to do something I should have done right away. But

257

there had been so many things to do, from the very first. It was not as if I had been nodding, as I saw it. I had assigned priorities and acted on them. Now, though . . .

I crossed the garden, out of the shade and into the slanting sunlight. I swung up the wide, curving stair. A guard snapped to attention as I entered the palace. I made for the rear stairway, then up to the second floor. Then the third.

From the right, my brother Random stepped out of his suite and into the hallway.

"Corwin!" he said, studying my face. "What's the matter? I saw you from the balcony and—"

"Inside," I said, gesturing with my eyes. "We are going to have a private conference. Now."

He hesitated, regarding my burden.

"Let's make it two rooms up," he said. "Okay? Vialle's in here."

"All right."

He led the way, opened the door. I entered the small sitting room, sought a likely spot, dropped the body.

Random stared at the bundle.

"What am I supposed to do?" he asked.

"Unwrap the goodies," I said, "and take a look."

He knelt and undid the cloak. He folded it back.

"Dead all right," he observed. "What's the problem?"

"You did not look closely enough," I said. "Peel back an eyelid. Open the mouth and look at the teeth. Feel the spurs on the backs of the hands. Count the joints in the fingers. Then you tell me about the problem."

He began doing these things. As soon as he looked at the hands he stopped and nodded.

"All right," he said. "I remember."

"Remember out loud."

"It was back at Flora's place . . ."

"That was where I first saw anyone like this," I said. "They were after you, though. I never did find out why."

"That's right," he said. "I never got a chance to tell you about it. We weren't together all that long. Strange . . . Where did this one come from?"

I hesitated, torn between pushing him from his story and telling him mine. Mine won out because it was mine and very immediate.

I sighed and sank into a chair.

"We've just lost us another brother," I said. "Caine is dead. I got there a bit too late. That thing—person—did it. I wanted it alive, for obvious reasons. But it put up quite a fight. I didn't have much of a choice."

He whistled softly, seated himself in the chair opposite me.

"I see," he said very softly.

I studied his face. Was that the faintest of smiles waiting in the wings to enter and meet my own? Quite possibly.

"No," I said flatly. "If it were otherwise, I would have arranged for a lot less doubt as to my innocence. I'm telling you what really happened."

"All right," he said. "Where is Caine?"

"Under a layer of sod, near the Grove of the Unicorn."

"That looks suspicious right there," he said. "Or will. To the others."

I nodded.

"I know. I had to hide the body and cover it in the meantime, though. I couldn't just bring him back and start parrying questions. Not when there were important facts waiting for me, in your head."

"Okay," he said. "I don't know how important they are, but they're yours. But don't leave me hanging, huh? How did this thing happen?"

"It was right after lunch," I said. "I had eaten down at the harbor with Gérard. Afterward, Benedict brought me topside through his Trump. Back in my rooms, I found a note which apparently had been slipped in under the door. It requested a private meeting, later in the afternoon, at the Grove of the Unicorn. It was signed 'Caine.' "

"Have you still got the note?"

"Yes." I dug it out of my pocket and passed it to him. "Here."

He studied it and shook his head.

"I don't know," he said. "It *could* be his writing—if he were in a hurry— but I don't think it is."

I shrugged. I took the note back, folded it, put it away.

"Whatever, I tried to reach him with his Trump, to save myself the ride. But he wasn't receiving. I guessed it was to maintain secrecy as to his where-abouts, if it was all that important. So I got a horse and rode on down."

"Did you tell anyone where you were going?"

"Not a soul. I did decide to give the horse a workout, though, so I rode along at a pretty good clip. I didn't see it happen, but I saw him lying there as I came into the wood. His throat had been cut, and there was a disturbance off in the bushes some distance away. I rode the guy down, jumped him, fought with him, had to kill him. We didn't engage in any conversation while this was going on."

"You're sure you got the right guy?"

"As sure as you can be under such circumstances. His trail went back to Caine. He had fresh blood on his garments."

"Might have been his own."

"Look again. No wounds. I broke his neck. Of course I remembered where I had seen his like before, so I brought him right to you. Before you tell me about it, though, there was one more thing—just for a clincher." I withdrew the second note, passed it over. "The creature had this on its person. I presume it had removed it from Caine."

Random read it, nodded, and handed it back.

"From you, to Caine, asking to be met there. Yes, I see. Needless to say . . ."

"Needless to say," I finished. "And it does look a bit like my writing—at first glance, anyway."

"I wonder what would have happened if you had gotten there first?"

"Probably nothing," I said. "Alive and looking bad—that seems how they wanted me. The trick was to get us there in the proper order, and I didn't hurry quite enough to miss what was bound to follow."

He nodded.

"Granting the tight scheduling," he said, "it had to be someone on the scene, here in the palace. Any ideas?"

I chuckled and reached for a cigarette. I lit it and chuckled again.

"I'm just back. You have been here all along," I said. "Which one hates me the most these days?"

"That is an embarrassing question, Corwin," he stated. "Everyone's down on you for something. Ordinarily, I would nominate Julian. Only it doesn't seem to hold up here."

"Why not?"

"He and Caine got along very well. For years now. They had been looking out for each other, hanging around together. Pretty thick. Julian is cold and petty and just as nasty as you remember. But if he liked anybody, he liked Caine. I don't think he'd do it to him, not even to get at you. After all, he probably could have found plenty of other ways if that was all he wanted."

I sighed.

"Who's next?"

"I don't know. I just don't know."

"Okay. How do you read the reactions to this?"

"You're screwed, Corwin. Everyone is going to think you did it, no matter what you say."

I nodded at the corpse. Random shook his head.

"That could easily be some poor clod you dug up out of Shadow to take the blame."

"I know," I said. "Funny, coming back to Amber as I did, I arrived at an ideal time for positioning myself advantageously."

"A perfect time," Random agreed. "You didn't even have to kill Eric to get what you wanted. That was a stroke of luck."

"Yes. Still, it is no secret that that is what I came to do, and it is only a matter of time before my troops—foreign, specially armed, and quartered here—are going to start provoking some very bad feelings. Only the presence of an external threat has saved me from that so far. And then there are the things I am suspected of having done before my return—like murdering Benedict's retainers. Now this . . ."

"Yes," Random said, "I saw it coming as soon as you told me. When you and Bleys attacked years ago, Gérard deployed part of the fleet so that it was out of your way. Caine, on the other hand, engaged you with his vessels and scuttled you. Now that he is gone, I imagine you will put Gérard in command of the entire fleet."

"Who else? He is the only man for the job."

"Nevertheless . . ."

"Nevertheless. Admitted. If I were going to kill any one person to strengthen my position, Caine would be the logical choice. That's the real, damning truth."

"How do you propose handling this?"

"Tell everyone what happened and try to discover who was behind it. Have you any better suggestions?"

"I've been trying to think how I could alibi you. But it does not look promising."

I shook my head.

"You are too close to me. No matter how good we made it sound, it would probably have the opposite effect."

"Have you considered admitting to it?"

"Yes. But self-defense is out. With a cut throat, it had to be a matter of surprise. And I have no stomach for starting off with the alternative: hoke up some evidence that he was up to something rotten and say I did it for the good of Amber. I flatly refuse to take on fake guilt under those terms. I'd wind up with a bad odor that way, too."

"But with a real tough reputation."

"It's the wrong kind of tough for the sort of show I want to run. No, that's out."

"That covers everything, then—just about."

"What do you mean 'just about'?"

He studied his left thumbnail through slitted eyes.

"Well, it occurs to me that if there is anyone else you are anxious to get out of the picture, now is the time to consider that a frame can often be shifted."

I thought about it and finished my cigarette.

"Not bad," I said, "but I can't spare any more brothers at the moment. Not even Julian. Anyhow, he's the least frameable."

"It need not be family," he said. "Plenty of noble Amberites around with possible motives. Take Sir Reginald—"

"Forget it, Random The reframing is out, too."

"Okay. I've exhausted my little gray cells, then."

"Not the ones in charge of memory, I hope."

"All right."

He sighed. He stretched. He got to his feet, stepped over the room's other occupant, and made his way to the window. Drawing back the drapes, he stared out for a time.

"All right," he repeated. "There's a lot to tell. . . ."

Then he remembered out loud.

TWO

While sex heads a great number of lists, we all have other things we like to do in between. With me, Corwin, it's drumming, being up in the air, and gambling—in no special order. Well, maybe soaring has a little edge—in gliders, balloons, and certain variations—but mood has a lot to do with that too, you know. I mean, ask me another time and I might say one of the others. Depends on what you want most at the moment.

Anyway, I was here in Amber some years ago. Not doing much of anything. Just visiting and being a nuisance. Dad was still around, and when I noticed that he was getting into one of his grumpy moods, I decided it was time to take a walk. A long one. I had often noticed that his fondness for me tended to increase as an inverse function of my proximity. He gave me a fancy riding crop for a going-away present—to hasten the process of affection, I suppose. Still, it was a very nice crop—silver-chased, beautifully tooled— and I made good use of it. I had decided to go looking for an assemblage of all my simple pleasures in one small nook of Shadow.

It was a long ride—I will not bore you with the details—and it was pretty far from Amber, as such things go. This time, I was not looking for a place where I would be especially important. That can get either boring or difficult fairly quickly, depending on how responsible you want to be. I wanted to be an irresponsible nonentity and just enjoy myself.

Texorami was a wide open port city, with sultry days and long nights, lots of good music, gambling around the clock, duels every morning and in-between mayhem for those who couldn't wait. And the air currents were fabulous. I had a little red sail plane I used to go sky surfing in, every couple of days. It was the good life. I played drums till all hours in a basement spot up the river where the walls sweated almost as much as the customers and the smoke used to wash around the lights like streams of milk. When I was done playing I'd go find some action, women, or cards, usually. And that was it for the rest of the night. Damn Eric, anyway! That reminds me again . . . He once accused me of cheating at cards, did you know that? And that's about the only thing I wouldn't cheat at. I take my card playing seriously. I'm good and I'm also lucky. Eric was neither. The trouble with him was that he was good at so many things he wouldn't admit even to himself that there were some things other people could do better. If you kept beating him at anything you had to be cheating. He started a nasty argument over it one night—could have gotten serious—but Gérard and Caine broke it up. Give Caine that. He took my part that time. Poor guy . . . Hell of a way to go, you know? His throat . . . Well, anyhow, there I was in Texorami, making music and women, winning at cards and jockeying around the sky. Palm trees and night-blooming wall-flowers. Lots of good port smells—spices, coffee, tar, salt—you know. Gentlefolk, merchants, and peons—the same straights as in most other places. Sailors and assorted travelers passing in and out. Guys like me living around the edges of things. I spent a little over two years in Texor-ami, happy. Really. Not much contact with the others. Sort of postcardlike hellos via the Trumps every now and then, and that was about it. Amber was pretty much off my mind. All this changed one night when I was sitting there with a full house and the guy across from me was trying to make up his mind whether or not I was bluffing.

The Jack of Diamonds began talking to me.

Yes, that is how it started. I was in a weird frame of mind anyway. I had just finished a couple very hot sets and was still kind of high. Also, I was physically strung out from a long day's gliding and not much sleep the night before. I decided later that it must be our mental quirk associated with the Trumps that made me see it that way when someone was trying to reach me and I had cards in my hand—any cards. Ordinarily, of course, we get the message empty-handed, unless we are doing the calling. It could have been that my subconscious—which was kind of footloose at the time—just seized on the available props out of habit. Later, though, I had cause to wonder. Really, I just don't know.

The Jack said, "Random." Then its face blurred and it said, "Help me." I began getting a feel of the personality by then, but it was weak. The whole thing was very weak. Then the face rearranged itself and I saw that I was right. It was Brand. He looked like hell, and he seemed to be chained or tied to something. "Help me," he said again.

"I'm here," I said. "What's the matter?"

". . . prisoner," he said, and something else that I couldn't make out.

"Where?" I asked.

He shook his head at that.

"Can't bring you through," he said. "No Trumps, and I am too weak. You will have to come the long way around. . . ."

I did not ask him how he was managing it without my Trump. Finding out where he was seemed of first importance. I asked him how I could locate him.

"Look very closely," he said. "Remember every feature. I may only be able to show you once. Come armed, too. . . ."

Then I saw the landscape—over his shoulder, out a window, over a battlement, I can't be sure. It was far from Amber, somewhere where the shadows go mad. Farther than I like to go. Stark, with shifting colors. Fiery. Day without a sun in the sky. Rocks that glided like sailboats across the land. Brand there in some sort of tower—a small point of stability in that flowing scene. I remembered it, all right. And I remembered the presence coiled about the base of that tower. Brilliant. Prismatic. Some sort of watch-thing, it seemed—too bright for me to make out its outline, to guess its proper size. Then it all just went away. Instant off. And there I was, staring at the Jack of Diamonds again, with the guy across from me not knowing whether to be mad at my long distraction or concerned that I might be having some sort of sick spell.

I closed up shop with that hand and went home. I lay stretched out on my bed, smoking and thinking. Brand had still been in Amber when I had departed. Later, though, when I had asked after him, no one had any idea as to his whereabouts. He had been having one of his melancholy spells, had snapped out of it one day and ridden off. And that was that. No messages either—either way. He wasn't answering, he wasn't talking.

I tried to figure every angle. He was smart, damn smart. Possibly the best mind in the family. He was in trouble and he had called me. Eric and Gérard were more the heroic types and would probably have welcomed the adventure.

Caine would have gone out of curiosity, I think. Julian, to look better than the rest of us and to score points with Dad. Or, easiest of all, Brand could have called Dad himself. Dad would have done something about it. But he had called me. Why?

It occurred to me then that maybe one or more of the others had been responsible for his circumstances. If, say, Dad was beginning to favor him . . . Well. You know. Eliminate the positive. And if he did call Dad, he would look like a weakling.

So I suppressed my impulse to yell for reinforcements. He had called me, and it was quite possible that I would be cutting his throat by letting anyone back in Amber in on the fact that he had gotten the message out. Okay. What was in it for me?

If it involved the succession and he had truly become fair-haired, I figured that I could do a lot worse than give him this to remember me by. And if it did not . . . There were all sorts of other possibilities. Perhaps he had stumbled onto something going on back home, something it would be useful to know about. I was even curious as to the means he had employed for bypassing the Trumps. So it was curiosity, I'd say, that made me decide to go it alone and try to rescue him.

I dusted off my own Trumps and tried reaching him again. As you might expect, there was no response. I got a good night's sleep then and tried one more time in the morning. Again, nothing. Okay, no sense waiting any longer.

I cleaned up my blade, ate a big meal, and got into some rugged clothes. I also picked up a pair of dark, polaroid goggles. Didn't know how they would work there, but that warden-thing had been awfully bright—and it never hurts to try anything extra you can think of. For that matter, I also took a gun. I had a feeling it would be worthless, and I was right. But, like I said, you never know till you try.

The only person I said good-bye to was another drummer, because I stopped to give him my set before I left. I knew he'd take good care of them.

Then I went on down to the hangar, got the sail plane ready, went aloft, and caught a proper current. It seemed a neat way to do it.

I don't know whether you've ever glided through Shadow, but—No? Well, I headed out over the sea till the land was only a dim line to the north. Then I had the waters go cobalt beneath me, rear up and shake sparkly beards. The wind shifted. I turned. I raced the waves shoreward beneath a darkening sky. Texorami was gone when I returned to the rivermouth, replaced by miles of swamp. I rode the currents inward, crossing and recrossing the river at new twists and kinks it had acquired. Gone were the piers, the trails, the traffic. The trees were high.

Clouds massed in the west, pink and pearl and yellow. The sun phased from orange through red to yellow. You shake your head? The sun was the price of the cities, you see. In a hurry, I depopulate—or, rather, go the elemental route. At that altitude artifacts would have been distracting. Shading and texture becomes everything for me. That's what I meant about gliding it being a bit different.

So, I bore to the west till the woods gave way to surface green, which quickly faded, dispersed, broke to brown, tan, yellow. Light and crumbly then, splotched. The price of that was a storm. I rode it out as much as I could, till the lightnings forked nearby and I feared that the gusts were getting to be too much for the little glider. I toned it down fast then, but got more green below as a result. Still, I pulled it out of the storm with a yellow sun firm and bright at my back. After a time, I got it to go desert beneath me again, stark and rolling.

Then the sun shrank and strands of cloud whipped past its face, erasing it bit by bit. That was the shortcut that took me farther from Amber than I had been in a long while.

No sun then, but the light remained, just as bright but eerie now, directionless. It tricked my eyes, it screwed up perspective. I dropped lower, limiting my range of vision. Soon large rocks came into view, and I fought for the shapes I remembered. Gradually, these occurred.

The buckling, flowing effect was easier to achieve under these conditions, but its production was physically disconcerting. It made it even more difficult to judge my effectiveness in guiding the glider. I got lower than I thought I was and almost collided with one of the rocks. Finally, though, the smokes rose and flames danced about as I remembered them—conforming to no particular pattern, just emerging here and there from crevasses, holes, cave mouths. Colors began to misbehave as I recalled from my brief view. Then came the actual motion of the rocks—drifting, sailing, like rudderless boats in a place where they wring out rainbows.

By then, the air currents had gone crazy. One updraft after another, like fountains, I fought them as best I could, but knew I could not hold things together much longer at that altitude. I rose a considerable distance, forgetting everything for a time while trying to stabilize the craft. When I looked down again, it was like viewing a free-form regatta of black icebergs. The rocks were racing around, clashing together, backing off, colliding again, spinning, arcing across the open spaces, passing among one another. Then I was slammed about, forced down, forced up—and I saw a strut give way. I gave the shadows their final nudge, then looked again. The tower had appeared in the distance, something brighter than ice or aluminum stationed at its base.

That final push had done it. I realized that just as I felt the winds start a particularly nasty piece of business. Then several cables snapped and I was on my way down—like riding a waterfall. I got the nose up, brought it in low and wild, saw where we were headed, and jumped at the last moment. The poor glider was pulverized by one of those peripatetic monoliths. I felt worse about that than I did about the scrapes, rips, and lumps I collected.

Then I had to move quickly, because a hill was racing toward me. We both veered, fortunately in different directions. I hadn't the faintest notion as to their motive force, and at first I could see no pattern to their movements. The ground varied from warm to extremely hot underfoot, and along with the smoke and occasional jets of flame, nasty-smelling gases were escaping from numerous openings in the ground. I hurried toward the tower, following a necessarily irregular course.

It took a long while to cover the distance. Just how long, I was uncertain, as I had no way of keeping track of the time. By then, though, I was beginning to notice some interesting regularities. First, the larger stones moved at a greater velocity than the smaller ones. Second, they seemed to be orbiting one another—cycles within cycles within cycles, larger about smaller, none of them ever still. Perhaps the prime mover was a dust mote or a single molecule—somewhere. I had neither time nor desire to indulge in any attempt to determine the center of the affair. Keeping this in mind, I did manage to observe as I went, though, enough so that I was able to anticipate a number of their collisions well in advance.

So Childe Random to the dark tower came, yeah, gun in one hand, blade in the other. The goggles hung about my neck. With all the smoke and confused lighting, I wasn't about to don them until it became absolutely necessary.

Now, whatever the reason, the rocks avoided the tower. While it seemed to stand on a hill, I realized as I approached that it would be more correct to say that the rocks had scooped out an enormous basin just short of it. I could not tell from my side, however, whether the effect was that of an island or a peninsula.

I dashed through the smoke and rubble, avoiding the jets of flame that leaped from the cracks and holes. Finally I scrambled up the slope, removing myself from the courseway. Then for several moments I clung at a spot just below any line of sight from the tower. I checked my weapons, controlled my breathing, and put on the goggles. Everything set, I went over the top and came up into a crouch.

Yes, the shades worked. And yes, the beast was waiting.

It was a fright all right, because in some ways it was kind of beautiful. It had a snake body as big around as a barrel, with a head sort of like a massive claw hammer, but kind of tapered to the snout end. Eyes of a very pale green. And it was clear as glass, with very faint, fine lines seeming to indicate scales. Whatever flowed in its veins was reasonably clear, also. You could look right into it and see its organs—opaque or cloudy as the case might be. You could almost be distracted by watching the thing function. And it had a dense mane, like bristles of glass, about the head and collaring its gullet. Its movement when it saw me, raised that head and slithered forward, was like flowing water—living water, it seemed, a bedless river without banks. What almost froze me, though, was that I could see into its stomach. There was a partly digested man in it.

I raised the gun, aimed at the nearest eye, and squeezed the trigger.

I already told you it didn't work. So I threw the gun, leaped to my left, and sprang in on its right side, going for its eye with my blade.

You know how hard it can be to kill things built along reptilian lines. I decided immediately to try to blind the thing and hack off its tongue as the first order of business. Then, being more than a little fast on my feet, I might have any number of chances to lay in some good ones about the head until I decapitated it. Then let it tie itself in knots till it stopped. I was hoping, too, that it might be sluggish because it was still digesting someone.

If it was sluggish then, I was glad that I hadn't stopped by earlier. It drew its head out of the path of my blade and snapped down over it while I was still off balance. That snout glanced across my chest, and it did feel as if I had been hit by a massive hammer. It knocked me sprawling.

I kept on rolling to get out of range, coming up short near the edge of the embankment. I recovered my footing there while it unwound itself, dragged a lot of weight in my direction, and then reared up and cocked its head again, about fifteen feet above me.

I know damn well that Gérard would have chosen that moment to attack. The big bastard would have strode forward with that monster blade of his and cut the thing in half. Then it probably would have fallen on him and writhed all over him, and he'd have come away with a few bruises. Maybe a bloody nose. Benedict would not have missed the eye. He would have had one in each pocket by then and be playing football with the head while composing a footnote to Clausewitz. But they are genuine hero types. Me, I just stood there holding the blade point upward, both hands on the hilt, my elbows on my hips, my head as far back out of the way as possible. I would much rather have run and called it a day. Only I knew that if I tried it, that head would drop down and smear me.

Cries from within the tower indicated that I had been spotted, but I was not about to look away to see what was going on. Then I began cursing the thing. I wanted it to strike and get it over with, one way or the other.

When it finally did, I shuffled my feet, twisted my body, and swung the point into line with my target.

My left side was partly numbed by the blow, and I felt as if I had been driven a foot into the ground. Somehow I managed to remain upright. Yes, I had done everything perfectly. The maneuver had gone exactly as I had hoped and planned.

Except for the beast's part. It wasn't cooperating by producing the appropriate death throes.

In fact, it was beginning to rise.

It took my blade with it, too. The hilt protruded from its left eye socket, the point emerged like another bristle amid the mane on the back of its head. I had a feeling that the offensive team had had it.

At that moment, figures began to emerge—slowly, cautiously—from an opening at the base of the tower. They were armed and ugly-looking, and I had a feeling that they were not on my side of the disagreement.

Okay. I know when it is time to fold and hope for a better hand another day.

"Brand!" I shouted. "It's Random! I can't get through! Sorry!"

Then I turned, ran, and leaped back over the edge, down into the place where the rocks did their unsettling things. I wondered whether I had chosen the best time to descend.

Like so many things, the answer was yes and no.

It was not the sort of jump I would make for many reasons other than those which prevailed. I came down alive, but that seemed the most that could be said for it. I was stunned, and for a long while I thought I had broken my ankle.

The thing that got me moving again was a rustling sound from above and the rattle of gravel about me. When I readjusted the goggles and looked up, I saw that the beast had decided to come down and finish the job. It was winding its phantom way down the slope, the area about its head having darkened and opaqued since I had skewered it upstairs.

I sat up. I got to my knees. I tried my ankle, couldn't use it. Nothing around to serve as a crutch, either. Okay. I crawled then. Away. What else was there to do? Gain as much ground as I could and think hard while I was about it.

Salvation was a rock—one of the smaller, slower ones, only about the size of a moving van. When I saw it approaching, it occurred to me that here was transportation if I could make it aboard. Maybe some safety, too. The faster, really massive ones appeared to get the most abuse.

This in mind, I watched the big ones that accompanied my own, estimated their paths and velocities, tried to gauge the movement of the entire system, readied myself for the moment, the effort. I also listened to the approach of the beast, heard the cries of the troops from the edge of the bluff, wondered whether anyone up there was giving odds on me and what they might be if they were.

When the time came, I went. I got past the first big one without any trouble, but had to wait for the next one to go by. I took a chance in crossing the path of the final one. Had to, to make it in time.

I made it to the right spot at the right moment, caught on to the holds I had been eyeing, and was dragged maybe twenty feet before I could pull myself up off the ground. Then I hauled my way to its uncomfortable top, sprawled there, and looked back.

It had been close. Still was, for that matter, as the beast was pacing me, its one good eye following the spinning big ones.

From overhead I heard a disappointed wail. Then the guys started down the slope, shouting what I took to be encouragement to the creature. I commenced massaging my ankle. I tried to relax. The brute crossed over, passing behind the first big rock as it completed another orbit.

How far could I shift through Shadow before it reached me? I wondered. True, there was constant movement, a changing of textures . . .

The thing waited for the second rock, slithered by behind it, paced me again, drew nearer.

Shadow, Shadow, on the wing—

The men were almost to the base of the slope by then. The beast was waiting for its opening—the next time around—past the inner satellite. I knew that it was capable of rearing high enough to snatch me from my perch.

—Come alive and smear that thing!

As I spun and glided I caught hold of the stuff of Shadow, sank into the feel of it, worked with the textures, possible to probable to actual, felt it coming with the finest twist, gave it that necessary fillip at the appropriate moment . . .

It came in from the beast's blind side, of course. A big mother of a rock, careening along like a semi out of control . . .

It would have been more elegant to mash it between two of them. However, I hadn't the time for finesse. I simply ran it over and left it there, thrashing in the granite traffic.

Moments later, however, inexplicably, the mashed and mangled body rose suddenly above the ground and drifted skyward, twisting. It kept going, buffeted by the winds, dwindling, dwindling, gone.

My own rock bore me away, slowly, steadily. The entire pattern was drifting. The guys from the tower then went into a huddle and decided to pursue me. They moved away from the base of the slope, began to make their way across the plain. But this was no real problem, I felt. I would ride my stony mount through Shadow, leaving them worlds away. This was by far the easiest course of action open to me. They would doubtless have been more difficult to take by surprise than the beast. After all, this was their land; they were wary and unmaimed.

I removed the goggles and tested my ankle again. I stood for a moment. It was very sore, but it bore my weight. I reclined once more and turned my thoughts to what had occurred. I had lost my blade and I was now in less than top shape. Rather than go on with the venture under these conditions, I knew that I was doing the safest, wisest thing by getting the hell out. I had gained enough knowledge of the layout and the conditions for my chances to be better next time around. All right . . .

The sky brightened above me, the colors and shadings lost something of their arbitrary, meandering habit. The flames began to subside about me. Good. Clouds started to find their ways across the sky. Excellent. Soon a localized glow began behind a cloudbank. Superb. When it went away, a sun would hang once again in the heavens.

I looked back and was surprised to see that I was still being pursued. However, it could easily be that I had not dealt properly with their analogues for this slice of Shadow. It is never good to assume that you have taken care of everything when you are in a hurry. So . . .

I shifted again. The rock gradually altered its course, shifted its shape, lost its satellites, moved in a straight line toward what was to become the west. Above me, the clouds dispersed and a pale sun shone down. We picked up speed. That should have taken care of everything right there. I had positively come into a different place.

But it had not. When I looked again, they were still coming. True, I had gained some distance on them. But the party trooped right along after me.

Well, all right. Things like that can sometimes happen. There were of course two possibilities. My mind still being more than a little disturbed from all that had just occurred, I had not performed ideally and had drawn them along with me. Or, I had maintained a constant where I should have suppressed a variable—that is, shifted into a place and unconsciously required that the pursuit element be present. Different guys then, but still chasing me.

I rubbed my ankle some more. The sun brightened toward orange. A wind out of the north raised a screen of dust and sand and hung it at my back, removing the gang from my sight. I raced on into the west, where a line of mountains had now grown up. Time was in a distortion phase. My ankle felt a little better.

I rested a while. Mine was reasonably comfortable, as rocks go. No sense turning it into a hellride when everything seemed to be proceeding smoothly. I stretched out, hands behind my head, and watched the mountains draw nearer. I thought about Brand and the tower. That was the place all right. Everything was just as it had been in the glimpse he had given me. Except for the guards, of course. I decided that I would cut through the proper piece of Shadow, recruit a cohort of my own, then go back and give them hell. Yes, then everything would be fine. . . .

After a time, I stretched, rolled over onto my stomach, and looked back. Damned if they weren't still following me! They had even gained some.

Naturally, I got angry. To hell with flight! They were asking for it, and it was time they got it.

I rose to my feet. My ankle was only half sore, a little numb. I raised my arms and looked for the shadows I wanted. I found them.

Slowly the rock swung out from its straight course into an arc, turning off to the right. The curve tightened. I swung through a parabola and headed back toward them, my velocity gradually increasing as I went. No time to raise a storm at my back, though I thought that would have been a nice touch if I could have managed it.

As I swept down upon them—there were maybe two dozen—they prudently began to scatter. A number of them didn't make it, though. I swung through another curve and returned as soon as I could.

I was shaken by the sight of several corpses rising into the air, dripping gore, two of them already high above me.

I was almost upon them on that second pass when I realized that a few of them had jumped aboard as I had gone through. The first one over the edge drew his blade and rushed me. I blocked his arm, took the weapon away from him, and threw him back down. I guess it was then that I became aware of those spurs on the backs of their hands. I had been slashed by his.

By that time I was the target of a number of curiously shaped missiles from below, two more guys were coming over the edge, and it looked as if several more might have made it aboard.

Well, even Benedict sometimes retreats. I had at least given the survivors something to remember.

I let go of the shadows, tore a barbed wheel from my side, another from my thigh, hacked off a guy's swordarm and kicked him in the stomach, dropped to my knees to avoid a wild swing from the next one, and caught him across the legs with my riposte. He went over, too.

There were five more on the way up and we were sailing westward once again, leaving perhaps a dozen live ones to regroup on the sand at my back, a sky full of oozing drifters above them.

I had the advantage with the next fellow because I caught him just partway over the edge. So much for him, and then there were four.

While I had been dealing with him, though, three more had arisen, simultaneously, at three different points.

I rushed the nearest and dispatched him, but the other two made it over and were upon me while I was about it. As I defended myself from their attack, the final one came up and joined them.

They were not all that good, but it was getting crowded and there were a lot of points and sharp edges straying about me. I kept parrying and moving, trying to get them to block one another, get in each other's way. I was partly successful, and when I had the best lineup I thought I was going to get, I rushed them, taking a couple of cuts—I had to lay myself open a bit to do it—but splitting one skull for my pains. He went over the edge and took the second one with him in a tangle of limbs and gear.

Unfortunately, the inconsiderate lout had carried off my blade, snagged in some bony cleft or other he had chosen to interpose when I swung. It was obviously my day for losing blades, and I wondered if my horoscope would have mentioned it if I had thought to look before I'd set out.

Anyhow, I moved quickly to avoid the final guy's swing. In doing so, I slipped on some blood and went skidding toward the front of the rock. If I went down that way, it would plow right over me, leaving a very flat Random there, like an exotic rug, to puzzle and delight future wayfarers.

I clawed for handholds as I slid, and the guy took a couple of quick steps toward me, raising his blade to do unto me as I had his buddy.

I caught hold of his ankle, though, and it did the trick of braking me very nicely—and damned if someone shouldn't choose that moment to try to get hold of me via the Trumps.

"I'm busy!" I shouted. "Call back later!" and my own motion was arrested as the guy toppled, clattered, and went sliding by.

I tried to reach him before he fell to rugdom, but I was not quite quick enough. I had wanted to save him for questioning. Still, my unegged beer was more than satisfactory. I headed back top and center to observe and muse.

The survivors were still following me, but I had a sufficient lead. I did not at the moment have to worry about another boarding party. Good enough. I was headed toward the mountains once again. The sun I had conjured was beginning to bake me. I was soaked with sweat and blood. My wounds were giving me trouble. I was thirsty. Soon, soon, I decided, it would have to rain. Take care of that before anything else.

So I began the preliminaries to a shift in that direction: clouds massing, building, darkening. . . .

I drifted off somewhere along the line, had a disjointed dream of someone trying to reach me again but not making it. Sweet darkness.

I awakened to the rain, sudden and hard-driving. I could not tell whether the darkness in the sky was from storm, evening, or both. It was cooler, though, and I spread my cloak and just lay there with my mouth open. Periodically I wrung moisture from the cloak. My thirst was eventually slaked and I began feeling clean again. The rock had also become so slick-looking that I was afraid to move about on it. The mountains were much nearer, their peaks limned by frequent lightnings. Things were too dark in the opposite direction for me to tell whether my pursuers were still with me. It would have been pretty rough trekking for them to have kept up, but then it is seldom good policy to rely on assumptions when traveling through strange shadows. I was a bit irritated with myself for going to sleep, but since no harm had come of it I drew my soggy cloak about me and decided to forgive myself. I felt around for some cigarettes I had brought along and found that about half of them had survived. After the eighth try, I juggled shadows enough to get a light. Then I just sat there, smoking and being rained on. It was a good feeling and I didn't move to change anything else, not for hours.

When the storm finally let up and the sky came clear, it was a night full of strange constellations. Beautiful though, the way nights can be on the desert. Much later, I detected a gentle upward sloping and my rock started to slow. Something began happening in terms of whatever physical rules controlled the situation. I mean, the slope itself did not seem so pronounced that it would affect our velocity as radically as it had. I did not want to tamper with Shadow in a direction that would probably take me out of my way. I wanted to get back onto more familiar turf as soon as possible—find my way to a place where my gut anticipations of physical events had more of a chance of being correct.

So I let the rock grind to a halt, climbed down when it did, and continued on up the slope, hiking. As I went, I played the Shadow game we all learned as children. Pass some obstruction—a scrawny tree, a stand of stone—and have the sky be different from one side to the other. Gradually I restored familiar constellations. I knew that I would be climbing down a different mountain from the one I ascended. My wounds still throbbed dully, but my ankle had stopped bothering me except for a little stiffness. I was rested. I knew that I could go for a long while. Everything seemed to be all right again.

It was a long hike, up the gradually steepening way. But I hit a trail eventually, and that made things easier. I trudged steadily upward under the now familiar skies, determined to keep moving and make it across by morning. As I went, my garments altered to fit the shadow—denim trousers and jacket now, my wet cloak a dry serape. I heard an owl nearby, and from a great distance below and behind came what might have been the yipyip-howl of a coyote. These signs of a more familiar place made me feel somewhat secure, exorcised any vestiges of desperation that remained with my flight.

An hour or so later, I yielded to the temptation to play with Shadow just a bit. It was not all that improbable for a stray horse to be wandering in these hills, and of course I found him. After ten or so minutes of becoming friendly, I was mounted bareback and moving toward the top in a more congenial fashion. The wind sowed frost in our path. The moon came and sparked it to life.

To be brief, I rode all night, passing over the crest and commencing my downward passage well before dawn. As I descended, the mountain grew even more vast above me, which of course was the best time for this to occur. Things were green on this side of the range, and divided by neat highways, punctuated by occasional dwellings. Everything therefore was proceeding in accordance with my desire.

Early morning. I was into the foothills and my denim had turned to khaki and a bright shirt. I had a light sport jacket slung before me. At a great height, a jetliner poked holes in the air, moving from horizon to horizon. There were birdsongs about me, and the day was mild, sunny.

It was about then that I heard my name spoken and felt the touch of the Trump once more. I drew up short and responded.

"Yes?"

It was Julian.

"Random, where are you?" he asked.

"Pretty far from Amber," I replied. "Why?"

"Have any of the others been in touch with you?"

"Not recently," I said. "But someone did try to get hold of me yesterday. I was busy though, and couldn't talk."

"That was me," he said. "We have a situation here that you had better know about."

"Where are you?" I asked.

"In Amber. A number of things have happened recently."

"Like what?"

"Dad has been gone for an unusually long time. No one knows where."

"He's done that before."

"But not without leaving instructions and making delegations. He always provided them in the past."

"True," I said. "But how long is 'long'?"

"Well over a year. You weren't aware of this at all?"

"I knew that he was gone. Gérard mentioned it some time back."

"Then add more time to that."

"I get the idea. How have you been operating?"

"That is the problem. We have simply been dealing with affairs as they arise. Gérard and Caine had been running the navy anyway, on Dad's orders. Without him, they have been making all their own decisions. I took charge of the patrols in Arden again. There is no central authority though, to arbitrate, to make policy decisions, to speak for all of Amber."

"So we need a regent. We can cut cards for it, I suppose."

"It is not that simple. We think Dad is dead."

"Dead? Why? How?"

"We have tried to raise him on his Trump. We have been trying every day for over half a year now. Nothing. What do you think?"

I nodded.

"He may be dead," I said. "You'd think he would have come across with something. Still, the possibility of his being in some trouble—say, a prisoner somewhere—is not precluded."

"A cell can't stop the Trumps. Nothing can. He would call for help the minute we made contact."

"I can't argue with that," I said. But I thought of Brand as I said it. "Perhaps he is deliberately resisting contact, though."

"What for?"

"I have no idea, but it is possible. You know how secretive he is about some things."

"No," Julian said, "it doesn't hold up. He would have given some operating instructions, somewhere along the line."

"Well, whatever the reasons, whatever the situation, what do you propose doing now?"

"Someone has to occupy the throne," he said.

I had seen it coming throughout the entire dialogue, of course—the opportunity it had long seemed would never come to pass.

"Who?" I asked.

"Eric seems the best choice," he replied. "Actually, he has been acting in that capacity for months now. It simply becomes a matter of formalizing it."

"Not just as regent?"

"Not just as regent."

"I see . . . Yes, I guess that things have been happening in my absence. What about Benedict as a choice?"

"He seems to be happy where he is, off somewhere in Shadow."

"What does he think of the whole idea?"

"He is not entirely in favor of it. But we do not believe he will offer resistance. It would disrupt things too much."

"I see," I said again. "And Bleys?"

"He and Eric had some rather heated discussions of the issue, but the troops do not take their orders from Bleys. He left Amber about three months ago. He could cause some trouble later. But then, we are forewarned."

"Gérard? Caine?"

"They will go along with Eric. I was wondering about yourself."

"What about the girls?"

He shrugged.

"They tend to take things lying down. No problem."

"I don't suppose Corwin . . ."

"Nothing new. He's dead. We all know it. His monument has been gathering dust and ivy for centuries. If not, then he has intentionally divorced himself from Amber forever. Nothing there. Now I am wondering where you stand."

I chuckled.

"I am hardly in a position to possess forceful opinions," I said.

"We need to know now."

I nodded.

"I have always been able to detect the quarter of the wind," I said. "I do not sail against it."

He smiled and returned my nod.

"Very good," he said.

"When is the coronation? I assume that I am invited."

"Of course, of course. But the date has not yet been set. There are still a few minor matters to be dealt with. As soon as the affair is calendared, one of us will contact you again."

"Thank you, Julian."

"Good-bye for now, Random."

And I sat there being troubled for a long while before I started on downward again. How long had Eric spent engineering it? I wondered. Much of the politicking back in Amber could have been done pretty quickly, but the setting up of the situation in the first place seemed the product of long-term thinking and planning. I was naturally suspicious as to his involvement in Brand's predicament. I also could not help but give some thought to the possibility of his having a hand in Dad's disappearance. That would have taken some doing and have required a really foolproof trap. But the more I thought of it, the less I was willing to put it past him. I even dredged up some old speculations as to his part in your own passing, Corwin. But, offhand, I could not think of a single thing to do about any of it. Go along with it, I figured, if that's where the power was. Stay in his good graces.

Still . . . One should always get more than one angle on a story. I tried to make up my mind as to who would give me a good one. While I was thinking along these lines, something caught my eye as I glanced back and up, appreciating anew the heights from which I had not quite descended.

There were a number of riders up near the top. They had apparently traversed the same trail I had taken. I could not get an exact nose count, but it seemed suspiciously close to a dozen—a fairly sizable group to be out riding at just that place and time. As I saw that they were proceeding on down the same way that I had come, I had a prickly feeling along the base of my neck. What if. . . ? What if they were the same guys? Because I felt that they were.

Individually, they were no match for me. Even a couple of them together had not made that great a showing. That was not it. The real chiller was that if that's who it was, then we were not alone in our ability to manipulate Shadow in a very sophisticated fashion. It meant that someone else was capable of a stunt that for all my life I had thought to be the sole property of our family. Add to this the fact that they were Brand's wardens, and their designs on the family—at least part of it—did not look all that clement. I perspired suddenly at the notion of enemies who could match our greatest power.

Of course, they were too far off for me to really know just then whether that was truly who it was. But you have to explore every contingency if you want to keep winning the survival game. Could Eric have found or trained or created some special beings to serve him in this particular capacity? Along with you and Eric, Brand had one of the firmest claims on the succession. . . . not to take anything away from your case, damn it! Hell! You know what I mean. I have to talk about it to show you how I was thinking at the time. That's all. So, Brand had had the basis for a pretty good claim if he had been in a position to press it. You being out of the picture, he was Eric's chief rival when it came to adding a legal touch to things. Putting that together with his plight and the ability of those guys to traverse Shadow, Eric came to look a lot more sinister to me. I was more scared by that thought than I was by the riders themselves, though they did not exactly fill me with delight. I decided that I had better do several things quickly: talk to someone else in Amber, and have him take me through the Trump.

Okay. I decided quickly. Gérard seemed the safest choice. He is reasonably open, neutral. Honest about most things. And from what Julian had said, Gérard's role in the whole business seemed kind of passive. That is, he was not going to resist Eric's move actively. He would not want to cause a lot of trouble. Didn't mean he approved. He was probably just being safe and conservative old Gérard. That decided, I reached for my deck of Trumps and almost howled. They were gone.

I searched every pocket in every garment about me. I had taken them along when I'd left Texorami. I could have lost them at any point in the previous day's action. I had certainly been battered and thrown about a lot. And it had been a great day for losing things. I composed a complicated litany of curses and dug my heels into the horse's sides. I was going to have to move fast and think faster now. The first thing would be to get into a nice, crowded, civilized place where an assassin of the more primitive sort would be at a disadvantage.

As I hurried downhill, heading for one of the roads, I worked with the stuff of Shadow—quite subtly this time, using every bit of skill I could muster. There were just two things I desired at the moment: a final assault on my possible trackers and a fast path to a place of sanctuary.

The world shimmered and did a final jig, becoming the California I had been seeking. A rasping, growling noise reached my ears, for the final touch I had intended. Looking back, I saw a section of cliff face come loose, almost in slow motion, and slide directly toward the horsemen. A while later, I had dismounted and was walking in the direction of the road, my garments even fresher and of better quality. I was uncertain as to the time of year, and I wondered what the weather was like in New York.

Before very long, the bus that I had anticipated approached and I flagged it down. I located a window seat, smoked for a while, and watched the countryside. After a time, I dozed.

I did not wake until early afternoon, when we pulled into a terminal. I was ravenous by then, and decided I had better have something to eat before getting a cab to the airport. So I bought three cheeseburgers and a couple of malts with a few of my quondam Texorami greenbacks. Getting served and eating took me maybe twenty minutes. Leaving the snack bar, I saw that there were a number of taxis standing idle at the stand out front. Before I picked one up, though, I decided to make an important stop in the men's room.

At the very damnedest moment you can think of, six stalls flew open behind my back and their occupants rushed me. There was no mistaking the spurs on the backs of their hands, the oversized jaws, the smoldering eyes. Not only had they caught up with me, they were now clad in the same acceptable garb as anyone else in the neighborhood. Gone were any remaining doubts as to their power over Shadow.

Fortunately, one of them was faster than the others. Also, perhaps because of my size, they still might not have been fully aware of my strength. I seized that first one high up on the arm, avoiding those hand bayonets he sported, pulled him over in front of me, picked him up, and threw him at the others. Then I just turned and ran. I broke the door on the way out. I didn't even pause to zip up until I was in a taxi and had the driver burning rubber.

Enough. It was no longer simple sanctuary that I had in mind. I wanted to get hold of a set of Trumps and tell someone else in the family about those guys. If they were Eric's creatures, the others ought to be made aware of them. If they were not, then Eric ought to be told, too. If they could make their way through Shadow like that, perhaps others could, also. Whatever they represented might one day constitute a threat to Amber herself. Supposing— just supposing—that no one back home was involved? What if Dad and Brand were the victims of a totally unsuspected enemy? Then there was something big and menacing afoot, and I had stepped right into it. That would be an excellent reason for their hounding me this thoroughly. They would want me pretty badly. My mind ran wild. They might even be harrying me toward some sort of a trap. No need for the visible ones to be the only ones about.

I brought my emotions to heel. One by one, you must deal with those things that come to hand, I told myself. That is all. Divorce the feelings from the speculations, or at least provide for separate maintenance. This is sister Flora's shadow. She lives on the other edge of the continent in a place called Westchester. Get to a phone, get hold of information, and call her. Tell her it is urgent and ask for sanctuary. She can't refuse you that, even if she does hate your guts. Then jump a jet and get the hell over there. Speculate on the way if you want, but keep cool now.

So I telephoned from the airport and you answered it, Corwin. That was the variable that broke all the possible equations I had been juggling—you suddenly showing up at that time, that place, that point in events. I grabbed for it when you offered me protection, and not just because I wanted protection. I could probably have taken those six guys out by myself. But that was no longer it. *I thought they were yours.* I figured you had been lying low all along, waiting for the right moment to move in. Now, I thought, you were ready. This explains everything. You had taken our Brand and you were about to use your Shadow-walking zombies for purposes of going back and catching Eric with his pants down. I wanted to be on your side because I hated Eric and because I knew you were a careful planner and you usually get what you go after. I mentioned the pursuit by guys out of Shadow to see what you would say. The fact that you said nothing didn't really prove anything, though. Either you were being cagey, I figured, or you had no way of knowing where I had been. I also thought of the possibility of walking into a trap of your devising, but I was already in trouble and did not see that I was so important to the balance of power that you would want to dispose of me. Especially if I offered my support, which I was quite willing to do. So I flew on out. And damned if those six didn't board later and follow me. Is he giving me an escort? I wondered. Better not start making more assumptions. I shook them again when we landed, and headed for Flora's place. Then I acted as if none of my guesses had occurred, waiting to see what you would do. When you helped me dispose of the guys, I was really puzzled. Were you genuinely surprised, or was it a put-on, with you sacrificing a few of the troops to keep me ignorant of something? All right, I decided, be ignorant, cooperate, see what he has in mind. I was a perfect setup for that act you pulled to cover the condition of your memory. When I did learn the truth, it was simply too late. We were headed for Rebma and none of this would have meant anything to you. Later, I didn't care to tell Eric anything after his coronation. I was his prisoner then and not exactly kindly disposed toward him. It even occurred to me that my information might be worth something one day—at least, my freedom again—if that threat ever materialized. As for Brand, I doubt anyone would have believed me; and even if someone did, I was the only one who knew how to reach that shadow. Could you see Eric buying that as a reason for releasing me? He would have laughed and told me to come up with a better story. And I never heard from Brand again. None of the others seem to have heard from him either. Odds are he's dead by now—I'd say. And that is the story I never got to tell you. You figure out what it all means.

THREE

I studied Random, remembering what a great card player he was. By looking at his face, I could no more tell whether he was lying, in whole or in part, than I could learn by scrutinizing the Jack of, say, Diamonds. Nice touch, that part, too. There was enough of that kind of business to his story to give it some feel of verisimilitude.

"To paraphrase Oedipus, Hamlet, Lear, and all those guys," I said, "I wish I had known this some time ago."

"This was the first chance I really had to tell you," he said.

"True," I agreed. "Unfortunately, it not only fails to clarify things, it complicates the puzzle even more. Which is no mean trick. Here we are with a black road running up to the foot of Kolvir. It passes through Shadow, and things have succeeded in traversing it to beset Amber. We do not know the exact nature of the forces behind it, but they are obviously malign and they seem to be growing in strength. I have been feeling guilty about it for some while now, because I see it as being tied in with my curse. Yes, I laid one on us. Curse or no curse, though, everything eventually resolves into some sort of tangibility that can be combatted. Which is exactly what we are going to do. But all week long I have been trying to figure out Dara's part in things.

Who is she really? What is she? Why was she so anxious to try the Pattern? How is it that she managed to succeed? And that final threat of hers . . . 'Amber will be destroyed,' she said. It seems more than coincidental that this occurred at the same time as the attack over the black road. I do not see it as a separate thing, but as a part of the same cloth. And it all seems to be tied in with the fact that there is a traitor somewhere here in Amber—Caine's death, the notes . . . Someone here is either abetting an external enemy or is behind the whole thing himself. Now you link it all up with Brand's disappearance, by way of this guy." I nudged the corpse with my foot. "It makes it look as if Dad's death or absence is also a part of it. If that is the case, though, it makes for a major conspiracy—with detail after detail having been carefully worked out over a period of years."

Random explored a cupboard in the corner, produced a bottle and a pair of goblets. He filled them and brought me one, then returned to his chair. We drank a silent toast to futility.

"Well," he said, "plotting is the number-one pastime around here, and everyone *has* had plenty of time, you know. We are both too young to remember brothers Osric and Finndo, who died for the good of Amber. But the impression I get from talking with Benedict—"

"Yes," I said, "—that they had done more than wishful thinking about the throne, and it became necessary that they die bravely for Amber. I've heard that, too. Maybe so, maybe not. We'll never know for sure. Still . . . Yes, the point is well taken, though almost unnecessary. I do not doubt that it has been tried before. I do not put it past a number of us. Who, though? We will be operating under a severe handicap until we find out. Any move that we make externally will probably only be directed against a limb of the beast. Come up with an idea."

"Corwin," he said, "to be frank about it, I could make a case for it being anyone here—even myself, prisoner status and all. In fact, something like that would be a great blind for it. I would have taken genuine delight in looking helpless while actually pulling the strings that made all the others dance. Any of us would, though. We all have our motives, our ambitions. And over the years we all have had time and opportunity to lay a lot of groundwork. No, that is the wrong way to go about it, looking for suspects. Everyone here falls into that category. Let us decide instead what it is that would distinguish such an individual, aside from motives, apart from opportunities. I would say, let's look at the methods involved."

"All right. Then you start."

"Some one of us knows more than the rest of us about the workings of Shadow—the ins and the outs, the whys and the hows. He also has allies, obtained from somewhere fairly far afield. This is the combination he has brought to bear upon Amber. Now, we have no way of looking at a person and telling whether he possesses such special knowledge and skills. But let us consider where he could have obtained them. It could be that he simply learned something off in Shadow somewhere, on his own. Or he could have been studying all along, here, while Dworkin was still alive and willing to give lessons."

I stared down into my glass. Dworkin could *still* be living. He had provided my means of escape from the dungeons of Amber—how long ago? I had told no one this, and was not about to. For one thing, Dworkin was quite mad—which was apparently why Dad had had him locked away. For another, he had demonstrated powers I did not understand, which convinced me he could be quite dangerous. Still, he had been kindly disposed toward me after a minimum of flattery and reminiscence. If he were still around, I suspected that with a bit of patience I might be able to handle him. So I had kept the whole business locked away in my mind as a possible secret weapon. I saw no reason for changing that decision at this point.

"Brand did hang around him a lot," I acknowledged, finally seeing what he was getting at. "He was interested in things of that sort."

"Exactly," Random replied. "And he obviously knew more than the rest of us, to be able to send me that message without a Trump."

"You think he made a deal with outsiders, opened the way for them, then discovered that they no longer needed him when they hung him out to dry?"

"Not necessarily. Though I suppose that is possible, too. My thinking runs more like this—and I don't deny my prejudice in his favor: I think he had learned enough about the subject so that he was able to detect it when someone did something peculiar involving the Trumps, the Pattern, or that area of Shadow most adjacent to Amber. Then he slipped up. Perhaps he underestimated the culprit and confronted him directly, rather than going to Dad or Dworkin. What then? The guilty party subdued him and imprisoned him in that tower. Either he thought enough of him not to want to kill him if he did not have to, or he had some later use of him in mind."

"You make that sound plausible, too," I said, and I would have added, "and it fits your story nicely" and watched his poker face again, except for one thing. Back when I was with Bleys, before our attack on Amber, I had had a momentary contact with Brand while fooling with the Trumps. He had indicated distress, imprisonment, and then the contact had been broken. Random's story did fit, to that extent. So, instead, I said, "If he can point the finger, we have got to get him back and set him to pointing."

"I was hoping you would say that," Random replied.

"I hate to leave a bit of business like that unfinished."

I went and fetched the bottle, refilled our glasses. I sipped. I lit another cigarette.

"Before we get into that, though," I said, "I have to decide on the best way of breaking the news about Caine. Where is Flora, anyway?"

"Down in town, I think. She was here this morning. I can find her for you, I'm pretty sure."

"Do it, then. She is the only other one I know of who has seen one of these guys, back when they broke into her place in Westchester. We might as well have her handy for that much corroboration as to their nastiness. Besides, I have some other things I want to ask her."

He swallowed his drink and rose.

"All right. I'll go do that now. Where should I bring her?"

"My quarters. If I'm not there, wait."

He nodded.

I rose and accompanied him into the hall.

"Have you got the key to this room?" I asked.

"It's on a hook inside."

"Better get it and lock up. We wouldn't want a premature unveiling."

He did that and gave me the key. I walked with him as far as the first landing and saw him on his way.

From my safe, I removed the Jewel of Judgment, a ruby pendant which had given Dad and Eric control over the weather in the vicinity of Amber. Before he died, Eric had told me the procedure to be followed in tuning it to my own use. I had not had time to do it, though, and did not really have the time now. But during my conversation with Random I had decided that I was going to have to take the time. I had located Dworkin's notes, beneath a stone near Eric's fireplace. He had given me that much information also, that last time. I would have liked to know where he had come across the notes in the first place, though, for they were incomplete. I fetched them from the rear of the safe and regarded them once again. They did agree with Eric's explanation as to how the attunement was to be managed.

But they also indicated that the stone had other uses, that the control of meteorological phenomena was almost an incidental, though spectacular, demonstration of a complex of principles which underlay the Pattern, the Trumps, and the physical integrity of Amber herself, apart from Shadow. Unfortunately, the details were lacking. Still, the more I searched my memory, the more something along these lines did seem indicated. Only rarely had Dad produced the stone; and though he had spoken of it as a weather changer, the weather had not always been especially altered on those occasions when he had sported it. And he had often taken it along with him on his little trips. So I was ready to believe that there was more to it than that. Eric had probably reasoned the same way, but he had not been able to dope out its other uses either. He had simply taken advantage of its obvious powers when Bleys and I had attacked Amber; and he had used it the same way this past week when the creatures had made their assault from the black road. It had served him well on both occasions, even if it had not been sufficient to save his life. So I had better get hold of its power myself, I decided, now. Any extra edge was important. And it would be good to be seen wearing the thing, too, I judged. Especially now.

I put the notes back into the safe, the jewel in my pocket. I left then and headed downstairs. Again, as before, to walk those halls made me feel as if I had never been away. This was home, this was what I wanted. Now I was its defender. I did not even wear the crown, yet all its problems had become my own. It was ironic. I had come back to claim the crown, to wrest it from Eric, to hold the glory, to reign. Now, suddenly, things were falling apart. It had not taken long to realize that Eric had behaved incorrectly. If he had indeed done Dad in, he had no right to the crown. If he had not, then he had acted prematurely. Either way, the coronation had served only to fatten his already obese ego. Myself, I wanted it and I knew that I could take it. But it would be equally irresponsible to do so with my troops quartered in Amber, suspicious of Caine's murder about to descend upon me, the first signs of a fantastic plot suddenly displayed before me, and the continuing possibility that Dad was still alive. On several occasions it seemed we had been in contact, briefly—and at one such time, years ago, that he had okayed my succession. But there was so much deceit and trickery afoot that I did not know what to believe. He had not abdicated. Also, I had had a head injury, and I was well aware of my own desires. The mind is a funny place. I do not even trust my own. Could it be that I had manufactured that whole business? A lot had happened since. The price of being an Amberite, I suppose, is that you cannot even trust yourself. I wondered what Freud would have said. While he had failed to pierce my amnesia, he had come up with some awfully good guesses as to what my father had been like, what our relationship had been, even though I had not realized it at the time. I wished that I could have one more session with him.

I made my way through the marble dining hall and into the dark, narrow corridor that lay behind. I nodded to the guard and walked on back to the door. Through it then, out onto the platform, across and down. The interminable spiral stairway that leads into the guts of Kolvir. Walking. Lights every now and then. Blackness beyond.

It seemed that a balance had shifted somewhere along the way, and that I was no longer acting but being acted upon, being forced to move, to respond. Being herded. And each move led to another. Where had it all begun? Maybe it had been going on for years and I was only just now becoming aware of it. Perhaps we were all victims, in a fashion and to a degree none of us had realized. Great victuals for morbid thought. Sigmund, where are you now? I had wanted to be king—still wanted to be king—more than anything else. Yet the more I learned and the more I thought about what I had learned, the more all of my movements actually seemed to amount to Amber Pawn to King Four. I realized then that this feeling had been present for some time, growing, and I did not like it at all. But nothing that has ever lived has gotten by without making some mistake, I consoled myself. If my feeling represented actuality, my personal Pavlov was getting closer to my fangs with each ringing of the bell. Soon now, soon, I felt that it had to be soon, I would have to see that he came very near. Then it would be mine to see that he neither went away nor ever came again.

Turning, turning, around and down, light here, light there, these my thoughts, like thread on a spool, winding or unwinding, hard to be sure. Below me the sound of metal against stone. A guard's scabbard, the guard rising. A ripple of light from a lantern raised.

"Lord Corwin . . ."

"Jamie."

At bottom, I took a lantern from the shelf. Putting a light to it, I turned and headed toward the tunnel, pushing the darkness on ahead of me, a step at a time.

Eventually the tunnel, and so up it, counting side passages. It was the seventh that I wanted. Echoes and shadows. Must and dust.

Coming to it, then. Turning there. Not too much farther.

Finally, that great, dark, metal-bound door. I unlocked it and pushed hard. It creaked, resisted, finally moved inward.

I set down the lantern, just to the right, inside. I had no further need of it, as the Pattern itself gave off sufficient light for what I had to do.

For a moment I regarded the Pattern—a shining mass of curved lines that tricked the eye as it tried to trace them—imbedded there, huge, in the floor's slick blackness. It had given me power over Shadow, it had restored most of my memory. It would also destroy me in an instant if I were to essay it improperly. What gratitude the prospect did arouse in me was therefore not untinged with fear. It was a splendid and cryptic old family heirloom which belonged right where it was, in the cellar.

I moved off to the corner where the tracery began. There I composed my mind, relaxed my body, and set my left foot upon the Pattern. Without pausing, I strode forward then and felt the current begin. Blue sparks outlined my boots. Another step. There was an audible crackling this time and the beginning of resistance. I took the first curvelength, striving to hurry, wanting to reach the First Veil as quickly as possible. By the time I did, my hair was stirring and the sparks were brighter, longer.

The strain increased. Each step required more effect than the previous one. The crackling grew louder and the current intensified. My hair rose and I shook off sparks. I kept my eyes on the fiery lines and did not stop pushing.

Suddenly the pressure abated. I staggered but kept moving. I was through the First Veil and into the feeling of accomplishment that that entailed. I recalled the last time that I had come this way, in Rebma, the city under the sea. The maneuver I had just completed was what had started the return of my memories. Yes. I pushed ahead and the sparks grew and the currents rose once again, setting my flesh to tingling.

The Second Veil . . . The angles . . . It always seemed to tax the strength to its limits, to produce the feeling that one's entire being was transformed into pure Will. It was a driving, relentless sensation. At the moment, the negotiation of the Pattern was the only thing in the world that meant anything to me. I had always been there, striving, never been away, always would be there, contending, my will against the maze of power. Time had vanished. Only the tension held.

The sparks were up to my waist. I entered the Grand Curve and fought my way along it. I was continually destroyed and reborn at every step of its length, baked by the fires of creation, chilled by the cold at entropy's end.

Out and onward, turning. Three more curves, a straight line, a number of arcs. Dizziness, a sensation of fading and intensifying as though I were oscillating into and out of existence. Turn after turn after turn after turn . . . A short, sharp arc . . . The line that led to the Final Veil . . . I imagine I was gasping and drenched with sweat by then. I never seem to remember for sure. I could hardly move my feet. The sparks were up to my shoulders. They came into my eyes and I lost sight of the Pattern itself between blinks. In, out, in, out . . . There it was. I dragged my right foot forward, knowing how Benedict must have felt, his legs snared by the black grass. Right before I rabbit-punched him. I felt bludgeoned myself—all over. Left foot, forward . . . So slowly it was hard to be certain it was actually moving. My hands were blue flames, my legs pillars of fire. Another step. Another. Yet another.

I felt like a slowly animated statue, a thawing snowman, a buckling girder. . . . Two more . . . Three . . . Glacial, my movements, but I who directed them had all of eternity and a perfect constancy of will that would be realized. . . .

I passed through the Veil. A short arc followed. Three steps to cross it into blackness and peace. They were the worst of all.

A *coffee break for Sisyphus!* That was my first thought as I departed the Pattern. *I've done it again!* was my second. And, *Never again!* was my third.

I allowed myself the luxury of a few deep breaths and a little shaking. Then I unpocketed the jewel and raised it by its chain. I held it before my eye.

Red inside, of course—a deep cherry-red, smoke-shot, fulgent. It seemed to have picked up something extra of light and glitter during the trip through the Pattern. I continued to stare, thinking over the instructions, comparing them with things I already knew.

Once you have walked the Pattern and reached this point, you can cause it to transport you to any place that you can visualize. All that it takes is the desire and an act of will. Such being the case, I was not without a moment's trepidation. If the effect proceeded as it normally did, I could be throwing myself into a peculiar sort of trap. But Eric had succeeded. He had not been locked into the heart of a gem somewhere off in Shadow. The Dworkin who had written those notes had been a great man, and I had trusted him.

Composing my mind, I intensified my security of the stone's interior.

There was a distorted reflection of the Pattern within it, surrounded by winking points of light, tiny flares and flashes, different curves and paths. I made my decision, I focused my will. . . .

Redness and slow motion. Like sinking into an ocean of high viscosity. Very slow, at first. Drifting and darkening, all the pretty lights far, far ahead. Faintly, my apparent velocity increased. Flakes of light, distant, intermittent. A trifle faster then, it seemed. No scale. I was a point of consciousness of indeterminate dimensions. Aware of movement, aware of the configuration toward which I advanced, now almost rapidly. The redness was nearly gone, as was the consciousness of any medium. Resistance vanished. I was speeding. All of this, now, seemed to have taken but a single instant, was still taking that same instant. There was a peculiar, timeless quality to the entire affair. My velocity relative to what now seemed my target was enormous. The little, twisted maze was growing, was resolving into what appeared a three-dimensional variation of the Pattern itself. Punctuated by flares of colored light, it grew before me, still reminiscent of a bizarre galaxy half raveled in the middle of the ever-night, haloed with a pale shine of dust, its streamers composed of countless flickering points. And it grew or I shrank, or it advanced or I advanced, and we were near, near together, and it filled all of space now, top to bottom, this way to that, and my personal velocity still seemed, if anything, to be increasing. I was caught, overwhelmed by the blaze, and there was a stray streamer which I knew to be the beginning. I was too close—lost, actually—to apprehend its over-all configuration any longer, but the buckling, the flickering, the weaving of all that I could see of it, everywhere about me, made me wonder whether three dimensions were sufficient to account for the senses-warping complexities with which I was confronted. Rather than my galactic analogy, something in my mind shifted to the other extreme, suggesting the infinitely dimensioned Hilbert space of the subatomic. But then, it was a metaphor of desperation. Truly and simply, I did not understand anything about it. I had only a growing feeling—Pattern-conditioned? Instinctive?—that I had to pass through this maze also to gain the new degree of power that I sought.

Nor was I incorrect. I was swept on into it without any slackening of my apparent velocity. I was spun and whirled along blazing ways, passing through substanceless clouds of glitter and shine. There were no areas of resistance, as in the Pattern itself, my initial impetus seeming sufficient to bear me throughout. A whirlwind tour of the Milky Way? A drowning man swept among canyons of coral? An insomniac sparrow passing over an amusement park of a July Fourth evening? These my thoughts as I recapitulated my recent passage in this transformed fashion.

. . . And out, through, over, and done, in a blaze of ruddy light that found me regarding myself holding the pendant beside the Pattern, then regarding the pendant, Pattern within it, within me, everything within me, me within it, the redness subsiding, down, gone. Then just me, the pendant, the Pattern, alone, subject-object relationships reestablished—only an octave higher, which I feel is about the best way there is to put it. For a certain empathy now existed. It was as though I had acquired an extra sense, and an additional means of expression. It was a peculiar sensation, satisfying.

Anxious to test it, I summoned my resolve once again and commanded the Pattern to transport me elsewhere.

I stood then in the round room, atop the highest tower in Amber. Crossing it, I passed outside, onto a very small balcony. The contrast was powerful, coming so close to the supersensory voyage I had just completed. For several long moments I simply stood there, looking.

The sea was a study in textures, as the sky was partly overcast and getting on toward evening. The clouds themselves showed patterns of soft brightness and rough shading. The wind made its way seaward, so that the salt smell was temporarily denied me. Dark birds dotted the air, swinging and hovering at a great distance out over the water. Below me, the palace yards and the terraces of the city lay spread in enduring elegance out to Kolvir's rim. People were tiny on the thoroughfares, their movements discountable. I felt very alone.

Then I touched the pendant and called for a storm.

FOUR

Random and Flora were waiting in my quarters when I returned. Random's eyes went first to the pendant, then to my own. I nodded.

I turned toward Flora, bowing slightly.

"Sister," I said, "it has been a while, and then a while."

She looked somewhat frightened, which was all to the good. She smiled and took my hand, though.

"Brother," she said. "I see that you have kept your word."

Pale gold, her hair. She had cut it, but retained the bangs. I could not decide whether I liked it that way or not. She had very lovely hair. Blue eyes, too, and tons of vanity to keep everything in her favorite perspective. At times she seemed to behave quite stupidly, but then at other times I have wondered.

"Excuse me for staring," I said, "but the last time that we met I was unable to see you."

"I am very happy that the situation has been corrected," she said. "It was quite—There was nothing that I could do, you know."

"I know," I said, recalling the occasional lilt of her laughter from the other side of the darkness on one of the anniversaries of the event. "I know."

I moved to the window and opened it, knowing that the rain would not be coming in. I like the smell of a storm.

"Random, did you learn anything of interest with regard to a possible postman?" I asked.

"Not really," he said. "I made some inquiries. No one seems to have seen anyone else in the right place at the right time."

"I see," I said. "Thank you. I may see you again later."

"All right," he said. "I'll be in my quarters all evening, then."

I nodded, turned, leaned back against the sill, watched Flora. Random closed the door quietly as he left. I listened to the rain for half a minute or so.

"What are you going to do with me?" she said finally.

"Do?"

"You are in a position to call for a settlement on old debts. I assume that things are about to begin."

"Perhaps," I said. "Most things depend on other things. This thing is no different."

"What do you mean?"

"Give me what I want, and we'll see. I have even been known to be a nice guy on occasion."

286

"What is it that you want?"

"The story, Flora. Let's start with that. Of how you came to be my shepherdess there on that shadow, Earth. All pertinent details. What was the arrangement? What was the understanding? Everything. That's all."

She sighed.

"The beginning . . ." she said. "Yes . . . It was in Paris, a party, at a certain Monsieur Focault's. This was about three years before the Terror—"

"Stop," I said. "What were you doing there?"

"I had been in that general area of Shadow for approximately five of their years," she said. "I had been wandering, looking for something novel, something that suited my fancy. I came upon that place at that time in the same way we find anything. I let my desires lead me and I followed my instincts."

"A peculiar coincidence."

"Not in light of all the time involved—and considering the amount of travel in which we indulge. It was, if you like, my Avalon, my Amber surrogate, my home away from home. Call it what you will, I was there, at that party, that October night, when you came in with the little redheaded girl—Jacqueline, I believe, was her name."

That brought it back, from quite a distance, a memory I hadn't called for in a long, long while. I remembered Jacqueline far better than I did Focault's party, but there had been such an occasion.

"Go ahead."

"As I said," she went on, "I was there. You arrived later. You caught my attention immediately, of course. Still, if one exists for a sufficiently long period of time and travels considerably, one does occasionally encounter a person greatly resembling someone else one has known. That was my first thought after the initial excitement faded. Surely it had to be a double. So much time had passed without a whisper. Yet we all have secrets and good reasons for having them. This could be one of yours. So I saw that we were introduced and then had a devil of a time getting you away from that little redheaded piece for more than a few minutes. And you insisted your name was Fenneval—Cordell Fenneval. I grew uncertain. I could not tell whether it was a double or you playing games. The third possibility did cross my mind, though—that you had dwelled in some adjacent area of Shadow for a sufficient time to cast shadows of yourself. I might have departed still wondering had not Jacqueline later boasted to me concerning your strength. Now this is not the commonest subject of conversation for a woman, and the way in which she said it led me to believe that she had actually been quite impressed by some things you had done. I drew her out a bit and realized that they were all of them feats of which you were capable. That eliminated the notion of it being a double. It had to be either you or your shadow. This in mind, even if Cordell was not Corwin he was a clue, a clue that you were or had been in that shady neighborhood—the first real clue I had come across concerning your whereabouts. I had to pursue it. I began keeping track of you then, checking into your past. The more people I questioned, the more puzzling it became. In fact, after several months I was still unable to decide.

There were enough smudgy areas to make it possible. Things were resolved for me the following summer, though, when I revisited Amber for a time. I mentioned the peculiar affair to Eric . . ."

"Yes?"

"Well . . . he was—somewhat—aware—of the possibility."

She paused and rearranged her gloves on the seat beside her.

"Uh-huh," I said. "Just what did he tell you?"

"That it might be the real you," she said. "He told me there had been— an accident."

"Really?"

"Well, no," she admitted. "Not an accident. He said there had been a fight and he had injured you. He thought you were going to die, and he did not want the blame. So he transported you off into Shadow and left you there, in that place. After a long while, he decided that you must be dead, that it was finally all over between you. My news naturally disturbed him. So he swore me to secrecy and sent me back to keep you under surveillance. I had a good excuse for being there, as I had already told everyone how much I liked the place."

"You didn't promise to keep silent for nothing, Flora. What did he give you?"

"He gave me his word that should he ever come into power here in Amber, I would not be forgotten."

"A little risky," I said. "After all, that would still leave you with something on him—knowledge of the whereabouts of a rival claimant, and of his part in putting him there."

"True. But things sort of balanced out, and I would have to admit having become an accomplice in order to talk about it."

I nodded.

"Tight, but not impossible," I agreed. "But did you think he would let me continue living if he ever did get a chance at the throne?"

"That was never discussed. Never."

"It must have crossed your mind, though."

"Yes, later," she said, "and I decided that he would probably do nothing. After all, it was beginning to seem likely that you had been deprived of your memory. There was no reason to do anything to you so long as you were harmless."

"So you stayed on to watch me, to see that I remained harmless?"

"Yes."

"What would you have done had I shown signs of recovering my memory?"

She looked at me, then looked away.

"I would have reported it to Eric."

"And what would he have done then?"

"I don't know."

I laughed a little, and she blushed. I could not remember the last time I had seen Flora blush.

"I will not belabor the obvious," I said. "All right, you stayed on, you watched me. What next? What happened?"

"Nothing special. You just went on leading your life and I went on keeping track of it."

"All of the others knew where you were?"

"Yes. I'd make no secret of my whereabouts. In fact, all of them came around to visit me at one time or another."

"That includes Random?"

She curled her lip.

"Yes, several times," she said.

"Why the sneer?"

"It is too late to start pretending I like him," she said. "You know. I just don't like the people he associates with—assorted criminals, jazz musicians. . . . I had to show him family courtesy when he was visiting my shadow, but he put a big strain on my nerves, bringing those people around at all hours—jam sessions, poker parties. The place usually reeked for weeks afterward and I was always glad to see him go. Sorry. I know you like him, but you wanted the truth."

"He offended your delicate sensibilities. Okay. I now direct your attention to the brief time when I was your guest. Random joined us rather abruptly. Pursuing him were half a dozen nasty fellows whom we dispatched in your living room."

"I recall the event quite vividly."

"Do you recall the guys responsible—the creatures we had to deal with?"

"Yes."

"Sufficiently well to recognize one if you ever saw another?"

"I think so."

"Good. Had you ever seen one before?"

"No."

"Since?"

"No."

"Had you ever heard them described anywhere?"

"Not that I can remember. Why?"

I shook my head.

"Not yet. This is my inquisition, remember? Now I want you to think back for a time before that evening. Back to the event that put me in Greenwood. Maybe even a little earlier. What happened, and how did you find out about it? What were the circumstances? What was your part in things?"

"Yes," she said. "I knew you would ask me that sooner or later. What happened was that Eric contacted me the day after it occurred—from Amber, via my Trump." She glanced at me again, obviously to see how I was taking it, to study my reactions. I remained expressionless. "He told me you had been in a bad accident the previous evening, and that you were hospitalized. He told me to have you transferred to a private place, one where I could have more say as to the course of your treatment."

"In other words, he wanted me to stay a vegetable."

"He wanted them to keep you sedated."

"Did he or did he not admit to being responsible for the accident?"

"He did not say that he had had someone shoot out your tire, but he did know that that was what had happened. How else could he have known? When I learned later that he was planning to take the throne, I assumed that he had finally decided it was best to remove you entirely. When the attempt failed, it seemed logical that he would do the next most effective thing: see that you were kept out of the way until after the coronation."

"I was not aware that the tire had been shot out," I said.

Her face changed. She recovered.

"You told me that you knew it was not an accident—that someone had tried to kill you. I assumed you were aware of the specifics."

I was treading on slightly mucky ground again for the first time in a long while. I still had a bit of amnesia, and I had decided I probably always would. My memories of the few days prior to the accident were still spotty. The Pattern had restored the lost memories of my entire life up until then, but the trauma appeared to have destroyed recollection of some of the events immediately preceding it. Not an uncommon occurrence. Organic damage rather than simple functional distress, most likely. I was happy enough to have all the rest back, so those did not seem especially lamentable. As to the accident itself, and my feelings that it had been more than an accident, I did recall the gunshots. There had been two of them. I might even have glimpsed the figure with the rifle—fleetingly, too late. Or maybe that was pure fantasy. It seemed that I had, though. I had had something like that in mind when I had headed out for Westchester. Even at this late time, though, when I held the power in Amber, I was loath to admit this single deficiency. I had faked my way with Flora before with a lot less to go on. I decided to stick with a winning combination.

"I was in no position to get out and see what had been hit," I said. "I heard the shots. I lost control. I had assumed that it was a tire, but I never knew for sure. The only reason I raised the question was because I was curious as to how you knew it was a tire."

"I already told you that Eric told me about it."

"It was the way that you said it that bothered me. You made it sound as if you already knew all the details before he contacted you."

She shook her head.

"Then pardon my syntax," she said. "That sometimes happens when you look at things after the fact. I am going to have to deny what you are implying. I had nothing to do with it and I had no prior knowledge that it had occurred."

"Since Eric is no longer around to confirm or deny anything, we will simply have to let it go," I said, "for now," and I said it to make her look even harder to her defense, to direct her attention away from any possible slip, either in word or expression, from which she might infer the small flaw which still existed in my memory. "Did you later become aware of the identity of the person with the gun?" I asked.

"Never," she said. "Most likely some hired thug. I don't know."

"Have you any idea how long I was unconscious before someone found me, took me to a hospital?"

She shook her head again.

Something was bothering me and I could not quite put my finger on it.

"Did Eric say what time I had been taken into the hospital?"

"No."

"When I was with you, why did you try walking back to Amber rather than using Eric's Trump?"

"I couldn't raise him."

"You could have called someone else to bring you through," I said. "Flora, I think you are lying to me."

It was really only a test, to observe her reaction. Why not?

"About what?" she asked. "I couldn't raise anyone else. They were all otherwise occupied. Is that what you mean?"

She studied me.

I raised my arm and pointed at her and the lightning flashed at my back, just outside the window. I felt a tingle, a mild jolt. The thunderclap was also impressive.

"You sin by omission," I tried.

She covered her face with her hands and began to weep.

"I don't know what you mean!" she said. "I answered all your questions! What do you want? I don't know where you were going or who shot at you or what time it occurred! I just know the facts I've given you, damn it!"

She was either sincere or unbreakable by these means, I decided. Whichever, I was wasting my time and could get nothing more this way. Also, I had better switch us away from the accident before she began thinking too much about its importance to me. If there was something there that I was missing, I wanted to find it first.

"Come with me," I said.

"Where are we going?"

"I have something I want you to identify. I will tell you why after you see it."

She rose and followed me. I took her up the hall to see the body before I gave her the story on Caine. She regarded the corpse quite dispassionately. She nodded.

"Yes," she said, and, "Even if I did not know it I would be glad to say that I did, for you."

I grunted a noncommittal. Family loyalty always touches me, somewhere. I could not tell whether she believed what I had said about Caine. But things sort of equal to equal things sort of being equal to each other, it didn't much seem to matter. I did not tell her anything about Brand and she did not seem to possess any new information concerning him. Her only other comment when everything I'd had to say was said, was, "You wear the jewel well. What about the headpiece?"

"It is too soon to talk of such things," I told her.

"Whatever my support may be worth . . ."

"I know," I said. "I know."

My tomb is a quiet place. It stands alone in a rocky declivity, shielded on three sides against the elements, surrounded by transported soil wherein a pair of scrubby trees, miscellaneous shrubs, weeds, and great ropes of mountain ivy are rooted, about two miles down, in back of the crest of Kolvir. It is a long, low building with two benches in front, and the ivy has contrived to cover it to a great extent, mercifully masking most of a bombastic statement graven on its face beneath my name. It is, understandably, vacant most of the time.

That evening, however, Ganelon and I repaired thither, accompanied by a good supply of wine and some loaves and cold cuts.

"You weren't joking!" he said, having dismounted, crossed over, and parted the ivy, able to read by the moon's light the words that were rendered there.

"Of course not," I said, climbing down and taking charge of the horses. "It's mine all right."

Tethering our mounts to a nearby shrub, I unslung our bags of provisions and carried them to the nearest bench. Ganelon joined me as I opened the first bottle and poured us a dark, deep pair.

"I still don't understand," he said, accepting his.

"What's there to understand? I'm dead and buried there," I said. "It's my cenotaph, is what it is—the monument that gets set up when the body has not been recovered. I only just learned about mine recently. It was raised several centuries ago, when it was decided I wasn't coming back."

"Kind of spooky," he said. "What's inside then?"

"Nothing. Though they did thoughtfully provide a niche and a casket, just in case my remains put in an appearance. You cover both bets that way."

Ganelon made himself a sandwich.

"Whose idea was it?" he asked.

"Random thinks it was Brand's or Eric's. No one remembers for sure. They all seemed to feel it was a good idea at the time."

He chuckled, an evil noise that perfectly suited his creased, scarred, and red-bearded self.

"What's to become of it now?"

I shrugged.

"I suppose some of them think it's a shame to waste it this way and would like to see me fill it. In the meantime, though, it's a good place to come and get drunk. I hadn't really paid my respects yet."

I put together a pair of sandwiches and ate them both. This was the first real breather I had had since my return, and perhaps the last for some time to come. It was impossible to say. But I had not really had a chance to speak with Ganelon at any length during the past week, and he was one of the few persons I trusted. I wanted to tell him everything. I had to. I had to talk with someone who was not a part of it in the same way as the rest of us. So I did.

The moon moved a considerable distance and the shards of broken glass multiplied within my crypt.

"So how did the others take it?" he asked me.

"Predictably," I answered. "I could tell that Julian did not believe a word of it even though he said that he did. He knows how I feel about him, and he is in no position to challenge me. I don't think Benedict believes me either, but he is a lot harder to read. He is biding his time, and I hope giving me the benefit of the doubt while he is about it. As for Gérard, I have the feeling that this was the final weight, and whatever trust he had left for me has just collapsed. Still, he will be returning to Amber early tomorrow, to accompany me to the grove to recover Caine's body. No sense in turning it into a safari, but I did want another family member present. Deirdre now— she seemed happy about it. Didn't believe a word, I'm sure. But no matter. She has always been on my side, and she has never liked Caine. I'd say she is glad that I seem to be consolidating my position. I can't really tell whether Llewella believed me or not. She doesn't much give a damn what the rest of us do to one another, so far as I can see. As to Fiona, she simply seemed amused at the whole business. But then, she has always had this detached, superior way of regarding things. You can never be certain what represents her real thinking."

"Did you tell them the business about Brand yet?"

"No. I told them about Caine and I told them I wanted them all to be in Amber by tomorrow evening. That is when the subject of Brand will be raised. I've an idea I want to try out."

"You contacted all of them by means of the Trumps?"

"That's right."

"There is something I have been meaning to ask you about that. Back on the shadow world we visited to obtain the weapons, there are telephones. . . ."

"Yes?"

"I learned about wiretaps and such while we were there. Is it possible, do you think, that the Trumps could be bugged?"

I began to laugh, then caught myself as some of the implications of his suggestion sank in. Finally, "I don't really know," I said. "So much concerning Dworkin's work remains a mystery—the thought just never occurred to me. I've never tried it myself. I wonder, though. . . ."

"Do you know how many sets there are?"

"Well, everyone in the family has a pack or two and there were a dozen or so spares in the library. I don't really know whether there are any others."

"It seems to me that a lot could be learned just by listening in."

"Yes. Dad's deck, Brand's, my original pack, the one Random lost—Hell! There are quite a number unaccounted for these days. I don't know what to do about it. Start an inventory and try some experiments, I guess. Thanks for mentioning it."

He nodded and we both sipped for a while in silence.

Then, "What are you going to do, Corwin?" he asked.

"About what?"

"About everything. What do we attack now, and in what order?"

"My original intention was to begin tracing the black road toward its origin as soon as things were more settled here in Amber," I said. "Now, though, I have shifted my priorities. I want Brand returned as soon as possible, if he is still living. If not, I want to find out what happened to him."

"But will the enemy give you the breathing time? He might be preparing a new offensive right now."

"Yes, of course. I have considered that. I feel we have some time, since they were defeated so recently. They will have to pull themselves together again, beef up their forces, reassess the situation in light of our new weapons. What I have in mind for the moment is to establish a series of lookout stations along the road to give us advance warning of any new movements on their part. Benedict has already agreed to take charge of the operation."

"I wonder how much time we have."

I poured him another drink, as it was the only answer I could think of.

"Things were never this complicated back in Avalon—our Avalon, I mean."

"True," I said. "You are not the only one who misses those days. At least, they seem simpler now."

He nodded. I offered him a cigarette, but he declined in favor of his pipe. In the flamelight, he studied the Jewel of Judgment which still hung about my neck.

"You say you can really control the weather with that thing?" he asked.

"Yes," I said.

"How do you know?"

"I've tried it. It works."

"What did you do?"

"That storm this afternoon. It was mine."

"I wonder . . ."

"What?"

"I wonder what I would have done with that sort of power. What I would do with it."

"The first thing that crossed my mind," I said, slapping the wall of my tomb, "was to destroy this place by lightning—strike it repeatedly and reduce it to rubble. Leave no doubt in anyone's mind as to my feelings, my power."

"Why didn't you?"

"Got to thinking about it a bit more then. Decided—Hell! They might really have a use for the place before too long, if I'm not smart enough or tough enough or lucky enough. Such being the case, I tried to decide where I would like them to dump my bones. It caught me then that this is really a pretty good spot—up high, clean, where the elements still walk naked. Nothing in sight but rock and sky. Stars, clouds, sun, moon, wind, rain . . . better company than a lot of other stiffs. Don't know why I should have to lie beside anyone I wouldn't want next to me now, and there aren't many."

"You're getting morbid, Corwin. Or drunk. Or both. Bitter, too. You don't need that."

"Who the hell are you to say what I need?"

I felt him stiffen beside me, then relax.

"I don't know," he finally said. "Just saying what I see."

"How are the troops holding up?" I asked.

"I think they are still bewildered, Corwin. They came to fight a holy war on the slopes of heaven. They think that's what the shooting was all about last week. So they are happy on that count, seeing as we won. But now this waiting, in the city . . . They don't understand the place. Some of the ones they thought to be enemies are now friends. They are confused. They know they are being kept ready for combat, but they have no idea against whom, or when. As they have been restricted to the billets the whole time, they have not yet realized the extent to which their presence is resented by the regulars and the population at large. They will probably be catching on fairly soon, though. I had been waiting to raise the subject, but you've been so busy lately. . . ."

I sat smoking for a time.

Then, "I guess I had better have a talk with them," I said. "Won't have a chance tomorrow, though, and something should be done soon. I think they should be moved—to a bivouac area in the Forest of Arden. Tomorrow, yes. I'll locate it for you on the map when we get back. Tell them it is to keep them close to the black road. Tell them that another attack could come that way at any time—which is no less than the truth. Drill them, maintain their fighting edge. I'll come down as soon as I can and talk to them."

"That will leave you without a personal force in Amber."

"True. It may prove a useful risk, though, both as a demonstration of confidence and a gesture of consideration. Yes, I think it will turn out to be a good move. If not . . ." I shrugged.

I poured and tossed another empty into my tomb.

"By the way," I said, "I'm sorry."

"What for?"

"I just noticed that I am morbid and drunk and bitter. I don't need that."

He chuckled and clicked his glass against my own.

"I know," he said. "I know."

So we sat there while the moon fell, till the last bottle was interred among its fellows. We talked for a time of days gone by. At length we fell silent and my eyes drifted to the stars above Amber. It was good that we had come to this place, but now the city was calling me back. Knowing my thoughts, Ganelon rose and stretched, headed for the horses. I relieved myself beside my tomb and followed him.

FIVE

The Grove of the Unicorn lies in Arden to the southwest of Kolvir, near to that jutting place where the land begins its final descent into the valley called Garnath. While Garnath had been cursed, burned, invaded, and fought through in recent years, the adjacent highlands stood unmolested. The grove where Dad claimed to have seen the unicorn ages before and to have experienced the peculiar events which led to his adopting the beast as the patron of Amber and placing it on his coat of arms, was, as near as we could tell, a spot now but slightly screened from the long view across Garnath to the sea—twenty or thirty paces in from the upper edge of things: an asymmetrical glade where a small spring trickled from a mass of rock, formed a clear pool, brimmed into a tiny creek, made its way off toward Garnath and on down.

It was to this place that Gérard and I rode the following day, leaving at an hour that found us halfway down our trail from Kolvir before the sun skipped flakes of light across the ocean, then cast its whole bucketful against the sky. Gérard drew rein as it was doing this. He dismounted then and motioned to me to do the same. I did, leaving Star and the pack horse I was leading there beside his own huge piebald. I followed him off perhaps a dozen paces into a basin half-filled with gravel. He halted and I came up beside him.

"What is it?" I asked.

He turned and faced me and his eyes were narrow and his jaw clamped tight. He unfastened his cloak, folded it, and placed it on the ground. He unclapped his swordbelt and lay it atop the cloak.

"Get rid of your blade and your cloak," he said. "They will only get in the way."

I had an inkling of what was coming, and I decided I had better go along with it. I folded my cloak, placed the Jewel of Judgment beside Grayswandir, and faced him once again. I said only one word.

"Why?"

"It has been a long time," he said, "and you might have forgotten."

He came at me slowly, and I got my arms out in front of me and backed away. He did not swing at me. I used to be faster than he was. We were both crouched, and he was making slow, pawing movements with his left hand, his right hand nearer to his body, twitching slightly.

If I had had to choose a place to fight with Gérard, this would not have been it. He, of course, was aware of this. If I had to fight with Gérard at all, I would not have chosen to do so with my hands. I am better than Gérard with a blade or a quarterstaff. Anything that involved speed and strategy and gave me a chance to hit him occasionally while keeping him at bay would permit me to wear him down eventually and provide openings for heavier and heavier assaults. He, of course, was aware of this also. That is why he had trapped me as he had. I understood Gérard, though, and I had to play by his rules now.

I brushed his hand away a couple of times as he stepped up his movements, pressing nearer to me with every pace. Finally I took a chance, ducked and swung. I landed a fast, hard left just a little above his middle. It would have broken a stout board or ruptured the insides of a lesser mortal. Unfortunately, time had not softened Gérard. I heard him grunt, but he blocked my right, got his right hand under my left arm, and caught my shoulder from behind.

I closed with him fast then, anticipating a shoulder lock I might not be able to break; and, turning, driving forward, catching his left shoulder in a similar fashion, I hooked my right leg behind his knee and was able to cast him backward to the ground.

He maintained his grip, though, and I came down atop him. I released my own hold and was able to drive my right elbow into his left side as we hit. The angle was not ideal and his left hand went up and across, reaching to grasp his right somewhere behind my head.

I was able to duck out of it, but he still had my arm. For a moment I had a clear shot at his groin with my right, but I restrained myself. It is not that I have any qualms about hitting a man below his belt. I knew that if I did it to Gérard just then his reflexes would probably cause him to break my shoulder. Instead, scraping my forearm on the gravel, I managed to twist my left arm up behind his head, while at the same time sliding my right arm between his legs and catching him about the left thigh. I rolled back as I did this, attempting to straighten my legs as soon as my feet were beneath me. I wanted to raise him off the ground and slam him down again, driving my shoulder into his middle for good measure.

But Gérard scissored his legs and rolled to the left, forcing me to somersault across his body. I let go my hold on his head and pulled my left arm free as I went over. I scrambled clockwise then, dragging my right arm away and going for a toehold.

But Gérard would have none of that. He had gotten his arms beneath him by then. With one great heave he tore himself free and twisted his way back to his feet. I straightened myself and leaped backwards. He began moving toward me immediately, and I decided that he was going to maul the hell out of me if I just kept grappling with him. I had to take a few chances.

I watched his feet, and at what I judged to be the best moment I dove in beneath his extended arms just as he was shifting his weight forward onto his left foot and raising his right. I was able to catch hold of his right ankle and hoist it about four feet high behind him. He went over and down, forward and to his left.

He scrambled to get to his feet and I caught him on the jaw with a left that knocked him down again. He shook his head and blocked with his arms as he came up once more. I tried to kick him in the stomach, but missed as he pivoted, catching him on the hip. He maintained his balance and advanced again.

I threw jabs at his face and circled. I caught him twice more in the stomach and danced away. He smiled. He knew I was afraid to close with him. I snapped a kick at his stomach and connected. His arms dropped sufficiently for me to chop him alongside the neck, just above the collarbone. At that moment, however, his arms shot forward and locked about my waist. I slammed his jaw with the heel of my hand, but it did not stop him from tightening his grip and raising me above the ground. Too late to hit him again. Those massive arms were already crushing my kidneys. I sought his carotids with my thumbs, squeezed.

But he kept raising me, back, up over his head. My grip loosened, slipped away. Then he slammed me down on my back in the gravel, as peasant women do their laundry on rocks.

There were exploding points of light and the world was a jittering, half-real place as he dragged me to my feet again. I saw his fist—

The sunrise was lovely, but the angle was wrong . . . By about ninety degrees . . .

Suddenly I was assailed by vertigo. It canceled out the beginning awareness of a roadmap of pains that ran along my back and reached the big city somewhere in the vicinity of my chin.

I was hanging high in the air. By turning my head slightly I could see for a very great distance, down.

I felt a set of powerful clamps affixed to my body—shoulder and thigh. When I turned to look at them, I saw that they were hands. Twisting my neck even farther, I saw that they were Gérard's hands. He was holding me at full arm's length above his head. He stood at the very edge of the trail, and I could see Garnath and the terminus of the black road far below. If he let go, part of me might join the bird droppings that smeared the cliff face and the rest would come to resemble washed-up jellyfish I had known on beaches past.

"Yes. Look down, Corwin," he said, feeling me stir, glancing up, meeting my eyes. "All that I need to do is open my hands."

"I hear you," I said softly, trying to figure a way to drag him along with me if he decided to do it.

"I am not a clever man," he said. "But I had a thought—a terrible thought. This is the only way that I know to do something about it. My thought was that you had been away from Amber for an awfully long while. I have no way of knowing whether the story about your losing your memory is entirely true. You have come back and you have taken charge of things, but you do not yet truly rule here. I was troubled by the deaths of Benedict's servants, as I am troubled now by the death of Caine. But Eric has died recently also, and Benedict is maimed. It is not so easy to blame you for this part of things, but it has occurred to me that it might be possible—if it should be that you are secretly allied with our enemies of the black road."

"I am not," I said.

"It does not matter, for what I have to say," he said. "Just hear me out. Things will go the way that they will go. If, during your long absence, you arranged this state of affairs—possibly even removing Dad and Brand as part of your design—then I see you as out to destroy all family resistance to your usurpation."

"Would I have delivered myself to Eric to be blinded and imprisoned if this were the case?"

"Hear me out!" he repeated. "You could easily have made mistakes that led to that. It does not matter now. You may be as innocent as you say or as guilty as possible. Look down, Corwin. That is all. Look down at the black road. Death is the limit of the distance you travel if that is your doing. I have shown you my strength once again, lest you have forgotten. I can kill you, Corwin. Do not even be certain that your blade will protect you, if I can get my hands on you but once. And I will, to keep my promise. My promise is only that if you are guilty I will kill you the moment I learn of it. Know also that my life is insured, Corwin, for it is linked now to your own."

"What do you mean?"

"All of the others are with us at this moment, via my Trump, watching, listening. You cannot arrange my removal now without revealing your intentions to the entire family. That way, if I die forsworn, my promise can still be kept."

"I get the point," I said. "And if someone else kills you? They remove me, also. That leaves Julian, Benedict, Random, and the girls to man the barricades. Better and better—for whoever it is. Whose idea was this, really?"

"Mine! Mine alone!" he said, and I felt his grip tighten, his arms bend and grow tense. "You are just trying to confuse things! Like you always do!" he groaned. "Things didn't go bad till you came back! Damn it, Corwin! I think it's your fault!"

Then he hurled me into the air.

"Not guilty, Gérard!" was all I had time to shout.

Then he caught me—a great, shoulder-wrenching grab—and snatched me back from the precipice. He swung me in and around and set me on my feet. He walked off immediately, heading back to the gravelly area where we had fought. I followed him and we collected our things.

As he was clasping his big belt he looked up at me and looked away again.

"We'll not talk about it any more," he said.

"All right."

I turned and walked back to the horses. We mounted and continued on down the trail.

The spring made its small music in the grove. Higher now, the sun strung lines of light through the trees. There was still some dew on the ground. The sod that I had cut for Caine's grave was moist with it.

I fetched the spade that I had packed and opened the grave. Without a word, Gérard helped me move the body onto a piece of sailcloth we had brought for that purpose. We folded it about him and closed it with big, loose stitches.

"Corwin! Look!" It was a whisper, and Gérard's hand closed on my elbow as he spoke.

I followed the direction of his gaze and froze. Neither of us moved as we regarded the apparition: a soft, shimmering white encompassed it, as if it were covered with down rather than fur and maning; its tiny, cloven hooves were golden, as was the delicate, whorled horn that rose from its narrow head. It stood atop one of the lesser rocks, nibbling at the lichen that grew there. Its eyes, when it raised them and looked in our direction, were a bright, emerald green. It joined us in immobility for a pair of instants. Then it made a quick, nervous gesture with its front feet, pawing the air and striking the stone, three times. And then it blurred and vanished like a snowflake, silently, perhaps in the woods to our right.

I rose and crossed to the stone. Gérard followed me. There, in the moss, I traced its tiny hoofmarks.

"Then we really did see it," Gérard said.

I nodded.

"We saw something. Did you ever see it before?"

"No. Did you?"

I shook my head.

"Julian claims he once saw it," he said, "in the distance. Says his hounds refused to give chase."

"It was beautiful. That long, silky tail, those shiny hooves . . ."

"Yes. Dad always took it as a good omen."

"I'd like to myself."

"Strange time for it to appear . . . All these years . . ."

I nodded again.

"Is there a special observance? It being our patron and all . . . is there something we should do?"

"If there is, Dad never told me about it," I said. I patted the rock on which it had appeared. "If you herald some turn in our fortunes, if you bring us some measure of grace—thanks, unicorn," I said. "And even if you do not, thanks for the brightness of your company at a dark time."

We went and drank from the spring then. We secured our grim parcel on the back of the third horse. We led our mounts until we were away from the place, where, save for the water, things had become very still.

SIX

Life's incessant ceremonies leap everlasting, humans spring eternal on hope's breast, and frying pans without fires are often far between: the sum of my long life's wisdom that evening, tendered in a spirit of creative anxiety, answered by Random with a nod and a friendly obscenity.

We were in the library, and I was seated on the edge of the big desk. Random occupied a chair to my right. Gérard stood at the other end of the room, inspecting some weapons that hung on the wall. Or maybe it was Rein's etching of the unicorn he was looking at. Whichever, along with ourselves, he was also ignoring Julian, who was slouched in an easy chair beside the display cases, right center, legs extended and crossed at the ankles, arms folded, staring down at his scaley boots. Fiona—five-two, perhaps, in height—green eyes fixed on Flora's own blue as they spoke, there beside the fireplace, hair more than compensating for the vacant hearth, smoldering, reminded me, as always, of something from which the artist had just drawn back, setting aside his tools, questions slowly forming behind his smile. The place at the base of her throat where his thumb had notched the collarbone always drew my eyes as the mark of a master craftsman, especially when she raised her head, quizzical or imperious, to regard us taller others. She smiled faintly, just then, doubtless aware of my gaze, an almost clairvoyant faculty the acceptance of which has never deprived of its ability to disconcert. Llewella, off in a corner, pretending to study a book, had her back to the rest of us, her green tresses bobbed a couple of inches above her dark collar. Whether her withdrawal involved animus, self-conscious in her alienation, or simple caution, I could never be certain. Probably something of all these. Hers was not that familiar a presence in Amber.

. . . And the fact that we constituted a collection of individuals rather than a group, a family, at a time when I wanted to achieve some over-identity, some will to cooperate, was what led to my observations and Random's acknowledgement.

I felt a familiar presence, heard a "Hello, Corwin" and there was Deirdre, reaching toward me. I extended my hand, clasped her own, raised it. She took a step forward, as if to the first strain of some formal dance, and moved close, facing me. For an instant a grilled window had framed her head and shoulders and a rich tapestry had adorned the wall to her left. Planned and posed, of course. Still, effective. She held my Trump in her left hand. She smiled. The others glanced our way as she appeared and she hit them all with that smile, like the Mona Lisa with a machine gun, turning slowly.

"Corwin," she said, kissing me briefly and withdrawing, "I fear I am early."

"Never," I replied, turning toward Random, who had just risen and who anticipated me by seconds.

"May I fetch you a drink, sister?" he asked, taking her hand and nodding toward the sideboard.

"Why, yes. Thank you," and he led her off and poured her some wine, avoiding or at least postponing, I suppose, her usual clash with Flora. At least, I assumed most of the old frictions were still alive as I remembered them. So if it cost me her company for the moment it also maintained the domestic-tranquility index, which was important to me just then. Random can be good at such things when he wants to.

I drummed the side of the desk with my fingertips, I rubbed my aching shoulder, I uncrossed and recrossed my legs, I debated lighting a cigarette. . . .

Suddenly he was there. At the far end of the room, Gérard had turned to his left, said something, and extended his hand. An instant later, he was clasping the left and only hand of Benedict, the final member of our group.

All right. The fact that Benedict had chosen to come in on Gérard's Trump rather than mine was his way of expressing his feelings toward me. Was it also an indication of an alliance to keep me in check? It was at least calculated to make me wonder. Could it have been Benedict who had put Gérard up to our morning's exercise? Probably.

At that moment Julian rose to his feet, crossed the room, gave Benedict a word and a handclasp. This activity attracted Llewella. She turned, closing her book and laying it aside. Smiling then, she advanced and greeted Benedict, nodded to Julian, said something to Gérard. The impromptu conference warmed, grew animated. All right again, and again.

Four and three. And two in the middle . . .

I waited, staring at the group across the room. We were all present, and I could have asked them for attention and proceeded with what I had in mind. However . . .

It was too tempting. All of us could feel the tension, I knew. It was as if a pair of magnetic poles had suddenly been activated within the room. I was curious to see how all the filings would fall.

Flora gave me one quick glance. I doubted that she had changed her mind overnight—unless, of course, there had been some new development. No, I felt confident that I had anticipated the next move.

Nor was I incorrect. I overheard her mentioning thirst and a glass of wine. She turned partway and made a move in my direction, as if expecting Fiona to accompany her. She hesitated for a moment when this did not occur, suddenly became the focus of the entire company's attention, realized this fact, made a quick decision, smiled, and moved in my direction.

"Corwin," she said, "I believe I would like a glass of wine."

Without turning my head or removing my gaze from the tableau before me, I called back over my shoulder, "Random, pour Flora a glass of wine, would you?"

"But of course," he replied, and I heard the necessary sounds.

Flora nodded, unsmiled, and passed beyond me to the right.

Four and four, leaving dear Fiona burning brightly in the middle of the room. Totally self-conscious and enjoying it, she immediately turned toward the oval mirror with the dark, intricately carved frame, hanging in the space between the two nearest tiers of shelves. She proceeded to adjust a stray strand of hair in the vicinity of her left temple.

Her movement produced a flash of green and silver among the red and gold geometries of the carpet, near to the place where her left foot had rested.

I had simultaneous desires to curse and to smile. The arrant bitch was playing games with us again. Always remarkable, though . . . Nothing had changed. Neither cursing nor smiling, I moved forward, as she had known I would.

But Julian too approached, and a trifle more quickly than I. He had been a bit nearer, may have spotted it a fraction of an instant sooner.

He scooped it up and dangled it gently.

"Your bracelet, sister," he said pleasantly. "It seems to have forsaken your wrist, foolish thing. Here—allow me."

She extended her hand, giving him one of those lowered-eyelash smiles while he unfastened her chain of emeralds. Completing the business, he folded her hand within both of his own and began to turn back toward his corner, from whence the others were casting sidelong glances while attempting to seem locally occupied.

"I believe you would be amused by a witticism we are about to share," he began.

Her smile grew even more delightful as she disengaged her hand.

"Thank you, Julian," she replied. "I am certain that when I hear it I will laugh. Last, as usual, I fear." She turned and took my arm. "I find that I feel a greater desire," she said, "for a glass of wine."

So I took her back with me and saw her refreshed. Five and four.

Julian, who dislikes showing strong feelings, reached a decision a few moments later and followed us over. He poured himself a glass, sipped from it, studied me for ten or fifteen seconds, then said, "I believe we are all present now. When do you plan to proceed with whatever you have in mind?"

"I see no reason for further delay," I said, "now that everyone has had his turn." I raised my voice then and directed it across the room. "The time has come. Let us get comfortable."

The others drifted over. Chairs were dragged up and settled into. More wine was poured. A minute later we had an audience.

"Thank you," I said when the final stirrings had subsided. "I have a number of things I would like to say, and some of them might even get said. The course of it all will depend on what goes before, and we will get into that right now. Random, tell them what you told me yesterday."

"All right."

I withdrew to the seat behind the desk and Random moved to occupy the edge of it. I leaned back and listened again to the story of his communication with Brand and his attempt to rescue him. It was a condensed version, bereft of the speculations which had not really strayed from my consciousness since Random had put them there. And despite their omission, a tacit awareness of the implications was occurring within all the others. I knew that. It was the main reason I had wanted Random to speak first. Had I simply come out with an attempt to make a case for my suspicions, I would almost certainly have been assumed to be engaged in the time-honored practice of directing attention away from myself—an act to be followed immediately by the separate, sharp, metallic clicks of minds snapping shut against me. This way, despite any thoughts that Random would say whatever I wanted him to say, they would hear him out, wondering the while. They would toy with the ideas, attempting to foresee the point of my having called the assembly in the first place. They would allow the time that would permit the premises to take root contingent upon later corroboration. And they would be wondering whether we could produce the evidence. I was wondering that same thing myself.

While I waited and wondered I watched the others, a fruitless yet inevitable exercise. Simple curiosity, more than suspicion even, required that I search these faces for reactions, clues, indications—the faces that I knew better than any others, to the limits of my understanding such things. And of course they told me nothing. Perhaps it is true that you really only look at a person the first time you see him, and after that you do a quick bit of mental shorthand each time you recognize him. My brain is lazy enough to give that its likelihood, using its abstracting powers and a presumption of regularity to avoid work whenever possible. This time I forced myself to see, though, and it still did not help. Julian maintained his slightly bored, slightly amused mask. Gérard appeared alternately surprised, angry, and wistful. Benedict just looked bleak and suspicious. Llewella seemed as sad and inscrutable as ever. Deirdre looked distracted, Flora acquiescent, and Fiona was studying everyone else, myself included, assembling her own catalog of reactions.

The only thing that I could tell, after some time, was that Random was making an impression. While no one betrayed himself, I saw the boredom vanish, the old suspicion abate, the new suspicion come to life. Interest rose among my kin. Fascination, almost. Then everyone had questions. At first a few, then a barrage.

"Wait," I finally interrupted. "Let him finish. The whole thing. Some of these will answer themselves. Get the others afterward."

There were nods and growls, and Random proceeded through to the real end. That is, he carried it on to our fight with the beastmen at Flora's, indicating that they were of the same ilk as the one who had slain Caine. Flora endorsed this part.

Then, when the questions came, I watched them carefully. So long as they dealt with the matter of Random's story, they were all to the good. But I wanted to cut things short of speculation as to the possibility of one of us being behind it all. As soon as that came out, talk of me and the smell of red herrings would also drift in. This could lead to ugly words and the emergence of a mood I was not anxious to engender. Better to go for the proof first, save on later recriminations, corner the culprit right now if possible, and consolidate my position on the spot.

So I watched and waited. When I felt that the vital moment had ticked its way too near I stopped the clock.

"None of this discussion, this speculation, would be necessary," I said, "if we had all of the facts right now. And there may be a way to get them—right now. That is why you are here."

That did it. I had them. Attentive. Ready. Maybe even willing.

"I propose we attempt to reach Brand and bring him home," I said, "now."

"How?" Benedict asked me.

"The Trumps."

"It has been tried," said Julian. "He cannot be reached that way. No response."

"I was not referring to the ordinary usage," I said. "I asked you all to bring full sets of Trumps with you. I trust that you have them?"

There were nods.

"Good," I said. "Let us shuffle out Brand's Trump now. I propose that all nine of us attempt to contact him simultaneously."

"An interesting thought," Benedict said.

"Yes," Julian agreed, producing his deck and riffling through it. "Worth trying, at least. It may generate additional power. I do not really know."

I located Brand's Trump. I waited until all the others had found it. Then, "Let us coordinate things," I said. "Is everyone ready?"

Eight assents were spoken.

"Then go ahead. Try. Now."

I studied my card. Brand's features were similar to my own, but he was shorter and slenderer. His hair was like Fiona's. He wore a green riding suit. He rode a white horse. How long ago? How long ago was that? I wondered.

Something of a dreamer, a mystic, a poet, Brand was always disillusioned or elated, cynical or wholly trusting. His feelings never seemed to find a middle ground. Manic-depressive is too facile a term for his complex character, yet it might serve to indicate a direction of departure, multitudes of qualifications lining the roadway thereafter. Pursuant to this state of affairs, I must admit that there were times when I found him so charming, considerate, and loyal that I valued him above all my other kin. Other times, however, he could be so bitter, sarcastic, and downright savage that I tried to avoid his company for fear that I might do him harm. Summing up, the last time I had seen him had been one of the latter occasions, just a bit before Eric and I had had the falling out that led to my exile from Amber.

. . . And those were my thoughts and feelings as I studied his Trump, reaching out to him with my mind, my will, opening the vacant place I sought him to fill. About me, the others shuffled their own memories and did the same.

Slowly the card took on a dream-dust quality and acquired the illusion of depth. There followed that familiar blurring, with the sense of movement which heralds contact with the subject. The Trump grew colder beneath my fingertips, and then things flowed and formed, achieving a sudden verity of vision, persistent, dramatic, full.

He seemed to be in a cell. There was a stone wall behind him. There was straw on the floor. He was menacled, and his chain ran back through a huge ring bolt set in the wall above and behind him. It was a fairly long chain, providing sufficient slack for movement, and at the moment he was taking advantage of this fact, lying sprawled on a heap of straw and rags off in the corner. His hair and beard were quite long, his face thinner than I had ever before seen it. His clothes were tattered and filthy. He seemed to be sleeping. My mind went back to my own imprisonment—the smells, the cold, the wretched fare, the dampness, the loneliness, the madness that came and went. At least he still had his eyes, for they flickered and I saw them when several of us spoke his name; green they were, with a flat, vacant look.

Was he drugged? Or did he believe himself to be hallucinating?

But suddenly his spirit returned. He raised himself. He extended his hand. "Brothers!" he said. "Sisters . . ."

"I'm coming!" came a shout that shook the room.

Gérard had leaped to his feet, knocking over his chair. He dashed across the room and snatched a great battle ax from its pegs on the wall. He slung it at his wrist, holding the Trump in that same hand. For a moment he froze, studying the card. Then he extended his free hand and suddenly he was there, clasping Brand, who chose that moment to pass out again. The image wavered. The contact was broken.

Cursing, I sought through the pack after Gérard's own Trump. Several of the others seemed to be doing the same thing. Locating it, I moved for contact. Slowly, the melting, the turning, the re-forming occurred. There!

Gérard had drawn the chain taut across the stones of the wall and was attacking it with the ax. It was a heavy thing, however, and resisted his powerful blows for a long while. Eventually several of the links were mashed and scarred, but by then he had been at it for almost two minutes, and the ringing, chopping sounds had alerted the jailers.

For there were noises from the left—a rattling sound, the sliding of bolts, the creaking of hinges. Although my field of perception did not extend that far, it seemed obvious that the cell's door was being opened. Brand raised himself once more. Gérard continued to hack at the chain.

"Gérard! The door!" I shouted.

"I know!" he bellowed, wrapping the chain about his arm and yanking it. It did not yield.

Then he let go of the chain and swung the ax, as one of the horny-handed warriors rushed him, blade upraised. The swordsman fell, to be replaced by another. Then a third and a fourth crowded by them. Others were close on their heels.

There was a blur of movement at that moment and Random knelt within the tableau, his right hand clasped with Brand's, his left holding his chair before him like a shield, its legs pointing outward. He sprang to his feet and rushed the attackers, driving the chair like a battering ram amid them. They fell back. He raised the chair and swung it. One lay dead on the floor, felled by Gérard's ax. Another had drawn off to one side, clutching at the stump of his right arm. Random produced a dagger and left it in a nearby stomach, brained two more with the chair, and drove back the final man. Eerily, while this was going on, the dead man rose above the floor and slowly drifted upward, spilling and dripping the while. The one who had been stabbed collapsed to his knees, clutching at the blade.

In the meantime, Gérard had taken hold of the chain with both hands. He braced one foot against the wall and commenced to pull. His shoulders rose as the great muscles tightened across his back. The chain held. Ten seconds, perhaps. Fifteen . . .

Then, with a snap and a rattle, it parted. Gérard stumbled backward, catching himself with an outflung hand. He glanced back, apparently at Random, who was out of my line of sight at the moment. Seemingly satisfied, he turned away, stooped and raised Brand, who had fallen unconscious again. Holding him in his arms, he turned and extended one hand from beneath the limp form. Random leaped back into sight beside them, *sans* chair, and gestured to us also.

All of us reached for them, and a moment later they stood amid us and we crowded around.

A sort of cheer had gone up as we rushed to touch him, to see him, our brother who had been gone these many years and just now snatched back from his mysterious captors. And at last, hopefully, finally, some answers might also have been liberated. Only he looked so weak, so thin, so pale. . . .

"Get back!" Gérard shouted. "I'm taking him to the couch! Then you can look all you—"

Dead silence. For everyone had backed off, and then turned to stone. This was because there was blood on Brand, and it was dripping. And this was because there was a knife in his left side, to the rear. It had not been there moments before. Some one of us had just tried for his kidney and possibly succeeded. I was not heartened by the fact that the Random-Corwin Conjecture that it was One Of Us Behind It All had just received a significant boost. I had an instant during which to concentrate all my faculties in an attempt to mentally photograph everyone's position. Then the spell was broken. Gérard bore Brand to the couch and we drew aside; and we all knew that we all realized not only what had happened, but what it implied.

Gérard set Brand down in a prone position and tore away his filthy shirt.

"Get me clean water to bathe him," he said. "And towels. Get me saline solution and glucose and something to hang them from. Get me a whole medical kit."

Deirdre and Flora moved toward the door.

"My quarters are closest," said Random. "One of you will find a medical kit there. But the only IV stuff is in the lab on the third floor. I'd better come and help."

They departed together.

We all had had medical training somewhere along the line, both here and abroad. That which we learned in Shadow, though, had to be modified in Amber. Most antibiotics from the shadow worlds, for example, were ineffectual here. On the other hand, our personal immunological processes appear to behave differently from those of any other peoples we have studied, so that it is much more difficult for us to become infected—and if infected we deal with it more expeditiously. Then, too, we possess profound regenerative abilities.

All of which is as it must be, of course, the ideal necessarily being superior to its shadows. And Amberites that we are, and aware of these facts from an early age, all of us obtained medical training relatively early in life. Basically, despite what is often said about being your own physician, it goes back to our not unjustified distrust of virtually everyone, and most particularly of those who might hold our lives in their hands. All of which partly explains why I did not rush to shoulder Gérard aside to undertake Brand's treatment myself, despite the fact that I had been through a med school on the shadow Earth within the past couple of generations. The other part of the explanation is that Gérard was not letting anyone else near Brand. Julian and Fiona had both moved forward, apparently with the same thing in mind, only to encounter Gérard's left arm like a gate at a railway crossing.

"No," he had said. "I know that I did not do it, and that is all that I know. There will be no second chance for anyone else."

With any one of us sustaining that sort of wound while in an otherwise sound condition, I would say that if he made it through the first half hour he would make it. Brand, though . . . The shape he was in . . . There was no telling.

When the others returned with the materials and equipment, Gérard cleaned Brand, sutured the wound, and dressed it. He hooked up the IV, broke off the manacles with a hammer and chisel Random had located, covered Brand with a sheet and a blanket, and took his pulse again.

"How is it?" I asked.

"Weak," he said, and he drew up a chair and seated himself beside the couch. "Someone fetch me my blade—and a glass of wine. I didn't have any. Also, if there is any food left over there, I'm hungry."

Llewella headed for the sideboard and Random got him his blade from the rack behind the door.

"Are you just going to camp there?" Random asked, passing him the weapon.

"I am."

"What about moving Brand to a better bed?"

"He is all right where he is. I will decide when he can be moved. In the meantime, someone get a fire going. Then put out a few of those candles."

Random nodded.

"I'll do it," he said. Then he picked up the knife Gérard had drawn from Brand's side, a thin stiletto, its blade about seven inches in length. He held it across the palm of his hand.

"Does anyone recognize this?" he asked.

"Not I," said Benedict.

"Nor I," said Julian.

"No," I said.

The girls shook their heads.

Random studied it.

"Easily concealed—up a sleeve, in a boot or bodice. It took real nerve to use it that way. . . ."

"Desperation," I said.

". . . And a very accurate anticipation of our mob scene. Inspired, almost."

"Could one of the guards have done it?" Julian asked. "Back in the cell?"

"No," Gérard said. "None of them came near enough."

"It looks to be decently balanced for throwing," Deirdre said.

"It is," said Random, shifting it about his fingertips. "Only none of them had a clear shot or the opportunity. I'm positive."

Llewella returned, bearing a tray containing slabs of meat, half a loaf of bread, a bottle of wine, and a goblet. I cleared a small table and set it beside Gérard's chair. As Llewella deposited the tray, she asked, "But why? That only leaves us. Why would one of us want to do it?"

I sighed.

"Whose prisoner do you think he might have been?" I asked.

"One of us?"

"If he possessed knowledge which someone was willing to go to this length to suppress, what do you think? The same reason also served to put him where he was and keep him there."

Her brows tightened.

"That does not make sense either. Why didn't they just kill him and be done with it?"

I shrugged.

"Must have had some use for him," I said. "But there is really only one person who can answer that question adequately. When you find him, ask him."

"Or her," Julian said. "Sister, you seem possessed of a superabundance of naïveté, suddenly."

Her gaze locked with Julian's own, a pair of icebergs reflecting frigid infinities.

"As I recall," she said, "you rose from your seat when they came through, turned to the left, rounded the desk, and stood slightly to Gérard's right. You leaned pretty far forward. I believe your hands were out of sight, below."

"And as I recall," he said, "you were within striking distance yourself, off to Gérard's left—and leaning forward."

"I would have had to do it with my left hand—and I am right-handed."

"Perhaps he owes what life he still possesses to that fact."

"You seem awfully anxious, Julian, to find that it was someone else."

"All right," I said. "All right! You know this is self-defeating. Only one of us did it, and this is not the way to smoke him out."

"Or her," Julian added.

Gérard rose, towered, glared.

"I will not have you disturbing my patient," he said. "And, Random, you said you were going to see to the fire."

"Right away," Random said, and moved to do it.

"Let us adjourn to the sitting room off the main hall," I said, "downstairs. Gérard, I will post a couple of guards outside the door here."

"No," Gérard said. "I would rather that anyone who wishes to try it get this far. I will hand you his head in the morning."

I nodded.

"Well, you can ring for anything you need—or call one of us on the Trumps. We will fill you in in the morning on anything that we learn."

Gérard seated himself, grunted, and began eating. Random got the fire going and extinguished some lights. Brand's blanket rose and fell, slowly but regularly. We filed quietly from the room and headed for the stairway, leaving them there together with the flare and the crackle, the tubes and the bottles.

SEVEN

Many are the times I have awakened, sometimes shaking, always afraid, from the dream that I occupied my old cell, blind once more, in the dungeons beneath Amber. It is not as if I were unfamiliar with the condition of imprisonment. I have been locked away on a number of occasions, for various periods of time. But solitary, plus blindness with small hope of recovery, made for a big charge at the sensory-deprivation counter in the department store of the mind. That, with the sense of finality to it all, had left its marks. I generally keep these memories safely tucked away during waking hours, but at night, sometimes, they come loose, dance down the aisles and frolic round the notions counter, one, two, three. Seeing Brand there in his cell had brought them out again, along with an unseasonal chill; and that final thrust served to establish a more or less permanent residence for them. Now, among my kin in the shield-hung sitting room, I could not avoid the thought that one or more of them had done unto Brand as Eric had done unto me. While this capacity was in itself hardly a surprising discovery, the matter of occupying the same room with the culprit and having no idea as to his identity was more than a little disturbing. My only consolation was that each of the others, according to his means, must be disturbed also. Including the guilty, now that the existence theorem had shown a positive. I knew then that I had been hoping all along that outsiders were entirely to blame. Now, though . . . On the one hand I felt even more restricted than usual in what I could say. On the other, it seemed a good time to press for information, with everyone in an abnormal state of mind. The desire to cooperate for purposes of dealing with the threat could prove helpful. And even the guilty party would want to behave the same as everyone else. Who knew but that he might slip up while making the effort?

"Well, have you any other interesting little experiments you would care to conduct?" Julian asked me, clasping his hands behind his head and leaning back in my favorite chair.

"Not at the moment," I said.

"Pity," he replied. "I was hoping you would suggest we go looking for Dad now in the same fashion. Then, if we are lucky, we find him and someone puts him out of the way with more certainty. After that, we could all play Russian roulette with those fine new weapons you've furnished— winner take all."

"Your words are ill-considered," I said.

"Not so. I considered every one of them," he answered. "We spend so much time lying to one another that I decided it might be amusing to say what I really felt. Just to see whether anyone noticed."

"Now you see that we have. We also notice that the real you is no improvement over the old one."

"Whichever you prefer, both of us have been wondering whether you have any idea what you are going to do next."

"I do," I said. "I now intend to obtain answers to a number of questions dealing with everything that is plaguing us. We might as well start with Brand and his troubles." Turning toward Benedict, who was sitting gazing into the fire, I said, "Back in Avalon, Benedict, you told me that Brand was one of the ones who searched for me after my disappearance."

"That is correct," Benedict answered.

"All of us went looking," Julian said.

"Not at first," I replied. "Initially, it was Brand, Gérard, and yourself, Benedict. Isn't that what you told me?"

"Yes," he said. "The others did have a go at it later, though. I told you that, too."

I nodded.

"Did Brand report anything unusual at that time?" I asked.

"Unusual? In what way?" said Benedict.

"I don't know. I am looking for some connection between what happened to him and what happened to me."

"Then you are looking in the wrong place," Benedict said. "He returned and reported no success. And he was around for ages after that, unmolested."

"I gathered that much," I said. "I understand from what Random has told me, though, that his final disappearance occurred approximately a month before my own recovery and return. That almost strikes me as peculiar. If he did not report anything special after his return from the search, did he do so prior to his disappearance? Or in the interim? Anyone? Anything? Say it if you've got it!"

There followed some mutual glancing about. The looks seemed more curious than suspicious or nervous, though.

Finally, then, "Well," Llewella said, "I do not know. Do not know whether it is significant, I mean."

All eyes came to rest upon her. She began to knot and unknot the ends of her belt cord, slowly, as she spoke.

"It was in the interim, and it may have no bearing," she went on. "It is just something that struck me as peculiar. Brand came to Rebma long ago—"

"How long ago?" I asked.

She furrowed her brow.

"Fifty, sixty, seventy years . . . I am not certain."

I tried to summon up the rough conversion factor I had worked out during my long incarceration. A day in Amber, it seemed, constituted a bit over two and a half days on the shadow Earth where I had spent my exile. I wanted to relate events in Amber to my own time-scale whenever possible, just in case any peculiar correspondences turned up. So Brand had gone to Rebma sometime in what was, to me, the nineteenth century.

"Whatever the date," she said, "he came and visited me. Stayed for several weeks." She glanced at Random then. "He was asking about Martin."

Random narrowed his eyes and cocked his head.

"Did he say why?" he asked her.

"Not exactly," she said. "He implied that he had met Martin somewhere in his travels, and he gave the impression that he would like to get in touch with him again. I did not realize until some time after his departure that finding out everything he could concerning Martin was probably the entire reason for his visit. You know how subtle Brand can be, finding out things without seeming to be after them. It was only after I had spoken with a number of others whom he had visited that I began to see what had occurred. I never did find out why, though."

"That is—most peculiar," Random observed. "For it brings to mind something to which I had never attached any significance. He once questioned me at great length concerning my son—and it may well have been at about the same time. He never indicated that he had met him, however—or that he had any desire to do so. It started out as a bit of banter on the subject of bastards. When I took offense he apologized and asked a number of more proper questions about the boy, which I assumed he then put for the sake of politeness—to leave me with a softer remembrance. As you say, though, he had a way of drawing admissions from people. Why is it you never told me of this before?"

She smiled prettily.

"Why should I have?" she said.

Random nodded slowly, his face expressionless.

"Well, what did you tell him?" he said. "What did he learn? What do you know about Martin that I don't?"

She shook her head, her smile fading.

"Nothing—actually," she said. "To my knowledge, no one in Rebma ever heard from Martin after he took the Pattern and vanished. I do not believe that Brand departed knowing any more than he did when he arrived."

"Strange . . ." I said. "Did he approach anyone else on the subject?"

"I don't remember," Julian said.

"Nor I," said Benedict.

The others shook their heads.

"Then let us note it and leave it for now," I said. "There are other things I also need to know. Julian, I understand that you and Gérard attempted to follow the black road a while back, and that Gérard was injured along the way. I believe you both stayed with Benedict for a time after that, while Gérard recuperated. I would like to know about that expedition."

"It seems as if you already do," Julian replied. "You have just stated everything that occurred."

"Where did you learn of this, Corwin?" Benedict inquired.

"Back in Avalon," I said.

"From whom?"

"Dara," I said.

He rose to his feet, came over, stood before me, glared down.

"You still persist in that absurd story about the girl!"

I sighed.

"We have been round and round on this too many times," I said. " By now I have told you everything that I know on the subject. Either you accept it or you do not. She is the one who told me, though."

"Apparently, then, there were some things you did not tell me. You never mentioned that part before."

"Is it true or isn't it? About Julian and Gérard."

"It is true," he said.

"Then forget the source for now and let us get on with what happened."

"Agreed," Benedict said. "I may speak candidly, now that the reason for secrecy is no longer with us. Eric, of course. He was unaware of my whereabouts, as were most of the others. Gérard was my main source of news in

Amber. Eric grew more and more apprehensive concerning the black road and finally decided to send scouts to trace it through Shadow to its source. Julian and Gérard were selected. They were attacked by a very strong party of its creatures at a point near Avalon. Gérard called to me, via my Trump, for assistance and I went to their aid. The enemy was dispatched. As Gérard had sustained a broken leg in the fighting and Julian was a bit battered himself, I took them both home with me. I broke my silence with Eric at that time, to tell him where they were and what had become of them. He ordered them not to continue their journey, but to return to Amber after they had recovered. They remained with me until they did. Then they went back."

"That is all?"

"That is all."

But it wasn't. Dara had also told me something else. She had mentioned another visitor. I remembered it quite distinctly. That day, beside the stream, a tiny rainbow in the mist above the waterfall, the mill wheel turning round and round, delivering dreams and grinding them, that day we had fenced and talked and walked in Shadow, had passed through a primordial wood, coming to a spot beside a mighty torrent where turned a wheel fit for the granary of the gods, that day we had picnicked, flirted, gossiped, she had told me many things, some of them doubtless false. But she had not lied concerning the journey of Julian and Gérard, and I believed it possible that she had also spoken truly when she said that Brand had visited Benedict in Avalon. "Frequently" was the word she had used.

Now, Benedict made no secret of the fact that he distrusted me. I could see this alone as sufficient reason for his withholding information on anything he judged too sensitive to become my business. Hell, buying his story, I would not have trusted me either if our situations were reversed. Only a fool would have called him on it at that moment, though. Because of the other possibilities.

It could be that he planned to tell me later, in private, of the circumstances surrounding Brand's visits. They could well have involved something he did not wish to discuss before the group, and especially before Brand's would-be killer.

Or—There was, of course, the possibility that Benedict himself was behind it all. I did not even like to think about the consequences. Having served under Napoleon, Lee, and MacArthur, I appreciated the tactician as well as the strategist. Benedict was both, and he was the best I had ever known. The recent loss of his right arm had in no way diminished him in this, or for that matter impaired his personal fighting skills. Had I not been very lucky recently he could easily have turned me into a pile of scallops over our misunderstanding. No, I did not want it to be Benedict, and I was not about to grope after whatever he had at that moment seen fit to conceal. I only hoped that he was just saving it for later.

So I settled for his, "That is all," and decided to move on to other matters.

"Flora," I said, "back when I first visited you, after my accident, you said something which I still do not quite understand. In that I had ample time relatively soon thereafter in which to review many things, I came across it in my memories and occasionally puzzled over it. I still do not understand it. So would you please tell me what you meant when you said that the shadows contained more horrors than any had thought?"

"Why, I do not properly recall saying it," Flora said. "But I suppose that I must have, if it made such an impression. You know the effect that I was referring to: that Amber seems to act as something of a magnet on adjacent shadows, drawing things across from them; the nearer you get to Amber the easier the road becomes, even for shadow-things. While there always seems to be some exchange of materials among adjacent shadows themselves, the effect is more forceful and also more of a one-way process when it comes to Amber. We have always been alert for peculiar things slipping through. Well, for several years prior to your recovery, more such things than usual seemed to be showing up in the vicinity of Amber. Dangerous things, almost invariably. Many were recognizable creatures from nearby realms. After a time, though, things kept coming in from farther and farther afield. Eventually, some which were totally unknown made it through. No reason could be found for this sudden transportation of menaces, although we sought fairly far for disturbances which might be driving them this way. In other words, highly improbable penetrations of Shadow were occurring."

"This actually began while Dad was still around?"

"Oh yes. It started several years before your recovery—as I said."

"I see. Did anyone consider the possibility of there being a connection between this state of affairs and Dad's departure?"

"Certainly," Benedict replied. "I still feel that that was the reason for it. He went off to investigate, or to seek a remedy."

"But that is purely conjecture," Julian said. "You know how he was. He gave no reasons."

Benedict shrugged.

"It is a reasonable inference, though," he said. "I understand that he had spoken of his concern over the—monster migrations, if you like—on numerous occasions."

I withdrew my cards from their case, having recently gotten into the habit of carrying a set of Trumps with me at all times. I raised Gérard's Trump and regarded it. The others were silent, watching me as I did this. Moments later, there was contact.

Gérard was still seated in his chair, his blade across his knees. He was still eating. He swallowed when he felt my presence and said, "Yes, Corwin? What do you want?"

"How is Brand?"

"Sleeping," he said. "His pulse is a little stronger. His breathing is the same—regular. It's still too early—"

"I know," I said. "I mainly wanted to check your recollection of something: Near the end there, did you get the impression from anything he might have said or done that Dad's going away might have been connected with the increased number of Shadow beings that were slipping through into Amber?"

"That," said Julian, "is what is known as a leading question."

Gérard wiped his mouth.

"There could have been a connection, yes," he said. "He seemed disturbed, preoccupied with something. And he did talk about the creatures. But he never really said that that was his main concern—or whether it was something entirely different."

"Like what?"

He shook his head.

"Anything. I—yes . . . yes, there is something you probably ought to know, for whatever it is worth. Some time after his disappearance, I did make an effort to find out one thing. That was, whether I was indeed the last person to see him before his departure. I am fairly certain that I was. I had been here in the palace all evening, and I was preparing to return to the flagship. Dad had retired about an hour earlier, but I had stayed on in the guard room, playing draughts with Captain Thoben. As we were sailing the following morning, I decided to take a book with me. So I came up here to the library. Dad was seated at the desk." He gestured with his head. "He was going through some old books, and he had not yet changed his garments. He nodded to me when I entered, and I told him I had just come up for a book. He said, 'You've come to the right place,' and he kept on reading. While I was looking over the shelves, he said something to the effect that he could not sleep. I found a book, told him good night, he said, 'Good sailing,' and I left." He lowered his eyes again. "Now I am positive he was wearing the Jewel of Judgment that night, that I saw it on him then as plainly as I see it on you now. I am equally certain that he had not had it on earlier that evening. For a long while after, I thought that he had taken it along with him, wherever he went. There was no indication in his chambers that he had later changed his clothing. I never saw the stone again until you and Bleys were defeated in your assault on Amber. Then, Eric was wearing it. When I questioned him he claimed that he had found it in Dad's chambers. Lacking evidence to the contrary, I had to accept his story. But I was never happy with it. Your question—and seeing you wearing it—has brought it all back. So I thought you had better know about it."

"Thanks," I said, and another question occurred to me but I decided against asking it at that moment. For the benefit of the others, I closed off by saying, "So do you think he needs any more blankets? Or anything else?"

Gérard raised his glass to me, then took a drink.

"Very good. Keep up the good work," I said, and I passed my hand over his card.

"Brother Brand seems to be doing all right," I said, "and Gérard does not recollect Dad's saying anything that would directly connect Shadow slippage and his departure. I wonder how Brand will recall things, when he comes around?"

"*If* he comes around," Julian said.

"I think that he will," I said. "We have all taken some pretty bad beatings.

Our vitality is one of the few things we have come to trust. My guess is that he will be talking by morning."

"What do you propose doing with the guilty party," he asked, "if Brand names him?"

"Question him," I said.

"Then I would like to do the questioning. I am beginning to feel that you may be right this time, Corwin, and that the person who stabbed him may also be responsible for our intermittent state of siege, for Dad's disappearance, and for Caine's killing. So I would enjoy questioning him before we cut his throat, and I would like to volunteer for that last part also."

"We will keep it in mind," I said.

"You are not excluded from the reckoning, Corwin."

"I was aware of that."

"I have something to say," said Benedict, smothering a rejoinder from Julian. "I find myself troubled both by the strength and the apparent objective of the opposition. I have encountered them now on several occasions, and they *are* out for blood. Accepting for the moment your story of the girl Dara, Corwin, her final words do seem to sum up their attitude: 'Amber will be destroyed.' Not conquered, subjugated, or taught a lesson. Destroyed. Julian, you wouldn't mind ruling here, would you?"

Julian smiled.

"Perhaps next year this time," he said. "Not today, thank you."

"What I am getting at is that I could see you—or any of us—employing mercenaries or obtaining allies to effect a takeover. I cannot see you employing a force so powerful that it would represent a grave problem itself afterward. Not a force that seems bent on destruction rather than conquest. I cannot see you, me, Corwin, the others as actually trying to destroy Amber, or willing to gamble with forces that would. That is the part I do not like about Corwin's notion that one of us is behind this."

I had to nod. I was not unaware of the weakness of that link in my chain of speculations. Still, there were so many unknowns. . . . I could offer alternatives, such as Random then did, but guesses prove nothing.

"It may be," Random said, "that one of us made the deal but underestimated his allies. The guilty party may now be sweating this thing as much as the rest of us. He may not be in a position to turn things off now, even if he wants to."

"We could offer him the opportunity," Fiona said, "to betray his allies to us now. If Julian could be persuaded to leave his throat uncut and the rest of us were willing to do the same, he might come around—if Random's guess is correct. He would not claim the throne, but he was obviously not about to have it before. He would have his life and he could save Amber quite a bit of trouble. Is anyone willing to commit himself to a position on this?"

"I am," I said. "I will give him life if he will come across, with the understanding that it will be spent in exile."

"I will go along with that," Benedict said.

"So will I," said Random.

"On one condition," Julian said. "If he was not personally responsible for Caine's death, I will go along with it. Otherwise, no. And there would have to be evidence."

"Life, in exile," Deirdre said. "All right. I agree."

"So do I," said Flora.

"And I," Llewella followed.

"Gérard will probably agree too," I said. "But I really wonder whether Brand will feel the same as the rest of us. I've a feeling he may not."

"Let us check with Gérard," Benedict said. "If Brand makes it and proves the only holdout, the guilty party will know he has only one enemy to avoid— and they can always work out their own terms on that count."

"All right," I said, smothering a few misgivings, and I recontacted Gérard, who agreed also.

So we rose to our feet and swore that much by the Unicorn of Amber— Julian's oath having an extra clause to it—and swore to enforce exile on any of our own number who violated the oath. Frankly, I did not think it would net us anything, but it is always nice to see families doing things together.

After that, everyone made a point of mentioning that he would be remaining in the palace overnight, presumably to indicate that no one feared anything Brand might have to say in the morning—and especially to indicate that no one had a desire to get out of town, a thing that would not be forgotten, even if Brand gave up the ghost during the night. In that I had no further questions to put to the group and no one had sprung forward to own up to the misdeeds covered by the oath, I leaned back and listened for a time after that. Things came apart, falling into a series of conversations and exchanges, one of the main topics being an attempted reconstruction of the library tableau, each of us in his own place and, invariably, why each of us was in a position to have done it, except for the speaker. I smoked; I said nothing on the subject. Deirdre did spot an interesting possibility, however. Namely, that Gérard could have done the stabbing himself while we were all crowded around, and that his heroic efforts were not prompted by any desire to save Brand's neck, but rather to achieve a position where he could stop his tongue—in which case Brand would never make it through the night. Ingenious, but I just couldn't believe it. No one else bought it either. At least, no one volunteered to go upstairs and throw Gérard out.

After a time Fiona drifted over and sat beside me.

"Well, I've tried the only thing I could think of," she said. "I hope some good comes of it."

"It may," I said.

"I see that you have added a peculiar piece of ornamentation to your wardrobe," she said, raising the Jewel of Judgment between her thumb and forefinger and studying it.

Then she raised her eyes.

"Can you make it do tricks for you?" she asked.

"Some," I said.

"Then you knew how to attune it. It involves the Pattern, doesn't it?"

"Yes. Eric told me how to go about it, right before he died."

"I see."

She released it, settled back into her seat, regarded the flames.

"Did he give you any cautions to go along with it?" she asked.

"No," I said.

"I wonder whether that was a matter of design or circumstance?"

"Well, he was pretty busy dying at the time. That limited our conversation considerably."

"I know. I was wondering whether his hatred for you outweighed his hopes for the realm, or whether he was simply ignorant of some of the principles involved."

"What do you know about it?"

"Think again of Eric's death, Corwin. I was not there when it occurred, but I came in early for the funeral. I was present when his body was bathed, shaved, dressed—and I examined his wounds. I do not believe that any of them were fatal, in themselves. There were three chest wounds, but only one looked as if it might have run into the mediastinal area—"

"One's enough, if—"

"Wait," she said. "It was difficult, but I tried judging the angle of the puncture with a thin glass rod. I wanted to make an incision, but Caine would not permit it. Still, I do not believe that his heart or arteries were damaged. It is still not too late to order an autopsy, if you would like me to check further on this. I am certain that his injuries and the general stress contributed to his death, but I believe it was the jewel that made the difference."

"Why do you think this?"

"Because of some things that Dworkin said when I studied with him— and things that I noticed afterward, because of this. He indicated that while it conferred unusual abilities, it also represented a drain on the vitality of its master. The longer you wear it, the more it somehow takes out of you. I paid attention after that, and I noticed that Dad wore it only seldom and never kept it on for long periods of time."

My thoughts returned to Eric, the day he lay dying on the slopes of Kolvir, the battle raging about him. I remembered my first look at him, his face pale, his breath labored, blood on his chest. . . . And the Jewel of Judgment, there on its chain, was pulsing, heartlike, among the moist folds of his garments. I had never seen it do that before, or since. I recalled that the effect had grown fainter, weaker. And when he died and I folded his hands atop it, the phenomenon had ceased.

"What do you know of its function?" I asked her.

She shook her head.

"Dworkin considered that a state secret. I know the obvious—weather control—and I inferred from some of Dad's remarks that it has something to do with a heightened perception, or a higher perception. Dworkin had mentioned it primarily as an example of the pervasiveness of the Pattern in everything that gives us power—even the Trumps contain the Pattern, if you look closely, look long enough—and he cited it as an instance of a conservation principle: all of our special powers have their price. The greater the power, the larger the investment. The Trumps are a small matter, but there is still an element of fatigue involved in their employment. Walking through Shadow, which is an exercise of the image of the Pattern which exists within us, is an even greater expenditure. To essay the Pattern itself, physically, is a massive drain on one's energies. But the jewel, he said, represents an even higher octave of the same thing, and its cost to its employer is exponentially greater."

Thus, if correct, another ambiguous insight into the character of my late and least favored brother. If he were aware of this phenomenon and had donned the jewel and worn it overlong anyhow, in the defense of Amber, it made him something of a hero. But then, seen in this light, his passing it along to me, without warnings, became a deathbed effort at a final piece of vengeance. But he had exempted me from his curse, he'd said, so as to spend it properly on our enemies in the field. This, of course, only meant that he hated them a little more than he hated me and was deploying his final energies as strategically as possible, for Amber. I thought then of the partial character of Dworkin's notes, as I had recovered them from the hiding place Eric had indicated. Could it be that Eric had acquired them intact and had purposely destroyed that portion containing the cautions so as to damn his successor? That notion did not strike me as quite adequate, for he had had no way of knowing that I would return when I did, as I did, that the course of battle would run as it had, and that I would indeed be his successor. It could just as easily have been one of his favorites that followed him to power, in which case he would certainly not have wanted him to inherit any booby traps. No. As I saw it, either Eric was not really aware of this property of the stone, having acquired only partial instructions for its use, or someone had gotten to those papers before I had and removed sufficient material to leave me with a mortal liability. It may well have been the hand of the real enemy, once again.

"Do you know the safety factor?" I asked.

"No," she said. "I can give you only two pointers, for whatever they may be worth. The first is that I do not recall Dad's ever wearing it for long periods of time. The second, I pieced together from a number of things that he said, beginning with a comment to the effect that 'when people turn into statues you are either in the wrong place or in trouble.' I pressed him quite a bit on that, over a long period of time, and I eventually got the impression that the first sign of having worn it too long is some sort of distortion of your time sense. Apparently it begins speeding up the metabolism—everything—with a net effect that the world seems to be slowing down around you. This must take quite a toll on a person. That is everything that I know about it, and I admit that a large part of the last is guesswork. How long have you been wearing it?"

"A while now," I said, taking my mental pulse and glancing about to see whether things seemed to be slowing down any.

I could not really tell, though of course I did not feel in the best of shape. I had assumed it was totally Gérard's doing, though. I was not about to yank it off, however, just because another family member had suggested it, even if it was clever Fiona in one of her friendlier moods. Perversity, cussedness . . . No, independence. That was it. That and purely formal distrust. I had only put it on for the evening a few hours before, anyway. I'd wait.

"Well, you have made your point in wearing it," she was saying. "I simply wanted to advise you against prolonged exposure until you know more about it.

"Thanks, Fi. I'll have it off soon, and I appreciate your telling me. By the way, whatever became of Dworkin?"

She tapped her temple.

"His mind finally went, poor man. I like to think that Dad had him put away in some restful retreat in Shadow."

"I see what you mean," I said. "Yes, let us think that. Poor fellow."

Julian rose to his feet, concluding a conversation with Llewella. He stretched, nodded to her, and strolled over.

"Corwin, have you thought of any more questions for us?" he said.

"None that I'd care to ask just now."

He smiled.

"Anything more that you want to tell us?"

"Not at the moment."

"Any more experiments, demonstrations, charades?"

"No."

"Good. Then I'm going to bed. Good night."

"Night."

He bowed to Fiona, waved to Benedict and Random, nodded to Flora and Deirdre as he passed them on the way to the door. He paused on the threshold, turned back and said, "Now you can all talk about me," and went on out.

"All right," Fiona said. "Let's. I think he's the one."

"Why?" I asked.

"I'll go down the list, subjective, intuitive, and biased as it is. Benedict, in my opinion, is above suspicion. If he wanted the throne, he'd have it by now, by direct, military methods. With all the time he has had, he could have managed an attack that would have succeeded, even against Dad. He is that good, and we all know it. You, on the other hand, have made a number of blunders which you would not have made had you been in full possession of your faculties. That is why I believe your story, amnesia and all. No one gets himself blinded as a piece of strategy. Gérard is well on the way to establishing his own innocence. I almost think he is up there with Brand now more for that reason than from any desire to protect Brand. At any rate, we will know for sure before long—or else have some new suspicions. Random has simply been watched too closely these past years to have had the opportunity to engineer everything that has been happening. So he is out. Of us more delicate sorts, Flora hasn't the brains, Deirdre lacks the guts, Llewella hasn't the motivations, as she is happy elsewhere but never here, and I, of course, am innocent of all but malice. That leaves Julian. Is he capable? Yes. Does he want the throne? Of course. Has he had time and opportunity? Again, yes. He is your man."

"Would he have killed Caine?" I asked. "They were buddies."

She curled her lip.

"Julian has no friends," she said. "That icy personality of his is thawed only by thoughts of himself. Oh, in recent years he *seemed* closer to Caine than to anyone else. But even that . . . even that could have been a part of it. Shamming a friendship long enough to make it seem believable, so that he would not be suspect at this time. I can believe Julian capable of that because I cannot believe him capable of strong emotional attachments."

I shook my head.

"I don't know," I said. "His friendship with Caine is something that occurred during my absence, so everything I know concerning it is second-hand. Still, if Julian were looking for friendship in the form of another person-ality close to his own, I can see it. They were a lot alike. I tend to think it was real, because I don't think anybody is capable of deceiving someone about his friendship for years. Unless the other party is awfully stupid, which is something Caine was not. And—well, you say your reasoning was subjective, intuitive, and biased. So is mine, on something like this. I just don't like to think anybody is such a miserable wretch that he would use his only friend that way. That's why I think there is something wrong with your list."

She sighed.

"For someone who has been around for as long as you have, Corwin, you say some silly things. Were you changed by your long stay in that funny little place? Years ago you would have seen the obvious, as I do."

"Perhaps I have changed, for such things no longer seem obvious. Or could it be that you have changed, Fiona? A trifle more cynical than the little girl I once knew. It might not have been all that obvious to you, years ago."

She smiled softly.

"Never tell a woman she has changed, Corwin. Except for the better. You used to know that, too. Could it be that you are really only one of Corwin's shadows, sent back to suffer and intimidate here on his behalf? Is the real Corwin somewhere else, laughing at us all?"

"I am here, and I am not laughing," I said.

She laughed.

"Yes, that is it!" she said. "I have just decided that you are not yourself!

"Announcement, everybody!" she cried, springing to her feet. "I have just noticed that this is not really Corwin! It has to be one of his shadows! It has just announced a belief in friendship, dignity, nobility of spirit, and those other things which figure prominently in popular romances! I am obviously onto something!"

The others stared at her. She laughed again, then sat down abruptly.

I heard Flora mutter "drunk" and return to her conversation with Deirdre. Random said, "Let's hear it for shadows," and turned back to a discussion with Benedict and Llewella.

"See?" she said.

"What?"

"You're insubstantial," she said, patting my knee. "And so am I, now that I think about it. It has been a bad day, Corwin."

"I know. I feel like hell, too. I thought I had such a fine idea for getting Brand back. Not only that, it worked. A lot of good it did him."

"Don't overlook those bits of virtue you've acquired," she said. "You're not to blame for the way it turned out."

"Thanks."

"I believe that Julian might have had the right idea," she said. "I don't feel like staying awake any longer."

I rose with her, walked her to the door.

"I'm all right," she said. "Really."

"Sure?"

She nodded sharply.

"See you in the morning then."

"I hope so," she said. "Now you can talk about me."

She winked and went out.

I turned back, saw that Benedict and Llewella were approaching.

"Turning in?" I asked.

Benedict nodded.

"Might as well," Llewella said, and she kissed me on the cheek.

"What was that for?"

"A number of things," she said. "Good night."

"Good night."

Random was crouched on the hearth, poking at the fire. Deirdre turned to him and said, "Don't throw on more wood just for us. Flora and I are going too."

"Okay." He set the poker aside and rose. "Sleep well," he called after them.

Deirdre gave me a sleepy smile and Flora a nervous one. I added my good nights and watched them leave.

"Learn anything new and useful?" Random asked.

I shrugged.

"Did you?"

"Opinions, conjectures. No new facts," he said. "We were trying to decide who might be next on the list."

"And . . . ?"

"Benedict thinks it's a toss-up. You or him. Providing you are not behind it all, of course. He also thinks your buddy Ganelon ought to watch his step."

"Ganelon . . . Yes, that's a thought—and it should have been mine. I think he is right about the toss-up, too. It may even be slightly weighted against him, since they know I'm alert because of the attempted frameup."

"I would say that all of us are now aware that Benedict is alert himself. He managed to mention his opinion to everyone. I believe that he would welcome an attempt."

I chuckled.

"That balances the coin again. I guess it *is* a toss-up."

"He said that, too. Naturally, he knew I would tell you."

"Naturally, I wish he would start talking to me again. Well . . . not much I can do about it now," I said. "The hell with everything. I'm going to bed."

He nodded.

"Look under it first."

We left the room, headed up the hall.

"Corwin, I wish you'd had the foresight to bring some coffee back with you, along with the guns," he said. "I could use a cup."

"Doesn't it keep you awake?"

"No. I like a couple of cups in the evening."

"I miss it mornings. We'll have to import some when this mess is all settled."

"Small comfort, but a good idea. What got into Fi, anyhow?"

"She thinks Julian is our man."

"She may be right."

"What about Caine?"

"Supposing it was not a single individual," he said as we mounted the stair. "Say it was two, like Julian *and* Caine. They finally had a falling out, Caine lost, Julian disposed of him and used the death to weaken your position as well. Former friends make the worst enemies."

"It's no use," I said. "I get dizzy when I start sorting the possibilities. We are either going to have to wait for something more to happen, or make something happen. Probably the latter. But not tonight—"

"Hey! Wait up!"

"Sorry." I paused at the landing. "Don't know what got into me. Finishing spurt, I guess."

"Nervous energy," he said, coming abreast of me once more. We continued on up, and I made an effort to match his pace, fighting down a desire to hurry.

"Well, sleep well," he said finally.

"Good night, Random."

He continued on up the stair and I headed off along the corridor toward my quarters. I was feeling jittery by then, which must be why I dropped my key.

I reached and plucked it out of the air before it had fallen very far. Simultaneously, I was struck by the impression that its motion was somewhat slower than it should have been. I inserted it in the lock and turned it.

The room was dark, but I decided against lighting a candle or an oil lamp. I had gotten used to the dark a long time ago. I locked and bolted the door. My eyes were already half adjusted to the gloom, from the dim hallway. I turned. There was some starlight leaking in about the drapes, too. I crossed the room, unfastening my collar.

He was waiting in my bed chamber, to the left of the entrance. He was perfectly positioned and he did nothing to give himself away. I walked right into it. He had the ideal station, he held the dagger ready, he had the element of total surprise going for him. By rights I should have died—not in my bed, but just there at its foot.

I caught a glimpse of the movement, realized the presence and its significance as I stepped over the threshold.

I knew that it was too late to avoid the thrust even as I raised my arm to try to block it. But one peculiarity struck me before the blade itself did: my assailant seemed to be moving too slowly. Quick, with all the tension of his weight behind it, that is how it should have been. I should never have known it was occurring until after the act, if then. I should not have had time to turn partway and swing my arm as far as I did. A ruddy haze filled my vision and I felt my forearm strike the side of the outflung arm at about the same moment as the steel touched my belly and bit. Within the redness there seemed a faint tracing of that cosmic version of the Pattern I had followed earlier in the day. As I doubled and fell, unable to think but still for a moment conscious, it came clearer, came nearer, the design. I wanted to flee, but my body stumbled. I was thrown.

EIGHT

Out of every life a little blood must spill. Unfortunately, it was my turn again, and it felt like more than a little. I was lying, doubled up, on my right side, both arms clutching at my middle. I was wet, and every now and then something trickled along the creases of my belly. Front, lower left, just above the beltline, I felt like a casually opened envelope. These were my first sensations as consciousness came around again. And my first thought was, "What is he waiting for?" Obviously, the *coup de grâce* had been withheld. Why?

I opened my eyes. They had taken advantage of whatever time had elapsed to adjust themselves to the darkness. I turned my head. I did not see anyone else in the room with me. But something peculiar had occurred and I could not quite place it. I closed my eyes and let my head fall back to the mattress once more.

Something was wrong, yet at the same time right. . . .

The mattress . . . Yes, I was lying on my bed. I doubted my ability to have gotten there unassisted. But it would be absurd to knife me and then help me to bed.

My bed . . . It was my bed, yet it was not.

I squeezed my eyes tight. I gritted my teeth. I did not understand. I knew that my thinking could not be normal there on the fringes of shock, by blood pooling in my guts and then leaking out. I tried to force myself to think clearly. It was not easy.

My bed. Before you are fully aware of anything else, you are aware whether you are awakening in your own bed. And I was, but—

I fought down an enormous impulse to sneeze, because I felt it would tear me apart. I compressed my nostrils and breathed in short gasps through my mouth. The taste, smell and feel of dust was all about me.

The nasal assault subsided and I opened my eyes. I knew then where I was. I did not understand the why and how of it, but I had come once more to a place I had never expected to see again.

I lowered my right hand, used it to raise myself.

It was my bedroom in my house. The old one. The place which had been mine back when I was Carl Corey. I had been returned to Shadow, to that world heavy with dust. The bed had not been made up since the last time I had slept in it, over half a decade before. I knew the state of the house fully, having looked in on it only a few weeks earlier.

I pushed myself further, managed to slide my feet out over the edge of the bed and down. Then I doubled up again and sat there. It was bad.

While I felt temporarily safe from further assault, I knew that I required more than safety just then. I had to have help, and I was in no position to help myself. I was not even certain how much longer I might remain conscious. So I had to get down and get out. The phone would be dead, the nearest house was not too close by. I would have to get down to the road, at least. I reflected grimly that one of my reasons for locating where I had was that it was not a well-traveled road. I enjoy my solitude, at least some of the time.

With my right hand I drew up the nearest pillow and slipped off its case. I turned it inside out, tried to fold it, gave up, wadded it, slipped it beneath my shirt, and pressed it against my wound. Then I sat there, just holding it in place. It had been a major exertion and I found it painful to take too deep a breath.

After a time, though, I drew the second pillow to me, held it across my knees and let it slip out of its case. I wanted the pillowslip to wave at a passing motorist, for my garments, as usual, were dark. Before I could draw it through my belt, though, I was confounded by the behavior of the pillow itself. It had not yet reached the floor. I had released it, nothing was supporting it, and it *was* moving. But it was moving quite slowly, descending with a dreamlike deliberation.

I thought of the fall of the key as I had dropped it outside my room. I thought of my unintended quickness on mounting the stair with Random. I thought of Fiona's words, and of the Jewel of Judgment, which still hung about my neck now pulsating in time with the throbbing of my side. It might have saved my life, at least for the moment; yes, it probably had, if Fiona's notions were correct. It had probably given me a moment or so more than would otherwise have been my due when the assailant struck, letting me turn, letting me swing my arm. It might, somehow, even have been responsible for my sudden transportation. But I would have to think about such things at another time, should I succeed in maintaining a meaningful relationship with the future. For now, the jewel had to go—in case Fiona's fears concerning it were also correct—and I had to get moving.

I tucked away the second pillow cover, then tried to stand, holding on to the footboard. No good! Dizziness and too much pain. I lowered myself to the floor, afraid of passing out on the way down. I made it. I rested. Then I began to move, a slow crawl.

The front door, as I recalled, was now nailed shut. All right. Out the back, then.

I made it to the bedroom and halted, leaning against its frame. As I rested there I removed the Jewel of Judgment from my neck and wrapped its chain about my wrist. I had to cache it someplace, and the safe in my study was too far out of the way. Besides, I believed that I was leaving a trail of blood. Anyone finding and following it might well be curious enough to investigate and spring the small thing. And I lacked the time and the energy. . . .

I made my way out, around, and through. I had to rise and exert myself to get the back door open. I made the mistake of not resting first.

When I regained consciousness, I was lying across the threshold. The night was raw and clouds filled much of the sky. A mean wind rattled branches above the patio. I felt several drops of moisture on the back of my outflung hand.

I pushed up and crawled out. The snow was about two inches deep. The icy air helped to revive me. With something near panic, I realized just how foggy my mind had been during much of my course from the bedroom. It was possible that I might go under at any time.

I started immediately for the far corner of the house, deviating only to reach the compost heap, tear my way into it, drop the jewel, and reposition the clump of dead grasses I had broken loose. I brushed snow over it and continued on.

Once I made it about the corner, I was shielded from the wind and headed down a slight incline. I reached the front of the house and rested once more. A car had just passed and I watched its taillights dwindle. It was the only vehicle in sight.

Icy crystals stung my face as I moved again. My knees were wet and burning cold. The front yard sloped, gently at first, then dropped sharply toward the road. There was a dip about a hundred yards to the right, where motorists generally hit their brakes. It seemed that this might give me a few moments more in the headlights of anyone coming from that direction—one of those small assurances the mind always seeks when things get serious, an aspirin for the emotions. With three rest stops, I made it down to the roadside, then over to the big rock that bore my house number. I sat on it and leaned back against the icy embankment. I hauled out the second pillow case and draped it across my knees.

I waited. I knew that my mind was fuzzy. I believe that I drifted into and out of consciousness a number of times. Whenever I caught myself at it, I attempted to impose some version of order on my thoughts, to assess what had happened in the light of everything else that had just happened, to seek other safety measures. The former effort proved too much, however. It was simply too difficult to think beyond the level of responding to circumstance. With a sort of numb enlightenment, though, it occurred to me that I was still in possession of my Trumps. I could contact someone in Amber, have him transport me back.

But who? I was not so far gone that I failed to realize I might be contacting the one responsible for my condition. Would it be better to gamble that way, or to take my chances here? Still, Random or Gérard—

I thought that I heard a car. Faint, distant . . . The wind and my pulsebeat were competing with perception, though. I turned my head. I concentrated.

There . . . Again. Yes. It was an engine. I got ready to wave the cloth.

Even then, my mind kept straying. And one thought that flitted through was that I might already be unable to muster sufficient concentration to manipulate the Trumps.

The sound grew louder. I raised the cloth. Moments later, the farthest visible point along the road to my right was touched with light. Shortly after, I saw the car at the top of the rise. I lost sight of it once more as it descended the hill. Then it climbed again and came on, snowflakes flashing through its headbeams.

I began waving as it approached the dip. The lights caught me as it came up out of it, and the driver could not have missed seeing me. He went by, though, a man in a late model sedan, a woman in the passenger seat. The woman turned and looked at me, but the driver did not even slow down.

A couple of minutes later another car came by, a bit older, a woman driving, no visible passengers. It did slow down, but only for a moment. She must not have liked my looks. She stepped on the gas and was gone in an instant.

I sagged back and rested. A prince of Amber can hardly invoke the brotherhood of man for purposes of moral condemnation. At least not with a straight face, and it hurt too much to laugh just then.

Without strength, concentration, and some ability to move, my power over Shadow was useless. I would use it first, I decided, to get to some warm place. . . . I wondered whether I could make it back up the hill, to the compost heap. I had not thought of trying to use the jewel to alter the weather. Probably I was too weak for that too, though. Probably the effort would kill me. Still . . .

I shook my head. I was drifting off, more than half a dream. I had to stay awake. Was that another car? Maybe. I tried to raise the cloth and dropped it. When I leaned forward to retrieve it, I just had to rest my head on my knees for a moment. Deirdre . . . I would call my dear sister. If anyone would help me, Deirdre would. I would get out her Trump and call her. In a minute. If only she weren't my sister . . . I had to rest. I am a knave, not a fool. Perhaps, sometimes, when I rest, I am even sorry for things. Some things. If only it were warmer . . . But it wasn't too bad, bent over this way . . . Was that a car? I wanted to raise my head but found that I could not. It would not make that much difference in being seen, though, I decided.

I felt light on my eyelids and I heard the engine. Now it was neither advancing nor retreating. Just a steady cycling of growls. Then I heard a shout. Then the click-pause-chunk of a car door opening and closing. I felt that I could open my eyes but I did not want to. I was afraid that I would look only on the dark and empty road, that the sounds would resolve into pulse-beats and wind once more. It was better to keep what I had than to gamble.

"Hey! What's the matter? You hurt?"

Footsteps . . . This was real.

I opened my eyes. I forced myself up once again.

"Corey! My God! It's *you!*"

I forced a grin, cut my nod short of a topple.

"It's me, Bill. How've you been?"

"What happened?"

"I'm hurt," I said. "Maybe bad. Need a doctor."

"Can you walk if I help? Or should I carry you?"

"Let's try walking," I said.

He got me to my feet and I leaned on him. We started for his car. I only remember the first few steps.

When that low-swinging sweet chariot turned sour and swung high once more, I tried to raise my arm, realized that it was restrained, settled for a consideration of the tube affixed thereto, and decided that I was going to live. I had sniffed hospital smells and consulted my internal clock. Having made it this far, I felt that I owed it to myself to continue. And I was warm, and as comfortable as recent history allowed. That settled, I closed my eyes, lowered my head, and went back to sleep.

Later, when I came around again, felt more fit and was spotted by a nurse, she told me that it was seven hours since I had been brought in and that a doctor would be by to talk with me shortly. She also got me a glass of water and told me that it had stopped snowing. She was curious as to what had happened to me.

I decided that it was time to start plotting my story. The simpler the better. All right. I was coming home after an extended stay abroad. I had hitchhiked out, gone on in, and been attacked by some vandal or drifter I had surprised inside. I crawled back out and sought help. Finis.

When I told it to the doctor I could not tell at first whether he believed me. He was a heavy man whose face had sagged and set long ago. His name was Bailey, Morris Bailey, and he nodded as I spoke and then asked me, "Did you get a look at the fellow?"

I shook my head.

"It was dark," I said.

"Did he rob you too?"

"I don't know."

"Were you carrying a wallet?"

I decided I had better say yes to that one.

"Well, you didn't have it when you came in here, so he must have taken it."

"Must have," I agreed.

"Do you remember me at all?"

"Can't say that I do. Should I?"

"You seemed vaguely familiar to me when they brought you in. That was all, at first . . ."

"And . . . ?" I asked.

"What sort of garments were you wearing? They seemed something like a uniform."

"Latest thing, Over There, these days. You were saying that I looked familiar?"

"Yes," he agreed. "Where is Over There, anyway? Where did you come from? Where have you been?"

"I travel a lot," I said. "You were going to tell me something a moment ago."

"Yes," he said. "We are a small clinic, and some time ago a fast-talking salesman persuaded the directors to invest in a computerized medical-records system. If the area had developed more and we had expanded a lot, it might have been worthwhile. Neither of these things happened, though, and it is an expensive item. It even encouraged a certain laziness among the clerical help. Old files just don't get purged the way they used to, even for the emergency room. Space there for a lot of useless backlog. So, when Mr. Roth gave me your name and I ran a routine check on you, I found something and I realized why you looked familiar. I had been working the emergency room that night too, around seven years ago, when you had your auto accident. I remembered working on you then—and how I thought you weren't going to make it. You surprised me, though, and you still do. I can't even find the scars that *should* be there. You did a nice job of healing up."

"Thanks. A tribute to the physician, I'd say."

"May I have your age, for the record?"

"Thirty-six," I said. That's always safe.

He jotted it somewhere in the folder he held across his knees.

"You know, I would have sworn—once I got to checking you over and remembering—that that's about what you looked the last time I saw you."

"Clean living."

"Do you know about your blood type?"

"It's an exotic. But you can treat it as an AB positive for all practical purposes. I can take anything, but don't give mine to anybody else."

He nodded.

"The nature of your mishap is going to require a police report, you know."

"I had guessed that."

"Just thought you might want to be thinking about it."

"Thanks," I said. "So you were on duty that night, and you patched me up? Interesting. What else do you recall about it?"

"What do you mean?"

"The circumstances under which I was brought in that time. My own memory is a blank from right before the accident until some time after I had been transferred up to the other place—Greenwood. Do you recall how I arrived?"

He frowned, just when I had decided he had one face for all occasions. "We sent an ambulance," he said.

"In response to what? Who reported the accident? How?"

"I see what you mean," he said. "It was the State Patrol that called for the ambulance. As I recollect, someone had seen the accident and phoned their headquarters. They then radioed a car in the vicinity. It went to the lake, verified the report, gave you first aid, and called for the ambulance. And that was it."

"Any record of who called in the report in the first place?"

He shrugged.

"That's not the sort of thing we keep track of," he said. "Didn't your insurance company investigate? Wasn't there a claim? They could probably—"

"I had to leave the country right after I recovered," I said. "I never pursued the matter. I suppose there would have been a police report, though."

"Surely. But I have no idea how long they keep them around." He chuckled. "Unless, of course, that same salesman got to them, too. . . . It is rather late to be talking about that though, isn't it? It seems to me there is a statute of limitations on things of that sort. Your friend Roth will tell you for sure—"

"It isn't a claim that I have in mind," I said. "Just a desire to know what really happened. I have wondered about it on and off for a number of years now. You see, I have this touch of retrograde amnesia going."

"Have you ever talked it over with a psychiatrist?" he said, and there was something about the way he said it that I did not like. Came one of those little flashes of insight then: Could Flora have managed to get me certified insane before my transfer to Greenwood? Was that on my record here? And was I still on escape status from that place? A lot of time had passed and I knew nothing of the legalities involved. If this was indeed the case, however, I imagined they would have no way of knowing whether I had been certified sane again in some other jurisdiction. Prudence, I guess it was, cautioned me to lean forward and glance at the doctor's wrist. I seemed possessed of a subliminal memory that he had consulted a calendar watch when taking my pulse. Yes, he had, I squinted. All right. Day and month: November 28. I did a quick calculation with my two-and-a-half-to-one conversion and had the year. It *was* seven, as he had indicated.

"No, I haven't," I said. "I just assumed it was organic rather than functional and wrote the time off as a loss."

"I see," he said. "You use such phrases rather glibly. People who've been in therapy sometimes do that."

"I know," I said. "I've read a lot about it."

He sighed. He stood.

"Look," he said. "I am going to call Mr. Roth and let him know you are awake. It is probably best."

"What do you mean by that?"

"I mean that with your friend being an attorney, there might be things you want to discuss with him before you talk to the police."

He opened the folder wherein he had somewhere jotted my age, raised his pen, furrowed his brow, and said, "What's the date, anyway?"

I wanted my Trumps. I imagined my belongings would be in the drawer of the bedside table, but getting at it involved too much twisting and I did not want to put the strain on my sutures. It was not all that urgent, though. Eight hours' sleep in Amber would come to around twenty hours here, so everyone should still have been respectably retired back home. I wanted to get hold of Random, though, to come up with some sort of cover story for my not being there in the morning. Later.

I did not want to look suspicious at a time like this. Also, I wanted to know immediately whatever Brand had to say. I wanted to be in a position to act on it. I did a quick bit of mental juggling. If I could do the worst of my recovering here in Shadow, it would mean less wasted time for me back in Amber. I would have to budget my time carefully and avoid complications on this end. I hoped that Bill would arrive soon. I was anxious to know what the picture was in this place.

Bill was a native of the area, had gone to school in Buffalo, come back, married, joined the family firm, and that was that. He had known me as a retired Army officer who sometimes traveled on vague business. We both belonged to the country club, which was where I had met him. I had known him for over a year without our exchanging more than a few words. Then one evening I happened to be next to him in the bar and it had somehow come out that he was hot on military history, particularly the Napoleonic Wars. The next thing we knew, they were closing up the place around us. We were close friends from then on, right up until the time of my difficulties. I had occasionally wondered about him since. In fact, the only thing that had prevented me from seeing him the last time I had passed through was that he would doubtless have had all sorts of questions as to what had become of me, and I had had too many things on my mind to deal with them all that gracefully and still enjoy myself. I had even thought once or twice of coming back and seeing him if I could, when everything was finally settled in Amber. Next to the fact that this was not the case, I regretted not being able to meet him in the club lounge.

He arrived within the hour, short, heavy, ruddy, a bit grayer on the sides, grinning, nodding. I had propped myself up by then, already tried a few deep breaths and decided they were premature. He clasped my hand and took the bedside chair. He had his briefcase with him.

"You scared the hell out of me last night, Carl. Thought I was seeing a ghost," he said.

I nodded.

"A bit later, and I might have been one," I said. "Thanks. How have you been?"

Bill sighed.

"Busy. You know. The same old stuff, only more of it."

"And Alice?"

"She's fine. And we've got two new grandsons—Bill Jr.'s—twins. Wait a minute."

He fished out his wallet and located a photo.

"Here."

I studied it, noted the family resemblances.

"Hard to believe," I said.

"You don't look much worse for the years."

I chuckled and patted my abdomen.

"Subtracting that, I mean," he said. "Where have you been?"

"God! Where haven't I been!" I said. "So many places I've lost count."

He remained expressionless, caught my eyes and stared.

"Carl, what kind of trouble are you in?" he asked.

I smiled.

"If you mean am I in trouble with the law, the answer is no. My troubles actually involve another country, and I am going to have to go back there shortly."

His face relaxed again, and there was a small glint behind his bifocals.

"Are you some sort of military adviser in that place?"

I nodded.

"Can you tell me where?"

I shook my head.

"Sorry."

"That I can sort of understand," he said. "Dr. Roth told me what you said had happened last night. Off the record now, was it connected with whatever you have been doing?"

I nodded again.

"That makes things a little clearer," he said. "Not much, but enough. I won't even ask you which agency, or even if there is one. I have always known you to be a gentleman, and a rational one at that. That was why I grew curious at the time of your disappearance and did some investigating. I felt a bit officious and self-conscious about it. But your civil status was quite puzzling, and I wanted to know what had happened. Mainly, because I was concerned about you. I hope that doesn't disturb you."

"Disturb me?" I said. "There aren't that many people who care what happens to me. I'm grateful. Also, curious what you discovered. I never had the time to look into it, you know, to straighten things out. How about telling me what you learned?"

He opened the briefcase and withdrew a manila folder. Spreading it across his knees, he shuffled out several sheets of yellow paper covered with neat handwriting. Raising the first of these, he regarded it a moment, then said, "After you escaped from the hospital in Albany and had your accident, Brandon apparently dropped out of the picture and—"

"Stop!" I said, raising my hand, trying to sit up.

"What?" he asked.

"You have the order wrong, also the place," I said. "First came the accident, and Greenwood is not in Albany."

"I know," he said. "I was referring to the Porter Sanitarium, where you spent two days and then escaped. You had your accident that same day, and you were brought here as a result of it. Then your sister Evelyn entered the picture. She had you transferred to Greenwood, where you spent a couple of weeks before departing on your own motion once again. Right?"

"Partly," I said. "Namely, the last part. As I was telling the doctor earlier, my memory is shot for a couple of days prior to the accident. This business about a place in Albany *does* sort of seem to ring a bell, but only very faintly. Do you have more on it?"

"Oh yes," he said. "It may even have something to do with the state of your memory. You were committed on a bum order—"

"By whom?"

He shook the paper and peered.

" 'Brother, Brandon Corey; attendant physician, Hillary B. Rand, psychiatrist,' " he read. "Hear any more bells?"

"Quite possibly," I said. "Go ahead."

"Well, an order got signed on that basis," he said. "You were duly certified, taken into custody, and transported. Then, concerning your memory . . ."

"Yes?"

"I don't know that much about the practice and its effects on the memory, but you were subjected to electroshock therapy while you were at Porter. Then, as I said, the record indicates that you escaped after the second day. You apparently recovered your car from some unspecified locale and were heading back this way when you had the accident."

"That seems right," I said. "It does." For a moment, when he had begun talking, I had had a wild vision of having been returned to the wrong shadow—one where everything was similar, but not congruent. Now, though, I did not believe this to be the case. I was responding to this story on some level.

"Now, about that order," he said. "It was based on false evidence, but there was no way of the court's knowing it at the time. The real Dr. Rand was in England when everything happened, and when I contacted him later he had never heard of you. His office had been broken into while he was away, though. Also, peculiarly, his middle initial is not B. He had never heard of Brandon Corey either."

"What did become of Brandon?"

"He simply vanished. Several attempts were made to contact him at the time of your escape from Porter, but he could not be found. Then you had the accident, were brought here and treated. At that time, a woman named Evelyn Flaumel, who represented herself as your sister, contacted this place, told them you had been probated and that the family wanted you transferred to Greenwood. In the absence of Brandon, who had been appointed your guardian, her instructions were followed, as the only available next of kin. That was how it came about that you were sent to the other place. You escaped again, a couple of weeks later, and that is where my chronology ends."

"Then what is my legal status right now?" I asked.

"Oh, you've been made whole," he said. "Dr. Rand went down after I talked with him and gave the court an affidavit reciting these facts. The order was vacated."

"Then why is the doctor here acting as if I might be a psycho case?"

"Oh my! That *is* a thought. It hadn't occurred to me. All their records here would show is that one time you apparently were. I had better see him on the way out. I have a copy of the journal entry in here, too. I can show it to him."

"How long was it after I left Greenwood that things were set right with the court?"

"The following month," he said. "It was several weeks before I could bring myself to get nosy."

"You couldn't know how happy I am that you did," I said. "And you have given me several pieces of information I think are going to prove extremely important."

"It is nice to be able to help a friend sometime," he said, closing the folder and replacing it in his briefcase. "One thing . . . When this is all over—whatever you are doing—if you are permitted to talk about it, I would like to hear the story."

"I can't promise," I said.

"I know. Just thought I'd mention it. By the way, what do you want to do about the house?"

"Mine? Do I still hold title to it?"

"Yes, but it will probably be sold this year for back taxes if you don't do anything about it."

"I'm surprised that hasn't already happened."

"You gave the bank power of attorney for paying your bills."

"I never thought of that. I'd just set it up for utilities and my charge accounts. Stuff like that."

"Well, the account is nearly empty now," he said. "I was talking to McNally over there the other day. That means the house will go next year if you don't do anything."

"I've got no use for it now," I said. "They can do whatever they want with it."

"Then you might as well sell it and realize what you can."

"I won't be around that long."

"I could handle it for you. Send the money wherever you want."

"All right," I said. "I'll sign anything necessary. Pay my hospital bill out of it and keep the rest."

"I couldn't do that."

I shrugged.

"Do whatever you think best, but be sure and take a good fee."

"I'll put the balance in your account."

"All right. Thanks. By the way, before I forget, would you look in the drawer of that table and see if there is a deck of cards there? I can't reach it yet, and I'll be wanting them later."

"Surely."

He reached over, opened it.

"A big brown envelope," he said. "Kind of bulgy. They probably put whatever was in your pockets in it."

"Open it."

"Yes, here's a pack of cards," he said, reaching inside. "Say! That's a beautiful case! May I?"

"I—" What could I say?

He slipped the case.

"Lovely . . ." he murmured. "Some kind of tarots . . . Are they antique?"

"Yes."

"Cold as ice . . . I never saw anything like these. Say, that's you! Dressed up like some kind of knight! What's their purpose?"

"A very complicated game," I said.

"How could that be you if they are antique?"

"I didn't say it was me. You did."

"Yes, so I did. Ancestor?"

"Sort of."

"Now that's a good-looking gal! But so is the red-head. . . ."

"I think . . ."

He squared the deck and replaced it in the case. He passed it to me.

"Nice unicorn, too," he added. "I shouldn't have looked at them, should I?"

"That's all right."

He sighed and leaned back in the chair, clasping his hands behind his head.

"I couldn't help it," he said. "It is just that there is something very strange about you, Carl, beyond any hush-hush work you may be doing—and mysteries intrigue me. I've never been this close to a real puzzler before."

"Because you just slipped yourself a cold deck of tarots?" I asked.

"No, that just adds atmosphere," he said. "While what you have been doing all these years is admittedly none of my business, there is one recent incident I am unable to comprehend."

"What is that?"

"After I brought you here and took Alice home last night, I went back to your place, hoping to get some sort of idea as to what had happened. The snow had let up by then, though it started in again later, and your track was still clearly visible, going around the house and down the front yard."

I nodded.

"But there were no tracks going in—nothing to indicate your arrival. And for that matter, there were no other tracks departing—nothing to show the flight of your assailant."

I chuckled.

"You think the wound was self-inflicted?"

"No, of course not. There wasn't even a weapon in sight. I followed the bloodstains back to the bedroom, to your bed. I had only my flashlight to see by, of course, but what I saw gave me an eerie feeling. It seemed as if you had just suddenly appeared there on the bed, bleeding, and then gotten up and made your way out."

"Impossible, of course."

"I wonder about the lack of tracks, though."

"The wind must have blown snow over them."

"And not the others?" He shook his head. "No, I don't think so. I just want to go on the record as interested in the answer to that one too, if you ever do want to tell me about things."

"I will remember," I said.

"Yes," he said. "But I wonder . . . I've a peculiar feeling that I may never see you again. It is as if I were one of those minor characters in a melodrama who gets shuffled offstage without ever learning how things turn out."

"I can appreciate the feeling," I said. "My own role sometimes makes me want to strangle the author. But look at it this way: inside stories seldom live up to one's expectations. Usually they are grubby little things, reducing down to the basest of motives when all is known. Conjectures and illusions are often the better possessions."

He smiled.

"You talk the same as always," he said, "yet I have known occasions when you have been tempted to virtue. Several of them . . ."

"How did we get from the footprints to me?" I said. "I was about to tell you that I suddenly recalled having approached the house by exactly the same route as I left it. My departure obviously obliterated the signs of my arrival."

"Not bad," he said. "And your attacker followed the same route?"

"Must have."

"Pretty good," he acknowledged. "You know how to raise a reasonable doubt. But I still feel that the preponderance of evidence indicates the weird."

"Weird? No. Peculiar, perhaps. A matter of interpretation."

"Or semantics. Have you read the police report on your accident?"

"No. Have you?"

"Uh-huh. What if it was more than peculiar? Then will you grant me my word, as I used it: 'weird'?"

"Very well."

". . . And answer one question?"

"I don't know. . . ."

"A simple yes-or-no question. That's all."

"Okay, it's a deal. What did it say?"

"It said that they received report of the accident and a patrol car proceeded to the scene. There they encountered a strangely garbed man in the process of giving you first aid. He stated that he had pulled you from the wrecked car in the lake. This seemed believable in that he was also soaking wet. Average height, light build, red hair. He had on a green outfit that one of the officers said looked like something out of a Robin Hood movie. He refused to identify himself, to accompany them or to give a statement of any sort. When they insisted that he do so, he whistled and a white horse came trotting up. He leaped onto its back and rode off. He was not seen again."

I laughed. It hurt, but I couldn't help it.

"I'll be damned!" I said. "Things are starting to make sense."

Bill just stared at me for a moment. Then, "Really?" he said.

"Yes, I think so. It may well have been worth getting stabbed and coming back for what I learned today."

"You put the two in peculiar order," he said, massaging his chin.

"Yes, I do. But I am beginning to see some order where I had seen nothing before. This one may have been worth the price of admission, all unintended."

"All because of a guy on a white horse?"

"Partly, partly . . . Bill, I am going to be leaving here soon."

"You are not going anywhere for a while."

"Just the same—those papers you mentioned . . . I think I had better get them signed today."

"All right. I'll get them over this afternoon. But I don't want you doing anything foolish."

"I grow more cautious by the moment," I said, "believe me."

"I hope so," he said, snapping his briefcase shut and rising. "Well, get your rest. I'll clear things up with the doctor and have those papers sent over today."

"Thanks again."

I shook his hand.

"By the way," he said, "you did agree to answer a question."

"I did, didn't I? What is it?"

"Are you human?" he asked, still gripping my hand, no special expression on his face.

I started in on a grin, then threw it away.

"I don't know. I—I like to think so. But I don't really—Of course I am! That's a silly . . . Oh hell! You really mean it, don't you? And I said I'd be honest. . . ." I chewed my lip and thought for a moment. Then, "I don't think so," I said.

"Neither do I," he said, and he smiled. "It doesn't make any real difference to me, but I thought it might to you—to know that someone knows you are different and doesn't care."

"I'll remember that, too," I said.

"Well . . . see you around."

"Right."

NINE

It was just after the state patrolman left . . . Late afternoon. I was lying there feeling better, and feeling better that I felt better. Lying there, reflecting on the hazards involved in living in Amber. Brand and I were both laid up by means of the family's favorite weapon. I wondered who had gotten it worse.

Probably he had. It might have reached his kidney, and he was in poor condition to begin with.

I had stumbled across the room and back again twice before Bill's clerk came over with the papers for me to sign. It was necessary that I know my limits. It always is. Since I tended to heal several times faster than those about me in that shadow, I felt that I ought to be able to stand and walk some, to perform in the same fashion as one of these after, say, a day and a half, maybe two. I established that I could. It did hurt, and I was dizzy the first time, less dizzy the second. That was something, anyway. So I lay there feeling better.

I had fanned the Trumps dozens of times, dealt private solitaires, read ambiguous fortunes among familiar faces. And each time I had restrained myself, suppressing my desire to contact Random, to tell him what had happened, to inquire after new developments. Later, I kept telling myself. Each additional hour they sleep is two and a half for you, here. Each two and a half for you, here, is the equivalent of seven or eight for some lesser mortal, here. Abide. Think. Regenerate.

And so it came to pass that a little after dinnertime, just as the sky was darkening again, I was beaten to the punch. I had already told a well-starched young member of the State Patrol everything that I was going to tell him. I have no idea whether he believed me, but he was polite and he did not stay long. In fact, it was only moments after he left that things began to happen.

Lying there, feeling better, I was waiting for Dr. Bailey to stop by and check whether I was still oriented. Lying there, assessing all of the things Bill had told me, trying to fit them together with other things that I knew or had guessed at. . . .

Contact! I had been anticipated. Someone in Amber was an early riser.

"Corwin!"

It was Random, agitated.

"Corwin! Get up! Open the door! Brand's come around, and he's asking for you."

"Have you been pounding on that door, trying to get me up?"

"That's right."

"Are you alone?"

"Yes."

"Good. I am not inside. You have reached me in Shadow."

"I do not understand."

"Neither do I. I am hurt, but I will live. I will give you the story later. Tell me about Brand."

"He woke up just a little while ago. Told Gérard he had to talk to you right away. Gérard rang up a servant, sent him to your room. When he couldn't rouse you, he came to me. I just sent him back to tell Gérard I'd be bringing you along shortly."

"I see," I said, stretching slowly and sitting up. "Get in some place where you can't be seen, and I'll come through. I will need a robe or something. I am missing some clothes."

"It could probably be best if I went back to my rooms, then."

"Okay. Go ahead."

"A minute, then."

And silence.

I moved my legs slowly. I sat on the edge of the bed. I gathered up my Trumps and replaced them in their case. I felt it important that I mask my injury back in Amber. Even in normal times one never advertises one's vulnerability.

I took a deep breath and stood, holding on to the bed frame. My practice had paid off. I breathed normally and relaxed my grip. Not bad, if I moved slowly, if I did not exert myself beyond the barest essentials required for appearances' sake . . . I might be able to carry it until my strength really returned.

Just then I heard a footfall, and a friendly nurse was framed in the doorway, crisp, symmetrical, differing from a snowflake mainly in that they are all of them alike.

"Get back in that bed, Mr. Corey! You are not supposed to be up!"

"Madam," I said, "it is quite necessary that I be up. I have to go."

"You could have rung for a pan," she said, entering the room and advancing.

I gave my head a weary shake just as Random's presence reached me once more. I wondered how she would report this one—and if she would mention my prismatic afterimage as I trumped out. Another entry, I suppose, for the growing record of folklore I tend to leave behind.

"Think of it this way, my dear," I told her. "Ours has been a purely physical relationship all along. There will be others . . . many others. *Adieu!*"

I bowed and blew her a kiss as I stepped forward into Amber, leaving her to clutch at rainbows as I caught hold of Random's shoulder and staggered.

"Corwin! What the hell—"

"If blood be the price of admiralty, I've just bought me a naval commission," I said. "Give me something to wear."

He draped a long, heavy cloak about my shoulders and I fumbled to clasp it at my throat.

"All set," I said. "Take me to him."

He led me out the door, into the hall, toward the stair. I leaned on him heavily as we went.

"How bad is it?" he asked me.

"Knife," I said, and laid my hand on the spot. "Someone attacked me in my room last night."

"Who?"

"Well, it couldn't have been you, because I had just left you," I said, "and Gérard was up in the library with Brand. Subtract the three of you from the rest and start guessing. That is the best—"

"Julian," he said.

"His stock is definitely bearish," I said. "Fiona was just running him down for me the other night, and of course it is no secret that he is not my favorite."

"Corwin, he's gone. He cut out during the night. The servant who came to get me told me that Julian had departed. What does that look like to you?"

We reached the stair. I kept one hand on Random and rested there briefly.

"I don't know," I said. "It can sometimes be just as bad to extend the benefit of the doubt too far as not to grant it at all. But it does occur to me that if he thought he had disposed of me, he would look a lot better by staying here and acting surprised to learn of it than by getting the hell out. That *does* look suspicious. I am inclined to think he might have departed because he was afraid of what Brand would have to say when he came around."

"But you lived, Corwin. You got away from whoever attacked you, and he could not be certain he had done you in. If it were me, I would be worlds away by now."

"There is that," I acknowledged, and we started on down again. "Yes, you might well be right. Let us leave it academic for now. And no one is to know I have been injured."

He nodded.

"As you say. Silence beats a chamber pot in Amber."

"How's that?"

" 'Tis gilt, m'lord, like a royal flush."

"Your wit pains both wounded and unwounded parts, Random. Spend some figuring how the assailant entered my room."

"Your panel?"

"It secures from the inside. I keep it that way now. And the door's lock is a new one. Tricky."

"All right, I have it. My answer requires that it be a family member, too."

"Tell me."

"Someone was willing to psyche himself up and tough it through the Pattern again for a shot at you. He went below, walked it, projected himself into your room, and attacked you."

"That would be perfect except for one thing. We all left at pretty much the same time. The attack did not occur later on in the evening. It happened immediately on my entering. I do not believe there was sufficient time for one of us to get down to the chamber, let alone negotiate the Pattern. The attacker was already waiting. So if it was one of us, he had gotten in by some other means."

"Then he picked your lock, tricks and all."

"Possibly," I said as we reached the landing and continued on. "We will rest at the corner so that I can go on into the library unassisted."

"Sure thing."

We did that. I composed myself, drew the cloak completely about me, squared my shoulders, advanced, and knocked on the door.

"Just a minute." Gérard's voice.

Footsteps approaching the door . . .

"Who is it?"

"Corwin," I said. "Random's with me."

I heard him call back, "You want Random, too?" and I heard a soft "No" in reply.

The door opened.

"Just you, Corwin," Gérard said.

I nodded and turned to Random.

"Later," I told him.

He returned my nod and headed back in the direction from which we had come. I entered the library.

"Open your cloak, Corwin," Gérard ordered.

"That is not necessary," Brand said, and I looked over and saw that he was propped up by a number of cushions and showing a yellow-toothed smile.

"Sorry, I am not as trusting as Brand," Gérard said, "and I will not have my work wasted. Let's have a look."

"I said that it is not necessary," Brand repeated. "He is not the one who stabbed me."

Gérard turned quickly.

"How do you know he isn't?" he asked.

"Because I know who did, of course. Don't be an ass, Gérard. I wouldn't have asked for him if I had reason to fear him."

"You were unconscious when I brought you through. You couldn't know who did it."

"Are you certain of that?"

"Well . . . Why didn't you tell me, then?"

"I have my reasons, and they are valid ones. I want to speak with Corwin alone now."

Gérard lowered his head.

"You had better not be delirious," he said. He stepped to the door, opened it again. "I'll be within hailing distance," he added, and closed it behind him.

I moved nearer. Brand reached up and I clasped his hand.

"Good to see that you made it back," he said.

"Vice versa," I said, and then I took Gérard's chair, trying not to collapse into it.

"How do you feel now?" I asked.

"Rotten, in one sense. But better than I have in years, in another. It's all relative."

"Most things are."

"Not Amber."

I sighed.

"All right. I wasn't getting technical. What the hell happened?"

His gaze was most intense. He was studying me, looking for something. What? Knowledge, I'd guess. Or, more correctly, ignorance. Negatives being harder to gauge, his mind had to be moving fast, must have been from the moment he had come around. Knowing him, he was more interested in what I did not know than in what I knew. He wasn't going to give away anything if he could help it. He wanted to know the minimum enlightenment he need shed in order to get what he wanted. Not a watt more would he willingly spend. For this was his way, and of course he wanted something. Unless . . . More strongly in recent years than ever before I have tried to convince myself that people do change, that the passage of time does not serve merely to accentuate that which is already there, that qualitative changes do sometimes occur in people because of things they have done, seen, thought, and felt. It would provide some small solace in times such as these when everything else seems to be going wrong, not to mention pepping up my mundane philosophy no end. And Brand had probably been responsible for saving my life and my memory, whatever his reasons. Very well, I resolved to give him the doubt's benefit without exposing my back. A small concession here, my move against the simple psychology of humors which generally governs the openings of our games.

"Things are never what they seem, Corwin," he began. "Your friend today is your enemy tomorrow, and—"

"Cut it out!" I said. "Cards-on-the-table time is here. I do appreciate what Brandon Corey did for me, and it was my idea to try the trick we used to locate you and bring you back."

He nodded.

"I fancy there were good reasons for a recrudescence of fraternal sentiment after all this time."

"I might suppose you had additional reasons for helping me, also."

He smiled again, raised his right hand and lowered it.

"Then we are either even or in each other's debt, depending upon how one looks at these things. As it would seem we now have need of each other, it would be well to regard ourselves in the most flattering light."

"You are stalling, Brand. You are trying to psych me. You are also spoiling my day's effort at idealism. You got me out of bed to tell me something. Be my guest."

"Same old Corwin," he said, chuckling. Then he looked away. "Or are you? I wonder . . . Did it change you, do you think? Living all that while in Shadow? Not knowing who you really were? Being a part of something else?"

"Maybe," I said. "I don't know. Yes, I guess I did. I know that it shortened my temper when it comes to family politics."

"Plain-speaking, blunt, plain-dealing? You miss some of the fun that way. But then there is a value to such novelty. Keep everyone unbalanced with it . . . revert when they least expect it. . . . Yes, it might prove valuable. Refreshing, too. All right! Panic not. Thus end my preliminaries. All pleasantries are now exchanged. I'll bare the basics, bridle the beast Unreason, and wrest from murky mystery the pearl of sweetest sense. But one thing first, if you would. Have you anything smokable with you? It has been a number of years, and I'd like some foul weed or other—to celebrate my homecoming."

I started to say no. But I was sure there were some cigarettes in the desk, left there by me. I did not really want the exercise, but, "Just a minute," I said.

I tried to make my movements look casual rather than stiff as I rose and crossed the room. I attempted to make it seem as if I were resting my hand naturally upon the desktop as I rummaged through it, rather than leaning as heavily as I was. I masked my movements with my body and my cloak as much as possible.

I located the package and returned as I had come, stopping to light a pair at the hearth. Brand was slow in taking his from me.

"Your hand is rather shaky," he said. "What is the matter?"

"Too much partying last night," I said, returning to my chair.

"I hadn't thought of that. I imagine there would have been, wouldn't there? Of course. Everyone together in one room . . . Unexpected success in finding me, bringing me back . . . A desperate move on the part of a very nervous, very guilty person. . . . Half success there. Me injured and mum, but for how long? Then—"

"You said that you knew who did it. Were you kidding?"

"No, I was not."

"Who then?"

"In its place, dear brother. In its place. Sequence and order, time and stress—they are most important in this matter. Allow me to savor the drama of the event in safe retrospect. I see me punctured and all of you gathered round. Ah! what would I not give to witness that tableau! Could you possibly describe for me the expression on each face?"

"I'm afraid their faces were my least concern at the time."

He sighed and blew smoke.

"Ah, that is good," he said. "Never mind, I can see their faces. I've a vivid imagination, you know. Shock, distress, puzzlement—shading over into suspicion, fear. Then all of you departed, I'm told, and gentle Gérard my nursemaid here." He paused, stared into the smoke, and for a moment the note of mockery was absent. "He is the only decent one among us, you know."

"He's high on my list," I said.

"He took good care of me. He's always looked out for the rest of us." He chuckled suddenly. "Frankly, I can't see why he bothers. As I was musing, though—prompted by your recuperating self—you must have adjourned to talk things over. There is another party I'm sad I missed. All those emotions and suspicions and lies bouncing off one another—and no one wanting to be the first to say good night. It must have gotten shrill after a time. Everyone on his own best behavior, with an eye out to blacken the rest. Attempts to intimidate the one guilty person. Perhaps a few stones shied at scapegoats. But, all in all, nothing much really accomplished. Am I right?"

I nodded, appreciative of the way his mind worked, and resigned to letting him tell it his way.

"You know you're right," I said.

He gave me a sharp look at that, then went on. "But everyone did finally go off, to lie awake worrying, or to get together with an accomplice, to scheme. There were hidden turmoils in the night. It is flattering to know that my well-being was on everyone's mind. Some, of course, were for it, others against. And in the midst of it all, I rallied—nay, flourished—not wishing to disappoint my supporters. Gérard spent a long while bringing me up to date on recent history. When I had enough of this, I sent for you."

"In case you haven't noticed, I'm here. What did you want to tell me?"

"Patience, brother! Patience! Consider all the years you spent in Shadow, not even remembering—this." He gestured widely with his cigarette. "Consider all that time you waited, unknowing, until I succeeded in locating you and tried to remedy your plight. Surely a few moments now are not so priceless by contrast."

"I was told that you had sought me," I said. "I wondered at that, for we had not exactly parted on the best of terms the last time we were together."

He nodded.

"I cannot deny it," he said. "But I always get over such things, eventually."

I snorted.

"I have been deciding how much to tell you, and what you would believe," he continued. "I doubted you would accept it if I had simply come out and said that, save for a few small items, my present motives are almost entirely altruistic."

I snorted again.

"But this is true," he went on, "and to lay your suspicions, I add that it is because I have small choice in it. Beginnings are always difficult. Wherever I begin, something preceded it. You were gone for so long. If one must name a single thing, however, then let it be the throne. There. I have said it. We had thought of a way to take it, you see. This was just after your disappearance, and in some ways, I suppose, prompted by it. Dad suspected Eric of having slain you. But there was no evidence. We worked on this feeling, though—a word here and there, every now and then. Years passed, with you unreachable by any means, and it seemed more and more likely that you were indeed dead. Dad looked upon Eric with growing disfavor. Then, one night, pursuant to a discussion I had begun on a totally neutral matter—most of us present at the table—he said that no fratricide would ever take the throne, and he was looking at Eric as he said it. You know how his eyes could get. Eric grew bright as a sunset and could not swallow for a long while. But then Dad took things much further than any of us had anticipated or desired. In fairness to you, I do not know whether he spoke solely to vent his feelings, or whether he actually meant what he said. But he told us that he had more than half decided upon you as his successor, so that he took whatever misadventure had befallen you quite personally. He would not have spoken of it, but that he was convinced as to your passing. In the months that followed, we reared you a cenotaph to give some solid form to this conclusion, and we made certain that no one forgot Dad's feelings toward Eric. All along, after yourself, Eric was the one we felt had to be gotten around to reach the throne."

"We! Who were the others?"

"Patience, Corwin. Sequence and order, time and stress! Accent, emphasis . . . Listen." He took another cigarette, chain-lit it from the butt, stabbed the air with its burning tip. "The next step required that we get Dad out of Amber. This was the most crucial and dangerous part of it, and it was here that we disagreed. I did not like the idea of an alliance with a power I did not fully understand, especially one that gave them some hold on us.

Using shadows is one thing; allowing them to use you is ill-considered, whatever the circumstances. I argued against it, but the majority had it otherwise." He smiled. "Two to one. Yes, there were three of us. We went ahead then. The trap was set and Dad went after the bait—"

"Is he still living?" I asked.

"I do not know," Brand said. "Things went wrong afterward, and then I'd troubles of my own to concern me. After Dad's departure, though, our next move was to consolidate our position while waiting a respectable period of time for a presumption of death to seem warranted. Ideally, all that we required was the cooperation of one person. Either Caine or Julian—it did not matter which. You see, Bleys had already gone off into Shadow and was in the process of putting together a large military force—"

"Bleys! He was one of you?"

"Indeed. We intended him for the throne—with sufficient strings on him, of course, so that it would have amounted to a *de facto* triumvirate. So, he went off to assemble troops, as I was saying. We hoped for a bloodless takeover, but we had to be ready in the event that words proved insufficient to win our case. If Julian gave us the land route in, or Caine the waves, we could have transported the troops with dispatch and held the day by force of arms, should that have proven necessary. Unfortunately, I chose the wrong man. In my estimate, Caine was Julian's superior in matters of corruption. So, with measured delicacy I sounded him on the matter. He seemed willing to go along with things, at first. But he either reconsidered subsequently or deceived me quite skillfully from the beginning. Naturally, I prefer to believe that it was the former. Whatever, at some point he came to the conclusion that he stood to benefit more by supporting a rival claimant. To wit, Eric. Now Eric's hopes had been somewhat dashed by Dad's attitude toward him—but Dad was gone, and our intended move gave Eric the chance to act as defender of the throne. Unfortunately for us, such a position would also put him but a step away from the throne itself. To make matters darker, Julian went along with Caine in pledging the loyalty of his troops to Eric, as defender. Thus was the other trio formed. So Eric took a public oath to defend the throne, and the lines were thereby drawn. I was naturally in a somewhat embarrassing position at this time. I bore the brunt of their animosity, as they did not know who my fellows were. Yet they could not imprison or torture me, for I would immediately be trumped out of their hands. And if they were to kill me, they realized there might well be a reprisal by parties unknown. So it had to stand as a stalemate for a time. They also saw that I could no longer move directly against them. They kept me under heavy surveillance. So a more devious route was charted. Again I disagreed and again I lost, two to one. We were to employ the same forces we had called upon to deal with Dad, this time for purposes of discrediting Eric. If the job of defending Amber, so confidently assumed, were to prove too much for him and Bleys then came onto the scene and handled the situation with dispatch, why Bleys would even have popular support as he moved on to assume the role of defender himself and—

after a fit period of time—suffered the thrusting of sovereignty upon him, for the good of Amber."

"Question," I interrupted. "What about Benedict? I know he was off being discontent in his Avalon, but if something really threatened Amber . . ."

"Yes," he said, nodding, "and for that reason, a part of our deal was to involve Benedict with a number of problems of his own."

I thought of the harassment of Benedict's Avalon by the hellmaids. I thought of the stump of his right arm. I opened my mouth to speak again, but Brand raised his hand.

"Let me finish in my own fashion, Corwin. I am not unmindful of your thought processes as you speak. I feel the pain in your side, twin to my own. Yes, I know these things and many more." His eyes burned strangely as he took another cigarette into his hand and it lit of its own accord. He drew heavily upon it and spoke as he exhaled. "I broke with the others over this decision. I saw it as involving too great a peril, as placing Amber herself in jeopardy. Broke with them . . ." He watched the smoke for several moments before he continued. "But things were too far advanced that I might simply walk away. I had to oppose them, in order to defend myself as well as Amber. It was too late to swing over to Eric's side. He would not have protected me if he could have—and besides, I was certain he was going to lose. It was then that I decided to employ certain new abilities I had acquired. I had often wondered at the strange relationship between Eric and Flora, off on that shadow Earth she pretended so to enjoy. I had had a slight suspicion that there was something about that place which concerned him, and that she might be his agent there. While I could not get close enough to him to achieve any satisfaction on this count, I felt confident that it would not take too much in the way of investigation, direct and otherwise, to learn what Flora was about. And so I did. Then suddenly the pace accelerated. My own party was concerned as to my whereabouts. Then when I picked you up and shocked back a few memories, Eric learned from Flora that something was suddenly quite amiss. Consequently, both sides were soon looking for me. I had decided that your return would throw everyone's plans out the window and get me out of the pocket I was in long enough to come up with an alternative to the way things were going. Eric's claim would be clouded once again, you would have had supporters of your own, my party would have lost the purpose for its entire maneuver and I had assumed you would not be ungrateful to me for my part in things. Then you went and escaped from Porter, and things really got complicated. All of us were looking for you, as I later learned, for different reasons. But my former associates had something very extra going for them. They learned what was happening, located you, and got there first. Obviously, there was a very simple way to preserve the status quo, where they would continue to hold the edge. Bleys fired the shots that put you and your car into the lake. I arrived just as this was occurring. He departed almost immediately, for it looked as if he had done a thorough job. I dragged you out, though, and there was enough left to start treating. It was frustrating now that I think back on it, not knowing whether the treatment had really been effective, whether you would awaken as Corwin or Corey. It was frustrating afterward, also, still not knowing. . . . I hellrode out when help arrived. My associates caught up with me somewhat later and put me where you found me. Do you know the rest of the story?"

"Not all of it."

"Then stop me whenever we've caught up on this. I only obtained it later, myself. Eric's crowd learned of the accident, got your location, and had you transferred to a private place, where you could be better protected, and kept you heavily sedated, so that *they* could be protected."

"Why should Eric protect me, especially if my presence was going to wreck his plans?"

"By then, seven of us knew you were still living. That was too many. It was simply too late to do what he would have liked to do. He was still trying to live down Dad's words. If anything had happened to you once you were in his power, it would have blocked his movement to the throne. If Benedict ever got word of it, or Gérard . . . No, he'd not have made it. Afterward, yes. Before, no. What happened was that general knowledge of the fact of your existence forced his hand. He scheduled his coronation and resolved to keep you out of the way until it had occurred. An extremely premature bit of business, not that I see he had much of a choice. I guess you know what happened after that, since it happened to you."

"I fell in with Bleys, just as he was making his move. Not too fortunate."

He shrugged.

"Oh, it might have been—if you had won, and if you had been able to do something about Bleys. You hadn't a chance, though, not really. My grasp of their motivations begins to dissolve at this point, but I believe that that entire assault really constituted some sort of feint."

"Why?"

"As I said, I do not know. But they already had Eric just about where they wanted him. It should not have been necessary to call that attack."

I shook my head. Too much, too fast . . . Many of the facts sounded true, once I subtracted the narrator's bias. But still . . .

"I don't know . . ." I began.

"Of course," he said. "But if you ask me I will tell you."

"Who was the third member of your group?"

"The same person who stabbed me, of course. Would you care to venture a guess?"

"Just tell me."

"Fiona. The whole thing was her idea."

"Why didn't you tell me that right away?"

"Because you would not have sat still long enough to hear the rest of what I had to say. You would have dashed off to put her under restraint, discovered that she was gone, roused all the others, started an investigation, and wasted a lot of valuable time. You still may, but it at least provided me with your attention for a sufficient time for me to convince you that I know what I am about. Now, when I tell you that time is essential and that you must hear the rest of what I have to say as soon as possible—if Amber is to have any chance at all—you might listen rather than chase a crazy lady."

I had already half risen from my chair.

"I shouldn't go after her?" I said.

"The hell with her, for now. You've got bigger problems. You had better sit down again."

So I did.

TEN

A raft of moonbeams . . . the ghostly torchlight, like fires in black-and-white films . . . stars . . . a few fine filaments of mist . . .

I leaned upon the rail, I looked across the world. . . . Utter silence held the night, the dream-drenched city, the entire universe from here. Distant things—the sea, Amber, Arden, Garnath, the Lighthouse of Cabra, the Grove of the Unicorn, my tomb atop Kolvir . . . Silent, far below, yet clear, distinct . . . A god's eye view, I'd say, or that of a soul cut loose and drifting high . . . In the middle of the night . . .

I had come to the place where the ghosts play at being ghosts, where the omens, portents, signs, and animate desires thread the nightly avenues and palace high halls of Amber in the sky, Tir-na Nog'th . . .

Turning, my back to the rail and dayworld's vestiges below, I regarded the avenues and dark terraces, the halls of the lords, the quarters of the low. . . . The moonlight is intense in Tir-na Nog'th, silvers over the facing sides of all our imaged places. . . . Stick in hand, I passed forward, and the strangelings moved about me, appeared at windows, on balconies, on benches, at gates . . . Unseen I passed, for truly put, in this place I was the ghost to whatever their substance. . . .

Silence and silver . . . Only the tapping of my stick, and that mostly muted . . . More mists adrift toward the heart of things . . . The palace a white bonfire of it . . . Dew, like drops of mercury on the finely sanded petals and stems in the gardens by the walks . . . The passing moon as painful to the eye as the sun at midday, the stars outshone, dimmed by it . . . Silver and silence . . . The shine . . .

I had not planned on coming, for its omens—if that they truly be—are deceitful, its similarities to the lives and places below unsettling, its spectacle often disconcerting. Still, I had come. . . . A part of my bargain with time . . .

After I had left Brand to continue his recovery in the keeping of Gérard, I had realized that I required additional rest myself and sought to obtain it without betraying my disability. Fiona was indeed flown, and neither she nor Julian could be reached by means of the Trumps. Had I told Benedict and Gérard what Brand had told me, I was certain that they would have insisted we begin efforts at tracking her down, at tracking both of them. I was equally certain that such efforts would prove useless.

I had sent for Random and Ganelon and retired to my quarters, giving out that I intended to pass the day in rest and quiet thought in anticipation of spending the night in Tir-na Nog'th—reasonable behavior for any Amberite with a serious problem. I did not put much stock in the practice, but most of the others did. As it was the perfect time for me to be about such a thing, I felt that it would make my day's retirement believable. Of course, this obliged me to follow through on it that night. But this, too, was good. It gave me a day, a night, and part of the following day in which to heal sufficiently to carry my wound that much the better. I felt that it would be time well spent.

You've got to tell someone, though. I told Random and I told Ganelon. Propped in my bed, I told them of the plans of Brand, Fiona, and Bleys, and of the Eric-Julian-Caine cabal. I told them what Brand had said concerning my return and his own imprisonment by his fellow conspirators. They saw why the survivors of both factions—Fiona and Julian—had run off: doubtless to marshal their forces, hopefully to expend them on one another, but probably not. Not immediately, anyhow. More likely, one or the other would move to take Amber first.

"They will just have to take numbers and wait their turns, like everyone else," Random had said.

"Not exactly," I remembered saying. "Fiona's allies and the things that have been coming in on the black road are the same guys."

"And the Circle in Lorraine?" Ganelon had asked.

"The same. That was how it manifested itself in that shadow. They came a great distance."

"Ubiquitous bastards," Random had said.

Nodding, I had tried to explain.

. . . And so I came to Tir-na Nog'th. When the moon rose and the apparition of Amber came faintly into the heavens, stars showing through it, pale halo about its towers, tiny flecks of movement upon its walls, I waited, waited with Ganelon and Random, waited on the highest crop of Kolvir, there where the three steps are fashioned, roughly, out of the stone. . . .

When the moonlight touched them, the outline of the entire stairway began to take shape, spanning the great gulf to that point above the sea the vision city held. When the moonlight fell full upon it, the stair had taken as much of substance as it would ever possess, and I set my foot on the stone. . . . Random held a full deck of Trumps and I'd mine within my jacket. Grayswandir, forged upon this very stone by moonlight, held power in the city in the sky, and so I bore my blade along. I had rested all day, and I held a staff to lean upon. Illusion of distance and time . . . The stairs through the Corwin-ignoring sky escalate somehow, for it is not a simple arithmetic progression up them once motion has commenced. I was here, I was there, I was a quarter of the way up before my shoulder had forgotten the clasp of Ganelon's hand. . . . If I looked too hard at any portion of the stair, it lost its shimmering opacity and I saw the ocean far below as through a translucent lens. . . . I lost track of time, though it seems it's never long, afterward . . . As far beneath the waves as I'd soon be above them, off to my right, glittering and curling, the outline of Rebma appeared within the sea. I thought of Moire, wondered how she fared. What would become of our deepwater double should Amber ever fall? Would the image remain unshattered in its mirror? Or would building blocks and bones be taken and shaken alike, dice in the deepwater casino canyons our fleets fly over? No answer in the man-drowning, Corwin-confounding waters, though I felt a twinge in my side.

At the head of the stair, I entered, coming into the ghost city as one would enter Amber after mounting the great forestair up Kolvir's seaward face.

I leaned upon the rail, looked across the world.

The black road led off to the south. I could not see it by night. Not that it mattered. I knew now where it led. Or rather where Brand said that it led. As he appeared to have used up a life's worth of reasons for lying, I believed that I knew where it led.

All the way.

From the brightness of Amber and the power and clean-shining splendor of adjacent Shadow, off through the progressively darkening slices of image that lead away in any direction, farther, through the twisted landscapes, and farther still, on through places seen only when drunk, delirious, or dreamingly ill, and farther yet again, running beyond the place where I stop. . . . Where I stop . . .

How to put simply that which is not a simple thing . . . ? Solipsism, I suppose, is where we have to begin—the notion that nothing exists but the self, or, at least, that we cannot truly be aware of anything but our own existence and experience. I can find, somewhere, off in Shadow, anything I can visualize. Any of us can. This, in good faith, does not transcend the limits of the ego. It may be argued, and in fact has, by most of us, that we create the shadows we visit out of the stuff of our own psyches, that we alone truly exist, that the shadows we traverse are but projections of our own desires. . . . Whatever the merits of this argument, and there are several, it does go far toward explaining much of the family's attitude toward people, places, and things outside of Amber. Namely, we are toymakers and they, our playthings— sometimes dangerously animated, to be sure; but this, too, is part of the game. We are impresarios by temperament, and we treat one another accordingly. While solipsism does tend to leave one slightly embarrassed on questions of etiology, one can easily avoid the embarrassment by refusing to admit the validity of the questions. Most of us are, as I have often observed, almost entirely pragmatic in the conduct of our affairs. Almost . . .

Yet—yet there is a disturbing element in the picture. There is a place where the shadows go mad. . . . When you purposely push yourself through layer after layer of Shadow, surrendering—again, purposely—a piece of your understanding every step of the way, you come at last to a mad place beyond which you cannot go. Why do this? In hope of an insight, I'd say, or a new game . . . But when you come to this place, as we all have, you realize that you have reached the limit of Shadow or the end of yourself—synonymous terms, as we had always thought. Now, though . . .

Now I know that it is not so, now as I stand, waiting, without the Courts of Chaos, telling you what it was like, I know that it is not so. But I knew well enough then, that night, in Tir-na Nog'th, had known earlier, when I had fought the goat-man in the Black Circle of Lorraine, had known that day in the Lighthouse of Cabra, after my escape from the dungeons of Amber, when I had looked upon ruined Garnath. . . . I knew that that was not all there was to it. I knew because I knew that the black road ran beyond that point. It passed through madness into chaos and kept going. The things that traveled across it came from somewhere, but they were not my things. I had somehow helped to grant them this passage, but they did not spring from my version of reality. They were their own, or someone else's—small matter there—and they tore holes in that small metaphysic we had woven over the ages. They had entered our preserve, they were not of it, they threatened it, they threatened us. Fiona and Brand had reached beyond everything and found something, where none of the rest of us had believed anything to exist. The danger released was, on some level, almost worth the evidence obtained: we were not alone, nor were shadows truly our toys. Whatever our relationship with Shadow, I could nevermore regard it in the old light. . . .

All because the black road headed south and ran beyond the end of the world, where I stop.

Silence and silver . . . Walking away from the rail, leaning on my stick, passing through the fog-spun, mist-woven, moonlight-brushed fabric of vision within the troubling city . . . Ghosts . . . Shadows of shadows . . . Images of probability . . . Might-bes and might-have-beens . . . Probability lost . . . Probability regained . . .

Walking, across the promenade now . . . Figures, faces, many of them familiar . . . What are they about? Hard to say . . . Some lips move, some faces show animation. There are no words there for me. I pass among them, unnoted.

There . . . One such figure . . . Alone, but waiting . . . Fingers unknotting minutes, casting them away . . . Face averted, and I wish to see it . . . A sign that I will or should . . . She sits on a stone bench beneath a gnarly tree . . . She gazes in the direction of the palace . . . Her form is quite familiar . . . Approaching, I see that it is Lorraine . . . She continues to regard a point far beyond me, does not hear me say that I have avenged her death.

But mine is the power to be heard here. . . . It hangs in the sheath at my side.

Drawing Grayswandir, I raise my blade overhead where moonlight tricks its patterns into a kind of motion. I place it on the ground between us.

"Corwin!"

Her head snaps back, her hair rusts in the moonlight, her eyes focus.

"Where did you come from? You're early."

"You wait for me?"

"Of course. You told me to—"

"How did you come to this place?"

"This bench . . . ?"

"No. This city."

"Amber? I do not understand. You brought me yourself. I—"

"Are you happy here?"

"You know that I am, so long as I am with you."

I had not forgotten the evenness of her teeth, the hint of freckles beneath the soft light's veil. . . .

"What happened? It is very important. Pretend for a moment that I do not know, and tell me everything that happened to us after the battle of the Black Circle in Lorraine."

She frowned. She stood. She turned away.

"We had that argument," she said. "You followed me, drove away Melkin, and we talked. I saw that I was wrong and I went with you to Avalon. There, your brother Benedict persuaded you to talk with Eric. You were not reconciled, but you agreed to a truce because of something that he told you. He swore not to harm you and you swore to defend Amber, with Benedict to witness both oaths. We remained in Avalon while you obtained chemicals, and we went to another place later, a place where you purchased strange weapons. We won the battle, but Eric lies wounded now." She stood and faced me. "Are you thinking of ending the truce? Is that it, Corwin?"

I shook my head, and though I knew better I reached to embrace her. I wanted to hold her, despite the fact that one of us did not exist, could not exist, when that tiny gap of space between our skins was crossed, to tell her that whatever had happened or would happen—

The shock was not severe, but it caused me to stumble. I lay across Grayswandir. . . . My staff had fallen to the grass several paces away. Rising to my knees, I saw that the color had gone out of her face, her eyes, her hair. Her mouth shaped ghost words as her head turned, searching. Sheathing Grayswandir, recovering my staff, I rose once again. Her seeing passed through me and focused. Her face grew smooth, she smiled, started forward. I moved aside and turned, watching her run toward the man who approached, seeing her clasped in his arms, glimpsing his face as he bent it toward her own, lucky ghost, silver rose at the throat of his garment, kissing her, this man I would never know, silver on silence, and silver. . . .

Walking away . . . Not looking back . . . Crossing the promenade . . .

The voice of Random: "Corwin, are you all right?"

"Yes."

"Anything interesting happening?"

"Later, Random."

"Sorry."

And sudden, the gleaming stair before the palace grounds . . . Up it, and a turn to the right . . . Slow and easy now, into the garden . . . Ghost flowers throb on their stalks all about me, ghost shrubs spill blossoms like frozen firework displays. *Sans* colors, all . . . Only the essentials sketched in, degrees of luminosity in silver the terms of their claim on the eye. Only the essentials here. Is Tir-na Nog'th a special sphere of Shadow in the real world, swayed by the promptings of the id—a full-sized projective test in the sky, perhaps even a therapeutic device? Despite the silver, I'd say, if this is a piece of the soul, the night is very dark. . . . And silent . . .

Walking . . . By fountains, benches, groves, cunning alcoves in mazes of hedging . . . Passing along the walks, up an occasional step, across small bridges . . . Moving past ponds, among trees, by an odd piece of statuary, a boulder, a sundial (moondial, here?), bearing to my right, pressing steadily ahead, rounding, after a time, the northern end of the palace, swinging left then, past a courtyard overhung by balconies, more ghosts here and there upon them, behind them, within . . .

Circling around to the rear, just to see the back gardens this way, again, for they are lovely by normal moonlight in the true Amber.

A few more figures, talking, standing . . . No motion but my own is apparent.

. . . And feel myself drawn to the right. As one should never turn down a free oracle, I go.

. . . Toward a mass of high hedging, a small open area within, if it is not overgrown . . . Long ago there was . . .

Two figures, embracing, within. They part as I begin to turn away. None of my affair, but . . . Deirdre . . . One of them is Deirdre. I know who the man will be before he turns. It is a cruel joke by whatever powers rule that silver, that silence. . . . Back, back, away from that hedge . . . Turning, stumbling, rising again, going, away, now, quickly . . .

The voice of Random: "Corwin? Are you all right?"

"Later! Damn it! Later!"

"It is not too long till sunrise, Corwin. I felt I had better remind you—"

"Consider me reminded!"

Away, now, quickly . . . Time, too, is a dream in Tir-na Nog'th. Small comfort, but better than none. Quickly, now, away, going, again . . .

. . . Toward the palace, bright architecture of the mind or spirit, more clearly standing now than the real ever did . . . To judge perfection is to render a worthless verdict, but I must see what lies within. . . . This must be an end of sorts, for I am driven. I had not paused to recover my staff from where it had fallen this time, among the sparkling grasses. I know where I must go, what I must do. Obvious now, though the logic which has seized me is not that of the waking mind.

Hurrying, climbing, up to the rearward portal . . . The side-biting soreness comes home again . . . Across the threshold, in . . .

Into an absence of starshine and moonlight. The illumination is without direction, seeming almost to drift and to pool, aimlessly. Wherever it misses, the shadows are absolute, occulting large sections of room, hallway, closet, and stair.

Among them, through them, almost running now . . . Monochrome of my home . . . Apprehension overtakes me . . . The black spots seem like holes in this piece of reality now. . . . I fear to pass too near. Fall in and be lost . . .

Turning . . . Crossing . . . Finally . . . Entering . . . The throne room . . .

Bushels of blackness stacked where my eyes would drive down lines of seeing to the throne itself . . .

There, though, is movement.

A drifting, to my right, as I advance.

A lifting, with the drifting.

The boots on feet on legs come into view as forward pressing I near the place's base.

Grayswandir comes into my hand, finding its way into a patch of light, renewing its eyetricking, shapeshifting stretch, acquiring a glow of its own . . .

I place my left foot on the step, rest my left hand on my knee. Distracting but bearable, the throb of my healing gut. I wait for the blackness, the emptiness, to be drawn, appropriate curtain for the theatrics with which I am burdened this night.

And it slides aside, revealing a hand, an arm, a shoulder, the arm a glinting, metallic thing, its planes like the facets of a gem, its wrist and elbow wondrous weaves of silver cable, pinned with flecks of fire, the hand, stylized, skeletal, a Swiss toy, a mechanical insect, functional, deadly, beautiful in its way . . .

And it slides aside, revealing the rest of the man. . . .

Benedict stands relaxed beside the throne, his left and human hand laid lightly upon it. He leans toward the throne. His lips are moving.

And it slides aside, revealing the throne's occupant. . . .

"Dara!"

Turned toward her right, she smiles, she nods to Benedict, her lips move. I advance and extend Grayswandir till its point rests lightly in the concavity beneath her sternum. . . .

Slowly, quite slowly, she turns her head and meets my eyes. She takes on color and life. Her lips move again, and this time her words reach me.

"What are you?"

"No. That is my question. You answer it. Now."

"I am Dara. Dara of Amber, Queen Dara. I hold this throne by right of blood and conquest. Who are you?"

"Corwin. Also of Amber. Don't move! I did not ask *who* you are—"

"Corwin is dead these many centuries. I have seen his tomb."

"Empty."

"Not so. His body lies within."

"Give me your lineage!"

Her eyes move to her right, where the shade of Benedict still stands. A blade has appeared in his new hand, seeming almost an extension of it, but he holds it loosely, casually. His left hand now rests on her arm. His eyes seek me in back of Grayswandir's hilt. Failing, they go again to that which is visible—Grayswandir—recognizing its design. . . .

"I am the great-granddaughter of Benedict and the hellmaid Lintra, whom he loved and later slew." Benedict winces at this, but she continues. "I never knew her. My mother and my mother's mother were born in a place where time does not run as in Amber. I am the first of my mother's line to bear all the marks of humanity. And you, Lord Corwin, are but a ghost from a long dead past, albeit a dangerous shade. How you came here, I do not know. But it was wrong of you. Return to your grave. Trouble not the living."

My hand wavers. Grayswandir strays no more than half an inch. Yet that is sufficient.

Benedict's thrust is below my threshold of perception. His new arm drives the new hand that holds the blade that strikes Grayswandir, as his old arm draws his old hand, which has seized upon Dara, back across the arm of the throne. . . . This subliminal impression reaches me moments later, as I fall back, cutting air, recover and strike an *en garde*, reflexively. . . . It is ridiculous for a pair of ghosts to fight. Here, it is uneven. He cannot even reach me, whereas Grayswandir—

But no! His blade changes hands as he releases Dara and pivots, bringing them together, old hand and new. His left wrist rotates as he slides it forward and down, moving into what would be *corps à corps*, were we two facing mortal bodies. For a moment our guards are locked. That moment is enough. . . .

That gleaming, mechanical hand comes forward, a thing of moonlight and fire, blackness and smoothness, all angles, no curves, fingers slightly flexed, palm silver-scribbled with a half-familiar design, comes forward, comes forward and catches at my throat. . . .

Missing, the fingers catch my shoulder and the thumb goes hooking— whether for clavicle or larynx, I do not know. I throw one punch with my left, toward his midsection, and there is nothing there. . . .

The voice of Random: "Corwin! The sun is about to rise! You've got to come down now!"

I cannot even answer. A second or two and that hand would tear away whatever it held. That hand . . . Grayswandir and that hand, which strangely resembles it, are the only two things which seem to coexist in my world and the city of ghosts. . . .

"I see it, Corwin! Pull away and reach for me! The Trump—"

I spin Grayswandir out of the bind and bring it around and down in a long, slashing arc. . . .

Only a ghost could have beaten Benedict or Benedict's ghost with that maneuver. We stand too close for him to block my blade, but his countercut, perfectly placed, would have removed my arm, had there been an arm there to meet it. . . .

As there is not, I complete the stroke, delivering the blow with the full force of my right arm, high upon that lethal device of moonlight and fire, blackness and smoothness, near to the point where it is joined with him.

With an evil tearing at my shoulder, the arm comes away from Benedict and grows still. . . . We both fall.

"Get up! By the unicorn, Corwin, get up! The sun is rising! The city will come apart about you!"

The floor beneath me wavers to and from a misty transparency. I glimpse a light-scaled expanse of water. I roll to my feet, barely avoiding the ghost's rush to clutch at the arm he has lost. It clings like a dead parasite and my side is hurting again. . . .

Suddenly I am heavy and the vision of ocean does not fade. I begin to sink through the floor. Color returns to the world, wavering stripes of pink. The Corwin-spurning floor parts and the Corwin-killing gulf is opened. . . .

I fall. . . .

"This way, Corwin! Now!"

Random stands on a mountaintop and reaches for me. I extend my hand. . . .

ELEVEN

. . . And frying pans without fires are often far between . . .

We untangled ourselves and rose. I sat down again immediately, on the bottommost stair. I worked the metal hand loose from my shoulder—no blood there, but a promise of bruises to come—then cast it and its arm to the ground. The light of early morning did not detract from its exquisite and menacing appearance.

Ganelon and Random stood beside me.

"You all right, Corwin?"

"Yes. Just let me catch my breath."

"I brought food," Random said. "We could have breakfast right here."

"Good idea."

As Random began unpacking provisions, Ganelon nudged the arm with the toe of his boot.

"What the hell," he asked, "is that?"

I shook my head.

"I lopped it off the ghost of Benedict," I told him. "For reasons I do not understand, it was able to reach me."

He stooped and picked it up, studied it.

"A lot lighter than I thought it would be," he observed. He raked the air with it. "You could do quite a job on someone, with a hand like that."

"I know."

He worked the fingers.

"Maybe the real Benedict could use it."

"Maybe," I said. "My feelings are quite mixed when it comes to offering it to him, but possibly you're right. . . ."

"How's the side?"

I prodded it gently.

"Not especially bad, everything considered. I'll be able to ride after breakfast, so long as we take it nice and easy."

"Good. Say, Corwin, while Random is getting things ready, I have a question that may be out of order, but it has been bothering me all along."

"Ask it."

"Well, let me put it this way: I am all for you, or I would not be here. I will fight for you to have your throne, no matter what. But every time talk of the succession occurs, someone gets angry and breaks it off or the subject gets changed. Like Random did, while you were up there. I suppose that it is not absolutely essential for me to know the basis of your claim to the throne, or that of any of the others, but I cannot help being curious as to the reasons for all the friction."

I sighed, then sat silent for a time.

"All right," I said after a while, and then I chuckled. "All right. If we cannot agree on these things ourselves, I would guess that they must seem pretty confused to an outsider. Benedict is the eldest. His mother was Cymnea. She bore Dad two other sons, also—Osric and Finndo. Then—how does one put these things?—Faiella bore Eric. After that, Dad found some defect in his marriage with Cymnea and had it dissolved—*ab initio*, as they would say in my old shadow—from the beginning. Neat trick, that. But he was the king."

"Didn't that make all of them illegitimate?"

"Well, it left their status less certain. Osric and Finndo were more than a little irritated, as I understand it, but they died shortly thereafter. Benedict was either less irritated or more politic about the entire affair. He never raised a fuss. Dad then married Faiella."

"And that made Eric legitimate?"

"It would have, if he had acknowledged Eric as his son. He treated him as if he were, but he never did anything formal in that regard. It involved the smoothing-over process with Cymnea's family, which had become a bit stronger around that time."

"Still, if he treated him as his own . . ."

"Ah! But he later *did* acknowledge Llewella formally. She was born out of wedlock, but he decided to recognize her, poor girl. All of Eric's supporters hated her for its effect on his status. Anyway, Faiella was later to become my mother. I was born safely in wedlock, making me the first with a clean claim on the throne. Talk to one of the others and you may get a different line of reasoning, but those are the facts it will have to be based on. Somehow it does not seem quite as important as it once did, though, with Eric dead and Benedict not really interested. . . . But that is where I stand."

"I see—sort of," he said. "Just one more thing, then . . ."

"What?"

"Who is next? That is to say, if anything were to happen to you . . . ?"

I shook my head.

"It gets even more complicated there, now. Caine would have been next. With him dead, I see it as swinging over to Clarissa's brood—the redheads. Bleys would have followed, then Brand."

"Clarissa? What became of your mother?"

"She died in childbirth. Deirdre was the child. Dad did not remarry for many years after mother's death. When he did, it was a redheaded wench from a far southern shadow. I never liked her. He began feeling the same way after a time and started fooling around again. They had one reconciliation after Llewella's birth in Rebma, and Brand was the result. When they were finally divorced, he recognized Llewella to spite Clarissa. At least, that is what I think happened."

"So you are not counting the ladies in the succession?"

"No. They are neither interested nor fit. If I were, though, Fiona would precede Bleys and Llewella would follow him. After Clarissa's crowd, it would swing over to Julian, Gérard, and Random, in that order. Excuse me—count Flora before Julian. The marriage data is even more involved, but no one will dispute the final order. Let it go at that."

"Gladly," he said. "So now Brand gets it if you die, right?"

"Well . . . He is a self-confessed traitor and he rubs everybody the wrong way. I do not believe the rest of them would have him, as he stands now. But I do not believe he has by any means given up."

"But the alternative is Julian."

I shrugged.

"The fact that I do not like Julian does not make him unfit. In fact, he might even be a very effective monarch."

"So he knifed you for the chance to prove it," Random called out. "Come on and eat."

"I still don't think so," I said, getting to my feet and heading for the food. "First, I don't see how he could have gotten to me. Second, it would have been too damned obvious. Third, if I die in the near future Benedict will have the real say as to the succession. Everyone knows that. He's got the seniority, he's got the wits, and he's got the power. He could simply say, for example, 'The hell with all this bickering, I am backing Gérard,' and that would be it."

"What if he decided to reinterpret his own status and take it himself?" Ganelon asked.

We seated ourselves on the ground and took the tin dishes Random had filled.

"He could have had it long before this, had he wanted it," I said. "There are several ways of regarding the offspring of a void marriage, and the most favorable one would be the most likely in his case. Osric and Finndo rushed to judgment, taking the worst view. Benedict knew better. He just waited. So . . . It is possible. Unlikely, though, I'd say."

"Then—in the normal course of affairs—if anything happened to you, it could still be very much in the air?"

"Very much."

"But why was Caine killed?" Random asked. Then, between mouthfuls, he answered his own question. "So that when they got you, it would swing over to Clarissa's kids immediately. It has occurred to me that Bleys is probably still living, and he is next in line. His body was never found. My guess is this: He trumped off to Fiona during your attack and returned to Shadow to rebuild his forces, leaving you to what he hoped would be your death at the hands of Eric. He is finally ready to move again. So they killed Caine and tried for you. If they are really allied with the black-road horde, they could have arranged for another assault from that quarter. Then he could have done the same thing you did—arrive at the last hour, turn back the invaders, and move on in. And there he would be, next in line and first in force. Simple. Except that you survived and Brand has been returned. If we are to believe Brand's accusation of Fiona—and I see no reason why we should not—then it follows from their original program."

I nodded.

"Possibly," I said. "I asked Brand just those things. He admitted their possibility, but he disavowed any knowledge as to whether Bleys was still living. Personally, I think he was lying."

"Why?"

"It is possible that he wishes to combine revenge for his imprisonment and the attempt on his life with the removal of the one impediment, save for myself, to his own succession. I think he feels that I will be expended in a scheme he is evolving to deal with the black road. The destruction of his own cabal and the removal of the road could make him look pretty decent, especially after all the penance he has had thrust upon him. Then, maybe then, he would have a chance—or thinks that he would."

"Then you think Bleys is still living, too?"

"Just a feeling," I said. "But yes, I do."

"What is their strength, anyway?"

"An endorsement of higher education," I said. "Fiona and Brand paid attention to Dworkin while the rest of us were off indulging our assorted passions in Shadow. Consequently, they seem to have obtained a better grasp of principles than we possess. They know more about Shadow and what lies beyond it, more about the Pattern, more about the Trumps than we do. That is why Brand was able to send you his message."

"An interesting thought . . ." Random mused. "Do you think they might have disposed of Dworkin after they felt they had learned enough from him? It would certainly help to keep things exclusive, if anything happened to Dad."

"That thought had not occurred to me," I said.

And I wondered, could they have done something that had affected his mind? Something that left him as he was when last I had seen him? If so, were they aware that he was possibly still living, somewhere? Or might they have assumed his total destruction?

"Yes, an interesting thought," I said. "I suppose that it is possible."

The sun inched its way upward, and the food restored me. No trace of Tir-na Nog'th remained in the morning's light. My memories of it had already taken on the quality of images in a dim mirror. Ganelon fetched its only other token, the arm, and Random packed it away along with the dishes. By daylight, the first three steps looked less like stairs and more like jumbled rock.

Random gestured with his head.

"Take the same way back?" he asked.

"Yes," I said, and we mounted.

We had come by way of a trail that wound about Kolvir to the south. It was longer but less rugged than the route across the crest. I'd a humor to pamper myself so long as my side protested.

So we bore to the right, moving single file, Random in the lead, Ganelon to the rear. The trail ran gently upward, then cut back down again. The air was cool, and it bore the aromas of verdure and moist earth, a thing quite unusual in that stark place, at that altitude. Straying air currents, I reasoned, from the forest far below.

We let the horses pick their own casual pace down through the dip and up the next rise. As we neared its crest, Random's horse whinnied and began to rear. He controlled it immediately, and I glanced about but saw nothing that might have startled it.

When he reached its summit, Random slowed and called back, "Take a look at that sunrise now, will you?"

It would have been rather difficult to avoid doing so, though I did not remark on the fact. Random was seldom given to sentimentality over vegetation, geology, or illumination.

I almost drew rein myself as I topped the rise, for the sun was a fantastic golden ball. It seemed half again its normal size, and its peculiar coloration was unlike anything I remembered having seen before. It did marvelous things to the band of ocean that had come into view above the next rise, and the tints of cloud and sky were indeed singular. I did not halt, though, for the sudden brightness was almost painful.

"You're right," I called out, following him down into the next declivity. Behind me, Ganelon snorted an appreciative oath.

When I had blinked away the aftereffects of that display I noticed that the vegetation was heavier than I had remembered in this little pocket in the sky. I had thought there were several scrubby trees and some patches of lichen, but there were actually several dozen trees, larger than I recalled, and greener, with a clutch of grasses here and there and a vine or two softening the outlines of the rocks. However, since my return I had only passed this way after dark. And now that I thought of it, it was probably the source of the aromas that had come to me earlier.

Passing through, it seemed that the little hollow was also wider than I recalled it. By the time we had crossed and were ascending once more, I was certain of it.

"Random," I called out, "has this place changed recently?"

"Hard to say," he answered. "Eric didn't let me out much. It seems to have grown up a bit."

"It seems bigger—wider."

"Yes, it does. I had thought that that was just my imagination."

When we reached the next crest I was not dazzled again because the sun was blocked by foliage. The area ahead of us contained many more trees than the one we had just departed—and they were larger and closer together. We drew rein.

"I don't remember this," he said. "Even passing through at night, it would have registered. We must have taken a wrong turn."

"I don't see how. Still, we know about where we are. I would rather go ahead than go back and start again. We should keep aware of conditions around Amber, anyway."

"True."

He headed down toward the wood. We followed.

"It's kind of unusual, at this altitude—a growth like this," he called back.

"There also seems to be a lot more soil than I recall."

"I believe you are right."

The trail curved to the left as we entered among the trees. I could see no reason for this deviation from the direct route. We stayed with it, however, and it added to the illusion of distance. After a few moments it swung suddenly to the right again. The prospect on cutting back was peculiar. The trees seemed even taller and were now so dense as to puzzle the eye that sought their penetration. When it turned once more it broadened, and the way was straight for a great distance ahead. Too great, in fact. Our little dell just wasn't that wide.

Random halted again.

"Damn it, Corwin! This is ridiculous!" he said. "You are not playing games, are you?"

"I couldn't if I would," I said. "I have never been able to manipulate Shadow anywhere on Kolvir. There isn't supposed to be any to work with here."

"That has always been my understanding, too. Amber casts Shadow but is not of it. I don't like this at all. What do you say we turn back?"

"I've a feeling we might not be able to retrace our way," I said. "There has to be a reason for this, and I want to know it."

"It occurs to me that it might be some sort of a trap."

"Even so," I said.

He nodded and we rode on, down that shaded way, under trees now grown more stately. The wood was silent about us. The ground remained level, the trail straight. Half consciously, we pushed the horses to a greater pace.

About five minutes passed before we spoke again. Then Random said, "Corwin, this can't be Shadow."

"Why not?"

"I have been trying to influence it and nothing happens. Have you tried?"

"No."

"Why don't you?"

"All right."

A rock could jut beyond the coming tree, a morning glory twine and bell within that shrubby stand. . . . There ought a patch of sky come clear, a wispy cloud upon it. . . . Then let there be a fallen limb, a stair of fungus up its side. . . . A scummed-over puddle . . . A frog . . . Falling feather, drifting seed . . . A limb that twists just so . . . Another trail upon our way, fresh-cut, deep-marked, past the place the feather should have fallen . . .

"No good," I said.

"If it is not Shadow, what is it?"

"Something else, of course."

He shook his head and checked again to see that his blade was loose in its scabbard. Automatically, I did the same. Moments later, I heard Ganelon's make a small clicking noise behind me.

Ahead, the trail began to narrow, and shortly thereafter it commenced to wander. We were forced to slow our pace once again, and the trees pressed nearer with branches sweeping lower than at any time before. The trail became a path. It jogged, it curved, it gave a final twist and then quit.

Random ducked a limb, then raised his hand and halted. We came up beside him. For as far as I could see ahead there was no indication of the trail's picking up again. Looking back, I failed to locate any sign of it either.

"Suggestions," he said, "are now in order. We do not know where we have been or where we are going, let alone where we are. My suggestion is the hell with curiosity. Let's get out of here the fastest way we know how."

"The Trumps?" Ganelon asked.

"Yes. What do you say, Corwin?"

"Okay. I don't like it either, and I can't think of anything better to try. Go ahead."

"Who should I try for?" he asked, producing his deck and uncasing it. "Gérard?"

"Yes."

He shuffled through his cards, located Gérard's, stared at it. We stared at him. Time went its way.

"I can't seem to reach him," he finally announced.

"Try Benedict."

"Okay."

Repeat performance. No contact.

"Try Deirdre," I said, drawing forth my own deck and searching out her Trump. "I'll join you. We will see whether it makes a difference with two of us trying."

And again. And again.

"Nothing," I said after a long effort.

Random shook his head.

"Did you notice anything unusual about your Trumps?" he asked.

"Yes, but I don't know what it is. They do seem different."

"Mine seem to have lost that quality of coldness they once possessed," he said.

I shuffled mine slowly. I ran my fingertips across them.

"Yes, you are right," I said. "That's it. But let us try again. Say, Flora."

"Okay."

The results were the same. And with Llewella. And Brand.

"Any idea what could be wrong?" Random asked.

"Not the slightest. They couldn't all be blocking us. They couldn't all be dead. . . . Oh, I suppose they could. But it is highly unlikely. Something seems to have affected the Trumps themselves, is what it is. And I never knew of anything that could do that."

"Well, they are not guaranteed one hundred percent," Random said, "according to the manufacturer."

"What do you know that I don't?"

He chuckled.

"You never forget the day you come of age and walk the Pattern," he said. "I remember it as though it were last year. When I had succeeded—all flushed with excitement, with glory—Dworkin presented me with my first set of Trumps and instructed me in their use. I distinctly recall asking him whether they worked everywhere. And I remember his answer: 'No,' he said. 'But they should serve in any place you will ever be.' He never much liked me, you know."

"But did you ask him what he meant by that?"

"Yes, and he said, 'I doubt that you will ever achieve a state where they will fail to serve you. Why don't you run along now?' And I did. I was anxious to go play with the Trumps all by myself."

" 'Achieve a state?' He didn't say 'reach a place'?"

"No. I have a very good memory for certain things."

"Peculiar—though not much help that I can see. Smacks of the metaphysical."

"I'd wager Brand would know."

"I've a feeling you're right, for all the good that does us."

"We ought to do something other than discuss metaphysics," Ganelon commented. "If you can't manipulate Shadow and you can't work the Trumps, it would seem that the next thing to do is determine where we are. And then go looking for help."

I nodded.

"Since we are not in Amber, I think it is safe to assume that we are in Shadow—a very special place, quite near to Amber, since the changeover was not abrupt. In that we were transported without active cooperation on our part, there had to be some agency and presumably some intent behind the maneuver. If it is going to attack us, now is as good a time as any. If there is something else it wants, then it is going to have to show us, because we aren't even in a position to make a good guess."

"So you propose we do nothing?"

"I propose we wait. I don't see any value in wandering about, losing ourselves further."

"I seem to remember your once telling me that adjacent shadows tend to be somewhat congruent," Ganelon said.

"Yes, I probably did. So what?"

"Then, if we are as near to Amber as you suppose, we need but ride toward the rising sun to come to a spot that parallels the city itself."

"It is not quite that simple. But supposing it were, what good would it do us?"

"Perhaps the Trumps would function again at the point of maximum congruity."

Random looked at Ganelon, looked at me.

"That may be worth trying," he said. "What have we got to lose?"

"Whatever small orientation we still possess," I said. "Look, it is not a bad idea. If nothing develops here, we will try it. However, looking back, it seems that the road behind us closes in direct proportion to the distance we advance. We are not simply moving in space. Under these circumstances, I am loath to wander until I am satisfied that we have no other option. If someone desires our presence at a particular location, it is up to him now to phrase the invitation a little more legibly. We wait."

They both nodded. Random began to dismount, then froze, one foot in the stirrup, one on the ground.

"After all these years," he said, and, "I never really believed it . . ."

"What is it?" I whispered.

"The option," he said, and he mounted again.

He persuaded his horse to move very slowly forward. I followed, and a moment later I glimpsed it, white as I had seen it in the grove, standing, half hidden, amid a clump of ferns: the unicorn.

It turned as we moved, and seconds later flashed ahead, to stand partly concealed once more by the trunks of several trees.

"I see it!" Ganelon whispered. "To think there really is such a beast . . . Your family's emblem, isn't it?"

"Yes."

"A good sign, I'd say."

I did not answer, but followed, keeping it in sight. That it was meant to be followed I did not doubt.

It had a way of remaining partly concealed the entire while—looking out from behind something, passing from cover to cover, moving with an incredible swiftness when it did move, avoiding open areas, favoring glade and shade. We followed, deeper and deeper into the wood which had given up all semblance of anything to be found on Kolvir's slopes. It resembled Arden now, more than anything else near Amber, as the ground was relatively level and the trees grew more and more stately.

An hour had passed, I guessed, and another had followed it, before we came to a small, clear stream and the unicorn turned and headed up it. As we rode along the bank, Random commented, "This is starting to look sort of familiar."

"Yes," I said, "but only sort of. I can't quite say why."

"Nor I."

We entered upon a slope shortly thereafter, and it grew steeper before very long. The going became more difficult for the horses, but the unicorn adjusted its pace to accommodate them. The ground became rockier, the trees smaller. The stream curved in its splashing course. I lost track of its twists and turns, but we were finally nearing the top of the small mount up which we had been traveling.

We achieved a level area and continued along it toward the wood from which the stream issued. At this point I caught an oblique view—ahead and to the right, through a place where the land fell away—of an icy blue sea, quite far below us.

"We're pretty high up," Ganelon said. "It seemed like lowland, but—"

"The Grove of the Unicorn!" Random interrupted. "That's what it looks like! See!"

Nor was he incorrect. Ahead lay an area strewn with boulders. Amid them a spring uttered the stream we followed. This place was larger and more lush, its situation incorrect in terms of my internal compass. Yet the similarity had to be more than coincidental. The unicorn mounted the rock nearest the spring, looked at us, then turned away. It might have been staring down at the ocean.

Then, as we continued, the grove, the unicorn, the trees about us, the stream beside us took on an unusual clarity, all, as though each were radiating some special illumination, causing it to quiver with the intensity of its color while at the same time wavering, slightly, just at the edges of perception. This produced in me an incipient feeling like the beginning of the emotional accompaniment to a hellride.

Then, then and then, with each stride of my mount, something went out of the world about us. An adjustment in the relationships of objects suddenly occurred, eroding my sense of depth, destroying perspective, rearranging the display of articles within my field of vision, so that everything presented its entire outer surface without simultaneously appearing to occupy an increased area: angles predominated, and relative sizes seemed suddenly ridiculous. Random's horse reared and neighed, massive, apocalyptic, instantly recalling *Guernica* to my mind. And to my distress I saw that we ourselves had not been untouched by the phenomenon—but that Random, struggling with his mount, and Ganelon, still managing to control Firedrake, had, like everything else, been transfigured by this cubist dream of space.

But Star was a veteran of many a hellride; Firedrake, also, had been through a lot. We clung to them and felt the movements that we could not accurately gauge. And Random succeeded, at last, in imposing his will upon his mount, though the prospect continued to alter as we advanced.

Light values shifted next. The sky grew black, not as night, but like a flat, nonreflecting surface. So did certain vacant areas between objects. The only light left in the world seemed to originate from things themselves, and all of it was gradually bleached. Various intensities of white emerged from the planes of existence, and brightest of all, immense, awful, the unicorn suddenly reared, pawing at the air, filling perhaps ninety percent of creation with what became a slow-motion gesture I feared would annihilate us if we advanced another pace.

Then there was only the light.

Then absolute stillness.

Then the light was gone and there was nothing. Not even blackness. A gap in existence, which might have lasted an instant or an eternity . . .

Then the blackness returned, and the light. Only they were reversed. Light filled the interstices, outlining voids that must be objects. The first sound that I heard was the rushing of water, and I knew somehow that we were halted beside the spring. The first thing that I felt was Star's quivering. Then I smelled the sea.

Then the Pattern came into view, or a distorted negative of it. . . .

I leaned forward and more light leaked around the edges of things. I leaned back; it went away. Forward again, this time farther than before . . .

The light spread, introduced various shades of gray into the scheme of things. With my knees then, gently, I suggested that Star advance.

With each pace, something returned to the world. Surfaces, textures, colors . . .

Behind me, I heard the others begin to follow. Below me, the Pattern surrendered nothing of its mystery, but it acquired a context which, by degrees, found its place within the larger reshaping of the world about us.

Continuing downhill, a sense of depth reemerged. The sea, now plainly visible off to the right, underwent a possibly purely optical separation from the sky, with which it seemed momentarily to have been joined in some sort of *Urmeer* of the waters above and the waters below. Unsettling upon reflection, but unnoted while in effect. We were heading down a steep, rocky incline which seemed to have taken its beginning at the rear of the grove to which the unicorn had led us. Perhaps a hundred meters below us was a perfectly level area which appeared to be solid, unfractured rock—roughly oval in shape, a couple of hundred meters along its major axis. The slope down which we rode swung off to the left and returned, describing a vast arc, a parenthesis, half cupping the smooth shelf. Beyond its rightward jutting there was nothing—that is to say the land fell away in steep descent toward that peculiar sea.

And, continuing, all three dimensions seemed to reassert themselves once more. The sun was that great orb of molten gold we had seen earlier. The sky was a deeper blue than that of Amber, and there were no clouds in it. That sea was a matching blue, unspecked by sail or island. I saw no birds, and I heard no sounds other than our own. An enormous silence lay upon this place, this day. In the bowl of my suddenly clear vision, the Pattern at last achieved its disposition upon the surface below. I thought at first that it was inscribed in the rock, but as we drew nearer I saw that it was contained within it—gold-pink swirls, like veining in an exotic marble, natural-seeming despite the obvious purpose to the design.

I drew rein and the others came up beside me, Random to my right, Ganelon to my left.

We regarded it in silence for a long while. A dark, rough-edged smudge had obliterated an area of the section immediately beneath us, running from its outer rim to the center.

"You know," Random finally said, "it is as if someone had shaved the top off Kolvir, cutting at about the level of the dungeons."

"Yes," I said.

"Then—looking for congruence—that would be about where our own Pattern lies."

"Yes," I said again.

"And that blotted area is to the south, from whence comes the black road."

I nodded slowly as the understanding arrived and forged itself into a certainty.

"What does it mean?" he asked. "It seems to correspond to the true state of affairs, but beyond that I do not understand its significance. Why have we been brought here and shown this thing?"

"It does not correspond to the true state of affairs," I said. "It *is* the true state of affairs."

Ganelon turned toward us.

"On that shadow Earth we visited—where you had spent so many years— I heard a poem about two roads that diverged in a wood," he said. "It ends, 'I took the one less traveled by, and that has made all the difference.' When I heard it, I thought of something you had once said—'All roads lead to Amber'—and I wondered then, as I do now, at the difference the choice may make, despite the end's apparent inevitability to those of your blood."

"You know?" I said. "You understand?"

"I think so."

He nodded, then pointed.

"That is the real Amber down there, isn't it?"

"Yes," I said. "Yes, it is."

BOOK FOUR
THE HAND OF OBERON

*To Jay Haldeman,
of fellowship and artichokes.*

ONE

A bright flash of insight, to match that peculiar sun . . .

There it was. . . . Displayed within that light, a thing I had only seen self-illuminated in darkness up until then: the Pattern, the great Pattern of Amber cast upon an oval shelf beneath/above a strange sky-sea.

. . . And I knew, perhaps by that within me which bound us, that this had to be the real one. Which meant that the Pattern in Amber was but its first shadow. Which meant—

Which meant that Amber itself was not carried over into places beyond the realm of Amber, Rebma, and Tir-na Nog'th. Meaning, then, that this place to which we had come was, by the law of precedence and configuration, the real Amber.

I turned to a smiling Ganelon, his beard and wild hair molten in the merciless light.

"How did you know?" I asked him.

"You know I am a very good guesser, Corwin," he replied, "and I recall everything you ever told me about how things work in Amber: how its shadow and those of your struggles are cast across the worlds. I often wondered, in thinking of the black road, whether anything could have cast such a shadow into Amber itself. And I imagined that such a something would have to be extremely basic, powerful, and secret." He gestured at the scene before us. "Like that."

"Continue," I said.

His expression changed and he shrugged.

"So there had to be a layer of reality deeper than your Amber," he explained, "where the dirty work was done. Your patron beast led us to what seems to be such a place, and that blot on the Pattern looks to be the dirty work. You agreed."

I nodded.

"It was your perceptiveness rather than the conclusion itself which stunned me so," I said.

"You beat me to it," admitted Random, off to my right, "but the feeling has found its way into my intestines—to put it delicately. I do believe that somehow that is the basis of our world down there."

"An outsider can sometimes see things better than one who is part of them," Ganelon offered.

Random glanced at me and returned his attention to the spectacle.

"Do you think things will change any more," he asked, "if we go down for a closer look?"

"Only one way to find out," I said.

"Single file, then," Random agreed. "I'll lead."

"All right."

Random guided his mount to the right, the left, the right, in a long series of switchbacks which zigged us and zagged us across most of the face of the wall. Continuing in the order we had maintained all day, I followed him and Ganelon came last.

"Seems stable enough now," Random called back.

"So far," I said.

"Some sort of opening in the rocks below."

I leaned forward. There was a cave mouth back to the right, on level with the oval plain. Its situation was such that it had been hidden from sight when we had occupied our higher position.

"We pass fairly near it," I said.

"—quickly, cautiously, and silently," Random added, drawing his blade.

I unsheathed Grayswandir, and one turn back above me Ganelon drew his own weapon.

We did not pass the opening, but turned leftward once more before we came to it. We moved within ten or fifteen feet of it, however, and I detected an unpleasant odor which I could not identify. The horses must have done a better job of it, though, or been pessimists by nature, because they flattened their ears, widened their nostrils, and made alarmed noises while turning against the reins. They calmed, however, as soon as we had made the turn and begun moving away once again. They did not suffer a relapse until we reached the end of our descent and moved to approach the damaged Pattern. They refused to go near it.

Random dismounted. He advanced to the edge of the design, paused and stared. After a time, he spoke without looking back.

"It follows that the damage was deliberate," he said, "from everything else that we know."

"It seems to follow," I said.

"It is also obvious that we were brought here for a reason."

"I'd say so."

"Then it does not take too much imagination to conclude that our purpose for being here is to determine how the Pattern was damaged and what might be done to repair it."

"Possibly. What is your diagnosis?"

"Nothing yet."

He moved along the perimeter of the figure, off to the right where the smear-effect began. I resheathed my blade and prepared to dismount. Ganelon reached over and took hold of my shoulder.

"I can make it myself—" I began.

But, "Corwin," he said, ignoring my words, "there does appear to be a small irregularity out toward the middle of the Pattern. It does not look like something that belongs . . ."

"Where?"

He pointed and I followed the gesture.

There was some foreign object near the center. A stick? A stone? A stray bit of paper . . . ? It was impossible to tell from this distance.

"I see it," I said.

We dismounted and headed toward Random, who by then was crouched at the extreme right of the figure, examining the discoloration.

"Ganelon's spotted something out toward the center," I said.

Random nodded.

"I've noticed it," he replied. "I was just trying to decide on the best way to head out for a better look. I do not relish the notion of walking a broken Pattern. On the other hand, I was wondering what I would be laying myself open to if I tried heading in across the blackened area. What do you think?"

"Walking what there is of the Pattern would take some time," I said, "if the resistance is on par with what it is at home. Also, we have been taught that it is death to stray from it—and this setup would force me to leave it when I reach the blot. On the other hand, as you say, I might be alerting our enemies by treading on the black. So—"

"So neither of you is going to do it," Ganelon interrupted. "I am."

Then, without waiting for a reply, he took a running leap into the black sector, raced along it toward the center, paused long enough to pick up some small object, turned and headed back.

Moments later, he stood before us.

"That was a risky thing to do," Random said.

He nodded.

"But you two would still be debating it if I hadn't." He raised his hand and extended it. "Now, what do you make of this?"

He was holding a dagger. Impaled on it was a rectangle of stained pasteboard. I took them from him.

"Looks like a Trump," Random said.

"Yes."

I worked the card loose, smoothed down the torn sections. The man I regarded upon it was half familiar—meaning of course that he was also half strange. Light, straight hair, a trifle sharp-featured, a small smile, somewhat slight of build.

I shook my head.

"I do not know him," I said.

"Let me see."

Random took the card from me, frowned at it.

"No," he said after a time. "I don't either. It almost seems as though I should, but . . . No."

At that moment, the horses renewed their complaints much more forcefully. And we needed but turn part way to learn the cause of their discomfort, in that it had chosen that moment to emerge from the cave.

"Damn," said Random.

I agreed with him.

Ganelon cleared his throat, took forth his blade.

"Anyone know what it is?" he asked quietly.

My first impression of the beast was that it was snake-like, both from its movements and because of the fact that its long thick tail seemed more a continuation of its long thin body than a mere appendage. It moved on four double-jointed legs, however, large-footed and wickedly clawed. Its narrow head was beaked, and it swung from side to side as it advanced, showing us one pale blue eye and then the other. Large wings were folded against its sides, purple and leathery. It possessed neither hair nor feathers, though there were scaled areas across its breast, shoulders, back, and along the length of its tail. From beak-bayonet to twisting tail-tip it seemed a little over three meters. There was a small tinkling sound as it moved, and I caught a flash of something bright at its throat.

"Closest thing I know," said Random, "is a heraldic beast—the griffin. Only this one is bald and purple."

"Definitely not our national bird," I added, drawing Grayswandir and swinging its point into line with the creature's head.

The beast darted a red, forked tongue. It raised its wings a few inches, then let them fall. When its head swung to the right its tail moved to the left, then left and right, right and left—producing a near-hypnotic, flowing effect as it advanced.

It seemed more concerned with the horses than with us, however, for its course was directed well past us toward the spot where our mounts stood quivering and stamping. I moved to interpose myself.

At that point, it reared.

Its wings went up and out, spreading like a pair of slack sails suddenly caught by a gust of wind. It was back on its hind legs and towering above us, seeming to occupy at least four times the space it had previously. And then it shrieked, a god-awful, hunting scream or challenge that left my ears ringing. With that, it snapped those wings downward and sprang, becoming temporarily airborne.

The horses bolted and ran. The beast was beyond our reach. It was only then that I realized what the bright flash and the tinkling had represented. The thing was tethered, by means of a long chain running back into the cave. The exact length of its leash was immediately a question of more than academic interest.

I turned as it passed, hissing, flapping, and falling, beyond us. It had not possessed sufficient momentum to obtain true flight in that brief rush upward. I saw that Star and Firedrake were retreating toward the far end of the oval. Random's mount Iago, on the other hand, had bolted in the direction of the Pattern.

The beast touched ground again, turned as if to pursue Iago, appeared to study us once more, and froze. It was much nearer this time—under four meters—and it cocked its head, showing us its right eye, then opened its beak and made a soft cawing noise.

"What say we rush it now?" said Random.

"No. Wait. There is something peculiar about its behavior."

It had dropped its head while I was speaking, spreading its wings downward. It struck the ground three times with its beak and looked up again. Then it drew its wings part way back toward its body. Its tail twitched once, then swung more vigorously from side to side. It opened its beak and repeated the cawing sound.

At that moment we were distracted.

Iago had entered the Pattern, well to the side of the darkened area. Five or six meters into it, standing obliquely across the lines of power, he was caught near one of the Veil points like an insect on a piece of flypaper. He cried loudly as the sparks came up about him and his mane rose and stood erect.

Immediately, the sky began to darken directly overhead. But it was no cloud of water vapor which had begun to coalesce. Rather, it was a perfectly circular formation which had appeared, red at the center, yellow nearer the edges, turning in a clockwise direction. A sound like a single bell chime followed by the growl of a bull-roarer suddenly came to our ears.

Iago continued his struggles, first freeing his right front foot, then entangling it again as he freed the left, neighing wildly the while. The sparks were up to his shoulders by then, and he shook them like raindrops from his body and neck, his entire form taking on a soft, buttery glow.

The roaring increased in volume and small lightnings began to play at the heart of the red thing above us. A rattling noise caught my attention at that moment, and I glanced downward to discover that the purple griffin had slithered past and moved to interpose itself between us and the loud red phenomenon. It crouched like a gargoyle, facing away from us, watching the spectacle.

Just then, Iago freed both front feet and reared. There was something insubstantial about him by then, what with his brightness and the spark-shot indistinctness of his outline. He might have neighed at that moment, but all other sounds were submerged by the incessant roar from above.

A funnel descended from the noisy formation—bright, flashing, wailing now, and tremendously fast. It touched the rearing horse, and for a moment his outline expanded enormously, becoming increasingly tenuous in direct proportion to this effect. And then he was gone. For a brief interval, the funnel remained stationary, like a perfectly balanced top. Then the sound began to diminish.

The trunk raised itself, slowly, to a point but a small distance—perhaps the height of a man—above the Pattern. Then it snapped upward as quickly as it had descended.

The wailing ceased. The roaring began to subside. The miniature lightnings faded within the circle. The entire formation began to pale and slow. A moment later, it was but a bit of darkness; another moment and it was gone.

No trace of Iago remained anywhere that I could see.

"Don't ask me," I said when Random turned toward me. "I don't know either."

He nodded, then directed his attention toward our purple companion, who was just then rattling his chain.

"What about Charlie here?" he asked, fingering his blade.

"I had the distinct impression he was trying to protect us," I said, taking a step forward. "Cover me. I want to try something."

"You sure you can move fast enough?" he asked. "With that side . . ."

"Don't worry," I said, a trifle more heartily than necessary, and I kept moving.

He was correct about my left side, where the healing knife wound still ached dully and seemed to exercise a drag on my movements. But Grayswandir was still in my right hand and this was one of those occasions when my trust in my instincts was running high. I had relied on this feeling in the past with good results. There are times when such gambles just seem to be in order.

Random moved ahead and to the right. I turned sidewise and extended my left hand as you would in introducing yourself to a strange dog, slowly. Our heraldic companion had risen from its crouch and was turning.

It faced us again and studied Ganelon, off to my left. Then it regarded my hand. It lowered its head and repeated the ground-striking movement, cawed very softly—a small, bubbling sound—raised its head and slowly extended it. It wagged its great tail, touched my fingers with its beak, then repeated the performance. Carefully, I placed my hand on its head. The wagging increased; its head remained motionless. I scratched it gently about the neck and it turned its head slowly then, as if enjoying it. I withdrew my hand and dropped back a pace.

"I think we're friends," I said softly. "Now you try it, Random."

"Are you kidding?"

"No, I'm sure you're safe. Try it."

"What will you do if you are wrong?"

"Apologize."

"Great."

He advanced and offered his hand. The beast remained friendly.

"All right," he said half a minute or so later, still stroking its neck, "what have we proved?"

"That he is a watchdog."

"What is he watching?"

"The Pattern, apparently."

"Offhand then," said Random, moving back, "I would say that his work leaves something to be desired." He gestured at the dark area. "Which is understandable, if he is this friendly to anyone who doesn't eat oats and whinny."

"My guess is that he is quite selective. It is also possible that he was set here after the damage was done, to defend against further unappreciated activity."

"Who set him?"

"I'd like to know myself. Someone on our side, apparently."

"You can now test your theory further by letting Ganelon approach him." Ganelon did not move.

"It may be you have a family smell about you," he finally said, "and he only favors Amberites. So I will pass, thank you."

"All right. It is not that important. Your guesses have been good so far. How do you interpret events?"

"Of the two factions out for the throne," he said, "that composed of Brand, Fiona, and Bleys was, as you said, more aware of the nature of the forces that play about Amber. Brand did not supply you with particulars — unless you omitted some incidents he might have related—but my guess is that this damage to the Pattern represents the means by which their allies gained access to your realm. One or more of them did that damage, which provided the dark route. If the watchdog here responds to a family smell or some other identifying information you all possess, then he could actually have been here all along and not seen fit to move against the despoilers."

"Possibly," Random observed. "Any idea how it was accomplished?"

"Perhaps," he replied. "I will let you demonstrate it for me, if you are willing."

"What does it involve?"

"Come this way," he said, turning and heading over to the edge of the Pattern.

I followed him. Random did the same. The watchgriffin slunk at my side. Ganelon turned and extended his hand.

"Corwin, may I trouble you for that dagger I fetched us?"

"Here," I said, drawing it from my belt and passing it over.

"I repeat, what does it involve?" Random inquired.

"The blood of Amber," Ganelon replied.

"I am not so sure I like this idea," Random said.

"All you have to do is prick your finger with it," he said, extending the blade, "and let a drop fall upon the Pattern."

"What will happen?"

"Let's try it and see."

Random looked at me.

"What do you say?" he asked.

"Go ahead. Let's find out. I'm intrigued."

He nodded.

"Okay."

He received the blade from Ganelon and nicked the tip of his left little finger. He squeezed the finger then, holding it above the Pattern. A tiny red bead appeared, grew larger, quivered, fell.

Immediately, a wisp of smoke rose from the spot where it struck, accompanied by a tiny crackling noise.

"I'll be damned!" said Random, apparently fascinated.

A tiny stain had come into being, gradually spreading to about the size of a half dollar.

"There you are," said Ganelon. "That is how it was done."

The stain was indeed a miniature counterpart of the massive blot further to our right. The watchgriffin gave forth a small shriek and drew back, rapidly turning his head from one of us to the other.

"Easy, fellow. Easy," I said, reaching out and calming him once more.

"But what could have caused such a large—" Random began, and then he nodded slowly.

"What indeed?" said Ganelon. "I see no mark to show where your horse was destroyed."

"The blood of Amber," Random said. "You are just full of insights today, aren't you?"

"Ask Corwin to tell you of Lorraine, the place where I dwelled for so long," he said, "the place where the dark circle grew. I am alert to the effects of those powers, though I knew them then only at a distance. These matters have become clearer to me with each new thing I have learned from you. Yes, I have insights now that I know more of these workings. Ask Corwin of the mind of his general."

"Corwin," Random said, "give me the pierced Trump."

I withdrew it from my pocket and smoothed it. The stains seemed more ominous now. Another thing also struck me. I did not believe that it had been executed by Dworkin, sage, mage, artist, and one-time mentor to the children of Oberon. It had not occurred to me until that moment that anyone else might be capable of producing one. While the style of this one did seem somehow familiar, it was not his work. Where had I seen that deliberate line before, less spontaneous than the master's, as though every movement had been totally intellectualized before the pen touched the paper? And there was something else wrong with it—a quality of idealization of a different order from that of our own Trumps, almost as if the artist had been working with old memories, glimpses, or descriptions rather than a living subject.

"The Trump, Corwin. If you please," Random said.

There was that about the way in which he said it to make me hesitate. It gave rise to the feeling that he was somehow a jump ahead of me on something important, a feeling which I did not like at all.

"I've petted old ugly here for you, and I've just bled for the cause, Corwin. Now let's have it."

I handed it over, my uneasiness increasing as he held it in his hand and furrowed his brow. Why was I suddenly the stupid one? Does a night in Tir-na Nog'th slow cerebration? Why—

Random began to curse, a string of profanities unsurpassed by anything encountered in my long military career.

Then, "What is it?" I said. "I don't understand."

"The blood of Amber," he finally said. "Whoever did it walked the Pattern first, you see. Then they stood there at the center and contacted him via this Trump. When he responded and a firm contact was achieved, they stabbed him. His blood flowed upon the Pattern, obliterating that part of it, as mine did here."

He was silent for the space of several deep breaths.

"It smacks of a ritual," I said.

"Damn rituals!" he said. "Damn all of them! One of them is going to die, Corwin. I am going to kill him—or her."

"I still do not—"

"I am a fool," he said, "for not seeing it right away. Look! Look closely!"

He thrust the pierced Trump at me. I stared. I still did not see.

"Now look at me!" he said. "See me!"

I did. Then I looked back at the card.

I realized what he meant.

"I was never anything to him but a whisper of life in the darkness. But they used my son for this," he said. "That has to be a picture of Martin."

TWO

Standing there beside the broken Pattern, regarding a picture of the man who may or may not have been Random's son, who may or may not have died of a knife wound received from a point within the Pattern, I turned and took a giant step back within my mind for an instant replay of the events which had brought me to this point of peculiar revelation. I had learned so many new things recently that the occurrences of the past few years seemed almost to constitute a different story than they had while I was living them. Now this new possibility and a number of things it implied had just shifted the perspective again.

I had not even been aware of my name when I had awakened in Greenwood, that private hospital in upstate New York where I had spent two totally blank weeks subsequent to my accident. It was only recently that I had been told that the accident itself had been engineered by my brother Bleys, immediately following my escape from the Porter Sanitarium in Albany. I got this story from my brother Brand, who had railroaded me into Porter in the first place, by means of fake psychiatric evidence. At Porter, I had been subjected to electroshock therapy over the span of several days, results ambiguous but presumably involving the return of a few memories. Apparently, this was what had scared Bleys into making the attempt on my life at the time of my escape, shooting out a couple of my tires on a curve above a lake. This doubtless would have resulted in my death, had Brand not been a step behind Bleys and out to protect his insurance investment, me. He said he had gotten word to the cops, dragged me out of the lake, and administered first aid until help arrived. Shortly after that, he was captured by his former partners—Bleys and our sister Fiona—who confined him in a guarded tower in a distant place in Shadow.

There had been two cabals, plotting and counter-plotting after the throne, treading on one another's heels, breathing down one another's necks, and doing anything else to one another that might suggest itself at that range. Our brother Eric, backed by brothers Julian and Caine, had been preparing to take the throne, long left vacant by the unexplained absence of our father, Oberon. Unexplained to Eric, Julian, and Caine, that is. To the other group, consisting of Bleys, Fiona, and—formerly—Brand, it was not unexplained because they were responsible for it. They had arranged for this state of affairs to come into being in order to open the way for Bleys's accession to the throne. But Brand had committed a tactical error in attempting to obtain Caine's assistance in their play for the throne, in that Caine decided a better deal obtained in upholding Eric's part. This left Brand under close scrutiny, but did not immediately result in the betrayal of his partners' identities. At about that time, Bleys and Fiona decided to employ their secret allies against Eric. Brand had demurred in this, fearing the strength of those forces, and as a result had been rejected by Bleys and Fiona. With everyone on his back then, he had sought to upset the balance of powers completely by journeying to the shadow Earth where Eric had left me to die centuries before. It was only later that Eric had learned that I had not died but was possessed of total amnesia, which was almost as good, had set sister Flora to watch over my exile, and hoped that that was the last of it. Brand later told me he had gotten me committed to Porter in a desperate move to restore my memory as a preliminary to my return to Amber.

While Fiona and Bleys had been dealing with Brand, Eric had been in touch with Flora. She had arranged for my transfer to Greenwood from the clinic to which the police had taken me, with instructions to keep me narcotized, while Eric began arrangements for his coronation in Amber. Shortly thereafter, our brother Random's idyllic existence in Texorami was broken when Brand managed to send him a message outside the normal family channels—i.e., the Trumps—requesting deliverance. While Random, who was blissfully nonpartisan in the power struggle, was about this business, I managed to deliver myself from Greenwood, still relatively unmemoried. Having obtained Flora's address from Greenwood's frightened director, I betook myself to her place in Westchester, engaged in some elaborate bluffing, and moved in as a house guest. Random, in the meantime, had been less than successful in his attempt to rescue Brand. Slaying the snaky warden of the tower, he had had to flee its inner guards, utilizing one of the region's strangely mobile rocks. The guards, a hardy band of not quite human guys, had succeeded in pursuing him through Shadow, however, a feat normally impossible for most non-Amberites. Random had fled then to the shadow Earth where I was guiding Flora along the paths of misunderstanding while attempting to locate the proper route to enlightenment as to my own circumstances. Crossing the continent in response to my assurance that he would be under my protection, Random had come believing that his pursuers were my own creatures. When I helped him destroy them he was puzzled but unwilling to raise the issue while I seemed engaged in some private maneuver throneward. In fact, he had easily been tricked into conveying me back to Amber through Shadow.

This venture had proved beneficial in some respects while much less satisfactory in others. When I had finally revealed the true state of my personal situation, Random and our sister Deirdre, whom we had encountered along the way, conducted me to Amber's mirror-city within the sea, Rebma. There I had walked the image of the Pattern and recovered the bulk of my memories as a result—thereby also settling the issue as to whether I was the real Corwin or merely one of his shadows. From Rebma I had traveled into Amber, utilizing the power of the Pattern to effect an instantaneous journey home. After fighting an inconclusive duel with Eric, I had fled via the Trumps into the keeping of my beloved brother and would-be assassin, Bleys.

I joined with Bleys in an attack on Amber, a mismanaged affair which we had lost. Bleys vanished during the final engagement, under circumstances which looked likely to prove fatal but, the more that I learned and thought about it, probably had not. This left me to become Eric's prisoner and an unwilling party to his coronation, after which he had had me blinded and locked away. A few years in the dungeons of Amber had seen a regeneration of my eyes, in direct proportion to the deterioration of my state of mind. It was only the accidental appearance of Dad's old adviser Dworkin, worse off mentally than myself, which had led to a way of escape.

After that, I set about recovering and I resolved to be more prudent the next time I went after Eric. I journeyed through Shadow toward an old land where I had once reigned—Avalon—with plans to obtain there a substance of which I alone among Amberites was aware, a chemical unique in its ability to undergo detonation in Amber. En route, I had passed through the land of Lorraine, there encountering my old exiled Avalonian general Ganelon, or someone very much like him. I remained because of a wounded knight, a girl, and a local menace peculiarly similar to a thing occurring in the vicinity of Amber herself—a growing black circle somehow related to the black road our enemies traveled, a thing for which I held myself partly responsible because of a curse I had pronounced at the time of my blinding. I won the battle, lost the girl, and traveled on to Avalon with Ganelon.

The Avalon we reached, we quickly learned, was under the protection of my brother Benedict, who had been having troubles of his own with a situation possibly akin to the black circle/black road menaces. Benedict had lost his right arm in the final engagement, but had been victorious in his battle with the hell-maids. He had warned me to keep my intentions toward Amber and Eric pure, and had then allowed us the hospitality of his manor while he remained for a few days more in the field. It was at his place that I met Dara.

Dara told me she was Benedict's great-granddaughter, whose existence had been kept secret from Amber. She drew me out as far as she could on Amber, the Pattern, the Trumps, and our ability to walk in Shadow. She was also an extremely skilled fencer. We indulged in a bit of casual lovemaking on my return from a hellride to a place where I obtained a sufficient quantity of rough diamonds to pay for the things I was going to need for my assault on Amber. The following day, Ganelon and I picked up our supply of the necessary chemicals and departed for the shadow Earth where I had spent my exile, there to obtain automatic weapons and ammunition manufactured to my specifications.

En route, we had some difficulties along the black road, which seemed to have extended its scope of influence among the worlds of Shadow. We were equal to the troubles it presented, but I almost perished in a duel with Benedict, who had pursued us through a wild hellride. Too angry for argument, he had fought me through a small wood—still a better man than I, even wielding his blade left-handed. I had only managed to best him by means of a trick involving a property of the black road of which he was unaware. I had been convinced that he wanted my blood because of the affair with Dara. But no. In the few words that passed between us he denied any knowledge of the existence of such a person. Instead, he had come after us convinced that I had murdered his servants. Now, Ganelon had indeed located some fresh corpses in the wood at Benedict's place, but we had agreed to forget about them, having no idea as to their identities and no desire to complicate our existence any further.

Leaving Benedict in the care of brother Gérard, whom I had summoned via his Trump from Amber, Ganelon and I proceeded to the shadow Earth, armed ourselves, recruited a strike force in Shadow, and headed off to attack Amber. But upon our arrival we discovered that Amber was already under attack by creatures which had come in along the black road. My new weapons quickly turned the tide in Amber's favor, and my brother Eric died in that battle, leaving me his problems, his ill will, and the Jewel of Judgment—a weather-controlling weapon he had used against me when Bleys and I had attacked Amber.

At that point, Dara showed up, swept on by us, rode into Amber, found her way to the Pattern, and proceeded to walk it—prima-facie evidence that we were indeed somehow related. During the course of this ordeal, however, she had exhibited what appeared to be peculiar physical transformations. Upon completion of the Pattern, she announced that Amber would be destroyed. Then she had vanished.

About a week later, brother Caine was murdered, under conditions arranged to show me as the culprit. The fact that I had slain his slayer was hardly satisfactory evidence of my innocence, in that the guy was necessarily in no condition to talk about it. Realizing, however, that I had seen his like before, in the persons of those creatures who had pursued Random into Flora's home, I finally found time to sit down with Random and hear the story of his unsuccessful attempt to rescue Brand from his tower.

Random, subsequent to my leaving him in Rebma years before, when I had journeyed to Amber to fight my duel with Eric, had been forced by Rebma's queen, Moire, to marry a woman of her court: Vialle, a lovely blind girl. This was partly intended as a punishment for Random, who years before had left Moire's late daughter Morganthe pregnant with Martin, the apparent subject of the damaged Trump Random now held in his hands. Strangely, for Random, he appeared to have fallen in love with Vialle, and he now resided legendary unicorn of Amber.

After I left Random, I fetched the Jewel of Judgment and took it down to the chamber of the Pattern. There, I followed the partial instructions I had received for purposes of attuning it to my use. I underwent some unusual sensations during the process and was successful in obtaining control of its most obvious function: the ability to direct meteorological phenomena. After that, I questioned Flora concerning my exile. Her story seemed reasonable and jibed with those facts I did possess, although I had the feeling she was holding back somewhat on events at the time of my accident. She did promise to identify Caine's slayer as one of the same sort as those individuals Random and I had fought at her home in Westchester, however, and she assured me of her support in anything I might currently be about.

At the time I had heard Random's story, I was still unaware of the two factions and their machinations. I decided then that if Brand were still living, his rescue was of first importance, if for no other reason than the fact that he obviously possessed information that someone did not want circulated. I hit on a scheme for achieving this, the trial of which was only postponed for the time required by Gérard and myself for returning Caine's body to Amber. Part of this time, however, was appropriated by Gérard for purposes of beating me unconscious, just in case I had forgotten he was capable of the feat, to add weight to his words when he informed me that he would personally kill me should it turn out that I was the author of Amber's present woes. It was the most exclusive closed circuit fight I knew of, viewed by the family via Gérard's Trump—an act of insurance should I actually be the culprit and have a mind to erase his name from the list of the living because of his threat. We journeyed on to the Grove of the Unicorn then and exhumed Caine. At that time, we actually caught a brief glimpse of the legendary unicorn of Amber.

That evening we met in the library of the palace in Amber—we being Random, Gérard, Benedict, Julian, Deirdre, Fiona, Flora, Llewella, and myself. There, we tested my idea for finding Brand. It amounted to all nine of us simultaneously attempting to reach him via his Trump. And we succeeded.

We contacted him and were successful in transporting him back to Amber. In the midst of the excitement, however, with all of us crowded about as Gérard bore him through, someone planted a dagger in Brand's side. Gérard immediately elected himself attending physician and cleared the room.

The rest of us moved to a downstairs sitting room, there to backbite and discuss events. During this time, Fiona advised me that the Jewel of Judgment might represent a hazard in situations of prolonged exposure, suggesting the possibility that it, rather than his wounds, might have been the cause of Eric's death. One of the first signs, she believed, was a distortion of one's time-sense—an apparent slowdown of temporal sequence, actually representing a speed-up of physiological events. I resolved to be more cautious with it, in that she was more conversant with these matters than the rest of us, having once been an advanced pupil of Dworkin's.

And perhaps she was correct. Perhaps there was such an effect in operation later that evening when I returned to my own quarters. At least, it seemed as if the person who attempted to kill me was moving a trifle more slowly than I would have myself under similar circumstances. At that, the stroke was almost successful. The blade caught me in the side and the world went away.

Leaking life, I awoke in my old bed in my old home on the shadow Earth where I had dwelled for so long as Carl Corey. How I had been returned, I had no idea. I crawled outside and into a blizzard. Clinging precariously to consciousness, I cached the Jewel of Judgment in my old compost heap, for the world did indeed seem to be slowing down about me. Then I made it to the road, to try flagging down a passing motorist.

It was a friend and former neighbor, Bill Roth, who found me there and drove me to the nearest clinic. There, I was treated by the same doctor who had attended me years before, at the time of my accident. He suspected I might be a psychiatric case, as the old record did reflect that faked state of affairs.

Bill showed up later, however, and set a number of things right. An attorney, he had grown curious at the time of my disappearance and done some investigating. He had learned about my fake certification and my successive escapes. He even possessed details on these matters and on the accident itself. He still felt there was something strange about me, but it did not really bother him that much.

Later, Random contacted me via my Trump and advised me that Brand had come around and was asking for me. With Random's assistance, I returned to Amber. I went to see Brand. It was then that I learned of the nature of the power struggle which had been going on about me, and the identities of the participants. His story, together with what Bill had told me back on the shadow Earth, finally brought some sense and coherence to occurrences of the past several years. He also told me more concerning the nature of the danger we currently faced.

I did nothing the following day, ostensibly for purposes of preparing myself for a visit to Tir-na Nog'th, actually to buy additional time in which to recover from my injury. This commitment made, however, it had to be kept. I did journey to the city in the sky that night, encountering a confusing collection of signs and portents, signifying perhaps nothing, and collecting a peculiar mechanical arm from the ghost of my brother Benedict while I was about it.

Returned from this excursion on high, I breakfasted with Random and Ganelon before setting out across Kolvir to return home. Slowly, bewilderingly, the trail began to change about us. It was as though we were walking in Shadow, a well-nigh impossible feat this near to Amber. When we reached this conclusion, we tried to alter our course, but neither Random nor I was able to affect the changing scene. About that time, the unicorn put in an appearance. It seemed to want us to follow it. We did.

It had led us through a kaleidoscopic series of changes, until finally we arrived at this place, where it abandoned us to our present devices. Now, with this entire sequence of events tumbling through my head, my mind moved about the peripheries, pushed its way forward, returned to the words Random had just spoken. I felt that I was slightly ahead of him once more. For how long this state of affairs might last, I did not know, but I realized where I had seen work by the same hand which had executed the pierced Trump.

Brand had often painted when he was entering one of his melancholy periods, and his favorite techniques came to mind as I recalled canvas after canvas he had brightened or darkened. Add to this his campaign of years before to obtain recollections and descriptions from everyone who had known Martin. While Random had not recognized his style, I wondered how long it might be before he began thinking as I just had about the possible ends of Brand's information gathering. Even if his hand had not actually propelled the blade, Brand was party to the act by providing the means. I knew Random well enough to know that he meant what he had said. He would try to kill Brand as soon as he saw the connection. This was going to be more than awkward.

It had nothing to do with the fact that Brand had probably saved my life. I figured I had squared accounts with him by getting him out of that damned tower. No. It was neither indebtedness nor sentiment that caused me to cast about for ways to mislead Random or slow him down. It was the naked, frigid fact that I needed Brand. He had seen to that. My reason for saving him was no more altruistic than his had been in dragging me out of the lake. He possessed something I needed now: information. He had realized this immediately and he was rationing it—his life's union dues.

"I do see the resemblance," I said to Random, "and you may well be right about what happened."

"Of course I am right."

"It is the card that was pierced," I said.

"Obviously. I don't—"

"He was not brought through on the Trump, then. The person who did it therefore made contact, but was unable to persuade him to come across."

"So? The contact had progressed to a point of sufficient solidity and proximity that he was able to stab him anyway. He was probably even able to achieve a mental lock and hold him where he was while he bled. The kid probably hadn't had much experience with the Trumps."

"Maybe yes, maybe no," I said. "Llewella or Moire might be able to tell us how much he knew about the Trumps. But what I was getting at was the possibility that contact could have been broken before death. If he inherited your regenerative abilities he might have survived."

"Might have? I don't want guesses! I want answers!"

I commenced a balancing act within my mind. I believed I knew something that he did not, but then my source was not the best. Also, I wanted to keep quiet about the possibility because I had not had a chance to discuss it with Benedict. On the other hand, Martin was Random's son, and I did want to direct his attention away from Brand.

"Random, I may have something," I said.

"What?"

"Right after Brand was stabbed," I said, "when we were talking together in the sitting room, do you remember when the conversation turned to the subject of Martin?"

"Yes. Nothing new came up."

"I had something I might have added at that time, but I restrained myself because everyone was there. Also, because I wanted to pursue it in private with the party concerned."

"Who?"

"Benedict."

"Benedict? What has he to do with Martin?"

"I do not know. That is why I wanted to keep it quiet until I found out. And my source of information was a touchy one, at that."

"Go ahead."

"Dara. Benedict gets mad as hell whenever I mention her name, but so far a number of things she told me have proved correct—things like the journey of Julian and Gérard along the black road, their injury, their stay in Avalon. Benedict admitted these things had happened."

"What did she say about Martin?"

Indeed. How to phrase it without giving away the show on Brand . . . ? Dara had said that Brand had visited Benedict a number of times in Avalon, over a span of years. The time differential between Amber and Avalon is such that it seemed likely, now that I thought about it, that the visits fell into the period when Brand was so actively seeking information on Martin. I had wondered what kept drawing him back there, since he and Benedict had never been especially chummy.

"Only that Benedict had had a vistor named Martin, whom she thought was from Amber," I lied.

"When?"

"Some while back. I'm not sure."

"Why didn't you tell me this before?"

"It is not really very much—and besides, you had never seemed especially interested in Martin."

Random shifted his gaze to the griffin, crouched and gurgling on my right, then nodded.

"I am now," he said. "Things change. If he is still alive, I would like to get to know him. If he is not . . ."

"Okay," I said. "The best way to be about either one is to start figuring a way to get home. I believe we have seen what we were supposed to see and I would like to clear out."

"I was thinking about that," he said, "and it occurred to me that we could probably use this Pattern for that purpose. Just head out to the center and transfer back."

"Going in along the dark area?" I asked.

"Why not? Ganelon has already tried it and he's okay."

"A moment," said Ganelon. "I did not say that it was easy, and I am positive you could not get the horses to go that route."

"What do you mean?" I said.

"Do you remember that place where we crossed the black road—back when we were fleeing Avalon?"

"Of course."

"Well, the sensations I experienced in retrieving the card and the dagger were not unlike the upset that came over us at that time. It is one of the reasons I was running so fast. I would favor trying the Trumps again first, under the theory that this point is congruent with Amber."

I nodded.

"All right. We might as well try making it as easy as we can. Let's collect the horses first."

We did this, learning the length of the griffin's leash while we were about it. He was drawn up short about thirty meters from the cave mouth, and immediately set up a bleating complaint. This did not make the job of pacifying the horses any easier, but it did give rise to a peculiar notion which I decided to keep to myself.

Once we had things under control, Random located his Trumps and I brought out my own.

"Let's try for Benedict," he said.

"All right. Any time now."

I noticed immediately that the cards felt cold again, a good sign. I shuffled out Benedict's and began the preliminaries. Beside me, Random did the same.

Contact came almost at once.

"What is the occasion?" Benedict asked, his eyes moving over Random, Ganelon, and the horses, then meeting with my own.

"Will you bring us through?" I said.

"Horses, too?"

"The works."

"Come ahead."

He extended his hand and I touched it. We all moved toward him. Moments later, we stood with him in a high, rocky place, a chill wind ruffling our garments, the sun of Amber past midday in a sky full of clouds. Benedict wore a stiff leather jacket and buckskin leggings. His shirt was a faded yellow. An orange cloak concealed the stump of his right arm. He tightened his long jaw and peered down at me.

"Interesting spot you hie from," he said. "I glimpsed something of the background."

I nodded.

"Interesting view from this height, also," I said, noting the spyglass at his belt at the same time that I realized we stood on the wide ledge of rock from which Eric had commanded battle on the day of his death and my return. I moved to regard the dark swath through Garnath, far below and stretching off to the horizon.

"Yes," he said. "The black road appears to have stabilized its boundaries at most points. At a few others though, it is still widening. It is almost as if it is nearing a final conformity with some—pattern. . . . Now tell me, from what point have you journeyed?"

"I spent last night in Tir-na Nog'th," I said, "and this morning we went astray in crossing Kolvir."

"Not an easy thing to do," he said. "Getting lost on your own mountain. You keep heading east, you know. That is the direction from which the sun has been known to take its course."

I felt my face flush.

"There was an accident," I said, looking away. "We lost a horse."

"What sort of accident?"

"A serious one—for the horse."

"Benedict," said Random, suddenly looking up from what I realized to be the pierced Trump, "what can you tell me concerning my son Martin?"

Benedict studied him for several moments before he spoke. Then, "Why the sudden interest?" he asked.

"Because I have reason to believe he may be dead," he said. "If that is the case, I want to avenge it. If it is not the case—well, the thought that it might be has caused me some upset. If he is still living, I would like to meet him and talk with him."

"What makes you think he might be dead?"

Random glanced at me. I nodded.

"Start with breakfast," I said.

"While he is doing that, I'll find us lunch," said Ganelon, rummaging in one of the bags.

"The unicorn showed us the way . . ." Random began.

THREE

We sat in silence. Random had finished speaking and Benedict was staring skyward over Garnath. His face betrayed nothing. I had long ago learned to respect his silence.

At length, he nodded, once, sharply, and turned to regard Random.

"I have long suspected something of this order," he stated, "from things that Dad and Dworkin let fall over the years. I had the impression there was a primal Pattern which they had either located or created, situating our Amber but a shadow away to draw upon its forces. I never obtained any notion as to how one might travel to that place, however." He turned back toward Garnath, gesturing with his chin. "And that, you tell me, corresponds to what was done there?"

"It seems to," Random replied.

". . . Brought about by the shedding of Martin's blood?"

"I think so."

Benedict raised the Trump Random had passed him during his narration. At that time, Benedict had made no comment.

"Yes," he said now, "this is Martin. He came to me after he departed Rebma. He stayed with me a long while."

"Why did he go to you?" Random asked.

Benedict smiled faintly.

"He had to go somewhere, you know," he said. "He was sick of his position in Rebma, ambivalent toward Amber, young, free, and just come into his power through the Pattern. He wanted to get away, see new things, travel in Shadow—as we all did. I had taken him to Avalon once when he was a small boy, to let him walk on dry land of a summer, to teach him to ride a horse, to have him see a crop harvested. When he was suddenly in a position to go anywhere he would in an instant, his choices were still restricted to the few places of which he had knowledge. True, he might have dreamed up a place in that instant and gone there—creating it, as it were. But he was also aware that he still had many things to learn, to ensure his safety in Shadow. So he elected to come to me, to ask me to teach him. And I did. He spent the better part of a year at my place. I taught him to fight, taught him of the ways of the Trumps and of Shadow, instructed him in those things an Amberite must know if he is to survive."

"Why did you do all these things?" Random asked.

"Someone had to. It was me that he came to, so it was mine to do," Benedict replied. "It was not as if I were not very fond of the boy, though," he added.

Random nodded.

"You say that he was with you for almost a year. What became of him after that?"

"That wanderlust you know as well as I. Once he had obtained some confidence in his abilities, he wanted to exercise them. In the course of instructing him, I had taken him on journeys in Shadow myself, had introduced him to people of my acquaintance at various places. But there came a time when he wanted to make his own way. One day then, he bade me good-by and fared forth."

"Have you seen him since?" Random asked.

"Yes. He returned periodically, staying with me for a time, to tell me of his adventures, his discoveries. It was always clear that it was just a visit. After a time, he would get restless and depart again."

"When was the last time you saw him?"

"Several years ago, Avalon time, under the usual circumstances. He showed up one morning, stayed for perhaps two weeks, told me of the things he had seen and done, talked of the many things he wanted to do. Later, he set off once more."

"And you never heard from him again?"

"On the contrary. There were messages left with mutual friends when he would pass their way. Occasionally, he would even contact me via my Trump—"

"He had a set of the Trumps?" I broke in.

"Yes, I made him a gift of one of my extra decks."

"Did you have a Trump for him?"

He shook his head.

"I was not even aware that such a Trump existed, until I saw this one," he said, raising the card, glancing at it, and passing it back to Random. "I haven't the art to prepare one. Random, have you tried reaching him with this Trump?"

"Yes, any number of times since we came across it. Just a few minutes ago, as a matter of fact. Nothing."

"Of course that proves nothing. If everything occurred as you guessed and he did survive it, he may have resolved to block any future attempts at contact. He does know how to do that."

"Did it occur as I guessed? Do you know more about it?"

"I have an idea," Benedict said. "You see, he did show up injured at a friend's place—off in Shadow—some years ago. It was a body wound, caused by the thrust of a blade. They said he came to them in very bad shape and did not go into details as to what had occurred. He remained for a few days— until he was able to get around again—and departed before he was really fully recovered. That was the last they heard of him. The last that I did, also."

"Weren't you curious?" Random asked. "Didn't you go looking for him?"

"Of course I was curious. I still am. But a man should have the right to lead his own life without the meddling of relatives, no matter how well-intentioned. He had pulled through the crisis and he did not attempt to contact me. He apparently knew what he wanted to do. He did leave a message for me with the Tecys, saying that when I learned of what had happened I was not to worry, that he knew what he was about."

"The Tecys?" I said.

"That's right. Friends of mine off in Shadow."

I refrained from saying the things that I might. I had thought them just another part of Dara's story, for she had so twisted the truth in other areas. She had mentioned the Tecys to me as if she knew them, as if she had stayed with them—all with Benedict's knowledge. The moment did not seem appropriate, however, to tell him of my previous night's vision in Tir-na Nog'th and the things it had indicated concerning his relationship to the girl. I had not yet had sufficient time to ponder the matter and all that it implied.

Random stood, paced, paused near the ledge, his back to us, fingers knotted behind him. After a moment, he turned and stalked back.

"How can we get in touch with the Tecys?" he asked Benedict.

"No way," said Benedict, "except to go and see them."

Random turned to me.

"Corwin, I need a horse. You say that Star's been through a number of hellrides . . ."

"He's had a busy morning."

"It wasn't that strenuous. It was mostly fright, and he seems okay now. May I borrow him?"

Before I could answer, he turned toward Benedict.

"You'll take me, won't you?" he said.

Benedict hesitated.

"I do not know what more there is to learn—" he began.

"Anything! Anything at all they might remember—possibly something that did not really seem important at the time but is now, knowing what we know."

Benedict looked to me. I nodded.

"He can ride Star, if you are willing to take him."

"All right," Benedict said, getting to his feet. "I'll fetch my mount."

He turned and headed off toward the place where the great striped beast was tethered.

"Thanks, Corwin," Random said.

"I'll let you do me a favor in return."

"What?"

"Let me borrow Martin's Trump."

"What for?"

"An idea just hit me. It is too complicated to get into if you want to get moving. No harm should come of it, though."

He chewed his lip.

"Okay. I want it back when you are done with it."

"Of course."

"Will it help find him?"

"Maybe."

He passed me the card.

"You heading back to the palace now?" he asked.

"Yes."

"Would you tell Vialle what has happened and where I have gone? She worries."

"Sure. I'll do that."

"I'll take good care of Star."

"I know that. Good luck."

"Thanks."

I rode Firedrake. Ganelon walked. He had insisted. We followed the route I had taken in pursuing Dara on the day of the battle. Along with recent developments, that is probably what made me think of her again. I dusted off my feelings and examined them carefully. I realized then that despite the games she had played with me, the killings she had doubtless been privy or party to, and her stated designs upon the realm, I was still attracted to her by something more than curiosity. I was not really surprised to discover this. Things had looked pretty much the same the last time I had pulled a surprise inspection in the emotional barracks. I wondered then how much of truth there might have been to my final vision of the previous night, wherein her possible line of descent from Benedict had been stated. There was indeed a physical resemblance, and I was more than half-convinced. In the ghost city, of course, the shade of Benedict had conceded as much, raising his new, strange arm in her defense . . .

"What's funny?" Ganelon asked, from where he strode to my left.

"The arm," I said, "that came to me from Tir-na Nog'th—I had worried over some hidden import, some unforeseen force of destiny to the thing, coming as it had into our world from that place of mystery and dream. Yet it did not even last the day. Nothing remained when the Pattern destroyed Iago. The entire evening's visions come to nothing."

Ganelon cleared his throat.

"Well, it wasn't exactly the way you seem to think," he said.

"What do you mean?"

"That arm device was not in Iago's saddlebag. Random stowed it in your bag. That's where the food was, and after we had eaten he returned the utensils to where they had been in his own bag, but not the arm. There was no space."

"Oh," I said. "Then—"

Ganelon nodded.

"—So he has it with him now," he finished.

"The arm and Benedict both. Damn! I've small liking for that thing. It tried to kill me. No one has ever been attacked in Tir-na Nog'th before."

"But Benedict, Benedict's okay. He's on our side, even if you have some differences at the moment. Right?"

I did not answer him.

He reached up and took Firedrake's reins, drawing him to a halt. He stared up then, studying my face.

"Corwin, what happened up there, anyway? What did you learn?"

I hesitated. In truth, what had I learned in the city in the sky? No one was certain as to the mechanism behind the visions of Tir-na Nog'th. It could well be, as we have sometimes suspected, that the place simply served to objectify one's unspoken fears and desires, mixing them perhaps with unconscious guesswork. Sharing conclusions and reasonably based conjectures was one thing. Suspicions engendered by something unknown were likely better retained than given currency. Still, that arm was solid enough . . .

"I told you," I said, "that I had knocked that arm off the ghost of Benedict. Obviously, we were fighting."

"You see it then as an omen that you and Benedict will eventually be in conflict?"

"Perhaps."

"You were shown a reason for it, weren't you?"

"Okay," I said, finding a sigh without trying. "Yes. It was indicated that Dara was indeed related to Benedict—a thing which may well be correct. It is also quite possible, if it is true, that he is unaware of it. Therefore, we keep quiet about it until we can verify it or discount it. Understood?"

"Of course. But how could this thing be?"

"Just as she said."

"Great-granddaughter?"

I nodded.

"By whom?"

"The hellmaid we knew only by reputation—Lintra, the lady who cost him his arm."

"But that battle was only a recent thing."

"Time flows differently in different realms of Shadow, Ganelon. In the farther reaches—It would not be impossible."

He shook his head and relaxed his grip on the reins.

"Corwin, I really think Benedict should know about this," he said. "If it is true, you ought to give him a chance to prepare himself rather than let him discover it of a sudden. You people are such an infertile lot that paternity seems to hit you harder than it does others. Look at Random. For years, he had disowned his son, and now—I've a feeling he'd risk his life for him."

"So do I," I said. "Now forget the first part but carry the second one a step further in the case of Benedict."

"You think he would take Dara's side against Amber?"

"I would rather avoid presenting him with the choice by not letting him know that it exists—if it exists."

"I think you do him a disservice. He is hardly an emotional infant. Get hold of him on the Trump and tell him your suspicions. That way, at least, he can be thinking about it, rather than have him risk some sudden confrontation unprepared."

"He would not believe me. You have seen how he gets whenever I mention Dara."

"That in itself may say something. Possibly he suspects what might have happened and rejects it so vehemently because he would have it otherwise."

"Right now it would just widen a rift I am trying to heal."

"Your holding back on him now may serve to rupture it completely when he finds out."

"No. I believe I know my brother better than you do."

He released the reins.

"Very well," he said. "I hope you are right."

I did not answer, but started Firedrake to moving once more. There was an unspoken understanding between us that Ganelon could ask me anything he wanted, and it also went without saying that I would listen to any advice he had to offer me. This was partly because his position was unique. We were not related. He was no Amberite. The struggles and problems of Amber were his only by choice. We had been friends and then enemies long ago, and finally, more recently, friends again and allies in a battle in his adopted

land. That matter concluded, he had asked to come with me, to help me deal
with my own affairs and those of Amber. As I saw it, he owed me nothing
now, nor I him—if one keeps a scoreboard tally on such matters. Therefore, it
was friendship alone that bound us, a stronger thing than bygone debts and
points of honor: in other words, a thing which gave him the right to bug me
on matters such as this, where I might have told even Random to go to hell
once I had made up my mind. I realized I should not be irritated when
everything that he said was tendered in good faith. Most likely it was an old
military feeling, going back to our earliest relationship as well as being tied in
with the present state of affairs: I do not like having my decisions and orders
questioned. Probably, I decided, I was irritated even more by the fact that he
had made some shrewd guesses of late, and some fairly sound suggestions based
upon them—things I felt I ought to have caught myself. No one likes to admit
to a resentment based on something like that. Still . . . was that all? A simple
projection of dissatisfaction over a few instances of personal inadequacy? An
old army reflex as to the sanctity of my decisions? Or was it something deeper
that had been bothering me and was just now coming to the surface?

"Corwin," Ganelon said, "I've been doing some thinking . . ."

I sighed.

"Yes?"

". . . about Random's son. The way your crowd heals, I suppose it is
possible that he might have survived and still be about."

"I would like to think so."

"Do not be too hasty."

"What do you mean?"

"I gather he had very little contact with Amber and the rest of the family,
growing up in Rebma the way that he did."

"That is the way I understand it, too."

"In fact, outside of Benedict—and Llewella, back in Rebma—the only
other one he apparently had contact with would have been the one who
stabbed him—Bleys, Brand, or Fiona. It has occurred to me that he probably
has a pretty distorted view of the family."

"Distorted," I said, "but maybe not unwarranted, if I see what you are
getting at."

"I think you do. It seems conceivable that he is not only afraid of the
family, but may have it in for the lot of you."

"It is possible," I said.

"Do you think he could have thrown in with the enemy?"

I shook my head.

"Not if he knows they are the tools of the crowd that tried to kill him."

"But are they? I wonder . . . ? You say Brand got scared and tried to back
out of whatever arrangement they had with the black road gang. If they are
that strong, I wonder whether Fiona and Bleys might not have become *their*
tools? If this were the case, I could see Martin angling for something which
gave him power over them."

"Too elaborate a structure of guesses," I said.

"The enemy seems to know a lot about you."

"True, but they had a couple traitors to give them lessons."

"Could they have given them everything you say Dara knew?"

"That is a good point," I said, "but it is hard to say." Except for the business about the Tecys, which occurred to me immediately. I decided to keep that to myself for the moment though, to find out what he was leading up to, rather than going off on a tangent. So, "Martin was hardly in a position to tell them much about Amber," I said.

Ganelon was silent for a moment. Then, "Have you had a chance to check on the business I asked you about that night at your tomb?" he said.

"What business?"

"Whether the Trumps could be bugged," he said. "Now that we know Martin had a deck . . ."

It was my turn to be silent while a small family of moments crossed my path, single file, from the left, sticking their tongues out at me.

"No," I said then. "I haven't had a chance."

We proceeded on for quite a distance before he said, "Corwin, the night you brought Brand back . . . ?"

"Yes?"

"You say you accounted for everyone later, in trying to figure out who it was that stabbed you, and that any of them would have been hard put to pull the stunt in the time involved."

"Oh," I said, "and oh."

He nodded.

"Now you have another relative to think about. He may lack the family finesse only because he is young and unpracticed."

Sitting there in my mind, I gestured back at the silent parade of moments that crossed between Amber and then.

FOUR

She asked who it was when I knocked and I told her.

"Just a moment."

I heard her footsteps and then the door swung in. Vialle is only a little over five feet tall and quite slim. Brunette, fine-featured, very soft-spoken. She was wearing red. Her sightless eyes looked through me, reminding me of darkness past, of pain.

"Random," I said, "asked me to tell you that he would be delayed a little longer, but that there was nothing to worry about."

"Please come in," she said, stepping aside and drawing the door the rest of the way open.

I did. I did not want to, but I did. I had not intended to take Random's request literally—that I tell her what had happened and where he had gone. I had meant simply to tell her what I had already said, nothing more. It was not until we had ridden our separate ways that I realized exactly what Random's request had amounted to: He had just asked me to go tell his wife, to whom I had never spoken more than half a dozen words, that he had taken off to go looking for his illegitimate son—the lad whose mother, Morganthe, had committed suicide, a thing for which Random had been punished by being forced to marry Vialle. The fact that the marriage had somehow worked beautifully was something which still amazed me. I had no desire to dispense a load of awkward tidings, and as I moved into the room I sought alternatives.

I passed a bust of Random set on a high shelf on the wall to my left. I had actually gone by before it registered that my brother was indeed the subject. Across the room, I saw her workbench. Turning back, I studied the bust.

"I did not realize that you sculpted," I said.

"Yes."

Casting my gaze about the apartment, I quickly located other examples of her work.

"Quite good," I said.

"Thank you. Won't you sit down?"

I lowered myself into a large, high-armed chair, which proved more comfortable than it had looked. She seated herself on a low divan to my right, curling her legs beneath her.

"May I get you something to eat, or to drink?"

"No thanks. I can only stay a short while. What it is, is that Random, Ganelon, and I had gotten a bit side-tracked on the way home, and after that delay we met with Benedict for a time. The upshot of it was that Random and Benedict had to make another small journey."

"How long will he be away?"

"Probably overnight. Maybe a bit longer. If it is going to be much longer he will probably call back on someone's Trump, and we'll let you know."

My side began to throb and I rested my hand upon it, massaging it gently.

"Random has told me many things about you," she said.

I chuckled.

"Are you certain you would not care for something to eat? It would be no trouble."

"Did he tell you that I am always hungry?"

She laughed.

"No. But if you have been as active as you say, I would guess that you did not take time for lunch."

"In that you would be only half-correct. All right. If you've a spare piece of bread lying about it might do me some good to gnaw on it."

"Fine. Just a moment."

She rose and departed into the next room. I took the opportunity to scratch heartily all about my wound where it was suddenly itching fit to kill. I had accepted her hospitality partly for this reason and partly because of the realization that I actually was hungry. Only a little later it struck me that she could not have seen me attacking my side as I was. Her sure movements, her confident manner, had relaxed my awareness of her blindness. Good. It pleased me that she was able to carry it so well.

I heard her humming a tune: "The Ballad of the Water Crossers," the song of Amber's great merchant navy. Amber is not noted for manufacture, and agriculture has never been our forte. But our ships sail the shadows, plying between anywhere and anywhere, dealing in anything. Just about every male Amberite, noble or otherwise, spends some time in the fleet. Those of the blood laid down the trade routes long ago that other vessels might follow, the seas of a double dozen worlds in every captain's head. I had assisted in this in times gone by, and though my involvement had never been so deep as Gérard's or Caine's, I had been mightily moved by the forces of the deep and the spirit of the men who crossed it.

After a while, Vialle came in bearing a tray heavy with bread, meat, cheese, fruit, and a flask of wine. She set it upon a table near at hand.

"You mean to feed a regiment?" I asked.

"Best to be safe."

"Thanks. Won't you join me?"

"A piece of fruit, perhaps," she said.

Her fingers sought for a second, located an apple. She returned to the divan.

"Random tells me you wrote that song," she said.

"That was a very long time ago, Vialle."

"Have you composed any recently?"

I began to shake my head, caught myself, said, "No. That part of me is . . . resting."

"Pity. It is lovely."

"Random is the real musician in the family."

"Yes, he is very good. But performance and composition are two different things."

"True. One day when things have eased up . . . Tell me, are you happy here in Amber? Is everything to your liking? Is there anything that you need?" She smiled.

"All that I need is Random. He is a good man."

I was strangely moved to hear her speak of him in this fashion.

"Then I am happy for you," I said. And, "Younger, smaller . . . he might have had it a bit rougher than the rest of us," I went on. "Nothing quite as useless as another prince when there is already a crowd of them about. I was as guilty as the rest. Bleys and I once stranded him for two days on an islet to the south of here . . ."

". . . And Gérard went and got him when he learned of it," she said.

"Yes, he told me. It must bother you if you remember it after all this time."

"It must have made an impression on him, too."

"No, he forgave you long ago. He told it as a joke. Also, he drove a spike through the heel of your boot—pierced your foot when you put it on."

"Then it *was* Random! I'll be damned! I had always blamed Julian for that one."

"That one bothers Random."

"How long ago all of this was . . ." I said.

I shook my head and continued eating. Hunger seized me and she gave me several minutes of silence in which to get the upper hand on it. When I had, I felt compelled to say something.

"That is better. Much better," I began. "It was a peculiar and trying night that I spent in the sky-city."

"Did you receive omens of a useful nature?"

"I do not know how useful they might prove. On the other hand, I suppose I'd rather have had them than not. Have there been any interesting happenings hereabouts?"

"A servant tells me your brother Brand continues to rally. He ate well this morning, which is encouraging."

"True," I said. "True. It would seem he is out of danger."

"Likely. It—it is a terrible series of happenings to which you have all been subjected. I am sorry. I was hoping you might obtain some indication of an upturn in your affairs during the night you spent in Tir-na Nog'th."

"It does not matter," I said. "I am not that sure of the value of the thing."

"Then why—Oh."

I studied her with renewed interest. Her face still betrayed nothing, but her right hand twitched, tapping and plucking at the material of the divan. Then, as with a sudden awareness of its eloquence, she stilled it. She was obviously a person who had answered her own question and wished now she had done it in silence.

"Yes," I said, "I was stalling. You are aware of my injury."

She nodded.

"I am not angry with Random for having told you," I said. "His judgment has always been acute and geared to defense. I see no reason not to rely on it myself. I must inquire as to how much he has told you, however, both for your own safety and my peace of mind. For there are things I suspect but have not yet spoken."

"I understand. It is difficult to assess a negative—the things he might have left out, I mean—but he tells me most things. I know your story and most of the others'. He keeps me aware of events, suspicions, conjectures."

"Thank you," I said, taking a sip of the wine. "It makes it easier for me to speak then, seeing how things are with you. I am going to tell you everything that happened from breakfast till now . . ."

So I did.

She smiled occasionally as I spoke, but she did not interrupt. When I had finished, she asked, "You thought that mention of Martin would upset me?"

"It seemed possible," I told her.

"No," she said. "You see, I knew Martin in Rebma, when he was but a small boy. I was there while he was growing up. I liked him then. Even if he were not Random's son he would still be dear to me. I can only be pleased with Random's concern and hope that it has come in time to benefit them both."

I shook my head.

"I do not meet people like you too often," I said. "I am glad that I finally have."

She laughed, then said, "You were without sight for a long while."

"Yes."

"It can embitter a person, or it can give him a greater joy in those things which he does have."

I did not have to think back over my feelings from those days of blindness to know that I was a person of the first sort, even discounting the circumstances under which I had suffered it. I am sorry, but that is the way that I am, and I am sorry.

"True," I said. "You are fortunate."

"It is really only a state of mind—a thing a Lord of Shadow can easily appreciate."

She rose.

"I have always wondered as to your appearance," she said. "Random has described you, but that is different. May I?"

"Of course."

She approached and placed her finger tips upon my face. Delicately, she traced my features.

"Yes," she said, "you are much as I had thought you would be. And I feel the tension in you. It has been there for a long while, has it not?"

"In some form or other, I suppose, ever since my return to Amber."

"I wonder," she said, "whether you might have been happier before you regained your memory."

"It is one of those impossible questions," I said. "I might also be dead if I had not. But putting that part aside for a moment, in those times there was still a thing that drove me, that troubled me every day. I was constantly looking for ways to discover who I really was, what I was."

"But were you happier, or less happy, than you are now?"

"Neither," I said. "Things balance out. It is, as you suggested, a state of mind. And even if it were not so, I could never go back to that other life, now that I know who I am, now that I have found Amber."

"Why not?"

"Why do you ask me these things?"

"I want to understand you," she said. "Ever since I first heard of you back in Rebma, even before Random told me stories, I wondered what it was that drove you. Now I've the opportunity—no right, of course, just the opportunity—I felt it worth speaking out of turn and order beyond my station simply to ask you."

A half-chuckle caught me.

"Fairly taken," I said. "I will see whether I can be honest. Hatred drove me at first—hatred for my brother Eric—and my desire for the throne. Had you asked me on my return which was the stronger, I would have said that it was the summons of the throne. Now, though . . . now I would have to admit that it was actually the other way around. I had not realized it until this moment, but it is true. But Eric is dead and there is nothing left of what I felt then. The throne remains, but now I find that my feelings toward it are mixed. There is a possibility that none of us has a right to it under present circumstances, and even if all family objections were removed I would not take it at this time. I would have to see stability restored to the realm and a number of questions answered first."

"Even if these things showed that you may not have the throne?"

"Even so."

"Then I begin to understand."

"What? What is there to understand?"

"Lord Corwin, my knowledge of the philosophical basis of these things is limited, but it is my understanding that you are able to find anything you wish within Shadow. This has troubled me for a long while, and I never fully understood Random's explanations. If you wished, could not each of you walk in Shadow and find yourself another Amber—like this one in all respects, save that you ruled there or enjoyed whatever other status you might desire?"

"Yes, we can locate such places," I said.

"Then why is this not done, to have an end of strife?"

"It is because a place could be found which *seemed* to be the same—but that would be all. We are a part of this Amber as surely as it is a part of us. Any shadow of Amber would have to be populated with shadows of ourselves to seem worth while. We could even except the shadow of our own person should we choose to move into a ready realm. However, the shadow folk would not be exactly like the other people here. A shadow is never precisely like that which casts it. These little differences add up. They are actually worse than major ones. It would amount to entering a nation of strangers. The best mundane comparison which occurs to me is an encounter with a person who strongly resembles another person you know. You keep expecting him to act like your acquaintance; worse yet, you have a tendency to act toward him as you would toward that other. You face him with a certain mask and his responses are not appropriate. It is an uncomfortable feeling. I never enjoy meeting people who remind me of other people. Personality is the one thing we cannot control in our manipulations of Shadow. In fact, it is the means by which we can tell one another from shadows of ourselves. This is why Flora could not decide about me for so long, back on the shadow Earth: my new personality was sufficiently different."

"I begin to understand," she said. "It is not just Amber for you. It is the place plus everything else."

"The place plus everything else . . . *That* is Amber," I agreed.

"You say that your hate died with Eric and your desire for the throne has been tempered by the consideration of new things you have learned."

"That is so."

"Then I think I do understand what it is that moves you."

"The desire for stability moves me," I said, "and something of curiosity— and revenge on our enemies . . ."

"Duty," she said. "Of course."

I snorted.

"It would be comforting to put such a face on it," I said. "As it is, however, I will not be a hypocrite. I am hardly a dutiful son of Amber or of Oberon."

"Your voice makes it plain that you do not wish to be considered one."

I closed my eyes, closed them to join her in darkness, to recall for a brief while the world where other messages than light waves took precedence. I knew then that she had been right about my voice. Why had I trodden so heavily on the idea of duty as soon as it was suggested? I like credit for being good and clean and noble and high-minded when I have it coming, even sometimes when I do not—the same as the next person. What bothered me about the notion of duty to Amber? Nothing. What was it then?

Dad.

I no longer owed him anything, least of all duty. Ultimately, he was responsible for the present state of affairs. He had fathered a great brood of us without providing for a proper succession, he had been less than kind to all of our mothers and he then expected our devotion and support. He played favorites and, in fact, it even seemed he played us off against one another. He then got suckered into something he could not handle and left the kingdom in a mess. Sigmund Freud had long ago anesthetized me to any normal, generalized feelings of resentment which might operate within the family unit. I have no quarrel on those grounds. Facts are another matter. I did not dislike my father simply because he had given me no reason to like him; in truth, it seemed that he had labored in the other direction. Enough. I realized what it was that bothered me about the notion of duty: its object.

"You are right," I said, opening my eyes, regarding her, "and I am glad that you told me of it."

I rose.

"Give me your hand," I said.

She extended her right hand and I raised it to my lips.

"Thank you," I said. "It was a good lunch."

I turned and made my way to the door. When I looked back she had blushed and was smiling, her hand still partly raised, and I began to understand the change in Random.

"Good luck to you," she said, the moment my footsteps ceased.

". . . And you," I said, and went out quickly.

I had been planning to see Brand next, but just could not bring myself to do it. For one thing, I did not want to encounter him with my wits dulled by fatigue. For another, talking with Vialle was the first pleasant thing which had happened to me in some time, and just this once I was going to quit while I was ahead.

I mounted the stairs and walked the corridor to my room, thinking, of course, of the night of the knifings as I fitted my new key to my new lock. In my bedchamber, I drew the drapes against the afternoon's light, undressed, and got into bed. As on other occasions of rest after stress with more stress pending, sleep eluded me for a time. For a long while I tossed and twisted, reliving events of the past several days and some from even farther back. When finally I slept, my dreams were an amalgam of the same material, including a spell in my old cell, scraping away at the door.

It was dark when I awoke and I actually felt rested. The tension gone out of me, my reverie was much more peaceful. In fact, there was a tiny charge of pleasant excitement dancing through the back of my head. It was a tip-of-the-tongue imperative, a buried notion that—

Yes!

I sat up. I reached for my clothes, began to dress. I buckled on Grayswandir. I folded a blanket and tucked it under my arm. Of course . . .

My mind felt clear and my side had stopped throbbing. I had no idea how long I had slept, and it was hardly worth checking at this point. I had something far more important to look into, something which should have occurred to me a long while ago—had occurred, as a matter of fact. I had actually been staring right at it once, but the crush of time and events had ground it from my mind. Until now.

I locked my room behind me and headed for the stairs. Candles flickered, and the faded stag who had been dying for centuries on the tapestry to my right looked back on the faded dogs who had been pursuing him for approximately as long. Sometimes my sympathies are with the stag; usually though, I am all dog. Have to have the thing restored one of these days.

The stairs and down. No sounds from below. Late, then. Good. Another day and we're still alive. Maybe even a trifle wiser. Wise enough to realize there are many more things we still need to know. Hope, though. There's that. A thing I lacked when I squatted in that damned cell, hands pressed against my ruined eyes, howling. Vialle . . . I wish I could have spoken with you for a few moments in those days. But I learned what I learned in a nasty school, and even a milder curriculum would probably not have given me your grace. Still . . . hard to say. I have always felt I am more dog than stag, more hunter than victim. You might have taught me something that would have blunted the bitterness, tempered the hate. But would that have been for the best? The hate died with its object and the bitterness, too, has passed— but looking back, I wonder whether I would have made it without them to sustain me. I am not at all certain that I would have survived my internment without my ugly companions to drag me back to life and sanity time and again. Now I can afford the luxury of an occasional stag-thought, but then it might have been fatal. I do not truly know, kind lady, and I doubt that I ever will.

Stillness on the second floor. A few noises from below. Sleep well, lady. Around, and down again. I wondered whether Random had uncovered anything of great moment. Probably not, or he or Benedict should have contacted me by now. Unless there was trouble. But no. It is ridiculous to shop for worries. The real thing makes itself felt in due course, and I'd more than enough to go around.

The ground floor.

"Will," I said, and, "Rolf."

"Lord Corwin."

The two guards had assumed professional stances on hearing my footsteps. Their faces told me that all was well, but I asked for the sake of form.

"Quiet, Lord. Quiet," replied the senior.

"Very good," I said, and I continued on, entering and crossing the marble dining hall.

It would work, I was sure of that, if time and moisture had not totally effaced it. And then . . .

I entered the long corridor, where the dusty walls pressed close on either side. Darkness, shadows, my footsteps . . .

I came to the door at the end, opened it, stepped out onto the platform. Then down once more, that spiraling way, a light here, a light there, into the caverns of Kolvir. Random had been right, I decided then. If you had gouged out everything, down to the level of that distant floor, there would be a close correspondence between what was left and the place of that primal Pattern we had visited this morning.

. . . On down. Twisting and winding through the gloom. The torch and lantern-lit guard station was theatrically stark within it. I reached the floor and headed that way.

"Good evening, Lord Corwin," said the lean, cadaverous figure who rested against a storage rack, smoking his pipe, grinning around it.

"Good evening, Roger. How are things in the nether world?"

"A rat, a bat, a spider. Nothing much else astir. Peaceful."

"You enjoy this duty?"

He nodded.

"I am writing a philosophical romance shot through with elements of horror and morbidity. I work on those parts down here."

"Fitting, fitting," I said. "I'll be needing a lantern."

He took one from the rack, brought it to flame from his candle.

"Will it have a happy ending?" I inquired.

He shrugged.

"I'll be happy."

"I mean, does good triumph and hero bed heroine? Or do you kill everybody off?"

"That's hardly fair," he said.

"Never mind. Maybe I'll read it one day."

"Maybe," he said.

I took the lantern and turned away, heading in a direction I had not taken in a long while. I discovered that I could still measure the echoes in my mind.

Before too long, I neared the wall, sighted the proper corridor, entered it. It was simply a matter of counting my paces then. My feet knew the way.

The door to my old cell stood partly ajar. I set down the lantern and used both hands to open it fully. It gave way grudgingly, moaning as it moved. Then I raised the lantern, held it high, and entered.

My flesh tingled and my stomach clenched itself within me. I began to shiver. I had to fight down a strong impulse to bolt and run. I had not anticipated such a reaction. I did not want to step away from that heavy brassbound door for fear that it would be slammed and bolted behind me. It was an instant close to pure terror that the small dirty cell had aroused in me. I forced myself to dwell on particulars—the hole which had been my latrine, the blackened spot where I had built my fire on that final day. I ran my left hand over the inner surface of the door, finding and tracing there the grooves I had worn while scraping away with my spoon. I remembered what the activity had done to my hands. I stooped to examine the gouging. Not nearly so deep as it had seemed at the time, not when compared to the total thickness of the door. I realized how much I had exaggerated the effects of that feeble effort toward freedom. I stepped past it and regarded the wall.

Faint. Dust and moisture had worked to undo it. But I could still discern the outlines of the lighthouse of Cabra, bordered by four slashes of my old spoon handle. The magic was still there, that force which had finally transported me to freedom. I felt it without calling upon it.

I turned and faced the other wall.

The sketch which I now regarded had fared less well than that of the lighthouse, but then it had been executed with extreme haste by the light of my last few matches. I could not even make out all of the details, though my memory furnished a few of those which were hidden: It was a view of a den or library, bookshelves lining the walls, a desk in the foreground, a globe beside the desk. I wondered whether I should risk wiping it clean.

I set my lantern on the floor, returned to the sketch on the other wall. With a corner of my blanket, I gently wiped some dust from a point near the base of the lighthouse. The line grew clearer. I wiped it again, exerting a little more pressure. Unfortunate. I destroyed an inch or so of outline.

I stepped back and tore a wide strip from the edge of the blanket. I folded what remained into a pad and seated myself on it. Slowly, carefully then, I set to work on the lighthouse. I had to get an exact feeling for the work before I tried cleaning the other one.

Half an hour later I stood up and stretched, bent and massaged life back into my legs. What remained of the lighthouse was clean. Unfortunately, I had destroyed about 20 per cent of the sketch before I developed a sense of the wall's texture and an appropriate stroke across it. I doubted that I was going to improve any further.

The lantern sputtered as I moved it. I unfolded the blanket, shook it out, tore off a fresh strip. Making up a new pad, I knelt before the other sketch and set to work.

A while later I had uncovered what remained of it. I had forgotten the skull on the desk until a careful stroke revealed it once again—and the angle of the far wall, and a tall candlestick. . . . I drew back. It would be risky to do any more rubbing. Probably unnecessary, also. It seemed about as entire as it had been.

The lantern was flickering once again. Cursing Roger for not checking the kerosene level, I stood and held the light at shoulder level off to my left. I put everything from my mind but the scene before me.

It gained something of perspective as I stared. A moment later and it was totally three-dimensional and had expanded to fill my entire field of vision. I stepped forward then and rested the lantern on the edge of the desk.

I cast my eyes about the place. There were bookshelves on all four walls. No windows. Two doors at the far end of the room, right and left, across from one another, one closed, the other partly ajar. There was a long, low table covered with books and papers beside the opened door. Bizarre curios occupied open spaces on the shelves and odd niches and recesses in the walls— bones, stones, pottery, inscribed tablets, lenses, wands, instruments of unknown function. The huge rug resembled an Ardebil. I took a step toward that end of the room and the lantern sputtered again. I turned and reached for it. At that moment, it failed.

I growled an obscenity and lowered my hand. Then I turned, slowly, to check for any possible light sources. Something resembling a branch of coral shone faintly on a shelf across the room and a pale line of illumination occurred at the base of the closed door. I abandoned the lantern and crossed the room.

I opened the door as quietly as I could. The room it let upon was deserted, a small, windowless living place faintly lit by the still smoldering embers in its single, recessed hearth. The room's walls were of stone and they arched above me. The fireplace was a possibly natural niche in the wall to my left. A large, armored door was set in the far wall, a big key partly turned in its lock.

I entered, taking a candle from a nearby table, and moved toward the fireplace to give it a light. As I knelt and sought a flame among the embers, I heard a soft footfall in the vicinity of the doorway.

Turning, I saw him just beyond the threshold. About five feet in height, hunchbacked. His hair and beard were even longer than I remembered. Dworkin wore a nightshirt which reached to his ankles. He carried an oil lamp, his dark eyes peering across its sooty chimney.

"Oberon," he said, "is it finally time?"

"What time is that?" I asked softly.

He chuckled.

"What other? Time to destroy the world, of course!"

FIVE

I kept the light away from my face, kept my voice low.

"Not quite," I said. "Not quite."

He sighed.

"You remain unconvinced."

He looked forward and cocked his head, peering down at me.

"Why must you spoil things?" he said.

"I've spoiled nothing."

He lowered the lamp. I turned my head again, but he finally got a good look at my face. He laughed.

"Funny. Funny, funny, funny," he said. "You come as the young Lord Corwin, thinking to sway me with family sentiment. Why did you not choose Brand or Bleys? It was Clarissa's lot served us best."

I shrugged and stood.

"Yes and no," I said, determined now to feed him ambiguities for so long as he'd accept them and respond. Something of value might emerge, and it seemed an easy way to keep him in a good humor. "And yourself?" I continued. "What face would you put on things?"

"Why, to win your good will I'll match you," he said, and then he began to laugh.

He threw his head back, and as his laughter rang about me a change came over him. His stature seemed to increase, and his face luffed like a sail cut too close to the wind. The hump on his back was diminished as he straightened and stood taller. His features rearranged themselves and his beard darkened. By then it was obvious that he was somehow redistributing his body mass, for the nightshirt which had reached his ankles was now midway up his shins. He breathed deeply and his shoulders widened. His arms lengthened, his bulging abdomen narrowed, tapered. He reached shoulder height on me, then higher. He looked me in the eye. His garment reached only to his knees. His hump was totally resorbed. His face gave a final twist, his features steadied, were reset. His laughter fell to a chuckle, faded, closed with a smirk.

I regarded a slightly slimmer version of myself.

"Sufficient?" he inquired.

"Not half bad," I said. "Wait till I toss a couple logs on the fire."

"I will help you."

"That's all right."

I drew some wood from a rack to the right. Any stall served me somewhat, buying reactions for my study. As I was about the work, he crossed to a chair and seated himself. When I glanced at him I saw that he was not looking at me, but staring into the shadows. I drew out the fire-building, hoping that he would say something, anything. Eventually, he did.

"Whatever became of the grand design?" he asked.

I did not know whether he was speaking of the Pattern or of some master plan of Dad's to which he had been privy. So, "You tell me," I said.

He chuckled again.

"Why not? You changed your mind, that is what happened," he said.

"From what to what—as you see it?"

"Don't mock me. Even you have no right to mock me," he said. "Least of all, you."

I got to my feet.

"I was not mocking you," I said.

I crossed the room to another chair and carried it over to a position near the fire, across from Dworkin. I seated myself.

"How did you recognize me?" I asked.

"My whereabouts are hardly common knowledge."

"That is true."

"Do many in Amber think me dead?"

"Yes, and others suppose you might be traveling off in Shadow."

"I see."

"How have you been—feeling?"

He gave me an evil grin.

"Do you mean am I still mad?"

"You put it more bluntly than I care to."

"There is a fading, there is an intensifying," he said. "It comes to me and it departs again. For the moment I am almost myself—almost, I say. The shock of your visit, perhaps . . . Something is broken in my mind. You know that. It cannot be otherwise, though. You know that, too."

"I suppose that I do," I said. "Why don't you tell me all about it, all over again? Just the business of talking might make you feel better, might give me something I've missed. Tell me a story."

Another laugh.

"Anything you like. Have you any preferences? My flight from Chaos to this small sudden island in the sea of night? My meditations upon the abyss? The revelation of the Pattern in a jewel hung round the neck of a unicorn? My transcription of the design by lightning, blood, and lyre while our fathers raged baffled, too late come to call me back while the poem of fire ran that first route in my brain, infecting me with the will to form? Too late! Too late . . . Possessed of the abominations born of the disease, beyond their aid, their power, I planned and built, captive of my new self. Is that the tale you'd hear again? Or rather I tell you of its cure?"

My mind spun at the implications he had just scattered by the fistful. I could not tell whether he spoke literally or metaphorically or was simply sharing paranoid delusions, but the things that I wanted to hear, had to hear, were things closer to the moment. So, regarding the shadowy image of myself from which that ancient voice emerged, "Tell me of its cure," I said.

He braced his finger tips together and spoke through them.

"I am the Pattern," he said, "in a very real sense. In passing through my mind to achieve the form it now holds, the foundation of Amber, it marked me as surely as I marked it. I realized one day that I am both the Pattern and myself, and it was forced to become Dworkin in the process of becoming itself. There were mutual modifications in the birthing of this place and this time, and therein lay our weakness as well as our strength. For it occurred to me that damage to the Pattern would be damage to myself, and damage to myself would be reflected within the Pattern. Yet I could not be truly harmed because the Pattern protects me, and who but I could harm the Pattern? A beautiful closed system, it seemed, its weakness totally shielded by its strength."

He fell silent. I listened to the fire. I do not know what he listened to.

Then, "I was wrong," he said. "Such a simple matter, too . . . My blood, with which I drew it, could deface it. But it took me ages to realize that the blood of my blood could also do this thing. You could use it, you could also change it—yea, unto the third generation."

It did not come to me as a surprise, learning that he was grandsire to us all. Somehow, it seemed that I had known all along, had known but never voiced it. Yet . . . if anything, this raised more questions than it answered. *Collect one generation of ancestry. Proceed to confusion.* I had less idea now than ever before as to what Dworkin really was. Add to this the fact which even he acknowledged: It was a tale told by a madman.

"But to repair it . . . ?" I said.

He smirked, my own face twisting before me.

"Have you lost your taste to be a lord of the living void, a king of chaos?" he asked.

"Mayhap," I replied.

"By the Unicorn, thy mother, I knew it would come to this! The Pattern is as strong in you as is the greater realm. What then is your desire?"

"To preserve the realm."

He shook his/my head.

" 'Twould be simpler to destroy everything and try a new start—as I have told you so often before."

"I'm stubborn. So tell me again," I said, attempting to simulate Dad's gruffness.

He shrugged.

"Destroy the Pattern and we destroy Amber—and all of the shadows in polar array about it. Give me leave to destroy myself in the midst of the Pattern and we will obliterate it. Give me leave by giving me your word that you will then take the Jewel which contains the essence of order and use it to create a new Pattern, bright and pure, untainted, drawing upon the stuff of your own being while the legions of chaos attempt to distract you on every side. Promise me that and let me end it, for broken as I am, I would rather die for order than live for it. What say you now?"

"Would it not be better to try mending the one we've got than to undo the work of eons?"

"Coward!" he cried, leaping to his feet. "I knew you would say that again!"

"Well, wouldn't it?"

He began to pace.

"How many times have we been through this?" he asked. "Nothing has changed! You are afraid to try it!"

"Perhaps," I said. "But do you not feel that something for which you have given so much is worth some effort—some additional sacrifice—if there is even a possibility of saving it?"

"You still do not understand," he said. "I cannot but think that a damaged thing should be destroyed—and hopefully replaced. The nature of my personal injury is such that I cannot envision repair. I am damaged in just this fashion. My feelings are foreordained."

"If the Jewel can create a new Pattern, why will it not serve to repair the old one, end our troubles, heal your spirit?"

He approached and stood before me.

"Where is your memory?" he said. "You know that it would be infinitely more difficult to repair the damage than it would be to start over again. Even the Jewel could more easily destroy it than repair it. Have your forgotten what it is like out there?" He gestured toward the wall behind him. "Do you want to go and look at it again?"

"Yes," I said. "I would like that. Let's go."

I rose and looked down at him. His control over his form had begun slipping when he had grown angry. He had already lost three or four inches in height, the image of my face was melting back into his gnome-like features, and a noticeable bulge was growing between his shoulders, had already been visible when he had gestured.

His eyes widened and he studied my face.

"You really mean it," he said after a moment. "All right, then. Let us go."

He turned and moved toward the big metal door. I followed him. He used both hands to turn the key. Then he threw his weight against it. I moved to help him, but he brushed me aside with extraordinary strength before giving the door a final shove. It made a grating noise and moved outward into a fully opened position. I was immediately struck by a strange, somehow familiar odor.

Dworkin stepped through and paused. He located what looked to be a long staff leaning against the wall off to his right. He struck it several times against the ground and its upper end began to glow. It lit up the area fairly well, revealing a narrow tunnel into which he now advanced. I followed him and it widened before too long, so that I was able to come abreast of him. The odor grew stronger, and I could almost place it. It had been something fairly recent . . .

It was close to eighty paces before our way took a turn to the left and upward. We passed then through a little appendixlike area. It was strewn with broken bones, and a large metal ring was set in the rock a couple of feet above the floor. Affixed thereto was a glittering chain, which fell to the floor and trailed on ahead like a line of molten droplets cooling in the gloom.

Our way narrowed again after that and Dworkin took the lead once more. After a brief time, he turned an abrupt corner and I heard him muttering. I nearly ran into him when I made the turn myself. He was crouched down and groping with his left hand inside a shadowy cleft. When I heard the soft cawing noise and saw that the chain vanished into the opening I realized what it was and where we were.

"Good Wixer," I heard him say. "I am not going far. It is all right, good Wixer. Here is something to chew on."

From where he had fetched whatever he tossed the beast, I do not know. But the purple griffin, which I had now advanced far enough to glimpse as it stirred within its lair, accepted the offering with a toss of its head and a series of crunching noises.

Dworkin grinned up at me.

"Surprised?" he asked.

"At what?"

"You thought I was afraid of him. You thought I would never make friends with him. You set him out here to keep me in there—away from the Pattern."

"Did I ever say that?"

"You did not have to. I am not a fool."

"Have it your way," I said.

He chuckled, rose, and continued on along the passageway.

I followed and it grew level underfoot once again. The ceiling rose and the way widened. At length, we came to the cave mouth. Dworkin stood for a moment silhouetted, staff raised before him. It was night outside, and a clean salt smell swept the musk from my nostrils.

Another moment, and he moved forward once more, passing into a world of sky-candles and blue velours. Continuing after him, I had gasped briefly at that amazing view. It was not simply that the stars in the moonless, cloudless sky blazed with a preternatural brilliance, nor that the distinction between sky and sea had once again been totally obliterated. It was that the Pattern glowed an almost acetylene blue by that sky-sea, and all of the stars above, beside, and below were arrayed with a geometric precision, forming a fantastic, oblique latticework which, more than anything else, gave the impression that we hung in the midst of a cosmic web where the Pattern was the true center, the rest of the radiant meshwork a precise consequence of its existence, configuration, position.

Dworkin continued on down to the Pattern, right up to the edge beside the darkened area. He waved his staff over it and turned to look at me just as I came near.

"There you are," he announced, "the hole in my mind. I can no longer think through it, only around it. I no longer know what must be done to repair something I now lack. If you think that you can do it, you must be willing to lay yourself open to instant destruction each time you depart the Pattern to cross the break. Not destruction by the dark portion. Destruction by the Pattern itself when you break the circuit. The Jewel may or may not sustain you. I do not know. But it will not grow easier. It will become more difficult with each circuit, and your strength will be lessening all the while. The last time we discussed it you were afraid. Do you mean to say you have grown bolder since then?"

"Perhaps," I said. "You see no other way?"

"I know it can be done starting with a clean slate, because once I did it so. Beyond that, I see no other way. The longer you wait the more the situation worsens. Why not fetch the Jewel and lend me your blade, son? I see no better way."

"No," I said. "I must know more. Tell me again how the damage was done."

"I still do not know which of your children shed our blood on this spot, if this is what you mean. It was done. Let it go at that. Our darker natures came forth strongly in them. It must be that they are too close to the chaos from which we sprang, growing without the exercises of will we endured in defeating it. I had thought that the ritual of traveling the Pattern might suffice for them. I could think of nothing stronger. Yet it failed. They strike out against everything. They seek to destroy the Pattern itself."

"If we succeed in making a fresh start, might not these events simply repeat themselves?"

"I do not know. But what choice have we other than failure and a return to chaos?"

"What will become of them if we try for a new beginning?"

He was silent for a long while. Then he shrugged.

"I cannot tell."

"What would another generation have been like?"

He chuckled.

"How can such a question be answered? I have no idea."

I withdrew the mutilated Trump and passed it to him. He regarded it near the blaze of his staff.

"I believe it is Random's son Martin," I said, "he whose blood was spilled here. I have no idea whether he still lives. What do you think he might have amounted to?"

He looked back out over the Pattern.

"So this is the object which decorated it," he said. "How did you fetch it forth?"

"It was gotten," I said. "It is not your work, is it?"

"Of course not. I have never set eyes on the boy. But this answers your question, does it not? If there is another generation, your children will destroy it."

"As we would destroy them?"

He met my eyes and peered.

"Is it that you are suddenly becoming a doting father?" he asked.

"If you did not prepare that Trump, who did?"

He glanced down and flicked it with his fingernail.

"My best pupil. Your son Brand. That is his style. See what they do as soon as they gain a little power? Would any of them offer their lives to preserve the realm, to restore the Pattern?"

"Probably," I said. "Probably Benedict, Gérard, Random, Corwin . . ."

"Benedict has the mark of doom upon him, Gérard possesses the will but not the wit, Random lacks courage and determination. Corwin . . . Is he not out of favor and out of sight?"

My thoughts returned to our last meeting, when he had helped me to escape from my cell to Cabra. It occurred to me that he might have had second thoughts concerning that, not having been aware of the circumstances which had put me there.

"Is that why you have taken his form?" he went on. "Is this some manner of rebuke? Are you testing me again?"

"He is neither out of favor nor sight," I said, "though he has enemies among the family and elsewhere. He would attempt anything to preserve the realm. How do you see his chances?"

"Has he not been away for a long while?"

"Yes."

"Then he might have changed. I do not know."

"I believe he is changed. I know that he is willing to try."

He stared at me again, and he kept staring.

"You are not Oberon," he said at length.

"No."

"You are he whom I see before me."

"No more, no less."

"I see. . . . I did not realize that you knew of this place."

"I didn't, until recently. The first time that I came here I was led by the unicorn."

His eyes widened.

"That is—very—interesting," he said. "It has been so long . . ."

"What of my question?"

"Eh? Question? What question?"

"My chances. Do you think I might be able to repair the Pattern?"

He advanced slowly, and reaching up, placed his right hand on my shoulder. The staff tilted in his other hand as he did so; its blue light flared within a foot of my face, but I felt no heat. He looked into my eyes.

"You have changed," he said, after a time.

"Enough," I asked, "to do the job?"

He looked away.

"Perhaps enough to make it worth trying," he said, "even if we are foredoomed to failure."

"Will you help me?"

"I do not know," he said, "that I will be able. This thing with my moods, my thoughts—it comes and it goes. Even now, I feel some of my control slipping away. The excitement, perhaps. . . . We had best get back inside."

I heard a clinking noise at my back. When I turned, the griffin was there, his head swinging slowly from left to right, his tail from right to left, his tongue darting. He began to circle us, halting when he came to a position between Dworkin and the Pattern.

"He knows," Dworkin said. "He can sense it when I begin to change. He will not let me near the Pattern then. . . . Good Wixer. We are returning now. It is all right. . . . Come, Corwin."

We headed back toward the cave mouth and Wixer followed, a clink for every pace.

"The Jewel," I said, "the Jewel of Judgment . . . you say that it is necessary for the repair of the Pattern?"

"Yes," he said. "It would have to be borne the entire distance through the Pattern, reinscribing the original design in the places where it has been broken. This could only be done by one who is attuned to the Jewel, though."

"I am attuned to the Jewel," I said.

"How?" he asked, halting.

Wixer made a cackling noise behind us, and we resumed walking.

"I followed your written instructions—and Eric's verbal ones," I said. "I took it with me to the center of the Pattern and projected myself through it."

"I see," he said. "How did you obtain it?"

"From Eric, on his deathbed."

We entered the cave.

"You have it now?"

"I was forced to cache it in a place off in Shadow."

"I would suggest you retrieve it quickly and bring it here or take it back to the palace. It is best kept near the center of things."

"Why is that?"

"It tends to have a distorting effect on shadows if it lies too long among them."

"Distorting? In what fashion?"

"There is no way to tell, in advance. It depends entirely upon the locale."

We rounded a corner, continued on back through the gloom.

"What does it mean," I said, "when you are wearing the Jewel and everything begins to slow down about you? Fiona warned me that this was dangerous, but she was not certain why."

"It means that you have reached the bounds of your own existence, that your energies will shortly be exhausted, that you will die unless you do something quickly."

"What is that?"

"Begin to draw power from the Pattern itself—the primal Pattern within the Jewel."

"How is this achieved?"

"You must surrender to it, release yourself, blot out your identity, erase the bounds which separate you from everything else."

"It sounds easier said than done."

"But it can be done, and it is the only way."

I shook my head. We moved on, coming at last to the big door. Dworkin extinguished the staff and leaned it against the wall. We entered and he secured the door. Wixer had stationed himself just outside.

"You will have to leave now," Dworkin said.

"But there are many more things that I must ask you, and some that I would like to tell you."

"My thoughts grow meaningless, and your words would be wasted. Tomorrow night, or the next, or the next. Hurry! Go!"

"Why the rush?"

"I may harm you when the change comes over me. I am holding it back by main will now. Depart!"

"I do not know how. I know how to get here, but—"

"There are all manner of special Trumps in the desk in the next room. Take the light! Go anywhere! Get out of here!"

I was about to protest that I hardly feared any physical violence he could muster, when his features began to flow like melting wax and he somehow seemed much larger and longer-limbed than he had been. Seizing the light, I fled the room, a sudden chill upon me.

. . . To the desk. I tore open the drawer and snatched at some Trumps which lay scattered within it. I heard footsteps then, of something entering the room behind me, coming from the chamber I had just departed. They did not seem like the footsteps of a man. I did not look back. Instead, I raised the cards before me and regarded the one on top. It was an unfamiliar scene, but I opened my mind immediately and reached for it. A mountain crag, something indistinct beyond it, a strangely stippled sky, a scattering of stars to the left . . . The card was alternately hot and cold to my touch, and a heavy wind seemed to come blowing through it as I stared, somehow rearranging the prospect.

From right behind me then, the heavily altered but still recognizable voice of Dworkin spoke: "Fool! You have chosen the land of your doom!"

A great clawlike hand—black, leathery, gnarled—reached over my shoulder, as if to snatch the card away. But the vision seemed ready, and I rushed forward into it, turning the card from me as soon as I realized I had made my escape. Then I halted and stood stockstill, to let my senses adjust to the new locale.

I knew. From snatches of legend, bits of family gossip, and from a general feeling which came over me, I knew the place to which I had come. It was with full certainty as to identity that I raised my eyes to look upon the Courts of Chaos.

SIX

Where? The senses are such uncertain things, and now mine were strained beyond their limits. The rock on which I stood . . . If I attempted to fix my gaze upon it, it took on the aspect of a pavement on a hot afternoon. It seemed to shift and waver, though my footing was undisturbed. And it was undecided as to the portion of the spectrum it might call home. It pulsated and flashed like the skin of an iguana. Looking upward, I beheld a sky such as I had never before set eyes upon. At the moment, it was split down the middle—half of it of deepest night-black, and the stars danced within it. When I say danced, I do not mean twinkled; they cavorted and they shifted magnitudes; they darted and they circled; they flared to nova brilliance, then faded to nothing. It was a frightening spectacle to behold, and my stomach tightened within me as I experienced a profound acrophobia. Yet, shifting my gaze did little to improve the situation. The other half of the sky was like a bottle of colored sands, continuously shaken; belts of orange, yellow, red, blue, brown, and purple turned and twisted; patches of green, mauve, gray, and dead white came and went, sometimes snaking into belthood, replacing or joining the other writhing entities. And these, too, shimmered and wavered, creating impossible sensations of distance and nearness. At times, some or all seemed literally sky-high, and then again they came to fill the air before me, gauzy, transparent mists, translucent swaths or solid tentacles of color. It was not until later that I realized that the line which separated the black from the color was advancing slowly from my right while retreating to my left. It was as if the entire celestial mandala were rotating about a point directly overhead. As to the light source of the brighter half, it simply could not be determined. Standing there, I looked down upon what at first seemed a valley filled with countless explosions of color; but when the advancing darkness faced this display away the stars danced and burned within its depths as well as above, giving them the impression of a bottomless chasm. It was as if I stood at the end of the world, the end of the universe, the end of everything. But far, far out from where I stood, something hovered on a mount of sheerest black—a blackness itself, but edged and tempered with barely perceptible flashes of light. I could not guess at its size, for distance, depth, perspective, were absent here. A single edifice? A group? A city? Or simply a place? The outline varied each time that it fell upon my retina. Now faint and misty sheets drifted slowly between us, twisting, as if long strands of gauze were buoyed by heated air. The mandala ceased its turning when it had exactly reversed itself. The colors were behind me now, and imperceptible unless I turned my head, an action I had no desire to take. It was pleasant standing there, staring at the formlessness from which all things eventually emerged. . . . Before the Pattern, even, this thing was. I knew this, dimly but surely, at the very center of my consciousness. I knew this, because I was certain that I had been here before. Child of the man I had become, it seemed that I had been brought here in some distant day—whether by Dad or Dworkin, I could not now recall—and had stood or been held in this place or one very near to it, looking out upon the same scene with, I am certain, a similar lack of comprehension, a similar sense of apprehension. My pleasure was tinged with a nervous excitement, a sense of the forbidden, a feeling of dubious anticipation. Peculiarly, at that moment, there rose in me a longing for the Jewel I had had to abandon in my compost heap on the shadow Earth, the thing Dworkin had made so much of. Could it be that some part of me sought a defense or at least a symbol of resistance against whatever was out there? Probably.

As I continued to stare, fascinated, across the chasm, it was as if my eyes adjusted or the prospect shifted once again, subtly. For now I discerned tiny, ghostly forms moving within that place, like slow-motion meteors along the gauzy strands. I waited, regarding them carefully, courting some small understanding of the actions in which they were engaged. At length, one of the strands drifted very near. Shortly thereafter I had my answer.

There was a movement. One of the rushing forms grew larger, and I realized that it was following the twisting way that led toward me. In only a few moments, it took on the proportions of a horseman. As it came on, it assumed a semblance of solidity without losing that ghostly quality which seemed to cling to everything which lay before me. A moment later, I beheld a naked rider on a hairless horse, both deathly pale, rushing in my direction. The rider brandished a bone-white blade; his eyes and the eyes of the horse both flashed red. I did not really know whether he saw me, whether we existed on the same plane of reality, so unnatural was his mien. Yet I unsheathed Grayswandir and took a step backward as he approached.

His long white hair shed tiny sparkling motes, and when he turned his head I knew that he was coming for me, for then I felt his gaze like a cold pressure across the front of my body. I turned sidewise and raised my blade to guard.

He continued, and I realized that both he and the horse were big, bigger even than I had thought. They came on. When they reached the point nearest me—some ten meters, perhaps—the horse reared as the rider drew it to a halt. They regarded me then, bobbing and swaying as if on a raft in a gently swelling sea.

"Your name!" the rider demanded. "Give me your name, who comes to this place!"

His voice produced a crackling sensation in my ears. It was all of one sound level, loud and without inflection.

I shook my head.

"I give my name when I choose, not when I am ordered to," I said. "Who are you?"

He gave three short barks, which I took to be a laugh.

"I will hale you down and about, where you will cry it out forever."

I pointed Grayswandir at his eyes.

"Talk is cheap," I said. "Whisky costs money."

I felt a faint cool sensation just then, as if someone were toying with my Trump, thinking of me. But it was dim, weak, and I had no attention to spare, for the rider had passed some signal to his mount and the beast reared. The distance is too great, I decided. But this thought belonged to another shadow. The beast plunged ahead toward me, departing the tenuous roadway that had been its course.

Its leap bore it to a point far short of my position. But it did not fall from there and vanish, as I had hoped. It resumed the motions of galloping, and although its progress was not fully commensurate with the action, it continued to advance across the abyss at about half-speed.

While this was occurring, I saw that in the distance from which it had come another figure appeared to be headed my way. Nothing to do but stand my ground, fight, and hope that I could dispatch this attacker before the other was upon me.

As the rider advanced, his ruddy gaze flicked over my person and halted when it fell upon Grayswandir. Whatever the nature of the mad illumination at my back, it had tricked the delicate tracery on my blade to life once more, so that that portion of the Pattern it bore swam and sparkled along its length. The horseman was very near by then, but he drew back on the reins and his eyes leaped upward, meeting my own. His nasty grin vanished.

"I know you!" he said. "You are the one called Corwin!"

But we had him, me and my ally momentum.

His mount's front hoofs fell upon the ledge and I rushed forward. The beast's reflexes caused it to seek equal footing for its hind legs despite the drawn reins. The rider swung his blade into a guard position as I came on, but I cross-stepped and attacked from his left. As he moved his blade cross-body, I was already lunging. Grayswandir sheared through his pale hide, entering beneath the sternum and above the guts.

I wrenched my blade free and gouts of fire poured like blood from his wound. His sword arm sagged and his mount uttered a shriek that was almost a whistle as the blazing stream fell upon its neck. I danced back as the rider slumped forward and the beast, now fully footed, plunged on toward me, kicking. I cut again, reflexively, defensively. My blade nicked its left foreleg, and it, too, began to burn.

I side-stepped once again as it turned and made for me a second time. At that moment, the rider erupted into a pillar of light. The beast bellowed, wheeled, and rushed away. Without pausing, it plunged over the edge and vanished into the abyss, leaving me with the memory of the smoldering head of a cat which had addressed me long ago and the chill which always accompanied the recollection.

I was backed against rock, panting. The wispy road had drifted nearer—ten feet, perhaps, from the ledge. I had developed a cramp in my left side. The second rider was rapidly approaching. He was not pale like the first. His hair was dark and there was color in his face. His mount was a properly maned sorrel. He bore a cocked and bolted crossbow. I glanced behind me and there was no retreat, no crevice into which I might back.

I wiped my palm on my trousers and gripped Grayswandir by the forte of the blade. I turned sideways, so as to present the narrowest target possible. I raised my blade between us, hilt level with my head, point toward the ground, the only shield I possessed.

The rider came abreast of me and halted at the nearest point on the gauzy strip. He raised the crossbow slowly, knowing that if he did not drop me instantly with his single shot, I might be able to hurl my blade like a spear. Our eyes met.

He was beardless, slim. Possibly light-eyed within the squint of his aim. He managed his mount well, with just the pressure of his legs. His hands were big, steady. Capable. A peculiar feeling passed over me as I beheld him.

The moment stretched beyond the point of action. He rocked backward and lowered the weapon slightly, though none of the tension left his stance.

"You," he called out. "Is that the blade Grayswandir?"

"Yes," I answered, "it is."

He continued his appraisal, and something within me looked for words to wear, failed, ran naked away through the night.

"What do you want here?" he asked.

"To depart," I said.

There was a *chish-chá*, as his bolt struck the rock far ahead and to the left of me.

"Go then," he said. "This is a dangerous place for you."

He turned his mount back in the direction from which he had come.

I lowered Grayswandir.

"I won't forget you," I said.

"No," he answered. "Do not."

Then he galloped away, and moments later the gauze drifted off also.

I resheathed Grayswandir and took a step forward. The world was beginning to turn about me again, the light advancing on my right, the dark retreating to my left. I looked about for some way to scale the rocky prominence at my back. It seemed to rise only thirty or forty feet higher, and I wanted the view that might be available from its summit. My ledge extended to both my right and my left. On inspection, the way to the right narrowed quickly, however, without affording a suitable ascent. I turned and made my way to the left.

I came upon a rougher spot in a narrow place beyond a rocky shoulder. Running my gaze up its height, an ascent seemed possible. I checked behind me after the approach of additional threats. The ghostly roadway had drifted farther away; no new riders advanced. I commenced climbing.

The going was not difficult, though the height proved greater than it had seemed from below. Likely a symptom of the spatial distortion which seemed to have affected my sight of so much else in this place. After a time, I hauled myself up and stood erect at a point which afforded a better view in the direction opposite the abyss.

Once again, I beheld the chaotic colors. From my right, the darkness herded them. The land they danced above was rock-cropped and cratered, no sign of any life within it. Passing through its midst, however, from the far horizon to a point in the mountains somewhere to the right, inky and serpentine, ran what could only be the black road.

Another ten minutes of climbing and maneuvering, and I had positioned myself to view its terminus. It swept through a broad pass in the mountains and ran right to the very edge of the abyss. There, its blackness merged with that which filled the place, noticeable now only by virtue of the fact that no stars shone through it. Using this occlusion to gauge it, I obtained the impression that it continued on to the dark eminence about which the misty strips drifted.

I stretched out on my belly, so as to disturb the outline of the low crest as little as possible to whatever unseen eyes might flick across it. Lying there, I thought upon the opening of this way. The damage to the Pattern had laid Amber open to this access, and I believed that my curse had provided the precipitating element. I felt now that it would have come to pass without me, but I was certain that I had done my part. The guilt was still partly mine though no longer entirely so, as I had once believed. I thought then of Eric, as he lay dying on Kolvir. He had said that as much as he hated me, he was saving his dying curse for the enemies of Amber. In other words, this, and these. Ironic. My efforts were now entirely directed toward making good on my least-liked brother's dying wish. His curse to cancel my curse, me as the agent. Fitting though, perhaps, in some larger sense.

I sought, and was pleased not to discover, ranks of glowing riders setting forth or assembling upon that road. Unless another raiding party was already under way Amber was still temporarily safe. A number of things immediately troubled me, however. Mainly, if time did indeed behave as peculiarly in that place as Dara's possible origin indicated, then why had there not been another attack? They had certainly had ample time in which to recover and prepare for another assault. Had something occurred recently, by Amber's time, that is, to alter the nature of their strategy? If so, what? My weapons? Brand's recovery? Or something else? I wondered, too, how far Benedict's outposts reached. Certainly not this far, or I should have been informed. Had he ever been to this place? Had any of the others, within recent memory, stood where I had just stood, looking upon the Courts of Chaos, knowing something that I did not know? I resolved to question Brand and Benedict in this regard as soon as I returned.

All of which led me to wonder how time was behaving with me, at that moment. Better not to spend any more time here than I had to, I decided. I scanned the other Trumps I had removed from Dworkin's desk. While they were all of them interesting, I was familiar with none of the scenes depicted. I slipped my own case then and riffled through to Random's Trump. Perhaps he was the one who had tried to contact me earlier. I raised his card and regarded it.

Shortly, it swam before my eyes and I looked upon a blurred kaleidoscope of images, the impression of Random in their midst. Motion, and twisting perspectives . . .

"Random," I said. "This is Corwin."

I felt his mind, but there was no response from it. It struck me then that he was in the middle of a hellride, all his concentration bent on wrapping the stuff of Shadow about him. He could not respond without losing control. I blocked the Trump with my hand, breaking the contact.

I cut to Gèrard's card. Moments later, there was contact. I stood.

"Corwin, where are you?" he inquired.

"At the end of the world," I said. "I want to come home."

"Come ahead."

He extended his hand. I reached out and clasped it, stepped forward.

We were on the ground floor of the palace in Amber, in the sitting room to which we had all adjourned on the night of Brand's return. It seemed to be early morning. There was a fire going on the grate. No one else was present.

"I tried to reach you earlier," he said. "I think Brand did, too. But I can't be sure."

"How long have I been away?"

"Eight days," he said.

"Glad I hurried. What's happening?"

"Nothing untoward," he said. "I do not know what Brand wants. He kept asking for you, and I could not reach you. Finally, I gave him a deck and told him to see whether he could do any better. Apparently, he could not."

"I was distracted," I said, "and the time-flow differential was bad."

He nodded.

"I have been avoiding him now that he is out of danger. He is in one of his black moods again, and he insists he can take care of himself. He is right, in that, and it is just as well."

"Where is he now?"

"Back in his own quarters, and he was still there as of perhaps an hour ago—brooding."

"Has he been out at all?"

"A few brief walks. But not for the past several days."

"I guess I had best go see him then. Any word on Random?"

"Yes," he said. "Benedict returned several days ago. He said they had found a number of leads concerning Random's son. He helped him check on a couple of them. One led further, but Benedict felt he had best not be away from Amber for too long, things being as uncertain as they are. So he left Random to continue the search on his own. He gained something in the venture, though. He came back sporting an artificial arm—a beautiful piece of work. He can do anything with it that he could before."

"Really?" I said. "It sounds strangely familiar."

He smiled, nodded.

"He told me you had brought it back for him from Tir-na Nog'th. In fact, he wants to speak with you about it as soon as possible."

"I'll bet," I said. "Where is he now?"

"At one of the outposts he has established along the black road. You would have to reach him by Trump."

"Thanks," I said. "Anything further on Julian or Fiona?"

He shook his head.

"All right," I said, turning toward the door. "I guess I will go see Brand first."

"I am curious to know what it is that he wants," he said.

"I will remember that," I told him.

I left the room and headed for the stairs.

SEVEN

I rapped on Brand's door.

"Come in, Corwin," he said.

I did, deciding as I crossed the threshold that I would not ask him how he had known who it was. His room was a gloomy place, candles burning despite the fact that it was daytime and he had four windows. The shutters were closed on three of them. The fourth was only part way open. Brand stood beside this one, staring out toward the sea. He was dressed all in black velvet with a silver chain about his neck. His belt was also of silver—a fine, linked affair. He played with a small dagger, and did not look at me as I entered. He was still pale, but his beard was neatly trimmed and he looked well scrubbed and a bit heavier than he had when last I had seen him.

"You are looking better," I said. "How are you feeling?"

He turned and regarded me, expressionless, his eyes half-closed.

"Where the hell have you been?" he said.

"Hither and yon. What did you want to see me about?"

"I asked you where you've been."

"And I heard you," I said, reopening the door behind me. "Now I am going to go out and come back in. Supposing we start this conversation over again?"

He sighed.

"Wait a minute. I am sorry," he said. "Why are we all so thin-skinned? I do not know. . . . All right. It may be better if I do start over again."

He sheathed his dagger and crossed to sit in a heavy chair of black wood and leather.

"I got to worrying about all the things we had discussed," he said, "and some that we had not. I waited what seemed an appropriate time for you to have concluded your business in Tir-na Nog'th and returned. I then inquired after you and was told you had not yet come back. I waited longer. First I was impatient, and then I grew concerned that you might have been ambushed by our enemies. When I inquired again later, I learned that you had been back only long enough to speak with Random's wife—it must have been a conversation of great moment—and then to take a nap. You then departed once more. I was irritated that you had not seen fit to keep me posted as to events, but I resolved to wait a bit longer. Finally, I asked Gérard to get hold of you with your Trump. When he failed, I was quite concerned. I tried it myself then, and while it seemed that I touched you on several occasions I could not get through. I feared for you, and now I see that I had nothing to fear all along. Hence, I was abrupt."

"I see," I said, taking a seat off to his right. "Actually, time was running faster for me than it was for you, so from where I am sitting I have hardly been away. You are probably further recuperated from your puncture than I am from mine."

He smiled faintly and nodded.

"That is something, anyway," he said, "for my pains."

"I have had a few pains myself," I said, "so don't give me any more. You wanted me for something. Let's have it."

"Something is bothering you," he said. "Perhaps we ought to discuss that first."

"All right," I said. "Let's."

I turned and looked at the painting on the wall beside the door. An oil, a rather somber rendering of the well at Mirata, two men standing beside their horses nearby, talking.

"You've a distinctive style," I said.

"In all things," he replied.

"You stole my next sentence," I said, locating Martin's Trump and passing it to him.

He remained expressionless as he examined it, gave me one brief, sidelong look and then nodded.

"I cannot deny my hand," he said.

"It executed more than that card, your hand. Didn't it?"

He traced his upper lip with the tip of his tongue.

"Where did you find it?" he asked.

"Right where you left it, at the heart of things—in the real Amber."

"So . . ." he said, rising from the chair and returning to the window, holding up the card as if to study it in a better light. "So," he repeated, "you are aware of more than I had guessed. How did you learn of the primal Pattern?"

I shook my head.

"You answer my question first: Did you stab Martin?"

He turned toward me once again, stared a moment, then nodded sharply. His eyes continued to search my face.

"Why?" I asked.

"Someone had to," he explained, "to open the way for the powers we needed. We drew straws."

"And you won."

"Won? Lost?" He shrugged. "What does any of this matter now? Things did not come about as we had intended. I am a different person now than I was then."

"Did you kill him?"

"What?"

"Martin, Random's son. Did he die as a result of the wound you inflicted?"

He turned his hands palms upward.

"I do not know," he said. "If he did not, it was not because I did not try. You need look no further. You have found your guilty party. Now that you have, what are you going to do?"

I shook my head.

"I? Nothing. For all I know, the lad may still be living."

"Then let us move on to matters of greater moment. For how long have you known of the existence of the true Pattern?"

"Long enough," I said. "Its origin, its functions, the effect of the blood of Amber upon it—long enough. I paid more attention to Dworkin than you might have thought. I saw no gain to be had in damaging the fabric of existence, though. So I let Rover lie sleeping for a long, long while. It did not even occur to me until I spoke with you recently that the black road might have been connected with such foolishness. When I went to inspect the Pattern I found Martin's Trump and all the rest."

"I was not aware that you were acquainted with Martin."

"I have never set eyes on him."

"Then how were you aware he was the subject of the Trump?"

"I was not alone in that place."

"Who was with you?"

I smiled.

"No, Brand. It is still your turn. You told me when last we talked that the enemies of Amber hied all the way from the Courts of Chaos, that they have access to the realm via the black road because of something you and Bleys and Fiona had done back when you were of one mind as to the best way to take the throne. Now I know what it is that you did. Yet Benedict has been watching the black road and I have just looked upon the Courts of Chaos. There is no new massing of forces, no movement toward us upon that road. I know that time flows differently in that place. They should have had more than enough time to ready a new assault. I want to know what is holding them back. Why have they not moved? What are they waiting for, Brand?"

"You credit me with more knowledge than I possess."

"I don't think so. You are the resident expert on the subject. You have dealt with them. That Trump is evidence that you have been holding back on other matters. Don't weasel, just talk."

"The Courts . . ." he said. "You have been busy. Eric was a fool not to have killed you immediately—if he was aware you had knowledge of these things."

"Eric was a fool," I acknowledged. "You are not. Now talk."

"But I am a fool," he said, "a sentimental one, at that. Do you recall the day of our last argument, here in Amber, so long ago?"

"Somewhat."

"I was sitting on the edge of my bed. You were standing by my writing desk. As you turned away and headed toward the door, I resolved to kill you. I reached beneath my bed, where I keep a cocked crossbow with a bolt in it. I actually had my hand on it and was about to raise it when I realized something which stopped me."

He paused.

"What was that?" I asked.

"Look over there by the door."

I looked, I saw nothing special. I began to shake my head, just as he said, "On the floor."

Then I realized what it was—russet and olive and brown and green, with a small geometric pattern.

He nodded.

"You were standing on my favorite rug. I did not want to get blood on it. Later, my anger passed. So I, too, am a victim of emotion and circumstance."

"Lovely story—" I began.

"—but now you want me to stop stalling. I was not stalling, however. I was attempting to make a point. We are all of us alive by one another's sufferance and an occasional fortunate accident. I am going to propose suspending that sufferance and eliminating the possibility of accident in a couple of very important cases. First though, to answer your question, while I do not know for certain what is holding them back, I can venture a very good guess. Bleys has assembled a large strike force for an attack on Amber. It will be nowhere near the scale of the one on which you accompanied him, however. You see, he will be counting on the memory of that last attack to have conditioned the response to this one. It will probably also be preceded by attempts to assassinate Benedict and yourself. The entire affair will be a feint, though. I would guess that Fiona has contacted the Courts of Chaos—may even be there right now—and has prepared them for the real attack, which might be expected any time after Bleys's diversionary foray. Therefore—"

"You say this is a very good guess," I interrupted. "But we do not even know for certain that Bleys is still living."

"Bleys is alive," he said. "I was able to ascertain his existence via his Trump—even a brief assessment of his current activities—before he became aware of my presence and blocked me out. He is very sensitive to such surveillance. I found him in the field with troops he intends to employ against Amber."

"And Fiona?"

"No," he said, "I did no experimenting with her Trump, and I would advise you not to either. She is extremely dangerous, and I did not want to lay myself open to her influence. My estimate of her current situation is based on deduction rather than direct knowledge. I would be willing to rely on it, though."

"I see," I said.

"I have a plan."

"Go ahead."

"The manner in which you retrieved me from durance was quite inspired, combining the forces of everyone's concentration as you did. The same principle could be utilized again, to a different end. A force such as that would break through a person's defense fairly easily—even someone like Fiona, if the effort is properly directed."

"That is to say, directed by yourself?"

"Of course. I propose that we assemble the family and force our way through to Bleys and Fiona, wherever they may be. We hold them, locked in the full, in the flesh, just for a moment or so. Just long enough for me to strike."

"As you did Martin?"

"Better, I trust. Martin was able to break free at the last moment. That should not occur this time, with all of you helping. Even three or four would probably be sufficient."

"You really think you can pull it off that easily?"

"I know we had better try. Time is running. You will be one of the ones executed when they take Amber. So will I. What do you say?"

"If I become convinced that it is necessary. Then I would have no choice but to go along with it."

"It is necessary, believe me. The next thing is that I will need the Jewel of Judgment."

"What for?"

"If Fiona is truly in the Courts of Chaos, the Trump alone will probably be insufficient to reach her and hold her—even with all of us behind it. In her case, I will require the Jewel to focus our energies."

"I suppose that could be arranged."

"Then the sooner we are about it the better. Can you set things up for tonight? I am sufficiently recovered to handle my end of it."

"Hell, no," I said, standing.

"What do you mean?" He clenched the arms of the chair, half-rising. "Why not?"

"I said I would go along with it if I became convinced that it was necessary. You have admitted that a lot of this is conjecture. That alone is sufficient to keep me from being convinced."

"Forget about being convinced then. Can you afford to take the chance? The next attack is going to be a lot stronger than the last, Corwin. They are aware of your new weapons. They are going to allow for this in their planning."

"Even if I agreed with you, Brand, I am certain I could not convince the others that the executions are necessary."

"Convince them? Just tell them! You've got them all by the throat, Corwin! You are on top right now. You want to stay there, don't you?"

I smiled and moved toward the door.

"I will, too," I said, "by doing things my way. I will keep your suggestion on file."

"Your way is going to get you dead. Sooner than you think."

"I am standing on your rug again," I said.

He laughed.

"Very good. But I was not threatening you. You know what I meant. You are responsible for all of Amber now. You have to do the right thing."

"And you know what I meant. I am not going to kill a couple more of us because of your suspicions. I would need more than that."

"When you get it, it may be too late."

I shrugged.

"We'll see."

I reached toward the door.

"What are you going to do now?"

I shook my head.

"I don't tell anybody everything that I know, Brand. It is a kind of insurance."

"I can appreciate that. I only hope that you know enough."

"Or perhaps you fear that I know too much," I said.

For a moment a wary look danced on the muscles beneath his eyes. Then he smiled.

"I am not afraid of you, brother," he said.

"It is good to have nothing to fear," I said.

I opened the door.

"Wait," he said.

"Yes?"

"You neglected to tell me who was with you when you discovered Martin's Trump, in the place where I had left it."

"Why, it was Random," I said.

"Oh. Is he aware of the particulars?"

"If you mean, does he know that you stabbed his son," I said, "the answer is no, not yet."

"I see. And of Benedict's new arm? I understand that you somehow got it for him in Tir-na Nog'th. I would like to know more about this."

"Not now," I said. "Let's save something for our next get-together. It won't be all that long."

I went on out and closed the door, my silent regards to the rug.

EIGHT

After visiting the kitchens, compiling an enormous meal and demolishing it, I headed for the stables, where I located a handsome young sorrel which had once belonged to Eric. I made friends with him in spite of this, and a short while later we were moving toward the trail down Kolvir which would take us to the camp of my Shadow forces. As I rode and digested, I tried to sort out the events and revelations of what, to me, had been the past few hours. If Amber had indeed arisen as the result of Dworkin's act of rebellion within the Courts of Chaos, then it followed that we were all of us related to the very forces which now threatened us. It was, of course, difficult to decide how far anything Dworkin said might now be trusted. Yet, the black road did run to the Courts of Chaos, apparently as a direct result of Brand's ritual, a thing which he had based on principles learned from Dworkin. Fortunately, for now, the parts of Dworkin's narrative which required the greatest credulity were those things which were not of any great moment, from an immediate, practical standpoint. Still, I had mixed feelings about being descended from a unicorn—

"Corwin!"

I drew rein. I opened my mind to the sending and the image of Ganelon appeared.

"I am here," I said. "Where did you get hold of a set of Trumps? And learn how to use them?"

"I picked up a pack from the case in the library a while back. Thought it a good idea to have a way of getting in touch with you in a hurry. As for using them, I just did what you and the others seem to do—study the Trump, think about it, concentrate on getting in touch with the person."

"I should have gotten you a pack long ago," I said. "It was an oversight on my part which I am glad you've remedied. Are you just testing them now, or did something come up?"

"Something," he said. "Where are you?"

"As chance would have it, I am on my way down to see you."

"You are all right?"

"Yes."

"Fine. Come ahead then. I'd rather not try bringing you through this thing, the way you people do. It is not that urgent. I will see you by and by."

"Yes."

He broke the contact and I rustled the reins and continued on. For a moment, I had been irritated that he had not simply asked me for a deck. Then I recalled that I had been away for over a week, by Amber's time. He had probably been getting worried, didn't trust any of the others to do it for him. Perhaps rightly so.

The descent went quickly, as did the balance of the journey to the camp. The horse—whose name, by the way, was Drum—seemed happy to be going somewhere and had a tendency to pull away at the least excuse. I gave him his head at one point to tire him a bit, and it was not too long afterward that I sighted the camp. I realized at about that time that I missed Star.

I was the subject of stares and salutes as I rode into camp. A silence followed me and all activity ceased as I passed. I wondered whether they believed I had come to deliver a battle order.

Ganelon emerged from his tent before I had dismounted.

"Fast," he observed, clasping my hand as I came down. "Pretty horse, that."

"Yes," I agreed, turning the reins over to his orderly. "What news have you?"

"Well . . ." he said. "I've been talking to Benedict . . ."

"Something stirring on the black road?"

"No, no. Nothing like that. He came to see me after he returned from those friends of his—the Tecys—to tell me that Random was all right, that he was following a lead as to Martin's whereabouts. We got to talking of other matters after that, and finally he asked me to tell him everything I knew about Dara. Random had told him about her walking the Pattern, and he had decided then that too many people other than yourself were aware of her existence."

"So what did you tell him?"

"Everything."

"Including the guesswork, the speculation after Tir-na Nog'th?"

"Just so."

"I see. How did he take this?"

"He seemed excited about it. Happy, I'd even say. Come talk with him yourself."

I nodded and he turned toward his tent. He pushed back the flap and stepped aside. I entered.

Benedict was seated on a low stool beside a foot locker atop which a map had been spread. He was tracing something on the map with the long metal finger of the glinting, skeletal hand attached to the deadly, silver-cabled, fire-pinned mechanical arm I had brought back from the city in the sky, the entire device now attached to the stump of his right arm a little below the point where the sleeve had been cut away from his brown shirt, a transformation which halted me with a momentary shudder, so much did he resemble the ghost I had encountered. His eyes rose to meet my own and he raised the hand in greeting, a casual, perfectly executed gesture, and he smiled the broadest smile I had ever seen crease his face.

"Corwin!" he said, and then he rose and extended that hand.

I had to force myself to clasp the device which had almost killed me. But Benedict looked more kindly disposed toward me than he had in a long while. I shook the new hand and its pressures were perfect. I tried to disregard its coldness and angularity and almost succeeded, in my amazement at the control he had acquired over it in such a brief time.

"I owe you an apology," he said. "I have wronged you. I am very sorry."

"It's all right," I said. "I understand."

He clasped me for a moment, and my belief that things had apparently been set right between us was darkened only by the grip of those precise and deadly fingers on my shoulder.

Ganelon chuckled and brought up another stool, which he set at the other end of the locker. My irritation at his having aired the subject I had not wanted mentioned, whatever the circumstances, was submerged by the sight of its effects. I could not remember having seen Benedict in better spirits; Ganelon was obviously pleased at having effected the resolution of our differences.

I smiled myself and accepted a seat, unbuckling my sword belt and hanging Grayswandir on the tent pole. Ganelon produced three glasses and a bottle of wine. As he set the glasses before us and poured, he remarked, "To return the hospitality of your tent, that night, back in Avalon."

Benedict took up his glass with but the faintest of clicks.

"There is more ease in this tent," he said. "Is that not so, Corwin?"

I nodded and raised my glass.

"To that ease. May it always prevail."

"I have had my first opportunity in a long while," he said, "to talk with Random at some length. He has changed quite a bit."

"Yes," I agreed.

"I am more inclined to trust him now than I was in days gone by. We had the time to talk after we left the Tecys."

"Where were you headed?"

"Some comments Martin had made to his host seemed to indicate that he was going to a place I knew of further off in Shadow—the block city of Heerat. We journeyed there and found this to be correct. He had passed that way."

"I am not familiar with Heerat," I said.

"A place of adobe and stone—a commercial center at the junction of several trade routes. There, Random found news which took him eastward and probably deeper into Shadow. We parted company at Heerat, for I did not want to be away from Amber overlong. Also, there was a personal matter I was anxious to pursue. He told me how he had seen Dara walk the Pattern on the day of the battle."

"That's right," I said. "She did. I was there, too."

He nodded.

"As I said, Random had impressed me. I was inclined to believe he was telling the truth. If this were so, then it was possible that you were also. Granting this, I had to pursue the matter of the girl's allegations. You were not available, so I came to Ganelon—this was several days ago—and had him tell me everything he knew about Dara."

I glanced at Ganelon, who inclined his head slightly.

"So you now believe you have uncovered a new relative," I said, "a mendacious one, to be sure, and quite possibly an enemy—but a relative, nevertheless. What is your next move?"

He took a sip of wine.

"I would like to believe in the relationship," he said. "The notion somehow pleases me. So I would like to establish it or negate it to a certainty. If it turns out that we are indeed related, then I would like to understand the motives behind her actions. And I would like to learn why she never made her existence known to me directly." He put down his glass, raised his new hand and flexed the fingers. "So I would like to begin," he continued, "by learning of those things you experienced in Tir-na Nog'th which apply to me and to Dara. I am also extremely curious about this hand, which behaves as if it were made for me. I have never heard of a physical object being obtained in the city in the sky." He made a fist, unclenched it, rotated the wrist, extended the arm, raised it, lowered it gently to his knee. "Random performed a very effective piece of surgery, don't you think?" he concluded.

"Very," I agreed.

"So, will you tell me the story?"

I nodded and took a sip of my wine.

"It was in the palace in the sky that it occurred," I said. "The place was filled with inky, shifting shadows. I felt impelled to visit the throne room. I did this, and when the shadows moved aside, I saw you standing to the right of the throne, wearing that arm. When things cleared further, I saw Dara seated upon the throne. I advanced and touched her with Grayswandir, which made me visible to her. She declared me dead these several centuries and bade me return to my grave. When I demanded her lineage, she said she was descended of you and of the hellmaid Lintra."

Benedict drew a deep breath but said nothing. I continued:

"Time, she said, moved at such a different rate in the place of her birth, that several generations had passed there. She was the first of them possessed of regular human attributes. She again bade me depart. During this time, you had been studying Grayswandir. You struck then to remove her from danger, and we fought. My blade could reach you and your hand could reach me. That was all. Otherwise, it was a confrontation of ghosts. As the sun began to rise and the city to fade, you had me in a grip with that hand. I struck it free of the arm with Grayswandir and escaped. It was returned with me because it was still clasping my shoulder."

"Curious," Benedict said. "I have known that place to render false prophecies—the fears and hidden desires of the visitor, rather than a true picture of what is to be. But then, it often reveals unknown truths as well. And as in most other things, it is difficult to separate the valid from the spurious. How did you read it?"

"Benedict," I said, "I am inclined to believe the story of her origin. You have never seen her, but I have. She does resemble you in some ways. As for the rest . . . it is doubtless as you said—that which is left after the truth has been separated out."

He nodded slowly, and I could tell that he was not convinced but did not want to push the matter. He knew as well as I did what the rest implied. If he were to pursue his claim to the throne and succeed in achieving it, it was possible that he might one day step aside in favor of his only descendant.

"What are you going to do?" I asked him.

"Do?" he said. "What is Random now doing about Martin? I shall seek her, find her, have the story from her own lips, and then decide for myself. This will have to wait, however, until the matter of the black road is settled. That is another matter I wish to discuss with you."

"Yes?"

"If time moves so differently in their stronghold, they have had more than they need in which to mount another attack. I do not want to keep waiting to meet them in indecisive encounters. I am contemplating following the black road back to its source and attacking them on their home ground. I would like to do it with your concurrence."

"Benedict," I said, "have you ever looked upon the Courts of Chaos?"

He raised his head and stared at the blank wall of the tent.

"Ages ago, when I was young," he said, "I hellrode as far as I might go, to the end of everything. There, beneath a divided sky, I looked upon an awesome abyss. I do not know if the place lies there or if the road runs that far, but I am prepared to take that way again, if such is the case."

"Such is the case," I said.

"How can you be certain?"

"I am just returned from that land. A dark citadel hovers within it. The road goes to it."

"How difficult was the way?"

"Here," I said, taking out the Trump and passing it to him. "This was Dworkin's. I found it among his things. I only just tried it. It took me there. Time is already rapid at that point. I was attacked by a rider on a drifting roadway, of a sort not shown on the card. Trump contact is difficult there, perhaps because of the time differential. Gérard brought me back."

He studied the card.

"It seems the place I saw that time," he said at length. "This solves our logistics problems. With one of us on either end of a Trump connection we can transport the troops right through, as we did that day from Kolvir to Garnath."

I nodded.

"That is one of the reasons I showed it to you, to indicate my good faith. There may be another way, involving less risk than running our forces into the unknown. I want you to hold off on this venture until I have explored my way further."

"I will have to hold off in any event, to obtain some intelligence concerning that place. We do not even know whether your automatic weapons will function there, do we?"

"No, I did not have one along to test."

He pursed his lips.

"You really should have thought to take one and try it."

"The circumstances of my departure did not permit this."

"Circumstances?"

"Another time. It is not relevant here. You spoke of following the black road to its source . . ."

"Yes?"

"That is not its true source. Its real source lies in the true Amber, in the defect in the primal Pattern."

"Yes, I understand that. Both Random and Ganelon have described your journey to the place of the true Pattern, and the damage you discovered there. I see the analogy, the possible connection—"

"Do you recall my flight from Avalon, and your pursuit?"

In answer, he only smiled faintly.

"There was a point where we crossed the black road," I said. "Do you recall it?"

He narrowed his eyes.

"Yes," he said. "You cut a path through it. The world had returned to normal at that point. I had forgotten."

"It was an effect of the Pattern upon it," I said, "one which I believe can be employed upon a much larger scale."

"How much larger?"

"To wipe out the entire thing."

He leaned back and studied my face.

"Then why are you not about it?"

"There are a few preliminaries I must undertake."

"How much time will they involve?"

"Not too much. Possibly as little as a few days. Perhaps a few weeks."

"Why didn't you mention all of this sooner?"

"I only learned how to go about it recently."

"How *do* you go about it?"

"Basically, it amounts to repairing the Pattern."

"All right," he said. "Say you succeed. The enemy will still be out there." He gestured toward Garnath and the black road. "Someone gave them passage once."

"The enemy has always been out there," I said. "And it will be up to us to see that they are not given passage again—by dealing properly with those who provided it in the first place."

"I go along with you on that," he said, "but that is not what I meant. They require a lesson, Corwin. I want to teach them a proper respect for Amber, such a respect that even if the way is opened again they will fear to use it. That is what I meant. It is necessary."

"You do not know what it would be like to carry a battle to that place, Benedict. It is—literally—indescribable."

He smiled and stood.

"Then I guess I had best go see for myself," he said. "I will keep this card for a time, if you don't mind."

"I don't mind."

"Good. Then you be on with your business about the Pattern, Corwin, and I will be about my own. This will take me some time, too. I must go give my commanders orders concerning my absence now. Let us agree that neither of us commence anything of a final nature without checking first with the other."

"Agreed," I said.

We finished our wine.

"I will be under way myself, very soon now," I said. "So, good luck."

"To you, also." He smiled again. "Things are better," he said, and he clasped my shoulder as he passed to the entrance.

We followed him outside.

"Bring Benedict's horse," Ganelon directed the orderly who stood beneath a nearby tree; and turning, he offered Benedict his hand. "I, too, want to wish you luck," he said.

Benedict nodded and shook his hand.

"Thank you, Ganelon. For many things."

Benedict withdrew his Trumps.

"I can bring Gérard up to date," he said, "before my horse arrives."

He riffled through them, withdrew one, studied it.

"How do you go about repairing the Pattern?" Ganelon asked me.

"I have to get hold of the Jewel of Judgment again," I said. "With it, I can reinscribe the damaged area."

"Is this dangerous?"

"Yes."

"Where is the Jewel?"

"Back on the shadow Earth, where I left it."

"Why did you abandon it?"

"I feared that it was killing me."

He contorted his features into a near-impossible grimace.

"I don't like the sound of this, Corwin. There must be another way."

"If I knew a better way, I'd take it."

"Supposing you just followed Benedict's plan and took them all on? You said yourself that he could raise infinite legions in Shadow. You also said that he is the best man there is in the field."

"Yet the damage would remain in the Pattern, and something else would come to fill it. Always. The enemy of the moment is not as important as our own inner weakness. If this is not mended we are already defeated, though no foreign conqueror stands within our walls."

He turned away.

"I cannot argue with you. You know your own realm," he said. "But I still feel you may be making a grave mistake by risking yourself on what may prove unnecessary at a time when you are very much needed."

I chuckled, for it was Vialle's word and I had not wanted to call it my own when she had said it.

"It is my duty," I told him.

He did not reply.

Benedict, a dozen paces away, had apparently reached Gérard, for he would mutter something, then pause and listen. We stood there, waiting for him to conclude his conversation so that we could see him off.

". . . Yes, he is here now," I heard him say. "No, I doubt that very much. But—"

Benedict glanced at me several times and shook his head.

"No, I do not think so," he said. Then, "All right, come ahead."

He extended his new hand, and Gérard stepped into being, clasping it. Gérard turned his head, saw me, and immediately moved in my direction.

He ran his eyes up and down and back and forth across my entire person, as if searching for something.

"What is the matter?" I said.

"Brand," he replied. "He is no longer in his quarters. At least, most of him isn't. He left some blood behind. The place is also broken up enough to show there had been a fight."

I glanced down at my shirt front and trousers.

"And you are looking for bloodstains? As you can see, these are the same things I had on earlier. They may be dirty and wrinkled, but that's all."

"That does not really prove anything," he said.

"It was your idea to look. Not mine. What makes you think I—"

"You were the last one to see him," he said.

"Except for the person he had a fight with—if he really did."

"What do you mean by that?"

"You know his temper, his moods. We had a small argument. He might have started breaking things up after I left, maybe cut himself, gotten disgusted, trumped out for a change of scene— Wait! His rug! Was there any blood on that small, fancy rug before his door?"

"I am not sure—no, I don't think so. Why?"

"Circumstantial evidence that he did it himself. He was very fond of that rug. He avoided messing it."

"I don't buy it," Gérard said, "and Caine's death still looks peculiar—

and Benedict's servants, who could have found out you wanted gunpowder. Now Brand—"

"This could well be another attempt to frame me," I said, "and Benedict and I have come to better terms."

He turned toward Benedict, who had not moved from where he stood a dozen paces away, regarding us without expression, listening.

"Has he explained away those deaths?" Gérard asked him.

"Not directly," Benedict answered, "but much of the rest of the story now stands in a better light. So much so, that I am inclined to believe all of it."

Gérard shook his head and glared down at me again.

"Still unsettled," he said. "What were you and Brand arguing about?"

"Gérard," I said, "that is our business, till Brand and I decide otherwise."

"I dragged him back to life and watched over him, Corwin. I didn't do it just to see him killed in a squabble."

"Use your brains," I told him. "Whose idea was it to search for him the way that we did? To bring him back?"

"You wanted something from him," he said. "You finally got it. Then he became an impediment."

"No. But even if that were the case, do you think I would be so damned obvious about it? If he has been killed, then it is on the same order as Caine's death—an attempt to frame me."

"You used the obviousness excuse with Caine, too. It seems to me it could be a kind of subtlety—a thing you are good at."

"We have been through this before, Gérard . . ."

". . . And you know what I told you then."

"It would be difficult to have forgotten."

He reached forward and seized my right shoulder. I immediately drove my left hand into his stomach and pulled away. It occurred to me then that perhaps I should have told him what Brand and I had been talking about. But I didn't like the way he had asked me.

He came at me again. I side-stepped and caught him with a light left near the right eye. I kept jabbing after that, mainly to keep his head back. I was in no real shape to fight him again, and Grayswandir was back in the tent. I had no other weapon with me.

I kept circling him. My side hurt if I kicked with my left leg. I caught him once on the thigh with my right, but I was slow and off-balance and could not really follow through. I continued to jab.

Finally, he blocked my left and managed to drop his hand on my biceps. I should have pulled away then, but he was open. I stepped in with a heavy right to his stomach, all of my strength behind it. It bent him forward with a gasp, but his grip tightened on my arm. He blocked my attempted uppercut with his left, continuing its forward motion until the heel of his hand slammed against my chest, at the same time jerking my left arm backward and to the side with such force that I was thrown to the ground. If he came down on me, that was it.

He dropped to one knee and reached for my throat.

NINE

I moved to block his hand, but it halted in midreach. Turning my head, I saw that another hand had fallen upon Gérard's arm, was now grasping it, was holding it back.

I rolled away. When I looked up again, I saw that Ganelon had caught hold of him. Gérard jerked his arm forward, but it did not come free.

"Stay out of this, Ganelon," he said.

"Get going, Corwin!" Ganelon said. "Get the Jewel!"

Even as he called out, Gérard was beginning to rise. Ganelon crossed with his left and connected with Gérard's jaw. Gérard sprawled at his feet. Ganelon moved in and swung a kick toward his kidney, but Gérard caught his foot and heaved him over backward. I scrambled back into a crouch, supporting myself with one hand.

Gérard came up off the ground and rushed Ganelon, who was just recovering his feet. As he was almost upon him, Ganelon came up with a double-fisted blow to Gérard's midsection, which halted him in his tracks. Instantly, Ganelon's fists were moving like pistons against Gérard's abdomen. For several moments, Gérard seemed too dazed to protect himself, and when he finally bent and brought his arms in, Ganelon caught him with a right to the jaw that staggered him backward. Ganelon immediately rushed forward, throwing his arms about Gérard as he slammed into him and hooking his right leg behind Gérard's own. Gérard toppled and Ganelon fell upon him. He straddled Gérard then and drove his right fist against his jaw. When Gérard's head rolled back, Ganelon crossed with his left.

Benedict suddenly moved to intervene, but Ganelon chose that moment to rise to his feet. Gérard lay unconscious, bleeding from his mouth and nose.

I got shakily to my own feet, dusted myself off.

Ganelon grinned at me.

"Don't stay around," he said. "I don't know how I would do in a rematch. Go find the trinket."

I glanced at Benedict and he nodded. I returned to the tent for Grayswandir. When I emerged, Gérard still had not moved, but Benedict stood before me.

"Remember," he said, "you've my Trump and I've yours. Nothing final without a conference."

I nodded. I was going to ask him why he had seemed willing to help

433

Gérard, but not me. But second thoughts had me and I decided against spoiling our fresh-minted amity.

"Okay."

I headed toward the horses. Ganelon clapped me on the shoulder as I came up to him.

"Good luck," he said. "I'd go with you, but I am needed here—especially with Benedict trumping off to Chaos."

"Good show," I said. "I shouldn't have any trouble. Don't worry."

I went off to the paddock. Shortly, I was mounted and moving. Ganelon threw me a salute as I passed and I returned it. Benedict was kneeling beside Gérard.

I headed for the nearest trail into Arden. The sea lay at my back, Garnath and the black road to the left, Kolvir to my right. I had to gain some distance before I could work with the stuff of Shadow. The day lay clear once Garnath was lost to sight, several rises and dips later. I struck the trail and followed its long curve into the wood, where moist shadows and distant bird songs reminded me of the long periods of peace we had known of old and the silken, gleaming presence of the maternal unicorn.

My aches faded into the rhythm of the ride, and I thought once again of the encounter I had departed. It was not difficult to understand Gérard's attitude, since he had already told me of his suspicions and issued me a warning. Still, it was such bad timing for whatever had happened with Brand that I could not but see it as another action intended either to slow me or to stop me entirely. It was fortunate that Ganelon had been on hand, in good shape, and able to put his fists in the right places at the proper times. I wondered what Benedict would have done if there had only been the three of us present. I'd a feeling he would have waited and intervened only at the very last moment, to stop Gérard from killing me. I was still not happy with our accord, though it was certainly an improvement over the previous state of affairs.

All of which made me wonder again what had become of Brand. Had Fiona or Bleys finally gotten to him? Had he attempted his proposed assassinations singlehanded and been met with a counterthrust, then dragged through his intended victim's Trump? Had his old allies from the Courts of Chaos somehow gotten through to him? Had one of his horny-handed guardians from the tower finally been able to reach him? Or had it been as I had suggested to Gérard—an accidental self-injury in a fit of rage, followed by an ill-tempered flight from Amber to do his brooding and plotting elsewhere?

When that many questions arise from a single event the answer is seldom obtainable by pure logic. I had to sort out the possibilities though, to have something to reach for when more facts did turn up. In the meantime, I thought carefully over everything he had told me, regarding his allegations in light of those things which I now knew. With one exception, I did not doubt most of the facts. He had built too cleverly to have the edifice simply toppled—but then, he had had a lot of time to think these things over. No, it was in his manner of presenting events that something had been hidden by misdirection. His recent proposal practically assured me of that.

The old trail twisted, widened, narrowed again, swung to the northwest and downward, into the thickening wood. The forest had changed very little. It seemed almost the same trail a young man had ridden centuries before, riding for the sheer pleasure of it, riding to explore that vast green realm which extended over most of the continent, if he did not stray into Shadow. It would be good to be doing it again for no reason other than this.

After perhaps an hour, I had worked my way well back into the forest, where the trees were great dark towers, what sunlight I glimpsed caught like phoenix nests in their highest branches, an always moist, twilight softness smoothing the outlines of stumps and boles, logs and mossy rocks. A deer bounded across my path, not trusting to the excellent concealment of a thicket at the right of the trail. Bird notes sounded about me, never too near. Occasionally, I crossed the tracks of other horsemen. Some of these were quite fresh, but they did not stay long with the trail. Kolvir was well out of sight, had been for some time.

The trail rose again, and I knew that I would shortly reach the top of a small ridge, pass among rocks, and head downward once more. The trees thinned somewhat as we climbed, until finally I was afforded a partial view of the sky. It was enlarged as I continued, and when I came to the summit I heard the distant cry of a hunting bird.

Glancing upward, I saw a great dark shape, circling and circling, high above me. I hurried past the boulders and shook the reins for a burst of speed as soon as the way was clear. We plunged downward, racing to get under cover of the larger trees once again.

The bird cried out as we did this, but we won to the shade, to the dimness, without incident. I slowed gradually after that and continued to listen, but there were no untoward sounds on the air. This part of the forest was pretty much the same as that we had left beyond the ridge, save for a small stream we picked up and paralleled for a time, finally crossing it at a shallow ford. Beyond, the trail widened and a little more light leaked through and flowed with us for half a league. We had almost come a sufficient distance for me to begin those small manipulations of Shadow which would bear me to the pathway back to the shadow Earth of my former exile. Yet, it would be difficult to begin here, easier farther along. I resolved to save the strain on myself and my mount by continuing to a better beginning. Nothing of a threatening nature had really occurred. The bird could be a wild hunter, probably was.

Only one thought nagged at me as I rode.

Julian . . .

Arden was Julian's preserve, patrolled by his rangers, sheltering several encampments of his troops at all times—Amber's inland border guard, both against incursions natural and against those things which might appear at the boundaries of Shadow.

Where did Julian go when he had departed the palace so suddenly on the night of Brand's stabbing? If he wished simply to hide, there was no necessity for him to flee farther than this. Here he was strong, backed by his own men, moving in a realm he knew far better than the rest of us. It was quite possible that he was not, right now, too far away. Also, he liked to hunt. He had his hellhounds, he had his birds . . .

A half mile, a mile . . .

Just then, I heard the sound that I feared most. Piercing the green and the shade, there came the notes of a hunting horn. They came from some distance behind me, and I think from the left of the trail.

I urged my mount to a gallop and the trees rushed to a blur on either side. The trail was straight and level here. We took advantage of this.

Then from behind, I heard a roar—a kind of deep-chested coughing, growling sound backed by a lot of resonant lung space. I did not know what it was that had uttered it, but it was no dog. Not even a hellhound sounded like that. I glanced back, but there was no pursuit in sight. So I kept low and talked to Drum a bit.

After a time, I heard a crashing noise in the woods off to my right, but the roar was not repeated just then. I looked again, several times, but I was unable to make out what it was that was causing the disturbance. Shortly thereafter, I heard the horn once more, much nearer, and this time it was answered by the barks and the baying which I could not mistake. The hellhounds were coming—swift, powerful, vicious beasts Julian had found in some shadow and trained to the hunt.

It was time, I decided, to begin the shift. Amber was still strong about me, but I laid hold of Shadow as best I could and started the movement.

The trail began to curve to the left, and as we raced along it the trees at either hand diminished in size, fell back. Another curve, and the trail led us through a clearing, perhaps two hundred meters across. I glanced up then and saw that that damned bird was still circling, much nearer now, close enough to be dragged with me through Shadow.

This was more complicated than I had intended. I wanted an open space in which to wheel my mount and swing a blade freely if it came to that. The occurrence of such a place, however, revealed my position quite clearly to the bird, whom it was proving difficult to lose.

All right. We came to a low hill, mounted it, started downward, passing a lone, lightning-blasted tree as we did. On its nearest branch sat a hawk of gray and silver and black. I whistled to it as we passed, and it leaped into the air, shrieking a savage battle cry.

Hurrying on, I heard the individual voices of the dogs clearly now, and the thud of the horses' hoofs. Mixed in with these sounds there was something else, more a vibration, a shuddering of the ground. I looked back again, but none of my pursuit had yet topped the hill. I bent my mind toward the way away and clouds occluded the sun. Strange flowers appeared along the trail— green and yellow and purple—and there came a rumble of distant thunders. The clearing widened, lengthened. It became completely level.

I heard once again the sound of the horn. I turned for another look.

It bounded into view then, and I realized at that instant that I was not the object of the hunt, that the riders, the dogs, the bird, were pursuing the thing that ran behind me. Of course, this was a rather academic distinction, in that I was in front, and quite possibly the object of *its* hunt. I leaned forward, shouting to Drum and digging in with my knees, realizing even as I did that the abomination was moving faster than we could. It was a panic reaction.

I was being pursued by a manticora.

The last time I had seen its like was on the day before the battle in which Eric died. As I had led my troops up the rearward slopes of Kolvir, it had appeared to tear a man named Rall in half. We had dispatched it with automatic weapons. The thing proved twelve feet in length, and like this one it had worn a human face on the head and shoulders of a lion; it, too, had had a pair of eaglelike wings folded against its sides and the long pointed tail of a scorpion curving in the air above it. A number of them had somehow wandered in from Shadow to devil our steps as we headed for that battle. There was no reason to believe all of them had been accounted for, save that none had been reported since that time and no evidence of their continued existence in the vicinity of Amber had come to light. Apparently, this one had wandered down into Arden and been living in the forest since that time.

A final glance showed me that I might be pulled down in moments if I did not make a stand. It also showed me a dark avalanche of dogs rushing down the hill.

I did not know the intelligence or psychology of the manticora. Most fleeing beasts will not stop to attack something which is not bothering them. Self-preservation is generally foremost in their minds. On the other hand, I was not certain that the manticora even realized that it was being pursued. It might have started out on my trail and only had its own picked up afterward. It might have only the one thing on its mind. It was hardly a time to pause and reflect on all the possibilities.

I drew Grayswandir and turned my mount to the left, pulling back on the reins immediately as he made the turn.

Drum screamed and rose high onto his hind legs. I felt myself sliding backward, so I jumped to the ground and leaped to the side.

But I had, for the moment, forgotten the speed of the storm-hounds, had also forgotten how easily they had once overtaken Random and myself in Flora's Mercedes, had also forgotten that unlike ordinary dogs chasing cars, they had begun tearing the vehicle apart.

Suddenly, they were all over the manticora, a dozen or more dogs, leaping and biting. The beast threw back its head and uttered another cry as they struck at it. It swept that vicious tail through them, sending one flying, stunning or killing two others. It reared then and turned, striking out with its forelegs as it descended.

But even as it did this, a hound attached itself to its left foreleg, two more were at its haunches and one had scrambled onto its back, biting at its shoulder and neck. The others were circling it now. As soon as it would go after one, the others would dart in and slash at it.

It finally caught the one on its back with its scorpion sting and disembowled the one gnawing at its leg. However, it was running blood from a double dozen wounds by then. Shortly, it became apparent that the leg was giving it trouble, both for striking purposes and for bearing its weight when it struck with the others. In the meantime, another dog had mounted its back and was tearing at its neck. It seemed to be having a more difficult time getting at this one. Another came in from its right and shredded its ear. Two more plied its haunches, and when it reared again one rushed in and tore at its belly. Their barks and growls also seemed to be confusing it somewhat, and it began striking wildly at the ever-moving gray shapes.

I had caught hold of Drum's bridle and was trying to calm him sufficiently to remount and get the hell out of there. He kept trying to rear and pull away, and it took considerable persuasion even to hold him in place.

In the meantime, the manticora let out a bitter, wailing cry. It had struck wildly at the dog on its back and driven its sting into its own shoulder. The dogs took advantage of this distraction and rushed in wherever there was an opening, snapping and tearing.

I am certain the dogs would have finished it, but at that moment the riders topped the hill and descended. There were five of them, Julian in the lead. He had on his scaled white armor and his hunting horn hung about his neck. He rode his gigantic steed Morgenstern, a beast which has always hated me. He raised the long lance that he bore and saluted with it in my direction. Then he lowered it and shouted orders to the dogs. Grudgingly, they dropped away from the prey. Even the dog on the manticora's back loosened its grip and leaped to the ground. All of them drew back as Julian couched the lance and touched his spurs to Morgenstern's sides.

The beast turned toward him, gave a final cry of defiance, and leaped ahead, fangs bared. They came together, and for a moment my view was blocked by Morgenstern's shoulder. Another moment, however, and I knew from the horse's behavior that the blow had been a true one.

A turning, and I saw the beast stretched out, great gouts of blood upon its breast, flowering about the dark stem of the lance.

Julian dismounted. He said something to the other riders which I did not overhear. They remained mounted. He regarded the still-twitching manticora, then looked at me and smiled. He crossed and placed his foot upon the beast, seized the lance with one hand, and wrenched it from the carcass. Then he drove it into the ground and tethered Morgenstern to its shaft. He reached up and patted the horse's shoulder, looked back at me, turned, and headed in my direction.

When he came up before me he said, "I wish you hadn't killed Bela."

"Bela?" I repeated.

He glanced at the sky. I followed his gaze. Neither bird was now in sight.

"He was one of my favorites."

"I am sorry," I said. "I misunderstood what was going on."

He nodded.

"All right. I've done something for you. Now you can tell me what happened after I left the palace. Did Brand make it?"

"Yes," I said, "and you're off the hook on that. He claimed Fiona stabbed him. And she was not around to question either. She departed during the night, also. It's a wonder you didn't bump into one another."

He smiled.

"I'd have guessed as much," he said.

"Why did you flee under such suspicious circumstances?" I asked. "It made it look bad for you."

He shrugged.

"It would not be the first time I've been falsely accused, suspected. And for that matter, if intent counts for anything, I am as guilty as our little sister. I'd have done it myself if I could. In fact, I'd a blade ready the night we fetched him back. Only, I was crowded aside."

"But why?" I asked.

He laughed.

"Why? I am afraid of the bastard, that's why. For a long while, I had thought he was dead, and certainly hoped so—finally claimed by the dark powers he dealt with. How much do you really know about him, Corwin?"

"We had a long talk."

"And . . . ?"

"He admitted that he and Bleys and Fiona had formed a plan to claim the throne. They would see Bleys crowned, but each would share the real power. They had used the forces you referred to, to assure Dad's absence. Brand said that he had attempted to win Caine to their cause, but that Caine had instead gone to you and to Eric. The three of you then formed a similar cabal to seize power before they could, by placing Eric on the throne."

He nodded.

"The events are in order, but the reason is not. We did not want the throne, at least not that abruptly, nor at that time. We formed our group to oppose their group, because it had to be opposed to protect the throne. At first, the most we could persuade Eric to do was to assume a Protectorship. He was afraid he would quickly turn up dead if he saw himself crowned under those conditions. Then you turned up, with your very legitimate claim. We could not afford to let you press it at that time, because Brand's crowd was threatening out-and-out war. We felt they would be less inclined to make this move if the throne were already occupied. We could not have seated you, because you would have refused to be a puppet, a role you would have had to play since the game was already in progress and you were ignorant on too many fronts. So we persuaded Eric to take the risk and be crowned. That was how it happened."

"So when I did arrive he put out my eyes and threw me in the dungeon for laughs."

Julian turned away and looked back at the dead manticora.

"You are a fool," he finally said. "You were a tool from the very beginning. They used you to force our hand, and either way you lost. If that half-assed attack of Bleys's had somehow succeeded, you wouldn't have lasted long enough to draw a deep breath. If it failed, as it did, Bleys disappeared, as he did, leaving you with your life forfeit for attempted usurpation. You had served your purpose and you had to die. They left us small choice in the matter. By rights, we should have killed you—and you know it."

I bit my lip. There were many things I might say. But if he was telling something approximating the truth, he did have a point. And I did want to hear more.

"Eric," he said, "figured that your eyesight might eventually be restored— knowing the way we regenerate—given time. It was a very delicate situation. If Dad were to return, Eric could step down and justify all of his actions to anyone's satisfaction—except for killing you. That would have been too patent a move to ensure his own continued reign beyond the troubles of the moment. And I will tell you frankly that he simply wanted to imprison you and forget you."

"Then whose idea was the blinding?"

He was silent again for a long while. Then he spoke very softly, almost a whisper: "Hear me out, please. It was mine, and it may have saved your life. Any action taken against you had to be tantamount to death, or their faction would have tried for the real thing. You were no longer of any use to them, but alive and about you possessed the potentiality of becoming a danger at some future time. They could have used your Trump to contact you and kill you, or they could have used it to free you in order to sacrifice you in yet another move against Eric. Blinded, however, there was no need to slay you and you were of no use for anything else they might have in mind. It saved you by taking you out of the picture for a time, and it saved us from a more egregious act which might one day be held against us. As we saw it, there was no choice. It was the only thing we could do. There could be no show of leniency either, or we might be suspected of having some use for you ourselves. The moment you assumed any such semblance of value you would have been a dead man. The most we could do was look the other way whenever Lord Rein contrived to comfort you. That was all that could be done."

"I see," I said.

"Yes," he agreed, "you saw too soon. No one had guessed you would recover your sight that quickly, nor that you would be able to escape once you did. How did you manage it?"

"Does Macy's tell Gimbel's?" I said.

"Beg pardon?"

"I said—never mind. What do you know of Brand's imprisonment, then?"

He regarded me once more.

"All I know is that there was some sort of falling out within his group. I lack the particulars. For some reason, Bleys and Fiona were afraid to kill him and afraid to let him run loose. When we freed him from their compromise— imprisonment—Fiona was apparently more afraid of having him free."

"And you said you feared him enough to have made ready to kill him. Why now, after all this time, when all of this is history and the power has shifted again? He was weak, virtually helpless. What harm could he do now?"

He sighed.

"I do not understand the power that he possesses," he said, "but it is considerable. I know that he can travel through Shadow with his mind, that he can sit in a chair, locate what he seeks in Shadow, and then bring it to him by an act of will without moving from the chair; and he can travel through Shadow physically in a somewhat similar fashion. He lays his mind upon the place he would visit, forms a kind of mental doorway, and simply steps through. For that matter, I believe he can sometimes tell what people are thinking. It is almost as if he has himself become some sort of living Trump. I know these things because I have seen him do them. Near the end, when we had him under surveillance in the palace he had eluded us once in this fashion. This was the time he traveled to the shadow Earth and had you placed in Bedlam. After his recapture, one of us remained with him at all times. We did not yet know that he could summon things through Shadow, however. When he became aware that you had escaped your confinement, he summoned a horrid beast which attacked Caine, who was then his body-guard. Then he went to you once again. Bleys and Fiona apparently got hold of him shortly after that, before we could, and I did not see him again until that night in the library when we brought him back. I fear him because he has deadly powers which I do not understand."

"In such a case, I wonder how they managed to confine him at all?"

"Fiona has similar strengths, and I believe Bleys did also. Between the two of them, they could apparently annul most of Brand's power while they created a place where it would be inoperative."

"Not totally," I said. "He got a message to Random. In fact, he reached me once, weakly."

"Obviously not totally, then," he said. "Sufficiently, however. Until we broke through the defenses."

"What do you know of all their byplay with me—confining me, trying to kill me, saving me."

"That I do not understand," he said, "except that it was part of the power struggle within their own group. They had had a falling out amongst themselves, and one side or the other had some use for you. So, naturally, one side was trying to kill you while the other fought to preserve you. Ultimately, of course, Bleys got the most mileage out of you, in that attack he launched."

"But he was the one who tried to kill me, back on the shadow Earth," I said. "He was the one who shot out my tires."

"Oh?"

"Well, that is what Brand told me, but it jibes with all sorts of second-ary evidence."

He shrugged.

"I cannot help you on that," he said. "I simply do not know what was going on among them at that time."

"Yet you countenance Fiona in Amber," I said. "In fact, you are more than a little cordial to her whenever she is about."

"Of course," he said, smiling. "I have always been very fond of Fiona. She is certainly the loveliest, most civilized of us all. Pity Dad was always so dead-set against brother-sister marriages, as well you know. It bothered me that we had to be adversaries for so long as we were. Things returned pretty much to normal after Bleys's death, your imprisonment, and Eric's coronation, though. She accepted their defeat gracefully, and that was that. She was obviously as frightened at the prospect of Brand's return as I was."

"Brand told things differently," I said, "but then, of course, he would. For one thing, he claims that Bleys is still living, that he hunted him down with his Trump and knows that he is off in Shadow, training another force for another strike at Amber."

"I suppose this is possible," Julian said. "But we are more than adequately prepared, are we not?"

"He claims further that the strike will be a feint," I continued, "and that the real attack will then come direct from the Courts of Chaos, over the black road. He says that Fiona is off preparing the way for this right now."

He scowled.

"I hope he was simply lying," he said. "I would hate to see their group resurrected and at us again, this time with help from the dark direction. And I would hate to see Fiona involved."

"Brand claimed he was out of it himself, that he had seen the error of his ways—and suchlike penitent noises."

"Ha! I'd sooner trust that beast I just slew than take Brand at his word. I hope you've had the sense to keep him well guarded—though this might not be of much avail if he has his old powers back."

"But what game could he be playing now?"

"Either he has revived the old triumvirate, a thought I like not at all, or he has a new plan all his own. But mark me, he has a plan. He has never been satisfied to be a mere spectator at anything. He is always scheming. I'd take an oath he even plots in his sleep."

"Perhaps you are right," I said. "You see, there has been a new development, whether for good or ill, I cannot yet tell. I just had a fight with Gérard. He thinks I have done Brand some mischief. This is not the case, but I was in no position to prove my innocence. I was the last person I know of to see Brand, earlier today. Gérard visited his quarters a short time ago. He says the place is broken up, there are blood smears here and there, and Brand is missing. I don't know what to make of it."

"Neither do I. But I hope it means someone has done the job properly this time."

"Lord," I said, "it's tangled. I wish I had known all of these things before."

"There was never a proper time to tell you," he said, "until now. Certainly not when you were a prisoner and could still be reached, and after that you were gone for a long while. When you returned with your troops and your new weapons, I was uncertain as to your full intentions. Then things happened quickly and Brand was back again. It was too late. I had to get out to save my skin. I am strong here in Arden. Here, I can take anything he can throw at me. I have been maintaining the patrols at full battle force and awaiting word of Brand's death. I wanted to inquire of one of you whether he was still around. But I could not decide whom to ask, thinking myself still suspect should he have died. As soon as I did get word, though, should it prove he was still living, I was resolved to have a try at him myself. Now this . . . state of affairs . . . What are you going to do now, Corwin?"

"I am off to fetch the Jewel of Judgment from a place where I cached it in Shadow. There is a way it can be used to destory the black road. I intend to try it."

"How can this be done?"

"That is too long a story, for a horrible thought has just occurred to me."

"What is that?"

"Brand wants the Jewel. He was asking about it, and now— This power of his to find things in Shadow and fetch them back. How good is it?"

Julian looked thoughtful.

"He is hardly omniscient, if that is what you mean. You can find anything you want in Shadow the normal way we go about it—by traveling to it. According to Fiona, he just cuts out the footwork. It is therefore *an* object, not a particular object that he summons. Besides, that Jewel is a very strange item from everything Eric told me about it. I think Brand would have to go after it in person, once he finds out where it is."

"Then I must get on with my hellride. I have to beat him to it."

"I see you are riding Drum," Julian observed. "He is a good beast, a sturdy fellow. Been through many a hellride."

"Glad to hear that," I said. "What are *you* going to do now?"

"Get in touch with someone in Amber and get up to date on everything we haven't had a chance to talk about—Benedict, probably."

"No good," I said. "You will not be able to reach him. He is off to the Courts of Chaos. Try Gérard, and convince him I am an honorable man while you are about it."

"The redheads are the only magicians in this family, but I will try. . . . You *did* say the Courts of Chaos?"

"Yes, but again, the time is too valuable now."

"Of course. Get you gone. We will have our leisure later—I trust."

He reached out and clasped my arm. I glanced at the manticora, at the dogs seated in a circle about it.

"Thanks, Julian. I— You are a difficult man to understand."

"Not so. I think the Corwin I hated must have died centuries ago. Ride now, man! If Brand shows up around here, I'll nail his hide to a tree!"

He shouted an order to his dogs as I mounted, and they fell upon the carcass of the manticora, lapping at its blood and tearing out huge chunks and strips of flesh. As I rode past that strange, massive, manlike face, I saw that its eyes were still open, though glazed. They were blue, and death had not robbed them of a certain preternatural innocence. Either that, or the look was death's final gift—a senseless way of passing out ironies, if it was.

I took Drum back to the trail and began my hellride.

TEN

Moving along the trail at a gentle pace, clouds darkening the sky and Drum's whinny of memory or anticipation. . . . A turn to the left, and uphill. . . . The ground is brown, yellow, back to brown again. . . . The trees squat down, draw apart. . . . Grasses wave between them in the cool and rising breeze. . . . A quick fire in the sky. . . . A rumble shakes loose raindrops. . . .

Steep and rocky now. . . . The wind tugs at my cloak. . . . Up. . . . Up to where the rocks are streaked with silver and the trees have drawn their line. . . . The grasses, green fires, die down in the rain. . . . Up, to the craggy, sparkling, rain-washed heights, where the clouds rush and boil like a mud-gorged river at flood crest. . . . The rain stings like buckshot and the wind clears its throat to sing. . . . We rise and rise and the crest comes into view, like the head of a startled bull, horns guarding the trail. . . . Lightnings twist about their tips, dance between them. . . . The smell of ozone as we reach that place and rush on through, the rain suddenly blocked, the wind shunted away. . . .

Emerging on the farther side. . . . There is no rain, the air is still, the sky smoothed and darkened to a proper star-filled black. . . . Meteors cut and burn, cut and burn, cauterizing to afterimage scars, fading, fading. . . . Moons, cast like a handful of coins. . . . Three bright dimes, a dull quarter, a pair of pennies, one of them tarnished and scarred. . . . Down then, that long, winding way. . . . Hoof clops clear and metallic in the night air. . . . Somewhere, a catlike cough. . . . A dark shape crossing a lesser moon, ragged and swift. . . .

Downward. . . . The land drops away at either hand. . . . Darkness below. . . . Moving along the top of an infinitely high, curved wall, the way itself bright with moonlight. . . . The trail buckles, folds, grows transparent. . . . Soon it drifts, gauzy, filamentous, stars beneath as well as above. . . . Stars below on either side. . . . There is no land. . . . There is only the night, night and the thin, translucent trail I had to try to ride, to learn how it felt, against some future use. . . .

It is absolutely silent now, and the illusion of slowness attaches to every movement. . . . Shortly, the trail falls away, and we move as if swimming underwater at some enormous depth, the stars bright fish. . . . It is freedom, it is the power of the hellride that brings an elation, like yet unlike the recklessness that sometimes comes in battle, the boldness of a risky feat well learned, the rush of rightness following the finding of the poem's proper word. . . . It is these and the prospect itself, riding, riding, riding, from nowhere to nowhere perhaps, across and among the minerals and fires of the void, free of earth and air and water. . . .

We race a great meteor, we touch upon its bulk. . . . Speeding across its pitted surface, down, around, then up again. . . . It stretches into a great plain, it lightens, it yellows. . . .

It is sand, sand now beneath our movement. . . . The stars fade out as the darkness is diluted to a morning full of sunrise. . . . Swaths of shade ahead, desert trees within them. . . . Ride for the dark. . . . Crashing through. . . . Bright birds burst forth, complain, resettle. . . .

Among the thickening trees. . . . Darker the ground, narrower the way. . . . Palm fronds shrink to hand size, barks darken. . . . A twist to the right, a widening of the way. . . . Our hoofs striking sparks from cobblestones. . . . The lane enlarges, becomes a tree-lined street. . . . Tiny row houses flash by. . . . Bright shutters, marble steps, painted screens, set back beyond flagged walks. . . . Passing, a horse-drawn cart, loaded with fresh vegetables. . . . Human pedestrians turning to stare. . . . A small buzz of voices. . . .

On. . . . Passing beneath a bridge. . . . Coursing the stream till it widens to river, taking it down to the sea. . . .

Thudding along the beach beneath a lemon sky, blue clouds scudding. . . . The salt, the wrack, the shells, the smooth anatomy of driftwood. . . . White spray off the lime-colored sea. . . .

Racing, to where the place of waters ends at a terrace. . . . Mounting, each step crumbling and roaring down behind, losing its identity, joined with the boom of the surf. . . . Up, up to the flattopped, tree-grown plain, a golden city shimmering, miragelike, at its end. . . .

The city grows, darkens beneath a shadowy umbrella, its gray towers stretch upward, glass and metal flashing light through the murk. . . . The towers begin to sway. . . .

The city falls in upon itself, soundlessly, as we pass. . . . Towers topple, dust boils, rises, is pinked by some lower glow. . . . A gentle noise, as of a snuffed candle, drifting by. . . .

A dust storm, quickly falling, giving place to fog. . . . Through it, the sounds of automobile horns. . . . A drift, a brief lift, a break in the gray-white, pearl-white, shifting. . . . Our hoofprints on a shoulder of highway. . . . To the right, endless rows of unmoving vehicles. . . . Pearl-white, gray-white, drifting again. . . .

Directionless shrieks and wailings. . . . Random flashes of light. . . .

Rising once more. . . . The fogs lower and ebb. . . . Grass, grass, grass. . . . Clear now the sky, and delicate blue. . . . A sun racing to set. . . . Birds. . . . A cow in the field, chewing, staring and chewing. . . .

Leaping a wooden fence to ride a country road. . . . A sudden chill beyond the hill. . . . The grasses are dry and snow's on the ground. . . . Tin-roofed farmhouse atop a rise, curl of smoke above it. . . .

On. . . . The hills grow up, the sun rolls down, darkness dragged behind. . . . A sprinkle of stars. . . . Here a house, set far back. . . . There another, long driveway wound among old trees. . . . Headlights. . . .

Off to the side of the road. . . . Draw rein and let it pass. . . .

I wiped my brow, dusted my shirt front and sleeves. I patted Drum's neck. The oncoming vehicle slowed as it neared me, and I could see the driver staring. I gave the reins a gentle movement and Drum began walking. The car braked to a halt and the driver called something after me, but I kept going. Moments later, I heard him drive off.

It was country road for a time after that. I traveled at an easy pace, passing familiar landmarks, recalling other times. A few miles later and I came to another road, wider and better. I turned there, staying off on the shoulder to the right. The temperature continued to drop, but the cold air had a good clean taste to it. A sliced moon shone above the hills to my left. There were a few small clouds passing overhead, touched to the moon's quarter with a soft, dusty light. There was very little wind; an occasional stirring of branches, no more. After a time, I came to a series of dips in the road, telling me I was almost there.

A curve and a couple more dips. . . . I saw the boulder beside the driveway, I read my address upon it.

I drew rein then and looked up the hill. There was a station wagon in the driveway and a light on inside the house. I guided Drum off the road and across a field into a stand of trees. I tethered him behind a pair of evergreens, rubbed his neck, and told him I would not be long.

I returned to the road. No cars in sight. I crossed over and walked up the far side of the driveway, passing behind the station wagon. The only light in the house was in the living room, off to the right. I made my way around the left side of the house to the rear.

I halted when I reached the patio, looking around. Something was wrong.

The back yard was changed. A pair of decaying lawn chairs which had been leaning against a dilapidated chicken coop I had never bothered to remove were gone. So, for that matter, was the chicken coop. They had been present the last time I had passed this way. All of the dead tree limbs which had previously been strewn about, as well as a rotting mass of them I had long ago heaped to cut for firewood, were also gone.

The compost heap was missing.

I moved to the space where it had been. All that was there was an irregular patch of bare earth of the approximate shape of the heap itself.

But I had discovered in attuning myself to the Jewel that I could make myself feel its presence. I closed my eyes for a moment and tried to do so.

Nothing.

I looked again, searching carefully, but there was no tell-tale glitter anywhere in sight. Not that I had really expected to see anything, not if I could not feel it nearby.

There had been no curtains in the lighted room. Studying the house now, I saw that none of the windows had curtains, shades, shutters, or blinds. Therefore . . .

I passed around the other end of the house. Approaching the first lighted window, I glanced in quickly. Dropcloths covered much of the floor. A man in cap and coveralls was painting the far wall.

Of course.

I had asked Bill to sell the place. I had signed the necessary papers while a patient in the local clinic, when I had been projected back to my old home—probably by some action of the Jewel—on the occasion of my stabbing. That would have been several weeks ago, local time, using the Amber to shadow Earth conversion factor of approximately two and a half to one and allowing for the eight days the Courts of Chaos had cost me in Amber. Bill, of course, had gone ahead on my request. But the place had been in bad shape, abandoned as it had been for a number of years, vandalized. . . . It needed some new windowpanes, some roofing work, new guttering, painting, sanding, buffing. And there had been a lot of trash to haul away, outside as well as inside. . . .

I turned away and walked down the front slope to the road, recalling my last passage this way, half-delirious, on my hands and knees, blood leaking from my side. It had been much colder that night and there had been snow on the ground and in the air. I passed near the spot where I'd sat, trying to flag down a car with a pillow case. The memory was slightly blurred, but I still recalled the ones that had passed me by.

I crossed the road, made my way through the field to the trees. Unhitching Drum, I mounted.

"We've some more riding ahead," I told him. "Not too far this time."

We headed back to the road and started along it, continuing on past my house. If I had not told Bill to go ahead and sell the place, the compost heap would still have been there, the Jewel would still have been there. I could be on my way back to Amber with the ruddy stone hung about my neck, ready to have a try at what had to be done. Now, now I had to go looking for it, when I'd a feeling time was beginning to press once again. At least, I had a favorable ratio here with respect to its passage in Amber. I clucked at Drum and shook the reins. No sense wasting it, even so.

A half hour, and I was into town, riding down a quiet street in a residential area, houses all about me. The lights were on at Bill's place. I turned up his driveway. I left Drum in his back yard.

Alice answered my knock, stared a moment, then said, "My God! Carl!"

Minutes later, I was seated in the living room with Bill, a drink on the table to my right. Alice was out in the kitchen, having made the mistake of asking me whether I wanted something to eat.

Bill studied me as he lit his pipe.

"Your ways of coming and going still tend to be colorful," he said.

I smiled.

"Expediency is all," I said.

"That nurse at the clinic . . . scarcely anyone believed her story."

"Scarcely anyone?"

"The minority I refer to is, of course, myself."

"What was her story?"

"She claimed that you walked to the center of the room, became two-dimensional, and just faded away, like the old soldier that you are, with a rainbowlike accompaniment."

"Glaucoma can cause the rainbow symptom. She ought to have her eyes checked."

"She did," he said. "Nothing wrong."

"Oh. Too bad. The next thing that comes to mind is neurological."

"Come on, Carl. She's all right. You know that."

I smiled and took a sip of my drink.

"And you," he said, "you look like a certain playing card I once commented on. Complete with sword. What's going on, Carl?"

"It's still complicated," I said. "Even more than the last time we talked."

"Which means you can't give me that explanation yet?"

I shook my head.

"You have won an all-expense tour of my homeland, when this is over," I said, "if I still have a homeland then. Right now, time is doing terrible things."

"What can I do to help you?"

"Information, please. My old house. Who is the guy you have fixing the place up?"

"Ed Wellen. Local contractor. You know him, I think. Didn't he put in a shower for you, or something?"

"Yes, yes he did. . . . I remember."

"He's expanded quite a bit. Bought some heavy equipment. Has a number of fellows working for him now. I handled his incorporation."

"Do you know who he's got working at my place—now?"

"Offhand, no. But I can find out in just a minute." He moved his hand to rest on the telephone on the side table. "Shall I give him a ring?"

"Yes," I said, "but there is a little more to it than that. There is only one thing in which I am really interested. There was a compost heap in the back yard. It was there the last time I passed this way. It is gone now. I have to find out what became of it."

He cocked his head to the right and grinned around his pipe.

"You serious?" he finally said.

"Sure as death," I said. "I hid something in that heap when I crawled by, decorating the snow with my precious bodily fluids. I've got to have it back now."

"Just what is it?"

"A ruby pendant."

"Priceless, I suppose."

"You're right."

He nodded, slowly.

"If it were anyone else, I would suspect a practical joke," he said. "A treasure in a compost heap. . . . Family heirloom?"

"Yes. Forty or fifty carats. Simple setting. Heavy chain."

He removed his pipe and whistled softly.

"Mind if I ask why you put it there?"

"I'd be dead now if I hadn't."

"Pretty good reason."

He reached for the phone again.

"We've had some action on the house already," he remarked. "Pretty good, since I haven't advertised yet. Fellow'd heard from someone who'd heard from someone else. I took him over this morning. He's thinking about it. We may move it pretty quick."

He began to dial.

"Wait," I said. "Tell me about him."

He cradled the phone, looked up.

"Thin guy," he said. "Redhead. Had a beard. Said he was an artist. Wants a place in the country."

"Son of a bitch!" I said, just as Alice came into the room with a tray.

She made a *tsking* sound and smiled as she delivered it to me.

"Just a couple hamburgers and some leftover salad," she said. "Nothing to get excited about."

"Thank you. I was getting ready to eat my horse. I'd have felt bad afterward."

"I don't imagine he'd have been too happy about it himself. Enjoy," she said, and returned to the kitchen.

"Was the compost heap still there when you took him over?" I asked.

He closed his eyes and furrowed his brow.

"No," he said after a moment. "The yard was already clear."

"That's something, anyway," I said, and I began eating.

He made the call, and he talked for several minutes. I got the drift of things from his end of the conversation, but I listened to the entire thing after he had hung up, while I finished the food and washed it down with what was left in my glass.

"He hated to see good compost go to waste," Bill said. "So he pitched the heap into his pickup just the other day and took it out to his farm. He dumped it next to a plot he intends to cultivate, and he has not had a chance to spread it yet. Says he did not notice any jewelry, but then he could easily have missed it."

I nodded.

"If I can borrow a flashlight, I had better get moving."

"Sure. I will drive you out," he said.

"I do not want to be parted from my horse at this point."

"Well, you will probably want a rake, and a shovel or a pitchfork. I can drive them out and meet you there, if you know where the place is."

"I know where Ed's place is. He must have tools, though."

Bill shrugged and smiled.

"All right," I said. "Let me use your bathroom, and then we had better get moving."

"You seemed as if you knew the prospective buyer."

I put the tray aside and rose to my feet.

"You heard of him last as Brandon Corey."

"The guy who pretended to be your brother and got you committed?"

" 'Pretended' hell! He is my brother. No fault of mine, though. Excuse me."

"He was there."

"Where?"

"Ed's place, this afternoon. At least a bearded redhead was."

"Doing what?"

"Said he was an artist. Said he wanted permission to set up his easel and paint in one of the fields."

"And Ed let him?"

"Yes, of course. Thought it was a great idea. That is why he told me about it. Wanted to brag."

"Get the stuff. I will meet you there."

"Right."

The second thing I took out in the bathroom was my Trumps. I had to reach someone in Amber soonest, someone strong enough to stop him. But who? Benedict was on his way to the Courts at Chaos, Random was off looking for his son, I had just parted with Gérard on somewhat less than amicable terms. I wished that I had a Trump for Ganelon.

I decided that I would have to try Gérard.

I drew forth his card, performed the proper mental maneuvers. Moments later, I had contact.

"Corwin!"

"Just listen, Gérard! Brand is alive, if that is any consolation. I'm damn sure of that. This is important. Life and death. You've got to do something—fast!"

His expressions had changed rapidly while I had spoken—anger, surprise, interest . . .

"Go ahead," he said.

"Brand could be coming back very soon. In fact, he may already be in Amber. You haven't seen him yet, have you?"

"No."

"He must be stopped from walking the Pattern."

"I do not understand. But I can post a guard outside the chamber of the Pattern."

"Put the guard inside the chamber. He has strange ways of coming and going now. Terrible things may happen if he walks the Pattern."

"I will watch it personally then. What is happening?"

"No time now. Here is the next thing: Is Llewella back in Rebma?"

"Yes, she is."

"Get hold of her with her Trump. She's got to warn Moire that the Pattern in Rebma has to be guarded also."

"How serious is this, Corwin?"

"It could be the end of everything," I said. "I have to go now."

I broke the contact and headed for the kitchen and the back door, stopping only long enough to thank Alice and say good night. If Brand had got hold of the Jewel and attuned himself to it, I was not certain what he would do, but I had a pretty strong hunch.

I mounted Drum and turned him toward the road. Bill was already backing out of the driveway.

ELEVEN

I cut through fields in many places where Bill had to follow the roads, so I was not all that far behind him. When I drew up, he was talking with Ed, who was gesturing toward the southwest.

As I dismounted, Ed was studying Drum.

"Nice horse, that," he said.

"Thanks."

"You've been away."

"Yes."

We shook hands.

"Good to see you again. I was just telling Bill that I don't really know how long that artist stayed around. I just figured he would go away when it got dark, and I didn't pay too much attention. Now, if he was really looking for something of yours and knew about the compost heap, he could still be out there for all I know. I'll get my shotgun, if you like, and go with you."

"No," I said, "thanks. I think I know who it was. The gun will not be necessary. We'll just walk over and do a little poking around."

"Okay," he said. "Let me come along and give you a hand."

"You don't have to do that," I said.

"How about your horse, then? What say I give him a drink and something to eat, clean him up a bit?"

"I'm sure he'd be grateful. I know I would."

"What's his name?"

"Drum."

He approached Drum and began making friends with him.

"Okay," he said. "I'll be back in the barn for a while. If you need me for anything, just holler."

"Thanks."

I got the tools out of Bill's car and he carried the electric lantern, leading me off to the southwest where Ed had been pointing earlier.

As we crossed the field, I followed the beam of Bill's light, searching for the heap. When I saw what might be the remains of one, I drew a deep breath, involuntarily. Someone must have been at it, the way the clods were strewn about. The mass would not have been dumped from a truck to fall in such a dispersed fashion.

Still . . . the fact that someone had looked did not mean he had located what he had been seeking.

"What do you think?" Bill said.

"I don't know," I told him, lowering the tools to the ground and approaching the largest aggregate in sight. "Give me some light here."

I scanned what remained of the heap, then fetched a rake and began taking it apart. I broke each clod and spread it upon the ground, running the tines through it. After a time, Bill set the lantern at a good angle and moved to help me.

"I've got a funny feeling . . ." he said.

"So do I."

". . . that we may be too late."

We kept pulverizing and spreading, pulverizing and spreading. . . .

I felt the tingle of a familiar presence. I straightened and waited. Contact came moments later.

"Corwin!"

"Here, Gérard."

"What'd you say?" said Bill.

I raised my hand to silence him and gave my attention to Gérard. He stood in shadow at the bright beginning of the Pattern, leaning upon his great blade.

"You were right," he said. "Brand did show up here, just a moment ago. I am not sure how he got in. He stepped out of the shadows off to the left, there." He gestured. "He looked at me for a moment, then turned around and walked back. He did not answer when I hailed him. So I turned up the lantern, but he was nowhere in sight. He just disappeared. What do you want me to do now?"

"Was he wearing the Jewel of Judgment?"

"I could not tell. I only had sight of him for a moment, in this bad light."

"Are they watching the Pattern in Rebma now?"

"Yes. Llewella's alerted them."

"Good. Stay on guard, then. I will be in touch again."

"All right. Corwin—about what happened earlier . . ."

"Forget it."

"Thanks. That Ganelon is one tough fellow."

"Indeed," I said. "Stay awake."

His image faded as I released the contact, but a strange thing happened then. The sense of contact, the path, remained with me, objectless, open, like a switched-on radio not tuned to anything.

Bill was looking at me peculiarly.

"Carl, what is happening?"

"I don't know. Wait a minute."

Suddenly, there was contact again, though not with Gérard. She must have been trying to reach me while my attention was diverted.

"Corwin, it is important . . ."

"Go ahead, Fi."

"You will not find what you are looking for there. Brand has it."

"I was beginning to suspect as much."

"We have to stop him. I do not know how much you know—"

"Neither do I any more," I said, "but I have the Pattern in Amber and the one in Rebma under guard. Gérard just told me that Brand appeared at the one in Amber, but was scared off."

She nodded her small, fine-featured face. Her red tresses were unusually disarrayed. She looked tired.

"I am aware of this," she said. "I have him under surveillance. But you have forgotten another possibility."

"No," I said. "According to my calculations, Tir-na Nog'th should not be attainable yet—"

"That is not what I was referring to. He is headed for the primal Pattern itself."

"To attune the Jewel?"

"The first time through," she said.

"To walk it, he would have to pass through the damaged area. I gather that is more than a little difficult."

"So you do know about it," she said. "Good. That saves time. The dark area would not trouble him the way it would another of us. He has come to terms with that darkness. We must stop him, now."

"Do you know any short cuts to that place?"

"Yes. Come to me. I will take you there."

"Just a minute. I want Drum with me."

"What for?"

"No telling. That is why I want him."

"Very well. Then bring me through. We can as easily depart from there as from here."

I extended my hand. In a moment, I held hers. She stepped forward.

"Lord!" said Bill, drawing back. "You were giving me doubts about your sanity, Carl. Now it's mine I wonder about. She—she's on one of the cards, too, isn't she?"

"Yes. Bill, this is my sister Fiona. Fiona, this is Bill Roth, a very good friend."

Fi extended her hand and smiled, and I left them there while I went back to fetch Drum. A few minutes later, I led him forth.

"Bill," I said, "I am sorry to have wasted your time. My brother has the thing. We are going after him now. Thanks for helping me."

I shook his hand. He said, "Corwin." I smiled.

"Yes, that is my name."

"We have been talking, your sister and I. Not much I could learn in a few minutes, but I know it is dangerous. So good luck. I still want the whole story one day."

"Thanks," I said. "I will try to see that you get it."

I mounted, leaned down, and drew Fiona up before me.

"Good night, Mr. Roth," she said. Then, to me, "Start riding, slowly, across the field."

I did.

"Brand says you are the one who stabbed him," I said, as soon as we had gone far enough to feel alone.

"That's right."

"Why?"

"To avoid all this."

"I talked with him for a long while. He claimed it was originally you, Bleys, and himself, together in a scheme to seize power."

"That is correct."

"He told me he had approached Caine, trying to win him to your side, but that Caine would have none of it, that Caine had passed the word along to Eric and Julian. And this led to their forming their own group, to block your way to the throne."

"That is basically correct. Caine had ambitions of his own—long-term ones—but ambitions nevertheless. He was in no position to pursue them, however. So he decided that if his lot was to be a lesser one, he would rather serve it under Eric than under Bleys. I can see his point, too."

"He also claimed that the three of you had a deal going with the powers at the end of the black road, in the Courts of Chaos."

"Yes," she said, "we did."

"You use the past tense."

"For myself and for Bleys, yes."

"That is not the way Brand tells it."

"He wouldn't."

"He said you and Bleys wanted to continue exploiting that alliance, but that he had had a change of heart. Because of this, he claims you turned on him and imprisoned him in that tower."

"Why didn't we just kill him?"

"I give up. Tell me."

"He was too dangerous to be allowed his freedom, but we could not kill him either because he held something vital."

"What?"

"With Dworkin gone, Brand was the only one who knew how to undo the damage he had done to the primal Pattern."

"You had a long time to get that information out of him."

"He possesses unbelievable resources."

"Then why did you stab him?"

"I repeat, to avoid all this. If it became a question of his freedom or his death, it were better he died. We would have to take our chances on figuring the method of repairing the Pattern."

"This being the case, why did you consent to cooperate in bringing him back?"

"First, I was not co-operating, I was trying to impede the attempt. But there were too many trying too hard. You got through to him in spite of me. Second, I had to be on hand to try to kill him in the event you succeeded. Too bad things worked out the way they did."

"You say that you and Bleys had second thoughts about the alliance, but that Brand did not?"

"Yes."

"How did your second thoughts affect your desire for the throne?"

"We thought we could manage it without any additional outside help."

"I see."

"Do you believe me?"

"I'm afraid that I am beginning to."

"Turn here."

I entered a cleft in a hillside. The way was narrow and very dark, with only a small band of stars above us. Fiona had been manipulating Shadow while we had talked, leading us from Ed's field downward, into a misty, moorlike place, then up again, to a clear and rocky trail among mountains. Now, as we moved through the dark defile, I felt her working with Shadow again. The air was cool but not cold. The blackness to our left and our right was absolute, giving the illusion of enormous depths, rather than nearby rock cloaked in shadow. This impression was reinforced, I suddenly realized, by the fact that Drum's hoofbeats were not producing any echoes, aftersounds, overtones.

"What can I do to gain your trust?" she said.

"That's asking quite a bit."

She laughed.

"Let me rephrase it. What can I do to convince you I am telling the truth?"

"Just answer one question."

"What?"

"Who shot out my tires?"

She laughed again.

"You've figured it out, haven't you?"

"Maybe. You tell me."

"Brand," she said. "He had failed in his effort to destroy your memory, so he decided he had better do a more thorough job."

"The version I had of the story was that Bleys had done the shooting and left me in the lake, that Brand had arrived in time to drag me out and save my life. In fact, the police report seemed to indicate something to that effect."

"Who called the police?" she asked.

"They had it listed as an anonymous call, but—"

"Bleys called them. He couldn't reach you in time to save you, once he realized what was happening. He hoped that they could. Fortunately, they did."

"What do you mean?"

"Brand did not drag you out of the wreck. You did it yourself. He waited around to be certain you were dead, and you surfaced and pulled yourself ashore. He went down and was checking you over, to decide whether you would die if he just left you there or whether he should throw you back in again. The police arrived about then and he had to clear out. We caught up with him shortly afterward and were able to subdue him and imprison him in the tower. That took a lot of doing. Later, I contacted Eric and told him what had happened. He then ordered Flora to put you in the other place and see that you were held until after his coronation."

"It fits," I said. "Thanks."

"What does it fit?"

"I was only a small-town GP in simpler times than these, and I never had much to do with psychiatric cases. But I do know that you don't give a person electroshock therapy to restore memories. EST generally does just the opposite. It destroys some of the short-term ones. My suspicions began to stir when I learned that that was what Brand had had done to me. So I came up with my own hypothesis. The auto wreck did not restore my memories, and neither did the EST. I had finally begun recovering them naturally, not as the result of any particular trauma. I must have done something or said something to indicate that this was occurring. Word of it somehow got to Brand and he decided that this would not be a good thing to have happen at that time. So he journeyed to my shadow and managed to get me committed and subjected to treatment which he hoped would wipe out those things I had recently recovered. This was just partly successful, in that its only lasting effect was to fuzz me up for the few days surrounding the sessions. The accident may have contributed, too. But when I escaped from Porter and lived through his attempt to kill me, the process of recovery continued after I regained consciousness in Greenwood and left the place. I was remembering more and more when I was staying at Flora's. The recovery was accelerated by Random's taking me to Rebma, where I walked the Pattern. If this had not occurred, however, I am convinced now that it would all have come back, anyway. It might have taken somewhat longer, but I had broken through and the remembering was an ongoing process, coming faster and faster near the end. So I concluded that Brand was trying to sabotage me, and that is what fits the things you just told me."

The band of stars had narrowed, and it finally vanished above us. We advanced through what seemed a totally black tunnel now, with perhaps the tiniest flickering of light a great distance ahead of us.

"Yes," she said in the darkness before me, "you guessed correctly. Brand was afraid of you. He claimed he had seen your return one night in Tir-na Nog'th, to the undoing of all our plans. I paid him no heed at the time, for I was not even aware you still lived. It must have been then that he set out to find you. Whether he divined your whereabouts by some arcane means or simply saw it in Eric's mind, I do not know. Probably the latter. He is occasionally capable of such a feat. However he located you, you now know the rest."

"It was Flora's presence in that place and her strange liasion with Eric that first made him suspicious. Or so he said. Not that it matters, now. What do you propose doing with him if we get our hands on him?"

She chuckled.

"You are wearing your blade," she said.

"Brand told me, not all that long ago, that Bleys is still alive. Is this true?"

"Yes."

"Then why am I here, rather than Bleys?"

"Bleys is not attuned to the Jewel. You are. You interact with it at near distances, and it will attempt to preserve your life if you are in imminent danger of losing it. The risk, therefore, is not as great," she said. Then, moments later, "Don't take it for granted, though. A swift stroke can still beat its reaction. You can die in its presence."

The light ahead grew larger, brighter, but there were no drafts, sounds, or smells from that direction. Advancing, I thought of the layers upon layers of explanations I had received since my return, each with its own complex of motivations, justifications for what had happened while I was away, for what had happened since, for what was happening now. The emotions, the plans, the feelings, the objectives I had seen swirled like floodwater through the city of facts I was slowly erecting on the grave of my other self, and though an act is an act, in the best Steinian tradition, each wave of interpretation that broke upon me shifted the position of one or more things I had thought safely anchored, and by this brought about an alteration of the whole, to the extent that all of life seemed almost a shifting interplay of Shadow about the Amber of some never to be attained truth. Still, I could not deny that I knew more now than I had several years earlier, that I was closer to the heart of matters than I had been before, that the entire action in which I had been caught up upon my return seemed now to be sweeping toward some final resolution. And what did I want? A chance to find out what was right and a chance to act on it! I laughed. Who is ever granted the first, let alone the second of these? A workable approximation of truth, then. That would be enough. . . . And a chance to swing my blade a few times in the right direction: The highest compensation I could receive from a one o'clock world for the changes wrought since noon. I laughed again and made sure my blade was loose in the sheath.

"Brand said that Bleys had raised another army—" I began.

"Later," she said, "later. There is no more time."

And she was right. The light had grown large, become a circular opening. It had approached at a rate out of proportion to our advance, as though the tunnel itself were contracting. It seemed to be daylight that was rushing in through what I chose to regard as the cave mouth.

"All right," I said, and moments later we reached the opening and passed through it.

I blinked my eyes as we emerged. To my left was the sea, which seemed to merge with the same-colored sky. The golden sun which floated/hung above/within it, bounced beams of brilliance from all directions. Behind me, now, there was nothing but rock. Our passage to this place had vanished without a sign. Not too far below and before me—perhaps a hundred feet distant—lay the primal Pattern. A figure was negotiating the second of its outer arcs, his attention so confined by this activity that he had apparently not yet noted our presence. A flash of red as he took a turn: the Jewel, hanging now from his neck as it had hung from mine, from Eric's, from Dad's. The figure, of course, was Brand's.

I dismounted. I looked up at Fiona, small and distraught, and I placed Drum's reins in her hand.

"Any advice, other than to go after him?" I whispered.

She shook her head.

Turning then, I drew Grayswandir and strode forward.

"Good luck," she said softly.

As I walked toward the Pattern, I saw the long chain leading from the cave mouth to the now still form of the griffin Wixer. Wixer's head lay on the ground several paces to the left of his body. Body and head both leaked a normal-colored blood upon the stone.

As I approached the beginning of the Pattern, I did a quick calculation. Brand had already taken several turns about the general spiral of the design. He was approximately two and a half laps into it. If we were only separated by one winding, I could reach him with my blade once I achieved a position paralleling his own. The going, however, got rougher the further one penetrated the design. Consequently, Brand was moving at a steadily decreasing pace. So it would be close. I did not have to catch him. I just had to pick up a lap and a half and obtain a position across from him.

I placed my foot upon the Pattern and moved forward, as fast as I was able. The blue sparks began about my feet as I rushed through the first curve against the rising resistance. The sparks grew quickly. My hair was beginning to rise when I hit the First Veil, and the crackling of the sparks was quite audible now. I pushed on against the pressure of the Veil, wondering whether Brand had noticed me yet, unable to afford the distraction of a glance in his direction just then. I met the resistance with increased force, and several steps later I was through the Veil and moving more easily again.

I looked up. Brand was just emerging from the terrible Second Veil, blue sparks as high as his waist. He was grinning a grin of resolve and triumph as he pulled free and took a clear step forward. Then he saw me.

The grin went away and he hesitated, a point in my favor. You never stop on the Pattern if you can help it. If you do, it costs a lot of extra energy to get moving again.

"You are too late!" he called out.

I did not answer him. I just kept going. Blue fires fell from the Pattern tracery along Grayswandir's length.

"You will not make it through the black," he said.

I kept going. The dark area was just ahead of me now. I was glad that it had not occurred over one of the more difficult portions of the Pattern this time around. Brand moved forward and slowly began his movement toward the Grand Curve. If I could catch him there, it would be no contest. He would not have the strength or the speed to defend himself.

As I approached the damaged portion of the Pattern, I recalled the means by which Ganelon and I had cut the black road on our flight from Avalon. I had succeeded in breaking the power of the road by holding the image of the Pattern in my mind as we had gone across. Now, of course, I had the Pattern itself all around me, and the distance was not nearly so great. While my first thought had been that Brand was simply trying to rattle me with his threat, it occurred to me that the force of the dark place might well be much stronger here at its source. As I came up to it, Grayswandir blazed with a sudden intensity which outshone its previous light. On an impulse, I touched its point to the edge of the blackness, at the place where the Pattern ended.

Grayswandir clove to the blackness and could not be raised above it. I continued forward, and my blade sliced the area before me, sliding ahead in what seemed an approximation of the original tracery. I followed. The sun seemed to darken as I trod the dark ground. I was suddenly conscious of my heartbeat, and perspiration formed on my brow. A grayish cast fell over everything. The world seemed to dim, the Pattern to fade. It seemed it would be easy to step amiss in this place, and I was not certain whether the result would be the same as a misstep within the intact portions of the Pattern. I did not want to find out.

I kept my eyes low, following the line Grayswandir was inscribing before me, the blade's blue fire now the only thing of color left to the world. Right foot, left foot . . .

Then suddenly I was out of it and Grayswandir swung free in my hand once again, the fires partly diminished, whether by contrast with the reilluminated prospect or for some other reasons I did not know.

Looking about, I saw that Brand was approaching the Grand Curve. As for me, I was working my way toward the Second Veil. We would both be involved in the strenuous efforts these entailed in a few more minutes. The Grand Curve is more difficult, more prolonged than the Second Veil, however. I should be free and moving more quickly again before he worked his way through his barrier. Then I would have to cross the damaged area another time. He might be free by then, but he would be moving more slowly than I would, for he would be into the area where the going becomes even more difficult.

A steady static arose with each step that I took, and a tingling sensation permeated my entire body. The sparks rose to midthigh as I moved. It was like striding through a field of electric wheat. My hair was at least partly risen by then. I could feel its stirring. I glanced back once to see Fiona, still mounted, unmoving, watching.

I pressed ahead to the Second Veil.

Angles . . . short, sharp turns. . . . The force rose and rose against me, so that all of my attention, all of my strength, was now occupied in striving against it. There came again that familiar sense of timelessness, as though this was all I had ever done, all that I ever would do. And will . . . a focusing of desire to such an intensity that everything else was excluded . . . Brand, Fiona, Amber, my own identity. . . . The sparks rose to even greater heights as I struggled, turned, labored, each step requiring more effort than the previous one.

I pushed through. Right into the black area again.

Reflexively, I moved Grayswandir down and ahead once more. Again, the grayness, the monochrome fog, cut by the blue of my blade opening the way before me like a surgical incision.

When I emerged into normal light, I sought Brand. He was still in the western quadrant, struggling with the Grand Curve, about two thirds of the way through it. If I pushed hard, I might be able to catch him just as he was coming out of it. I threw all of my strength into moving as quickly as possible.

As I made it to the north end of the Pattern and into the curve leading back, it struck me suddenly what I was about to do.

I was rushing to spill more blood upon the Pattern.

If it came to a simple choice between further damage to the Pattern and Brand's destroying it utterly, then I knew what I had to do. Yet, I felt there had to be another way. Yes . . .

I slowed my pace just a trifle. It was going to be a matter of timing. His passage was a lot rougher than mine just then, so I had an edge in that respect. My entire new strategy involved arranging our encounter at just the right point. Ironically, at that moment, I recalled Brand's concern for his rug. The problem of keeping this place clean was a lot trickier, though.

He was nearing the end of the Grand Curve, and I paced him while calculating the distance to the blackness. I had decided to let him do his bleeding over the area which had already been damaged. The only disadvantage I seemed to possess was that I would be situated to Brand's right. To minimize the benefit this would give him when we crossed blades, I would have to remain somewhat to the rear.

Brand struggled and advanced, all of his movements in slow motion. I struggled too, but not as hard. I kept the pace. I wondered as I went, about the Jewel, about the affinity we had shared since the attunement. I could feel its presence, there to my left and ahead, even though I could not see it now upon Brand's breast. Would it really act to save me across that distance should Brand gain the upper hand in our coming conflict? Feeling its presence, I could almost believe that it would. It had torn me from one assailant and found, somehow, within my mind, a traditional place of safety—my own bed—and had transported me there. Feeling it now, almost seeing the way before Brand was through it, I felt some assurance that it would attempt to function on my behalf once again. Recalling Fiona's words, however, I was determined not to rely on it. Still, I considered its other functions, speculated upon my ability to operate it without contact . . .

Brand had almost completed the Grand Curve. I reached out from some level of my being and made contact with the Jewel. Laying my will upon it, I called for a storm of the red tornado variety which had destroyed Iago. I did not know whether I could control that particular phenomenon in this particular place, but I called for it nevertheless and directed it toward Brand. Nothing happened immediately, though I felt the Jewel functioning to achieve something. Brand came to the end, offered a final exertion, and passed from the Grand Curve.

I was right there behind him.

He knew it, too—somehow. His blade was out the instant the pressure was off, he gained a couple feet faster than I thought he could, got his left foot ahead of him, turned his body, and met my gaze over the lines of our blades.

"Damned if you didn't make it," he said, touching the tip of my blade with his own. "You would never have gotten here this soon if it weren't for the bitch on the horse, though."

"Nice way to talk about our sister," I said, feinting and watching him move to parry.

We were hampered, in that neither of us could lunge without departing the Pattern. I was further hampered in not wanting to make him bleed, yet. I faked a stop thrust and he drew back, sliding his left foot along the design to his rear. He withdrew his right then, stamped it, and tried a head cut without preliminaries. Damn it! I parried and then riposted by pure reflex. I did not want to catch him with the chest cut I had thrown back at him, but the tip of Grayswandir traced an arc beneath his sternum. I heard a humming in the air above us. I could not afford to take my eyes off Brand, though. He glanced downward and backed some more. Good. A red line now decorated his shirt front where my cut had taken him. So far, the material seemed to be absorbing it. I stamped, feinted, thrust, parried, stop thrust, bound, and unbound—everything I could think of to keep him retreating. I had the psychological edge on him in that I had the greater reach and we both knew I could do more things with it, more quickly. Brand was nearing the dark area. Just a few more paces. . . . I heard a sound like a single bell chime, followed by a great roaring. A shadow suddenly fell upon us, as though a cloud had just occluded the sun.

Brand glanced up. I think I could have gotten him just then, but he was still a couple of feet too far from the target area.

He recovered immediately and glared at me.

"Damn you, Corwin! That's yours, isn't it?" he cried, and then he attacked, discarding what caution he still possessed.

Unfortunately, I was in a bad position, as I had been edging up on him, preparing to press him the rest of the way back. I was exposed and slightly off-balance. Even as I parried, I realized it would not be sufficient, and I twisted and fell back.

I struggled to keep my feet in place as I went down. I caught myself with my right elbow and my left hand. I cursed, as the pain was too much and my elbow slid to the side, dropping me to my right shoulder.

But Brand's thrust had gone by me, and within blue halos my feet still touched the line. I was out of Brand's reach for a death thrust, though he could still hamstring me.

I raised my right arm, still clutching Grayswandir, before me. I began to sit up. As I did, I saw that the red formation, yellow about the edges, was now spinning directly above Brand, crackling with sparks and small lightnings, its roar now changed to a wailing.

Brand took hold of his blade by the forte and raised it above his shoulder like a spear, pointed in my direction. I knew that I could not parry it, that I could not dodge it.

With my mind, I reached out to the Jewel and up to the formation in the sky . . .

There came a bright flash as a small finger of lightning reached down and touched his blade . . .

The weapon fell from his hand and his hand flew to his mouth. With his left hand, he clutched at the Jewel of Judgment, as if he realized what I was doing and sought to nullify it by covering the stone. Sucking his fingers, he looked upward, all of the anger draining from his face to be replaced by a look of fear verging on terror. The cone was beginning to descend.

Turning then, he stepped onto the blackened area, faced south, raised both his arms and cried out something I could not hear above the wailing.

The cone fell toward him, but he seemed to grow two-dimensional as it approached. His outline wavered. He began to shrink—but it did not seem a function of actual size, so much as an effect of distancing. He dwindled, dwindled, was gone, a bare instant before the cone licked across the area he had occupied.

With him went the Jewel, so that I was left with no way of controlling the thing above me. I did not know whether it was better to maintain a low profile or to resume a normal stance on the Pattern. I decided on the latter, because the whirlwind seemed to go for things which broke the normal sequence. I got back into a sitting position and edged over to the line. Then I leaned forward into a crouch, by which time the cone began to rise. The wailing retreated down the scale as it withdrew. The blue fires about my boots had subsided completely. I turned and looked at Fiona. She motioned me to get up and go on.

So I rose slowly, seeing that the vortex above me continued to dissipate as I moved. Advancing upon the area where Brand had so recently stood, I once again used Grayswandir to guide me through. The twisted remains of Brand's blade lay near the far edge of the dim place.

I wished there were some easy way out of the Pattern. It seemed pointless to complete it now. But there is no turning back once you have set foot upon it, and I was extremely leery of trying the dark route out. So I headed on toward the Grand Curve. To what place, I wondered, had Brand taken himself? If I knew, I could command the Pattern to send me after him, once I reached the center. Perhaps Fiona had an idea. Still, he would probably head for a place where he had allies. It would be senseless to pursue him alone.

At least I had stopped the attunement, I consoled myself.

Then I entered the Grand Curve. The sparks shot up about me.

TWELVE

Late afternoon on a mountain: the westering sun shone full on the rocks to my left, tailored long shadows for those to the right; it filtered through the foilage about my tomb; it countered to some extent the chill winds of Kolvir. I released Random's hand and turned to regard the man who sat on the bench before the mausoleum.

It was the face of the youth on the pierced Trump, lines now drawn above the mouth, brow heavier, a general weariness in eye movement and set of jaw which had not been apparent on the card.

So I knew it before Random said, "This is my son Martin."

Martin rose as I approached him, clasped my hand, said, "Uncle Corwin." His expression changed but slightly as he said it. He scrutinized me.

He was several inches taller than Random, but of the same light build. His chin and cheekbones had the same general cut to them, his hair was of a similar texture.

I smiled.

"You have been away a long while," I said. "So was I."

He nodded.

"But I have never really been in Amber proper," he said. "I grew up in Rebma—and other places."

"Then let me welcome you, nephew. You come at an interesting time. Random must have told you about it."

"Yes," he said. "That is why I asked to meet you here, rather than there."

I glanced at Random.

"The last uncle he met was Brand," Random said, "and under very nasty circumstances. Do you blame him?"

"Hardly. I ran into him myself a bit earlier. Can't say it was the most rewarding encounter."

"Ran into him?" said Random. "You've lost me."

"He has left Amber and he has the Jewel of Judgment with him. If I had known earlier what I know now, he would still be in the tower. He is our man, and he is very dangerous."

Random nodded.

"I know," he said. "Martin confirmed all our suspicions on the stabbing—and it was Brand. But what is this about the Jewel?"

"He beat me to the place where I had left it on the shadow Earth. He has to walk the Pattern with it and project himself through it, though, to attune it to his use. I just stopped him from doing that on the primal Pattern in the real Amber. He escaped, however. I was just over the hill with Gérard, sending a squad of guards through to Fiona in that place, to prevent his returning and trying again. Our own Pattern and that in Rebma are also under guard because of him."

"Why does he want so badly to attune it? So he can raise a few storms? Hell, he could take a walk in Shadow and make all the weather he wants."

"A person attuned to the Jewel could use it to erase the Pattern."

"Oh? What happens then?"

"The world as we know it comes to an end."

"Oh," Random said again. Then, "How the hell do you know?"

"It is a long story and I haven't the time, but I had it from Dworkin and I believe that much of what he said."

"He's still around?"

"Later," I said.

"Okay. But Brand would have to be mad to do something like that."

I nodded.

"I believe he thinks he could then cast a new Pattern, redesign the universe with himself as chief executive."

"Could this be done?"

"Theoretically, perhaps. But even Dworkin has certain doubts that the feat could be repeated effectively now. The combination of factors was unique. . . . Yes, I believe Brand is somewhat mad. Looking back over the years, recalling his personality changes, his cycles of moods, it seems there was something of a schizoid pattern there. I do not know whether the deal he made with the enemy pushed him over the edge or not. It does not really matter. I wish he were back in his tower. I wish Gérard were a worse physician."

"Do you know who stabbed him?"

"Fiona. You can get the story from her, though."

He leaned against my epitaph and shook his head.

"Brand," he said. "Damn him. Any one of us might have killed him on a number of occasions—in the old days. Just when he would get you mad enough, though, he would change. After a while, you would get to thinking he wasn't such a bad guy after all. Too bad he didn't push one of us just a little harder at the wrong time . . ."

"Then I take it he is now fair game?" said Martin.

I looked at him. The muscles in his jaws had tightened and his eyes narrowed. For a moment, all of our faces fled across his, like a riffling of the family cards. All of our egoism, hatred, envy, pride, and abuse seemed to flow by in that instant—and he had not even set foot in Amber yet. Something snapped inside me and I reached out and seized him by the shoulders.

"You have good reason to hate him," I said, "and the answer to your question is 'yes.' The hunting season is open. I see no way to deal with him other than to destroy him. I hated him myself for so long as he remained an abstraction. But—now—it is different. Yes, he must be killed. But do not let that hatred be your baptism into our company. There has been too much of it among us. I look at your face—I don't know. . . . I am sorry, Martin. Too much is going on right now. You are young. I have seen more things. Some of them bother me—differently. That's all."

I released my grip and stepped back.

"Tell me about yourself," I said.

"I was afraid of Amber for a long while," he began, "and I guess that I still am. Ever since he attacked me, I have been wondering whether Brand might catch up with me again. I have been looking over my shoulder for years. I have been afraid of all of you, I suppose. I knew most of you as pictures on cards—with bad reputations attached. I told Random—Dad—that I did not want to meet you all at once, and he suggested that I see you first. Neither of us realized at the time that you would be particularly interested in certain things that I know. After I mentioned them though, Dad said I had to see you as soon as possible. He has been telling me all about what has been going on and—you see, I know something about it."

"I had a feeling that you might—when a certain name cropped up not too long ago."

"The Tecys?" Random said.

"The same."

"It is difficult, deciding where to start . . ." Martin said.

"I know that you grew up in Rebma, walked the Pattern, and then used your power over Shadow to visit Benedict in Avalon," I said. "Benedict told you more about Amber and Shadow, taught you the use of the Trumps, coached you in weaponry. Later, you departed to walk in Shadow by yourself. And I know what Brand did to you. That is the sum of my knowledge."

He nodded, stared off into the west.

"After I left Benedict's, I traveled for years in Shadow," he said. "Those were the happiest times I have known. Adventure, excitement, new things to see, to do. . . . In the back of my mind, I always had it that one day when I was smarter and tougher—more experienced—I would journey to Amber and meet my other relatives. Then Brand caught up with me. I was camped on a little hillside, just resting from a long ride and taking my lunch, on my way to visit my friends the Tecys. Brand contacted me then. I had reached Benedict with his Trump, when he was teaching me how to use them, and other times when I had traveled. He had even transported me through occasionally, so I knew what it felt like, knew what it was all about. This felt the same way, and for a moment, I thought that somehow·it was Benedict calling me. But no. It was Brand—I recognized him from his picture in the deck. He was standing in the midst of what seemed to be the Pattern. I was curious. I did not know how he had reached me. So far as I knew, there was no Trump for me. He talked for a minute—I forget what he said—and when everything was firm and clear, he—he stabbed me. I pushed him and pulled away then. He held the contact somehow. It was hard for me to break it—and when I did, he tried to reach me again. But I was able to block him. Benedict had taught me that. He tried again, several times, but I kept blocking. Finally, he stopped. I was near to the Tecys. I managed to get onto my horse and make it to their place. I thought I was going to die, because I had never been hurt that badly before. But after a time, I began to recover. Then I grew afraid once again, afraid that Brand would find me and finish what he had begun."

"Why didn't you contact Benedict," I asked him, "and tell him what had happened, tell him of your fears?"

"I thought of that," he said, "and I also thought of the possibility that Brand believed he had succeeded, that I was indeed dead. I did not know what sort of power struggle was going on in Amber, but I decided that the attempt on my life was probably part of such a thing. Benedict had told me enough about the family that this was one of the first things to come to mind. So I decided that perhaps it would be better to remain dead. I left the Tecys before I was completely recovered and rode off to lose myself in Shadow.

"I happened upon a strange thing then," he continued, "a thing I had never before encountered, but which now seemed virtually omnipresent: In nearly all of the shadows through which I passed, there was a peculiar black road existing in some form or other. I did not understand it, but since it was the only thing I had come across which seemed to traverse Shadow itself, my curiosity was aroused. I resolved to follow it and learn more about it. It was dangerous. I learned very quickly not to tread the thing. Strange shapes seemed to travel it at night. Natural creatures which ventured upon it sickened and died. So I was careful. I went no nearer than was necessary to keep it in sight. I followed it through many places. I quickly learned that everywhere it ran there was death, desolation, or trouble nearby. I did not know what to make of it.

"I was still weak from my wound," he went on, "and I made the mistake of pressing myself, of riding too far, too fast, in a day's time. That evening, I fell ill and I lay shivering in my blanket through the night and much of the next day. I was into and out of delirium during this time, so I do not know exactly when she appeared. She seemed like part of my dream much of the while. A young girl. Pretty. She took care of me while I recovered. Her name was Dara. We talked interminably. It was very pleasant. Having someone to talk with like that . . . I must have told her my whole life story. Then she told me something of herself. She was not a native of the area in which I had collapsed. She said that she had traveled there through Shadow. She could not yet walk through it as we do, though she felt she could learn to do this, as she claimed descent from the House of Amber through Benedict. In fact, she wanted very badly to learn how it was done. Her means of travel then was the black road itself. She was immune to its noxious effects, she said, because she was also related to the dwellers at its farther end, in the Courts of Chaos. She wanted to learn our ways though, so I did my best to instruct her in those things that I did know. I told her of the Pattern, even sketched it for her. I showed her my Trumps—Benedict had given me a deck—to show her the appearance of her other relatives. She was particularly interested in yours."

"I begin to understand," I said. "Go on."

"She told me that Amber, in the fullness of its corruption and presumption, had upset a kind of metaphysical balance between itself and the Courts of Chaos. Her people now had the job of redressing the matter by laying waste to Amber. Their own place is not a shadow of Amber, but a solid entity in its own right. In the meantime, all of the intervening shadows are suffering because of the black road. My knowledge of Amber being what it was, I could only listen. At first, I accepted everything that she said. Brand, to me, certainly fit her description of evil in Amber. But when I mentioned him, she said no. He was some sort of hero back where she hied from. She was uncertain as to the particulars, but it did not trouble her all that much. It was then that I realized how oversure she seemed about everything—there was a ring of the fanatic when she talked. Almost unwillingly, I found myself trying to defend Amber. I thought of Llewella and of Benedict—and of Gérard, whom I had met a few times. She was eager to learn of Benedict, I discovered. That proved the soft spot in her armor. Here I could speak with some knowledge, and here she was willing to believe the good things I had to say. So, I do not know what the ultimate effect of all this talk was, except that she seemed somewhat less sure of herself near the end . . ."

"The end?" I said. "What do you mean? How long was she with you?"

"Almost a week," he replied. "She had said she would take care of me until I was recovered, and she did. Actually, she remained several days longer. She said that was just to be sure, but I think it was really that she wanted to continue our conversations. Finally though, she said that she had to be moving on. I asked her to stay with me, but she said no. I offered to go with her, but she said no to that, too. She must have realized that I planned to follow her then, because she slipped away during the night. I could not ride the black road, and I had no idea what shadow she would travel to next on her way to Amber. When I awoke in the morning and realized she had gone, I thought for a time of visiting Amber myself. But I was still afraid. Perhaps some of the things she had said had reinforced my own fears. Whatever, I decided to remain in Shadow. And so I traveled on, seeing things, trying to learn things—until Random found me and told me he wanted me to come home. He brought me here first though, to meet you, because he wanted you to hear my story before any of the others. He said that you knew Dara, that you wanted to learn more about her. I hope that I have helped."

"Yes," I said. "Thank you."

"I understand that she did finally walk the Pattern."

"Yes, she succeeded in that."

"And afterward declared herself an enemy of Amber."

"That, too."

"I hope," he said, "that she comes to no harm from all this. She was kind to me."

"She seems quite able to take care of herself," I said. "But . . . yes, she is a likable girl. I cannot promise you anything concerning her safety, because I still know so little about her, so little of her part in everything that is going on. Yet, what you have told me has been helpful. It makes her someone I would still like to grant doubt's benefit, as far as I can."

He smiled.

"I am glad to hear that."

I shrugged.

"What are you going to do now?" I asked.

"I am taking him to see Vialle," Random said, "and then to meet the others, as time and opportunity permit. Unless, of course, something new has developed and you need me now."

"There have been new developments," I said, "but I do not really need you now. I had better bring you up to date, though. I still have a little time."

As I filled Random in on events since his departure, I thought about Martin. He was still an unknown quantity so far as I was concerned. His story might be perfectly true. In fact, I felt that it was. On the other hand, I had a feeling that it was not complete, that he was intentionally leaving something out. Maybe something harmless. Then again, maybe not. He had no real reason to love us. Quite the contrary. And Random could be bringing home a Trojan Horse. Probably though, it was nothing like that. It is just that I never trust anyone if there is an alternative available.

Still, nothing that I was telling Random could really be used against us, and I strongly doubted that Martin could do us much damage if that was his intention. No, more likely he was being as cagey as the rest of us, and for pretty much the same reasons: fear and self-preservation. On a sudden inspiration, I asked him, "Did you ever run into Dara again after that?"

He flushed.

"No," he said, too quickly. "Just that time. That's all."

"I see," I said, and Random was too good a poker player not to have noticed; so I had just bought us a piece of instant insurance at the small price of putting a father on guard against his long-lost son.

I quickly shifted our talk back to Brand. It was while we were comparing notes on psychopathology that I felt the tiny tingle and the sense of presence which heralds a Trump contact. I raised my hand and turned aside.

In a moment the contact was clear and Ganelon and I regarded one another.

"Corwin," he said, "I decided it was time to check. By now, you have the Jewel, Brand has the Jewel, or you are both still looking. Which one is it?"

"Brand has the Jewel," I said.

"More's the pity," he said. "Tell me about it."

So I did.

"Then Gérard had the story right," he said.

"He's already told you all this?"

"Not in such detail," Ganelon replied, "and I wanted to be sure I was getting it straight. I just finished speaking with him." He glanced upward. "It would seem you had best be moving then, if my memories of moonrise serve me right."

I nodded.

"Yes, I will be heading for the stairway shortly. It is not all that far from here."

"Good. Now here is what you must be ready to do—"

"I know what I have to do," I said. "I have to get up to Tir-na Nog'th before Brand does and block his way to the Pattern. Failing that, I have to chase him through it again."

"That is not the way to go about it," he said.

"You have a better idea?"

"Yes, I do. You have your Trumps with you?"

"Yes."

"Good. First, you would not be able to get up there in time to block his way to the Pattern—"

"Why not?"

"You have to make the ascension, then you have to walk to the palace and make your way down to the Pattern. That takes time, even in Tir-na Nog'th—especially in Tir-na Nog'th, where time tends to play tricks anyway. For all you know, you may have a hidden death wish slowing you down. I don't know. Whatever the case, he would have commenced walking the Pattern by the time you arrived. It may well be that he would be too far into it for you to reach him this time."

"He will probably be tired. That should slow him some."

"No. Put yourself in his place. If you were Brand, wouldn't you have headed for some shadow where the time flow was different? Instead of an afternoon, he could well have taken several days to rest up for this evening's ordeal. It is safest to assume that he will be in good shape."

"You are right," I said. "I can't count on it. Okay. An alternative I had entertained but would rather not try if it could be avoided, would be to kill him at a distance. Take along a crossbow or one of our rifles and simply shoot him in the midst of the Pattern. The thing that bothers me about it is the effect of our blood on the Pattern. It may be that it is only the primal Pattern that suffers from it, but I don't know."

"That's right. You do not know," he said. "Also, I would not want you to rely on normal weapons up there. That is a peculiar place. You said yourself it is like a strange piece of Shadow drifting in the sky. While you figured how to make a rifle fire in Amber, the same rules may not apply up there."

"It is a risk," I acknowledged.

"As for the crossbow—supposing a sudden gust of wind deflected the bolt each time you shot one?"

"I am afraid I do not follow you."

"The Jewel. He walked it part way through the primal Pattern, and he has had some time to experiment with it since then. Do you think it possible that he is partly attuned to it now?"

"I do not know. I am not at all that sure how the process works."

"I just wanted to point out that if it does work that way, he may be able to use it to defend himself. The Jewel may even have other properties you are not aware of. So what I am saying is that I would not want you to count on being able to kill him at a distance. And I would not even want you to rely on being able to pull the trick you did with the Jewel again—not if he may have gained some measure of control over it."

"You do make things look a little bleaker than I had them."

"But possibly more realistic," he said.

"Conceded. Go on. You said you had a plan."

"That is correct. My thinking is that Brand must not be allowed to reach the Pattern at all, that once he sets foot upon it the probability of disaster goes way up."

"And you do not think I can get there in time to block him?"

"Not if he can really transport himself around almost instantaneously while you have to take a long walk. My bet is that he is just waiting for moonrise, and as soon as the city takes form he will be inside, right next to the Pattern."

"I see the point, but not the answer."

"The answer is that you are not going to set foot in Tir-na Nog'th tonight."

"Hold on a minute!"

"Hold on, hell! You imported a master strategist, you'd better listen to what he has to say."

"Okay, I am listening."

"You have agreed that you probably cannot reach the place in time. But someone else can."

"Who and how?"

"All right. I have been in touch with Benedict. He has returned. At this moment, he is in Amber, down in the chamber of the Pattern. By now, he should have finished walking it and be standing there at its center, waiting. You proceed to the foot of the stairs to the sky-city. There you await the rising of the moon. As soon as Tir-na Nog'th takes form, you will contact Benedict via his Trump. You tell him that all is ready, and he will use the power of the Pattern in Amber to transport himself to the place of the Pattern in Tir-na Nog'th. No matter how fast Brand travels, he cannot gain much on that."

"I see the advantages," I said. "That is the fastest way to get a man up there and Benedict is certainly a good man. He should have no trouble dealing with Brand."

"Do you really think Brand will make no other preparations?" Ganelon said. "From everything I've heard about the man, he's smart even if he is daft. He just may anticipate something like this."

"Possibly. Any idea what he might do?"

He made a sweeping gesture with one hand, slapped his neck and smiled.

"A bug," he said. "Pardon me. Pesky little things."

"You still think—"

"I think you had better remain in contact with Benedict the entire time he is up there, that is what I think. If Brand gets the upper hand, you may need to pull Benedict back immediately to save his life."

"Of course. But then—"

"But then we would have lost a round. Admitted. But not the game. Even with the Jewel fully attuned, he would have to get to the primal Pattern to do his real damage with it—and you have that under guard."

"Yes," I said. "You seem to have everything figured. You surprised me, moving so fast."

"I've had a lot of time on my hands recently, which can be a bad thing unless you use it for thinking. So I did. What I think now is that you had best move fast. The day isn't getting any longer."

"Agreed," I said. "Thanks for the good counsel."

"Save your thanks till we see what comes of it," he said, and then he broke the contact.

"That one sounded important," Random said. "What's up?"

"Appropriate question," I answered, "but I am all out of time now. You will have to wait till morning for the story."

"Is there anything I can do to help?"

"As a matter of fact," I said, "yes, if you'll either ride double or go back to Amber on a Trump. I need Star."

"Sure," Random said. "No trouble. Is that all?"

"Yes. Haste is all."

We moved toward the horses.

I patted Star a few times and then mounted.

"We'll see you in Amber," Random said. "Good luck."

"In Amber," I said. "Thanks."

I turned and headed toward the place of the stairway, treading my tomb's lengthening shadow eastward.

THIRTEEN

On the highest ridge of Kolvir there is a formation which resembles three steps. I sat on the lowest of these and waited for more to occur above me. It takes night and moonlight to do this, so half of the requirements had been met.

There were clouds to the west and northeast. I was leery of those clouds. If they massed sufficiently to block all moonlight, Tir-na Nog'th faded back to nothingness. This was one reason why it was always advisable to have a backup man on the ground, to Trump you to safety should the city vanish about you.

The sky overhead was clear, however, and filled with familiar stars. When the moon came up and its light fell upon the stone at which I rested, the stairway in the sky would come into being, sweeping upward to a great height, taking its way to Tir-na Nog'th, the image of Amber that rode the night's middle air.

I was weary. Too much had occurred in too brief a time. Suddenly to be at rest, to remove my boots and rub my feet, to lean back and rest my head, even against stone, was a luxury, a pure animal pleasure. I drew my cloak together before me against the growing chill. A hot bath, a full meal, a bed would be very good things. But these assumed an almost mythic quality from that vantage. It was more than sufficient simply to rest as I was, to let my thoughts move more slowly, drifting, spectatorlike, back over the day's happenings.

So much . . . but now, at least, I had some answers to some of my questions. Not all of them, certainly. But enough to slake my mind's thirst for the moment . . . I now had some idea as to what had been going on during my absence, a better understanding of what was happening now, a knowledge of some of the things that had to be done, of what I had to do. . . . And I felt, somehow, that I knew more than I realized, consciously, that I already possessed pieces that would fit the growing picture before me, if I were only to jiggle them, flip them, rotate them properly. The pace of recent events, particularly today's, had not allowed me a moment's reflection. Now, though, some of the pieces seemed to be turning at odd angles. . . .

I was distracted by a stirring above my shoulder, a tiny effect of brightening in the higher air. Turning, then standing, I regarded the horizon. A preliminary glow had occurred out over the sea at the point where the moon would ascend. As I watched, a minute arc of light came into view. The clouds had shifted slightly also, though not enough to cause concern. I glanced up then, but the overhead phenomenon had not yet begun. I withdrew my Trumps, however, riffled them, and cut out Benedict's.

Lethargy forgotten, I stared, watching the moon expand above the water, casting a trail of light over the waves. A faint form was suddenly hovering on the threshold of visibility high overhead. As the light grew, a spark limned it here and there. The first lines, faint as spider webbing, appeared above the rock. I studied Benedict's card, I reached for contact. . . .

His cold image came alive. I saw him in the chamber of the Pattern, standing at the designs' center. A lighted lantern glowed beside his left foot. He became aware of my presence.

"Corwin," he said, "is it time?"

"Not quite," I told him. "The moon is rising. The city is just beginning to take form. So it will only be a little longer. I wanted to be certain you were ready."

"I am ready," he said.

"It is good that you came back when you did. Did you learn anything of interest?"

"Ganelon called me back," he said, "as soon as he learned what had happened. His plan seemed a good one, which is why I am here. As for the Courts of Chaos, yes. I believe I have learned a few things—"

"A moment," I said.

The moonbeam strands had assumed a more tangible appearance. The city overhead was now clear in outline. The stairway was visible in its entirety, though fainter in some places than in others. I stretched forth enough to slake my mind's thirst for the moment. . . .

Cool, soft, I encountered the fourth stair. It seemed to give somewhat beneath my push, however.

"Almost," I said to Benedict. "I am going to try the stairs. Be ready."

He nodded.

I mounted the stone stairs, one, two, three. I raised my foot then and lowered it upon the fourth, ghostly one. It yielded gently to my weight. I was afraid to raise my other foot, so I waited, watching the moon. I breathed the cool air as the brightness increased, as the path in the waters widened. Glancing upward, I saw Tir-na Nog'th lose something of its transparency. The stars behind it grew dimmer. As this occurred, the stair became firmer beneath my foot. All resiliency went out of it. I felt that it might bear my full weight. Casting my eyes along its length, I now saw it in its entirety, here translucent, there transparent, sparkling, but continuous all the way up to the silent city that drifted above the sea. I raised my other foot and stood on the fourth stair. If I'd the mind, a few more steps would send me along that celestial escalator into the place of dreams made real, walking neuroses and dubious prophecy, into a moonlit city of ambiguous wish fulfillment, twisted time, and pallid beauty. I stepped back down and glanced at the moon, now balanced on the world's wet rim. I regarded Benedict's Trump in its silvery glow.

"The stair is solid, the moon is up," I said.

"All right. I am going."

I watched him there at the center of the Pattern. He raised the lantern in his left hand and for a moment stood unmoving. An instant later he was gone, and so was the Pattern. Another instant, and he stood within a similar chamber, this time outside the Pattern, next to the point where it begins. He raised the lantern high and looked all around the room. He was alone.

He turned, walked to the wall, set the lantern beside it. His shadow stretched toward the Pattern, changed shape as he turned on his heel, moved back to his first position.

This Pattern, I noted, glowed with a paler light than the one in Amber—silvery white, without the hint of blue with which I was familiar. Its configuration was the same, but the ghost city played strange tricks with perspective. There were distortions—narrowings, widenings—which seemed to shift for no particular reason across its surface, as though I viewed the entire tableau through an irregular lens rather than Benedict's Trump.

I retreated down the stairs, settled once again on the lowest step. I continued to observe.

Benedict loosened his blade in its scabbard.

"You know about the possible effect of blood on the Pattern?" I asked.

"Yes. Ganelon told me."

"Did you ever suspect—any of this?"

"I never trusted Brand," he told me.

"What of your journey to the Courts of Chaos? What did you learn?"

"Later, Corwin. He could come any time now."

"I hope no distracting visions show up," I said, recalling my own journey to Tir-na Nog'th and his own part in my final adventure there.

He shrugged.

"One gives them power by paying them heed. My attention is reserved for one matter tonight."

He turned through a full circle, regarding every part of the chamber, halted when he had finished.

"I wonder if he knows you are there?" I said.

"Perhaps. It does not matter."

I nodded. If Brand did not show up, we had gained a day. The guards would ward the other Patterns, Fiona would have a chance to demonstrate her own skill in matters arcane by locating Brand for us. We would then pursue him. She and Bleys had been able to stop him once before. Could she do it alone now? Or would we have to find Bleys and try to convince him to help? Had Brand found Bleys? What the hell did Brand want this kind of power for anyhow? A desire for the throne I could understand. Yet . . . The man was mad, leave it at that. Too bad, but that's the way it was. Heredity or environment? I wondered wryly. We were all of us, to some degree, mad after his fashion. To be honest, it had to be a form of madness, to have so much and to strive so bitterly for just a little more, for a bit of an edge over the others. He carried this tendency to its extreme, that is all. He was a caricature of this mania in all of us. In this sense, did it really matter which of us was the traitor?

Yes, it did. He was the one who had acted. Mad or not, he had gone too far. He had done things Eric, Julian, and I would not have done. Bleys and Fiona had finally backed away from his thickening plot. Gérard and Benedict were a notch above the rest of us—moral, mature, whatever—for they had exempted themselves from the zero-sum power game. Random had changed, quite a bit, in recent years. Could it be that the children of the unicorn took ages in which to mature, that it was slowly happening to the rest of us but had somehow passed Brand by? Or could it be that by his actions Brand was causing it in the rest of us? Like most such questions, the benefit of these was in the asking, not the answering. We were enough like Brand that I knew a particular species of fear nothing else could so provoke. But yes, it did matter. Whatever the reason, he was the one who had acted.

The moon was higher now, its vision superimposed upon my inward viewing of the chamber of the Pattern. The clouds continued to shift, to boil nearer the moon. I thought of advising Benedict, but it would serve no other end than distraction. Above me, Tir-na Nog'th rode like some supernatural ark upon the seas of night.

. . . And suddenly Brand was there.

Reflexively, my hand went to Grayswandir's hilt, despite the fact that a part of me realized from the very first that he stood across the Pattern from Benedict in a dark chamber high in the sky.

My hand fell again. Benedict had become aware of the intruding presence immediately, and he turned to face him. He made no move toward his weapon, but simply stared across the Pattern at our brother.

My earliest fear had been that Brand would contrive to arrive directly behind Benedict and stab him in the back. I would not have tried that though, because even in death Benedict's reflexes might have been sufficient to dispatch his assailant. Apparently, Brand wasn't that crazy either.

Brand smiled.

"Benedict," he said. "Fancy . . . You . . . Here."

The Jewel of Judgment hung fiery upon his breast.

"Brand," Benedict said, "don't try it."

Still smiling, Brand unclasped his sword belt and let his weapon fall to the floor. When the echoes died, he said, "I am not a fool, Benedict. The man hasn't been born who can go up against you with a blade."

"I don't need the blade, Brand."

Brand began walking, slowly, about the edge of the Pattern.

"Yet you wear it as a servant of the throne, when you could have been king."

"That has never been high on my list of ambitions."

"That is right." He paused, only part way about the Pattern. "Loyal, self-effacing. You have not changed at all. Pity Dad conditioned you so well. You could have gone so much further."

"I have everything that I want," Benedict said.

". . . To have been stifled, cut off, so early."

"You cannot talk your way past me either, Brand. Do not make me hurt you."

The smile still on his face, Brand began moving again, slowly. What was it he was trying to do? I could not figure his strategy.

"You know I can do certain things the others cannot," Brand said. "If there is anything at all that you want and think that you cannot have, now is your chance to name it and learn how wrong you were. I have learned things you would scarcely believe."

Benedict smiled one of his rare smiles.

"You have chosen the wrong line," he said. "I can walk to anything that I want."

"Shadows!" Brand snorted, halting again. "Any of the others can clutch a phantom! I am talking of reality! Amber! Power! Chaos! Not daydreams made solid! Not second best!"

"If I had wanted more than I have, I knew what to do. I did not do it."

Brand laughed, began walking again. He had come a quarter of the way about the Pattern's periphery. The Jewel burned more brightly. His voice rang.

"You are a fool, to wear your chains willingly! But if things do not call out to you to possess them and if power holds no attraction, what of knowledge? I learned the last of Dworkin's lore. I have gone on since then and paid dark prices for greater insight into the workings of the universe. This you could have without that price tag."

"There would be a price," Benedict said, "one that I will not pay."

Brand shook his head and tossed his hair. The image of the Pattern wavered for a moment then, as a wisp of cloud crossed the moon. Tir-na Nog'th faded slightly, returned to normal focus.

"You mean it, you really mean it," Brand said, apparently not aware of the moment of fading. "I shan't test you further then. I had to try." He halted again, staring. "You are too good a man to waste yourself on that mess in

Amber, defending something that is obviously falling apart. I am going to win, Benedict. I am going to erase Amber and build it anew. I am going to rub out the old Pattern and draw my own. You can be with me. I want you on my side. I am going to raise up a perfect world, one with more direct access to and from Shadow. I am going to merge Amber with the Courts of Chaos. I am going to extend this realm directly through all of Shadow. You will command our legions, the mightiest military forces ever assembled. You—"

"If your new world would be as perfect as you say, Brand, there would be no need for legions. If, on the other hand, it is to reflect the mind of its creator, then I see it as something less than an improvement over the present state of affairs. Thank you for your offer, but I hold with the Amber which already exists."

"You are a fool, Benedict. A well-meaning one, but a fool nevertheless."

He began to move again, casually. He was within forty feet of Benedict. Thirty. . . . He kept moving. He finally paused about twenty feet away, hooked his thumbs behind his belt, and simply stared. Benedict met his gaze. I checked the clouds again. A long mass of them continued a moonward slide. I could pull Benedict out at any time, though. It was hardly worth disturbing him at the moment.

"Why don't you come and cut me down then?" Brand finally said. "Unarmed as I am, it should not be difficult. The fact that the same blood flows in both our veins makes no difference, does it? What are you waiting for?"

"I already told you that I do not wish to hurt you," Benedict said.

"Yet you stand ready to, if I attempt to pass your way."

Benedict simply nodded.

"Admit that you fear me, Benedict. All of you are afraid of me. Even when I approach you weaponless like this, something must be twisting your guts. You see my confidence and you do not understand it. You must be afraid."

Benedict did not reply.

". . . And you fear my blood on your hands," Brand went on, "you fear my death curse."

"Did you fear Martin's blood on your own?" Benedict asked.

"That bastard puppy!" Brand said. "He was not truly one of us. He was only a tool."

"Brand, I have no desire to kill a brother. Give me that trinket you wear about your neck and come back with me now to Amber. It is not too late to set matters right."

Brand threw back his head and laughed.

"Oh, nobly spoken! Nobly spoken, Benedict! Like a true lord of the realm! You would shame me with your excessive virtue! And what is the sticking point of this all?" He reached down and stroked the Jewel of Judgment. "This?" He laughed again and strode forward. "This bauble? Would its surrender buy us peace, amity, order? Would it ransom my life?"

He halted once more, ten feet from Benedict now. He raised the Jewel between his fingers and looked down at it.

"Do you realize the full powers of this thing?" he asked.

"Enough of th—" Benedict began, and his voice cracked in his throat.

Brand hurriedly took another step forward. The Jewel was bright before him. Benedict's hand had begun to move toward his blade, but it did not reach it. He stood stiffly now, as if suddenly transformed into a statue. Then I began to understand, but by then it was too late.

Nothing that Brand had been saying had really mattered. It had simply been a running line of patter, a distraction thrown up before him while he sought cautiously after the proper range. He was indeed partly attuned to the Jewel, and the limited control this gave him was still sufficient to enable him to produce effects with it, effects which I was unaware it could produce, but of which he had known all along. Brand had carefully contrived his arrival a good distance from Benedict, tried the Jewel, moved a little nearer, tried again, kept up this movement, this testing, until he found the point where it could affect Benedict's nervous system.

"Benedict," I said, "you had better come to me now," and I exerted my will, but he did not budge nor did he reply. His Trump was still functioning, I felt his presence, I observed events because of it, but I could not reach him. The Jewel was obviously affecting more than his motor system.

I looked to the clouds again. They were still growing, they were reaching for the moon. It seemed they might come across it soon. If I could not pull Benedict out when it happened, he would fall to the sea as soon as the light was fully blocked, the city disrupted. Brand! If he became aware of it, he might be able to use the Jewel to dissipate the clouds. But to do that, he would probably have to release Benedict. I did not think he would do it. Still . . . The clouds seemed to be slowing now. This entire line of reasoning could become unnecessary. I thumbed out Brand's Trump though, and set it aside.

"Benedict, Benedict," said Brand, smiling, "of what use is the finest swordsman alive if he cannot move to take up his blade? I told you that you were a fool. Did you think I would walk willingly to my slaughter? You should have trusted the fear you must have felt. You should have known that I would not enter this place helpless. I meant it when I said that I was going to win. You were a good choice though, because you are the best. I really wish that you had accepted my offer. But it is not that important now. I cannot be stopped. None of the others has a chance, and with you gone things are going to be much easier."

He reached beneath his cloak and produced a dagger.

"Bring me through, Benedict!" I cried, but it was no use. There was no response, no strength to trump me up there.

I seized Brand's Trump. I recalled my Trump battle with Eric. If I could hit Brand through his Trump, I might be able to break his concentration sufficiently for Benedict to come free. I turned all of my faculties upon the card, preparing for a massive mental assault.

But nothing. The way was frozen and dark.

It had to be that his concentration on the task at hand, his mental involvement with the Jewel, was so complete that I simply could not reach him. I was blocked at every turn.

Suddenly, the stairway grew paler above me and I cast a quick glance at the moon. A limb of cumulus now covered a portion of its face. Damn!

I returned my attention to Benedict's Trump. It seemed slow, but I did recover the contact, indicating that somewhere, inside it all, Benedict was still conscious. Brand had moved a pace nearer and was still taunting him. The Jewel on its heavy chain burned with the light of its use. They stood perhaps three paces apart now. Brand toyed with the dagger.

". . . Yes, Benedict," he was saying, "you probably would have preferred to die in battle. On the other hand, you might look upon this as a kind of honor— a signal honor. In a way, your death will allow the birth of a new order . . ."

For a moment, the Pattern faded behind them. I could not tear my eyes from the scene to examine the moon, however. There, within the shadows and the flickering light, his back to the Pattern, Brand did not seem to notice. He took another step forward.

"But enough of this," he said. "There are things to be done, and the night grows no younger."

He stepped nearer and lowered the blade.

"Good night, sweet Prince," he said, and he moved to close with him.

At that instant, Benedict's strange mechanical right arm, torn from this place of shadow and silver and moonlight, moved with the speed of a striking snake. Thing of glinting, metallic planes like the facets of a gem, wrist a wondrous weave of silver cable, pinned with flecks of fire, stylized, skeletal, a Swiss toy, a mechanical insect, functional, deadly, beautiful in its way, it shot forward with a speed that I could not follow, while the rest of his body remained steady, a statue.

The mechanical fingers caught the Jewel's chain about Brand's neck. Immediately, the arm moved upward, raising Brand high above the floor. Brand dropped the dagger and clutched at his throat with both hands.

Behind him, the Pattern faded once again. It returned with a much paler glow. Brand's face in the lantern light was a ghastly, twisted apparition. Benedict remained frozen, holding him on high, unmoving, a human gallows.

The Pattern grew dimmer. Above me, the steps began to recede. The moon was half-occluded.

Writhing, Brand raised his arms above his head, catching at the chain on either side of the metal hand that held it. He was strong, as all of us are. I saw his muscles bunch and harden. By then, his face was dark and his neck a mass of straining cables. He bit his lip; the blood ran into his beard as he drew upon the chain.

With a sharp snap followed by a rattling, the chain parted and Brand fell to the floor gasping. He rolled over once, clutching at his throat with both hands.

Slowly, very slowly, Benedict lowered his strange arm. He still held the chain and the Jewel. He flexed his other arm. He sighed deeply.

The Pattern grew even dimmer. Above me, Tir-na Nog'th became transparent. The moon was almost gone.

"Benedict!" I cried. "Can you hear me?"

"Yes," he said, very softly, and he began to sink through the floor.

"The city is fading! You've got to come to me right away!"

I extended my hand.

"Brand . . ." he said, turning.

But Brand was sinking also, and I saw that Benedict could not reach him. I clasped Benedict's left hand and jerked. Both of us fell to the ground beside the high outcrop.

I helped him to his feet. Then we both seated ourselves on the stone. For a long while, we did not say anything. I looked again and Tir-na Nog'th was gone.

I thought back over everything that had happened, so fast, so sudden, that day. A great weight of weariness lay upon me now, and I felt that my energies must be at their end, that shortly I must sleep. I could scarcely think straight. Life had simply been too crowded recently. I leaned my back against the stone once more, regarding cloud and star. The pieces . . . the pieces which it seemed should fit, if only the proper jiggle, twist, or flip were applied. . . . They were jiggling, twisting, and flipping now, almost of their own accord. . . .

"Is he dead, do you think?" Benedict asked, pulling me back from a half-dream of emerging forms.

"Probably," I said. "He was in bad shape when things fell apart."

"It was a long way down. He might have had time to work some escape along the lines of his arrival."

"Right now it does not really matter," I said. "You've drawn his fangs."

Benedict grunted. He was still holding the Jewel, a much dimmer red than it had been so recently.

"True," he finally said. "The Pattern is safe now. I wish   I wish that some time, long ago, something had not been said that was said, or something done that was not done. Something, had we known, which might have let him grow differently, something which would have seen him become another man than the bitter, bent thing I saw up there. It is best now if he is dead. But it is a waste of something that might have been."

I did not answer him. What he had said might or might not be right. It did not matter. Brand might have been borderline psychotic, whatever that means, and then again maybe not. There is always a reason. Whenever anything has been mucked up, whenever anthing outrageous happens, there is a reason for it. You still have a mucked-up, outrageous situation on your hands, however, and explaining it does not alleviate it one bit. If someone does something really rotten, there is a reason for it. Learn it, if you care, and you learn why he is a son of a bitch. The fact is the thing that remains, though. Brand had acted. It changed nothing to run a posthumous psychoanalysis. Acts and their consequences are the things by which our fellows judge us. Anything else, and all that you get is a cheap feeling of moral superiority by thinking how you would have done something nicer if it had been you. So as for the rest, leave it to heaven. I'm not qualified.

"We had best get back to Amber," Benedict said, "There are a great number of things that must be done."

"Wait," I said.

"Why?"

"I've been thinking."

When I did not elaborate, he finally said, "And . . . ?"

I riffled slowly through my Trumps, replacing his, replacing Brand's.

"Haven't you wondered yet about the new arm you wear?" I asked him.

"Of course. You brought it from Tir-na Nog'th, under unusual circumstances. It fits. It works. It proved itself tonight."

"Exactly. Isn't the last a lot of weight to dump on poor coincidence? The one weapon that gave you a chance up there, against the Jewel. And it just happened to be a part of you—and you just happened to be the person who was up there, to use it? Trace things back and trace them forward again. Isn't there an extraordinary—no, preposterous—chain of coincidences involved?"

"When you put it that way . . ." he said.

"I do. And you must realize as well as I do that there has to be more to it than that."

"All right. Say that. But how? How was it done?"

"I have no idea," I said, withdrawing the card I had not looked upon in a long, long while, feeling its coldness beneath my finger tips, "but the method is not important. You asked the wrong question."

"What should I have asked?"

"Not 'How?' but 'Who?'"

"You think that a human agency arranged that entire chain of events, up through the recovery of the Jewel?"

"I don't know about that. What's human? But I do think that someone we both know has returned and is behind it all."

"All right. Who?"

I showed him the Trump that I held.

"Dad? That *is* ridiculous! He must be dead. It's been so long."

"You know he could have engineered it. He's that devious. We never understood all of his powers."

Benedict rose to his feet. He stretched. He shook his head.

"I think you have been out in the cold too long, Corwin. Let's go home now."

"Without testing my guess? Come on! That is hardly sporting. Sit down and give me a minute. Let's try his Trump."

"He would have contacted someone by now."

"I don't think so. In fact—Come on. Humor me. What have we got to lose?"

"All right. Why not?"

He sat down beside me. I held the Trump where both of us could make it out. We stared at it. I relaxed my mind, I reached for contact. It came almost immediately.

He was smiling as he regarded us.

"Good evening. That was a fine piece of work," Ganelon said. "I am pleased that you brought back my trinket. I'll be needing it soon."

BOOK FIVE

THE COURTS OF CHAOS

To Carl Yoke, First Reader—

From Lucetania to Euclid Park,
Sarcobatus Flats to Cygnus X-1—
May you live another ten thousand years.
May your lair be safe from trendeltiles.
May the diminutive deities
break their collective leg.

ONE

Amber: high and bright atop Kolvir in the middle of the day. A black road: low and sinister through Garnath from Chaos to the south. Me: Cursing, pacing and occasionally reading in the library of the palace in Amber. The door to that library: closed and barred.

The mad prince of Amber seated himself at the desk, returned his attention to the opened volume. There was a knock on the door.

"Go away!" I said.

"Corwin. It's me—Random. Open up, huh? I even brought lunch."

"Just a minute."

I got to my feet again, rounded the desk, crossed the room. Random nodded when I opened the door. He carried a tray, which he took to a small table near the desk.

"Plenty of food there," I said.

"I'm hungry, too."

481

"So do something about it."

He did. He carved. He passed me some meat on a slab of bread. He poured wine. We seated ourselves and ate.

"I know you are still mad . . ." he said, after a time.

"Aren't you?"

"Well, maybe I am more used to it. I don't know. Still . . . Yes. It was sort of abrupt, wasn't it?"

"Abrupt?" I took a large swallow of wine. "It is just like the old days. Worse even. I had actually come to like him when he was playing at being Ganelon. Now that he is back in control he is just as peremptory as ever, he has given us a set of orders he has not bothered to explain and he has disappeared again."

"He said he would be in touch soon."

"I imagine he intended that last time, too."

"I'm not so sure."

"And he explained nothing about his other absence. In fact, he has not really explained anything."

"He must have his reasons."

"I am beginning to wonder, Random. Do you think his mind might finally be going?"

"He was still sharp enough to fool you."

"That was a combination of low animal cunning and shapeshifting ability."

"It worked, didn't it?"

"Yes. It worked."

"Corwin, could it be that you do not want him to have a plan that might be effective, that you do not want him to be right?"

"That is ridiculous. I want this mess cleared up as much as any of us."

"Yes, but wouldn't you rather the answer came from another quarter?"

"What are you getting at?"

"You do not want to trust him."

"I will admit that. I have not seen him—as himself—in a hell of a long time, and . . ."

He shook his head.

"That is not what I mean. You are angry that he is back, aren't you? You hoped that we had seen the last of him."

I looked away.

"There is that," I finally said. "But not for a vacant throne, or not *just* for it. It is him, Random. Him. That's all."

"I know," he said. "But you have to admit he suckered Brand, which is not an easy thing to do. He pulled a stunt I still do not understand, getting you to bring that arm back from Tir-na Nog'th, somehow getting me to pass it along to Benedict, seeing to it that Benedict was in the right place at the proper moment, so that everything worked and he got the Jewel back. He is also still better than we are at Shadow play. He managed it right on Kolvir when he took us to the primal Pattern. I cannot do that. Neither can you.

And he was able to whip Gérard. I do not believe that he is slowing down. I think he knows exactly what he is doing, and whether we like it or not, I think he is the only one who can deal with the present situation."

"You are trying to say that I should trust him?"

"I am trying to say that you have no choice."

I sighed.

"I guess you've put your finger on it," I said. "No sense in my being bitter. Still . . ."

"The attack order bothers you, doesn't it?"

"Yes, among other things. If we could wait longer, Benedict could field a greater force. Three days is not much time to get ready for something like this. Not when we are so uncertain about the enemy."

"But we may not be. He spoke in private with Benedict for a long while."

"And that is the other thing. These separate orders. This secrecy . . . He is not trusting us any more than he has to."

Random chuckled. So did I.

"All right," I said. "Maybe I would not either. But three days to launch a war." I shook my head. "He had better know something we don't."

"I get the impression that it is more a peremptory strike than a war."

"Only he did not bother to tell us what we are preempting."

Random shrugged, poured more wine.

"Perhaps he will say when he gets back. You did not get any special orders, did you?"

"Just to stand and wait. What about you?"

He shook his head.

"He said that when the time comes, I will know. At least with Julian, he told him to have his troops ready to move on a moment's notice."

"Oh? Aren't they staying in Arden?"

He nodded.

"When did he say this?"

"After you left. He trumped Julian up here to give him the message, and they rode off together. I heard Dad say that he would ride partway back with him."

"Did they take the eastern trail over Kolvir?"

"Yes. I saw them off."

"Interesting. What else did I miss?"

He shifted in his seat.

"The part that bothers me," he said. "After Dad had mounted and waved a good-bye, he looked back at me and said, 'And keep an eye on Martin.'"

"That is all?"

"That is all. But he was laughing as he said it."

"Just natural suspicion at a newcomer, I guess."

"Then why the laugh?"

"I give up."

I cut a piece of cheese and ate it.

"Might not be a bad idea, though. It might not be suspicion. Maybe he feels Martin needs to be protected from something. Or both. Or neither. You know how he sometimes is."

Random stood.

"I had not thought through to the alternative. Come with me now, huh?" he said. "You have been up here all morning."

"All right." I got to my feet, buckled on Grayswandir. "Where is Martin, anyway?"

"I left him down on the first floor. He was talking with Gérard."

"He is in good hands, then. Is Gérard going to be staying here, or will he be returning to the fleet?"

"I do not know. He would not discuss his orders."

We left the room. We headed for the stairway.

On the way down, I heard some small commotion from below and I quickened my pace.

I looked over the railing and saw a throng of guards at the entrance to the throne room, along with the massive figure of Gérard. All of them had their backs to us. I leaped down the final stairs. Random was not far behind me.

I pushed my way through.

"Gérard, what is happening?" I asked.

"Damned if I know," he said. "Look for yourself. But there is no getting in."

He moved aside and I took a step forward. Then another. And that was it. It was as if I were pushing against a slightly resilient, totally invisible wall. Beyond was a sight that tied my memory and feelings into a knot. I stiffened, as fear took hold of me by the neck, clasped my hands. No mean trick, that.

Martin, smiling, still held a Trump in his left hand, and Benedict— apparently recently summoned—stood before him. A girl was nearby, on the dais, beside the throne, facing away. Both men appeared to be speaking, but I could not hear the words.

Finally, Benedict turned and seemed to address the girl. After a time, she appeared to be answering him. Martin moved off to her left. Benedict mounted the dais as she spoke. I could see her face then. The exchange continued.

"That girl looks somewhat familiar," said Gérard, who had moved forward and now stood at my side.

"You might have gotten a glimpse of her as she rode past us," I told him, "the day Eric died. It's Dara."

I heard his sudden intake of breath.

"Dara!" he said. "Then you . . ." His voice faded.

"I was not lying," I said. "She is real."

"Martin!" cried Random, who had moved up on my right. "Martin! What's going on!"

There was no response.

"I don't think he can hear you," Gérard said. "This barrier seems to have cut us off completely."

Random strained forward, his hands pushing against something unseen. "Let's all of us give it a shove," he said.

So I tried again. Gérard also threw his weight against the invisible wall. After half a minute without success, I eased back.

"No good," I said. "We can't move it."

"What is the damned thing?" Random asked. "What is holding—"

I'd had a hunch—only that, though—as to what might be going on. And only because of the *déjà vu* character of the entire piece. Now, though . . . Now I clasped my hand to my scabbard, to assure myself that Grayswandir still hung at my side.

It did.

Then how could I explain the presence of my distinctive blade, its elaborate tracery gleaming for all to see, hanging where it had suddenly appeared, without support, in the air before the throne, its point barely touching Dara's throat?

I could not.

But it was too similar to what had happened that night in the dream city in the sky, Tir-na Nog'th, to be a coincidence. Here were none of the trappings—the darkness, the confusion, the heavy shadows, the tumultuous emotions I had known—and yet the piece was set much as it had been that night. It was very similar. But not precisely so. Benedict's stance seemed somewhat off—farther back, his body angled differently. While I could not read her lips, I wondered whether Dara was asking the same strange questions. I doubted it. The tableau—like, yet unlike, that which I had experienced—had probably been colored at the other end—that is, if there were any connection at all— by the effects of Tir-na Nog'th's powers upon my mind at that time.

"Corwin," Random said, "that looks like Grayswandir hanging in front of her."

"It does, doesn't it?" I said. "But as you can see, I am wearing my blade."

"There can't be another just like it . . . can there? Do you know what is happening?"

"I am beginning to feel as if I may," I said. "Whatever, I am powerless to stop it."

Benedict's blade suddenly came free and engaged the other, so like my own. In a moment, he was fighting an invisible opponent.

"Give him hell, Benedict!" Random shouted.

"It is no use," I said. "He is about to be disarmed."

"How can you know?" Gérard asked.

"Somehow, that is me in there, fighting with him," I said. "This is the other end of my dream in Tir-na Nog'th. I do not know how he managed it, but this is the price for Dad's recovering the Jewel."

"I do not follow you," he said.

I shook my head.

"I do not pretend to understand how it is being done," I told him. "But we will not be able to enter until two thing have vanished from that room."

"What two things?"

"Just watch."

Benedict's blade had changed hands, and his gleaming prosthesis shot forward and fixed itself upon some unseen target. The two blades parried one another, locked, pressed, their points moving toward the ceiling. Benedict's right hand continued to tighten.

Suddenly, the Grayswandir blade was free, and moving past the other. It struck a terrific blow to Benedict's right arm at the place where the metal portion joined it. Then Benedict turned and the action was blocked to our view for several moments.

Then the sight was clear again, as Benedict dropped to one knee, turning. He clutched at the stump of his arm. The mechanical hand/arm hung in the air near Grayswandir. It was moving away from Benedict and descending, as was the blade. When both reached the floor, they did not strike it but passed on through, vanishing from sight.

I lurched forward, recovering my balance, moved ahead. The barrier was gone.

Martin and Dara reached Benedict before we did. Dara had already torn a strip from her cloak and was binding Benedict's stump when Gérard, Random and I got there.

Random seized Martin by the shoulder and turned him.

"What happened?" he asked.

"Dara . . . Dara told me she wanted to see Amber," he said. "Since I live here now, I agreed to bring her through and show her around. Then—"

"Bring her through? You mean on a Trump?"

"Well, yes."

"Yours or hers?"

Martin raked his lower lip with his teeth.

"Well, you see . . ."

"Give me those cards," said Random, and he snatched the case from Martin's belt. He opened it and began going through them.

"Then I thought to tell Benedict, since he was interested in her," Martin went on. "Then Benedict wanted to come and see—"

"What the hell!" Random said. "There is one of you, one of her, and one of a guy I've never even seen before! Where did you get these?"

"Let me see them," I said.

He passed me the three cards.

"Well?" he said. "Was it Brand? He is the only one I know who can make Trumps now."

"I would not have anything to do with Brand," Martin replied, "except to kill him."

But I already knew they were not from Brand. They were simply not in his style. Nor were they in the style of anyone whose work I knew. Style was not foremost in my mind at that moment, however. Rather, it was the features of the third person, the one whom Random had said he had never seen before. I had. I was looking at the face of the youth who had confronted me with a crossbow before the Courts of Chaos, recognized me and then declined to shoot.

I extended the card.

"Martin, who is this?" I asked.

"The man who made these extra Trumps," he said. "He drew one of himself while he was about it, I do not know his name. He is a friend of Dara's."

"You are lying," Random said.

"Then let Dara tell us," I said, and I turned to her.

She still knelt beside Benedict, though she had finished bandaging him and he was now sitting up.

"How about it?" I said, waving the card at her. "Who is this man?"

She glanced at the card, then up at me. She smiled.

"You really do not know?" she said.

"Would I be asking if I did?"

"Then look at it again and go look in mirror. He is your son as much as mine. His name is Merlin."

I am not easily shocked, but this had nothing of ease about it. I felt dizzy. But my mind moved quickly. With the proper time differential the thing was possible.

"Dara," I said, "what is it that you want?"

"I told you when I walked the Pattern," she said, "that Amber must be destroyed. What I want is to have my rightful part in it."

"You will have my old cell," I said. "No, the one next to it. Guards!"

"Corwin, it is all right," Benedict said, getting to his feet. "It is not as bad as it sounds. She can explain everything."

"Then let her start now."

"No. In private. Just family."

I motioned back the guards who had come at my call.

"Very well. Let us adjourn to one of the rooms up the hall."

He nodded, and Dara took hold of his left arm. Random, Gérard, Martin and I followed them out. I looked back once to the empty place where my dream had come true. Such is the stuff.

TWO

I rode up over the crest of Kolvir and dismounted when I came to my tomb. I went inside and opened the casket. It was empty. Good. I was beginning to wonder. I had half-expected to see myself laid out before me, evidence that despite signs and intuitions I had somehow wandered into the wrong shadow.

I went back outside and rubbed Star's nose. The sun was shining and the breeze was chill. I had a sudden desire to go to sea. I seated myself on the bench instead and fumbled with my pipe.

We had talked. Seated with her legs beneath her on the brown sofa, Dara had smiled and repeated the story of her descent from Benedict and Lintra, the hellmaid, growing up in and about the Courts of Chaos, a grossly non-Euclidean realm where time itself presented strange distribution problems.

"The things you told me when we met were lies," I said. "Why should I believe you now?"

She had smiled and regarded her fingernails.

"I had to lie to you then," she explained, "to get what I wanted from you."

"That being . . . ?"

"Knowledge, of the family, the Pattern, the Trumps, of Amber. To gain your trust. To have your child."

"The truth would not have served as well?"

"Hardly. I come from the enemy. My reasons for wanting these things were not the sort of which you would approve."

"Your swordplay . . . ? You told me then that Benedict had trained you."

She smiled again and her eyes showed dark fires.

"I learned from the great Duke Borel himself, a High Lord of Chaos."

". . . and your appearance," I said. "It was altered on a number of occasions when I saw you walk the Pattern. How? Also, why?"

"All whose origins involve Chaos are shapeshifters," she replied.

I thought of Dworkin's performance the night he had impersonated me. Benedict nodded.

"Dad fooled us with his Ganelon disguise."

"Oberon is a son of Chaos," Dara said, "a rebel son of a rebel father. But the power is still there."

"Then why is it we cannot do it?" Random asked.

She shrugged.

"Have you ever tried? Perhaps you can. On the other hand, it may have died out with your generation. I do not know. As to myself, however, I have certain favored shapes to which I revert in times of stress. I grew up where this was the rule, where the other shape was actually sometimes dominant. It is still a reflex with me. This is what you witnessed—that day."

"Dara," I said, "why did you want the things that you said you wanted—knowledge of the family, the Pattern, the Trumps, Amber? And a son?"

"All right." She sighed. "All right. You are by now aware of Brand's plans—the destruction and rebuilding of Amber . . . ?"

"Yes."

"This involved our consent and co-operation."

"Including the murder of Martin?" Random asked.

"No," she said. "We did not know who he intended to use as the—agent."

"Would it have stopped you had you known?"

"You are asking a hypothetical question," she said. "Answer it yourself. I am glad that Martin is still alive. That is all that I can say about it."

"All right," Random said. "What about Brand?"

"He was able to contact our leaders by methods he had learned from

Dworkin. He had ambitions. He needed knowledge, power. He offered a deal."

"What sort of knowledge?"

"For one thing, he did not know how to destroy the Pattern—"

"Then you *were* responsible for what he did," Random said.

"If you choose to look at it that way."

"I do."

She shrugged, looked at me.

"Do you want to hear this story?"

"Go ahead." I glanced at Random and he nodded.

"Brand was given what he wanted," she said, "but he was not trusted. It was feared that once he possessed the power to shape the world as he would, he would not stop with ruling over a revised Amber. He would attempt to extend his dominion over Chaos as well. A weakened Amber was what was desired, so that Chaos would be stronger than it now is—the striking of a new balance, giving to us more of the shadowlands that lie between our realms. It was realized long ago that the two kingdoms can never be merged, or one destroyed, without also disrupting all the processes that lie in flux between us. Total stasis or complete chaos would be the result. Yet, though it was seen what Brand had in mind, our leaders came to terms with him. It was the best opportunity to present itself in ages. It had to be seized. It was felt that Brand could be dealt with, and finally replaced, when the time came."

"So you were also planning a double-cross," Random said.

"Not if he kept his word. But then, we knew that he would not. So we provided for the move against him."

"How?"

"He would be allowed to accomplish his end and then be destroyed. He would be succeeded by a member of the royal family of Amber who was also of the first family of the Courts, one who had been raised among us and trained for the position. Merlin even traces his connection with Amber on both sides, through my forebear Benedict and directly from yourself—the two most favored claimants to your throne."

"You are of the royal house of Chaos?"

She smiled.

I rose. Strode away. Stared at the ashes on the grate.

"I find it somewhat distressing to have been involved in a calculated breeding project," I said, at length. "But be that as it may, and accepting everything you have said as true—for the moment—why are you telling us all of these things now?"

"Because," she said, "I fear that the lords of my realm would go as far for their vision as Brand would for his. Farther, perhaps. That balance I spoke of. Few seem to appreciate what a delicate thing it is. I have traveled in the shadowlands near to Amber, and I have walked in Amber herself. I also have known the shadows that lie by Chaos' side. I have met many people and seen many things. Then, when I encountered Martin and spoke with him, I began to feel that the changes I had been told would be for the better would not simply result in a revision of Amber more along the lines of my elders' liking. They would, instead, turn Amber into a mere extension of the Courts, most of the shadows would boil away to join with Chaos. Amber would become an island. Some of my seniors who still smart at Dworkin's having created Amber in the first place are really seeking a return to the days before this happened. Total Chaos, from which all things arose. I see the present condition as superior and I wish to preserve it. My desire is that neither side emerge victorious in any conflict."

I turned in time to see Benedict shaking his head.

"Then you are on neither side," he stated.

"I like to think that I am on both."

"Martin," I said, "are you in this with her?"

He nodded.

Random laughed.

"The two of you? Against both Amber and the Courts of Chaos? What do you hope to achieve? How do you plan to further this notion of balance?"

"We are not alone," she said, "and the plan is not ours."

Her fingers dipped into her pocket. Something glittered when she withdrew them. She turned it in the light. It was our father's signet ring that she held.

"Where did you get that?" Random asked.

"Where else?"

Benedict stepped toward her and held out his hand. She gave it to him. He scrutinized it.

"It *is* his," he said. "It has the little markings on the back that I've seen before. Why do you have it?"

"First, to convince you that I am acting properly when I convey his orders," she said.

"How is it that you even know him?" I asked.

"I met him during his—difficulties—some time back," she told us. "In fact, you might say that I helped to deliver him from them. This was after I had met Martin, and I was inclined to be more sympathetic toward Amber. But then, your father is also a charming and persuasive man. I decided that I could not simply stand by and see him remain prisoner to my kin."

"Do you know how he was captured in the first place?"

She shook her head.

"I only know that Brand effected his presence in a shadow far enough from Amber that he could be taken there. I believe it involved a fake quest for a nonexistent magical tool which might heal the Pattern. He realizes now that only the Jewel can do it."

"Your helping him to get away . . . How did this affect your relations with your own people?"

"Not too damned well," she said. "I am temporarily without a home."

"And you want one here?"

She smiled again.

"It depends on how things turn out. If my people have their way, I would as soon go back—or stay with what shadows remain."

I withdrew a Trump, glanced at it.

"What of Merlin? Where is he now?"

"They have him," she said. "I fear he may be their man now. He knows his parentage, but they have had charge of his education for a long while. I do not know whether he could be gotten away."

I raised the Trump, stared at it.

"No good," she said. "It will not function between here and there."

I recalled how difficult Trump communication had been when I had been to the fringes of that place. I tried anyway.

The card grew cold in my hand and I reached out. There was the faintest flicker of a responding presence. I tried harder.

"Merlin, this is Corwin," I said. "Do you hear me?"

I seemed to hear a reply. It seemed to be, "I cannot—" And then there was nothing. The card lost its coldness.

"Did you reach him?" she asked.

"I am not sure," I said. "But I think so. Just for a moment."

"Better than I thought," she said. "Either conditions are good or your minds are very similar."

"When you began waving Dad's signet around you spoke of orders," Random said. "What orders? And why is he sending them through you?"

"It is a matter of timing."

"Timing? Hell! He just left here this morning!"

"He had to finish one thing before he was ready for another. He had no idea how long it would take. But I was just in touch with him before I came here—though I was hardly prepared for the reception I walked into—and he is now ready to begin the next phase."

"Where did you speak with him?" I asked. "Where is he?"

"I have no idea where he is. He contacted me."

"And . . . ?"

"He wants Benedict to attack immediately."

Gérard finally stirred from the huge armchair in which he had sat listening. He rose to his feet, hooked his thumbs in his belt and looked down at her.

"An order like that would have to come directly from Dad."

"It did," she said.

He shook his head.

"It makes no sense. Why contact you—someone we have small reason to trust—rather than one of us?"

"I do not believe that he can reach you at the moment. On the other hand, he was able to reach me."

"Why?"

"He did not use a Trump. He does not have one for me. He used a reverberation effect of the black road, similar to the means by which Brand once escaped Corwin."

"You know a lot of what has been going on."

"I do. I still have sources in the Courts, and Brand transported himself there after your struggle. I hear things."

"Do you know where our father is right now?" Random asked.

"No, I do not know. But I believe that he has journeyed to the real Amber, to take counsel with Dworkin and to re-examine the damage to the primal Pattern."

"To what end?"

"I do not know. Probably to decide on the course of action he will take. The fact that he reached me and ordered the attack most likely means that he has decided."

"How long ago was this communication?"

"Just a few hours—my time. But I was far from here in Shadow. I do not know what the time differential is. I am too new at this."

"So it could be something extremely recent. Possibly only moments ago," Gérard mused. "Why did he talk with you rather than one of us? I do not believe that he could not reach us if he wished to."

"Perhaps to show that he looks upon me with favor." she said.

"All of this may be entirely true," Benedict stated. "But I am not moving without a confirmation of that order."

"Is Fiona still at the primal Pattern?" Random asked.

"Last I heard," I told him, "she had set up camp there. I see what you mean. . . ."

I shuffled out Fi's card.

"It took more than one of us to get through from there," he observed.

"True. So give me a hand."

He rose, came to my side. Benedict and Gérard also approached.

"This is not really necessary," Dara protested.

I ignored her and concentrated on the delicate features of my red-haired sister. Moments later, we had contact.

"Fiona," I asked, seeing from the background that she was still in residence at the heart of things, "is Dad there?"

"Yes," she said, smiling tightly. "He is inside with Dworkin."

"Listen, urgency prevails. I do not know whether or not you know Dara, but she is here—"

"I know who she is, but I have never met her."

"Well, she claims she has an attack order for Benedict, from Dad. She has his signet to back it up, but he did not speak of this earlier. Do you know anything about it?"

"No," she said. "All we did was exchange greetings when he and Dworkin were out here earlier to look at the Pattern. I had some suspicions then, though, and this confirms them."

"Suspicions? What do you mean?"

"I think Dad is going to try to repair the Pattern. He has the Jewel with him, and I overheard some of the things he said to Dworkin. If he makes the attempt, they will be aware of it in the Courts of Chaos the moment that he begins. They will try to stop him. He would want to strike first to keep them occupied. Only . . ."

"What?"

"It is going to kill him, Corwin. I know that much about it. Whether he succeeds or fails, he will be destroyed in the process."

"I find it hard to believe."

"That a king would give up his life for the realm?"

"That Dad would."

"Then either he has changed or you never really knew him. But I do believe he is going to try it."

"Then why send his latest order by someone he knows we do not really trust?"

"To show that he wants you to trust her, I would guess, once he has confirmed it."

"It seems a roundabout way of doing things, but I agree that we should not act without that confirmation. Can you get it for us?"

"I will try. I will get back to you as soon as I have spoken with him."

She broke the contact.

I turned toward Dara, who had heard only our side of the conversation.

"Do you know what Dad is going to do right now?" I asked her.

"Something involving the black road," she said. "He had indicated that much. What, though, or how, he did not say."

I turned away. I squared my cards and encased them. I did not like this turning of events. This entire day had started badly, and things had been going downhill ever since. It was only a little past lunchtime, too. I shook my head. When I had spoken with him, Dworkin had described the results of any attempt to repair the Pattern, and they had sounded pretty horrendous to me. Supposing Dad tried it, failed, and got himself killed in the attempt? Where would we be then? Right where we were now, only without a leader, on the eve of battle—and with the succession problem stirring again. That whole ghastly business would be in the back of our minds as we rode to the wars, and we would all begin our private arrangements to fight one another once more as soon as the current enemy was dealt with. There had to be another way of handling things. Better Dad alive and on the throne than a revival of the succession in intrigues.

"What are we waiting for?" Dara asked. "Confirmation?"

"Yes," I replied.

Random began to pace. Benedict seated himself and tested the dressing on his arm. Gérard leaned against the mantelpiece. I stood and thought. An idea came to me just then. I pushed it away immediately, but it returned. I did not like it, but that had nothing to do with practicalitics. I would have to move quickly, though, before I had a chance to talk myself around to another viewpoint. No. I would stick with this one. Damn it!

There came a stirring of contact. I waited. Moments later, I regarded Fiona again. She stood in a familiar place that it took me several seconds to recognize: Dworkin's sitting room, on the other side of the heavy door at the back of the cave. Dad and Dworkin were both with her. Dad had dropped his Ganelon disguise and was his old self once again. I saw that he wore the Jewel.

"Corwin," Fiona said, "it is true. Dad did send the attack order with Dara, and he expected this call for confirmation. I—"

"Fiona, bring me through."

"What?"

"You heard me. Now!"

I extended my right hand. She reached forward and we touched.

"Corwin!" Random shouted. "What's happening!"

Benedict was on his feet, Gérard already moving toward me.

"You will hear about it shortly," I said, and I stepped forward.

I squeezed her hand before I released it and I smiled.

"Thanks, Fi. Hello, Dad. Hi, Dworkin. How's everything?"

I glanced once at the heavy door, saw that it stood open. Then I passed around Fiona and moved toward them. Dad's head was lowered, his eyes narrowed. I knew that look.

"What is this, Corwin? You are here without leave," he said. "I have confirmed that damned order, now I expect it to be carried out."

"It will be," I said, nodding. "I did not come here to argue about that."

"What, then?"

I moved nearer, calculating my words as well as the distance. I was glad that he had remained seated.

"For a time we rode as comrades," I said. "Damned if I did not come to like you then. I never had before, you know. Never had guts enough to say that before either, but you know it is true. I like to think that that is how things could have been, if we had not been what we are to each other." For the barest moment, his gaze seemed to soften as I positioned myself. Then, "At any rate," I went on, "I am going to believe in you that way rather than this way, because there is something I would never have done for you otherwise."

"What?" he asked.

"This."

I seized the Jewel with an upward sweeping motion and snapped the chain up over his head. I pivoted on my heel then and raced across the room and through the door. I drew it shut behind me and snapped it to. I could see no way to bar it from the outside, so I ran on, retracing the route through the cave from that night I had followed Dworkin along it. Behind me, I heard the expected bellow.

I followed the twistings. I stumbled only once. Wixer's smell still hung heavy in his lair. I pounded on and a final turning brought me a view of daylight ahead.

I raced toward it, slipping the Jewel's chain over my head as I went. I felt it fall to my breast, I reached down into it with my mind. There were echoes in the cave behind me.

Outside!

I sprinted toward the Pattern, feeling through the Jewel, turning it into an extra sense. I was the only person other than Dad or Dworkin fully attuned to it. Dworkin had told me that the Pattern's repair might be effected by a person's walking the Grand Pattern in such a state of attunement, burning out the smear at each crossing, replacing it with stock from the image of the Pattern that he bore within him, wiping out the black road in the process. Better me than Dad, then. I still felt that the black road owed something of its final form to the strength my curse against Amber had given it. I wanted to wipe that out, too. Dad would do a better job of putting things together after the war than I ever could, anyway. I realized, at that moment, that I no longer wanted the throne. Even if it were available, the prospect of administering to the kingdom down all the dull centuries that might lie before me was overwhelming. Maybe I would be taking the easy way out if I died in this effort. Eric was dead, and I no longer hated him. The other thing that had driven me—the throne—seemed now to have been desirable only because I'd thought he had wanted it so. I renounced both. What was left? I had laughed at Vialle, then wondered. But she had been right. The old soldier in me was strongest. It was a matter of duty. But not duty alone. There was more. . . .

I reached the edge of the Pattern, quickly made my way toward its beginning. I glanced back at the cavemouth. Dad, Dworkin, Fiona—none of them had yet emerged. Good. They could never make it in time to stop me. Once I set foot on the Pattern, it would be too late for them to do anything but wait and watch. I thought for a fleeting instant of Iago's dissolution, pushed that thought away, strove to calm my mind to the level necessary for the undertaking, recalled my battle with Brand in this place and his strange departure, pushed that away, too, slowed my breathing, prepared myself.

A certain lethargy came upon me. It was time to begin, but I held back for a moment, trying to fix my mind properly on the grand task that lay before me. The Pattern swam for a moment in my vision. Now! Damn it! Now! No more preliminaries! Begin, I told myself. Walk!

Still, I stood, contemplating the Pattern as in a dream. I forgot about myself for long moments as I regarded it. The Pattern, with its long black smear to be removed . . .

It no longer seemed important that it might kill me. My mind drifted, considering the beauty of the thing. . . .

I heard a sound. It would be Dad, Dworkin, Fiona, coming. I had to do something before they reached me. I had to walk it, in a moment. . . .

I pulled my gaze away from the Pattern and glanced back toward the cavemouth. They had emerged, come partway down the slope and halted. Why? Why had they stopped?

What did it matter? I had the time I needed in which to begin. I began to raise my foot, to step forward.

I could barely move. I inched my foot ahead with a great effort of will. Taking this first step was proving worse than walking the Pattern itself, near to the end. But it did not seem so much an external resistance I fought against as it did the sluggishness of my own body. It was almost as if—

Then I had me an image of Benedict beside the Pattern in Tir-na Nog'th, Brand approaching, mocking, the Jewel burning upon his breast.

Before I looked down, I knew what I would see.

The red stone was pulsing in time with my heartbeat.

Damn them!

Either Dad or Dworkin—or both of them—reached through it at this instant, paralyzing me. I did not doubt that either of them could manage it alone. Still, at this distance, it was not worth surrendering without a fight.

I continued to push forward with my foot, sliding it slowly ahead toward the edge of the Pattern. Once I made it, I did not see how they . . .

Drowsing . . . I felt myself beginning to fall. I had been asleep for a moment. It happened again.

When I opened my eyes, I could see a portion of the Pattern. When I turned my head, I saw feet. When I looked up, I saw Dad holding the Jewel.

"Go away," he said to Dworkin and Fiona, without turning his head toward them.

They withdrew as he placed the Jewel about his own neck. He leaned forward then and extended his hand. I took it and he drew me to my feet.

"That was a damfool thing to do," he said.

"I almost made it."

He nodded.

"Of course, you would have killed yourself and not accomplished anything," he said. "But it was well done nevertheless. Come on, let's walk."

He took my arm, and we began to move about the periphery of the Pattern.

I watched that strange sky-sea, horizonless about us, as we went. I wondered what would have happened had I been able to begin the Pattern, what would be happening at that moment.

"You have changed," he finally said, "or else I never really knew you."

I shrugged.

"Something of both perhaps. I was about to say the same of you. Tell me something?"

"What?"

"How difficult was it for you, being Ganelon?"

He chuckled.

"Not hard at all," he said. "You may have had a glimpse of the real me."

"I liked him. Or, rather, you being him. I wonder whatever became of the real Ganelon?"

"Long dead, Corwin. I met him after you had exiled him from Avalon, long ago. He wasn't a bad chap. Wouldn't have trusted him worth a damn, but then I never trust anyone I don't have to."

"It runs in the family."

"I regretted having to kill him. Not that he gave me much choice. All this was very long ago, but I remembered him clearly, so he must have impressed me."

"And Lorraine?"

"The country? A good job, I thought. I worked the proper shadow. It grew in strength by my very presence, as any will if one of us stays around for long—as with you in Avalon, and later that other place. And I saw that I had a long while there by exercising my will upon its timestream."

"I did not know that could be done."

"You grow in strength slowly, beginning with your initiation into the Pattern. There are many things you have yet to learn. Yes, I strengthened Lorraine, and made it especially vulnerable to the growing force of the black road. I saw that it would lie in your path, no matter where you went. After your escape, all roads led to Lorraine."

"Why?"

"It was a trap I had set for you, and maybe a test. I wanted to be with you when you met the forces of Chaos. I also wanted to travel with you for a time."

"A test? What were you testing me for? And why travel with me?"

"Can you not guess? I have watched all of you over the years. I never named a successor. I purposely left the matter muddled. You are all enough like me for me to know that the moment I declared for one of you I would be signing his or her death warrant. No. I intentionally left things as they were until the very end. Now, though, I have decided. It is to be you."

"You communicated with me, as yourself, briefly, back in Lorraine. You told me then to take the throne. If you had made up your mind at that point why did you continue the masquerade?"

"But I had not decided then. That was merely a means to assure your continuing. I feared you might come to like that girl too much, and that land. When you emerged a hero from the Black Circle you might have decided to settle and stay there. I wanted to plant the notions that would cause you to continue your journey."

I was silent for a long while. We had moved a good distance about the Pattern.

Then, "There is something that I have to know," I said. "Before I came here I was speaking with Dara, who is in the process of trying to clear her name with us—"

"It is clear," he said. "I have cleared it."

I shook my head.

"I refrained from accusing her of something I have been thinking about for some time. There is a very good reason why I felt she cannot be trusted, despite her protests and your endorsement. Two reasons, in fact."

"I know, Corwin. But she did not kill Benedict's servants to manage her position at his house. I did it myself, to assure her getting to you as she did, at just the appropriate time."

"You? You were party to her whole plot? Why?"

"She will make you a good queen, son. I trust the blood of Chaos for strength. It was time for a fresh infusion. You will take the throne already provided with an heir. By the time he is ready for it, Merlin will long have been weaned from his upbringing."

We had come all the way around to the place of the black smear. I stopped. I squatted and studied it.

"You think this thing is going to kill you?" I finally asked.

"I know that it is."

"You are not above murdering innocent people to manipulate me. Yet you would sacrifice your life for the kingdom."

I looked at him.

"My own hands are not clean," I said, "and I certainly do not presume to judge you. A while back, though, when I made ready to try the Pattern, I thought how my feelings had changed—toward Eric, toward the throne. You do what you do, I believe, as a duty. I, too, feel a duty now, toward Amber, toward the throne. More than that, actually. Much more, I realized, just then. But I realized something else, also, something that duty does not require of me. I do not know when or how it stopped and I changed, but I do not want the throne, Dad. I am sorry it messes up your plans, but I do not want to be king of Amber. I am sorry."

I looked away then, back down at the smear. I heard him sigh.

Then, "I am going to send you home now," he said. "Saddle your horse and take provisions. Ride to a place outside Amber—any place, fairly isolated."

"My tomb?"

He snorted and chuckled faintly.

"That will do. Go there and wait my pleasure. I have some thinking to do."

I stood. He reached out and placed his right hand on my shoulder. The Jewel was pulsing. He looked into my eyes.

"No man can have everything he wants the way that he wants it," he said.

And there was a distancing effect, as of the power of a Trump, only working in reverse. I heard voices, then about me I saw the room I had earlier departed. Benedict, Gérard, Random and Dara were still there. I felt Dad release my shoulder. Then he was gone and I was among them once again.

"What is the story?" Random said. "We saw Dad sending you back. By the way, how did he do that?"

"I do not know," I said. "But he confirms what Dara has told us. He gave her the signet and the message."

"Why?" Gérard asked.

"He wanted us to learn to trust her," I said.

Benedict rose to his feet. "Then I will go and do as I have been bid."

"He wants you to attack, then fall back," Dara said. "After that, it will only be necessary to contain them."

"For how long?"

"He said only that this will become apparent."

Benedict gave one of his rare smiles and nodded. He managed his card case with his one hand, removed the deck, thumbed out the special Trump I had given him for the Courts.

"Good luck," Random said.

"Yes," Gérard agreed.

I added my wishes and watched him fade. When his rainbow afterimage had vanished I looked away and noticed that Dara was crying silently. I did not remark on it.

"I, too, have orders now—of a sort," I said. "I had best be moving."

"And I will get back to the sea," said Gérard.

"No," I heard Dara say as I was moving toward the door.

I halted.

"You are to remain here, Gérard, and see to the safety of Amber herself. No attack will come by sea."

"But I thought Random was in charge of the local defense."

She shook her head.

"Random is to join Julian in Arden."

"Are you sure?" Random asked.

"I am certain."

"Good," he said. "It is nice to know he at least thought of me. Sorry, Gérard. That's the breaks."

Gérard simply looked puzzled. "I hope he knows what he is doing," he said.

"We have been through that already," I told him. "Good-bye."

I heard a footfall as I left the room. Dara was beside me.

"What now?" I asked her.

"I thought I would walk with you, wherever you are going."

"I am just going up the hill to get some supplies. Then I am heading for the stables."

"I will go with you."

"I am riding alone."

"I could not accompany you, anyway. I still have to speak with your sisters."

"They're included, huh?"

"Yes."

We walked in silence for a time, then she said, "The whole business was not so cold-blooded as it seemed, Corwin."

We entered the supply room.

"What business?"

"You know what I mean."

"Oh. That. Well, good."

"I like you. It could be more than that one day, if you feel anything."

My pride handed me a snappy reply, but I bit it back. One learns a few things over the centuries. She had used me, true, but then it seemed she had not been entirely a free agent at the time. The worst that might be said, I suppose, was that Dad wanted me to want her. But I did not let my resentment on this interfere with what my own feelings really were, or could become.

So, "I like you, too," I said, and I looked at her. She seemed as if she needed to be kissed just then, so I did. "I had better get ready now."

She smiled and squeezed my arm. Then she was gone. I decided not to examine my feelings just then. I got some things together.

I saddled Star and rode back up over the crest of Kolvir until I came to my tomb. Seated outside it, I smoked my pipe and watched the clouds. I felt I had had a very full day, and it was still early afternoon. Premonitions played tag in the grottoes of my mind, none of which I would have cared to take to lunch.

THREE

Contact came suddenly as I sat drowsing. I was on my feet in an instant. It was Dad.

"Corwin, I have made my decisions and the time has come," he said. "Bare your left arm."

I did this, as his form continued to grow in substantiality, looking more and more regal the while, a strange sadness on his face, of a sort I had never seen there before.

He took hold of my arm with his left hand and drew his dagger with his right.

I watched as he cut my arm, then resheathed his blade. The blood came forth, and he cupped his left hand and caught it. He released my arm, covered his left hand with his right and drew away from me. Raising his hands to his face, he blew his breath into them and drew them quickly apart.

A crested red bird the size of a raven, its feathers all the color of my blood, stood on his hand, moved to his wrist, looked at me. Even its eyes were red, and there was a look of familiarity as it cocked its head and regarded me.

"He is Corwin, the one you must follow," he told the bird. "Remember him."

Then he transferred it to his left shoulder, from whence it continued to stare at me, making no effort to depart.

"You must go now, Corwin," he said, "quickly. Mount your horse and ride south, passing into Shadow as soon as you can. Hellride. Get as far away from here as possible."

"Where am I going, Father?" I asked him.

"To the Courts of Chaos. You know the way?"

"In theory. I have never ridden the distance."

He nodded slowly.

"Then get moving," he said. "I want you to create as great a time differential as you can between this place and yourself."

"All right," I said, "but I do not understand."

"You will, when the time comes."

"But there is an easier way," I protested. "I can get there faster and with a lot less bother simply by getting in touch with Benedict with his Trump and having him take me through."

"No good," Dad said. "It will be necessary for you to take the longer route because you will be carrying something which will be conveyed to you along the way."

"Conveyed? How?"

He reached up and stroked the red bird's feathers.

"By your friend here. He could not fly all the way to the Courts—not in time, that is."

"What will he bring me?"

"The Jewel. I doubt that I will be able to effect the transfer myself when I have finished what I have to do with it. Its powers may be of some benefit to us in that place."

"I see," I said. "But I still need not ride the entire distance. I can Trump through after I receive it."

"I fear not. Once I have done what must be done here, the Trumps will all become inoperative for a period of time."

"Why?"

"Because the entire fabric of existence will be undergoing an alteration. Move now, damn it! Get on your horse and ride!"

I stood and stared a moment longer.

"Father, is there no other way?"

He simply shook his head and raised his hand. He began to fade.

"Good-bye."

I turned and mounted. There was more to say, but it was too late. I turned Star toward the trail that would take me southward.

While Dad was able to play with the stuff of Shadow atop Kolvir, I had never been able to. I required a greater distance from Amber in order to work the shifts.

Still, knowing that it could be done, I felt that I ought to try. So, working my way southward across bare stone and down rocky passes where the wind howled, I sought to warp the fabric of being about me as I headed toward the trail that led to Garnath.

. . . A small clump of blue flowers as I rounded a stony shoulder.

I grew excited at this, for they were a modest part of my working. I continued to lay my will upon the world to come beyond each twisting of my way.

A shadow from a triangular stone, across my path . . . A shifting of the wind . . .

Some of the smaller ones were indeed working. A backward twist to the trail . . . A crevice . . . An ancient bird's nest, high on a rocky shelf . . . More of the blue flowers . . .

Why not? A tree . . . Another . . .

I felt the power moving within me. I worked more changes.

A thought came to me then, concerning my newfound strength. It seemed possible that it might have been purely psychological reasons which had barred me from performing such manipulations earlier. Until very recently I had considered Amber herself the single, immutable reality from which all shadows took their form. Now I realized she was but first among shadows, and that the place where my father stood represented the higher reality. Therefore, while the proximity made it difficult it did not make it impossible to effect changes in this place. Yet, under other circumstances I would have saved my strength until I had reached a point where it was easier to shift things about.

Now, now though, the need for haste lay upon me. I would have to exert myself, to rush, to do my father's bidding.

By the time I reached the trail leading down the southern face of Kolvir, the character of the land had already changed. I looked upon a series of gentle slopes, rather than the steep descent which normally marked the way. I was already entering the shadowlands.

The black road still lay like a dark scar to my left as I headed downward, but the Garnath through which it had been cut was in slightly better shape than that which I knew so well. Its lines were softer, from flocks of greenery which lay somewhat nearer the dead swath. It was as though my curse upon the land were slightly mitigated. Illusion of feeling, of course, for this was no longer exactly my Amber. But, *I am sorry for my part in this,* I addressed everything mentally, half-prayerlike. *I ride now to try to undo it. Forgive me, O spirit of this place.* My eyes moved in the direction of the Grove of the Unicorn, but it was too far to the west, masked by too many trees, for me even to glimpse that sacred glade.

The slope grew more level as I descended, becoming a series of gentle foothills. I let Star move faster as we crossed them, bearing to the southwest, then finally the south. Lower, lower. At a great distance to my left the sea sparkled and shone. Soon the black road would come between us, for I was descending into Garnath in its direction. No matter what I did with Shadow, I would not be able to erase that ominous presence. In fact, the fastest course I could follow would be one that paralleled it.

We came at last to the floor of the valley. The Forest of Arden towered far to my right, sweeping westward, immense and venerable. I rode on, working what changes I could to bear me even farther from my home.

While keeping the black road on hand, I stayed a good distance from it. I had to, since it was the one thing I could not change. I kept shrubs, trees and low hills between us.

I reached out then, and the texture of the land changed.

Veins of agate . . . Heaps of schist . . . A darkening of the greenery . . .

Clouds swimming across the sky . . . The sun shimmering and dancing . . .

We increased our pace. The land sank lower still. Shadows lengthened, merged. The forest retreated. A rocky wall grew to my right, another to my left. . . . A cold wind pursued me down a rough canyon. Strata streaks—red, gold, yellow and brown—flashed by. The floor of the canyon grew sandy. Dust devils spun about us. I leaned farther forward as the way began to rise once again. The walls slanted inward, grew closer together.

The way narrowed, narrowed. I could almost touch either wall. . . .

Their tops came together. I rode through a shadowy tunnel, slowing as it darkened. . . . Phosphorescent designs burst into being. The wind made a moaning noise.

Out then!

The light from the walls was blinding, and giant crystals rose all about us. We plunged past, following an upward trail that led away from this region and through a series of mossy dells where small, perfectly circular pools lay still as green glass.

Tall ferns appeared before us and we made our way among them. I heard a distant trumpeting noise.

Turning, pacing . . . Red now the ferns, wider and lower . . . Beyond, a great plain, pinking into evening . . .

Forward, over pale grasses . . . The smell of fresh earth . . . Mountains or dark clouds far ahead . . . A rush of stars from my left . . . A quick spray of moisture . . . A blue moon leaps into the sky . . . Flickerings among the dark masses . . . Memories and a rumbling noise . . . Stormsmell and rushing air . . .

A strong wind . . . Clouds across the stars . . . A bright fork spearing a shattered tree to my right, turning it to flame . . . A tingling sensation . . . The smell of ozone . . . Sheets of water upon me . . . A row of lights to my left . . .

Clattering down a cobbled street . . . A strange vehicle approaching . . . Cylindrical, chugging . . . We avoid one another . . . A shout pursues me . . . Through a lighted window the face of a child . . .

Clattering . . . Splashing . . . Storefronts and homes . . . The rain lets up, dies down, is gone . . . A fog blows by, lingers, deepens, is pearled by a growing light to my left . . .

The terrain softens, grows red . . . The light within the mist brightens . . . A new wind, from behind, a growing warmth . . . The air breaks apart . . .

Sky of pale lemon . . . Orange sun rushing toward noon . . .

A shudder! A thing not of my doing, totally unanticipated . . . The ground moves beneath us, but there is more to it than that. The new sky, the new sun, the rusty desert I have just now entered—all of them expand and contract, fade and return. There comes a cracking sound, and with each fading I find Star and myself alone, amid a white nothingness—characters without a setting. We tread upon nothing. The light comes from everywhere and illuminates only ourselves. A steady cracking noise, as of the spring thaw come upon a Russian river I had once ridden beside, fills my ears. Star, who has paced many shadows, emits a frightened sound.

I look all about me. Blurred outlines appear, sharpen, grow clear. My environment is restored, though with a somewhat washed-out look to it. A bit of the pigment has been drained from the world.

We wheel to the left, racing for a low hill, mounting it, halting finally at its summit.

The black road. It too seems denatured—but even more so than the rest. It ripples beneath my gaze, almost seems to undulate as I watch. The cracking noise continues, grows louder. . . .

A wind comes out of the north, gentle at first but increasing in force. Looking in that direction, I see a mass of dark clouds building.

I know that I must move as I have never moved before. Ultimates of destruction and creation are occurring at the place I visited—when? No matter. The waves move outward from Amber and this, too, may pass away—and me along with it. If Dad cannot put it all back together again.

I shake the reins. We race southward.

A plain . . . Trees . . . Some broken buildings . . . Faster . . .

The smoke of a forest afire . . . A wall of flame . . . Gone . . .

Yellow sky, blue clouds . . . An armada of dirigibles crossing . . .

Faster . . .

The sun drops like a piece of hot iron into a bucket of water, stars become streaks . . . A pale light upon a straight trail . . . Sounds dopplered from dark smears, the wailing . . . Brighter the light, fainter the prospect . . . Gray, to my right, my left . . . Brighter now . . . Nothing but the trail my eyes to ride . . . The wailing heightens to a shriek . . . Forms run together . . . We race through a tunnel of Shadow . . . It begins to revolve. . . .

Turning, turning . . . Only the road is real . . . The worlds go by . . . I have released my control of the sets and ride now the thrust of the power itself, aimed only to remove me from Amber and hurl me toward Chaos . . . There is wind upon me and the cry in my ears . . . Never before have I pushed my power over Shadow to its limit . . . The tunnel grows as slick and seamless as glass . . . I feel I am riding down a vortex, a maelstrom, the heart of a tornado . . . Star and I are drenched with sweat . . . There is a wild feeling of flight upon me, as though I am pursued . . . The road is become an abstraction . . . My eyes sting as I try to blink away the perspiration . . . I cannot hold this ride much longer . . . There comes a throbbing at the base of my skull. . . .

I draw back gently upon the reins and Star begins to slow. . . .

The walls of my tunnel of light grow grainy . . . Blotches of gray, black, white, rather than a uniformity of shading . . . Brown . . . A hint of blue . . . Green . . . The wailing descends to a hum, a rumble, fading . . . Gentler the wind . . . Shapes comes and go. . . .

Slowing, slowing . . .

There is no path. I ride on mossy earth. The sky is blue, the clouds are white. I am very light-headed, I draw rein. I—

Tiny.

I was shocked as I lowered my eyes. I stood at the outskirts of a toy village. Houses I could hold in the palm of my hand, minuscule roads, tiny vehicles crawling along them. . . .

I looked back. We had crushed a number of these diminutive residences. I looked all around. There were fewer to the left. I guided Star carefully in that direction, kept moving until we had left that place. I felt bad about it—whatever it was—whoever dwelled there. But there was not a thing that I could do.

I moved again, passing through Shadow, until I came to what seemed a deserted quarry beneath a greenish sky. I felt heavier here. I dismounted, took a drink of water, walked around a bit.

I breathed deeply of the damp air that engulfed me. I was far from Amber now, about as far as one ever need go, and well on my way to Chaos. I had seldom come this far before. While I had chosen this place for a rest stop because it represented the nearest thing to normalcy I could catch hold of, the changes would soon be getting more and more radical.

I was stretching my cramped muscles when I heard the shriek, high in the air above me.

I looked up and saw the dark form descending, Grayswandir coming by reflex into my hand. But the light caught it at a proper angle as it came down, and the winged form took fire on its way.

My familiar bird circled, circled, descended to my outstretched arm. Those frightening eyes regarded me with a peculiar intelligence, but I did not spare them the attention I might have on another occasion. Instead, I sheathed Grayswandir and reached for the thing the bird bore.

The Jewel of Judgment.

I knew by this that Dad's effort, whatever it had amounted to, was finished. The Pattern had either been repaired or botched. He was either alive or dead. Choose a couple from either column. The effects of his act would be spreading outward from Amber through Shadow now, like the ripples in the proverbial pond. I would learn more of them soon enough. In the meantime, I had my orders.

I drew the chain over my head and let the Jewel fall upon my breast. I remounted Star. My bloodbird emitted a short cry and rose into the air.

We moved again.

. . . Over a landscape where the sky whitened as the ground darkened. Then the land flared and the sky grew black. Then the reverse. And again . . . with each stride the effect shifted, and as we moved faster it built to a stroboscopic series of still-shots about us, gradually growing to a jerky animation, then the hyperactive quality of a silent film. Finally, all was a blur.

Points of light flashed past, like meteors or comets. I began to feel a throbbing sensation, as of a cosmic heartbeat. Everything began to turn about me, as though I had been caught up in a whirlwind.

Something was going wrong. I seemed to be losing control. Could it be that the effects of Dad's doings had already reached the area of Shadow through which I passed? It seemed hardly likely. Still . . .

Star stumbled. I clung tightly as we went down, not wishing to be separated in Shadow. I struck my shoulder on a hard surface and lay there for a moment, stunned.

When the world came together about me again, I sat up and looked around.

A uniform twilight prevailed, but there were no stars. Instead, large rocks of various shapes and sizes drifted and hovered in the air. I got to my feet and looked all about.

It was possible, from what I could see of it, that the irregular stony surface on which I stood was itself but a mountain-sized boulder drifting with the others. Star rose and stood shivering at my side. An absolute silence contained us. The still air was cool. There was not another living thing in sight. I did not like this place. I would not have halted here of my own volition. I knelt to inspect Star's legs. I wanted to leave as soon as possible, preferably mounted.

As I was about this, I heard a soft chuckle which might have come from a human throat.

I paused, resting my hand upon Grayswandir's hilt and seeking the source of the sound.

Nothing. Nowhere.

Yet I had heard it. I turned slowly, looking in every direction. No . . .

Then it came again. Only this time, I realized that it had its source overhead.

I scanned the floating rocks. Shadow-draped, it was difficult to distinguish—

There!

Ten meters above the ground and thirty or so to my left, what appeared to be a human form stood atop a small island in the sky, regarding me. I considered it. Whatever it was, it seemed too far off to pose a threat. I was certain that I could be gone before it could reach me. I moved to mount Star.

"No good, Corwin," called the voice I least wanted to hear just then. "You are locked here. There is no way you can depart without my leave."

I smiled as I mounted, then drew Grayswandir.

"Let's find out," I said. "Come bar my way."

"Very well," he replied, and flames sprang from the bare rock, towering full circle about me, licking, sprawling, soundless.

Star went wild. I slammed Grayswandir back into the scabbard, whipped a corner of my cloak across Star's eyes, spoke soothing words. As I did this, the circle enlarged, the fires receding toward the edges of the great rock on which we stood.

"Convinced?" came the voice. "This place is too small. Ride in any direction. Your mount will panic again before you can shift into Shadow."

"Good-bye, Brand," I said, and I began to ride.

I rode in a large counterclockwise circle about the rocky surface, shielding Star's right eye from the flames about the periphery of things. I head Brand chuckle again, not realizing what I was doing.

A pair of large rocks . . . Good. I rode on by, continuing the course. Now a jagged hedge of stone to my left, a rise, a dip . . . A mess of shadow the fires cast, across my path . . . There. Down . . . Up. A touch of green to that patch of light . . . I could feel the shifting begin.

The fact that it is easier for us to take a straight course does not make it the only way. We all pursue it so much of the time, though, that we tend to forget that one can also make progress by going around in circles. . . .

I could feel the shift more strongly as I neared the two large rocks again. Brand caught on about then, also.

"Hold it, Corwin!"

I threw him a finger and cut between the rocks, heading down into a narrow canyon speckled with points of yellow light. According to specifications.

I drew my cloak away from Star's head and shook the reins. The canyon cut abruptly to the right. We followed it into a better-lighted avenue which widened and brightened as we went.

. . . Beneath a jutting overhang, sky of milk shading to pearl on its other side.

Riding deeper, faster, farther . . . A jagged cliff crowned the upper talus to my left, greening in twisted sign of shrubbery beneath a pink-touched sky.

I rode until the greenery was bluery beneath a yellow sky, till the canyon rose to meet a lavender plain where orange rocks rolled as the ground was shaken beneath us in time with our hoofbeats. I crossed there under wheeling comets, coming to the shore of a blood-red sea in a place of heavy perfumes. I rode a large green sun and a small bronze one out of the sky as I paced that shore, while skeletal navies clashed and serpents of the deep circled their orange and blue-sailed vessels. The Jewel pulsed upon me and I drew strength from it. A wild wind came up and lofted us through a copper-clouded sky above a wailing chasm which seemed to extend forever, black-bottomed, spark-shot, fuming with heady scents. . . .

At my back, the sound of thunder, ceaseless . . . Fine lines, like the craquelure of an old painting, abreast of us, advancing, everywhere . . . Cold, a fragrance-killing wind pursues . . .

Lines . . . The cracks widen, blackness flows to fill . . . Dark streaks race by, up, down, back upon themselves . . . The settling of a net, the labors of a giant, invisible spider, world trapping . . .

Down, down and down . . . The ground again, wrinkled and leathery as a mummy's neck . . . Soundless, our throbbing passage . . . Softer the thunder, falling the wind . . . Dad's last gasp? Speed now and away . . .

A narrowing of lines, to the fineness of an etching, fading then in the three suns' heat . . . And faster yet . . .

A rider, approaching . . . Hand to hilt in time to my own . . . Me. Myself coming back? Simultaneous, our salutes . . . Through one another, somehow, the air like a sheet of water that one dry instant . . . What Caroll mirror, what Rebma, Tir-na Nog'th effect . . . Yet far, far to my left, a black thing writhing . . . We pace the road . . . It leads me on . . .

White sky, white ground and no horizon . . . Sunless and cloudless the prospect . . . Only that thread of black, far off, and gleaming pyramids everywhere, massive, disconcerting . . .

We tire. I do not like this place . . . But we have outrun whatever process pursues. Draw rein.

I was tired, but I felt a strange vitality within me. It seemed as though it arose from within my breast . . . The Jewel. Of course. I made an effort to draw upon this power again. I felt it flow outward through my limbs, barely halting at my extremities. It was almost as if—

Yes. I reached out and lay my will upon my blank and geometrical surroundings. They began to alter.

It was a movement. The pyramids shuffled by, darkening as they passed. They shrank, they merged, they passed to gravel. The world turned upside down and I stood as on the underside of a cloud, watching landscapes flash by beneath/above.

Light streamed upward past me, from a golden sun beneath my feet. This, too, passed, and the fleecy ground darkened, firing waters upward to erode the passing land. Lightnings jumped up to strike the world overhead, to break it apart. In places it shattered and its pieces fell about me.

They began to swirl as a wave of darkness passed.

When the light came again, bluish this time, it held no point source and described no land.

. . . Golden bridges cross the void in great streamers, one of them flashing beneath us even now. We wind along its course, standing the while still as a statue . . . For an age, perhaps, this goes on. A phenomenon not unrelated to highway hypnosis enters through my eyes, lulls me dangerously.

I do what I can to accelerate our passage. Another age goes by.

Finally, far ahead, a dusky, misty blotch, our terminus, growing very slowly despite our velocity.

By the time we reach it, it is gigantic—an island in the void, forested over with golden, metallic trees. . . .

I stop the motion which has borne us thus far and we move forward under our own power, entering that wood. Grass like aluminum foil crunches beneath us as we pass among those trees. Strange fruit, pale and shiny, hangs about me. There are no animal sounds immediately apparent. Working our way inward, we come to a small clearing through which a quicksilver stream flows. There, I dismount.

"Brother Corwin," comes that voice again. "I have been waiting for you."

FOUR

I faced the wood, watched him emerge from it. I did not draw my own weapon, as he had not drawn his. I reached down into the Jewel with my mind, though. After the exercise I had just completed, I realized that I could do a lot more than control weather with it. Whatever Brand's power, I felt I'd a weapon now with which to confront it directly. The Jewel pulsed more deeply as I did this.

"Truce," Brand said. "Okay? May we talk?"

"I do not see that we have anything more to say to one another," I told him.

"If you do not give me a chance you will never know for certain, will you?"

He came to a halt about seven meters away, flung his green cloak back over his left shoulder and smiled.

"All right. Say it, whatever it is," I said.

"I tried to stop you," he said, "back there, for the Jewel. It is obvious that you know what it is now, that you realize how important it is."

I said nothing.

"Dad has already used it," he continued, "and I am sorry to report that he has failed in what he set out to do with it."

"What? How could you know?"

"I can see through Shadow, Corwin. I would have thought our sister had filled you in more thoroughly on these matters. With a little mental effort, I can perceive whatever I choose now. Naturally, I was concerned with the outcome of this affair. So I watched. He is dead, Corwin. The effort was too much for him. He lost control of the forces he was manipulating and was blasted by them a little over halfway through the Pattern."

"You lie!" I said, touching the Jewel.

He shook his head.

"I admit that I am not above lying to gain my ends, but this time I am telling the truth. Dad is dead. I saw him fall. The bird brought you the Jewel then, as he had willed it. We are left in a universe without a Pattern."

I did not want to believe him. But it was possible that Dad had failed. I had the assurance of the only expert in the business, Dworkin, as to the difficulty of the task.

"Granting for the moment what you have said, what happens next?" I asked.

"Things fall apart," he replied. "Even now, Chaos wells up to fill the vacuum back at Amber. A great vortex has come into being, and it grows. It spreads ever outward, destroying the shadow worlds, and it will not stop until it meets with the Courts of Chaos, bringing all of creation full circle, with Chaos once more to reign over all."

I felt dazed. Had I struggled from Greenwood, through everything, to here, to have it end this way? Would I see everything stripped of meaning, form, content, life, when things had been pushed to a kind of completion?

"No!" I said. "It cannot be so."

"Unless . . ." Brand said softly.

"Unless what?"

"Unless a new Pattern is inscribed, a new order created to preserve form."

"You mean ride back into that mess and try to complete the job? You just said that the place no longer exists."

"No. Of course not. The location is unimportant. Wherever there is a Pattern there is a center. I can do it right here."

"You think that you can succeed where Dad failed?"

"I have to try. I am the only one who knows enough about it and has sufficient time before the waves of Chaos arrive. Listen, I admit to everything Fiona has doubtless told you about me. I have schemed and I have acted. I have dealt with the enemies of Amber. I have shed our blood. I tried to burn out your memory. But the world as we know it is being destroyed now, and I live here too. All of my plans—everything!—will come to nothing if some measure of order is not preserved. Perhaps I have been duped by the Lords of Chaos. It is difficult for me to admit that, but I see the possibility now. It is not too late to foil them, though. We can build the new bastion of order right here."

"How?"

"I need the Jewel—and your assistance. This will be the site of the new Amber."

"Supposing—*arguendo*—I give it to you. Would the new Pattern be exactly like the old one?"

He shook his head.

"It could not be, any more than the one Dad was attempting to create would have been like Dworkin's. No two authors can render the same story in the same fashion. Individual stylistic differences cannot be avoided. No matter how hard I might try to duplicate it, my version would be slightly different."

"How could you do this," I asked, "when you are not fully attuned to the Jewel? You would need a Pattern to complete the process of attunement— and, as you say, the Pattern has been destroyed. What gives?"

Then, "I said that I would need your help," he stated. "There is another way to attune a person to the Jewel. It requires the assistance of someone who is already attuned. You would have to project yourself through the Jewel once more, and take me with you—into and through the primary Pattern that lies beyond."

"And then?"

"Why, when the ordeal is past I will be attuned, you give me the Jewel, I inscribe a new Pattern and we are back in business. Things hold together. Life goes on."

"What of Chaos?"

"The new Pattern will be unmarred. They will no longer have the road giving them access to Amber."

"With Dad dead, how would the new Amber be run?"

He smiled crookedly.

"I ought to have something for my pains, oughtn't I? I will be risking my life with this, and the odds are not all that good."

I smiled back at him.

"Considering the payoff, what is to prevent me from taking the gamble myself?" I said.

"The same thing that prevented Dad from succeeding—all the forces of Chaos. They are summoned by a kind of cosmic reflex when such an act is begun. I have had more experience with them than you. You would not have a chance. I might."

"Now let us say that you are lying to me, Brand. Or let us be kind and say that you did not see clearly through all the turmoil. Supposing Dad did succeed? Supposing there is a new Pattern in existence right now? What would happen if you were to do another, here, now?"

"I . . . It has never been done before. How should I know?"

"I wonder," I said. "Might you still get your own version of reality that way? Might it represent the splitting off of a new universe—Amber and Shadow—just for you? Might it negate ours? Or would it simply stand apart? Or would there be some overlapping? What do you think, given that situation?"

He shrugged his shoulders.

"I have already answered that. It has never been done before. How should I know?"

"But I think that you do know, or can make a very good guess at it. I think that that is what you are planning, that that is what you want to try—because that is all you have left now. I take this action on your part as an indication that Dad has succeeded and that you are down to your last card. But you need me and you need the Jewel for it. You cannot have either."

He sighed.

"I had expected more of you. But all right. You are wrong, but leave it at that. Listen, though. Rather than see everything lost, I will split the realm with you."

"Brand," I said, "get lost. You cannot have the Jewel, or my help. I have heard you out, and I think that you are lying."

"You are afraid," he said, "afraid of me. I do not blame you for not wanting to trust me. But you are making a mistake. You need me now."

"Nevertheless, I have made my choice."

He took a step toward me. Another . . .

"Anything you want, Corwin. I can give you anything you care to name."

"I was with Benedict in Tir-na Nog'th," I said, "looking through his eyes, listening with his ears, when you made him the same offer. Shove it, Brand. I am going on with my mission. If you think that you can stop me, now is as good a time as any."

I began walking toward him. I knew that I would kill him if I reached him. I also felt that I would not reach him.

He halted. He took a step backward.

"You are making a big mistake," he said.

"I do not think so. I think that I am doing exactly the right thing."

"I will not fight with you," he said hastily. "Not here, not above the abyss. You have had your chance, though. The next time that we meet, I will have to take the Jewel from you."

"What good will it be to you, unattuned?"

"There might still be a way for me to manage it—more difficult, but possible. You have had your chance. Good-bye."

He retreated into the wood. I followed after, but he had vanished.

I left that place and rode on, along a road over nothing. I did not like to consider the possibility that Brand might have been telling the truth, or at least a part of it. But the things he had said kept returning to plague me. Supposing Dad had failed? Then I was on a fool's errand. Everything was already over, and it was just a matter of time. I did not like looking back, just in case something was gaining on me. I passed into a moderately paced hellride. I wanted to get to the others before the waves of Chaos reached that far, just to let them know that I had kept faith, to let them see that in the end I had tried my best. I wondered then how the actual battle was going. Or had it even begun yet, within the time frame?

I swept along the bridge, which widened now beneath a brightening sky. As it assumed the aspect of a golden plain, I considered Brand's threat. Had he said what he had said simply to raise doubts, increase my discomfort and impair my efficiency? Possibly. Yet, if he required the Jewel he would have to ambush me. And I had a respect for that strange power he had acquired over Shadow. It seemed almost impossible to prepare for an attack by someone who could watch my every move and transport himself instantaneously to the most advantageous spot. How soon might it come? Not too soon, I guessed. First, he would want to frazzle my nerves—and I was already tired and more than a little punchy. I would have to rest, to sleep, sooner or later. It was impossible for me to go that great distance in a single stretch, no matter how accelerated the hellride.

Fogs of pink and orange and green fled past, swirled about me, filling up the world. The ground rang beneath us like metal. Occasional musical tones, as of rung crystal, occurred overhead. My thoughts danced. Memories of many worlds came and went in random fashion. Ganelon, my friend-enemy, and my father, enemy-friend, merged and parted, parted and merged. Somewhere one of them asked me who had a right to the throne. I had thought it was Ganelon, wanting to know our several justifications. Now I knew that it had been Dad, wanting to know my feelings. He had judged. He had made his decision. And I was backing out. Whether it was arrested development, the desire to be free of such an encumbrance, or a matter of sudden enlightenment based on all that I had experienced in recent years, growing slowly within me, granting me a more mature view of the onerous role of monarch apart from its moments of glory, I do not know. I remembered my life on the shadow Earth, following orders, giving them. Faces swam before me— people I had known over the centuries—friends, enemies, wives, lovers, relatives. Lorraine seemed to be beckoning me on, Moire laughing, Deirdre weeping. I fought again with Eric. I recalled my first passage through the Pattern, as a boy, and the later one when, step by step, my memory was given back to me. Murders, thieveries, knaveries, seductions returned because, as Mallory said, they were there. I was unable, even, to place them all correctly in terms of time. There was no great anxiety because there was no great guilt. Time, time, and more time had softened the edges of harsher things, had worked its changes on me. I saw my earlier selves as different people, acquaintances I had outgrown. I wondered how I could ever have been some of them. As I rushed onward, scenes from my past seemed to solidify in the mists about me. No poetic license here. Battles in which I had taken part assumed tangible form, save for a total absence of sound—the flare of weapons, the colors of uniforms, banners and blood. And people—most of them now long dead— moved from my memory into silent animation about me. None of these were members of my family, but all of them were people who had once meant something to me. Yet there was no special pattern to it. There were noble deeds as well as shameful; enemies as well as friends—and none of the persons involved took note of my passage; all were caught up in some long-past sequence of actions. I wondered then at the nature of the place through which I rode. Was it some watered-down version of Tir-na Nog'th, with some mind-sensitive substance in the vicinity that drew from me and projected about me this "This Is Your Life" panorama? Or was I simply beginning to hallucinate? I was tired, anxious, troubled, distressed, and I passed along a way which provided a monotonous, gentle stimulation of the senses of the sort leading to reverie. . . . In fact, I realized that I had lost control over Shadow sometime back and was now simply proceeding in a linear fashion across this landscape, trapped in a kind of externalized narcissism by the spectacle. . . . I realized then that I had to stop and rest—probably even sleep a little—though I feared doing so in this place. I would have to break free and make my way to a more sedate, deserted spot. . . .

I wrenched at my surroundings. I twisted things about. I broke free.

Soon I was riding in a rough, mountainous area, and shortly thereafter I came to the cave that I desired.

We passed within, and I tended to Star. I ate and drank just enough to take the edge off my hunger. I built no fire. I wrapped myself in my cloak and in a blanket I had brought. I held Grayswandir in my right hand. I lay facing the darkness beyond the cavemouth.

I felt a little sick. I knew that Brand was a liar, but his words bothered me anyway.

But I had always been good at going to sleep. I closed my eyes and was gone.

FIVE

I was awakened by a sense of presence. Or maybe it was a noise and a sense of presence. Whatever, I was awake and I was certain that I was not alone. I tightened my grip on Grayswandir and opened my eyes. Beyond that, I did not move.

A soft light, like moonlight, came in through the cavemouth. There was a figure, possibly human, standing just inside. The lighting was such that I could not tell whether it faced me or faced outward. But then it took a step toward me.

I was on my feet, the point of my blade toward its breast. It halted.

"Peace," said a man's voice, in Thari. "I have but taken refuge from the storm. May I share your cave?"

"What storm?" I asked.

As if in answer, there came a roll of thunder followed by a gust of wind with the smell of rain within it.

"Okay, that much is true," I said. "Make yourself comfortable."

He sat down, well inside, his back against the right-hand wall of the cave. I folded my blanket for a pad and seated myself across from him. About four meters separated us. I located my pipe and filled it, then tried a match which had been with me from the shadow Earth. It lit, saving me a lot of trouble. The tobacco had a good smell, mixed with the damp breeze. I listened to the sounds of the rain and regarded the dark outline of my nameless companion. I thought over some possible dangers, but it had not been Brand's voice which had addressed me.

"This is no natural storm," the other said.

"Oh? How so?"

"For one thing, it is coming out of the north. They never come out of the north, here, this time of year."

"That's how records are made."

"For another, I have never seen a storm behave this way. I have been watching it advance all day—just a steady line, moving slowly, front like a sheet of glass. So much lightning, it looks like a monstrous insect with hundreds of shiny legs. Most unnatural. And behind it, things have grown very distorted."

"That happens in the rain."

"Not that way. Everything seems to be changing its shape. Flowing. As if it is melting the world—or stamping away its forms."

I shuddered. I had thought that I was far enough ahead of the dark waves that I could take a little rest. Still, he might be wrong, and it could just be an unusual storm. But I did not want to take the chance. I rose and turned to the rear of the cave. I whistled.

No response. I went back and groped around.

"Something the matter?"

"My horse is gone."

"Could it have wandered off?"

"Must have. I'd have thought Star'd have better sense, though."

I went to the cavemouth but could see nothing. I was half-drenched in the instant I was there. I returned to my position beside the left wall.

"It seems like an ordinary enough storm to me," I said. "They sometimes get pretty bad in the mountains."

"Perhaps you know this country better than I do?"

"No, I am just traveling through—a thing I had better be continuing soon, too."

I touched the Jewel. I reached into it, then through it, out and up, with my mind. I felt the storm about me and ordered it away, with red pulses of energy corresponding to my heartbeats. Then I leaned back, found another match and relit my pipe. It would still take a while for the forces I had manipulated to do their work, against a stormfront of this size.

"It will not last too long," I said.

"How can you tell?"

"Privileged information."

He chuckled.

"According to some versions, this is the way that the world ends—beginning with a strange storm from out of the north."

"That's right," I said, "and this is it. Nothing to worry about, though. It will be all over, one way or the other, before too long."

"That stone you are wearing . . . It is giving off light."

"Yes."

"You were joking about this being the end, though—were you not?"

"No."

"You make me think of that line from the Holy Book—*The Archangel Corwin shall pass before the storm, lightning upon his breast. . . .* You would not be named Corwin, would you?"

"How does the rest of it go?"

"*. . . When asked where he travels, he shall say, 'To the ends of the Earth,' where he goes not knowing what enemy will aid him against another enemy, nor whom the Horn will touch.*"

"That's all?"

"All there is about the Archangel Corwin."

"I have run into this difficulty with Scripture in the past. It tells you enough to get interested, but never enough to be of any immediate use. It is as though the author gets his kicks by tantalizing. One enemy against another? The Horn? Beats me."

"Where *do* you travel?"

"Not too far, unless I can find my horse."

I returned to the cavemouth. It was letting up now, with a glow like a moon behind some clouds to the west, another to the east. I looked both ways along the trail and down the slope to the valley. No horses anywhere in sight. I turned back to the cave. Just as I did, however, I heard Star's whinny far below me.

I called back to the stranger in the cave, "I have to go. You can have the blanket."

I do not know whether he replied, for I moved off into the drizzle then, picking my way down the slope. Again, I exerted myself through the Jewel, and the drizzle halted, to be replaced by a mist.

The rocks were slippery, but I made it halfway down without stumbling. I paused then, both to catch my breath and to get my bearings. From that point, I was not certain as to the exact direction from which Star's whinny had come. The moon's light was a little stronger, visibility a bit better, but I saw nothing as I studied the prospect before me. I listened for several minutes.

Then I heard the whinny once more—from below, to my left, near a dark boulder, cairn or rocky outcrop. There did seem to be some sort of turmoil in the shadows at its base. Moving as quickly as I dared, I laid my course in that direction.

As I reached level ground and hurried toward the place of the action, I passed pockets of ground mist, stirred slightly by a breeze from out of the west, snaking silvery, about my ankles. I heard a grating, crunching sound, as of something heavy being pushed or rolled over a rocky surface. Then I caught sight of a gleam of light, low on the dark mass I was approaching.

Drawing nearer, I saw small, manlike forms outlined in a rectangle of light, struggling to move a great rocky slab. Faint echoes of a clattering sound and another whinny came from their direction. Then the stone began to move, swinging like the door that it probably was. The lighted area diminished, narrowed to a sliver, vanished with a booming sound, all of the struggling figures having first passed within.

When I finally reached that rocky mass all was silent once again. I pressed my ear to the stone, but heard nothing. But, whoever they were, they had taken my horse. I had never liked horse thieves, and I had killed my share in the past. And right now, I needed Star as I had seldom needed a horse. So I groped about, seeking the edges of that stony gate.

It was not too difficult to describe its outlines with my fingertips. I probably located it sooner than I would have by daylight, when everything would have blended and merged more readily to baffle the eye. Knowing its situation, I sought further then after some handhold by which I might draw it. They had seemed to be little guys, so I looked low.

I finally discovered what might have been the proper place and seized hold of it. I pulled then, but it was stubborn. Either they were disproportionately strong or there was a trick to it that I was missing.

No matter. There is a time for subtlety and a time for brute force. I was both angry and in a hurry, so the decision was made.

I began to draw upon the slab once again, tightening the muscles in my arms, my shoulders, my back, wishing Gérard were nearby. The door creaked. I kept pulling. It moved slightly—an inch, perhaps—and stuck. I did not slacken, but increased my effort. It creaked again.

I leaned backward, shifted my weight and braced my left foot against the rocky wall at the side of the portal. I pushed with it as I drew back. There was more creaking and some grinding as it moved again—another inch or so. Then it stopped and I could not budge it.

I released my grip and stood, flexing my arms. Then I put my shoulder to it and pushed the door back to its fully closed position. I took a deep breath and seized it again.

I put my left foot back where it had been. No gradual pressure this time. I yanked and shoved simultaneously.

There was a snapping sound and a clattering from within, and the door came forward about half a foot, grinding as it moved. It seemed freer now, though, so I got to my feet, reversed my position—back to wall—and found sufficient purchase to push it outward.

It moved more easily this time, but I could not resist placing my foot against it as it began to swing and thrusting forward as hard as I could. It shot through a full hundred and eighty degrees, slammed back against the rock on the other side with a great booming noise, fractured in several places, swayed, fell and struck the ground with a crash that made it shudder, breaking off more fragments when it hit.

Grayswandir was back in my hand before it struck, and I had dropped into a crouch and stolen a quick look about the corner.

Light . . . There was illumination beyond . . . From little lamps depending from hooks along the wall . . . Beside the stairway . . . Going down . . . To a place of greater light and some sounds . . . Like music . . .

There was no one in sight. I would have thought that the godawful din I had raised would have caught someone's attention, but the music continued. Either the sound—somehow—had not carried, or they did not give a damn. Either way . . .

I rose and stepped over the threshold. My foot struck against a metal object. I picked it up and examined it. A twisted bolt. They had barred the door after themselves. I tossed it back over my shoulder and started down the stair.

The music—fiddles and pipes—grew louder as I advanced. From the breaking of the light, I could see that there was some sort of hall off to my right, from the foot of the stair. They were small steps and there were a lot of them. I did not bother with stealth, but hurried down to the landing.

When I turned and looked into the hall, I beheld a scene out of some drunken Irishman's dream. In a smoky, torchlit hall, hordes of meter-high people, red-faced and green clad, were dancing to the music or quaffing what appeared to be mugs of ale while stamping their feet, slapping tabletops and each other, grinning, laughing and shouting. Huge kegs lined one wall, and a number of the revelers were queued up before the one which had been tapped. An enormous fire blazed in a pit at the far end of the room, its smoke being sucked back through a crevice in the rock wall, above a pair of cave-mouths running anywhere. Star was tethered to a ring in the wall beside that pit, and a husky little man in a leather apron was grinding and honing some suspicious-looking instruments.

Several faces turned in my direction, there were shouts and suddenly the music stopped. The silence was almost complete.

I raised my blade to an overhand, épée en garde position, pointed across the room toward Star. All faces were turned in my direction by then.

"I have come for my horse," I said. "Either you bring him to me or I come and get him. There will be a lot more blood the second way."

From off to my right, one of the men, larger and grayer than most of the others, cleared his throat.

"Begging your pardon," he began, "but how did you get in here?"

"You will be needing a new door," I said. "Go and look if you care to, if it makes any difference—and it may. I will wait."

I stepped aside and put the wall to my back.

He nodded.

"I will do that."

And he darted by.

I could feel my anger-born strength flowing into and back out of the Jewel. One part of me wanted to cut and slash and stab my way across the room, another wanted a more humane settlement with people so much smaller than myself; and a third and perhaps wiser part suggested that the little guys might not be such pushovers. So I waited to see how my door-opening feat impressed their spokesman.

Moments later, he returned, giving me wide berth.

"Bring the man his horse," he said.

A sudden flurry of conversation occurred within the hall. I lowered my blade.

"My apologies," said the one who had given the order. "We desire no trouble with the like of you. We will be foraging elsewhere. No hard feelings, I hope?"

The man in the leather apron had untethered Star and started in my direction. The revelers drew back to make way as he led my mount through the hall.

I sighed.

"I will just call it a day and forgive and forget," I said.

The little man seized a flagon from a nearby table and passed it to me. Seeing my expression, he sipped from it himself.

"Join us in a drink, then?"

"Why not?" I said, and I took it and quaffed it as he did the same with the second one.

He gave a gentle belch and grinned.

" 'Tis a mighty small draught for a man of your size," he said then. "Let me fetch you another, for the trail."

It was a pleasant ale, and I was thirsty after my efforts.

"All right," I said.

He called for more as Star was delivered to me.

"You can wrap the reins around this hook here," he said, indicating a low projection near the doorway, "and he will be safe out of the way."

I nodded and did that as the butcher withdrew. No one was staring at me any longer. A pitcher of the brew arrived and the little man refilled our flagons from it. One of the fiddlers struck up a fresh tune. Moments later, another joined him.

"Sit a spell," said my host, pushing a bench in my direction with his foot. "Keep your back to the wall as you would. There will be no funny business."

I did, and he rounded the table and seated himself across from me, the pitcher between us. It was good to sit for a few moments, to take my mind from my journey for just a little while, to drink the dark ale and listen to a lively tune.

"I will not be apologizing again," said my companion, "nor explaining either. We both know it was no misunderstanding. But you have got the right on your side, it is plain to see." He grinned and winked. "So I am for calling it a day, too. We will not starve. We will just not feast tonight. 'Tis a lovely jewel you are wearing. Tell me about it?"

"Just a stone," I said.

The dancing resumed. The voices grew louder. I finished my drink and he refilled the flagon. The fire undulated. The night's cold went out of my bones.

"Cozy place you've got here," I said.

"Oh, that it is. Served us for time out of mind, it has. Would you be liking the grand tour?"

"Thank you, no."

"I did not think so, but 'twas my hostly duty to offer. You are welcome to join in the dancing, too, if you wish."

I shook my head and laughed. The thought of my cavorting in this place brought me images out of Swift.

"Thanks anyway."

He produced a clay pipe and proceeded to fill it. I cleaned my own and did the same. Somehow all danger seemed past. He was a genial enough little fellow, and the others seemed harmless now with their music and their stepping.

Yet . . . I knew the stories from another place, far, so far from here . . . To awaken in the morning, naked, in some field, all traces of this spot vanished . . . I knew, yet . . .

A few drinks seemed small peril. They were warming me now, and the keening of the pipes and the wailings of the fiddles were pleasant after the brain-numbing twistings of the hellride. I leaned back and puffed smoke. I watched the dancers.

The little man was talking, talking. Everyone else was ignoring me. Good. I was hearing some fantastic yarn of knights and wars and treasures. Though I gave it less than half an ear, it lulled me, even drew a few chuckles.

Inside, though, my nastier, wiser self was warning me: All right, Corwin, you have had enough. Time to take your leave . . .

But, magically it seemed, my glass had been refilled, and I took it and sipped from it. One more, one more is all right.

No, said my other self, he is laying a spell on you. Can't you feel it?

I did not feel that any dwarf could drink me under the table. But I was tired, and I had not eaten much. Perhaps it would be prudent . . .

I felt myself nodding. I placed my pipe on the table. Each time that I blinked it seemed to take longer to reopen my eyes. I was pleasantly warm now, with just the least bit of delicious numbness in my tired muscles.

I caught myself nodding, twice. I tried to think of my mission, of my personal safety, of Star. . . . I mumbled something, still vaguely awake behind closed eyelids. It would be so good, just to remain this way for half a minute more. . . .

The little man's voice, musical, grew monotonous, dropped to a drone. It did not really matter what he was say—

Star whinnied.

I sat bolt upright, eyes wide, and the tableau before me swept all sleep from my mind.

The musicians continued their performance, but now no one was dancing. All of the revelers were advancing quietly upon me. Each held something in his hand—a flask, a cudgel, a blade. The one in the leather apron brandished his cleaver. My companion had just fetched a stout stick from where it had leaned against the wall. Several of them lofted small pieces of furniture. More of them had emerged from the caves near the fire pit, and they bore stones and clubs. All traces of gaiety had vanished, and their faces were now either expressionless, twisted into grimaces of hate or smiling very nasty smiles.

My anger returned, but it was not the white-heat thing I had felt earlier. Looking at the horde before me, I had no wish to tackle it. Prudence had come to temper my feelings. I had a mission. I should not risk my neck here if I could think of another way of handling things. But I was certain that I could not talk my way out of this one.

I took a deep breath. I saw that they were getting ready to rush me, and I thought suddenly of Brand and Benedict in Tir-na Nog'th, Brand not even fully attuned to the Jewel. I drew strength from that fiery stone once again, growing alert and ready to lay about me if it came to that. But first, I would have a go at their nervous systems.

I was not certain how Brand had managed it, so I simply reached out through the Jewel as I did when influencing the weather. Strangely, the music was still playing as though this action of the little people was but some grisly continuation of their dance.

"Stand still." I said it aloud and I willed it, rising to my feet. "Freeze. Turn to statues. All of you."

I felt a heavy throbbing within/upon my breast. I felt the red forces move outward, exactly as on those other occasions when I had employed the Jewel.

My diminutive assailants were poised. The nearest ones stood stock-still, but there were still some movements among those to the rear. Then the pipes let out a crazy squeal and the fiddles fell silent. Still, I did not know whether I had reached them or whether they had halted of their own accord on seeing me stand.

Then I felt the great waves of force which flowed out from me, embedding the entire assembly in a tightening matrix. I felt them all trapped within this expression of my will, and I reached out and untethered Star.

Holding them with a concentration as pure as anything I used when passing through Shadow, I led Star to the doorway. I turned then for a final look at the frozen assembly and pushed Star on ahead of me up the stair. As I followed, I listened, but there were no sounds of renewed activity from below.

When we emerged, dawn was already paling the east. Strangely, as I mounted, I heard the distant sounds of fiddles. Moments later, the pipes came in on the tune. It seemed as though it mattered not at all whether they succeeded or failed in their designs against me; the party was going to go on.

As I headed us south, a small figure hailed me from the doorway I had so recently quitted. It was their leader with whom I had been drinking. I drew rein, to better catch his words.

"And where do you travel?" he called after me.

Why not?

"To the ends of the Earth!" I shouted back.

He broke into a jig atop his shattered door.

"Fare thee well, Corwin!" he cried.

I waved to him. Why not, indeed? Sometimes it's damned hard to tell the dancer from the dance.

SIX

I rode fewer than a thousand meters to what had been the south, and everything stopped—ground, sky, mountains. I faced a sheet of white light. I thought then of the stranger in the cave and his words. He had felt that the world was being blotted out by that storm, that it corresponded to something out of a local apocalyptic legend. Perhaps it had. Perhaps it had been the wave of Chaos of which Brand had spoken, moving this way, passing over, destroying, disrupting. But this end of the valley was untouched. Why should it remain?

Then I recalled my actions on rushing out into the storm. I had used the Jewel, the power of the Pattern within it, to halt the storm over this area. And if it had been more than an ordinary storm? The Pattern had prevailed over Chaos before. Could this valley where I had stopped the rainfall be but a small island in a sea of Chaos now? If so, how was I to continue?

I looked to the east, from whence the day brightened. No sun stood new-risen in the heavens, but rather a great, blindingly burnished crown, a gleaming sword hanging through it. From somewhere I heard a bird singing, notes almost like laughter. I leaned forward and covered my face with my hands. Madness . . .

No! I had been in weird shadows before. The farther one traveled, the stranger they sometimes grew. Until . . . What was it I'd thought that night in Tir-na Nog'th?

Two lines from a story of Isak Dinesen's returned to me, lines which had troubled me sufficiently to cause me to memorize them, despite the fact that I had been Carl Corey at the time: ". . . Few people can say of themselves that they are free of the belief that this world which they see around them is in reality the work of their own imagination. Are we pleased with it, proud of it, then?" A summation of the family's favorite philosophical pastime. Do we make the Shadow worlds? Or are they there, independent of us, awaiting our footfalls? Or is there an unfairly excluded middle? Is it a matter of more or less, rather than either-or? A dry chuckle arose suddenly as I realized that I might never know the answer for certain. Yet, as I had thought that night, there is a place, a place where there comes an end to Self, a place where solipsism is no longer the plausible answer to the locales we visit, the things that we find. The existence of this place, these things, says that here, at least, there is a difference, and if here, perhaps it runs back through our shadows, too, informing them with the not-self, moving our egos back to a smaller stage. For this, I felt, was such a place, a place where the "Are we pleased with it, proud of it, then?" need not apply, as the rent vale of Garnath and my curse might have nearer home. Whatever I ultimately believed, I felt that I was about to enter the land of the completely not-I. My powers over Shadow might well be canceled beyond this point.

I sat up straight and squinted against the glare. I spoke a word to Star and shook the reins. We moved ahead.

For a moment, it was like riding into a fog. Only it was enormously brighter, and there was absolutely no sound. Then we were falling.

Falling, or drifting. After the initial shock, it was difficult to say. At first, there was a feeling of descent—perhaps intensified by the fact that Star panicked when it began. But there was nothing to kick against, and after a time Star ceased all movement save for shivering and heavy breathing.

I held the reins with my right hand and clutched the Jewel with my left. I do not know what I willed or how I reached with it, exactly, but that I wanted passage through this place of bright nothingness, to find my way once more and move on to the journey's end.

I lost track of time. The feeling of descent had vanished. Was I moving, or merely hovering? No way to say. Was the brightness really brightness, still? And that deadly silence . . . I shuddered. Here was even greater sensory silence . . . I shuddered. Here was even greater sensory deprivation than in the days of my blindness, in my old cell. Here was nothing—not the sound of a scuttling rat nor the grinding of my spoon against the door; no dampness, no chill, no textures. I continued to reach . . .

Flicker.

It seemed there had been some momentary breaking of the visual field to my right, near subliminal in its brevity. I reached out and felt nothing.

It had been so brief a thing that I was uncertain whether it had really occurred. It could easily have been an hallucination.

But it seemed to happen again, this time to my left. How long the interval between, I could not say.

Then I heard something like a groan, directionless. This, too, was very brief.

Next—and for the first time, I was certain—there came a gray and white landscape like the surface of the moon. There and gone, perhaps a second's worth, in a small area of my visual field, off to my left. Star snorted.

To my right appeared a forest—gray and white—tumbling, as though we passed one another at some impossible angle. A small-screen fragment, less than two seconds' worth.

Then pieces of a burning building beneath me . . . Colorless . . .

Snatches of wailing, from overhead . . .

A ghostly mountain, a torchlit procession ascending a switchback trail up its nearest face . . .

A woman hanging from a tree limb, taut rope about her neck, head twisted to the side, hands tied behind her back . . .

Mountains, upside down, white; black clouds beneath . . .

Click. A tiny thrill of vibration, as if we had momentarily touched something solid—Star's hoof on stone, perhaps. Then gone . . .

Flicker.

Heads, rolling, dripping black gore . . . A chuckle from nowhere . . . A man nailed to a wall, upside down . . .

The white light again, rolling and heaving, wavelike . . .

Click. Flicker.

For one pulsebeat, we trod a trail beneath a stippled sky. The moment it was gone, I reached for it again, through the Jewel.

Click. Flicker. Click. Rumble.

A rocky trail, approaching a high mountain pass . . . Still monochrome, the world . . . At my back, a crashing like thunder . . .

I twisted the Jewel like a focus knob as the world began to fade. It came back again. . . . Two, three, four . . . I counted hoofbeats, heartbeats against the growling background. . . . Seven, eight, nine . . . The world grew brighter. I took a deep breath and sighed heavily. The air was cold.

Between the thunder and its echoes, I heard the sound of rain. None fell upon me, though.

I glanced back.

A great wall of rain stood perhaps a hundred meters to the rear. I could distinguish only the dimmest of mountain outlines through it. I clucked to Star and we moved a little faster, climbing to an almost level stretch that led between a pair of peaks like turrets. The world ahead was still a study in black and white and gray, the sky before me divided by alternate bands of darkness and light. We entered the pass.

I began to tremble. I wanted to draw rein, to rest, eat, smoke, dismount and walk around. Yet, I was still too close to that stormscreen to so indulge myself.

Star's hoofbeats echoed within the pass, where rock walls rose sheer on either hand beneath that zebra sky. I hoped these mountains would break this stormfront, though I felt that they could not. This was no ordinary storm, and I had a sick feeling that it stretched all the way back to Amber, and that I would have been trapped and lost forever within it but for the Jewel.

As I watched that strange sky, a blizzard of pale flowers began to fall about me, brightening my way. A pleasant odor filled the air. The thunder at my back softened. The rocks at my sides were shot with silver streaks. The world was possessed of a twilight feeling to match the illumination, and as I emerged from the pass, I saw down into a valley of quirked perspective, distance impossible to gauge, filled with natural-seeming spires and minarets reflecting the moon-like light of the sky-streaks, reminiscent of a night in Tir-na Nog'th, interspersed with silvery trees, spotted with mirror-like pools, traversed by drifting wraiths, almost terraced-seeming in places, natural and rolling in others, cut by what appeared to be an extension of the line of trail I followed, rising and falling, hung over by an elegiac quality, sparked with inexplicable points of glitter and shine, devoid of any signs of habitation.

I did not hesitate, but began my descent. The ground about me here was chalky and pale as bone—and was that the faintest line of a black road far off to my left? I could just about make it out.

I did not hurry now, as I could see that Star was tiring. If the storm did not come on too quickly, I felt that we might take a rest beside one of the pools in the valley below. I was tired and hungry myself.

I kept a lookout on the way down, but saw no people, no animals. The wind made a soft, sighing noise. White flowers stirred on vines beside the trail when I reached the lower levels where regular foliage began. Looking back, I saw that the stormfront still had not passed the mountain crest, though the clouds continued to pile behind it.

I made my way on down into that strange place. The flowers had long before ceased to fall about me, but a delicate perfume hung in the air. There were no sounds other than our own and that of the constant breeze from my right. Oddly shaped rock formations stood all about me, seeming almost sculpted in their purity of line. The mists still drifted. The pale grasses sparkled damply.

As I followed the trail toward the valley's wooded center, the perspectives continued to shift about me, skewing distances, bending prospects. In fact, I turned off the trail to the left to approach what appeared to be a nearby lake and it seemed to recede as I advanced. When I finally came upon it, however, dismounted and dipped a finger to taste, the water was icy but sweet.

Tired, I sprawled after drinking my fill, to watch Star graze while I began a cold meal from my bag. The storm was still fighting to cross the mountains. I looked for a long while, wondering about it. If Dad had failed, then those were the growls of Armageddon and this whole trip was meaningless. It did me no good to think that way, for I knew that I had to go on, whatever. But I could not help it. I might arrive at my destination, I might see the battle won, and then see it all swept away. Pointless . . . No. Not pointless. I would have tried, and I would keep on trying to the end. That was enough, even if everything was lost. Damn Brand, anyway! For starting—

A footfall.

I was into a crouch and I was turned in that direction with my hand on my blade in an instant.

It was a woman that I faced, small, clad in white. She had long, dark hair and wild, dark eyes, and she was smiling. She carried a wicker basket, which she placed on the ground between us.

"You must be hungry, Knight at arms," she said in strangely accented Thari. "I saw you come. I brought you this."

I smiled and assumed a more normal stance.

"Thank you," I said. "I am. I am called Corwin. Yourself?"

"Lady," she said.

I quirked an eyebrow. "Thank you—Lady. You make your home in this place?"

She nodded and knelt to uncover the basket.

"Yes, my pavilion is farther back, along the lake." She gestured with her head, eastward—in the direction of the black road.

"I see," I said.

The food and the wine in the basket looked real, fresh, appetizing, better than my traveler's fare. Suspicion was with me, of course. "You will share it with me?" I asked.

"If you wish."

"I wish."

"Very well."

She spread a cloth, seated herself across from me, removed the food from the basket and arranged it between us. She served it then, and quickly sampled each item herself. I felt a trifle ignoble at this, but only a trifle. It was a peculiar location for a woman to be residing, apparently alone, just waiting around to succor the first stranger who happened along. Dara had fed me on our first meeting, also; and as I might be nearing the end of my journey, I was closer to the enemy's places of power. The black road was too near at hand, and I caught Lady eyeing the Jewel on several occasions.

But it was an enjoyable time, and we grew more familiar as we dined. She was an ideal audience, laughing at all my jokes, making me talk about myself. She maintained eye contact much of the time, and somehow our fingers met whenever anything was passed. If I were being taken in in some way, she was being very pleasant about it.

As we had dined and talked, I had also kept an eye on the progress of that inexorable-seeming stormfront. It had finally breasted the mountain crest and crossed over. It had begun its slow descent of the high slope. As she cleared the cloth, Lady saw the direction of my gaze and nodded.

"Yes, it is coming," she said, placing the last of the utensils in the basket and seating herself beside me, bringing the bottle and our cups. "Shall we drink to it?"

"I will drink with you, but not to that."

She poured.

"It does not matter," she said. "Not now," and she placed her hand on my arm and passed me my cup.

I held it and looked down at her. She smiled. She touched the rim of my cup with her own. We drank.

"Come to my pavilion now," she said, taking my hand, "where we will wile pleasurably the hours that remain."

"Thanks," I said. "Another time and that wiling would have been a fine dessert to a grand meal. Unfortunately, I must be on my way. Duty nags, time rushes. I've a mission."

"All right," she said. "It is not that important. And I know all about your mission. It is not all that important either, now."

"Oh? I must confess that I fully expected you to invite me to a private party which would result in me alone and palely loitering on the cold side of some hill sometime hence if I were to accept."

She laughed.

"And I must confess that it was my intention to so use you, Corwin. No longer, though."

"Why not?"

She gestured toward the advancing line of disruption.

"There is no need to delay you now. I see by this that the Courts have won. There is nothing anyone can do to halt the advance of the Chaos."

I shuddered briefly and she refilled our cups.

"But I would rather you did not leave me at this time," she went on. "It will reach us here in a matter of hours. What better way to spend this final time than in one another's company? There is no need even to go as far as my pavilion."

I bowed my head, and she drew up close against me. What the hell. A woman and a bottle—that was how I had always said I wanted to end my days. I took a sip of the wine. She was probably right. Yet, I thought of the woman-thing which had trapped me on the black road as I was leaving Avalon. I had gone at first to aid her, succumbed quickly to her unnatural charms— then, when her mask was removed, saw that there was nothing at all behind it. Damned frightening, at the time. But, not to get too philosophical, everybody has a whole rack of masks for different occasions. I have heard pop psychologists inveigh against them for years. Still, I have met people who impressed me favorably at first, people whom I came to hate when I learned what they were like underneath. And sometimes they were like that woman-thing—with nothing much really there. I have found that the mask is often far more acceptable than its alternative. So . . . This girl I held to me might really be a monster inside. Probably was. Aren't most of us? I could think of worse ways to go if I wanted to give up at this point. I liked her.

I finished my wine. She moved to pour me more and I stayed her hand. She looked up at me. I smiled.

"You almost persuaded me," I said.

Then I closed her eyes with kisses four, so as not to break the charm, and I went and mounted Star. The sedge was not withered, but he was right about the no birds. Hell of a way to run a railroad, though.

"Good-bye, Lady."

I headed south as the storm boiled its way down into the valley. There were more mountains before me, and the trail led toward them. The sky was still streaked, black and white, and these lines seemed to move about a bit; the over-all effect was still that of twilight, though no stars shone within the black areas. Still the breeze, still the perfume about me—and the silence, and the twisted monoliths and the silvery foliage, still dew-damp and glistening. Rag ends of mist blew before me. I tried to work with the stuff of Shadow, but it was difficult and I was tired. Nothing happened. I drew strength from the Jewel, trying to transmit some of it to Star, also. We moved at a steady pace until finally the land tilted upward before us, and we were climbing toward another pass, a more jagged thing than the one by which we had entered. I halted to look back, and perhaps a third of the valley now lay behind the shimmering screen of that advancing stormthing. I wondered about Lady and her lake, her pavilion. I shook my head and continued.

The way steepened as we neared the pass, and we were slowed. Overhead, the white rivers in the sky took on a reddish cast which deepened as we rode. By the time I reached the entrance, the whole world seemed tinged with blood. Passing within that wide, rocky avenue, I was struck by a heavy wind. Pushing on against it, the ground grew more level beneath us, though we continued to climb and I still could not see beyond the pass.

As I rode, something rattled in the rocks to my left. I glanced that way, but saw nothing. I dismissed it as a falling stone. Half a minute later, Star jerked beneath me, let out a terrible neigh, turned sharply to the right, then began to topple, leftward.

I leaped clear, and as we both fell I saw that an arrow protruded from behind Star's right shoulder, low. I hit the ground rolling, and when I halted I looked up in the direction from which it must have come.

A figure with a crossbow stood atop the ridge to my right, about ten meters above me. He was already cranking the weapon back to prepare for another shot.

I knew that I could not reach him in time to stop him. So I cast about for a stone the size of a baseball, found one at the foot of the escarpment to my rear, hefted it and tried not to let my rage interfere with the accuracy of my throw. It did not, but it may have contributed some extra force.

The blow caught him on the left arm, and he let out a cry, dropping the crossbow. The weapon clattered down the rocks and landed on the other side of the trail, almost directly across from me.

"You son of a bitch!" I cried. "You killed my horse! I'm going to have your head for it!"

As I crossed the trail, I looked for the fastest way up to him and saw it off to my left. I hurried to it and commenced climbing. An instant later, the light and the angle were proper and I had a better view of the man, bent nearly double, massaging his arm. It was Brand, his hair even redder in the sanguine light.

"This is it, Brand," I said. "I only wish someone had done it a long time ago."

He straightened and watched me climb for a moment. He did not reach for his blade. Just as I got to the top, perhaps seven meters away from him, he crossed his arms on his breast and lowered his head.

I drew Grayswandir and advanced. I admit that I was prepared to kill him in that or any other position. The red light had deepened until we seemed bathed in blood. The wind howled about us, and from the valley below came a rumble of thunder.

He simply faded before me. His outline grew less distinct, and by the time I reached the place where he had been standing he had vanished entirely.

I stood for a moment, cursing, remembering the story that he had somehow been transformed into a living Trump, capable of transporting himself anywhere in a very brief time.

I heard a noise from below. . . .

I rushed to the edge and looked down. Star was still kicking and blowing blood, and it tore my heart to see it. But that was not the only distressing sight.

Brand was below. He had picked up the crossbow and begun preparing it once more.

I looked about for another stone, but there was nothing at hand. Then I spotted one farther back, in the direction from which I had come. I hurried to it, resheathed my blade and raised the thing. It was about the size of a watermelon. I returned with it to the edge and sought Brand.

He was nowhere in sight,

Suddenly, I felt very exposed. He could have transported himself to any vantage and be sighting in on me at that instant. I dropped to the ground, falling across my rock. A moment later, I heard the bolt strike to my right. The sound was followed by Brand's chuckle.

I stood again, knowing it would take him at least a little while to recock his weapon. Looking in the direction of the laughter, I saw him, atop the ledge across the pass from me—about five meters higher than I was, and about twenty meters distant.

"Sorry about the horse," he said. "I was aiming for you. But those damned winds . . ."

By then I had spotted a niche and I made for it, taking the rock with me for a shield. From that wedge-shaped fissure, I watched him fit the bolt.

"A difficult shot," he called out, raising the weapon, "a challenge to my marksmanship. But certainly worth the effort. I've plenty more quarrels."

He chuckled, sighted and fired.

I bent low, holding the rock before my middle, but the bolt struck about two feet to my right.

"I had sort of guessed that might happen," he said, beginning to prepare his weapon once again. "Had to learn the windage, though."

I looked about for smaller stones to use for ammunition as I had earlier. There were none nearby. I wondered about the Jewel then. It was supposed to act to save me in the presence of immediate peril. But I had a funny feeling that this involved close proximity, and that Brand was aware of this and was taking advantage of the phenomenon. Still, mightn't there be something else I could do with the Jewel to thwart him? He seemed too far away for the paralysis trick, but I had beaten him once before by controlling the weather. I wondered how far off the storm was. I reached for it. I saw that it would take minutes I did not possess in order to set up the conditions necessary to draw lightning upon him. But the winds were another matter. I reached out for them, felt them. . . .

Brand was almost ready to shoot again. The wind began to scream through the pass.

I do not know where his next shot landed. Nowhere near me, though. He fell to readying his weapon again. I began setting up the factors for a lightningstroke. . . .

When he was ready, when he raised the weapon this time, I raised the winds once more. I saw him sight, I saw him draw a breath and hold it. Then he lowered the bow and stared at me.

"It just occurred to me," he called out, "you've got that wind in your pocket, haven't you? That is cheating, Corwin." He looked all about. "I should be able to find a footing where it will not matter, though. Aha!"

I kept working to set things up to blast him, but conditions were not ready yet. I looked up at that red- and black-streaked sky, something cloud-like forming above us. Soon, but not yet . . .

Brand faded and vanished again. Wildly, I sought him everywhere.

Then he faced me. He had come over to my side of the pass. He stood about ten meters to the south of me, with the wind at his back. I knew that I could not shift it in time. I wondered about throwing my rock. He would probably duck and I would be throwing away my shield. On the other hand . . .

He raised the weapon to his shoulder.

Stall! cried my own voice within my mind, while I continued to tamper with the heavens.

"Before you shoot, Brand, tell me one thing. All right?"

He hesitated, then lowered the weapon a few inches.

"What?"

"Were you telling me the truth about what happened—with Dad, the Pattern, the coming of Chaos?"

He threw back his head and laughed, a series of short barks.

"Corwin," he stated then, "it pleases me more than I can say to see you die not knowing something that means that much to you."

He laughed again and began to raise the weapon. I had just moved to hurl my rock and rush him. But neither of us completed either action.

There came a great shriek from overhead, and a piece of the sky seemed to detach itself and fall upon Brand's head. He screamed and dropped the crossbow. He raised his hands to tear at the thing that assailed him. The red bird, the Jewel bearer, born of my blood from my father's hand, had returned, to defend me.

I let go the rock and advanced upon him, drawing my blade as I went. Brand struck the bird and it flapped away, gaining altitude, circling for another dive. He raised both arms to cover his face and head, but not before I saw the blood that flowed from his left eye socket.

He began to fade again even as I rushed toward him. But the bird descended like a bomb and it talons struck Brand about the head once again. Then the bird, too, began to fade. Brand was reaching for his ruddy assailant and being slashed by it as they both disappeared.

When I reached the place of the action the only thing that remained was the fallen crossbow, and I smashed it with my boot.

Not yet, not yet the end, damn it! How long will you plague me, brother? How far must I go to bring it to an end between us?

I climbed back down to the trail. Star was not yet dead and I had to finish the job. Sometimes I think I'm in the wrong business.

SEVEN

A bowl of cotton candy.

Having traversed the pass, I regarded the valley that lay before me. At least, I assumed that it was a valley. I could see nothing below its cover of cloud/mist/fog.

In the sky, one of the red streaks was turning yellow; another, green. I was slightly heartened by this, as the sky had behaved in somewhat similar fashion when I had visited the edge of things, across from the Courts of Chaos.

I hitched up my pack and began hiking down the trail. The winds diminished as I went. Distantly, I heard some thunder from the storm I was fleeing. I wondered where Brand had gone. I had a feeling that I would not be seeing him again for a time.

Partway down, with the fog just beginning to creep and curl about me, I spotted an ancient tree and cut myself a staff. The tree seemed to shriek as I severed its limb.

"Damn you!" came something like a voice from within it.

"You're sentient?" I said. "I'm sorry . . ."

"I spent a long time growing that branch. I suppose you are going to burn it now?"

"No," I said. "I needed a staff. I've a long walk before me."

"Through this valley?"

"That's right."

"Come closer, that I may better sense your presence. There is something about you that glows."

I took a step forward.

"Oberon!" it said. "I know thy Jewel."

"Not Oberon," I said. "I am his son. I wear it on his mission, though."

"Then take my limb, and have my blessing with it. I've sheltered your father on many a strange day. He planted me, you see."

"Really? Planting a tree is one of the few things I never saw Dad do."

"I am no ordinary tree. He placed me here to mark a boundary."

"Of what sort?"

"I am the end of Chaos and of Order, depending upon how you view me. I mark a division. Beyond me other rules apply."

"What rules?"

"Who can say? Not I. I am only a growing tower of sentient lumber. My staff may comfort you, however. Planted, it may blossom in strange climes. Then again, it may not. Who can say? Bear it with you, however, son of Oberon, into the place where you journey now. I feel a storm approaching. Good-bye."

"Good-bye," I said. "Thank you."

I turned and walked on down the trail into the deepening fog. The pinkness was drained from it as I went. I shook my head as I thought about the tree, but its staff proved useful for the next several hundred meters, where the going was particularly rough.

Then things cleared a bit. Rocks, a stagnant pool, some small, dreary trees festooned with ropes of moss, a smell of decay . . . hurried by. A dark bird was watching me from one of the trees.

It took wing as I regarded it, flapping in a leisurely fashion in my direction. Recent events having left me a little bird-shy, I drew back as it circled my head. But then it fluttered to rest on the trail before me, cocked its head and viewed me with its left eye.

"Yes," it announced then. "You are the one."

"The one what?" I said.

"The one I will accompany. You've no objection to a bird of ill omen following you, have you, Corwin?"

It chuckled then, and executed a little dance.

"Offhand, I do not see how I can stop you. How is it that you know my name?"

"I've been waiting for you since the beginning of Time, Corwin."

"Must have been a bit tiresome."

"It has not been all that long, in this place. Time is what you make of it."

I resumed walking. I passed the bird and kept going. Moments later, it flashed by me and landed atop a rock off to my right.

"My name is Hugi," he stated. "You are carrying a piece of old Ygg, I see."

"Ygg?"

"The stuffy old tree who waits at the entrance to this place and won't let anyone rest on his branches. I'll bet he yelled when you whacked it off." He emitted peals of laughter then.

"He was quit decent about it."

"I'll bet. But then, he hadn't much choice once you'd done it. Fat lot of good it will do you."

"It's doing me fine," I said, swinging it lightly in his direction.

He fluttered away from it.

"Hey! That was not funny!"

I laughed.

"I thought it was."

I walked on by.

For a long while, I made my way through a marshy area. An occasional gust of wind would clear the way nearby. Then I would pass it, or the fogs would shift over it once again. Occasionally, I seemed to hear a snatch of music—from what direction, I could not tell—slow, and somewhat stately, produced by a steel-stringed instrument.

As I slogged along, I was hailed from somewhere to my left:

"Stranger! Halt and regard me!"

Wary, I halted. Couldn't see a damned thing through that fog, though.

"Hello," I said. "Where are you?"

Just then, the fogs broke for a moment and I beheld a huge head, eyes on a level with my own. They belonged to what seemed a giant body, sunk up to the shoulders in a quag. The head was bald, the skin pale as milk, with a stony texture to it. The dark eyes probably seemed even darker than they really were by way of contrast.

"I see," I said then. "You are in a bit of a fix. Can you free your arms?"

"If I strain mightily," came the reply.

"Well, let me check about for something stable you can grab onto. You ought to have a pretty good reach there."

"No. That is not necessary."

"Don't you want to get out? I thought that was why you hollered."

"Oh, no. I simply wanted you to regard me."

I moved nearer and stared, for the fog was beginning to shift again.

"All right," I said. "I have seen you."

"Do you feel my plight?"

"Not particularly, if you will not help yourself or accept help."

"What good would it do me to free myself?"

"It is your question. You answer it."

I turned to go.

"Wait! Where do you travel?"

"South, to appear in a morality play."

Just then, Hugi flew out of the fog and landed atop the head. He pecked at it and laughed.

"Don't waste your time, Corwin. There is much less here than meets the eye," he said.

The giant lips shaped my name. Then: "He is indeed the one?"

"That's him, all right," Hugi replied.

"Listen, Corwin," said the sunken giant. "You are going to try to stop the Chaos, aren't you?"

"Yes."

"Do not do it. It is not worth it. I want things to end. I desire a release from this condition."

"I already offered to help you out. You turned me down."

"Not that sort of release. An end to the whole works."

"That is easily done," I said. "Just duck your head and take a deep breath."

"It is not only personal termination that I desire, but an end to the whole foolish game."

"I believe there are a few other folks around who would rather make their own decisions on the matter."

"Let it end for them, too. There will come a time when they are in my position and will feel the same way."

"Then they will possess the same option. Good day."

I turned and walked on.

"You will, too!" he called after me.

As I hiked along, Hugi caught up with me and perched on the end of my staff.

"It's neat to sit on old Ygg's limb now he can't—Yikes!"

Hugi sprang into the air and circled.

"Burned my foot! How'd he do that?" he cried.

I laughed.

"Beats me."

He fluttered for a few moments, then made for my right shoulder.

"Okay if I rest here?"

"Go ahead."

"Thanks." He settled. "The Head is really a mental basket case, you know."

I shrugged my shoulders and he spread his wings for balance.

"He is groping after something," he went on, "but proceeding incorrectly by holding the world responsible for his own failings."

"No. He would not even grope to get out of the mud," I said.

"I meant philosophically."

"Oh, that sort of mud. Too bad."

"The whole problem lies with the self, the ego, and its involvement with the world on the one hand and the Absolute on the other."

"Oh, is that so?"

"Yes. You see, we are hatched and we drift on the surface of events. Sometimes, we feel that we actually influence things, and this gives rise to striving. This is a big mistake, because it creates desires and builds up a false ego when just being should be enough. That leads to more desires and more striving and there you are, trapped."

"In the mud?"

"So to speak. One needs to fix one's vision firmly on the Absolute and learn to ignore the mirages, the illusions, the fake sense of identity which sets one apart as a false island of consciousness."

"I had a fake identity once. It helped me a lot in becoming the absolute that I am now—me."

"No, that's fake, too."

"Then the me that may exist tomorrow will thank me for it, as I do that other."

"You are missing the point. That you will be fake, too."

"Why?"

"Because it will still be full of those desires and strivings that set you apart from the Absolute."

"What is wrong with that?"

"You remain alone in a world of strangers, the world of phenomena."

"I like being alone. I am quite fond of myself. I like phenomena, too."

"Yet the Absolute will always be there, calling to you, causing unrest."

"Good, then there is no need to hurry. But yes, I see what you mean. It takes the form of ideals. Everyone has a few. If you are saying that I should pursue them, I agree with you."

"No, they are distortions of the Absolute, and what you are talking about is more striving."

"That is correct."

"I can see that you have a lot to unlearn."

"If you are talking about my vulgar instinct for survival, forget it."

The trail had been leading upward, and we came now to a smooth, level place, almost paved-seeming, though strewn lightly with sand. The music had grown louder and continued to do so as I advanced. Then, through the fog, I saw dim shapes moving, slowly, rhythmically. It took several moments for me to realize that they were dancing to the music.

I kept moving until I could view the figures—human-seeming, handsome folk, garbed in courtly attire—treading to the slow measures of invisible musicians. It was an intricate and lovely dance that they executed, and I halted to watch some of it.

"What is the occasion," I asked Hugi, "for a party out here in the middle of nowhere?"

"They dance," he said, "to celebrate your passage. They are not mortals, but the spirits of Time. They began this foolish show when you entered the valley."

"Spirits?"

"Yes. Observe."

He left my shoulder, flew above them and defecated. The dropping passed through several dancers as if they were holograms, without staining a brocaded sleeve or a silken shirt, without causing any of the smiling figures to miss a measure. Hugi cawed several times then and flew back to me.

"That was hardly necessary," I said. "It is a fine performance."

"Decadent," he said, "and you should hardly take it as a compliment, for they anticipate your failure. They but wish to get in a final celebration before the show is closed."

I watched for a time anyway, leaning upon my staff, resting. The figure described by the dancers slowly shifted, until one of the women—an auburn-haired beauty—was quite near to me. Now, none of the dancers' eyes at any time met my own. It was as if I were not present. But that woman, in a perfectly timed gesture, cast with her right hand something which landed at my feet.

I stooped and found it substantial. It was a silver rose—my own emblem—that I held. I straightened and fixed it at the collar of my cloak. Hugi looked the other way and said nothing. I had no hat to doff, but I did bow to the lady. There might have been a slight twitch at her right eye as I turned to go.

The ground lost its smoothness as I walked, and finally the music faded. The trail grew rougher, and whenever the fogs cleared the only views were of rocks or barren plains. I drew strength from the Jewel when I would otherwise have collapsed, and I noted that each such fix was of shorter duration now.

After a time, I grew hungry and I halted to eat what rations I had left. Hugi stood on the ground nearby and watched me eat.

"I will admit to a certain small admiration for your persistence," he said, "and even for what you implied when you spoke of ideals. But that is about it. Earlier, we were talking about the futility of desire and of striving—"

"You were. It was not a major concern in my life."

"It should be."

"I have had a long life, Hugi. You insult me by assuming I have never considered these footnotes to sophomore philosophy. The fact that you find consensus reality barren tells me more about you than it does about that state of affairs. To wit, if you believe what you say I feel sorry for you, in that you must for some inexplicable reason be here desiring and striving to influence this false ego of mine rather than free of such nonsense and on your way to your Absolute. If you do not believe it, then it tells me that you have been set to hinder and discourage me, in which case you are wasting your time."

Hugi made a gargling noise. Then: "You are not so blind that you deny the Absolute, the beginning and end of everything?"

"It is not indispensable to a liberal education."

"You admit the possibility?"

"Perhaps I know it better than you, bird. The ego, as I see it, exists at an intermediate stage between rationality and reflex existence. Blotting it out is a retreat, though. If you come from that Absolute—of a self-canceling All— why do you wish to go back home? Do you so despise yourself that you fear mirrors? Why not make the trip worthwhile? Develop. Learn. Live. If you have been sent on a journey why do you wish to cop out and run back to your point of departure? Or did your Absolute make a mistake in sending something of your caliber? Admit that possibility and that is the end of the news."

Hugi glared at me, then sprang into the air and flew off. Going to consult his manual, perhaps. . . .

I heard a peal of thunder as I rose to my feet. I began walking. I had to try to keep ahead of things.

The trail narrowed and widened a number of times before it vanished completely, leaving me to wander across a gravelly plain. I felt more and more depressed as I traveled, trying to keep my mental compass set in the proper direction. I almost came to welcome the sounds of the storm, for they at least gave me a rough idea as to which way was north. Of course, things were a bit confusing in the fog, so that I could not be absolutely certain. And they were growing louder. . . . Damn.

. . . And I had been grieved by the loss of Star, troubled by Hugi's futilitarianism. This was definitely not a good day. I began to doubt that I was going to complete my journey. If some nameless denizen of this dark place did not ambush me before too long, there was a strong possibility that

I would wander here until my strength failed or the storm caught me. I did not know whether I would be able to beat back that canceling storm another time. I began to doubt it.

I tried using the Jewel to disperse the fog, but its effects seemed blunted. By my own sluggishness, perhaps. I could clear a small area, but my rate of travel quickly bore me through it. My sense of Shadow was dulled in this place which seemed in some way the essence of Shadow.

Sad. It would have been nice to go out with opera—in a big Wagnerian finale beneath strange skies, against worthy opponents—not scrabbling about in a foggy wasteland.

I passed a familiar-seeming outcrop of stone. Could I have been moving in a circle? There is a tendency to do that when completely lost. I listened for the thunder, to take my bearings again. Perversely, all was silent. I moved to the outcrop and seated myself on the ground, resting my back against it. No sense to merely wandering. I would wait a time for the thunder's signal. I withdrew my Trumps as I sat there. Dad had said that they would be out of commission for a time, but I had nothing better to do.

One by one, I went through them all, trying to reach everyone, save for Brand and Caine. Nothing. Dad had been right. The cards lacked the familiar coldness. I shuffled the entire deck then and cast my fortune, there on the sand. I got an impossible reading and put them all away again. I leaned back and wished I had some water left. For a long while, I listened for the storm. There were a few growls, but they were directionless. The Trumps made me think of my family. They were up ahead—wherever that might be—waiting for me. Waiting for what? I was transporting the Jewel. To what end? At first, I had assumed that its powers might be necessary in the conflict. If so, and if I were indeed the only one who could employ them, then we were in bad shape. I thought of Amber then, and I was shaken with remorse and a kind of dread. Things must not end for Amber, ever. There had to be a way to roll back the Chaos. . . .

I threw away a small stone I had been toying with. Once I released it, it moved very slowly.

The Jewel. Its slowdown effect again . . .

I drew more energy and the stone shot away. It seemed that I had just taken strength from the Jewel a little while ago. While this treatment energized my body, my mind still felt fogged up. I needed sleep—with lots of rapid eye movements. This place might seem a lot less unusual if I were rested.

How close was I to my destination? Was it just beyond the next mountain range, or an enormous distance farther? And what chance had I of staying ahead of that storm, no matter what the distance? And the others? Supposing the battle was already concluded and we had lost? I had visions of arriving too late, to serve only as grave-digger. . . . Bones and soliloquies, Chaos . . .

And where was that damned black road now that I finally had a use for it? If I could locate it, I could follow it. I had a feeling that it was somewhere off to my left. . . .

I reached out once again, parting the fogs, rolling them back. . . . Nothing . . .

A shape? Something moving?

It was an animal, a large dog perhaps, moving to remain within the fog. Was it stalking me?

The Jewel began to pulse as I moved the fog even farther back. Exposed, the animal seemed to shrug itself. Then it moved straight toward me.

EIGHT

I stood as it came near. I could see then that it was a jackal, a big one, its eyes fixed on my own.

"You are a little early," I said. "I was only resting."

It chuckled.

"I have come merely to regard a Prince of Amber," the beast said. "Anything else would be a bonus."

It chuckled again. So did I.

"Then feast your eyes. Anything else, and you will find that I have rested sufficiently."

"Nay, nay," said the jackal. "I am a fan of the House of Amber. And that of Chaos. Royal blood appeals to me, Prince of Chaos. And conflict."

"You have awarded me an unfamiliar title. My connection with the Courts of Chaos is mainly a matter of genealogy."

"I think of the images of Amber passing through the shadows of Chaos. I think of the waves of Chaos washing over the images of Amber. Yet at the heart of the order Amber represents moves a family most chaotic, just as the House of Chaos is serene and placid. Yet you have your ties, as well as your conflicts."

"At the moment," I said, "I am not interested in paradox hunting and terminology games. I am trying to get to the Courts of Chaos. Do you know the way?"

"Yes," said the jackal. "It is not far, as the carrion bird flies. Come, I will set you in the proper direction."

It turned and began walking away. I followed.

"Do I move too fast? You seem tired."

"No. Keep going. It is beyond this valley certainly, is it not?"

"Yes. There is a tunnel."

I followed it, out across sand and gravel and dry, hard ground. There was nothing growing at either hand. As we walked, the fogs thinned and took on a greenish cast—another trick of that stippled sky, I assumed.

After a time, I called out, "How much farther is it?"

"Not too far now," it said. "Do you grow tired? Do you wish to rest?"

It looked back as it spoke. The greenish light gave to its ugly features an even more ghastly cast. Still, I needed a guide; and we were heading uphill, which seemed to be proper.

"Is there water anywhere near about?" I asked.

"No. We would have to backtrack a considerable distance."

"Forget it. I haven't the time."

It shrugged and chuckled and walked on. The fog cleared a little more as we went, and I could see that we were entering the low range of hills. I leaned on my staff and kept up the pace.

We climbed steadily for perhaps half an hour, the ground growing stonier, the angle of ascent steeper. I found myself beginning to breathe heavily.

"Wait," I called to hm. "I do want to rest now. I thought you said that it was not far."

"Forgive me," it said, halting, "for jackalocentrism. I was judging in terms of my own natural pace. I erred in this, but we *are* almost there now. It lies among the rocks just ahead. Why not rest there?"

"All right," I replied, and I resumed walking.

Soon we reached a stony wall which I realized was the foot of a mountain. We picked our way among the rocky debris which lined it and came at last to an opening which led back into darkness.

"There you have it," said the jackal. "The way is straight, and there are no troublesome side branches. Take your passage through, and good speed to you."

"Thank you," I said, giving up thoughts of rest for the moment and stepping inside. "I appreciate this."

"My pleasure," he said from behind me.

I took several more steps and something crunched beneath my feet and rattled when kicked aside. It was a sound one does not readily forget. The floor was strewn with bones.

There came a soft, quick sound from behind me, and I knew that I did not have time to draw Grayswandir. So I spun, raising my staff before me and thrusting with it.

This maneuver blocked the beast's leap, striking it on the shoulder. But it also knocked me over backward, to roll among the bones. The staff was torn from my hands by the impact, and in the split second of decision allowed me by my opponent's own fall I chose to draw Grayswandir rather than grope after it.

I managed to get my blade unsheathed, but that was all. I was still on my back with the point of my weapon to my left when the jackal recovered and leaped again. I swung the pommel with all of my strength into its face.

The shock ran down my arm and up into my shoulder. The jackal's head snapped back and its body twisted to my left. I brought the point into line immediately, gripping the hilt with both hands, and I was able to rise to my right knee before it snarled and lunged once more.

As soon as I saw that I had it on target, I threw my weight behind it, driving the blade deep into the jackal's body. I released it quickly and rolled away from those snapping jaws.

The jackal shrieked, struggled to rise, dropped back. I lay panting where I had fallen. I felt the staff beneath me and seized it. I brought it around to guard and drew myself back against the cave wall. The beast did not rise again, however, but lay there thrashing. In the dim light, I could see that it was vomiting. The smell was overpowering.

Then it turned its eyes in my direction and lay still.

"It would have been so fine," it said softly, "to eat a Prince of Amber. I always wondered—about royal blood."

Then the eyes closed and the breathing stopped and I was left with the stink.

I rose, back still against the wall, staff still before me, and regarded it. It was a long while before I could bring myself to retrieve my blade.

A quick exploration showed me that I was in no tunnel, but only a cave. When I made my way out, the fog had grown yellow, and it was stirred now by a breeze from the lower reaches of the valley.

I leaned against the rock and tried to decide which way to take. There was no real trail here.

Finally, I struck off to my left. That way seemed somewhat steeper, and I wanted to get above the fog and into the mountains as soon as I could. The staff continued to serve me well. I kept listening for the sound of running water, but there was none about.

I struggled along, always continuing upward, and the fogs thinned and changed color. Finally, I could see that I was climbing toward a wide plateau. Above it, I began to catch glimpses of the sky, many-colored and churning.

There were several sharp claps of thunder at my back, but I still could not see the disposition of the storm. I increased my pace then, but began to grow dizzy after a few minutes. I stopped and seated myself on the ground, panting. I was overwhelmed with a sense of failure. Even if I made it up to the plateau, I had a feeling that the storm would roar right across it. I rubbed my eyes with the heels of my hands. What was the use of going on if there was no way I could make it?

A shadow moved through the pistachio mists, dropped toward me. I raised my staff, then saw that it was only Hugi. He braked himself and landed at my feet.

"Corwin," he said, "you have come a good distance."

"But maybe not good enough," I said. "The storm seems to be getting nearer."

"I believe that it is. I have been meditating and would like to give you the benefit of—"

"If you want to benefit me at all," I said, "I could tell you what to do."

."What is that?"

"Fly back and see how far off the storm really is, and how fast it seems to be moving. Then come and tell me."

Hugi hopped from one foot to the other. Then, "All right," he said, and leaped into the air and batted his way toward what I felt to be the northwest.

I leaned on the staff and rose. I might as well keep climbing at the best pace I could manage. I drew upon the Jewel again, and strength came into me like a red lightning flash.

As I mounted the slope, a damp breeze sprang up from the direction in which Hugi had departed. There came another thunderclap. No more growls and rumbles.

I made the most of the influx of energy, climbing quickly and efficiently for several hundred meters. If I were going to lose, I might as well make it up to the top first. I might as well see where I was and learn whether there was anything at all left for me to try.

My view of the sky grew more and more clear as I climbed. It had changed considerably since last I had regarded it. Half of it was of uninterrupted blackness and the other half those masses of swimming colors. And the entire heavenly bowl seemed to be rotating about a point directly overhead. I began to grow excited. This was the sky I was seeking, the sky which had covered me that time I had journeyed to Chaos. I struggled higher. I wanted to utter something heartening, but my throat was too dry.

As I neared the rim of the plateau, I heard a flapping sound and Hugi was suddenly on my shoulder.

"The storm is about ready to crawl up your arse," he said. "Be here any minute."

I continued climbing, reached level ground and hauled myself up to it. I stood for a moment then, breathing heavily. The wind must have kept the area clear of fog, for it was a high, smooth plain, and I could see the sky for a great distance ahead. I advanced, to find a point from which I could see beyond the farther edge. As I moved, the sounds of the storm came to me more clearly.

"I do not believe you will make it across," Hugi said, "without getting wet."

"You know that is no ordinary storm," I croaked. "If it were, I'd be thankful for the chance of getting a drink."

"I know. I was speaking figuratively."

I growled something vulgar and kept going.

Gradually, the vista before me enlarged. The sky still did its crazy veil dance, but the illumination was more than sufficient. When I reached a position where I was positive what lay before me, I halted and sagged against my staff.

"What is the matter?" Hugi asked.

But I could not speak. I simply gestured at the great wasteland which commenced somewhere below the farther lip of the plateau to sweep on for at least forty miles before butting up against another range of mountains. And far off to the left and still running strong went the black road.

"The waste?" he said. "I could have told you it was there. Why didn't you ask me?"

I made a noise halfway between a groan and a sob and sank slowly to the ground.

How long I remained so, I am not certain. I felt more than a little delirious. In the midst of it I seemed to see a possible answer, though something within me rebelled against it. I was finally roused by the noises of the storm and Hugi's chattering.

"I can't beat it across that place," I whispered. "There is no way."

"You say you have failed," Hugi said. "But this is not so. There is neither failure nor victory in striving. It is all but an illusion of the ego."

I rose slowly to my knees.

"I did not say that I had failed."

"You said that you cannot go on to your destination."

I looked back, to where lightnings now flashed as the storm climbed toward me.

"That's right, I cannot do it that way. But if Dad failed, I have got to attempt something that Brand tried to convince me only he could do. I have to create a new Pattern, and I have to do it right here."

"You? Create a new Pattern? If Oberon failed, how could a man who can barely stay on his feet do it? No, Corwin. Resignation is the greatest virtue you might cultivate."

I raised my head and lowered the staff to the ground. Hugi fluttered down to stand beside it and I regarded him.

"You do not want to believe any of the things that I said, do you?" I told him. "It does not matter, though. The conflict between our views is irreducible. I see desire as hidden identity and striving as its growth. You do not." I moved my hands forward and rested them on my knees. "If for you the greatest good is union with the Absolute, then why do you not fly to join it now, in the form of the all-pervading Chaos which approaches? If I fail here, it will become Absolute. As for me, I must try, for so long as there is breath within me, to raise up a Pattern against it. I do this because I am what I am, and I am the man who could have been king in Amber."

Hugi lowered his head.

"I'll see you eat crow first," he said, and he chuckled.

I reached out quickly and twisted his head off, wishing that I had time to build a fire. Though he made it look like a sacrifice, it is difficult to say to whom the moral victory belonged, since I was planning on doing it anyway.

NINE

. . . Cassis, and the smell of the chestnut blossoms. All along the Champs-Elysées the chestnuts were foaming white. . . .

I remembered the play of the fountains in the Place de la Concorde. . . . And down the Rue de la Seine and along the quais, the smell of the old books, the smell of the river. . . . The smell of chestnut blossoms . . .

Why should I suddenly remember 1905 and Paris on the shadow Earth, save that I was very happy that year and I might, reflexively, have sought an antidote for the present? Yes . . .

White absinthe, Amer Picon, grenadine . . . Wild strawberries, with Crème d'Isigny . . . Chess at the Café de la Régence with actors from the Comédie Française, just across the way . . . The races at Chantilly . . . Evenings at the Boîte à Fursy on the Rue Pigalle . . .

I placed my left foot firmly before my right, my right before my left. In my left hand, I held the chain from which the Jewel depended—and I carried it high, so that I could stare into the stone's depths, seeing and feeling there the emergence of the new Pattern which I described with each step. I had screwed my staff into the ground and left it to stand near the Pattern's beginning. Left . . .

The wind sang about me and there was thunder near at hand. I did not meet with the physical resistance that I did on the old Pattern. There was no resistance at all. Instead—and in many ways worse—a peculiar deliberation had come over all my movements, slowing them, ritualizing them. I seemed to expend more energy in preparing for each step—perceiving it, realizing it and ordering my mind for its execution—than I did in the physical performance of the act. Yet the slowness seemed to require itself, was exacted of me by some unknown agency which determined precision and an adagio tempo for all my movements. Right . . .

. . . And, as the Pattern in Rebma had helped to restore my faded memories, so this one I was now striving to create stirred and elicited the smell of the chestnut trees, of the wagonloads of vegetables moving through the dawn toward the Halles. . . . I was not in love with anyone in particular at the time, though there were many girls—Yvettes and Mimis and Simones, their faces merge—and it was spring in Paris, with Gipsy bands and cocktails at Louis'. . . . I remembered, and my heart leaped with a kind of Proustian joy while Time tolled about me like a bell. . . . And perhaps this was the reason for the recollection, for this joy seemed transmitted to my movements, informed my perceptions, empowered my will. . . .

I saw the next step and I took it. . . . I had been around once now, creating the perimeter of my Pattern. At my back, I could feel the storm. It must have mounted to the plateau's rim. The sky was darkening, the storm blotting the swinging, swimming, colored lights. Flashes of lightning splayed about, and I could not spare the energy and the attention to try to control things.

Having gone completely around, I could see that as much of the new Pattern as I had walked was now inscribed in the rock and glowing palely, bluely. Yet, there were no sparks, no tingles in my feet, no hair-raising currents—only the steady law of deliberation, upon me like a great weight. . . . Left . . .

. . . Poppies, poppies and cornflowers and tall poplars along country roads, the taste of Normandy cider . . . And in town again, the smell of the chestnut blossoms . . . The Seine full of stars . . . The smell of the old brick houses in the Place des Vosges after a morning's rain . . . The bar under the Olympia Music Hall . . . A fight there . . . Bloodied knuckles, bandaged by a girl who took me home . . . What was her name? Chestnut blossoms . . . A white rose . . .

I sniffed then. The odor was all but gone from the remains of the rose at my collar. Surprising that any of it had survived this far. It heartened me. I pushed ahead, curving gently to my right. From the corner of my eye, I saw the advancing wall of the storm, slick as glass, obliterating everything it passed. The roar of its thunder was deafening now.

Right, left . . .

The advance of the armies of the night . . . Would my Pattern hold against it? I wished that I might hurry, but if anything I was moving with increasing slowness as I went on. I felt a curious sense of bilocation, almost as if I were within the Jewel tracing the Pattern there myself while I moved out here, regarding it and mimicking its progress. Left . . . Turn . . . Right . . . The storm was indeed advancing. Soon it would reach old Hugi's bones. I smelled the moisture and the ozone and wondered about the strange dark bird who had said he'd been waiting for me since the beginning of Time. Waiting to argue with me or to be eaten by me in this place without history? Whatever, considering the exaggeration usual in moralists, it was fitting that, having failed to leave me with my heart all laden with rue over my spiritual condition, he be consumed to the accompaniment of theatrical thunder. . . . There was distant thunder, near thunder and more thunder now. As I turned in that direction once more, the lightning flashes were nearly blinding. I clutched my chain and took another step. . . .

The storm pushed right up to the edge of my Pattern, and then it parted. It began to creep around me. Not a drop fell upon me or the Pattern. But slowly, gradually, we came to be totally engulfed within it.

It seemed as if I were in a bubble at the bottom of a stormy sea. Walls of water encircled me and dark shapes darted by. It seemed as if the entire universe were pressing in to crush me. I concentrated on the red world of the Jewel. Left . . .

The chestnut blossoms . . . A cup of hot chocolate at a sidewalk café . . . A band concert in the Tuileries Gardens, the sounds climbing through the sunbright air . . . Berlin in the twenties, the Pacific in the thirties—there had been pleasures there, but of a different order. It may not be the true past, but images of the past that rush to comfort or torment us later, man or nation. No matter. Across the Pont Neuf and down the Rue Rivoli, buses and fiacres . . . Painters at their easels in the Luxembourg Gardens . . . If all were to fall well, I might seek a shadow like this again one day . . . It ranked with my Avalon. I had forgotten . . . The details . . . The touches that make for life . . . The smell of the chestnuts . . .

Walking . . . I completed another circuit. The wind screamed and the storm roared on, but I was untouched. So long as I did not permit it to distract me, so long as I kept moving and maintained my focus on the Jewel. . . . I had to hold up, had to keep taking these slow, careful steps, never to stop, slower and slower but constantly moving. . . . Faces . . . It seemed that rows of faces regarded me from beyond the Pattern's edge. . . . Large, like the Head, but twisted—grinning, jeering, mocking me, waiting for me to stop or step wrongly. . . . Waiting for the whole thing to come apart around me. . . .

There was lightning behind their eyes and in their months, their laughter was the thunder. . . . Shadows crawled among them. . . . Now they spoke to me, with words like a gale from off a dark ocean. . . . I would fail, they told me, fail and be swept away, this fragment of a Pattern dashed to pieces behind me and consumed. . . . They cursed me, they spat and vomited toward me, though none of it reached. . . . Perhaps they were not really there. . . . Perhaps my mind had been broken by the strain. . . . Then what good were my efforts? A new Pattern to be shaped by a madman? I wavered, and they took up the chorus, "Mad! Mad! Mad!" in the voices of the elements.

I drew a deep breath and smelled what was left of the rose and thought of chestnuts once again, and days filled with the joys of life and organic order. The voices seemed to soften as my mind raced back through the events of that happy year. . . . And I took another step. . . . And another. . . . They had been playing on my weaknesses, they could feel my doubts, my anxiety, my fatigue. . . . Whatever they were, they seized what they saw and tried to use it against me. . . . Left . . . Right . . . Now let them feel my confidence and wither, I told myself. I have come this far. I will continue. Left . . .

They swirled and swelled about me, still mouthing discouragements. But some of the force seemed gone out of them. I made my way through another section of arc, seeing it grow before me in my mind's red eye.

I thought back to my escape from Greenwood, to my tricking Flora out of information, to my encounter with Random, our fight with his pursuers, our journey back to Amber. . . . I thought of our flight to Rebma and my walking of the reversed Pattern there for a restoration of much of my memory. . . Of Random's shotgun wedding and my sojourn to Amber, where I fought with Eric and fled to Bleys. . . . Of the battles that followed, my blinding, my recovery, my escape, my journey to Lorraine and then to Avalon. . . .

Moving into even higher gear, my mind skimmed the surface of subsequent events. . . . Ganelon and Lorraine . . . The creatures of the Black Circle . . . Benedict's arm . . . Dara . . . The return of Brand and his stabbing . . . My stabbing . . . Bill Roth . . . Hospital records . . . My accident . . .

. . . Now, from the very beginning at Greenwood, through it all, to this moment of my struggle to assure each perfect maneuver as it appeared to me, I felt the growing sense of anticipation I had known—whether my actions were directed toward the throne, vengeance, or my conception of duty—felt it, was aware of its continuous existence across those years up until this moment, when it was finally accompanied by something else. . . . I felt that the waiting was just about over, that whatever I had been anticipating and struggling toward was soon to occur.

Left . . . Very, very slowly . . . Nothing else was important. I threw all of my will into the movements now. My concentration became total. Whatever lay beyond the Pattern, I was now oblivious to it. Lightnings, faces, winds . . . It did not matter. There was only the Jewel, the growing Pattern and myself— and I was barely aware of myself. Perhaps this was the closest I would ever come to Hugi's ideal of merging with the Absolute. Turn . . . Right foot . . . Turn again . . .

Time ceased to have meaning. Space was restricted to the design I was creating. I drew strength from the Jewel without summoning it now, as part of the process in which I was engaged. In a sense, I suppose, I was obliterated. I became a moving point, programed by the Jewel, performing an operation which absorbed me so totally that I had no attention available for self-consciousness. Yet, at some level, I realized that I was a part of the process, also. For I knew, somehow, that if anyone else were doing it, it would be a different Pattern emerging.

I was vaguely aware that I had passed the halfway point. The way had become trickier, my movements even slower. Despite the matter of velocity, I was somehow reminded of my experiences on originally becoming attuned to the Jewel, in that strange, many-dimensional matrix which seemed to be the source of the Pattern itself.

Right . . . Left . . .

There was no drag. I felt very light, despite the deliberation. A boundless energy seemed to wash constantly through me. All of the sounds about me had merged into a white noise and vanished.

Suddenly then, I no longer seemed to be moving slowly. It did not seem as if I had passed a Veil or barrier, but rather that I had undergone some internal adjustment.

It felt as if I were moving at a more normal pace now, winding my way through tighter and tighter coils, approaching what would soon be the design's terminus. Mainly, I was still emotionless, though I knew intellectually that at some level a sense of elation was growing and would soon burst through. Another step . . . Another . . . Perhaps half a dozen more paces . . .

Suddenly, the world went dark. It seemed that I stood within a great void, with only the faint light of the Jewel before me and the glow of the Pattern like a spiral nebula through which I was striding. I wavered, but only for an instant. This must be the last trial, the final assault. I would have to be sufficient to the distraction.

The Jewel showed me what to do and the Pattern showed me where to do it. The only thing missing was a view of myself. Left . . .

I continued, executing each move with all of my attention. An opposing force began to rise against me finally, as on the old Pattern. But for this, I was prepared by years of experience. I struggled for two more steps against the mounting barrier.

Then, within the Jewel, I saw the ending of the Pattern. I would have gasped at the sudden realization of its beauty, but at this point even my breath was regulated by my efforts. I threw all of my strength into the next step, and the void seemed to shake about me. I completed it, and the next was even more difficult. I felt as if I were at the center of the universe, treading on stars, struggling to impart some essential motion by what was basically an act of will.

My foot slowly advanced, though I could not see it. The Pattern began to brighten. Soon its blaze was almost blinding.

Just a little farther . . . I strove harder than I ever had on the old Pattern, for now the resistance seemed absolute. I had to oppose it with a firmness and constancy of will that excluded everything else, though I seemed not to be moving at all now, though all of my energies seemed diverted into the brightening of the design. At least, I would go out with a splendid backdrop. . . .

Minutes, days, years . . . I do not know how long this went on. It felt like forever, as if I had been engaged in this single act for all of eternity. . . .

Then I moved, and how long that took I do not know. But I completed the step and began another. Then another . . .

The universe seemed to reel about me. I was through.

The pressure was gone. The blackness was gone. . . .

For an instant, I stood at the center of my Pattern. Without even regarding it, I fell forward onto my knees and bent double, my blood pounding in my ears. Head swimming, I panted. I began to shake, all over. I had done it, I realized dimly. Come whatever may, there was a Pattern. And it would endure. . . .

I heard a sound where there should have been none, but my jaded muscles refused to respond, even reflexively, until it was too late. Not until the Jewel was jerked from my limp fingers did I raise my head and roll back onto my haunches. No one had been following me through the Pattern—I was certain that I would have been aware of it. Therefore . . .

The light was almost normal, and blinking against it, I looked up into Brand's smiling face. He wore a black eyepatch now, and he held the Jewel in his hand. He must have teleported himself in.

He struck me just as I raised my head, and I fell onto my left side. He kicked me in the stomach then, hard.

"Well, you've done it," he said. "I did not think you could. Now I have another Pattern to destroy before I set things right. I need this to turn the battle at the Courts first, though." He waved the Jewel. "Good-bye for now."

And he vanished.

I lay there gasping and clutching at my stomach. Waves of blackness rose and fell, like a surf, within me, though I did not completely succumb to unconsciousness. A feeling of enormous despair washed over me, and I closed my eyes and moaned. There was no Jewel for me to draw upon now, either.

The chestnut trees . . .

TEN

As I lay there hurting, I had visions of Brand appearing on the battlefield where the forces of Amber and Chaos fought, the Jewel pulsing about his neck. Apparently his control over it was sufficient, as he saw it, to enable him to turn things against us. I saw him lashing out with lightning bolts among our troops. I saw him summoning great winds and hailstorms to strike at us. I almost wept. All of this, when he could still redeem himself by coming in on our side. Just winning was not enough for him now, though. He had to win for himself, and on his own terms. And I? I had failed. I had thrown up a Pattern against the chaos, a thing I had never thought I could do. Yet, this would be as nothing if the battle was lost and Brand returned and wiped out my work. To have come this close, passing through everything that I had, and then to fail here. . . . It made me want to cry "Injustice!" though I knew the universe did not run in accordance with my notions of equity. I gnashed my teeth and spat some dirt I had mouthed. I had been charged by our father to take the Jewel to the place of battle. I had almost made it.

A sense of strangeness came over me then. Something was calling for my attention. What?

The silence.

The raging winds and the thunder had ceased. The air was still. In fact, the air felt cool and fresh. And on the other side of my eyelids, I knew that there was light.

I opened my eyes. I saw a sky of a bright, uniform white. I blinked, I turned my head. There was something off to my right. . . .

A tree. A tree stood where I had planted the staff I had cut from old Ygg. It was already far taller than the staff itself had been. I could almost see it growing. And it was green with leaves and white with a sprinkling of buds; a few blossoms had opened. From that direction, the breeze brought me a faint and delicate scent which offered me some comfort.

I felt along my sides. I did not seem to have any broken ribs, though my guts still felt knotted from the kick I had taken. I rubbed my eyes with my knuckles and ran my hands through my hair. I sighed heavily then and rose to one knee.

Turning my head, I regarded the prospect. The plateau was the same, yet somehow not the same. It was still bare but was no longer harsh. Likely an effect of the new illumination. No, there was more to it than that. . . .

I had continued to turn, completing my scanning of the horizon. It was not the same place where I had commenced my walk. There were differences both subtle and gross: altered rock formations, a dip where there had been a rise, a new texture to the stone beneath and near me, in the distance what appeared to be soil. I stood and it seemed that now, from somewhere, I caught the scent of the sea. This place had an entirely different feeling to it than the one to which I had mounted—so long ago, it seemed. It was too much of a change for that storm to have wrought. It reminded me of something.

I sighed again, there at the Pattern's center, and continued to consider my surroundings. Somehow, in spite of myself, my despair was slipping away and a feeling of—"refreshment" seems somehow the best word—was rising within me. The air was so clean and sweet, and the place had a new, unused feeling about it. I—

Of course. It was like the place of the primal Pattern. I turned back to the tree and regarded it again, higher already. Like, yet unlike . . . There was something new in the air, the ground, the sky. This was a new place. A new primal Pattern. Everything about me then was a result of the Pattern in which I stood.

I suddenly realized that I was feeling more than refreshment. It was now a sense of elation, a kind of joy that was moving through me. This was a clean, fresh place and I was somehow responsible for it.

Time passed. I just stood there watching the trees, looking around me, enjoying the euphoria that had come over me. Here was some kind of victory, anyway—until Brand came back to wipe it out.

Suddenly, I was sober again. I had to stop Brand, I had to protect this place. I was at the center of a Pattern. If this one behaved like the other, I could use its power to project me anywhere I desired. I could use it to go and join the others now.

I dusted myself off. I loosened my blade in the scabbard. Things might not be as hopeless as they had seemed earlier. I had been told to convey the Jewel to the place of battle. So Brand had done it for me; it would still be there. I would simply have to go and take it back from him, somehow, to make things turn the way they were supposed to have fallen.

I looked all around me. I would have to return here, to investigate this new situation at another time, if I survived what was to come. There was mystery here. It hung in the air and drifted on the breeze. It could take ages to unravel what had occurred when I had drawn the new Pattern.

I saluted the tree. It seemed to stir as I did so. I adjusted my rose and pushed it back into shape. It was time to move again. There was a thing I had yet to do.

I lowered my head and closed my eyes. I tried to recall the lay of the land before the final abyss at the Courts of Chaos. I saw it then, beneath that wild sky, and I peopled it with my relatives, with troops. I seemed to hear the sounds of a distant battle as I did this. The scene adjusted itself, came clearer. I held the vision an instant longer, then charged the Pattern to take me there.

. . . A moment later, it seemed, I stood upon a hilltop beside a plain, a cold wind whipping my cloak about me. The sky was that crazy, turning, stippled thing I remembered from last time—half-black, half-psychedelic rainbows. There were unpleasant fumes in the air. The black road was off to the right now, crossing that plain and passing beyond it over the abyss toward that nighted citadel, firefly gleams flickering about it. Gauzy bridges drifted in the air, extending from far in that darkness, and strange forms traveled upon them as well as upon the black road. Below me on the field was what seemed to be the main concentration of troops. At my back, I heard something other than Time's winged chariot.

Turning toward what must have been north by a succession of previous reckonings regarding its course, I beheld the advance of that devil-storm through distant mountains, flashing and growling, coming on like a skyhigh glacier.

So I had not stopped it with the creation of a new Pattern. It seemed that it had simply passed by my protected area and would continue until it got to wherever it was going. Hopefully then, the thing would be succeeded by whatever constructive impulses were now spreading outward from the new Pattern, with the reimposition of order throughout the places of Shadow. I wondered how long it would take for the storm to get here.

I heard the sound of hoofs and turned, drawing my blade. . . .

A horned rider on a great black horse was bearing down upon me, something like firelight glowing in his eyes.

I adjusted my position and waited. He seemed to have descended from one of the gauzy roadways which had drifted in this direction. We were both fairly far removed from the main scene of action. I watched as he mounted the hill. Good horse, that. Nice chest. Where the hell was Brand? I wasn't looking for just any fight.

I watched the rider as he came on, and the crooked blade in his right hand. I repositioned myself as he moved in to cut me down. When he swung, I was ready with a parry that pulled his arm within reach. I caught hold of it and dragged him from his mount.

"That rose . . ." he said as he fell to the ground. I do not know what else he might have said, because I cut his throat, and his words and everything else about him were lost with the fiery slash.

I whirled then, drawing Grayswandir away, sprinted several paces and had hold of the black charger's bridle. I spoke with the horse to calm him and led him away from the flames. After a couple of minutes we were on better terms, and I mounted.

He was skittish at first, but I just had him pace the hilltop lightly while I continued to observe. The forces of Amber appeared to be on the offense. Smoldering corpses were all over the field. The main force of our enemies was drawn back onto a height near the lip of the abyss. Lines of them, not yet broken but hard pressed, were falling back slowly toward it. On the other hand, more troops were crossing that abyss and joining the others who held the heights. Estimating their growing numbers and their position quickly, I judged that these might be readying an offense of their own. Brand was nowhere in sight.

Even if I had been rested and wearing armor I would have had second thoughts about riding down and joining in the fray. My job right now was to locate Brand. I doubted that he would be directly involved in the fighting. I looked off to the sides of the battle proper, seeking a lone figure. No . . . Perhaps the far side of the field. I would have to circle to the north. There was too much that I could not see to the west.

I turned my mount and made my way down the hill. It would be so pleasant to collapse, I decided. Just to fall down in a heap and sleep. I sighed. Where the hell was Brand?

I reached the bottom of the hill and turned to cut through a culvert. I needed a better view—

"Lord Corwin of Amber!"

He was waiting for me as I rounded a bend in the depression, a big, corpse-colored guy with red hair and a horse to match. He wore coppery armor with greenish tracings, and he sat facing me, still as a statue.

"I saw you on the hilltop," he said. "You are not mailed, are you?"

I slapped my chest.

He nodded sharply. Then he reached up, first to his left shoulder, then to his right, then to his sides, opening fastenings upon his breastplate. When he had them undone, he removed it, lowered it toward the ground on his left side and let it fall. He did the same with his greaves.

"I have long wanted to meet you," he said. "I am Borel. I do not want it said that I took unfair advantage of you when I killed you."

Borel . . . The name was familiar. Then I remembered. He had Dara's respect and affection. He had been her fencing teacher, a master of the blade. Stupid, though, I saw. He had forfeited my respect by removing his armor. Battle is not a game, and I had no desire to make myself available to any presumptuous ass who thought otherwise. Especially a skilled ass, when I was feeling beat. If nothing else, he could probably wear me down.

"Now we shall resolve a matter which has long troubled me," he said.

I replied with a quaint vulgarism, wheeled my black and raced back the way I had come. He gave chase immediately.

As I passed back along the culvert, I realized that I did not have a sufficient lead. He would be upon me in matter of moments with my back all exposed, to cut me down or force me to fight. However, while limited, my choices included a little more than that.

"Coward!" he cried. "You flee combat! Is this the great warrior of whom I have heard so much?"

I reached up and unfastened my cloak. At either hand, the culvert's lip was level with my shoulders, then my waist.

I rolled out of the saddle to my left, stumbled once and found my footing. The black went on. I moved to my right, facing the draw.

Catching my cloak in both hands, I swung it in a reverse-veronica maneuver a second or two before Borel's head and shoulders came abreast of me. It swept over him, drawn blade and all, muffling his head and slowing his arms.

I kicked then, hard. I was aiming for his head, but I caught him on the left shoulder. He was spilled from his saddle, and his horse, too, went by.

Drawing Grayswandir, I leaped after him. I caught him just as he had brushed my cloak aside and was struggling to rise. I skewered him where he sat and saw the startled expression on his face as the wound began to flame.

"Oh, basely done!" he cried. "I had hoped for better of thee!"

"This isn't exactly the Olympic Games," I said, brushing some sparks from my cloak.

I chased down my horse then and mounted. This took me several minutes. As I continued northward, I achieved higher ground. From there, I spotted Benedict directing the battle, and in a draw far to the rear, I caught a glimpse of Julian at the head of his troops from Arden. Benedict was apparently holding them in reserve.

I kept going, toward the advancing storm, beneath the half-dark, half-painted, revolving sky. I soon reached my goal, the highest hill in sight, and began to mount it. I halted several times on the way up, to look back.

I saw Deirdre in black armor, swinging an ax; Llewella and Flora were among the archers. Fiona was nowhere in sight. Gérard was not there either. Then I saw Random on horseback, swinging a heavy blade, leading an assault toward the enemy's high ground. Near him was a knight clad in green whom I did not recognize. The man swung a mace with deadly efficiency. He wore a bow upon his back, and he'd a quiver of gleaming arrows at his hip.

The sounds of the storm came louder as I reached the summit of my hill. The lightning flickered with the regularity of a neon tube and the rain sizzled down, a fiberglass curtain that had now passed over the mountains.

Below me, both beasts and men—and more than a few beast-men—were woven in knots and strands of battle. A cloud of dust hung over the field. Assessing the distribution of forces, however, it did not appear to me that the growing forces of the enemy could be pushed much farther. In fact, it seemed that it was just about time for the counterattack. They appeared to be ready up in their craggy places, and just waiting for the order.

I was about a minute and a half off. They advanced, sweeping down the slope, reinforcing their lines, pushing our troops back, driving ahead. And more were arriving from beyond the dark abyss. Our own troops began a reasonably orderly retreat. The enemy pressed harder, and when things seemed about ready to be turned into a rout an order must have been given.

I heard the sound of Julian's horn, and shortly thereafter I saw him stride Morgenstern leading the men of Arden onto the field. This balanced the opposing forces almost exactly and the noise level rose and rose while the sky turned above us.

I watched the conflict for perhaps a quarter of an hour, as our own forces slowly withdrew across the field. Then I saw a one-armed figure on a fiery striped horse suddenly appear atop a distant hill. He bore a raised blade in his hand and he was faced away from me, toward the west. He stood unmoving for several long moments. Then he lowered the blade.

I heard trumpets in the west, and at first I saw nothing. Then a line of cavalry came into view. I started. For a moment, I thought Brand was there. Then I realized it was Bleys leading his troops to strike at the enemy's exposed flank.

And suddenly, our troops in the field were no longer retreating. They were holding their line. Then, they were pressing forward.

Bleys and his riders came on, and I realized that Benedict had the day again. The enemy was about to be ground to pieces.

Then a cold wind swept over me from out of the north, and I looked that way again.

The storm had advanced considerably. It must have started moving faster just recently. And it was darker now than it had been, with brighter flashes and louder roars. And this cold, wet wind was increasing in intensity.

I wondered then . . . would it simply sweep over the field like an annihilating wave and that be that? What of the effects of the new Pattern? Would these follow, to restore everything? Somehow, I doubted this. If this storm smashed us, I'd a feeling we would stay smashed. It would require the force of the Jewel to permit us to ride it out until order was restored. And what would be left if we survived it? I simply could not guess.

So what was Brand's plan? What was he waiting for? What was he going to do?

I looked out over the battlefield once more. . . .

Something.

In a shadowy place on the heights where the enemy had regrouped, been reinforced, and down which it had stormed . . . something.

A tiny flash of red . . . I was sure I had seen it.

I kept watching, waiting. I had to see it again, to pinpoint it. . . .

A minute passed. Two, perhaps . . .

There! And again.

I wheeled the black charger. It looked possible to make it around the enemy's near flank and up to that supposedly vacant height. I raced down the hill and began that course.

It had to be Brand with the Jewel. He had chosen a good, safe spot, from which he commanded a view of the entire battlefield as well as the approaching storm. From there, he could direct its lightning into our troops as the front advanced. He would signal a retreat at the proper moment, hit us with the storm's strange furies, then sidetrack the thing to bypass the side he was backing. It seemed the simplest and most effective use of the Jewel under the circumstances.

I would have to get close fast. My control of the stone was greater than his, but it diminished with distance, and he would have the Jewel on his person. My best bet would be to charge right into him, to get within control range at all costs, take over command of the stone and use it against him. But he might have a bodyguard up there with him. That troubled me, because dealing with it could slow me disastrously. And if he did not, what was to prevent him from teleporting himself away if the going got too rough? Then what could I do? I would have to start all over, hunting him again. I wondered whether I could use the Jewel to keep him from transporting himself. I did not know. I resolved to try.

It might not have been the best of plans, but it was the only one I had. There was no longer time to plot.

As I rode, I saw that there were others headed for that height, also. Random, Deirdre and Fiona, mounted and accompanied by eight horsemen, had made their way through the enemy lines, with a few other troops—friends or foes, I could not tell—maybe both—riding had behind them. The knight clad in green seemed to be moving the fastest, gaining on them. I did not recognize him—or her, as the case might be. I did not doubt the objective of the vanguard, however—not with Fiona there. She must have detected Brand's presence and be leading the others to him. A few drops of hope fell upon my heart. She might be able to neutralize Brand's powers, or minimize them. I leaned forward, still bearing to my left, hurrying my horse along. The sky kept turning. The wind whistled about me. A terrific clap of thunder rolled by. I did not look back.

I was racing them. I did not want them to get there before me, but I feared that they would. The distance was just too great.

If only they would turn and see me coming, they would probably wait. I wished there had been some way of giving them a sign of my presence earlier. I cursed the fact that the Trumps no longer worked.

I began shouting. I screamed after them, but the wind blew my words away and the thunder rolled over them.

"Wait for me! Damn it! It's Corwin!"

Not even a glance in my direction.

I passed the nearest engagements and rode along the enemy's flank out of range of missiles and arrows. They seemed to be retreating faster now and our troops were spreading out over a larger area. Brand must be getting ready to strike. Part of the rotating sky was covered by a dark cloud which had not been above the field minutes before.

I turned toward my right, behind the retreating forces, racing on toward those hills the others were already mounting.

The sky continued to darken as I neared the foot of the hills, and I feared for my kinsmen. They were getting too close to him. He would have to do something. Unless Fiona was strong enough to stop him. . . .

The horse reared and I was thrown to the ground at the blinding flash which had occurred before me. The thunder cracked before I hit the earth.

I lay there for several moments, dazed. The horse had run off, was perhaps fifty meters away, before he halted and began to move about uncertainly. I rolled onto my stomach and looked up the long slope. The other riders were also down. Their group had apparently been struck by the discharge. Several were moving, more were not. None had yet risen. Above them, I saw the red glow of the Jewel, back beneath an underhang, brighter and steadier now, and the shadowy outline of the figure who wore it.

I began crawling forward, upward and to my left. I wanted to get out of the line of sight with that figure before I risked rising. It would take too long to reach him crawling, and I was going to have to skirt the others now, because his attention would be with them.

I made my way carefully, slowly, using every bit of cover in sight, wondering whether the lightning would be striking in the same place again soon — and if not, when he would begin pulling disaster down upon our troops. Any minute now, I judged. A glance back showed me our forces spread over the far end of the field, with the enemy pulled back and coming this way. Before too long, in fact, it seemed I might have them to worry about, too.

I made it into a narrow ditch and wormed my way south for perhaps ten meters. Out again then on the far side, to take advantage of a rise, then some rocks.

When I raised my head to take stock of the situation, I could no longer see the glow of the Jewel. The cleft from which it had shone was blocked by its own eastern shoulder of stone.

I kept crawling, though, near to the lip of the great abyss itself, before I bore to my right once more. I reached a point where it seemed safe to rise, and I did so. I kept expecting another flash, another thunderclap—nearby or on the field—but none came. I began to wonder . . . why not? I reached out, trying to sense the presence of the Jewel, but I could not. I hurried toward the place where I had seen the glow.

I glanced back over the abyss to be sure that no new menaces were approaching from that direction. I drew my blade. When I reached my goal, I stayed close to the escarpment and worked my way northward. I dropped low when I came to its edge and peered around.

There was no red glow. No shadowy figure either. The stony recess appeared to be empty. There was nothing suspicious anywhere in the vicinity. Could he have teleported again? And if so, why?

I rose and passed about the rocky rise. I continued moving in that direction. I tried once more to feel the Jewel, and this time I made a faint contact with it—somewhere off to my right and above, it seemed.

Silent, wary, I moved that way. Why had he left his shelter? He had been perfectly situated for what he had been about. Unless . . .

I heard a scream and a curse. Two different voices. I began to run.

ELEVEN

I passed the niche and kept going. Beyond it, there was a natural trail winding upward. I mounted this.

I could see no one as yet, but my sense of the Jewel's presence grew stronger as I moved. I thought that I heard a single footfall from off to my right and I whirled in that direction, but there was no one in sight. The Jewel did not feel that near either, so I continued.

As I neared the top of the rise, the black drop of Chaos hanging behind, I heard voices. I could not distinguish what was being said, but the words were agitated.

I slowed as I neared the crest, lowered myself and peered around the side of a rock.

Random was a small distance ahead of me and Fiona was with him, as were Lords Chantris and Feldane. All, save Fiona, held weapons as if ready to use them, but they stood perfectly still. They were staring toward the edge of things—a shelf of rock slightly above their level and perhaps fifteen meters distant—the place where the abyss began.

Brand stood in that place, and he was holding Deirdre before him. She was unhelmed, her hair blowing wild, and he had a dagger at her throat. It appeared that he had already cut her slightly. I dropped back.

I heard Random say softly, "Is there nothing more you can do, Fi?"

"I can hold him here," she said, "and at this range, I can slow his efforts at weather control. But that is all. He's got some attunement with it and I do not. He also has proximity going for him. Anything else I might try, he can counter."

Random gnawed his lower lip.

"Put down your weapons," Brand called out. "Do it now, or Deirdre's dead."

"Kill her," Random said, "and you lose the only thing that's keeping you alive. Do it, and I'll show you where I'll put my weapon."

Brand muttered something under his breath. Then: "Okay. I will start by mutilating her."

Random spat.

"Come on!" he said. "She can regenerate as well as the rest of us. Find a threat that means something, or shut up and fight it out!"

Brand was still. I thought it better not to reveal my presence. There must be something I could do. I ventured another look, mentally photographing the terrain before I dropped back. There were some rocks way off to the left, but they did not extend far enough. I saw no way that I might sneak up on him.

"I think we are going to have to rush him and chance it," I heard Random say. "I don't see anything else. Do you?"

Before anyone answered him, a strange thing occurred. The day began to grow brighter.

I looked all about me for the source of the illumination, then sought it overhead.

The clouds were still there, the crazy sky doing its tricks beyond them. The brightness was in the clouds, however. They had paled and were now glowing, as if they masked a sun. Even as I watched, there was a perceptible brightening.

"What is he up to now?" Chantris asked.

"Nothing that I can tell," Fiona said. "I do not believe it is his doing."

"Whose then?"

There was no answer that I could overhear.

I watched the clouds grow brighter. The largest and brightest of them seemed to swirl then, as if stirred. Forms tossed within it, settled. An outline began to take shape.

Below me, on the field, the sounds of battle lessened. The storm itself was muted as the vision grew. Something was definitely forming in the bright place above our heads—the lines of an enormous face.

"I do not know, I tell you," I heard Fiona say in response to something mumbled.

Before it finished taking form, I realized that it was my father's face in the sky. Neat trick, that. And I had no idea what it represented either.

The face moved, as if he were regarding us all. There were lines of strain there, and something of concern to his expression. The brightness grew a little further. His lips moved.

When his voice came down to me it was somehow at an ordinary conversational level, rather than the vast booming I had expected:

"I send you this message," he said, "before undertaking the repair of the Pattern. By the time you receive it, I will already have succeeded or failed.

It will precede the wave of Chaos which must accompany my endeavor. I have reason to believe the effort will prove fatal to me."

His eyes seemed to sweep across the field.

"Rejoice or mourn, as you would," he went on, "for this is either the beginning or the end. I will send the Jewel of Judgment to Corwin as soon as I have finished with it. I have charged him to bear it to the place of conflict. All of your efforts there will be as nothing if the wave of Chaos cannot be averted. But with the Jewel, in that place, Corwin should be able to preserve you until it passes."

I heard Brand's laugh. He sounded quite mad now.

"With my passing," the voice continued, "the problem of the succession will be upon you. I had wishes in this regard, but I see now that these were futile. Therefore, I have no choice but to leave this on the horn of the Unicorn.

"My children, I cannot say that I am entirely pleased with you, but I suppose this works both ways. Let it be. I leave you with my blessing, which is more than a formality. I go now to walk the Pattern. Good-bye."

Then his face began to fade and the brightness drained out of the cloudbank. A little while, and it was gone. A stillness lay upon the field.

". . . and, as you can see," I heard Brand saying, "Corwin does not have the Jewel. Throw down your weapons and get the hell out of here. Or keep them and get out. I do not care. Leave me alone. I have things to do."

"Brand," Fiona said, "can you do what he wanted of Corwin? Can you use it to make that thing miss us?"

"I could if I would," he said. "Yes, I could turn it aside."

"You will be a hero if you do," she said gently. "You will earn our gratitude. All past wrongs will be forgiven. Forgiven and forgotten. We—"

He began to laugh wildly.

"*You* forgive *me?*" he said. "You, who left me in that tower, who put the knife into my side? Thank you, sister. It is very kind of you to offer to forgive me, but excuse me if I decline."

"All right," Random said, "what *do* you want? An apology? Riches and treasure? An important appointment? All of these? They are yours. But this is a stupid game you are playing. Let us end it and go home, pretend it was all a bad dream."

"Yes, let us end it," Brand replied. "You do that by throwing down your weapons first. Then Fiona releases me from her spell, you all do an about-face and march north. You do it or I kill Deirdre."

"Then I think you had better go ahead and kill her and be ready to fight it out with me," he said, "because she will be dead in a little while anyway, if we let you have your way. All of us will."

I heard Brand's chuckle.

"Do you honestly think I am going to let you die? I need you—as many of you as I can save. Hopefully Deirdre, too. You are the only ones who can appreciate my triumph. I will preserve you through the holocaust that is about to begin."

"I do not believe you," Random said.

"Then take a moment and think about it. You know me well enough to know that I will want to rub your noses in it. I want you as witnesses to what I do. In this sense, I require your presence in my new world. Now, get out of here."

"You will have everything you want plus our gratitude," Fiona began, "if you will just—"

"Go!"

I knew that I could delay no longer. I had to make my move. I also knew that I could not reach him in time. I had no choice but to try using the Jewel as a weapon against him.

I reached out and felt its presence. I closed my eyes and summoned my powers.

Hot. Hot, I thought. It is burning you, Brand. It is causing every molecule in your body to vibrate faster and faster. You are about to become a human torch—

I heard him scream.

"Corwin!" he bellowed. "Stop it! Wherever you are! I'll kill her! Look!"

Still willing the Jewel to burn him, I rose to my feet. I glared at him across the distance that separated us. His clothing was beginning to smolder.

"Stop it!" he cried, and he raised the knife and slashed Deirdre's face.

I screamed and my eyes swam. I lost control of the Jewel. But Deirdre, her left cheek bloody, sank her teeth into his hand as he moved to cut her again. Then her arm was free, and she jabbed her elbow into his ribs and tried to pull away.

As soon as she moved, as soon as her head dropped, there was a silver flash. Brand gasped and let go the dagger. An arrow had pierced his throat. Another followed an instant later and stood out from his breast, a little to the right of the Jewel.

He stepped backward and made a gurgling noise. Only there was no place to which he might step, from the edge of the abyss.

His eyes went wide as he began to topple. Then his right hand shot forward and caught hold of Deirdre's hair. I was running by then, shouting, but I knew that I could not reach them in time.

Deirdre howled, a look of terror on her bloodstreaked face, and she reached out to me. . . .

Then Brand, Deirdre and the Jewel were over the edge and falling, vanished from sight, gone. . . .

I believe that I tried to throw myself after them, but Random caught hold of me. Finally, he had to hit me, and it all went away.

When I came around, I lay upon the stony earth farther back from the edge of that place where I had fallen. Someone had folded my cloak into a pillow for me. My first vision was of the turning sky, reminding me somehow of my dream of the wheel the day I had met Dara. I could feel the others about me, hear their voices, but I did not at first turn my head. I just lay there and regarded the mandala in the heavens and thought upon my loss. Deirdre . . . she had meant more to me than all the rest of the family put together. I cannot help it. That is how it was. How many times had I wished she were not my sister. Yet, I had reconciled myself to the realities of our situation. My feelings would never change, but . . . now she was gone, and this thought meant more to me than the impending destruction of the world.

Yet, I had to see what was happening now. With the Jewel gone, everything was over. Yet . . . I reached out, trying to feel its presence, wherever it might be, but there was nothing. I began to rise then, to see how far the wave had advanced, but a sudden arm pushed me back.

"Rest, Corwin." It was Random's voice. "You're beat. You look as if you have just crawled through hell. There is nothing you can do now. Take it easy."

"What difference does the state of my health make?" I replied. "In a little while, it will not matter."

I made to rise again, and this time the arm moved to support me.

"All right, then," he said. "Not that much worth seeing, though."

I suppose that he was right. The fighting appeared to be over except for a few isolated pockets of resistance by the enemy, and these were rapidly being enveloped, their combatants slain or captured, everyone moving in this direction, withdrawing before the advancing wave which had reached the far end of the field. Soon our height would be crowded with all of the survivors from both sides. I looked behind us. No new forces were approaching from the dark citadel. Could we retreat to that place when the wave finally reached us here? Then what? The abyss seemed the ultimate answer. "Soon," I muttered, thinking of Deirdre. "Soon . . ." Why not?

I watched the stormfront, flashing, masking, transforming. Yes, soon. With the Jewel gone along with Brand—

"Brand . . ." I said. "Who was it finally got him?"

"I claim that distinction," said a familiar voice which I could not place.

I turned my head and stared. The man in green was seated on a rock. His bow and quiver lay beside him on the ground. He flashed an evil smile in my direction.

It was Caine.

"I'll be damned," I said, rubbing my jaw. "A funny thing happened to me on the way to your funeral."

"Yes. I heard about it." He laughed. "You ever kill yourself, Corwin?"

"Not recently. How'd you manage it?"

"Walked to the proper shadow," he said, "waylaid the shadow of myself there. He provided the corpse." He shuddered. "An eerie feeling, that. Not one I'd care to repeat."

"But why?" I said. "Why fake your death and try to frame me for it?"

"I wanted to get to the root of the trouble in Amber," he said, "and destroy it. I thought it best to go underground for that. What better way than by convincing everyone that I was dead? I finally succeeded, too, as you saw."

He paused. "I'm sorry about Deirdre, though. But I had no choice. It was our last chance. I did not really think he would take her with him."

I looked away.

"I had no choice," he repeated. "I hope you can see that."

I nodded.

"But why did you try to make it look as if I had killed you?" I asked.

Just then Fiona approached with Bleys. I greeted them both and turned back to Caine for my answer. There were things I wanted to ask Bleys, too, but they could wait.

"Well?" I said.

"I wanted you out of the way," he said. "I still thought you might be behind the whole thing. You or Brand. I had it narrowed down that far. I thought it might even be the two of you in it together—especially with him struggling to bring you back."

"You have that wrong," said Bleys. "Brand was trying to keep him away. He had learned that his memory was returning and—"

"I gather," Caine replied, "but at the time it looked that way. So I wanted Corwin back in a dungeon while I searched for Brand. I lay low then and listened in on the Trumps to everything everyone said, hoping for a clue as to Brand's whereabouts."

"That's what Dad meant," I said.

"What?" Caine asked.

"He implied there was an eavesdropper on the Trumps."

"I do not see how he could have known. I had learned to be completely passive about it. I had taught myself to deal them all out and touch all of them lightly at the same time, waiting for a stirring. When it came, I would shift my attention to the speakers. Taking you one at a time, I even found I could sometimes get into your minds when you were not using the Trumps yourselves—if you were sufficiently distracted and I allowed myself no reaction."

"Yet he knew," I said.

"It is entirely possible. Likely, even," said Fiona, and Bleys nodded.

Random drew nearer.

"What did you mean when you asked about Corwin's side?" he inquired. "How could you even know about it unless—"

Caine merely nodded. I saw Benedict and Julian together in the distance, addressing their troops. At Caine's silent movement, I forgot them.

"You?" I croaked. "You stabbed me?"

"Have a drink, Corwin," Random said, passing me his flask. It was a dilute wine. I gulped it. My thirst was immense, but I stopped after several good swigs.

"Tell me about it," I said.

"All right. I owe you that," he said. "When I learned from Julian's mind that you had brought Brand back to Amber, I decided that an earlier guess had been correct—that you and Brand were in it together. That meant you both had to be destroyed. I used the Pattern to project myself into your chambers that night. There, I tried to kill you, but you moved too fast and you somehow managed to Trump out before I got a second chance."

"Well, damn your eyes," I said. "If you could touch our minds couldn't you have seen that I was not the man you were looking for?"

He shook his head.

"I could pick up only surface thoughts and reactions to your immediate environment. Not always that, even. And I had heard your curse, Corwin. And it was coming true. I could see it all around us. I felt that we would all be a lot safer with you and Brand both out of the way. I knew what he could do, from his actions back before your return. I could not get at him just then, though, because of Gérard. Then he began to grow stronger. I made one effort later, but it failed."

"When was that?" Random asked.

"That was the one Corwin got blamed for. I masked myself. In case he managed to get away as Corwin had, I did not want him knowing I was still around. I used the Pattern to project myself into his chambers and tried to finish him off. We were both hurt—there was a lot of blood around—but he managed to Trump away, too. Then I got in touch with Julian a while back and joined him for this battle, because Brand just had to show up here. I had some silver-tipped arrows made because I was more than half convinced that he was no longer like the rest of us. I wanted to kill him fast and do it from a distance. I practiced my archery and came looking for him. I finally found him. Now everyone tells me I was wrong about you, so I guess your arrow will go unused."

"Thanks a lot."

"I might even owe you an apology."

"That would be nice."

"On the other hand, I thought that I was right. I was doing it to save the rest—"

I never did get Caine's apology, because just then a trumpet blast seemed to shake the entire world—directionless, loud, prolonged. We cast about, seeking its source.

Caine stood and pointed.

"There!" he said.

My eyes followed his gesture. The curtain of the stormfront was broken off to the northwest, at the point where the black road emerged from it. There, a ghostly rider on a black horse had appeared and was winding his horn. It was a while before more of its notes reached us. Moments later, two more trumpeters—also pale, and mounted on black steeds—joined him. They raised their horns and added to the sound.

"What can it be?" Random asked.

"I think I know," Bleys said, and Fiona nodded.

"What, then?" I asked.

But they did not answer me. The horsemen were beginning to move again, passing along the black road, and more were emerging behind them.

TWELVE

I watched. There was a great silence on the heights about me. All of the troops had halted and were regarding the procession. Even the prisoners from the Courts, hemmed by steel, turned their attention that way.

Led by the pale trumpeters came a mass of horsemen mounted on white steeds, bearing banners, some of which I did not recognize, behind a man-thing who bore the Unicorn standard of Amber. These were followed by more musicians, some of them playing upon instruments of a sort I had never seen before.

Behind the musicians marched horned man-shaped things in light armor, long columns of them, and every twentieth or so bore a great torch before him, reaching high above his head. A deep noise came to us then—slow, rhythmic, rolling beneath the notes of the trumpets and the sounds of the musicians—and I realized that the foot soldiers were singing. A great deal of time seemed to pass as this body advanced along that black way across the distant track below us, yet none of us stirred and none of us spoke. They passed, with the torches and the banners and the music and the singing, and they finally came to the edge of the abyss and continued over the near-invisible extension of that dark highway, their torches flaring against the blackness now, lighting their way. The music grew stronger, despite the distance, with more and more voices added to that chorus, as the guard continued to emerge from that flashing stormcurtain. An occasional roll of thunder passed by, but this could not drown it; nor did the winds which assailed the torches extinguish any so far as I could see. The movement had a hypnotic effect. It seemed that I had been watching the procession for countless days, years perhaps, listening to the tune I now recognized.

Suddenly, a dragon sailed through the stormfront, and another, and another. Green and golden and black as old iron, I watched them soar on the winds, turning their heads to trail pennons of fire. The lightning flashed behind them and they were awesome and magnificent and of incalculable size. Beneath them came a small herd of white cattle, tossing their heads and blowing, beating the ground with their hoofs. Riders passed beside and among these, cracking long black whips.

Then came a procession of truly bestial troops from a shadow with which Amber sometimes has commerce—heavy, scaled, taloned—playing upon instruments like bagpipes, whose skirling notes came to us with vibrance and pathos.

These marched on, and there were more torch bearers and more troops with their colors—from shadows both distant and near. We watched them pass and wind their way into the far sky, like a migration of fireflies, their destination that black citadel called the Courts of Chaos.

There seemed no end to it. I had lost all track of time. But the stormfront, strangely, was not advancing as all this went on. I had even lost something of my sense of person, to be caught up in the procession which passed us. This, I knew, was an event which could never be repeated. Bright flying things darted above the columns and dark ones floated, higher.

There were ghostly drummers, beings of pure light and a flock of floating machines; I saw horsemen, clad all in black, mounted on a variety of beasts; a wyvern seemed to hang in the sky for a moment, like part of a fireworks display. And the sounds—of hoofbeats and footfalls, of singing and skirling, of drumming and trumpeting—mounted to a mighty wave that washed over us. And on, on, on out over the bridge of darkness, wound the procession, its lights lining the great span for a vast distance now.

Then, as my eyes drifted back along those lines, another shape emerged from the glistening curtain. It was a cart draped all in black and drawn by a team of black horses. At each corner rose a staff which glowed with blue fire, and atop it rested what could only be a casket, draped with our Unicorn flag. The driver was a hunchback clad in purple and orange garments, and I knew even at that distance that it was Dworkin.

It is thus, then, I thought. *I do not know why, but somehow it is fitting that it be the Old Country to which you travel now. There were many things that I might have said while you lived. Some of them I did say, but few of the right words were ever spoken. Now it is over, for you are dead. As dead as all of those who have gone before you into that place where the rest of us soon may follow. I am sorry. It was only after all these years, on your assuming another face and form, that I finally knew you, respected you, even came to like you—though you were a crochety old bastard in that form, too. Was the Ganelon self the real you all along, or was it only another form adopted for convenience's sake, Old Shapeshifter? I will never know, but I like to think that I finally saw you as you were, that I met someone I liked, someone I could trust, and that it was you. I wish that I might have known you even better, but I am grateful for this much. . . .*

"Dad . . . ?" Julian said softly.

"He wanted to be taken beyond the Courts of Chaos and into the final darkness when his time came at last," Bleys said. "So Dworkin once told me. Beyond Chaos and Amber, to a place where none reigned."

"And so it is," Fiona said. "But is there order somewhere beyond that wall they come through? Or does the storm go on forever? If he succeeded, it is but a passing matter and we are in no danger. But if he did not . . ."

"It does not matter," I said, "whether or not he succeeded, because I did."

"What do you mean?" she asked.

"I believe that he failed," I said, "that he was destroyed before he could repair the old Pattern. When I saw this storm coming—actually, I experienced a part of it—I realized that I could not possibly make it here in time with the Jewel, which he had sent to me after his efforts. Brand had been trying to get it from me all along the way—to create a new Pattern, he said. Later, that gave me the idea. When I saw that all else was failing, I used the Jewel to create a new Pattern. It was the most difficult thing I ever did, but I succeeded. Things should hold together after this wave passes, whether we survive it or not. Brand stole the Jewel from me just as I completed it. When I recovered from his attack I was able to use the new Pattern to project me here. So there is still a Pattern, no matter what else happens."

"But Corwin," she said, "what if Dad succeeded?"

"I do not know."

"It is my understanding," Bleys said, "from things that Dworkin told me, that two distinct Patterns could not exist in the same universe. Those in Rebma and Tir-na Nog'th do not count, being but reflections of our own. . . ."

"What would happen?" I said.

"I think there would be a splitting off, the founding of a new existence—somewhere."

"Then what would its effect be upon our own?"

"Either total catastrophe or no effect whatsoever," Fiona said. "I can make a case for its going either way."

"Then we are right back where we started," I said. "Either things are going to fall apart shortly or they are going to hold."

"So it would seem," Bleys said.

"It does not matter, if we are not going to be around after that wave gets to us," I said. "And it will."

I turned my attention back to the funeral cortege. More horsemen had emerged behind the wagon, followed by marching drummers. Then pennons and torches and a long line of foot soldiers. The singing still came to us, and far, far out over the abyss it seemed the procession might finally have reached that dark citadel.

. . . I hated you for so long, blamed you for so many things. Now it is over, and none of these feelings remain. Instead, you had even wanted me to be king, a job for which—I see now—I am not fitted. I see that I must have meant something to you after all. I will never tell the others. It is enough to know it myself. But I can never think of you in the same fashion again. Already your image blurs. I see Ganelon's face where yours should be. He was my companion. He risked his neck for me. He was you, but a different you—a you that I had not known. How many wives and enemies had you outlived? Were there many friends? I think not. But there were so many things about you of which we knew nothing. I never thought that I would see your passing. Ganelon—Father—old friend and enemy, I bid you farewell. You join Deirdre, whom I have loved. You have preserved your mystery. Rest in peace, if that be your will. I give you this withered rose I have borne through hell, casting it into the abyss. I leave you the rose and the twisted colors in the sky. I will miss you. . . .

Finally, the long line came to an end. The last marchers emerged from the curtain and moved away. The lightning still flared, the rain still poured and the thunder rumbled. No member of the procession that I could recall had seemed wet, however. I had been standing at the edge of the abyss, watching them pass. There was a hand on my arm. How long it had been there, I could not tell. Now that the passage was complete, I realized that the stormfront was advancing again.

The rotation of the sky seemed to be bringing more darkness upon us. There were voices off to my left. It seemed they had been talking for a long while, but I had not been hearing their words. I realized that I was shaking, that I ached all over, that I could barely stand.

"Come and lie down," Fiona said. "The family has shrunken enough for one day."

I let her lead me away from the edge.

"Would it really make any difference?" I asked. "How much longer do you think we have?"

"We do not have to stay here and wait for it," she said. "We will cross the dark bridge into the Courts. We have already broken their defense. The storm may not reach that far. It may be stopped here by the abyss. We ought to see Dad off, anyway."

I nodded.

"It would seem we have small choice but to be dutiful unto the end."

I eased myself down and sighed. If anything, I felt even weaker now.

"Your boots . . ." she said.

"Yes."

She pulled them off. My feet throbbed.

"Thanks."

"I'll get you some rations."

I closed my eyes. I dozed. Too many images played within my head to make for a coherent dream. How long this lasted, I do not know, but an old reflex drew me to wakefulness at the sound of an approaching horse. Then a shadow passed over my eyelids.

I looked up and beheld a muffled rider, silent, still. I was regarded.

I looked back. No threatening gesture had been made, but there was a feeling of antipathy in that cold gaze.

"There lies the hero," said a soft voice.

I said nothing.

"I could slay you easily now."

I recognized the voice then, though I had no idea as to the reason behind the sentiment.

"I came upon Borel before he died," she said. "He told me how ignobly you had bested him."

I could not help it, I could not control it. A dry chuckle rose in my throat. Of all the stupid things to get upset about. I might have told her that Borel had been far better equipped and far fresher than I, and that he had come to me looking for a fight. I might have told her that I do not recognize rules when my life is at stake, or that I do not consider war a game. I could have said a great number of things, but if she did not know them already or did not choose to understand them, they would not have made a bit of difference. Besides, her feelings were already plain.

So I simply said one of the great trite truths: "There is generally more than one side to a story."

"I will settle for the one I have," she told me.

I thought about shrugging, but my shoulders were too sore.

"You have cost me two of the most important persons in my life," she said then.

"Oh?" I said. "I'm sorry, for you."

"You are not what I was led to believe. I had seen you as a truly noble figure—strong, yet understanding and sometimes gentle. Honorable . . ."

The storm, much closer now, was flaring at her back. I thought of something vulgar and said it. She let it pass as if she had not heard me.

"I am going now," she said, "back to my own people. You have won the day thus far—but that way lay Amber." She gestured toward the storm. I could only stare. Not at the raging elements. At her. "I doubt there is anything of my new allegiance left for me to renounce," she continued.

"What about Benedict?" I asked softly.

"Don't . . ." she said, and she turned away. There was a silence. Then, "I do not believe that we will ever meet again," she said, and her horse carried her off to my left, in the direction of the black road.

A cynic might have decided that she had simply chosen to toss in her lot with what she now saw as the winning side, as the Courts of Chaos would likely survive. I simply did not know. I could think only of what I had seen when she had gestured. The cowling had slipped away and I had gotten a glimpse of what she had become. It had not been a human face, there within the shadows. But I turned my head and watched until she was gone. With Deirdre, Brand and Dad gone, and now a parting with Dara on these terms, the world was much emptier—whatever was left of it.

I lay back and sighed. Why not just remain here when the others departed, wait for the storm to wash over me, and sleep . . . dissolve? I thought of Hugi. Had I digested his flight from life as well as his flesh? I was so tired that it seemed the easiest course. . . .

"Here, Corwin."

I had been dozing again, though only for a moment. Fiona was beside me once more, with rations and a flask. Someone was with her.

"I did not wish to interrupt your audience," she said. "So I waited."

"You heard?" I asked.

"No, but I can guess," she said, "since she is gone. Here."

I swallowed some wine, turned my attention to the meat, the bread. Despite my state of mind, they tasted good to me.

"We will be moving soon," Fiona said, casting a glance at the raging stormfront. "Can you ride?"

"I think so," I said.

I took another drink of the wine.

"But too much has happened, Fi," I told her. "I have gone numb emotionally. I broke out of a sanitarium on a shadow world. I have tricked people and I've killed people. I have calculated and I have fought. I won back my memory and I have been trying to straighten out my life. I have found my family, and found that I love it. I have been reconciled with Dad. I have fought for the kingdom. I have tried everything I know to hold things together. Now it appears that it has all come to nothing, and I have not enough spirit left to mourn further. I have gone numb. Forgive me."

She kissed me.

"We are not yet beaten. You will be yourself again," she said.

I shook my head.

"It is like the last chapter of *Alice*," I said. "If I shout, 'You are only a pack of cards!' I feel we will all fly into the air, a hand of painted pasteboards. I am not going with you. Leave me here. I am only the Joker, anyway."

"Right now, I am stronger than you are," she said. "You are coming."

"It is not fair," I said softly.

"Finish eating," she said. "There is still some time."

As I did, she went on, "Your son Merlin is waiting to see you. I would like to call him up here now."

"Prisoner?"

"Not exactly. He was not a combatant. He just arrived a little while ago, asking to see you."

I nodded and she went away. I abandoned my rations and took another swig of wine. I had just become nervous. What do you say to a grown son you only recently learned existed? I wondered about his feelings toward me. I wondered whether he knew of Dara's decision. How should I act with him?

I watched him approach from a place where my relatives were clustered, far off to the left. I had wondered why they had left me by myself this way. The more visitors I received the more apparent it became. I wondered whether they were holding up the withdrawal because of me. The storm's moist winds were growing stronger. He was staring at me as he advanced, no special expression on that face so much like my own. I wondered how Dara felt now that her prophecy of the destruction seemed to have been fulfilled. I wondered how her relationship with the boy actually stood. I wondered . . . many things.

He leaned forward to clasp my hand.

"Father . . ." he said.

"Merlin." I looked into his eyes. I rose to my feet, still holding his hand.

"Do not get up."

"It is all right." I clasped him to me, then released him. "I am glad," I said. Then: "Drink with me." I offered him the wine, partly to cover my lack of words.

"Thank you."

He took it, drank some and passed it back.

"Your health," I said and took a sip myself. "Sorry I cannot offer you a chair."

I lowered myself to the ground. He did the same.

"None of the others seemed to know exactly what you have been doing," he said, "except for Fiona, who said only that it had been very difficult."

"No matter," I said. "I am glad to have made it this far, if for no other reason than this. Tell me of yourself, son. What are you like? How has life treated you?"

He looked away.

"I have not lived long enough to have done too much," he said.

I was curious whether he possessed the shapeshifting ability, but restrained myself from asking at this point. No sense in looking for our differences when I had just met him.

"I have no idea what it was like," I said, "growing up in the Courts."

He smiled for the first time.

"And I have no idea what it would have been like anywhere else," he responded. "I was different enough to be left to myself a lot. I was taught the usual things a gentleman should know—magic, weapons, poisons, riding, dancing. I was told that I would one day rule in Amber. This is not true anymore, is it?"

"It does not seem too likely in the foreseeable future," I said.

"Good," he replied. "This is the one thing I did not want to do."

"What do you want to do?"

"I want to walk the Pattern in Amber as Mother did and gain power over Shadow, so that I might walk there and see strange sights and do different things. Do you think I might?"

I took another sip and I passed him the wine.

"It is quite possible," I said, "that Amber no longer exists. It all depends on whether your grandfather succeeded in something he attempted—and he is no longer around to tell us what happened. However, one way or the other, there is a Pattern. If we live through this demon storm, I promise you that I will find you a Pattern, instruct you and see you walking it."

"Thanks," he said. "Now will you tell me of your journey here?"

"Later," I told him. "What did they tell you of me?"

He looked away.

"I was taught to dislike many of the things about Amber," he finally said. Then, after a pause: "You, I was taught to respect, as my father. But I was reminded that you were of the party of the enemy." Another pause. "I remember that time on patrol, when you had come to this place and I found you, after your fight with Kwan. My feelings were mixed. You had just slain someone I had known, yet—I had to admire the stance you took. I saw my face in your own. It was strange. I wanted to know you better."

The sky had rotated completely and the darkness was now above us, the colors passing over the Courts. The steady advance of the flashing stormfront was emphasized by this. I leaned forward and reached for my boots, began pulling them on. Soon it would be time to begin our retreat.

"We will have to continue our conversation on your home ground," I said. "It is about time to fly the storm."

He turned and considered the elements, then looked back out over the abyss.

"I can summon a filmy if you wish."

"One of those drifting bridges such as you rode on the day we met?"

"Yes," he answered. "They are most convenient. I—"

There had been a shout from the direction of my assembled relatives. Nothing threatening seemed to be about when I regarded them. So I got to my feet and took a few steps toward them, Merlin rising to follow me.

Then I saw her. A white form, pawing air it seemed, and rising out of the abyss. Her front hooves finally struck its brink, and she came forward and then stood still, regarding us all: our Unicorn.

THIRTEEN

For a moment, my aches and my fatigue fell away. I felt a tiny twinge of something like hope as I considered the dainty white form which stood before us. A part of me wanted to rush forward, but something much stronger kept me motionless, waiting.

How long we stood thus, I could not tell. Below, on the slopes, the troops had been readying themselves for travel. The prisoners had been bound, horses loaded, equipment secured. But this vast army in the process of march, ordering its gear had suddenly halted. It was not natural that they should have become aware so quickly, but every head that I could see was turned in this direction, toward the Unicorn on the brink, limned against that wild sky.

I was suddenly aware that the wind at my back had grown still, though the thunder continued to rumble and explode and the lightning flares threw dancing shadows before me.

I thought of the other time I had seen the Unicorn—at the recovery of the Shadow-Caine's body, the day I had lost a fight with Gérard. I thought of the stories I had heard. . . . Could she really help us?

The Unicorn took a step forward and halted.

She was such a lovely thing that somehow I was heartened just by looking upon her. It was a kind of aching feeling that she aroused, though; hers was a beauty of the sort to be taken in small doses. And I could somehow sense the unnatural intelligence within that snowy head. I wanted very badly to touch her, but knew that I could not.

She cast her gaze all about. Her eyes lighted upon me, and I would have looked away if I had been able. This was not possible, however, and I returned that gaze in which I read an understanding beyond my own. It was as if she knew everything about me, and in this instant had comprehended all of my recent trials—seeing, understanding, possibly sympathizing. For a moment, I felt that I saw something of pity and a strong love reflected there—and perhaps a touch of humor.

Then her head turned and the gaze was broken. I sighed involuntarily.

At that moment, in the lightning's glare, I thought I caught a glimpse of something shining at the side of her neck.

She advanced another step, and now she was looking upon the crowd of my kinsmen toward which I had been moving. She lowered her head and made a small whickering noise. She tapped at the earth with her right front hoof.

I felt Merlin at my side. I thought upon things I would be losing if it all ended here.

She took several dancing steps forward. She tossed her head and lowered it. It seemed that she did not like the notion of approaching so large a group of people.

At her next step, I saw the glitter again, and more. A tiny spark of red shone through her fur farther down on her neck. She was wearing the Jewel of Judgment. How she had retrieved it, I had no idea. And it did not matter. If she would just deliver it, I felt that I could break the storm—or at least shield us from this section of it until it had passed.

But that one glance had been enough. She paid me no more heed. Slowly, carefully, as if ready to bolt at the slightest disturbance, she advanced upon the spot where Julian, Random, Bleys, Fiona, Llewella, Benedict and several nobles stood.

I should have realized then what was occurring, but I did not. I simply watched the sleek beast's movements as she picked her way forward, passing about the periphery of the group.

She halted once again and lowered her head. Then she shook her mane and dropped to her front knees. The Jewel of Judgment hung suspended from her twisted, golden horn. The tip of her horn was almost touching the person before whom she knelt.

Suddenly, in my mind's eye, I saw our father's face in the heavens, and his words came back to me: "With my passing, the problem of the succession will be upon you. . . . I have no choice but to leave this on the horn of the Unicorn."

A murmur moved through the group, as I realized this same thought must be occurring to the others. The Unicorn did not stir at this disturbance, however, but remained a soft, white statue, not even seeming to breathe.

Slowly, Random reached forward and removed the Jewel from her horn. His whisper carried to me.

"Thank you," he said.

Julian unsheathed his blade and placed it at Random's feet as he knelt. Then Bleys and Benedict and Caine, Fiona and Llewella. I went and joined them. So did my son.

Random stood silent for a long while. Then, "I accept your allegiance," he said. "Now get up, all of you."

As we did, the Unicorn turned and bolted. She raced down the slope and was out of sight in a matter of moments.

"I had never expected anything like this to happen," Random said, still holding the Jewel at eye level. "Corwin, can you take this thing and stop that storm?"

"It is yours now," I said, "and I do not know how extensive the disturbance is. It occurs to me that in my present condition I might not be able to hold up long enough to keep us all safe. I think it is going to have to be your first regal act."

"Then you are going to have to show me how to work it. I thought we needed a Pattern to perform the attunement."

"I think not. Brand indicated that a person who was already attuned could attune another. I have given it some thought since then, and I believe I know how to go about it. Let's get off to one side somewhere."

"Okay. Come on."

Already, something new had come into his voice and posture. The sudden role had begun working its change immediately, it seemed. I wondered what sort of king and queen he and Vialle would become. Too much. My mind felt disassociated. Too much had happened too recently. I could not contain all of the latest events in one big piece of thinking. I just wanted to crawl off somewhere and sleep around the clock. Instead, I followed him to a place where a small cooking fire still smoldered.

He poked at the fire and tossed a handful of sticks onto it. Then he seated himself close to it and nodded to me. I went over and sat down beside him.

"About this king business," he said. "What am I going to do, Corwin? It caught me totally unprepared."

"Do? Probably a very good job," I replied.

"Do you think there were many hard feelings?"

"If there were, they did not show," I said. "You were a good choice, Random. So much has happened recently . . . Dad sheltered us actually, maybe more than was good for us. The throne is obviously no plum. You have a lot of hard work ahead of you. I think the others have come to realize this."

"And yourself?"

"I wanted it only because Eric did. I did not realize it at the time, but it is true. It was the winning counter in a game we had been playing across the years. The end of a vendetta, really. And I would have killed him for it. I am glad now that he found another way to die. We were more alike than we were different, he and I. I did not realize that until much later either. But after his death, I kept finding reasons for not taking the throne. Finally, it dawned on me that it was not really what I wanted. No. You are welcome to it. Rule well, brother. I am sure that you will."

"If Amber still exists," he said after a time, "I will try. Come, let us be about this business with the Jewel. That storm is getting uncomfortably near."

I nodded and took the stone from his fingers. I held it by its chain with the fire behind it. The light came through; its insides seemed clear.

"Lean closer and stare into the Jewel with me," I directed.

He did this, and while we both regarded the stone, I told him, "Think of the Pattern," and I commenced thinking of it myself, trying to summon to mind its loops and swirls, its palely glowing lines.

I seemed to detect a slight flaw near to the stone's center. I considered it as I thought upon the twistings, the turns, the Veils. . . . I imagined the current which swept through me every time I essayed that complex way.

The imperfection in the stone grew more distinct.

I lay my will upon it, summoning it into fullness, clarity. A familiar feeling came over me as this occurred. It was that which had taken me on the day I had attuned myself to the Jewel. I only hoped that I was strong enough now to go through the experience once again.

I reached out and clasped Random by the shoulder.

"What do you see?" I asked him.

"Something like the Pattern," he said, "only it seems to be three dimensional. It lies at the bottom of a red sea. . . ."

"Come with me then," I said. "We must go to it."

Again, that feeling of movement, drifting at first, then falling with increasing velocity toward the never fully seen sinuosities of the Pattern within the Jewel. I willed us ahead, feeling my brother's presence beside me, and the ruby glow which surrounded us darkened, becoming the blackness of a clean night sky. This special Pattern grew with each thudding heartbeat. Somehow, the process seemed easier than it had before—perhaps because I was already attuned.

Feeling Random beside me, I drew him along as that familiar shape grew and its starting point became apparent. As we were moved in that direction, I once again tried to encompass the totality of this Pattern and was lost once more in what seemed its extra-dimensional convolutions. Great curves and spirals and knotted-seeming traceries wound before us. The sense of awe I had felt earlier swept over me, and from somewhere nearby I was aware of this in Random, also.

We progressed to the section of the beginning and were swept into it. There was a shimmering brightness all about us flashed through with sparks as we were woven into the matrix of light. This time, my mind was entirely absorbed by the process and Paris seemed far away. . . .

A subconscious memory reminded me of the more difficult sections, and here I employed my desire—my will, if you like—to hurry us along the dazzling route, recklessly drawing strength from Random to accelerate the process.

It was as if we negotiated the luminous interior of an enormous and elaborately convoluted seashell. Only our passage was soundless, and we ourselves disembodied points of sentience.

Our velocity seemed to increase constantly, as did a mental aching I did not recall from the previous traversal of the design. Perhaps it was related to my fatigue, or to my efforts to hurry things so. We crashed through the barriers; we were surrounded by steady, flowing walls of brightness. I felt myself growing faint, dizzy, now. But I could not afford the luxury of unconsciousness, nor could I permit us to move more slowly with the storm as near as I remembered it. Again, regretfully, I drew strength from Random—this time just to keep us in the game. We sped ahead.

This time, I did not experience the tingling, fiery sensation of somehow being shaped. It must have been an effect of my attunement. My previous passage through it might have rendered me some small immunity in this regard.

After a timeless interval, it seemed that I felt Random falter. Perhaps I represented too great a drain upon his energies. I began to wonder whether I would leave him with sufficient strength to manipulate the storm if I leaned upon him any further. I resolved not to draw upon his resources any more than I already had. We were well along the way. He should be able to continue without me, if it came to that. I would simply have to hang on as best I could now. Better for me to be lost here than both of us.

We swept on, my sense rebelling, the dizziness recurring. I set my will to our progress and forced everything else from my mind. It seemed we were nearing the terminus when a darkening began which I knew was not a part of the experience. I fought down panic.

It was no good. I felt myself slipping away. So close! I was certain we were almost finished. It would be so easy to—

Everything swam away from me. My last sensation was a knowledge of Random's concern.

It was flickering orange and red between my feet. Was I trapped in some astral hell? I continued to stare as my mind slowly cleared. The light was surrounded by darkness and . . .

There were voices, familiar . . .

Things cleared. I was lying on my back, feet toward a campfire.

"It is all right, Corwin. It is all right."

It was Fiona who had spoken. I turned my head. She was seated on the ground above me.

"Random . . . ?" I said.

"He is all right, also—Father."

Merlin was seated off to the right.

"What happened?"

"Random bore you back," Fiona said.

"Did the attunement work?"

"He thinks so."

I struggled to sit up. She tried to push me back, but I sat up anyway.

"Where is he?"

She gestured with her eyes.

I looked and I saw Random. He was standing with his back to us about thirty meters away, on a shelf of rock, facing the storm. It was very close now, and a wind whipped his garments. Lightning trails crissed and crossed before him. The thunder boomed almost constantly.

"How long—has he been there?" I asked.

"Only a few minutes," Fiona replied.

"That is how long it has been—since our return?"

"No," she said. "You have been out for a fairly long while. Random talked with the others first, then ordered a troop withdrawal. Benedict has taken them all to the black road. They are crossing over."

I turned my head.

There was movement along the black road, a dark column heading out toward the citadel. Gossamer strands drifted between us; there were a few sparks at the far end, about the nighted hulk. Overhead, the sky had completely reversed itself, with us between the darkened half. Again, I felt that strange feeling of having been here long, long ago, to see that this, rather than Amber, was the true center of creation. I grasped after the ghost of a memory. It vanished.

I searched the lightning-shot gloom about me.

"All of them—gone?" I said to her. "You, me, Merlin, Random—we're the only ones left here?"

"Yes," Fiona said. "Do you wish to follow them now?"

I shook my head.

"I am staying here with Random."

"I knew you would say that."

I got to my feet as she did. So did Merlin. She clapped her hands and a white horse came ambling up to her.

"You have no further need for my ministrations," she said. "So I will go and join the others in the Courts of Chaos. There are horses for you tethered by those rocks." She gestured. "Are you coming, Merlin?"

"I will stay with my father, and the king."

"So be it. I hope to see you there soon."

"Thanks, Fi," I said.

I helped her to mount and watched her ride off.

I went over and sat down by the fire again. I watched Random, who stood unmoving, facing the storm.

"There are plenty of rations and wine," Merlin said. "May I fetch you some?"

"Good idea."

The storm was so close that I could have walked down to it in a couple of minutes. I could not tell yet whether Random's efforts were having any effect. I sighed heavily and let my mind drift.

Over. One way or another, all of my efforts since Greenwood were over. No need for revenge any longer. No. We had an intact Pattern, maybe even two. The cause of all our troubles, Brand, was dead. Any residuum of my curse was bound to be wiped out by the massive convulsions sweeping through Shadow. And I had done my best to make up for it. I had found a friend in my father and come to terms with him as himself before his death. We had a new king, with the apparent blessing of the Unicorn, and we had pledged him our loyalty. It seemed sincere to me. I was reconciled with my entire family. I felt that I had done my duty. Nothing drove me now. I had run out of causes and was as close as I might ever be to peace. With all this behind me, I felt that if I had to die now, it was all right. I would not protest quite so loudly as I would have at any other time.

"You are far from here, Father."

I nodded, then smiled. I accepted some food and began eating. As I did, I watched the storm. Still too early to be certain, but it seemed that it was no longer advancing.

I was too tired to sleep. Or something like that. My aches had all subsided and a wondrous numbness had come over me. I felt as if I were embedded in warm cotton. Events and reminiscences kept the mental clockwork turning within me. It was, in many ways, a delicious feeling.

I finished eating and built up the fire. I sipped the wine and watched the storm, like a frosted window set before a fireworks display. Life felt good. If Random succeeded in pulling this one off, I would be riding into the Courts of Chaos tomorrow. What might await me there, I could not tell. Perhaps it might be a gigantic trap. An ambush. A trick. I dismissed the thought. Somehow, right now, it did not matter.

"You had begun telling me of yourself, Father."

"Had I? I do not recall what I said."

"I would like to get to know you better. Tell me more."

I made a popping noise with my lips and shrugged.

"Then this." He gestured. "This whole conflict. How did it get started? What was your part in it? Fiona told me that you had dwelled in Shadow for many years without your memory. How did you get it back and locate the others, and return to Amber?"

I chuckled. I regarded Random and the storm once more. I took a drink of wine and drew up my cloak against the wind.

"Why not?" I said then. "If you've a stomach for long stories, that is. . . . I suppose that the best place to begin is at Greenwood Private Hospital, on the shadow Earth of my exile. Yes . . ."

FOURTEEN

The sky turned, and turned again as I spoke. Standing against the storm, Random prevailed. It broke before us, parting as if cloven by a giant's axblade. It rolled back at either hand, finally sweeping off to the north and the south, fading, diminishing, gone. The landscape it had masked endured, and with it went the black road. Merlin tells me that this is no problem, though, for he will summon a strand of gossamer when the time comes for us to cross over.

Random is gone now. The strain upon him was immense. In repose, he no longer looked as once he did—the brash younger brother we delighted in tormenting—for there were lines upon his face which I had never noticed before, signs of some depth to which I had paid no heed. Perhaps my vision has been colored by recent events, but he seemed somehow nobler and stronger. Does a new role work some alchemy? Appointed by the Unicorn, anointed by the storm, it seems that he had indeed assumed a kingly mien, even in slumber.

I have slept—even as Merlin now dozes—and it pleases me to be, for this brief while before his awakening, the only spot of sentience on this crag at the rim of Chaos, looking back upon a surviving world, a world that has been scoured, a world which endures. . . .

We may have missed Dad's funeral, his drifting into some nameless place beyond the Courts. Sad, but I lacked the strength to move. And yet, I have seen the pageant of his passing, and I bear much of his life within me. I have said my good-byes. He would understand. And good-bye, Eric. After all this time I say it, in this way. Had you lived so long, it would have been over between us. We might even one day have become friends, all our causes for strife passed. Of them all, you and I were more alike than any other pair within the family. Save, in some ways, Deirdre and myself . . . But tears on this count were shed long ago. Good-bye again, though, dearest sister, you will always live somewhere in my heart.

And you Brand . . . With bitterness do I regard your memory, mad brother. You almost destroyed us. You nearly toppled Amber from her lofty perch on the breast of Kolvir. You would have shattered all of Shadow. You almost broke the Pattern and redesigned the universe in your own image. Your were mad and evil, and you came so close to realizing your desires that I tremble even now. I am glad that you are gone, that the arrow and the abyss have claimed you, that you sully no more the places of men with your presence nor walk in the sweet airs of Amber. I wish that you had never been born and, failing that, that you had died sooner. Enough! It diminishes me to reflect so. Be dead and trouble my thinking no more.

I deal you out like a hand of cards, my brothers and sisters. It is painful as well as self-indulgent to generalize like this, but you—I—we—seem to have changed, and before I move into the traffic again I require a final look.

Caine, I never liked you and I still do not trust you. You have insulted me, betrayed me and even stabbed me. Forget that. I do not like your methods, though I cannot fault your loyalty this time around. Peace, then. Let the new reign begin with a clean slate between us.

Llewella, you possess reserves of character the recent situation did not call upon you to exercise. For this, I am grateful. It is sometimes pleasant to emerge from a conflict untested.

Bleys, you are still a figure clad in light to me—valiant, exuberant and rash. For the first, my respect, for the second, my smile. And the last seems to have at least been tempered in recent times. Good. Stay away from conspiracies in the future. They do not suit you well.

Fiona, you have changed the most. I must substitute a new feeling for an old one, princess, as we have become for the first time friends. Take my fondness, sorceress. I owe you.

Gérard, slow, faithful brother, perhaps we have not all changed. You stood rock-like and held to what you believed. May you be less easily gulled. May

I never wrestle you again. Go down to your sea in your ships and breathe the clean salt air.

Julian, Julian, Julian . . . Is it that I never really knew you? No. Arden's green magic must have softened that old vanity during my long absence, leaving a juster pride and something I would fain call fairness—a thing apart from mercy, to be sure, but an addition to your armory of traits I'll not disparage.

And Benedict, the gods know you grow wiser as time burns its way to entropy, yet you still neglect single examples of the species in your knowledge of people. Perhaps I'll see you smile now this battle's done. Rest, warrior.

Flora . . . Charity, they say, begins at home. You seem no worse now than when I knew you long ago. It is but a sentimental dream to regard you and the others as I do, toting up my balance sheets, looking for credits. We are not enemies, any of us, now, and that should be sufficient.

And the man clad in black and silver with a silver rose upon him? He would like to think that he has learned something of trust, that he has washed his eyes in some clear spring, that he has polished an ideal or two. Never mind. He may still be only a smart-mouthed meddler, skilled mainly in the minor art of survival, blind as ever the dungeons knew him to the finer shades of irony. Never mind, let it go, let it be. I may never be pleased with him.

Carmen, *voulez-vous venir avec moi?* No? Then good-bye to you too, Princess of Chaos. It might have been fun.

The sky is turning once more, and who can say what deeds its stained-glass light might shine upon? The solitaire has been dealt and played. Where there had been nine of us now there are seven and one a king. Yet Merlin and Martin are with us, new players in the ongoing game.

My strength returns as I stare into the ashes and consider the path I have taken. The way ahead intrigues me, from hell to hallelujah. I have back my eyes, my memories, my family. And Corwin will always be Corwin, even on Judgment Day.

Merlin is stirring now, and this is good. It is time to be about. There are things to do.

Random's last act after defeating the storm was to join with me, drawing power from the Jewel, to reach Gérard through his Trump. They are cold once more, the cards, and the shadows are themselves again. Amber stands. Years have passed since we departed it, and more may elapse before I return. The others may already have Trumped home, as Random has done, to take up his duties. But I must visit the Courts of Chaos now, because I said that I would, because I may even be needed there.

We ready our gear now, Merlin and I, and soon he will summon a wispy roadway.

When all is done in that place, and when Merlin has walked his Pattern and gone to claim his worlds, there is a journey that I must make. I must ride to the place where I planted the limb of old Ygg, visit the tree it has grown to. I must see what has become of the Pattern I drew to the sound of pigeons on the Champs-Elysées. If it leads me to another universe, as I now believe it will, I must go there, to see how I have wrought.

The roadway drifts before us, rising to the Courts in the distance. The time has come. We mount and move forward.

We are riding now across the blackness on a road that looks like cheese-cloth. Enemy citadel, conquered nation, trap, ancestral home . . . We shall see. There is a faint flickering from battlement and balcony. We may even be in time for a funeral. I straighten my back and I loosen my blade. We will be there before much longer.

Good-bye and hello, as always.

BOOK SIX
TRUMPS OF DOOM

Again, Judy

ONE

It is a pain in the ass waiting around for someone to try to kill you. But it was April 30, and of course it would happen as it always did. It had taken me a while to catch on, but now I at least knew when it was coming. In the past, I'd been too busy to do anything about it. But my job was finished now. I'd only stayed around for this. I felt that I really ought to clear the matter up before I departed.

I got out of bed, visited the bathroom, showered, brushed my teeth, et cetera. I'd grown a beard again, so I didn't have to shave. I was not jangling with strange apprehensions, as I had been on that April 30 three years ago when I'd awakened with a headache and a premonition, thrown open the windows, and gone to the kitchen to discover all of the gas burners turned on and flameless. No. It wasn't even like the April 30 two years ago in the other apartment when I awoke before dawn to a faint smell of smoke to learn that the place was on fire. Still, I stayed out of direct line of the light fixtures in case the bulbs were filled with something flammable, and I flipped all of the switches rather than pushing them. Nothing untoward followed these actions.

Usually, I set up the coffee maker the night before with a timer. This morning, though, I didn't want coffee that had been produced out of my sight. I set a fresh pot going and checked my packing while I waited for it to brew. Everything I valued in this place resided in two medium-sized crates—clothing, books, paintings, some instruments, a few souvenirs, and so forth. I sealed the cases. A change of clothing, a sweatshirt, a good paperback, and a wad of traveler's checks went into the backpack. I'd drop my key off at the manager's on the way out, so he could let the movers in. The crates would go into storage.

No jogging for me this morning.

As I sipped my coffee, passing from window to window and pausing beside each for sidelong surveys of the streets below and the buildings across the way (last year's attempt had been by someone with a rifle), I thought back to the first time it had happened, seven years ago. I had simply been walking down the street on a bright spring afternoon when an oncoming truck had swerved, jumped the curb, and nearly combined me with portions of a brick wall. I was able to dive out of the way and roll. The driver never regained consciousness. It had seemed one of those freak occurrences that occasionally invade the lives of us all.

The following year to the day, however, I was walking home from my lady friend's place late in the evening when three men attacked me—one with a knife, the other two with lengths of pipe—without even the courtesy of first asking for my wallet.

I left the remains in the doorway of a nearby record store, and while I thought about it on the way home it did not strike me until the following day that it had been the anniversary of the truck crash. Even then, I dismissed it as an odd coincidence. The matter of the mail bomb that had destroyed half of another apartment the following year did cause me to begin wondering whether the statistical nature of reality might not be under a strain in my vicinity at that season. And the events of subsequent years served to turn this into a conviction.

Someone enjoyed trying to kill me once a year, it was as simple as that. The effort failing, there would be another year's pause before an attempt was made again. It seemed almost a game.

But this year I wanted to play, too. My main concern was that he, she, or it seemed never to be present when the event occurred, favoring stealth and gimmicks or agents. I will refer to this person as S (which sometimes stands for "sneak" and sometimes for "shithead" in my private cosmology), because X has been overworked and because I do not like to screw around with pronouns with disputable antecedents.

I rinsed my coffee cup and the pot and set them in the rack. Then I picked up my bag and departed. Mr. Mulligan wasn't in, or was sleeping, so I left my key in his mailbox before heading up the street to take my breakfast at a nearby diner.

Traffic was light, and all of the vehicles well behaved. I walked slowly, listening and looking. It was a pleasant morning, promising a beautiful day. I hoped to settle things quickly, so I could enjoy it at my leisure.

I reached the diner unmolested. I took a seat beside the window. Just as the waiter came to take my order I saw a familiar figure swinging along the street—a former classmate and later fellow employee—Lucas Raynard: six feet tall, red-haired, handsome in spite, or perhaps because, of an artistically broken nose, with the voice and manner of the salesman he was.

I knocked on the window and he saw me, waved, turned and entered,

"Merle, I was right," he said, coming up to the table, clasping my shoulder briefly, seating himself and taking the menu out of my hands. "Missed you at your place and guessed you might be here."

He lowered his eyes and began reading the menu.

"Why?" I asked.

"If you need more time to consider, I'll come back," the waiter said.

"No," Luke answered and read off an enormous order. I added my own. Then: "Because you're a creature of habit."

"Habit?" I replied. "I hardly eat here anymore."

"I know," he answered, "but you usually did when the pressure was on. Like, right before exams—or if something was bothering you."

"Hm," I said. There did seem to be something to that, though I had never before realized it. I spun the ashtray with its imprint of a unicorn's head, a smaller version of the stained-glass one that stood as part of a partition beside the doorway. "I can't say why," I finally stated. "Besides what makes you think something's bothering me?"

"I remembered that paranoid thing you have about April 30, because of a couple of accidents."

"More than a couple. I never told you about all of them."

"So you still believe it?"

"Yes."

He shrugged. The waiter came by and filled our coffee cups.

"Okay," he finally agreed. "Have you had it yet today?"

"No."

"Too bad. I hope it doesn't pall your thinking."

I took a sip of coffee.

"No problem," I told him.

"Good." He sighed and stretched. "Listen, I just got back to town yesterday . . ."

"Have a good trip?"

"Set a new sales record."

"Great."

"Anyhow . . . I just learned when I checked in that you'd left."

"Yeah. I quit about a month ago."

"Miller's been trying to reach you. But with your phone disconnected he couldn't call. He even stopped by a couple of times, but you were out."

"Too bad."

"He wants you back."

"I'm finished there."

"Wait'll you hear the proposition, huh? Brady gets kicked upstairs and you're the new head of Design—for a twenty percent pay hike. That's what he told me to tell you."

I chuckled softly.

"Actually, it doesn't sound bad at all. But, like I said, I'm finished."

"Oh." His eyes glistened as he gave me a sly smile. "You *do* have something lined up someplace else. He was wondering. Okay, if that's the case he told me to tell you to bring him whatever the other guys offered. He'll try like hell to top it."

I shook my head.

"I guess I'm not getting through," I said. "I'm finished. Period. I don't want to go back. I'm not going to work for anyone else either. I'm done with this sort of thing. I'm tired of computers."

"But you're really good. Say, you going to teach?"

"Nope."

"Well, hell! You've got to do something. Did you come into some money?"

"No. I believe I'll do some traveling. I've been in one place too long."

He raised his coffee cup and drained it. Then he leaned back, clasped his hands across his stomach, and lowered his eyelids slightly. He was silent for a time.

Finally: "You said you were finished. Did you just mean the job and your life here, or something else as well?"

"I don't follow you."

"You had a way of disappearing—back in college, too. You'd be gone for a while and then just as suddenly turn up again. You always were vague about it, too. Seemed like you were leading some sort of double life. That have anything to do with it?"

"I don't know what you mean."

He smiled.

"Sure you do," he said. When I did not reply, he added, "Well, good luck with it—whatever."

Always moving, seldom at rest, he fidgeted with a key ring while we had a second cup of coffee, bouncing and jangling keys and a blue stone pendant. Our breakfasts finally arrived and we ate in silence for a while.

Then he asked, "You still have the *Starburst*?"

"No. Sold her last fall," I told him. "I'd been so busy I just didn't have time to sail. Hated to see her idle."

He nodded.

"That's too bad," he said. "We had a lot of fun with her, back in school. Later, too. I'd have liked to take her out once more, for old times' sake."

"Yes."

"Say, you haven't seen Julia recently."

"No, not since we broke up. I think she's still going with some guy named Rick. Have you?"

"Yeah. I stopped by last night."

"Why?"

He shrugged.

"She was one of the gang—and we've all been drifting apart."

"How was she?"

"Still looking good. She asked me about you. Gave me this to give to you, too."

He withdrew a sealed envelope from inside his jacket and passed it to me. It bore my name, in her handwriting. I tore it open and read:

> Merle,
>
> *I was wrong. I know who you are and there is danger. I have to see you. I have something you will need. It is very important. Please call or come by as soon as you can.*
>
> Love,
> Julia

"Thanks," I said, opening my pack and filing it.

It was puzzling as well as unsettling. In the extreme. I'd have to decide what to do about it later. I still liked her more than I cared to think about, but I wasn't sure I wanted to see her again. But what did she mean about knowing who I am?

I pushed her out of my mind, again.

I watched the traffic for a time and drank coffee and thought about how I'd first met Luke, in our freshman year, in the Fencing Club. He was unbelievably good.

"Still fence?" I asked him.

"Sometimes. How about you?"

"Occasionally."

"We never really did find out who was better."

"No time now," I said.

He chuckled and poked his knife at me a few times.

"I guess not. When are you leaving?"

"Probably tomorrow—I'm just cleaning up a few odds and ends. When that's done I'll go."

"Where are you heading?"

"Here and there. Haven't decided on everything yet."

"You're crazy."

"Um-hm. *Wanderjahr* is what they used to call it. I missed out on mine and I want it now."

"Actually it does sound pretty nice. Maybe I ought to try it myself sometime."

"Maybe so. I thought you took yours in installments, though."

"What do you mean?"

"I wasn't the only one who used to take off a lot."

"Oh, that." He dismissed it with the wave of a hand. "That was business, no pleasure. Had to do some deals to pay the bills. You going to see your folks?"

Strange question. Neither of us had ever spoken of our parents before, except in the most general terms.

"I don't think so," I said. "How're yours?"

He caught my gaze and held it, his chronic smile widening slightly.

"Hard to say," he replied. "We're kind of out of touch."

I smiled, too.

"I know the feeling."

We finished our food, had a final coffee.

"So you won't be talking to Miller?" he asked.

"No."

He shrugged again. The check came by and he picked it up.

"This one's on me," he said. "After all, I'm working."

"Thanks. Maybe I can get back at you for dinner. Where're you staying?"

"Wait." He reached into his shirt pocket, took out a matchbook, tossed it to me. "There. New Line Motel," he said.

"Say I come by about six?"

"Okay."

He settled up and we parted on the street.

"See you," he said.

"Yeah."

Bye-bye, Luke Raynard. Strange man. We'd known each other for almost eight years. Had some good times. Competed in a number of sports. Used to jog together almost every day. We'd both been on the track team. Dated the same girls sometimes. I wondered about him again—strong, smart, and as private a person as myself. There was a bond between us, one that I didn't fully understand.

I walked back to my apartment's parking lot and checked under my car's hood and frame before I tossed my pack inside and started the engine. I drove slowly, looking at things that had been fresh and new eight years before, saying good-bye to them now. During the past week I had said it to all of the people who had mattered to me. Except for Julia.

It was one of those things I felt like putting off, but there was no time. It was either now or not at all, and my curiosity had been piqued. I pulled into a shopping mall's lot and located a pay phone, but there was no answer when I rang her number. I supposed she could be working full-time on a dayshift again, but she could also be taking a shower or be out shopping. I decided to drive on over to her place and see. It wasn't that far. And whatever it was that she had for me, picking it up would be a good excuse for seeing her this one last time.

I cruised the neighborhood for several minutes before I located a parking space. I locked the car, walked back to the corner, and turned right. The day had grown slightly warmer. Somewhere, dogs were barking.

I strolled on up the block to that huge Victorian house that had been converted into apartments. I couldn't see her windows from the front. She was on the top floor, to the rear. I tried to suppress memories as I passed on up the front walk, but it was no good. Thoughts of our times together came rushing back along with a gang of old feelings. I halted. It was silly coming here. Why bother, for something I hadn't even missed. Still . . .

Hell. I *wanted* to see her one more time. I wasn't going to back out now. I mounted the steps and crossed the porch. The door was open a crack so I walked in.

Same foyer. Same tired-looking potted violet, dust on its leaves, on the chest before the gilt-framed mirror—the mirror that had reflected our embrace, slightly warped, many times. My face rippled as I went by.

I climbed the green-carpeted stairs. A dog began howling somewhere out back.

The first landing was unchanged. I walked the short hallway, past the drab etchings and the old end table, turned and mounted the second staircase. Halfway up I heard a scratching noise from overhead and a sound like a bottle or vase rolling on a hardwood floor. Then silence again, save for a few gusts of wind about the eaves. A faint apprehension stirred within me and I quickened my pace. I halted at the head of the stairway and nothing looked to be out of order, but with my next inhalation a peculiar odor came to me. I couldn't place it—sweat, must, damp dirt perhaps—certainly something organic.

I moved then to Julia's door and waited for several moments. The odor seemed stronger there, but I heard no new sounds.

I rapped softly on the dark wood. For a moment it seemed that I heard someone stirring within, but only for a moment. I knocked again.

"Julia?" I called out. "It's me—Merle."

Nothing. I knocked louder.

Something fell with a crash. I tried the doorknob. Locked.

I twisted and jerked and tore the doorknob, the lock plate, and the entire locking mechanism free. I moved immediately to my left then, past the hinged edge of the door and the frame. I extended my left hand and applied gentle pressure to the upper panel with my fingertips.

I moved the door a few inches inward and paused. No new sounds ensued, and nothing but a slice of wall and floor came into my view, with narrow glimpses of a watercolor, the red sofa, the green rug. I eased the door open a little farther. More of the same. And the odor was even stronger.

I took a half-step to my right and applied a steady pressure.

Nothingnothingnothing . . .

I snatched my hand away when she came into view. Lying there. Across the room. Bloody . . .

There was blood on the floor, the rug, a bloody disarray near the corner off to my left. Upset furniture, torn cushions . . .

I suppressed an impulse to rush forward.

I took one slow step and then another, all of my senses alert. I crossed the threshold. There was nothing else/no one else in the room. Frakir tightened about my wrist. I should have said something then, but my mind was elsewhere.

I approached and knelt at her side. I felt sick. From the doorway I had not been able to see that half of her face and her right arm were missing. She was not breathing and her carotid was silent. She had on a torn and bloodied peach-colored robe; there was a blue pendant about her neck.

The blood that had spilled beyond the rug onto the hardwood floor was smeared and tracked. They were not human footprints, however, but large, elongated, three-toed things, well padded, clawed.

A draft of which I had been only half-consciously aware—coming from the opened bedroom door at my back—was suddenly diminished, as the odor intensified. There came another quick pulsing at my wrist. There was no sound, though. It was absolutely silent, but I knew that it was there.

I spun up out of my kneeling position into a crouch, turning—

I saw a large mouthful of big teeth, bloody lips curled back around them. They lined the muzzle belonging to several hundred pounds of doglike creature covered with coarse, moldy-looking yellow fur. Its ears were like clumps of fungi, its yellow-orange eyes wide and feral.

As I had no doubt whatever concerning its intentions I hurled the doorknob, which I had been clutching half-consciously for the past minute. It glanced off the bony ridge above its left eye without noticeable effect. Still soundless, the thing sprang at me.

Not even time for a word to Frakir . . .

People who work in slaughterhouses know that there is a spot on an animal's forehead to be found by drawing an imaginary line from the right ear to the left eye and another from the left ear to the right eye. They aim the killing blow an inch or two above the junction of this X. My uncle taught me that. He didn't work in a slaughterhouse, though. He just knew how to kill things.

So I spun forward and to the side as it sprang, and I struck a hammer blow at the death spot. It moved even faster than I'd anticipated, however, and when my fist struck it, it was already rushing by. Its neck muscles helped it to absorb the force of my blow.

This drew the first sound from it, though—a yelp. It shook its head and turned with great speed then, and it was at me again. Now a low, rumbling growl came up from its chest and its leap was high. I knew that I was not going to be able to sidestep this one.

My uncle had also taught me how to grab a dog by the flesh on the sides of its neck and under the jaws. You need a good grip if it's a big one, and you've got to get it just right. I had no real choice at the moment. If I tried a kick and missed it would probably take off my foot.

My hands shot forward and snaked upward and I braced myself when we met. I was sure it outweighed me and I had to meet its momentum as well.

I'd had visions of losing fingers or a hand, but I got in under the jaw, caught hold and squeezed. I kept my arms extended and leaned into the impact. I was shaken by the force of its lunge, but I was able to maintain my grip and absorb it.

As I listened to the growls and regarded the slavering muzzle a foot or so away from my face I realized that I hadn't thought much beyond this point. With a dog, you might be able to bash its head against anything hard and handy; its carotids are too deeply buried to rely on direct pressure to take it out. But this thing was strong and my grip was already beginning to slip against its frantic twisting. As I held its jaws away from me and kept pushing it upward, I also realized that it was taller than I was when extended along the vertical. I could try for a kick at its soft underside, but I would probably go off balance as well as lose my grip, and then my groin would be exposed to its teeth.

But it twisted free of my left hand, and I had no choice but to use my right or lose it. So I pushed as hard as I could and retreated again. I had been looking for a weapon, any weapon, but there was nothing handy that would serve.

It lunged again, coming for my throat, coming too fast and high for me to manage a kick to its head. I couldn't get out of its way either.

Its forelegs were level with my midriff, and I hoped that my uncle had been right about this one too, as I seized them and twisted backward and inward with all of my strength, dropping to one knee to avoid those jaws, chin lowered to protect my throat, my head drawn back. Bones popped and crunched as I twisted and its head lowered almost immediately to attack my wrists. But by then I was already rising, thrusting forward, springing up.

It went over backward, twisted, and almost caught itself. When its paws struck the floor, however, it made a sound halfway between a whimper and a snarl and collapsed forward.

I was about to try for another blow to the skull when it recovered its footing, moving faster than I'd thought it could. It raised its right foreleg immediately upon standing and balanced itself on three legs, still growling, eyes fixed on my own, saliva dampening its lower jaws. I moved slightly to my left, certain that it was about to rush me yet again, angling my body, positioning myself in a way that no one had taught me, because I do occasionally have original thoughts.

It was a little slower when it came for me this time. Maybe I could have gone for the skull and gotten it. I don't know because I didn't try. I seized it once more by the neck, and this time it was familiar territory. It would not pull away as it had before in the few moments I needed. Without breaking its momentum I turned and dropped low and thrust and pulled, adding some guidance to its trajectory.

It turned in midair, its back striking the window. With a shattering, splintering sound it passed through, taking most of the frame, the curtain and the curtain rod along with it.

I heard it hit three stories below. When I rose and looked out I saw it twitch a few times and grow still, there on the concrete patio where Julia and I had often had a midnight beer.

I returned to Julia's side and held her hand. I began to realize my anger. Someone had to be behind this. Could it be S again? Was this my April 30 present for this year? I'd a feeling that it was and I wanted to do unto S as I had just done unto the creature that had performed the act. There had to be a reason. There ought to be a clue.

I rose, went to the bedroom, fetched a blanket, and covered Julia with it. Mechanically, I wiped my fingerprints from the fallen doorknob as I began my search of the apartment.

I found them on the mantelpiece between the clock and a stack of paperbacks dealing with the occult. The moment I touched them and felt their coldness I realized that this was even more serious than I had thought. They had to be the thing of mine she'd had that I would be needing—only they were not really mine, though as I riffled through I recognized them on one level and was puzzled by them on another. They were cards, Trumps, like yet unlike any I had ever seen before.

It was not a complete deck. Just a few cards, actually, and strange. I slipped them into my side pocket quickly when I heard the siren. Time for solitaire later.

I tore down the stairs and out the back door, encountering no one. Fido still lay where he had fallen and all the neighborhood dogs were discussing it. I vaulted fences and trampled flowerbeds, cutting through backyards on my way over to the side street where I was parked.

Minutes later I was miles away, trying to scrub the bloody pawprints from my memory.

TWO

I drove away from the bay until I came to a quiet, well-treed area. I stopped the car and got out and walked.

After a long while I located a small, deserted park. I seated myself on one of the benches, took out the Trumps and studied them. A few seemed half familiar and the rest were totally puzzling. I stared too long at one and seemed to hear a siren song. I put them down. I did not recognize the style. This was extremely awkward.

I was reminded of the story of a world-famous toxicologist who inadvertently ingested a poison for which there was no antidote. The question foremost in his mind was, Had he taken a lethal dose? He looked it up in a classic textbook that he himself had written years before. According to his own book he had had it. He checked another, written by an equally eminent professional. According to that one he had taken only about half the amount necessary to do in someone of his body mass. So he sat down and waited, hoping he'd been wrong.

I felt that way because I am an expert on these things. I thought that I knew the work of everyone who might be capable of producing such items. I picked up one of the cards, which held a peculiar, almost familiar fascination for me—depicting a small grassy point jutting out into a quiet lake, a sliver of something bright, glistening, unidentifiable, off to the right. I exhaled heavily upon it, fogging it for an instant, and struck it with my fingernail. It rang like a glass bell and flickered to life. Shadows swam and pulsed as the scene inched into evening. I passed my hand over it and it grew still once again— back to lake, grasses, daytime.

Very distant. Time's stream flowed faster there in relationship to my present situation. Interesting.

I groped for an old pipe with which I sometimes indulge myself, filled it, lit it, puffed it, and mused. The cards were functional all right, not some clever imitations, and though I did not understand their purpose, that was not my main concern at the moment.

Today was April 30, and I had faced death once again. I had yet to confront the person who had been playing with my life. S had again employed a proxy menace. And that was no ordinary dog I had destroyed. And the cards . . . where had Julia gotten them and why had she wanted me to have them? The cards and the dog indicated a power beyond that of an ordinary person. All along I had thought I'd been the subject of the unwelcome attention of some psycho, whom I could deal with at my leisure. But this morning's events put an entirely different complexion on the case. It meant that I had one hell of an enemy somewhere.

I shuddered. I wanted to talk to Luke again, get him to reconstruct their conversation of the previous evening, see whether Julia had said anything that might provide me with a clue. I'd like to go back and search her apartment more carefully, too. But that was out of the question. The cops had pulled up in front of the place as I was driving away. There'd be no getting back in for some time.

Rick. There was Rick Kinsky, the guy she'd begun seeing after we'd broken up. I knew him on sight—a thin, mustached, cerebral sort, thick glasses and all. He managed a bookstore I'd visited once or twice. I didn't know him beyond that, though. Perhaps he could tell me something about the cards and how Julia might have gotten into whatever situation it was that had cost her her life.

I brooded a little longer, then put the cards away. I wasn't about to fool with them any further. Not yet. First, I wanted as much information as I could get.

I headed back for the car. As I walked I reflected that this April 30 wasn't over. Suppose S didn't really consider this morning's encounter as aimed directly at me? In that case there was plenty of time for another attempt. I also had a feeling that if I began getting close S would forget about dates and go for my throat whenever there was an opening. I resolved not to let my guard down at all henceforth, to live as in a state of siege until this matter was settled. And all of my energies were now going to be directed toward settling it. My well-being seemed to require the destruction of my enemy, very soon.

Should I seek counsel? I wondered. And if so, from whom? There was an awful lot I still didn't know about my heritage . . .

No. Not yet, I decided. I had to make every effort to handle things myself.

Besides the fact that I wanted to, I needed the practice. It's necessary to be able to deal with nasty matters where I come from.

I drove, looking for a pay phone and trying not to think of Julia as I had last seen her. A few clouds blew in from the west. My watch ticked on my wrist, next to unseen Frakir. The news on the radio was international and cheerless.

I stopped in a drugstore and used a phone there to try to reach Luke at his motel. He wasn't in. So I had a club sandwich and a milkshake in the dining area and tried again afterward. Still out.

Okay. Catch him later. I headed into town. The Browserie, as I recalled, was the name of the bookstore where Rick worked.

I drove by and saw that the place was open. I parked a couple of blocks up the street and walked back. I had been alert all of the way across town, but could not detect any sign that I was being followed.

A cool breeze touched me as I walked, hinting of rain. I saw Rick through the store's window, seated at his high counter reading a book. There was no one else in sight in the place.

A small bell jangled above the door as I entered, and he looked up. He straightened and his eyes widened as I approached.

"Hi," I said, pausing then for a moment. "Rick, I don't know whether you remember me."

"You're Merle Corey," he stated softly.

"Right." I leaned on the counter and he drew back. "I wondered whether you might be able to help me with a little information."

"What kind of information?"

"It's about Julia," I said.

"Look," he answered, "I never went near her until after you two had broken up."

"Huh? No, no, you don't understand. I don't care about that. It's more recent information that I need. She'd been trying to get in touch with me this past week and—"

He shook his head.

"I haven't heard from her for a couple of months."

"Oh?"

"Yeah, we stopped seeing each other. Different interests, you know?"

"Was she okay when you—stopped seeing each other?"

"I guess so."

I stared straight into his eyes and he winced. I didn't like that. "I guess so." I could see that he was a little afraid of me so I decided to push it.

"What do you mean 'different interests' " I asked.

"Well, she got a little weird, you know?" he said.

"I don't know. Tell me."

He licked his lips and looked away.

"I don't want any trouble," he stated.

"I'd rather not indulge either. What was the matter?"

"Well," he said, "she was scared."

"Scared? Of what?"

"Uh—of you."

"Me? That's ridiculous. I never did anything to frighten her. What did she say?"

"She never said it in so many words, but I could tell, whenever your name came up. Then she developed all these funny interests."

"You've lost me," I said. "Completely. She got weird? She got funny interests? What kind? What was going on? I really don't understand, and I'd like to."

He got to his feet and headed for the rear of the store, glancing at me as if I should follow him. I did.

He slowed when he reached a section full of books on natural healing and organic farming and martial arts and herbal remedies and having babies at home, but he went on past it into the hardcore occult section.

"Here," he said, halting. "She borrowed a few of these, brought them back, borrowed a few more."

I shrugged.

"That's all? That's hardly weird."

"But she really got into it."

"So do a lot of people."

"Let me finish," he went on. "She started with theosophy, even attended meetings of a local group. She got turned off on it fairly quick, but by then she'd met some people with different connections. Pretty soon she was hanging around with Sufis, Gurdjieffians, even a shaman."

"Interesting," I said. "No yoga?"

"No yoga. When I asked her that same thing she said that it was power she was after, not samadhi. Anyhow, she just kept finding stranger and stranger acquaintances. The atmosphere got too rarefied for me, so I said good-bye."

"I wonder why?" I mused.

"Here," he said, "take a look at this one."

He tossed me a black book and stepped back. I caught it. It was a copy of the Bible. I opened it to the publishing credits page.

"Something special about this edition?" I asked.

He sighed.

"No. I'm sorry."

He took it back and replaced it on the shelf.

"Just a minute," he said.

He returned to the counter and took a cardboard sign from a shelf beneath it. It read JUST STEPPED OUT. WE'LL REOPEN AT and there was a clock face beneath it with movable hands. He set them to indicate a time a half hour hence and went and hung the sign in the door's window. Then he shot the bolt and gestured for me to follow him to a room in the rear.

The back office contained a desk, a couple of chairs, cartons of books. He seated himself behind the desk and nodded toward the nearest chair. I took it. He switched on a telephone answering machine then, removed a stack of forms and correspondence from the blotter, opened a drawer and took out a bottle of Chianti.

"Care for a glass?" he asked.

"Sure, thanks."

He rose and stepped through the opened door of a small lavatory. He took a pair of glasses from a shelf and rinsed them. He brought them back, set them down, filled both, and pushed one in my direction. They were from the Sheraton.

"Sorry I tossed the Bible at you," he said, raising his glass and taking a sip.

"You looked as if you expected me to go up in a puff of smoke."

He nodded.

"I am really convinced that the reason she wants power has something to do with you. Are you into some form of occultism?"

"No."

"She talked sometimes as if you might even be a supernatural creature yourself."

I laughed. He did, too, after a moment.

"I don't know," he said then. "There're lots of strange things in the world. They can't all be right, but . . ."

I shrugged.

"Who knows? So you think she was looking for some system that would give her power to defend herself against me?"

"That was the impression I got."

I took a drink of the wine.

"That doesn't make sense," I told him.

But even as I said it I knew that it was probably true. And if I had driven her into the path of whatever had destroyed her, then I was partly responsible for her death. I suddenly felt the burden along with the pain.

"Finish the story," I said.

"That's pretty much it," he answered. "I got tired of people who wanted to discuss cosmic crap all the time and I split."

"And that's all? Did she find the right system, the right guru? What happened?"

He took a big drink and stared at me.

"I really liked her," he said.

"I'm sure."

"The Tarot, Caballa, Golden Dawn, Crowley, Fortune—that's where she went next."

"Did she stay?"

"I don't know for sure. But I think so. I only heard this after a while."

"Ritual magic, then?"

"Probably."

"Who does it?"

"Lots of people."

"I mean who did she find? Did you hear that?"

"I think it was Victor Melman."

He looked at me expectantly. I shook my head.

"I'm sorry. I don't know the name."

"Strange man," he mused, taking a sip and leaning back in his chair, clasping his hands behind his neck and bringing his elbows forward. He stared off into the lavatory. "I—I've heard it said—by a number of people, some of them fairly reliable—that he really has something going for him, that he has a hold on a piece of something, that he's known a kind of enlightenment, has been initiated, has a sort of power and is sometimes a great teacher. But he's got these ego problems, too, that seem to go along with that sort of thing. And there's a touch of the seamy side there. I've even heard it said that that's not his real name, that he's got a record, and there's more of Manson to him that Magus. I don't know. He's nominally a painter—actually a pretty good one. His stuff does sell."

"You've met him?"

A pause, then, "Yes."

"What were your own impressions?"

"I don't know. Well . . . I'm prejudiced. I can't really say."

I swirled the wine in my glass.

"How come?"

"Oh, I wanted to study with him once. He turned me down."

"So you were into this, too. I thought—"

"I'm not into anything," he snapped. "I tried everything at some time or other, I mean. Everybody goes through phases. I wanted to develop, expand, advance. Who doesn't? But I never found it." He unbent and took another gulp of wine. "Sometimes I felt that I was close, that there was some power, some vision that I could almost touch or see. Almost. Then it was gone. It's all a lot of crap. You just delude yourself. Sometimes I even thought I had it. Then a few days would go by and I realized that I was lying to myself again."

"All of this was before you met Julia?"

He nodded.

"Right. That might be what held us together for a while. I still like to talk about all this bullshit, even if I don't believe it anymore. Then she got too serious about it, and I didn't feel like going that route again."

"I see."

He drained his glass and refilled it.

"There's nothing to any of it," he said. "There are an infinite number of ways of lying to yourself, of rationalizing things into something they are not. I guess that I wanted magic, and there is no real magic in the world."

"That why you threw the Bible at me?"

He snorted.

"It could as easily have been the Koran or the Vedas, I suppose. It would have been neat to see you vanish in a flash of fire. But no go."

I smiled.

"How can I find Melman?"

"I've got it here somewhere," he said, lowering his eyes and opening a drawer. "Here."

He withdrew a small notebook and flipped through it. He copied out an address on an index card and handed it to me. He took another drink of wine.

"Thanks."

"It's his studio, but he lives there, too," he added.

I nodded and set down my glass.

"I appreciate everything you told me."

He raised the bottle.

"Have another drink?"

"No, thanks."

He shrugged and topped off his own. I rose.

"You know, it's really sad," he said.

"What?"

"That there's no magic, that there never was, there probably never will be."

"That's the breaks," I said.

"The world would be a lot more interesting place."

"Yeah."

I turned to go.

"Do me a favor," he said.

"What?"

"On the way out, set that sign for three o'clock and let the bolt in the door snap shut again."

"Sure."

I left him there and did those things. The sky had grown a lot darker, the wind a bit more chill. I tried again to reach Luke, from a phone on the corner, but he was still out.

We were happy. It had been a terrific day. The weather was perfect, and everything we did had worked out right. We went to a fun party that evening and afterward had a late dinner at a really good little place we'd stumbled upon by accident. We lingered over drinks, hating for the day to end. We decided then to prolong a winning streak, and we drove to an otherwise deserted beach where we sat around and splashed around and watched the moon and felt the breezes. For a long while. I did something then that I had sort of promised myself I would not. Hadn't Faust thought a beautiful moment worth a soul?

"Come on," I said, aiming my beer can at a trash bin and catching hold of her hand. "Let's take a walk."

"Where to?" she asked, as I drew her to her feet.

"Fairy land," I replied. "The fabled realms of yore. Eden. Come on."

Laughing, she let me lead her along the beach, toward a place where it narrowed, squeezing by high embankments. The moon was generous and yellow, the sea sang my favorite song.

We strolled hand in hand past the bluffs, where a quick turning of the way took us out of sight of our stretch of sand. I looked for the cave that should be occurring soon, high and narrow . . .

"A cave," I announced moments later. "Let's go in."

"It'll be dark."

"Good," I said, and we entered.

The moonlight followed us for about six paces. By then, though, I had spotted the turnoff to the left.

"This way," I stated.

"It *is* dark!"

"Sure. Just keep hold of me a little longer. It'll be okay."

Fifteen or twenty steps and there was a faint illumination to the right. I led her along that turning and the way brightened as we advanced.

"We may get lost," she said softly.

"I don't get lost," I answered her.

It continued to brighten. The way turned once more, and we proceeded along that last passage to emerge at the foot of a mountain in sight of a low forest, the sun standing at midmorning height above its trees.

She froze, blue eyes wide.

"It's daytime!" she said.

"Tempus fugit," I replied. "Come on."

We walked through the woods for a time, listening to the birds and the breezes, dark-haired Julia and I, and I led her after a while through a canyon of colored rocks and grasses, beside a stream that flowed into a river.

We followed the river until we came, abruptly to a precipice from whence it plunged a mighty distance, casting rainbows and fogs. Standing there, staring out across the great valley that lay below, we beheld a city of spires and cupolas, gilt and crystal, through morning and mist.

"Where—are we?" she asked.

"Just around the corner," I said. "Come."

I led her to the left, then down a trail that took us back along the face of the cliff, passing finally behind the cataract. Shadows and diamond beads . . . a roaring to approach the power of silence . . .

We passed at last into a tunnel, damp at first but drying as it rose. We followed it to a gallery, open to our left and looking out upon night and stars, stars, stars. . . . It was an enormous prospect, blazing with new constellations, their light sufficient to cast our shadows onto the wall behind us. She leaned over the low parapet, her skin some rare polished marble, and she looked downward.

"They're down there, too," she said. "And to both sides! There is nothing below but more stars. And to the sides . . ."

"Yes. Pretty things, aren't they?"

We remained there for a long while, watching, before I could persuade her to come away and follow the tunnel farther. It bore us out again to behold a ruined classical ampitheater beneath a late afternoon sky. Ivy grew over broken benches and fractured pillars. Here and there lay a shattered statue, as if cast down by earthquake. Very picturesque. I'd thought she'd like it, and I was right. We took turns seating ourselves and speaking to each other. The acoustics were excellent.

We walked away then, hand in hand, down myriad ways beneath skies of many colors, coming at last in sight of a quiet lake with a sun entering evening upon its farther shore. There was a glittering mass of rock off to my right. We walked out upon a small point cushioned with mosses and ferns.

I put my arms around her and we stood there for a long time, and the wind in the trees was lute song counterpointed by invisible birds. Later still, I unbuttoned her blouse.

"Right here?" she said.

"I like it here. Don't you?"

"It's beautiful. Okay. Wait a minute."

So we lay down and loved till the shadows covered us. After a time she slept, as I desired.

I set a spell upon her to keep her asleep, for I was beginning to have second thoughts over the wisdom of making this journey. Then I dressed both of us and picked her up to carry her back. I took a shortcut.

On the beach from which we'd started I put her down and stretched out beside her. Soon I slept also.

We did not awaken till after the sun was up, when the sound of bathers roused us.

She sat up and stared at me.

"Last night," she said, "could not have been a dream. But it couldn't have been real either. Could it?"

"I guess so," I said.

She furrowed her brow.

"What did you just agree to?" she asked.

"Breakfast," I said. "Let's go get some. Come on."

"Wait a minute." She put a hand on my arm. "Something unusual happened. What was it?"

"Why destroy the magic by talking about it? Let's go eat."

She questioned me a lot in the days that followed, but I was adamant in refusing to talk about it. Stupid, the whole thing was stupid. I should never have taken her on that walk. It contributed to that final argument that set us permanently apart.

And now, driving, as I thought about it, I realized something more than my stupidity. I realized that I had been in love with her, that I still loved her. Had I not taken her on that walk, or had I acknowledged her later accusation that I was a sorcerer, she would not have taken the route that she took, seeking power on her own—probably for self-protection. She would be alive.

I bit my lip and cried out. I cut around the braking car in front of me and crashed a light. If I had killed the thing I loved, I was certain that the opposite was not going to be true.

THREE

Grief and anger shrink my world, and I resent this. They seem to paralyze my memory of happier times, of friends, places, things, options. Squeezed by the grip of intense, unsettling emotion, I grow smaller in my single-mindedness. I suppose it is partly because I have discarded a range of choices, impairing in some measure my freedom of will. I don't like this, but after a point I have small control over it. It makes me feel that I have surrendered to a kind of determinism, which irritates me even more. Then, vicious cycle, this feeds back into the emotion that drives me and intensifies it. The simple way of ending this situation is the headlong rush to remove its object. The difficult way is more philosophical, a drawing back, the reestablishment of control. As usual, the difficult way is preferable. A headlong rush may also result in a broken neck.

I parked in the first place that I saw, opened the window, lit my pipe. I vowed not to depart until I had grown calm. All of my life I have had a tendency to overreact to things. It seems to run in my family. But I did not want to be like the others. They made a lot of trouble for themselves that way. The full-scale, all-or-nothing reaction may be all right if you always win, but that way also lies high tragedy or at least opera if you happen to be up against something extraordinary. And I did have indications that this was the case. Therefore, I was a fool. I told myself this till I believed it.

Then I listened to my calmer self as it agreed that I was indeed a fool— for not having seen my own feelings when I could have done something about them, for having displayed a power and denied its consequences, for not having at least guessed at the strange nature of my enemy in all these years, for my present simplification of the coming encounter. It would not do to seize Victor Melman on sight and try to beat the truth out of him. I resolved to proceed carefully, covering myself at all times. Life is never simple, I told myself. Sit still and gather, regroup.

Slowly, I felt the tension go out of me. Slowly, too, my world grew again, and I saw within it the possibility that S really knew me, knew me well, and may even have arranged events so that I would dispense with thinking and surrender to the moment. No, I would not be like the others . . .

I sat there and thought for a long while before I started the engine again and drove on slowly.

*   *   *

It was a grimy brick building situated on a corner. It was four stories in height, with occasional spray-painted obscenities on the alley side and on the wall facing the narrower street. I discovered the graffiti, a few broken windows and the fire escape as I strolled slowly about the place, looking it over. By then a light rain was just beginning to fall. The lower two stories were occupied by the Brutus Storage Company, according to a sign beside the stairs in a small hallway I entered. The place smelled of urine, and there was an empty Jack Daniels bottle lying on the dusty windowsill to my right. Two mailboxes hung upon the flaking wall. One said "Brutus Storage," the other bore the legend "V.M." Both were empty.

I mounted the stair, expecting it to creak. It did not.

There were four knobless doors letting upon the second-floor hallway, all of them closed. The outlines of what might be cartons were visible through several of the frosted panes in their upper sections. There were no sounds from within.

I surprised a black cat dozing on the next stairway. She arched her back, showed me her teeth, made a hissing noise, then turned and bounded up the stairs and out of sight.

The next landing also had four doors—three of them apparently nonfunctional, the fourth dark-stained and shellacked shiny. It bore a small brass plate that read "Melman." I knocked.

There was no answer. I tried again several times, with the same result. No sounds from within either. It seemed likely that these were his living quarters and that the fourth floor, with the possibility of a skylight, held his studio. So I turned away and took the final flight.

I reached the top and saw that one of the four doors there was slightly ajar. I halted and listened for a moment. From beyond it came faint sounds of movement. I advanced and gave it a few knocks. I heard a sudden intake of breath from somewhere inside. I pushed on the door.

He stood about twenty feet away beneath a large skylight and he had turned to face me—a tall, broad-shouldered man with dark beard and eyes. He held a brush in his left hand and a palette in his right. He wore a paint-smeared apron over his Levi's and had on a plaid sport shirt. The easel at his back held the outlines of what could be a madonna and child. There were a great many other canvases about, all of them facing the walls or covered.

"Hello," I said. "You are Victor Melman?"

He nodded, neither smiling nor frowning, placed his palette on a nearby table, his brush into a jar of solvent. He picked up a damp-looking cloth then and wiped his hands with it.

"And yourself?" he asked, tossing the cloth aside and facing me again.

"Merle Corey. You knew Julia Barnes."

"I don't deny it," he said. "Your use of the past tense would seem to indicate—"

"She's dead all right. I want to talk to you about it."

"All right," he said, untying his apron. "Let's go downstairs then. No place to sit up here."

He hung the apron upon a nail near the door and stepped outside. I followed him. He turned back and locked the studio before proceeding down the stairs. His movements were smooth, almost graceful. I could hear the rain on the roof.

He used the same key to unlock the dark door on the third floor. He drew the door open and stood aside, gesturing for me to enter. I did, traversing a hallway that led past a kitchen, its counters covered with empty bottles, stacks of dishes, pizza cartons. Bursting bags of trash leaned against cupboards; the floor looked sticky here and there and the place smelled like a spice factory next door to a slaughterhouse.

The living room, which I came to next, was large, with a comfortable-looking pair of black sofas, facing each other across a battlefield of Oriental carpets and miscellaneous tables, each of which bore several overflowing ashtrays. There was a beautiful concert-sized piano in the far corner, before a wall covered with heavy red drapery. There were numerous low bookcases filled with occult materials, stacks of magazines beside them, atop them, and alongside a few easy chairs. What could be the corner of a pentacle protruded slightly from beneath the largest rug. The stale smells of incense and pot lingered in patches. To my right, there was an archway leading to another room, a closed door to my left. Paintings of a semireligious nature—which I took to be his work—were hung on several of the walls. There was a Chagall-like quality to them. Quite good.

"Have a seat."

He gestured toward an easy chair and I took it.

"Care for a beer?"

"Thank you, no."

He seated himself on the nearer sofa, clasped his hands, and stared at me.

"What happened?" he asked.

I stared back at him.

"Julia Barnes got interested in occult systems," I said. "She came to you to learn more about them. She died this morning under very unusual circumstances."

The left corner of his mouth twitched slightly. He made no other movement.

"Yes, she was interested in such matters," he said. "She came to me for instruction and I provided it."

"I want to know why she died."

He continued to stare.

"Her time was up," he said. "It happens to everybody, in the long run."

"She was killed by an animal that should not exist here. Do you know anything about it?"

"The universe is a stranger place than most of us can imagine."

"Do you know or don't you?"

"I know you," he said, smiling for the first time. "She spoke of you, of course."

"What does that mean?"

"It means," he answered, "that I know you are more than a little aware of such matters yourself."

"And so?"

"The Arts have a way of bringing the right people together at the proper moment when there is work in progress."

"And that's what you think this is all about?"

"I know it."

"How?"

"It was promised."

"So you were expecting me?"

"Yes."

"Interesting. Would you care to tell me more about it?"

"I'd rather show you."

"You say that something was promised. How? By whom?"

"All of that will become clear shortly."

"And Julia's death?"

"That, too, I'd say."

"How do you propose rendering me this enlightenment?"

He smiled. "I just want you to take a look at something," he said.

"All right. I'm willing. Show me."

He nodded and rose.

"It's in here," he explained, turning and heading toward the closed door. I got to my feet and followed him across the room.

He reached into his shirtfront and drew up a chain. He lifted it over his head and I could see that it bore a key. He used it to unlock the door.

"Go in," he said, pushing it open and stepping aside.

I entered. It was not a large room, and it was dark. He flipped a switch and a blue light of small wattage came on within a plain fixture overhead. I saw then that there was one window, directly across from me, and that all of its panes had been painted black. There were no furnishings save for a few cushions scattered here and there across the floor. A portion of the wall to my right was covered with black drapery. The other walls were unadorned.

"I'm looking," I said.

He chuckled.

"A moment, a moment," he advised me. "Have you any idea of my major concern in the occult arts?"

"You're a cabalist," I stated.

"Yes," he admitted. "How could you tell?"

"People in Eastern disciplines tend to run a tight ship," I stated. "But cabalists always seem to be slobs."

He snorted.

"It is all a matter of what is really important to you," he said then.

"Exactly."

He kicked a cushion into the middle of the floor.

"Have a seat," he said.

"I'll stand."

He shrugged.

"Okay," he said, and he began muttering softly.

I waited. After a time, still speaking quietly, he moved to the black curtain. He opened it with a single quick movement and I stared.

A painting of the cabalistic Tree of Life was revealed, showing the ten sephira in some of their qlipphotic aspects. It was beautifully executed, and the sense of recognition that struck me as I regarded it was unsettling. It was no standard item from some head shop, but rather an original painting. It was not, however, in the style of any of the works hanging in the other room. Still, it was familiar to me.

As I studied it I had no doubt whatsoever that it had been painted by the same person who had done the Trumps I had found in Julia's apartment.

Melman continued his incantation as I regarded the painting.

"Is this your work?" I asked him.

He did not answer me. Instead, he advanced and pointed, indicating the third sephiroth, the one called Binah. I studied it. It seemed to represent a wizard before a dark altar, and—

No! I couldn't believe it. It shouldn't—

I felt a contact with that figure. It was not just symbolic. He was real, and he was summoning me. He loomed larger, grew three-dimensional. The room began to fade about me. I was almost—

There.

It was a place of twilight, a small glade in a twisted wood. An almost bloody light illuminated the slab before me. The wizard, his face hidden by cowl and shadow, manipulated objects upon the stone, his hands moving too rapidly for me to follow. From somewhere, I still seemed to hear the chanting, faintly.

Finally, he raised a single object in his right hand and held it steady. It was a black, obsidian dagger. He laid his left arm upon the altar and brushed it across the surface, sweeping everything else to the ground.

He looked at me for the first time.

"Come here," he said then.

I began to smile at the stupid simplicity of the request. But then I felt my feet move without my willing them to do so, and I knew that a spell lay upon me in this dark shadow.

I thanked another uncle, who dwelled in the most distant place imaginable, as I began to speak in Thari, a spell of my own.

A piercing cry, as of some swooping night bird, rent the air.

The wizard was not distracted, nor my feet freed, but I was able to raise my arms before me. I kept them at the proper level, and when they reached the forward edge of the altar I cooperated with the summoning spell, increasing the force of each automatonlike step that I took. I let my elbows bend.

The wizard was already swinging the blade toward my fingers, but it didn't matter. I put all of my weight behind it and heaved at the stone.

The altar toppled backward. The wizard scurried to avoid it, but it struck one—perhaps both—of his legs. Immediately, as he fell to the ground, I felt the spell depart from me. I could move properly again and my mind was clear.

He drew his knees up to his chest and began to roll even as I leaped over the wrecked altar and reached toward him. I moved to follow as he somersaulted down a small slope and passed between two standing stones and into the darkened wood.

As soon as I reached the clearing's edge I saw eyes, hundreds of feral eyes blazing from the darkness at many levels. The incanting grew louder, seemed nearer, seemed to be coming from behind me.

I turned quickly.

The altar was still in wreckage. Another cowled figure stood behind it, much larger than the first. This one was doing the chanting, in a familiar masculine voice. Frakir pulsed upon my wrist. I felt a spell building about me, but this time I was not unprepared. The opposite of my walk, a summons, brought an icy wind that swept the spell away like so much smoke. My garments were lashed about me, changing shape and color. Purple, gray . . . light the trousers and dark the cloak, the shirtfront. Black my boots and wide belt, my gauntlets tucked behind, my silver Frakir woven into a bracelet about my left wrist, visible now and shining. I raised my left hand and shielded my eyes with my right, as I summoned a flash of light.

"Be silent," I said then. "You offend me."

The chanting ceased.

The cowl was blown back from his head and I regarded Melman's frightened face.

"All right. You wanted me," I stated, "and now you have me, heaven help you. You said that everything would become clear to me. It hasn't. Make it clear."

I took a step forward.

"Talk!" I said. "It can be easy or it can be hard. But you will talk. The choice is yours."

He threw back his head and bellowed: "Master!"

"Summon your master then, by any means," I said. "I will wait. For he, too, must answer."

He called out again, but there was no answer. He bolted then, but I was ready for this with a major summoning. The woods decayed and fell before he could reach them, and then they moved, were swept up in a mighty wind where there should be stillness. It circled the glade, gray and red, building an impenetrable wall to infinites above and below. We inhabited a circular island in the night, several hundred meters across, its edges slowly crumbling.

"He is not coming," I said, "and you are not going. He cannot help you. No one will help you. This is a place of high magic and you profane it with your presence. Do you know what lies beyond the advancing winds? Chaos. I will give you to it now, unless you tell me about Julia and your master and why you dared to bring me here."

He drew back from the Chaos and turned to face me.

"Take me back to my apartment and I will tell you everything," he said.

I shook my head.

"Kill me and you will never know."

I shrugged.

"In that case, you will tell me in order to stop the pain. Then I will give you to the Chaos."

I moved toward him.

"Wait!" He raised his hand. "Give me my life for what I am about to tell you."

"No bargain. Talk."

The winds swirled around us and our island shrank. Half-heard, half-intelligible voices babbled within the wind and fragments of forms swam there. Melman drew back from the crumbling edge of things.

"All right," he said, speaking loudly. "Yes, Julia came to me, as I had been told she would, and I taught her some things—not the things I would have taught her even a year ago, but pieces of some new things I had only learned myself more recently. I had been told to teach her in this manner, also."

"By whom? Name your master."

He grimaced.

"He was not so foolish as to give me his name," he said, "that I might seek some control over him. Like yourself, he is not human, but a being from some other plane."

"He gave you the painting of the Tree?"

Melman nodded.

"Yes, and it actually transported me to each sephiroth. Magic worked in those places. I gained powers."

"And the Trumps? He did those, too? He gave them to you to give to her?"

"I don't know anything about any Trumps," he answered.

"These!" I cried, drawing them from beneath my cloak, spreading them like a conjurer's fan and advancing toward him. I thrust them at him and let him stare for a few moments, withdrawing them before he got the idea that they might represent a means of escape.

"I never saw them before," he said.

The ground continued its steady erosion toward us. We withdrew to a point nearer the center.

"And you sent the creature that slew her?"

He shook his head vehemently.

"I did not. I knew that she was going to die, for he had told me that that was what would bring you to me. He told me, too, that it would be a beast from Netzach that would slay her—but I never saw it and I had no part in its summoning."

"And why did he want you to meet me, to bring me here?"

He laughed wildly.

"Why?" he repeated. "To kill you, of course. He told me that if I could sacrifice you in this place I would gain your powers. He said that you are

Merlin, son of Hell and Chaos, and that I would become the greatest mage of all could I slay you here."

Our world was at best a hundred meters across now, and the rate of its shrinkage was accelerating.

"Was it true?" he asked. "Would I have gained had I succeeded?"

"Power is like money," I said. "You can usually get it if you're competent and it's the only thing you want in life. Would you have gained by it, though? I don't think so."

"I'm talking about the meaning of life. You know that."

I shook my head.

"Only a fool believes that life has but one meaning," I said. "Enough of this! Describe your master."

"I never saw him."

"What?"

"I mean, I saw him but I don't know what he looks like. He always wore a hood and a black trench coat. Gloves, too. I don't even know his race."

"How did you meet?"

"He appeared one day in my studio. I just turned around and he was standing there. He offered me power, said that he would teach me things in return for my service."

"How did you know he could deliver?"

"He took me on a journey through places not of this world."

"I see."

Our island of existence was now about the size of a large living room. The voices of the wind were mocking, then compassionate, frightened, sad and angry, too. Our wraparound vision shifted constantly. The ground trembled without letup. The light was still baleful. A part of me wanted to kill Melman right then, but if he had not really been the one who had hurt Julia . . .

"Did your master tell you why he wanted me dead?" I asked him.

He licked his lips and glanced back at the advancing Chaos.

"He said that you were his enemy," he explained, "but he never told me why. And he said that it was going to happen today, that he wanted it to happen today."

"Why today?"

He smiled briefly.

"I suppose because it's Walpurgisnacht," he replied, "though he never actually said that."

"That's all?" I said. "He never mentioned where he was from?"

"He once referred to something called the Keep of the Four Worlds as if it were important to him."

"And you never felt that he was simply using you?"

He smiled. "Of course he was using me," he replied. "We all use somebody. That is the way of the world. But he paid for this use with knowledge and power. And I think his promise may yet be fulfilled."

He seemed to be glancing at something behind me. It was the oldest trick in the world, but I turned. There was no one there. Immediately, I spun back to face him.

He held the black dagger. It must have been up his sleeve. He lunged at me, thrusting, mouthing fresh incantations.

I stepped back and swirled my cloak at him. He disengaged himself, sidestepping and slashing, turned and advanced again. This time he came in low, trying to circle me, his lips still moving. I kicked at the knifehand, but he snapped it back. I caught up the left edge of my cloak then, wrapped it about my arm. When he struck again, I blocked the thrust and seized his biceps. Dropping lower as I drew him forward, I caught hold of his left thigh with my right hand, then straightened, raising him high in the air, and threw him.

As I turned my body, completing the throw, I realized what I had done. Too late. With my attention focused on my adversary I had not kept track of the rapid, grinding advance of the destroying winds. The edge of Chaos was much nearer than I had thought, and Melman had time for only the most abbreviated of curses before death took him where he would incant no more.

I cursed, too, because I was certain there was still more information that I could have gotten from him; and I shook my head, there at the center of my diminishing world.

The day was not yet over and it was already my most memorable Walpurgisnacht ever.

FOUR

It was a long walk back. I changed my clothes on the way.

My exit from the labyrinth took the form of a narrow alleyway between a pair of dirty brick buildings. It was still raining and the day had made its way into evening. I saw my parked car across the street at the edge of a pool of light cast by one of the unbroken streetlamps. I thought wistfully for a moment of my dry garments in the trunk, then I headed back toward the Brutus Storage sign.

A small light burned within the first-floor office, spilling a little illumination into the otherwise dark entranceway. I trudged on up the stairs, terminally moist and reasonably alert. The apartment door opened when I turned the knob and pushed. I switched on the light and entered, bolting the door behind me.

A quick prowl showed me that the place was deserted, and I changed out of my wet shirt into one from Melman's closet. His trousers were too big in the waist and a bit long for me, though. I transferred my Trumps to a breast pocket to keep them dry.

Step two. I began a systematic ransacking of the place. After a few minutes, I came across his occult diary in a locked drawer in his bedside table. It was as messy as the rest of the place, with misspellings, crossed-out words, and a few beer and coffee stains. It seemed to contain a lot of derivative stuff mixed with the usual subjective business—dreams and meditations. I flipped farther along in it, looking for the place where he'd met his master. I came to it and skimmed along. It was lengthy, and seemed mostly comprised of enthusiastic ejaculations over the workings of the Tree he had been given. I decided to save it for later and was about to stow it when a final riffling of the pages brought a brief poem into view. Swinburnian, overly allusive and full of rapture, the lines that first caught my eye were, "—the infinite shadows of Amber, touched with her treacherous taint." Too much alliteration, but it was the thought that counted. It revived my earlier feeling of vulnerability and caused me to ransack faster. I suddenly wanted only to get out, get far away and think.

The room held no further surprises. I departed it, gathered an armload of strewn newspapers, carried them to the john, tossed them into the bathtub, and set fire to them, opening the window on the way out. I visited the sanctum then, fetched out the Tree of Life painting, brought it back and added it to the blaze. I switched off the bathroom light and closed the door as I left. I'm one hell of an art critic.

I headed for the stacks of miscellaneous papers on the bookshelves then and began a disappointing search among them. I was halfway through my second heap when the telephone rang.

The world seemed to freeze as my thoughts sprinted. Of course. Today was the day when I was supposed to find my way here and be killed. Chances seemed decent that if it were going to happen it would have happened by now. So this could well be S, calling to learn whether my obituary had been posted. I turned and located the phone, back on the shadowy wall near the bedroom. I had known immediately that I was going to answer it. Moving toward it, I was allowing two to three rings—twelve to eighteen seconds—in which to decide whether my response was to consist of a wisecrack, an insult and a threat, or whether I was going to try to fake it and see what I might learn. As satisfying as the former could be, spoilsport prudence dictated the latter course and also suggested I confine myself to low monosyllables and pretend to be injured and out of breath. I raised the receiver, ready to hear S's voice at last and find out whether I knew him.

"Yes?" I said.

"Well? Is it done?" came the response.

Damn pronoun. It was a woman. Wrong gender but a rightsounding question. One out of two isn't bad, though.

I exhaled heavily, then: "Yeah."

"What's the matter?"

"I'm hurt," I croaked.

"Is it serious?"

"Think so. Got something—here—though. Better come—see."

"What is it? Something of his?"

"Yeah. Can't talk. Getting dizzy. Come."

I cradled the phone and smiled. I thought it very well played. I'd a feeling I'd taken her in completely.

I crossed the living room to the same chair I had occupied earlier, drew up one of the small tables bearing a large ashtray, seated myself, and reached for my pipe. Time to rest, cultivate patience, think a bit.

Moments later I felt a familiar, almost electrical tingling. I was on my feet in an instant, snatching up the ashtray, butts flying like bullets around me, cursing my stupidity yet again as I looked frantically about the room.

There! Before the red drapes, beside the piano. Taking form . . .

I waited for the full outline, then hurled the ashtray as hard as I could.

An instant later she was there—tall, russet-haired, dark-eyed, holding what looked like a .38 automatic.

The ashtray hit her in the stomach and she doubled forward with a gasp.

I was there before she could straighten.

I jerked the gun out of her hand and threw it across the room. Then I seized both her wrists, spun her around and seated her hard in the nearest chair. In her left hand she still held a Trump. I snatched it away. It was a representation of this apartment, and it was done in the same style as the Tree and the cards in my pockct.

"Who are you?" I snarled.

"Jasra," she spat back, "dead man!"

She opened her mouth wide and her head fell forward. I felt the moist touch of her lips upon the back of my left forearm, which still held her own right wrist against the chair's arm. Seconds later I felt an excruciating pain there. It was not a bite, but rather felt as if a fiery nail had been driven into my flesh.

I let go her wrist and jerked my arm away. The movement was strangely slow, weakened. A cold, tingling sensation moved down into the hand and up along the arm. My hand dropped to my side and seemed to go away. She extricated herself easily from my grip, smiled, placed her fingertips lightly upon my chest and pushed.

I fell backward. I was ridiculously weak and I couldn't control my movements. I felt no pain when I struck the floor, and it was a real effort to turn my head to regard her as she rose to her feet.

"Enjoy it," she stated. "After you awaken, the remainder of your brief existence will be painful."

She passed out of my line of sight, and moments later I heard her raise the telephone receiver.

I was certain she was phoning S, and I believed what she had just said. At least, I would get to meet the mysterious artist . . .

Artist! I twitched the fingers of my right hand. They still functioned, albeit slowly. Straining every bit of will and anatomy that remained under my control, I tried then to raise the hand to my chest. The movement that followed was a jerky, slow-motion thing. At least I had fallen upon my left side, and my back masked this feeble activity from the woman who had done me in.

My hand was trembling and seemed to be slowing even more when it came to the breast pocket. For ages after, I seemed to pick at the edges of pieces of pasteboard. Finally, one came free and I was able to twitch it high enough to view it. By then I was very dizzy and my vision was beginning to blur. I wasn't certain I could manage the transfer. From across a vast distance I would hear Jasra's voice as she conversed with someone, but I was unable to distinguish the words.

I focused what remained of my attention upon the card. It was a sphinx, crouched upon a blue, rocky ledge. I reached for it. Nothing. My mind felt as if it were embedded in cotton. I possessed barely enough consciousness for one more attempt.

I felt a certain coldness and seemed to see the sphinx move slightly upon its stony shelf. I felt as if I were falling forward into a black wave that was rushing upward.

And that was all.

I was a long time coming around. My consciousness dribbled back, but my limbs were still leaden and my vision clouded. The lady's sting seemed to have delivered a neurotropic toxin. I tried flexing my fingers and toes and could not be certain whether I'd succeeded. I tried to speed up and deepen my breathing. That worked, anyway.

After a time, I heard what seemed a roaring sound. It stepped itself down a little later, and I realized it was my own rushing blood in my ears. A while after that I felt my heartbeat, and my vision began to clear. Light and dark and shapelessness resolved into sand and rocks. I felt little areas of chill, all over. Then I began to shiver, and this passed and I realized that I could move. But I felt very weak, so I didn't. Not for a while.

I heard noises—rustlings, stirrings—coming from somewhere above and before me. I also became aware of a peculiar odor.

"I say, are you awake?" This from the same direction as the sounds of movement.

I decided that I was not entirely ready to qualify for that state, so I did not answer. I waited for more life to slow back into my limbs.

"I really wish you'd let me know whether you can hear me," the voice came again. "I'd like to get on with it."

My curiosity finally overcame my judgment and I raised my head.

"There! I knew it!"

On the blue-gray ledge above me was crouched a sphinx, also blue—lion body, large feathered wings folded tight against it, a genderless face looking down upon me. It licked its lips and revealed a formidable set of teeth.

"Get on with what?" I asked, raising myself slowly into a sitting position and drawing several deep breaths.

"The riddling," it answered, "the thing I do best."

"I'll take a rain check," I said, waiting for the cramps in my arms and legs to pass.

"Sorry. I must insist."

I rubbed my punctured forearm and glared at the creature. Most of the stories I recalled about sphinxes involved their devouring people who couldn't answer riddles. I shook my head.

"I won't play your game," I said.

"In that case, you lose by forfeit," it replied, shoulder muscles beginning to tighten.

"Hold on," I said, raising my hand. "Give me a minute or two to recover and I'll probably feel differently."

It settled back and said, "Okay. That would make it more official. Take five. Let me know when you're ready."

I climbed to my feet and began swinging my arms and stretching. While I was about it, I surveyed the area quickly.

We occupied a sandy arroyo, punctuated here and there with orange, gray, and blue rocks. The stony wall whose ledge the sphinx occupied rose steeply before me to a height of perhaps twenty-five feet; another wall of the same height lay at about that distance to my rear. The wash rose steeply to my right, ran off in a more level fashion to my left. A few spiky green shrubs inhabited rifts and crevices. The hour seemed verging upon dusk. The sky was a weak yellow with no sun in sight. I heard a distant wind but did not feel it. The place was cool but not chill.

I spotted a rock the size of a small dumbbell on the ground nearby. Two ambling paces—as I continued swinging my arms and stretching—and it lay beside my right foot.

The sphinx cleared its throat.

"Are you ready?" it asked.

"No," I said. "But I'm sure that won't stop you."

"You're right."

I felt an uncontrollable desire to yawn and did so.

"You seem to lack something of the proper spirit," it observed. "But here it is: I rise in flame from the earth. The wind assails me and waters lash me. Soon I will oversee all things."

I waited. Perhaps a minute passed.

"Well?" the sphinx finally said.

"Well what?"

"Have you the answer?"

"To what?"

"The riddle, of course!"

"I was waiting. There was no question, only a series of statements. I can't answer a question if I don't know what it is."

"It's a time-honored format. The interrogative is implied by the context. Obviously, the question is, 'What am I?'"

"It could just as easily be, 'Who is buried in Grant's tomb?' But okay. What is it? The phoenix, of course—nested upon the earth, rising in flames above it, passing through the air, the clouds, to a great height—"

"Wrong."

It smiled and began to stir.

"Hold on," I said. "It is not wrong. It fits. It may not be the answer you want, but it is an answer that meets the requirements."

It shook its head.

"I am the final authority on these answers. I do the defining."

"Then you cheat."

"I do not!"

"I drink off half the contents of a flask. Does that make it half full or half empty?"

"Either. Both."

"Exactly. Same thing. If more than one answer fits, you have to buy them all. It's like waves and particles."

"I don't like that approach," it stated. "It would open all sorts of doors to ambiguity. It could spoil the riddling business."

"Not my fault," I said, clenching and unclenching my hands.

"But you do raise an interesting point."

I nodded vigorously.

"But there *should* only be one correct answer."

I shrugged.

"We inhabit a less than ideal world," I suggested.

"Hm."

"We could just call it a tie," I offered. "Nobody wins, nobody loses."

"I find that esthetically displeasing."

"It works okay in lots of other games."

"Also, I've grown a bit hungry."

"The truth surfaces."

"But I am not unfair. I serve the truth, in my fashion. Your mention of a tie raises the possibility of a solution."

"Good. I'm glad you see things—"

"That being a tie breaker. Ask me your riddle."

"This is silly," I said. "I don't have any riddles."

"Then you'd better come up with one fast. Because it's the only way out of our deadlock—that, or I judge you the loser."

I swung my arms and did a few deep kneebends. My body felt as if it were afire. It also felt stronger.

"Okay," I said. "Okay. Just a second."

What the hell . . .

"What's green and red and goes round and round and round?"

The sphinx blinked twice, then furrowed its brow. I used the time that followed for some more deep breathing and some running in place. The fires subsided, my head grew clearer, my pulse steadied . . .

"Well?" I said some minutes later.

"I'm thinking."

"Take your time."

I did a little shadowboxing. Did some isometrics, too. The sky had darkened a bit more and a few stars were now visible off to my right.

"Uh, I hate to rush you," I said, "but—"

The sphinx snorted. "I'm still thinking."

"Maybe we should set a time limit."

"It shouldn't be much longer."

"Mind if I rest?"

"Go ahead."

I stretched out on the sand and closed my eyes, muttering a guard word to Frakir before I slept.

I woke with a shiver, light in my eyes and a breeze upon my face. It took me several moments to realize that it was morning. The sky was brightening to my left, stars were fading to my right. I was thirsty. Hungry, too.

I rubbed my eyes. I got to my feet. I located my comb and ran it through my hair. I regarded the sphinx.

". . . and goes round and round and round," it muttered.

I cleared my throat. No reaction. The beast was staring past me. I wondered whether I might simply be able to slip off . . .

No. The gaze shifted to me.

"Good morning," I said cheerfully.

There was a brief gnashing of teeth.

"All right," I said, "you've taken a lot longer than I did. If you haven't got it by now I don't care to play any longer."

"I don't like your riddle," it said at last.

"Sorry."

"What is the answer?"

"You're giving up?"

"I must. What is the answer?"

I raised a hand.

"Hold on," I said. "These things should be done in proper order. I should have the preferred answer to yours before I tell you mine."

It nodded.

"There is some justice in that. All right—the Keep of the Four Worlds."

"What?"

"That is the answer. The Keep of the Four Worlds."

I thought of Melman's words. "Why?" I asked.

"It lies at the crossroads of the worlds of the four elements, where it rises from the earth in flames, assailed by the winds and waters."

"What about the business of overseeing all things?"

"It could refer to the view, or to its master's imperialistic designs. Or both."

"Who is its master?"

"I don't know. That information is not essential to the answer."

"Where'd you pick up this riddle, anyhow?"

"From a traveler, a few months back."

"Why'd you choose this one, of all the riddles you must know, to ask me?"

"It stopped me, so it had to be good."

"What became of the traveler?"

"He went on his way, uneaten. He'd answered my riddle."

"He had a name?"

"He wouldn't say."

"Describe him, please."

"I can't. He was well muffled."

"And he said nothing more about the Keep of the Four Worlds?"

"No."

"Well," I said. "I believe I'll follow his example and take a walk myself."
I turned and faced the slope to my right.

"Wait!"

"What?" I asked.

"Your riddle," it stated. "I've given you the answer to mine. You must
now tell me what it is that is green and red and goes round and round
and round."

I glanced downward, scanned the ground. Oh, yes, there it was—my
dumbbell-shaped stone. I took several steps and stood beside it.

"A frog in a Cuisinart," I said.

"What?"

Its shoulder muscles bunched, its eyes narrowed and its many teeth became very apparent. I spoke a few words to Frakir and felt her stir as I squatted
and caught hold of the stone with my right hand.

"That's it," I said, rising. "It's one of those visual things—"

"That's a rotten riddle!" the sphinx answered.

With my left index finger I made two quick movements in the air before me.

"What are you doing?" it asked.

"Drawing lines from your ears to your eyes," I said.

Frakir became visible at about that moment, sliding from my left wrist to
my hand, twining among my fingers. The sphinx's eyes darted in that direction. I raised the stone level with my right shoulder. One end of Frakir fell
free and hung writhing from my extended hand. She began to brighten, then
glowed like a hot silver wire.

"I believe the contest is a draw," I stated. "What do you think?"

The sphinx licked its lips.

"Yes," it finally said, sighing. "I suppose you are right."

"Then I will bid you good day," I said.

"Yes. Pity. Very well. Good day. But before you go may I have your
name—for the record?"

"Why not?" I said. "I am Merlin, of Chaos."

"Ah," it said, "then someone would have come to avenge you."

"It's possible."

"Then a draw is indeed best. Go."

I backed farther off before turning and proceeding up the slope to my
right. I remained on guard until I was out of that place, but there was no
pursuit.

I began jogging. I was thirsty and hungry, but I wasn't likely to turn up breakfast in this desolate, rocky place under a lemon sky. Frakir recoiled and faded. I began drawing deep breaths as I headed away from the risen sun.

Wind in my hair, dust in my eyes . . . I bore toward a cluster of boulders, passed among them. Seen from amid their shadows the sky grew greenish above me. Emerging, I came upon a softer plain, glitters in the distance, a few clouds rising to my left.

I maintained a steady pace, reaching a small rise, mounting it, descending its farther side where sparse grasses waved. A grove of mop-topped trees in the distance . . . I headed for them, startling a small orange-furred creature that sprang across my path and tore away to the left. Moments later, a dark bird flashed by, uttering a wailing note, headed in the same direction. I ran on, and the sky continued to darken.

Green the sky and thicker the grasses, green the grasses, too . . . Heavy gusts of wind at irregular intervals . . . Nearer the trees . . . A singing sound emerges from their branches . . . The clouds sweep onward . . .

A tightness goes out of my muscles and a familiar fluidity enters . . . I pass the first tree, treading upon long, fallen leaves . . . I pass among hairy-barked boles . . . The way I follow is hard-packed, becomes a trail, strange foot marks cast within it . . . It drops, curves, widens, narrows again . . . The ground rises at either hand . . . the trees sound bass viol notes . . . Patches of sky amid the leaves are the color of Morinci turquoise . . . Streamers of cloud snake forward like silver rivers . . . Small clusters of blue flowers appear on the trail walls . . . The walls rise higher, passing above my head . . . The way grows rocky . . . I run on . . .

My path widens, widens, descending steadily . . . Even before I see or hear it, I smell the water . . . Carefully now, among the stones . . . A bit slower here . . . I turn and see the stream, high, rocky banks at either hand, a meter or two of shoreline before the rise . . .

Slower still, beside the gurgling, sparkling flow . . . To follow its meandering . . . Bends, curves, trees high overhead, exposed roots in the wall to my right, gray and yellow talus-fall along the flaky base . . .

My shelf widens, the walls lower . . . More sand and fewer rocks beneath my feet . . . Lowering, lowering . . . Head-height, shoulder-height . . . Another bending of the way, slope descending . . . Waist high . . . Green-leafed trees all about me, blue sky overhead, off to the right a hard-packed trail . . . I mount the slope, I follow it . . .

Trees and shrubs, bird notes and cool breeze . . . I suck the air, I lengthen my stride . . . I cross a wooden bridge, footfalls echoing, creek flowing to the now-masked stream, moss-grown boulders beside its cool . . . Low stone wall to my right now . . . Wagon ruts ahead . . .

Wildflowers at either hand . . . A sound of distant laughter, echoing . . . The neigh of a horse . . . Creak of a cart . . . Turn left . . . Widening of the way . . . Shadow and sunlight, shadow and sunlight . . . Dapple, dapple . . . River to the left, wider now, sparkling . . . Haze of smoke above the next hill . . .

I slow as I near the summit. I reach it walking, dusting my garments, brushing my hair into place, limbs tingling, lungs pumping, bands of perspiration cooling me. I spit grit. Below me and to the right lies a country inn, some tables on its wide, rough-hewn porch, facing the river, a few in a garden nearby. Bye-bye, present tense. I am arrived.

I walked on down and located a pump at the far side of the building, where I washed my face, hands and arms, my left forearm still sore and slightly inflamed where Jasra had attacked me. I made my way to the porch then and took a small table, after waving to a serving woman I saw within. After a time, she brought me porridge and sausages and eggs and bread and butter and strawberry preserves and tea. I finished it all quickly and ordered another round of the same. The second time through a feeling of returning normalcy occurred, and I slowed and enjoyed it and watched the river go by.

It was a strange way to wind up the job. I had been looking forward to some leisurely travel, to a long lazy vacation, now my work had been done. The small matter of S had been all that stood in my way—a thing I had been certain I could settle quickly. Now I was in the middle of something I did not understand, something dangerous and bizarre. Sipping my tea and feeling the day warm about me, I could be lulled into a momentary sense of peace. But I knew it for a fleeting thing. There could be no true rest, no safety for me, until this matter was settled. Looking back over events, I saw that I could no longer trust my reactions alone for my deliverance, for a resolution of this affair. It was time to formulate a plan.

The identity of S and S's removal were high on my list of things that needed knowing and doing. Higher still was the determination of S's motive. My notion that I was dealing with a simple-minded psycho had dissolved. S was too well organized and possessed some very unusual abilities. I began searching my past for possible candidates. But though I could think of quite a few capable of managing what had occurred thus far, none of these were particularly ill-disposed toward me. However, Amber *had* been mentioned in that strange diary of Melman's. Theoretically, this made the whole thing a family matter and I suppose put me under some obligation to call it to the attention of the others. But to do so would be like asking for help, giving up, saying that I couldn't manage my own affairs. And threats on my life were my own affair. Julia was my affair. The vengeance on this one was to be mine. I had to think about it some more . . .

Ghostwheel?

I mulled it over, dismissed it, thought about it again. Ghostwheel . . . No. Untried. Still developing. The only reason it had occurred to me at all was because it was my pet, my major accomplishment in life, my surprise for the others. I was just looking for an easy way out. I would need a lot more data to submit, which meant I had to go after it, of course.

Ghostwheel . . .

Right now I needed more information. I had the cards and the diary. I didn't want to fool with the Trumps any more at this point, since the first one had seemed something of a trap. I would go through the diary soon, though my initial impression had been that it was too subjective to be of much help. I ought to go back to Melman's for a final look around, though, in case there was anything I had missed. Then I ought to look up Luke and see whether he could tell me anything more—even some small remark—that might be of value. Yes . . .

I sighed and stretched. I watched the river a little longer and finished my tea. I ran Frakir over a fistful of money and selected sufficient transformed coinage to pay for my meal. Then I returned to the road. Time to run on back.

FIVE

I came jogging up the street in the light of late afternoon and halted when I was abreast of my car. I'd almost failed to recognize it. It was covered with dust, ashes, and water stains. How long had I been away, anyhow? I hadn't tried to reckon the time differential between here and where I'd been, but my car looked as if it had been standing exposed for over a month. It seemed intact, though. It had not been vandalized and—

My gaze had drifted past the hood and on ahead. The building that had housed the Brutus Storage Company and the late Victor Melman no longer stood. A burnt-out, collapsed skeleton of the place occupied the corner, parts of two walls standing. I headed toward it.

Walking about it, I studied what was left. The charred remains of the place were cold and settled. Gray streaks and sooty fairy circles indicated that water had been pumped into it, had since evaporated. The ashy smell was not particularly strong.

Had I started it, with that fire in the bathtub? I wondered. I didn't think so. Mine had been a small enough blaze, and well confined, with no indication of its spreading while I was waiting.

A boy on a green bicycle pedaled past while I was studying the ruin. Several minutes later he returned and halted about ten feet from me. He looked to be about ten years old.

"I saw it," he announced. "I saw it burn."

"When was that?" I asked him.

"Three days ago."

"They know how it started?"

"Something in the storage place, something flam—"

"Flammable?"

"Yeah," he said through a gap-toothed smile. "Maybe on purpose. Something about insurance."

"Really?"

"Uh-huh. My dad said maybe business was bad."

"It's been known to happen," I said. "Was anybody hurt in the fire?"

"They thought maybe the artist who lived upstairs got burned up because nobody could find him. But they didn't see any bones or anything like that. It was a good fire. Burned a long time."

"Was it nighttime or daytime?"

"Nighttime. I watched from over there." He pointed to a place across the street and back in the direction from which I had come. "They put a lot of water on it."

"Did you see anyone come out of the building?"

"No," he said. "I got here after it was burning pretty good."

I nodded and turned back toward my car.

"You'd think bullets would explode in all that fire, wouldn't you?" he said.

"Yes," I answered.

"But they didn't."

I turned back.

"What do you mean?" I asked.

He was already digging in a pocket.

"Me and some of my friends were playing around in there yesterday," he explained, "and we found a mess of bullets."

He opened his hand to display several metallic objects.

As I moved toward him, he squatted and placed one of the cylinders on the sidewalk. He reached out suddenly, picked up a nearby rock and swung it toward it.

"Don't!" I cried.

The rock struck the shell and nothing happened.

"You could get hurt that way—" I began, but he interrupted.

"Naw. No way these suckers will explode. You can't even set that pink stuff on fire. Got a match?"

"Pink stuff?" I said as he moved the rock to reveal a mashed shell casing and a small trailing of pink powder.

"That," he said, pointing. "Funny, huh? I thought gunpowder was gray."

I knelt and touched the substance. I rubbed it between my fingers. I sniffed it. I even tasted it. I couldn't tell what the hell it was.

"Beats me," I told him. "Won't even burn, you say?"

"Nope. We put some on a newspaper and set the paper on fire. It'll melt and run, that's all."

"You got a couple of extras?"

"Well . . . yeah."

"I'll give you a buck for them," I said.

He showed me his teeth and spaces again as his hand vanished into the side of his jeans. I ran Frakir over some odd Shadow cash and withdrew a dollar from the pile. He handed me two sootstreaked double 30's as he accepted it.

"Thanks," he said.

"My pleasure. Anything else interesting in there?"

"Nope. All the rest is ashes."

I got into my car and drove. I ran it through the first car wash I came to, since the wipers had only smeared the crap on the windshield. As the rubbery tentacles slapped at me through a sea of foam, I checked to see whether I still had the matchbook Luke had given me. I did. Good. I'd seen a pay phone outside.

"Hello. New Line Motel," a young, male voice answered.

"You had a Lucas Raynard registered there a couple days ago," I said. "I want to know whether he left a message for me. My name's Merle Corey."

"Just a minute."

Pause. Shuffle.

Then: "Yes, he did."

"What does it say?"

"It's in a sealed envelope. I'd rather not—"

"Okay. I'll come by."

I drove over. I located the man matching the voice at the desk in the lobby. I identified myself and claimed the envelope. The clerk—a slight, blond fellow with a bristly mustache—stared for a moment, then: "Are you going to see Mr. Raynard?"

"Yes."

He opened a drawer and withdrew a small brown envelope, its sides distended. Luke's name and room number were written on it.

"He didn't leave a forwarding address," he explained, opening the envelope, "and the maid found this ring on the bathroom counter after he'd checked out. Would you give it to him?"

"Sure," I said, and he passed it to me.

I seated myself in a lounge area off to the left. The ring was of pink gold and sported a blue stone. I couldn't recall ever having seen him wear it. I slipped it on the ring finger of my left hand and it fit perfectly. I decided to wear it until I could give it to him.

I opened the letter, written on motel stationery, and read:

> Merle,
>
> Too bad about dinner. I did wait around. Hope everything's okay. I'm leaving in the morning for Albuquerque. I'll be there three days. Then up to Santa Fe for three more. Staying at the Hilton in both towns. I did have some more things I wanted to talk about. Please get in touch.
>
> Luke

Hm.

I phoned my travel agent and discovered that I could be on an afternoon flight to Albuquerque if I hustled. In that I wanted a face-to-face rather than a phone talk, I did that thing. I stopped by the office, picked up my ticket, paid cash for it, drove to the airport and said good-bye to my car as I parked it. I doubted I would ever see it again. I hefted my backpack and walked to the terminal.

The rest was smooth and easy. As I watched the ground drop away beneath me, I knew that a phase of my existence had indeed ended. Like so many things, it was not at all the way I had wanted it to be. I'd thought to wind up the matter of S pretty quickly or else decide to forget about it, and then visit people I'd been meaning to see for some time and stop at a few places I'd long been curious about. Then I would take off through Shadow for a final check on Ghostwheel, heading back to the brighter pole of my existence after that. Now, my priorities had been shuffled—all because S and Julia's death were somehow connected, and because it involved a power from elsewhere in Shadow that I did not understand.

It was the latter consideration that troubled me most. Was I digging my grave as well as jeopardizing friends and relatives because of my pride? I wanted to handle this myself, friendly skies, but the more I thought about it the more impressed I became with the adversary powers I had encountered and the paucity of my knowledge concerning S. It wasn't fair not to let the others know—not if they might be in danger, too. I'd love to wrap the whole thing up by myself and give it to them for a present. Maybe I would, too, but—

Damn it. I *had* to tell them. If S got me and turned on them, they needed to know. If it were a part of something larger, they needed to know. As much as I disliked the idea, I would have to tell them.

I leaned forward and my hand hovered above my backpack beneath the seat in front of me. It wouldn't hurt, I decided, to wait until after I'd spoken with Luke. I was out of town and probably safe now. There was the possibility of picking up a clue or two from Luke. I'd rather have more to give them when I told my story. I'd wait a little longer.

I sighed. I got a drink from the stewardess and sipped it. Driving to Albuquerque in a normal fashion would have taken too long. Short-cutting through Shadow would not work, because I'd never been there before and didn't know how to find the place. Too bad. I'd like to have my car there. Luke was probably in Santa Fe by now.

I sipped and I looked for shapes in the clouds. The things I found matched my mood, so I got out my paperback and read until we began our descent. When I looked again ranks of mountains filled my prospect for a time. A crackly voice assured me that the weather was pleasant. I wondered about my father.

I hiked in from my gate, passed a gift shop full of Indian jewelry, Mexican pots, and gaudy souvenirs, located a telephone, and called the local Hilton. Luke had already checked out, I learned. I phoned the Hilton in Santa Fe then. He had checked in there but was not in his room when they rang it for me. I made a reservation for myself and hung up. A woman at an information counter told me that I could catch a Shuttlejack to Santa Fe in about half an hour and sent me in the proper direction to buy a ticket. Santa Fe is one of the few state capitals without a major airport, I'd read somewhere.

While we were heading north on I-25, somewhere among lengthening shadows in the vicinity of Sandia Peak, Frakir tightened slightly upon my wrist and released the pressure a moment later. Again. Then once again. I glanced quickly about the small bus, seeking the danger against which I had just been warned.

I was seated in the rear of the vehicle. Up near the front was a middle-aged couple, speaking with Texas accents, wearing an ostentatious quantity of turquoise and silver jewelry; near the middle were three older women, talking about things back in New York; across the aisle from them was a young couple, very absorbed in each other; two young men with tennis racquets sat diagonally to the rear of them, talking about college; behind them was a nun, reading. I looked out the window again and saw nothing particularly threatening on the highway or near it. I did not want to draw to myself the attention that any location practices would involve either.

So I spoke a single word in Thari as I rubbed my wrist, and the warnings ceased. Even though the rest of the ride was uneventful, it bothered me, though an occasional false warning was possible just because of the nature of nervous systems. As I watched red shale and red and yellow earth streak by, bridged arroyos, viewed distant mountains and nearer slopes dotted with piñon, I wondered. S? Is S back there somewhere, somehow, watching, waiting? And if so, why? Couldn't we just sit down and talk about it over a couple of beers? Maybe it was based on some sort of misunderstanding.

I'd a feeling it was not a misunderstanding. But I'd settle for just knowing what was going on, even if nothing were resolved. I'd even pay for the beers.

The light of the setting sun touched flashes of brightness from streaks of snow in the Sangre de Cristos as we pulled into town; shadows slid across gray-green slopes; most of the buildings in sight were stuccoed. It felt about ten degrees cooler when I stepped down from the bus in front of the Hilton than it had when I'd boarded in Albuquerque. But then, I'd gained about two thousand feet in altitude and it was an hour and a quarter further along in the direction of evening.

I registered and found my room. I tried phoning Luke, but there was no answer. I showered then and changed into my spare outfit. Rang his room once more then, but still no answer. I was getting hungry and I'd hoped to have dinner with him.

I decided to find the bar and nurse a beer for a while, then try again. I hoped he didn't have a heavy date.

A Mr. Brazda, whom I approached in the lobby and asked for directions, turned out to be the manager. He asked about my room, we exchanged a few pleasantries and he showed me the corridor leading off to the lounge. I started in that direction, but didn't quite make it.

"Merle! What the hell are you doing here?" came a familiar voice.

I turned and regarded Luke, who had just entered the lobby. Sweaty and smiling, he was wearing dusty fatigues and boots, a fatigue cap, and a few streaks of grime. We shook hands and I said, "I wanted to talk to you." Then: "What'd you do, enlist in something?"

"No, I've been off hiking in the Pecos all day," he answered. "I always do that when I'm out this way. It's great."

"I'll have to try it sometime," I said. "Now it seems it's my turn to buy dinner."

"You're right," he answered. "Let me catch a shower and change clothes. I'll meet you in the bar in fifteen, twenty minutes. Okay?"

"Right. See you."

I headed up the corridor and located the place. It was medium-sized, dim, cool and relatively crowded, divided into two widely connected rooms, with low, comfortable-looking chairs and small tables.

A young couple was just abandoning a corner table off to my left, drinks in hand, to follow a waitress into the adjacent dining room. I took the table. A little later a cocktail waitress came by, and I ordered a beer.

Sitting there, several minutes later, sipping, and letting my mind drift over the perversely plotted events of the past several days, I realized that one of the place's passing figures had failed to pass. It had come to a halt at my side—just far enough to the rear to register only as a dark peripheral presence.

It spoke softly: "Excuse me. May I ask you a question?"

I turned my head, to behold a short, thin man of Spanish appearance, his hair and mustache flecked with gray. He was sufficiently well dressed and groomed to seem a local business type. I noted a chipped front tooth when he smiled so briefly—just a twitch—as to indicate nervousness.

"My name's Dan Martinez," he said, not offering to shake hands. He glanced at the chair across from me. "Could I sit down a minute?"

"What's this about? If you're selling something, I'm not interested. I'm waiting for somebody and—"

He shook his head.

"No, nothing like that. I know you're waiting for someone—a Mr. Lucas Raynard. It involves him, actually."

I gestured at the chair.

"Okay. Sit down and ask your question."

He did so, clasping his hands and placing them on the table between us. He leaned forward.

"I overheard you talking in the lobby," he began, "and I got the impression you knew him fairly well. Would you mind telling me for about how long you've known him?"

"If that's all you want to know," I answered, "for about eight years. We went to college together, and we worked for the same company for several years after that."

"Grand Design," he stated, "the San Francisco computer firm. Didn't know him before college, huh?"

"It seems you already know quite a bit," I said. "What did you want, anyway? Are you some kind of cop?"

"No," he said, "nothing like that. I assure you I'm not trying to get your friend into trouble. I am simply trying to save myself some. Let me just ask you—"

I shook my head.

"No more freebies," I told him. "I don't care to talk to strangers about my friends without some pretty good reasons."

He unclasped his hands and spread them wide.

"I'm not being underhanded," he said, "when I know you'll tell him about it. In fact, I want you to. He knows me. I want him to know I'm asking around about him, okay? It'll actually be to his benefit. Hell, I'm even asking a friend, aren't I? Someone who might be willing to lie to help him out. And I just need a couple simple facts—"

"And I just need one simple reason: why do you want this information?"

He sighed. "Okay," he said. "He offered me—tentatively, mind you—a very interesting investment opportunity. It would involve a large sum of money. There is an element of risk, as in most ventures involving new companies in a highly competitive area, but the possible returns do make it tempting."

I nodded.

"And you want to know whether he's honest."

He chuckled. "I don't really care whether he's honest," he said. "My only concern is whether he can deliver a product with no strings on it."

Something about the way this man talked reminded me of someone. I tried, but couldn't recall who it was.

"Ah," I said, taking a sip of beer. "I'm slow today. Sorry. Of course this deal involves computers."

"Of course."

"You want to know whether his present employer can nail him if he goes into business out here with whatever he's bringing with him."

"In a word, yes."

"I give up," I said. "It would take a better man than me to answer that. Intellectual properties represent a tricky area of the law. I don't know what he's selling and I don't know where it comes from—he gets around a lot. But even if I did know, I have no idea what your legal position would be."

"I didn't expect anything beyond that," he said, smiling.

I smiled back.

"So you've sent your message," I said.

He nodded and began to rise.

"Oh, just one thing more," he began.

"Yes?"

"Did he ever mention places," he said, staring full into my eyes, "called Amber or the Courts of Chaos?"

He could not have failed to note my startled reaction, which had to have given him a completely false impression. I was sure that he was sure I was lying when I answered him truthfully.

"No, I never heard him refer to them. Why do you ask?"

He shook his head as he pushed his chair back and stepped away from the table. He was smiling again.

"It's not important. Thank you, Mr. Corey. *Nus a dhabzhun dhuilsha.*"

He practically fled around the corner.

"Wait!" I called out, so loudly that there was a moment of silence and heads turned in my direction.

I got to my feet and started after him, when I heard my name called.

"Hey, Merle! Don't run off! I'm here already!"

I turned. Luke had just come in through the entrance behind me, hair still shower-damp. He advanced, clapped me on the shoulder, and lowered himself into the seat Martinez had just vacated. He nodded at my half-finished beer as I sat down again.

"I need one of those," he said. "Lord, am I thirsty!" Then, "Where were you off to when I came in?"

I found myself reluctant to describe my recent encounter, not least because of its strange conclusion. Apparently, he had just missed seeing Martinez.

So: "I was heading for the john."

"It's back that way," he told me, nodding in the direction from which he had entered. "I passed it on the way in."

His eyes shifted downward.

"Say, that ring you have on—"

"Oh, yeah," I said. "You left it at the New Line Motel. I picked it up for you when I collected your message. Here, let me . . ."

I tugged at it, but it wouldn't come off.

"Seems to be stuck," I noted. "Funny. It went on easy enough."

"Maybe your finger's swollen," he remarked. "It could have something to do with the altitude. We're up pretty high."

He caught the waitress's attention and ordered a beer, while I kept twisting at the ring.

"Guess I'll just have to sell it to you," he said. "Give you a good deal."

"We'll see," I told him. "Back in a minute."

He raised one hand limply and let it fall as I headed toward the rest room.

There was no one else in the facility, and so I spoke the words that released Frakir from the suppression spell I had uttered back aboard the Shuttlejack. There followed immediate movement. Before I could issue another command, Frakir became shimmeringly visible in the act of uncoiling, crept across the back of my hand and wound about my ring finger. I watched, fascinated, as the finger darkened and began to ache beneath a steady tightening.

A loosening followed quickly, leaving my finger looking as if it had been threaded. I got the idea. I unscrewed the ring along the track that had been pressed into my flesh. Frakir moved again as if to snag it and I stroked her.

"Okay," I said. "Thanks. Return."

There seemed a moment of hesitation, but my will proved sufficient without a more formal command. She retreated back across my hand, rewound herself about my wrist, and faded.

I finished up in there and returned to the bar. I passed Luke his ring as I seated myself, and took a sip of beer.

"How'd you get it off?" he asked.

"A bit of soap," I answered.

He wrapped it in his handkerchief and put it in his pocket.

"Guess I can't take your money for it, then."

"Guess not. Aren't you going to wear it?"

"No, it's a present. You know, I hardly expected you to make the scene here," he commented, scooping a handful of peanuts from a bowl that had appeared in my absence. "I thought maybe you'd just call when you got my message, and we could set something up for later. Glad you did, though. Who knows when later might have been. See, I had some plans that started moving faster than I'd thought they would—and that's what I wanted to talk to you about."

I nodded.

"I had a few things I wanted to talk to you about, too."

He returned my nod.

I had decided back in the lavatory definitely to refrain from mentioning Martinez yet, and the first things he had said and implied. Although the entire setup did not sound as if it involved anything in which I had any interest any longer, I always feel more secure in talking with anyone—even friends—when I have at least a little special information they don't know I have. So I decided to keep it that way for now.

"So let's be civilized and hold everything important till after dinner," he said, slowly shredding his napkin and wadding the pieces, "and go somewhere we can talk in private then."

"Good idea," I agreed. "Want to eat here?"

He shook his head.

"I've been eating here. It's good, but I want a change. I had my heart set on eating at a place around the corner. Let me go and see if they've got a table."

"Okay."

He gulped the rest of his drink and departed.

. . . And then the mention of Amber. Who the hell was Martinez? It was more than a little necessary that I learn this, because it was obvious to me that he was something other than he appeared to be. His final words had been in Thari, my native tongue. How this could be and why it should be, I had no idea. I cursed my own inertia, at having let the S situation slide for so long. It was purely a result of my arrogance. I'd never anticipated the convoluted mess the affair would become. Served me right, though I didn't appreciate the service.

"Okay," Luke said, rounding the corner, digging into his pocket, and tossing some money on the table. "We've got a reservation. Drink up, and let's take a walk."

I finished, stood and followed him. He led me through the corridors and back to the lobby, then out and along a hallway to the rear. We emerged into a balmy evening and crossed the parking lot to the sidewalk that ran along Guadaloupe Street. From there it was only a short distance to the place where it intersected with Alameda. We crossed twice there and strolled on past a big church, then turned right at the next corner. Luke pointed out a restaurant called La Tertulia across the street a short distance ahead.

"There," he said.

We crossed over and found our way to the entrance. It was a low adobe building, Spanish, venerable, and somewhat elegant inside. We went through a pitcher of sangria, orders of pollo adova, bread puddings, and many cups of coffee, keeping our agreement not to speak of anything serious during dinner.

During the course of the meal Luke was greeted twice, by different guys passing through the room, both of whom paused at the table to pass a few pleasantries.

"You know everybody in this town?" I asked him a bit later.

He chuckled. "I do a lot of business here."

"Really? It seems a pretty small town."

"Yes, but that's deceptive. It *is* the state capital. There're a lot of people here buying what we're selling."

"So you're out this way a lot?"

He nodded. "It's one of the hottest spots on my circuit."

"How do you manage all this business when you're out hiking in the woods?"

He looked up from the small battle formation he was creating from things on the table. He smiled.

"I've got to have a little recreation," he said. "I get tired of cities and offices. I have to get away and hike around, or canoe or kayak or something like that—or I'd go out of my gourd. In fact, that's one of the reasons I built up the business in this town—quick access to a lot of good places for that stuff."

He took a drink of coffee.

"You know," he continued, "it's such a nice night we ought to take a drive, let you get a feeling of what I mean."

"Sounds good," I said, stretching my shoulders and looking for our waiter. "But isn't it too dark to see much?"

"No. The moon'll be up, the stars are out, the air's real clear. You'll see."

I got the tab, paid up, and we strolled out. Sure enough, the moon had risen.

"Car's in the hotel lot," he said as we hit the street. "This side."

He indicated a station wagon once we were back in the parking lot, unlocked it, and waved me aboard. He drove us out, turned at the nearest corner, and followed the Alameda to the Paseo, took a right leading uphill on a street called Otero and another onto Hyde Park Road. From then on traffic was very light. We passed a sign indicating that we were heading toward a ski basin.

As we worked our way through many curves, heading generally upward, I felt a certain tension going out of me. Soon we had left all signs of habitation behind us, and the night and the quiet settled fully. No streetlights here. Through the opened window I smelled pine trees. The air was cool. I rested, away from S and everything else.

I glanced at Luke. He stared straight ahead, brow furrowed. He felt my gaze, though, because he seemed to relax suddenly and he shot me a grin.

"Who goes first?" he asked.

"Go ahead," I answered.

"Okay. When we were talking the other morning about your leaving Grand D, you said you weren't going to work anywhere else and you weren't planning on teaching."

"That's right."

"You said you were just going to travel around."

"Yep."

"Something else did suggest itself to me a little later on."

I remained silent as he glanced my way.

"I was wondering," he said after a time, "whether you might not be shopping around—either for backing in getting your own company going, or for a buyer for something you have to sell. You know what I mean?"

"You think I came up with something—innovative—and didn't want Grand Design to have it."

He slapped the seat beside him.

"Always knew you were no fool," he said. "So you're screwing around now, to allow decent time for its development. Then you hunt up the buyer with the most bread."

"Makes sense," I said, "if that were the case. But it isn't."

He chuckled.

"It's okay," he said. "Just because I work for Grand D doesn't make me their fink. You ought to know that."

"I do know it."

"And I wasn't asking just to pry. In fact, I had other intentions completely. I'd like to see you make out with it, make out big."

"Thanks."

"I might even be of some assistance—valuable assistance—in the matter."

"I begin to get the drift, Luke, but—"

"Just hear me out, huh? But answer one thing first, though, if you would: You haven't signed anything with anybody in the area, have you?"

"No."

"Didn't think so. It would seem a little premature."

The roadside trees were larger now, the night breeze a bit more chill. The moon seemed bigger, more brilliant up here than it had in the town below. We rounded several more curves, eventually commencing a long series of switchbacks that bore us higher and higher. I caught occasional glimpses of sharp drops to the left. There was no guard rail.

"Look," he said, "I'm not trying to cut myself in for nothing. I'm not asking you for a piece of the action for old times' sake or anything like that. That's one thing and business is another—though it never hurts to do a deal with someone you know you can trust. Let me tell you some of the facts of life. If you've got some really fantastic design, sure, you can go sell it for a bundle to lots of people in the business—if you're careful, damn careful. But that's it. Your golden opportunity's flown then. If you really want to clean up, you start your own outfit. Look at Apple. If it really catches on you can always sell out then, for a lot more than you'd get from just peddling the idea. You may be a whiz at design, but I know the marketplace. And I know people— all over the country—people who'd trust me enough to bankroll us to see it off the ground and out on the street. Shit! I'm not going to stay with Grand D all my life. Let me in and I'll get us the financing. You run the shop and I'll run the business. That's the only way to go with something big."

"Oh, my," I sighed. "Man, it actually sounds nice. But you're following a bum scent. I don't have anything to sell."

"Come one!" he said. "You know you can level with me. Even if you absolutely refuse to go that way, I'm not going to talk about it. I don't screw my buddies. I just think you're making a mistake if you don't develop it yourself."

"Luke, I mean what I said."

He was silent for a little while. Then I felt his gaze upon me again. When I glanced his way I saw that he was smiling.

"What," I asked him, "is the next question?"

"What is Ghostwheel?" he said.

"What?"

"Top secret, hush-hush, Merle Corey project. Ghostwheel," he answered. "Computer design incorporating shit nobody's ever seen before. Liquid semi-conductors, cryogenic tanks, plasma—"

I started laughing.

"My God!" I said. "It's a joke, that's what it is. Just a crazy hobby thing. It was a design game—a machine that could never be built on Earth. Well, maybe most of it could. But it wouldn't function. It's like an Escher drawing— looks great on paper, but it can't be done in real life." Then after a moment's reflection, I asked, "How is it you even know about it? I've never mentioned it to anyone."

He cleared his throat as he took another turn. The moon was raked by treetops. A few beads of moisture appeared upon the windshield.

"Well, you weren't all that secret about it," he answered. "There were designs and graphs and notes all over your work table and drawing board any number of times I was at your place. I could hardly help but notice. Most of them were even labeled 'Ghostwheel.' And nothing anything like it ever showed up at Grand D, so I simply assumed it was your pet project and your ticket to security. You never impressed me as the impractical dreamer type. Are you sure you're giving this to me straight?"

"If we were to sit down and build as much as could be constructed of that thing right here," I replied honestly, "it would just sit there and look weird and wouldn't do a damned thing."

He shook his head.

"That sounds perverse," he said. "It's not like you, Merle. Why the hell would you waste your time designing a machine that doesn't function?"

"It was an exercise in design theory—" I began.

"Excuse me, but that sounds like bullshit," he said. "You mean to say there's no place in the universe that damn machine of yours would kick over?"

"I didn't say that. I was trying to explain that I designed it to operate under bizarre hypothetical conditions."

"Oh. In other words, if I find a place like that on another world we can clean up?"

"Uh, yeah."

"You're weird, Merle. You know that?"

"Uh-huh."

"Another dream shot to shit. Oh, well . . . Say, is there anything unusual about it that could be adapted to the here and now?"

"Nope. It couldn't perform its functions here."

"What's so special about its functions, anyhow?"

"A lot of theoretical crap involving space and time and some notions of some guys named Everett and Wheeler. It's only amendable to a mathematical explanation."

"You sure?"

"What difference does it make, anyhow? I've got no product, we've got no company. Sorry. Tell Martinez and associates it was a blind alley."

"Huh? Who's Martinez?"

"One of your potential investors in Corey and Raynard, Inc.," I said. "Dan Martinez—middle-aged, a bit short, kind of distinguished-looking, chipped front tooth . . ."

His brow furrowed. "Merle, I don't know who the hell you're talking about."

"He came up to me while I was waiting for you in the bar. Seemed to know an awful lot about you. Started asking questions on what I can now see as the potential situation you just described. Acted as if you'd approached him to invest in the thing."

"Uh-uh," he said. "I don't know him. How come you didn't tell me sooner?"

"He beat it, and you said no business till after dinner. Didn't seem all that important, anyway. He even as much as asked me to let you know he'd been inquiring about you."

"What, specifically, did he want to know?"

"Whether you could deliver an unencumbered computer property and keep the investors out of court, was what I gathered."

He slapped the wheel. "This makes no sense at all," he said. "It really doesn't."

"It occurs to me that he might have been hired to investigate a bit—or even just to shake you up some and keep you honest—by the people you've been sounding out to invest in this thing."

"Merle, do you think I'm so damn stupid I'd waste a lot of time digging up investors before I was even sure there was something to put the money into? I haven't talked to anybody about this except you, and I guess I won't be now either. Who do you think he could have been? What did he want?"

I shook my head, but I was remembering those words in Thari.

Why not?

"He also asked me whether I'd ever heard you refer to a place called Amber."

He was looking in the rearview mirror when I said it, and he jerked the wheel to catch a sudden curve.

"Amber? You're kidding."

"No."

"Strange. It has to be a coincidence—"

"What?"

"I did hear a reference to a kind of dreamland place called Amber, last week. But I never mentioned it to anybody. It was just drunken babbling."

"Who? Who said it?"

"A painter I know. A real nut, but a very talented guy. Name's Melman. I like his work a lot, and I've bought several of his paintings. I'd stopped by to see whether he had anything new this last time I was in town. He didn't, but I stayed pretty late at his place anyway, talking and drinking and smoking some stuff he had. He got pretty high after a while and he started talking about magic. Not card tricks, I mean. Ritual stuff, you know?"

"Yes."

"Well, after a time he started doing some of it. If it weren't that I was kind of stoned myself I'd swear that it worked—that he levitated, summoned sheets of fire, conjured and banished a number of monsters. There had to've been acid in something he gave me. But damn! It sure seemed real."

"Uh-huh."

"Anyway," he went on, "he mentioned a sort of archetypal city. I couldn't tell whether it sounded more like Sodom and Gomorrah or Camelot—all the adjectives he used. He called the place Amber, and said that it was run by a half-mad family, with the city itself peopled by their bastards and folks whose ancestors they'd brought in from other places ages ago. Shadows of the family and the city supposedly figure in most major legends and such—whatever that means. I could never be sure whether he was talking in metaphor, which he did a lot, or just what the hell he meant. But that's where I heard the place mentioned."

"Interesting," I said. "Melman is dead. His place burned down a few days ago."

"No, I didn't know." He glanced into the mirror again. "Did you know him?"

"I met him—after you left this last time. Kinsky told me Julia'd been seeing him, and I looked the guy up to see what he could tell me about her. You see—well, Julia's dead."

"How'd it happen? I just saw her last week."

"In a very bizarre fashion. She was killed by a strange animal."

"Lord!"

He braked suddenly and pulled off the road onto a wide shoulder to the left. It looked upon a steep, tree-filled drop. Above the trees I could see the tiny lights of the city across a great distance.

He killed the engine and the headlights. He took a Durham's bag from his pocket and began rolling a cigarette. I caught him glancing upward and ahead.

"You've been checking that mirror a lot."

"Yes," he replied. "I was just about sure a car had been following us all the way from the parking lot down at the Hilton. It was a few turns behind us for the longest while. Now it seems to have disappeared."

He lit his cigarette and opened the door.

"Let's get some air."

I followed him and we stood for a few moments staring out across the big spaces, the moonlight strong enough to cast the shadows of some trees near to us. He threw down the cigarette and stamped on it.

"Shit!" he said. "This is getting too involved! I knew Julia was seeing Melman, okay? I went to see her the night after I'd seen him, okay? I even delivered a small parcel he'd asked me to take her, okay?"

"Cards," I said.

He nodded.

I withdrew them from my pocket and held them toward him. He barely glanced at them there in the dim light, but he nodded again.

"Those cards," he said. Then: "You still liked her, didn't you?"

"Yes, I guess I did."

"Oh, hell," he sighed. "All right. There are some things I'm going to have to tell you, old buddy. Not all of them nice. Give me just a minute to sort it all out. You've just given me one big problem—or I've given it to myself, because I've just decided something."

He kicked a patch of gravel and the stones rattled down the hillside.

"Okay," he said. "First, give me those cards."

"Why?"

"I'm going to tear them into confetti."

"The hell you are. Why?"

"They're dangerous."

"I already know that. I'll hang onto them."

"You don't understand."

"So explain."

"It's not that easy. I have to decide what to tell you and what not to."

"Why not just tell me everything?"

"I can't. Believe me—"

I hit the ground as soon as I heard the first shot, which ricocheted off a boulder to our right. Luke didn't. He began running in a zigzag pattern toward a cluster of trees off to our left, from which two more shots were fired. He had something in his hand and he raised it.

Luke fired three times. Our assailant got off one more round. After Luke's second shot I heard someone gasp. I was on my feet by then and running toward him, a rock in my hand. After his third shot I heard a body fall.

I reached him just as he was turning the body over, in time to see what seemed a faint cloud of blue or gray mist emerge from the man's mouth past his chipped tooth and drift away.

"What he hell was that?" Luke asked as it blew away.

"You saw it too? I don't know."

He looked down at the limp form with the dark spot growing larger on its shirtfront, a .38 revolver still clutched in the right hand.

"I didn't know you carried a gun," I said.

"When you're on the road as much as I am, you go heeled," he answered. "I pick up a new one in each city I hit and sell it when I leave. Airline security. Guess I won't be selling this one. I never saw this guy, Merle. You?"

I nodded.

"That's Dan Martinez, the man I was telling you about."

"Oh, boy," he said. "Another damn complication. Maybe I should just join a Zen monastery someplace and persuade myself it doesn't matter. I—"

Suddenly, he raised his left fingertips to his forehead.

"Oh-oh," he said then. "Merle, the keys are in the ignition. Get in the car and drive back to the hotel right away. Leave me here. Hurry!"

"What's going on? What—"

He raised his weapon, a snub-nosed automatic, and pointed it at me.

"Now! Shut up and go!"

"But—"

He lowered the muzzle and put a bullet into the ground between my feet. Then he aimed it squarely at my abdomen.

"Merlin, son of Corwin," he said through clenched teeth, "if you don't start running right now you're a dead man!"

I followed his advice, raising a shower of gravel and laying some streaks of rubber coming out of the U-turn I spun the wagon through. I roared down the hill and skidded around the curve to my right. I braked for the next one to my left. Then I slowed.

I pulled off to the left, at the foot of a bluff, near some shrubbery. I killed the engine and the lights and put on the parking brake. I opened the door quietly and did not close it fully after I'd slipped out. Sounds carry too well in places like this.

I started back, keeping to the darker, righthand side of the road. It was very quiet. I rounded the first turn and headed for the next one. Something flew from one tree to another. An owl, I think. I moved more slowly than I wanted to, for the sake of silence, as I neared the second turning.

I made my way around that final corner on all fours, taking advantage of the cover provided by rocks and foliage. I halted then and studied the area we had occupied. Nothing in sight. I advanced slowly, cautiously, ready to freeze, drop, dive, or spring up into a run as the situation required.

Nothing stirred, save branches in the wind. No one in sight.

I rose into a crouch and continued, still more slowly, still hugging the cover.

Not there. He had taken off for somewhere. I moved nearer, halted again and listened for at least a minute. No sounds betrayed any moving presences.

I crossed to the place where Martinez had fallen. The body was gone. I paced about the area but could locate nothing to give me any sort of clue as to what might have occurred following my departure. I could think of no reason for calling out, so I didn't.

I walked back to the car without misadventure, got in and headed for town. I couldn't even speculate as to what the hell was going on.

I left the wagon in the hotel lot, near to the spot where it had been parked earlier. Then I went inside, walked to Luke's room, and knocked on the door. I didn't really expect a response, but it seemed the proper thing to do preparatory to breaking and entering.

I was careful to snap only the lock, leaving the door and the frame intact, because Mr. Brazda had seemed a nice guy. It took a little longer, but there was no one in sight. I reached in and turned on the light, did a quick survey, then slipped inside quickly. I stood listening for a few minutes but heard no sounds of activity from the hall.

Tight ship. Suitcase on luggage rack, empty. Clothing hung in closet— nothing in the pockets except for two matchbooks, and a pen and pencil. A few other garments and some undergarments in a drawer, nothing with them. Toiletries in shaving kit or neatly arrayed on countertop. Nothing peculiar there. A copy of B. H. Liddell Hart's *Strategy* lay upon the bedside table, a bookmark about three-quarters of the way into it.

His fatigues had been thrown onto a chair, his dusty boots stood next to it, socks beside them. Nothing inside the boots but a pair of blousing bands. I checked the shirt pockets, which at first seemed empty, but my fingertips then discovered a number of small white paper pellets in one of them. Puzzled, I unfolded a few. Bizarre secret messages? No . . . No sense getting completely paranoid, when a few brown flecks on a paper answered the question. Tobacco. They were pieces of cigarette paper. Obviously he stripped his butts when he was hiking in the wilderness. I recalled a few past hikes with him. He hadn't always been that neat.

I went through the trousers. There was a damp bandanna in one hip pocket and a comb in the other. Nothing in the right front pocket, a single round of ammo in the left. On an impulse, I pocketed the shell, then went on to look beneath the mattress and behind the drawers. I even looked in the toilet's flush box. Nothing. Nothing to explain his strange behavior.

Leaving the car keys on the bedside table I departed and returned to my own room. I did not care that he'd know I'd broken in. In fact, I rather liked the idea. It irritated me that he'd poked around in my Ghostwheel papers. Besides, he owed me a damned good explanation for his behavior on the mountain.

I undressed, showered, got into bed, and doused my light. I'd have left him a note, too, except that I don't like to create evidence and I had a strong feeling that he wouldn't be coming back.

SIX

He was a short, heavy-set man with a somewhat florid complexion, his dark hair streaked with white and perhaps a bit thin on top. I sat in the study of his semirural home in upstate New York, sipping a beer and telling him my troubles. It was a breezy, star-dotted night beyond the window and he was a good listener.

"You say that Luke didn't show up the following day," he said. "Did he send a message?"

"No."

"What exactly did you do that day?"

"I checked his room in the morning. It was just as I'd left it. I went by the desk. Nothing, like I said. Then I had breakfast and checked again. Nothing again. So I took a long walk around the town. Got back a little after noon, had lunch, and tried the room again. It was the same. I borrowed the car keys then and drove back up to the place we'd been the night before. No sign of anything unusual there, looking at it in the light of day. I even climbed down the slope and hunted around. No body, no clues. I drove back, replaced the keys, hung around the hotel till dinnertime, ate, then called you. After you told me to come on up, I made a reservation and went to bed early. Caught the Shuttlejack this morning and flew here from Albuquerque."

"And you checked again this morning?"

"Yeah. Nothing new."

He shook his head and relit his pipe.

His name was Bill Roth, and he had been my father's friend as well as his attorney, back when he'd lived in this area. He was possibly the only man on Earth Dad had trusted, and I trusted him, too. I'd visited him a number of times during my eight years—most recently, unhappily, a year and a half earlier, at the time of his wife, Alice's, funeral. I had told him my father's story, as I heard it from his own lips, outside the Court of Chaos, because I'd gotten the impression that he wanted Bill to know what had been going on, felt he'd owed him sort of explanation for all the help he'd given him. And Bill actually seemed to understand and believe it. But then, he'd known Dad a lot better than I did.

"I've remarked before on the resemblance you bear your father."

I nodded.

"It goes beyond the physical," he continued. "For a while there he had a habit of showing up like a downed fighter pilot behind enemy lines. I'll never forget the night he arrived on horseback with a sword at his side and had me trace a missing compost heap for him." He chuckled. "Now you come along with a story that makes me believe Pandora's box has been opened again. Why couldn't you just want a divorce like any sensible young man? Or a will written or a trust set up? A partnership agreement? Something like that? No, this sounds more like one of Carl's problems. Even the other stuff I've done for Amber seems pretty sedate by comparison."

"Other stuff? You mean the Concord—the time Random sent Fiona with a copy of the Patternfall Treaty with Swayvil, King of Chaos, for her to translate and you to look at for loopholes?"

"That, yes," he said, "though I wound up studying your language myself before I was done. Then Flora wanted her library recovered—no easy job— and then an old flame traced—whether for reunion or revenge I never learned. Paid me in gold, though. Bought the place in Palm Beach with it. Then— Oh, hell. For a while there, I thought of adding 'Counsel to the Court of Amber' to my business card. But that sort of work was understandable. I do similar things on a mundane level all the time. Yours, though, has that black magic and sudden-death quality to it that seemed to follow your father about. It scares the hell out of me, and I wouldn't even know how to go about advising you on it."

"Well, the black magic and sudden-deaths parts are my area, I guess," I observed. "In fact, they may color my thinking too much. You're bound to look at things a lot differently than I do. A blind spot by definition is something you're not aware of. What might I be missing?"

He took a sip of his beer, lit his pipe again.

"Okay." He said. "Your friend Luke—where's he from?"

"Somewhere in the Midwest, I believe he said: Nebraska, Iowa, Ohio— one of those places."

"Mm-hm. What line of work is his old man in?"

"He never mentioned it."

"Does he have any brothers or sisters?"

"I don't know. He never said."

"Doesn't that strike you as somewhat odd—that he never mentioned his family or talked about his home town in the whole eight years you've known him?"

"No. After all, I never talked about mine either."

"It's not natural, Merle. You grew up in a strange place that you *couldn't* talk about. You had every reason to change the subject, avoid the issues. He obviously did, too. And then, back when you came you weren't even certain how most people here behaved. But didn't you ever wonder about Luke?"

"Of course. But he respected my reticence. I could do no less for him. You might say that we had a sort of tacit agreement that such things were off limits."

"How'd you meet him?"

"We were freshman together, had a lot of the same classes."

"And you were both strangers in town, no other friends. You hit it off right from the beginning . . ."

"No. We barely talked to each other. I thought he was an arrogant bastard who felt he was ten times better than anybody he'd ever met. I didn't like him, and he didn't like me much either."

"Why not?"

"He felt the same way about me."

"So it was only gradually that you came to realize you were both wrong?"

"No. We were both right. We got to know each other by trying to show each other up. If I'd do something kind of—outstanding—he'd try to top it. And vice versa. We got so we'd go out for the same sport, try to date the same girls, try to beat each other's grades."

"And . . . ?"

"Somewhere along the line I guess we started to respect each other. When we both made the Olympic finals something broke. We started slapping each other on the back and laughing, and we went out and had dinner and sat up all night talking and he said he didn't give a shit about the Olympics and I said I didn't either. He said he'd just wanted to show me he was a better man and now he didn't care anymore. He'd decided we were both good enough, and he'd just as soon let the matter stand at that. I felt exactly the same way and told him so. That was when we got to be friends."

"I can understand that," Bill said. "It's a specialized sort of friendship. You're friends in certain places."

I laughed and took a drink.

"Isn't everyone?"

"At first, yes. Sometimes always. Nothing wrong with that. It's just that yours seems a much more highly specialized friendship than most."

I nodded slowly. "Maybe so."

"So it still doesn't make sense. Two guys as close as you got to be—with no pasts to show each other."

"I guess you're right. What does it mean?"

"You're not a normal human being."

"No, I'm not."

"I'm not so sure Luke is either."

"What, then?"

"That's your department."

I nodded.

"Apart from that issue," Bill continued, "something else has been bothering me."

"What?"

"This Martinez fellow. He followed you out to the boondocks, stopped when you did, stalked you, then opened fire. Who was he after? Both of you? Just Luke? Or just you?"

"I don't know. I'm not sure which of us that first shot was aimed for. After that, he was firing at Luke—because by then Luke was attacking and he was defending himself."

"Exactly. If he were S—or S's agent—why would he even have bothered with that conversation with you in the bar?"

"I now have the impression that the whole thing was an elaborate buildup to that final question of his, as to whether Luke knew anything about.Amber."

"And your reaction, rather than your answer, led him to believe that he did."

"Well, apparently Luke does—from the way he addressed me right there at the end. You think he was really gunning for someone from Amber?"

"Maybe. Luke is no Amberite, though?"

"I never heard of anyone like him in the time I spent there after the war. And I got plenty of lectures on genealogy. My relatives are like a sewing circle when it comes to keeping track of such matters—a lot less orderly about it than they are in Chaos—can't even decide exactly who's oldest, because some of them were born in different time streams—but they're pretty thorough—"

"Chaos! That's right! You're also lousy with relatives on that side! Could—?"

I shook my head. "No way. I have an even more extensive knowledge of the families there. I believe I'm acquainted with just about all of the ones who can manipulate Shadow, traverse it. Luke's not one of them and—"

"Wait a minute! There are people in the Courts who can walk in Shadows, also?"

"Yes. Or stay in one place and bring things from Shadow to them. It's a kind of reverse—"

"I thought you had to walk the Pattern to gain that power?"

"They have a sort of equivalent called the Logrus. It's a kind of chaotic maze. Keeps shifting about. Very dangerous. Unbalances you mentally, too, for a time. No fun."

"So you've done it?"

"Yes."

"And you walked the Pattern as well?"

I licked my lips, remembering.

"Yes. Damn near killed me. Suhuy'd thought it would, but Fiona thought I could make it if she helped. I was—"

"Who's Suhuy?"

"He's Master of the Logrus. He's an uncle of mine, too. He felt that the Pattern of Amber and the Logrus of Chaos were incompatible, that I couldn't bear the images of both inside me. Random, Fiona, and Gérard had taken me down to show me the Pattern. I got in touch with Suhuy then and gave him a look at it. He said that they seemed antithetical, and that I would either be destroyed by the attempt or the Pattern would drive the image of the Logrus from me—probably the former. But Fiona said that the Pattern should be able to encompass anything, even the Logrus, and from what she understood of the Logrus it should be able to work its way around anything, even the Pattern. So they left it up to me, and I knew that I had to walk it. So I did. I made it, and I still bear the Logrus as well as the Pattern. Suhuy acknowledged that Fi had been right, and he speculated that it had to do with my mixed parentage. She disagreed, though—"

Bill raised his hand. "Wait a minute. I don't understand how you got your uncle Suhuy down into the basement of Amber Castle on a moment's notice."

"Oh, I have a set of Chaos Trumps as well as a set of Amber Trumps, for my relatives back in the Courts."

He shook his head. "All of this is fascinating, but we're straying from the point. Is there anyone else who can walk in Shadow? Or are there other ways of doing it?"

"Yes, there are different ways it could be done. There are a number of magical beings, like the Unicorn, who can just wander wherever they want. And you can follow a Shadow walker or a magical being through Shadow for so long as you can keep track of it, no matter who you are. Kind of like Thomas Rhymer in the ballad. And one Shadow walker could lead an army through. And then there are the inhabitants of the various Shadow kingdoms nearest to Amber and to Chaos. Those at both ends breed mighty sorcerers, just because of their proximity to the two power centers. Some of the good ones can become fairly adept at it—but their images of the Pattern or the Logrus are imperfect, so they're never quite as good as the real thing. But on either end they don't even need an invitation to wander on in. The Shadow interfaces are thinnest there. We even have commerce with them, actually. And established routes become easier and easier to follow with time. Going outward is harder, though. But large attacking forces have been known to come through. That's why we maintain patrols. Julian in Arden, Gérard at sea, and so forth."

"Any other ways?"

"A Shadow-storm perhaps."

"What's that?"

"It's a natural but not too well-understood phenomenon. The best comparison I can think of is a tropical storm. One theory as to their origin has to do with the beat frequencies of waves that pulse outward from Amber and from the Courts, shaping the nature of shadows. Whatever, when such a storm rises it can flow through a large number of shadows before it plays itself out. Sometimes they do a lot of damage, sometimes very little. But they often transport things in their progress."

"Does that include people?"

"It's been known to happen."

He finished his beer. I did the same with mine.

"What about the Trumps?" he asked. "Could anybody learn to use them?"

"Yes."

"How many sets are there kicking around?"

"I don't know."

"Who makes them?"

"There are a number of experts in the Courts. That's where I learned. And there are Fiona and Bleys back in Amber—and I believe they were teaching Random—"

"Those sorcerers you spoke of—from the adjacent kingdoms . . . Could any of them do up a set of Trumps?"

"Yes, but theirs would be less than perfect. It is my understanding that you have to be an initiate of either the Pattern or the Logrus to do them properly. Some of them could do a sort of half-assed set, though, one you'd be taking your chances on using—maybe winding up dead or in some limbo, sometimes getting where you were headed."

"And the set you found at Julia's place . . . ?"

"They're the real thing."

"How do you account for them?"

"Someone who knew how to do it taught someone else who was able to learn it, and I never heard about it. That's all."

"I see."

"I'm afraid none of this is too productive."

"But I need it all to think with," he replied. "How else can I come up with lines of inquiry? You ready for another beer?"

"Wait."

I closed my eyes and visualized an image of the Logrus—shifting, ever shifting. I framed my desire and two of the swimming lines within the eidolon increased in brightness and thickness. I moved my arms slowly, imitating their undulations, their jerkings. Finally, the lines and my arms seemed to be one, and I opened my hands and extended the lines outward, outward through Shadow.

Bill cleared his throat.

"Uh—what are you doing, Merle?"

"Looking for something," I replied. "Just a minute."

The lines would keep extending through an infinitude of Shadow till they encountered the objects of my desire—or until I ran out of patience or concentration. Finally, I felt the jerks, like bites on a pair of fishing lines.

"There they are," I said, and I reeled them in quickly.

An icy bottle of beer appeared in each of my hands. I grasped them as they did and passed one to Bill.

"That's what I meant by the reverse of Shadow walk," I said, breathing deeply a few times. "I sent out to Shadow for a couple of beers. Saved you a trip to the kitchen."

He regarded the orange label with the peculiar green script on it.

"I don't recognize the brand," he said, "let alone the language. You sure it's safe?"

"Yes, I ordered real beer."

"Uh—you didn't happen to pick up an opener, too, did you?"

"Oops!" I said. "Sorry I'll—"

"That's all right."

He got up, walked out to the kitchen, and came back a little later with an opener. When he opened the first one it foamed a bit and he had to hold it over the wastebasket till it settled. The same with the other.

"Things can get a bit agitated when you pull them in fast the way I did," I explained. "I don't usually get my beer that way and I forgot—"

"That's okay," Bill said, wiping his hands on his handkerchief . . .

He tasted his beer then.

"At least it's good beer," he observed. "I wonder . . . Naw."

"What?"

"Could you send out for a pizza?"

"What do you want on it?" I asked.

The next morning we took a long walk beside a wandering creek, which we met at the back of some farmland owned by a neighbor and client of his. We strolled slowly, Bill with a stick in his hand and a pipe in his mouth, and he continued the previous evening's questioning.

"Something you said didn't really register properly at the time," he stated, "because I was more interested in other aspects of the situation. You said that you and Luke actually made it up to the finals for the Olympics and then dropped out?"

"Yes."

"What area?"

"Several different track and field events. We were both runners and—"

"And his time was close to yours?"

"Damn close. And sometimes it was mine that was close to his."

"Strange."

"What?"

The bank grew steeper, and we crossed on some stepping-stones to the other side where the way was several feet wider and relatively flat, with a well-trod path along it.

"It strikes me as more than a little coincidental," he said, "that this guy should be about as good as you are in sports. From all I've heard, you Amberites are several times stronger than a normal human being, with a fancy metabolism giving you unusual stamina and recuperative and regenerative powers. How come Luke should be able to match you in high-level performances?"

"He's a fine athlete and keeps himself in good shape," I answered. "There are other people like that here—very strong and fast."

He shook his head as we started out along the path.

"I'm not arguing that," he said. "It's just that it seems like one coincidence too many. This guy hides his past the same way you do, and then it turns out that he really knows who you are anyhow. Tell me, is he really a big art buff?"

"Huh?"

"Art. He really cared enough about art to collect it?"

"Oh. Yes. We used to hit gallery openings and museum exhibits fairly regularly."

He snorted and swung his stick at a pebble, which splashed into the stream.

"Well," he observed, "that weakens one point, but hardly destroys the pattern."

"I don't follow . . ."

"It seemed odd that he also knew that crazy occultist painter. Less odd, though, when you say that the guy was good and that Luke really did collect art."

"He didn't have to tell me that he knew Melman."

"True. But all of this plus his physical abilities . . . I'm just building a circumstantial case, or course, but I feel that guy is very unusual."

I nodded.

"I've been over it in my mind quite a few times since last night," I said. "If he's not really from here, I don't know where the hell he's from."

"Then we may have exhausted this line of inquiry," Bill said, leading me around a bend and pausing to watch some birds take flight from a marshy area across the water. He glanced back in the direction from which we had came, then, "Tell me—completely off the subject—what's your—uh, rank?" he asked.

"What do you mean?"

"You're the son of a Prince of Amber. What does that make you?"

"You mean titles? I'm Duke of the Western Marches and Earl of Kolvir."

"What does that mean?"

"It means I'm not a Prince of Amber. Nobody has to worry about me scheming, no vendettas involving the succession—"

"Hm."

"What do you mean, 'Hm'?"

He shrugged. "I've read to much history. Nobody's safe."

I shrugged myself. "Last I heard, everything was peaceful on the home front."

"Well, that's good news, anyway."

A few more turnings brought us to a wide area of pebbles and sand, rising gently for perhaps thirty feet to the place where it met an abrupt embankment seven or eight feet in height. I could see the high water line and a number of exposed roots from trees that grew along the top. Bill seated himself on a boulder back in their shade and relit his pipe. I rested on one nearby, to his left. The water splashed and rippled in a comfortable key, and we watched it sparkle for a time.

"Nice," I said, a bit later. "Pretty place."

"Uh-huh."

I glanced at him. Bill was looking back the way we'd come.

I lowered my voice. "Something there?"

"I caught a glimpse a little earlier," he whispered, "of someone else taking a walk this way—some distance behind us. Lost sight of him in all the turnings we took."

"Maybe I should take a stroll back."

"Probably nothing. It's a beautiful day. A lot of people do like to hike around here. Just thought that if we waited a few minutes he'd either show up or we'd know he'd gone somewhere else."

"Can you describe him?"

"Nope. Caught only a barest glimpse. I don't think it's anything to get excited about. It's just that thinking about your story made me a little wary—or paranoid. I'm not sure which."

I found my own pipe and packed it and lit it and we waited. For fifteen minutes or so we waited. But no one showed.

Finally, Bill rose and stretched. "False alarm," he said.

"I guess."

He started walking again and I fell in step beside him.

"Then that Jasra lady bothers me," he said. "You say she seemed to trump in—and then she had that sting in her mouth that knocked you for a loop?"

"Right."

"Ever encounter anyone like her before?"

"No."

"Any guesses?"

I shook my head.

"And why the Walpurgisnacht business? I can see a certain date having significance for a psycho, and I can see people in various primitive religions placing great importance on the turning of seasons. But S seems almost too well organized to be a mental case. And as for the other—"

"Melman thought it was important."

"Yes, but he was into that stuff. I'd be surprised if he didn't come up with a correspondence, whether it was intended or not. He admitted that his master had never told him that that was the case. It was his own idea. But you're the one with the background in the area. Is there any special significance or any real power that you know of to be gained by slaying someone of your blood at this particular time of the year?"

"None that I ever heard of. But of course there are a lot of things I don't know about. I'm very young compared to most of the adepts. But which way are you trying to go on this? You say you don't think it's a nut, but you don't buy the Walpurgis notion either."

"I don't know. I'm just thinking out loud. They both sound shaky to me, that's all. For that matter, the French Foreign Legion gave everyone leave on April 30 to get drunk, and a couple of days after that to sober up. It's the anniversary of the battle of Camerone, one of their big triumphs. But I doubt that figures in this either.

"And why the sphinx?" he said suddenly. "Why a Trump that takes you someplace to trade dumb riddles or get your head bitten off?"

"I'd a feeling it was more the latter that was intended."

"I sort of think so, too. But it's certainly bizarre. You know what? I'll bet they're all that way—traps of some kind."

"Could be."

I put my hand in my pocket, reaching for them.

"Leave them," he said. "Let's not look for trouble. Maybe you should ditch them, at least for a while. I could put them in my safe, down at the office."

I laughed.

"Safes aren't all that safe. No thanks. I want them with me. There may be a way of checking them out without any risk."

"You're the expert. But tell me, could someone sneak through from the scene on the card without you—"

"No. They don't work that way. They require your attention to operate. More than a little of it."

"That's something, anyway. I—"

He looked back again. Someone is coming. I flexed my fingers, involuntarily.

Then I heard him let go a big breath.

"It's okay," he said. "I know him. It's George Hansen. He's the son of the guy who owns the farm we're behind. Hi, George!"

The approaching figured waved. He was of medium height and stocky build. Had sandy hair. He wore Levi's and a Grateful Dead T-shirt, a pack of cigarettes twisted into its left sleeve. He looked to be in his twenties.

"Hi," he answered, drawing near. "Swell day, huh?"

"Sure is," Bill answered. "That's why we're out walking in it, instead of sitting at home."

George's gazed shifted to me.

"Me, too," he said, raking his teeth over his lower lip. "Real good day."

"This is Merle Corey. He's visiting me."

"Merle Corey," George repeated, and he stuck out his hand. "Hi, Merle."

I took it and shook it. It was a little clammy.

"Recognize the name?"

"Uh—Merle Corey," he said again.

"You knew his dad."

"Yeah? Oh, sure!"

"Sam Corey," Bill finished, and he shot me a glance over George's shoulder.

"Sam Corcy," George repeated. "Son of a gun! Good to know you. You going to be here long?"

"A few days, I guess," I replied. "I didn't realize you'd known my father."

"Fine man," he said. "Where you from?"

"California, but it's time for a change."

"Where you headed?"

"Out of the country, actually."

"Europe?"

"Farther."

"Sounds great. I'd like to travel sometime."

"Maybe you will."

"Maybe. Well, I'll be moving on. Let you guys enjoy your walk. Nice meeting you, Merle."

"My pleasure."

He backed away, waved, turned, and walked off.

I glanced at Bill then and noticed that he was shaking.

"What's the matter?" I whispered.

"I've known that boy all his life," he said. "Do you think he's on drugs?"

"Not the kind you have to make holes in your arms for. I didn't see any tracks. And he didn't seem particularly spacey."

"Yeah, but you don't know him the way I do. He seemed very—different. It was just on impulse that I used the name Sam for you dad, because something didn't seem right. His speech patterns have changed, his posture, his gait . . . Intangibles. I was waiting for him to correct me, and then I could have made a joke about premature senility. But he didn't. He picked up on it instead. Merle, this is scary! He knew your father real well—as Carl Corey. Your dad liked to keep his place nice, but he was never much for weeding and mowing or raking leaves. George did his yard work for him for years while he was in school. He knew his name wasn't Sam."

"I don't understand."

"Neither do I," he said, "and I don't like it."

"So he's acting weird—and you think he was following us?"

"Now I do. This is too much of a coincidence, timed with your arrival." I turned.

"I'm going after him," I said. "I'll find out."

"No. Don't."

"I won't hurt him. There are other ways."

"It might be better to let him think he's got us fooled. It might encourage him to do something or say something later that could prove useful. On the other hand, anything you do—even something subtle or magical—might let him, or something, know that we're on to him. Let it ride, be grateful you're warned and be wary."

"You've got a point there." I agreed. "Okay."

"Let's head on back and drive into town for lunch. I want to stop by the office and pick up some papers and make some phone calls. Then I have to see a client at two o'clock. You can take the car and knock around while I'm doing that."

"Fine."

As we strolled back I did some wondering. There were a number of things I had not told Bill. For instance, there had been no reason to tell him that I wore an invisible strangling cord possessed of some rather unusual virtues, woven about my left wrist. One of the virtues is that it generally warns me of nasty intentions aimed in my direction, as it had done in Luke's presence for almost two years until we became friends. Whatever the reason for George Hansen's unusual behavior, Frakir had not given me any indication that he meant me harm.

Funny, though . . . there was something about the way he talked, the way he said his words . . .

I went for a drive after lunch while Bill took care of his business. I headed out to the place where my father had lived years ago. I'd been by it a number of times in the past, but I'd never been inside. No real reason to, I guess, anyway. I parked up the road on a rise, off on the shoulder, and regarded it. A young couple lived there now, Bill had told me, with some kids—a thing I could see for myself from some scattered toys off to the side of the yard. I wondered what it would have been like, growing up in a place like that. I suppose that I could have. The house looked well kept, sprightly even. I imagined that the people were happy there.

I wondered where he was—if he were even among the living. No one could reach him via Trump, though that didn't necessarily prove anything. There are a variety of ways in which a Trump sending can be blocked. In fact one these situations was even said to apply in his case, though I didn't like to think about it.

One rumor had it that Dad had been driven mad in the Courts of Chaos by a curse placed upon him by my mother, and that he now wandered aimlessly through Shadow. She refused even to comment on this story. Another was that he had entered the universe of his own creation and never returned, which it seemed possible could remove him from the reach of the Trumps. Another was simply that he had perished at some point after his departure from the Courts—and a number of my relatives there assured me that they had seen him leave after his sojourn. So, if the rumor of his death were correct, it did not occur in the Courts of Chaos. And there were others who claimed to have seen him at widely separated sites afterward, encounters invariably involving bizarre behavior on his part. I had been told by one that he was traveling in the company of a mute dancer—a tiny, lovely lady with whom he communicated by means of sign language—and that he wasn't talking much himself either. Another reported him as roaring drunk in a raucous cantina, from which he eventually expelled all the other patrons in order to enjoy the music of the band without distraction. I could not vouch for the authenticity of any of these accounts. It had taken me a lot of searching just to come up with this handful of rumors. I could not locate him with a Logrus summoning either, though I had tried many times. But of course if he were far enough afield my powers of concentration may simply have been inadequate.

In other words, I didn't know where the hell my father, Corwin of Amber, was, and nobody else seemed to know either. I regretted this sorely, because my only long encounter with him had been on the occasion of hearing his lengthy story outside the Courts of Chaos on the day of the Patternfall Battle. This had changed my life. It had given me the resolve to depart the Court, with the determination to seek experience and education in the shadow world where he had dwelled for so long. I'd felt a need to understand it if I were to understand him better. I believed that I had now achieved something of this, and more. But he was no longer available to continue our conversation.

I believed that I was about ready to attempt a new means of locating him—now that the Ghostwheel project was almost off the ground—when the most recent fecal missile met the rotating blades. Following my cross-country trip, scheduled to wind up at Bill's place a month or two from now, I was going to head off to my personal anomaly of a place and begin the work.

Now . . . other things had crowded in. The matters at hand would have to be dealt with before I could get on with the search.

I drove past the house slowly. I could hear the sounds of stereo music through open windows. Better not to know exactly what it was like inside. Sometimes a little mystery is best.

That evening after dinner I sat on the porch with Bill, trying to think of anything else I should run through his mind. As I kept drawing blanks, he was the first to renew our serial conversation:

"Something else," he began.

"Yes?"

"Dan Martinez struck up his conversation with you by alluding to Luke's attempts to locate investors for some sort of computer company. You later felt that the whole thing could simply have been a ploy, to get you off guard and then hit you with that question about Amber and Chaos."

"Right."

"But then Luke really did raise the matter of doing something along those lines. He insisted, though, that he had not been in touch with potential investors and that he had never heard of Dan Martinez. When he saw the man dead later he still maintained that he'd had never met him."

I nodded.

"Then either Luke was lying, or Martinez had somehow learned his plans."

"I don't think Luke was lying," I said. "In fact, I've been thinking about that whole business some more. Just knowing him as I do, I don't believe Luke *would* have gone around looking for investors until he was sure there was something to put money into. I think he was telling the truth on that, too. It seems more likely to me that this might have been the only real coincidence in everything that's happened so far. I have the feeling that Martinez knew a lot about Luke and just wanted that one final piece of information—about his knowledge of Amber and the Courts. I think he was very shrewd, and on the basis of what he knew already he was able to concoct something that seemed plausible to me, knowing I'd worked for the same company as Luke."

"I suppose it's possible," he said. "But then when Luke really did—"

"I'm beginning to believe," I interrupted, "that Luke's story was phoney, too."

"I don't follow you."

"I think he put it together the same way as Martinez did, and for similar reasons—to sound plausible to me so that he could get some information he wanted."

"You've lost me. What information?"

"My Ghostwheel. He wanted to know what it was."

"And he was disappointed to learn that it was just an exercise in exotic design, for other reasons than building a company?"

Bill caught my smile as I nodded.

"There's more?" he said. Then: "Wait. Don't tell me. You were lying, too. It's something real."

"Yes."

"I probably shouldn't even ask—unless you think it's material and want to tell me. If it's something big and very important it could be gotten out of me, you know. I have a low tolerance for pain. Think about it."

I did. I sat there for some time, musing.

"I suppose it could be," I said finally, "in a sort of peripheral way I'm sure you're not referring to. But I don't see how it could be—as you say—material. Not to Luke or to anyone else—because nobody even knows what it is but me. No. I can't see how it enters the equation beyond Luke's curiosity about it. So I think I'll follow your suggestion and just keep it off the record."

"Fine with me," he said. "Then there is the matter of Luke's disappearance—"

Within the house, a telephone rang.

"Excuse me," Bill said.

He rose and went into the kitchen.

After a few moments, I heard him call, "Merle, it's for you!"

I got up and went inside. I gave him a questioning look as soon as I entered and he shrugged and shook his head. I thought fast and recalled the location of two other phones in the house. I pointed at him, pointed in the direction of his study and pantomimed the motion of picking up a receiver and holding it to one's ear. He smiled slightly and nodded.

I took the receiver and waited a while, till I heard the click, only beginning to speak then, hoping the caller would think I'd picked up an extension to answer.

"Hello," I said.

"Merle Corey?"

"That's me."

"I need some information I think you might have."

It was a masculine voice, sort of familiar but not quite.

"Who am I talking to?" I asked.

"I'm sorry. I can't tell you that."

"Then that will probably be my answer to your question, too."

"Will you at least let me ask?"

"Go ahead," I said

"Okay. You and Luke Raynard are friends."

He paused.

"You could say that," I said, to fill in the space.

"You have heard him speak of places called Amber and the Courts of Chaos."

Again, a statement rather than a question.

"Maybe," I said.

"Do you know anything of these places yourself?"

Finally a question.

"Maybe," I said again.

"Please. This is serious. I need something more than a 'maybe.'"

"Sorry. 'Maybe' is all you're going to get, unless you tell me who you are and why you want to know."

"I can be of great service to you if you will be honest with me."

I bit back a reply just in time and felt my pulse begin to race. That statement had been spoken in Thari. I maintained my silence.

Then: "Well, that didn't work, and I still don't really know."

"What? What don't you know?" I said.

"Whether he's from one of those places or whether it's you."

"To be blunt as possible, what's it to you?" I asked him.

"Because one of you may be in great danger."

"The one who is from such a place or the one who is not?" I asked.

"I can't tell you that. I can't afford another mistake."

"What do you mean? What was your last one about?"

"You won't tell me—either for purposes of self-preservation, or to help a friend?"

"I might," I said, "if I knew that that were really the case. But for all I know, it might be you that's the danger."

"I assure you I am only trying to help the right person."

"Words, words, words," I said. "Supposing we were both from such places?"

"Oh, my!" he said. "No. That couldn't be."

"Why not?"

"Never mind. What do I have to do to persuade you?"

"Mm. Wait a minute. Let me think," I answered. "All right. How about this? I'll meet you someplace. You name the place. I get a good look at you and we trade information, one piece at a time, till all the cards are on the table."

There was a pause.

Then: "That's the only way you'll do it?"

"Yes."

"Let me think about it. I'll be back in touch soon."

"One thing—"

"What?"

"If it is me, am I in danger right now?"

"I think so. Yes, you probably are. Good-bye."

He hung up.

I managed to sigh and swear at the same time as I recradled the phone. People who knew about us seemed to be coming out of the woodwork.

Bill came into the kitchen, a very puzzled expression on his face.

"How'd whoever-the-hell-he-is even know you're here?" were his first words.

"That was my question," I said. "Think up another."

"I will. If he wants to set something up, are you really going?"

"You bet. I suggested it because I want to meet this guy."

"As you pointed out, he may be the danger."

"That's okay by me. He's going to be in a lot of danger, too."

"I don't like it."

"I'm not so happy with it myself. But it's the best offer I've had so far."

"Well, it's your decision. It's too bad there isn't some way of locating him beforehand."

"That passed through my mind, too."

"Listen, why not push him a little?"

"How?"

"He sounded a little nervous, and I don't think he liked your suggestion any more than I do. Let's not be here when he calls back. Don't let him think you're just sitting around waiting for the phone to ring. Make him wait a little. Go conjure up some fresh clothes and we'll drive over to the country club for a couple of hours. It'll beat raiding the icebox."

"Good idea," I said. "This was supposed to be a vacation, one time. That's probably the closest I'll get. Sounds fine."

I renewed my wardrobe out of Shadow, trimmed my beard, showered, and dressed. We drove to the club then and had a leisurely meal on the terrace. It was a good evening for it, balmy and star-filled, running with moonlight like milk. By mutual consent we refrained from discussing my problems any further. Bill seemed to know almost everyone there, so it seemed a friendly place to me. It was the most relaxed evening I'd spent in a long while. Afterward we stopped for drinks in the club bar, which I gathered had been one of my dad's favorite watering spots, strains of dance music drifting through from the room next door.

"Yeah, it was a good idea," I said. "Thanks."

"*De nada,*" he said. "I had a lot of good times here with your old man. You haven't, by any chance—?"

"No, no news of him."

"Sorry."

"I'll let you know when he turns up."

"Sure. Sorry."

The drive back was uneventful, and no one followed us. We got in a little after midnight, said good night, and I went straight to my room. I shrugged out of my new jacket and hung it in the closet, kicked off my new shoes and left them there, too. As I walked back into the room, I noticed the white rectangle on the pillow of my bed.

I crossed to it in two big steps and snatched it up.

SORRY YOU WERE NOT IN WHEN I CALLED BACK, it said, in block capitals. BUT I SAW YOU AT THE CLUB AND CAN CERTAINLY UNDERSTAND YOUR WANTING A NIGHT OUT. IT GAVE ME AN IDEA. LET'S MEET IN THE BAR THERE, TOMORROW NIGHT, AT TEN. I'D FEEL BETTER WITH LOTS OF PEOPLE AROUND BUT NONE OF THEM LISTENING.

Damn. My first impulse was to go and tell Bill. My first thought following the impulse, though, was that there was nothing he could do except lose more sleep over it, a thing he probably needed a lot more than I did. So I folded the note and stuck it in my shirt pocket, then hung up the shirt.

*   *   *

Not even a nightmare to liven my slumber. I slept deeply and well, knowing Frakir would rouse me in the event of danger. In fact, I overslept, and it felt good. The morning was sunny and birds were singing.

I made my way downstairs to the kitchen after splashing and combing myself into shape and raiding Shadow for fresh slacks and a shirt. There was a note on the kitchen table. I was tired of finding notes, but this one was from Bill, saying he'd had to run into town to his office for a while and I should go ahead and help myself to anything that looked good for breakfast. He'd be back a little later.

I checked out the refrigerator and came up with some English muffins, a piece of cantaloupe and a glass of orange juice. Some coffee I'd started first thing was ready shortly after I finished, and I took a cup with me out onto the porch.

As I sat there, I began to think I ought to leave a note of my own and move on. My mysterious correspondent—conceivably S—had phoned here once and broken in once. How S had known I was here was immaterial. It was a friend's house, and though I did not mind sharing some of my problems with friends, I did not like the idea of exposing them to danger. But then, it was daylight now and the meeting was set for this evening. Not that much longer till some sort of resolution was achieved. Almost silly to depart at this point. In fact, it was probably better that I hang around till then. I could keep an eye on things, protect Bill if anything came up today—

Suddenly, I had a vision of someone forcing Bill to write that note at gunpoint, then whisking him away as a hostage to pressure me into answering questions.

I hurried back to the kitchen and phoned his office. Horace Crayper, his secretary, answered on the second ring.

"Hi, this is Merle Corey," I said. "Is Mr. Roth in?"

"Yes," he replied, "but he's with a client right now. Could I have him call you back?"

"No, it's not that important," I said, "and I'll be seeing him later. Don't bother him. Thanks."

I poured myself another cup of coffee and returned to the porch. This sort of thing was bad for the nerves. I decided that if everything wasn't squared away this evening I would leave.

A figure rounded the corner of the house.

"Hi, Merle."

It was George Hansen. Frakir gave me the tiniest of pulses, as if beginning a warning and then reconsidering it. Ambiguous. Unusual.

"Hi, George. How's it going?"

"Pretty well. Is Mr. Roth in?"

"Afraid not. He had to go into town for a while. I imagine he'll be back around lunchtime or a little after."

"Oh. A few days ago he'd asked me to stop by when I was free, about some work he wanted done."

He came nearer, put his foot on the step.

I shook my head.

"Can't help you. He didn't mention it to me. You'll have to catch him later."

He nodded, unwound his pack of cigarettes, shook one out and lit it, then rewound the pack in his shirt sleeve. This T-shirt was a Pink Floyd.

"How are you enjoying your stay?" he asked.

"Real well. You care for a cup of coffee?"

"Don't mind if I do."

I rose and went inside.

"With a little cream and sugar," he called after me.

I fixed him one and when I returned with it he was seated in the other chair on the porch.

"Thanks."

After he'd tasted it, he said, "I know your dad's name's Carl even though Mr. Roth said Sam. His memory must've slipped."

"Or his tongue," I said.

He smiled.

What was it about the way he talked? His voice could almost be the one I'd heard on the phone last night, though that one had been very controlled and slowed just enough to neutralize any number of speech clues. It wasn't that comparison that was bothering me.

"He was a retired military officer, wasn't he? And some sort of government consultant?"

"Yes."

"Where is he now?"

"Doing a lot of traveling—overseas."

"You going to see him on your own trip?"

"I hope so."

"That'll be nice," he said, taking a drag on his cigarette and another sip of coffee. "Ah! That's good!"

"I don't remember seeing you around," he said suddenly then. "You never lived with your dad, huh?"

"No, I grew up with my mother and other relatives."

"Pretty far from here, huh?"

I nodded. "Overseas."

"What was her name?"

I almost told him. I'm not certain why. But I changed it to "Dorothy" before it came out.

I glanced at him in time to see him purse his lips. He had been studying my face as I spoke.

"Why do you ask?" I said.

"No special reason. Or genetic nosiness, you might say. My mother was the town gossip."

He laughed and gulped coffee.

"Will you be staying long?" he asked then.

"Hard to say. Probably not real long, though."

"Well, I hope you have a good time of it." He finished his coffee and set the cup on the railing. He rose then, stretched and added, "Nice talking to you."

Partway down the stairs he paused and turned.

"I've a feeling you'll go far," he told me. "Good luck."

"You may, too," I said. "You've a way with words."

"Thanks for the coffee. See you around."

"Yes."

He turned the corner and was gone. I simply didn't know what to make of him, and after several attempts I gave up. When inspiration is silent reason tires quickly.

I was making myself a sandwich when Bill returned, so I made two. He went and changed clothes while I was doing this.

"I'm supposedly taking it easy this month," he said while we were eating, "but that was an old client with some pressing business, so I had to go in. What say we follow the creek in the other direction this afternoon?"

"Sure."

As we hiked across the field I told him of George's visit.

"No," he said, "I didn't tell him I had any jobs for him."

"In other words—"

"I guess he came by to see you. It would have been easy enough to see me leave, from their place."

"I wish I knew what he wanted."

"If it's important enough he'll probably wind up asking you, in time."

"But time is running," I said. "I've decided to leave tomorrow morning, maybe even tonight."

"Why?"

As we made our way down the creek, I told him of last night's note and this evening's rendezvous. I also told him my feelings about exposing him to stray shots, or intended ones.

"It may not be that serious," he began.

"My mind's made up, Bill. I hate to cut things short when I haven't seen you for so long, but I hadn't counted on all this trouble. And if I go away you know that it will, too."

"Probably so, but . . ."

We continued in this vein for a while as we followed the watercourse. Then we finally dropped the matter as settled and returned to a fruitless rehashing of my puzzles. As we walked I looked back occasionally but did not see anyone behind us. I did hear a few sounds within the brush on the opposite bank at infrequent intervals, but it could easily have been an animal disturbed by our voices.

We had hiked for over an hour when I had the premonitory feeling that someone was picking up my Trump. I froze.

Bill halted and turned to me.

"What—"

I raised my hand.

"Long distance call," I said.

A moment later I felt the first movement of contact. I also heard the noise in the bushes again, across the water.

"Merlin."

It was Random's voice, calling to me. A few seconds later I saw him, seated at a desk in the library of Amber.

"Yes?" I answered.

The image came into solidity, assumed full reality, as if I were looking through an archway into an adjacent room. At the same time, I still possessed my vision of the rest of my surroundings, though it was growing more and more peripheral by the moment. For example, I saw George Hansen start up from among the bushes across the creek, staring at me.

"I want you back in Amber right away," Random stated.

George began to move forward, splashing down into the water.

Random raised his hand, extended it.

"Come on through," he said.

By now my outline must have begun shimmering, and I heard George cry out, "Stop! Wait! I have to come with—!"

I reached out and grasped Bill's shoulder.

"I can't leave you with this nut," I said. "Come on!"

With my other hand I clasped Random's.

"Okay," I said, moving forward.

"Stop!" George cried.

"The hell you say," I replied, and we left him to clasp a rainbow.

SEVEN

Random looked startled as the two of us came through into the library. He rose to his feet, which still left him shorter than either of us, and he shifted his attention to Bill.

"Merlin, who's this?" he asked.

"Your attorney, Bill Roth," I said. "You've always dealt with him through agents in the past. I thought you might like to—"

Bill began dropping to one knee, "Your Majesty," on his lips, but Random caught him by the shoulders.

"Cut the crap," he said. "We're not in Court." He clasped his hand, then said, "Call me Random. I've always intended to thank you personally for the work you did on that treaty. Never got around to it, though. Good to meet you."

I'd never seen Bill at a loss for words before, but he just stared, at Random, at the room, out of the window at a distant tower.

Finally, "It's real . . ." I heard him whisper moments later.

"Did I not see someone springing toward you?" Random said to me, running a hand through his unruly brown hair. "And surely your last words back there were not addressed to me?"

"We were having a little problem," I answered. "That's the real reason I brought Bill along. You see, someone's been trying to kill me, and —"

Random raised his hand. "Spare me the details for the moment. I'll need them all later, but—but let it be later. There is more nastiness than usual afoot at the moment, and yours may well be a part of it. But I've got to breathe a bit."

It was only then that some deepened lines in his naturally youthful face registered and I began to realize that he was under a strain.

"What's the matter?" I asked.

"Caine is dead. Murdered," he replied. "This morning."

"How did it happen?"

"He was off in Shadow Deiga—a distant port with which we have commerce. He was with Gérard, to renegotiate an old trade agreement. He was shot, through the heart. Died instantly."

"Did they catch the bowman?"

"Bowman, hell! It was a rifleman, on a rooftop. And he got away."

"I thought gunpowder didn't work around here."

He made a quick palms-up gesture.

"Deiga may be far enough off in Shadow for it to work. Nobody here can remember ever testing any there. For that matter, though, your father once came up with a compound that worked here."

"True. I'd almost forgotten."

"Anyway, the funeral is tomorrow—"

"Bill! Merlin!"

My aunt Flora—who had turned down Rossetti's offers, one of them being to model for him—had entered the room. Tall, slim and burnished, she hurried forward and kissed Bill on the cheek. I had never seen him blush before. She repeated the act for me, too, but I was less moved, recalling that she had once been my father's warden.

"When did you get in?" Her voice was lovely, too.

"Just now," I said.

She immediately linked arms with both of us and attempted to lead us off.

"We have so much to talk about," she began.

"Flora!" This from Random.

"Yes, brother?"

"You may give Mr. Roth the full tour, but I require Merlin's presence for a time."

She pouted slightly for a moment, then released my arm.

"Now you know what an absolutely monarchy is," she explained to Bill. "You can see how power corrupts."

"I was corrupt before I had power," Random said, "and rich is better. You have my leave to depart, sister."

She sniffed and led Bill away.

"It's always quieter around here when she finds a boyfriend off somewhere in Shadow," Random observed. "Unfortunately, she's been home for the better part of a year this time."

I made a tsking sound.

He gestured toward a chair and I took it. He crossed to a cabinet then.

"Wine?" he asked.

"Don't mind if I do."

He poured two glasses, brought me one, and seated himself in a chair to my left, a small table between us.

"Someone also took a shot at Bleys," he said, "this afternoon, in another shadow. Hit him, too, but not bad. Gunman got away. Bleys was just on a diplomatic mission to a friendly kingdom."

"Same person, you think?"

"Sure. We've never had rifle sniping in the neighborhood before. Then two, all of a sudden? It must be the same person. Or the same conspiracy."

"Any clues?"

He shook his head and tasted the wine.

"I wanted to talk to you alone," he said then, "before any of the others got to you. There are two things I'd like you to know."

I sipped the wine and waited.

"The first is that this really scares me. With the attempt on Bleys it no longer appears to have been simply a personal thing directed at Caine. Somebody seems to have it in for us—or at least some of us. Now you say there's someone after you, too."

"I don't know whether there's any connection—"

"Well, neither do I. But I don't like the possible pattern I see developing. My worst fear is that it may be one or more of us behind it."

"Why?"

He glowered into his goblet.

"For centuries the personal vendetta has been our way of settling disagreements, not necessarily proceeding inevitably to death—though that was always a possibility—but certainly characterized by intrigues, to the end of embarrassing, disadvantaging, maiming, or exiling the other and enhancing one's own position. This reached its latest peak in the scramble for the succession. I thought everything was pretty much settled, though, when I wound up with the job, which I certainly wasn't looking for. I had no real axes to grind, and I've tried to be fair. I know how touchy everyone here is. I don't think it's me, though, and I don't think it's the succession. I haven't had any bad vibes from any of the others. I'd gotten the impression they had decided I was the lesser of all possible evils and were actually cooperating to make it work. No, I don't believe any of the others is rash enough to want my crown. There was actually amity, goodwill, after the succession was settled. But what I'm wondering now is whether the old pattern might be recurring—that some of the others might have taken up the old game again to settle personal grievances. I really don't want to see that happen—all the suspicion, precautions, innuendoes, mistrust, double dealings. It weakens us, and there's always some possible threat or other against which we should be strong. Now, I've spoken with everyone privately, and of course they all deny any knowledge of current cabals, intrigues, and vendettas, but I could see that they're getting suspicious of each other. It's become a habit of thought. And it wasn't at all difficult for them to dig up some old grudge each of the others might still have had against Caine, despite the fact that he saved all our asses by taking out Brand. And the same with Bleys—everyone could find motives for everyone else."

"So you want the killer fast, because of what he's done to morale?"

"Certainly. I don't need all this backbiting and grudge-hunting. It's all still so close to the surface that we're likely to have real cabals, intrigues, and vendettas before long, if we don't already, and some little misunderstanding could lead to violence again."

"*Do* you think it's one of the others?"

"Shit! I'm the same as they are. I get suspicious by reflex. It well may be, but I haven't really seen a bit of evidence."

"Who else could it be?"

He uncrossed and recrossed his legs. He took another drink of wine.

"Hell! Our enemies are legion. But most of them wouldn't have the guts. They all know the kind of reprisal they could expect once we found them out."

He clasped his hands behind his head and stared at the row of books.

"I don't know how to say this," he began after a time, "but I have to."

I waited again. Then he said quickly, "There's talk it's Corwin, but I don't believe it."

"No," I said softly.

"I told you I don't believe it. Your father means a lot to me."

"Why would anybody believe it?"

"There's a rumor he's gone crazy. You've heard it. What if he's reverted to some past state of mind, from the days when his relations with Caine and Bleys were a lot less than cordial—or with any of us, for that matter? That's what they're saying."

"I don't believe it."

"I just wanted you to be aware that it's being kicked around."

"Nobody'd better kick it in my direction."

He sighed. "Don't *you* start. Please. They're upset. Don't look for trouble." I took a drink of wine.

"Yes, you're right," I said.

"Now I have to listen to your story. Go ahead, complicate my life some more."

"Okay. At least I'm fresh on it," I told him.

So I ran through it again. It took a long while, and it was getting dark by the time I finished. He had interrupted me only for occasional clarifications and had not indulged in the exploration of contingencies the way Bill had when he'd heard it.

When I had finished, he rose and lit a few oil lamps. I could almost hear him thinking.

Finally he said, "No, you've got me on Luke. He doesn't ring any bells at all. The lady with the sting bothers me a bit, though. It seems I might have heard something about people like that, but I can't recall the circumstances. It'll come to me. I want to know more about this Ghostwheel project of yours, though. Something about it troubles me."

"Sure," I said. "But there is something else I am reminded to tell you first."

"What's that?"

"I covered everything for you pretty much the way I did when I was talking to Bill. In fact, my just having been through it recently made me almost use it like a rehearsal. But there was something I didn't mention to Bill because it didn't seem important at the time. I might even have forgotten it entirely in the light of everything else, till this business about the sniper came up—then you reminded me that Corwin once developed a substitute for gunpowder that will work here."

"Everybody remembered it, believe me."

"I forgot about two rounds of ammunition I have in my pocket that came from the ruins of that warehouse where Melman had his studio."

"So?"

"They don't contain gunpowder. There's some kind of pink stuff in them instead—and it won't even burn. At least back on that shadow Earth . . ."

I dug one out.

"Looks like a 30-30," he said.

"I guess so."

Random rose and drew upon a braided cord that hung beside one of the bookshelves.

By the time he'd returned to his seat there was a knock on the door.

"Come in," he called.

A liveried servant entered, a young blond fellow.

"That was quick," Random said.

The man looked puzzled.

"Your Majesty, I do not understand . . ."

"What's to understand? I rang. You came."

"Sire, I was not on duty in the quarters. I was sent to tell you that dinner is ready to be served, awaiting your pleasure."

"Oh. Tell them I'll be along shortly. As soon as I've spoken with the person I've called."

"Very good, Sire."

The man departed backward with a quick bow.

"I thought that was too good to be true," Random muttered.

A little later another guy appeared, older and less elegantly garbed.

"Rolf, would you run down to the armory and talk to whoever's on duty?" Random said. "Ask him to go through that collection of rifles we have from the time Corwin came to Kolvir with them, the day Eric died. See if he can dig up a 30-30 for me, in good shape. Have him clean it and send it up. We're going down to dinner now. You can just leave the weapon in the corner over there."

"30-30, Sire?"

"Right."

Rolf departed, Random rose and stretched. He pocketed the round I'd given him and gestured toward the door.

"Let's go eat."

"Good idea."

There were eight of us at dinner: Random, Gérard, Flora, Bill, Martin—who had been called back a little earlier in the day, Julian—who had just arrived from Arden, Fiona—who had also just come in, from some distant locale, and myself. Benedict was due in the morning, and Llewella later this evening.

I sat to Random's left, Martin to his right. I hadn't seen Martin in a long while and was curious what he'd been about. But the atmosphere was not conducive to conversation. As soon as anyone spoke everyone else evinced unusually acute attention—far beyond the dictates of simple politeness. I found it rather unnerving, and I guess Random did, too, because he sent for Droppa MaPantz, the court jester, to fill the heavy silences.

Droppa had a rough time at first. He began by juggling some food, eating it as it moved by until it was gone, wiped his mouth on a borrowed napkin, then insulted each of us in turn. After that, he commenced a stand-up routine I found very funny.

Bill, who was at my left, commented softly, "I know enough Thari to catch most of it, and that's a George Carlin shtick! How—"

"Oh, whenever Droppa's stuff starts sounding stale, Random sends him off to various clubs in Shadow," I explained, "to pick up new material. I understand he's a regular at Vegas. Random even accompanies him sometimes, to play cards."

He did start getting laughs after a while which loosened things up a bit. When he knocked off for a drink it became possible to talk without being the center of attention, as separate conversations had sprung up. As soon as this happened, a massive arm passed behind Bill and fell upon my shoulder. Gérard was leaning back in his chair and sideward toward me.

"Merlin," he said, "good to see you again. Listen, when you get a chance I'd like to have a little talk with you in private."

"Sure," I said, "but Random and I have to take care of something after dinner."

"When you get a chance," he repeated.

I nodded.

A few moments later I had the feeling that someone was trying to reach me via my Trump.

"Merlin!"

It was Fiona. But she was just sitting at the other end of the table . . .

Her image came clear, however, and I answered her, "Yes?" and then I glanced down the table and saw that she was staring into her handkerchief. She looked up at me then, smiled, and nodded.

I still retained the mental image of her, simultaneously, and I heard it say, *"I dislike raising my voice, for a number of reasons. I'm certain that you will be rushed off after dinner, and I just wanted to let you know that we ought to take a walk, or row out on one of the ponds, or Trump out to Cabra or go look at the Pattern together sometime soon. You understand?"*

"I understand," I said. "I'll be in touch."

"Excellent."

The contact was broken then, and when I glanced her way she was folding her handkerchief and studying her plate.

Random did not linger, but rose quickly after he had finished his dessert, bidding the others a good night and gesturing for Martin and me to accompany him as he departed.

Julian brushed by me on the way out, trying to look somewhat less than sinister and almost succeeding.

"We must go riding together in Arden," he said, "soon."

"Good idea," I told him. "I'll be in touch."

We departed the dining room. Flora caught me in the hall. She still had Bill in tow.

"Stop by my room for a nightcap," she said, "before you turn in. Or come by for tea tomorrow."

"Thank you," I said. "We'll get together. It all depends on how things run, as to just when."

She nodded and hit me with the smile that had caused numerous duels and Balkan crises in the past. Then she moved on and we did too.

As we mounted the stair on the way to the library, Random asked, "Is that everyone?"

"What do you mean?" I said.

"Have they all set up assignations with you by now?"

"Well, they're all tentative things, but yes."

He laughed. "Didn't think they'd waste any time. You'll get everybody's pet suspicions that way. Might as well collect them. Some might come in handy later. They're probably all looking for allies, too—and you should seem a pretty safe choice."

"I do want to visit with all of them. It's just a shame it has to be this way."

He gestured as we came to the top of the stairs. We turned up the hallway and headed toward the library.

"Where are we going?" Martin asked.

Although he resembled Random, Martin looked a little less sneaky, and he was taller. Still, he was not a really big guy.

"To pick up a rifle," Random said.

"Oh. Why?"

"I want to test some ammo Merlin brought back. If it actually fires, our lives have just acquired an additional complication."

We entered the library. The oil lamps were still burning. The rifle was standing in a corner. Random went to it, dug the shell out of his pocket, and loaded it.

"Okay. What should we try it on?" he mused.

He stepped back out into the hall and looked around.

"Ah! Just the thing!"

He shouldered it, aimed at a suit of armor up the hall, and squeezed the trigger. There followed a sharp retort and the ringing of metal. The armor shook.

"Holy shit!" Random said. "It worked! Why me, Unicorn? I was looking for a peaceful reign."

"May I try it, father," Martin asked. "I've always wanted to."

"Why not?" Random said. "You still got that other round, Merlin?"

"Yes," I said, and I rummaged about in my pocket and brought out two. I passed them to Random. "One of these shouldn't work, anyway," I said. "It just got mixed in with the other two."

"All right."

Random accepted both, loaded one. He passed the weapon to Martin then and began explaining its operation. In the distance I heard the sounds of alarm.

"We're about to have the entire palace guard descend upon us," I observed.

"Good," Random answered, as Martin raised the piece to his shoulder. "A little realistic drill every now and then never hurts."

The rifle roared and the armor rang a second time. Martin looked startled and quickly passed the weapon back to Random. Random glanced at the shell in his hand, said, "What the hell!", loaded the final round and fired without sighting.

There was a third report, followed by sounds of a ricochet, just as the guard reached the top of the stair.

"I guess I just don't live right," Random remarked.

After Random had thanked the guard for their prompt response to a training exercise and I overheard a mutter about the king being in his cups, we returned to the library and he asked me the question.

"I found the third one in the pocket of Luke's field jacket," I answered, and I proceeded to explain the circumstances.

"I can no longer afford *not* to know about Luke Raynard," he finally said. "Tell me how you read what just happened."

"The building that burned down," I began. "Upstairs was Melman who wanted to sacrifice me. Downstairs was the Brutus Storage Company. Brutus apparently was storing ammo of this sort. Luke admitted that he knew Melman. I had no idea that there might be some connection with Brutus and the ammunition, also. The fact that they were located in the same building is too much, though."

"If they're turning it out in such quantities that it requires warehousing, then we're in big trouble," Random said. "I want to know who owned that building—and who owned the company, if it's a different person."

"It shouldn't be too difficult to check."

"Who should I send to do it?" he mused. Then he snapped his fingers and smiled. "Flora is about to undertake an important mission for the Crown."

"Inspired," I said.

Martin smiled at that and then shook his head. "I'm afraid I don't under-stand what's going on," he told us, "and I want to."

"Tell you what," Random said. "You fill him in while I go give Flora her assignment. She can leave right after the funeral."

"Yes," I said as he departed, and I began telling my tale once again, editing for brevity.

Martin had no fresh insights and no new information, not that I had expected any of him. He had spent the past few years off in a more pastoral setting, I learned. I got the impression that he was more fond of the country-side than of cities.

"Merlin," he said. "You should have brought this whole mess home to Amber sooner. We're all affected."

And what of the Courts of Chaos? I wondered. Would that rifle have fired there? Still, it had been Caine and Bleys who had been targets. No one had summoned me back to the Courts to brief me on any incidents. Still . . . perhaps I ought to bring my other relatives aboard at some point.

"But up until a few days ago matters were a lot simpler," I told Martin, "and then when things began developing fast I was too caught up in them."

"But all those years . . . those attempts on your life . . ."

I said, "I don't call home whenever I stub my toe. Nobody else does either. I couldn't see any connection, all that time."

But I knew that he was right and I was wrong. Fortunately, Random returned about then.

"I couldn't quite get her to believe it was an honor," he said, "but she'll do it."

We talked for a while then about more general matters, mostly what we had been doing for the past several years. I recalled Random's curiosity about Ghostwheel and mentioned the project to him. He changed the subject imme-diately, giving the impression he wanted to save it for a fully private conversa-tion. After a time, Martin began to yawn and it was contagious. Random decided to bid us good night and rang for a servant to show me to my room.

I asked Dik, who had led me to my quarters, to find me some drawing materials. It took him about ten minutes to turn up everything that I needed.

It would have been a long, difficult walk back and I was tired. So I seated myself beside a table and commenced the construction of a Trump for the bar at the country club Bill had taken me to the previous evening. I worked for perhaps twenty minutes before I was satisfied.

Now it was just a matter of time differential, a thing that was subject to variation, the 2.5-to-1 ratio being only a rule of thumb between Amber and the shadow I had recently inhabited. It was quite possible that I had missed my rendezvous with the nameless housebreaker.

I set everything aside except for the Trump. I rose to my feet.

There came a knock on my door. I was tempted not to answer it, but my curiosity won out. I crossed the room, unbolted the door, and opened it.

Fiona stood there, her hair down for a change. She had on an attractive green evening dress and a small jeweled pin that matched her hair perfectly.

"Hello, Fi," I said. "What brings you around?"

"I felt you working with certain forces," she answered, "and I didn't want anything happening to you before we had our talk. May I come in?"

"Of course," I said, stepping aside. "But I am in a hurry."

"I know, but perhaps I can be of help."

"How?" I asked, closing the door.

She looked about the room and spotted the Trump I'd just finished. She shot the bolt on the door and crossed to the table.

"Very nice," she observed, studying my handiwork. "So that's where you're headed? Where is it?"

"The bar at a country club in the place I just came form," I replied. "I'm supposed to meet an unknown party there at ten, local time. Hopefully, I will obtain information as to who has been trying to kill me, and why, and possibly even learn something of others matters that have been troubling me."

"Go," she said, "and leave the Trump behind. That way, I can use it to spy, and if you should suddenly need help I will be in a position to provide it."

I reached out and squeezed her hand. Then I took up a position beside the table and focused my attention.

After several moments, the scene took on depth and color. I sank into the emerging textures, and everything advanced toward me, growing larger, crowding out my immediate surroundings. My gaze sought the wall clock I remembered, to the right of the bar . . .

9:48. I couldn't have cut things much closer.

I could see the patrons now, hear the sounds of their voices. I looked for the best point of arrival. Actually, there was no one at the right end of the bar, near that clock. Okay . . .

I was there. Trying to look as if I had been, all along. Three of the patrons snapped glances in my direction. I smiled and nodded. Bill had introduced me to one of the men the previous evening. The other I had seen, but not spoken with at that time. Both of them returned my nod, which seemed to satisfy the third that I was real, as he immediately turned his attention back to the woman he was with.

Shortly, the bartender came up to me. He recalled me from last night, also, because he asked whether Bill was around.

I had a beer from him and retired with it to the most secluded table, where I sat and nursed it, my back to the wall, glancing occasionally at the clock, watching the room's two entrances between times. If I tried I could feel Fiona's presence.

Ten o'clock came and went. So did a few patrons, new and old. None of them seemed particularly interested in me, though my own attention was drawn to an unescorted young lady with pale hair and a cameolike profile, which ends the resemblance because cameos don't smile much and she did the second time she glanced at me, right before she looked away. Damn, I thought, why did I have to be wrapped up in a life-and-death situation? Under almost any other circumstances I would have finished the beer, walked over for another, passed a few pleasantries, then asked her whether she'd care to join me. In fact . . .

I glanced at the clock.

10:20.

How much longer should I give the mystery voice? Should I just assume it had been George Hansen, and that he'd given up on tonight when he'd seen me fade? How much longer might the lady hang around?

I growled softly. Stick to business. I studied the narrowness of her waist, the swell of her hips, the tension of her shoulders . . .

10:25.

I noticed that my mug was empty. I took it over for a refill. Dutifully, I watched the progress of the mug.

"I saw you sitting there," I heard her say. "Waiting for someone?"

She smelled strongly of a strange perfume.

"Yes," I said. "But I'm beginning to think it's too late."

"I've a similar problem," she said, and I turned toward her. She was smiling again. "We could wait together," she concluded.

"Please join me," I said. "I'd much rather pass the time with you."

She picked up her drink and followed me back to the table.

"My name's Merle Corey," I told her, as soon as we were seated.

"I'm Meg Devlin. I haven't seen you around before."

"I'm just visiting. You, I take it, are not?"

She shook her head slightly.

"Afraid not. I live in the new apartment complex a couple of miles up the road."

I nodded as if I knew where it was located.

"Where are you from?" she wanted to know.

"The center of the universe," I said, then hastily added, "San Francisco."

"Oh, I've spent a lot of time there. What do you do?"

I resisted a sudden impulse to tell her that I was a sorcerer, and instead described my recent employment at Grand Design. She, I learned in turn, had been a model, a buyer for a large store, and later manager of a boutique.

I glanced at the clock. It was 10:45. She caught the look.

"I think we've both been stood up," she said.

"Probably," I agreed, "but we ought to give them till eleven to be decent about it."

"I suppose."

"Have you eaten?"

"Earlier."

"Hungry?"

"Some. Yes. Are you?"

"Uh-huh, and I noticed some people had food in here earlier. I'll check."

I learned we could get sandwiches, so we got two, with some salad on the side.

"I hope your date didn't include a late supper," I said suddenly.

"It wasn't mentioned, and I don't care," she replied, taking a bite.

Eleven o'clock came and went. I'd finished my drink and the food, and I didn't really want another.

"At least the evening wasn't a total loss," she said, crumpling her napkin and setting it aside.

I watched her eyelashes because it was a pleasant thing to do. She wore very little or very pale makeup. It didn't matter at all. I was about to reach out and cover her hand with my own, but she beat me.

"What were you going to do tonight?" I asked her.

"Oh, dance a bit, have a few drinks, maybe take a walk in the moonlight. Silly things like that."

"I hear music in the next room. We could stroll on over."

"Yes, we could," she said. "Why don't we?"

As we were leaving the bar, I heard Fiona, like a whisper: *"Merlin! If you leave the scene on the Trump you will be out of range to me."*

"Hold on a minute," I answered.

"What?" Meg asked me.

"Uh—I want to visit the rest room first," I said.

"Good idea. I'll do the same. Meet you in the hall here in a couple of minutes."

The place was vacant, but I took a stall in case anyone wandered in. I located Fiona's Trump in the packet I carried. Moments later, I reached Fiona.

"Listen, Fi," I said. "Obviously, no one's going to show. But the rest of the evening promises to shape up nicely, and I might as well have a little fun while I'm here. So thanks for your help. I'll just wander on back later."

"I don't know," she said. *"I don't like you going with a stranger, under the circumstances. There may still be danger around there for you, somewhere."*

"There isn't," I replied. "I have a way of knowing, and it doesn't register for her. Besides, I'm sure it was a fellow I'd met here and that he gave up when I trumped out. I'll be all right."

"I don't like it," she said.

"I'm a big boy. I can take care of myself."

"I suppose so. Call me immediately if there are any problems."

"There won't be. You might as well turn in."

"And call when you're ready to come back. Don't worry about waking me. I want to bring you home personally."

"Okay, I'll do that. Good night."

"Stay wary."

"I always am."

"Good night, then."

She broke the contact.

A few minutes later we were on the dance floor, turning and listening and touching. Meg had a strong tendency to lead. But what the hell, I can be led. I even tried being wary occasionally but there was nothing more threatening than loud music and sudden laughter.

At eleven-thirty we checked the bar. There were several couples there, but her date wasn't. And no one even gave me a nod. We returned to the music.

We looked again a little after midnight with similar results. We seated ourselves then and ordered a final drink.

"Well, it was fun," she said, resting her hand where I could cover it with my own. So I did.

"Yes," I replied. "I wish we could do it more often. But I'm going to be leaving tomorrow."

"Where are you headed?"

"Back to the center of the universe."

"A pity," she said. "Do you need a ride anywhere?"

I nodded. "Anywhere you're going."

She smiled and squeezed my hand.

"All right," she agreed. "Come on over and I'll make you a cup of coffee."

We finished our drinks and headed out to the parking lot, pausing a few times to embrace along the way. I even tried being wary again, but we seemed to be the only people in the lot. Her car was a neat little red Porsche convertible with the top down.

"Here we are. You care to drive?" she asked.

"No, you do it and I'll watch for headless horsemen."

"What?"

"It's a lovely night, and I've always wanted a chauffeur who looked exactly like you."

We got in and she drove. Fast, of course. It just seemed to follow. The roads were deserted and a feeling of exhilaration swept over me. I raised one hand and summoned a lighted cigar from Shadow. I took a few puffs and tossed it away as we roared over a bridge. I regarded the constellations, which had grown familiar to me these past eight years. I drew a deep breath and let it out slowly. I tried to analyze my feelings and realized that I was happy. I hadn't felt that way in a long while.

A mess of light occurred beyond a fringe of trees up ahead. A minute later we rounded a curve and I saw that it came from a small apartment complex off to the right. She slowed and turned there when we reached it.

She parked in a numbered slot, from whence we made our way along a shrub-lined walk to the building's entrance. She let us in and we crossed the lobby to the elevators. The ride up was over too soon, and once we reached her apartment she really did make coffee.

Which was fine with me. It was good coffee, and we sat together and sipped it. Plenty of time . . .

One thing finally did lead to another. We found ourselves in the bedroom a bit later, our clothes on a nearby chair, and I was congratulating myself that the meeting for which I had returned had not come off. She was smooth and soft and warm, and there was just enough of her in all the right places. A vise in velvet, with honey . . . the scent of her perfume . . .

We lay there, much later, in that peaceful state of temporary fatigue on which I will not waste metaphors. I was stroking her hair when she stretched, turning her head slightly, and regarded me through half-lidded eyes.

"Tell me something," she said.

"Sure."

"What was your mother's name?"

I felt as if something prickly had just been rolled along my spine. But I wanted to see where this was leading.

"Dara," I told her.

"And your father?"

"Corwin."

She smiled.

"I thought so," she said, "but I had to be sure."

"Do I get some questions now? Or can only one play?"

"I'll save you the trouble. You want to know why I asked."

"You're on the ball."

"Sorry," she said, moving her leg.

"I take it their names mean something to you?"

"You are Merlin," she stated, "Duke of Kolvir and Prince of Chaos."

"Damn!" I observed. "It seems everybody in this shadow knows who I am! Do you all belong to a club or something?"

"Who else knows?" she asked quickly, her eyes suddenly wide.

"A fellow named Luke Raynard, a dead man named Dan Martinez, a local man named George Hansen, probably—and another dead man named Victor Melman . . . Why? These name ring any bells?"

"Yes, the dangerous one is Luke Raynard. I brought you here to warn you about him, if you were the right one."

"What do you mean 'the right one'?"

"If you were who you are—the son of Dara."

"So warn me."

"I just did. Don't trust him."

I sat up and propped a pillow behind me.

"What's he after? My stamp collection? My traveler's checks? Could you be a little more specific?"

"He tried several times to kill you, years ago—"

"What? How?"

"The first time it involved a truck that almost ran you down. Then the next year—"

"Gods! You really do know! Give me the dates, the dates he tried it."

"April 30, always April 30."

"Why? Do you know why?"

"No."

"Shit. How do you know all of this?"

"I was around. I was watching."

"Why didn't you do something about it?"

"I couldn't. I didn't know which of you was which."

"Lady, you've lost me completely. Who the hell are you, and what's your part in this?"

"Like Luke, I am not what I seem," she began.

There came a sharp buzzing around from the next room.

"Oh my!" she said and sprang out of bed.

I followed her, arriving in the foyer as she pushed a button beside a small grating and said, "Hello?"

"Honey, it's me," came the reply. "I got home a day early. Buzz me in, will you? I'm carrying a bunch of packages."

Oh-oh.

She released the one button and pushed another, turning toward me as she did so.

"The husband," she said, suddenly breathless. "You've got to leave now. Please! Take the steps!"

"But you haven't told me anything yet!"

"I've told you enough. Please don't make trouble!"

"Okay," I said, hurrying back to the bedroom, pulling on my pants and slipping my feet into my loafers.

I stuffed my socks and underwear into my hip pockets and drew on my shirt.

"I'm not satisfied," I said. "You know more and I want it."

"Is that all you want?"

I kissed her cheek quickly.

"Not really. I'll be back," I said.

"Don't," she told me. "It won't be the same. We shall meet again, when the time is right.

I headed for the door.

"That's not good enough," I said as I opened it.

"It will have to be."

"We'll see."

I tore off up the hall and pushed open the door beneath the EXIT sign. I buttoned my shirt and tucked it in on my way down the steps. I paused at the bottom to draw on my socks. I ran a hand through my hair then and opened the door to the lobby.

No one in sight. Good.

As I left the building and headed down the walk a black sedan pulled up in front of me and I heard the hum of a power window and saw a flash of red.

"Get in, Merlin," came a familiar voice.

"Fiona!"

I opened the door and slid inside. We began moving immediately.

"Well, was she?" she asked me.

"Was she what?" I said.

"The one you went to the club to meet."

I hadn't thought of it that way until she said it.

"You know," I said a little later. "I think maybe she was."

She turned onto the road and drove back in the direction from which we had come earlier.

"What kind of game was she playing?" Fiona asked.

"I'd give a lot to know," I answered.

"Tell me about it," she said, "and feel free to edit certain portions."

"Well, all right," I said, and I let her have it.

We were back in the country club parking lot before I was finished.

"Why are we here again?" I asked.

"This is where I got the car. It might belong to a friend of Bill's. I thought I'd be nice and bring it back."

"You used the Trump I'd made to go through to the bar in there?" I asked, gesturing.

"Yes, right after you went in to dance. I watched you for about an hour, mostly from the terrace. And I'd told you to be wary."

"Sorry, I was smitten."

"I'd forgotten they don't serve absinthe here. I had to make do with a frozen marguerita."

"Sorry about that, too. Then you hot-wired a car and followed us when we left?"

"Yes. I waited in her parking lot and maintained the most peripheral of touches with you via your Trump. If I'd felt danger I would have come in after you."

"Thanks. How peripheral?"

"I am not a voyeur, if that's what you mean. Very well, we're up to date."

"There's a lot more to the story than this last part."

"Keep it," she said, "for now. There is only one thing I am curious about at the moment. Would you happen to have a picture of this Luke Raynard?"

"I might," I told her, reaching for my wallet. "Yes, I think I do."

I withdrew my shorts form my hip pocket and explored further.

"At least you don't wear jockeys," she remarked.

I withdrew my wallet and turned on the overhead light. As I flipped the wallet open she leaned toward me, resting her hand on my arm. Finally, I found a clear colored photo of Luke and me at the beach, with Julia and a girl named Gail whom Luke used to date.

I felt her grip tighten as she drew in a short, sharp breath.

"What is it?" I asked. "You know him?"

She shook her head too quickly.

"No. No," she said. "Never saw him before in my life."

"You're a lousy liar, Auntie. Who is it?"

"I don't know," she said.

"Come on! You nearly broke my arm when you saw him."

"Don't push me," she said.

"It involves my life."

"It involves more than your life, I think."

"So?"

"Let it be, for now."

"I'm afraid I can't do that. I must insist."

She turned more fully and both of her hands came up between us. Smoke began to rise from her well-manicured fingertips. Frakir throbbed upon my wrist, which meant she was sufficiently pissed off to lean on me if it came to that.

I made a warding gesture and decided to back off.

"Okay, let's call it a day and head home."

She flexed her fingers and the smoke fled. Frakir became still. She withdrew a packet of Trumps from her purse and shuffled out the one for Amber.

"But sooner or later I'm going to have to know," I added.

"Later," she said, as the vision of Amber grew before us.

One thing I always liked about Fiona: she didn't believe in hiding her feelings.

I reached up and switched off the dome light as Amber came on all around us.

EIGHT

I guess that my thoughts at funerals are typical. Like Bloom in *Ulysses*, I think the most mundane things about the deceased and the current goings-on. The rest of the time my mind wanders.

On the wide strand of shoreline at the southern foot of Kolvir there is a small chapel dedicated to the Unicorn, one of several such throughout the realm at places where she has been sighted. This one seemed most appropriate for Caine's service in that—like Gérard—he had once expressed a desire to be laid to rest in one of the sea caves at the mountain's foot, facing the waters he had sailed so long, so often. One such had been prepared for him, and there would be a procession after the service to inter him there. It was a windy, misty, sea-cool morning with only a few sails in sight, moving to or from the port over half a league westward of us.

Technically, I suppose Random should have officiated, since his kingship automatically made him high priest, but aside from reading an opening and closing passage on the Passing of Princes from the Book of the Unicorn, he turned the service over to Gérard to perform in his stead, as Caine had gotten along with Gérard better than anyone else in the family. So Gérard's booming voice filled the small stone building, reading long sections involving the sea and mutability. It was said that Dworkin himself had penned the Book in his saner days, and that long passages had come direct from the Unicorn. I don't know. I wasn't there. It is also said that we are descended of Dworkin and the Unicorn, which gives rise to some unusual mental images. Origins of anything tend to fade off into myth, though. Who knows? I wasn't around then.

". . . And all things return to the sea," Gérard was saying. I looked about me. Besides the family, there were perhaps forty or fifty people present, mostly nobility from the town, a few merchants with whom Caine had been friendly, representatives of realms in several adjacent shadows where Caine had spent time on both official and personal business, and of course Vinta Bayle. Bill had expressed a desire to be present, and he stood to my left. Martin was at my right. Neither Fiona nor Bleys was present. Bleys had pleaded his injury and excused himself from the service. Fiona had simply vanished. Random had been unable to locate her this morning. Julian departed partway through the service, to check on the guard he had posted along the strand, someone having pointed out that a would-be assassin could rack up a high score with that many of us together in one small space. Consequently, Julian's foresters, with short sword, dagger, and longbow or lance, were spotted strategically all over the place—and every now and then we'd hear the baying of one of his hellhounds, to be answered almost immediately by several others, a mournful, unnerving thing, counterpointing waves, wind, and reflections upon mortality. Where had she gotten off to? I wondered. Fiona? Fear of a trap? Or something to do with last night? And Benedict . . . he had sent regrets and regards, mentioning sudden business that precluded his making it back in time. Llewella simply hadn't shown, and could not be reached by Trump. Flora stood ahead and to the left of me, knowing she looked lovely in dark colors, too. Perhaps I do her an injustice. I don't know. But she seemed more fidgety than contemplative.

At the conclusion of the service we filed out, four seamen bearing Caine's casket, and we formed up into a procession that would lead to the cave and his sarcophagus. A number of Julian's troops came up to pace us as an armed escort.

As we walked along, Bill nudged me and gestured upward with his head, toward Kolvir. I looked in that direction and beheld a black-cloaked and cowled figure standing upon a ledge in the shadow of a rocky projection. Bill leaned close so that I could hear him above the sound of the pipes and strings that were now playing.

"Is that one some part of the ceremony?" he asked.

"Not that I know of," I answered.

I broke out of line and moved forward. In another minute or so we would pass directly beneath the figure.

I caught up with Random and put my hand on his shoulder. When he looked back I pointed upward. He halted and stared, squinting.

His right hand rose to his breast, where he wore the Jewel of Judgement, as on most state occasions. Instantly, the winds rose.

"Halt!" Random called out. "Stop the procession! Everyone stay where you are!"

The figure moved then, slightly, head turning as if to stare at Random. In the sky, as if by trick photography, a cloud blew itself together, growing above Kolvir. A red pulsing glow emerged from beneath Random's hand.

Suddenly, the figure looked upward and a hand flashed beneath the cloak, emerging moments later to perform a quick casting movement. A tiny black object hung in the air, then began its decent.

"Everybody down!" Gérard called out.

Random did not move as the others of us dropped. He remained standing, watching, as lightning emerged from the cloud and played across the face of the cliff.

The thunder that followed coincided almost exactly with the explosion that occurred high overhead. The distance had been too great. The bomb had gone off before it reached us—though it would probably have scored had we continued as we were, to pass beneath the ledge and have it dropped directly upon us. When the spots stopped dancing before my eyes, I regarded the cliff again. The dark figure was gone.

"Did you get him?" I asked Random.

He shrugged as he lowered his hand. The Jewel had ceased its pulsing.

"Everybody on your feet!" he called out. "Let's get on with this funeral!"

And we did. There were no more incidents, and the business was concluded as planned.

My thoughts, and probably everyone else's, were already playing family games as the box was being fitted into the vault. Might the attacker have been one of our absent kin? And if so, which one? What motives might each of them possess for the act? Where were they now? And what were their alibis? Could there have been a coalition involved? Or could it have been an outsider? If so, how was access obtained to the local supply of explosives? Or was this imported stuff? Or had someone local come up with the proper formula? If it were an outsider, what was the motive and where was the person from? Had one of us imported an assassin? Why?

As we filed past the vault I did think fleetingly of Caine, but more as part of the puzzle picture than as an individual. I had not known him all that well. But then, several of the others had told me early on that he was not the easiest person to get to know. He was tough and cynical and had a streak of cruelty in his nature. He had made quite a few enemies over the years and seemed even to be proud of this fact. He had always been decent enough with me, but then we'd never been at cross-purposes over anything. So my feelings did not run as deep for him as they did for most of the others. Julian was another of this cut, but more polished on the surface. And no one could be certain what lay beneath that surface on any given day. Caine . . . I wish I'd gotten to know you better. I am certain that I am diminished by your passing in ways that I do not even understand.

Departing, afterward, heading back to the palace for food and drink, I wondered, not for the first time, how my problems and everyone else's were connected. For I felt they were. I don't mind small coincidences, but I don't trust big ones.

And Meg Devlin? Did she know something of this business, too? It seemed possible that she might. Husband or no husband, I decided, we had a date. Soon.

Later, in the big dining hall, amid the buzz of conversation and the rattle of cutlery and crockery, one vague possibility occurred to me and I resolved to pursue it immediately. Excusing myself from the cold but attractive company of Vinta Bayle, third daughter of some minor nobility and apparently Caine's last mistress, I made my way to the far end of the hall and the small knot of people surrounding Random. I was standing there for several minutes, wondering how to break in, when he spotted me. He excused himself from the others immediately, advanced upon me, and caught hold of my sleeve.

"Merlin," he said, "I don't have time now, but I just wanted to let you know that I don't consider our conversation concluded. I want to get together with you again later this afternoon or this evening—as soon as I'm free. So don't go running off anywhere till we've talked, okay?"

I nodded.

"One quick question," I said, as he began turning back toward the others.

"Shoot," he said.

"Are there any Amberites currently in residence on the shadow Earth I just departed—agents of any sort?"

He shook his head.

"I don't have any, and I don't believe any of the others do just now. I have a number of contacts there in different places, but they're all natives— like Bill."

His eyes narrowed. "Something new come up?" he asked then.

I nodded again.

"Serious?"

"Possibly."

"I wish I had the time to hear it, but it'll just have to keep till we talk later."

"I understand."

"I'll send for you," he said, and he returned to his companions.

That shot down the only explanation I could think of for Meg Devlin. It also foreclosed the possibility of my taking off to see her as soon as I could leave the gathering.

I consoled myself with another plate of food. After a time, Flora entered the hall, studied all the knots of humanity, then made her way among them to settle beside me on the window seat.

"No way of talking to Random right now without an audience," she said.

"You're right," I replied. "May I get you something to eat or drink?"

"Not now. Maybe you can help. You're a sorcerer."

I didn't like that opening, but I asked, "What's the problem?"

"I went to Bleys' room, to see whether he wanted to come down and join us. He's gone."

"Wasn't his door locked? Most people do that around here."

"Yes, from the inside. So he must have trumped out. I broke in when he didn't answer, since there'd been one attempt on his life already."

"And what would you want of a sorcerer?"

"Can you trace him?"

"Trumps don't leave tracks," I said. "But even if I could, I'm not so sure that I would. He knows what he's doing, and he obviously wants to be left alone."

"But what if he's involved? He and Caine had been on opposite sides in the past."

"If he's mixed up in something dangerous to the rest of us you should be happy to see him go."

"So you can't help—or won't?"

I nodded. "Both, I guess. Any decision to seek him out should really come from Random, don't you think?"

"Maybe."

"I'd suggest keeping it to yourself till you can talk to Random. No use stirring up fruitless speculations among the others. Or I'll tell him, if you'd like. I'm going to be talking with him a bit later."

"What about?"

Ouch.

"Not sure," I said. "It's something he wants to tell me, or ask me."

She studied me carefully.

"We haven't really had our own little talk yet," she said then.

"Looks like we're having it now."

"Okay. May I hear about your problems in one of my favorite shadows?"

"Why not?" I said, and I launched into a synopsis of the damned thing again. I felt that this would be the final time, though. Once Flora knew it I was confident it would make the rounds.

She had no information bearing upon my case that she cared to share. We chatted for a while then—local gossip—and she finally decided to get something to eat. She departed in the direction of the food and did not return.

I talked with a few of the others, too—about Caine, about my father. I did not hear anything that I did not already know. I was introduced to a number of people I had not met before. I memorized a mess of names and relationships since I had nothing better to do.

When things finally broke up, I kept an eye on Random and contrived to depart at about the same time he did.

"Later," he said as we passed, and he went off with a couple of guys he'd been talking with.

So I went back to my rooms and stretched out on the bed. When things are brewing you take your rest whenever you can.

After a time I slept, and I dreamed . . .

I was walking in the formal garden behind the palace. Someone else was with me, but I did not know who it was. This did not seem to matter. I heard a familiar howling. Suddenly, there were growling noises near at hand. The first time I looked about I saw nothing. But then, abruptly, they were there—three huge, doglike creatures similar to the one I had slain in Julia's apartment. They were racing toward me across the garden. The howling continued, but they were not its authors. They restricted themselves to growling and slavering as they came on. Just as suddenly, I realized that this was a dream and that I had dreamt it several times before only to lose track of it upon awakening. The knowledge that it was a dream, however, in no way detracted from the feeling of a menace as they rushed toward me. All three of them were surrounded by a kind of light—pale, distorting. Looking past them, through their haloes, I did not see the garden but caught glimpses of a forest.

When they drew near and sprang to attack it was as if they had encountered a glass wall. They fell back, rose and dashed toward me once more only to be blocked again. They leaped and growled and whined and tried again. It was as if I stood beneath a bell jar or within a magic circle, though. They could not get at me. Then the howling came louder, came nearer and they turned their attention away from me.

"Wow!" Random said. "I should charge you something for pulling you out of a nightmare."

. . . And I was awake and lying on my bed and there was darkness beyond my window—and I realized that Random had called me via my Trump and tuned in on my dream when he'd made contact.

I yawned and thought him my answer; *Thanks.*

"Finish waking up and let's have our talk," he said.

"Yes. Where are you?"

"Downstairs. The little sitting room off the main hall to the south. Drinking coffee. We've got it to ourselves."

"See you in five."

"Check."

Random faded. I sat up, swung my feet over the side of the bed, and rose. I crossed the room to the window and flung it wide. I inhaled the crisp evening air of autumn. Spring on the shadow Earth, fall here in Amber—my two favorite seasons. I should be heartened, uplifted. Instead—a trick of the night, the tag-end of the dream—it seemed for a moment that I heard the final note of the howling. I shuddered and closed the window. Our dreams are too much with us.

I hiked down to the designated room and took a seat on one of its sofas. Random let me get through half a cup of coffee before he said, "Tell me about the Ghostwheel."

"It's a kind of—paraphysical surveillance device and library."

Random put down his cup and cocked his head to one side.

"Could you be more specific?" he said.

"Well, my work with computers led me to speculate that basic data-processing principles could be employed with interesting results in a place where computer mechanics themselves would not operate," I began. "In other words, I had to locate a shadow environment where the operations would remain pretty much invariant but where the physical construct, all of the peripherals, the programming techniques and the energy inputs would be of a different nature."

"Uh, Merlin," Random said. "You've lost me already."

"I designed and built a piece of data-processing equipment in a shadow where no ordinary computer could function," I replied, "because I used different materials, a radically different design, a different power source. I also chose a place where different physical laws apply, so that it could operate along different lines. I was then able to write programs for it which would not have operated on the shadow Earth where I'd been living. In doing so, I believe that I created a unique artifact. I called it the Ghostwheel because of certain aspects of its appearance."

"And it's a surveillance device and a library. What do you mean by that?"

"It riffles through Shadow like the pages of a book—or a deck of cards," I said. "Program it for whatever you want checked out and it will keep an eye on it for you. I was planning it as a surprise. You could, say, use it to determine whether any of our potential enemies are mobilizing, or to follow the progress of Shadow-storms, or—"

"Wait a minute," he said, raising a hand. "How? How does it flip through shadows that way? What makes it work?"

"In effect," I explained, "it creates the equivalent of multitudes of Trumps in an instant, then—"

"Stop. Back up. How can you write a program for the creation of Trumps? I thought they could only be done by a person who had an initiate of either the Pattern or the Logrus."

"But in this case," I said, "the machine itself is of that same class of magical objects as Dad's blade, Grayswandir. I incorporated elements of the Pattern itself into its design."

"And you were going to surprise us with this?"

"Yes, once it's ready."

"When will that be?"

"I'm not sure. It had to gather certain critical amounts of data before its programs could become fully operational. I set it to do that a while back, and I haven't had a chance to check on it recently."

Random poured some more coffee, took a drink.

"I don't see where it would save that much in the way of time and effort," he said a little later. "Say I'm curious about something in Shadow. I go and investigate, or I send someone. Now, say that instead I want to use this thing to check it out. I still have to spend the time going to the place where you keep it."

"No," I told him. "You summon a remote terminal."

"Summon? A terminal?"

"Right."

I unearthed my Amber Trumps and dealt myself the one off the bottom. It showed a silver wheel against a dark background. I passed it to Random and he studied it.

"How do you use it?" he asked.

"Same as the others. You want to call it to you?"

"You do it," he said. "I want to watch."

"Very well," I answered. "But while I've set it to gathering data across the shadows it still won't know a whole lot that's useful at this point."

"I don't want to question it so much as I want to see it."

I raised the card and stared, seeing through it with my mind's eye. After a few moments, there was contact. I called it to me.

There followed a small crackling sound and a feeling of ionization in the air as a glowing wheel about eight feet in diameter materialized before me.

"Diminish terminal size," I ordered.

It shrank down to about a third of what it had been and I ordered it to halt at that point. It looked like a pale picture frame, occasional sparks dancing within it, the view across the room constantly rippling as seen through its center.

Random began to extend a hand.

"Don't," I said. "You might get a shock. I still don't have all the bugs out."

"It can transmit energy?"

"Well, it could. No big deal."

"If you ordered to transmit energy . . .?"

"Oh, sure. It has to be able to transmit energy here to sustain the terminal, and through Shadow to operate its scanners."

"I mean, could it discharge it at this end?"

"If I told it to it could build up a charge and let it go. Yes."

"What are its limits in this?"

"Whatever it has available."

"And what does it have available?"

"Well, in theory an entire planet. But—"

"Supposing you ordered it to appear beside someone here, build up a large charge and discharge it into that person. Could it do an electrocution?"

"I guess so," I said. "I don't see why not. But that's not its purpose—"

"Merlin, your surprise is certainly a surprise. But I'm not sure I like it."

"It's safe," I explained. "No one knows where it's located. No one goes there. This Trump I have is the only one. Nobody else can reach it. I was going to make one more card, just for you, and then show you how to operate the thing when it was ready."

"I'm going to have to think about this . . ."

"Ghost, within five thousand Shadow veils, this location—how many Shadow-storms are currently in existence?"

The words came as if spoken within the hoop: "Seventeen."

"Sounds like—"

"I gave it my voice," I told him. "Ghost, give us some pictures of the biggest one."

A scene of chaotic fury filled the hoop.

"Another thought just occurred to me," Random stated. "Can it transport things?"

"Sure, just like a regular Trump."

"Was the original size of that circle its maximum size?"

"No, we could make it a lot larger if you wanted. Or smaller."

"I don't. But supposing you made it larger—and then told it to transmit that storm, or as much of it as it could manage?"

"Wow! I don't know. It would try. It would probably be like opening a giant window onto it."

"Merlin, shut it down. It's dangerous."

"Like I said, nobody knows where it is but me, and the only other way to reach it is—"

"I know, I know. Tell me, could anybody access it with the proper Trump, or just by finding it?"

"Well, yes. I didn't bother with any security codes because of its inaccessibility."

"That thing could be an awesome weapon, kid. Shut it down. Now."

"I can't."

"What do you mean?"

"You can't dump its memory or kill its power from a remote terminal. I would actually have to travel to the site itself to do that."

"Then I suggest you get going. I want it turned off until there are a lot more safeguards built into it. Even then—well, we'll see. I don't trust a power like that. Not when I don't have any defenses against it. It could strike almost without warning. What were you thinking of when you built that thing?"

"Data-processing. Look, we're the only ones—"

"There's always a possibility someone will get wise to it and find a way to get at it. I know, I know—you're in love with your handiwork—and I appreciate what you had in mind. But it's got to go."

"I have done nothing to offend you." It was my voice, but it came from the wheel.

Random stared at it, looked at me, looked back at it.

"Uh—that's not the point," he addressed it. "It's your potential that I'm concerned about.

"Merlin, turn off the terminal!"

"End transmission," I said. "Withdraw terminal."

It wavered a moment, then was gone.

"Had you anticipated that comment from the thing?" Random asked me.

"No. I was surprised."

"I'm beginning to dislike surprises. Maybe that shadow environment is actually altering the thing in subtle ways. You know my wishes. Give it a rest."

I bowed my head. "Whatever you say, sir."

"Cut it out. Don't be a martyr. Just do it."

"I still think it's just a matter of installing a few safeguards. No reason to crash the whole project."

"If things were quieter," he said, "maybe I'd go along with it. But there's too much shit coming down right now, with snipers and bombers and all the things you've been telling me about. I don't need another worry."

I got to my feet. "Okay. Thanks for the coffee," I said. "I'll let you know when it's done."

He nodded. "Good night, Merlin."

"Good night."

As I was stalking out through the big entrance hall I saw Julian, in a green dressing gown, talking with two of his men. On the floor between them lay a large dead animal. I halted and stared. It was one of those same damned dog things I had just dreamed about, like at Julia's.

I approached. "Hi, Julian. What is it?" I asked gesturing.

He shook his head. "Don't know. But the hellhounds just killed three of them in Arden. I trumped these guys up with one of the carcasses, to show Random. You wouldn't know where he is, would you?"

I stabbed with my thumb back over my shoulder. "In the sitting room."

He walked off in that direction. I went nearer and prodded the animal with my toe. Should I go back and tell Random I'd met one before?

The hell with it, I decided. I couldn't see how the information would be of any vital use.

I returned to my rooms and washed up and changed my clothes. Then I stopped by the kitchen and filled my backpack with food. I didn't feel like saying good-bye to anyone, so I just headed for the back and took the big rear staircase down into the gardens.

Dark. Starry. Cool. Walking, I felt a sudden chill as I neared the spot where, in my dream, the dogs had appeared.

No howls, no growls. Nothing. I passed through that area and continued on my way to the rear of that well-kept site, to the place where a number of trails led off through a more natural landscape. I took the second one from the left. It was a slightly longer route than another I might have chosen—with which it intersected later, anyway—but was easier going, a thing I felt I needed in the night. I was still not all that familiar with the irregularities of the other way.

I hiked the crest of Kolvir for the better part of an hour before I located the downward trail I was seeking. I halted then, took a drink of water and rested for a few minutes before I began the descent.

It is very difficult to walk in Shadow on Kolvir. One has to put some distance between oneself and Amber in order to do it properly. So all I could do at this point was hike—which was fine with me, because it was a good night for walking.

I was well on my way down before a glow occurred overhead and the moon crested a shoulder of Kolvir and poured its light upon my twisting trail. I increased my pace somewhat after that. I did want to make it off the mountain by morning.

I was angry with Random for not giving me a chance to justify my work. I hadn't really been ready to tell him about it. If it hadn't been for Caine's funeral I would not have returned to Amber until I'd had the thing perfected. And I wasn't even going to mention Ghostwheel this time around, except that it had figured in a small way in the mystery that had engulfed me and Random had wanted to know about it in order to have the whole story. Okay. He didn't like what he'd seen, but the preview had been premature. Now, if I shut it down as I'd been ordered I would ruin a lot of work that had been in progress for some time now. Ghostwheel was still in a Shadow-scanning, self-education phase. I would have been checking on it about now, anyway, to see how it was coming along and to correct any obvious flaws that had crept into the system.

I thought about it as the trail grew steeper and curved on Kolvir's western face. Random had not exactly ordered me to dump everything it had accumulated thus far. He'd simply told me to shut it down. Viewed the way I chose to view it, that meant I could exercise my own judgment as to means. I decided that gave me leeway to check everything out first, reviewing systems functions and revising programs until I was satisfied that everything was in order. Then I could transfer everything to a more permanent status before shutting it down. Then nothing would be lost; its memory would be intact when the time came to restore its functions again.

Maybe . . .

What if I did everything to make it shipshape, including throwing in a few—as I saw it—unnecessary safeguards to make Random happy? Then, I mused, supposing I got in touch with Random, showed him what I'd done, and asked him whether he was happy with it that way? If he weren't, I could always shut it down then. But perhaps he'd reconsider. Worth thinking about . . .

I played over imaginary conversations with Random until the moon had drifted off to my left. I was more than halfway down Kolvir by then and the going was becoming progressively easier. I could already feel the force of the Pattern as somewhat diminished.

I halted a couple more times on the way down, for water and once for a sandwich. The more I thought about it, the more I felt that Random would just get angry if I proceeded along the lines I had been thinking and probably wouldn't even give me a full hearing. On the other hand, I was angry myself.

But it was a long journey with a few shortcuts. I'd have plenty of time to mull it over.

The sky was growing lighter when I crossed the last rocky slope to reach the wide trail at the foot of Kolvir to the northwest. I regarded a stand of trees across the way, one large one a familiar landmark—

With a dazzling flash that seemed to sizzle and a bomb-like report of thunder the tree was split, not a hundred meters away. I'd flung up both hands at the lightning stroke, but I could still hear cracking wood and the echo of the blast for several seconds afterward.

Then a voice cried out, "Go back!"

I assumed I was the subject of this conversational gambit. "May we talk this over?" I responded.

There was no reply.

I stretched out in a shallow declivity beside the trail, then crawled along it for several body lengths to a place where the cover was better. I was listening and watching the while, hoping that whoever had pulled that stunt would betray his position in some fashion.

Nothing happened, but for the next half minute I surveyed the grove and a portion of the slope down which I had come. From that angle their proximity gave me a small inspiration.

I summoned the image of the Logrus, and two of its lines became my arms. I reached then, not through Shadow but up the slope to where a fairly good-sized rock was poised above a mass of others.

Seizing hold, I drew upon it. It was too heavy to topple easily, so I began rocking it. Slowly, at first. Finally, I got it to the tipping point and it tumbled. It fell among the others and a small cascade began. I withdrew further as they struck and sent new ones bouncing. Several big ones began to roll. A fracture line gave way when they fell upon its edge at a steeper place. An entire sheet of stone groaned and cracked, began to slide.

I could feel the vibration as I continued my withdrawal. I had not anticipated setting off anything this spectacular. The rocks bounced, slid and flew into the grove. I watched the trees sway, saw some of them go down. I heard the crunching, the pinging, the breaking.

I gave it an extra half minute after what seemed its end. There was much dust in the air and half of the grove was down. Then I rose to my feet, Frakir dangling from my left hand, and I advanced upon the grove.

I searched carefully, but there was no one there. I climbed upon the trunk of a fallen tree.

"I repeat, do you care to talk about it?" I called out.

No answer.

"Okay, be that way," I said, and I headed north into Arden.

I heard the sound of horses occasionally as I hiked through that ancient forest. If I was being followed, though, the horsemen showed no interest in closing with me. Most likely, I was passing in the vicinity of one of Julian's patrols.

Not that it mattered. I soon located a trail and began the small adjustments that bore me farther and farther from them.

A lighter shade, from brown to yellow, and slightly shorter trees . . . Fewer breaks in the leafy canopy . . . Odd bird note, strange mushroom . . .

Little by little, the character of the wood was altered. And the shifting grew easier and easier the farther this took me from Amber.

I began to pass sunny clearings. The sky grew a paler blue . . . The trees were all green now, but most of them saplings . . .

I broke into a jog.

Masses of clouds came into view, the spongy earth grew firmer, drier . . .

I stepped up my pace, heading downhill. Grasses were more abundant. The trees were divided into clusters now, islands in a waving see of those pale grasses. My view took in a greater distance. A flapping, beaded curtain off to my right: rain.

Rumbles of thunder came to me, though sunlight continued to light my way. I breathed deeply of the clean damp air and ran on.

The grasses fell away, ground fissured, sky blackened . . . Waters rushed through canyons and arroyos all about me . . . Torrents poured from overhead onto the rocking terrain . . .

I began slipping. I cursed each time I picked myself up, for my overeagerness in the shifting.

The clouds parted like a theater curtain, to where a lemon sun poured warmth and light from a salmon-colored sky. The thunder halted in midrumble and a wind rose . . .

I made my way up a hillside, looked down upon a ruined village. Long-abandoned, partly overgrown, strange mounds lined its broken main street.

I passed through it beneath a slate-colored sky, picked my way slowly across an icy pond, faces of those frozen beneath me staring sightlessly in all directions . . .

The sky was soot-streaked, the snow hard-packed, my breath feathery as I entered the skeletal wood where frozen birds perched: an etching.

Slipping downhill, rolling, sliding into melting and spring . . . Movement again, about me . . . Mucky ground and clumps of green . . . Strange cars on distant highway . . .

A junkyard, smelling, oozing, rusting, smoldering . . . Threading my way amid acres of heaps . . . Rats scurrying . . .

Away . . . Shifting faster, breathing harder . . . Skyline beneath smog cap . . . Delta bottom . . . Seashore . . . Golden pylons along the road . . . Countryside with lakes . . . Brown grasses beneath green sky . . .

Slowing . . . Rolling grassland, river and lake . . . Slowing . . . Breeze and grass, sealike . . . Mopping my brown on my sleeve . . . Sucking air . . . Walking now . . .

I moved through the field at a normal pace, preferring to do my resting in a congenial spot such as this, where I could see for a good distance. The wind made soft noises as it passed among the grasses. The nearest lake was a deep lime color. Something in the air smelled sweet.

I thought I saw a brief flash of light off to my right, but when I looked that way there was nothing unusual to be seen. A little later, I was certain that I heard a distant sound of hoofbeats. But again, I saw nothing. That's the trouble with shadows—you don't always know what's natural there; you're never certain what to look for.

Several minutes passed, and then I smelled it before I saw anything. Smoke.

The next instant there was a rush of fire. A long line of flame cut across my path.

And again the voice: "I told you to go back!"

The wind was behind the fire, pushing it toward me. I turned to head away and saw that it was already flanking me. It takes a while to build up the proper mental set for shadow-shifting, and I had let mine go. I doubted I could set it up again in time.

I began running.

The line of flame was curving about me, as if to describe a huge circle. I did not pause to admire the precision of the thing, however, as I could feel the heat by then and the smoke was getting thicker.

Above the fire's crackling it seemed that I could still hear the drumming of hoofs. My eyes were beginning to water, though, and streams of smoke further diminished my vision. And again, I detected no sign of the person who had sprung the trap.

Yet—definitely—the ground was shaking with the rapid progress of a hooved creature headed in my direction. The flames flashed higher, drew nearer as the circle rushed toward closure.

I was wondering what new menace was approaching, when a horse and rider burst into view through the gap in the fiery wall. The rider drew back the reins, but the horse—a chestnut—was not too happy at the nearness of the flames. It bared its teeth, biting at the bit, and tried several times to rear.

"Hurry! Behind me!" the rider cried, and I rushed to mount.

The rider was a dark-haired woman. I caught only a glimpse of her features. She managed to turn the horse back in the direction from which she had come, and she shook the reins. The chestnut started forward, and suddenly it reared. I managed to hang on.

When its front hooves struck the ground, the beast wheeled and tore off toward the light. It was almost into the flames when it wheeled again.

"Damn!" I heard the rider say, as she worked almost frantically with the reins.

The horse turned again, neighing loudly. Bloody spittle dripped from its mouth. And by then the circle was closed, the smoke was heavy and the flames very near. I was in no position to help, beyond giving it a pair of sharp kicks in the flanks when it began moving in a straight line again.

It plunged into the flames to our left, almost screaming as it went. I had no idea how wide the band of fire was at that point. I could feel a searing along my legs, though, and I smelled burning hair.

Then the beast was roaring again, the rider was screaming back at it, and I found that I could no longer hold on. I felt myself sliding backward just as we broke through the ring of fire and into a charred, smoldering area where the flames had already passed. I fell amid hot black clumps; ashes rose about me. I rolled frantically to my left, and I coughed and squeezed my eyes shut against the cloud of ashes that assailed my face.

I heard the woman scream and I scrambled to my feet, rubbing my eyes. My vision came clear in time for me to see the chestnut rising from where he had apparently fallen atop his rider. The horse immediately tore off, to be lost among clouds of smoke. The woman lay very still and I rushed to her side. Kneeling, I brushed sparks from her clothing and checked for breathing and a pulse. Her eyes opened while I was doing this.

"Back's—broken—I think," she said, coughing. "Don't feel—much. . . . Escape—if you can. . . . Leave me. I'll die—anyway."

"No way," I said. "But I've got to move you. There's a lake nearby, if I remember right."

I removed my cloak where it was tied about my waist and I spread it out beside her. I inched her onto it as carefully as I could, folded it over her to protect her against the flames and began dragging her in what I hoped was the proper direction.

We made it through a shifting patchwork of fire and smoke. My throat was raw, my eyes watering steadily and my trousers on fire when I took a big step backward and felt my heel squish downward into mud. I kept going.

Finally, I was waist deep in the water and supporting her there. I leaned forward, pushed a flap of the cloak back from her face. Her eyes were still open, but they looked unfocused and there was no movement. Before I could feel for a carotid pulse, however, she made a hissing noise, then she spoke my name.

"Merlin," she said hoarsely, "I'm—sorry—"

"You helped me and I couldn't help you," I said. "*I'm* sorry."

"Sorry—I didn't last—longer," she continued. "No good—with horses. They're—following you."

"Who?" I asked.

"Called off—the dogs, though. But the—fire—is—someone—else's. Don't know—whose."

"I don't know what you're talking about."

I splashed a little water onto her cheeks to cool them. Between the soot and her singed, disheveled hair it was difficult to judge her appearance.

"Someone—behind—you," she said, her voice growing fainter. "Someone—ahead—too. Didn't—know—about—that one. Sorry."

"Who?" I asked again. "And who are you? How do you know me? Why—"

She smiled faintly. ". . . Sleep with you. Can't now. Going . . ."

Her eyes closed.

"No!" I cried.

Her face contorted and she sucked in a final breath. She expelled it then, using it to form the whispered words. "Just—let me—sink here. G'bye . . ."

A cloud of smoke blew across her face. I held my breath and shut my eyes as a larger billow followed, engulfing us.

When the air finally cleared again, I studied her. Her breathing had ceased and there was no pulse, no heartbeat. There was no nonburning, nonmarshy area available for even an attempt at CPR. She was gone. She'd known she was going.

I wrapped my cloak about her carefully, turning it into a shroud. Last of all, I folded a flap over her face. I fixed everything into place with the clasp I'd used to close it at my neck when I'd worn it. Then I waded out into deeper water. "Just let me sink here." Sometimes the dead sink quickly, sometimes they float . . .

"Good-bye, lady," I said. "Wish I knew your name. Thanks again."

I released my hold upon her. The waters swirled. She was gone. After a time, I looked away then moved away. Too many questions and no answers.

Somewhere, a maddened horse was screaming . . .

NINE

Several hours and many shadows later I rested again, in a place with a clear sky and not much tinder about. I bathed in a shallow stream and afterward summoned fresh clothing out of Shadow. Clean and dry then, I rested on the bank and made myself a meal.

It seemed as if every day were now an April 30. It seemed as if everyone I met knew me, and as if everyone were playing an elaborate double-game. People were dying all about me and disasters were becoming a common occurrence. I was beginning to feel like a figure in a video game. What would be next? I wondered. A meteor shower?

There had to be a key. The nameless lady who had given her life to pull me out of the fire had said that someone was following me and that there was someone ahead of me, also. What did that mean? Should I wait for my pursuer to catch up and simply ask him, her, or it what the hell was going on? Or should I push on fast, hopefully catch the other party and make inquiry there? Would either give me the same answer? Or were there two different answers involved? Would a duel satisfy someone's honor? I'd fight it, then. Or a bribe. I'd pay it. All I wanted was an answer followed by a little peace and quiet. I chuckled. That sounded like a description of death— though I wasn't that sure about the answer part.

"Shit!" I commented, to no one in particular, and I tossed a stone into the stream.

I got to my feet and crossed the water. Written in the sand on its opposite shore were the words GO BACK. I stepped on them and broke into a run.

The world spun about me as I touched the shadows. Vegetation fell away. The rocks grew into boulders, lightening, taking on a sparkle . . .

I ran through a valley of prisms beneath an awesome purple sky . . . Wind among rainbow stones, singing, Aeolian music . . .

Garments lashed by gales . . . Purple to lavender above . . . Sharp cries within the strains of sound . . . Earth cracking . . .

Faster.

I am giant. Same landscape, infinitesimal now . . . Cyclopean, I grind the glowing stones beneath my feet . . . Dust of rainbows upon my boots, puffs of cloud above my shoulders . . .

Atmosphere thickening, thickening, almost to liquid, and green . . . Swirling . . . Slow motion, my best efforts . . .

Swimming in it . . . Castles fit for aquaria drift by . . . Bright missiles like fireflies assail me . . . I feel nothing . . .

Green to blue . . . Thinning, thinning . . . Blue smoke and air like incense . . . The reverberation of a million invisible gongs, incessant . . . I clench my teeth.

Faster.

Blue to pink, spark-shot . . . A catlick of fire . . . Another . . . Heatless flames dance like sea plants . . . Higher, rising higher . . . Walls of fire buckle and crackle . . .

Footfalls at my back.

Don't look. Shift.

Sky split down the middle, by sun a comet streaking . . . Here and gone . . . Again. Again. Three days in as many heartbeats . . . I breathe the air spicy . . . Swirl the fires, descend to purple earth . . . Prism in the sky . . .

I race the course of a glowing river across a field of fungus color of blood, spongy . . . Spores that turn to jewels, fall like bullets . . .

Night on a plain of brass, footfalls echoing to eternity . . . Knobbed machinelike plants clanking, metal flowers retracting back to metal stalks, stalks to consoles . . . Clank, clank, sigh . . . Echoes only, at my back?

I spin once.

Was that a dark figure ducking behind a windmill tree? Or only the dance of shadows in my shadow-shifting eyes?

Forward. Through glass and sandpaper, orange ice, landscape of pale flesh . . .

There is no sun, only pale light . . . There is no earth . . . Only thin bridges and islands in the air . . . The world is crystal matrix . . .

Up, down, around . . . Through a hole in the air and down a chute . . .

Sliding . . . To a cobalt beach beside a still copper sea . . . Twilight without stars . . . Faint glow everywhere . . . Dead, dead this place . . . Blue rocks . . . Broken statues of inhuman beings . . . Nothing stirring . . .

Stop.

I drew a magic circle about me in the sand and invested it with the forces of Chaos. I spread my new cloak then at its center, stretched out and went to sleep. I dreamed that the waters rose up to wash away a portion of the circle, and that a green, scaly being with purple hair and sharp teeth crept out of the sea and came to me to drink my blood.

When I awoke, I saw that the circle was broken and a green, scaly being with purple hair and sharp teeth lay dead upon the beach a half-dozen yards from me, Frakir knotted tightly about its throat and the sand disturbed all around. I must have slept very deeply.

I retrieved my strangling cord and crossed another bridge over infinity.

On the next leg of my journey I was nearly caught up in a flash flood the first time I paused to rest. I was no longer unwary, however, and I kept ahead of it long enough to shift away. I received another warning—in burning letters on the face of an obsidian mountain—suggesting I withdraw, retire, go home. My shouted invitation to a conference was ignored.

I traveled till it was time to sleep again, and I camped then in the Blackened Lands—still, gray, musty, and foggy. I found myself an easily defended cleft, warded it against magic and slept.

Later—how much later, I am uncertain—I was awakened from a dreamless slumber by the pulsing of Frakir upon my wrist.

I was instantly awake, and then I wondered why. I heard nothing and I saw nothing untoward within my limited field of vision. But Frakir—who is not 100 percent perfect—always has a reason when she does give an alarm. I waited, and I recalled my image of the Logrus while I did so. When it was fully before me, I fitted my hand within it as if it were a glove and I reached . . .

I seldom carry a blade above the length of a middle-sized dagger. It's too damned cumbersome having several feet of steel hanging at my side, bumping into me, catching onto bushes, and occasionally even tripping me up. My father, and most of the others in Amber and the Courts, swear by the heavy, awkward things, but they are probably made of sterner stuff than myself. I've nothing against them in principle. I love fencing, and I've had a lot of training in their use. I just find carrying one all the time to be a nuisance. The belt even rubs a raw place on my hip after a while. Normally, I prefer Frakir and improvisation. However . . .

This, I was willing to admit, might be a good time to be holding one. For now I heard bellowslike hissing sounds and scrambling noises from somewhere outside and to my left.

I extended through Shadow, seeking a blade. I extended, I extended . . .

Damn. I had come far from any metalworking culture of the appropriate anatomy and at the proper phase in its historical development.

I continued to reach, sweat suddenly beading my brow. Far, very far. And the sounds came nearer, louder, faster.

There came rattling, stamping and spitting noises. A roar.

Contact!

I felt the haft of the weapon in my hand. Seize and summon! I called it to me, and I was thrown against the wall by the force of its delivery. I hung there a moment before I could draw it from the sheath in which it was still encased. In that moment, things grew silent outside.

I waited ten seconds. Fifteen. Half a minute . . .

Nothing now.

I wiped my palms on my trousers. I continued to listen. Finally, I advanced.

There was nothing immediately before the opening save a light fog, and as the peripheral lines of sight opened there was still nothing to behold.

Another step . . .

No.

Another.

I was right at the threshold now. I leaned forward and darted a quick glance in either direction.

Yes. There was something off to the left—dark, low, unmoving, half masked by the fog. Crouched? Ready to spring at me?

Whatever it was, it did not stir and it kept total silence. I did the same. After a time, I noticed another dark form of the same general outline beyond it—and possibly a third even farther away. None of them showed any inclination to raise the sort of hell I had been listening to but minutes before.

I continued my vigil.

Several minutes must have passed before I stepped outside. Nothing was roused by my movement. I took another step and waited. Then another.

Finally, moving slowly, I approached the first form. An ugly brute, covered with scales the color of dried blood. A couple of hundred pounds' worth of creature, long and sinuous . . . Nasty teeth, too, I noted, when I opened its mouth with the point of my weapon. I knew it was safe to do this, because its head was almost completely severed from the rest of it. A very clean cut. A yellow-orange liquid still flowed from the wound.

And I could see from where I stood that the other two forms were creatures of the same sort. In all ways. They were dead, too. The second one I examined had been run through several times and was missing one leg. The third had been hacked to pieces. All of them oozed, and they smelled faintly of cloves.

I inspected the well-trampled area. Mixed in with that strange blood and the dew were what seemed to be the partial impressions of a boot, human-scale. I sought farther and I came across one intact footprint. It was pointed back in the direction from which I had come.

My pursuer? S, perhaps? The one who had called off the dogs? Coming to my aid?

I shook my head. I was tired of looking for sense where there wasn't any. I continued to search, but there were no more full tracks. I returned to the cleft then and picked up my blade's sheathe. I fitted the weapon into it and hung it from my belt. I fastened it over my shoulders so that it hung down my back. The hilt would protrude just above my backpack once I'd shouldered that item. I couldn't see how I could jog with it at my side.

I ate some bread and the rest of the meat. Drank some water, too, and a mouthful of wine. I resumed my journey.

I ran much of the next day—though "day" is something of a misnomer beneath unchanging stippled skies, checkered skies, skies lit by perpetual pin-wheels and fountains of light. I ran until I was tired, and I rested and ate and ran some more. I rationed my food, for I'd a feeling I'd have to send far for more and such an act places its own energy demands upon the body. I eschewed shortcuts, for flashy shadows-spanning hellruns also have their price and I did not want to be all whacked out when I arrived. I checked behind me often. Usually, I saw nothing suspicious. Occasionally, though, I thought that I glimpsed distant pursuit. Other explanations were possible, however, considering some of the tricks the shadows can play.

I ran until I knew that I was finally nearing my destination. There came no new disaster followed by an order to turn back. I wondered fleetingly whether this was a good sign, or if the worst were yet to come. Either way, I knew that one more sleep and a little more journeying would put me where I wanted to be. Add a little caution and a few precautions and there might even be reason for optimism.

I ran through a vast, forestlike stand of crystalline shapes. Whether they were truly living things or represented some geological phenomenon, I did not know. They distorted perspectives and made shifting difficult. However, I saw no signs of living things in that glossy, glassy place, which led me to consider making my final campsite there.

I broke off a number of the limbs and drove them into the pink ground, which had the consistency of partly set putty. I constructed a circular palisade standing to about shoulder height, myself at its center. I unwound Frakir from my wrist, then voiced the necessary instructions as I placed her atop my rough and shining wall.

Frakir elongated, stretching herself as thin as a thread and twining among the shardlike branches. I felt safe. I did not believe anything could cross that barrier without Frakir's springing loose and twining herself to deathly tightness about it.

I spread my cloak, lay down, and slept. For how long, I am not certain. And I recall no dreams. There were no disturbances either.

When I woke I moved my head to reorient it, but the view was the same. In every direction but down the view was filled with interwoven crystal branches. I climbed slowly to my feet and pressed against them. Solid. They had become a glass cage.

Although I was able to break off some lesser branches, they were mainly from overhead, and it did nothing to work my release. Those which I had planted initially had thickened considerably, having apparently rooted themselves solidly. They would not yield to my strongest kicks.

The damned thing infuriated me. I swung my blade and glassy chips flew all about. I muffled my face with my cloak then and swung several times more. Then I noticed that my hand felt wet. When I looked at it, I saw that it was running with blood. Some of those splinters were very sharp. I desisted with the blade and returned to kicking at my enclosure. The walls creaked occasionally and made chiming noises, but they held.

I am not normally claustrophobic and my life was not in imminent peril, but something about this shining prison annoyed me out of all proportion to the situation itself. I raged for perhaps ten minutes before I forced myself to sufficient calmness that I might think clearly.

I studied the tangle until I discerned the uniform color and texture of Frakir running through it. I placed my fingertips on her and spoke an order. Her brightness increased and she ran through the spectrum and settled into a red glow. The first creaking sound occurred a few seconds later.

I quickly withdrew to the center of the enclosure and wrapped myself fully in my cloak. If I crouched, I decided, some of the overhead pieces would fall a greater distance, striking me with more force. So I stood upright, protecting my head and neck with my arms and hands as well as with the cloak.

The creaking sounds became cracking sounds, followed by rattling, snapping, breaking. I was suddenly struck across the shoulder, but I maintained my footing.

Ringing and crunching, the edifice began to fall about me. I held my ground, though I was struck several times more.

When the sounds ceased and I looked again I saw that the roof had been removed, and I stood calf-deep amid fallen branches of the hard, corallike material. Several of the side members had splintered off at near to ground level. Others now stood at unnatural angles, and this time a few well-placed kicks brought them down.

My cloak was torn in a number of places, and Frakir coiled now about my left ankle and began to migrate to my wrist. The stuff crunched underfoot as I departed.

I shook out my cloak and brushed myself off. I traveled for perhaps half an hour then, leaving the place far behind me, before I halted and took my breakfast in a hot, bleak valley smelling faintly of sulfur.

As I was finishing, I heard a crashing noise. A horned and tusked purple thing went racing along the ridge to my right pursued by a hairless orange-skinned creature with long claws and a forked tail. Both were wailing in different keys.

I nodded. It was just one damned thing after another.

I made my way through frozen lands and burning lands, under skies both wild and placid. Then at last, hours later, I saw the low range of dark hills, and aurora streaming upward from behind them. That was it. I needed but approach and pass through and I would see my goal beyond the last and most difficult barrier of all.

I moved ahead. It would be good to finish this job and get on with more important matters. I would trump back to Amber when I was finished there, rather than retracing my steps. I could not have trumped in to my destination, though, because the place could not be represented on a card.

In that I was jogging, I first thought that the vibrations were my own. I was disabused of this notion when small pebbles began to roll aimlessly about the ground before me.

Why not?

I'd been hit with just about everything else. It was as if my strange nemesis were working down through a checklist and had just now come to "Earthquake." All right. At least there was nothing high near at hand to fall on me.

"Enjoy yourself, you son of a bitch!" I called out. "One day real soon it won't be so funny!"

As if in response the shaking grew more violent, and I had to halt or be thrown from my feet. As I watched, the ground began to subside in places, tilt in still others. I looked about quickly, trying to decide whether to advance, retreat, or stay put. Small fissures had begun to open, and now I could hear a growling, grinding sound.

The earth dropped abruptly beneath me—perhaps six inches—and the nearest crevices widened. I turned and began sprinting back the way I had come. The ground seemed less disturbed there.

A mistake perhaps. A particularly violent tremor followed, knocking me from my feet. Before I could rise a large crack appeared within reaching distance. It continued to widen even as I watched. I sprang to my feet, leapt across it, stumbled, rose again, and beheld another opening rift—widening more rapidly than the one I had been fleeing.

I sprang once more, onto a tilting tabletop of land. The ground seemed torn everywhere now with the dark lightning strokes of rifts, heaving themselves open widely to the accompaniment of awful groans and screechings. Big sections of ground slipped from sight into abysses. My small island was already going.

I leaped again, and again, trying to make it over to what appeared to be a more stable area.

I didn't quite manage it. I missed my footing and fell. But I managed to catch hold of the edge. I dangled a moment then and began to draw myself upward. The edge began to crumble. I clawed at it and caught a fresh hold. Then I dangled again, coughing and cursing.

I sought for footholds in the clayey wall against which I hung. It yielded somewhat beneath the thrusting of my boots and I dug in, blinking dirt from my eyes, trying for a firmer hold overhead. I could feel Frakir loosening, tightening into a small loop, one end free and flowing over my knuckles, hopefully to locate something sufficiently firmset to serve as an anchor.

But no. My lefthand hold gave way again. I clung with my right and groped for another. Loose earth fell about me as I failed, and my right hand was beginning to slip.

Dark shadow above me, through dust and swimming eyes.

My right hand fell loose. I thrust with my legs for another try.

My right wrist was clasped as it sped upward and forward once again. A big hand with a powerful grip held me. Moments later, it was joined by another and I was drawn upward, quickly, smoothly. I was over the edge and seeking my footing in an instant. My wrist was released. I wiped my eyes.

"Luke!"

He was dressed in green, and blades must not have bothered him the way they do me, for a good-sized one hung at his right side. He seemed to be using a rolled cloak for a backpack, and he wore its clasp like a decoration upon his left breast—an elaborate thing, a golden bird of some sort.

"This way," he said, turning, and I followed him.

He led me a course back and to the left, tangent to the route I had taken on entering the valley. The footing grew steadier as we hurried that way, mounting at last a low hill that seemed completely out of range in the disturbance. Here we paused to look back.

"Come no farther!" a great voice boomed from that direction.

"Thanks, Luke," I panted. "I don't know how you're here or why but—"

He raised a hand. "Right now I just want to know one thing," he said, rubbing at a short beard he seemed to have grown in an amazingly brief time, and causing me to note that he was wearing the ring with the blue stone.

"Name it," I told him.

"How come whatever it was that just spoke has your voice?" he asked.

"Uh-oh. I knew it sounded familiar."

"Come on!" he said. "You must know. Every time you're threatened and it warns you back it's your voice that I hear doing it—echolike."

"How long have you been following me, anyhow?"

"Quite a distance."

"Those dead creatures outside the cleft where I'd camped—"

"I took them out for you. Where are you going, and what is that thing?"

"Right now I have only suspicions as to exactly what's going on, and it's a long story. But the answer should lie beyond that next range of hills."

I gestured toward the aurora.

He stared off in that direction, then nodded.

"Let's get going," he said.

"There is an earthquake in progress," I observed.

"It seems pretty much confined to this valley," he stated. "We can cut around it and proceed."

"And quite possibly encounter its continuance."

He shook his head. "It seems to me," he said, "that whatever it is that's trying to bar your way exhausts itself after each effort and takes quite a while to recover sufficiently to make another attempt."

"But the attempts are getting closer together," I noted, "and more spectacular each time."

"Is it because we're getting closer to their source?" he asked.

"Possibly."

"Then let's hurry."

We descended the far side of the hill, then went up and down another. The tremors, by that time, had already subsided to an occasional shuddering of the ground and shortly these, too, ceased.

We made our way into and along another valley, which for a while headed us far to the right of our goal, then curved gently back in the proper direction, toward the final range of barren hills, lights flickering beyond them against the low, unmoving base of a cloudlike line of white under a mauve to violet sky. No fresh perils were presented.

"Luke," I asked after a time, "what happened on the mountain, that night in New Mexico?"

"I had to go away—fast," he answered.

"What about Dan Martinez's body?"

"Took it with me."

"Why?"

"I don't like leaving evidence lying about."

"That doesn't really explain much."

"I know," he said, and he broke into a jog.

I paced him.

"And you know who I am," I continued.

"Yes."

"How?"

"Not now," he said. "Not now."

He increased his pace. I matched it.

"And why were you following me?"

"I saved your ass, didn't I?"

"Yeah, and I'm grateful. But it still doesn't answer the question."

"Race you to that leaning stone," he said, and he put on a burst of speed.

I did, too, and I caught him. Try as I could I couldn't pass him, though. And we were breathing too hard by then to ask or answer questions.

I pushed myself, ran faster. He did, too, keeping up. The leaning stone was still a good distance off. We stayed side by side and I saved my reserve for the final sprint. It was crazy, but I'd run against him too many times. It was almost a matter of habit by now. That, and the old curiosity. Had he gotten a little faster? Had I? Or a little slower?

My arms pumped, my feet thudded. I got control of my breathing, maintained it in an appropriate rhythm. I edged a little ahead of him and he did nothing about it. The stone was suddenly a lot nearer.

We held our distance for perhaps half a minute, and then he cut loose. He was abreast of me, he was past me. Time to dig in.

I drove my legs faster. The blood thudded in my ears. I sucked air and pushed with everything I had. The distance between us began to narrow again. The leaning rock was looking bigger and bigger . . .

I caught him before we reached it, but try as I might I could not pull ahead. We raced past it side by side and collapsed together.

"Photo finish," I gasped.

"Got to call it a tie," he paused. "You always surprise me—right at the end."

I groped out my water bottle and passed it to him. He took a swig and handed it back. We emptied it that way, a little at a time.

"Damn," he said then, getting slowly to his feet. "Let's see what's over those hills."

I got up and went along.

When I finally recovered my breath the first thing I said was, "You seem to know a hell of a lot more about me than I do about you."

"I think so," he said after a long pause, "and I wish I didn't."

"What does that mean?"

"Now now," he replied. "Later. You don't read *War and Peace* on your coffee break."

"I don't understand."

"Time," he said. "There's always either too much time or not enough. Right now there's not enough."

"You've lost me."

"Wish I could."

The hills were nearer and the ground remained firm beneath our feet. We trudged steadily onward.

I thought of Bill's guesswork, Random's suspicions, and Meg Devlin's warning. I also thought of that round of strange ammunition I'd found in Luke's jacket.

"That thing we're heading toward," he said, before I could frame a fresh question of my own. "That's your Ghostwheel, isn't it?"

"Yes."

He laughed. Then: "So you were telling the truth back in Santa Fe when you told me it required a peculiar environment What you didn't say was that you'd found that environment and built the thing there."

I nodded. "What about your plans for a company?" I asked him.

"That was just to get you to talk about it."

"And what about Dan Martinez—the things he said?"

"I don't know. I really didn't know him. I still don't know what he wanted, or why he came at us shooting."

"Luke, what is it that you want, anyhow?"

"Right now I just want to see that damned thing," he said. "Did building it out here in the boonies endow it with some sort of special properties?"

"Yes."

"Like what?"

"Like a few I didn't even think of—unfortunately," I answered.

"Name one."

"Sorry," I said. "Question and answer is a two-way game."

"Hey, I'm the guy who just pulled you out of a hole in the ground."

"I gather you're also the guy who tried to kill me on a bunch of April thirtieths."

"Not recently," he said. "Honest."

"You mean you really did?"

"Well . . . yeah. But I had reasons. It's a long story and—"

"Jesus, Luke! Why? What did I ever do to you?"

"It's not that simple," he answered.

We reached the base of the nearest hill and he started climbing it.

"Don't," I called to him. "You can't go over."

He halted. "Why not?"

"The atmosphere ends thirty or forty feet up."

"You're kidding."

I shook my head.

"And it's worse on the other side," I added. "We have to find a passage through. There's one farther to the left."

I turned and headed in that direction. Shortly, I heard his footfalls.

"So you gave it your voice," he said.

"So?"

"So I see what you're up to and what's been going on. It's become sentient in that crazy place you built it. It went wild, and you're heading to shut it down. It knows it and it's got the power to do something about it. It's your Ghosthwheel that's been trying to get you to turn back, isn't it?"

"Probably."

"Why didn't you just trump in?"

"You can't construct a Trump for a place that keeps changing. What do you know about Trumps, anyway?"

"Enough," he said.

I saw the passage I was seeking up ahead.

I approached the place and I halted before I entered it.

"Luke," I said, "I don't know what you want or why or how you got here, and you don't seem to care to tell me. I will tell you something for free, though. This could be very dangerous. Maybe you ought to go back to wherever you came from and let me handle it. There's no reason to place you in jeopardy."

"I think there is," he said. "Besides, I might be useful."

"How?"

He shrugged. "Let's get on with it, Merlin. I want to see that thing."

"Okay. Come on."

I led the way into the narrow place where the stone had been riven.

TEN

The passage was long and dark and occasionally tight, growing progressively colder as we advanced, but at length we emerged onto the wide, rocky shelf that faced the steaming pit. There was an ammonialike odor in the air, and my feet were cold and my face flushed, as usual. I blinked hard several times, studying the latest outlines of the maze through the shifting mist. A pearl-gray pall hung over the entire area. Intermittent orange flashes penetrated the gloom.

"Uh—where is it?" Luke inquired.

I gestured straight ahead, toward the site of the latest flicker. "Out there," I told him.

Just then, the mists were swept away, revealing file upon file of dark, smooth ridges separated by black declivities. The ridges zigged and zagged their way out toward a fortresslike island, a low wall running about it, several metallic structures visible beyond.

"It's a—maze," he remarked. "Do we travel it down in the passages or up on top of the walls?"

I smiled as he studied it.

"It varies," I said. "Sometimes up and sometimes down."

"Well, which way do we go?"

"I don't know yet. I have to study it each time. You see, it keeps changing, and there's a trick to it."

"A trick?"

"More than one, actually. The whole damn thing is floating on a lake of liquid hydrogen and helium. The maze moves around. It's different each time. And then there's a matter of the atmosphere. If you were to walk upright along the ridges you would be above it in most places. You wouldn't last long. And the temperature ranges from horribly cold to roasting hot over a range of a few feet in elevation. You have to know when to crawl and when to climb and when to do other things—as well as which way to go."

"How do you tell?"

"Un-uh," I said. "I'll take you in, but I'm not giving you the secret."

The mists began to rise again from the depths and to collect into small clouds.

"I see now why you can't make a Trump for it," he began.

I continued to study the layout.

"All right," I said then. "This way."

"What if it attacks us while we're in the maze?" he asked.

"You can stay behind if you want."

"No. Are you really going to shut it down?"

"I'm not sure. Come on."

I took several steps ahead and to the right. A faint circle of light appeared in the air before me, grew brighter. I felt Luke's hand upon my shoulder.

"What—?" he began.

"No farther!" the voice I now recognized as my own said to me.

"I think we can work something out," I responded. "I have several ideas and—"

"No!" it answered. "I heard what Random said."

"I am prepared to disregard his order," I said, "if there is a better alternative."

"You're trying to trick me. You want to shut me down."

"You're making things worse with all these power displays," I said. "I'm coming in now and—"

"No!"

A heavy gust of wind blew out of the circle and struck against me. I was staggered by it. I saw my sleeve turn brown, then orange. It began to fray even as I watched.

"What are you doing? I have to talk to you, explain—"

"Not here! Not now! Never!"

I was hurled back again Luke, who caught me, dropping to one knee as he did so. An arctic blast assailed us and icy crystals danced before my eyes. Bright colors began to flash then, half blinding me.

"Stop!" I cried, but nothing did.

The ground seemed to tilt beneath us and suddenly there was no ground. It did not feel as if we were falling, however. It seemed rather as if we hung suspended in the midst of a blizzard of light.

"Stop!" I called out once again, but the words were swept away.

The circle of light vanished, as if retreating down a long tunnel. I realized, however, through the sensory overload, that it was Luke and I who were receding from the light, that we had already been blasted a great enough distance to drive us halfway through the hill. But there was nothing solid in any direction about us.

A faint buzzing sound began. It grew into a humming, then a dull roar. In the distance, I seemed to see a tiny steam locomotive negotiating a mountainside at an impossible angle, then an upside-down waterfall, a skyline beneath green waters. A park bench passed us quickly, a blue-skinned woman seated upon it, clutching at it, a horrified expression on her face.

I dug frantically within my pocket, knowing we might be destroyed at any moment.

"What," Luke screamed into my ear, his grip now almost dislocating my arm, "is it?"

"Shadow-storm!" I cried back. "Hang on!" I added unnecessarily.

A batlike creature was blown into my face, was gone an instant later, leaving a wet slash upon my right cheek. Something struck against my left foot.

An inverted mountain range flowed past us, buckling and rippling. The roaring increased in volume. The light seemed to pulse by us now, in wide bands of color, touching us with a near-physical force. Heat lamps and wind chimes . . .

I heard Luke cry out as if he had been struck, but I was unable to turn to his aid. We traversed a region of lightninglike flashes where my hair stood on end and my skin tingled.

I gripped the packet of cards within my pocket and withdrew it. At this point we were beginning to spin and I was afraid they would be torn from my hand. I held them tightly, fearing to sort through them, keeping them close to my body. I drew them upward slowly, carefully. Whichever one lay on top would have to be our exit.

Dark bubbles formed and broke about us, discharging noxious fumes.

I saw, as I raised my hand, that my skin was gray in appearance, sparkling with fluorescent swirls. Luke's hand upon my arm looked cadaverous, and when I glanced back at him a grinning death's head met my gaze.

I looked away, turned my attention back to the cards. It was hard to focus my vision, through the grayness, through a peculiar distancing effect. But it finally came clear. It was a grassy spit of land I had regarded—how long ago?—quiet waters about it, the edge of something crystalline and bright jutting into view off toward the right.

I held it within my attention. Sounds from beyond my shoulder indicated that Luke was trying to address me, but I could not distinguish his words. I continued to regard the Trump and it grew clearer. But slowly, slowly. Something struck me hard, below the right side of my rib cage. I forced myself to ignore it and continued to concentrate.

At last the scene on the card seemed to move toward me, to grow larger. There was a familiar sense of coldness to it now as the scene engulfed me and I it. An almost elegiac feeling of stillness hung over that little lake.

I fell forward into the grass, my heart pounding, my side throbbing. I was gasping, and the subjective sense of worlds rushing by me was still present, like the afterimages of highways upon closing one's eyes at the end of a long day's drive.

Smelling sweet water, I passed out.

I was vaguely aware of being dragged, carried, then helped, stumbling along. There followed a spell of full unconsciousness, shading over into sleep and dreaming.

. . . I walked the streets of a ruined Amber beneath a lowering sky. A crippled angel with a fiery sword stalked the heights above me, slashing. Wherever its blade fell, smoke, dust, and flame rose up. Its halo was my Ghostwheel, pouring forth mighty winds ridden by abominations that streamed past the angel's face like a dark, living veil, working disorder and ruin wherever they fell. The palace was half collapsed, and there were gibbets nearby where my relatives hung, twisting in the gusts. I'd a blade in one hand and Frakir dangled from the other. I was climbing now, going up to meet and do battle with the bright-dark nemesis. An awful feeling lay upon me as I mounted my rocky way, as if my imminent failure was a thing foregone. Even so, I decided, the creature was going to leave here with wounds to lick.

It took note of me as I drew near, turning in my direction. Its face was still hidden as it raised its weapon. I rushed forward, regretting only that I had not had time to envenom my blade. I spun twice as I went in, feinting, to strike somewhere in the vicinity of its left knee.

There followed a flash of light and I was falling, falling, bits of flame descending about me, like a burning blizzard.

I fell so for what seemed an age and a half, coming to rest at last upon my back atop a large stone table marked out like a sundial, its stylus barely missing impaling me—which seemed crazy even in a dream. There were no sundials in the Courts of Chaos, for there is no sun there. I was located at the edge of a courtyard beside a high, dark tower, and I found myself unable to move, let alone rise. Above me, my mother, Dara, stood upon a low balcony in her natural form, looking down at me in her awful power and beauty.

"Mother!" I cried. "Free me!"

"I have sent one to help you," she answered.

"And what of Amber?"

"I do not know."

"And my father?"

"Speak not to me of the dead."

The stylus turned slowly, positioned itself above my throat, began a gradual but steady descent.

"Help me!" I cried. "Hurry!"

"Where are you?" she called out, head turning, eyes darting. "Where have you gone?"

"I'm still here!" I yelled.

"Where are you?"

I felt the stylus touch the side of my neck—

The vision broke and fell apart.

My shoulders were propped against something unyielding, my legs were stretched out before me. Someone had just squeezed my shoulder, the hand brushing against my neck.

"Merle, you okay? Want a drink?" a familiar voice was asking.

I took a deep breath and sighed it out. I blinked several times. The light was blue, the world a field of lines and angles. A dipper of water appeared before my mouth.

"Here." It was Luke's voice.

I drank it all.

"Want another?"

"Yes."

"Just a minute."

I felt his weight shift, heard his footsteps recede. I regarded the diffusely illuminated wall six or seven feet before me. I ran my hand along the floor. It seemed to be of the same material.

Shortly, Luke returned, smiling, and passed me the dipper. I drained it and handed it back.

"Want more?" he asked.

"No. Where are we?"

"In a cave—a big, pretty place."

"Where'd you get the water?"

"In a side cavern, up that way." He gestured. "Several barrels of it in there. Also lots of food. Want something to eat?"

"Not yet. Are you okay?"

"Kind of beat," he replied, "but intact. You don't seem to have any broken bones, and that cut on your face has stopped bleeding."

"That's something, anyway," I said.

I climbed slowly to my feet, the final strands of dreams withdrawing slowly as I rose. I saw then that Luke had turned and was walking away. I followed him for several paces before I thought to inquire, "Where are you going?"

"In there," he answered, pointing with the dipper.

I followed him through an opening in the wall and into a cold cavern about the size of my old apartment's living room. Four large wooden barrels stood along the wall to my left, and Luke proceeded to hang the dipper upon the upper edge of the nearest. Against the far wall were great stacks of cartons and piles of sacks.

"Canned goods," he announced. "Fruit, vegetables, ham, salmon, biscuits, sweets. Several cases of wine. A Coleman stove. Plenty of Sterno. Even a bottle or two of cognac."

He turned and brushed quickly past me, headed on up the hall again.

"Now where?" I asked.

But he was moving fast and did not reply. I had to hurry to catch up. We passed several branches and openings before he halted at another, nodding.

"Latrine in there. Just a hole with some boards over it. Good idea to keep it covered, I'd say."

"What the hell is this?" I asked.

He raised his hand. "It will all become clear in a minute. This way."

He swung around a sapphire corner and vanished. Almost completely disoriented, I moved in that direction. After several turns and one cutback, I felt totally lost. Luke was nowhere in sight.

I halted and listened. Not a sound except for my own breathing.

"Luke! Where are you?" I called.

"Up here," he answered.

The voice seemed to be coming from overhead and somewhere off to my right. I ducked beneath a low arch and came into a bright blue chamber of the same crystalline substance as the rest of the place. I saw a sleeping bag and a pillow in one corner. Light streamed in from a small opening about eight feet overhead.

"Luke?" I asked again.

"Here," came his reply.

I moved to position myself beneath the hole, squinting against the brightness as I stared upward. Finally, I shaded my eyes. Luke's head and shoulders were limned above me, his hair a crown of coppery flame in what could be the light of early morning or of evening. He was smiling again.

"That, I take it, is the way out," I said.

"For me," he answered.

"What do you mean?"

There followed a grating noise and the view was partly occluded by the edge of a large boulder.

"What are you doing?"

"Moving this stone into a position where I can block the opening quickly," he replied, "and stick in a few wedges afterward."

"Why?"

"There are sufficient tiny openings for air so that you shan't suffocate," he went on.

"Great. Why am I hear, anyway?"

"Let's not get existential just now," he said. "This isn't a philosophy seminar."

"Luke! Damn it! What's going on?"

"It should be obvious that I'm making you a prisoner," he said. "The blue crystal, by the way, will block any Trump sendings and negate your magical abilities that rely on things beyond the walls. I need you alive and fangless for now, in a place where I can get to you in a hurry."

I studied the opening and the nearby walls.

"Don't try it," he said. "I have the advantage of position."

"Don't you think you owe me an explanation?"

He stared at me for a moment, then nodded.

"I have to go back," he said finally, "and try to get control of the Ghostwheel. Any suggestions?"

I laughed. "It's not on the best terms with me at the moment. I'm afraid I can't help you."

He nodded again. "I'll just have to see what I can do. God, what a weapon! If I can't swing it myself I'll have to come back and pick your brains for some ideas. You be thinking about it, okay?"

"I'll be thinking about a lot of things, Luke. You're not going to like some of them."

"You're not in a position to do much."

"Not yet," I said.

He caught hold of the boulder, began to move it.

"Luke!" I cried.

He paused, studied me, his expression changing to one I had never seen before.

"That's not really my name," he stated, after a moment.

"What, then?"

"I am your cousin Rinaldo," he said slowly. "I killed Caine, and I came close with Bleys. I missed with the bomb at the funeral, though. Someone spotted me. I will destroy the House of Amber with or without your

Ghostwheel—but it would make things a lot easier if I had that kind of power."

"What's your bitch, Luke? . . . Rinaldo? Why the vendetta?"

"I went after Caine first," he continued, "because he's the one who actually killed my father."

"I—didn't know." I stared at the flash of the Phoenix clasp upon his breast. "I didn't know that Brand had a son," I finally said.

"You do now, old buddy. That's another reason why I can't let you go, and why I have to keep you in a place like this. Don't want you warning the others."

"You're not going to be able to pull this off."

He was silent for several seconds, then he shrugged.

"Win or lose, I have to try."

"Why April 30?" I said suddenly. "Tell me that."

"It was the day I got the news of my dad's death."

He drew upon the boulder and it slid into the hole, blocking it fully. There followed some brief hammerings.

"Luke!"

He did not answer. I could see his shadow through the translucent stone. After a while it straightened, then dropped from sight. I heard his boots strike the ground outside.

"Rinaldo!"

He did not answer and I heard his retreating footsteps.

I count the days by the lightening and darkening of the blue crystal walls. It has been over a month since my imprisonment, though I do not know how slowly or rapidly time flows here in relation to other shadows. I have paced every hall and chamber of this great cave, but I have found no way out. My Trumps do not work here, not even the Trumps of Doom. My magic is useless to me, limited as it is by the walls the color of Luke's ring. I begin to feel that I might enjoy even the escape of temporary insanity, but my reason refuses to surrender to it, there being too many puzzles to trouble me: Dan Martinez, Meg Devlin, my Lady of the Lake . . . Why? And why did he spend all of that time in my company, Luke, Rinaldo, my enemy? I have to find a way to warn the others. If he succeeds in turning Ghostwheel upon them then Brand's dream—my nightmare of vengeance—will be realized. I see now that I have made many mistakes . . . Forgive me, Julia . . . I will pace the measure of my confinement yet again. Somewhere there must be a gap in the icy blue logic that surrounds me, against which I hurl my mind, my cries, my bitter laughter. Up this hall, down the tunnel. The blue is everywhere. The shadows will not bear me away, for there are no shadows here. I am Merlin the pent, son of Corwin the lost, and my dream of light has been turned against me. I stalk my prison like my own ghost. I cannot let it end this way. Perhaps the next tunnel, or the next . . .

BOOK SEVEN

BLOOD OF AMBER

For Kirby McCauley

REFLECTIONS IN A CRYSTAL CAVE

My life had been relatively peaceful for eight years—not count-ing April thirtieths, when someone invariably tried to kill me. Outside of that, my academic career with its concentration on computer science went well enough and my four years' employment at Grand Design proved a rewarding experience, letting me use what I'd learned in a situation I liked while I labored on a project of my own on the side. I had a good friend in Luke Raynard, who worked for the same company, in sales. I sailed my little boat, I jogged regularly—

It all fell apart this past April 30, just when I thought things were about to come together. My pet project, Ghostwheel, was built; I'd quit my job, packed my gear and was ready to move on to greener shadows. I'd stayed in town this long only because that morbidly fascinating day was near, and this time I intended to discover who was behind the attempts on my life and why.

At breakfast that morning, Luke appeared with a message from my former girlfriend, Julia. Her note said that she wanted to see me again. So I stopped by her place, where I found her dead, apparently killed by the same doglike beast which then attacked me. I succeeded in destroying the creature. A quick search of the apartment before I fled the scene turned up a slim packet of strange playing cards, which I took

699

along with me. They were too much like the magical Tarots of Amber and Chaos for a sorcerer such as myself not to be interested in them.

Yes. I am a sorcerer. I am Merlin, son of Corwin of Amber and Dara of the Courts of Chaos, known to local friends and acquaintances as Merle Corey: bright, charming, witty, athletic. . . . Go read Castiglione and Lord Byron for particulars, as I'm modest, aloof and reticent, as well.

The cards proved to be genuine magical objects, which seemed appropriate once I learned that Julia had been keeping company with an occultist named Victor Melman after we had broken up. A visit to this gentleman's studio resulted in his attempting to kill me in a ritual fashion. I was able to free myself from the constraints of the ceremony and question him somewhat, before local conditions and my enthusiasm resulted in his death. So much for rituals.

I'd learned enough from him to realize that he'd been but a cat's-paw. Someone else had apparently put him up to the sacrifice bit—and it seemed quite possible that the other person was the one responsible for Julia's death and my collection of memorable April thirtieths.

I had small time to reflect upon these matters, though, because I was bitten (yes, bitten) shortly thereafter by an attractive red-haired woman who materialized in Melman's apartment, following my brief telephone conversation with her in which I'd tried to pose as Melman. Her bite paralyzed me, but I was able to depart before it took full effect by employing one of the magical cards I'd found at Julia's place. It bore me into the presence of a sphinx, which permitted me to recover so that it could play that silly riddle game sphinxes love so well because they get to eat you when you lose. All I can say about it is that this particular sphinx was a bad sport.

Anyhow, I returned to the shadow Earth where I'd been making my home to discover that Melman's place had burned down during my absence. I tried phoning Luke, because I wanted to have dinner with him, and learned that he had checked out of his motel, leaving me a message indicating that he had gone to New Mexico on business and telling me where he'd be staying. The desk clerk also gave me a blue-stone ring Luke had left behind, and I took it with me to return when I saw him.

I flew to New Mexico, finally catching up with Luke in Santa Fe. While I waited in the bar for him to get ready for dinner, a man named Dan Martinez questioned me, giving the impression that Luke had proposed some business deal and that he wanted to be assured Luke was reliable and could deliver. After dinner, Luke and I went for a drive in the mountains. Martinez followed us and started shooting as we stood admiring the night. Perhaps he'd decided Luke was not reliable or couldn't deliver. Luke surprised me by drawing a weapon of his own and shooting Martinez. Then an even stranger thing happened. Luke called me by name—my real name, which I'd never told him—and cited my parentage and told me to get into the car and get the hell out. He emphasized his point by placing a shot in the ground near my feet. The matter did not seem open to discussion so I departed. He also told me to destroy those strange Trumps that had saved my life once already. And I'd learned on the way up that he'd known Victor Melman. . . .

I didn't go far. I parked downhill and returned on foot. Luke was gone. So was Martinez's body. Luke did not return to the hotel, that night or the next day, so I checked out and departed. The only person I was sure I could trust, and who actually might have some good advice for me, was Bill Roth. Bill was an attorney who lived in upstate New York, and he had been my father's best friend. I went to visit him, and I told him my story.

Bill got me wondering even more about Luke. Luke, by the way, is a big, smart, red-haired natural athlete of uncanny prowess—and though we'd been friends for many years I knew next to nothing (as Bill pointed out) concerning his background.

A neighboring lad named George Hansen began hanging out near Bill's place, asking strange questions. I received an odd phone call, asking similar questions. Both interrogators seemed curious as to my mother's name. Naturally, I lied. The fact that my mother is a member of the dark aristocracy of the Courts of Chaos was none of their business. But the caller spoke my language, Thari, which made me curious enough to propose a meeting and a trade-off of information that evening in the bar of the local country club.

But my Uncle Random, King of Amber, called me home before that, while Bill and I were out hiking. George Hansen, it turned out, was following us and wanted to come along as we shifted away across the shadows of reality. Tough; he wasn't invited. I took Bill along because I didn't want to leave him with anyone acting that peculiar.

I learned from Random that my Uncle Caine was dead, of an assassin's bullet, and that someone had also tried to kill my Uncle Bleys but only succeeded in wounding him. The funeral service for Caine would be the following day.

I kept my date at the country club that evening, but my mysterious interrogator was nowhere in sight. All was not lost, however, as I made the acquaintance of a pretty lady named Meg Devlin—and, one thing leading to another, I saw her home and we got to know each other a lot better. Then, at a moment when I would have judged her thoughts to be anywhere but there, she asked me my mother's name. So, what the hell, I told her. It did not come to me until later that she might really have been the person I'd gone to the bar to meet.

Our liaison was terminated prematurely by a call from the lobby—from a man purportedly Meg's husband. I did what any gentleman would do. I got the hell out fast.

My Aunt Fiona, who is a sorceress (of a different style from my own), had not approved of my date. And apparently she approved even less of Luke, because she asked me whether I had a picture of him after I'd told her somewhat concerning him. I showed her a photo I had in my wallet, which included Luke in the group. I'd have sworn she recognized him from somewhere, though she wouldn't admit it. But the fact that she and her brother Bleys both disappeared from Amber that night would seem more than coincidental.

The pace of events was accelerated even more after that. A crude attempt at knocking off most of the family with a thrown bomb was made the next day, following Caine's funeral. The would-be assassin escaped. Later, Random was upset at a brief demonstration on my part of the power of the Ghostwheel, my pet project, my hobby, my avocation during those years at Grand Design. Ghostwheel is a—well, it started out as a computer that required a different set of physical laws to operate than those I'd learned in school. It involved what might be called magic. But I found a place where it could be built and operated, and I'd constructed it there. It was still programming itself when I'd left it. It seemed to have gone sentient, and I think it scared Random. He ordered me to go and turn it off. I didn't much like the idea, but I departed.

I was followed in my passage through Shadow; I was harassed, threatened and even attacked. I was rescued from a fire by a strange lady who later died in a lake. I was protected from vicious beasts by a mysterious individual and saved from a bizarre earthquake by the same person—who turned out to be Luke. He accompanied me to the final barrier, for a confrontation with Ghostwheel. My creation was a bit irritated with me and banished us by means of a shadow-storm—a thing it is not fun to be caught in, with or without an umbrella. I delivered us from the vicissitudes by means of one of the Trumps of Doom, as I'd dubbed the odd pasteboards from Julia's apartment.

We wound up outside a blue crystal cave, and Luke took me in. Good old Luke. After seeing to my needs he proceeded to imprison me. When he told me who he was, I realized that it was a resemblance to his father which had upset Fiona when she'd seen his photo. For Luke was the son of Brand, assassin and arch traitor, who had damn near destroyed the kingdom and the rest of the universe alone with it some years back. Fortunately, Caine had killed him before he'd accomplished his designs. Luke, I learned then, was the one who'd killed Caine, to avenge his father. (And it turned out he'd gotten the news of his father's death on an April thirtieth and had had a peculiar way of observing its anniversary over the years.) Like Random, he too had been impressed by my Ghostwheel, and he told me that I was to remain his prisoner, as I might become necessary in his efforts to gain control of the machine, which he felt would be the perfect weapon for destroying the rest of the family.

He departed to pursue the matter, and I quickly discovered that my powers were canceled by some peculiar property of the cave, leaving me with no one to talk to but you, Frakir, and no one here for you to strangle. . . .

Would you care to hear a few bars of "Over the Rainbow"?

ONE

I threw the hilt away after the blade had shattered. The weapon had done me no good against that blue sea of a wall in what I had taken to be its thinnest section. A few small chips of stone lay at my feet. I picked them up and rubbed them together. This was not the way out for me. The only way out seemed to be the way I had come in and it wasn't working.

I walked back to my quarters, meaning that section of the caves where I had cast my sleeping bag. I sat down on the bag, a heavy brown one, uncorked a wine bottle and took a drink. I had worked up a sweat hacking away at the wall.

Frakir stirred upon my wrist then, unwound herself partway and slithered into the palm of my left hand, to coil around the two blue chips I still held. She knotted herself about them, then dropped to hang and swing pendulum-like. I put the bottle aside and watched. The arc of her swing paralleled the lengthwise direction of the tunnel I now called home. The swinging continued for perhaps a full minute. Then she withdrew upward, halting when she came to the back of my hand. She released the chips at the base of my third finger and returned to her normal hidden position about my wrist.

I stared. I raised the flickering oil lamp and studied the stones. Their color. . . .

Yes.

Seen against skin, they were similar in appearance to the stone in that ring of Luke's I had picked up at the New Line Motel some time ago. Coincidence? Or was there a connection? What had my strangling cord been trying to tell me? And where had I seen another such stone?

Luke's key ring. He'd a blue stone on it, mounted on a piece of metal. . . . And where might I have seen another?

The caverns in which I was imprisoned had the power to block the Trumps and my Logrus magic. If Luke carried stones from these walls about with him, there was probably a special reason. What other properties might they possess?

I tried for perhaps an hour to learn something concerning their nature, but they resisted my Logrus probes. Finally, disgusted, I pocketed them, ate some bread and cheese and took another swallow of wine.

Then I rose and made the rounds once more, inspecting my traps. I'd been a prisoner in this place for what seemed at least a month now. I had paced all these tunnels, corridors, grottoes, seeking an exit. None of them proved a way out. There were times when I had run manic through them and bloodied my knuckles upon their cold sides. There were times when I had moved slowly, seeking after cracks and fault lines. I had tried on several occasions to dislodge the boulder that barred the entranceway—to no avail. It was wedged in place, and I couldn't budge it. It seemed that I was in for the duration.

My traps. . . .

They were all as they had been the last time I had checked—deadfalls, boulders nature had left lying about in typical careless fashion, propped high and ready now to be released from their wedging when someone tripped any of the shadow-masked lengths of packing cord I'd removed from crates in the storeroom.

Someone?

Luke, of course. Who else? He was the one who'd imprisoned me. And if he returned—no, *when* he returned—the booby traps would be waiting. He was armed. He would have me at a disadvantage from the overhead position of the entrance if I merely waited for him below. No way. I would not be there. I would make him come in after me—and then—

Vaguely troubled, I returned to my quarters.

Hands behind my head, I lay there and reviewed my plans. The deadfalls could kill a man, and I did not want Luke dead. This had nothing to do with sentiment, though I had thought of Luke as a good friend until fairly recently—up until the time I learned that he had killed my Uncle Caine and seemed intent upon destroying the rest of my relatives in Amber as well. This was because Caine had killed Luke's father—my Uncle Brand—a man whom any of the others would gladly have done in also. Yes, Luke—or Rinaldo, as I now knew him—was my cousin, and he had a reason for engaging in one of our in-family vendettas. Still, going after everybody struck me as a bit intemperate.

But neither consanguinity nor sentiment bade me dismantle my traps. I wanted him alive because there were too many things about the entire situation that I did not understand and might never understand were he to perish without telling me.

Jasra . . . the Trumps of Doom . . . the means by which I had been tracked so easily through Shadow . . . the entire story of Luke's relationship with the painter and mad occultist Victor Melman . . . anything he knew about Julia and her death. . . .

I began again. I dismantled the deadfalls. The new plan was a simple one, and it drew upon something of which I believed Luke had no knowledge.

I moved my sleeping bag to a new position, in the tunnel just outside the chamber whose roof held the blocked entranceway. I shifted some of the food stores there, also. I was determined to remain in its vicinity for as much of the time as possible.

The new trap was a very basic thing: direct and just about unavoidable. Once I'd set it there was nothing to do but wait. Wait, and remember. And plan. I had to warn the others. I had to do something about my Ghostwheel. I needed to find out what Meg Devlin knew. I needed to . . . lots of things.

I waited. I thought of Shadow storms, dreams, strange Trumps and the Lady in the Lake. After a long spell of drifting, my life had become very crowded in a matter of days. Then this long spell of doing nothing. My only consolation was that this time line probably outpaced most of the others that were important to me right now. My month here might only be a day back in Amber, or even less. If I could deliver myself from this place soon, the trails I wished to follow might be relatively fresh.

Later, I put out the lamp and went to sleep. Sufficient light filtered through the crystal lenses of my prison, brightening and waning, for me to distinguish day from night in the outside world, and I kept my small series of routines in accord with its rhythms.

During the next three days I read through Melman's diary again—a thing heavy in allusion and low in useful information—and just about succeeded in convincing myself that the Hooded One, as he referred to his visitor and teacher, had probably been Luke. Except for a few references to androgyny, which puzzled me. References to the sacrifice of the Son of Chaos near the end of the volume were something I could take personally, in light of my present knowledge of Melman's having been set up to destroy me. But if Luke had done it, how to explain his ambiguous behavior on the mountain in New Mexico, when he had advised me to destroy the Trumps of Doom and had driven me away almost as if to protect me from something? And then he had admitted to several of the earlier attempts on my life, but denied the later ones. No reason to do that if he were indeed responsible for all of them. What else might be involved? Who else? And how? There were obviously missing pieces to the puzzle, but I felt as if they were minor, as if the smallest bit of new information and the slightest jiggling of the pattern would suddenly cause everything to fall into place, with the emerging picture to be something I should have seen all along.

I might have guessed that the visitation would be by night. I might have, but I didn't. Had it occurred to me, I would have changed my sleep cycle and been awake and alert. Even though I felt fairly confident of my trap's efficiency, every little edge is important in truly crucial matters.

I was deeply asleep, and the grating of rock upon rock was a distant thing. I stirred but slowly as the sounds continued, and it was several seconds more before the proper circuits closed and I realized what was occurring. Then I sat up, my mind still dusty, and moved into a crouch beside the wall of the chamber nearest the entranceway, knuckling my eyes, brushing back my hair, seeking lost alertness on sleep's receding shore.

The first sounds I heard must have accompanied the removal of the wedges, which apparently had entailed some rocking or tipping of the boulder. The continuing sounds were muffled, echoless—external.

So I ventured a quick glance into the chamber. There was no opened adit, showing stars. The overhead vibrations continued. The rocking sounds were now succeeded by a steady crunching, grating noise. A ball of light with a diffuse halo shone through the translucent stone of the chamber's roof. A lantern, I guessed. Too steady to be a torch. And a torch would be impractical under the circumstances.

A crescent of sky appeared, holding two stars near its nether horn. It widened, and I heard the heavy breathing and grunts of what I took to be two men.

My extremities tingled as I felt additional adrenaline doing its biological trick within me. I hadn't counted on Luke's bringing anyone with him. My foolproof plan might not be proof against this—meaning I was the fool.

The boulder rolled more quickly now, and there was not even time for profanity as my mind raced, focused upon a course of action and assumed its appropriate stance.

I summoned the image of the Logrus and it took shape before me. I rose to my feet, still leaning against the wall, and began moving my arms to correspond with the random-seeming movements of two of the eidolon's limbs.

By the time I achieved a satisfactory conjunction, the sounds from overhead had ceased.

The opening was now clear. Moments later the light was raised and moved toward it.

I stepped into the chamber and extended my hands. As the men, short and dark, came into view above me my original plan was canceled completely. They both carried unsheathed poignards in their right hands. Neither of them was Luke.

I reached out with my Logrus gauntlets and took hold of each of them by the throat. I squeezed until they collapsed within my grip. I squeezed a little longer, then released them.

As they dropped from sight I hooked the high lip of the entrance with my glowing lines of force and drew myself upward with them. As I reached the opening I paused to recover Frakir, who was coiled about its underside. That had been my trap. Luke, or anyone else, would have been passing through a noose to enter, a noose ready to tighten instantly upon anything moving through.

Now, though. . . .

A trail of fire ran down the slope to my right. The fallen lantern had shattered, its spilled fuel become a burning rivulet. The men I had choked lay sprawled at either hand. The boulder that had blocked this opening rested to the left and somewhat to the rear of me. I remained where I was—head and shoulders above the opening, resting on my elbows—with the image of the Logrus dancing between my eyes, the warm tingling of its power lines yet a part of my arms, Frakir moving from my left shoulder down to my biceps.

It had been almost too easy. I couldn't see Luke trusting a couple of lackeys to question, kill or transport me—whichever of these had been their mission. This is why I had not emerged fully, but scanned the nighted environs from my vantage of relative security.

Prudent, for a change. For someone else shared the night with me. It was sufficiently dark, even with the dwindling fire trail, that my ordinary vision did not serve to furnish me this intelligence. But when I summon the Logrus, the mental set that grants me vision of its image permits me to view other nonphysical manifestations as well.

So it was that I detected such a construct beneath a tree to my left, amid shadows where I would not have seen the human figure before which it hovered. And a strange pattern at that, reminiscent of Amber's own; it turned like a slow pinwheel, extending tendrils of smoke-shot yellow light. These drifted toward me across the night and I watched, fascinated, knowing already what I would do when the moment came.

There were four big ones and they came on slowly, probing. When they were within several yards of me they halted, gained slack, then struck like cobras. My hands were together and slightly crossed, Logrus limbs extended. I separated them with a single sweeping motion, tilting them slightly forward as I did so. They struck the yellow tendrils, casting them away to be thrown back upon their pattern. I felt a tingling sensation in my forearms as this occurred. Then, using my right-hand extension as if it were a blade, I struck at the now-wavering pattern as if it were a shield. I heard a short sharp cry as that image grew dim, and I struck again quickly, hauled myself out of my hole and started down the slope, my arm aching.

The image—whatever it had been—faded and was gone. By then, however, I could make out more clearly the figure leaning against the tree trunk. It appeared to be that of a woman, though I could not distinguish her features because of some small object she had raised and now held before her near to eye level. Fearing that it was a weapon, I struck at it with a Logrus extension, hoping to knock it from her hand.

I stumbled then, for there was a recoil which jolted my arm with considerable force. It would seem to have been a potent sorcerous object which I had struck. At least I had the pleasure of seeing the lady sway also. She uttered a short cry, too, but she hung on to the object.

A moment later a faint polychrome shimmering began about her form and I realized what the thing was. I had just directed the force of the Logrus against a Trump. I had to reach her now, if only to find out who she was.

But as I rushed ahead I realized that I could not get to her in time. Unless . . .

I plucked Frakir from my shoulder and cast her along the line of the Logrus force, manipulating her in the proper direction and issuing my commands as she flew.

From my new angle of view and by the faint rainbow halo that now surrounded her I finally saw the lady's face. It was Jasra, who had damn near killed me with a bite back in Melman's apartment. In a moment she would be gone, taking with her my chance of obtaining some answers on which my life might depend.

"Jasra!" I cried, trying to break her concentration.

It didn't work, but Frakir did. My strangling cord, glowing silver now, caught her about the throat, whipping out with a free end to lash tightly about the branch that hung near, to Jasra's left.

The lady began to fade, apparently not realizing that it was too late. She couldn't trump out without decapitating herself.

She learned it quickly. I heard her gurgling cry as she stepped back, grew solid, lost her halo, dropped her Trump and clawed at the cord encircling her throat.

I came up beside her, to lay my hand upon Frakir, who uncoiled one end from the tree limb and rewound it about my wrist.

"Good evening, Jasra," I said, jerking her head back. "Try the poison bite again and you'll need a neck brace. You understand?"

She tried to talk but couldn't. She nodded.

"I'm going to loosen my cord a bit," I said, "so you can answer my questions."

I eased Frakir's grip upon her throat. She began coughing, then, and gave me a look that would have turned sand to glass. Her magical construct had faded completely, so I let the Logrus slip away also.

"Why are you after me?" I asked. "What am I to you?"

"Son of perdition!" she said, and she tried to spit at me but her mouth must have been too dry.

I jerked lightly on Frakir and she coughed again.

"Wrong answer," I said. "Try again."

But she smiled then, her gaze shifting to a point beyond me. I kept the slack out of Frakir and chanced a glance. The air was beginning to shimmer, behind me and to the right, in obvious preparation to someone's trumping in.

I did not feel ready to take on an additional threat at this time, and so I dipped my free hand into my pocket and withdrew a handful of my own Trumps. Flora's was on top. Fine. She'd do.

I pushed my mind toward her, through the feeble light, beyond the face of the card. I felt her distracted attention, followed by a sudden alertness.

Then, *Yes, . . . ?*

"Bring me through! Hurry!" I said.

Is it an emergency? she asked.

"You'd better believe it," I told her.

Uh—okay. Come on.

I had an image of her in bed. It grew clearer, clearer. She extended her hand.

I reached out and took it. I moved forward just as I heard Luke's voice ring out, crying, "Stop!"

I continued on through, dragging Jasra after me. She tried to draw back and succeeded in halting me as I stumbled against the side of the bed. It was then I noted the dark-haired, bearded man regarding me with wide eyes from the bed's farther side.

"Who—? What—?" he began as I smiled bleakly and regained my balance.

Luke's shadowy form came into view beyond my prisoner. He reached forward and seized Jasra's arm, drawing her back away from me. She made a gurgling noise as the movement drew Frakir more tightly about her throat.

Damn! What now?

Flora rose suddenly, her face contorted, the scented lavender sheet falling away as she drove a fist forward with surprising speed.

"You bitch!" she cried. "Remember me?"

The blow fell upon Jasra's jaw, and I barely managed to free Frakir in time to keep from being dragged backward with her into Luke's waiting arms.

Both of them faded, and the shimmer was gone.

The dark-haired guy in the meantime had scrambled out of the bed and was snatching up articles of clothing. Once he had them all in his grasp he did not bother to don any, but simply held them in front of him and backed quickly toward the door.

"Ron! Where are you going?" Flora asked.

"Away!" he answered, and he opened the door and passed through it.

"Hey! Wait!"

"No way!" came the reply from the next room.

"Damn!" she said, glaring at me. "You have a way of messing up a person's life." Then, "Ron! What about dinner?" she called.

"I have to see my analyst," came his voice, followed shortly by the slamming of another door.

"I hope you realize what a beautiful thing you just destroyed," Flora told me.

I sighed. "When did you meet him?" I asked.

She frowned. "Well, yesterday," she replied. "Go ahead and smirk. These things are not always a mere function of time. I could tell right away that it was going to be something special. Trust someone crass like you or your father to cheapen a beautiful—"

"I'm sorry," I said. "Thanks for pulling me through. Of course he'll be back. We just scared the hell out of him. But how could he fail to return once he's known you?"

She smiled. "Yes, you *are* like Corwin," she said. "Crass, but perceptive." She rose and crossed to the closet, took out a lavender robe and donned it.

"What," she said, belting it about her, "was that all about?"

"It's a long story—"

"Then I'd better hear it over lunch. Are you hungry?" she asked.

I grinned.

"It figures. Come on."

She led me out through a French Provincial living room and into a large country kitchen full of tiles and copper. I offered to help her, but she pointed at a chair beside the table and told me to sit.

As she was removing numerous goodies from the refrigerator, I said, "First—"

"Yes?"

"Where are we?"

"San Francisco," she replied.

"Why have you set up housekeeping here?"

"After I finished that business of Random's I decided to stay on. The town looked good to me again."

I snapped my fingers. I'd forgotten she's been sent to determine the ownership of the warehouse where Victor Melman had had his apartment and studio, and where Brutus Storage had a supply of ammo that would fire in Amber.

"So who owned the warehouse?" I asked.

"Brutus Storage," she replied. "Melman rented from them."

"And who owns Brutus Storage?"

"J. B. Rand, Inc."

"Address?"

"An office in Sausalito. It was vacated a couple of months ago."

"Did the people who owned the place have a home address for the renter?"

"Just a post office box. It's been abandoned too."

I nodded. "I'd a feeling it would be something like that," I said. "Now tell me about Jasra. Obviously you know the lady."

She sniffed. "No lady," she said. "A royal whore is what she was when I knew her."

"Where?"

"In Kashfa."

"Where's that?"

"An interesting little shadow kingdom, a bit over the edge of the Golden Circle of those with which Amber has commerce. Shabby barbaric splendor and all that. It's kind of a cultural backwater."

"How is it you know it at all, then?"

She paused a moment in stirring something in a bowl.

"Oh, I used to keep company with a Kashfan nobleman I'd met in a wood one day. He was out hawking and I happened to have twisted my ankle—"

"Uh," I interjected, lest we be diverted by details. "And Jasra?"

"She was consort to the old king Menillan. Had him wrapped around her finger."

"What have you got against her?"

"She stole Jasrick while I was out of town."

"Jasrick?"

"My nobleman. Earl of Kronklef."

"What did His Highness Menillan think of these goings-on?"

"He never knew. He was on his deathbed at the time. Succumbed shortly thereafter. In fact, that's why she really wanted Jasrick. He was chief of the palace guard and his brother was a general. She used them to pull off a coup when Menillan expired. Last I heard, she was queen in Kashfa and she'd ditched Jasrick. Served him proper, I'd say. I think he had his eye on the throne, but she didn't care to share it. She had him and his brother executed for treason of one sort or another. He was really a handsome fellow. . . . Not too bright, though.

"Do the people of Kashfa have any—uh—unusual physical endowments?" I asked.

She smiled. "Well, Jasrick was one hell of a fellow. But I wouldn't use the word 'unusual' to—"

"No, no," I interrupted. "What I meant was some sort of anomaly of the mouth—retractable fangs or a sting or something of that sort."

"Un-uh," she said, and I could not tell whether her heightened coloring came from the heat of the stove. "Nothing like that. They're built along standard lines. Why do you ask?"

"When I told you my story back in Amber I omitted the part where Jasra bit me, and I was barely able to trump out because of some sort of poison she seemed to have injected. It left me numb, paralyzed and very weak for a long while."

She shook her head. "Kashfans can't do anything like that. But then, of course, Jasra is not a Kashfan."

"Oh? Where's she from?"

"I don't know. But she's a foreigner. Some say a slaver brought her in from a distant land. Others say she just wandered in herself one day and caught Menillan's eye. It was rumored she was a sorceress. I don't know."

"I do. That rumor's right."

"Really? Perhaps that's how she got Jasrick?"

I shrugged. "How long ago was your—experience—with her?"

"Thirty or forty years, I'd guess."

"And she is still queen in Kashfa?"

"I don't know. It's been a long time since I've been back that way."

"Is Amber on bad terms with Kashfa?"

She shook her head. "No special terms at all, really. As I said, they're a bit out of the way. Not as accessible as a lot of other places, with nothing greatly desirable for trade."

"No real reason then for her to hate us?"

"No more than for hating anyone else."

Some delightful cooking odors began to fill the room. As I sat there sniffing them and thinking of the long, hot shower I would head for after lunch, Flora said what I had somehow known she would say.

"That man who dragged Jasra back. . . . He looked familiar. Who was he?"

"He was the one I told you about back in Amber," I replied. "Luke. I'm curious whether he reminds you of anyone."

"He seems to," she said, after a pause. "But I can't say just who."

As her back was to me I said, "If you're holding anything that might break or spill if you drop it, please put it down."

I heard something set to rest on the countertop. Then she turned, a puzzled expression on her face.

"Yes?"

"His real name is Rinaldo, and he's Brand's son," I told her. "I was his prisoner for over a month in another shadow. I just now escaped."

"Oh, my," she whispered. Then, "What does he want?"

"Revenge," I answered.

"Against anyone in particular?"

"No. All of us. But Caine, of course, was first."

"I see."

"Please don't burn anything," I said. "I've been looking forward to a good meal for a long time."

She nodded and turned away. After a while she said, "You knew him for a pretty long time. What's he like?"

"He always seemed to be a fairly nice guy. If he's crazy, like his dad, he hid it well."

She uncorked a wine bottle, poured two glasses and brought them over. Then she began serving the meal.

After a few bites she paused with her fork half raised and stared at nothing in particular.

"Who'd have thought the son of a bitch would reproduce?" she remarked.

"Fiona, I think," I told her. "The night before Caine's funeral she asked me whether I had a photo of Luke. When I showed her one I could tell that something was bothering her, but she wouldn't say what."

"And the next day she and Bleys were gone," Flora said. "Yes. Now I think of it, he does look somewhat the way Brand did when he was very young—so long ago. Luke seems bigger and heavier, but there is a resemblance."

She resumed eating.

"By the way, this is very good," I said.

"Oh, thanks." She sighed then. "That means I have to wait till you're finished eating to hear the whole story."

I nodded, because my mouth was full. Let the empire totter. I was starved.

TWO

Showered, trimmed, manicured and garbed in fresh-conjured finery, I got a number out of Information and placed a call to the only Devlin listed in Bill Roth's area. The voice of the woman who answered did not possess the proper timbre, though I still recognized it.

"Meg? Meg Devlin?" I said.

"Yes," came the reply. "Who is this?"

"Merle Corey."

"Who?"

"Merle Corey. We spent an interesting night together some time back—"

"I'm sorry," she said. "There must be some mistake."

"If you can't talk freely now I can call whenever you say. Or you can call me."

"I don't know you," she said, and she hung up.

I stared at the receiver. If her husband were present I'd assumed she'd play it a bit cagey but would at least give some indication that she knew me and would talk another time. I had held off on getting in touch with Random because I'd a feeling he'd summon me back to Amber immediately, and I'd wanted to talk to Meg first. I certainly couldn't spare the time to go and visit her. I could not understand her response, but for now at least I was stuck with it. So I tried the only other thing that occurred to me. I got hold of Information again and obtained the number for Bill's next-door neighbors, the Hansens.

It was answered on the third ring—a woman's voice I recognized as Mrs. Hansen's. I had met her in the past, though I had not seen her on my most recent trip to the area.

"Mrs. Hansen," I began. "It's Merle Corey."

"Oh, Merle. . . .You were just up here a while ago, weren't you?"

"Yes. Couldn't stay long, though. But I did finally get to meet George.

Had several long talks with him. In fact, I'd like to speak with him right now if he's handy."

The silence ran several beats too long before she responded.

"George. . . .Well, George is over at the hospital just now, Merle. Is it something you could tell me?"

"Oh, it's not urgent," I said. "What happened to George?"

"It—it's nothing real bad. He's just an outpatient now, and today's his day to get checked over and pick up some medication. He had a—sort of—breakdown last month. Has a couple days' worth of amnesia, and they can't seem to figure what caused it."

"I'm sorry to hear that."

"Well, the X-rays didn't show any damage—like he'd hit his head or anything. And he seems okay now. They say he'll probably be fine. But they want to keep an eye on him a little longer. That's all." Suddenly, as if struck by inspiration, she asked, "How'd he seem when you were talking with him, anyway?"

I'd seen it coming, so I didn't hesitate.

"He seemed fine when I talked with him," I answered. "But of course I hadn't known him before, so I couldn't tell whether he was acting any different."

"I see what you mean," she said. "Do you want him to call you back when he gets in?"

"No. I'm going to be going out," I said, "and I'm not sure when I'll be getting back. It was nothing really important. I'll get in touch again one of these days."

"Okay, then. I'll tell him you called."

"Thanks. G'bye."

That one I'd almost expected. After Meg. George's behavior had been overtly weird, at the end there. What had bothered me was that he'd seemed to know who I really was and to know about Amber—and he even wanted to follow me through a Trump. It was if he and Meg had both been subjected to some strange manipulation.

Jasra came to mind immediately in this regard. But then she was Luke's ally, it seemed, and Meg had warned me against Luke. Why would she do that if Jasra were controlling her in some fashion? It didn't make sense. Who else did I know who might be capable of causing such phenomena?

Fiona, for one. But then she'd been party to my later return to this shadow from Amber and had even picked me up after my evening with Meg. And she'd seemed just as puzzled about the course of events as I was.

Shit. Life is full of doors that don't open when you knock, equally spaced amid those that open when you don't want them to.

I went back and knocked on the bedroom door, and Flora told me to come in. She was seated before a mirror, applying makeup.

"How'd it go?" she asked.

"Not too well. Totally unsatisfactory, actually." I summarized the results of my calls.

"So what are you going to do now?" she inquired.

"Get in touch with Random," I said, "and bring him up to date. I've got a feeling he'll call me back to hear it all. So I wanted to say good-bye, and thanks for helping me. Sorry if I broke up your romance."

She shrugged, her back still to me, as she studied herself in the mirror.

"Don't worry—"

I did not hear the remainder of her sentence, though she continued talking. My attention was snatched away by what seemed the beginning of a Trump contact. I made myself receptive and waited. The feeling grew stronger but the caller's presence did not become manifest. I turned away from Flora.

"Merle, what is it?" I heard her say then.

I raised one hand to her as the feeling intensified. I seemed to be staring down a long black tunnel with nothing at its farther end.

"I don't know," I said, summoning the Logrus and taking control of one of its limbs. "Ghost? Is that you? Are you ready to talk?" I asked.

There was no reply. I felt a chill as I remained receptive, waiting. I had never experienced anything quite like this before. I'd a strong feeling that if I but moved forward I would be transported somewhere. Was this a challenge? A trap? Whatever, I felt that only a fool would accept such an invitation from the unknown. For all I knew, it might deliver me back to the crystal cave.

"If there is something you want," I said, "you are going to have to make yourself known and ask. I've given up on blind dates."

A sense of presence trickled through, then, but no intimations of identity.

"All right," I said. "I'm not coming and you have no message. The only other thing I can think of is that you're asking to come to me. If that's the case, come ahead."

I extended both of my apparently empty hands, my invisible strangling cord writhing into position in my left, an unseen Logrus death bolt riding my right. It was one of those times when courtesy demanded professional standards.

A soft laughter seemed to echo within the dark tunnel. It was purely a mental projection, however, cold and genderless.

Your offer is, of course, a trick, came to me then. *For you are not a fool. Still, I grant your courage, to address the unknown as you do. You do not know what you face, yet you await it. You even invite it.*

"The offer is still good," I said.

I never thought of you as dangerous.

"What do you want?"

To regard you.

"Why?"

There may come a time when I will face you on different terms.

"What terms?"

I feel that our purposes will be crossed.

"Who are you?"

Again, the laughter.

No. Not now. Not yet. I would merely look upon you, and observe your reactions.

"Well?" Have you seen enough?"

Almost.

"If our purposes are crossed, let the conflict be now," I said. "I'd like to get it out of the way so I can get on with some important business."

I appreciate arrogance. But when the time comes the choice will not be yours.

"I'm willing to wait," I said, as I cautiously extended a Logrus limb out along the dark way.

Nothing. My probe encountered nothing. . . .

I admire your performance. Here!

Something came rushing toward me. My magical extension informed me that it was soft—too soft and loose to do me any real harm—a large, cool mass showing bright colors. . . .

I stood my ground and extended through it—beyond, far, farther—reaching for the source. I encountered something tangible but yielding: a body perhaps, perhaps not; too—too big to snap back in an instant.

Several small items, hard and of sufficiently low mass, recommended themselves to my lightning search. I seized upon one, tore it free of whatever held it and called it to me.

A wordless impulse of startlement reached me at the same time as the rushing mass and the return of my Logrus summoning.

It burst about me like fireworks: flowers, flowers, flowers. Violets, anemones, daffodils, roses. . . . I heard Flora gasp as hundreds of them rained into the room. The contact was broken immediately. I was aware that I held something small and hard in my right hand, and the heady odors of the floral display filled my nostrils.

"What the hell," said Flora, "happened?"

"I'm not sure," I answered, brushing petals from my shirtfront. "You like flowers? You can have these."

"Thanks, but I prefer a less haphazard arrangement," she said, regarding the bright mound that lay at my feet. "Who sent them?"

"A nameless person at the end of a dark tunnel."

"Why?"

"Down payment on a funeral display, maybe. I'm not sure. The tenor of the whole conversation was somewhat threatening."

"I'd appreciate it if you'd help me pick them up before you go."

"Sure," I said.

"There are vases in the kitchen and the bathroom. Come on."

I followed her and collected several. On the way, I studied the object I had brought back from the other end of the sending. It was a blue button mounted in a gold setting, a few navy blue threads still attached. The cut stone bore a curved, four-limbed design. I showed it to Flora and she shook her head.

"It tells me nothing," she said.

I dug into my pocket and produced the chips of stone from the crystal cave. They seemed to match. Frakir stirred slightly when I passed the button near her, then lapsed again in quiescence, as if having given up on warning me about blue stones when I obviously never did anything about them.

"Strange," I said.

"I'd like some roses on the night table," Flora told me, "and a couple of mixed displays on the dresser. You know, no one's ever sent *me* flowers this way. It's a rather intriguing introduction. Are you sure they were for you?"

I growled something anatomical or theological and gathered rosebuds.

Later, as we sat in the kitchen drinking coffee and musing, Flora remarked, "This thing's kind of spooky."

"Yes."

"Maybe you ought to discuss it with Fi after you've talked with Random."

"Maybe."

"Speaking of whom, shouldn't you be calling Random?"

"Maybe."

"What do you mean, 'maybe'? He's got to be warned."

"True. But I've a feeling that being safe won't get any questions answered for me."

"What do you have in mind, Merle?"

"Do you have a car?"

"Yes, I just got it a few days back. Why?"

I withdrew the button and the stones from my pocket, spread them on the table and regarded them again. "It just occurred to me while we were picking up flowers where I might have seen another of these."

"Yes?"

"There is a memory I must have been blocking, because it was very distressing: Julia's appearance when I found her. I seem to recall now that she had on a pendant with a blue stone. Maybe it's just a coincidence, but—"

She nodded. "Could be. But even so, the police probably have it now."

"Oh, I don't want the thing. But it reminds me that I didn't really get to look over her apartment as well as I might have if I hadn't had to leave in a hurry. I want to see it again before I go back to Amber. I'm still puzzled as to how that—creature—got in."

"What if the place has been cleaned out? Or rented again?"

I shrugged. "Only one way to find out."

"Okay, I'll drive you there."

A few minutes later we were in her car and I was giving her directions. It was perhaps a twenty-minute drive beneath a sunny late-afternoon sky, stray clouds passing. I spent much of the time making certain preparations with Logrus forces, and I was ready by the time we reached the proper area.

"Turn here and go around the block," I said, gesturing. "I'll show you where to park if there's a place."

There was, close to the spot where I'd parked on that day.

When we were stopped beside the curb she glanced at me. "Now what? Do we just go up to the place and knock?"

"I'm going to make us invisible," I told her, "and I'm going to keep us that way till we're inside. You'll have to stay close to me in order for us to see each other, though."

She nodded.

"Dworkin did it for me once," she said, "when I was a child. Spied on a lot of people then." She chuckled. "I'd forgotten."

I put the finishing touches to the elaborate spell and laid it upon us, the world growing dimmer beyond the windshield as I did. It was as if I regarded our surroundings through gray sunglasses as we slipped out the passenger side of the car. We walked slowly up to the corner and turned right.

"Is this a hard spell to learn?" she asked me. "It seems a very handy one to know."

"Unfortunately, yes," I said. "Its biggest drawback is that you can't just do it at a moment's notice if you don't have it hanging ready—and I didn't. So, starting from scratch, it takes about twenty minutes to build."

We turned up the walk to the big old house.

"Which floor?" she asked me.

"Top."

We climbed to the front door and found it locked. No doubt they were more particular about such matters these days.

"Break it?" Flora whispered.

"Too noisy," I answered.

I placed my left hand upon the doorknob and gave Frakir a silent command. She unwound two turnings of her coil from about my wrist, coming into view as she moved across the lock plate and slithered into the keyhole. There followed a tightening, a stiffening and several rigid movements.

A soft click meant the bolt was drawn, and I turned the knob and pulled gently. The door opened. Frakir returned to bracelethood and invisibility.

We entered, closing the door quietly behind us. We were not present in the wavery mirror. I led Flora up the stairs.

There were soft voices from one of the rooms on the second floor. That was all. No wind. No excited dogs. And the voices grew still before we reached the third floor.

I saw that the entire door to Julia's apartment had been replaced. It was slightly darker than the other and it sported a bright new lock. I tapped upon it gently and we waited. There was no response, but I knocked again after perhaps half a minute and we awaited again.

No one came. So I tried it. It was locked, but Frakir repeated her trick and I hesitated. My hand shook as I recalled my last visit. I knew her mutilated corpse was no longer lying there. I knew no killer beast was waiting to attack me. Yet the memory held me for several seconds.

"What's the matter?" Flora whispered.

"Nothing," I said, and I pushed the door open.

The place had been partly furnished, as I recalled. The part that had come with it remained—the sofa and end tables, several chairs, a larger table—but all Julia's own stuff was gone. There was a new rug on the floor, and the floor itself had been buffed recently. It did not appear that the place had been re-let, as there were no personal items of any sort about.

We entered and I closed the door, dropping the spell that had cloaked us as I began my circuit through the rooms. The place brightened perceptibly as our magic veils faded.

"I don't think you're going to find anything," Flora said. "I can smell wax and disinfectant and paint. . . ."

I nodded.

"The more mundane possibilities seem to be excluded," I said. "But there is something else I want to try."

I calmed my mind and called up the Logrus-seeing. If there were any remaining traces of a magical working, I hoped I could spot them in this fashion. I wandered slowly then, through the living room, regarding everything from every possible angle. Flora moved off, conducting her own investigation, which consisted mainly in looking under everything. The room flickered slightly for me as I scanned at those wavelengths where such a manifestation was most likely to be apparent—at least, that was the best way to describe the process in this shadow.

Nothing, large or small, escaped my scrutiny. But nothing was revealed to it. After long minutes, I moved into the bedroom.

Flora must have heard my sudden intake of breath, because she was into the room and at my side in seconds, and staring at the chest of drawers before which I stood.

"Something in it?" she inquired, reaching forward, then withdrawing her hand.

"No. Behind it," I said.

The chest of drawers had been moved in the course of purging the apartment. It used to occupy a space several feet farther to the right. That which I now saw was visible to its left and above it, with more of it obviously blocked to my sight. I took hold of the thing and pushed it back to the right, to the position it had formerly occupied.

"I still don't see anything," Flora said.

I reached out and caught hold of her hand, extending the Logrus force so that she, too, saw what I saw.

"Why"—she raised her other hand and traced the faint rectangular outline on the wall—"it looks like a . . . doorway," she said.

I studied it—a dim line of faded fire. The thing was obviously sealed and had been for some time. Eventually it would fade completely and be gone.

"It *is* a doorway," I answered.

She pulled me back into the other room to regard the opposite side of the wall.

"Nothing here," she observed. "It doesn't go through."

"Now you've got the idea," I said. "It goes somewhere else."

"Where?"

"Wherever the thing that killed Julia came from."

"Can you open it?"

"I am prepared to stand in front of it for as long as I have to," I told her, "and try."

I returned to the other room and studied it once again.

"Merlin," she said, as I released her hand and raised mine before me, "don't you think this is the point where you should get in touch with Random, tell him exactly what has been happening and perhaps have Gérard standing next to you if you succeed in opening that door?"

"I probably should," I agreed, "but I'm not going to."

"Why not?"

"Because he might tell me not to."

"He might be right, too."

I lowered my hands and turned toward her. "I have to admit you have a point," I said. "Random has to be told everything, and I've probably put it off too long already. So here is what I would like you to do: Go back to the car and wait. Give me an hour. If I'm not out by then, get in touch with Random, tell him everything I told you and tell him about this, too."

"I don't know," she said. "If you don't show, Random's going to be mad at me."

"Just tell him I insisted and there was nothing you could do. Which is actually the case, if you stop to think about it."

She pursed her lips. "I don't like leaving you—though I'm not anxious to stay either. Care to take along a hand grenade?"

She raised her purse and began to open it.

"No. Thanks. Why do you have it, anyway?"

She smiled. "I always carry them in this shadow. They sometimes come in handy. But okay, I'll go wait."

She kissed me lightly on the cheek and turned away.

"And try to get hold of Fiona," I said, "if I don't show. Tell her the whole story, too. She might have a different angle on this."

She nodded and departed. I waited until I heard the door close, then focused my attention fully upon the bright rectangle. Its outline seemed fairly uniform, with only a few slightly thicker, brighter areas and a few finer, dimmer ones. I traced the lines slowly with the palm of my right hand at a height of about an inch above the wall's surface. I felt a small prickling, a heatlike sensation as I did this. Predictably, it was greater above the brighter areas. I took this as an indication that the seal was slightly less perfect in these spots. Very well. I would soon discover whether the thing could be forced, and these would be my points of attack.

I twisted my hands deeper into the Logrus until I wore the limbs I desired as fine-fingered gauntlets, stronger than metals, more sensitive than tongues in the places of their power. I moved my right hand to the point nearest it, on a level with my hip. I felt the pulse of an old spell when I touched that spot of greater brightness. I narrowed my extension as I pushed, making it finer and finer until it slipped through. The pulsing then became a steady thing. I repeated the exercise on a higher area to my left.

I stood there, feeling the force that had sealed it, my fine filament extensions throbbing within its matrix. I tried moving them, first upward, then down. The right one slid a little farther than the left, in both directions, before a tightness and resistance halted it. I summoned more force from the body of the Logrus, which swam specterlike within and before me, and I poured this energy into the gauntlets, the pattern of the Logrus changing form again as I did so. When I tried once more to move it, the right one slid downward for perhaps a foot before the throbbing trapped it; when I pushed it upward it rose nearly to the top. I tried again on the left. It moved all the way to the top, but it only passed perhaps six inches below the starting point when I drew it downward.

I breathed deeply and felt myself beginning to perspire. I pumped more power into the gauntlets and forced their extensions farther downward. The resistance was even greater there, and the throbbing passed up my arms and into the very center of my being. I paused and rested, then raised the force to an even higher level of intensity. The Logrus writhed again and I pushed both hands all the way to the floor, then knelt there panting before I began working my way along the bottom. The portal was obviously meant never to be opened again. There was no artistry for this, only brute force.

When my forces met in the middle, I withdrew and regarded the work. To the right, to the left and along the bottom, the fine red lines had now become broad fiery ribbons. I could feel their pulsation across the distance that separated us.

I stood and raised my arms. I began to work along the top, starting at the corners, moving inward. It was easier than it had been earlier. The forces from the opened areas seemed to add a certain pressure, and my hands just flowed to the middle. When they met I seemed to hear something like a soft sighing sound. I dropped them and considered my work. The entire outline flared now. But more than that. It seemed almost as if the bright line were flowing, around and around. . . .

I stood there for several minutes, regrouping, relaxing, settling. Working up my nerve. All I knew was that the door would lead to a different shadow. That could mean anything. When I opened it something could, I suppose, leap out and attack me. But then, it had been sealed for some time. More probably any trap would be of a different sort. Most likely, I would open it and nothing would happen. I would then have a choice of merely looking around from where I stood or entering. And there probably wouldn't be very much to see, just standing there, looking. . . .

So I extended my Logrus members once again, taking hold of the door at either side, and I pushed. A yielding occurred on the side to my right, so I released my hold on the left. I continued my pressure on the right and the whole thing suddenly swung inward and away. . . .

I was looking down a pearly tunnel, which appeared to widen after a few paces. Beyond that was a ripple effect, as of distant heat patterns above the road on a hot summer day. Patches of redness and indeterminate dark shapes swam within it. I waited for perhaps half a minute, but nothing approached.

I prepared Frakir for trouble. I maintained my Logrus connection. I advanced, extending probes before me. I passed within.

A sudden change in the pressure gradient at my back caused me to cast a quick glance in that direction. The doorway had closed and dwindled, now appearing to me in the distance as a tiny red cube. My several steps could, of course, have borne me a great distance also, should the rules of this space so operate.

I continued, and a hot wind flowed toward me, engulfed me, stayed with me. The sides of my passageway receded, the prospect before me continued to shimmer and dance, and my pace became more labored, as if I were suddenly walking uphill. I heard something like a grunt from beyond the place where my vision misbehaved, and my left Logrus probe encountered something that it jolted slightly. Frakir began to throb simultaneous with my sensing an aura of menace through the probe. I sighed. I hadn't expected this was going to be easy. If I'd been running the show I wouldn't have let things go with just sealing the door.

"All right, asshole! Hold it right there!" a voice boomed from ahead.

I continued to trudge forward.

It came again. "I said halt!"

Things began to swim into place as I advanced, and suddenly there were rough walls to my right and left and a roof overhead, narrowing, converging—

A huge rotund figure barred my way, looking like a purple Buddha with bat ears. Details resolved themselves as I drew nearer: protruding fangs, yellow eyes that seemed to be lidless, long red claws on its great hands and feet. It was seated in the middle of the tunnel and made no effort to rise. It wore no clothing, but its great swollen belly rested upon its knees, concealing its sex. Its voice had been gruffly masculine, however, and its odor generically foul.

"Hi," I said. "Nice day, wasn't it?"

It growled and the temperature seemed to rise slightly. Frakir had grown frantic and I calmed her mentally.

The creature leaned forward and with one bright nail inscribed a smoking line in the stone of the floor. I halted before it.

"Cross that line, sorcerer, and you've had it," it said.

"Why?" I asked.

"Because I said so."

"If you're collecting tolls," I suggested, "name the price."

It shook its head. "You can't buy your way past me."

"Uh—what makes you think I'm a sorcerer?"

It opened the dingy cavern of its face, displaying even more lurking teeth than I'd suspected, and it did something like the rattling of a tin sheet way down deep in back.

"I felt that little probe of yours," it said. "It's a sorcerer's trick. Besides, nobody but a sorcerer could have gotten to the place where you're standing."

"You do not seem to possess a great deal of respect for the profession."

"I eat sorcerers," it told me.

I made a face, thinking back over some of the old farts I've known in the business.

"To each, his, or her or its own, I guess," I told it. "So what's the deal? A passage is no good unless you can get through it. How do I get by here?"

"You don't."

"Not even if I answer a riddle?"

"That won't do it for me," it said. But a small gleam came into its eye. "Just for the hell of it, though, what's green and red and goes round and round and round?" it asked.

"You know the sphinx!"

"Shit!" it said. "You've heard it."

I shrugged. "I get around."

"Not here, you don't."

I studied it. It had to have some special defense against magical attacks if it were set to stop sorcerers. As for physical defense it was fairly imposing. I wondered how fast it was. Could I just dive past and start running? I decided that I did not wish to experiment along that line.

"I really do have to get through," I tried. "It's an emergency."

"Tough."

"Look, what do you get out of this, anyway? It seems like a pretty crummy job, sitting here in the middle of a tunnel."

"I love my work. I was created for it."

"How come you let the sphinx come and go?"

"Magical beings don't count."

"Hm."

"And don't try to tell me you're really a magical being, and then pull some sorcerous illusion. I can see right through that stuff."

"I believe you. What's your name, anyhow?"

It snorted. "You can call me Scrof, for conversational purposes. Yourself?"

"Call me Corey."

"Okay, Corey. I don't mind sitting here bullshitting with you, because that's covered by the rules. It's allowed. You've got three choices and one of them would be real stupid. You can turn around and go back the way you came and be none the worse for wear. You can also camp right where you are for as long as you like and I won't lift a finger so long as you behave. The dumb thing to do would be to cross this line I've drawn. Then I'd terminate you. This is the Threshold and I am the Dweller on it. I don't let anybody get by."

"I appreciate your making it clear."

"It's part of the job. So what'll it be?"

I raised my hands and the lines of force twisted like knives at each fingertip. Frakir dangled from my wrist and began to swing in an elaborate pattern.

Scrof smiled. "I not only eat sorcerers, I eat their magic, too. Only a being torn from the primal Chaos can make that claim. So come ahead, if you think you can face that."

"Chaos, eh? Torn from the primal Chaos?"

"Yep. There's not much can stand against it."

"Except maybe a Lord of Chaos," I replied, as I shifted my awareness to various points within my body. Rough work. The faster you do it the more painful it is.

Again, the rattling of the tin sheet.

"You know what the odds are against a Chaos Lord coming this far to go two out of three with a Dweller?" Scrof said.

My arms began to lengthen and I felt my shirt tear across my back as I leaned forward. The bones in my face shifted about and my chest expanded and expanded. . . .

"One out of one should be enough," I replied, when the transformation was complete.

"Shit," Scrof said as I crossed the line.

THREE

I stood just within the mouth of the cave for some time, my left shoulder hurting and my right leg sore also. If I could get the pain under control before I retransformed myself there was a chance that much of it would fade during the anatomical reshuffling. The process itself would probably leave me pretty tired, however. It takes a lot of energy, and switching twice this close together could be somewhat prostrating, following my bout with the Dweller. So I rested within the cave into which the pearly tunnel had eventually debouched, and I regarded the prospect before me.

Far down and to my left was a bright blue and very troubled body of water. White-crested waves expired in kamikaze attacks on the gray rocks of the shore; a strong wind scattered their spray and a piece of rainbow hung within the mist.

Before me and below me was a pocked, cracked and steaming land which trembled periodically, as it swept for well over a mile toward the high dark walls of an amazingly huge and complex structure, which I immediately christened Gormenghast. It was a hodgepodge of architectural styles, bigger even than the palace at Amber and somber as all hell. Also, it was under attack.

There were quite a few troops in the field before the walls, most of them in a distant nonscorched area of more normal terrain and some vegetation, though the grasses were well trampled and many trees shattered. The besiegers were equipped with scaling ladders and a battering ram, but the ram was idle at the moment and the ladders were on the ground. What appeared to have been an entire village of outbuildings smoldered darkly at the wall's base. Numerous sprawled figures were, I assumed, casualties.

Moving my gaze even farther to the right, I encountered an area of brilliant whiteness beyond that great citadel. It looked to be the projecting edge of a massive glacier, and gusts of snow or ice crystals were whipped about it in a fashion similar to the sea mists far to my left.

The wind seemed a constant traveler through these parts. I heard it cry out high above me. When I finally stepped outside to look upward, I found that I was only about halfway up a massive stone hillside—or low mountainside, depending on how one regards such matters—and the whining note of the wind came down even more loudly from those broken heights. There was also a *thump* at my back, and when I turned I could no longer locate the cave mouth. My journey along the route from the fiery door had been completed once I exited the cave, and its spell had apparently clamped down and closed the way immediately. I supposed that I could locate the outline upon the steep wall if I wanted to, but at the moment I had no such desire. I made a little pile of stones before it, and then I looked about again, studying details.

A narrow trail curved off to my right and back among some standing stones. I headed in that direction. I smelled smoke. Whether it was from the battle site or the area of vulcanism below I could not tell. The sky was a patchwork of cloud and light above me. When I halted between two of the stones and turned to regard the scene below once again, I saw that the attackers had formed themselves into new groups and that the ladders were being borne toward the walls. I also saw what looked like a tornado rise on the far side of the citadel and begin a slow counterclockwise movement about the walls. If it continued on its route it would eventually reach the attackers. Neat trick. Fortunately, it was their problem and not mine.

I worked my way back into a stony declivity and settled myself upon a low ledge. I began the troublesome shape-shifting work, which I paced to take me half an hour or so. Changing from something nominally human to something rare and strange—perhaps monstrous to some, perhaps frightening—and then back again is a concept some may find repugnant. They shouldn't. We all of us do it every day in many different ways, don't we?

When the transformation was completed I lay back, breathing deeply, and listened to the wind. I was sheltered from its force by the stones and only its song came down to me. I felt vibrations from distant tremors of the earth and chose to take them as a gentle message, soothing. . . . My clothes were in tatters, and for the moment I was too tired to summon a fresh outfit. My shoulder seemed to have lost its pain, and there was only the slightest twinge in my leg, fading, fading. . . . I closed my eyes for a few moments.

Okay, I'd made it through, and I'd a strong feeling that the answer to the matter of Julia's killer lay in the besieged citadel below. Offhand, I didn't see any easy way into the place at the moment, to make inquiry. But that was not the only way I might proceed. I decided to wait where I was, resting, until it grew dark—that is, if things here proceeded in a normal dark-light fashion. Then I'd slip downstairs, kidnap one of the besiegers and question him. Yes. And if it didn't get dark? Then I'd think of something else. Right now, though, just drifting felt best. . . .

For how long I dozed, I was uncertain. What roused me was the clicking of pebbles, from somewhere off to the right. I was instantly alert, though I didn't stir. There was no effort at stealth, and the pattern of approaching sounds—mainly slapping footfalls, as of someone wearing loose sandals—convinced me that only a single individual was moving in this direction. I tensed and relaxed my muscles and drew a few deep breaths.

A very hairy man emerged from between two of the stones to my right. He was about five and a half feet in height, very dirty, and he wore a dark animal skin about his loins; also, he had on a pair of sandals. He stared at me for several seconds before displaying the yellow irregularities of his smile.

"Hello. Are you injured?" he asked, in a debased form of Thari that I did not recall ever having heard before.

I stretched to make sure and then stood. "No," I replied. "Why do you ask that?"

The smile persisted. "I thought maybe you'd had enough of the fighting below and decided to call it quits."

"Oh, I see. No, it's not exactly like that. . . .

He nodded and stepped forward. "Dave's my name. What's yours?"

"Merle," I said, clasping his grimy hand.

"Not to worry, Merle," he told me. "I wouldn't turn in anybody who decided to take a walk from a war, unless maybe there was a reward—and there ain't on this one. Did it myself years ago and never regretted it. Mine was goin' the same way this one seems to be goin', and I had sense enough to get out. No army's ever taken that place down there, and I don't think one ever will."

"What place is it?"

He cocked his head and squinted, then shrugged. "Keep of the Four Worlds," he said. "Didn't the recruiter tell you anything?"

I sighed. "Nope," I said.

"Wouldn't have any smokin' stuff on you, would you?"

"No," I answered, having used all my pipe tobacco back in the crystal cave. "Sorry."

I moved past him to a point where I could look downward from between the stones. I wanted another look at the Keep of the Four Worlds. After all, it was the answer to a riddle as well as the subject of numerous cryptic references in Melman's diary. Fresh bodies were scattered all over before its walls, as if cast about by the whirlwind, which was now circling back toward the point whence it had risen. But a small party of besiegers had apparently made it to the top of the wall despite this. And a fresh party had formed below and was headed for the ladders. One of its members bore a banner I could not place, but which seemed vaguely familiar—black and green, with what might be a couple of heraldic beasts having a go at each other. Two ladders were still in place, and I could see some fierce fighting going on behind the battlements.

"Some of the attackers seem to have gotten in," I said.

Dave hurried up beside me and stared. I immediately moved upwind.

"You're right," he acknowledged. "Now, that's a first. If they can get that damn gate open and let the others in they might even have a chance. Never thought I'd live to see it."

"How long ago was it," I asked, "when the army you were with attacked the place?"

"Must be eight, nine—maybe ten years," he muttered. "Those guys must be pretty good."

"What's it all about?" I asked.

He turned and studied me. "You really don't know?"

"Just got here," I said.

"Hungry? Thirsty?"

"As a matter of fact, yes."

"Come on, then." He took hold of my arm and steered me back between the stones, then led me along a narrow trail.

"Where are we headed?" I asked.

"I live nearby. I make it a point to feed deserters, for old times' sake. I'll make an exception for you."

"Thanks."

The trail split after a short while, and he took the right-hand branch, which involved some climbing. Eventually this led us to a series of rocky shelves, the last of which receded for a considerable distance. There were a number of clefts at its rear, into one of which he ducked. I followed him a short distance along it, and he halted before a low cave mouth. A horrible odor of putrefaction drifted forth, and I could hear the buzzing of flies within.

"This is my place," he announced. "I'd invite you in, but it's a little—uh—"

"That's okay," I said. "I'll wait."

He ducked inside, and I realized that my appetite was rapidly vanishing, especially when it came to anything he might have stored in that place.

Moments later he emerged, a duffel bag slung over his shoulder. "Got some good stuff in here," he announced.

I started walking back along the cleft. "Hey! Where are you headed?"

"Air," I said. "I'm gong back out on the shelf. It's a bit close back there."

"Oh. Okay," he said, and he fell into step behind me.

He had two unopened bottles of wine, several canteens of water, a fresh-looking loaf of bread, some tinned meat, a few firm apples and an uncut head of cheese in the bag, I discovered, after we'd seated ourselves on a ledge out in the open and he'd gestured for me to open the thing and serve myself. Having prudently remained upwind, I took some water and an apple for openers.

"Place has a stormy history," he stated, withdrawing a small knife from his girdle and cutting himself a piece of cheese. "I'm not sure who built it or how long it's been there."

When I saw that he was about to dig the cork out of a wine bottle with the knife I halted him and essayed a small and surreptitious Logrus sending. The response was quick, and I passed him the corkscrew immediately. He handed me the entire bottle after he'd uncorked it and opened the other for himself. For reasons involving public health I was grateful, though I wasn't in the mood for that much wine.

"That's what I call being prepared," he said, studying the corkscrew. "I've needed one of these for some time. . . ."

"Keep it," I told him. "Tell me more about that place. Who lives there? How did you come to be part of an invading army? Who's attacking it now?"

He nodded and took a swig of wine.

"The earliest boss of the place that I know of was a wizard named Sharu Garrul. The queen of my country departed suddenly and came here." He paused and stared off into the distance for a time, then snorted. "Politics! I don't even know what the given reason for the visit was at the time. I'd never heard of the damned place in those days. Anyhow, she stayed a long while and people began to wonder: Was she a prisoner? Was she working out an alliance? Was she having an affair? I gather she sent back messages periodi-cally, but they were the usual bland crap that didn't say anything—unless of course there were also secret communications folks like me wouldn't have heard about. She had a pretty good-sized retinue with her, too, with an honor guard that was not just for show. These guys were very tough veterans, even though they dressed pretty. So it was kind of debatable what was going on at that point."

"A question, if I may," I said. "What was your king's part in all this? You didn't mention him, and it would seem he ought to know—"

"Dead," he announced. "She made a lovely widow, and there was a lot of pressure on her to remarry. But she just took a succession of lovers and played the different factions off against each other. Usually her men were military leaders or powerful nobles, or both. She'd left her son in charge when she made this trip, though."

"Oh, so there was a prince old enough to sit in control?"

"Yes. In fact, he started the damned war. He raised troops and wasn't happy with the muster, so he got in touch with a childhood friend, a man generally considered an outlaw, but who commanded a large band of merce-naries. Name of Dalt—"

"Stop!" I said.

My mind raced as I recalled a story Gérard had once told me, about a strange man named Dalt who had led a private army against Amber, unusually effectively. Benedict himself had to be called to oppose him. The man's forces had been defeated at the foot of Kolvir, and Dalt himself severely wounded. Though no one ever saw his body, it was assumed he would have died of such injuries. But there was more.

"Your home," I said. "You never named it. Where are you from, Dave?"

"A place called Kashfa," he replied.

"And Jasra was your queen?"

"You've heard of us. Where're you from?"

"San Francisco," I said.

He shook his head. "Don't know the place."

"Who does? Listen, how good are your eyes?"

"What do you mean?"

"A little while ago, when we looked down on the fighting, could you make out the flag the attackers were carrying?"

"Eyes ain't what they used to be," he said.

"It was green and black with some sort of animals on it."

He whistled. "A lion rending a unicorn, I'll bet. Sounds like Dalt's."

"What is the significance of that device?"

"He hates them Amberites, is what it means. Even went up against them once."

I tasted the wine. Not bad.

The same man, then. . . .

"You know why he hates them?" I asked.

"I understand they killed his mother," he said. "Had something to do with border wars. They get real complicated. I don't know the details."

I pried open a tin of meat, broke off some bread and made myself a sandwich.

"Please go ahead with your story," I said.

"Where was I?"

"The prince got hold of Dalt because he was concerned about his mother, and he needed more troops in a hurry."

"That's right, and I was picked up for Kashfan service about that time — foot soldier. The prince and Dalt led us through dark ways till we came to that place below. Then we did just what them guys downstairs were doing."

"And what happened?"

He laughed. "Went bad for us at first," he said. "I think it's somehow easy for whoever's in charge down there to control the elements—like that twister you saw a while ago. We got an earthquake and a blizzard and lightning. But we pressed on to the walls anyhow. Saw my brother scalded to death with boiling oil. That's when I decided I'd had enough. I started running and climbed on up here. Nobody chased me, so I waited around and watched. Probably shouldn't have, but I didn't know how things would go. More of the same, I'd figgered. But I was wrong, and it was too late to go back. They'd have whacked off my head or some other valuable parts if I did."

"What happened?"

"I got the impression that the attack forced Jasra's hand. She'd apparently been planning to do away with Sharu Garrul all along and take over the place herself. I think she'd been setting him up, gaining his confidence before she struck. I believe she was a little afraid of the old man. But when her army appeared on the doorstep she had to move, even though she wasn't ready. She took him on in a sorcerous duel while her guard held his men at bay. She won, though I gather she was somewhat injured. Mad as hell, too, at her son—for bringing in an army without her ordering it. Anyway, her guard opened the gates to them, and she took over the Keep. That's what I meant about no army taking the place. That one was an inside job."

"How did you learn all this?"

"Like I said, when deserters head this way I feed 'em and get the news."

"You gave me the impression that there have been other attempts to take the place. These would have had to be after she'd taken over."

He nodded and took another drink of wine.

"Yup. There was apparently a coup back in Kashfa, with both her and her kid away—a noble named Kasman, brother of one of her dead lovers, a fellow named Jasrick. This Kasman took over, and he wanted her and the prince out of the way. Must've attacked this place half a dozen times. Never could get in. Finally resigned himself to a standoff, I think. She sent her son off somewhere later, maybe to raise another army and try to win back her throne. I don't know. That was long ago."

"What about Dalt?"

"They paid him off with some loot from the Keep—there was apparently a lot of good stuff in there—and he took his troops and went back to wherever he hangs out."

I took another sip of wine myself and cut off a piece of the cheese. "How come you've stayed around all these years? It seems like a hard life."

He nodded. "Truth of it is, I don't know the way home. Those were strange trails they brought us in on. I thought I knew where they were, but when I went lookin' I couldn't never find 'em. I suppose I could have just taken off, but then I'd probably get lost more than ever. Besides, I know I can make it out here. A few weeks and those outbuildings will be rebuilt and the peasants will move back in, no matter who wins. And they think I'm a holy man, prayin' up here and meditatin'. Any time I wander down that way they come out for a blessin' and give me enough food and drink to hold me for a long while."

"Are you a holy man?" I asked.

"I just pretend," he said. "Makes them happy and keeps me fed. Don't go tellin' that, though."

"Of course not. They wouldn't believe me, anyway."

He laughed again. "You're right."

I got to my feet and walked back along the trail a little way, so that I could see the Keep once again. The ladders were on the ground, and I beheld even more scattered dead. I saw no signs of the struggle within.

"Is the gate open yet?" Dave called.

"No. I don't think the ones who got in were sufficient to the task."

"Is that green and black banner anywhere in sight?"

"I can't see it anywhere."

He rose and came over, carrying both bottles. He passed me mine and we both took a drink. The ground troops began to fall back from the area before the wall.

"Think they're giving up or re-forming for another rush?" he asked me.

"Can't say yet," I told him.

"Whichever it is, there should be a lot of good loot down there tonight. Stick around and you'll have all you can carry."

"I'm curious," I said, "why Dalt would be attacking again, if he's on good terms with the queen and her son."

"I think it's just the son," he said, "and he's gone. The old lady's supposed to be a real bitch. And after all, the guy *is* a mercenary. Maybe Kasman hired him to go after her."

"Maybe she's not even in there," I said, having no idea how this time stream ran, but thinking of my recent encounter with the lady. The image of it, though, caused a strange train of thought. "What's the prince's name, anyway?" I asked.

"Rinaldo," he answered. "He's a big red-haired guy."

"She's his mother!" I said involuntarily.

He laughed. "That's how you get to be a prince," he said. "Have the queen be your mother."

But then, that would mean. . . .

"Brand!" I said. Then, "Brand of Amber."

He nodded. "You've heard the story."

"Not really. Just that much," I replied. "Tell it to me."

"Well, she snared herself an Amberite—the prince called Brand," he said. "Rumor had it they met over some magical operation and it was love at first blood. She wanted to keep him, and I've heard it said they actually were married in a secret ceremony. But he wasn't interested in the throne of Kashfa, though he was the only one she might have been willing to see on it. He traveled a lot, was away for long stretches of time. I've heard it said that he was responsible for the Days of Darkness years ago, and that he died in a great battle between Chaos and Amber at that time, at the hands of his kinsmen."

"Yes," I said, and Dave gave me a strange look, half puzzlement, half scrutiny. "Tell me more about Rinaldo," I said quickly.

"Not much to say," he replied. "She bore him, and I've heard she taught him something of her Arts. He didn't know his father all that well, Brand being away so much. Kind of a wild kid. Ran away any number of times and hung out with a brand of outlaws—"

"Dalt's people?" I asked.

He nodded. "Rode with them, they say—even though his mother'd placed bounties on many of their heads at that time."

"Wait a minute. You say that she really hated these outlaws and mercenaries—"

" 'Hate' may be the wrong word. She'd never bothered about them before, but when her son got friendly with them I think she just got mad."

"She thought they were a bad influence?"

"No, I think she didn't like it that he'd run to them and they'd take him in whenever he had a falling out with her."

"Yet you say that she saw Dalt paid off out of the Keep's treasure and allowed him to ride away, after they'd forced her hand against Sharu Garrul."

"Yup. Big argument at the time, too, between Rinaldo and his mom, over just that point. And she finally gave in. That's the way I heard it from a couple of guys who were there. One of the few times the boy actually stood up to her and won, they say. In fact, that's why the guys deserted. She ordered all witnesses to their argument executed, they told me. They were the only ones managed to get away."

"Tough lady."

"Yup."

We walked on back to the area where we'd been seated and ate some more food. The song of the wind rose in pitch and a storm began out at sea. I asked Dave about big dog-like creatures, and he told me that packs of them would probably be feasting on the battle's victims tonight. They were native to the area.

"We divide the spoils," he said. "I want rations, the wine and any valuables. They just want the dead."

"What good are the valuables to you?" I said.

He looked suddenly apprehensive, as if I were considering the possibility of robbing him.

"Oh, it don't really amount to much. It's just that I've always been a thrifty person," he said, "and I make it sound more important than it is."

"You never can tell," he added.

"That's true," I agreed.

"How'd you get here anyway, Merle?" he asked quickly, as if to get my mind off the subject of his loot.

"Walked," I said.

"That don't sound right. Nobody comes here willingly."

"I didn't know I was coming here. Don't think I'll be staying long either," I said, as I saw him take up the small knife and begin toying with it. "No sense going below and begging after hospitality at a time like this."

"That's true," he remarked.

Was the old coot actually thinking of attacking me, to protect his cache? He could be more than a little mad by now, living up here alone in his stinking cave, pretending to be a saint.

"Would you be interested in returning to Kashfa," I said, "if I could set you on the right trail?"

He gave me a crafty look. "You don't know that much about Kashfa," he said, "or you wouldn't have been asking me all those questions. Now you say you can send me home?"

"I take it you're not interested?"

He sighed. "Not really, not anymore. It's too late now. This is my home. I enjoy being a hermit."

I shrugged. "Well, thanks for feeding me, and thanks for all the news." I got to my feet.

"Where are you going now?" he asked.

"I think I'll look around some, then head for home." I backed away from that small lunatic glow in his eyes.

He raised the knife, his grip tightened on it. Then he lowered it and cut another piece of cheese.

"Here, you can take some of the cheese with you if you want," he said.

"No, that's okay. Thanks."

"Just trying to save you some money. Have a good trip."

"Right. Take it easy."

I heard his chuckling all the way back to the trail. Then the wind drowned it.

I spent the next several hours reconnoitering. I moved around in the hills. I descended into the steaming, quaking lands. I walked along the seashore. I passed through the rear of the normal-seeming area and crossed the neck of the ice field. In all of this, I stayed as far from the Keep itself as possible. I wanted to fix the place as firmly in mind as I could, so that I could find my way back through Shadow rather than crossing a threshold the hard way. I saw several packs of wild dogs on my journey, but they were more intent upon the battle's corpses than anything that moved.

There were oddly inscribed boundary stones at each topographical border, and I found myself wondering whether they were mapmakers' aids or something more. Finally, I wrestled one from the burning land over about fifteen feet into a region of ice and snow. I was knocked down almost immediately by a heavy tremor; I was able to scramble away in time, however, from the opening of a crevice and the spewing of geysers. The hot area claimed that small slice of the cold land in less than half an hour. Fortunately, I moved quickly to get out of the way of any further turmoil, and I observed the balance of these phenomena from a distance. But there was more to come.

I crouched back among the rocks, having reached the foothills of the range from which I had started by crossing through a section of the volcanic area. There, I rested and watched for a time while that small segment of terrain rearranged itself and the wind smeared smoke and steam across the land. Rocks bounced and rolled; dark carrion birds went out of their way to avoid what had to be some interesting thermals.

Then I beheld a movement which I first assumed to be seismic in origin. The boundary stone I had shifted rose slightly and jogged to the side. A moment later, however, and it was elevated even farther, appearing almost as if it had been levitated slightly above the ground. Then it drifted across the blasted area, moving in a straight line at a uniform speed, until—as nearly as I could judge—it had recovered its earlier position. And there it settled. Moments later the turmoil recommenced, and this time it was a jolting shrug of the ice sheet, jerking back, reclaiming the invaded area.

I called up my Logrus sight, and was able to make out a dark glow surrounding the stone. This was connected by a long, straight, steady stream of light of the same general hue, extending from a high rear tower of the Keep. Fascinating. I would have given a lot for a view of the interior of that place.

Then, born with a sigh, maturing to a whistle, a whirlwind rose from the disputed area, growing, graying, swaying, to advance suddenly toward me like the swung proboscis of some cloudy, sky-high elephant. I turned and climbed higher, weaving my way amid rocks and around the shoulders of hillsides. The thing pursued, as if there were an intelligence guiding its movements.

And the way it hung together while traversing that irregular terrain indicated an artificial nature, which in this place most likely meant magic.

It takes some time to determine an appropriate magical defense, and even more time to bring it into being. Unfortunately, I was only about a minute ahead of the posse, and that margin was probably dwindling.

When I spotted the long narrow crevice beyond the next turning, jagged as a limb of lightning, I paused only an instant to peer into its depth, and then I was descending, my tattered garments lashed about me, the windy tower a rumbling presence at my back. . . .

The way ran deep and so did I, following its jogs, its twistings. The rumble rose to a roar, and I coughed at the cloud of dust that engulfed me. A hailstorm of gravel assailed me. I threw myself flat then, about eight feet below the surface of the land, and covered my head with my arms, for I believed that the thing was about to pass directly above me.

I muttered warding spells as I lay there, despite their minuscule parrying effect at this distance against such an energy-intensive manifestation.

I did not jump up when the silence came. It could be that the tornado's driver had withdrawn support and collapsed the funnel on seeing that I might be out of reach. It could also be the eye of the storm, with more to come, by and by.

While I did not jump up, I did look up, because I hate to miss educational opportunities.

And there was the face—or, rather, the mask—at the center of the storm, regarding me. It was a projection, of course, larger than life and not fully substantial. The head was cowled; the mask was full and cobalt bright and strongly reminiscent of the sort worn by goalies in ice hockey; there were two vertical breathing slits from which pale smoke emerged—a touch too theatrical for my taste; a lower series of random punctures was designed to give the impression of a sardonically lopsided mouth. A distorted sound of laughter came down to me from it.

"Aren't you overdoing it a bit?" I said, coming up into a crouch and raising the Logrus between us. "For a kid on Halloween, yes. But we're all adults here, aren't we? A simple domino would probably serve—"

"You moved my stone!" it said.

"I've a certain academic interest in such matters," I offered, easing myself into the extensions. "Nothing to get upset about. Is that you, Jasra? I—"

The rumbling began again, softly at first, then building once more.

"I'll make a deal," I said. "You call off the storm, and I'll promise not to move any more markers."

Again, the laughter as the storm sounds rose. "Too late," came the reply. "Too late for you. Unless you're a lot tougher than you look."

What the hell! The battle is not always to the strong, and nice guys tend to win because they're the ones who get to write their memoirs. I'd been fiddling with the Logrus projections against the insubstantiality of the mask until I found the link, the opening leading back to its source. I stabbed through it—a thing on the order of an electrical discharge—at whatever lay behind.

There came a scream. The mask collapsed, the storm collapsed, and I was on my feet and running again. When whatever I'd hit recovered I did not want to be in the same place I had been because that place might be subject to sudden disintegration.

I had a choice of cutting off into Shadow or seeking an even faster path of retreat. If a sorcerer were to tag me as I started shadow-slipping I could be followed. So I dug out my Trumps and shuffled forth Random's. I rounded the next turning of the way then, and I would have had to halt there anyway, I saw, because it narrowed to a width impossible for me to pass. I raised the card and reached with my mind.

There followed contact, almost immediately. But even as the images solidified I felt a probe. I was certain that it was my blue-masked nemesis seeking me once more.

But Random came clear, seated before a drum set, sticks in hand. He set aside the drumsticks and rose.

"It's about time," he said, and he extended his hand.

Even as I reached I felt something rushing toward me. As our fingers touched and I stepped forward, they burst about me like a giant wave.

I passed through into the music room in Amber. Random had opened his mouth to speak again when the cascade of flowers fell upon us.

Brushing violets from his shirtfront, he regarded me. "I'd rather you said it with words," he remarked.

FOUR

Portrait of the artists, purposes crossed, temperature falling. . . .

Sunny afternoon, and walking through small park following light lunch, us, prolonged silences and monosyllabic responses to conversational sallies indicating all's not well at either end of communication's taut line. Upon bench, seated then, facing flower beds, souls catch up with bodies, words with thoughts. . . .

"Okay, Merle. What's the score?" she asks.

"I don't know what game you're talking about, Julia."

"Don't get cute. All I want's a straight answer."

"What's the question?"

"That place you took me, from the beach, that night. . . . Where was it?"

"It was—sort of a dream."

"Bullshit!" She turns sideways to face me fully, and I must meet those flashing eyes without my face giving anything away. "I've been back there, several times, looking for the way we took. There is no cave. There's nothing! What happened to it? What's going on?"

"Maybe the tide came in and—"

"Merle! What kind of an idiot do you take me for? That walk we took isn't on the maps. Nobody around here's ever heard of anything like those places. It was geographically impossible. The times of day and the seasons kept shifting. The only explanation is supernatural or paranormal—whatever you want to call it. What happened? You owe me an answer and you know it. What happened? Where were you?"

I look away, past my feet, past the flowers.

"I—can't say."

"Why not?"

"I—" What could I say? It was not only that telling her of Shadow would disturb, perhaps destroy, her view of reality. At the heart of my problem lay the realization that it would also require telling her how I knew this, which would mean telling her who I am, where I am from, what I am—and I was afraid to give her this knowledge. I told myself that it would end our relationship as surely as telling her nothing would; and if it must end either way, I would rather we parted without her possessing this knowledge. Later, much later, I was to see this for the rationalization it was; my real reason for denying her the answers she desired was that I was not ready to trust her, or anyone, so close to me as I really am. Had I known her longer, better—another year, say—I might have answered her. I don't know. We never used the word "love," though it must have run through her mind on occasion, as it did through mine. It was, I suppose, that I didn't love her enough to trust her, and then it was too late. So, "I can't tell you," were my words.

"You have some power that you will not share."

"Call it that, then."

"I would do whatever you say, promise whatever you want promised."

"There is a reason, Julia."

She is on her feet, arms akimbo. "And you won't even share that."

I shake my head.

"It must be a lonely world you inhabit, magician, if even those who love you are barred from it."

At that moment it seems she is simply trying her last trick for getting an answer from me. I screw my resolve yet tighter. "I didn't say that."

"You didn't have to. It is your silence that tells me. If you know the road to Hell too, why not head that way? Good-bye!"

"Julia. Don't. . . ."

She chooses not to hear me.

Still life with flowers. . . .

Awakening. Night. Autumn wind beyond my window. Dreams. Blood of life without the body . . . swirling. . . .

I swung my feet out of bed and sat rubbing my eyes, my temples. It had been sunny and afternoon when I'd finished telling Random my story, and he'd sent me to get some shuteye afterward. I was suffering from shadow lag and felt completely turned around at the moment, though I was not certain exactly what the hour might be.

I stretched, got up, repaired myself and donned fresh clothing. I knew that I would not be able to get back to sleep; also, I was feeling hungry. I took a warm cloak with me as I departed my quarters. I felt like going out rather than raiding the larder. I was in the mood for some walking, and I hadn't been outside the palace and into town in—years, I guessed.

I made my way downstairs, then cut through a few chambers and a big hall, connecting up at the rear with a corridor I could have followed all the way from the stair if I'd cared to, but then I'd have missed a couple of tapestries I'd wanted to say hello to: an idyllic sylvan scene, with a couple making out following a picnic lunch; and a hunting scene of dogs and men pursuing a magnificent stag, which looks as if it might yet have a chance of getting away, if it will dare a stupendous leap that lies ahead. . . .

I passed through and made my way up the corridor to a postern, where a bored-looking guard named Jordy suddenly strove to seem attentive when he heard me coming. I stopped to pass the time with him and learned that he didn't get off duty till midnight, which was almost two hours away.

"I'm heading down into town," I said. "Where's a good place to eat this time of night?"

"What've you got a taste for?"

"Seafood," I decided.

"Well, Fiddler's Green—about two thirds of the way down the Main Concourse—is very good for seafood. It's a fancy place . . ."

I shook my head. "I don't want a fancy place," I said.

"The Net's still supposed to be good—down near the corner of the Smiths and Ironmongers Street. It's not real fancy."

"But you wouldn't go there yourself?"

"Used to," he replied. "But a number of the nobles and big merchants discovered it recently. I'd feel kind of uncomfortable there these days. It's gotten sort of clubby."

"Hell! I don't want conversation or atmosphere. I just want some nice fresh fish. Where would you go for the best?"

"Well, it's a long walk. But if you go all the way down to the docks, at the base of the cove, it's a little to the west. . . . But maybe you shouldn't. It's kind of late, and that isn't the best neighborhood after dark."

"Is that by any chance Death Alley?"

"They do sometimes call it that, sir, as bodies are occasionally found there of a morning. Maybe you'd better go to the Net, seeing as you're alone."

"Gérard took me through that area once, during the day. I think I could find my way around it, all right. What's the name of the place?"

"Uh, Bloody Bill's."

"Thanks. I'll say hi to Bill for you."

He shook his head. "Can't. It was renamed after the manner of his demise. His cousin Andy runs it now."

"Oh. What was it called before?"

"Bloody Sam's."

Well, what the hell. I bade him a good night and set out walking. I took the path to the short stairway down the slope, which led to the walkway through a garden and over to a side gate, where another guard let me out. It was a cool night with the breezed smells of autumn burning down the world about me. I drew it into my lungs and sighed it out again as I headed for the Main Concourse, the distant, almost-forgotten, slow clopping sounds of hoofs on cobbles coming to me like something out of dream or memory. The night was moonless but filled with stars, and the concourse below flanked by globes of phosphorescent liquid set atop high poles, long-tailed mountain moths darting about them.

When I reached the avenue I strolled. A few closed carriages rolled by as I passed along the way. An old man walking a tiny green dragon on a chain leash touched his hat to me as I passed and said, "Good evening." He had seen the direction from which I had come, though I was sure he did not recognize me. My face is not that well-known about town. My spirits loosened a bit after a time, and I felt a spring come into my step.

Random had not been as angry as I'd thought he might. Since Ghostwheel had not been stirring up any trouble, he had not charged me to go after it immediately and try again for a shutdown. He had merely told me to think about it and come up with the best course of action we might pursue. And Flora had been in touch earlier and told him who Luke was—a thing that seemed to have eased his mind somehow, knowing the identity of the enemy. Though I'd asked, he would not tell me what plans he might have formulated for dealing with him. He did allude to the recent dispatch of an agent to Kashfa, though, to obtain certain unspecified information. The thing that seemed to trouble him the most, actually, was the possibility that the outlaw Dalt was still to be numbered among the living.

"Something about that man . . ." Random began.

"What?" I'd asked.

"For one thing, I saw Benedict run him through. That generally tends to terminate a person's career."

"Tough son of a bitch," I said. "Or damn lucky. Or both."

"If he is the same man, he's the son of the Desacratrix. You've heard of her?"

"Deela," I said. "Wasn't that her name? Some sort of religious fanatic? Militant?"

Random nodded. "She caused a lot of trouble out around the periphery of the Golden Circle—mostly near Begma. You ever been there?"

"No."

"Well, Begma's the nearest point on the circle to Kashfa, which is what makes your story particularly interesting. She'd raided a lot in Begma and they couldn't handle her by themselves. They finally reminded us of the protection alliance we have with almost all the Circle kingdoms—and Dad decided to go in personally and teach her a lesson. She'd burned one Unicorn shrine too many. He took a small force, defeated her troops, took her prisoner and hanged a bunch of her men. She escaped, though, and a couple of years later when she was all but forgotten she came back with a fresh force and started the same crap all over. Begma screamed again, but Dad was busy. He sent Bleys in with a large force. There were several inconclusive engagements—they were raiders, not a regular army—but Bleys finally cornered them and wiped them out. She died that day, leading her troops."

"And Dalt's her son?"

"That's the story, and it makes some sense, because he did everything he could to harass us for a long time. He was after revenge, pure and simple, for his mother's death. Finally, he put together a fairly impressive fighting force and tried to raid Amber. Got a lot farther than you'd think, right up to Kolvir. But Benedict was waiting, his pet regiment at his back. Benedict cut them into pieces, and it sure looked as if he'd wounded Dalt mortally. A few of his men were able to carry him off the field, so we never saw the body. But hell! Who cared?"

"And you think he could be the same guy who was Luke's friend when he was a kid—and later?"

"Well, the age is about right and he seems to hail from the same general area. I suppose it's possible."

I mused as I strolled. Jasra hadn't really liked the guy, according to the hermit. So what was his part in things now? Too many unknowns, I decided. It would take knowledge rather than reasoning to answer that one. So let it ride and go enjoy dinner. . . .

I continued on down the concourse. Near to its farther end I heard laughter and saw where some hardy drinkers still occupied a few tables at a sidewalk café. One of them was Droppa, but he didn't spot me and I passed on. I did not feel like being amused. I turned onto Weavers Street, which would take me over to where West Vine wound its way up from the harbor district. A tall masked lady in a silver cloak hurried by and into a waiting carriage. She glanced back once and smiled beneath her domino. I was certain that I didn't know her, and I found myself wishing I did. It was a pretty smile. Then a gust of wind brought me the smokesmell of someone's fireplace and rattled a few dead leaves as it went by. I wondered where my father was.

Down along the street then and left on West Vine. . . . Narrower here than the concourse, but still wide; a greater distance between lights, but still sufficiently illuminated for night travelers. A pair of horsemen clopped slowly by, singing a song I did not recognize. Something large and dark passed overhead a bit later, to settle upon a roof across the street. A few scratching noises came from that direction, then silence. I followed a curve to the right, then another to the left, entering what I knew to be a long series of switchbacks. My way grew gradually steeper. A harbor breeze came up at some point a little later, bearing me my first salt sea smells of the evening. A short while afterward—two turns, I believe—and I had a view of the sea itself, far below: bobbing lights on a sparkling, swelling slickness over black, pent by the curving line of bright dots, Harbor Street. To the east the sky was powdered slightly. A hint of horizon appeared at the edge of the world. I thought I caught a glimpse of the distant light of Cabra minutes later, then lost it again with another turning of the way.

A puddle of light like spilled milk pulsed on the street to my right, outlining a ghostly gridwork of cobbles at its farthest downhill reach; the stippled pole above it might advertise some spectral barbershop; the cracked globe at its top still showed a faint phosphorescence, skull-on-a-stick style, reminding me of a game we used to play as kids back in the Courts. A few lighted footprints proceeded downhill away from it, faint, fainter, gone. I passed on, and across the distance I heard the cries of sea birds. Autumn's smells were submerged in the ocean's. The powdered light beyond my left shoulder rose higher above the water, drifted forward across the wrinkled face of the deep. Soon. . . .

My appetite grew as I walked. Ahead, I beheld another dark-cloaked stroller on the other side of the street, a slight glowing at the edges of the boots. I thought of the fish I would soon be eating and hurried, breasting the figure and passing. A cat in a doorway paused at licking her asshole to watch me go by, hind leg held vertical the while. Another horseman passed, this one headed up the hill. I heard the fringes of an argument between a man and a woman from upstairs in one of the darkened buildings. Another turning and the shoulder of the moon came into sight like some magnificent beast surfacing, shrugging droplets from bright bathic grottoes. . . .

Ten minutes later I had reached the port district and found my way over to Harbor Road, its lack of all but occasional globes supplemented by window spillage, a number of buckets of burning pitch and the glow of the now-risen moon. The smells of salt and sea-wrack were more intense here, the road more cluttered with trash, the passersby more colorfully garbed and noisier than any on the concourse, unless you counted Droppa. I made my way to the rear of the cove, where the sounds of the sea came to me more strongly: the rushing, building advances of waves, then their crashing and splashing out beyond the breakwater; the gentler falls and slopping withdrawals nearer at hand; the creaking of ships, the rattling of chains, the bumping of some smaller vessel at pier or moor post. I wondered where the Starburst, my old sailboat, might be now.

I followed the curve of the road over to the western shore of the harbor. A pair of rats chased a black cat across my path as I wandered briefly, checking several sidestreets for the one I sought. The smells of barf as well as solid and liquid human waste mingled with other odors here, and I heard the cries, crashes and thuds of a struggle from somewhere nearby, leading me to believe that I was in the proper neighborhood. From somewhere distant a buoy bell rattled; from somewhere nearby I heard an almost bored-sounding string of curses preceding a pair of sailors who rounded the nearest corner to my right, reeling, staggered on past me, grinning, and broke into song moments later, receding. I advanced and checked the sign on that corner. SEABREEZE LANE, it read.

That was it, the stretch commonly called Death Alley. I turned there. It was just a street like any other. I didn't see any corpses or even collapsed drunks for the first fifty paces, though a man in a doorway tried to sell me a dagger and a mustachioed stock character offered to fix me up with something young and tight. I declined both, and learned from the latter that I wasn't all that far from Bloody Bill's. I walked on. My occasional glances showed me three dark-cloaked figures far to the rear which, I supposed, could be following me; I had seen them back on Harbor Road too. Also, they might not. In that I was not feeling particularly paranoid, I reflected that they could be anybody going anywhere and decided to ignore them. Nothing happened. They kept to themselves, and when I finally located Bloody Bill's and entered they passed on by, crossing the street and going into a small bistro a little farther down along the way.

I turned and regarded Bill's. The bar was to my right, tables to my left, suspicious-looking stains on the floor. A board on the wall suggested I give my order at the bar and say where I was sitting. The day's catch was chalked beneath this.

So I went over and waited, collecting glances, until a heavy-set man with gray and amazingly shaggy brows came over and asked what I wanted. I told him the blue sea scut and pointed at an empty table to the rear. He nodded and shouted my order back through a hole in the wall, then asked me whether I wanted a bottle of Bayle's Piss to go with it. I did, he got it for me, and a glass, uncorked it and passed it over. I paid up there, headed back to the table I had chosen and seated myself with my back to the wall.

Oil flames flickered through dirty chimneys in brackets all about the place. Three men—two young, one middle-aged—played cards at the corner table in the front and passed a bottle. An older man sat alone at the table to my left, eating. He had a nasty-looking scar running both above and below his left eye, and there was a long wicked blade about six inches out of its scabbard resting on the chair to his right. He, too, had his back to the wall. Men with musical instruments rested at another table: between numbers, I guessed. I poured some of the yellow wine into my glass and took a sip: a distinctive taste I remembered from across the years. It was okay for quaffing. Baron Bayle owned a number of vineyards about thirty miles to the east. He was the official vintner to the Court, and his red wines were generally excellent. He was less successful with the whites, though, and often wound up dumping a lot of second-rate stuff onto the local market. It bore his emblem and a picture of a dog—he liked dogs—so it was sometimes called Dog Piss and sometimes Bayle's Piss, depending on who you talked to. Dog lovers sometimes take offense at the former appellation.

About the time my food arrived I noticed that two young men near the front of the bar were glancing in my direction more than occasionally, exchanging a few indistinguishable words and laughing and smiling a lot. I ignored them and turned my attention to my meal. A little later the scarred man at the next table said softly, without leaning or looking toward me, his lips barely moving, "Free advice. I think those two guys at the bar noticed you're not wearing a blade, and they've marked you for trouble."

"Thanks," I said.

Well. . . , I was not overly concerned about my ability to deal with them, but given a choice I'd rather avoid the occasion entirely. If all that it required was a visible blade, that was easily remedied.

A moment's meditation and the Logrus danced before me. Shortly thereafter, I was reaching through it in search of the proper weapon—neither too long nor too heavy, properly balanced, with a comfortable grip—with a wide dark belt and scabbard. It took me close to three minutes, partly because I was so fussy about it, I suppose—but hell, if prudence required one, I wanted comfort—and partly because it is harder reaching through Shadow in the vicinity of Amber than it is almost anywhere else.

When it came into my hands I sighed and mopped my brow. Then I brought it up slowly from beneath the table, belt and all, drew it about half a foot from its scabbard, to follow a good example, and placed it on the seat to my right. The two guys at the bar caught the performance and I grinned back at them. They had a quick consultation, and this time they weren't laughing. I poured myself a fresh glass of wine and drank it off at a single draught. Then I returned to my fish, about which Jordy had been right. The food here was very good.

"Neat trick, that," the man at the next table said. "I don't suppose it's an easy one to learn?"

"Nope."

"It figures. Most good things aren't, or everybody'd do 'em. They may still go after you, though, seeing as you're alone. Depends on how much they drink and how reckless they get. You worried?"

"Nope."

"Didn't think so. But they'll hit someone tonight."

"How can you tell?"

He looked at me for the first time and grinned a nasty grin. "They're generic, like wind-up toys. See you around."

He tossed a coin onto the table, stood, buckled on his sword belt, picked up a dark, feathered hat and headed for the door.

"Take care."

I nodded.

" 'Night."

As he passed out of the place the two guys began whispering again, this time glancing after him rather than at me. Some decision reached, they rose and departed quickly. For a moment I was tempted to follow, but something restrained me. A little later, I heard the sounds of a scuffle from up the street. Not too long after that, a figure appeared in the doorway, hovered a moment, then fell forward. It was one of the two drinkers. His throat had been cut.

Andy shook his head and dispatched his waiter to inform the local constabulary. Then he took hold of the body by the heels and dragged it outside, so as not to impede the flow of customers.

Later, when I was ordering another fish, I asked Andy about the occurrence. He smiled grimly.

"It is not good to mess with an emissary of the Crown," he said. "They tend to pick them tough."

"That guy who was sitting next to me works for Random?"

He studied my face, then nodded. "Old John worked for Oberon, too. Whenever he passes through he eats here."

"I wonder what sort of mission he was on?"

He shrugged. "Who knows? But he paid me in Kashfan currency, and I know he ain't from Kashfa."

As I worked on my second platter I pondered that one. Whatever it was that Random had wanted from Kashfa was probably on its way to the castle right now, unless of course it was unavailable. It would almost have to concern Luke and Jasra. I wondered what it was, and of what benefit it might be.

I sat there for a long while after that, thinking, and the place was a lot less noisy than it had been for most of an hour, even when the musicians began a fresh set. Had it been John the guys had been watching all along, with both of us misinterpreting their gazes as directed toward me? Or had they simply decided to go after the first person who left alone? I realized from these reflections that I was beginning to think like an Amberite again—seeking plots everywhere—and I hadn't been back all that long. Something in the atmosphere, I guessed. Probably it was a good thing that my mind was moving along these lines once more, since I was involved in so much already and it seemed an investment in self-preservation.

I finished my glass of wine and left the bottle on the table with a few drinks still in it. It occurred to me that I shouldn't be fogging my senses any further, all things considered. I rose and buckled on my sword belt.

As I passed the bar Andy nodded. "If you run into anyone from the palace," he said softly, "you might mention that I didn't know that was going to happen."

"You knew them?"

"Yeah. Sailors. Their ship came in a couple of days ago. They've been in trouble here before. Blow their pay fast, then look for some more the quick way."

"Do you think they might be professionals at—removing people?"

"Because of John's being what he is, you mean? No. They got caught once too often, mainly for being stupid. Sooner or later they were bound to run into someone who knew what he was doing and end up this way. I don't know anyone who'd hire them for something serious."

"Oh, he got the other one too?"

"Yep. Up the street a way. So you might mention that they just happened to be in the wrong place at the wrong time."

I stared at him and he winked.

"I saw you down here with Gérard, several years ago. I make it a point never to forget a face that might be worth remembering."

I nodded. "Thanks. You serve a good meal."

Outside, it was cooler than it had been earlier. The moon hung higher and the sea was noisier. The street was deserted in my immediate vicinity. Loud music poured from one of the places back toward Harbor Street, with accompanying sounds of laughter. I glanced within as I passed it and saw where a tired-looking woman on a small stage appeared to be giving herself a gynecological examination. From somewhere nearby I heard a sound of breaking glass. A drunk reeled toward me from between two buildings, one hand outstretched. I walked on. The wind sighed amid masts in the harbor, and I found myself wishing Luke were at my side—like in the old days, before things got complicated—someone of my own age and cast of mind to talk to. All my relatives here had too many centuries of cynicism or wisdom for us to see things and feel them in much the same way.

Ten paces later, Frakir pulsed wildly upon my wrist. In that there was no one anywhere near me at the moment, I did not even draw my new blade. I threw myself flat, then rolled toward the shadows to my right. Simultaneous with this, I heard a *thunk* from the side of the building across the street. The first glance I could spare in that direction showed me an arrow protruding from a wall, its height and position such that had I not taken the dive it might well have hit me. Its angle also indicated that I had just cast myself in the direction from which it had been discharged.

I raised myself enough to draw my blade and looked to my right. There were no opened windows or doors in the immediately adjacent building, a darkened place, its front wall only about six feet away now. But there was a gap between it and the buildings on either side, and geometry told me that the arrow had come from the open area ahead of me.

I rolled again, bringing myself up beside the low, roofed porch which ran the full width of the place. I scrambled up onto it before I rose fully. Staying near the wall I advanced, cursing the slowness silence demanded. I was almost near enough to the opening to be able to rush any archer who might step out, before he could release another arrow. The possibility of his circling and catching me from behind did pass through my mind, though, and I flattened myself against the wall, blade extended forward, and cast quick glances behind as I moved. Frakir writhed into my left hand and hung ready.

If I reached the corner and no one emerged I was uncertain what I would do next. The situation seemed to demand a magical offensive. But unless the spells were already hung—and I'd been remiss in this—one can seldom spare the attention it requires in life-and-death situations. I halted. I controlled my breathing. I listened. . . .

He was being careful, but I heard faint sounds of movement from the roof, coming forward. But this did not preclude another, or even several, being around the corner. I had no idea how many persons might be involved in this ambush, though it was beginning to strike me as a little too sophisticated for a simple robbery. In such a case, I doubted there would be only one. And their forces might be split several ways. I held my position, my mind racing. When the attack came, it would be concerted, I was certain of that. I imagined an archer around the corner, arrow nocked, waiting for a signal. The one on the roof would most likely have a blade. I guessed at blades for any others, too. . . .

I pushed aside any questions as to who might be after me and how they had located me here—if it were indeed me, personally, whom they were after.

Such considerations made no difference at this point. I would be just as dead were they random thugs seeking my purse as I would be if they were assassins, should they succeed in the present enterprise..

Again. A sound from above. Someone was directly overhead. Any moment now. . . .

With a shuffling noise and a great cry a man leaped from the roof to the street before me. His shout was apparently the signal to the archer, also, for there was immediate movement at the corner of the building, accompanied by the sounds of rapid footfalls from the building's other corner, to my rear.

Before his feet even struck the ground I had cast Frakir at the man from the roof with a command to kill. And I was rushing the archer before he had even rounded the corner completely, my blade already swinging. My cut passed through his bow, his arm and his lower abdomen. On the minus side, there was a man with a drawn blade right behind him and someone was running toward me along the porch.

I placed my left foot upon the folding archer's chest and propelled him backward into the man behind him. I used the recoiling momentum from the push to spin, my blade sweeping through a wide, wild parry which I had to adjust immediately to stop a head cut from the man who had crossed the porch. As I riposted to his chest and had my own cut parried I became peripherally aware of the one from the roof kneeling now in the street and tearing at his throat, in evidence that Frakir was doing her job.

The man somewhere to my rear made my back feel very exposed. I had to do something fast or his blade would be in me within seconds. So. . . .

Rather than riposting, I pretended to stumble, actually gathering my weight, positioning myself.

He lunged, cutting downward. I sprang to the side and thrust with a twisting movement of my body. If he were able to adjust the angle of that cut as I moved I would feel it in seconds. Dangerous, but I couldn't see any other choice.

Even as my blade entered his chest I did not know whether he had connected with me. Not that it mattered now. Either he had or he hadn't. I had to keep moving until I stopped or was stopped.

I used my blade like a lever, turning him as I continued my counterclockwise movement, him at its center, hoping to position him between that fourth man and myself.

The maneuver was partly successful. It was too late to interpose my skewered and sagging adversary fully, but in time at least to cause a small collision between him and the other. Time enough, I hoped, as the other stumbled to the side, stepping down from the porch. All I needed do now was wrench my blade free, and it would be one-on-one.

I yanked at it. . . .

Damn, damn, damn. The thing was wedged into bone and wouldn't come free. And the other man had regained his footing. I kept turning the body to keep it between us while with my left hand I tried to free my most recent adversary's own blade from his still-clenched right fist.

Ditto the damns. It was locked in a death grip, his fingers like metal cables about the haft.

The man in the street gave me a nasty smile while moving his blade about, looking for an opening. It was then that I caught the flash of the blue-stone ring he wore, answering my question as to whether it was me in particular who had been sought, here, tonight.

I bent my knees as I moved and positioned my hands low upon the dead man's body.

Situations such as this are, for me, sometimes videotaped into memory — a total absence of conscious thought and a great mass of instant perceptions — timeless, yet only subject to serial review when the mind indulges in later replay.

There were cries from various places along the street, from within and without. I could hear people rushing in my direction. There was blood on the boards all around me, and I recall cautioning myself not to slip on it. I could see the archer and his bow, both of them broken, on the ground past the far edge of the porch. The garroted swordsman was sprawled in the street, off to the right of the man who menaced me now. The body I steered and positioned had become dead weight. To my small relief I saw that no more attackers had emerged from anywhere to join the final man I faced. And that man was sidestepping and feinting, getting ready to make his rush.

Okay. Time.

I propelled the corpse toward my attacker with all my strength and did not wait to observe the result of my action. The risk I was about to take granted me no time for such indulgence.

I dove into the street and did a shoulder roll past the supine figure, who had dropped his blade in trying to use his hands against Frakir. As I moved I heard the sound of some impact followed by a grunt from above and somewhere to the rear, indicating that I had been at least partly on target when I'd pushed the dead man toward the other. How effectively this would serve me still remained to be seen.

My right hand snaked out as I went by, catching the hilt of the fallen man's blade. I rolled to my feet, facing back in the direction from which I had come, extending the blade, crossing my legs and springing backward. . . .

Barely in time. He was upon me with a strong series of attacks, and I backed away fast, parrying wildly. He was still smiling, but my first riposte slowed his advance and my second one stopped it.

I settled and stood my ground. He was strong, but I could see that I was faster. There were people near at hand now, watching us. A few shouts of useless advice reached me. To which of us it was directed, I could not say. It didn't matter, though. He stood for a few moments as I began to press my attack, and then he began to give ground, slowly, and I was sure that I could take him.

I wanted him alive, though, which would make things a little more difficult. That blue-stoned ring flashing and retreating before me held a mystery to which he had the answer, and I needed that answer. Therefore, I had to keep pressing him, to wear him down. . . .

I tried turning him, a little at a time, as subtly as I could. I was hoping to press him into stumbling over the dead man to his rear. It almost worked, too.

When his rear foot fell upon the arm of the sprawled man, he shifted his weight forward to maintain his balance. In one of those instants of inspiration on which one must act immediately without thinking, he turned this movement into a rush, seeing that my blade was out of line in preparation for the heavy rush I was about to give him as he stumbled. Wrong of me to have anticipated that much, I guess.

He beat my blade cross-body with a heavy swing, throwing his own weapon way out of line also and bringing us *corps á corps*, with him turning in the same direction I was facing and unfortunately providing him with the opportunity to drive his left fist into my right kidney with the full force of his momentum.

Immediately, his left foot shot out to trip me, and the impact of the blow as we came together showed me that he was going to succeed. The best thing I could manage was to catch hold of my cloak with my left hand, spinning it out and dragging it back, entangling both our blades as we fell, while I tried hard to turn on the way down, so as to land on top of him. I did not succeed in falling upon him. We came down side by side, still facing each other, and the guard of someone's blade—my own, I think—hit me hard in the ribs on my left side.

My right hand was caught beneath me and my left was still tangled in my cloak. His left was free, though, and high. He clawed at my face with it, and I bit his hand but couldn't hold it. In the meantime, I finally managed to drag my own left hand free and I thrust it into his face. He turned his head away, tried to knee me and hit my hip, then thrust stiff fingers toward my eyes. I caught his wrist and held it. Both of our right hands were still pinned and our weights seemed about equal. So all that I had to do was squeeze.

The bones of his wrist crunched within my grip, and for the first time he cried out. Then I simply pushed him away, rolled into a kneeling position and started to rise, dragging him up along with me. End of the game. I had won.

He slumped suddenly against me. For a moment, I thought it a final trick, and then I saw the blade protruding from his back, the hand of the grim-faced man who had put it there already tightening to pull it out again.

"You son of a bitch!" I cried in English—though I'm sure the meaning came through—and I dropped my burden and drove my fist into the stranger's face, knocking him over backward, his blade remaining in place. "I needed him!"

I caught hold of my former adversary and raised him into the most comfortable position I could manage.

"Who sent you?" I asked him. "How did you find me?"

He grinned weakly and dribbled blood. "No freebies here," he said. "Ask somebody else," and he slumped forward and got blood on my shirtfront.

I drew the ring from his finger and added it to my collection of god-damned blue stones. Then I rose and glared at the man who had stabbed him. Two other figures were helping him to his feet.

"Just what the hell did you do that for?" I asked, advancing upon them.

"I saved your damn life," the man growled.

"The hell you did! You might have just cost me it! I needed that man alive!"

Then the figure to his left spoke, and I recognized the voice. She placed her hand lightly upon the arm I did not even realize I had raised to strike the man again.

"He did it on my orders," she said. "I feared for your life, and I did not understand that you wanted him prisoner."

I stared at her pale proud features within the dark cloak's raised cowl. It was Vinta Bayle, Caine's lady, whom I had last seen at the funeral. She was also the third daughter of the Baron Bayle, to whom Amber owed many a bibulous night.

I realized that I was shaking slightly. I drew a deep breath and caught control of myself.

"I see," I said at last. "Thank you."

"I am sorry," she told me.

I shook my head. "You didn't know. What's done is done. I'm grateful to anybody who tries to help me."

"I can still help you," she said. "I might have misread this one, but I believe you may still be in danger. Let's get away from here."

I nodded. "A moment, please."

I went and retrieved Frakir from about the neck of the other dead man. She disappeared quickly into my left sleeve. The blade I had been using fit my scabbard after a fashion, so I pushed it home and adjusted the belt, which had pulled toward the rear.

"Let's go," I said to her.

The four of us strode back toward Harbor Street. Interested bystanders got out of our way quickly. Someone was probably already robbing the dead behind us. Things fall apart; the center cannot hold. But what the hell, it's home.

FIVE

Walking, with the Lady Vinta and two servingmen of the House of Bayle, my side still hurting from its encounter with a sword hilt, beneath a moon-bright, starbright sky, through a sea mist, away from Death Alley. Lucky, actually, that a bump on the side was all I acquired in my engagement with those who would do me harm. How they had located me so quickly upon my return, I could not say. But it seemed as if Vinta might have some idea about this, and I was inclined to trust her, both because I knew her somewhat and because she had lost her man, my Uncle Caine, to my former friend Luke, from whose party anything involving a blue stone seemed to have its origin.

When we turned onto a seaward side way off Harbor Street, I asked her what she had in mind.

"I thought we were heading for Vine," I said.

"You know you are in danger," she stated.

"I guess that's sort of obvious."

"I could take you to my father's place up in town," she said, "or we could escort you back to the palace, but someone knows you are here and it didn't take long to reach you."

"True."

"We have a boat moored down this way. We can sail along the coast and reach my father's country place by morning. You will have disappeared. Anyone seeking you in Amber will be foiled."

"You don't think I'd be safe back in the palace?"

"Perhaps," she said. "But your whereabouts may be known locally. Come with me and this won't be the case."

"I'll be gone and Random will learn from one of the guards that I was heading for Death Alley. This will cause considerable consternation and a huge brouhaha."

"You can reach him by Trump tomorrow and tell him that you're in the country—if you have your cards with you."

"True. How did you know where to find me this evening? You can't persuade me that we met by coincidence."

"No, we followed you. We were in the place across the way from Bill's."

"You anticipated tonight's happenings?"

"I saw the possibility. If I'd known everything, of course I'd have prevented it."

"What's going on? What do you know about all of this, and what's your part in it?"

She laughed, and I realized it was the first time I had ever heard her do it. It was not the cold, mocking thing I would have guessed at from Caine's lady.

"I want to sail while the tide is high," she said, "and you want a story that will take all night. Which will it be, Merlin? Security or satisfaction?"

"I'd like both, but I'll take them in order."

"Okay," she said, then turned to the smaller of the two men, the one I had hit. "Jarl, go home. In the morning, tell my father that I decided to go back to Arbor House. Tell him it was a nice night and I wanted to sail, so I took the boat. Don't mention Merlin."

The man touched his cap to her. "Very good, m'lady."

He turned and headed back along the way we had come.

"Come on," she said to me then, and she and the big fellow—whose name I later learned was Drew—led me down among the piers to where a long sleek sailboat was tied up. "Do much sailing?" she asked me.

"Used to," I said.

"Good enough. You can give us a hand."

Which I did. We didn't talk much except for business while we were getting unbuttoned and rigged and casting off. Drew steered and we worked the sails. Later, we were able to take turns for long spells. The wind wasn't tricky. In fact, it was just about perfect. We slid away, rounded the breakwater and made it out without any problems. Having stowed our cloaks, I saw that she wore dark trousers and a heavy shirt. Very practical, as if she'd planned for something like this ahead of time. The belt she stowed bore a real, full-length blade, not some jeweled dagger. And just from watching the way she moved, I'd a feeling she might be able to use the thing pretty well. Also, she reminded me of someone I couldn't quite place. It was more a matter of mannerisms of gesture and voice than it was of appearance. Not that it mattered. I had more important things to think about as soon as we settled into routine and I had a few moments to stare across the dark waters and do some quick reviewing.

I was familiar with the general facts of her life, and I had encountered her a number of times at social gatherings. I knew she knew that I was Corwin's son and that I had been born and raised in the Courts of Chaos, being half of that bloodline which was linked anciently with Amber's own. In our conversation the last time we met, it became apparent that she was aware that I had been off in Shadow for some years, going native and trying to pick up something of an education. Presumably, Uncle Caine had not wanted her ignorant of family matters—which led me to wonder how deeply their relationship might have run. I'd heard that they had been together for several years. So I wondered exactly how much she knew about me. I felt relatively safe with her, but I had to decide how much I was willing to tell her in exchange for the information she obviously possessed concerning those who were after me locally. This, because I had a feeling it would probably be a trade-off. Other than doing a favor for a member of the family, which generally comes in handy, there was no special reason for her having an interest in me personally. Her motivation in the whole matter pretty much had to be a desire for revenge, so far as I could see, for Caine's killing. With this in mind, I was willing to deal. It is always good to have an ally. But I had to decide how much I was willing to give her of the big picture. Did I want her messing around in the entire complex of events that surrounded me? I doubted it, even as I wondered how much she would be asking. Most likely she just wanted to be in on the kill, whatever that might be. When I glanced over to where moonlight accentuated the planes of her angular face, it was not difficult to superimpose a mask of Nemesis upon those features.

Out from shore, riding the sea breeze east, passing the great rock of Kolvir, the lights of Amber like jewels in her hair, I was taken again by an earlier feeling of affection. Though I had grown up in darkness and exotic lighting amid the non-Euclidean paradoxes of the Courts, where beauty was formed of more surreal elements, I felt more and more drawn to Amber every time I visited her, until at last I realized she was a part of me, until I began to think of her, too, as home. I did not want Luke storming her slopes with riflemen, or Dalt performing commando raids in her vicinity. I knew that I would be willing to fight them to protect her.

Back on the beach, near the place where Caine had been laid to rest, I thought I saw a flash of prancing whiteness, moving slowly, then quickly, then vanishing within some cleft of the slope. I would have said it was a Unicorn, but with the distance and the darkness and the quickness of it all, I could never be certain.

We picked up a perfect wind a little later, for which I was grateful. I was tired, despite my day-long slumber. My escape from the crystal cave, my encounter with the Dweller, and the pursuit by the whirlwind and its masked master all flowed together in my mind as the nearly continuous action that they were. And now the postadrenal reaction from my latest activity was settling in. I wanted nothing more than to listen to the lapping of the waves while I watched the black and craggy shoreline slide by to port or turned to regard the flickering sea to starboard. I did not want to think, I did not want to move. . . .

A pale hand upon my arm.

"You're tired," I heard her say.

"I guess so," I heard myself say.

"Here's your cloak. Why don't you put it on and rest? We're holding steady. The two of us can manage easily now. We don't need you."

I nodded as I drew it about me. "I'll take you up on that. Thanks."

"Are you hungry or thirsty?"

"No. I had a big meal back in town."

Her hand remained on my arm. I looked up at her. She was smiling. It was the first time I had seen her smile. With the fingertips of her other hand she touched the bloodstain on my shirtfront.

"Don't worry. I'll take care of you," she said.

I smiled back at her because it seemed she wanted me to. She squeezed my shoulder and left me then, and I stared after her and wondered whether there were some element I had omitted from my earlier equation concerning her. But I was too tired now to solve for a new unknown. My thinking machinery was slowing, slowing. . . .

Back braced against the port gunwale, rocked gently by the swells, I let my head nod. Through half-closed eyes I saw the dark blot she had indicated upon my white shirtfront. Blood. Yes, blood. . . .

"First blood!" Despil had cried. "Which is sufficient! Have you satisfaction?"

"No!" Jurt had shouted. "I barely scratched him!" and he spun on his stone and waved the triple claws of his *trisp* in my direction as he prepared to have at me again.

The blood oozed from the incision in my left forearm and formed itself into beads which rose into the air and drifted away from me like a handful of scattered rubies. I raised my *fandon* into a high guard position and lowered my *trisp*, which I held far out to the right and angled forward. I bent my left knee and rotated my stone 90 degrees on our mutual axis. Jurt corrected his own position immediately and dropped a half-dozen feet. I turned another 90 degrees, so that each of us seemed to be hanging upside down in relation to the other.

"Bastard son of Amber!" he cried, and the triple lances of light raked toward me from his weapon, to be shattered into bright, mothlike fragments by the sweep of my *fandon*, to fall, swirling, downward into the Abyss of Chaos above which we rode.

"Up yours," I replied, and squeezed the haft of my *trisp*, triggering the pulsed beams from its three hair-fine blades. I extended my arm above my head as I did so, slashing at his shins.

He swept the beams away with his *fandon*, at almost the full extent of their eight-foot effective range. There is about a three-second recharge pause on a *trisliver*, but I feinted a dead cut toward his face, before which he raised *fand* reflexively, and I triggered the *trisp* for a swirl cut at his knees. He broke the one-second pulse in low *fand*, triggered a thrust at my face and spun over backward through a full 360, counting on the recharge time to save his back and coming up, *fandon* high, to cut at my shoulder.

But I was gone, circling him, dropping and rotating erect. I cut at his own exposed shoulder but was out of range. Despil, on his beachball-sized stone, was circling also, far to my right, while my own second—Mandor—high above, was dropping quickly. We clung to our small stones with shape-shifted feet, there on an outer current of Chaos, drifting, as at the whirlpool's rim. Jurt rotated to follow me, keeping his left forearm—to which the *fandon* is attached, elbow and wrist—horizontal, and executing a slow circular movement with it. Its three-foot length of filmy mesh, *mord*-weighted at the bottom, glittered in the balefire glow, which occurred at random intervals from many directions. He held his *trisp* in middle attack position, and he showed his teeth but was not smiling as I moved and he moved at opposite ends of the diameter of a ten-foot circle which we described over and over, looking for an opening.

I tilted the plane of my orbit and he adjusted his own immediately to keep me company. I did it again, and so did he. Then I did the dive—90 degrees forward, *fandon* raised and extended—and I turned my wrist and dropped my elbow, angling my raking cut upward beneath his guard.

He cursed and cut, but I scattered his light, and three dark lines appeared upon his left thigh. The *trisliver* only cuts to a depth of about three quarters of an inch through flesh, which is why the throat, eyes, temples, inner wrists and femoral arteries are particularly favored targets in a serious encounter. Still, enough cuts anywhere and you eventually wave good-bye to your opponent as he spins downward in a swarm of red rubbles into that place from whence no traveler returns.

"Blood!" Mandor cried, as the beads formed upon Jurt's leg and drifted. "Is there satisfaction, gentlemen?"

"I'm satisfied," I answered.

"I'm not!" Jurt replied, turning to face me as I drifted to his left and rotated to my right. "Ask me again after I've cut his throat!"

Jurt had hated me from sometime before he had learned to walk, for reasons entirely his own. While I did not hate Jurt, liking him was totally beyond my ability. I had always gotten along reasonably well with Despil, though he tended to take Jurt's side more often than my own. But that was understandable. They were full brothers, and Jurt was the baby.

Jurt's *trisp* flashed and I broke the light and riposted. He scattered my beams and spun off to the side. I followed. Our *trisps* flared simultaneously, and the air between us was filled with flakes of brilliance as both attacks were shattered. I struck again, this time low, as soon as I had recharge. His came in high, and again both attacks died in *fand*. We drifted nearer.

"Jurt," I said, "if either of us kills the other, the survivor will be outcast. Call it off."

"It will be worth it," he said. "Don't you think I've thought about it?"

Then he slashed an attack at my face. I raised both arms reflexively, *fandon* and *trisp*, and triggered an attack as shattered light showered before me. I heard him scream.

When I lowered my *fandon* to eye level I saw that he was bent forward, and his *trisp* was drifting away. So was his left ear, trailing a red filament that quickly beaded itself and broke apart. A flap of scalp had also come loose, and he was trying to press it back into place.

Mandor and Despil were already spiraling in.

"We declare the duel ended!" they were shouting, and I twisted the head of my *trisp* into a safety-lock position.

"How bad is it?" Despil asked me.

"I don't know."

Jurt let him close enough to check, and a little later Despil said, "He'll be all right. But Mother is going to be mad."

I nodded. "It was his idea," I said.

"I know. Come on. Let's get out of here."

He helped Jurt steer toward an outcropping of the Rim, *fandon* trailing like a broken wing. I lingered behind. Sawall's son Mandor, my stepbrother, put his hand on my shoulder.

"You didn't even mean him that much," he said. "I know."

I nodded and bit my lip. Despil had been right about the Lady Dara, our mother, though. She favored Jurt, and somehow he'd have her believing this whole thing was my fault. I sometimes felt she liked both of her sons by Sawall, the old Rim Duke she'd finally married after giving up on Dad, better than me. I'd once overheard it said that I reminded her of my father, whom I'd been told I resembled more than a little. I wondered again about Amber and about other places, out in Shadow, and felt my customary twinge of fear as this recalled to me the writhing Logrus, which I knew to be my ticket to other lands. I knew that I was going to try it sooner than I had originally intended.

"Let's go see Suhuy," I said to Mandor, as we rose up out of the Abyss together. "There are more things I want to ask him."

When I finally went off to college I did not spend a lot of time writing home.

". . .home," Vinta was saying, "pretty soon now. Have a drink of water," and she passed me a flask.

I took several long swallows and handed it back. "Thanks."

I stretched my cramped muscles and breathed the cold sea air. I looked for the moon and it was way back behind my shoulder.

"You were really out," she said.

"Do I talk in my sleep?"

"No."

"Good."

"Bad dreams?"

I shrugged. "Could be worse."

"Maybe you made a little noise, right before I woke you."

"Oh."

Far ahead I saw a small light at the end of a dark promontory. She gestured toward it.

"When we've passed the point," she said, "we will come into sight of the harbor at Baylesport. We'll find breakfast there, and horses."

"How far is it from Arbor House?"

"About a league," she replied. "An easy ride."

She stayed by me in silence for a while, watching the coastline and the sea. It was the first time we had simply sat together, my hands unoccupied and my mind free. And my sorcerer's sense was stirred in that interval. I felt as if I were in the presence of magic. Not some simple spell or the aura of some charmed object she might be bearing, but something very subtle. I summoned my vision and turned it upon her. There was nothing immediately obvious, but prudence suggested I check further. I extended my inquiry through the Logrus. . . .

"Please don't do that," she said.

I had just committed a faux pas. It is generally considered somewhat gauche to probe a fellow practitioner in such a fashion.

"I'm sorry," I said. "I didn't realize you were a student of the Art."

"I am not," she answered, "but I am sensitive to its operations."

"In that case, you would probably make a good one."

"My interests lie elsewhere," she said.

"I thought perhaps someone had laid a spell upon you," I stated. "I was only trying to—"

"Whatever you saw," she said, "belongs. Let it be."

"As you would. Sorry."

She must have known I couldn't let it rest at that, though, when unknown magic represents possible danger. So she went on, "It is nothing that can do you harm, I assure you. Quite the contrary."

I waited, but she did not have anything further to say on the matter. So I had to let it drop, for the moment. I shifted my gaze back to the lighthouse. What was I getting into with her, anyhow? How had she even known that I was back in town, let alone that I would visit Death Alley when I did? She must have known that the question would occur to me, and if there was to be good faith on both our parts she should be willing to explain it.

I turned back toward her, and she was smiling again.

"The wind changes in the lee of the light," she said, and she rose. "Excuse me. I've got work to do."

"May I give you a hand?"

"In a bit. I'll call you when I need you."

I watched her move away, and as I did I had the eerie feeling that she was watching me also, no matter where she was looking. I realized, too, that this feeling had been with me for some time, like the sea.

By the time we had docked and put everything in order and headed up a hill along a wide cobbled way toward an inn with smoke snaking from its chimney, the sky was growing pale in the east. After a hearty breakfast, morning's light lay full upon the world. We walked then to the livery stable where three quiet mounts were obtained for the ride to her father's estate.

It was one of those clear crisp autumn days which become rarer and dearer as the year winds down. I finally felt somewhat rested, and the inn had had coffee—which is not that common in Amber, outside the palace—and I enjoy my morning cup. It was good to move through the countryside at a leisurely pace and to smell the land, to watch the moisture fade from sparkling fields and turning leaves, to feel the wind, to hear and watch a flock of birds southbound for the Isles of the Sun. We rode in silence, and nothing happened to break my mood. Memories of sorrow, betrayal, suffering and violence are strong but they do fade, whereas interludes such as this, when I close my eyes and regard the calendar of my days, somehow outlast them, as I see myself riding with Vinta Bayle under morning skies where the houses and fences are stone and stray seabirds call, there in the wine country to the east of Amber, and the scythe of Time has no power in this corner of the heart.

When we arrived at Arbor House we gave the horses into the care of Bayle's grooms, who would see to their eventual return to town. Drew departed for his own quarters then, and I walked with Vinta to the huge hilltop manor house. It commanded far views of rocky valleys and hillsides where the grapes were grown. A great number of dogs approached and tried to be friendly as we made our way to the house, and once we had entered their voices still reached us on occasion. Wood and wrought iron, gray flagged floors, high beamed ceilings, clerestory windows, family portraits, a couple of small tapestries of salmon, brown, ivory and blue, a collection of old weapons showing a few touches of oxidation, soot smudges on the gray stone about the hearth. . . . We passed through the big front hall and up a stair.

"Take this room," she said, opening a darkwood door, and I nodded as I entered and looked about. It was spacious, with big windows looking out over the valley to the south. Most of the servants were at the Baron's place in town for the season. "There is a bath in the next room," she told me, indicating a door to my left.

"Great. Thanks. Just what I need."

"So repair yourself as you would." She crossed to the window and looked downward. "I'll meet you on that terrace in about an hour, if that is agreeable."

I went over and looked down upon a large flagged area, well shaded by ancient trees—their leaves now yellow, red and brown, many of them dotting the patio—the place bordered by flower beds, vacant now, a number of tables and chairs arranged upon it, a collection of potted shrubs well disposed among them.

"Fine."

She turned toward me. "Is there anything special you would like?"

"If there is any coffee about, I wouldn't mind another cup or two when I meet you out there."

"I'll see what I can do."

She smiled and seemed to sway slightly toward me for a moment. It almost seemed in that instant as if she wanted me to embrace her. But if she did not, it could be slightly awkward. And under the circumstances I wanted no familiarity with her anyway, having no idea as to the sort of game she was playing. So I returned her smile, reached out and squeezed her arm, said, "Thank you," and stepped away. "I guess I'll see about that bath now."

I saw her to the door and led her out.

It was good to get my boots off. It was far better to soak, for a long, warm time.

Later, in fresh-conjured attire, I made my way downstairs and located a side door that led off the kitchen onto the patio. Vinta, also scrubbed and refitted, in brown riding pants and loose tan blouse, sat beside a table at the east end of the patio. Two places were set upon it, and I saw a coffeepot and tray of fruit and cheeses. I crossed over, leaves crunching beneath my feet, and sat down.

"Did you find everything to your satisfaction?" she asked me.

"Entirely," I replied.

"And you've notified Amber of your whereabouts?"

I nodded. Random had been a bit irritated at my taking off without letting him know, but then he had never told me not to. He was less irritated, however, when he learned that I hadn't gone all that far, and he even acknowledged finally that perhaps I had done a prudent thing in disappearing following such a peculiar attack. "Keep your eyes open and keep me posted," were his final words.

"Good. Coffee?"

"Please."

She poured and gestured toward the tray. I took an apple and took a bite.

"Things have begun happening," she said ambiguously, as she filled her own cup.

"I can't deny it," I acknowledged.

"And your troubles have been manifold."

"True."

She took a sip of coffee. "Would you care to tell me about them?" she finally said.

"They're a little too manifold," I replied. "You said something last night about your story being a long one, too."

She smiled faintly. "You must feel you have no reason to trust me more than necessary at this point," she said. "I can see that. Why trust anyone you don't have to when something dangerous is afoot, something you do not completely understand? Right?"

"It does strike me as a sound policy."

"Yet I assure you that your welfare is of the highest concern to me."

"Do you think I may represent a means of getting at Caine's killer?"

"Yes," she said, "and insofar as they may become your killers I would like to get at them."

"Are you trying to tell me that revenge is not your main objective?"

"That's right. I would rather protect the living than avenge the dead."

"But that part becomes academic if it's the same individual in both cases. Do you think it is?"

"I am not certain," she said, "that it was Luke who sent those men after you last night."

I placed my apple beside my cup and took a long drink of coffee. "Luke?" I said. "Luke who? What do you know of any Luke?"

"Lucas Raynard," she said steadily, "who trained a band of mercenaries in the Pecos Wilderness in northern New Mexico, issued them supplies of a special ammunition that will detonate in Amber, and sent them all home with it to await his orders to muster and be transported here—to attempt something your father once tried years ago."

"Holy shit!" I said.

That *would* explain a lot—like Luke's showing up in fatigues back at the Hilton in Santa Fe, with his story about liking to hike around in the Pecos, with that round of peculiar ammunition I'd found in his pocket; and all the other trips he'd been making there—more, actually, than seemed absolutely necessary on his sales route. . . .That angle had never occurred to me, but it made a lot of sense in light of everything I'd since learned.

"Okay," I acknowledged, "I guess you know Luke Raynard. Mind telling me how you came by this?"

"Yes."

"Yes?"

"Yes, I mind. I'm afraid I'm going to have to play this game your way and trade you information a piece at a time. Now that I think of it, it will probably make me feel more comfortable too. How does that sound to you?"

"Either one of us can call it quits at any time?"

"Which stops the trading, unless we can negotiate it."

"All right."

"So you owe me one. You just returned to Amber the other day. Where had you been?"

I sighed and took another bite of the apple. "You're fishing," I said finally. "That's a big question. I've been to a lot of places. It all depends on how far back you want to go."

"Let's take it from Meg Devlin's apartment to yesterday," she said.

I choked on a piece of apple. "Okay, you've made the point—you have some damn good sources of information," I observed. "But it has to be Fiona for that one. You're in league with her some way, aren't you?"

"It's not your turn for a question," she said. "You haven't answered mine yet."

"Okay, Fi and I came back to Amber after I left Meg's place. The next day Random sent me on a mission, to turn off a machine I'd built called Ghostwheel. I failed in this but I ran into Luke along the way. He actually helped me out of a tight spot. Then, following a misunderstanding with my creation, I used a strange Trump to take both Luke and myself to safety. Luke subsequently imprisoned me in a crystal cave—"

"Aha!" she said.

"I should stop here?"

"No, go on."

"I was a prisoner for a month or so, though it amounted to only a few days, Amber time. I was released by a couple of fellows working for a lady named Jasra, had an altercation with them and with the lady herself and trumped out to San Francisco, to Flora's place. There, I revisited an apartment where a murder had occurred—"

"Julia's place?"

"Yes. In it, I discovered a magical gateway which I was able to force open. I passed through it to a place called the Keep of the Four Worlds. A battle was in progress there, the attackers probably being led by a fellow named Dalt, of some small notoriety hereabouts at one time. Later, I was pursued by a magical whirlwind and called names by a masked wizard. I trumped out and came home—yesterday."

"And that's everything?"

"In capsule form, yes."

"Are you leaving out anything?"

"Sure. For instance, there was a Dweller on the threshold of the gateway, but I was able to get by."

"No, that's part of the package. Anything else?"

"Mm. Yes, there were two peculiar communications, ending in flowers."

"Tell me about them."

So I did.

She shook her head when I'd finished. "You've got me there," she said.

I finished my coffee and the apple. She refilled my cup.

"Now it's my turn," I said. "What did you mean by that 'Aha!' when I mentioned the crystal cave?"

"It was blue crystal, wasn't it? And it blocked your powers."

"How'd you know?"

"It was the color of the stone in the ring you took from that man last night."

"Yes."

She got to her feet and moved around the table, stood a moment, then pointed to the vicinity of my left hip.

"Would you empty that pocket onto the table, please?"

I smiled. "Sure. How'd you know?"

She didn't answer that one, but then it was a different question. I removed the assortment of blue stones from my pocket—the chips from the cave, the carved button I'd snatched, the ring—and placed them upon the table.

She picked up the button, studied it, then nodded.

"Yes, that's one also," she stated.

"One what?"

She ignored the query and dipped her right forefinger into a bit of spilled coffee within her saucer. She then used it to trace three circles around the massed stones, widdershins. Then she nodded again and returned to her seat. I'd summoned the vision in time to see her build a cage of force about them. Now, as I continued to watch, it seemed as if they were exhaling faint wisps of blue smoke that remained within the circle.

"I thought you said you weren't a sorcerer."

"I'm not," she replied.

"I'll save the question. But continue answering the last one. What is the significance of the blue stones?"

"They have an affinity for the cave, and for each other," she told me. "A person with very little training could hold one of them and simply begin walking, following the slight psychic tugging. It would eventually lead him to the cave."

"Through Shadow, you mean?"

"Yes."

"Intriguing, but I fail to see any great value to it."

"But that is not all. Ignore the pull of the cave, and you will become aware of secondary tugging. Learn to distinguish the signature of the proper stone, and you can follow its bearer anywhere."

"That does sound a little more useful. Do you think that's how those guys found me last night, because I had a pocket full of the things?"

"Probably, from a practical standpoint, they helped. Actually though, in your case, they should not even have been necessary at this point."

"Why not?"

"They have an additional effect. Anyone who has one in his possession for a time becomes attuned to the thing. Throw it away and the attunement remains. You can still be tracked then, just as if you had retained the stone. You would possess a signature of your own."

"You mean that even now, without them, I'm marked?"

"Yes."

"How long does it take to wear off?"

"I am not certain that it ever does."

"There must be some means of deattunement."

"I do not know for certain, but I can think of a couple of things that would probably do it."

"Name them."

"Walking the Pattern of Amber or negotiating the Logrus of Chaos. They seem almost to break a person apart and do a reassemblement into a purer form. They have been known to purge many strange conditions. As I recall, it was the Pattern that restored your father's memory."

"Yes—and I won't even ask you how you know about the Logrus—you may well be right. As with so much else in life, it seems enough of a pain in the ass to be good for me. So, you think they could be zeroing in on me right now, with or without the stones?"

"Yes."

"How do you know all this?" I asked.

"I can sense it—and that's an extra question. But I'll give you a free one in the interests of expedition."

"Thanks. I guess it's your turn now."

"Julia was seeing an occultist named Victor Melman before she died. Do you know why?"

"She was studying with him, looking for some sort of development—at least, that's what I was told by a guy who knew her at the time. This was after we broke up."

"That is not exactly what I meant," she said. "Do you know why she desired this development?"

"Sounds like an extra question to me, but maybe I owe you one. The fellow I'd spoken with told me that I had scared her, that I'd given her to believe that I possessed unusual abilities, and that she was looking for some of her own in self-defense."

"Finish it," she said.

"What do you mean?"

"That's not a complete answer. *Did* you actually give her cause to believe that and to be afraid of you?"

"Well, I guess I did. Now my question: How could you possibly know anything about Julia in the first place?"

"I was there," she answered. "I knew her."

"Go ahead."

"That's it. Now it's my turn."

"That's hardly complete."

"But it's all you're getting on that one. Take it or leave it."

"According to our agreement I can call it quits over that."

"True. Will you?"

"What do you want to know next?"

"Did Julia develop the abilities she sought?"

"I told you that we'd stopped seeing each other before she got involved in that sort of thing. So I have no way of knowing."

"You located the portal in her apartment from which the beast that slew her had presumably emerged. Two questions now—not for you to answer for me, just for you to think over: Why would anyone want her dead in the first place? And does it not seem a very peculiar way to have gone about it? I can think of a lot simpler ways of disposing of a person."

"You're right," I agreed. "A weapon is a hell of a lot easier to manage than magic any day. As for why, I can only speculate. I had assumed it was a trap for me, and that she had been sacrificed as part of the package—my annual April thirtieth present. Do you know about them, too?"

"Let's save that business for later. You are obviously aware that sorcerers have styles, the same as painters, writers, musicians. When you succeeded in locating that gateway in Julia's apartment, was there anything about it which we might refer to as the author's signature?"

"Nothing special that I can recall. Of course, I was in a hurry to force it. I wasn't there to admire the aesthetics of the thing. But, no, I can't associate it with anyone with whose work I am familiar. What are you getting at?"

"I just wondered whether it were possible that she might have developed some abilities of her own along these lines, and in the course of things opened that gateway herself and suffered those consequences."

"Preposterous!"

"All right. I am just trying to turn up some reasons. I take it then that you never saw any indication that she might possess latent abilities for sorcery?"

"No, I can't recall any instances."

I finished my coffee, poured a refill.

"If you don't think Luke is after me now, why not?" I asked her then.

"He set up some apparent accidents for you, years ago."

"Yes. He admitted that recently. He also told me that he quit doing it after the first few times."

"That is correct."

"You know, it's maddening—not knowing what you know and what you do not."

"That is why we're talking, isn't it? It was your idea to go about it this way."

"It was not! You suggested this trade-off!"

"This morning, yes. But the idea was originally yours, some time ago. I am thinking of a certain telephone conversation, at Mr. Roth's place—"

"You? That disguised voice on the phone? How could that be?"

"Would you rather hear about that or about Luke?"

"That! No, Luke! Both, damn it!"

"So it would seem there is a certain wisdom in keeping to the format we've agreed upon. There is much to be said for orderliness."

"Okay, you've made another point. Go on about Luke."

"It seemed to me, as an observer, that he quit that business as soon as he got to know you better."

"You mean back about the time we became friendly—that wasn't just an act?"

"I couldn't tell for sure then—and he certainly countenanced the years of attacks on you—but I believe that he actually sabotaged some of them."

"Who was behind them after he quit?"

"A red-haired lady with whom he seemed to be associated."

"Jasra?"

"Yes, that was her name—and I still don't know as much about her as I'd like to. Do you have anything there?"

"I think I'll save that for a big one," I said.

For the first time, she directed a narrow-eyed, teeth-clenched expression toward me.

"Can't you see that I'm trying to help you, Merlin?"

"Really, what I see is that you want information I have," I said, "and that's okay. I'm willing to deal because you seem to know things I want, too. But I've got to admit that your reasons are murky to me. How the hell did you get to Berkeley? What were you doing calling me at Bill's place? What is this power of yours you say isn't sorcery? How—"

"That's three questions," she said, "and the beginning of a fourth. Would you prefer to write them all out, and have me do the same for you? Then we can both go off to our rooms and decide which ones we want to answer?"

"No," I replied. "I'm willing to play the game. But you are aware of my reason for wanting to know these things. It's a matter of self-preservation to me. I thought at first that you wanted information that would help you to nail the man who killed Caine. But you said no, and you didn't give me anything to put in its place."

"I did, too! I want to protect you!"

"I appreciate the sentiment. But why? When it comes down to it, you hardly know me."

"Nevertheless, that is my reason and I don't feel like going behind it. Take it or leave it."

I got to my feet and began pacing the patio. I didn't like the thought of giving away information that could be vital to my security, and ultimately that of Amber—though I had to admit I was getting a pretty good return for what I'd given. Her stuff did sound right. For that matter, the Bayles had a long history of loyalty to the Crown, for whatever that was worth. The thing that bothered me the most, I decided, was her insistence that it was not actually revenge that she was after. Apart from this being a very un-Amberlike attitude, if she were any judge at all as to what would go over with me she need but have agreed that blood was what she wanted in order to make her concern intelligible. I would have bought it without looking any further. And what did she offer in its place? Airy nothings and classified motives. . . .

Which could well mean she was telling the truth. Disdaining the use of a workable lie and offering something more cumbersome in its place would seem the mark of genuine honesty. And she did, apparently, have more answers that I wanted—

I heard a small rattling sound from the table. I thought at first that she might be drumming on it with her fingertips as a sign of her irritation with me. But when I glanced back I saw that she was sitting perfectly still, not even looking at me.

I drew nearer, seeking the source. The ring, the pieces of blue stone and even the button were jiggling about on the tabletop, as of their own accord.

"Something you're doing?" I asked.

"No," she replied.

The stone in the ring cracked and fell out of its setting.

"What, then?"

"I broke a link," she said. "I believe something may be trying to reestablish it and failing."

"Even so, if I'm still attuned they don't need them in order to locate me, do they?"

"There may be more than one party involved," she observed. "I think I should have a servant ride back to town and throw the things into the ocean. If someone wished to follow them there, fine."

"The chips should just lead back to the cave, and the ring to the dead man," I said. "But I'm not ready to throw the button away."

"Why not? It represents a big unknown."

"Exactly. But these things would have to work both ways, wouldn't they? That would mean that I could learn to use the button to find my way to the flower thrower."

"That could be dangerous."

"And not doing it could prove more dangerous in the long run. No, you can throw the rest of them into the sea, but not the button."

"All right. I'll keep it pent for you."

"Thanks. Jasra is Luke's mother."

"You're joking!"

"Nope."

"That explains why he didn't lean on her directly about the later April thirtieths. Fascinating! It opens up a whole new lane of speculation."

"Care to share them?"

"Later, later. In the meantime, I'll take care of these stones right now."

She scooped them all out of the circle and they seemed, for a moment, to dance in her hand. She stood.

"Uh—the button?" I said.

"Yes."

She put the button into her pocket and kept the others in her hand.

"You're going to get attuned yourself if you keep the button that way, aren't you?"

"No," she said, "I won't."

"Why not?"

"There's a reason. Excuse me while I find a container for the others, and someone to transport them."

"Won't that person get attuned?"

"It takes a while."

"Oh."

"Have some more coffee—or something."

She turned and left. I ate a piece of cheese. I tried to figure out whether I'd gotten more answers or more new questions during the course of our conversation. I tried to fit some of the new pieces into the old puzzle.

"Father?"

I turned to see who had spoken. There was no one in sight.

"Down here."

A coin sized disk of light lay within a nearby flower bed, otherwise empty save for a few dry stalks and leaves. The light caught my attention when it moved slightly.

"Ghost?" I asked.

"Uh-huh," came the reply from among the leaves. "I was waiting to catch you when you were alone. I'm not sure I trust that woman."

"Why not?"

"She doesn't scan right, like other people. I don't know what it is. But that's not what I wanted to talk to you about."

"What then?"

"Uh—well, did you mean what you said about not really intending to turn me off?"

"Jeez! After all the sacrifices I made for you! Your education and everything. . . . And lugging all your damn components out to a place like that where you'd be safe! How can you ask me that?"

"Well, I heard Random tell you to do it—"

"You don't do everything you're told either, do you? Especially when it comes to assaulting me when I just wanted to check out a few programs? I deserve a little more respect than that!"

"Uh—yeah. Look, I'm sorry."

"You ought to be. I went through a lot of crap because of you."

"I looked for you for several days, and I couldn't find you."

"Crystal caves are no fun."

"I don't have much time now. . . ." The light flickered, faded almost to the point of vanishing, returned to full brilliance. "Will you tell me something fast?"

"Shoot."

"That fellow who was with you when you came out this way—and when you left—the big red-haired man?"

"Luke. Yes?"

The light grew dimmer again.

"Is it okay to trust him?" Ghost's voice came faintly, weakly.

"No!" I shouted. "That would be damn stupid."

Ghost was gone, and I couldn't tell whether he'd heard my answer.

"What's the matter?" Vinta's voice, from above me.

"Argument with my imaginary playmate," I called out.

Even from that distance I could see the expression of puzzlement on her face. She sought in all directions about the patio and then, apparently persuading herself that I was indeed alone, she nodded.

"Oh," she said. Then, "I'll be along in a little while."

"No hurry," I answered.

Where shall wisdom be found, and where is the place of understanding? If I knew, I'd walk over and stand there. As it was, I felt as if I stood in the midst of a large map, surrounded by vague areas wherein were penned the visages of particularly nasty-looking random variables. A perfect place for a soliloquy, if one had anything to say.

I went back inside to use the john. All that coffee.

SIX

Well, maybe.

With Julia, I mean.

I sat alone in my room, thinking by candlelight.

Vinta had stirred a few sunken memories to the surface.

It was later on, when we weren't seeing much of each other. . . .

I'd met Julia first in a Computer Science course I was taking. We'd started seeing each other occasionally, just coffee after class and like that, at first. Then more and more frequently, and pretty soon it was serious.

Now it was ending as it had started, a little more each time. . . .

I felt her hand on my shoulder as I was leaving the supermarket with a bag of groceries. I knew it was her and I turned and there was no one there. Seconds later, she hailed me from across the parking lot. I went over and said hello, asked her if she were still working at the software place where she'd been. She said that she wasn't. I recalled that she was wearing a small silver pentagram on a chain about her neck. It could easily—and more likely should—have been hanging down inside her blouse. But of course I wouldn't have seen it then, and her body language indicated that she wanted me to see it. So I ignored it while we exchanged a few generalities, and she turned me down on dinner and a movie, though I asked after several nights.

"What are you doing now?" I inquired.

"I'm studying a lot."

"What?"

"Oh, just—different things. I'll surprise you one of these days."

Again, I didn't bite, though an over-friendly Irish setter approached us about then. She placed her hand on its head and said, "Sit!" and it did. It became still as a statue at her side, and remained when we left later. For all I know, there's a dog skeleton still crouched there, near the car return area, like a piece of modern sculpture.

It didn't really seem that important at the time. But in retrospect, I wondered. . . .

We had ridden that day, Vinta and I. Seeing my growing exasperation of the morning, she must have felt a break was in order. She was right. Following a light lunch, when she made the suggestion that we take a ride about the estate, I agreed readily. I had wanted a little more time in which to think before continuing our cross-examination and discourse game. And the weather was good, the countryside attractive.

We made our way along a curling trail through arbors, which led at length into the northern hills from where we were afforded long views across the rugged and cross-hatched land down to the sun-filled sea. The sky was full of winds and wisps of cloud, passing birds. . . . Vinta seemed to have no special destination in mind, which was all right with me. As we rode, I recalled a visit to a Napa Valley winery, and the next time we drew rein to rest the horses I asked her, "Do you bottle the wine here at the estate? Or is that done in town? Or in Amber?"

"I don't know," she said.

"I thought you grew up here."

"I never paid attention."

I bit back a remark about patrician attitudes. Unless she were joking, I couldn't see how she'd fail to know something like that.

She caught my expression, though, and added immediately, "We've done it various ways at various times. I've been living in town for several years now. I'm not sure where the principal bottling has been done recently."

Nice save, because I couldn't fault it. I hadn't intended my question as any sort of trap, but felt as if I had just touched on something. Possibly, from the fact that she didn't let it go at that. She went on to say that they shipped large casks all over the place and often sold them in that fashion. On the other hand, there were smaller customers who wanted the product bottled. . . . I stopped listening after a time. On the one hand, I could see it, coming from a vinter's daughter. On the other, it was all stuff I could have made up myself on the spot. There was no way for me to check on any of it. I got the feeling that she was trying to snow me, to cover something. But I couldn't figure what.

"Thanks," I said when she paused for breath, and she gave me a strange look but took the hint and did not continue.

"You have to speak English," I said in that language, "if the things you told me earlier are true."

"Everything I told you is true," she replied, in unaccented English.

"Where'd you learn it?"

"On the shadow Earth where you went to school."

"Would you care to tell me what you were doing there?"

"I was on a special mission."

"For your father? For the Crown?"

"I'd rather not answer you at all than lie to you."

"I appreciate that. Of course, I must speculate."

She shrugged.

"You said you were in Berkeley?" I asked.

A hesitation, then, "Yes."

"I don't remember ever seeing you around."

Another shrug. I wanted to grab her and shake her. Instead I said, "You knew about Meg Devlin. You said you were in New York—"

"I believe you're getting ahead of me on questions."

"I didn't know we were playing the game again. I thought we were just talking."

"All right, then: Yes."

"Tell me one more thing and perhaps I can help you."

She smiled. "I don't need any help. You're the one with problems."

"May I, anyway?"

"Go ahead and ask. Every time you question me you tell me things I wish to know."

"You knew about Luke's mercenaries. Did you visit New Mexico, too?"

"Yes, I've been there."

"Thanks," I said.

"That's all?"

"That's all."

"You've come to some conclusion?"

"Perhaps."

"Care to tell me what it is?"

I smiled and shook my head.

I left it at that. A few oblique queries on her part as we rode on led me to believe that I had her wondering what I might have guessed or suddenly seen. Good. I was determined to let it smolder. I needed something to balance her reticence on those points about which I was most curious, to lead hopefully to a full trade of information. Besides, I *had* reached a peculiar conclusion concerning her. It was not complete, but if it were correct I would require the rest of the answer sooner or later. So it was not exactly as if I were setting up a bluff.

The afternoon was golden, orange, yellow, red about us, with an autumn-damp smell behind the cool nips of the breezes. The sky very blue, like certain stones. . . .

Perhaps ten minutes later I asked her a more neutral question. "Could you show me the road to Amber?"

"You don't know it?"

I shook my head. "I've never been this way before. All I know is that there are overland routes coming through here that lead to the Eastern Gate."

"Yes," she said. "A bit farther to the north, I believe. Let's go find it."

She headed back to a road we had followed for a time earlier and we turned right on it, which seemed logical. I did not remark on her vagueness, though I expected a comment from her before too long in that I had not elaborated on my plans and I'd a feeling she was hoping that I would.

Perhaps three quarters of a mile later we came to a crossroads. There was a low stone marker at the far left corner giving the distance to Amber, the distance back to Baylesport, the distance to Baylecrest in the east and to a place called Murn, straight ahead.

"What's Murn?" I asked.

"A little dairy village."

No way I could check that, without traveling six leagues.

"You plan on riding back to Amber?" she asked.

"Yes."

"Why not just use a Trump?"

"I want to get to know the area better. It's my home. I like it here."

"But I explained to you—about the danger. The stones have marked you. You can be tracked."

"That doesn't mean I *will* be tracked. I doubt that whoever sent the ones I met last night would even be aware this soon that they'd found me and failed. They'd still be lurking about if I hadn't decided to go out for dinner. I'm sure I have a few days' grace in which to remove the markings you spoke of."

She dismounted and let her horse nibble a few blades of grass. I did the same. Dismounted, that is.

"You're probably right. I just don't like to see you taking *any* chances," she said. "When are you planning on heading back?"

"I don't know. I suppose that the longer I wait the more likely it is that the person behind last night's business will get restless and maybe send more muscle."

She took hold of my arm and turned, so that she was suddenly pressed against me. I was somewhat surprised by the act, but my free arm automatically moved to hold the lady as it tends to on such occasions.

"You weren't planning on leaving now, were you? Because if you are, I'm going with you."

"No," I answered truthfully. Actually, I'd been thinking of departing the following morning, following a good night's sleep.

"When, then? We still have a lot of things to talk about."

"I think we've pushed the question-and-answer business about as far as you're willing to let it go."

"There are some things—"

"I know."

Awkward, this. Yes, she was desirable. And no, I didn't care to have anything to do with her that way. Partly because I felt she wanted something else as well—what, I wasn't sure—and partly because I was certain she possessed a peculiar power to which I did not wish to expose myself at intimate range. As my Uncle Suhuy used to say, speaking technically as a sorcerer, "If you don't understand it, don't screw around with it." And I had a feeling that anything beyond a friendly acquaintanceship with Vinta could well turn into a duel of energies.

So I kissed her quickly to stay friendly and disengaged myself.

"Maybe I'll head back tomorrow," I told her.

"Good. I was hoping you'd spend the night. Perhaps several. I will protect you."

"Yes, I'm still very tired," I said.

"We'll have to feed you a good meal and build up your strength."

She brushed my cheek with her fingertips then, and I suddenly realized that I did know her from somewhere. Where? I couldn't say. And that, too, frightened me. More than a little. As we mounted and headed back toward Arbor House I began making my plans for getting out of there that night.

So, sitting in my room, sipping a glass of my absent host's wine (the red) and watching the candles flicker in the breeze from an opened window, I waited—first for the house to grow quiet (which it had), then for a goodly time to pass. My door was latched. I had mentioned how tired I felt several times during dinner, and then I had retired early. I am not so egotistically male that I feel myself constantly lusted after, but Vinta had given indication that she might stop by and I wanted the excuse of heavy sleeping. Least of all did I wish to offend her. I had problems enough without turning my strange ally against me.

I wished I still had a good book about, but I'd left my last one at Bill's place, and if I were to summon it now I did not know but that Vinta might sense the sending, just as Fiona had once known I was creating a Trump, and come pounding on the door to see what the hell was going on.

But no one came pounding, and I listened to the creaking of a quiet house and the night sounds without. The candles shortened themselves and the shadows on the wall behind the bed ebbed and flowed like a dark tide beyond their swaying light. I thought my thoughts and sipped my wine. Pretty soon. . . .

An imagining? Or had I just heard my name whispered from some undetectable place?

"Merle. . . ."

Again.

Real, but—

My vision seemed to swim for a moment, then I realized it for what it was: a very weak Trump contract.

"Yes," I said, opening and extending. "Who is it?"

"Merle, baby. . . .Give me a hand or I've had it. . . ."

Luke!

"Right here," I said, reaching, reaching, as the image grew clear, solidified.

He was leaning, his back against a wall, shoulders slumped, head hanging.

"If this is a trick, Luke, I'm ready for it," I told him. I rose quickly and, crossing to the table where I had laid my blade, I drew it and held it ready.

"No trick. Hurry! Get me out of here!"

He raised his left hand. I extended my left hand and caught hold of it. Immediately he slumped against me, and I staggered. For an instant I thought it was an attack, but he was dead weight and I saw that there was blood all over him. He still clutched a bloody blade in his right hand.

"Over here. Come on."

I steered him and supported him for several paces, then deposited him on the bed. I pried the blade from his grip, then placed it along with mine on a nearby chair.

"What the hell happened to you?"

He coughed and shook his head weakly. He drew several deep breaths, then, "Did I see a glass of wine," he asked, "as we passed a table?"

"Yeah. Hold on."

I fetched it, brought it back, propped him and held it to his lips. It was still over half full. He sipped it slowly, pausing for deep breaths.

"Thanks," he said when he'd finished, then his head turned to the side. He was out. I took his pulse. It was fast but kind of weak.

"Damn you, Luke!" I said. "You've got the worst timing. . . ."

But he didn't hear a word. He just lay there and bled all over the place.

Several curses later I had him undressed and was going over him with a wet towel to find out where, under all that blood, the injuries lay. There was a nasty chest wound on the right, which might have hit the lung. His breathing was very shallow, though, and I couldn't tell. If so, I was hoping he'd inherited the regenerative abilities of Amber in full measure. I put a compress on it and laid his arm on top to hold it in place while I checked elsewhere. I suspected he had a couple of fractured ribs, also. His left arm was broken above the elbow and I set it and splinted it, using loose slats from a chair I'd noticed in the back of the closet earlier, and I strapped it to him. There were over a dozen lacerations and incisions of various degrees of severity on his thighs, right hip, right arm and shoulder, his back. None of them, fortunately, involved arterial bleeding. I cleaned all of these and bound them, which left him looking like an illustration in a first-aid handbook. Then I checked his chest wound again and covered him up.

I wondered about some of the Logrus healing techniques I knew in theory but had never had a chance to practice. He was looking pretty pale, so I decided I had better try them. When I'd finished, some time later, it seemed as if his color had returned to his face. I added my cloak to the blanket which covered him. I took his pulse again and it felt stronger. I cursed again, just to stay in practice, removed our blades from the chair and sat down on it.

A little later my conversation with Ghostwheel returned to trouble me. Had Luke been trying to do a deal with my creation? He'd told me he wanted Ghost's power, to prosecute his designs against Amber. Then Ghost had asked me earlier today whether Luke was to be trusted, and my answer had been emphatically negative.

Had Ghost terminated negotiations with Luke in the fashion I saw before me?

I fetched forth my Trumps and shuffled out the bright circle of the Ghostwheel. I focused on it, setting my mind for contact, reaching out, calling, summoning.

Twice I felt near to something—agitated—during the several minutes I devoted to the effort. But it was as if we were separated by a sheet of glass. Was Ghost occupied? Or just not inclined to talk with me?

I put my cards away. But they had served to push my thoughts into another channel.

I gathered Luke's gory clothing and did a quick search. I turned up a set of Trumps in a side pocket, along with several blank cards and a pencil— and yes, they seemed to be rendered in the same style as the ones I had come to call the Trumps of Doom. I added to the packet the one depicting myself, which Luke had been holding in his hand when he had trumped in.

His were a fascinating lot. There was one of Jasra, and one of Victor Melman. There was also one of Julia, and a partly completed one of Bleys. There was one for the crystal cave, another for Luke's old apartment. There were several duplicated from the Trumps of Doom themselves, one for a palace I did not recognize, one for one of my old pals, one for a rugged-looking blond guy in green and black, another of a slim, russet-haired man in brown and black, and one of a woman who resembled this man so closely it would seem they must be related. These last two, strangely, were done in a different style; even by a different hand, I'd say. The only unknown one I felt relatively certain about was the blond fellow, who, from his colors, I would assume to be Luke's old friend, Dalt, the mercenary. There were also three separate attempts at something resembling Ghostwheel—none of them, I would guess, completely successful.

I heard Luke growl something, and I saw that his eyes were open and darting.

"Take it easy," I said. "You're safe."

He nodded and closed his eyes. A few moments later, he opened them again.

"Hey! My cards," he said weakly.

I smiled. "Nice work," I remarked. "Who did them?"

"Me," he answered. "Who else?"

"Where'd you learn?"

"My dad. He was real good at it."

"If you can do them, you must have walked the Pattern."

He nodded.

"Where?"

He studied me a moment, then performed a weak shrug and winced. "Tir-na Nog'th."

"Your father took you, saw you through it?"

Again, a nod.

Why not push it, since I seemed to be on a roll? I picked up a card.

"And here's Dalt," I said. "You used to be Cub Scouts together, didn't you?"

He did not reply. When I looked up I saw narrowed eyes and a furrowed brow.

"I've never met him," I added. "But I recognize the colors, and I know he's from out your way—around Kashfa."

Luke smiled. "You always did your homework back in school, too," he said.

"And usually on time," I agreed. "But with you I've been running late. Like, I can't find a Trump for the Keep of the Four Worlds. And here's someone I don't know."

I picked up the slim lady's card and waved it at him.

He smiled. "Gettin' weak and losin' my breath again," he said. "You been to the Keep?"

"Yep."

"Recently?"

I nodded.

"Tell you what," he said at last. "Tell me what you saw at the Keep and how you learned some of that stuff about me and I'll tell you who she is."

I thought quickly. I could say things so that I probably wouldn't be telling him anything he didn't already know.

So, "The other way around," I said.

"Okay. The lady," he stated, "is Sand."

I stared so hard that I felt the beginnings of a contact. I smothered it.

"The long-lost," he added.

I raised the card depicting the man who resembled her. "Then this must be Delwin," I said.

"Right."

"You didn't do these two cards. They're not your style, and you probably wouldn't have known what they looked like to begin with."

"Perceptive. My father drew them, back in the time of the troubles—for all the good it did him. They wouldn't help him either."

"Either?"

"They weren't interested in helping me, despite their disaffection with this place. Count them as out of the game."

"This place?" I said. "Where do you think you are, Luke?"

His eyes widened. He cast his gaze about the room. "The camp of the enemy," he answered. "I had no choice. These are your quarters in Amber, right?"

"Wrong," I replied.

"Don't bait me, Merle. You've got me. I'm your prisoner. Where am I?"

"Do you know who Vinta Bayle is?"

"No."

"She was Caine's mistress. This is her family's place, way out in the country. She's just up the hall somewhere. Might even stop by. I think she's got a crush on me."

"Uh-oh. She a tough lady?"

"Very."

"What are you doing making out with her this soon after the funeral? That's hardly decent."

"Huh! If it weren't for you there wouldn't have been any funeral."

"Don't give me that indignation crap, Merle. If it had been *your* dad, Corwin, he'd killed, wouldn't you have gone after him?"

"That's not fair. My father wouldn't have done all those things Brand did."

"Maybe, maybe not. But supposing he had? Even then. Wouldn't you have gone after Caine?"

I turned away. "I don't know," I said finally. "It's too damned hypothetical."

"You'd have done it. I know you, Merle. I'm sure you would have."

I sighed. "Maybe," I said. "Well, okay. Maybe I might have. But I would have stopped there. I wouldn't have gone after the others too. I don't want to make you feel any worse than you do about it, but your old man was psycho; you must know that. And you're not. I know you as well as you know me. I've been thinking about this for some time. You know, Amber recognizes the personal vendetta. You've got an arguable case there for one. And the death didn't even occur within Amber, if Random were really looking for an out for you."

"Why should he be?"

"Because I'd be vouching for your integrity in other matters."

"Come on, Merle—"

"You've got a classic vendetta defense—a son avenging his father's death."

"I don't know. . . . Hey, you trying to get out of telling me the stuff you promised to?"

"No, but—"

"So you made it to the Keep of the Four Worlds. What did you learn there and how did you learn it?"

"Okay. You think about what I said, though," I replied.

His expression remained unchanged.

Then, "There was an old hermit named Dave," I began.

Luke fell asleep before I finished. I just let my voice trail off and sat there. After a time, I rose and located the wine bottle and poured a little into the glass, since Luke had drunk most of mine. I took it with me to the window and stared down and out across the patio, where the wind was rattling leaves. I wondered about what I'd said to Luke. It wasn't a full picture I'd given him, partly because I hadn't had time to go into it thoroughly, mainly because he hadn't seemed interested. But even if Random did let him off the hook officially in the matter of Caine's death, Julian or Gérard would probably be looking to kill him under the same vendetta code I'd been talking about. I didn't really know what to do. I was obliged to tell Random about him, but I'd be damned if I'd do it yet. There were still too many things I had to learn from him, and getting at him might be a lot harder if he were a prisoner back in Amber. Why had he ever gotten himself born as Brand's son, anyway?

I returned to the bedside seat, near which I had left our weapons and Luke's Trumps. I moved these items across the room to where I seated myself in the more comfortable chair I had occupied earlier. I studied his cards again. Amazing. A whole bunch of history in my hand. . . .

When Oberon's wife Rilga had shown less hardihood than many by aging rapidly and retiring to a reclusive life at a country shrine, he had gone off and remarried, somewhat to the chagrin of their children—Caine, Julian and Gérard. But to confuse genealogists and sticklers for family legality, he had done it in a place where time flowed far more rapidly than in Amber. Interesting arguments both for and against the bigamous nature of his marriage to Harla may be made. I'm in no position to judge. I had the story from Flora years ago, and in that she'd never gotten along too well with Delwin and Sand, the offspring of that union, she was inclined to the pro-bigamy interpretation. I'd never seen pictures of Delwin or Sand until now. There weren't any hanging around the palace, and they were seldom mentioned. But they had lived in Amber for the relatively short time Harla was queen there. Following her death, they grew unhappy with Oberon's policies toward her homeland—which they visited often—and after a time they departed, vowing not to have anything to do with Amber again. At least that's the way I'd heard it. There could easily have been all sorts of sibling politicking involved, too. I don't know.

But here were two missing members of the royal family, and obviously Luke had learned of them and approached them, hoping to revive old resentments and gain allies. He admitted that it hadn't worked. Two centuries is a long time to hold a grudge at high pitch. That's about how long it had been since their departure, as I understood it. I wondered fleetingly whether I should get in touch with them, just to say hello. If they weren't interested in helping Luke I didn't suppose they'd be interested in helping the other side either, now they were aware there was another side. It did seem proper that I should introduce myself and pay my respects, as a family member they'd never met. I decided that I would do it sometime, though the present moment was hardly appropriate. I added their Trumps to my own collection, along with good intentions.

And then there was Dalt—sworn enemy of Amber, I gathered. I studied his card again, and I wondered. If he were indeed such a good friend of Luke's, perhaps I should let him know what had happened. He might even know of the circumstances involved and mention something I could use. In fact, the more I thought about it—recalling his recent presence at the Keep of the Four Worlds—the more tempting it became to try to reach him. It seemed possible I could even pick up something about what was now going on in that place.

I gnawed a knuckle. Should I or shouldn't I? I couldn't see any harm that could come of it. I wasn't planning on giving anything away. Still, there were a few misgivings.

What the hell, I decided finally. Nothing ventured. . . .

Hello, hello. Reaching out through the suddenly cold card. . . .

A startled moment somewhere, and the sense of an *Aha!*

Like a portrait come to life, my vision stirred.

"Who are you?" the man asked, hand on hilt, blade half drawn.

"My name is Merlin," I said, "and we've a mutual acquaintance named Rinaldo. I wanted to tell you that he'd been badly injured."

By now, we both hovered between our two realities, solid and perfectly clear to each other. He was bigger than I'd thought from his representation, and he stood at the center of a stone-walled room, a window to his left showing a blue sky and a limb of cloud. His green eyes, at first wide, were now narrowed and the set of his jaw seemed a bit truculent.

"Where is he?" he inquired.

"Here. With me," I answered.

"How fortunate," he replied, and the blade was in his hand and he moved forward.

I flipped the Trump away, which did not sever the contact. I had to summon the Logrus to do that—and it fell between us like the blade of a guillotine and jerked me back as if I had just touched a live wire. My only consolation was that Dalt had doubtless felt the same thing.

"Merle, what's going on?" Luke's voice came hoarsely. "I saw—Dalt. . . ."

"Uh, yeah. I just called him."

He raised his head slightly. "Why?"

"To tell him about you. He's your friend, isn't he?"

"You asshole!" he said. "He's the one that did this to me!"

Then he began coughing and I rushed to his side.

"Get me some water, huh?" he said.

"Coming up."

I went off to the bathroom and fetched him a glass. I propped him and he sipped it for a time.

"Maybe I should have told you," he said finally. "Didn't think—you'd play games—that way, though—when you don't know—what's going on. . . ."

He coughed again, drank more water.

"Hard to know what to tell you—and what not to," he continued, a while later.

"Why not tell me everything?" I suggested.

He shook his head slightly. "Can't. Probably get you killed. More likely both of us."

"The way things have been going, it seems as if it could happen whether you tell me or not."

He smiled faintly and took another drink.

"Parts of this thing are personal," he said then, "and I don't want anyone else involved."

"I gather that your trying to kill me every spring for a while there was kind of personal, too," I observed, "yet somehow I felt involved."

"Okay, okay," he said, slumping back and raising his right hand. "I told you I cut that out a long time ago."

"But the attempts went on."

"They weren't my doing."

Okay, I decided. Try it. "It was Jasra, wasn't it?"

"What do you know about her?"

"I know she's your mother, and I gather this is her war, too."

He nodded. "So you know. . . . All right. That makes it easier." He paused to catch his breath. "She started me doing the April thirtieth stuff for practice. When I got to know you better and quit, she was mad."

"So she continued it herself?"

He nodded.

"She wanted you to go after Caine," I said.

"So did I."

"But the others? She's leaning on you about them, I'll bet. And you're not so sure they have it coming."

Silence.

"Are you?" I said.

He shifted his gaze away from my own and I heard his teeth grind together.

"You're off the hook," he said at last. "I've no intention of hurting you. I won't let her do it either."

"And what about Bleys and Random and Fiona and Flora and Gérard and—"

He laughed, which cost him a wince and a quick clutch at his chest.

"They've nothing to worry about from us," he said, "right now."

"What do you mean?"

"Think," he told me. "I could have trumped back to my old apartment, scared hell out of the new tenants and called an ambulance. I could be in an emergency room right now."

"Why aren't you?"

"I've been hurt worse than this, and I've made it. I'm here because I need your help."

"Oh? For what?"

He looked at me, then looked away again. "She's in bad trouble, and we've got to rescue her."

"Who?" I asked, already knowing the answer.

"My mother," he replied.

I wanted to laugh, but I couldn't when I saw the expression on his face. It took real balls to ask me to help rescue the woman who'd tried to kill me—not once, but many times—and whose big aim in life seemed to be the destruction of my relatives. Balls, or—

"I've no one else to turn to," he said.

"If you talk me into this one, Luke, you'll deserve the Salesman of the Year Award," I said. "But I'm willing to listen."

"Throat's dry again," he said.

I went and refilled the glass. As I returned with it, it seemed there was a small noise in the hall. I continued listening while I helped Luke to a few more sips.

He nodded when he was finished, but I had heard another sound by then. I raised my finger to my lips and glanced at the door. I put down the glass, rose and crossed the room, retrieving my blade as I did so.

Before I reached the door, however, there was a gentle knock.

"Yes?" I said, advancing to it.

"It's me," came Vinta's voice. "I know that Luke is in there, and I want to see him."

"So you can finish him off?" I said.

"I told you before that that is not my intention."

"Then you're not human," I said.

"I never claimed I was."

"Then you're not Vinta Bayle," I said.

There followed a long silence, then, "Supposing I'm not?"

"Then tell me who you are."

"I can't."

"Then meet me halfway," I said, drawing upon all of my accumulated guesswork concerning her, "and tell me who you were."

"I don't know what you mean."

"Yes, you do. Pick one—any one. I don't care."

There was another silence, then, "I dragged you from the fire," she said, "but I couldn't control the horse. I died in the lake. You wrapped me in your cloak. . . ."

That was not an answer I had anticipated. But it was good enough.

With the point of my weapon I raised the latch. She pushed the door open and glanced at the blade in my hand.

"Dramatic," she remarked.

"You've impressed me," I said, "by the perils with which I am beset."

"Not sufficiently, it would seem." She entered, smiling.

"What do you mean?" I asked.

"I didn't hear you ask him anything about the blue stones and what he might have homing in on you as a consequence of your attunement."

"You've been eavesdropping."

"A lifetime habit," she agreed.

I turned toward Luke and introduced her. "Luke, this is Vinta Bayle—sort of."

Luke raised his right hand, his eyes never leaving her face. "I just want to know one thing," he began.

"I'll bet you do," she replied. "Am I going to kill you or aren't I? Keep wondering. I haven't decided yet. Do you remember the time you were low on gas north of San Luis Obispo and you discovered your wallet was missing? You had to borrow money from your date to get back home. She had to ask you twice, before you paid her back."

"How could you know that?" he whispered.

"You got in a fight with three bikers one day," she went on. "You almost lost an eye when one of them wrapped a chain around your head. Seems to have healed up nicely. Can't see the scar—"

"And I won," he added.

"Yes. Not too many people can pick up a Harley and throw it like you did."

"I have to know," he said, "how you learned these things."

"Maybe I'll tell you that too, sometime," she said. "I just mentioned them to keep you honest. Now I'm going to ask you some questions, and your life is going to depend on giving me honest answers. Understand—"

"Vinta," I interrupted, "you told me that you weren't interested in killing Luke."

"It's not at the top of my list," she replied, "but if he's in the way of what is, he goes."

Luke yawned. "I'll tell you about the blue stones," he muttered. "I don't have anybody on a blue-stone detail after Merle now."

"Might Jasra have someone tracking him that way?"

"Possible. I just don't know."

"What about the ones who attacked him in Amber last night?"

"First I've heard of it," he said, and he closed his eyes.

"Look at this," she ordered, removing the blue button from her pocket. He opened his eyes and squinted at it.

"Recognize it?"

"Nope," he said, and closed his eyes again.

"And you don't mean Merle any harm now?"

"That's right," he answered, his voice drifting off.

She opened her mouth again and I said, "Let him sleep. He's not going anywhere."

She gave me an almost angry look, then nodded. "You're right," she said.

"So what are you going to do now—kill him while he's out?"

"No," she replied. "He was telling the truth."

"And does it make a difference?"

"Yes," she told me, "for now."

SEVEN

I actually did get a fairly decent night's sleep despite everything, including a distant dogfight and a lot of howling. Vinta had been disinclined to continue at questions and answers, and I hadn't wanted her bothering Luke any more. I persuaded her to leave and let us rest. I sacked out on the comfortable chair, with my feet propped on the other one. I was hoping to continue my conversation with Luke in private. I remember chuckling right before I fell asleep as I tried to decide which of them I distrusted less.

I was awakened by the first brightening of the sky and a few arguments of birds. I stretched several times then and made my way to the bathroom. Half an ablution later I heard Luke cough and then whisper my name.

"Unless you're hemorrhaging, wait a minute," I replied, and I dried myself off. "Need some water?" I asked while I was doing it.

"Yeah. Bring some."

I threw the towel over my shoulder and took him a drink.

"Is she still around?" he asked me.

"No."

"Give me a glass and go check the hall, will you? I'll manage."

I nodded and passed it to him. I kept it quiet as I eased the door open. I stepped out into the hall, walked up to the corner. There was no one in sight.

"All clear," I whispered as I came back into the room.

Luke was gone. A moment later I heard him in the bathroom.

"Damn! I'd have helped you!" I said.

"I can still take a leak by myself," he replied, staggering back into the room, his good hand on the wall. "Had to see whether I could negotiate," he added, lowering himself to the edge of the bed. He put his hand against his rib cage and panted. "Shit! that smarts!"

"Let me help you lie back."

"Okay. Listen, don't let her know I can do even that much."

"Okay," I said. "Take it easy now. Rest."

He shook his head. "I want to tell you as much as I can before she comes busting back in here," he said, "and she will, too—believe me."

"You know that for a fact?"

"Yes. She's not human, and she's more attuned to both of us than any blue stone ever was. I don't understand your style of magic, but I've got my own and I know what it tells me. It was your question about who she was that got me to working on the problem, though. Have you figured her out yet?"

"Not completely, no."

"Well, I know she can switch bodies like changing clothes—and she can travel through Shadow."

"Do the names Meg Devlin or George Hansen mean anything to you?" I asked.

"No. Should they?"

"Didn't think so. But she was both of them, I'm sure."

I'd left out Dan Martinez, not because he'd shot it out with Luke and telling Luke would raise his distrust of her even further, but because I didn't want him to know that I was aware of the New Mexico guerrilla operation—and I could see that it might lead in that direction.

"She was also Gail Lampron."

"Your old girlfriend, back in school?" I said.

"Yes. I thought there was something familiar about her immediately. But it didn't hit me till later. She has all of Gail's little mannerisms—the way she turns her head, the way she uses her hands and eyes when she's talking. Then she mentioned two events to which there had only been a single common witness—Gail."

"It sounds as if she wanted you to know."

"I believe she did," he agreed.

"Why didn't she just come out and say it then, I wonder?"

"I don't think she can. There's something could be a spell on her, only it's hard to judge, her not being human and all." He glanced furtively at the door as he said this. Then, "Check again," he added.

"Still clear," I said. "Now what about—"

"Another time," he said. "I've got to get out of here."

"I can see your wanting to get away from her—" I began.

He shook his head. "That's not it," he said. "I've got to hit the Keep of the Four Worlds—soon."

"The shape you're in—"

"That's it. That's what I mean. I've got to get out of here so I can be in shape soon. I think old Sharu Garrul's gotten loose. That's the only way I can figure what happened."

"What *did* happen?"

"I got a distress call from my mother. She'd gone back to the Keep after I'd gotten her away from you."

"Why?"

"Why, what?"

"Why'd she head for the Keep?"

"Well, the place is a power center. The way the four worlds come together there releases an awful lot of free power, which an adept can tap into—"

"Four worlds actually do come together there? You mean you're in a different shadow depending on the direction you might take off in?"

He studied me for a moment. "Yes," he finally said, "but I'll never get this thing told if you want all the details."

"And I won't understand it if too much gets left out. So she went to the Keep to raise some power and got in trouble instead. She called you to come help her. What did she want that power for, anyway?"

"Mm. Well, I'd been having trouble with Ghostwheel. I thought I almost had him talked into coming over to our side, but she probably thought I wasn't making progress fast enough and apparently decided to try binding him with a massive spell after—"

"Wait a minute. You were talking to Ghost? How did you get in touch? Those Trumps you drew are no good."

"I know. I went in."

"How'd you manage it?"

"In scuba gear. I wore a wet suit and oxygen tanks."

"Son of a gun. That's an interesting approach."

"I wasn't Grand D's top salesman for nothing. I almost had him convinced, too. But she'd learned where I'd stashed you, and she decided to try expediting matters by putting you under control, then using you to clinch the deal—as if you'd come over to our side. Anyhow, when that plan fell through and I had to go and get her away from you, we split up again. I thought she was headed for Kashfa, but she went to the Keep instead. Like I said, I think it was to try a massive working against Ghostwheel. I believe something that she did there inadvertently freed Sharu, and he took the place over again and captured her. Anyhow, I got this frantic sending from her, so—"

"Uh, this old wizard," I said, "had been locked up there for—how long?"

Luke began to shrug, thought better of it. "Hell, I don't know. Who cares? He's been a cloak rack since I was a boy."

"A cloak rack?"

"Yeah. He lost a sorcerous duel. I don't really know whether she beat him or whether it was Dad. Whoever it was, though, caught him in mid-invocation, arms outspread and all. Froze him like that, stiff as a board. He got moved to a place near an entranceway later. People would hang cloaks and hats on him. The servants would dust him occasionally. I even carved my name on his leg when I was little, like on a tree. I'd always thought of him as furniture. But I learned later that he'd been considered pretty good in his day."

"Did this guy ever wear a blue mask when he worked?"

"You've got me. I don't know anything about his style. Say, let's not get academic or she'll be here before I finish. In fact, maybe we ought to go now, and I can tell you the rest later."

"Uh-uh," I said. "You are, as you noted last night, my prisoner. I'd be nuts to let you go anywhere without knowing a hell of a lot more than I do. You're a threat to Amber. That bomb you tossed at the funeral was pretty damn real. You think I want to give you another shot at us?"

He smiled, then lost it. "Why'd you have to be born Corwin's son, anyway?" he said. Then, "Can I give you my parole on this?" he asked.

"I don't know. I'm going to be in a lot of trouble if they find out I had you and didn't bring you in. What terms are you talking? Will you swear off your war against Amber?"

He gnawed his lower lip. "There's no way I can do that, Merle."

"There are things you're not telling me, aren't there?"

He nodded. Then he grinned suddenly. "But I'll make you a deal you can't refuse."

"Luke, don't give me that hard-sell crap."

"Just give me a minute, okay? And you'll see why you can't afford to pass this one up."

"Luke, I'm not biting."

"Only one minute. Sixty seconds. You're free to say no when I'm done."

"All right," I said. "Tell me."

"Okay. I've got a piece of information vital to the security of Amber, and I'm certain nobody there has an inkling of it. I'll give it to you, after you've helped me."

"Why should you want to give us something like that? It sounds kind of self-defeating."

"I don't, and it is. But it's all I've got to offer. Help me get out of here to a place I have in mind where the time flow is so much faster that I'll be healed up in a day or so in terms of local time at the Keep."

"Or here, for that matter, I'd guess."

"True. Then—uh-oh!"

He sprawled on the bed, clutched at his chest with his good hand and began to moan.

"Luke!"

He raised his head, winked at me, glanced at the door and commenced moaning again.

Shortly, there came a knocking.

"Come in," I said.

Vinta entered and studied us both. For a moment, there seemed to be a look of genuine concern on her face as she regarded Luke. Then she advanced to the bed and placed her hands upon his shoulders. She stood there for about half a minute, then announced, "You're going to live."

"At the moment," Luke replied, "I don't know whether that's a blessing or a curse." Then he slipped his good arm around her, drew her to him suddenly and kissed her. "Hi, Gail," he said. "It's been a long time."

She drew away with less haste than she might have. "You seem improved already," she observed, "and I can see that Merle's worked something to help you along." She smiled faintly for an instant, then said, "Yes, it has been, you dumb jock. You still like your eggs sunny-side up?"

"Right," he acknowledged. "But not half a dozen. Maybe just two today. I'm out of sorts."

"All right," she said. "Come on, Merle. I'll need you to supervise."

Luke gave me a funny look, doubtless certain she wanted to talk with me about him. And for that matter, I wasn't certain I wanted to leave him alone even though I had all his Trumps in my pocket. I was still uncertain as to the extent of his abilities, and I knew a lot less concerning his intentions. So I hung back.

"Maybe someone should stay with the invalid," I told her.

"He'll be all right," she said, "and I might need your help if I can't scare up a servant."

On the other hand, maybe she had something interesting to tell me. . . .

I found my shirt and drew it on. I ran a hand through my hair.

"Okay," I said. "See you in a bit, Luke."

"Hey," he responded, "see if you can turn up a walking stick for me, or cut me a staff or something."

"Isn't that rushing things a bit?" Vinta asked.

"Never can tell," Luke replied.

So I fetched my blade and took it along. As I followed Vinta out and down the stairs, it occurred to me that when any two of us got together we would probably have something to say about the third.

As soon as we were out of earshot, Vinta remarked, "He took a chance, coming to you."

"Yes, he did."

"So things must be going badly for him, if he felt you were the only one he could turn to."

"I'd say that's true."

"Also, I'm sure he wants something besides a place to recover."

"Probably so."

"'Probably,' hell! He must have asked by now."

"Perhaps."

"Either he did or he didn't."

"Vinta, obviously you've told me everything you intend to tell me," I said.

"Well, vice versa. We're even. I don't owe you explanations. If I feel like trusting Luke, I will. Anyhow, I haven't decided yet."

"So he *has* made you a pitch. I might be able to help you decide if you'll let me know what it is."

"No, thanks. You're as bad as he is."

"It's your welfare I'm concerned with. Don't be so quick to spurn an ally."

"I'm not," I said. "But if you stop to think about it, I know a lot more about Luke than I do about you. I think I know the things on which I shouldn't trust him as well as I do the safe ones."

"I hope you're not betting your life on it."

I smiled. "That's a matter on which I tend to be conservative."

We entered the kitchen, where she spoke with a woman I hadn't met yet who seemed in charge there. She left our breakfast orders with her and led me out the side door and onto the patio. From there, she indicated a stand of trees off to the east.

"You ought to be able to find a good sapling in there," she said, "for Luke's staff."

"Probably so," I replied, and we began walking in that direction. "So you really were Gail Lampron," I said suddenly.

"Yes."

"I don't understand this body-changing bit at all."

"And I'm not about to tell you."

"Care to tell me why not?"

"Nope."

"Can't or won't?"

"Can't," she said.

"But if I already know something, would you be willing to add a bit?"

"Maybe. Try me."

"When you were Dan Martinez you took a shot at one of us. Which one was it?"

"Luke," she replied.

"Why?"

"I'd become convinced that he was not the one—that is, that he represented a threat to you—"

"—and you just wanted to protect me," I finished.

"Exactly."

"What did you mean 'that he was not the one'?"

"Slip of the tongue. That looks like a good tree over there."

I chuckled. "Too thick. Okay, be that way."

I headed on into the grove. There were a number of possibilities off to the right.

As I moved through the morning-lanced interstices, damp leaves and dew adhering to my boots, I became aware of some unusual scuffing along the way, a series of marks leading off farther to the right, where—

"What's that?" I said, kind of rhetorically, since I didn't think Vinta would know either, as I headed toward a dark mass at the shady foot of an old tree.

I reached it ahead of her. It was one of the Bayle dogs, a big brown fellow. Its throat had been torn open. The blood was dark and congealed. A few insects were crawling on it. Off farther to the right I saw the remains of a smaller dog. It had been disemboweled.

I studied the area about the remains. The marks of very large paws were imprinted in the damp earth. At least they were not the three-toed prints of the deadly doglike creatures I had encountered in the past. They seemed simply to be those of a very large dog.

"This must be what I heard last night," I remarked. "I thought it sounded like a dogfight."

"When was that?" she asked.

"Some time after you left. I was drowsing."

Then she did a strange thing. She knelt, leaned and sniffed the track. When she recovered there was a slightly puzzled expression on her face.

"What did you find?" I asked.

She shook her head, then stared off to the northeast. "I'm not sure," she finally said, "but it went that way."

I studied the ground further, rising and finally moving along the trail it had left. It did run off in that direction, though I lost it after several hundred feet when it departed the grove. Finally, I turned away.

"One of the dogs attacked the others, I guess," I observed. "We'd better find that stick and head back if we want our breakfasts warm."

Inside, I learned that Luke's breakfast had been sent up to him. I was torn. I wanted to take mine upstairs, to join him and continue our conversation. If I did, though, Vinta would accompany me and the conversation would not be continued. Nor could I talk further with her under those circumstances. So I would have to join her down here, which meant leaving Luke alone for longer than I liked.

So I went along with her when she said, "We will eat in here," and led me into a large hall. I guessed she had chosen it because my room with its open window was above the patio, and Luke could have heard us talking if we ate out there.

We sat at the end of a long darkwood table, where we were served. When we were alone again, she asked, "What are you going to do now?"

"What do you mean?" I asked, sipping some grape juice.

She glanced upward. "With him," she said. "Take him back to Amber?"

"It would seem the logical thing to do," I replied.

"Good," she said. "You should probably transport him soon. They have decent medical facilities at the palace."

I nodded. "Yes, they do."

We ate a few mouthfuls, then she asked, "That *is* what you intend doing, isn't it?"

"Why do you ask?"

"Because anything else would be absolutely foolish, and obviously he is not going to want to do it. Therefore, he will try to talk you into something else, something that will give him some measure of freedom while he recovers.

You know what a line of shit he has. He'll make it sound like a great idea, whatever it is. You must remember that he is an enemy of Amber, and when he is ready to move again you will be in the way."

"It makes sense," I said.

"I'm not finished."

"Oh?"

She smiled and ate a few more bites, to keep me wondering. Finally, "He came to you for a reason," she continued. "He could have crawled off to any of a number of places to lick his wounds. But he came to you because he wants something. He's gambling, but it's a calculated thing. Don't go for it, Merle. You don't owe him anything."

"I don't know why you think me incapable of taking care of myself," I replied.

"I never said that," she responded. "But some decisions are finely balanced things. A little extra weight this way or that sometimes makes the difference. You know Luke, but so do I. This is not a time to be giving him any breaks."

"You have a point there," I said.

"So you *have* decided to give him what he wants!"

I smiled and drank some coffee. "Hell, he hasn't been conscious long enough to give me the pitch," I said. "I've thought of these things, and I want to know what he's got in mind too."

"I never said you shouldn't find out as much as you can. I just wanted to remind you that talking with Luke can sometimes be like conversing with a dragon."

"Yeah," I acknowledged. "I know."

"And the longer you wait the harder it's going to be," she added.

I took a gulp of coffee; then, "Did you like him?" I asked.

"Like?" she said. "Yes, I did. And I still do. That is not material at this point, though."

"I don't know about that," I said.

"What do you mean?"

"You wouldn't harm him without a good reason."

"No, I wouldn't."

"He is no threat to me at the moment."

"He does not seem to be."

"Supposing I were to leave him here in your care while I went off to Amber to walk the Pattern and to prepare them for the news?"

She shook her head vigorously. "No," she stated. "I will not—I cannot— take that responsibility at this time."

"Why not?"

She hesitated.

"And please don't say again that you cannot tell me," I went on. "Find a way to tell me as much as you can."

She spoke slowly then, as if choosing her words very carefully. "Because it is more important for me to watch you than Luke. There is still danger for you which I do not understand, even though it no longer seems to be proceeding from him. Guarding you against this unknown peril is of higher priority than keeping an eye on him. Therefore, I cannot remain here. If you are returning to Amber, so am I."

"I appreciate your concern," I said, "but I will not have you dogging my footsteps."

"Neither of us has a choice."

"Supposing I simply trump out of here to some distant shadow?"

"I will be obliged to follow you."

"In this form, or another?"

She looked away. She poked at her food.

"You've already admitted that you can be other persons. You locate me in some arcane fashion, then you take possession of someone in my vicinity."

She took a drink of coffee.

"Perhaps something prevents you from saying it," I continued, "but that's the case. I know it."

She nodded once, curtly, and resumed eating.

"Supposing I did trump out right now," I said, "and you followed after in your peculiar fashion." I thought back to my telephone conversations with Meg Devlin and Mrs. Hansen. "Then the real Vinta Bayle would wake up in her own body with a gap in her memory, right?"

"Yes," she answered softly.

"And that would leave Luke here in the company of a woman who would be happy to destroy him if she had any inkling who he really is."

She smiled faintly. "Just so," she said.

We ate in silence for a time. She had attempted to foreclose all my choices, to force me a trump back to Amber and take Luke with me. I do not like being manipulated or coerced. My reflexive attempt to do something other than what is desired of me then feels forced also.

I refilled our coffee cups when I had finished eating. I regarded a collection of dog portraits that hung on the wall across from me. I sipped and savored. I did not speak because I could think of nothing further to say.

Finally, she did. "So what are you going to do?" she asked me.

I finished my coffee and rose. "I am going to take Luke his stick," I said.

I pushed my chair back into place and headed for the corner of the room where I had leaned the stick.

"And then?" she said. "What will you do?"

I glanced back at her as I hefted the staff. She sat very erect, her hands palms down on the table. The Nemesis look overlay her features once again, and I could almost feel electricity in the air.

"Whatever I must," I replied, and I headed for the door.

I increased my pace as soon as I was out of sight. When I hit the stairs and saw that she was not following, I took the steps two at a time. On the way up, I withdrew my cards and located the proper one.

When I entered the room, I saw that Luke was resting, his back against the bed's pillows. His breakfast tray was on the smaller chair, beside the bed. I dropped the latch on the door.

"What's the matter, man? We under attack or something?" Luke asked.

"Start getting up," I said.

I picked up his weapon then and crossed to the bed. I gave him a hand sitting up, thrust the staff and the blade at him.

"My hand has been forced," I said, "and I'm not about to turn you over to Random."

"That's a comfort," he observed.

"But we have to clear out—now."

"That's all right by me."

He leaned on the staff, got slowly to his feet. I heard a noise in the hall, but it was already too late. I'd raised the card and was concentrating.

There came a pounding on the door.

"You're up to something and I think it's the wrong thing," Vinta called out.

I did not reply. The vision was already coming clear.

The doorframe splintered from the force of a tremendous kick, and the latch was torn loose. There was a look of apprehension on Luke's face as I reached out and took hold of his arm.

"Come on," I said.

Vinta burst into the room as I led Luke forward, her eyes flashing, her hands extended, reaching. Her cry of "Fool!" seemed to change into a wail as she was washed by the spectrum, rippled and faded.

We stood in a patch of grass, and Luke let out a deep breath he had been holding.

"You believe in cutting things close, buddy-boy," he remarked, and then he looked around and recognized the place.

He smiled crookedly.

"What do you know," he said. "A crystal cave."

"From my own experience," I said, "the time flow here should be around what you were asking for."

He nodded and we began moving slowly toward the high blue hill.

"Still plenty of rations," I added, "and the sleeping bag should be where I left it."

"It will serve," he acknowledged.

He halted, panting, before we reached the foot. I saw his gaze drift toward a number of strewn bones off to our left. It would have been months since the pair who had removed the boulder had fallen there, long enough for scavengers to have done a thorough job. Luke shrugged, advanced a little, leaned against blue stone. He lowered himself slowly into a sitting position.

"Going to have to wait before I can climb," he said, "even with you helping."

"Sure," I said. "We can finish our conversation. As I recall you were going to make me an offer I couldn't refuse. I was to bring you to a place like this, where you could recover fast *vis-à-vis* the time flow at the Keep. You, in turn, had a piece of information vital to the security of Amber."

"Right," he agreed, "and you didn't hear the rest of my story either. They go together."

I hunkered across from him. "You told me that your mother had fled to the Keep, apparently gotten into trouble there and called to you for help."

"Yes," he acknowledged. "So I dropped the business with Ghostwheel and tried to help her. I got in touch with Dalt, and he agreed to come and attack the Keep."

"It's always good to know a band of mercenaries you can get hold of in a hurry," I said.

He gave me a quick, strange look but I was able to maintain an innocent expression.

"So we led them through Shadow and we attacked the place," he said then. "It had to be us that you saw when you were there."

I nodded slowly. "It looked as if you made it over the wall. What went wrong?"

"I still don't know," he said. "We were doing all right. Their defense was crumbling and we were pushing right along, when suddenly Dalt turned on me. We'd been separated for a time; then he appeared again and attacked me. At first I thought he'd made a mistake—we were all grimy and bloody—and I shouted to him that it was me. For a while I didn't want to strike back because I thought it was a misunderstanding and he'd realize his mistake in a few seconds."

"Do you think he sold you out? Or that it was something he'd been planning for a long time? Some grudge?"

"I don't like to think that."

"Magic, then?"

"Maybe. I don't know."

A peculiar thought occurred to me. "Did he know you'd killed Caine?" I asked.

"No, I make it a point never to tell anybody everything I'm about."

"You wouldn't kid me, would you?"

He laughed, moved as if to clap me on the shoulder, winced and thought better of it.

"Why do you ask?" he said then.

"I don't know. Just curious."

"Sure," he said. Then, "What say you give me a hand up and inside, so I can see what kind of supplies you've left me?"

"Okay."

I got to my feet and helped him to his. We moved around to the right to the slope of easiest ascent, and I guided him slowly to the top.

Once we'd achieved the summit he leaned on his staff and stared down into the opening.

"No really easy way down in," he said, "for me. At first I was thinking you could roll up a barrel from the larder, and I could get down to it and then down to the floor. But now I look at it, it's an even bigger drop than I remembered. I'd tear something open, for sure."

"Mm-hm," I said. "Hang on. I've got an idea."

I turned away from him and climbed back down. Then I made my way along the base of the blue rise to my right until I had rounded two shiny shoulders and was completely out of Luke's line of sight.

I did not care to use the Logrus in his presence if I did not have to. I did not wish for him to see how I went about things, and I did not want to give him any idea as to what I could or could not do. I'm not that comfortable letting people know too much about me, either.

The Logrus appeared at my summons, and I reached into it, extended through it. My desire was framed, became the aim. My sending extending sought the thought. Far, far. . . .

I kept extending for the damnedest long time. We really had to be out in the Shadow boonies. . . .

Contact.

I did not jerk, but rather exerted a slow and steady pressure. I felt it move toward me across the shadows.

"Hey, Merle! Everything okay?" I heard Luke call.

"Yeah," I answered and I did not elaborate.

Closer, closer. . . .

There!

I staggered when it arrived, because it came to me too near to one end. The far end bounced on the ground. So I moved to the middle and took a new grip. I hefted it and carried it back.

I set it against a steep area of the rise a bit in advance of Luke's position and I mounted quickly. I began drawing it up behind me then.

"Okay, where'd you get the ladder?" he asked.

"Found it," I said.

"Looks like wet paint on the side there."

"Maybe someone lost it just recently."

I began lowering it into the opening. Several feet protruded after it reached the bottom. I adjusted it for stability.

"I'll start down first," I said, "and stay right under you."

"Take my stick and my blade down first, will you?"

"Sure."

I did that thing. By the time I climbed back he had caught hold and gotten onto it, had begun his descent.

"You'll have to teach me that trick one of these days," he said, breathing heavily.

"Don't know what you're talking about," I answered.

He descended slowly, pausing to rest at each rung, and he was flushed and panting when he reached the bottom. He slumped to the floor immediately, pressing his right palm against his lower rib cage. After a time, he inched backward a bit and rested against the wall.

"You okay?" I asked.

He nodded. "Will be," he said, "in a few minutes. Being stabbed takes a lot out of you."

"Want a blanket?"

"No, thanks."

"Well, you rest here and I'll go check the larder and see whether anything's gotten at the supplies. Want me to bring you anything?"

"Some water," he said.

The supplies proved to be in good order, and the sleeping bag was still where I'd left it. I returned with a drink for Luke and a few ironic memories of the occasion when he'd done the same for me.

"Looks as if you're in business," I told him. "There's still plenty of stuff."

"You didn't drink all the wine, did you?" he asked between sips.

"No."

"Good."

"Now, you said you have a piece of information vital to the interests of Amber," I said. "Care to tell me about it?"

He smiled. "Not yet," he said.

"I thought that was our deal."

"You didn't hear the whole thing. We were interrupted."

I shook my head. But, "All right, we were interrupted," I acknowledged. "Tell me the rest."

"I've got to get back on my feet, so I can take the Keep and free my mother. . . ."

I nodded.

"The information is yours after we rescue her."

"Hey! Wait a minute! You're asking a hell of a lot!"

"Not for what I'm paying."

"Sounds like I'm buying a pig in a poke."

"Yes, I guess you are. But believe me, it'll be worth knowing."

"What if it becomes worth knowing while I'm waiting?"

"No, I've figured the timing on this. My recovery is only going to take a couple of days, Amber time. I can't see the matter coming up that fast."

"Luke, this is starting to sound like some sort of trick."

"It is," he said, "but it will benefit Amber as well as myself."

"That's another thing. I can't see you giving something like this away to the enemy."

He sighed. "It might even be enough to get me off the hook," he added.

"You're thinking of calling off your feud?"

"I don't know. But I've been doing a lot of thinking, and if I did decide to go that route it would make for a real good opener."

"And if you decided not to, you'd be screwing yourself. Wouldn't you?"

"I could live with it, though. It might make my job harder, but not impossible."

"I don't know," I said. "If word of this gets out and I've got nothing to show for letting you get away like this, I'll be in real hot water."

"I won't tell anybody if you won't."

"There's Vinta."

"And she keeps insisting that her big aim in life is to protect you. Besides, she won't be there if you go back. Or rather, there will be the real Vinta, having awakened as from a troubled sleep."

"How can you be so sure?"

"Because you've left. She's probably already off seeking you."

"Do you know what she really is?"

"No, but I'll help you speculate sometime."

"Not now?"

"No, I've got to sleep some more. It's catching up with me again."

"Then let's go over this deal one more time. What are you going to do, how do you intend to do it and what are you promising me?"

He yawned. "I stay here till I'm back in shape," he said. "Then when I'm ready to attack the Keep I get in touch with you. Which reminds me, you still have my Trumps."

"I know. Keep talking. How do you intend taking the Keep?"

"I'm working on it. I'll let you know that too. Anyhow, you can help us or not at that point, as you see fit. I wouldn't mind having another sorcerer with me, though. Once we're in and she's freed, I'll tell you what I promised and you can take it back to Amber."

"What if you lose?" I asked.

He looked away. "I guess there's always that possibility," he finally agreed. "Okay, how's this? I'll write the whole thing out and keep it with me. I'll give it to you—by Trump or in person—before we attack. Win or lose, I'll have paid my way with you."

He extended his good hand and I clasped it.

"Okay," I said.

"Then let me have my Trumps back, and I'll be talking to you as soon as I get moving again."

I hesitated. Finally, I drew out my pack, which was now grown quite thick. I shuffled out my own then—along with a number of his—and passed him what remained.

"What about the rest?"

"I want to study them, Luke. Okay?"

He shrugged weakly. "I can always make more. But give me back my mother's."

"Here."

He accepted it, then said, "I don't know what you've got in mind, but I'll give you a piece of advice: Don't screw around with Dalt. He's not the nicest of guys when he's normal, and I think there's something wrong with him right now. Keep away from him."

I nodded, then got to my feet.

"You're going now?" he asked.

"Right."

"Leave me the ladder."

"It's all yours."

"What are you going to tell them back in Amber?"

"Nothing—yet," I said. "Hey, you want me to bring some food up here before I go? Save you a trip."

"Yeah. Good idea. Bring me a bottle of wine, too."

I went back and got him a load of provisions. I dragged in the sleeping bag also.

I started up the ladder, then paused. "You don't know your own mind on this yet," I said, "do you?"

He smiled. "Don't be too sure of that."

When I got to the top I stared at the big boulder that had once sealed me in. Earlier, I'd thought of returning the favor. I could keep track of the time, come get him when he was back on his feet. That way, he couldn't pull a disappearing act on me. I had decided against it, though, not only because I was the only one who knew he was here and if something happened to me he'd be dead. Mainly, it was because he wouldn't be able to reach me with my Trump when he was ready to move, if I kept him fully confined. That's what I told myself, anyhow.

I stooped and caught hold of the boulder, anyway, and pushed it nearer the opening.

"Merle! What are you doing?"—from below.

"Looking for fishing bait," I answered.

"Hey, come on! Don't. . . ."

I laughed and pushed it a little nearer.

"Merle!"

"Thought you might want the door closed, in case it rains," I said. "But it's too damned heavy. Forget it. Take it easy."

I turned and jumped. I thought the extra adrenaline might do him some good.

EIGHT

When I hit the ground I kept going, back to the place from which I had conjured the ladder, out of sight from several directions.

I withdrew one of the blank cards. Time was running. When I fished out the pencil, I discovered that its point had broken. I unsheathed my blade, which was about the length of my arm. I'd found another use for the thing.

A minute or so later I had the card before me on a flat rock, and I was sketching my room back at the Arbor House, the forces of the Logrus moving through my hands. I had to work deliberately, getting the proper feeling of the place into the drawing. Finally, when it was finished, I stood. It was right, it was ready. I opened my mind and regarded my work until it became reality. Then I walked forward into the room. Just as I did I thought of something I wanted to ask Luke, but it was too late.

Beyond the window, the shadows of the trees were stretching to the east. I had obviously been gone for most of the day.

When I turned I saw a sheet of paper upon the now made-up bed, secured against breezes by the edge of a pillow. I crossed to it and picked it up, removing the small blue button which lay atop it before I did so.

The writing was in English. It said: PUT THE BUTTON IN A SAFE PLACE TILL YOU NEED IT. I WOULDN'T CARRY IT AROUND TOO MUCH. I HOPE YOU DID THE RIGHT THING. I GUESS I'LL FIND OUT PRETTY SOON. SEE YOU AROUND.

It was unsigned.

Safe or not, I couldn't just leave it there. So I wrapped the button in the note and put it in my pocket. Then I fetched my cloak from the closet and slung it over my arm.

I departed the room. The latch being broken, I left the door standing wide. I stopped in the hallway and listened, but I heard no voices, no sounds of movement.

I made my way to the stairs and headed down. I was almost to the bottom before I noticed her, so still did she sit, there beside the window to my right, a tray of bread and cheese, a bottle and a goblet on a small table at her side.

"Merlin!" she said suddenly, half rising. "The servants said you were here, but when I looked I couldn't find you."

"I was called away," I said descending the final stair and advancing. "How are you feeling?"

"How do you—what do you know about me?" she asked.

"You probably don't remember anything that happened during the past couple of days," I replied.

"You are right," she said. "Won't you sit down?"

She gestured at the empty chair at the other side of the small table.

"Please join me." She indicated the tray. "And let me get you some wine."

"That's all right," I said, seeing that she was drinking the white.

She rose and crossed the room to a cabinet, opened it and took out another goblet. When she returned she poured a healthy slug of Bayle's Piss into it and set it near my hand. I guessed it was possible they kept the good stuff for themselves.

"What can you tell me about my blackout?" she asked. "I'd been in Amber, and the next thing I knew I was back here and several days had gone by."

"Yes," I said, taking up a cracker and a bit of cheese. "About what time did you become yourself again?"

"This morning."

"It's nothing to worry about—now," I answered. "There shouldn't be a recurrence."

"But what was it?"

"Just something that's been going around," I said, trying the wine.

"It seems more like magic than the flu."

"Perhaps there was a touch of that too," I agreed. "You never know what might blow in out of Shadow. But almost everyone I know who's had it is okay now."

She furrowed her brow. "It was very strange."

I had a few more crackers and sips of the wine. They did keep the good stuff for themselves.

"There is absolutely nothing to worry about," I repeated.

She smiled and nodded. "I believe you. What are you doing here, anyhow?"

"Stopover. I'm on my way back to Amber," I said, "from elsewhere. Which reminds me—may I borrow a horse?"

"Certainly," she replied. "How soon will you be leaving?"

"As soon as I get the horse," I said.

She got to her feet. "I didn't realize you were in a hurry. I'll take you over to the stables now."

"Thanks."

I grabbed two more crackers and another piece of cheese on the way out and tossed off the rest of the wine. I wondered where the blue fog might be drifting now.

When I'd located a good horse, which she told me I could have delivered to their stable in Amber, I saddled him and fitted his bridle. He was a gray, named Smoke. I donned my cloak then and clasped Vinta's hands.

"Thanks for the hospitality," I said, "even if you don't recall it."

"Don't say good-bye yet," she told me. "Ride around to the kitchen door off the patio, and I'll give you a water bottle and some food for the road. We didn't have a mad affair that I don't remember, did we?"

"A gentleman never tells," I said.

She laughed and slapped my shoulder. "Come see me sometime when I'm in Amber," she told me, "and refresh my memory."

I grabbed a set of saddlebags, a bag of chow for Smoke and a longish tethering rope. I led him outside as Vinta headed back to the house. I mounted then and rose slowly after her, a few dogs capering about me. I circled the manor, taking the long way around, drew rein and dismounted near the kitchen. I considered the patio, wishing I had one just like it where I could sit and take coffee in the morning. Or had it just been the company?

After a time, the door opened and Vinta came out and passed me a bundle and a flask. As I was securing them, she said, "Let my father know that I'll be back in a few days, will you? Tell him that I came to the country because I wasn't feeling well, but that I'm all right now."

"Glad to," I said.

"I don't really know why you were here," she said. "But if it involves politics or intrigue I don't want to know."

"Okay," I said.

"If a servant took a meal to a big red-haired man who seemed to be pretty badly injured, this would be better forgotten?"

"I'd say."

"It will be, then. But one of these days I'd like the story."

"Me too," I said. "We'll see what we can do."

"So, have a good journey."

"Thanks. I'll try."

I clasped her hand, turned away and mounted.

"So long."

"See you in Amber," she said.

I mounted and continued my circuit of the house until I was back near the stables again. I headed past them then to a trail we had ridden that led off in the direction I wanted. Back toward the house, a dog began to howl and another joined it moments later. There was a breeze out of the south, and it carried a few leaves past me. I wanted to be on the road, far away and alone. I value my solitude because that is when I seem to do my best thinking, and right now I had many things to think over.

I rode to the northwest. About ten minutes later I came to a dirt road we had crossed the other day. This time I followed it westward, and it finally took me to the crossroads with the marker indicating that Amber lay straight ahead. I rode on.

It was a yellow dirt road that I traveled, showing the impress of many wagon wheels. It followed the contours of the land, passing between fallow fields bordered by low stone fences, a few trees at either hand. I could see the stark outlines of mountains far ahead, standing above the forested area I was soon to encounter. We moved along at an easy gait, and I let my mind drift over the events of the past few days.

That I had an enemy I did not doubt. Luke had assured me that it was no longer him, and I had found him to be more than a little persuasive. He need not have come to me to be patched up, as both he and Vinta had pointed out. And he could have found his own way to the crystal cave or some other sanctuary. And the business about my helping him to rescue Jasra could have waited. I was more than half convinced that he was trying to get back on better terms with me again quickly because I was his only contact with the Court of Amber, and his fortunes had taken a turn for the worse. I had a feeling that what he really wanted was an official determination as to his status with Amber, and that he had mentioned the piece of important information he would be willing to surrender both as a sign of good faith and as a bargaining chip. I was not at all certain that I, personally, would be very crucial to any plan he might have for rescuing Jasra. Not when he knew the Keep inside and out, was some kind of sorcerer himself and had a band of mercs he could transport from the shadow Earth. For all I knew, that fancy ammo of his would work there as well as in Amber. And whether that was true or not, why couldn't he just trump his attack force into the place? He wouldn't even really have to win a battle—just get in, grab Jasra and get out. No, I did not feel that I was really necessary to whatever operation he finally decided upon. I'd a feeling he'd waved a red herring at me, hoping that when the air cleared we would simply consider what he had and what he wanted and make him an offer.

I'd a feeling, too, that he might be willing to call it quits on the vendetta now that Caine was out of the way and family honor satisfied. And I'd a notion that Jasra was the stumbling block on his side. While I'd no idea what hold she might have over him, it had occurred to me that the piece of information to which he'd referred might represent some means of neutralizing her. If he got it to us quietly and it seemed to come from our side, he could save face with her as well as buying peace with us. Tantalizing. My problem now was to find the best way to present this at court without looking like a traitor for having let him go. Which meant I had to show that the profit would be worth the investment.

There were more trees at the roadside now, and the forest itself was nearer. I crossed a wooden bridge above a clear stream, and the gentle splashing sounds followed me for a time. There were brown fields and distant barns to my left, a wagon with a broken axle off to my right. . . .

And if I had read Luke wrong? Was there some way I might be able to pressure him and make my interpretation come out right anyway? A small idea began to form. I was not overjoyed with it, but I considered it nevertheless. Risk and speed were what it involved. It had its merits, though. I pushed it as far as I could, then put it aside and returned to my original train of thought.

Somewhere, there was an enemy. And if it wasn't Luke, who was it? Jasra seemed the most obvious candidate. She had made her feelings toward me pretty clear on the occasions of our two meetings. She could well be the one who had dispatched the assassins I had encountered in Death Alley. In that case, I was probably safe for a time—with her a prisoner back at the Keep—unless, of course, she had sent along a few more before she had been captured. That would have been redundant, though. Why waste all that manpower on me? I had only been a minor figure in the event she sought to avenge, and the men who came after me had been almost sufficient to the task.

And if it wasn't Jasra? Then I was still in jeopardy. The wizard in the blue mask, whom I assumed to be Sharu Garrul, had caused me to be pursued by a tornado, which seemed a far less friendly overture than the flowers that had followed. This latter, of course, identified him with the individual behind my peculiar experience at Flora's apartment back in San Francisco. In that instance, he had initiated the encounter, which meant that he had some designs on me. What was it he'd said? Something about the possibility of us being at cross-purposes at some future time. How interesting, in retrospect. For I could now see the possibility of such a situation's occurring.

But was it really Sharu Garrul who had sent the assassins? Despite his familiarity with the power of the blue stone that had guided them—as evidenced by the blue button in my pocket—it didn't seem to follow. For one thing, our purposes were not yet crossed. For another, it did not seem the proper style for a cryptic, flower-throwing master of elements. I could be dead wrong there, of course, but I expected something more in the nature of a sorcerous duel with that one.

The fields gave way to wilderness as I approached the verge of the forest. Something of twilight had already entered its brightleafed domain. It did not seem a dense, ancient wood like Arden, however; from the distance I had seen numerous gaps within its higher reaches. The road continued wide and well-kept. I drew my cloak more fully about me as I entered the shadowed coolness. It seemed an easy ride, if it were all to be like this. And I was in no hurry. I had too many thoughts that wanted thinking. . . .

If only I had been able to learn more from that strange, nameless entity who had, for a time, controlled Vinta. What her true nature might be, I still had no idea. "Her," yes. I somehow felt the entity to be more feminine than masculine in nature, despite its having controlled George Hansen and Dan Martinez. Perhaps this was only because I had made love to her as Meg Devlin. Difficult to say. But I had known Gail for some time, and the Lady in the Lake had seemed a real lady . . .

Enough. I'd decided on my pronoun. Other matters of greater importance were involved. Like, whatever she was, why was she following me about insisting that she wanted to protect me? While I appreciated the sentiment, I still had no insight into her motivation.

But there was something far more important to me than her motivation. Why she saw fit to guard me could remain her own business. The big question was: Against *what* did she feel I needed protection? She must have had a definite threat in mind, and she had not given me the slightest hint as to what it was.

Was this, then, the enemy? The real enemy? Vinta's adversary?

I tried reviewing everything I knew or had guessed about her.

There is a strange creature who sometimes takes the form of a small blue mist. She is capable of finding her way to me through Shadow. She possesses the power to take control of a human body, completely suppressing its natural ego. She hung around in my vicinity for a number of years without my becoming aware of her. Her earliest incarnation that I know of was as Luke's former girlfriend, Gail.

Why Gail? If she were guarding me, why go around with Luke? Why not become one of the women I'd dated? Why not be Julia? But no. She had decided upon Gail. Was that because Luke was the threat, and she wanted to keep a close watch on him? But she'd actually let Luke get away with a few attempts on my life. And then Jasra. She'd admitted that she'd known Jasra was behind the later ones. Why hadn't she simply removed them? She could have taken over Luke's body, stepped in front of a speeding car, drifted away from the remains, then gone and done the same with Jasra. She wasn't afraid to die in a host body. I'd seen her do it twice.

Unless she'd somehow known that all their attempts on my life would fail. Could she have sabotaged the letter bomb? Could she, in some way, have been behind my premonition on the morning of the opened gas jets? And perhaps something else with each of the others? Still, it would seem a lot simpler to go to the source and remove the problem itself. I knew that she had no compunction about killing. She'd ordered the slaying of my final assailant in Death Alley.

What, then?

Two possibilities came to mind immediately. One was that she'd actually come to like Luke—and that she'd simply found ways to neutralize him without destroying him. But then I thought of her as Martinez, and it fell apart. She'd actually been shooting that night in Santa Fe. Okay. Then there was the other possibility: Luke was not the real threat, and she'd liked him enough to let him go on living once he'd quit the April 30 games and she saw that we'd gotten friendly. Something happened in New Mexico that made her change her mind. As to what it was, I had no idea. She had followed me to New York, then, and been George Hansen and Meg Devlin in quick succession. Luke was, by that time, out of the picture, following his disappearing act on the mountain. He no longer represented a threat, yet she was almost frantic in her efforts to get in touch with me. Was something else impending? The real threat?

I racked my brains, but I could not figure what that threat might have been. Was I following a completely false trail with this line of reasoning?

She certainly was not omniscient. Her reason for spiriting me to Arbor House was as much to pump me for information as it was to remove me from the scene of the attack. And some of the things she'd wanted to know were as interesting as some of the things she knew.

My mind did a backward flip. What was the first question she had asked me?

Landing adroitly on my mental feet, back at Bill Roth's place, I heard the question several times. As George Hansen she had asked it causally and I had lied; as a voice on the telephone she had asked it and been denied; as Meg Devlin, in bed, she had finally gotten me to answer it honestly: What was your mother's name?

When I'd told her that my mother was named Dara she had finally begun speaking freely. She had warned me against Luke. It seemed that she might have been willing to tell me more then, too, save that the arrival of the real Meg's husband had cut short our conversation.

To what was this the key? It placed my origin in the Courts of Chaos, to which she had at no time referred. Yet it had to be important, somehow.

I had a feeling that I already had the answer but that I would be unable to realize it until I had formulated the proper question.

Enough. I could go no further. Knowing that she was aware of my connection with the Courts still told me nothing. She was also obviously aware of my connection with Amber, and I could not see how that figured in the pattern of events either.

So I would leave it at that point and come back to it later. I had plenty of other things to think about. At least, I now had lots of new questions to ask her the next time we met, and I was certain that we would meet again.

Then something else occurred to me. If she'd done any real protecting of me at all, it had taken place offstage. She had given me a lot of information, which I thought was probably correct but which I had had no opportunity to verify. From her phoning and lurking back in New York to her killing of my one possible source of information in Death Alley, she had really been more a bother than a help. It was conceivable that she could actually show up and encumber me with aid again, at exactly the wrong moment.

So instead of working on my opening argument for Random, I spent the next hour or so considering the nature of being capable of moving into a person and taking over the controls. There seemed only a certain number of ways it might be done, and I narrowed the field quickly, considering what I knew of her nature, by means of the technical exercises my uncle had taught me. When I thought I had it worked out I backtracked and mused over the forces that would have to be involved.

From the forces I worked my way through the tonic vibrations of their aspects. The use of raw power, while flashy, is wasteful and very fatiguing for the operator, not to mention aesthetically barbaric. Better to be prepared.

I lined up the spoken signatures and edited them into a spell. Suhuy would probably have gotten it down even shorter, but there is a point of diminishing returns on these things, and I had mine figured to where it should work if my main guesses were correct. So I collated it and assembled it. It was fairly long—too long to rattle off in its entirety if I were in the hurry I probably would be. Studying it, I saw that three linchpins would probably hold it, though four would be better.

I summoned the Logrus and extended my tongue into its moving pattern. Then I spoke the spell, slowing and clearly, leaving out the four key words I had chosen to omit. The woods grew absolutely still about me as the words rang out. The spell hung before me like a crippled butterfly of sound and color, trapped within the synesthetic web of my personal vision of the Logrus, to come again when I summoned it, to be released when I uttered the four omitted words.

I banished the vision and felt my tongue relax. Now she was not the only one capable of troublesome surprises.

I halted for a drink of water. The sky had grown darker and the small noises of the forest returned. I wondered whether Fiona or Bleys had been in touch, and how Bill was doing back in town. I listened to the rattling of branches. Suddenly, I had the feeling I was being watched—not the cold scrutiny of a Trump touch, but simply the sensation that there was a pair of eyes fixed upon me. I shivered. All those thoughts about enemies. . . .

I loosened my blade and rode on. The night was young, and there were more miles ahead than behind.

Riding through the evening I kept alert, but I neither heard nor saw anything untoward. Had I been wrong about Jasra, Sharu or even Luke? And was there a party of assassins at my back right now? Periodically, I drew rein and sat listening for a short while. But I heard nothing unusual on these occasions, nothing that could be taken as sounds of pursuit. I became acutely aware of the blue button in my pocket. Was it acting as a beacon for some sinister sending of the wizard's? I was loath to get rid of the thing because I could foresee a number of possible uses for it. Besides, if it had already attuned me—which it probably had—I could see no benefit in disposing of it now. I would secrete it someplace safe before I made my attempt to lose its vibes. Until such time, I could see no percentage in doing anything else with it.

The sky continued to darken, and a number of stars had put in hesitant appearances. Smoke and I slowed even more in our course, but the road remained good and its pale surface stayed sufficiently visible to present no hazard. I heard the call of an owl from off to the right and moments later saw its dark shape rush at middle height among the trees. It would have been a pleasant night to be riding if I were not creating my own ghosts and haunting myself with them. I love the smells of autumn and the forest, and I resolved to burn a few leaves in my campfire later on for that pungency unlike any other I know.

The air was clean and cool. Hoof sounds, our breathing and the wind seemed to be the only noises in the neighborhood until we flushed a deer a bit later and heard the diminishing crashes of its treat for some time afterward. We crossed a small but sturdy wooden bridge a little later, but no trolls were taking tolls. The road took a turn upward, and we wound our way slowly but steadily to a higher elevation. Now there were numerous stars visible through the weave of the branches, but no clouds that I could see. The deciduous trees grew barer as we gained a bit of altitude, and more evergreens began to occur. I felt the breezes more strongly now.

I began pausing more frequently, to rest Smoke, to listen, to nibble at my supplies. I resolved to keep going at least until moonrise—which I tried to calculate from its occurrence the other night, following my departure from Amber. If I made it to that point before I camped, the rest of the ride into Amber tomorrow morning would be pretty easy.

Frakir pulsed once, lightly on my wrist. But hell, that had often happened in traffic when I'd cut someone off. A hungry fox could have just passed, regarded me and wished itself a bear. Still, I waited there longer than I had intended, prepared for an attack and trying not to appear so.

But nothing happened, the warning as not repeated and after a time I rode on. I returned to my idea for putting the screws to Luke—and, for that matter, Jasra. I couldn't call it a plan yet, because it was lacking in almost all particulars. The more I thought of it, the crazier it seemed. For one thing, it was extremely tempting, as it held the potential for resolving a lot of problems. I wondered then why I had never created a Trump for Bill Roth. I felt a sudden need to talk to a good attorney. I might well want someone to argue my case before this was done. Too dark now to do any drawing, though . . . and not really necessary yet. Actually, I just wanted to talk with him, bring him up to date, get the views of someone not directly involved.

Frakir issued no further warnings during the next hour. We commenced a slightly downward course then, soon passing into a somewhat more sheltered area where the smell of pines came heavy. I mused on—about wizards and flowers, Ghostwheel and his problems, and the name of the entity who had recently occupied Vinta. There were lots of other musings, too, some of which went a long way back. . . .

Many stops later, with a bit of moonlight trickling through the branches behind me, I decided to call it quits and look for a place to bed down. I gave Smoke a brief drink at the next stream. About a quarter hour afterward, I thought I glimpsed what might be a promising spot off to the right, so I left the road and headed that way.

It turned out not to be as good a place as I'd thought, and I continued farther into the wood until I came across a small clear area that seemed adequate. I dismounted, unsaddled Smoke and tethered him, rubbed him down with his blanket and gave him something to eat. Then I scraped clear a small area of ground with my blade, dug a pit at its center and built a fire there. I used a spell to ignite it because I was feeling lazy, and threw on several clumps of leaves as I recalled my earlier reflections.

I seated myself on my cloak, my back against the bole of a middle-sized tree, and ate a cheese sandwich and sipped water while I worked up the ambition to pull my boots off. My blade lay upon the ground at my side. My muscles began to unkink. The smell of the fire was a nostalgic thing. I toasted my next sandwich over it.

I sat and thought of nothing for a long while. Gradually, in barely perceptible stages, I felt the gentle disengagements lassitude brings to the extremities. I had meant to gather firewood before I took my ease. But I didn't really need it. It wasn't all that cold. I'd wanted the fire mainly for company.

However. . . . I dragged myself to my feet and moved off into the woods. I did a long, slow reconnaissance about the area once I got moving. Though to be honest, my main reason for getting up had been to go and relieve myself. I halted in my circuit when I thought that I detected a small flicker of light far off to the northeast. Another campfire? Moonlight on water? A torch? There had been only a glimpse and I could not locate it again, though I moved my head about, retraced my most recent few paces and even struck off a small distance in that direction.

But I did not wish to chase after some will-o'-the-wisp and spend my night beating the bushes. I checked various lines of sight back to my camp. My small fire was barely visible even from this distance. I circled my camp, entered and sprawled again. The fire was already dying and I decided to let it burn out. I wrapped my cloak about me and listened to the soft sounds of the wind.

I fell asleep quickly. For how long I slept, I do not know. There were no dreams that I can recall.

I was awakened by Frakir's frantic pulsing. I opened my eyes the barest slits and tossed, as if in sleep, so that my right hand fell near the haft of my blade. I maintained my slow breathing pattern. I heard and felt that the wind had risen, and I saw that it had fanned the embers to the point where my fire flared once again. I saw no one before me, however. I strained my hearing after any sounds, but all I heard was the wind and popping of the fire.

It seemed as foolish to spring to my feet into a guard position when I did not know from which direction the danger was approaching as it did to remain a target. On the other hand, I had intentionally cast my cloak so that I lay with a large, low-limbed pine at my back. It would have been very difficult for someone to have approached me from the rear, let alone to have done so quietly. So it did not seem I was in danger of an imminent attack from that direction.

I turned my head slightly and studied Smoke, who had begun to seem a little uneasy. Frakir continued her now distracting warning till I willed her to be still.

Smoke was twitching his ears and moving his head about, nostrils dilated. As I watched, I saw that his attention seemed directed toward my right. He began edging his way across the camp, his long tether snaking behind him.

I heard a sound then, beyond the noise of Smoke's retreat, as of something advancing from the right. It was not repeated for a time, and then I heard it again. It was not a footfall, but a sound as of a body brushing against a branch which suddenly issued a weak protest.

I visualized the disposition of the trees and shrubs in that direction and decided to let the lurker draw nearer before I made my move. I dismissed the notion of summoning the Logrus and preparing a magical attack. It would take a bit more time than I thought I had remaining. Also, from Smoke's behavior and from what I had heard, it seemed that there was only a single individual approaching. I resolved, though, to lay in a decent supply of spells the first chance I got, both offensive and defensive, on the order of the one I had primed against my guardian entity. The trouble is that it can take several days of solitude to work a really decent array of them out properly, enact them and rehearse their releases to the point where you can spring them at a moment's notice—and then they have a tendency to start decaying after a week or so. Sometimes they last longer and sometimes less long, depending both on the amount of energy you're willing to invest in them and on the magical climate of the particular shadow in which you're functioning. It's a lot of bother unless you're sure you're going to need them within a certain period of time. On the other hand, a good sorcerer should have one attack, one defense and one escape spell hanging around at all times. But I'm generally somewhat lazy, not to mention pretty easygoing, and I didn't see any need for that sort of setup until recently. And recently, I hadn't had much time to be about it.

So any use I might make of the Logrus now, were I to summon it and situate myself within its ambit, would pretty much amount to blasting away with a raw power—which is very draining on the operator.

Let him come a little nearer, that's all, and it would be cold steel and a strangling cord that he would face.

I could feel the presence advancing now, hear the soft stirring of pine needles. A few more feet, enemy. . . . Come on. That's all I need. Come into range. . . .

He halted. I could hear a steady, soft breathing.

Then, "You must be aware of me by now, Magus," came a low whisper, "for we all have our little tricks, and I know the source of yours."

"Who are you?" I asked, as I clasped the haft of my blade and rolled into a crouch, facing the darkness, the point of my weapon describing a small circle.

"I am the enemy," was the reply. "The one you thought would never come."

NINE

Power.

I remembered the day I had stood atop a rocky prominence. Fiona—dressed in lavender, belted with silver—stood in a higher place before me and somewhat to my right. She held a silver mirror in her right hand, and she looked downward through the haze to the place where the great tree towered. There was a total stillness about us, and even our own small sounds became muffled. The upper portion of the tree disappeared into a low-hanging fog bank. The light that filtered through limned it starkly against another pile of fog which hung at its back, rising to join with the one overhead. A bright, seemingly self-illuminated line was etched into the ground near the base of the tree, curving off to vanish within the fog. Far to my left, a brief arc of a similar intensity was also visible, emerging from and returning to the billowing white wall.

"What is it, Fiona?" I asked. "Why did you bring me to this place?"

"You've heard of it," she replied. "I wanted you to see it."

I shook my head. "I've never heard of it. I've no idea what I'm looking at."

"Come," she said, and she began to descend.

She disdained my hand, moving quickly and gracefully, and we came down from the rocks and moved nearer to the tree. There was something vaguely familiar there, but I could not place it.

"From your father," she said at last. "He spent a long time telling you his story. Surely he did not omit this part."

I halted as understanding presented itself, tentatively at first.

"That tree," I said.

"Corwin planted his staff when he commenced the creation of the new Pattern," she said. "It was fresh. It took root."

I seemed to feel a faint vibration in the ground.

Fiona turned her back on the prospect, raised the mirror she carried and angled it so that she regarded the scene over her right shoulder.

"Yes," she said, after several moments. Then she extended the mirror to me. "Take a look," she told me, "as I just did."

I accepted it, held it, adjusted it and stared.

The view in the mirror was not the same as that which had presented itself to my unaided scrutiny. I was able to see beyond the tree now, through the fog, to discern most of the strange Pattern which twisted its bright way about the ground, working its passage inward to its off-center terminus, the only spot still concealed by an unmoving tower of white, within which tiny lights like stars seemed to burn.

"It doesn't look like the Pattern back in Amber," I said.

"No," she answered. "Is it anything like the Logrus?"

"Not really. The Logrus actually alters itself somewhat constantly. Still, it's more angular, whereas this is mostly curves and bends."

I studied it a little longer, then returned her looking glass.

"Interesting spell on the mirror," I commented, for I had been studying this also, while I held it.

"And much more difficult than you'd think," she responded, "for there's more than fog in there. Watch."

She advanced to the beginning of the Pattern, near the great tree, where she moved as if to set her foot upon the bright trail. Before it arrived, however, a small electrical discharge crackled upward and made contact with her shoe. She jerked her foot back quickly.

"It rejects me," she said. "I can't set foot on it. Try it."

There was something in her gaze I did not like, but I moved forward to where she had been standing.

"Why couldn't your mirror penetrate all the way to the center of the thing?" I asked suddenly.

"The resistance seems to go up the farther you go in. It is greatest there," she replied. "But as to why, I do not know."

I hesitated a moment longer. "Has anyone tried it other than yourself?"

"I brought Bleys here," she answered. "It rejected him too."

"And he's the only other one who's seen it?"

"No, I brought Random. Be he declined to try. Said he didn't care to screw around with it right then."

"Prudent, perhaps. Was he wearing the Jewel at the time?"

"No. Why?"

"Just curious."

"See what it does for you."

"All right."

I raised my right foot and lowered it slowly toward the line. About a foot above it, I stopped.

"Something seems to be holding me back," I said.

"Strange. There is no electrical discharge for you."

"Small blessing," I responded and I pushed my foot a couple of inches farther downward. Finally, I sighed. "Nope, Fi. I can't."

I read the disappointment in her features.

"I was hoping," she said as I drew back, "that someone other than Corwin might be able to walk it. His son seemed the most likely choice."

"Why is it so important that someone walk it? Just because it's there?"

"I think it's a menace," she said. "It has to be explored and dealt with."

"A menace? Why?"

"Amber and Chaos are the two poles of existence, as we understand it," she said, "housing as they do the Pattern and the Logrus. For ages there has been something of an equilibrium between them. Now, I believe, this bastard Pattern of your father's is undermining their balance."

"In what fashion?"

"There have always been wavelike exchanges between Amber and Chaos. This seems to be setting up some interference."

"It sounds more like tossing an extra ice cube into a drink," I said. "It should settle down after a while."

She shook her head. "Things are not settling. There have been far more shadow-storms since this thing was created. They rend the fabric of Shadow. They affect the nature of reality itself."

"No good," I said. "Another event a lot more important along these lines occurred at the same time. The original Pattern in Amber was damaged and Oberon repaired it. The wave of Chaos which came out of that swept through all of Shadow. Everything was affected. But the Pattern held and things settled again. I'd be more inclined to think of all those extra shadow-storms as being in the nature of aftershocks."

"It's a good argument," she said. "But what if it's wrong?"

"I don't think it is."

"Merle, there's some kind of power here—an immense amount of power."

"I don't doubt it."

"It has always been our way to keep an eye on power, to try to understand it, to control it. Because one day it might become a threat. Did Corwin tell you anything, anything at all, as to exactly what this represents and how we might get a handle on it?"

"No," I said. "Nothing beyond the fact that he made it in a hurry to replace the old one, which he'd figured Oberon might not have succeeded in repairing."

"If only we could find him."

"There still hasn't been any word?"

"Droppa claims that he saw him at the Sands, back on the shadow Earth you both favor. He said he was in the company of an attractive woman, and they were both having a drink and listening to a music group. He waved and headed toward them through a crowd, and he thought that Corwin saw him. When he got to their table, though, they were gone."

"That's all?"

"That's all."

"That's not much."

"I know. If he's the only one who can walk this damned thing, though, and if it *is* a menace, we could be in big trouble one day."

"I think you're being an alarmist, Aunty."

"I hope you're right, Merle. Come on, I'll take you home."

I studied the place once more, for details as well as feeling, because I wanted to be able to construct a Trump for it. I never told anyone that there had been no resistance as I had lowered my foot, because once you set foot into the Pattern or the Logrus there is no turning back. You either proceed to the end or are dstroyed by it. And as much as I love mysteries, my break was at its end and I had to get back to class.

Power.

We were together in a wood within the Black Zone, that area of Shadow with which Chaos holds commerce. We were hunting *zhind*, which are horned, short, black, fierce and carnivorous. I do not much like hunting because I do not much like killing things I don't really have to. However, it was Jurt's idea, and since it was possibly also my last chance to work some reconciliation with my brother before I departed, I had decided to take him up on the offer. Neither of us was that great an archer, and *zhind* are pretty fast. So with any luck at all nothing would get dead and we'd have some chance to talk and perhaps come away on better terms at the end of the hunt.

On one occasion when we'd lost the trail and were resting, we talked for a long time about archery, court politics, Shadow and the weather. He had been much more civil to me of late, which I took for a good sign. He'd let his hair grow in such a fashion as to cover the area of his missing left ear. Ears are hard to regenerate. We did not speak of our duel, or of the argument that led up to it. Because I would soon be out of his life, I felt perhaps he wished to close this chapter of his existence in a relatively friendly fashion, with both of us going our ways with a memory we could feel good about. I was half right, anyway.

Later, when we had halted for a cold trail lunch, he asked me, "So, what does it feel like?"

"What?" I said.

"The power," he answered "The Logrus power—to walk in Shadow, to work with a higher order of magic than the mundane."

I didn't really want to go into detail, because I knew he'd prepared himself to traverse the Logrus on three different occasions and had backed down at the last moment each time, when he'd looked into it. Perhaps the skeletons of failures that Suhuy keeps around had troubled him also. I don't think Jurt was aware that I knew about the last two times he'd changed his mind. So I decided to downplay my accomplishment.

"Oh, you don't really feel any different," I said, "until you're actually using it. Then it's hard to describe."

"I'm thinking of doing it soon myself," he said. "It would be good to see something of Shadow, maybe even find a kingdom for myself somewhere. Can you give me any advice?"

I nodded. "Don't look back," I said. "Don't stop to think. Just keep going."

He laughed. "Sounds like orders to an army," he said.

"I suppose there is a similarity."

He laughed again. "Let's go kill us a *zhind*," he said.

That afternoon, we lost a trail in a thicket full of fallen branches. We'd heard the *zhind* crash through it, but it was not immediately apparent which way it had gone. I had my back to Jurt and was facing the forward edge of the place, searching for some sign, when Frakir constricted tightly about my wrist, then came loose and fell to the ground.

I bent over to retrieve her, wondering what had happened, when I heard a *thunk* from overhead. Glancing upward, I saw an arrow protruding from the bole of the tree before me. Its height above the ground was such that had I remained standing it would have entered my back.

I turned quickly toward Jurt, not even straightening from my crouch. He was fitting another arrow to his bow.

He said, "Don't look back. Don't stop to think. Just keep going," and he laughed.

I dove toward him as he raised the weapon. A better archer would probably have killed me. I think when I moved he panicked and released the arrow prematurely, though, because it caught in the side of my leather vest and I didn't feel any pain.

I clipped him above the knees, and he dropped the bow as he fell over backward. He drew his hunting knife, rolled to the side and swung the weapon toward my throat. I caught his wrist with my left hand and was cast onto my back by the force of his momentum. I struck at his face with my right fist while holding the blade away from me. He blocked the punch and kneed me in the balls.

The point of the blade dropped to within inches of my throat as this blow collapsed a big piece of my resistance. Still aching, I was able to turn my hip to prevent another ball-buster, simultaneous with casting my right forearm beneath his wrist and cutting my hand in the process. Then I pushed with my right, pulled with my left and rolled to the left with the force of the turn. His arm was jerked free from my still-weakened grasp, and he rolled off to the side and I tried to recover—and then I heard him scream.

Coming up onto my knees, I saw that he lay upon his left side where he had come to a stop and the knife was several feet beyond him, caught in a tangle of broken branches. Both hands were raised to his face, and his cries were wordless, animal-like bleats.

I made my way over to him to see what had happened, with Frakir held ready to wrap about his throat in case it were some sort of trick he was playing.

But it was not. When I reached him I saw that a sharp limb of a fallen branch had pierced his right eye. There was blood on his cheek and the side of his nose.

"Stop jerking around!" I said. "You'll make it worse. Let me get it out."

"Keep your damn hands off me!" he cried.

Then, clenching his teeth and grimacing horribly, he caught hold of the limb with his right hand and drew his head back. I had to look away. He made a whimpering noise several moments later and collapsed, unconscious. I ripped off my left shirt sleeve, tore a strip from it, folded it into a pad and placed it over his damaged eye. With another strip, I tied it into place there. Frakir found her way back about my wrist, as usual.

Then I dug out the Trump that would take us home and raised him in my arms. Mom wasn't going to like this.

*　　*　　*

Power.

It was a Saturday. Luke and I had been hang gliding all morning. Then we met Julia and Gail for lunch, and afterward we took the Starburst out and sailed all afternoon. Later, we'd hit the bar and grill at the marina where I bought the beers while we waited for steaks, because Luke had slammed my right arm flat against the tabletop when we'd wrist wrestled to see who paid for drinks.

Someone at the next table said, "If I had a million dollars, tax free, I'd . . ." and Julia had laughed as she listened.

"What's funny?" I asked her.

"His wish list," she said. "I'd want a closet full of designer dresses and some elegant jewelry to go with them. Put the closet in a really nice house, and put the house someplace where I'd be important. . . ."

Luke smiled. "I detect a shift from money to power," he said.

"Maybe so," she replied. "But what's the difference, really?"

"Money buys things," Luke said. "Power makes things happen. If you ever have a choice, take the power."

Gail's usual faint smile had faded, and she wore a very serious expression.

"I don't believe power should be an end in itself," she said. "One has it only to use it in certain ways."

Julia laughed. "What's wrong with a power trip?" she asked. "It sounds like fun to me."

"Only till you run into a greater power," Luke said.

"Then you have to think big," Julia answered.

"That's not right," Gail said. "One has duties and they come first."

Luke was studying her now, and he nodded.

"You can keep morality out of it," Julia said.

"No, you can't," Luke responded.

"I disagree," she said.

Luke shrugged.

"She's right," Gail said suddenly. "I don't see that duty and morality are the same thing."

"Well, if you've got a duty," Luke said, "something you absolutely must do—a matter of honor, say—then that becomes your morality."

Julia looked at Luke, looked at Gail. "Does that mean we just agreed on something?" she asked.

"No," Luke said, "I don't think so."

Gail took a drink. "You're talking about a personal code that need not have anything to do with conventional morality."

"Right," Luke said.

"Then it's not really morality. You're just talking duty," she said.

"You're right on the duty," Luke answered. "But it's still morality."

"Morality is the values of a civilization," she said.

"There is no such thing as civilization," Luke replied. "The word just means the art of living in cities."

"All right, then. Of a culture," she said.

"Cultural values are relative things," Luke said, smiling, "and mine say I'm right."

"Where do yours come from?" Gail asked, studying him carefully.

"Let's keep this pure and philosophical, huh?" he said.

"Then maybe we should drop the term entirely," Gail said. "And just stick with duty."

"What happened to power?" Julia asked.

"It's in there somewhere," I said.

Suddenly Gail looked perplexed, as if our discussion were not something which had been repeated a thousand times in different forms, as if it had actually given rise to some new turn of thought.

"If they are two different things," she said slowly, "which one is more important?"

"They're not," Luke said. "They're the same."

"I don't think so," Julia told him. "But duties tend to be clear-cut, and it sounds as if you can choose your own morality. So if I had to have one I'd go with the morality."

"I like things that are clear-cut," Gail said.

Luke chugged his beer, belched lightly. "Shit!" he said. "Philosophy class isn't till Tuesday. This is the weekend. Who gets the next round, Merle?"

I placed my left elbow on the tabletop and opened my hand.

While we pushed together, the tension building and building between us, he said through clenched teeth, "I was right, wasn't I?"

"You were right," I said, just before I forced his arm all the way down.

Power.

I removed my mail from the little locked box in the hallway and carried it upstairs to my apartment. There were two bills, some circulars and something thick and first class without a return address on it.

I closed the door behind me, pocketed my keys and dropped my briefcase onto a nearby chair. I had started toward the sofa when the telephone in the kitchen rang.

Tossing the mail toward the coffee table, I turned and started for the kitchen. The blast that occurred behind me might or might not have been strong enough to knock me over. I don't know, because I dove forward of my own volition as soon as it occurred. I hit my head on the leg of the kitchen table. It dazed me somewhat, but I was otherwise undamaged. All the damage was in the other room. By the time I got to my feet the phone had stopped ringing.

I already knew there were lots of easier ways to dispose of junk mail, but I wondered for a long time afterward who it was that had been on the telephone.

I sometimes remembered the first of the series, too, the truck that had come rushing toward me. I had only caught a glimpse of the driver's face before I'd moved—inert, he was completely expressionless, as if he were dead, hypnotized, drugged or somehow possessed. Choose any of the above, I decided, and maybe more than one.

And then there was the night of the muggers. They had attacked me without a word. When it was all over and I was heading away, I had glanced back once. I thought I'd glimpsed a shadowy figure draw back into a doorway up the street—a smart precaution, I'd say, in light of what had been going on. But of course it could have been someone connected with the attack, too. I was torn. The person was too far off to have been able to give a good description of me. If I went back and it turned out to be an innocent bystander, there would then be a witness capable of identifying me. Not that I didn't think it was an open-and-shut case of self-defense, but there'd be a lot of hassle. So I said the hell with it, and I walked on. Another interesting April 30.

The day of the rifle. There had been two shots as I'd hurried down the street. They'd both missed me before I'd realized what was going on, chipping brickbats from the side of the building to my left. There was no third shot, but there was a thud and a splintering sound from the building across the street. A third-floor window stood wide open.

I hurried over. It was an old apartment house and the front door was locked, but I didn't slow down for niceties. I located the stair and mounted it. When I came to what I thought was the proper room, I decided to try the door the old-fashioned way and it worked. It was unlocked.

I stood to the side and pushed it open and saw that the place was unfurnished and empty. Unoccupied, too, it seemed. Could I have been wrong? But then I saw that the window facing the street stood wide and I saw what lay upon the floor. I entered and closed the door behind me.

A broken rifle lay in the corner. From markings on the stock I guessed that it had been swung with great force against a nearby radiator before it had been cast aside. Then I saw something else on the floor, something wet and red. Not much. Just a few drops.

I searched the place quickly. It was small. The one window in its single bedroom also stood open and I went to it. There was a fire escape beyond it, and I decided that it might be a good way for me to make my exit, too. There were a few more drops of blood on the black metal, but that was it. No one was in sight below, or in either direction.

Power. To kill. To preserve. Luke, Jasra, Gail. Who was responsible for what?

The more I thought of it, the more it seemed possible that there might have been a telephone call on the morning of the open gas jets, too. Could that be what had roused me to an awareness of danger? Each time I thought of these matters there seemed to be a slight shifting of emphasis. Things stood in a different light. According to Luke and the pseudo-Vinta, I was not in great danger in the later episodes, but it seemed that any of those things could have taken me out. Who was I to blame? The perpetrator? Or the savior who barely saved? And who was which? I remembered how my father's story had been complicated by that damned auto accident which played like *Last Year at Marienbad*—though his had seemed simple compared to everything that was coming down on me. At least he knew what he had to do most of the time. Could I be the inheritor of a family curse involving complicated plotting?

Power.

I remembered Uncle Suhuy's final lesson. He had spent some time following my completion of the Logrus in teaching me things I could not have learned before then. There came a time when I thought I was finished. I had been confirmed in the Art and dismissed. It seemed I had covered all the basics and anything more would be mere elaboration. I began making preparations for my journey to the shadow Earth. Then one morning Suhuy sent for me. I assumed that he just wanted to say good-bye and give me a few friendly words of advice.

His hair is white, he is somewhat stooped and there are days when he carries a staff. This was one of them. He had on his yellow caftan, which I had always thought of as a working garment rather than a social one.

"Are you ready for a short trip?" he asked me.

"Actually, it's going to be a long one," I said. "But I'm almost ready."

"No," he said. "That was not the journey I meant."

"Oh. You mean you want to go somewhere right now?"

"Come," he said.

So I followed him, and the shadows parted before us. We moved through increasing bleakness, passing at last into places that bore no sign of life whatsoever. Dark, sterile rock lay all about us, stark in the brassy light of a dim and ancient sun. This final place was chill and dry, and when we halted and I looked about, I shivered.

I waited, to see what he had in mind. But it was a long while before he spoke. He seemed oblivious of my presence for a time, simply staring out across the bleak landscape.

Finally, "I have taught you the ways of Shadow," he said slowly, "and the composition of spells and their working."

I said nothing. His statement didn't to seem to require a reply.

"So you know something of the ways of power," he continued. "You draw it from the Sign of Chaos, the Logrus, and you invest it in various ways."

He glanced at me at last, and I nodded.

"I understand that those who bear the Pattern, the Sign of Order, may do similar things in ways that may or may not be similar," he went on. "I do not know for certain, for I am not an initiate of the Pattern. I doubt the spirit could stand the strain of knowing the ways of both. But you should understand that there is another way of power, antithetical to our own."

"I understand," I said, for he seemed to be expecting an answer.

"But you have a resource available to you," he said, "which those of Amber do not. Watch!"

His final word did not mean that I should simply observe as he leaned his staff against the side of a boulder and raised his hands before him. It meant that I should have the Logrus before me so I could see what he was doing at that level. So I summoned my vision and watched him through it.

Now the vision that hung before him seemed a continuation of my own, stretched and twisting. I saw and felt it as he joined his hands with it and extended a pair of its jagged limbs outward across the distance to touch upon a boulder that lay downhill of us.

"Enter the Logrus now yourself," he said, "remaining passive. Stay with me through what I am about to do. Do not, at any time, attempt to interfere."

"I understand," I said.

I moved my hands into my vision, shifting them about, feeling after congruity, until they became a part of it.

"Good," he said, when I had settled them into place. "Now all you need do is observe, on all levels."

Something pulsed along the limbs he controlled, passing down to the boulder. I was not prepared for what came after.

The image of the Logrus turned black before me, becoming a seething blot of inky turmoil. An awful feeling of disruptive power surged through me, an enormous destructive force that threatened to overwhelm me, to carry me into the blissful nothingness of ultimate disorder. A part of me seemed to desire this, while another part was screaming wordlessly for it to cease. But Suhuy maintained control of the phenomenon, and I could see how he was doing it, just as I had seen how he had brought it into being in the first place.

The boulder became one with the turmoil, joined it and was gone. There was no explosion, no implosion, only the sensation of great cold winds and cacophonous sounds. Then my uncle moved his hands slowly apart, and the lines of seething blackness followed them, flowing out in both directions from that area of chaos which had been the boulder, producing a long dark trench wherein I beheld the paradox of both nothingness and activity.

Then he stood still, arresting it at that point. Moments later, he spoke.

"I could simply release it," he stated, "letting it run wild. Or I could give it a direction and then release it."

As he did not continue, I asked, "What would happen then? Would it simply continue until it had devastated the entire shadow?"

"No," he replied. "There are limiting factors. The resistance of Order to Chaos would build as it extended itself. There would come a point of containment."

"And if you remained as you are, and kept summoning more?"

"One would do a great deal of damage."

"And if we combined our efforts?"

"More extensive damage. But that is not the lesson I had in mind. I will remain passive now while you control it."

So I took over the Sign of the Logrus and ran the line of disruption back upon itself in a great circle, like a dark moat surrounding us.

"Banish it now," he said, and I did.

Still, the winds and the sounds continued to rage, and I could not see beyond the dark wall which seemed to be advancing slowly upon us from all sides.

"Obviously, the limiting factor has yet to be achieved," I observed.

He chuckled. "You're right. Even though you stopped, you exceeded a certain critical limit, so that it is now running wild."

"Oh," I said. "How long till those natural limitations you mentioned dampen it?"

"Sometime after it has completely annihilated the area on which we stand," he said.

"It is receding in all directions as well as heading this way?"

"Yes."

"Interesting. What *is* the critical mass?"

"I'll have to show you. But we'd better find a new place first. This one is going away. Take my hand."

I did, and he conducted me to another shadow. This time I summoned the Chaos and conducted the operations while he observed. This time I did not let it run wild.

When I had finished and I stood, shaken, staring into a small crater I had caused, he placed his hand on my shoulder and told me, "As you knew in theory, that is the ultimate power behind your spells. Chaos itself. To work with it directly is dangerous. But, as you have seen, it can be done. Now you know it, your training is complete."

It was more than impressive. It was awesome. And for most situations I could visualize it was rather like using nukes for skeet shooting. Offhand, I couldn't think of any circumstances under which I would care to employ the technique, until Victor Melman really pissed me off.

Power, in its many shapes, varieties, sizes and styles, continues to fascinate me. It has been so much a part of my life for so long that I feel very familiar with it, though I doubt that I will ever understand it fully.

TEN

"It's about time," I said, to whatever lurked in the shadows.

The sound that followed was not human. It was a low snarl. I wondered what manner of beast I confronted. I was certain an attack was imminent, but it did not come. Instead the growl died down, and whatever it was spoke again.

"Feel your fear," came the whisper.

"Feel your own," I said, "while you still can."

The sounds of its breathing came heavy. The flames danced at my back. Smoke had drawn as far away across the campsite as his lengthy tether permitted.

"I could have killed you while you slept," it said slowly.

"Foolish of you not to," I said. "It will cost you."

"I want to look at you, Merlin," it stated. "I want to see you puzzled. I want to see your fear. I want to see your anguish before I see your blood."

"Then I take it this is a personal rather than a business matter?"

There came a strange noise which it took me several moments to interpret as an inhuman throat trying to manage a chuckle.

Then, "Let us say that, magician," it responded. "Summon your Sign and your concentration will waver. I will know it and will rend you before you can employ it."

"Kind of you to warn me."

"I just wanted to foreclose that option in your thinking. The thing wound about your left wrist will not help you in time either."

"You have good vision."

"In these matters, yes."

"You wish perhaps to discuss the philosophy of revenge with me now?"

"I am waiting for you to break and do something foolish, to increase my pleasure. I have limited your actions to the physical, so you are doomed."

"Keep waiting, then," I said.

There was a sound of movement within the brush as something drew nearer. I still could not see it, though. I took a step to my left then, to allow firelight to reach that darkened area. At that, something shone, low. The light was reflected, yellow, from a single glaring eye.

I lowered the point of my weapon, directing it toward the eye. What the hell. Every creature I know of tries to protect its eyes.

"Banzai!" I cried as I lunged. The conversation seemed to have stagnated, and I was anxious to get on to other matters.

It rose instantly and with great power and speed rushed toward me, avoiding my thrust. It was a large, black, lop-eared wolf, and it slipped past a frantic slash I managed and went straight for my throat.

My left forearm came up automatically and I thrust it forward into the open jaws. At the same time, I brought the hilt of my blade across and slammed it against the side of its head. At this, the clamping force of the bite loosened even as I was borne over backward, but the grip remained, penetrating shirt and flesh. And I was turning and pulling before I hit the ground, wanting to land on top, knowing I wouldn't.

I landed on my left side, attempting to continue the roll, and added another belt of the pommel to the side of the beast's skull. It was then that fortune favored me, for a change, when I realized that we lay near the lip of my fire pit and were still turning in that direction. I dropped my weapon and sought its throat with my right hand. It was heavily muscled, and there was no chance of crushing the windpipe in time. But that was not what I was after.

My hand went up high and back beneath the lower jaw, where I commenced squeezing with all my strength. I scrabbled with my feet until I found purchase and then pushed with my legs as well as my arms. Our movement continued the short distance necessary to push its snarling head back into the fire.

For a moment nothing happened save the steady trickle of blood from my forearm into its mouth and out again. The grip of its jaws was still strong and painful.

Seconds later, my arm was released as the fur of its neck and head caught fire and it struggled to draw away from the flames. I was thrust aside as it rose and pulled free, an ear-piercing howl rising from its throat. I rolled to my knees and raised my hands, but it did not come at me again. Instead, it rushed past me into the woods in the opposite direction from which it had come.

I snatched up my blade and took off after it. No time to pause and pull on my boots; I was able to shapeshift the soles of my feet a bit to toughen them against the litter and irregularity of the forest floor. My adversary was still in sight, for its head still smoldered; though I might have been able to follow just from the howling, which was almost continuous. And strangely, the tone and character of the howls was changing, sounding more and more like human cries and less like the complaint of a wolf. Strangely, too, the beast was fleeing with something less than the speed and guile I would have expected from one of its kind. I heard it crashing through the shrubbery and running into trees. On several of these latter occasions, it even emitted sounds that seemed to bear the pattern of human cursing. So I was able to stay closer to it than I had any reason to expect, even gaining on it somewhat after the first few minutes.

Then, suddenly, I realized its apparent destination. I saw again that pale light I had noted earlier—brighter now and its source larger, as we moved toward it. Roughly rectangular in shape, I judged it as being eight or nine feet in height, perhaps five in width. I forgot about tracking the wolf by ear and headed for the light. That had to be its goal, and I wanted to reach it first.

I ran on. The wolf was ahead of me and to my left. Its hair had ceased to blaze now, though it still snarled and yipped as it rushed along. Before us, the light grew brighter still, and I was able to see into it—through it—and distinguish some of its features for the first time. I saw a hillside with a low stone building upon it, approached by a flagged walkway and a series of stone steps—framed like a picture within the rectangle—hazy at first, but coming clearer with each step. It was a cloudy afternoon within the picture, and the thing stood about twenty meters away now, in the midst of a clearing.

I realized as I saw the beast burst into the clearing that I was not going to be able to reach the place in time to snatch up the thing I knew must lie nearby. Still, I thought I might have a chance of catching the creature and halting its passage.

But it put on additional speed once it was in the clear. I could see the scene toward which it was headed more clearly than anything else in the vicinity. I shouted to distract it, but that did not work. My final burst of speed was not good enough. Then, on the ground, near the threshold, I saw what I was looking for. Too late. Even as I watched, the beast lowered its head and caught up in its teeth a flat rectangular object, without even breaking stride.

I halted and turned away as it plunged ahead, dropping my blade as I dove, rolling, continuing to roll.

I felt the force of the silent explosion, followed by the implosion and the small series of shock waves. I lay there thinking nasty thoughts until the turmoil and ceased; then I rose and retrieved my weapon.

The night was normal about me once again. Starlight. The wind in the pines. There was no need for me to turn, though I did, to know that the thing toward which I had been racing but moments before was now gone, without leaving any sign that it had been there, bright doorway to another place.

I hiked back to my camp and spent a while talking to Smoke, calming him. I donned my boots and cloak then, kicked dirt over the embers in my pit, and led the horse back to the road.

I mounted there and we moved on up the road toward Amber for the better part of an hour, before I settled upon a new campsite under a bone-white piece of moon.

The rest of my night was untroubled. I was awakened by increased light and morning bird calls through the pines. I took care of Smoke, breakfasted quickly on the remains of my rations, put myself in the best order I could and was on my way within half an hour.

It was a cool morning, with banks of cumulus far off to my left, clear skies overhead. I did not hurry. My main reason for riding back rather than trumping home was to learn a little more of what this area near Amber was like, and the other was to gain a bit of solitude for thinking. With Jasra a prisoner, Luke in sick bay and Ghostwheel occupied it seemed that any major threats to Amber or myself were in abeyance, and a small breathing spell could be justified. I felt that I was actually near to a point where I could handle everything personally with regard to Luke and Jasra, as soon as I'd worked out a few more details. And I was certain I could deal with Ghost after that, as I'd found our most recent conversation somewhat encouraging.

That was the big stuff. I could worry about loose ends later. A two-bit wizard like Sharu Garrul was only a pain when considered in conjunction with everything else that was troubling me. Dueling with him would be no problem when I'd had a bit of leisure—though I had to admit I was puzzled as to why he should be interested in me at all.

Then there was the matter of the entity which had for a time been Vinta. While I saw no real threat in it, there was certainly a mystery which affected my peace of mind, and which seemed ultimately to have something to do with my security. This, too, was a matter to be dealt with when that bit of leisure finally came along.

And Luke's offer to reveal a piece of information vital to Amber's security, once Jasra was rescued, troubled me. Because I believed him, and I believed he'd keep his word. I had a hunch, though, that he wouldn't be giving it away unless it was too late to do much about it. Guesswork was, of course, futile; there was no way of knowing what preparations would be appropriate. Was the offer itself, no matter how authentic, also a bit of psychological warfare? Luke had always been more subtle than his bluff exterior seemed to indicate. It had taken me a long time to learn that, and I wasn't about to forget it now.

I felt I could discount the business of the blue stones for the moment, and I planned soon to be rid of all traces of their vibes. No problem there, other than a mental string around the finger for extra wariness, just in case— and I was already in that frame of mind, had been for some time.

That left the business of last night's wolf to be fitted into the bigger picture.

Obviously, it had been no normal beast, and its intent had been apparent enough. Other matters concerning its visit were less than clear, however. Who or what was it? Was it a principal or an agent? And, if the latter, who had sent it? And finally, finally, why?

Its clumsiness indicated to me—since I had tried that sort of business myself in the past—that it was a shape-shifted human rather than a true wolf magically gifted with speech. Most people who daydream of transforming themselves into some vicious beast and going about tearing people's throats out, dismembering them, disfiguring them and perhaps devouring them tend mainly to dwell upon how much fun it would be and generally neglect the practicalities of the situation. When you find yourself quadruped, with a completely different center of gravity and a novel array of sensory input, it is not all that easy to get around for a time with any measure of grace. One is generally far more vulnerable than one's appearance would lead others to believe. And certainly one is nowhere near as lethal and efficient as the real thing with a lifetime of practice behind it. No. I've always tended to think of it more as a terrorist tactic than anything else.

Be that how it may, the manner of the beast's coming and going was actually the main cause of my trepidation concerning the entire affair. It had employed a Trump Gate, which is not a thing one does lightly—or at all, for that matter, if it can be avoided. It is a flashy and spectacular thing to make Trump contact with some distant place and then pour tons of power into the objectification of such a gateway as a form possessed for a time of an independent existence. It is exceedingly profligate of energy and effort—even a hellrun is much easier—to create one which will stand for even fifteen minutes. It can drain most of your resources for a long while. Yet this was what had occurred. The reason behind it did not trouble me, as much as the fact that it had happened at all. For the only people capable of the feat were genuine initiates of the Trumps. It couldn't be done by someone who just happened to come into possession of a card.

Which narrowed the field considerably.

I tried to picture the werebeast about its errand. First, it would have to locate me and—

Of course. I suddenly recalled the dead dogs in the grove near Arbor House and the large doglike tracks in the vicinity. The thing had spotted me sometime before, then, and had been watching, waiting. It had followed me when I set out yesterday evening, and when I made my camp it made its move. It set up—or was set up with—the Trump Gate, for a retreat that would brook no pursuit. Then it came to kill me. And I had no way of telling whether it involved Sharu Garrul, Luke's secret, the blue stones or the body-switching entity's mission. For now it would simply have to dangle as yet another loose end, while I concentrated on basics.

I overtook and passed a line of wagons headed for Amber. A few horsemen went by me headed in the other direction. No one I knew, though everyone waved. The clouds continued to mount to my left, but nothing resembling a storm took shape. The day remained cool and sunny. The road dipped and rose again, several times, though overall it rose more than it dipped. I stopped at a large, busy inn for lunch, had a quick, filling meal and did not linger. The road improved steadily after that, and it was not long before I caught distant glimpses of Amber atop Kolvir, sparkling in the noonday light.

Traffic grew heavier as the sun advanced through the heavens. I continued to make plans and indulge in whatever speculations came to mind as I rode on into afternoon. My uphill way took several turnings as the route passed through the heights, but Amber remained in sight most of the time.

I recognized no one along the way, and I reached the Eastern Gate—part of an ancient fortification—late in the afternoon. I made my way up East Vine and stopped at the Bayle town house, where I had once attended a party. I left Smoke with a groom at the stable in the rear, and they both seemed happy to see each other. I walked around to the front door then and knocked. A servant informed me that the Baron was out, so I identified myself and gave him Vinta's message, which he promised to deliver when his employer returned.

That duty out of the way, I proceeded up East Vine on foot. Near the top, but before the slope grew roughly level, I smelled food and discarded my plan of waiting to eat until I was back at the palace. I halted and cast about me for the source of the aromas. I located it up a side street to my right where the way widened into a large circle, a fountain at its center—in which a rearing copper dragon with a wonderful green patina pissed into a pink stone basin. The dragon faced a basement restaurant called the Pit, with ten outside tables enclosed by a low fence of copper pickets, potted plants along its inside perimeter. I crossed the circle. As I passed the fountain I saw a great number of exotic coins within its clear water, including a U.S. Bicentennial quarter. Crossing to the fenced area, I entered, made my way through and was about to descend the stair when I heard my name called.

"Merle! Over here!"

I looked about but did not see anyone I recognized at any of the four occupied tables. Then, as my eyes retraced their route, I realized that the older man at the corner table to my right was smiling.

"Bill!" I exclaimed.

Bill Roth rose to his feet—more a touch of display than any formality, I realized immediately. I hadn't recognized him at first because he now sported the beginnings of a grizzled beard and a mustache. Also, he had on brown trousers with a silver stripe running down their outside seams, vanishing into a pair of high brown boots. His shirt was silver with brown piping, and a black cloak lay folded upon the chair to his right. A wide black sword belt lay atop it and a sheathed blade of short-to-medium length was hung upon it.

"You've gone native. Also, you've lost some weight."

"True," he said, "and I'm thinking of retiring here. It agrees with me."

We seated ourselves.

"Did you order yet?" I asked him.

"Yes, but I see a waiter on the stair now," he said. "Let me catch him for you."

Which he did, and ordered for me too.

"Your Thari's much better," I said afterward.

"Lots of practice," he replied.

"What've you been doing?"

"I've sailed with Gérard. I've been to Deiga, and to one of Julian's camps in Arden. Visited Rebma, too. Fascinating place. I've been taking fencing lessons. And Droppa's been showing me around town."

"All the bars, most likely."

"Well, that's not all. In fact, that's why I'm here. He owns a half interest in the Pit, and I had to promise him I'd eat here a lot. A good place, though. When did you get back?"

"Just now," I said, "and I've another long story for you."

"Good. Your stories tend to be bizarre and convoluted," he said. "Just the thing for a cool autumn's eve. Let's hear it."

I talked throughout dinner and for a long while afterward. The day's-end chill began making it uncomfortable then, so we headed for the palace. I finally wound up my narrative over hot cider in front of the fireplace in one of the smaller rooms in the eastern wing.

Bill shook his head. "You do manage to stay busy," he finally said. "I have one question."

"What?"

"Why didn't you bring Luke in?"

"I already told you."

"It wasn't much of a reason. For some nebulous piece of information he says is important to Amber? And you've got to catch him to get it?"

"It's not like that at all."

"He's a salesman, Merle, and he sold you a line of shit. That's what I think."

"You're wrong, Bill. I know him."

"For a long time," he agreed. "But how well? We've been all through this before. What you don't know about Luke far outweighs what you do know."

"He could have gone elsewhere, but he came to me."

"You're part of his plan, Merle. He intends to get at Amber through you."

"I don't think so," I said. "It's not his style."

"I think he'll use anything that comes to hand—or anyone."

I shrugged. "I believe him. You don't. That's all."

"I guess so," he said. "What are you going to do now, wait and see what happens?"

"I've a plan," I said. "Just because I believe him doesn't mean I won't take out insurance. But I've a question for you."

"Yes?"

"If I brought him back here and Random decided the facts weren't clear enough and he wanted a hearing, would you represent Luke?"

His eyes widened, and then he smiled. "What kind of hearing?" he asked. "I don't know how such things are conducted here."

"As a grandson of Oberon," I explained, "he'd come under House Law. Random is head of the House now. It would be up to him whether to forget about a thing, render a summary judgment or call a hearing. As I understand it, such a hearing could be as formal or informal as Random wanted. There are books on the subject in the library. But a person has always had the right to be represented at one if he wanted."

"Of course I'd take the case," Bill said. "It doesn't sound like a legal experience that comes along too often.

"But it might look like a conflict of interest," he added, "since I have done work for the Crown."

I finished my cider and put the glass on the mantelpiece. I yawned.

"I have to go now, Bill."

He nodded; then, "This is all just hypothetical, isn't it?" he asked.

"Of course," I said. "It might turn out to be *my* hearing. G'night."

He studied me. "Uh—this insurance you were talking about," he said. "It probably involves something risky, doesn't it?"

I smiled.

"Nothing anyone could help you with, I suppose?"

"Nope."

"Well, good luck."

"Thanks."

"See you tomorrow?"

"Later in the day, maybe. . . ."

I went to my room and sacked out. I had to get some rest before I went about the business I had in mind. I don't recall any dreams, pro or con, on the matter.

It was still dark when I woke. Good to know that my mental alarm was working.

It would have been very pleasant to turn over and go back to sleep, but I couldn't allow myself the luxury. The day that lay ahead was to be an exercise in timing. Accordingly, I got up, cleaned up and dressed myself in fresh clothes.

I headed for the kitchen then, where I made myself some tea and toast and scrambled a few eggs with chilis and onions and a bit of pepper. I turned up some melka fruit from the Snelters, too—something I hadn't had in a long while.

Afterward, I went out through the rear and made my way into the garden. Dark it was, moonless and damp, with a few wisps of mist exploring invisible paths. I followed a path to the northwest. The world was a very quiet place. I let my thoughts get that way, too. It was to be a one-thing-at-a-time day, and I wanted to start it off with that habit of mind in place.

I walked until I ran out of garden, passing through a break in a hedge and continuing along the rough trail my path had become. It mounted slowly for the first few minutes, took an abrupt turn and grew immediately steeper. I paused at one jutting point and looked back, from where I was afforded a view of the dark outline of the palace, a few lighted windows within it. Some scatters of cirrus high above looked like raked starlight in the celestial garden over which Amber brooded. I turned away moments later. There was still a good distance to travel.

When I reached the crest I was able to discern a faint line of lightening to the east, beyond the forest I had traversed so recently. I hurried past the three massive steps of song and story and began my descent to the north. Slow at first, the way I followed steepened abruptly after a time and led off to the northeast, then into a gentler decline. When it swung back to the northwest there was another steep area followed by another easy one, and I knew the going would be fine after that. The high shoulder of Kolvir at my back blocked all traces of the pre-dawn light I had witnessed earlier, and the star-hung night lay before me and above, rubbing outlines to ambiguity on all but the nearest boulders. Still, I knew approximately where I was going, having been this way once before, though I'd only halted briefly at that time.

It was about two miles past the crest, and I slowed as I neared the area, searching. It was a large, somewhat horseshoe-shaped declivity, and when I finally located it I entered slowly, a peculiar feeling rising within me. I had not consciously anticipated all my reactions in this matter; but at some level I must have, I was certain.

As I moved into it, canyonlike walls of stone rising at either hand, I came upon the trail and followed it. It led me slightly downhill, toward a shadowy pair of trees, and then between them to where a low stone building stood, various shrubs and grasses grown wild about it. I understand that the soil was actually transported there to support the foliage, but afterward it was forgotten and neglected.

I seated myself on one of the stone benches in front of the building and waited for the sky to lighten. This was my father's tomb—well, cenotaph— built long ago when he had been presumed dead. It had amused him considerably to be able to visit the place later on. Now, of course, its status might well have changed. It could be the real thing now. Would this cancel the irony or increase it? I couldn't quite decide. It bothered me, though, more than I'd thought it would. I had not come here on a pilgrimage. I had come here for the peace and quiet a sorcerer of my sort needs in order to hang some spells. I had come here—

Perhaps I was rationalizing. I had chosen this spot because, real tomb or fake, it had Corwin's name on it, so it raised a sense of his presence, for me.

I had wanted to get to know him better, and this might be as close as I could ever come. I realized, suddenly, why I had trusted Luke. He had been right, back at the Arbor House. If I learned of Corwin's death and saw that blame could be fixed for it, I knew that I would drop everything else, that I would go off to present the bill and collect it, that I would have to close the account, to write the receipt in blood. Even had I not known Luke as I did, it was easy to see myself in his actions and too uncomfortable a thing to judge him.

Damn. Why must we caricature each other, beyond laughter or insight, into the places of pain, frustration, conflicting loyalties?

I rose. There was enough light now to show me what I was doing.

I went inside and approached the niche where the empty stone sarcophagus stood. It seemed an ideal safe deposit box, but I hesitated when I stood before it because my hands were shaking. It was ridiculous. I knew that he wasn't in there, that it was just an empty box with a bit of carving on it. Yet it was several minutes before I could bring myself to take hold of the lid and raise it. . . .

Empty, of course, like so many dreams and fears. I tossed in the blue button and lowered the lid again. What the hell. If Sharu wanted it back and could find it here, let him have the message that he was walking close to the grave when he played his games.

I went back outside, leaving my feelings in the crypt. It was time to begin. I'd a mess of spells to work and hang, for I'd no intention of going gently to the place where the wild winds blew.

ELEVEN

I stood on the rise above the garden, admiring the autumn foliage below. The wind played games with my cloak. A mellow afternoon light bathed the palace. There was a chill in the air. A flock of dead leaves rushed, lemming-like, past me and blew off the edge of the trail, rattling, into the air.

I had not really stopped to admire the view, however. I had halted while I blocked an attempted Trump contact—the day's second. The first had occurred earlier, while I was hanging a spell like a rope of tinsel on the image of Chaos. I figured that it was either Random—irritated that I was back in Amber and had not seen fit to bring him up to date on my most recent doings and my plans—or Luke, recovered now and wanting to request my assistance in his move against the Keep. They both came to mind because they were the two individuals I wished most to avoid; neither of them would much like what I was about to do, though for different reasons.

The call faded, was gone, and I descended the trail, passed through the hedge and entered the garden. I did not want to waste a spell to mask my passage, so I took a trail to the left, which led through a series of arbors where I was less exposed to the gaze of anyone who happened to glance out of a window. I could have avoided this by trumping in, but that card always delivers one to the main hall, and I had no idea who might be there.

Of course, I was headed that way. . . .

I went back the way I had come out, through the kitchen, helping myself to a sandwich and a glass of milk on the way. Then I took the back stairs up a flight, lurked a bit and made it to my rooms without being spotted. There, I buckled on the sword belt I had left hanging at the head of my bed, checked the blade, located a small dagger I had brought with me from Chaos—a gift from the Pit-diver Borquist, whom I'd once fixed up with an introduction that led to a patronage (he was a middling-good poet)—and hung it on the other side of my belt. I pinned a Trump to the inside of my left sleeve. I washed my hands and face and brushed my teeth, too. But then I couldn't think of any other ways to stall. I had to go and do something I feared. It was necessary to the rest of my plan. I was overwhelmed by a sudden desire to be off sailing. Just lying on the beach would do, actually. . . .

Instead, I departed my quarters and made my way back downstairs, returning the way I had come. I headed west along the back corridor, listening for footsteps and voices, retreating once into a closet to let some nameless parties pass. Anything to avoid official notice for just a little longer. Finally, I turned left, walked a few paces and waited the better part of minute before entering the major corridor, which led past the large marble dining hall. No one in sight. Good. I sprinted to the nearest entrance and peered within. Great. The place was not in use. It wasn't normally used every day, but I'd no way of knowing whether today was some state occasion—though this was not a normal dining hour either.

I entered and passed through. There is a dark, narrow corridor to its rear, with a guard normally posted somewhere near the passage's mouth or the door at its end. All members of the family have access there, though the guard would log our passage. His superior wouldn't have that information until the guard reported when he went off duty, though. By then it shouldn't matter to me.

Tod was short, stocky, bearded. When he saw me coming he presented arms with an ax that had been leaning against the wall moments before.

"At ease. Busy?" I asked.

"To tell the truth, no, sir."

"I'll be heading down. I hope there are some lanterns up here. I don't know that stairway as well as most."

"I checked a number inside when I came on duty, sir. I'll light you one."

Might as well save the energy that would have gone into the first spell, I decided. Every little bit helps. . . .

"Thanks."

He opened the door, hefted, successively, three lanterns which stood inside to the right, selected the second one. He took it back outside, where he lit it from the massive candle in its stand partway up the corridor.

"I'll be awhile," I said as I accepted it from him. "You'll probably be off duty before I'm finished."

"Very good sir. Watch your step."

"Believe me, I will."

The long spiraling stair turned round and round with very little visible in any direction but below, where a few chimneyed candles, sconced torches or hung lanterns flared along the central shaft, doing more for acrophobia than absolute blackness might, I suppose. There were just those little dots of light below me. I couldn't see the distant floor, or any walls. I kept one hand on the railing and held the lantern out in front with the other. Damp down here. Musty, too. Not to mention chilly.

Again, I tried counting the steps. As usual, I lost count somewhere along the way. Next time. . . .

My thoughts went back to that distant day when I had come this route believing I was headed for death. The fact that I hadn't died was small comfort now. It had still been an ordeal. And it was still possible that I could screw up on it this time and get fried or go up in a puff of smoke.

Around, around. Down, down. Night thoughts in the middle of the afternoon. . . .

On the other hand, I'd heard Flora say that it was easier the second time around. She'd been talking about the Pattern moments before, and I hoped that's what she was referring to.

The Grand Pattern of Amber, Emblem of Order. Matching in power the Great Logrus of the Courts, Sign of Chaos. The tensions between the two seem to generate everything that matters. Get involved with either, lose control—and you're done for. Just my luck to be involved with both. I've no one with whom to compare notes as to whether this makes things rougher, though it massages my ego to think that the mark of the one makes the other more difficult . . . and they do mark you, both of them. At some level you are torn apart and reassembled along the lines of vast cosmic principles when you undergo such an experience—which sounds noble, important, metaphysical, spiritual and lovely, but is mainly a pain in the ass. It is the price we pay for certain powers, but there is no cosmic principle requiring me to say I enjoy it.

Both the Pattern and the Logrus give to their initiates the ability to traverse Shadow unassisted—Shadow being the generic term for the possibly infinite collection of reality variations we play about in. And they also give us other abilities. . . .

Around and down. I slowed. I was feeling slightly dizzy, just like before. At least I wasn't planning on coming back this way. . . .

When the bottom finally came into sight I speeded up again. There was a bench, a table, a few racks and cases, a light to show them all. Normally, there was a guard on duty there, but I didn't see one. Could be off making rounds, though. There were cells somewhere to the left in which particularly unfortunate political prisoners might sometimes be found scrabbling about and going slowly out of their minds. I didn't know whether there were any such individuals doing time at the moment. I kind of hoped not. My father had once been one, and from his description of the experience it did not sound like easy time to do.

I halted when I reached the floor and called out a couple of times. I got back a suitably eerie echo, but no answer.

I moved to the rack and took up a filled lantern with my other hand. An extra one might come in handy. It was possible I would lose my way. I headed to the right then. The tunnel I wanted lay in that direction. After a long while, I stopped and raised a light, as it almost seemed I had come too far. There was still no tunnel mouth in sight. I looked back. The guard post was still in sight. I continued on, searching my memories of that last time.

Finally, there was a shifting of sounds—abrupt echoes of my footfalls. It would seem I was nearing a wall, an obstacle. I raised a lantern again.

Yes. Pure darkness ahead. Gray stone about it. I went that way.

Dark. Far. There was a continuous shadow-show as my light slid over rocky irregularities, as its beams glanced off specks of brightness in the stone walls. Then there was a side passage to my left. I passed it and kept going. It seemed there should be another fairly soon. Yes. Two. . . .

The third was farther along. Then there was a fourth. I wondered idly where they all led. No one had ever said anything about them to me. Maybe they didn't know either. Bizarre grottoes of indescribable beauty? Other worlds? Dead ends? Storerooms? One day, perhaps, when time and inclination came together. . . .

Five. . . .

And then another.

It was the seventh one I wanted. I halted when I came to it. It didn't go back all that far. I thought of the others who'd passed this way, and then I strode ahead, to the big, heavy, metal-bound door. There was a great key hanging from a steel hook that had been driven into the wall to my right. I took it down, unlocked the door and hung it back up again, knowing that the downstairs guard would check it and re-lock it at some point in his rounds; and I wondered—not for the first time—why it should be locked that way in the first place if the key was kept right there. It made it seem as if there were danger from something that might emerge from within. I had asked about that, but no one I'd questioned seemed to know. Tradition, I'd been told. Gérard and Flora had suggested, respectively, that I ask Random or Fiona. And *they* had both thought Benedict might know, but I'd never remembered to ask him.

I pushed hard and nothing happened. I put down the lanterns and tried again, harder. The door creaked and moved slowly inward. I recovered the lanterns and entered.

The door closed itself behind me, and Frakir—child of Chaos—pulsed wildly. I recalled my last visit and remembered why no one had brought an extra lantern upon that occasion: The bluish glow of the Pattern within the smooth, black floor lit the grotto well enough for one to see one's way about.

I lit the other lantern. I set the first one down at the near end of the Pattern and carried the other one with me about the periphery of the thing, setting it down at a point on its farther side. I did not care that the Pattern provided sufficient illumination to take care of the business at hand. I found the damned thing spooky, cold and downright intimidating. Having an extra natural light near at hand made me feel a lot better in its presence.

I studied that intricate mass of curved lines as I moved to the corner where they began. I had quieted Frakir but I had not entirely subdued my own apprehensions. If it were a response of the Logrus within me, I wondered whether my reaction to the Logrus itself would be worse were I to go back and essay it again, now that I bore the Pattern as well. Fruitless speculation. . . .

I tried to relax. I breathed deeply. I shut my eyes for a moment. I bent my knees. I lowered my shoulders. No use waiting any longer. . . .

I opened my eyes and set my foot upon the Pattern. Immediately, sparks rose about my foot. I took anther step. More sparks. A tiny crackling noise. Another step. A bit of resistance as I moved again. . . .

It all came back to me—everything I had felt the first time through: the chill, the small shocks, the easy areas and the difficult ones. There was a map of the Pattern somewhere inside me, and it was almost as if I read from it as I moved along that first curve, resistance rising, sparks flying, my hair stirring, the crackling, a kind of vibration. . . .

I reached the First Veil, and it was like walking in a wind tunnel. Every movement involved heavy effort. Resolve, though; that was all that it really took. If I just kept pushing I would advance, albeit slowly. The trick was not to stop. Starting again could be horrible, and in some places impossible. Steady pressure was all that was required just now. A few moments more and I would be through. The going would be easier. It was the Second Veil that was the real killer. . . .

Turn, turn. . . .

I was through. I knew the way would be easy now for a time. I began to stride with a bit of confidence. Perhaps Flora had been right. This part seemed a little less difficult than it had the first time. I negotiated a long curve, then a sharp switchback. The sparks reached up to my boottops now. My mind was flooded with April thirtieths, with family politics in the Courts, where people dueled and died as the succession to the succession to the succession wound and shifted its intricate way through blood rituals of status and elevation. No more. I was done with all that. Push it away. They might be a lot politer about it, but more blood was spilled there than in Amber, and for the damnedest small advantages over one's fellows. . . .

I gritted my teeth. It was hard to keep my mind focused on the task at hand. Part of the effect, of course. I remembered that too, now. Another step. . . . Tingling sensations all the way up my legs. . . . The crackling sounds as loud as a storm to me. . . . One foot in front of the other. . . . Pick them up, put them down. . . . Hair standing on end now. . . . turn. . . . Push. . . . Bringing the Starburst in before an autumn squall, Luke running the sails, wind like the breath of dragons at our back. . . . Three more steps and resistance rises. . . .

I am upon the Second Veil, and it is suddenly as if I am trying to push a car out of a muddy ditch. . . . All my strength goes forward, and the return of it is infinitesimal. I move with glacial slowness and the sparks are about my waist. I am blue flame. . . .

My mind is abruptly stripped of distraction. Even Time goes away and leaves me alone. There is only this pastless, nameless thing I am become, striving with its entire being against the inertia of all its days—an equation so finely balanced that I should be frozen here in mid-stride forever, save that this cancellation of masses and forces leaves the will unimpaired, purifies it in a way, so that the process of progress seems to transcend the physical striving. . . .

Another step, and another, and I am through, and ages older and moving again, and I know that I am going to make it despite the fact that I am approaching the Grand Curve, which is tough and tricky and long. Not at all like the Logrus. The power here is synthetic, not analytic. . . .

The universe seemed to wheel about me. Each step here made me feel as if I were fading and coming back into focus, being broken down and reassembled, scattered and gathered, dying and reviving. . . .

Outward. Onward. Three more curves then, followed by a straight line. I pushed ahead. Dizzy, nauseated. Soaking wet. End of the line. A series of arcs. Turn. Turn. Turn again. . . .

I knew that I was coming up to the Final Veil when the sparks rose to become a cage of lightnings and my feet began to drag again. The stillness and the terrible pushing. . . .

But this time I felt somehow fortified, and I drove onward knowing that I would win through. . . .

I made it, shaking, and only a single short arc remained. Those final three steps may well be the worst, however. It is as if, having gotten to know you this well, the Pattern is reluctant to release you. I fought it here, my ankles sore as at any race's end. Two steps. . . . Three—

Off. Standing still. Panting and shuddering. Peace. Gone the static. Gone the sparks. If that didn't wash off the blue stones' vibes I didn't know what would.

Now—well, in a minute—I could go anywhere. From this point, in this moment of empowerment, I could command the Pattern to transport me anywhere and I would be there delivered. Hardly a thing to waste to, say, save myself a walk up the spiral staircase and back to my rooms. No. I had other plans. In a minute. . . .

I adjusted my apparel, ran my hand through my hair, checked my weapons and my hidden Trump, waited for the pounding of my pulse to subside.

Luke had sustained his injuries in a battle at the Keep of the Four Worlds, fighting with his former friend and ally Dalt, the mercenary, son of the Desacratrix. Dalt meant little to me save as a possible obstacle, in that he now seemed in the employ of the keeper of the Keep. But even allowing for any time differential—which was probably not that great—I had seen him fairly soon following his fight with Luke. Which seemed to indicate that he was at the Keep when I had reached him via his Trump.

Okay.

I tried to recall it, my memory of the room where I had reached Dalt. It was pretty sketchy. What was the minimum amount of data the Pattern required in order to operate? I recalled the texture of the stone wall, the shape of the small window, a bit of worn tapestry upon the wall, strewn rushes on the floor; a low bench and a stool had come into view to his rear when Dalt had moved, a crack in the wall above them—and a bit of cobweb. . . .

I formed the image as sharply as I could. I willed myself there. I wanted to be in that place. . . .

And I was.

I turned around quickly, my hand on the hilt of my blade, but I was alone in the chamber. I saw a bed and an armoire, a small writing table, a storage chest, none of which had been in my line of sight during my brief view of the place. Daylight shone through the small window.

I crossed the room to its single door and stood there for a long while, listening. There was only silence on the other side. I opened it a crack—it swung to the left—and looked upon a long, empty hallway. I eased the door farther open. There was a stairway directly across from me, leading down. To my left was a blank wall. I stepped outside and closed the door. Go down or go right? There were several windows on both sides of the hallway. I moved to the nearest one, which was to my right, and looked out.

I saw that I was near to the lower corner of a rectangular courtyard, more buildings across the way and to my right and left, all of them connected at the corners save for an opening to the upper right which seemed as if it led to another courtyard where a very large structure rose beyond the buildings directly across from me. There were perhaps a dozen troops in the courtyard below, disposed near various entranceways, though not giving the appearance of being formally on guard—that is, they were engaged in cleaning and repairing their gear. Two of them were heavily bandaged. Still, most seemed in such a state that they could leap to service fairly quickly.

At the yard's far end was a strange bit of flotsam, looking like a large broken kite, which seemed somehow familiar. I decided to head along the hallway, which paralleled the courtyard, for it seemed that this would take me into those buildings along the farther edge of the perimeter and probably give me a view into the next yard.

I moved along the hallway, alert to any sounds of activity. There was nothing but silence as I advanced to the corner. I waited there for a long while, listening.

In that I heard nothing, I rounded the corner then, and froze. So did the man seated on the windowsill to the right. He wore a chain mail shirt, a leather cap, leather leggings and boots. There was a heavy blade at his side, but it was a dagger that he held in his hand, apparently giving himself a manicure. He looked as surprised as I felt when his head jerked in my direction.

"Who are you?" he asked.

His shoulders straightened and he lowered his hands as if to push himself from his perch and into a standing position.

Embarrassing to both of us. He seemed to be a guard. Whereas alertness or attempted stealth might have betrayed him to Frakir or myself, sloth had provided him with excellent concealment and me with a small dilemma. I was sure I couldn't bluff him, or trust to the result if I seemed to. I did not wish to attack him and create a lot of noise. This narrowed my choices. I could kill him quickly and silently with a neat little cardiac-arrest spell I had hanging in front of me. But I value life too highly to waste it when there is no need. So, as much as I hated to spend another spell that I carried this soon, I spoke the word that caused my hand to move reflexively through an accompanying gesture, and I had a glimpse of the Logrus as its force pulsed through me. The man closed his eyes and slumped back against the casement. I adjusted his position against slippage and left him snoring peacefully, the dagger still in his hand. Besides, I might have a greater need for the cardiac-arrest spell later.

The corridor entered some sort of gallery ahead, which seemed to bulge in both directions. In that I could not see what lay at either hand beyond a certain point, I knew that I would have to expend another spell sooner than I might wish. I spoke the word for my invisibility spell, and the world grew several shades darker. I had been hoping to get a little farther before I had to use it, since it was only good for about twenty minutes and I had no idea where my prize might lie. But I couldn't afford to take chances. I hurried along and passed into the gallery, which proved empty.

I learned a little more geography in that place, though. I had a view from there into the next courtyard, and it was gigantic. It contained the massive structure I had glimpsed from the other side. It was a huge, solidly built fortress; it appeared to have only one entrance, and that well guarded. From the opposite side of the gallery, I saw that there was also an outer courtyard, leading up to high, well-fortified walls.

I departed the gallery and sought a flight of stairs, almost certain that that hulking gray-stone structure was the place I should be searching. It had an aura of magic about it that I could feel down to my toes.

I jogged along the hallway, took a turn and saw a guard at the head of a stairway. If he felt anything of my passage it was only the breeze stirred by my cloak. I rushed down the stairs. There was an adit at its foot, leading to another corridor—a dark one—off to the left; and there was a heavy ironbound door directly before me, in the wall facing the inner courtyard.

I pushed the door open, passed through and stepped aside quickly, for a guard had turned, stared and was beginning to approach. I avoided him and moved toward the citadel. A focus of powers, Luke had said. Yes. I could feel this more strongly the closer I got to the place. I did not have time to try to figure out how to deal with them, to channel them. Anyway, I'd brought along my private stock.

When I neared the wall I cut to the left. A quick circuit was in order, for informational purposes. Partway around it, I saw that my guess that there was only one apparent entrance was correct. Also, there were no windows in its walls lower than about thirty feet. There was a high, spiked metal fence about the place, and a pit on the inside of the fence. The thing that most surprised me was not a feature of the structure, however. On its far side, near the wall, were two more of the large broken kites and three relatively intact ones. The matter of context no longer clouded my perception—not with the unbroken ones before me. They were hang gliders. I was eager to take a closer look at them, but time was running on my invisibility and I couldn't afford the detour. I hurried the rest of the way around and studied the gate.

The gate to the fence was closed and flanked by two guards. Several paces beyond it was a removable wooden bridge, reinforced with metal strapping, in place across the ditch. There were large eye bolts at its corners, and there was a winch built into the wall above the gate; the winch bore four chains terminating in hooks. I wondered how heavy the bridge was. The door to the citadel was recessed about three feet into the stone wall, and it was high, wide and plated, looking as if it could withstand a battering ram's pounding for a good long while.

I approached the gate to the fence and studied it. No lock on it—just a simple hand-operated latching mechanism. I could open it, run through, dash across the span and be at the big door before the guards had any idea as to what might be going on. On the other hand, considering the nature of the place, they might well have had some instruction as to the possibility of an unnatural attack. If so, it would not be necessary for them to see me if they responded quickly and cornered me in the alcove. And I'd a feeling the heavy door inside was not unlocked.

I mused for several moments, sorting through my spells. I also checked again on the position of the six or eight other people in the yard. None were too near, none moving in this direction. . . .

I advanced upon the guards quietly and placed Frakir on the shoulder of the man to my left with an order for a quick choke. Three rapid steps to the right, then, and I struck the other guard on the left side of his neck with the edge of my hand. I caught him beneath the armpits, to prevent the rattling a fall would produce, and lowered him to his rump, back against the fence, to the right of the gate. Behind me, though, I heard the clatter of the other man's scabbard against the fence as he slumped, clutching at his throat. I hurried to him, guided him the rest of the way to the ground and removed Frakir. A quick glance about showed me that two other men across the court-yard were not looking in this direction. Damn.

I unlatched the gate, slipped within, closed it and latched it behind me. I hurried across the bridge then and looked back. The two men I had noticed were now headed in this direction. Therefore, I was immediately presented with another choice. I decided to see how arduous the more strategically sound one might be.

Squatting, I caught hold of the nearest corner of the bridge—to my right. The ditch it spanned seemed something like twelve feet in depth, and it was almost twice that in width.

I began straightening my legs. Damned heavy, but the thing creaked and my corner rose several inches. I held it there for a moment, got control of my breathing and tried again. More creaking and a few more inches. Again. . . . My hands hurt where the edges pressed into them. My arms felt as if they were being slowly wrenched from their sockets. As I straightened my legs and strained upward with even greater exertion, I wondered how many people fail in robust undertakings because of sudden lower back problems. I guess they're the ones you don't hear about. I could feel my heart pounding as if it filled my entire chest. My corner was now about a foot above the ground, but the edge to my left was still touching. I strained again, feeling the perspiration appear as if by magic across my brow and under my arms. Breathe. . . . Up!

I went to knee level, then above. The corner to my left was finally raised. I heard the voices of the two approaching men—loud, excited—they were hurrying now. I began edging to my left, dragging the whole structure with me. The corner directly across from me moved outward as I did so. Good. I kept moving. The corner to my left was now a couple of feet out over the chasm. I felt fiery pains all the way up my arms and into my shoulders and neck. Farther. . . .

The men were at the gate now, but they paused to examine the fallen guards. Good, again. I still wasn't certain that the bridge might not catch and hold if I were to drop it. It had to slip into the chasm, or I was making myself a candidate for disk surgery for nothing. Left. . . .

It began swaying in my grip, tipping to the right. I could tell that it was going to slip from my control in a few moments. Left again, left . . . almost. . . . The men had turned their attention from the fallen guards to the moving bridge now and were fumbling at the latch. Two more were rushing to join them from across the way, and I heard a series of shouts. Another step. The thing was really slipping now. I wasn't going to be able to hold it. . . . One more step.

Let go and get back!

My corner crashed against the edge of the chasm, but the wood splintered and the edge gave way and I kept retreating. The span flopped over as it fell, struck against the far side twice and hit the bottom with a terrific crash. My arms hung at my sides, useless for the moment.

I turned and headed for the doorway. My spell was still holding, so at least I was not a target for any hurled missiles from the other side of the moat.

When I got to the door it took all that I had of effort to raise my arms to the big ring on the right-hand side and catch hold of it. But nothing happened when I pulled. The thing was secured. I had expected that, though, and was prepared. I'd had to try first, however. I do not spend my spells lightly.

I spoke the words, three of them this time—less elegant because it was a sloppy spell, though it possessed immense force.

My entire body shook as the door exploded inward as if kicked by a giant wearing a steel-toed boot. I entered immediately and was immediately confused as my eyes adjusted to the dimness. I was in a two-story-high hall. Stairways rose to the right and the left ahead of me, curving inward toward a railed landing, the terminus of a second-floor hallway. There was another hallway below it, directly across from me. Two stairways also headed downward, to the rear of those which ascended. Decisions, decisions. . . .

In the center of the room was a black stone fountain, spraying flames—

not water—into the air; the fire descended into the font's basin, where it swirled and danced. The flames were red and orange in the air, white and yellow below, rippling. A feeling of power filled the chamber. Anyone who could control the forces loose in this place would be a formidable opponent indeed. With luck, I might not have to discover how formidable.

I almost wasted a special attack when I became aware of the two figures in the corner, off to my right. But they hadn't stirred at all. They were unnaturally still. Statues, of course. . . .

I was trying to decide whether to go up, go down or move straight ahead, and I'd just about decided to descend, on the theory that there is some sort of instinct to imprison enemies in dank, below-ground quarters, when something about the two statues drew my attention again. My vision having adjusted somewhat, I could now make out that one was a white-haired man, the other a dark-haired woman. I rubbed my eyes, not realizing for several seconds that I had seen the outline of my hand. My invisibility spell was dissipating. . . .

I moved toward the figures. The fact that the old man was holding a couple of cloaks and hats should have been the tipoff. But I raised the skirt of his dark blue robe anyway. In the suddenly brighter light from the fountain I saw where the name RINALDO had been carved into his right leg. Nasty little kid, that.

The woman at his side was Jasra, saving me the problem of seeking her amid rodents below. Her arms were also outstretched, as in a warding gesture, and someone had hung a pale blue umbrella upon the left and a light gray London Fog raincoat upon the right; the matching rain hat was on her head, at a lopsided angle. Her face had been painted like a clown's and someone had pinned a pair of yellow tassels to the front of her green blouse.

The light behind me flared even more brightly, and I turned to see what was going on. The fountain, it turned out, was now spewing its liquid-like fires a full twenty feet into the air. They descended to overflow the basin and spread outward across the flagged floor. A major rivulet was headed in my direction. At that point, a soft chuckle caused me to look upward.

Wearing a dark robe, cowl and gauntlets, the wizard of the cobalt mask stood on the landing above me, one hand on the railing, the other pointed toward the fountain. In that I had anticipated our meeting on this expedition, I was not unprepared for the encounter. As the flames leaped even higher, forming a great bright tower that almost immediately began to bend and then topple toward me, I raised my arms in a wide gesture and spoke the word for the most appropriate of the three defensive spells I had hung earlier.

Air currents began to stir, powered by the Logrus, almost immediately achieving gale force and sending the flames back away from me. I adjusted my position then so that they were blown toward the wizard upstairs. Instantly, he gestured, and the flames fell back within the fountain, subsiding to the barest glowing trickle.

Okay. A draw. I had not come here to have it out with this guy. I had come to finesse Luke by rescuing Jasra on my own. Once she was my prisoner, Amber would sure as hell be safe from anything Luke had in mind. I found myself wondering, though, about this wizard, as my winds died down and the chuckle came again: Was he using spells, as I was? Or, living in the midst of a power source such as this, was he able to control the forces directly and shape them as he chose? If it were the latter, which I suspected, then he had a virtually inexhaustible source of tricks up his sleeve, so that in any full-scale competition on his turf I would eventually be reduced to flight or to calling in the nukes—that is, summoning Chaos itself to utterly reduce everything in the area—and this was a thing I was not about to do, destroying all the mysteries, including that of the wizard's identity, rather than solving them for answers that might be essential to Amber's well-being.

A shining metallic spear materialized in midair before the wizard, hung a moment, then flashed toward me. I used my second defensive spell, summoning a shield that turned it aside.

The only alternative I could see to my dueling with spells or blasting the place with Chaos would be for me to learn to control the forces here myself and try beating this guy at his own game. No time for practice now, though; I'd a job to do as soon as I could buy a few moments in which to get it done. Sooner or later, however, it seemed that we would have to have a full confrontation—since he seemed to have it in for me, and may well even have been the motive force behind the attack by the clumsy werewolf in the woods.

And I was not hot on taking chances to explore the power here further at this point—not if Jasra had been good enough to beat the original master of this place, Sharu Garrul, and then this guy had been good enough to beat Jasra. I'd give a lot, though, to know why he had it in for me. . . .

So, "What do you want, anyway?" I called out.

Immediately, that metallic voice replied, "Your blood, your soul, your mind and your body."

"What about my stamp collection?" I hollered back. "Do I get to keep the First Day Covers?"

I moved over beside Jasra and threw my right arm about her shoulders.

"What do you want with that one, funny man?" the wizard asked. "She is the most worthless property in this place."

"Then why should you object to my taking her off your hands?"

"You collect stamps. I collect presumptuous sorcerers. She's mine, and you're next."

I felt the power rising against me again even as I shouted, "What have you got against your brothers and sisters in the Art?"

There was no reply, but the air about me was suddenly filled with sharp, spinning shapes—knives, ax blades, throwing stars, broken bottles. I spoke the word for my final defense, the curtain of Chaos, raising a chittering, smoky screen about us. The sharp items hurtling in our direction were instantly reduced to cosmic dust on coming into contact with it.

Above the din of this engagement I cried out, "By what name shall I call you?"

"Mask!" was the wizard's immediate reply—not very original, I thought.

I'd half expected a John D. MacDonald appellation—Nightmare Mauve or Cobalt Casque, perhaps. Oh, well.

I had just used my last defensive spell. I had also just raised my left arm so that that portion of my sleeve bearing the Amber Trump now hung within my field of vision. I had cut things a bit fine, but I had not yet played my full hand. So far, I had run a completely defensive show, and I was rather proud of the spell I had kept in reserve.

"She'll do you no good, that one," Mask said, as both our spells subsided and he prepared to strike again.

"Have a nice day, anyway," I said, and I rotated my wrists, pointed my fingers to direct the flow and spoke the word that beat him to the punch.

"An eye for an eye!" I called out, as the contents of an entire florist shop fell upon Mask, completely burying him in the biggest damned bouquet I'd ever seen. Smelled nice, too.

There was silence and a subsidence of forces as I regarded the Trump, reached through it. Just as the contact was achieved there was a disturbance in the floral display and Mask rose through it, like the Allegory of Spring.

I was probably already fading from his view as he said, "I'll have you yet."

"And sweets to the sweet," I replied, then spoke the word that completed the spell, dropping a load of manure upon him.

I stepped through into the main hall of Amber, bearing Jasra with me. Martin stood near a sideboard, a glass of wine in his hand, talking with Bors, the falconer. He grew silent at Bors's wide-eyed stare in my direction, then turned and stared himself.

I set Jasra on her feet beside the doorway. I was not about to screw around with the spell on her right now—and I was not at all sure what I'd do with her if I released her from it. So I hung my cloak on her, went over to the sideboard and poured myself a glass of wine, nodding to Bors and Martin as I passed.

I drained the glass, put it down, then said to them, "Whatever you do, don't carve your initials on her." Then I went and found a sofa in a room to the east, stretched out on it and closed my eyes. Like a bridge over troubled waters. Some days are diamonds. Where have all the flowers gone?

Something like that.

TWELVE

There was a lot of smoke, a giant worm and many flashes of colored light. Every sound was born into form, blazed to its peak, faded as it waned. Lightninglike stabs of existence, these—called from, returning to, Shadow. The worm went on forever. The dog-headed flowers snapped at me but later wagged their leaves. The flowing smoke halted before a skyhooked traffic light. The worm—no, caterpillar—smiled. A slow, blinding rain began, and all the drifting drops were faceted. . . .

What is wrong with this picture? something within me asked.

I gave up, because I couldn't be sure. Though I'd a vague feeling the occasional landscape shouldn't be flowing the way that it did. . . .

"Oh, man! Merle. . . ."

What did Luke want now? Why wouldn't he get off my case? Always a new problem.

"Look at that, will you?"

I watched where a series of bright bounding balls—or maybe they were comets—wove a tapestry of light. It fell upon the forest of umbrellas.

"Luke—" I began, but one of the dog-headed flowers bit a hand I'd forgotten about, and everything nearby cracked as if it were painted on glass through which a shot had just passed. There was a rainbow beyond—

"Merle! Merle!"

It was Droppa shaking my shoulder, my suddenly opened eyes showed me. And there as a damp place on the sofa where my head was resting.

I propped myself on an elbow. I rubbed my eyes.

"Droppa. . . . What—?"

"I don't know," he told me.

"What don't you know? I mean. . . . Hell! What happened?"

"I was sitting in that chair," he said, with a gesture, "waiting for you to wake up. Martin had told me you were here. I was just going to tell you that Random wanted to see you when you got back."

I nodded, then noticed that my hand was oozing blood—from the place where the flower had bitten me.

"How long was I out?"

"Twenty minutes, maybe."

I swung my feet to the floor, sat up. "So why'd you decide to wake me?"

"You were trumping out," he said.

"Trumping out? While I was asleep? It doesn't work that way. Are you sure—"

"I am, unfortunately, sober at the moment," he said. "You got that rainbow glow and you started to soften around the edges and fade. Thought I'd better wake you then and ask if that's what you really had in mind. What've you been drinking, spot remover?"

"No," I said.

"I tried it on my dog once. . . ."

"Dreams," I said, massaging my temples, which had begun throbbing. "That's all. Dreams."

"The kind other people can see, too? Like DTs à deux?"

"That's not what I meant."

"We'd better go see Random." He started to turn toward the doorway.

I shook my head. "Not yet. I'm just going to sit here and collect myself. Something's wrong."

When I glanced at him I saw that his eyes were wide, and he was staring past me. I turned.

The wall at my back seemed to be melting, as if it were cast of wax and had been set too near a fire.

"It appears to be alarums and excursions time," Droppa remarked. "Help!"

And he was across the room and out of the door, screaming.

Three eyeblinks later the wall was normal again in every way, but I was trembling. What the hell was going on? Had Mask managed to lay a spell on me before I'd cut out? If so, where was it headed?

I rose to my feet and turned in a slow circle. Everything seemed to be in place now. I knew that it could not have been anything as simple as a hallucination born of all my recent stresses, since Droppa had seen it too. So I was not cracking up. This was something else—and whatever it was, I felt that it was still lurking nearby. There was a certain unnatural clarity to the air now, and every object seemed unusually vivid within it.

I made a quick circuit of the room, not knowing what I was really seeking. Not surprisingly, therefore, I did not find it. I stepped outside then. Whatever the problem, could it spring from something I had brought back with me? Might Jasra, stiff and gaudy, have been a Trojan horse?

I headed for the main hall. A dozen steps along the way, a lopsided gridwork of light appeared before me. I forced myself to continue, and it receded as I advanced, changing shape as it did so.

"Merle, come on!" Luke's voice, Luke himself nowhere in sight.

"Where?" I called out, not slowing.

No answer, but the gridwork split down the middle and its two halves swung away from me like a pair of shutters. They opened into a near-blinding light; within it, I thought I glimpsed a rabbit. Then, abruptly, the vision was gone, and the only thing that saved me from believing everything was normal again was several seconds' worth of Luke's sourceless laughter.

I ran. Was it really Luke who was the enemy, as I had been warned repeatedly? Had I somehow been manipulated through everything which had happened recently, solely for the purpose of freeing his mother from the Keep of the Four Worlds? And now that she was safe had he the temerity to invade Amber herself and summon me to a sorcerous duel the terms of which I did not even understand?

No, I could not believe it. I was certain he did not possess that sort of power. But even if he did, he wouldn't dare try it—not with Jasra as my hostage.

As I rushed along I heard him again—from everywhere, from nowhere. This time he was singing. He had a powerful baritone voice, and the song was "Auld Lang Syne." What sort of irony did this represent?

I burst into the main hall. Martin and Bors had departed. I saw their empty glasses on the sideboard near which they had been standing. And near the other door—? Yes, near the other door Jasra remained, erect, unchanged, still holding my cloak.

"Okay, Luke! Let's have it out!" I cried. "Cut the crap and let's settle this business!"

"Huh?"

The singing stopped abruptly.

I crossed slowly to Jasra, studying her as I went. Completely unchanged, save for a hat someone had added to her other hand. From somewhere else in the palace, I heard a shout. Maybe it was Droppa still alaruming.

"Luke, wherever you are," I said, "if you can hear me, if you can see me, take a good look and listen: I've got her here. See? Whatever you're planning, bear that in mind."

The room rippled violently, as if I were standing in the midst of an unframed painting someone had just decided to give a shake, to crinkle and then draw taut.

"Well?"

Nothing.

Then, a chuckle.

"My mother, the hat rack. . . . Well, well. Hey, thanks, buddy. Good show. Couldn't reach you earlier. Didn't know you'd gone in. They slaughtered us. Took some mercs in on hang gliders, rode the thermals. They were ready, though. Took us out. Don't remember exactly then. . . . Hurts!"

"You okay?"

There came something like a sob, just as Random and Droppa entered the hall, the lank form of Benedict silent as death at their back.

"Merle!" Random called to me. "What's going on?"

I shook my head. "Don't know," I said.

"Sure, I'll buy you a drink," Luke's voice came very faintly.

A fiery blizzard swept through the center of the hall. It lasted only a moment, and then a large rectangle appeared in its place.

"You're the sorcerer," Random said. "Do something!"

"I don't know what the hell it is," I replied. "I've never seen anything like it. It's like magic gone wild."

An outline began to appear within the rectangle, human. Its form settled and took on features, garments. . . . It was a Trump—a giant Trump—hanging in the middle of the air, solidifying. It was—

Me. I regarded my own features and they looked back at me. I noted that I was smiling.

"C'mon, Merle. Join the party," I heard Luke say, and the Trump began to rotate slowly upon its vertical axis.

Sounds, as of glass bells, filled the hall.

The huge card turned until I had viewed it edge-on, a black slash. Then the dark line widened with a ripple, like parting curtains, and I saw colored patches of intense light sliding beyond it. I also saw the caterpillar, puffing on a hookah, and fat umbrellas and a bright, shiny rail—

A hand emerged from the slit. "Right this way."

I heard a sharp intake of breath from Random.

Benedict's blade was suddenly pointed at the tableau. But Random laid his hand on his shoulder and said, "No."

There was a strange, disconnected sort of music hanging in the air now; it seemed somehow appropriate.

"C'mon, Merle."

"You coming or going?" I asked.

"Both."

"You made me a promise, Luke: a piece of information for your mother's rescue," I said. "Well, I've got her here. What's the secret?"

"Something vital to your well-being?" he asked slowly.

"Vital to the safety of Amber is what you'd said."

"Oh, *that* secret."

"I'd be glad to have the other one too."

"Sorry. One secret is all I'm selling. Which will it be?"

"The safety of Amber," I answered.

"Dalt," he replied.

"What of him?"

"Deela the Desacratrix was his mother—"

"I already know that."

"—and she'd been Oberon's prisoner nine months before he was born. He raped her. That's why Dalt's got it in for you guys."

"Bullshit!" I said.

"That's what I told him when I'd heard the story one time too many. I dared him to walk the Pattern in the sky then."

"And?"

"He did."

"Oh."

"I just learned that story recently," Random said, "from an emissary I'd sent to Kashfa. I didn't know about his taking the Pattern, though."

"If you knew, I still owe you," Luke said slowly, almost distractedly. "Okay, here's more: Dalt visited me on the shadow Earth after that. He's the one who raided my warehouse, stole a stock of weapons and special ammo. Burnt the place after that to cover the theft. I found witnesses, though. He'll be along—any time. Who knows when?"

"Another relative coming to visit," Random said. "Why couldn't I have been an only child?"

"Make what you will of it," Luke added. "We're square now. Give me a hand!"

"You coming through?"

He laughed, and the whole hall seemed to lurch. The opening in the air hung before me and the hand clasped my own. Something felt very wrong.

I tried to draw him to me, but felt myself drawn toward him instead. There was a mad power I could not fight, and the universe seemed to twist as it took hold of me. Constellations parted before me and I saw the bright railing again. Luke's booted foot rested upon it.

From some distant point to the rear I heard Random shouting, "B-twelve! B-twelve! And out!"

. . . And then I couldn't recall what the problem had been. It seemed a wonderful place. Silly of me to have mistaken the mushrooms for umbrellas, though. . . .

I put my own foot up on the rail as the Hatter poured me a drink and topped off Luke's. Luke gestured to his left and the March Hare got a refill too. Humpty was fine, balanced there near the end of things. Tweedledum, Tweedledee, and the Dodo and the Frog Footman kept the music moving. And the Caterpillar just kept puffing away.

Luke clapped me on the shoulder, and there was something I wanted to remember but it kept slipping out of sight.

"I'm okay now," Luke said. "Everything's okay."

"No, there's something. . . . I can't recall. . . ."

He raised his tankard, clanked it against my own. "Enjoy!" he said. "Life is a cabaret, old chum!"

The cat on the stool beside me just kept grinning.

BOOK EIGHT
SIGN OF CHAOS

To Phil Cleverley
and our seasons in the sun:
Thanks for all the kokyu nages.

ONE

I felt vaguely uneasy, though I couldn't say why. It did not seem all that unusual to be drinking with a White Rabbit, a short guy who resembled Bertrand Russell, a grinning Cat, and my old friend Luke Raynard, who was singing Irish ballads while a peculiar landscape shifted from mural to reality at his back. Well, I was impressed by the huge blue Caterpillar smoking the hookah atop the giant mushroom because I know how hard it is to keep a water pipe lit. Still, that wasn't it. It was a convivial scene, and Luke was known to keep pretty strange company on occasion. So why should I feel uneasy?

The beer was good and there was even a free lunch. The demons tormenting the red-haired woman tied to the stake had been so shiny they'd hurt to look at. Gone now, but the whole thing had been beautiful. Everything was beautiful. When Luke sang of Galway Bay it had been so sparkling and lovely that I'd wanted to dive in and lose myself there. Sad, too.

Something to do with the feeling. . . . Yes. Funny thought. When Luke sang a sad song I felt melancholy. When it was a happy one I was greatly cheered. There seemed an unusual amount of empathy in the air. No matter, I guess. The light show was superb. . . .

I sipped my drink and watched Humpty teeter, there at the end of the bar. For a moment I tried to remember when I'd come into this place, but that cylinder wasn't hitting. It would come to me, eventually. Nice party. . . .

I watched and listened and tasted and felt, and it was all great. Anything that caught my attention was fascinating. Was there something I'd wanted to ask Luke? It seemed there was, but he was busy singing and I couldn't think of it now, anyway.

What had I been doing before I'd come into this place? Trying to recall just didn't seem worth the effort either. Not when everything was so interesting right here and now.

It seemed that it might have been something important, though. Could that be why I felt uneasy? Might it be there was business I had left unfinished and should be getting back to?

I turned to ask the Cat but he was fading again, still seeming vastly amused. It occurred to me then that I, too, could do that. Fade, I mean, and go someplace else. Was that how I had come here and how I might depart? Possibly. I put down my drink and rubbed my eyes and my temples. Things seemed to be swimming inside my head, too.

I suddenly recalled a picture of me. On a giant card. A Trump. Yes. That was how I'd gotten here. Through the card. . . .

A hand fell upon my shoulder and I turned. It belonged to Luke, who grinned at me as he edged up to the bar for a refill.

"Great party, huh?" he said.

"Yeah, great. How'd you find this place?" I asked him.

He shrugged. "I forget. Who cares?"

He turned away, a brief blizzard of crystals swirling between us. The Caterpillar exhaled a purple cloud. A blue moon was rising.

What is wrong with this picture? I asked myself.

I had a sudden feeling that my critical faculty had been shot off in the war, because I couldn't focus on the anomalies I felt must be present. I knew that I was caught up in the moment, but I couldn't see my way clear.

I was caught up. . . .

I was caught. . . .

How?

Well. . . . It had all started when I'd shaken my own hand. No. Wrong. That sounds like Zen and that's not how it was. The hand I shook emerged from the space occupied by the image of myself on the card that went away. Yes, that was it. . . . After a fashion.

I clenched my teeth. The music began again. There came a soft scraping sound near to my hand on the bar. When I looked I saw that my tankard had been refilled. Maybe I'd had too much already. Maybe that's what kept getting in the way of my thinking. I turned away. I looked off to my left, past the place where the mural on the wall became the real landscape. Did that make me a part of the mural? I wondered suddenly.

No matter. If I couldn't think here. . . . I began running . . . to the left. Something about this place was messing with my head, and it seemed impossible to consider the process while I was a part of it. I had to get away in order to think straight, to determine what was going on.

I was across the bar and into that interface area where the painted rocks and trees became three-dimensional. I pumped my arms as I dug in. I heard the wind without feeling it.

Nothing that lay before me seemed any nearer. I was moving, but—

Luke began singing again.

I halted. I turned, slowly, because it sounded as if he were standing practically beside me. He was. I was only a few paces removed from the bar. Luke smiled and kept singing.

"What's going on?" I asked the Caterpillar.

"You're looped in Luke's loop," it replied.

"Come again?" I said.

It blew a blue smoke ring, sighed softly, and said, "Luke's locked in a loop and you're lost in the lyrics. That's all."

"How'd it happen?" I asked.

"I have no idea," it replied.

"Uh, how does one get unlooped?"

"Couldn't tell you that either."

I turned to the Cat, who was coalescing about his grin once again.

"I don't suppose you'd know—" I began.

"I saw him come in and I saw you come in later," said the Cat, smirking. "And even for this place your arrivals were somewhat . . . unusual—leading me to conclude that at least one of you is associated with magic."

I nodded.

"Your own comings and goings might give one pause," I observed.

"I keep my paws to myself," he replied. "Which is more than Luke can say."

"What do you mean?"

"He's caught in a contagious trap."

"How does it work?" I asked.

But he was gone again, and this time the grin went too.

Contagious trap? That seemed to indicate that the problem was Luke's, and that I had been sucked into it in some fashion. This felt right, though it still gave me no idea as to what the problem was or what I might do about it.

I reached for my tankard. If I couldn't solve my problem, I might as well enjoy it. As I took a slow sip I became aware of a strange pair of pale, burning eyes gazing into my own. I hadn't noticed them before, and the thing that made them strange was that they occupied a shadowy corner of the mural across the room from me—that, and the fact that they were moving, drifting slowly to my left.

It was kind of fascinating, when I lost sight of the eyes but was still able to follow whatever it was from the swaying of grasses as it passed into the area toward which I had been headed earlier. And far, far off to my right—beyond Luke—I now detected a slim gentleman in a dark jacket, palette and brush in hand, who was slowly extending the mural. I took another sip and returned my attention to the progress of whatever it was that had moved from flat reality to 3-D. A gunmetal snout protruded from between a rock and a shrub; the pale eyes blazed above it; blue saliva dripped from the dark muzzle and steamed upon the ground. It was either quite short or very crouched, and I couldn't make up my mind whether it was the entire crowd of us that it was studying or me in particular. I leaned to one side and caught Humpty by the belt or the necktie, whichever it was, just as he was about to slump to the side.

"Excuse me," I said. "Could you tell me what sort of creature that is?"

I pointed just as it emerged—many-legged, long-tailed, dark-scaled, undulating, and fast. Its claws were red, and it raised its tail as it raced toward us.

Humpty's bleary eyes moved toward my own, drifted past.

"I am not here, sir," he began, "to remedy your zoological ignor—My God! It's—"

It flashed across the distance, approaching rapidly. Would it reach a spot shortly where its running would become a treadmill operation—or had that effect only applied to me on trying to get away from this place?

The segments of its body slid from side to side, it hissed like a leaky pressure cooker, and steaming slaver marked its trail from the fiction of paint. Rather than slowing, its speed seemed to increase.

My left hand jerked forward of its own volition and a series of words rose unbidden to my lips. I spoke them just as the creature crossed the interface I had been unable to pierce earlier, rearing as it upset a vacant table and bunching its members as if about to spring.

"A Bandersnatch!" someone cried.

"A frumious Bandersnatch!" Humpty corrected.

As I spoke the final word and performed the ultimate gesture, the image of the Logrus swam before my inner vision. The dark creature, having just extended its foremost talons, suddenly drew them back, clutched with them against the upper left quadrant of its breast, rolled its eyes, emitted a soft moaning sound, exhaled heavily, collapsed, fell to the floor, and rolled over onto its back, its many feet extended upward into the air.

The Cat's grin appeared above the creature. The mouth moved.

"A *dead* frumious Bandersnatch," it stated.

The grin drifted toward me, the rest of the Cat occurring about it like an afterthought.

"That was a cardiac arrest spell, wasn't it?" it inquired.

"I guess so," I said. "It was sort of a reflex. Yeah, I remember now. I did still have that spell hanging around."

"I thought so," it observed. "I was sure that there was magic involved in this party."

The image of the Logrus which had appeared to me during the spell's operation had also served the purpose of switching on a small light in the musty attic of my mind. Sorcery. Of course.

I—Merlin, son of Corwin—am a sorcerer, of a variety seldom encountered in the areas I have frequented in recent years. Lucas Raynard—also known as Prince Rinaldo of Kashfa—is himself a sorcerer, albeit of a style different than my own. And the Cat, who seemed somewhat sophisticated in these matters, could well have been correct in assessing our situation as the interior of a spell. Such a location is one of the few environments where my sensitivity and training would do little to inform me as to the nature of my predicament. This, because my faculties would also be caught up in the manifestation and subject to its forces, if the thing were at all self-consistent. It struck me as something similar to color blindness. I could think of no way of telling for certain what was going on, without outside help.

As I mused over these matters, the King's horses and men arrived beyond the swinging doors at the front of the place. The men entered and fastened lines upon the carcass of the Bandersnatch. The horses dragged the thing off. Humpty had climbed down to visit the rest room while this was going on. Upon his return he discovered that he was unable to achieve his former position atop the barstool. He shouted to the King's men to give him a hand, but they were busy guiding the defunct Bandersnatch among tables and they ignored him.

Luke strolled up, smiling.

"So that was a Bandersnatch," he observed. "I'd always wondered what they were like. Now, if we could just get a Jabberwock to stop by—"

"Sh!" cautioned the Cat. "It must be off in the mural somewhere, and likely it's been listening. Don't stir it up! It may come whiffling through the tulgey wood after your ass. Remember the jaws that bite, the claws that catch! Don't go looking for troub—"

The Cat cast a quick glance toward the wall and phased into and out of existence several times in quick succession. Ignoring this, Luke remarked, "I was just thinking of the Tenniel illustration."

The Cat materialized at the far end of the bar, downed the Hatter's drink, and said, "I hear the burbling, and eyes of flame are drifting to the left."

I glanced at the mural, and I, too, saw the fiery eyes and heard a peculiar sound.

"It could be any of a number of things," Luke remarked.

The Cat moved to a rack behind the bar and reached high up on the wall to where a strange weapon hung, shimmering and shifting in shadow. He lowered the thing and slid it along the bar; it came to rest before Luke.

"Better have the Vorpal Sword in hand, that's all I can say."

Luke laughed, but I stared fascinated at the device which looked as if it were made of moth wings and folded moonlight.

Then I heard the burbling again.

"Don't just stand there in uffish thought!" said the Cat, draining Humpty's glass and vanishing again.

Still chuckling, Luke held out his tankard for a refill. I stood there in uffish thought. The spell I had used to destroy the Bandersnatch had altered my thinking in a peculiar fashion. It seemed for a small moment in its aftermath that things were beginning to come clear in my head. I attributed this to the image of the Logrus which I had regarded briefly. And so I summoned it again.

The Sign rose before me, hovered. I held it there. I looked upon it. It seemed as if a cold wind began to blow through my mind. Drifting bits of memory were drawn together, assembled themselves into an entire fabric, were informed with understanding. Of course. . . .

The burbling grew louder and I saw the shadow of the Jabberwock gliding among distant trees, eyes like landing lights, lots of sharp edges for biting and catching. . . .

And it didn't matter a bit. For I realized now what was going on, who was responsible, how and why.

I bent over, leaning far forward, so that my knuckles just grazed the toe of my right boot.

"Luke," I said, "we've got a problem."

He turned away from the bar and glanced down at me.

"What's the matter?" he asked.

Those of the blood of Amber are capable of terrific exertions. We are also able to sustain some pretty awful beatings. So, among ourselves, these things tend to cancel out to some degree. Therefore, one must go about such matters just right if one is to attend to them at all. . . .

I brought my fist up off the floor with everything I had behind it, and I caught Luke on the side of the jaw with a blow that lifted him above the ground as it turned him and sent him sprawling across a table which collapsed, to continue sliding backward the length of the entire serving area where he finally came to a crumpled halt at the feet of the quiet Victorian-looking gentleman—who had dropped his paintbrush and stepped away quickly when Luke came skidding toward him. I raised my tankard with my left hand and poured its contents over my right fist, which felt as if I had just driven it against a mountainside. As I did this the lights grew dim and there was a moment of utter silence.

Then I slammed the mug back onto the bartop. The entire place chose that moment in which to shudder, as if from an earth tremor. Two bottles fell from a shelf, a lamp swayed, the burbling grew fainter. I glanced to my left and saw that the eerie shadow of the Jabberwock had retreated somewhat within the tulgey wood. Not only that, the painted section of the prospect now extended a good deal farther into what had seemed normal space, and it looked to be continuing its advance in that direction, freezing that corner of the world into flat immobility. It became apparent from whiffle to whiffle that the Jabberwock was now moving away, to the left, hurrying ahead of the flatness. Tweedledum, Tweedledee, the Dodo, and the Frog began packing their instruments.

I started across the bar toward Luke's sprawled form. The Caterpillar was disassembling his hookah, and I saw that his mushroom was tilted at an odd angle. The White Rabbit beat it down a hole to the rear, and I heard Humpty muttering curses as he swayed atop the bar stool he had just succeeded in mounting.

I saluted the gentleman with the palette as I approached.

"Sorry to disturb you," I said. "But believe me, this is for the better."

I raised Luke's limp form and slung him over my shoulder. A flock of playing cards flew by me. I drew away from them in their rapid passage.

"Goodness! It's frightened the Jabberwock!" the man remarked, looking past me.

"What has?" I asked, not really certain that I wished to know.

"That," he answered, gesturing toward the front of the bar.

I looked and I staggered back and I didn't blame the Jabberwock a bit.

It was a twelve-foot Fire Angel that had just entered—russet-colored, with wings like stained-glass windows—and, along with intimations of mortality, it brought me recollections of a praying mantis, with a spiked collar and thorn-like claws protruding through its short fur at every suggestion of an angle. One of these, in fact, caught on and unhinged a swinging door as it came inside. It was a Chaos beast—rare, deadly, and highly intelligent. I hadn't seen one in years, and I'd no desire to see one now; also, I'd no doubt that I was the reason it was here. For a moment I regretted having wasted my cardiac arrest spell on a mere Bandersnatch—until I recalled that Fire Angels have three hearts. I glanced quickly about as it spied me, gave voice to a brief hunting wail, and advanced.

"I'd like to have had some time to speak with you," I told the artist. "I like your work. Unfortunately—"

"I understand."

"So long."

"Good luck."

I stepped down into the rabbit hole and ran, bent far forward because of the low overhead. Luke made my passage particularly awkward, especially on the turns. I heard a scrabbling noise far to the rear, with a repetition of the hunting wail. I was consoled, however, by the knowledge that the Fire Angel would actually have to enlarge sections of the tunnel in order to get by. The bad news was that it was capable of doing it. The creatures are incredibly strong and virtually indestructible.

I kept running till the floor dipped beneath my feet. Then I began falling. I reached out with my free hand to catch myself, but there was nothing to catch hold of. The bottom had fallen out. Good. That was the way I'd hoped and half-expected it would be. Luke uttered a single soft moan but did not stir.

We fell. Down, down, down, like the man said. It was a well, and either it was very deep or we were falling very slowly. There was twilight all about us, and I could not discern the walls of the shaft. My head cleared a bit further, and I knew that it would continue to do so for as long as I kept control of one variable: Luke. High in the air overhead I heard the hunting wail once again. It was followed immediately by a strange burbling sound. Frakir began pulsing softly upon my wrist again, not really telling me anything I didn't already know. So I silenced her again.

Clearer yet. I began to remember. . . . My assault on the Keep of the Four Worlds and my recovery of Luke's mother, Jasra. The attack of the werebeast. My odd visit with Vinta Bayle, who wasn't really what she seemed. . . . My dinner in Death Alley. . . . The Dweller, San Francisco, the crystal cave. . . . Clearer and clearer.

. . . And louder and louder the hunting wail of the Fire Angel above me. It must have made it through the tunnel and be descending now. Unfortunately, it possessed wings, while all I could do was fall.

I glanced upward. Couldn't make out its form, though. Things seemed darker up that way than down below. I hoped this was a sign that we were approaching something in the nature of a light at the end of the tunnel, as I couldn't think of any other way out. It was too dark to view a Trump or to distinguish enough of the passing scene to commence a shadow shift.

I felt we were drifting now, rather than falling, at a rate that might permit us to land intact. Should it seem otherwise when we neared the bottom, then a possible means of further slowing our descent came to mind—an adaptation of one of the spells I still carried with me. However, these considerations were not worth much should we be eaten on the way down—a distinct possibility, unless of course our pursuer were not all that hungry, in which case it might only dismember us. Consequently, it might become necessary to try speeding up to stay ahead of the beast—which of course would cause us to smash when we hit.

Decisions, decisions.

Luke stirred slightly upon my shoulder. I hoped he wasn't about to come around, as I didn't have time to mess with a sleep-spell and I wasn't really in a good position to slug him again. That pretty much left Frakir. But if he were borderline, then choking might serve to rouse him rather than send him back—and I did want him in decent shape. He knew too many things I didn't, things I now needed.

We passed through a slightly brighter area, and I was able to distinguish the walls of the shaft for the first time and to note that they were covered with graffiti in a language that I did not understand. I was reminded of a strange short story by Jamaica Kincaid, but it bore me no clues for deliverance. Immediately following our passage through that band of illumination, I distinguished a small spot of light far below. At almost the same moment I heard the wail once again, this time very near.

I looked up in time to behold the Fire Angel passing through the glow. But there was another shape close behind it, and it wore a vest and burbled. The Jabberwock was also on the way down, and it seemed to be making the best time of any of us. The question of its purpose was immediately prominent; as it gained, the circle of light grew and Luke stirred again. This question was quickly answered, however, as it caught up with the Fire Angel and attacked.

The whiffling, the wailing, and the burbling suddenly echoed down the shaft, along with hissing, scraping, and occasional snarls. The two beasts came together and tore at each other, eyes like dying suns, claws like bayonets, forming a hellish mandala in the pale light which now reached them from below. While this produced a round of activity too near at hand for me to feel entirely at ease, it did serve to slow them to the point where I felt I need not risk an ill-suited spell and an awkward maneuver to emerge from the tunnel in one piece.

"Argh!" Luke remarked, turning suddenly within my grasp.

"I agree," I said. "But lie still, will you? We're about to crash—"

"—and burn," he stated, twisting his head upward to regard the combatant monsters, then downward when he realized that we were falling, too. "What kind of trip is this?"

"A bad one," I answered, and then it hit me: That was exactly what it was.

The opening was even larger now, and our velocity sufficient for a bearable landing. Our reaction to the spell that I called the Giant's Slap would probably slow us to a standstill or even propel us backward. Better to collect a few bruises than become a traffic obstruction at this point.

A bad trip indeed. I was thinking of Random's words as we passed through the opening at a crazy angle, hit dirt, and rolled.

We had come to rest within a cave, near to its mouth. Tunnels ran off to the right and the left. The cave mouth was at my back. A quick glance showed it as opening upon a bright, possibly lush, and more than a little out-of-focus valley. Luke was sprawled unmoving beside me. I got to my feet immediately and caught hold of him beneath the armpits. I began dragging him back away from the dark opening from which we had just emerged. The sounds of the monstrous conflict were very near now.

Good that Luke seemed unconscious again. His condition was bad enough for any Amberite, if my guess were correct. But for one of sorcerous ability it represented a highly dangerous wild card of a sort I'd never encountered before. I wasn't at all certain how I should deal with it.

I dragged him toward the right-hand tunnel because it was the smaller of the two and would theoretically be a bit easier to defend. We had barely achieved its shelter when the two beasts fell through the opening, clutching and tearing at each other. They commenced rolling about the floor of the cave, claws clicking, uttering hisses and whistles as they tore at each other. They seemed to have forgotten us entirely, and I continued our retreat until we were well back in the tunnel.

I could only assume Random's guess to be correct. After all, he was a musician and he'd played all over Shadow. Also, I couldn't come up with anything better.

I summoned the Sign of the Logrus. When I had it clear and had meshed my hands with it, I might have used it to strike at the fighting beasts. But they were paying me no heed whatsoever, and I'd no desire to attract their attention. Also, I'd no assurance that the equivalent of being hit by a two-by-four would have much effect on them. Besides, my order was ready, and filling it took precedence.

So I reached.

It took an interminable time. There was an extremely wide area of Shadow to pass through before I found what I was looking for. Then I had to do it again. And again. There were a number of things I wanted, and none of them near.

In the meantime, the combatants showed no sign of slackening, and their claws struck sparks from the cave's walls. They had cut each other in countless places and were now covered with dark gore. Luke had awakened during all of this, propped himself, and was staring fascinated at the colorful conflict. How long it might hold his attention I could not tell. It would be important for me to have him awake very soon now, and I was pleased that he had not started thinking of other matters yet.

I was cheering, by the way, for the Jabberwock. It was just a nasty beast and need not have been homing in on me in particular when it was distracted by the arrival of its exotic nemesis. The Fire Angel had been playing an entirely different game. There was no reason for a Fire Angel to be stalking about this far from Chaos unless it had been sent. They're devilish hard to capture, harder to train, and dangerous to handle. So they represent a considerable expense and hazard. One does not invest in a Fire Angel lightly. Their main purpose in life is killing, and to my knowledge no one outside the Courts of Chaos has ever employed one. They've a vast array of senses— some of them, apparently, paranormal—and they can be used as Shadow bloodhounds. They don't wander through Shadow on their own, that I know of. But a Shadow-walker can be tracked, and Fire Angels seem to be able to follow a very cold trail once they've been imprinted with the victim's identity. Now, I had been trumped to that crazy bar, and I didn't know they could follow a Trump jump, but several other possibilities occurred to me—including someone's locating me, transporting the thing to my vicinity, and turning it loose to do its business. Whatever the means, though, the attempt had the mark of the Courts upon it. Hence, my quick conversion to Jabberwock fandom.

"What's going on?" Luke asked me suddenly, and the walls of the cave faded for a moment and I heard a faint strain of music.

"It's tricky," I said. "Listen, it's time for your medicine."

I dumped out a palmful of the vitamin B12 tabs I had just brought in and uncapped the water bottle I had also summoned.

"What medicine?" he asked as I passed them to him.

"Doctor's orders," I said. "Get you back on your feet faster."

"Well, okay."

He threw all of them into his mouth and downed them with a single big drink.

"Now these."

I opened the bottle of Thorazine. They were 200 milligrams each and I didn't know how many to give him, so I decided on three. I gave him some tryptophan, too, and some phenylalanine.

He stared at the pills. The walls faded again, the music returned. A cloud of blue smoke drifted past us. Suddenly the bar came into view, back to whatever passed for normal in that place. The upset tables had been righted, Humpty still teetered, the mural went on.

"Hey, the club!" Luke exclaimed. "We ought to head back. Looks like the party's just getting going."

"First, you take your medicine."

"What's it for?"

"You got some bad shit somewhere. This is to let you down easy."

"I don't feel bad. In fact, I feel real good—"

"Take it!"

"Okay! Okay!"

He tossed off the whole fistful.

The Jabberwock and the Fire Angel seemed to be fading now—and my latest exasperated gesture in the vicinity of the bartop had encountered some resistance, though the thing was not fully solid to me yet. Suddenly, then, I noticed the Cat, whose games with substantiality somehow at this point made it seem more real than anything else in the place.

"You coming or going?" it asked.

Luke began to rise. The light grew brighter, though more diffuse.

"Uh, Luke, look over there," I said, pointing.

"Where?" he asked, turning his head.

I slugged him again.

As he collapsed, the bar began to fade. The walls of the cave phased back into focus. I heard the Cat's voice. "Going . . ." it said.

The noises returned full blast, only this time the dominant sound was a bagpipelike squeal. It was coming from the Jabberwock, who was pinned to the ground and being slashed at. I decided then to use the Fourth of July spell I had left over from my assault on the citadel. I raised my hands and spoke the words. I moved in front of Luke to block his view as I did so, and I looked away and squeezed my eyes shut as I said them. Even through closed eyes I could tell there followed a brilliant flash of light. I heard Luke say, "Hey!" but all other sounds ceased abruptly. When I looked again I saw that the two creatures lay as if stunned, unmoving, toward the far side of the small cave.

I grabbed hold of Luke's hand and drew him up and over my shoulders in a fireman's carry. Then I advanced quickly into the cave, slipping only once on monster blood as I edged my way along the nearest wall, heading for the cave mouth. The creatures began to stir before I made it out, but their movements were more reflexive than directed. I paused at the opening where I beheld an enormous flower garden in full bloom. All of the flowers were at least as tall as myself, and a shifting breeze bore me an overpowering redolence.

Moments later I heard a more decisive movement at my back and I turned. The Jabberwock was drawing itself to its feet. The Fire Angel was still crouched and was making small piping noises. The Jabberwock staggered back, spreading its wings, then suddenly turned, beat the air, and fled back up the high hole in the cleft at the rear of the cave. Not a bad idea, I decided, as I hurried out into the garden.

Here the aromas were even stronger, the flowers, mostly in bloom, a fantastic canopy of colors as I rushed among them. I found myself panting after a short while, but I jogged on nevertheless. Luke was heavy, but I wanted to put as much distance as I could between ourselves and the cave. Considering how fast our pursuer could move, I wasn't sure there was sufficient time to fool with a Trump yet.

As I hurried along I began feeling somewhat woozy, and my extremities seemed extremely distant. It occurred to me immediately that the flower smells might be a bit narcotic. Great. That was all I needed, to get caught up in a drug high while trying to bring Luke back from one. I could make out a small, slightly elevated clearing in the distance, though, and I headed for it. Hopefully, we could rest there for a bit while I regained my mental footing and decided what to do next. So far, I could detect no sounds of pursuit.

Rushing on, I could feel myself beginning to reel. My equilibrium was becoming impaired. I suddenly felt a fear of falling, almost akin to acrophobia. For it occurred to me that if I fell I might not be able to rise again, that I might succumb to a drugged sleep and be discovered and dispatched by the creature of Chaos while I dozed. Overhead, the colors of the flowers ran together, flowing and tangling like a mass of ribbons in a bright stream. I tried to control my breathing, to take in as little of the effluvia as possible. But this was difficult, as winded as I was becoming.

But I did not fall, though I collapsed beside Luke at the center of the clearing after I'd lowered him to the ground. He remained unconscious, a peaceful expression on his face. A wind swept our hillock from the direction of its far side, where nasty-looking, spiked plants of a nonflowering variety grew. Thus, I no longer smelled the seductive odors of the giant flower field, and after a time my head began to clear. On the other hand, I realized that this meant that our own scents were being borne back in the direction of the cave. Whether the Fire Angel could unmask them within the heady perfumes, I did not know, but providing it with even that much of an opportunity made me feel uncomfortable.

Years ago, as an undergraduate, I had tried some LSD. It had scared me so badly that I'd never tried another hallucinogen since. It wasn't simply a bad trip. The stuff had affected my shadow-shifting ability. It is kind of a truism that Amberites can visit any place they can imagine, for everything is out there, somewhere, in Shadow. By combining our minds with motion we can tune for the shadow we desire. Unfortunately, I could not control what I was imagining. Also unfortunately, I was transported to those places. I panicked, and that only made it worse. I could easily have been destroyed, for I wandered through the objectified jungles of my subconscious and passed some time in places where the bad things dwell. After I came down I found my way back home, turned up whimpering on Julia's doorstep, and was a nervous wreck for days. Later, when I told Random about it, I learned that he had had some similar experiences. He had kept it to himself at first as a possible secret weapon against the rest of the family; but later, after they'd gotten back onto decent terms with each other, he had decided to share the information in the interest of survival. He was surprised to learn then that Benedict, Gérard, Fiona, and Bleys knew all about it—though their knowledge had come from other hallucinogens and, strangely, only Fiona had ever considered its possibility as an in-family weapon. She'd shelved the notion, though, because of its unpredictability. This had been sometime back, however, and in the press of other business in recent years it had slipped his mind; it simply had not occurred to him that a new arrival such as myself should perhaps be cautioned.

Luke had told me that his attempted invasion of the Keep of the Four Worlds, by means of a glider-borne commando team, had been smashed. Since I had seen the broken gliders at various points within the walls during my own visit to that place, it was logical to assume that Luke had been captured. Therefore, it seemed a fairly strong assumption that the sorcerer Mask had done whatever had been done to him to bring him to this state. It would seem that this simply involved introducing a dose of a hallucinogen to his prison fare and turning him loose to wander and look at the pretty lights. Fortunately, unlike myself, his mental travelings had involved nothing more threatening than the brighter aspects of Lewis Carroll. Maybe his heart was purer than mine. But the deal was weird any way you looked at it. Mask might have killed him or kept him in prison or added him to the coatrack collection. Instead, while what had been done was not without risk, it was something which would wear off eventually and leave him chastened but at liberty. It was more a slap on the wrist than a real piece of vengeance. This, for a member of the House which had previously held sway in the Keep and would doubtless like to do so again. Was Mask supremely confident? Or did he not really see Luke as much of a threat?

And then there is the fact that our shadow-shifting abilities and our sorcerous abilities come from similar roots—the Pattern or the Logrus. It had to be that messing with one also messed with the other. That would explain Luke's strange ability to summon me to him as by a massive Trump sending, when in actuality there was no Trump: His drug-enhanced abilities of visualization must have been so intense that the card's physical representation of me was unnecessary. And his skewed magical abilities would account for all of the preliminary byplay, all of the odd, reality-distorting experiences I'd had before he actually achieved contact. This meant that either of us could become very dangerous in certain drugged states. I'd have to remember that. I hoped he wouldn't wake up mad at me for hitting him, before I could talk to him a bit. On the other hand, the tranquilizer would hopefully keep him happy while the other stuff worked at detoxing him.

I massaged a sore muscle in my left leg and rose to my feet. I caught hold of Luke beneath the armpits and dragged him about twenty paces farther along into the clearing. Then I sighed and returned to the spot where I had rested. There was not sufficient time to flee farther. And as the wailing increased in volume and the giant flowers swayed in a line heading directly toward me—glimpses of a darker form becoming visible amid the stalks—I knew that with the Jabberwock fled the Fire Angel was back on the job, and since this confrontation seemed inevitable, this clearing was as good a place to meet it as any, and better than most.

TWO

I unfastened the bright thing at my belt and began to unfold it. It made a series of clicking noises as I did so. I was hoping that I was making the best choice available to me rather than, say, a bad mistake.

The creature took longer than I'd thought to pass among the flowers. This could mean it was having trouble following my trail amid its exotic surroundings. I was hoping, though, that it meant it had been sufficiently injured in its encounter with the Jabberwock that it had lost something of its strength and speed.

Whatever, the final stalks eventually swayed and were crushed. The angular creature lurched forward and halted to stare at me with unblinking eyes. Frakir panicked, and I calmed her. This was a little out of her league. I had a Fire Fountain spell left, but I didn't even bother with it. I knew it wouldn't stop the thing, and it might make it behave unpredictably.

"I can show you the way back to Chaos," I shouted, "if you're getting homesick!"

It wailed softly and advanced. So much for sentimentality.

It came on slowly, oozing fluids from a dozen wounds. I wondered if it were still capable of rushing me or if its present pace were the best it could manage. Prudence dictated I assume the worst, so I tried to stay loose and ready to match anything it attempted.

It didn't rush, though. It just kept coming, like a small tank with appendages. I didn't know where its vital spots were located. Fire Angel anatomy had not been high on my list of interests back home. I gave myself a crash course, however, in the way of gross observation as it approached. Unfortunately, this gave me to believe that it kept everything important well protected. Too bad.

I did not want to attack in case it was trying to sucker me into something. I was not aware of its combat tricks, and I did not care to expose myself unduly in order to learn them. Better to stay on the defense and let it make the first move, I told myself. But it just kept moving nearer and nearer. I knew that I'd be forced to do something soon, even if it were only to retreat. . . .

One of those long, folded front appendages flashed out toward me, and I spun to the side and cut. Snicker-snack! The limb lay on the ground, still moving. So I kept moving, also. One-two, one-two! Snicker-snack!

The beast toppled slowly to its left, for I had removed all of the limbs on that side of its body.

852

Then, overconfident, I passed too near in racing to round its head to reach the other side and repeat the performance while it was still traumatized and collapsing. Its other extensor flashed out. But I was too near and it was still toppling. Instead of catching me with its clawed extremity, it hit me with the equivalent of shin or forearm. The blow struck me across the chest and I was knocked backward.

As I scrambled away and drew my feet beneath me to rise, I heard Luke say, groggily, "Now what's going on?"

"Later," I called, without looking back.

Then, "Hey! You hit me!" he added.

"All in good fun," I answered. "Part of the cure," and I was up and moving again.

"Oh," I heard him say.

The thing was on its side now and that big limb struck wildly at me, several times. I avoided it and was able to gauge its range and striking angle.

Snicker-snack. The limb fell to the ground and I moved in.

I swung three blows which passed all the way through its head from different angles before I was able to sever it. It kept making clicking noises, though, and the torso kept pitching and scrabbling about on the remaining limbs.

I don't know how many times I struck after that. I just kept at it until the creature was literally diced. Luke had begun shouting "Olé!" each time that I struck. I was perspiring somewhat by then, and I noticed that heat waves or something seemed to be causing my view of the distant flowers to ripple in a disturbing fashion. I felt foresighted as all hell, though—the Vorpal Sword I'd appropriated back in the bar had proved a fine weapon. I swung it through a high arc, which I'd noted seemed to cleanse it entirely, and then I began folding it back into its original compact form. It was as soft as flower petals, and it still gave off a faint dusty glow. . . .

"Bravo!" said a familiar voice, and I turned until I saw the smile followed by the Cat, who was tapping his paws lightly together. "Callooh! Callay!" he added. "Well done, beamish boy!"

The background wavering grew stronger, and the sky darkened. I heard Luke say "Hey!" and when I glanced back I saw him getting to his feet, moving forward. When I looked again I could see the bar forming at the Cat's back, and I caught a glimpse of the brass rail. My head began to swim.

"There's normally a deposit on the Vorpal Sword," the Cat was saying. "But since you're returning it intact—"

Luke was beside me. I could hear music again, and he was humming along with it. Now it was the clearing, with its butchered Fire Angel, that seemed the superimposition, as the bar increased in solidity, taking on nuances of color and shading.

But the place seemed somehow smaller—the tables closer together, the music softer, the mural more compressed and its artist out of sight. Even the Caterpillar and his mushroom had retreated to a shadowy nook, and both seemed shrunken, the blue smoke less dense. I took this as a vaguely good sign, for if our presence there were a result of Luke's state of mind then perhaps the fixation was losing its hold on him.

"Luke?" I said.

He moved up to the bar beside me.

"Yeah?" he answered.

"You know you're on a trip, don't you?"

"I don't. . . . I'm not sure what you mean," he said.

"When Mask had you prisoner I think he slipped you some acid," I said. "Is that possible?"

"Who's Mask?" he asked me.

"The new head honcho at the Keep."

"Oh, you mean Sharu Garrul," he said. "I do remember that he had on a blue mask."

I saw no reason to go into an explanation as to why Mask wasn't Sharu. He'd probably forget, anyway. I just nodded and said, "The boss."

"Well . . . yes, I guess he could have given me something," he replied. "You mean that all this . . . ?" He gestured toward the room at large.

I nodded.

"Sure, it's real," I said. "But we can transport ourselves into hallucinations. They're all real somewhere. Acid'll do it."

"I'll be damned," he said.

"I gave you some stuff to bring you down," I told him. "But it may take a while."

He licked his lips and glanced about.

"Well, there's no hurry," he said. Then he smiled as a distant screaming began and the demons started in doing nasty things to the burning woman off in the mural. "I kind of like it here."

I placed the folded weapon back upon the bartop. Luke rapped on the surface beside it and called for another round of brews. I backed away, shaking my head.

"I've got to go now," I told him. "Someone's still after me, and he just came close."

"Animals don't count," Luke said.

"The one I just chopped up does," I answered. "It was sent."

I looked at the broken doors, wondering what might come through them next. Fire Angels have been known to hunt in pairs.

"But I've got to talk to you . . ." I continued.

"Not now," he said, turning away.

"You know it's important."

"I can't think right," he answered.

I supposed that had to be true, and there was no sense trying to drag him back to Amber or anywhere else. He'd just fade away and show up here again. His head would have to clear and his fixation dissipate before we could discuss mutual problems.

"You remember that your mother is a prisoner in Amber?" I asked.

"Yes."

"Call me when you've got your head together. We have to talk."

"I will."

I turned away and walked out the doors and into a bank of fog. In the distance I heard Luke begin singing again, some mournful ballad. Fog is almost as bad as complete darkness when it comes to shadow-shifting. If you can't see any referents while you're moving, there is no way to use the ability that allows you to slip away. On the other hand, I just wanted to be alone for a time to think, now my head was clear. If I couldn't see anybody in this stuff, nobody could see me either. And there were no sounds other than my own footfalls on a cobbled surface.

So what had I achieved? When I was awakened from a brief nap to attend Luke's unusual sending to Amber, I'd been dead tired following extraordinary exertions. I was transported into his presence, learned that he was tripping, fed him something I hoped would bring him off it sooner, hacked up a Fire Angel, and left Luke back where he had started.

I'd gotten two things out of it, I mused, as I strolled through the cottony mist: I'd stalemated Luke in any designs he might still have upon Amber. He was now aware that his mother was our prisoner, and I couldn't see him bringing any direct action against us under the circumstances. Aside from the technical problems involved in transporting Luke and keeping him in one place, this was the reason I was willing to leave him as I just had. I'm sure Random would have preferred him unconscious in a cell in the basement, but I was certain he would settle for a defanged Luke at large; especially so, when it was likely that Luke would be getting in touch with us sooner or later regarding Jasra. I was willing to let him come down and come around in his own good time. I had problems of my own in the waiting room, like Ghostwheel, Mask, Vinta . . . and the new specter which had just taken a number and a seat.

Maybe it had been Jasra who had been using the homing power of the blue stones to send assassins after me. She had the ability as well as a motive. It could also have been Mask, though, who I'd judge had the ability—and who seemed to have a motive, though I didn't understand it. Jasra was out of the way now, however; and while I intended to have things out with Mask eventually, I believed that I had succeeded in detuning myself from the blue stones. I also believed that I might have scared Mask somewhat in our recent encounter at the Keep. Whatever, it was extremely unlikely that Mask or Jasra, whatever their powers, would have had access to a trained Fire Angel. No, there's only one place Fire Angels come from, and shadow-sorcerers aren't on the customer list.

A puff of wind parted the fog for a moment and I caught sight of dark buildings. Good. I shifted. The fog moved again almost immediately, and they were not buildings but dark rock formations. Another parting and a piece of dawn or evening sky came into view, a foam of bright stars spilled across it. Before too long a wind whipped the fog away and I saw that I walked in a high rocky place, the heavens a blaze of starry light bright enough to read by. I followed a dark trail leading off to the edge of the world. . . .

The whole business with Luke, Jasra, Dalt, and Mask was somehow of a piece—completely understandable in some places and clouded in others. Given some time and legwork it would all hang together. Luke and Jasra seemed to be nullified now. Mask, an enigma of sorts, seemed to have it in for me personally but did not appear to represent any particular threat to Amber. Dalt, on the other hand, did, with his fancy new weaponry—but Random was aware of this situation and Benedict was back in town. So I was confident that everything possible was being done to deal with this.

I stood at the edge of the world and looked down into a bottomless rift full of stars. My mountain did not seem to grace the surface of a planet. However, there was a bridge to my left, leading outward to a dark, star-occluding shape—another floating mountain, perhaps. I strolled over and stepped out onto the span. Problems involving atmosphere, gravitation, temperature, meant nothing here, where I could, in a sense, make up reality as I went along. I walked out onto the bridge, and for a moment the angle was right and I caught a glimpse of another bridge on the far side of the dark mass, leading off to some other darkness.

I halted in the middle, able to see along it for a great distance in either direction. It seemed a safe and appropriate spot. I withdrew my packet of Trumps and riffled through them until I located one I hadn't used in a long, long time.

I held it before me and put the others away, studying the blue eyes and the young, hard, slightly sharp features beneath a mass of pure white hair. He was dressed all in black, save for a bit of white collar and sleeve showing beneath the glossy tight-fitting jacket. He held three dark steel balls in his gloved hand.

Sometimes it's hard to reach all the way to Chaos, so I focused and extended, carefully, strongly. The contact came almost immediately. He was seated on a balcony beneath a crazily stippled sky, the Shifting Mountains sliding to his left. His feet were propped on a small floating table and he was reading a book. He lowered it and smiled faintly.

"Merlin," he said softly. "You look tired."

I nodded.

"You look rested," I said.

"True," he answered, as he closed the book and set it on the table. Then, "There is trouble?" he asked.

"There is trouble, Mandor."

He rose to his feet.

"You wish to come through?"

I shook my head. "If you have any Trumps handy for getting back, I'd rather you came to me."

He extended his hand.

"All right," he said.

I reached forward, our hands clasped; he took a single step and stood beside me on the bridge. We embraced for a moment and then he turned and looked out and down into the rift.

"There is some danger here?" he asked.

"No. I chose this place because it seems very safe."

"Scenic, too," he replied. "What's been happening to you?"

"For years I was merely a student, and then a designer of certain sorts of specialized machinery," I told him. "Things were pretty uneventful until fairly recently. Then all hell broke loose—but most of it I understand, and much of it seems under control. That part's complicated and not really worth your concern."

He rested a hand on the bridge's side-piece.

"And the other part?" he asked.

"My enemies up until this point had been from the environs of Amber. But suddenly, when it seemed that most of that business was on its way to being settled, someone put a Fire Angel on my trail. I succeeded in destroying it just a little while ago. I've no idea why, and it's certainly not an Amber trick."

He made a clicking noise with his lips as he turned away, paced a few steps, and turned back.

"You're right, of course," he said. "I'd no idea it had come anywhere near this, or I'd have spoken with you some time ago. But let me differ with you as to orders of importance before I indulge in certain speculations on your behalf. I want to hear your entire story."

"Why?"

"Because you are sometimes appallingly naive, little brother, and I do not yet trust your judgment as to what is truly important."

"I may starve to death before I finish," I answered.

Smiling crookedly, my step-brother Mandor raised his arms. While Jurt and Despil are my half-brothers, borne by my mother, Jasra, to Prince Sawall the Rim Lord, Mandor was Sawall's son by an earlier marriage. Mandor is considerably older than I, and as a result he reminds me much of my relatives back in Amber. I'd always felt a bit of an outsider among the children of Dara and Sawall. In that Mandor was—in a more stable sense—not part of that particular grouping either, we'd had something in common. But whatever the impulse behind his early attentions, we'd hit it off and become closer, I sometimes think, than full blood brothers. He had taught me a lot of practical things over the years, and we had had many good times together.

The air was distorted between us, and when Mandor lowered his arms a dinner table covered with embroidered white linen came into sudden view between us, soundlessly, followed a moment later by a pair of facing chairs. The table bore numerous covered dishes, fine china, crystal, silverware; there was even a gleaming ice bucket with a dark twisted bottle within it.

"I am impressed," I stated.

"I've devoted considerable time to gourmet magic in recent years," he said. "Pray, be seated."

We made ourselves comfortable there on the bridge between two darknesses. I muttered appreciatively as I tasted, and it was some minutes before

I could begin a summary of the events that had brought me to this place of starlight and silence.

Mandor listened to my entire tale without interruption, and when I'd finished he nodded and said, "Would you care for another serving of dessert?"

"Yes," I agreed. "It's quite nice."

When I glanced up a few moments later, I saw that he was smiling.

"What's funny?" I asked.

"You," he replied. "If you recall, I told you before you left for that place to be discriminating when it came to giving your trust."

"Well? I told no one my story. If you're going to lecture me on being friendly with Luke without learning his, I've already heard it."

"And what of Julia?"

"What do you mean? She never learned. . . ."

"Exactly. And she seems like one you could have trusted. Instead, you turned her against you."

"All right! Maybe I used bad judgment there, too."

"You designed a remarkable machine, and it never occurred to you it might also become a potent weapon. Random saw that right away. So did Luke. You might have been saved from disaster on that front only by the fact that it became sentient and didn't care to be dictated to."

"You're right. I was more concerned with solving technical problems. I didn't think through all the consequences."

He sighed.

"What am I going to do with you, Merlin? You take risks when you don't even know you're taking risks."

"I didn't trust Vinta," I volunteered.

"I think you could have gotten more information out of her," he said, "if you hadn't been so quick to save Luke, who already appeared to be out of danger. She seemed to be loosening up considerably at the end of your dialogue."

"Perhaps I should have called you."

"If you encounter her again, do it, and I'll deal with her."

I stared. He seemed to mean it.

"You know what she is?"

"I'll unriddle her," he said, swirling the bright orange beverage in his glass. "But I've a proposal for you, elegant in its simplicity. I've a new country place, quite secluded, with all the amenities. Why not return to the Courts with me rather than bouncing around from hazard to hazard? Lie low for a couple of years, enjoy the good life, catch up on your reading. I'll see that you're well protected. Let everything blow over, then go about your business in a more peaceful climate."

I took a small sip of the fiery drink.

"No," I said. "What happened to those things you indicated earlier that you knew and I didn't?"

"Hardly important, if you accept my offer."

"Even if I were to accept, I'd want to know."

"Bag of worms," he said.

"You listened to my story. I'll listen to yours."

He shrugged and leaned back in his chair, looked up at the stars.

"Swayvill is dying," he said.

"He's been doing that for years."

"True, but he's gotten much worse. Some think it has to do with the death curse of Eric of Amber. Whatever, I really believe he hasn't much longer."

"I begin to see. . . ."

"Yes, the struggle for the succession has become more intense. People have been falling over left and right—poison, duels, assassinations, peculiar accidents, dubious suicides. A great number have also departed for points unknown. Or so it would seem."

"I understand, but I don't see where it concerns me."

"One time it would not have."

"But?"

"You are not aware that Sawall adopted you, formally, after your departure?"

"What?"

"Yes. I was never certain as to his exact motives. But you are a legitimate heir. You follow me but take precedence over Jurt and Despil."

"That would still leave me way in hell down on the list."

"True," he said slowly. "Most of the interest lies at the top. . . ."

"You say 'most.' "

"There are always exceptions," he answered. "You must realize that a time such as this is also a fine occasion for the paying off of old debts. One death more or less hardly rouses an eyebrow the way it would have in more placid times. Even in relatively high places."

I shook my head as I met his eyes.

"It really doesn't make sense in my case," I said.

He continued to stare until I felt uncomfortable.

"Does it?" I finally asked.

"Well . . ." he said. "Give it some thought."

I did. And just as the notion came to me, Mandor nodded as if he viewed the contents of my mind.

"Jurt," he said, "met the changing times with a mixture of delight and fear. He was constantly talking of the latest deaths and of the elegance and apparent ease with which some of them were accomplished. Hushed tones interspersed with a few giggles. His fear and his desire to increase his own capacity for mischief finally reached a point where they became greater than his other fear—"

"The Logrus. . . ."

"Yes. He finally tried the Logrus, and he made it through."

"He should be feeling very good about that. Proud. It was something he'd wanted for years."

"Oh, yes," Mandor answered. "And I'm sure he felt a great number of other things as well."

"Freedom," I suggested. "Power," and as I studied his half-amused expression, I was forced to add, "and the ability to play the game himself."

"There may be hope for you," he said. "Now, would you care to carry that through to its logical conclusion?"

"Okay," I responded, thinking of Jurt's left ear as it floated away following my cut, a swarm of blood-beads spreading about it. "You think Jurt sent the Fire Angel."

"Most likely," he replied. "But would you care to pursue that a little further?"

I thought of the broken branch piercing Jurt's eyeball as we wrestled in the glade. . . .

"All right," I said. "He's after me. It could be a part of the succession game, because I'm slightly ahead of him on that front, or just plain dislike and revenge—or both."

"It doesn't really matter which," Mandor said, "in terms of results. But I was thinking of that crop-eared wolf that attacked you. Only had one eye, too, it seemed. . . ."

"Yes," I said. "What does Jurt look like these days?"

"Oh, he's grown about half the ear back. It's pretty ragged and ugly-looking. Generally, his hair covers it. The eyeball is regenerated, but he can't see out of it yet. He usually wears a patch."

"That might explain recent developments," I said. "Hell of a time for it, though, with everything else that's been going on. Muddies the waters considerably."

"It's one of the reasons I suggest you simply drop out and let everything cool down. Too busy. With as many arrows as there seem to be in the air, one may well find your heart."

"I can take care of myself, Mandor."

"You could have fooled me."

I shrugged, got up, walked over to the rail, and looked down at the stars.

After a long while he called out to me, "Have you got any better ideas?" but I didn't answer him because I was thinking about that very matter. I was considering what Mandor had said about my tunnel vision and lack of preparedness and had just about concluded that he was right, that in nearly everything that had happened to me up to this point—with the exception of my going after Jasra—I had mainly been responding to circumstance. I had been far more acted upon than acting. Admittedly, it had all happened very quickly. But still, I had not formed any real plans for covering myself, learning about my enemies or striking back. It seemed that there were some things I might be doing. . . .

"If there is that much to worry about," he said, "you are probably better off playing it safe."

He was probably right, from the standpoints of reason, safety, caution. But he was strictly of the Courts, while I possessed an additional set of loyalties in which he did not participate. It was possible—if only through my connection with Luke—that I might be able to come up with some personal course of action that would further the security of Amber. So long as such a chance existed, I felt obliged to pursue matters. And beyond this, from a purely personal standpoint, my curiosity was too strong to permit me to walk away from the unanswered questions which abounded when I could be actively seeking some answers.

As I was considering how I might best phrase these matters in my reply to Mandor, I was again acted upon. I became aware of a faint feeling of inquiry, as of a cat scratching at the doors of my mind. It grew in force, thrusting aside other considerations, until I knew it as a Trump sending from some very distant place. I guessed that it might be from Random, anxious to discover what had transpired since my absence from Amber. So I made myself receptive, inviting the contact.

"Merlin, what's the matter?" Mandor asked, and I raised my hand to indicate I was occupied. At that, I saw him place his napkin upon the tabletop and rise to his feet.

My vision cleared slowly and I beheld Fiona, looking stern, rocks at her back, a pale green sky above her.

"Merlin," she said. "Where are you?"

"Far away," I answered. "It's a long story. What's going on? Where are you?"

She smiled bleakly.

"Far away," she replied.

"We seem to have chosen very scenic spots," I observed. "Did you pick the sky to complement your hair?"

"Enough!" she said. "I did not call you to compare travel notes."

At that moment Mandor came up beside me and placed his hand upon my shoulder, which was hardly in keeping with his character, as it is considered a gauche thing to do when a Trump communication is obviously in progress—on the order of intentionally picking up an extension phone and breaking in on someone's call. Nevertheless. . . .

"My! My!" he said. "Will you please introduce me, Merlin?"

"Who," Fiona asked, "is that?"

"This is my brother Mandor," I told her, "of the House of Sawall in the Courts of Chaos. Mandor, this is my Aunt Fiona, Princess of Amber."

Mandor bowed.

"I have heard of you, Princess," he said. "It is indeed a pleasure."

Her eyes widened for a moment.

"I know of the house," she replied, "but I'd no idea of Merlin's relationship with it. I am pleased to know you."

"I take it there's some problem, Fi?" I asked.

"Yes," she answered, glancing at Mandor.

"I will retire," he said. "Honored to have met you, Princess. I wish you lived a bit nearer the Rim."

She smiled.

"Wait," she said. "This does not involve any state secrets. You are an initiate of the Logrus?"

"I am," he stated.

". . . And I take it you two did not get together to fight a duel?"

"Hardly," I answered.

"In that case, I would welcome his view of the problem, also. Are you willing to come to me, Mandor?"

He bowed again, which I thought was hamming it a bit.

"Anyplace, Madam," he responded.

She said, "Come then," and she extended her left hand and I clasped it. Mandor reached out and touched her wrist. We stepped forward.

We stood before her in the rocky place. It was breezy and a bit chilly there. From somewhere distant there came a muted roar, as of a muffled engine.

"Have you been in touch with anyone in Amber recently?" I asked her.

"No," she stated.

"Your departure was somewhat abrupt."

"There were reasons."

"Such as your recognizing Luke?"

"His identity is known to you now?"

"Yes."

"And to the others?"

"I told Random," I answered, "and Flora."

"Then everyone knows," she said. "I departed quickly and took Bleys with me because we had to be next on Luke's list. After all, I tried killing his father and almost succeeded. Bleys and I were Brand's closest relatives, and we'd turned against him."

She turned a penetrating gaze upon Mandor, who smiled.

"I understand," he stated, "that right now Luke drinks with a Cat, a Dodo, a Caterpillar, and a White Rabbit. I also understand that with his mother a prisoner in Amber he is powerless against you."

She regarded me again.

"You *have* been busy," she said.

"I try."

". . . So that it is probably safe for you to return," Mandor continued.

She smiled at him, then glanced at me.

"Your brother seems well informed," she observed.

"He's family, too," I said, "and we've a lifelong habit of looking out for each other."

"His life or yours?" she asked.

"Mine," I replied. "He *is* my senior."

"What are a few centuries this way or that?" Mandor offered.

"I thought I felt a certain maturity of spirit," she noted. "I've a mind to trust you further than I'd intended."

"That's very sporting of you," he replied, "and I treasure the sentiment. . . ."

". . . But you'd rather I didn't overdo it?"

"Precisely."

"I've no intention of testing your loyalties to home and throne," she said, "on such short acquaintance. It does concern both Amber and the Courts, but I see no conflict in the matter."

"I do not doubt your prudence. I merely wanted to make my position clear."

She turned back toward me.

"Merlin," she said then, "I think you lied to me."

I felt myself frowning as I tried to recall an occasion when I might have misled her about something. I shook my head.

"If I did," I told her, "I don't remember."

"It was some years ago," she said, "when I asked you to try walking your father's Pattern."

"Oh," I answered, feeling myself blush and wondering whether it was apparent in this strange light.

"You took advantage of what I had told you—about the Pattern's resistance," she continued. "You pretended it was preventing you from setting your foot upon it. But there was no visible sign of the resistance, such as there was when I tried stepping onto it."

She looked at me, as if for confirmation.

"So?" I said.

"So," she replied, "it has become more important now than it was then, and I have to know: Were you faking it that day?"

"Yes," I said.

"Why?"

"Once I took one step upon it," I explained, "I'd have been committed to walking it. Who knows where it might have led me and what situation might have followed? I was near the end of my holiday and in a hurry to get back to school. I didn't have time for what might have turned into a lengthy expedition. Telling you there were difficulties seemed the most graceful way of begging off."

"I think there's more to it than that," she said.

"What do you mean?"

"I think Corwin told you something about it that the rest of us do not know—or that he left you a message. I believe you know more than you let on concerning the thing."

I shrugged.

"Sorry, Fiona. I have no control over your suspicions," I said. "Wish I could be of more help."

"You can," she replied.

"Tell me how."

"Come with me to the place of the new Pattern. I want you to walk it."

I shook my head.

"I've got a lot more pressing business," I told her, "than satisfying your curiosity about something my dad did years ago."

"It's more than just curiosity," she said. "I told you once before that I think it's what is behind the increased incidence of shadow storms."

"And I gave you a perfectly good reason for something else being the cause. I believe it's an adjustment to the partial destruction and recreation of the old Pattern."

"Would you come this way?" she asked, and she turned from me and began to climb.

I glanced at Mandor, shrugged, and followed her. He came along.

We mounted toward a jagged screen of rock. She reached it first and made her way onto a lopsided ledge which ran partway along it. She traversed this until she came to a place where the rock wall had broken down into a wide V-shaped gap. She stood there with her back to us then, the light from the green sky doing strange things to her hair.

I came up beside her and followed the direction of her gaze. On a distant plain, far below us and to the left, a large black funnel spun like a top. It seemed the source of the roaring sound we had been hearing. The ground appeared to be cracked beneath it. I stared for several minutes, but it did not change in form or position. Finally, I cleared my throat.

"Looks like a big tornado," I said, "not going anyplace."

"That's why I want you to walk the new Pattern," she told me. "I think it's going to get us unless we get it first."

THREE

If you had a choice between the ability to detect falsehood and the ability to discover truth, which one would you take? There was a time when I thought they were different ways of saying the same thing, but I no longer believe that. Most of my relatives, for example, are almost as good at seeing through subterfuge as they are at perpetrating it. I'm not at all sure, though, that they care much about truth. On the other hand, I'd always felt there was something noble, special, and honorable about seeking truth—a thing I'd attempted with Ghostwheel. Mandor had made me wonder, though. Had this made me a sucker for truth's opposite?

Of course, it's not as cut and dried as all that. I know that it is not a pure either/or situation with the middle excluded, but is rather a statement of attitude. Still, I was suddenly willing to concede that I might have gone to an extreme—to the point of foolhardiness—and that I had let certain of my critical faculties doze for far too long.

So I wondered about Fiona's request.

"What makes it such a threat?" I asked her.

"It is a shadow storm in the form of a tornado," she said.

"There have been such things before," I answered.

"True," she responded, "but they tend to move through Shadow. This one does have extension through an area of Shadow, but it is totally stationary. It first appeared several days ago, and it has not altered in any way since then."

"What's that come to in Amber-time?" I asked.

"Half a day, perhaps. Why?"

I shrugged. "I don't know. Just curious," I said. "I still don't see why it's a threat."

"I told you that such storms had proliferated since Corwin drew the extra Pattern. Now they're changing in character as well as frequency. That Pattern has to be understood soon."

A moment's quick reflection showed me that whoever gained control of Dad's Pattern could become master of some terrible forces. Or mistress.

So, "Supposing I walk it," I said. "Then what? As I understand it from Dad's story, I'd just wind up in the middle, the same as with the Pattern back home. What's to be learned from that?"

I studied her face for some display of emotion, but my relatives tend to have too much control for such simple self-betrayal.

"As I understand it," she said, "Brand was able to trump in when Corwin was at the middle."

"That's the way I understand it, too."

". . . So, when you reach the center, I can come in on a Trump."

"I suppose so. Then there will be two of us standing at the middle of the Pattern."

". . . And from there we will be in a position to go someplace we could not reach from any other point in existence."

"That being?" I asked.

"The primal Pattern which lies behind it."

"You're sure there is one?"

"There must be. It is in the nature of such a construct to be scribed at a more basic level of reality as well as the mundane."

"And our purpose in traveling to that place?"

"That is where its secrets dwell, where its deepest magics might be learned."

"I see," I told her. "Then what?"

"Why, there we might learn how to undo the trouble the thing is causing," she answered.

"That's all?"

Her eyes narrowed.

"We will learn whatever we can, of course. Power is power, and represents a threat until it is understood."

I nodded slowly.

"But right now there are a number of powers that are more pressing in the threat department," I said. "That Pattern is going to have to wait its turn."

"Even if it may represent the forces you need to deal with your other problems?" she asked.

"Even so," I said. "It might turn into a lengthy enterprise, and I don't believe I have the time for that."

"But you don't know that for certain."

"True. But once I set foot on it, there's no turning back."

I did not add that I'd no intention of taking her to the primal Pattern, then leaving her there on her own. After all, she had tried her hand at king-making once. And if Brand had made it to the throne of Amber in those days, she would have been standing right behind him, no matter what she had to say about it now. I think she was about to ask me to deliver her to the primal Pattern then but realized that I'd already considered it and rejected it. Not wanting to lose face by asking and being refused, she returned to her original argument.

"I suggest you make time now," she said, "if you do not wish to see worlds torn up about you."

"I didn't believe you the first time you told me that," I answered, "and I don't believe you now. I still think the increased shadow-storm activity is probably an adjustment to the damage and repair of the original Pattern. I also think that if we mess around with a new Pattern we don't know anything about, we stand a chance of making things worse, not better—"

"I don't want to mess around with it," she said. "I want to study—"

The Sign of the Logrus flashed between us suddenly. She must have seen it or felt it somehow, too, because she drew back at the same instant I did.

I turned my head with sure knowledge as to what I would see.

Mandor had mounted the battlementlike wall of stone. He stood as still as if he were a part of it, his arms upraised. I suppressed my first impulse, which was to shout to him to stop. He knew what he was doing. And I was certain that he would not pay me the slightest heed, anyway.

I advanced to the notch in which he had taken his position, and I looked past him at the swirling thing on the cracked plain far below. Through the image of the Logrus, I felt the dark, awful rush of power that Suhuy had revealed to me in his final lesson. Mandor was calling upon it now and pouring it into the shadow-storm. Did he not realize that the force of Chaos he was unleashing must spread until it had run a terrible course? Could he not see that if the storm were indeed a manifestation of Chaos then he was turning it into a truly monstrous thing?

It grew larger. Its roaring increased in volume. It became frightening to watch it.

From behind me, I heard Fiona gasp.

"I hope you know what you're doing," I called to him.

"We'll know in about a minute," he replied, lowering his arms.

The Sign of the Logrus winked out before me.

We watched the damned thing spin for some time, bigger and noisier.

Finally, "What have you proved?" I asked him.

"That you have no patience," he answered.

There was nothing particularly instructive to the phenomenon, but I continued to watch it anyway. Abruptly, the sound became a stutter. The dark apparition jerked about suddenly, shaking off bits of accumulated debris as it contracted. Soon it was restored to its former size, and it hit its earlier pitch and the sound grew steady once more.

"How did you do that?" I asked him.

"I didn't," he said. "It adjusted itself."

"It shouldn't have," Fiona stated.

"Exactly," he replied.

"You've lost me," I said.

"It should have gone roaring right on, stronger than ever, after he'd augmented it that way," Fiona said. "But whatever is controlling it had other plans. So it was readjusted."

". . . And it is a Chaos phenomenon," Mandor continued. "You could see that in the way it drew upon Chaos when I provided the means. But that pushed it past some limit, and there was a correction. Someone is playing with the primal forces themselves out there. Who or what or why, I cannot say. But I think it's strong testimony that the Pattern isn't involved. Not with Chaos games. So Merlin is probably correct. I think that this business has its origin elsewhere."

"All right," Fiona conceded. "All right. What does that leave us with?"

"A mystery," he said. "But hardly, I think, an imminent threat."

A faint firefly of an idea flitted through my mind. It could easily be dead wrong, though that was not the reason I decided against sharing it. It led into an area of thought I could not explore in an instant, and I don't like giving away pieces of things like that.

Fiona was glaring at me now, but I maintained a bland expression. Abruptly then, seeing that her cause was fruitless, she decided to change the subject:

"You said that you left Luke under somewhat unusual circumstances. Just where is he now?"

The last thing I wanted to do was to get her really mad at me. But I couldn't see turning her loose on Luke in his present condition. For all I knew, she might actually be up to killing him, just as a form of life insurance. And I did not want Luke dead. I'd a feeling he might be undergoing something of a change of attitude, and I wanted to give him every break I could. We still owed each other a few, even though it was hard keeping score; and there is something to be said for old times' sake. Considering what I'd judged his condition to be when I'd left him, it was going to be a while before he was in decent shape again. And then I had a number of things I wanted to talk to him about.

"Sorry," I said. "He's my province at the moment."

"I believe I have some interest in the matter," she replied levelly.

"Of course," I said, "but I feel that mine is greater and that we may get in each other's ways."

"I can judge these things for myself," she said.

"Okay," I told her. "He's on an acid trip. Any information you'd get out of him might be colorful, but it would also be highly disappointing."

"How did this happen?" she asked.

"A wizard named Mask apparently slipped him some chemicals when he had him prisoner."

"Where was this? I've never heard of Mask."

"A place called the Keep of the Four Worlds," I told her.

"It's been a long time since I heard the Keep mentioned," she said. "A sorcerer named Sharu Garrul used to hold it."

"He's a coatrack now," I stated.

"What?"

"Long story, but Mask has the place these days."

She stared at me, and I could tell she was just realizing that there was a lot she didn't know in the way of recent developments. I'd judge she was deciding which of several obvious questions to ask next when I decided to beat her to the punch while she was still off-balance.

"So how's Bleys?" I asked.

"He's much improved. I treated him myself and he's recovering quickly."

I was about to ask her where he was, which I knew she would refuse to answer, and hopefully we would both smile when she saw what I was driving at: no address for Bleys, no address for Luke; we keep our secrets and stay friends.

"Hello!" I heard Mandor say, and we both turned in the direction he was facing—back out through the notch.

The dark tornado-form had collapsed to half its former size, and even as we watched, it continued to diminish. It fell steadily in upon itself, shrinking and shrinking, and in about a half-minute it was gone, completely.

I could not suppress a smile, but Fiona did not even notice. She was looking at Mandor.

"Do you think it was because of what you did?" she asked him.

"I have no way of knowing," he replied, "but it may well be."

"But does it tell you anything?" she said.

"Perhaps whoever was responsible did not like having me tinker with his experiment."

"You really believe there's an intelligence behind it?"

"Yes."

"Someone from the Courts?"

"It seems more likely than someone from your end of the world."

"I suppose so . . . ," she agreed. "Have you any guesses as to the person's identity?"

He smiled.

"I understand," she said quickly. "Your business is your business. But a general threat is everybody's business. That's what I was really getting at."

"True," he acknowledged. "This is why I propose investigating it. I'm at loose ends at the moment. It might be amusing."

"It is awkward asking you to communicate your findings to me," she said, "when I do not know what interests might be involved."

"I appreciate your position," he replied, "but to the best of my knowledge the treaty provisions still hold and no one in the Courts is promoting any special designs against Amber. In fact. . . . If you like, we might pursue the matter together, at least part of the way."

"I've got the time," she said.

"I don't," I injected quickly. "I've some pressing business to attend to."

Mandor shifted his attention to me.

"About my offer . . . ," he said.

"I can't," I told him.

"Very well. Our conversation is not concluded, however. I'll be in touch later."

"Okay."

Fiona looked my way then, also.

"You will keep me posted on Luke's recovery, and his intentions," she stated.

"Of course."

"Good day, then."

Mandor gave me a small half-salute and I returned it. I began walking then, and as soon as I was out of sight I began shifting.

I found my way to a rocky slope, where I halted and withdrew my Trump for Amber. I raised it, focused my awareness, and transported myself as soon as I felt my way through. I was hoping the main hall would be empty, but at this point I didn't really care that much.

I came through near Jasra, who was holding an extra cloak over her outstretched left arm. I ducked out the doorway to my left into an empty corridor and made my way to the back stair. Several times I heard voices and I detoured to avoid the speakers. I was able to make it to my rooms without being discovered.

The only rest I had had in what seemed an age and a half had been a fifteen-minute nap before Luke's spaced-out sorcerous faculty had caused him to summon me to the Looking Glass Bar via a hallucinatory Trump. When? For all I knew, it could have been yesterday—which had been a very full day before that incident.

I barred the door and staggered to the bed, flinging myself down upon it without even removing my boots. Sure, there were all sorts of things I should be doing, but I was in no condition for any of them. I'd returned home because I still felt safest in Amber, despite the fact that Luke had reached me here once.

Someone with a high-powered subconscious might have had a brilliantly revelatory dream following as much crap as I'd been through recently, and then have awakened with a wonderful series of insights and answers detailing appropriate courses of action. I didn't. I woke once, in a small panic, not knowing where I was. But I opened my eyes and satisfied myself on that count, then went back to sleep. Later—much later, it seemed—I returned by degrees, like some piece of flotsam being pushed higher and higher onto a beach by wave following wave, until finally I was there. I saw no reason for going any further until I realized that my feet hurt. Then I sat up and pulled my boots off, which might have been one of the six greatest pleasures in my life. I removed my socks in a hurry then and threw them into the corner of the room. Why doesn't anyone else in my line of work seem to get sore feet? I filled the basin and soaked them for a time, then resolved to go barefoot for the next few hours.

Finally I rose, stripped, cleaned up, and put on a pair of Levi's and a purple flannel shirt of which I am fond. The hell with swords, daggers, and cloaks for a time. I opened the shutters and looked outside. It was dark. Because of clouds, I couldn't even guess from the stars whether it might be early evening, late night, or almost morning.

It was very quiet in the hall, and there were no sounds as I made my way down the back stair. The kitchen was deserted also, the big fires banked and smoldering low. I didn't want to stir things up beyond hanging a pot of water to warm for tea while I located some bread and fruit preserves. I turned up a jug of something like grapefruit juice, too, in one of the walk-in ice boxes.

As I sat warming my feet and working my way through the loaf, I began to feel uneasy. I was sipping my tea before I realized what it was. There seemed a great necessity that I be doing something, yet I had no idea what. Now I had something of a breather, and it felt strange. So I decided to start thinking again.

By the time I'd finished eating, I had a few small plans. The first thing I did was to make my way to the main hall, where I removed all of the hats and cloaks from Jasra and swept her off her feet. Later, as I was bearing her stiff form along the upstairs hallway in the direction of my room, a door opened partway and a bleary-eyed Droppa watched me go by.

"Hey, I'll take two!" he called after me.

"Reminds me of my first wife," he added then, and closed the door.

Once I had her installed in my quarters, I drew up a chair and seated myself before her. Garishly clad as part of a savage joke, her hard sort of beauty was not really diminished. She had placed me in extreme peril on one occasion, and I had no desire to free her at a time like this for a possible repeat performance. But the spell that held her claimed my attention for more than one reason, and I wanted to understand it fully.

Carefully then, I began exploring the construct which held her. It was not overcomplicated, but I could see that tracing all of its byways was going to take a while. All right. I wasn't about to stop now. I pushed on ahead into the spell, taking mental notes as I went.

I was busy for hours. After I had solved the spell, I decided to hang some more of my own, times being what they were. The castle came awake about me as I worked. I labored steadily as the day progressed, until everything was in place and I was satisfied with my work. I was also famished.

I moved Jasra off into a corner, pulled on my boots, departed my quarters, and headed for the stair. In that it seemed about lunchtime I checked out the several dining rooms in which the family generally ate. But all of them were deserted and none of them were set up for a meal yet to come. Nor did any of them show signs of a meal having recently been dispatched.

I suppose it was possible my time sense was still skewed and I was much too late or too early, but it did seem that it had been daylight long enough to bring me into the vicinity of the proper hour. Nobody, however, seemed to be eating, so something had to be wrong with this assumption. . . .

Then I heard it—the faint click of cutlery upon plate. I headed in the apparent direction of the sound. Obviously, the meal was taking place in a less frequented setting than usual. I turned right, then left. Yes, they had decided to set up in a drawing room. No matter.

I entered the room, where Llewella was seated with Random's wife, Vialle, on the red divan, dinner laid on a low table before them. Michael, who worked in the kitchen, stood nearby behind a cart loaded with dishes. I cleared my throat.

"Merlin," Vialle announced with a sensitivity that always gives me a small chill—she being completely blind. "How pleasant!"

"Hello," Llewella said. "Come and join us. We're anxious to hear what you've been doing."

I drew a chair up to the far side of the table and seated myself. Michael came over and laid a fresh setting before me. I thought about it quickly. Anything Vialle heard would doubtless get back to Random. So I gave them a somewhat edited version of recent events—leaving out all references to Mandor, Fiona, and anything having to do with the Courts. It made for a considerably shorter story and let me get to my food sooner.

"Everybody's been so busy lately," Llewella remarked when I'd finished talking. "It almost makes me feel guilty."

I studied the delicate green of her more-than-olive complexion, her full lips, her large catlike eyes.

"But not quite," she added.

"Where are they all, anyway?" I asked.

"Gérard," she said, "is down seeing to harbor fortifications, and Julian is in command of the army, which has now been equipped with some firearms and is set to defend the approaches to Kolvir."

"You mean Dalt has something in the field already? Coming this way?"

She shook her head. "No, it was a precautionary measure," she replied, "because of that message from Luke. Dalt's force had not actually been sighted."

"Does anyone even know where he is?" I asked.

"Not yet," she answered, "but we're expecting some intelligence on that soon." She shrugged. Then, "Perhaps Julian already has it," she added.

"Why is Julian in command?" I asked between nibbles. "I'd have thought Benedict would take charge of something like this."

Llewella looked away, glancing at Vialle, who seemed to feel the shifting of focus.

"Benedict and a small force of his men have escorted Random to Kashfa," Vialle said, softly.

"Kashfa?" I said. "Why would he want to do that? In fact, Dalt usually hangs out around Kashfa. The area could be dangerous right now."

She smiled faintly.

"That is why he wanted Benedict and his guard for escort," she said. "They may even be the intelligence-gathering expedition themselves, though that's not their reason for going right now."

"I don't understand," I said, "why the trip should be necessary at all."

She took a sip of water.

"A sudden political upheaval," she replied. "Some general had taken over in the absence of the queen and the crown prince. The general was just assassinated recently, and Random has succeeded in obtaining agreement for placing his own candidate—an older nobleman—on the throne."

"How'd he do that?"

"Everyone with an interest in the matter was even more interested in seeing Kashfa admitted to the Golden Circle of privileged trade status."

"So Random bought them off to see his own man in charge," I observed. "Don't these Golden Circle treaties usually give us the right to move troops through a client kingdom's territory with very little in the way of preliminaries?"

"Yes," she said.

I suddenly recalled that tough-looking emissary of the Crown I'd met at Bloody Bill's, who had paid his tab in Kashfan currency. I decided I did not really want to know how close in point of time that was to the assassination that had made this recent arrangement possible. What struck me with more immediate force was the picture that now emerged: It looked as if Random had just blocked Jasra and Luke from recovering their usurped throne—which, to be fair, I guess Jasra had usurped herself, years ago. With all that usurping going on, the equities of the thing were more than a little hazy to me. But if Random's ethics were no better than those which had gone before, they were certainly no worse. It looked now, though, as if any attempt on the part of Luke to regain his mother's throne would be met by a monarch who possessed a defense alliance with Amber. I suddenly felt willing to bet that the terms of the defense provisions of the alliance included Amber's assistance in internal troubles as well as help against outside aggressors.

Fascinating. It sounded as if Random were going to an awful lot of trouble to isolate Luke from his power base and any semblance of legitimacy as a head of state. I supposed the next step could be to get him outlawed as a pretender and a dangerous revolutionary, and to put a price on his head. Was Random overreacting? Luke didn't seem all that dangerous now, especially with his mother in our custody. On the other hand, I didn't really know how far Random intended to go. Was he just foreclosing all of the threatening options, or was he actually out to get Luke? The latter possibility bothered me in that Luke seemed on halfway good behavior at the moment and possibly in the throes of reconsidering his position. I did not want to see him needlessly thrown to the wolves as a result of overkill on Random's part.

So, "I suppose this has a lot to do with Luke," I said to Vialle.

She was silent for a moment, then replied, "It was Dalt that he seemed concerned about."

I shrugged mentally. It seemed that it would come down to the same thing in Random's mind, since he would see Dalt as the military force Luke would turn to to recover the throne. So I said, "Oh," and went on eating.

There were no new facts to be had beyond this, and nothing to clarify Random's thinking any further, so we lapsed into small talk while I considered my position once again. It still came down to a feeling that urgent action was necessary and uncertainty as to what form it should take. My course was determined in an unexpected fashion sometime during dessert.

A courtier named Randel—tall, thin, dark, and generally smiling—came into the room. I knew something was up because he was not smiling and he was moving faster than usual. He swept us with his gaze, fixed upon Vialle, advanced quickly and cleared his throat.

"M'lady Majesty . . . ?" he began.

Vialle turned her head slightly in his direction.

"Yes, Randel?" she said. "What is it?"

"The delegation from Begma has just arrived," he answered, "and I find myself without instructions as to the nature of their welcome and any special arrangements that would be suitable."

"Oh dear!" Vialle said, laying aside her fork. "They weren't due until the day after tomorrow, when Random will be back. He's the one they'll be wanting to complain to. What have you done with them?"

"I seated them in the Yellow Room," he replied, "and told them I would go and announce their arrival."

She nodded.

"How many of them are there?"

"The prime minister, Orkuz," he said, "his secretary, Nayda—who is also his daughter—and another daughter, Coral. There are also four servants—two men and two women."

"Go and inform the household staff, and be sure that appropriate quarters are made ready for them," she directed, "and alert the kitchen. They may not have had lunch."

"Very good, Your Highness," he said, beginning to back away.

". . . Then report to me in the Yellow Room, to let me know it's been done," she continued, "and I'll give you additional instructions at that time."

"Consider it done," he replied, and he hurried off.

"Merlin, Llewella," Vialle said, beginning to rise, "come help me entertain them while arrangements are being made."

I gulped my last bite of dessert and got to my feet. I did not really feel like talking to a diplomat and his party, but I was handy and it was one of life's little duties.

"Uh. . . . What are they here for, anyway?" I asked.

"Some sort of protest over what we've been doing in Kashfa," she replied. "They've never been friendly with Kashfa, but I'm not sure now whether they're here to protest Kashfa's possible admission to the Golden Circle or whether they're upset about our interfering in Kashfa's domestic affairs. It could be they're afraid they'll lose business with such a close neighbor suddenly enjoying the same preferred trade status they have. Or it may be they had different plans for Kashfa's throne and we just foreclosed them. Maybe both. Whatever. . . . We can't tell them anything we don't know."

"I just wanted to know what subjects to avoid," I said.

"All of the above," she answered.

"I was wondering the same thing myself," Llewella said. "I was also wondering, though, whether they might have any useful information on Dalt. Their intelligence service must keep a close eye on doings in and about Kashfa."

"Don't pursue that topic," Vialle said, moving toward the door. "If they let something slip or want to give something away, fine. Bring it home. But don't show them you'd like to know."

Vialle took my arm and I guided her out, heading toward the Yellow Room. Llewella produced a small mirror from somewhere and inspected her features. Obviously pleased, she put it away, then remarked, "Lucky you showed up, Merlin. An extra smiling face is always useful at times like this."

"Why don't I feel lucky?" I said.

We made our way to the room where the prime minister and his daughters waited. Their servants had already retired to the kitchen for refreshments. The official party was still hungry, which says something about protocol, especially since it seemed to take a long while before some trays of provender could be attractively assembled. Orkuz was of medium stature and stocky, his black hair tastefully streaked, the lines on his broad face seeming to indicate that he did a lot more frowning than smiling—a practice in which he indulged most of the while that afternoon. Nayda's was a more pleasingly sculpted version of his face, and though she showed the same tendency toward corpulence, it was held firmly in check at an attractive level of roundedness. Also, she smiled a lot and she had pretty teeth. Coral, on the other hand, was taller than either her father or sister, slender, her hair a reddish brown. When she smiled it seemed less official. Also, there was something vaguely familiar about her. I wondered whether I had met her at some boring reception years before. If I had, though, I felt I might have remembered.

After we had been introduced and wine had been poured, Orkuz made a brief comment to Vialle about "recent distressing news" concerning Kashfa. Llewella and I quickly moved to her side for moral support, but she simply said that such matters would have to be dealt with fully upon Random's return, and that for the moment she wished merely to see to their comfort. He was completely agreeable to this, even to the point of smiling. I had the impression he just wanted the purpose of his visit on the record immediately. Llewella quickly turned the conversation to the matter of his journey, and he graciously allowed the subject to be changed. Politicians are wonderfully programmed.

I learned later that the Begman ambassador wasn't even aware of his arrival, which would seem to indicate that Orkuz had come so quickly he had preceded any notification to their embassy. And he hadn't even bothered dropping in there, but had come straight to the palace and had a message sent over. I learned this a little later, when he asked to have the message delivered. Feeling somewhat supernumerary to Llewella's and Vialle's graceful cascades of neutral talk, I dropped back a pace to plan my escape. I was not at all interested in whatever game was being set up.

Coral backed off also and sighed. Then she glanced at me and smiled, surveyed the room quickly and came closer.

"I've always wanted to visit Amber," she said then.

"Is it the way you imagined it?" I asked.

"Oh, yes. So far. Of course, I haven't seen that much of it yet. . . ."

I nodded, and we withdrew a little farther from the others.

"Have I met you somewhere before?" I asked.

"I don't think so," she said. "I haven't traveled that much, and I don't believe you've been out our way. Have you?"

"No, though I've grown curious about it recently."

"I do know something of your background, though," she went on, "just from general gossip. I know you're from the Courts of Chaos, and I know you went to school on that Shadow world you Amberites seem to visit so frequently. I've often wondered what it was like."

I took the bait and I began telling her about school and my job, about a few places I'd visited and things I'd enjoyed doing. We made our way to a sofa across the room as I spoke, and we got more comfortable. Orkuz, Nayda, Llewella, and Vialle didn't seem to miss us, and if I had to be here I found talking with Coral more enjoyable than listening to them. Not to monopolize things, though, I asked her about herself.

She began telling me of a girlhood spent in and around Begma, of her fondness for the outdoors—of horses and of boating on the many lakes and rivers in that region—of books she had read, and of relatively innocent dabblings in magic. A member of the household staff came in just as she was getting around to a description of some interesting rites performed by members of the local farming community to insure the fertility of the crops, and she approached Vialle and told her something. Several more staff members were in view outside the doorway. Vialle then said something to Orkuz and Nayda, who nodded and moved toward the entrance. Llewella departed the group and came our way.

"Coral," she said, "your suite is ready. One of the staff will show you where it is. Perhaps you'd like to freshen up or rest after your journey."

We got to our feet.

"I'm not really tired," Coral said, looking at me rather than Llewella, a hint of a smile at the corners of her mouth.

What the hell. I suddenly realized I had been enjoying her company, so, "If you'd care to change into something simpler," I said, "I'll be glad to show you a bit of the town. Or the palace."

It became a full smile worth seeing.

"I'd much rather do that," she said.

"Then I'll meet you back here in about half an hour," I told her.

I saw her out, and accompanied her and the others as far as the foot of the big stairway. In that I still had on my Levi's and purple shirt, I wondered whether I should change into something more in keeping with local fashion. The hell with it, I decided then. We were just going to be knocking around. I'd simply add my swordbelt and weapons, a cloak, and my best boots. Might trim my beard, though, since I had a little time. And maybe a quick manicure. . . .

"Uh, Merlin. . . ."

It was Llewella, her hand on my elbow, steering me toward an alcove. I allowed myself to be steered.

Then, "Yes?" I said. "What's up?"

"Hm . . . ," she said. "Kind of cute, isn't she?"

"I suppose so," I replied.

"You got the hots for her?"

"Jeez, Llewella! I don't know. I just met the lady."

". . . And made a date with her."

"Come on! I deserve a break today. I enjoyed talking with her. I'd like to show her around a bit. I think we'd have a good time. What's wrong with that?"

"Nothing," she answered, "so long as you keep things in perspective."

"What perspective did you have in mind?"

"It strikes me as faintly curious," she said, "that Orkuz brought along his two good-looking daughters."

"Nayda *is* his secretary," I said, "and Coral's wanted to see the place for some time."

"Uh-huh, and it would be a very good thing for Begma if one of them just happened to latch onto a member of the family."

"Llewella, you're too damned suspicious," I said.

"It comes of having lived a long time."

"Well, I hope to live a long time myself, and I hope it doesn't make me look for an ulterior motive in every human act."

She smiled. "Of course. Forget I said anything," she told me, knowing I wouldn't. "Have a good time."

I growled politely and headed for my room.

FOUR

And so, in the midst of all manner of threats, intrigues, menaces, and mysteries, I decided to call a holiday and stroll about town with a pretty lady. Of all possible choices I might have made, it was certainly the most attractive. Whoever the enemy, whatever the power I faced, the ball was now in its court. I had no desire to hunt for Jurt, duel with Mask, or follow Luke about until he came down and told me whether or not he still wanted the family's scalps. Dalt was not my problem, Vinta was gone, Ghostwheel was silent, and the matter of my father's Pattern could await my leisure. The sun was shining and the breeze was gentle, though these could change quickly at this season.

It was a shame to waste what could well be the year's last good day on anything less than enjoyment. I hummed as I repaired myself, and I headed downstairs early for our meeting.

Coral had moved more quickly than I'd guessed, however, and was waiting for me. I approved of her sensible dark green breeches, heavy coppery shirt, and warm brown cloak. Her boots looked fine for walking, and she had on a dark hat that covered most of her hair. There were gloves and a dagger at her belt.

"All ready," she said when she saw me.

"Great," I replied, smiling, and I led her out into the hallway.

She started to turn in the direction of the main doorway, but I led her off to the right, then later to the left.

"Less conspicuous to use one of the side doors," I said.

"You people are certainly secretive," she said.

"Habit," I replied. "The less that outsiders know of your business the better."

"What outsiders? What are you afraid of?"

"Just now? A great number of things. But I don't really want to spend a nice day like this making lists."

She shook her head in what I took to be a mixture of awe and disgust.

"It's true what they say then?" she asked. "That your affairs are so complex you all carry scorecards?"

"Haven't had time for any affairs recently," I told her, "or even a simple score." Then, "Sorry," I added, when I saw her blush. "Life *has* been a bit complicated for me lately."

"Oh," she said, glancing at me, clearly asking for elaboration.

"Some other time," I said, forcing a laugh, flipping my cloak, and greeting a guard.

She nodded and, diplomatically, changed the subject:

"I guess I came at the wrong time of year to see your famous gardens."

"Yeah, they've pretty much had it for the season," I said, "except for Benedict's Japanese garden which is kind of far out back. Perhaps we can go and have a cup of tea there one day, but I thought we'd go into town now."

"Sounds fine," she agreed.

I told the postern guard to tell Henden, Amber's steward, that we were heading into town and weren't sure when we'd be back. He said that he would as soon as he got off duty, which would be pretty soon. My experience at Bloody Bill's had taught me the lesson of leaving such messages—not that I thought we were in any danger, or that Llewella's knowing wouldn't be sufficient.

Leaves crunched beneath our feet as we took one of the walks toward a side gate. With only a few strands of cirrus high overhead, the sun shone brightly. To the west, a flock of dark birds flapped its way toward the ocean, south.

"It's already snowed back home," she told me. "You're lucky."

"There's a warm current that gives us a break," I said, remembering something Gérard had once told me. "It moderates the climate considerably, compared to other places at equal latitude."

"You travel a lot?" she asked me.

"I've been traveling more than I care to," I said, "recently. I'd like to sit down and go to seed for about a year."

"Business or pleasure?" she asked me, as a guard let us out the gate and I quickly surveyed the environs for lurkers.

"Not pleasure," I answered as I took her elbow for a moment and steered her toward the way I had chosen.

When we reached civilized precincts, we followed the Main Concourse for a time. I pointed out a few landmarks and notable residences, including the Begman Embassy. She showed no inclination to visit the latter, though, saying she'd have to see her countrymen officially before she left, anyway. She did stop in a shop we found later, however, to buy a couple of blouses, having the bill sent to the embassy and the garments to the palace.

"My father promised me some shopping," she explained. "And I know he'll forget. When he hears about this, he'll know that I didn't."

We explored the streets of the various trades and stopped for a drink at a sidewalk cafe, watching pedestrians and horsemen pass. I had just turned toward her to relate an anecdote concerning one of the riders when I felt the beginning of a Trump contact. I waited for several seconds as the feeling grew stronger, but no identity took shape beyond the reaching. I felt Coral's hand upon my arm.

"What's the matter?" she asked.

I reached out with my mind, attempting to assist in the contact, but the other seemed to retreat as I did so. It was not the same as that lurking scrutiny when Mask had regarded me at Flora's place in San Francisco, though. Could it just be someone I knew trying to reach me and having trouble focusing? Injured, perhaps? Or—

"Luke?" I said. "Is that you?"

But there was no response and the feeling began to fade. Finally, it was gone.

"Are you all right?" Coral asked.

"Yeah, it's okay," I said. "I guess. Someone tried to reach me and then decided otherwise."

"Reach? Oh, you mean those Trumps you use?"

"Yes."

"But you said 'Luke' . . ." she mused. "None of your family is named—"

"You might know him as Rinaldo, Prince of Kashfa," I said.

She chuckled.

"Rinny? Sure I know him. He didn't like us to call him Rinny, though. . . ."

"You really *do* know him? Personally, I mean?"

"Yes," she replied, "though it's been a long time. Kashfa's pretty close to Begma. Sometimes we were on good terms, sometimes not so good. You know how it is. Politics. When I was little there were long spells when we were pretty friendly. There were lots of state visits, both ways. We kids would often get dumped together."

"What was he like in those days?"

"Oh, a big, gawky, red-haired boy. Liked to show off a lot—how strong he was, how fast he was. I remember how mad he got at me once because I beat him in a footrace."

"You beat Luke in a race?"

"Yes. I'm a very good runner."

"You must be."

"Anyway, he took Nayda and me sailing a few times, and on some long hikes. Where is he now, anyway?"

"Drinking with a Cheshire cat."

"What?"

"It's a long story."

"I'd like to hear it. I've been worried about him since the coup."

Mm. . . . I thought quickly about how to edit this so as not to tell the daughter of the Begman prime minister any state secrets, such as Luke's relationship to the House of Amber. . . . So, "I've known him for quite some time," I began. "He recently incurred the wrath of a sorcerer who drugged him and saw him banished to this peculiar bar. . . ."

I went on for a long while then, partly because I had to stop and summarize Lewis Carroll. I also had to promise her the loan of one of the Thari editions of *Alice* from the Amber library. When I finally finished, she was laughing.

"Why don't you bring him back?" she said then.

Ouch. I couldn't very well say that his shadow-shifting abilities would work against this until he came down. So, "It's part of the spell; it's working on his own sorcerous ability," I said. "He can't be moved till the drug wears off."

"How interesting," she observed. "Is Luke really a sorcerer himself?"

"Uh . . . yes," I said.

"How did he gain that ability? He showed no signs of it when I knew him."

"Sorcerers come by their skills in various ways," I explained. "But you know that," and I suddenly realized that she was smarter than that smiling, innocent expression indicated. I'd a strong feeling she was trying to steer this toward an acknowledgment of Pattern magic on Luke's part, which of course would say interesting things about his paternity. "And his mother, Jasra, is something of a sorceress herself."

"Really? I never knew that."

Damn! Coming and going. . . .

"Well, she'd learned it somewhere."

"What about his father?"

"I can't really say," I replied.

"Did you ever meet him?"

"Only in passing," I said.

A lie could make the matter seem really important if she had even a small idea as to the truth. So I did the only other thing I could think of. There was no one seated at the table behind her, and there was nothing beyond the table but a wall. I wasted one of my spells, with an out-of-sight gesture and a single mutter.

The table flipped over as it flew back and crashed against the wall. The noise was spectacular. There were loud exclamations from several other patrons, and I leaped to my feet.

"Is everyone all right?" I said, looking about as if for casualties.

"What happened?" she asked me.

"Freak gust of wind or something," I said. "Maybe we'd better be moving on."

"All right," she said, regarding the debris. "I'm not looking for trouble."

I tossed some coins onto our table, rose, and headed back outside, talking the while of anything I could think of to put some distance between us and the subject. This had the desired effect, because she did not attempt to retrieve the question.

Continuing our stroll, I headed us in the general direction of West Vine. When we reached it I decided to head downhill to the harbor, recalling her fondness for sailing. But she put her hand on my arm and halted me.

"Isn't there a big stairway up the face of Kolvir?" she asked. "I believe your father once tried to sneak troops up it and got caught and had to fight his way along."

I nodded. "Yes, that's true," I said. "Old thing. It goes way back. It's not used very much these days. But it's still in decent shape."

"I'd like to see it."

"All right."

I turned to the right and we headed back, uphill, toward the Main Concourse. A pair of knights wearing Llewella's livery passed us, headed in the other direction, saluting as they went by. I could not help but wonder whether they were on a legitimate errand or were following some standing order to keep an eye on my movements. The thought must have passed through Coral's mind, also, because she quirked an eyebrow at me. I shrugged and kept going. When I glanced back a bit later, they were nowhere to be seen.

We passed people in the garb of a dozen regions as we strolled, and the air was filled with the smells of cooking from open stalls, to satisfy a multitude of tastes. At various points in our career up the hill, we stopped for meat pies, yogurts, sweets. The stimuli were too overpowering for any but the most sated to ignore.

I noticed the lithe way she moved about obstacles. It wasn't just gracefulness. It was more a state of being—preparedness, I guess. Several times I noticed her glancing back in the direction from which we had come. I looked myself, but there was nothing unusual to see. Once, when a man stepped suddenly from a doorway we were approaching, I saw her hand flash toward the dagger at her belt, then drop away.

"There is so much activity, so much going on here . . . ," she commented after a time.

"True. Begma is less busy, I take it?"

"Considerably."

"Is it a pretty safe place to stroll about?"

"Oh, yes."

"Do the women as well as the men take military training there?"

"Not ordinarily. Why?"

"Just curious."

"I've had some training in armed and unarmed combat, though," she said.

"Why was that?" I asked.

"My father suggested it. Said it could come in handy for a relative of someone in his position. I thought he might be right. I think he really wanted a son."

"Did your sister do it, too?"

"No, she wasn't interested."

"You planning on a diplomatic career?"

"No. You're talking to the wrong sister."

"A wealthy husband?"

"Probably stodgy and boring."

"What, then?"

"Maybe I'll tell you later."

"All right. I'll ask if you don't."

We made our way southward along the Concourse, and the breezes picked up as we neared Land's End. It was a winter ocean that came into view across the distance, slate-gray and white-capped. Many birds wheeled far out over the waves, and one very sinuous dragon.

We passed through the Great Arch and came at last to the landing and looked downward. It was a vertiginous prospect, out across a brief, broad stair—the steep drop to the tan-and-black beach far below. I regarded the ripples in the sand left by the retreating tide, wrinkles in an old man's brow. The breezes were stronger here, and the damp, salty smell, which had been increasing as we approached, seasoned the air to a new level of intensity. Coral drew back for a moment, then advanced again.

"It looks a little more dangerous than I'd thought," she said, after a time. "Probably seems less so once you're on it."

"I don't know," I replied.

"You've never climbed it?"

"Nope," I said. "Never had any reason to."

"I'd think you'd have wanted to, after your father's doomed battle along it."

I shrugged. "I get sentimental in different ways."

She smiled. "Let's climb down to the beach. Please."

"Sure," I said, and we moved forward and started.

The broad stair took us down for perhaps thirty feet, then terminated abruptly where a much narrower version turned off to the side. At least the steps weren't damp and slippery. Somewhere far below, I could see where the stair widened again, permitting a pair of people to go abreast. For now, though, we moved single file, and I was irritated that Coral had somehow gotten ahead of me.

"If you'll scrunch over, I'll go past," I told her.

"Why?" she asked.

"So I can be ahead of you in case you slip."

"That's all right," she replied. "I won't."

I decided it wasn't worth arguing and let her lead.

The landings where the stairway switched back were haphazard affairs, hacked wherever the contours of the rock permitted such a turning. Consequently, some descending stretches were longer than others and our route wandered all over the face of the mountain. The winds were much stronger now than they were above, and we found ourselves staying as close to the mountain's side as its contours permitted. Had there been no wind, we probably would have done the same. The absence of any sort of guard railing made us shy back from the edge. There were places where the mountain's wall overhung us for a cavelike effect; other places, we followed a bellying of the rock and felt very exposed. My cloak blew up across my face several times and I cursed, recalling that natives seldom visit historical spots in their own neighborhoods. I began to appreciate their wisdom. Coral was hurrying on ahead, and I increased my pace to catch up with her. Beyond her, I could see that there was a landing which signaled the first turning of the way. I was hoping she'd halt there and tell me she'd reconsidered the necessity for this expedition. But she didn't. She turned and kept right on going. The wind stole my sigh and bore it to some storybook cave reserved for the plaints of the imposed-upon.

Still, I couldn't help but look down upon occasion; and whenever I did I thought of my father fighting his way up along these steps. It was not something I'd care to try—at least, not until I'd exhausted all of the more sneaky alternatives. I began to wonder how far we were below the level of the palace itself. . . .

When we finally came to the landing from which the stairway widened, I hurried to catch up with Coral so that we could walk abreast. In my haste, I snagged my heel and stumbled as I rounded the turn. It was no big deal. I was able to reach out and stabilize myself against the cliff's face as I jolted forward and swayed. I was amazed, though, at Coral's perception of my altered gait just on the basis of its sound, and by her reaction to it. She cast herself backward suddenly and twisted her body to the side. Her hands came in contact with my arm as she did this, and she thrust me to the side, against the rock.

"All right!" I said, from rapidly emptying lungs. "I'm okay."

She rose and dusted herself off as I recovered.

"I heard—" she began.

"I gather. But I just caught my heel. That's all."

"I couldn't tell."

"Everything's fine. Thanks."

We started down the stair side by side, but something was changed. I now harbored a suspicion I did not like but could not dispel. Not yet, anyway. What I had in mind was too dangerous, if I should prove correct.

So instead, "The rain in Spain stays mainly in the plain," I said.

"What?" she asked. "I didn't understand. . . ."

"I said, 'It's a fine day to be walking with a pretty lady.' "

She actually blushed.

Then, "What language did you say it in . . . the first time?"

"English," I replied.

"I've never studied it. I told you that when we were talking about *Alice*."

"I know. Just being whimsical," I answered.

The beach, nearer now, was tiger-striped and shiny in places. A froth of foam retreated along its slopes while birds cried and dipped to examine the waves' leavings. Sails bobbed in the offing, and a small curtain of rain rippled in the southeast, far out at sea. The winds had ceased their noise-making, though they still came upon us with cloak-wrapping force.

We continued in silence until we had reached the bottom. We stepped away then, moving a few paces onto the sand.

"The harbor's in that direction," I said, gesturing to my right, westward, "and there's a church off that way," I added, indicating the dark building where Caine's service had been held and where seamen sometimes came to pray for safe voyages.

She looked in both directions and also glanced behind us and upward.

"More people headed down," she remarked.

I looked back up and saw three figures near the top of the stairway, but they were standing still, as if they'd only come down a short distance to try the view. None of them wore Llewella's colors. . . .

"Fellow sightseers," I said.

She watched them a moment longer, then looked away.

"Aren't there caves along here somewhere?" she asked.

I nodded to my right.

"That way," I answered. "There's a whole series. People get lost in them periodically. Some are pretty colorful. Others just wander through darkness. A few are simply shallow openings."

"I'd like to see them," she said.

"Sure, easily done. Let's go."

I began walking. The people on the stair had not moved. They still appeared to be looking out to sea. I doubted they were smugglers. It doesn't seem like a daytime occupation for a place where anyone might wander by. Still, I was pleased that my faculty for suspicion was growing. It seemed appropriate in light of recent events. The object of my greatest suspicion, of course, was walking beside me, turning driftwood with the toe of her boot, scuffing bright pebbles, laughing—but there was nothing I was ready to do about it at the moment. Soon. . . .

She took my arm suddenly.

"Thanks for bringing me," she said. "I'm enjoying this."

"Oh, I am, too. Glad we came. You're welcome."

This made me feel slightly guilty, but if my guess were wrong no harm would be done.

"I think I would enjoy living in Amber," she remarked as we went along.

"Me, too," I replied. "I've never really done it for any great length of time."

"Oh?"

"I guess I didn't really explain how long I'd spent on the shadow Earth where I went to school, where I had that job I was telling you about . . . ," I began, and suddenly I was pouring out more autobiography to her—a thing I don't usually do. I wasn't certain why I was telling it at first, and then I realized that I just wanted someone to talk to. Even if my strange suspicion was correct, it didn't matter. A friendly-seeming listener made me feel better than I had in a long while. And before I realized it, I was telling her about my father—how this man I barely knew had rushed through a massive story of his struggles, his dilemmas, his decisions, as if he were trying to justify himself to me, as if that were the only opportunity he might have to do it, and how I had listened, wondering what he was editing, what he had forgotten, what he might be glossing over or dressing up, what his feelings were toward me. . . .

"Those are some of the caves," I told her, as they interrupted my now embarrassing indulgence in memory. She started to say something about my monologue, but I simply continued, "I've only seen them once."

She caught my mood and simply said, "I'd like to go inside one."

I nodded. They seemed a good place for what I had in mind.

I chose the third one. Its mouth was larger than the first two, and I could see back into it for a good distance.

"Let's try that one. It looks well lighted," I explained.

We walked into a shadow-hung chill. The damp sand followed us for a while, thinning only slowly to be replaced by a gritty stone floor. The roof dipped and rose several times. A turn to the left joined us with the passage of another opening, for looking back along it I could see more light. The other direction led more deeply into the mountain. We could still feel the echoing pulse of the sea from where we stood.

"These caves could lead back really far," she observed.

"They do," I replied. "They twist and cross and wind. I wouldn't want to go too far without a map and a light. They've never been fully charted, that I know of."

She looked about, studying areas of blackness within the darkness where side tunnels debouched into our own.

"How far back do you think they go?" she inquired.

"I just don't know."

"Under the palace?"

"Probably," I said, remembering the series of side tunnels I'd passed on my way to the Pattern. "It seems possible they cut into the big caves below it—somewhere."

"What's it like down there?"

"Under the palace? Just dark and big. Ancient. . . ."

"I'd like to see it."

"Whatever for?"

"The Pattern's down there. It must be pretty colorful."

"Oh, it is—all bright and swirly. Rather intimidating, though."

"How can you say that when you've walked it?"

"Walking it and liking it are two different things."

"I'd just thought that if it were in you to walk it, you'd feel some affinity, some deep resonant kinship with it."

I laughed, and the sounds echoed about us.

"Oh, while I was walking it I knew it was in me to do it," I said. "I didn't feel it beforehand, though. I was just scared then. And I never liked it."

"Strange."

"Not really. It's like the sea or the night sky. It's big and it's powerful and it's beautiful and it's there. It's a natural force and you make of it what you will."

She looked back along the passageway leading inward.

"I'd like to see it," she said.

"I wouldn't try to find my way to it from here," I told her. "Why do you want to see it, anyhow?"

"Just to see how I'd respond to something like that."

"*You're* strange," I said.

"Will you take me when we go back? Will you show it to me?"

This was not going at all the way I'd thought it would. If she were what I thought, I didn't understand the request. I was half-tempted to take her to it, to find out what she had in mind. However, I was operating under a system of priorities, and I'd a feeling she represented one concerning which I'd made myself a promise and some elaborate preparations.

"Perhaps," I mumbled.

"Please. I'd really like to see it."

She seemed sincere. But my guess felt near-perfect. Sufficient time had passed for that strange body-shifting spirit, which had dogged my trail in many forms, to have located a new host and then to have zeroed in on me again and be insinuating itself into my good graces once more. Coral was perfect for the role, her arrival appropriately timed, her concern for my physical welfare manifest, her reflexes fast. I'd have liked to keep her around for questioning, but I knew that she would simply lie to me in the absence of proof or an emergency situation. And I did not trust her. So I reviewed the spell I had prepared and hung on my way home from Arbor House, a spell I had designed to expel a possessing entity from its host. I hesitated a moment, though. My feelings toward her were ambivalent. Even if she were the entity, I might be willing to put up with her if I just knew her motive.

So, "What is it that you want?" I asked.

"Just to see it. Honestly," she answered.

"No, I mean that if you are what I think you really are, I'm asking the big question: Why?"

Frakir began to pulse upon my wrist.

Coral was silent for the space of an audible deep breath, then, "How could you tell?"

"You betrayed yourself in small ways discernible only to one who has recently become paranoid," I responded.

"Magic," she said. "Is that it?"

"It's about to be," I replied. "I could almost miss you, but I can't trust you."

I spoke the guide words to the spell, letting them draw my hands smoothly through the appropriate gestures.

There followed two horrible shrieks, and then a third. But they weren't hers. They came from around the corner in the passageway we had recently quitted.

"What—?" she began.

"—the hell!" I finished, and I rushed past her and rounded the corner, drawing my blade as I went.

Backlighted by the distant cavemouth I beheld three figures on the floor of the cave. Two of them were sprawled and unmoving. The third was seated and bent forward, cursing. I advanced slowly, the point of my weapon directed toward the seated one. His shadowy head turned in my direction, and he climbed to his feet, still bent forward. He clutched his left hand with his right, and he backed away until he came into contact with the wall. He halted there, muttering something I could not quite hear. I continued my cautious advance, all of my senses alert. I could hear Coral moving at my back, then I glimpsed her accompanying me on my left when the passage widened. She had drawn her dagger, and she held it low and near to her hip. No time now to speculate as to what my spell might have done to her.

I halted as I came to the first of the two fallen forms. I prodded it with the toe of my boot, ready to strike instantly should it spring into an attack. Nothing. It felt limp, lifeless. I used my foot to turn it over, and the head rolled back in the direction of the cavemouth. In the light that then fell upon it I beheld a half-decayed human face. My nose had already been informing me that this state was no mere illusion. I advanced upon the other one and turned him, also. He, too, bore the appearance of a decomposing corpse. While the first one clutched a dagger in his right hand, the second was weaponless. Then I noted another dagger—on the floor, near the live man's feet. I raised my eyes to him. This made no sense whatsoever. I'd have judged the two figures upon the floor to have been dead for several days, at least, and I had no idea as to what the standing man had been up to.

"Uh. . . . Mind telling me what's going on?" I inquired.

"Damn you, Merlin!" he snarled, and I recognized the voice.

I moved in a slow arc, stepping over the fallen ones. Coral stayed near to my side, moving in a similar fashion. He turned his head to follow our progress, and when the light finally fell upon his face, I saw that Jurt was glaring at me out of his one good eye—a patch covered the other—and I saw, too, that about half of his hair was missing, the exposed scalp covered with welts or scars, his half-regrown ear-stub plainly visible. From this side I could also see that a bandana suitable for covering most of this damage had slipped down around his neck. Blood was dripping from his left hand, and I suddenly realized that his little finger was missing.

"What happened to you?" I asked.

"One of the zombies hit my hand with his dagger as he fell," he said, "when you expelled the spirits that animated them."

My spell—to evict a possessing spirit. . . . They had been within range of it. . . .

"Coral," I asked, "are you all right?"

"Yes," she replied. "But I don't understand. . . ."

"Later," I told her.

I did not ask him about his head, as I recalled my struggle with the one-eyed werewolf in the wood to the east of Amber—the beast whose head I had forced into the campfire. I had suspected for some time that it had been Jurt in a shape-shifted form, even before Mandor had offered sufficient information to confirm it.

"Jurt," I began, "I have been the occasion of many of your ills, but you must realize that you brought them on yourself. If you would not attack me, I would have no need to defend myself—"

There came a clicking, grinding sound. It took me several seconds to realize that it was a gnashing of teeth.

"My adoption by your father meant nothing to me," I said, "beyond the fact that he honored me by it. I was not even aware until recently that it had occurred."

"You lie!" he hissed. "You tricked him some way, to get ahead of us in the succession."

"You've got to be kidding," I said. "We're all so far down on the list that it doesn't matter."

"Not for the Crown, you fool! For the House! Our father isn't all that well!"

"I'm sorry to hear that," I said. "But I'd never even thought of it that way. And Mandor's ahead of all of us, anyhow."

"And now you're second."

"Not by choice. Come on! I'll never see the title. You know that!"

He drew himself upright, and when he moved I became aware of a faint prismatic nimbus that had been clinging to his outline.

"That isn't the real reason," I continued. "You've never liked me, but you're not after me because of the succession. You're hiding something now. It's got to be something else, for all this activity on your part. By the way, you did send the Fire Angel, didn't you?"

"It found you that fast?" he said. "I wasn't even sure I could count on that. I guess it was worth the price after all. But. . . . What happened?"

"It's dead."

"You're very lucky. Too lucky," he replied.

"What is it that you want, Jurt? I'd like to settle this once and for all."

"Me, too," he answered. "You betrayed someone I love, and only your death will set things right."

"Who are you talking about? I don't understand."

He grinned suddenly.

"You will," he said. "In the last moments of your life I'll let you know why."

"I may have a long wait, then," I answered. "You don't seem to be very good at this sort of thing. Why not just tell me now and save us both a lot of trouble?"

He laughed, and the prism effect increased, and it occurred to me in that instant what it was.

"Sooner than you think," he said, "for shortly I will be more powerful than anything you ever met."

"But no less clumsy," I suggested, both to him and to whomever held his Trump, watching me through it, ready to snatch him away in an instant. . . .

"That *is* you, Mask, isn't it?" I said. "Take him back. You don't have to send him again either and watch him screw up. I'll promote you on my list of priorities and come calling soon, if you'll just give me an assurance that it's really you."

Jurt opened his mouth and said something, but I couldn't hear it because he faded fast and his words went away with him. Something flew toward me as this occurred; there was no need to parry it, but I couldn't stop the reflex.

Along with two moldering corpses and Jurt's little finger, a dozen or so roses lay scattered on the floor at my feet, there at the rainbow's end.

FIVE

As we walked along the beach in the direction of the harbor, Coral finally spoke:

"Does that sort of thing happen around here very often?"

"You should come by on a bad day," I said.

"If you don't mind telling me, I'd like to hear what it was all about."

"I guess I owe you an explanation," I agreed, "because I wronged you back there, whether you know it or not."

"You're serious."

"Yep."

"Go on. I'm really curious."

"It's a long story . . . ," I began again.

She looked ahead to the harbor, then up to Kolvir's heights.

". . . A long walk, too," she said.

". . . And you're a daughter of the prime minister of a country with which we have somewhat touchy relations at the moment."

"What do you mean?"

"Some of the things that are happening may represent kind of sensitive information."

She put her hand on my shoulder and halted. She stared into my eyes.

"I can keep a secret," she told me. "After all, you know mine."

I congratulated myself on having finally learned my relatives' trick of controlling facial expression even when puzzled as all hell. She *had* said something back in the cave when I had addressed her as if she were the entity, something that sounded as if she believed I had discovered a secret concerning her.

So I gave her a wry smile and nodded.

"Just so," I said.

"You're not planning on ravaging our country or anything like that, are you?" she asked.

"To my knowledge, no. And I don't think it likely either."

"Well, then. You can only speak from your knowledge, can't you?"

"True," I agreed.

"So let's hear the story."

"All right."

As we walked along the strand and I spoke, to the accompaniment of the waves' deep notes, I could not help but remember again my father's long narrative. Was it a family trait, I wondered, to go autobiographical at a time of troubles if the right listener turned up? For I realized I was elaborating my telling beyond the bounds of necessity. And why should she be the right listener, anyhow?

When we reached the port district, I realized I was hungry, anyway, and I still had a lot of telling to do. In that it was still daylight and doubtless considerably safer than when I'd made my nighttime visit, I found my way over to Harbor Street—which was even dirtier in strong light—and, having learned that Coral was hungry, too, I took us on around to the rear of the cove, pausing for a few minutes to watch a many-masted vessel with golden sails round the sea wall and head in. Then we followed the curving way to the western shore, and I was able to locate Seabreeze Lane without any trouble. It was still early enough that we passed a few sober sailors. At one point a heavy, black-bearded man with an interesting scar on his right cheek began to approach us, but a smaller man caught up with him first and whispered something in his ear. They both turned away.

"Hey," I said. "What did he want?"

"Nothin'," the smaller man said. "He don't want nothin'." He studied me for a moment and nodded. Then, "I saw you here the other night," he added.

"Oh," I said, as they continued to the next corner, turned it, and were gone.

"What was that all about?" Coral said.

"I didn't get to that part of the story yet."

But I remembered it vividly when we passed the place where it had occurred. No signs of that conflict remained.

I almost passed what had been Bloody Bill's, though, because a new sign hung above the door. It read "Bloody Andy's," in fresh green letters. The place was just the same inside, however, except for the man behind the counter, who was taller and thinner than the shaggy, crag-faced individual who had served me last time. His name, I learned, was Jak, and he was Andy's brother. He sold us a bottle of Bayle's Piss and put in our order for two fish dinners through the hole in the wall. My former table was vacant and we took it. I laid my sword belt on the chair to my right, with the blade partly drawn, as I had been taught etiquette required here.

"I like this place," she said. "It's . . . different."

"Uh . . . yes," I agreed, glancing at two passed-out drunks—one to the front of the establishment, one to the rear—and three shifty-eyed individuals conversing in low voices off in one corner. A few broken bottles and suspicious stains were upon the floor, and some not-too-subtle artwork of an amorous nature hung on the far wall. "The food's quite good," I added.

"I've never been in a restaurant like this," she continued, watching a black cat, who rolled in from a rear room, wrestling with an enormous rat.

"It has its devotees, but it's a well-kept secret among discriminating diners."

I continued my tale through a meal even better than the one I remembered. When the door opened much later to admit a small man with a bad limp and a dirty bandage about his head I noticed that daylight was beginning to wane. I had just finished my story and it seemed a good time to be leaving.

I said as much, but she put her hand on mine.

"You know I'm not your entity," she said, "but if you need any kind of help I can give you, I'll do it."

"You're a good listener," I said. "Thanks. We'd better be going now."

We passed out of Death Alley without incident and made our way along Harbor Street over to Vine. The sun was getting ready to set as we headed upward, and the cobbles passed through a variety of bright earth tones and fire colors. Street and pedestrian traffic was light. Cooking smells drifted on the air; leaves rattled along the road; a small yellow dragon rode the air currents high overhead; curtains of rainbow light rippled high in the north beyond the palace. I kept waiting, expecting more questions from Coral than the few she had asked. They never came. If I'd just heard my story, I think I'd have a lot of questions, unless I were totally overpowered by it or somehow understood it thoroughly.

"When we get back to the palace . . . ?" she said then.

"Yes?"

". . . You *will* take me to see the Pattern, won't you?"

I laughed.

. . . Or unless something else were occupying my mind.

"Right away? First thing in the door?" I asked.

"Yes."

"Sure," I said.

Then, that off her mind, "Your story changes my picture of the world," she said, "and I wouldn't presume to advise you. . . ."

"But—" I continued.

". . . It seems that the Keep of the Four Worlds holds the answers you want. Everything else may fall into place when you learn what's going on there. But I don't understand why you can't just do a card for it and trump in."

"Good question. There are parts of the Courts of Chaos to which no one can trump because they change constantly and cannot be represented in a permanent fashion. The same applies to the place where I situated Ghostwheel. Now, the terrain around the Keep fluctuates quite a bit, but I'm not positive that's the reason for the blockage. The place is a power center, and I think it possible that someone diverted some of that power into a shielding spell. A good enough magician might be able to drill through it with a Trump, but I've a feeling that the force required would probably set off some psychic alarm and destroy any element of surprise."

"What does the place look like, anyway?" she asked.

"Well . . . ," I began. "Here." I took my notebook and Scripto from my shirt pocket and sketched. "See, all of this area is volcanic." I scribbled in a few fumaroles and wisps of smoke. "And this part is Ice Age." More scribbles. "Ocean here, mountains here. . . ."

"Then it sounds as if your best bet is to use the Pattern again," she said, studying the drawing and shaking her head.

"Yes."

"Do you think you'll be doing it soon?"

"Possibly."

"How will you attack them?"

"I'm still working on that."

"If there's any sort of way that I can help you, I meant what I said."

"There isn't."

"Don't be so sure. I'm well trained. I'm resourceful. I even know a few spells."

"Thanks," I said. "But no."

"No discussion?"

"Nope."

"If you change your mind. . . ."

"I won't."

". . . Let me know."

We reached the Concourse, moved along it. The winds grew more blustery here and something cold touched my cheek. Then again. . . .

"Snow!" Coral announced, just as I realized that a few middle-sized flakes were drifting past us, vanishing immediately when they hit the ground.

"If your party had arrived at the proper time," I observed, "you might not have had your walk."

"Sometimes I'm lucky," she said.

It was snowing fairly hard by the time we reached the palace grounds. We used the postern gate again, pausing on the walkway to gaze back down over the light-dotted town, half-screened by falling flakes. I knew she kept looking longer than I did, because I turned to gaze at her. She appeared—

happy, I guess—as if she were pasting the scene in a mental scrapbook. So I leaned over and kissed her cheek, because it seemed like a good idea.

"Oh," she said, turning to face me. "You surprised me."

"Good," I told her. "I hate to telegraph these things. Let's get the troops in out of the cold."

She smiled and took my arm.

Inside, the guard told me, "Llewella wants to know whether you two will be joining them all for dinner."

"When *is* dinner?" I asked him.

"In about an hour and a half, I believe."

I glanced at Coral, who shrugged.

"I guess so," I said.

"Front dining room, upstairs," he told me. "Shall I pass the word to my sergeant—he's due by soon—and have him deliver it? Or do you want to—"

"Yes," I said. "Do that."

"Care to wash up, change clothes . . . ?" I began, as we walked away.

"The Pattern," she said.

"It would involve a lot more stairs," I told her.

She turned toward me, her face tightening, but saw that I was smiling.

"This way," I said, leading her to the main hall and through it.

I didn't recognize the guard at the end of the brief corridor that led up to the stair. He knew who I was, though, glanced curiously at Coral, opened the door, found us a lantern, and lit it.

"I'm told there's a loose step," he remarked as he passed me the light.

"Which one is it?"

He shook his head.

"Prince Gérard's reported it several times," he said, "but no one else seems to notice it."

"Okay," I said. "Thanks."

This time Coral didn't object to my going first. Of the two, this was more intimidating than the stairway on the cliff face, mainly because you can't see bottom and after a few paces you can't see much of anything beyond the shell of light within which you move as you wind your way down. And there's a heavy sense of vastness all about you. I've never seen the place illuminated, but I gather that the impression is not incorrect. It's a very big cavern, and you go round and round and down in the middle of it, wondering when you'll reach the bottom.

After a time, Coral cleared her throat, then, "Could we stop for a minute?" she asked.

"Sure," I said, halting. "Out of breath?"

"No," she said. "How much farther?"

"I don't know," I replied. "It seems a different distance each time I come this way. If you want to go back and have dinner, we can see it tomorrow. You've had a busy day."

"No," she answered. "But I wouldn't mind your holding me for a minute."

It seemed an awkward place to get romantic, so I cleverly deduced that there was another reason, said nothing, and obliged.

It took me a long while to realize that she was crying. She was very good at concealing it.

"What's the matter?" I finally asked.

"Nothing," she replied. "Nervous reaction, maybe. Primitive reflex. Darkness. Claustrophobia. Like that."

"Let's go back."

"No."

So we started down again.

About a half minute later I saw something white near the side of a lower step. I slowed. Then I realized that it was only a handkerchief. A little nearer, however, and I saw that it was held in place by a dagger. Also, there were markings upon it. I halted, reached out, flattened it, and read. "THIS ONE, DAMN IT!—GÉRARD," it said.

"Careful here," I said to Coral.

I prepared to step over it, but on an impulse I tested it lightly with one foot. No squeaks. I shifted more weight onto it. Nothing. It felt firm. I stood on it. The same. I shrugged.

"Careful, anyway," I said.

Nothing happened when she stepped on it either, and we kept going. A little later, I saw a flicker in the distance below. It was moving, and I guessed someone was doing a patrol. What for? I wondered. Were there prisoners to be tended and watched? Were certain cave mouths considered vulnerable points? And what about the business of locking the chamber of the Pattern and hanging the key on the wall near the door? Was there some possible danger from that quarter? How? Why? I realized that I ought to pursue these questions one of these days.

When we reached the bottom the guard was nowhere in sight, however. The table, the racks, and a few foot lockers—which constituted the guard station—were illuminated by a number of lanterns, but the guard was not at his post. Too bad. It would be interesting to ask what the orders called for in the event of an emergency—hopefully also specifying the possible natures of various emergencies. For the first time, though, I noticed a rope hanging down from the darkness into the dimness beside a weapons rack. I drew upon it ever so gently and it yielded, to be followed a moment later by a faint metallic sound from somewhere high overhead. Interesting. Obviously, this was the alarm.

"Which . . . way?" Coral asked.

"Oh, come on," I said, taking her hand, and I led her off to the right.

I kept waiting for echoes as we moved, but none came. Periodically, I raised the light. The darkness would recede a bit then, but nothing came into view beyond an additional area of floor.

Coral seemed to be slowing now, and I felt a certain tension in her arm as she hung back. I plodded on and she kept moving, however.

Finally, "It shouldn't be too much longer," I said, as the echoes began, very faintly.

"Good," she replied, but she did not increase her pace.

At last the gray wall of the cavern came into view, and far off to my left was the dark opening of the tunnel mouth I sought. I changed course and headed toward it. When we finally reached it and entered, I felt her flinch.

"If I'd known it would bother you this much—" I began.

"I'm really all right," she answered, "and I do want to see it. I just didn't realize that getting there would be this . . . involved."

"Well, the worst of it is over. Soon now," I said.

We came to the first side passage to the left fairly quickly and went on by. There was another shortly thereafter, and I slowed and extended the lantern toward it.

"Who knows?" I commented. "That could take you through some strange route back to the beach."

"I'd rather not check it out."

We walked for some time before we passed the third opening. I gave it a quick glance. There was a vein of some bright mineral partway back in it.

I speeded up and she kept pace, our footsteps ringing loudly now. We passed the fourth opening. The fifth. . . . From somewhere, it seemed I heard faint strains of music.

She glanced at me inquiringly when we neared the sixth passageway, but I just kept going. It was the seventh that I wanted, and when we finally came to it I turned, took a few paces, halted, and raised the lantern. We stood before a big metal-bound door.

I took the key down from the hook on the wall to my right, inserting it in the lock, turned it, withdrew it, and rehung it. Then I put my shoulder against the door and pushed hard. There followed a long moment of resistance, then slow movement accompanied shortly by a complaint from a tight hinge. Frakir tightened upon my wrist, but I kept pushing till the door was opened wide. Then I stood to the side and held it for Coral.

She moved a few steps past me into that strange chamber and halted. I stepped away and let the door swing shut, then came up beside her.

"So that's it," she remarked.

Roughly elliptical, the intricately wound oval form of the Pattern glowed blue-white within the floor. I set the lantern aside. It wasn't really necessary, the glow from the Pattern providing more than sufficient illumination. I stroked Frakir, calming her. A jet of sparks rose at the far end of the great design, subsided quickly, occurred again nearer to us. The chamber seemed filled with a half-familiar pulsing I had never consciously noted before. On an impulse—to satisfy a long-held point of curiosity—I summoned the Sign of the Logrus.

This was a mistake.

Immediately the image of the Logrus flared before me, sparks erupted along the entire length of the Pattern, and a high-pitched banshee wail rose from somewhere. Frakir went wild, my ears felt as if icicles had been driven into them, and the brightness of the writhing Sign hurt my eyes. I banished the Logrus in that instant, and the turmoil began to subside.

"What," she asked me, "was that?"

I tried to smile, didn't quite manage it.

"A little experiment I'd always meant to try," I told her.

"Did you learn anything from it?"

"Not to do it again, perhaps," I answered.

"Or at least not till the company's left," she said. "That hurt."

"Sorry."

She moved nearer to the edge of the Pattern, which had calmed itself again.

"Eerie," she observed. "Like a light in a dream. But it's gorgeous. And all of you have to walk it to come into your heritage?"

"Yes."

She moved slowly to the right, following its perimeter. I followed her as she strolled, her gaze roving across the bright expanse of arcs and turns, short straight lines, long sweeping curves.

"I assume it is difficult?"

"Yes. The trick is to keep pushing and not to stop trying even if you stop moving," I replied.

We walked on, to the right, circling slowly around to the rear. The design seemed to be within the floor rather than upon it, seen as through a layer of glass. But nowhere was the surface slippery.

We paused for a minute or so while she took its measure from a new angle.

"So how are you responding to it?" I finally asked.

"Esthetically," she said.

"Anything else?"

"Power," she said. "It seems to radiate something." She leaned forward and waved her hand above the nearest line. "It's almost a physical pressure," she added then.

We moved farther, passing along the back length of the grand design. I could see across the Pattern, to the place where the lantern glowed on the floor near to the entranceway. Its light was negligible beside the greater illumination we regarded now.

Shortly, Coral halted again. She pointed.

"What is this single line, which seems to end right here?" she asked.

"It's not the end," I said. "It's the beginning. That is the place where one commences the walking of the Pattern."

She moved nearer, passing her hand above it also.

"Yes," she said after a moment. "I can feel that it starts here."

For how long we stood there, I am uncertain. Then she reached out, took hold of my hand and squeezed it.

"Thanks," she said, "for everything."

I was about to ask her why that had such a final sound about it, when she moved forward and set her foot upon the line.

"No!" I cried. "Stop!"

But it was too late. Her foot was already in place, brightness outlining the sole of her boot.

"Don't move!" I said. "Whatever you do, stay still!"

She did as I said, holding her position. I licked my lips, which suddenly seemed very dry.

"Now, try to raise the foot you placed upon the line and draw it back. Can you do it?"

"No," she replied.

I knelt beside her and studied it. Theoretically, once you'd set foot upon the Pattern there was no turning back. You had no choice but to continue and either make it through or be destroyed somewhere along the way. On the other hand, she should already be dead. Theoretically, again, anyone not of the blood of Amber shouldn't be able to set foot upon it and live. So much for theory.

"Hell of a time to ask," I said. "But why'd you do it?"

"You indicated to me back in the cave that my guess was correct. You said that you knew what I was."

I recalled what I'd said, but that was with reference to my guess at her being the body-shifting entity. What could she have taken it to mean that had to do with the Pattern? But even as I sought after a spell that might free her from the Pattern's hold, the obvious answer to things drifted into my mind.

"Your connection with the House . . . ?" I said softly.

"King Oberon supposedly had an affair with my mother before I was born," she said. "The timing would have been right. It was only a rumor, though. I couldn't get anyone to provide details. So I was never certain. But I dreamed of it being true. I wanted it to be true. I hoped to find some tunnel that would bring me to this place. I wanted to sneak in and walk the Pattern and have the shadows unfold before me. But I was afraid, too, because I knew that if I were wrong I would die. Then, when you said what you said, you answered my dream. But I did not stop being afraid. I am still afraid. Only now I'm afraid that I won't be strong enough to make it."

That sense of familiarity I had felt when I first met her. . . . I suddenly realized that it was a general family resemblance that had caused it. Her nose and brow reminded me a bit of Fiona, her chin and cheekbones something of Flora. Her hair and eyes and height and build were her own, though. But she certainly did not resemble her nominal father or sister.

I thought again of a faintly leering portrait of my grandfather which I had often studied, in an upstairs hallway, to the west. The lecherous old bastard really got around. Giving him his due, though, he was a very good-looking man. . . .

I sighed and rose to my feet. I laid a hand upon her shoulder.

"Listen, Coral," I said. "All of us were well briefed before we tried it. I am going to tell you about it before you take another step, and while I speak you may feel energy flowing from me into you. I want you to be as strong as possible. When you take your next step I do not want you to stop again until you have reached the middle. I may call out instructions to you as you move along, also. Do whatever I say immediately, without thinking about it.

"First I will tell you about the Veils, the places of resistance. . . ."

For how long I spoke, I do not know.

I watched as she approached the First Veil.

"Ignore the chill and the shocks," I said. "They can't hurt you. Don't let the sparks distract you. You're about to hit major resistance. Don't start breathing rapidly."

I watched her push her way through.

"Good," I said, as she came onto an easier stretch, deciding against telling her that the next Veil was far worse. "By the way, don't think that you're going crazy. Shortly, it will begin playing head games with you—"

"It already has," she responded. "What should I do?"

"It's probably mostly memories. Just let them flow, and keep your attention on the path."

She continued, and I talked her through the Second Veil. The sparks reached almost to her shoulders before she was out of it. I watched her struggle through arc after arc, then tricky curves and long, sweeping ones, turns, reversals. There were times when she moved quickly, times when she was slowed almost to a standstill. But she kept moving. She had the idea, and it seemed she had the will. I did not think that she really needed me now. I was certain that I had nothing left to offer, that the outcome was entirely in her own hands.

So I shut up and watched, irritated with but unable to prevent my own leaning and turning, shifting and pressing, as if I were out there myself, anticipating, compensating.

When she came to the Grand Curve she was a living flame. Her progress was very slow, but there was a relentless quality to it. Whatever the outcome, I knew that she was being changed, had been changed already, that the Pattern was inscribing itself upon her, and that she was very near to the end of its statement. I almost cried out as she seemed to stop for a moment, but the words died in my throat as she shuddered once, then continued. I wiped my brow on my sleeve as she approached the Final Veil. Whatever the outcome, she had proved her suspicions. Only a child of Amber could have survived as she had.

I do not know how long it took her to pierce the last Veil. Her effort became timeless, and I was caught up in that protracted moment. She was a burning study in extreme slow motion, the nimbus that enshrouded her lighting up the entire chamber like a great blue candle.

And then she was through and onto that final short arc, the last three steps of which may well be the most difficult part of the entire Pattern. Some sort of psychic surface tension seems joined with the physical inertia one encounters just before the point of emergence.

Again, I thought she had stopped, but it was only an appearance. It was like watching someone doing tai chi, the painful slowness of that trio of paces.

But she completed it and moved again. If the final step didn't kill her, then she was home free. Then we could talk. . . .

That final moment went on and on and on. Then I saw her foot move forward and depart the Pattern. Shortly, the other foot followed and she stood panting at the center.

"Congratulations!" I shouted.

She waved weakly with her right hand while slowly raising her left to cover her eyes. She stood thus for the better part of a minute, and one who has walked the Pattern understands the feeling. I did not call out again, but let her recover, giving her the silence in which to enjoy her triumph.

The Pattern seemed to be glowing more brightly just then, as it often does immediately after being traversed. This gave a fairyland quality to the grotto—all blue light and shadow—and made a mirror of that small, still pool in the far corner where blind fish swim. I tried to think ahead to what this act might mean, for Coral, for Amber. . . .

She straightened suddenly.

"I'm going to live," she announced.

"Good," I replied. "You have a choice now, you know."

"What do you mean?" she asked.

"You are now in a position to command the Pattern to transport you anywhere," I explained. "So you could just have it deposit you back here again, or you could save yourself a long walk by having it return you to your suite right now. As much as I enjoy your company, I'd recommend the latter since you're probably pretty tired. Then you can soak in a nice warm bath and take your time dressing for dinner. I'll meet you in the dining room. Okay?"

I saw that she was smiling as she shook her head.

"I'm not going to waste an opportunity like this," she said.

"Listen, I know the feeling," I told her. "But I think you should restrain yourself. Rushing off someplace weird could be dangerous, and coming back could be tricky when you haven't had any training in shadow walking."

"It's just sort of a will and expectation thing, isn't it?" she asked. "You kind of impose images on the environment as you go along, don't you?"

"It's trickier than that," I said. "You have to learn to capitalize on certain features as points of departure. Normally, one is accompanied on one's first shadow walk by someone with experience—"

"Okay, I get the idea."

"Not enough," I said. "Ideas are fine, but there's feedback, too. There's a certain feeling you get when it begins working. That can't be taught. It has to be experienced—and until you're sure of it, you should have someone along for a guide."

"Seems like trial and error would do."

"Maybe," I answered. "But supposing you wound up in danger? That'd be a hell of a time to start learning. Kind of distracting—"

"All right. You made your point. Fortunately, I'm not planning on anything that would put me in such a position."

"What are you planning?"

She straightened and gestured widely.

"Ever since I learned about the Pattern, there's been something I wanted to try if I got this far," she said.

"What might that be?"

"I'm going to ask it to send me where I should go."

"I don't understand."

"I'm going to leave the choice up to the Pattern."

I shook my head.

"It doesn't work that way," I told her. "You have to give it an order to transport you."

"How do you know that?"

"It's just the way it works."

"Have you ever tried what I'm saying?"

"No. Nothing would happen."

"Has anyone you know of ever tried it?"

"It would be a waste of time. Look, you're talking as if the Pattern is somehow sentient, is capable of coming to a decision on its own and executing it."

"Yes," she replied. "And it must know me real well after what I've just been through with it. So I'm just going to ask its advice and—"

"Wait!" I said.

"Yes?"

"On the off chance that something happens, how do you plan on getting back?"

"I'll walk, I guess. So you're admitting that something could happen?"

"Yes," I said. "It's conceivable that you have an unconscious desire to visit a place, and that it will read that and take you there If you give a transport order. That won't prove that the Pattern is sentient—just that it's sensitive. Now, if it were me standing there, I'd be afraid to take a chance like that. Supposing I have suicidal tendencies I'm not aware of? Or—"

"You're reaching," she answered. "You're really reaching."

"I'm just counseling you to play it safe. You have your whole life to go exploring. It would be silly to—"

"Enough!" she said. "My mind's made up, and that's it. It feels right. See you later, Merlin."

"Wait!" I cried again. "All right. Do it if you must. But let me give you something first."

"What?"

"A means of getting out of a tight spot in a hurry. Here."

I withdrew my Trumps, shuffled out my own card. Then I unfastened my dagger and sheath from my belt. I wrapped my card around the haft and tied it there with my handkerchief.

"You have an idea how to use a Trump?"

"You just stare and think of the person till there's contact, don't you?"

"That'll do," I said. "Here's mine. Take it with you. Call me when you want to come home, and I'll bring you back."

I tossed it out across the Pattern, underhand. She caught it easily and hung it on her belt on the side opposite her own.

"Thanks," she said, straightening. "I guess I'll give it a try now."

"Just in case it really works, don't stay long. Okay?"

"Okay," she answered, and she closed her eyes.

An instant later she was gone. Oh, my.

I moved to the edge of the Pattern and held my hand above it until I could feel the forces stirring there.

"You'd better know what you're doing," I said. "I want her back."

A spark shot upward and tickled my palm.

"You trying to tell me you're really sentient?"

Everything swirled about me. The dizziness passed in an instant, and the first thing I noticed then was that the lantern was beside my right foot. When I looked about I realized that I was standing on the other side of the Pattern from where I had been and was now near the door.

"I was within your field and I'm already attuned," I said. "It was just my unconscious desire to get out."

Then I hefted the lantern, locked the door behind me, and hung the key back on its hook. I still didn't trust the thing. If it had really wanted to be helpful, it would have sent me directly to my quarters and saved me all those stairs.

I hurried along the tunnel. It was by far the most interesting first date I'd ever had.

SIX

As I passed out of the main hall and headed along the back hallway which would take me to any of a number of stairs, a fellow in black leathers and various pieces of rusty and shiny chain emerged from a corridor to my right, halted, and stared at me. His hair was of an orange Mohawk cut and there were several silver rings in his left ear near what looked like an electrical outlet of some sort.

"Merlin?" he said. "You okay?"

"For the moment," I replied as I drew nearer, trying to place him, there in the dimness.

"Martin!" I said. "You're . . . changed."

He chuckled.

"I'm just back from a very interesting shadow," he said. "Spent over a year there—one of those places where time runs like hell."

"I'd judge—just guessing—that it was high-tech, urban. . . ."

"Right."

"I thought you were a country boy."

"I got over it. Now I know why my dad likes cities and noise."

"You a musician, too?"

"Some. Different sounds, though. You going to be at dinner?"

"I was planning on it. As soon as I get cleaned up and changed."

"See you there, then. We've a lot of things to talk about."

"Sure thing, Cousin."

He clasped my shoulder and released it as I passed. His grip was still strong.

I walked on. Before I'd gone very far, I felt the beginning of a Trump contact. I halted and reached quickly, figuring it was Coral wanting to return. Instead, my eyes met those of Mandor, who smiled faintly.

"Ah, very good," he said. "You are alone and apparently safe."

As things came clearer I saw that Fiona was standing beside him, standing very close as a matter of fact.

"I'm okay," I said. "I'm back in Amber. You all right?"

"Intact," he said, looking past me, though there was not much to see beyond wall and a bit of tapestry.

"Would you care to come through?" I asked.

"I'd love to see Amber," he replied. "But that pleasure will have to await another occasion. We are somewhat occupied at the moment."

"You've discovered the cause of the disturbances?" I asked.

He glanced at Fiona, then back at me.

"Yes and no," he said. "We've some interesting leads but no certainty at the moment."

"Uh, what can I do for you then?" I asked.

Fiona extended her index finger and suddenly became much clearer. I realized that she must have reached out and touched my Trump for better contact.

"We've had an encounter with a manifestation of that machine you built," she said. "Ghostwheel."

"Yes?" I said.

"You're right, it's sentient—social AI as well as technical."

"I was already certain it could pass the Turing test."

"Oh, no doubt about that," she responded, "since by definition the Turing test requires a machine capable of lying to people and misleading them."

"What are you getting at, Fiona?" I asked.

"It's not just social AI. It's downright antisocial," she replied. "I think your machine is crazy."

"What did it do?" I asked. "Attack you?"

"No, nothing physical. It's wacky and mendacious and insulting, and we're too busy to go into details right now. I'm not saying it couldn't get nasty, though. I don't know. We just wanted to warn you not to trust it."

I smiled.

"That's it? End of message?" I said.

"For now," she answered, lowering her finger and growing dim.

I shifted my gaze to Mandor and was about to explain that I had built a host of safeguards into the thing, so that not just anybody could access it.

Mainly, though, I wanted to tell him about Jurt. But our communication was suddenly severed, as I felt another presence reaching toward me.

I was intrigued by the sensation. I had occasionally wondered what would occur if someone tried for a Trump contact when I was already in touch with someone else via a Trump. Would it turn into a conference call? Would someone get a busy signal? Would it put the other party on hold? I'd doubted I'd ever find out, though. It just seemed statistically unlikely. However. . . .

"Merlin, baby. I'm okay."

"Luke!"

Mandor and Fiona were definitely gone.

"I'm really okay now, Merle."

"You sure?"

"Yeah, as soon as I started coming down I switched to a fast lane. In this shadow it's been several days since I've seen you."

He was wearing sunglasses and green swim trunks. He was seated at a small table beside a swimming pool in the shade of a great umbrella, the remains of a large lunch spread before him. A lady in a blue bikini dived into the pool and passed from my line of sight.

"Well, I'm glad to hear about that and—"

"So what happened to me, anyhow? I remember you said something about someone slipping me some acid when I was a prisoner back at the Keep. Is that how it went?"

"It seems very likely."

"I guess that's what happens when you drink the water," he mused. "Okay. What's been going on while I've been out of it?"

Knowing how much to tell him was always a problem. So, "Where do we stand?" I asked.

"Oh. That," he said.

"Yeah."

"Well, I've had a chance to do a lot of thinking," he replied, "and I'm going to call it quits. Honor has been satisfied. It's pointless to keep pushing this thing against everybody else. But I'm not about to put myself in Random's hands for a kangaroo trial. Now it's your turn: Where do I stand so far as Amber's concerned? Should I be looking over my shoulder?"

"Nobody's said anything yet, one way or the other. But Random is out of town now and I just got back myself. I haven't really had a chance to learn what the others' feelings might be on this thing."

He removed his sunglasses and studied me.

"The fact that Random's out of town. . . ."

"No, I know he's not after you," I said, "because he's in Kash—" and I tried to stop it just a syllable too late.

"Kashfa?"

"So I understand."

"What the hell's he doing there? Amber was never interested in the place before."

"There's been a . . . death," I explained. "Some kind of shake-up going on."

"Ha!" Luke remarked. "That bastard finally bought it. Good! But. . . . Hey! Why's Amber moving in so suddenlike, huh?"

"Don't know," I said.

He chuckled. "Rhetorical question," he said. "I can see what's going on. I've got to admit Random's got style. Listen, when you find out who he puts on the throne let me know, will you? I like to keep abreast of doings in the old hometown."

"Oh, sure," I said, trying unsuccessfully to determine whether such information could be harmful. It would become public knowledge very soon, if it wasn't already.

"So what else is going on? That other person who was Vinta Bayle . . . ?"

"Gone," I said. "I don't know where."

"Very strange," he mused. "I don't think we've seen the last of her. She *was* Gail, too. I'm sure. Let me know if she comes back, will you?"

"Okay. You want to ask her out again?"

He shrugged, then smiled. "I could think of worse ways to spend some time."

"You're lucky she didn't try to take *you* out, literally."

"I'm not so sure she would've," he replied. "We always got along pretty well. Anyhow, none of this is the main reason I called. . . ."

I nodded, having already guessed as much.

"How's my mother doing?" he asked.

"Hasn't stirred," I answered. "She's safe."

"That's something," he said. "You know, it's kind of undignified for a queen to be in that position. A coatrack. Jeez!"

"I agree," I agreed. "But what's the alternative?"

"Well, I'd sort of like to . . . get her freed," he said. "What'll it take?"

"You raise a very thorny issue," I stated.

"I sort of figured that."

"I've a strong feeling she's the one behind this revenge business, Luke, that she's the one who put you up to going after everybody. Like with that bomb. Like encouraging you to set up that private army with modern weapons, to use against Amber. Like trying for a hit on me every spring. Like—"

"Okay, okay. You're right. I don't deny it. But things have changed—"

"Yeah. Her plans fell through and we've got her."

"That's not what I meant. I'm changed. I understand her now, and I understand myself better. She can't push me around that way anymore."

"Why is that?"

"That trip I was on. . . . It shook loose my thinking quite a bit. About her and me. I've had several days now to mull over what some of it meant, and I don't think she can pull the same crap on me that she used to."

I recalled the red-haired woman tied to the stake, tormented by demons. There was a resemblance, now I thought of it.

"But she's still my mother," he went on, "and I don't like leaving her in the position she's in. What kind of deal might be possible for turning her loose?"

"I don't know, Luke," I answered. "The matter hasn't come up yet."

"Well, she's *your* prisoner, actually."

"But her plans were directed against all of us."

"True, but I won't be helping her with them anymore. She really needs someone like me for carrying them out."

"Right. And if she doesn't have you to help, what's to prevent her from finding someone like you, as you put it? She'd still be dangerous if we let her go."

"But you know about her now. That would crimp her style quite a bit."

"It might just make her more devious."

He sighed. "I suppose there's some truth in that," he admitted. "But she's as venal as most people. It's just a matter of finding the right price."

"I can't see Amber buying someone off that way."

"I can."

"Not when that person is already a prisoner here."

"That does complicate matters a little," he acknowledged. "But I hardly think it's an insurmountable barrier. Not if she's more useful to you free than as a piece of furniture."

"You've lost me," I said. "What are you proposing?"

"Nothing yet. I'm just sounding you out."

"Fair enough. But offhand, I can't see a situation such as you describe arising. More valuable to us free than a prisoner. . . . I guess we'd go where the value lies. But these are just words."

"Just trying to plant a seed or two while I work on it. What is your greatest concern right now?"

"Me? Personally? You really want to know?"

"You bet."

"Okay. My mad brother Jurt has apparently allied himself with the sorcerer Mask back at the Keep. The two of them are out to get me. Jurt made an attempt just this afternoon, but I can see it's really a challenge from Mask. I'm going to take them on soon."

"Hey, I didn't know you had a brother!"

"Half-brother. I have a couple of others, too. But I can get along with them. Jurt's been after me for a long time."

"That's really something. You never mentioned them."

"We never talked family. Remember?"

"Yeah. But you've got me puzzled now. Who's this Mask? I seem to remember your mentioning him before. It's really Sharu Garrul, isn't it?"

I shook my head.

"When I brought your mother out of the citadel she left the company of a similarly stricken old guy with RINALDO carved on his leg. I was trading spells with Mask at the time."

"Most strange," Luke said. "Then he's a usurper. And he's the one slipped me the acid?"

"That seems most likely."

"Then I have a score to settle with him, too—apart from what he did to my mother. How tough is Jurt?"

"Well, he's nasty. But he's kind of clumsy, too. At least, he's screwed up whenever we've fought and left a piece of himself behind."

"He could also be learning from his mistakes, you know."

"That's true. And he said something kind of cryptic today, now you mention it. He talked as if he were about to become very powerful."

"Uh-oh," Luke said. "Sounds as if this Mask is using him as a guinea pig."

"For what?"

"The Fount of Power, man. There's a steady, pulsing source of pure energy inside the citadel, you know. Inter-Shadow stuff. Comes from the four worlds jamming together there."

"I know. I've seen it in action."

"I've got a feeling that this Mask is still in the process of getting a handle on it."

"He had a pretty good grip when we met."

"Yeah, but there's more to it than plugging into a wall outlet. There are all sorts of subtleties he's probably just becoming aware of and exploring."

"Such as?"

"Bathing a person in it will, if he's properly protected, do wonders for strength, stamina, and magical abilities. That part's easy for a person with some training to learn. I've been through it myself. But old Sharu's notes were in his lab, and there was something more in them—a way of replacing part of the body with energy, really packing it in. Very dangerous. Easily fatal. But if it works you get something special, a kind of superman, a sort of living Trump."

"I've heard that term before, Luke. . . ."

"Probably," he replied. "My father undertook the process, with himself as the subject—"

"That's it!" I said. "Corwin claimed that Brand had become some sort of living Trump. Made it almost impossible to nail him."

Luke gritted his teeth.

"Sorry," I said. "But that's where I heard about it. So *that* was the secret of Brand's power. . . ."

Luke nodded.

"I get the impression this Mask thinks he knows how it was done and is getting ready to try it on your brother."

"Shit!" I observed. "That's all I need. Jurt as a magical being or a natural force—or whatever the hell. This is serious. How much do you know about the process?"

"Oh, I know most of it, in theory. I wouldn't mess with it, though. I think it takes away something of your humanity. You don't much give a shit about other people or human values afterward. I think that's part of what happened to my father."

What could I say? Maybe that part was true and maybe it wasn't. I was sure Luke wanted to believe in some external cause for his father's treachery. I knew I'd never contradict him on it, even if I learned differently. And so I laughed.

"With Jurt," I said, "there'd be no way of telling the difference."

Luke smiled. Then, "You could get dead going up against a guy like that, along with a sorcerer, on their own turf."

"What choice have I got?" I asked. "They're after me. Better to move now. Jurt hasn't had the treatment yet. Does it take long?"

"Well, there are fairly elaborate preliminaries, but the subject doesn't have to be present for some of them. It all depends on how far along Mask is with the work."

"I'd better move pretty fast then."

"I won't have you going in there alone," he said. "It could be suicide. I know the place. I also have a small force of mercs bivouacked in Shadow and ready for action on short notice. If we can get them in, they can hold off the guards, maybe even take them out."

"Will that fancy ammo work there?"

"No. We tried it when I pulled the glider attack. It'll have to be hand to hand. Body armor and machetes, maybe. I'll have to work it out."

"We could use the Pattern to get in, but the troops can't . . . and Trumps aren't reliable for that place."

"I know. I'll have to work on that, too."

"Then it would be you and me against Jurt and Mask. If I tell any of the others here, they'll try to stop me till Random gets back, and that may be too late."

He smiled. "You know, my mother would really be useful in there," he said. "She knows more about the Fount than I do."

"No!" I said. "She tried to kill me."

"Easy, man. Easy," he said. "Hear me out."

"Besides, she lost to Mask last time they met. That's why she's a coatrack."

"All the more reason for her to be wary now. Anyway, it had to be trickery, not skill. She's good. Mask must have surprised her. She'd be a real asset, Merle."

"No! She wants all of us dead!"

"Details," he explained. "After Caine, the rest of you are just symbolic enemies. Mask is a real one, who took something away from her and still has it. Given the choice, she'll go after Mask."

"And if we're successful, she'll turn on Amber afterward."

"Not at all," he said. "That's the beauty of my plan."

"I don't want to hear about it."

"Because you already know you'll agree, right? I just figured a way to solve all your problems. Give her the Keep after it's liberated, as a kind of peace offering, to forget her differences with you guys."

"Just hand her this terrible power?"

"If she were going to use it against you, she'd have done it a long time ago. She's afraid to employ it in the extreme. With Kashfa down the tubes, she'll grab at the chance to salvage something. That's where the value lies."

"You really think so?"

"Better Queen of the Keep than a coatrack in Amber."

"Damn you, Luke. You always make the stupidest things sound sort of attractive."

"It's an art," he replied. "What do you say?"

"I've got to think about it," I said.

"Better think fast, then. Jurt may be bathing in that glow right now."

"Don't pressure me, man. I said I'll think about it. This is only one of my problems. I'm going to eat dinner now and mull things over."

"Want to tell me about your other problems, too? Maybe I can work them into the package some way."

"No, damn it! I'll call you back . . . soon. Okay?"

"Okay. But I'd better be around when you snap Mom out of it, to kind of smooth things over. You *have* figured out how to break the spell, haven't you?"

"Yes."

"Glad to know that. I wasn't sure how to do it, and I can stop working on it now. I'm going to finish here and go shape up the troops," he said, eyeing the lady in the bikini who had just emerged from the pool. "Call me."

"Okay," I said, and he was gone.

Damn. Amazing. No wonder Luke kept winning those sales awards. I had to admit it was a good pitch, despite my feelings about Jasra. And Random had not ordered me to keep her a prisoner. Of course, he had not had much opportunity to tell me anything the last time we had been together. Would she really behave as Luke said, though? It made a sort of sense, but then people seldom keep company with rationality at times when they should.

I passed along the hallway and decided to use the back stair. As I made the turn, I saw that there was a figure standing near the top. It was a woman, and she was looking the other way. She had on a full-length red-and-yellow gown. Her hair was very dark and she had lovely shoulders. . . .

She turned when she heard my tread, and I saw that it was Nayda. She studied my face.

"Lord Merlin," she said, "can you tell me where my sister is? I understand she went off with you earlier."

"She was admiring some art, and then she had a little errand she wanted to run afterward," I replied. "I'm not sure exactly where she was going, but she gave the impression she'd be back pretty soon."

"All right," she said. "It's just that it's getting near to dinnertime, and we'd expected her to be joining us. Did she enjoy her afternoon?"

"I believe she did," I said.

"She's been a bit moody recently. We were hoping this trip would cheer her up. She was looking forward to it quite a bit."

"She seemed pretty cheerful when I left her," I admitted.

"Oh, where was that?"

"Near here," I said.

"Where all did you go?"

"We had a long walk in and about town," I explained. "I showed her a bit of the palace, also."

"Then she's in the palace right now?"

"She was the last time I saw her. But she might have stepped out."

"I see," she said. "I'm sorry I didn't really get to talk to you at any length earlier. I feel as if I've known you for a long while."

"Oh?" I said. "Why is that?"

"I read through your file several times. It's kind of fascinating."

"File?"

"It's no secret that we keep files on people we're likely to encounter in our line of work. There's a file on everyone in the House of Amber, of course, even those who don't have much to do with diplomacy."

"I'd never thought about it," I said, "but it figures."

"Your early days are glossed over, of course, and your recent troubles are very confusing."

"They're confusing to me, too," I said. "You trying to update the file?"

"No, just curious. If your problems have ramifications that may involve Begma, we have an interest in them."

"How is it that you know of them at all?"

"We have very good intelligence sources. Small kingdoms often do."

I nodded.

"I won't press you on your sources, but we're not having a fire sale on classified data."

"You misunderstand me," she said. "I'm not trying to update that file either. I was trying to discover whether I might be able to offer you assistance."

"Thank you. I appreciate that," I told her. "I can't really think of any way you could help me, though."

She smiled, showing what seemed a set of perfect teeth.

"I can't be more precise without knowing more," she said. "But if you decide that you do want help—or if you just want to talk—come and see me."

"Well taken," I said. "I'll see you at dinner."

"Later, too, I hope," she said, as I passed her and turned down the hall.

What had she meant by that last bit? I wondered. Was she talking assignation? If so, her motives seemed awfully transparent. Or was she merely expressing her desire for information? I was not certain.

As I passed along the hallway in the direction of my rooms I noted an odd lighting phenomenon ahead of me: A bright white band about six or eight inches in width ran up both walls, across the ceiling, and over the floor. I slowed as I neared it, wondering whether someone had introduced a new method of illuminating the place in my absence.

As I stepped over the band on the floor, everything disappeared, except for the light itself, which resolved into a perfect circle, flipped once about me and settled on a level with my feet, myself at its center. The world appeared beyond the circle, suddenly, and it looked as if it were made of green glass formed into a dome. The surface on which I stood was reddish, irregular and moist in the pale light. It was not until a large fish swam by that I realized I might be underwater, standing on a ridge of coral.

"This is pretty as all hell," I said, "but I was trying to get to my apartment."

"Just showing off a bit," came a familiar voice which sounded eerily all about my magic circle. "Am I a god?"

"You can call yourself whatever you want," I said. "Nobody will disagree with you."

"It might be fun being a god."

"Then what does that make me?" I asked.

"That's a difficult theological question."

"Theological, my ass. I'm a computer engineer, and you know I built you, Ghost."

A sound like a sigh filled my submarine cell.

"It's hard to get away from one's roots."

"Why try? What's wrong with roots? All of the best plants have them."

"Pretty bloom above, mire and muck below."

"In your case it's metal and an interesting cryogenic setup—and quite a few other things—all of them very clean."

"Maybe it's mire and muck that I need, then."

"You feeling all right, Ghost?"

"I'm still trying to find myself."

"Everyone goes through phases like that. It'll pass."

"Really?"

"Really."

"When? How? Why?"

"It would be cheating to tell. Besides, it's different for everyone."

A whole school of fish swam by—little black-and-red-striped guys.

"I can't quite swing the omniscience business . . ." Ghost said after a time.

"That's okay. Who needs it?" I said.

". . . And I'm still working on omnipotence."

"That one's hard, too," I agreed.

"You're very understanding, Dad."

"I try. You got any special problems?"

"You mean, apart from the existential?"

"Yeah."

"No. I brought you here to warn you about a fellow named Mandor. He's—"

"He's my brother," I said.

There was silence.

Then, "That would make him my uncle, wouldn't it?"

"I guess so."

"How about the lady with him? She—"

"Fiona's my aunt."

"My great-aunt. Oh, my!"

"What's wrong?"

"It's bad form to speak ill of relatives, isn't it?"

"Not in Amber," I said. "In Amber we do it all the time."

The circle of light flipped again. We were back in the hallway.

"Now that we're in Amber," he said, "I want to speak ill of them. I wouldn't trust them if I were you. I think they're a little crazy. Also insulting and mendacious."

I laughed. "You're becoming a true Amberite."

"I am?"

"Yes. That's the way we are. Nothing to worry about. What came down between you, anyhow?"

"I'd rather work it out on my own, if you don't mind."

"Whatever you think is best."

"I don't really need to warn you about them?"

"No."

"Okay. That was my main concern. I guess I'll go and try the mire and muck bit now—"

"Wait!"

"What?"

"You seem pretty good at transporting things through Shadow these days."

"I seem to be improving, yes."

"What about a small band of warriors and their leader?"

"I think I could manage that."

"And me."

"Of course. Where are they and where do you want to go?"

I fished in my pocket, found Luke's Trump, held it up before me.

"But . . . He's the one you warned me not to trust," Ghost said.

"It's okay now," I told him. "Just for this matter. Nothing else, though. Things have changed a bit."

"I don't understand. But if you say so."

"Can you run him down and set things up?"

"I should be able to. Where do you want to go?"

"Do you know the Keep of the Four Worlds?"

"Yes. But that's a dangerous place, Dad. Very tricky coming and going. And that's where the red-haired lady tried to lay a power lock on me."

"Jasra."

"I never knew her name."

"She's Luke's mother," I explained, waving his Trump.

"Bad blood," Ghost stated. "Maybe we shouldn't have anything to do with either of them."

"She might be coming with us," I said.

"Oh, no. That's a dangerous lady. You don't want her along. Especially not in a place where she's strong. She might try to grab me again. She might succeed."

"She'll be too occupied with other matters," I said, "and I may need her. So start thinking of her as part of the package."

"Are you sure you know what you're doing?"

"I'm afraid so."

"When do you want to go there?"

"That depends in part on when Luke's troops will be ready. Why don't you go and find out?"

"All right. But I still think you might be making a mistake, going into that place with those people."

"I need someone who can help, and the die is damned well cast," I said. Ghost coalesced to a point and winked out.

I drew a deep breath, changed my mind about sighing, and moved on toward my nearest door, which was not that much farther up the hall. As I was reaching for it I felt the movement of a Trump contact. Coral?

I opened myself to it. Mandor appeared before me again.

"Are you all right?" he asked immediately. "We were cut off in such an odd fashion."

"I'm fine," I told him. "We were cut off in a once-in-a-lifetime fashion. Not to worry."

"You seem a trifle agitated."

"That's because it's an awfully long walk from downstairs to upstairs with all the powers of the universe converging to slow me."

"I don't understand."

"It's been a rough day," I said. "See you later."

"I did want to talk with you some more, about those storms and the new Pattern and—"

"Later," I said. "I'm waiting on an incoming call."

"Sorry. No rush. I'll check back."

He broke the contact and I reached for the latch. I wondered whether it would solve everybody's problems if I could turn Ghost into an answering service.

SEVEN

I hung my cloak on Jasra and my weapons belt on the bedpost. I cleaned my boots, washed my hands and face, hunted up a fancy ivory shirt—all ruffled, brocaded, frogged—and put it on, along with a pair of gray trousers. Then I brushed off my deep purple jacket, the one on which I'd once laid a spell to make the wearer seem a little more charming, witty, and trustworthy than is actually the case. It seemed a good occasion for getting some use out of it.

As I was brushing my hair there came a knock on the door.

"Just a minute," I called.

I finished up—which left me ready to go and also, probably, running late—then went to the door, unbarred it, and opened it.

Bill Roth stood there in browns and reds, looking like an aging condottiere.

"Bill!" I said, clasping his hand, arm, and shoulder and leading him in.

"Good to see you. I'm just back from some troubles and about to take off after more. I didn't know whether you were here in the palace now or what. I was going to look you up again as soon as things slowed a bit."

He smiled and punched my shoulder lightly.

"I'll be at dinner," he replied, "and Hendon said you'd be there, too. I thought I'd come up and walk over with you, though, since those Begman people will be there."

"Oh? You got some news?"

"Yes. Any fresh word on Luke?"

"I was just talking to him. He says the vendetta's off."

"Any chance of his wanting to justify himself at that hearing you asked me about?"

"Not from the way he sounded."

"Too bad. I've been doing a lot of research, and there are some good precendents for the vendetta defense—like, there was your uncle Osric, who took on the whole House of Karm over the death of a relative on his mother's side. Oberon was particularly friendly with Karm in those days, too, and Osric offed three of them. Oberon acquitted him at a hearing, though, basing his decision on earlier cases, and he even went further by stating a kind of general rule—"

"Oberon also sent him off to the front lines in a particularly nasty war," I interrupted, "from which he did not return."

"I wasn't aware of that part," Bill said, "but he did come off well in court."

"I'll have to mention it to Luke," I said.

"Which part?" he asked.

"Both," I answered.

"That wasn't the main thing I came to tell you," he went on. "There's something going on at a military level."

"What are you talking about?"

"It's even easier to show you," he explained. "It should only take a minute."

"Okay. Let's go," I agreed, and I followed him out into the hall.

He led the way down the back stair and turned left at its foot. We moved on past the kitchen and followed another hallway which turned off toward the rear. As we did, I heard some rattling sounds from up ahead. I glanced at Bill, who nodded.

"That's what I heard earlier," he told me, "when I was passing by. That's why I took a walk up this way. Everything around here makes me curious."

I nodded, understanding the feeling. Especially when I knew that the sounds were coming from the main armory.

Benedict stood in the midst of activity, peering at his thumbnail through a rifle barrel. He looked up immediately and our eyes met. Perhaps a dozen men moved about him, carrying weapons, cleaning weapons, stacking weapons.

"I thought you were in Kashfa," I said.

"Was," he replied.

I gave him a chance to continue, but nothing was forthcoming. Benedict has never been noted for loquacity.

"Looks like you're getting ready for something close to home," I remarked, knowing that gunpowder was useless here and that the special ammo we had only worked in the area of Amber and certain adjacent kingdoms.

"Always best to be safe," he said.

"Would you care to elaborate on that?" I asked.

"Not now," he answered, a reply twice as long as I'd anticipated and holding out hope of future enlightenment.

"Should we all be digging in?" I asked. "Fortifying the town? Arming ourselves? Raising—"

"It won't come to that," he said. "Just go on about your business."

"But—"

He turned away. I'd a feeling the conversation was over. I was sure of it when he ignored my next several questions. I shrugged and turned back to Bill.

"Let's go eat," I said.

As we walked back up the hall, Bill said softly, "Any idea what it means?"

"Dalt's in the neighborhood," I told him.

"Benedict was in Begma with Random. Dalt could be causing trouble there."

"I've a feeling he's nearer."

"If Dalt were to capture Random. . . ."

"Impossible," I said, feeling a slight chill at the idea. "Random can trump back here anytime he wants. No. When I talked about defending Amber, and Benedict said, 'It won't come to that,' I got the impression he was talking about something close at hand. Something he feels he can control."

"I see what you mean," he agreed. "But then he told you not to bother fortifying."

"If Benedict feels we don't need to fortify, then we don't need to fortify."

"Waltz and drink champagne while the cannons boom?"

"If Benedict says it's okay."

"You really trust that guy. What would you do without him?"

"Be more nervous," I said.

He shook his head. "Excuse me," he said. "I'm not used to being acquainted with legends."

"You don't believe me?"

"I shouldn't believe you, but I do believe you. That's the trouble." He was silent as we turned the corner and headed back toward the stair. Then he added, "It was that way whenever I was around your father, too."

"Bill," I said, as we began to climb. "You knew my dad back before he regained his memory, when he was just plain old Carl Corey. Maybe I've been going about this thing wrong. Is there anything you can recall about that phase of his life which might explain where he is now?"

He halted a moment and looked at me.

"Don't think I haven't thought about that angle, Merle. Many a time I've wondered whether he might have been involved in something as Corey that he'd have felt obliged to follow through on once his business here was finished. But he was a very secretive man, even in that incarnation. Paradoxical, too. He'd done a lot of hitches in a lot of different varieties of military, which seems logical enough. But he sometimes wrote music, which goes against that hard-ass image."

"He'd lived a long time. He'd learned a lot, felt a lot."

"Exactly, and that's what makes it hard to guess what he might have been involved in. Once or twice when he'd had a few drinks he'd mention people in the arts and sciences I'd never have guessed him to be acquainted with. He was never just plain Carl Corey. He had a few centuries' worth of Earth memory when I knew him. That makes for a character too complex to be easily predictable. I just don't know what he might have gone back to—if he went back."

We continued on up the stairway. Why did I feel that Bill knew more than he was telling me?

I heard music as we neared the dining room, and when we entered, Llewella gave me a nasty look. I saw that food was being kept warm at a serving table off against the far wall, and no one was seated yet. People stood about talking, drinks in hand, and most of them glanced in our direction as we entered. Three musicians were playing, off to my right. The dining table was to my left, near the big window in the south wall, providing a glorious view across the town below. It was still snowing lightly, casting a spectral veil over the entire bright prospect.

Llewella approached quickly.

"You've kept everybody waiting," she whispered. "Where's the girl?"

"Coral?"

"Who else?"

"I'm not sure where she's gotten off to," I said. "We parted company a couple of hours ago."

"Well, is she coming or isn't she?"

"I'm not sure."

"We can't keep things waiting any longer," she said. "And now the seating arrangement's screwed. What did you do, wear her out?"

"Llewella. . . ."

She muttered something I didn't understand in some lisping Rebman dialect. Just as well, probably. She turned away then and moved off toward Vialle.

"You in a heap of trouble, boy," Bill commented at my side. "Let's hit the bar while she's reassigning places."

But the wine steward was already approaching with a couple of drinks on a tray.

"Bayle's Best," he observed as we took them.

I sipped and saw that he was right, which heartened me a bit.

"I don't recognize all of these people," Bill said. "Who's that fellow with the red sash, over by Vialle?"

"That's Orkuz, the Begman prime minister," I told him, "and the rather attractive lady in the yellow-and-red dress who's talking to Martin is his daughter Nayda. Coral—the one I just got chewed out about—is her sister."

"Uh-huh. And who's the husky blond lady batting her eyes at Gérard?"

"I don't know," I said. "And I don't know that lady and the guy over to the right of Orkuz either."

We drifted inward, and Gérard, looking perhaps a trifle uncomfortable in layers of ruffled finery, introduced us to the lady he was with as Dretha Gannell, assistant to the Begman ambassador. The ambassador, it turned out, was the tall lady standing near Orkuz—and her name, I gathered, was Ferla Quist. The fellow with her was her secretary, whose name sounded something like Cade. While we were looking in that direction, Gérard tried slipping off and leaving us with Ferla. But she caught his sleeve and asked him something about the fleet. I smiled and nodded and moved away. Bill came along.

"Goodness! Martin's changed!" he announced suddenly. "He looks like a one-man rock video. I almost didn't recognize him. Just last week—"

"It's been over a year," I said, "for him. He's been off finding himself on some street scene."

"I wonder if he's finished?"

"Didn't get a chance to ask him that," I replied, but a peculiar thought occurred to me. I shelved it.

The music died just then, and Llewella cleared her throat and indicated Hendon, who announced the new seating arrangement. I was at the foot of the table, and I learned later that Coral was to have been seated to my left and Cade to my right. I also learned later that Llewella had tried to get hold of Flora at the last minute, to sit in Coral's place, but Flora wasn't taking any calls.

As it was, Vialle, at the head, had Llewella seated to her right and Orkuz to her left, with Gérard, Dretha, and Bill below Llewella, and Ferla, Martin, Cade, and Nayda below Orkuz. I found myself escorting Nayda to the table and seating her to my right, while Bill settled himself at my left.

"Fuss, fuss, fuss," Bill muttered softly, and I nodded, then introduced him to Nayda as counsel to the House of Amber. She looked impressed and asked him about his work. He proceeded to charm her with a story about once having represented the interests of a dog in an estate settlement, which had nothing to do with Amber but was a good story. Got her to laughing a bit, and also Cade, who was listening in.

The first course was served and the musicians began playing again, softly, which shortened the distance our voices carried and reduced conversation to a more intimate level. At this, Bill signaled he had something he wanted to tell me, but Nayda had beaten him by a second or two and I was already listening to her.

"About Coral," she said softly. "Are you sure she's all right? She wasn't feeling ill when you parted—or anything like that—was she?"

"No," I answered. "She seemed healthy enough."

"Strange," she said. "I had the impression she was looking forward to things like this dinner."

"She's obviously taking longer than she'd intended in whatever she's about," I observed.

"What exactly was she about?" Nayda asked. "Where did you part?"

"Here in the palace," I replied. "I was showing her around. She wanted to spend more time with certain features of the place than I could spare. So I came on ahead."

"I don't think she could have forgotten dinner."

"I think she got caught up by the power of an artistic piece."

"So she's definitely on the premises?"

"Now, that's hard to say. As I said before, a person can always step out."

"You mean you're not sure exactly where she is?"

I nodded.

"I'm not certain where she is at this moment," I said. "She could well be back in her room changing her clothes."

"I'll check after dinner," she said, "if she hasn't shown up by then. If that should be the case, will you help me find her?"

"I was planning on looking for her anyway," I answered, "if she doesn't put in an appearance soon."

She nodded and continued eating. Very awkward. Beyond the fact that I didn't want to distress her, I couldn't very well tell her what had happened without its becoming apparent that her sister was indeed an illegitimate daughter of Oberon. At a time such as this, when I had been cautioned about saying anything that might strain relations between Amber and Begma, I was not about to confirm to the daughter of the Begman prime minister the rumor that her mother had had an affair with the late king of Amber. Maybe it was an open secret back in Begma and nobody gave a damn. But maybe it wasn't. I didn't want to disturb Random for advice, partly because he might be extremely occupied in Kashfa just now, but mainly because he might also start asking me about my own immediate plans and problems, and I would not lie to him. That could get me into too much trouble. Such a conversation might well also result in his forbidding my attack on the Keep. The only other person I could tell about Coral and get some sort of official response from, as to how far I might go in informing her family, was Vialle. Unfortunately, Vialle was completely occupied as hostess at the moment.

I sighed and returned to my dinner.

Bill caught my attention and leaned a little in my direction. I leaned a little, too.

"Yes?" I said.

"There were some things I wanted to tell you," he began. "I was hoping for some leisure, some quiet, and some privacy, though."

I chuckled.

"Exactly," he continued. "I believe this is the best we're going to get for a time. Fortunately, voices don't seem to be carrying if one keeps them down. I couldn't make out what you and Nayda were talking about. So it's probably okay, so long as the musicians keep playing."

I nodded, took a few more bites.

"Thing is, the Begmans shouldn't hear about it, on the one hand. But on the other, I feel that perhaps you ought to know, because of your involvement with Luke and Jasra. So what's your schedule? I'd rather tell you later, but if you're going to be tied up, I can give you the gist of it now."

I glanced at Nayda and Cade. They seemed totally occupied with their food, and I didn't think they could overhear us. Unfortunately, I didn't have any sort of sheltering spells hung.

"Go ahead," I whispered from behind my wine glass.

"First," he said, "Random sent me a whole slew of papers to go over. They're the draft of an agreement whereby Amber will grant Kashfa privileged trade status, the same as Begma. So they'll definitely be coming into the Golden Circle."

"I see," I said. "That doesn't come as a complete surprise. But it's good to know for sure what's going on."

He nodded.

"There's a lot more to it, though," he said.

Just then the musicians stopped playing and I could hear voices from all around the table again. I glanced off to the right and saw that a steward had just taken the players a food tray and some wine. They were setting their instruments aside and taking a break. They had probably been playing for some time before I'd arrived and were doubtless due a rest.

Bill chuckled.

"Later," he said.

"Right."

There followed a funny little fruit dish with an amazing sauce. As I spooned it away, Nayda caught my attention with a gesture and I leaned toward her again.

"So what about tonight?" she whispered.

"What do you mean? I said I'd look for her if she doesn't show up."

She shook her head. "I wasn't referring to that," she said. "I meant later. Will you have time to stop by and talk?"

"About what?"

"According to your file you've been in a bit of trouble recently, with someone trying to get you."

I began wondering about that damned file. But, "It's out of date," I said. "Whatever's in there has already been cleared up."

"Really? Then nobody's after you just now?"

"I wouldn't say that," I replied. "The cast of characters keeps changing."

"So somebody still has you marked?"

I studied her face.

"You're a nice lady, Nayda," I said, "but I've got to ask, What is it to you? Everybody has problems. I just have more than usual at the moment. I'll work them out."

"Or die trying?"

"Maybe. I hope not. But what's your interest?"

She glanced at Cade, who seemed busy with his food.

"It is possible that I could help you."

"In what fashion?"

She smiled.

"A process of elimination," she stated.

"Oh? That refers to a person or persons?"

"Indeed."

"You have some special means of going about this sort of business?"

She continued to smile.

"Yes, it's good for removing problems caused by people," she continued. "All I'll need are their names and locations."

"Some sort of secret weapon?"

She glanced at Cade again, since I had raised my voice a bit.

"You might call it that," she answered.

"An interesting proposal," I said. "But you still haven't answered my first question."

"Refresh my memory."

We were interrupted by the wine steward, who came around topping off goblets, and then by another toast. The first had been to Vialle, led by Llewella. This one was proposed by Orkuz, to "the ancient alliance between Amber and Begma." I drank to that, and I heard Bill mutter, "It's going to get a bit more strained."

"The alliance?" I said.

"Yep."

I glanced at Nayda, who was staring at me, clearly expecting a resumption of our sotto voces. Bill noted this, too, and turned away. Just then Cade began talking to Nayda, however, so I finished what was on my plate and took a sip of wine while I waited. In a little while the plate was whisked away, to be replaced shortly by another.

I glanced at Bill who glanced at Nayda and Cade, then said, "Wait for the music."

I nodded. In a sudden moment of silence I overheard Dretha say, "Is it true that King Oberon's ghost is sometimes seen?" Gérard grunted something that sounded like an affirmative just as they were drowned out again. My mind being a lot fuller than my stomach, I kept eating. Cade, trying to be diplomatic or just conversational, turned my way a little later, addressed me and asked my views on the Eregnor situation. He jerked suddenly then and looked at Nayda. I'd a strong feeling she'd just kicked him under the table, which was fine with me because I didn't know what the hell the Eregnor situation was. I muttered something about there being things to be said for both sides of most matters, which seemed diplomatic enough for anything. If it were something barbed, I supposed I could have countered with an innocent-sounding observation about the Begman party's early arrival, but Eregnor might actually be some tedious conversation piece that Nayda didn't want to get into because it would cut off our own discussion. Also, I'd a feeling that Llewella might suddenly materialize and kick me under the table.

A thought hit suddenly then. Sometimes I'm a little slow. Obviously, they had known Random wasn't here, and from what I already knew and from what Bill had just said, they weren't too happy with whatever Random was about in the neighboring kingdom. Their early arrival seemed intended to embarrass us in some fashion. Did that mean that whatever Nayda was offering me was part of some scheme that fitted in with their general diplomatic strategy on this matter? If so, why me? I was a very poor choice, in that I had no say whatsoever concerning Amber's foreign policy. Were they aware of this? They must be, if their intelligence service were as good as Nayda had indicated. I was baffled, and I was half-tempted to ask Bill his views on the Eregnor situation. But then, he might have kicked me under the table.

The musicians, having finished snacking, resumed the entertainment with "Greensleeves," and Nayda and Bill both leaned toward me simultaneously, then glanced up, their gazes meeting. Both smiled.

"Ladies first," Bill said loudly.

She nodded to him.

Then, "Have a chance to think about my offer?" she asked me.

"Some," I said, "but I had a question. Remember?"

"What was it?"

"It's kind of you to want to do me a favor," I said, "but at times such as this, one must be excused for checking the price tag."

"What if I were to say that your good will would be sufficient?"

"What if I were to say that my good will isn't worth much at the policy level here?"

She shrugged. "Small price for a small return. I already knew that. But you're related to everybody in this place. Nothing may ever happen, but it's conceivable that someone might ask your opinion of us. I'd like you to know you have friends in Begma and to feel kindly disposed toward us if that occurred."

I studied her very serious expression. There was more to it than that, and we both knew it. Only I didn't know what might be on the horizon, and she obviously did.

I reached out and stroked her cheek once with the back of my hand.

"I am expected to say something nice about you folks if someone should ask me, that's all, and for this you will go out and kill someone for me if I just supply the particulars. Right?"

"In a word, yes," she replied.

"It makes me wonder why you think you can manage an assassination better than we could. We're old hands at it."

"We have, as you put it, a secret weapon," she said. "But I was thinking that this is a personal matter for you, not a state matter—and that you might not want any of the others involved. Also, I can provide a service that will not be traceable."

Bag of worms time again. Was she implying that she thought I did not trust all of the others here—or that I should not? What did she know that I didn't? Or was she just guessing, based on Amber's history of intrigue within the family? Or was she intentionally trying to stir up a generational conflict? Would that suit Begma's purpose in some fashion? Or. . . . Was she guessing that such a situation existed and offering to remove a family member for me? And if so, did she think I'd be stupid enough to get someone else to do the job? Or even to discuss such a notion and thereby give Begma a shot at sufficient evidence to have some kind of hold over me? Or. . . .

I drew back from the view. It pleased me that my thought processes were finally working properly for the company my family keeps. (Both my families, actually.) It had taken me a long while to get the hang of it. It felt good.

A simple refusal would foreclose all of the above. But, on the other hand, if I were to string her along a bit, she might prove a tantalizing source of information.

So, "Would you go after anyone I would name?" I said. "Anyone?"

She studied my face very carefully. Then, "Yes," she answered.

"You must excuse me again," I responded, "but doing it for such an intangible as my good will causes me to wonder about your good faith."

Her face reddened. Whether it was a simple blush or anger I could not be certain, because she looked away immediately. This didn't bother me, though, because I was certain it was a buyer's market.

I returned my attention to my food and was able to put away several mouthfuls before she was back again.

"Does this mean you won't be stopping by tonight?" she asked.

"I can't," I said. "I am going to be completely occupied."

"I can believe you are very busy," she said. "But does that mean we will not be able to talk at all?"

"It depends entirely on how things break," I said. "I have an awful lot going on just now, and I may be leaving town soon."

She started slightly. I was certain she considered asking me where I was going, but thought better of it.

Then, "This is awkward," she said. "Have you refused my offer?"

"Is the deal only good for this evening?" I asked.

"No, but it was my understanding you were in some peril. The sooner you move against your enemy, the sooner your sleep is untroubled."

"You feel I am in danger here in Amber?"

She hesitated a moment, then said, "No one is safe, anywhere, from an enemy of sufficient determination and skill."

"Do you feel the threat to be a local one?" I inquired.

"I asked you to name the party," she stated. "You are in the best position to know."

I drew back immediately. It was too simple an entrapment, and obviously she'd already smelled it.

"You've given me much to think about," I answered, and I returned to my food.

After a time, I saw that Bill was looking at me as if he wanted to say something. I gave him a minuscule shake of my head, which he seemed to understand.

"Breakfast, then?" I heard her say. "This trip you spoke of could represent a time of vulnerability. It would be good to settle this before you depart."

"Nayda," I said, as soon as I had swallowed, "I would like to be clear on the matter of my benefactors. If I were to discuss this with your father—"

"No!" she interrupted. "He knows nothing about it!"

"Thank you. You must admit my curiosity as to the level at which this plan originates."

"There is no need to look any further," she stated. "It is entirely my idea."

"Some of your earlier statements cause me to infer that you have special connections within the Begman intelligence community."

"No," she said, "only the ordinary ones. The offer is my own."

"But someone would have to . . . effectuate this design."

"That is the province of the secret weapon."

"I would have to know more about it."

"I've offered you a service and I've promised you total discretion. I will go no further as to means."

"If this idea is wholly your own, it would seem that you stand to benefit from it personally. How? What's in it for you?"

She looked away. She was silent for a long time.

"Your file," she said at last. "It was . . . fascinating reading it. You're one of the few people here close to my own age, and you've led such an interesting life. You can't imagine how dull most of the things I have to read are— agricultural reports, trade figures, appropriations studies. I have no social life whatsoever. I am always on call. Every party I attend is really a state function in one form or another. I read your file over and over and I wondered about you. I . . . I have something of a crush on you. I know it sounds silly, but it's true. When I saw some of the recent reports and realized that you might be in great danger, I decided I would help you if I could. I have access to all sorts of state secrets. One of them would provide me with the means of helping you. Using it would benefit you without damaging Begma, but it would be disloyal of me to discuss it further. I've always wanted to meet you, and I was very jealous of my sister when you took her out today. And I still wish you'd stop by later."

I stared at her. Then I raised my wineglass to her and took a drink.

"You are . . . amazing," I said. I couldn't think of anything else to say. It was either an on-the-spot fabrication or it was true. If it were true, it was somewhat pathetic; if not, I thought it a rather clever bit of quick thinking, calculated to hit me in that wonderfully vulnerable place, the ego. She deserved either my sympathy or my wariest admiration. So I added, "I'd like to meet the person who wrote the reports. There may be a great creative talent going to waste in a government office."

She smiled, raised her own glass and touched it to mine.

"Think about it," she said.

"I can honestly say I won't forget you," I told her.

We both returned to our food, and I spent the next five minutes or so catching up. Bill decently allowed me to do this. Also, I think, he was waiting to be certain that my conversation with Nayda was finally concluded.

At last he winked at me.

"Got a minute?" he asked.

"Afraid so," I said.

"I won't even ask whether it was business or pleasure going on on the other side."

"It was a pleasure," I said, "but a strange business. Don't ask or I'll miss dessert."

"I'll summarize," he said. "The coronation in Kashfa will take place tomorrow."

"Not wasting any time, are we?"

"No. The gentleman who will be taking the throne is Arkans, Duke of Shadburne. He's been in and out of various Kashfan governments in fairly responsible positions any number of times over the years. He actually knows how things work, and he's distantly related to one of the earlier monarchs. Didn't get along well with Jasra's crowd and pretty much stayed at his country place the whole time she was in power. He didn't bother her and she didn't bother him."

"Sounds reasonable."

"In fact, he actually shared her sentiments on the Eregnor situation, as the Begmans are well aware—"

"Just what," I asked, "is the Eregnor situation?"

"It's their Alsace-Lorraine," he said, "a large, rich area between Kashfa and Begma. It has changed hands back and forth so many times over the centuries that both countries make reasonable-sounding claims to it. Even the inhabitants of the area aren't all that firm on the matter. They have relatives in both directions. I'm not even sure they care which side claims them, so long as their taxes don't go up. I think Begma's claim might be a little stronger, but I could argue the case either way."

"And Kashfa holds it now, and Arkans says they'll damn well keep it."

"Right. Which is the same thing Jasra said. The interim ruler, however—Jaston was his name, military man—was actually willing to discuss its status with the Begmans, before his unfortunate fall from the balcony. I think he wanted to repair the treasury and was considering ceding the area in return for the settlement of some ancient war damage claims. Things were actually well along and headed in that direction."

"And. . . ?" I said.

"In the papers I got from Random, Amber specifically recognizes Kashfa as including the area of Eregnor. Arkans had insisted that go into the treaty. Usually—from everything I've been able to find in the archives—Amber avoids getting involved in touchy situations like this between allies. Oberon seldom went looking for trouble. But Random seems to be in a hurry, and he let this guy drive a hard bargain."

"He's overreacting," I said, "not that I blame him. He remembers Brand too well."

Bill nodded.

"I'm just the hired help," he said. "I don't want to have an opinion."

"Well, anything else I should know about Arkans?"

"Oh, there are lots of other things the Begmans don't like about him, but that's the big one—right when they thought they were making some headway on an issue that's been a national pastime for generations. They've even gone to war over the matter in the past. Don't doubt that that's why they came rushing to town. Govern yourself accordingly."

He raised his goblet and took a drink.

A little later Vialle said something to Llewella, rose to her feet, and announced that she had to see to something, that she'd be right back. Llewella started to get up also, but Vialle put a hand on her shoulder, whispered something, and departed.

"Wonder what that could be?" Bill said.

"Don't know," I answered.

He smiled.

"Shall we speculate?"

"My mind's on cruise control," I told him.

Nayda gave me a long stare. I met it and shrugged.

Another little while, and plates were cleared and more were coming. Whatever it was looked good. Before I could find out for certain, though, a member of the general house staff entered and approached.

"Lord Merlin," she said, "the queen would like to see you."

I was on my feet immediately.

"Where is she?"

"I'll take you to her."

I excused myself from my companions, borrowing the line that I'd be right back, wondering if it were true. I followed her out and around the corner to a small sitting room, where she left me with Vialle, who was seated in an uncomfortable-looking high-backed chair of dark wood and leather, held together with cast iron studs. If she'd wanted muscle, she'd have sent for Gérard. If she'd wanted a mind full of history and political connivance, Llewella would be here. So I was guessing it involved magic, since I was the authority in residence.

But I was wrong.

"I'd like to speak to you," she said, "concerning a small state of war in which we seem about to become engaged."

EIGHT

After a pleasant time with a pretty lady, a series of stimulating hallway conversations, and a relaxing dinner with family and friends, it seemed almost fitting that it be time for something different and distracting. The idea of a small war seemed, at least, better than a big one, though I did not say that to Vialle. A moment's careful thought, and I shaped the query:

"What's going on?"

"Dalt's men are dug in near the western edge of Arden," she said. "Julian's are strung out facing them. Benedict has taken Julian additional men and weapons. He says he can execute a flanking movement that will take Dalt's line apart. But I told him not to."

"I don't understand. Why not?"

"Men will die," she said.

"That's the way it is in war. Sometimes you have no choice."

"But we do have a choice, of sorts," she said, "one that I don't understand. And I do want to understand it before I give an order that will result in numerous deaths."

"What is the choice?" I asked.

"I came here to respond to a Trump message from Julian," she said. "He had just spoken with Dalt under a flag of truce. Dalt told him that his objective was not, at this time, the destruction of Amber. He pointed out that he could conduct an expensive attack, though, in terms of our manpower and equipment. He said he'd rather save himself and us the expense, however. What he really wants is for us to turn two prisoners over to him—Rinaldo and Jasra."

"Huh?" I said. "Even if we wanted to, we can't give him Luke. He's not here."

"That is what Julian told him. He seemed very surprised. For some reason, he believed we had Rinaldo in custody."

"Well, we're not obliged to provide the man with an education. I gather he's been something of a pain for years. I think Benedict has the right answer for him."

"I did not call you in for advice," she said.

"Sorry," I told her. "It's just that I don't like seeing someone trying to pull a stunt like this and actually believing he has a chance of success."

"He has no chance of success," Vialle stated. "But if we kill him now, we learn nothing. I would like to find out what is behind this."

"Have Benedict bring him in. I have spells that will open him up."

She shook her head.

"Too risky," she explained. "Once bullets start flying, there's the chance one might find him. Then we lose even though we win."

"I don't understand what it is that you want of me."

"He asked Julian to get in touch with us and relay his demand. He's promised to hold the truce until we give him some sort of official answer. Julian says he has the impression that Dalt would settle for either one of them."

"I don't want to give him Jasra either."

"Neither do I. What I do want very badly is to know what is going on. There would be small point in releasing Jasra and asking her, since this is a recent development. I want to know whether you have means of getting in touch with Rinaldo. I want to talk to him."

"Well, uh . . . yes," I said. "I have a Trump for him."

"Use it."

I got it out. I regarded it. I moved my mind into that special area of alertness and calling. The picture changed, came alive. . . .

It was twilight, and Luke stood near a campfire. He had on his green outfit, a light brown cloak about his shoulders clasped with that Phoenix pin.

"Merle," he said. "I can move the troops pretty fast. When do you want to hit the place and—"

"Put it on hold," I interrupted. "This is something different."

"What?"

"Dalt's at the gates, and Vialle wants to talk to you before we take him apart."

"Dalt? There? Amber?"

"Yes, yes, and yes. He says he'll go and play someplace else if we give him the two things he wants most in the world: you and your mother."

"That's crazy."

"Yeah. We think so, too. Will you talk to the queen about it?"

"Sure. Bring me thr—" He hesitated and looked into my eyes.

I smiled.

He extended his hand. I reached forward and took it. Suddenly, he was there. He looked about, saw Vialle. Immediately, he unclasped his sword belt and passed it to me. He approached her, dropped to his right knee, and lowered his head.

"Your Majesty," he said. "I've come."

She reached forward and touched him.

"Raise your head," she said.

He did, and her sensitive fingers slid over the planes and arches of his face.

"Strength," she said, "and sorrow. . . . So you're Rinaldo. You've brought us some grief."

"It works both ways, Your Majesty."

"Yes, of course," she replied. "Wrongs done and wrongs avenged have a way of spilling over on the innocent. How far will it go this time?"

"This thing with Dalt?" he asked.

"No. This thing with you."

"Oh," he said. "It's over. I've done with it. No more bombs or ambushes. I've already told Merlin that."

"You've known him for several years?"

"Yes."

"You've become friends?"

"He's one of the reasons I'm calling it off."

"You must trust him, to come here. I respect that," she said. "Take this."

She removed a ring she wore upon her right forefinger. The band was of gold, the stone a milky green; the prongs of its setting caught it in a fashion to suggest some mantic spider guarding dreamland treasures against the daybreak world.

"Your Majesty. . . ."

"Wear it," she said.

"I will," he replied, slipping it upon the little finger of his left hand. "Thank you."

"Rise. I want you to know exactly what has occurred."

He got to his feet, and she began telling him what she had told me, concerning Dalt's arrival, his forces' disposition, his demands, while I stood stunned at the implications of what she had done. She had just placed Luke under her protection. Everyone in Amber knew that ring. I wondered what Random would think. I realized then that there would not be a hearing. Poor Bill. I believe he was really looking forward to arguing Luke's case.

"Yes, I know Dalt," I heard him saying. "Once we shared . . . certain goals. But he's changed. He tried to kill me the last time we met. I'm not sure why. At first I thought the wizard of the Keep had taken control of him."

"And now?"

"Now, I just don't understand. I've a feeling he's on a leash, but I don't know who holds it."

"Why not the wizard?"

"It makes no sense to go to these lengths to claim me when he had me and let me go just a few days ago. He could simply have left me in my cell."

"True," she replied. "What is this wizard's name?"

"Mask," he answered. "Merlin knows more about him than I do."

"Merlin," she said. "Who is this Mask?"

"He's the wizard who took the Keep of the Four Worlds away from Jasra," I explained, "who, in turn, had taken it away from Sharu Garrul, who is now also a coatrack. Mask wears a blue mask and seems to draw power from a strange fountain in the citadel there. Doesn't seem to like me much either. That's about all I can tell you."

I'd omitted mentioning my plan to head that way for a showdown soon, because of Jurt's involvement, for the same reason I hadn't wanted Random to know about it. I was certain Luke had tossed me the question because he wasn't sure how far I wanted it taken.

"That doesn't really tell us much," she decided, "as to Dalt's involvement."

"There may not be a connection," I said. "I gather Dalt is a mercenary, and their relationship could have been a one-time thing. He could either be working for someone else now or pulling something on his own."

"I can't see why anybody wants us badly enough to go to such dramatic lengths," Luke said. "But I've a score to settle with that guy, and I'm going to combine business with pleasure."

"What do you mean?" she asked.

"I assume there's a way to get down there in a hurry," he said.

"One could always trump through to Julian," I said, "but what have you got in mind, Luke?"

"I want to talk to Dalt."

"It's too dangerous," she said, "since you're what he wants."

Luke grinned. "It could be a bit dangerous for Dalt, too," he replied.

"Wait a minute," I said. "If you've got more in mind than just talking, you could blow this truce. Vialle's trying to avoid a conflict here."

"There won't be any conflict," Luke said. "Look, I've known Dalt since we were kids, and I think he's bluffing. He does that sometimes. He hasn't got the kind of force to risk another attack on Amber. Your guys would slaughter him. If he wants Mom or me, I think he'd be willing to tell me why, and that's what we want to find out, isn't it?"

"Well, yes," I said. "But—"

"Let me go," he said to Vialle, "and I'll find a way to get him off your back. I promise."

"You tempt me," she told him. "But I don't like your talk of settling accounts with him at this time. As Merlin said, I want to avoid this conflict—for more than one reason."

"I promise not to let it go that far," he stated. "I can read the dice. I'm good at playing things by ear. I'm willing to postpone gratification."

"Merlin . . . ?" she said.

"He's right, in that," I answered. "He's the deadliest salesman in the southwest."

"I'm afraid I don't understand the concept."

"It's a highly specialized art, back on that Shadow Earth we both inhabited. In fact, he's using it on you right now."

"Do you think he can do what he says?"

"I think he's very good at getting what he wants."

"Exactly," Luke observed. "And since we both want the same thing here, I think the future looks bright for all of us."

"I see what you mean," she said, "How much danger would this put you near, Rinaldo?"

"I'll be as safe as I am right here in Amber," he said.

She smiled.

"All right, I'll speak to Julian," she agreed, "and you can go to him and see what you can learn from Dalt."

"A moment," I requested. "It's been snowing on and off, and that's a pretty nasty wind out there. Luke just came in from a more temperate clime, and it's a pretty flimsy-looking cloak he has on. Let me get him something warmer. I've a nice heavy one he can take, if he finds it suitable."

"Go ahead," she said.

"We'll be right back."

She pursed her lips, then nodded.

I passed Luke his weapons belt and he buckled it on. I knew that she knew I just wanted to talk to him alone for a few minutes. And she was certainly aware that I knew it. And we both knew she trusted me, which brightens my existence, as well as complicating it.

As we passed along the hallway toward my rooms, I'd intended to fill Luke in concerning the upcoming coronation in Kashfa, as well as a few other matters. I waited, however, till we were well away from the sitting room, because Vialle has inordinately acute hearing. This, though, gave Luke a foot in the door, and he began to speak first.

"What a strange development," he said. Then, "I like her, but I've a feeling she knows more than she's telling."

"Probably true," I answered. "I guess we're all like that."

"You, too?"

"These days, yes. It's gotten that way."

"You know anything more about this situation that I should be aware of?"

I shook my head. "This is very new, and she gave you the whole story I know. Would you, perchance, know something about it that we don't?"

"Nope," he said. "It came as a surprise to me, too. But I've got to pursue it."

"I guess so."

We were nearing my stretch of corridor now, and I felt obliged to prepare him.

"We'll be to my rooms in a minute," I said, "and I just wanted you to know your mother's in there. She's safe, but you won't find her too talkative."

"I'm familiar with the results of that spell," he said. "I also recall that you said you know how to lift it. So. . . . That leads into the next topic. I've been thinking. This interlude is slowing us down a bit in our plan for going after Mask and your brother."

"Not all that much," I responded.

"We don't really know how long this is going to take me, though," he went on. "Supposing it drags out a bit? Or supposing something happens to really slow me down?"

I gave him a quick glance.

"Like, what have you got in mind?" I asked.

"I don't know. I'm just supposing. Okay? I like to plan ahead. Say we get delayed on this attack. . . ."

"All right. Say that," I said, as we neared my door.

"What I'm getting at," he continued, "is, what if we get there too late? Supposing we arrive and your brother has already undergone the ritual that turns him into hell on wheels?"

I unlocked my door, opened it, and held it for him. I did not like entertaining the possibility he had just described, because I recalled my father's stories of the times he'd encountered Brand and faced that uncanny power.

Luke stepped inside. I snapped my fingers and a number of oil lamps came to life, their flames dancing for a moment before settling to a glowing steadiness.

Jasra was there in plain sight before him, holding a number of my garments on outstretched arms. I was concerned for a moment as to what his reaction might be.

He halted, studying her, then advanced, his speculations concerning Jurt forgotten. He regarded her for perhaps ten seconds, and I found myself growing uncomfortable. Then he chuckled.

"She always liked being decorative," he said, "but to combine it with being useful was generally beyond her. You've got to hand it to Mask, even though she probably won't catch the moral of it."

He turned away and faced me.

"No, she'll probably wake up mean as cat piss and looking for trouble," he reflected. Then, "She doesn't seem to be holding that cloak you mentioned."

"I'll get it."

I moved to an armoire, opened it, and fetched out a dark fur one. As we traded, he ran his hand over it.

"Manticore?" he asked.

"Dire wolf," I said.

I hung his within and closed the door while he donned mine.

"As I was saying when we came in here," he offered, "supposing I don't come back?"

"You weren't saying that," I corrected.

"Not in so many words," he admitted. "But whether it's a small delay or the big one, what difference does it make? The point is, what if Jurt goes through with the ritual and succeeds in obtaining the powers he's after before we can do anything about it? And supposing I'm not around right then to give you a hand?"

"That's a lot of supposing," I said.

"That's what separates us from the losers, man. Nice cloak."

He moved toward the door, glanced back at me, at Jasra.

"Okay," I said. "You go down there, Dalt cuts off your head and uses it for a football, then Jurt shows up ten feet tall and farting fire. I'm supposing. How does that separate us from the losers?"

He stepped out into the hall. I followed him, snapping my fingers again, leaving Jasra to the darkness.

"It's a matter of knowing your options," he told me, as I secured the door.

I fell into step beside him as he headed back down the hall.

"A person who acquires that kind of power also picks up a vulnerability, by way of its source," he said.

"What does that mean?" I asked.

"Specifically, I don't know," he told me. "But the power in the Keep can be used against a person who is empowered by the Keep. I learned that much in Sharu's notes. But Mom took them away before I read them all, and I never saw them again. Never trust—that's her motto, I think."

"You're saying. . . ?"

"I'm saying that if something happens to me and he comes up a winner in this game, I believe she knows some special way of destroying him."

"Oh."

"I'm also pretty sure that she'll have to be asked very nicely."

"Somehow, I think I already knew that."

He gave a humorless chuckle.

"So you tell her that I've ended the vendetta, that I'm satisfied, and then offer her the citadel in return for her help."

"What if she says that's not enough?"

"Hell! Turn her back into a coatrack then! It's not as if the guy can't be killed. My dad still died with an arrow through his throat, despite his fancy powers. A deathstroke is still a deathstroke. It's just that delivering it to a guy like that is a lot harder."

"You really think that'll be enough?" I said.

He halted and looked at me, frowning.

"She'll argue, but of course she'll agree," he said. "It'll be a step up in the world. And she'll want revenge on Mask as much as that piece of her former holdings. But to answer your question, don't trust her. No matter what she promises, she'll never be happy with less than she had before. She'll be scheming. She'll be a good ally till the job's done. Then you've got to think about protecting yourself against her. Unless. . . ."

"Unless what?"

"Unless I come up with something to sweeten the pot."

"Like what?"

"I don't know yet. But don't lift that spell until things are definitely settled between Dalt and me. Okay?"

He resumed walking.

"Wait a minute," I said "What are you planning?"

"Nothing special," he answered. "Like I told the queen, I'm just going to play things by ear."

"I sometimes get the feeling you're as devious as you make her out to be," I said.

"I hope so," he replied. "But there's a difference. I'm honest."

"I don't know that I'd buy a used car from you, Luke."

"Every deal I make is special," he said, "and for you it's always top of the line."

I glanced at him, saw that he kept his expression under control.

"What else can I say?" he added, indicating the sitting room with a quick gesture.

"Nothing, now," I answered, and we entered there.

Vialle turned her head in our direction as we came in, her expression as unreadable as Luke's.

"I take it you are properly attired now?" she asked.

"I am indeed," he answered.

"Then let's be about this," she said, raising her left hand, which I saw to contain a Trump. "Come over here, please."

Luke approached her and I followed him. I could see then that it was Julian's Trump that she held.

"Place your hand upon my shoulder," she told him.

"All right."

He did, and she reached, found Julian and began speaking to him. Shortly, Luke was party to the conversation, explaining what he intended to do. I overheard Vialle saying that the plan had her approval.

Moments later I saw Luke raise his free hand and extend it. I also saw the shadowy figure of Julian reaching forward, though I was not part of the

Trump nexus. This was because I had summoned my Logrus Sight and had become sensitive to such things. I needed it for the timing, not wanting Luke whisked away before I could move.

I let my hand fall upon his shoulder and I moved forward as he did.

"Merlin! What are you doing?" I heard Vialle call.

"I'd like to see what happens," I said. "I'll come right home when things are concluded," and the rainbow gate closed behind me.

We stood within the flickering light of oil lamps inside a large tent. From outside, I could hear the wind and the sounds of stirring branches. Julian stood facing us. He let Luke's hand fall and regarded him without expression.

"So you are Caine's killer," he said.

"I am," Luke replied.

And I was remembering that Caine and Julian had always been particularly close. If Julian were to kill Luke and cry vendetta, I was certain that Random would merely nod and agree. Perhaps he'd even smile. Hard to say. If I were Random, I would greet Luke's removal with a sigh of relief. In fact, that was one of the reasons I'd come along. Supposing this whole deal were a setup? I couldn't picture Vialle as a part of it, but she could easily have been deceived by Julian and Benedict. Supposing Dalt wasn't even out there?

Or suppose he were—and that what he'd really asked for was Luke's head? After all, he had tried to kill Luke fairly recently. I had to admit the possibility now, and I also had to admit that Julian was the most likely candidate to be a willing party to such a design. For the good of Amber.

Julian's gaze met mine, and I wore as affectless a mask as his own.

"Good evening, Merlin," he said. "Do you have a special part in this plan?"

"I'm an observer," I answered. "Anything else I may do will be dictated by circumstance."

From somewhere outside I heard the growling of a hellhound.

"So long as you keep out of the way," Julian said.

I smiled.

"Sorcerers have special ways of avoiding notice," I replied.

He studied me again, wondering, I am certain, whether that involved some sort of threat—to defend Luke or to avenge him.

Then he shrugged and turned away to where a small table held an unrolled map, weighted in place with a rock and a dagger. He indicated that Luke should join him there, and I followed when he did.

It was a map of the western fringe of Arden, and he pointed out our position on it. Garnath lay to our south-southwest, Amber to the southeast.

"Our troops are situated here," he said, with a movement of his finger. "And Dalt's are here." He described another line, roughly paralleling our own.

"What about Benedict's force?" I inquired.

He glanced at me, showing the slightest of frowns.

"It is good for Luke to know that there is such a force," he stated, "but not its size, location, or objective. That way, if Dalt were to capture and question him, he'd have a lot to worry about and nothing to act upon."

Luke nodded. "Good idea," he said.

Julian pointed again, to a spot midway between the lines. "This is the place where I met with him when we spoke earlier," he explained. "It is a clear, level area, in view of both sides during daylight. I'd suggest we use it again, for your meeting."

"All right," Luke said, and I noticed that as he spoke, Julian's fingertips caressed the handle of the dagger that lay before him. Then I saw that Luke's right hand, in casual movement, had come to rest upon his belt, slightly to the left and near to his own dagger.

Simultaneously, then, Luke and Julian smiled at each other, and held it several seconds too long. Luke was bigger than Julian, and I knew he was fast and strong. But Julian had centuries of experience with weapons behind him. I wondered how I would intervene if either made a move toward the other, because I knew that I would try to stop them. But they let their hands fall to their sides then, as if by sudden agreement, and Julian said, "Let me offer you a glass of wine."

"Don't mind if I do," Luke replied, and I wondered whether my presence had kept them from fighting. Probably not. I'd the feeling that Julian had just wanted to make his feelings clear, and Luke had wanted to let him know he didn't give a damn. I really don't know which one I'd have bet on.

Julian placed three cups upon the table, filled them with Bayle's Best, gestured for us to help ourselves as he corked the bottle, then picked up the remaining cup and took a swallow before either of us could do more than sniff ours. A quick assurance that we weren't being poisoned and that he wanted to talk business.

"When I met with him we each brought two retainers along," he said.

"Armed?" I asked.

He nodded.

"More for show, really."

"Were you mounted or on foot?" Luke asked.

"On foot," he replied. "We each left our lines at the same time and proceeded at the same pace till we met there in the middle, several hundred paces from either side."

"I see," Luke said. "No hitches?"

"None. We talked and returned."

"When was this?"

"Around sundown."

"Did he seem to be a man in a normal state of mind?"

"I'd say. I count a certain arrogant posturing and a few insults toward Amber as normal for Dalt."

"Understandable," Luke said. "And he wanted me or my mother, or both? And failing to get us, he threatened to attack?"

"Yes."

"Did he give any indication as to why he wants us?"

"None," Julian replied.

Luke took a sip of his wine.

"Did he specify whether he wanted us dead or alive?" he asked.

"Yes. He wants you alive," Julian answered.

"What are your impressions?"

"If I give you to him, I'm rid of you," Julian said. "If I spit in his eye and take him on in battle, I'm rid of him. Either way, I come out ahead. . . ."

Then his gaze moved to the wine cup, which Luke had picked up with his left hand, and for an instant his eyes widened. I realized he had just then noticed that Luke was wearing Vialle's ring.

"It looks as if I get to kill Dalt, anyway," he concluded.

"By impressions," Luke went on, unperturbed, "I meant, do you believe he will really attack? Do you have any idea where he came from? Any indication where he might be headed when he leaves here—if he leaves?"

Julian swirled his wine in his cup.

"I have to go under the assumption that he means what he says and plans to attack. When we first became aware of his troop movements, he was advancing from the general direction of Begma and Kashfa—probably Eregnor, since he hangs out there a lot. Your guess is as good as anyone's as to where he wants to go if he leaves here."

Luke took a quick swallow of wine a fraction of a second too late for it to conceal what appeared to be a sudden smile. No, I realized right then, Luke's guess was not as good as anyone else's. It was probably a hell of a lot better. I took a quick drink myself, though I'm not sure what expression I might have been concealing.

"You can sleep here," Julian said. "If you're hungry, I'll have some food brought in. We'll set up this meeting for you at daybreak."

Luke shook his head.

"Now," Luke said, with another subtle but obvious display of the ring. "We want it set up right away."

Julian studied him for several pulsebeats. Then, "You'll not be in the clearest sight of either side in the dark, especially with snow coming down," he said. "Some little misunderstanding could result in an attack, from either side."

"If both of my companions bore large torches—and if both of his did the same—" he suggested, "we ought to be visible to both sides at a few hundred yards."

"Possibly," Julian said. "All right. I'll have the message sent to his camp, and I'll choose two retainers to accompany you."

"I already know who I want to have with me," Luke said. "Yourself and Merlin here."

"You are a curious individual," Julian observed. "But yes, I agree. I would like to be there when whatever happens, happens."

Julian moved to the front of his tent, opened the flap, and summoned an officer with whom he spoke for several minutes. In this space, I asked, "You know what you're doing, Luke?"

"Certainly," he replied.

"I've a feeling this is a little more than playing it by ear," I said. "Any reason why you can't tell me your plan?"

He appraised me for a moment, then said, "I only recently realized that I, too, am a son of Amber. We've met, and we've seen that we're too much like each other. Okay. That's good. It means we can do business, right?"

I allowed myself to frown. I wasn't sure what he was trying to say.

He clasped my shoulder lightly.

"Don't worry," he said. "You can trust me. Not that you have a great deal of choice at this point. But you may a bit later. I want you to remember then that, whatever happens, you must not interfere."

"What do you think is going to happen?"

"We haven't the time or the privacy to speculate," he said. "So let it go, and remember everything I said this evening."

"As you said, I haven't much choice at this point."

"I want you to remember it later," he said, as Julian lowered the flap and turned toward us.

"I'll take you up on that meal," Luke called to him. "How about you, Merle? Hungry?"

"Lord, no!" I replied. "I just sat through a state dinner."

"Oh?" he inquired almost too casually. "What was the occasion?"

I began to laugh. It was too much for one day. I was about to tell him that we hadn't the time or the privacy. But Julian had just reopened the tent flap and was calling for an orderly, and I wanted to throw a few curve balls through Luke's broken field just to see what they did to his composure.

"Oh, it was for the Begman prime minister, Orkuz, and some of his staff," I explained.

He waited while I pretended to take a long drink of wine. Then I lowered it and said, "That's all."

"Come on, Merlin. What's it about? I've been relatively square with you recently."

"Oh?" I said.

For a minute I didn't think he'd see the humor in it, but then he began to laugh, too.

"Sometimes the mills of the gods grind too damned fast and we get buried in grist," he observed. "Look, how about giving me this one for free. I don't have anything brief to trade right now. What's he want?"

"You'll bear in mind that this is classified until tomorrow?"

"Okay. What happens tomorrow?"

"Arkans, Duke of Shadburne, gets crowned in Kashfa."

"Holy shit!" Luke said. He glanced at Julian, then back at me. "That was a damned clever choice on Random's part," he said after a time. "I didn't think he'd move this fast."

He stared off into some vanishing point for a long while. Then he said, "Thanks."

"Well, does it help or hurt?" I asked.

"Me, or Kashfa?" he said.

"I hadn't split it down that fine."

"That's okay, because I'm not sure how to take this. I need to do some thinking. Get the big picture."

I stared at him and he smiled again.

"It *is* interesting," he added. "You got anything else for me?"

"That's enough," I said.

"Yeah, probably you're right," he agreed. "Don't want to overload the systems. Think we're losing touch with the simple things, old buddy?"

"Not so long as we know each other," I said.

Julian dropped the flap, returned to us, and sought his wine cup.

"Your food will be along in a few minutes," he told Luke.

"Thanks."

"According to Benedict," he said, "you told Random that Dalt is a son of Oberon."

"I did," Luke acknowledged. "One who's walked the Pattern, at that. Does it make a difference?"

Julian shrugged.

"Won't be the first time I've wanted to kill a relative," he stated. "By the way, you're my nephew, aren't you?"

"Right . . . uncle."

Julian swirled the contents of his cup again.

"Well, welcome to Amber," he said. "I heard a banshee last night. I wonder if there's any connection?"

"Change," Luke said. "They mean things are changing and they wail for what's being lost."

"Death. They mean death, don't they?"

"Not always. Sometimes they just show up at turning points for dramatic effect."

"Too bad," Julian said. "But one can always hope."

I thought Luke was going to say something else, but Julian began again before he could.

"How well did you know your father?" he asked.

Luke stiffened slightly, but answered, "Maybe not as well as most. I don't know. He was like a salesman. Always coming and going. Didn't usually stay with us long."

Julian nodded.

"What was he like, near the end?" he inquired.

Luke studied his hands.

"Well, he wasn't exactly normal, if that's what you mean," he finally said. "Like I was telling Merlin earlier, I think the process he undertook to gain his powers might have unbalanced him some."

"I never heard that story."

Luke shrugged.

"The details aren't all that important—just the results."

"You're saying he wasn't a bad father before that?"

"Hell, I don't know. I never had another father to compare him to. Why do you ask?"

"Curiosity. It's a part of his life I knew nothing about."

"Well, what kind of brother was he?"

"Wild," Julian said. "We didn't get along all that well. So we pretty much stayed out of each other's ways. He was smart, though. Talented, too. Had a flare for the arts. I was just trying to figure how much you might take after him."

Luke turned his hands palms upward.

"Beats me," he said.

"Well, no matter," Julian replied, setting down his cup and turning toward the front of the tent again. "I believe your food is about to arrive."

He moved off in that direction. I could hear the tiny crystals of ice rattling against the canvas overhead, and a few growls from outside: concerto for wind and hellhound. No banshees, though. Not yet.

NINE

I walked a pace or so behind Luke, a couple of yards off to his left, trying to keep even with Julian, who was over to the right. The torch I bore was a big thing, about six tapering feet of pitchy wood, sharpened at its terminus to make it easy to drive into the ground. I held it at arm's distance, because the oily flames licked and lashed in all directions in accord with vagaries of the wind. Sharp, icy flakes fell upon my cheek, my forehead, my hands, with a few catching in my eyebrows and lashes. I blinked vigorously as the heat of the torch melted them and they ran into my eyes. The grasses beneath my feet were sufficiently cold to give a brittle, crunching sensation every time I took a step. Directly ahead I could see the slow advance of two other torches toward us, and the shadowy figure of a man who walked between them. I blinked and waited for the flow from one or the other of his torches to give me a better look. I'd only seen him once, very briefly, via Trump, back at Arbor House. His hair looked golden, or even coppery, by what light there was upon it; but I remembered it as a kind of dirty blond by natural light. His eyes, I recalled, were green, though there was no way I could see that now. I did begin to realize for the first time, however, that he was pretty big—either that or he had chosen fairly short torchbearers. He had been alone that one time I'd seen him, and I had had no standard for comparison. As the light from our torches reached him I saw that he had on a heavy, green sleeveless doublet without a collar, over something black and also heavy, with sleeves that extended down his arms to vanish within green gauntlets. His trousers were black, as were the high boots they entered; his cloak was black and lined with an emerald green that caught our light as the cloak furled about him in shifting, oily landscapes of yellow and red. He wore a heavy circular medallion, which looked to be gold, on a chain about his neck; and though I could not make out the details of its device, I was certain that it bore a Lion rending a Unicorn. He came to a halt about ten or twelve paces from Luke, who stopped an instant later. Dalt gestured, and his retainers drove the butts of their torches into the ground. Julian and I immediately did the same, and we remained near them, as Dalt's men were doing. Then Dalt nodded to Luke, and they both advanced again, meeting at the center of the box formed by the lights, clasping right forearms, staring into each other's eyes. Luke's back was to me, but I could see Dalt's face. He showed no signs of emotion, but his lips were already moving. I couldn't hear a word that was being said, between the wind and the fact that they seemed intentionally to be keeping it low. At least, I finally had a point of reference for Dalt's size. Luke is about six three, and I could see that Dalt was several inches taller. I glanced at Julian, but he was not looking my way. I wondered how many eyes regarded us from both sides of the field.

Julian is always a bad person to check for reactions. He was simply watching the two of them, expressionless, stolid. I cultivated the same attitude, and the minutes passed, the snow kept falling.

After a long while Luke turned away and headed back toward us. Dalt moved off toward one of his torchbearers. Luke stopped midway between us, and Julian and I moved to join him.

"What's up?" I asked him.

"Oh," he said, "I think I found a way of settling this without a war."

"Great," I said. "What did you sell him?"

"I sold him on the idea of fighting a duel with me to determine how this thing goes," he explained.

"God damn it, Luke!" I said. "That guy's a pro! And I'm sure he's got our genetic package for strength. And he's been living in the field all this time. He's probably in top shape. And he outweighs you and outreaches you."

Luke grinned.

"So, I might get lucky," he said. He looked at Julian. "Anyway, if you can get a message back to the lines and tell them not to attack when we start this thing, Dalt's side will be holding still for it, too."

Julian looked over to where one of Dalt's torchbearers had started back toward his lines. He turned toward his own side then and executed a number of hand signals. Shortly, a man emerged from cover and began jogging toward us.

"Luke," I said. "This is crazy. The only way you're going to win is to get Benedict for a second and then break a leg."

"Merle," he said, "let it go. This is between Dalt and me. Okay?"

"I've got a bunch of fairly fresh spells," I said. "We can let this thing start, and then I'll hit him with one at the right time. It'll look as if you did it."

"No!" he said. "This really is a matter of honor. So you've got to stay out of it."

"Okay," I said, "if that's how you want it."

"Besides, nobody's going to die," he explained. "Neither of us wants that right now, and it's part of the deal. We're too valuable to each other alive. No weapons. Strictly *mano a mano.*"

"Just what," Julian inquired, "*is* the deal?"

"If Dalt whips my ass," Luke replied, "I'm his prisoner. He'll withdraw his force and I'll accompany him."

"Luke, you're crazy!" I said.

Julian glared at me.

"Continue," he said.

"If I win, he's my prisoner," he went on. "He goes back with me to Amber, or anywhere else I care to transport him, and his officers withdraw his troops."

"The only way of assuring such a withdrawal," Julian said, "is to let them know that if they don't they're doomed."

"Of course," Luke said. "That's why I told him that Benedict is waiting in the wings to roll down on him. I'm sure it's the only reason he's agreed to do this."

"Most astute," Julian observed. "Either way, Amber wins. What are you trying to buy with this, Rinaldo, for yourself?"

Luke smiled.

"Think about it," he said.

"There is more to you than I'd thought, Nephew," he replied. "Move over there to my right, would you?"

"Why?"

"To block his view of me, of course. I've got to let Benedict know what's going on."

Luke moved while Julian located his Trumps and shuffled out the proper one. In the meantime the runner from our lines had come up and stood waiting. Julian put away all of the cards but one then, and commenced his communication. It lasted for a minute or so, then Julian paused to speak with the runner and send him back. Immediately, he continued the conversation with the card. When he finally stopped talking or seeming to listen, he did not restore the Trump to the inner pocket where he kept the others, but retained it in his hand out of sight. I realized then that the contact would not be broken, that he would stay in touch with Benedict until this business was finished, so that Benedict would know in an instant what it was that he must do.

Luke unfastened the cloak I'd lent him, came over, and handed it to me.

"Hold this till I'm done, will you?" he said.

"Yes," I agreed, accepting it. "Good luck."

He smiled briefly and turned away. Dalt was already moving toward the center of the square.

Luke advanced, also. He and Dalt both halted, facing each other, while there were still several paces separating them. Dalt said something I could not hear, and Luke's reply was lost to me, also.

Then they raised their arms. Luke struck a boxer's stance, and Dalt's hands came up in a wrestler's defense. Luke threw the first punch—or maybe it was just a feint; either way, it didn't land—toward Dalt's face. Dalt brushed at it and stepped back, and Luke moved in quickly and landed two blows on his midsection. Another shot at his face was blocked, though, and Luke began to circle, jabbing. Dalt tried rushing twice then and got clipped both times, a little trickle of blood coming from his lip after the second one. On his third rush, though, he sent Luke sprawling but was unable to crash down on top of him, as Luke was able to twist partly away and roll when he hit. He tried kicking Dalt in the right kidney, though, as soon as he'd scrambled to his feet, and Dalt caught his ankle and rose, bearing him over backward. Luke landed a kick on the side of his knee with his other foot as he went down, but Dalt kept hold of the foot, bearing down and beginning to twist. Luke bent forward then, grimacing, and managed to catch Dalt's right wrist with both hands and tear his foot free of the larger man's grip. He doubled and moved forward then, still holding the wrist, regaining his feet and straightening as he advanced, passing under Dalt's arm on his right side, turning, and dragging him face downward to the ground. He moved quickly then, bending the arm up into a hammerlock, holding it with his right hand and seizing a handful of Dalt's hair with his left. But as he drew Dalt's head backward— preparatory, I was certain, to slamming it a few times against the ground—I saw that it wasn't going to work. Dalt stiffened, and his arm started to move downward. He was straightening it against Luke's lock. Luke tried pushing Dalt's head forward several times then, without effect. It became apparent that if he released either hand he was in trouble, and he wasn't able to maintain the hold. Dalt was just too damned strong. Seeing this, Luke threw all of his weight against Dalt's back, pushed, and sprang up. He wasn't quite fast enough, however, because Dalt's freed arm swung around and clipped him across the left calf as he moved away. Luke stumbled. Dalt was up and swinging immediately. He caught Luke with a wild haymaker that knocked him over backward. This time, when he threw himself upon Luke, Luke was unable to roll free; he only managed to turn his body partly. Dalt landed with considerable force, twisting past a slow knee aimed toward his groin. Luke did not get his hands free in time to defend against a punch that caught him on the left side of the jaw. He turned with it and fell completely flat. Then his right hand snapped upward, its heel striking the point of Dalt's chin, fingers hooking toward the eyes. Dalt jerked his head back and slapped the hand away. Luke threw a hammer blow toward his temple with the other hand, and though it connected, Dalt was already moving his head to the side, and I couldn't see that it had any effect. Luke dropped both elbows to the ground and pushed himself up and forward, bowing. His forehead struck Dalt's face—where, I am not precisely certain—before he fell back. Moments later, Dalt's nose began bleeding as he reached out with his left hand to grasp Luke by the neck. His right hand, open, slapped Luke hard on the side of the head. I saw Luke's teeth just before it landed, as he tried biting at the incoming hand, but the grip on his neck prevented this. Dalt moved to repeat the blow, but this time Luke's left arm came up and blocked it, while his right hand caught hold of Dalt's left wrist in an effort to pull it away from his neck. Dalt's right hand snaked in past Luke's left then, to take hold, creating a two-handed grip on Luke's neck, thumbs moving to depress the windpipe.

I thought that might well be it. But Luke's right hand suddenly moved to Dalt's left elbow, his left hand crossed both of Dalt's arms to seize the left forearm, and Luke twisted his body and cranked the elbow skyward. Dalt went over to the left and Luke rolled to the right and regained his footing, shaking his head as he did so. This time he did not try kicking Dalt, who was already recovering. Dalt again extended his arms, Luke raised his fists, and they began circling once more.

The snow continued to fall, the wind to slacken and surge, sometimes driving the icy flakes hard against faces, other times permitting the snow to descend like a troubled curtain. I thought of all the troops about me and wondered for a moment whether I would find myself in the middle of a battlefield when this thing was finally over. The fact that Benedict was ready to swoop down from somewhere and wreak extra havoc did not exactly comfort me, even though it meant that my side would probably win. I remembered then that my being there was my own choice.

"Come on, Luke!" I yelled. "Flatten him!"

This produced a very odd effect. Immediately, Dalt's torchbearers began shouting encouragement to him. Our voices must have carried through the wind's lulls, for shortly there came waves of sound, which I at first took to be some distant part of the storm and only later realized to be shouting coming from both lines. Only Julian remained silent, inscrutable.

Luke continued to circle Dalt, throwing jabs and trying occasional combinations, and Dalt kept swatting away at them and trying to catch an arm. Both of them had blood on their faces and both seemed a bit slower than they had been earlier. I'd a feeling they'd both been hurt, though it was impossible to guess to what extent. Luke had opened a small cut high on Dalt's left cheek. Both of their faces were beginning to look puffy.

Luke connected with another body combination, but it was hard to say how much force there was behind the blows. Dalt took them stoically and found extra energy somewhere to rush forward and attempt to grapple. Luke was slow in withdrawing and Dalt managed to draw him into a clinch. Both tried kneeing the other; both turned their hips and avoided it. They kept tangling arms and twisting as Dalt continued reaching after a better grip and Luke kept defeating the efforts while attempting to free an arm and get in a punch. Both tried several forehead bashes and instep stompings, but all of these were avoided by the other. Finally, Luke succeeded in hooking Dalt's leg, driving him backward to the ground.

Half kneeling atop him then, Luke caught him with a left cross and followed it immediately with a right. He tried for another left then, and Dalt caught his fist, surged upward and threw him back to the ground. As Dalt hurled himself upon him again, his face a half mask of blood and dirt, Luke was somehow able to strike him beneath the heart, but this did not stop Dalt's right fist which came down like a falling rock on the side of Luke's jaw. Dalt followed it with a weak left to the other side, a weak right, paused to suck in a great breath, then landed a solid left. Luke's head rolled to the side and he did not move.

Dalt crouched there atop him, panting like a dog, studying his face as if suspecting some trick, his right hand twitching as if he were contemplating striking again.

But nothing happened. They remained in that position for ten or fifteen seconds before Dalt slowly drew himself erect, eased off of Luke to Luke's left, then rose carefully to his feet, swayed for a second and straightened fully.

I could almost taste the death spell I had hung earlier. It would only take a few seconds to nail him, and no one would be certain how he had died. But I wondered what would happen if he were to collapse now, too. Would both sides attack? It was neither this nor humanitarian considerations that finally restrained me, however. Instead, it was Luke's words, "This really is a matter of honor. So you've got to stay out of it," and, "Nobody's going to die. . . . We're too valuable to each other alive."

Okay. There was still no sound of trumpets. No rush of men to combat. It seemed that things might actually go as had been agreed. This was the way Luke had wanted it. I was not going to interfere.

I watched as Dalt knelt and began to raise Luke from the ground. Immediately, he lowered him, then called to his two torchmen to come and carry him. Dalt rose again and faced Julian as the men advanced.

"I call upon you to observe the rest of our agreement," he said loudly.

Julian inclined his head slightly.

"We will, provided you do," he answered. "Have your men out of here by daybreak."

"We leave now," Dalt replied, and he began to turn away.

"Dalt!" I called out.

He turned back and regarded me.

"My name is Merlin," I said. "We've met, though I don't know whether you remember."

He shook his head.

I raised my right arm and pronounced my most useless and at the same time flashiest spell. The ground erupted before him, showering him with dirt and gravel. He stepped back and wiped his face, then looked down into the rough trench that had appeared.

"That is your grave," I said, "if Luke's death comes of this."

He studied me again.

"Next time I'll remember you," he said, and he turned and followed the men who were carrying Luke back to his lines.

I looked over at Julian, who was watching me. He turned away and uprooted his torch. I did the same. I followed him back the way we had come.

Later, in his tent, Julian observed, "That solves one problem. Possibly two."

"Maybe," I said.

"It takes care of Dalt for the moment."

"I guess."

"Benedict tells me the man is already breaking camp."

"I don't think we've seen the last of him."

"If that's the best he can manage for an army these days, it won't matter."

"Don't you get the impression this was an impromptu mission?" I asked. "I'd guess he pulled his force together very fast. It makes me think he had a tight schedule."

"You may be right there. But he really gambled."

"And he won."

"Yes, he did. And you shouldn't have shown him your power, there at the end."

"Why not?"

"You'll have a wary enemy if you ever go after him."

"He needed warning."

"A man like that lives with risks. He calculates and he acts. However he figures you, he won't change his plans at this point. Besides, you haven't seen the last of Rinaldo either. He's the same way. Those two understand each other."

"You may be right."

"I am."

"If the fight had gone the other way, do you think his army would have stood for it?" I asked.

Julian shrugged. "He knew mine would if he won, because he knew I stood to gain by it. That was sufficient."

I nodded.

"Excuse me," he said. "I have to report this business to Vialle now. I assume you'll want to trump through when I've finished?"

"Yes."

He produced a card and set about the business. And I found myself wondering, not for the first time, just what it was that Vialle sensed when it came to a Trump contact. I always see the other person myself, and all of the others say that they do, too. But Vialle, as I understood it, had been blind from birth. I've always felt it would be impolite to ask her, and for that matter it's occurred to me that her answer probably wouldn't make much sense to a sighted person. I'll probably always wonder, though.

As Julian addressed her shadowy presence, I turned my mind to the future. I was going to have to do something about Mask and Jurt soon, and it looked now as if I'd be doing it without Luke. Did I really want to follow his advice and try to talk Jasra into an alliance against them? Would the benefits really be worth the risk? And if I didn't, how would I manage the thing? Maybe I should make my way back to that strange bar and see about renting the Jabberwock. Or the Vorpal Sword. Or both. Maybe—

I heard my name mentioned, and I drifted back to the present moment, present problems. Julian was explaining something to Vialle, but I knew there wasn't all that much to explain. So I got to my feet, stretched, and summoned the Logrus Sight.

I saw her ghostly form clearly when I directed my vision toward the area before Julian. She was in that same stiff chair where I had last seen her. I wondered whether she had remained there the entire while or had just returned. I hoped she'd had a chance to go back and eat that dessert I hadn't had a shot at.

Julian glanced at me, then, "If you're ready to go, she's ready to take you through," he said.

I crossed over and stood beside him, dropping the Logrus vision as I did so. I had decided it was not a good idea to bring the forces of the Logrus and the Pattern into too great a proximity. I reached out and touched the card, and Vialle's image sprang into full focus. A moment, and it was no longer an image.

"Anytime," she said, extending a hand.

I reached out and took hold of it gently.

"So long, Julian," I said, as I stepped forward.

He did not reply. Or if he did, I didn't catch it.

"I did not mean for things to go this way," she told me immediately, not releasing my hand.

"There was no way of foreseeing what happened," I said.

"Luke knew," she replied. "It makes sense now, doesn't it? Some of those little remarks he made? He planned the challenge all along."

"I guess so," I said.

"He's gambling on something. I wish I knew what."

"I can't help you on that," I answered. "He didn't say anything to me about it."

"But you will be the one with whom he will get in touch, eventually," she said. "I want to know immediately when you hear from him."

"All right," I agreed.

She released my hand.

"It would seem there is nothing more to say, for the moment."

"Well," I began, "there is another matter I think you ought to know about."

"Oh?"

"It concerns Coral's not being present at dinner this evening."

"Go on," she said.

"You are aware that we took a long walk about town today?"

"I am," she said.

"We wound up below," I continued, "in the chamber of the Pattern. She'd expressed a desire to see it."

"Many visitors do. It is pretty much a matter of judgment whether to take them. Often they lose interest, though, when they learn about the stairway."

"I did tell her about it," I said, "but it didn't discourage her. When she got there, she set foot upon the Pattern—"

"No!" she cried. "You should have watched her more closely! All that other trouble with Begma . . . and now this! Where is her body?"

"Good question," I responded. "I don't know. But she was alive the last time I saw her. You see, she claimed Oberon was her father, and then she proceeded to walk the Pattern. When she'd finished, she had it transport her somewhere. Now, her sister—who is aware that we went off together—is concerned. She was pestering me through dinner as to where Coral might be."

"What did you tell her?"

"I told her that I'd left her sister enjoying some of the beauties of the palace and that she might be a bit late to dinner. As things wore on, though, she seemed to grow more concerned and made me promise to search for her tonight if she didn't turn up. I didn't want to talk about what had really happened because I didn't want to go into the business of Coral's parentage."

"Understandable," she replied. "Oh, my."

I waited, but she said nothing more. I continued to wait.

Finally, "I was not aware of the late king's affair in Begma," she said, "so it is difficult to assess the impact of this revelation. Did Coral give you any indication as to how long she intended to stay away? And for that matter, did you provide her with any means of return?"

"I gave her my Trump," I said, "but she hasn't been in touch. I got the impression she didn't intend to be away for too long, though."

"This could be serious," Vialle decided, "for reasons other than the obvious. How does Nayda strike you?"

"She seemed quite sensible," I said. "Also, I believe she rather likes me."

Vialle brooded a moment, then said, "If word of this gets to Orkuz, he could well get the impression that we are holding her hostage against his proper performance in any negotiations which might arise out of the situation in Kashfa."

"You're right. I hadn't thought of that."

"He will. People tend to think of such matters when dealing with us. So what we need to do is buy some time and try to turn her up before this begins looking suspicious."

"I understand," I said.

"Most likely, he will send to her quarters soon—if he hasn't already done so—to discover why she was not present at dinner. If he can be satisfied now, you will have the entire night in which to try to locate her."

"How?"

"You're the magician. You figure it out. In the meantime, you say that Nayda is sympathetic?"

"Very much so."

"Good. It seems to me that the best course of action then would be to attempt to enlist her aid. I trust you to be tactful and do this in the least distressing manner possible, of course—"

"Naturally—" I began.

"—because of her recent illness," she went on. "All we need to do now is give the second daughter a heart attack."

"Illness?" I inquired. "She hadn't mentioned anything about that."

"I'd imagine the memory is still distressing. She was apparently quite close to death until very recently, then rallied suddenly and insisted on accompanying her father on this mission. He's the one who told me about it."

"She seemed fine at dinner," I said lamely.

"Well, try to keep her that way. I want you to go to her immediately, tell her what happened as diplomatically as possible, and try to get her to cover for her sister while you search for her. There is, of course, the risk that she will not believe you and that she will go directly to Orkuz. Perhaps you might employ a spell to prevent this. But we have no other choice that I can see. Tell me whether I'm wrong."

"You're not wrong," I said.

"Then I suggest you be about it . . . and report back to me immediately if there are any problems, or any progress, no matter what the hour."

"I'm on my way," I said.

I departed the room in a hurry but shortly came to a halt. It occurred to me that while I knew the general area of the palace in which the Begman party was quartered, I did not really know where Nayda's rooms were located. I did not want to go back and ask Vialle because it would make me look stupid for not having found out during dinner.

It took me the better part of ten minutes to turn up a member of the palace staff able to give me directions—along with a smirk—and then to follow them at a jog until I stood before Nayda's door.

I ran my hand through my hair, brushed off my trousers and jacket, wiped my boots on the backs of my pants legs, took a deep breath, smiled, exhaled, and knocked.

The door opened a few moments later. It was Nayda. She returned my smile and stepped aside.

"Come in," she said.

"I was expecting the maid," I told her as I entered. "You surprised me."

"Since I was expecting you, I sent her off to bed early," she replied.

She had changed into an outfit that looked like a gray sweat suit with a black sash. She also had on a pair of black slippers, and she had removed most of her makeup. Her hair was now drawn back severely and tied with a black ribbon. She gestured toward a couch, but I did not move to seat myself.

I clasped her shoulder lightly and stared into her eyes. She moved nearer.

"How are you feeling?" I asked.

"Find out," she said softly.

I could not even permit myself a sigh. Duty called. I slipped my arms around her, drew her to me, and kissed her. I held the pose for several seconds, then drew away, smiled again, and said, "You feel fine to me. Listen, there are some things I did not tell you—"

"Shall we sit down?" she said, taking my hand and leading me toward the couch.

Vialle had told me to be diplomatic, so I followed her. Immediately, she continued our embrace and began to add refinements. Damn! And me constrained to rush her out to cover for Coral. If she would, I'd be happy to cover her afterward. Or any other interesting position Begmans might go in for. I'd better ask quickly, though, I decided. A couple of minutes more and it would be very undiplomatic to begin talking about her sister. Today was just a bad day when it came to timing.

"Before we get too involved here," I said, "I've got to ask a favor of you."

"Ask me anything," she said.

"I think there's going to be a delay in turning up your sister," I explained, "and I'd hate to worry your father. Do you know whether he's sent to her rooms yet, or been by them, to check on her?"

"I don't believe so. He strolled off with Gérard and Mr. Roth after dinner. I don't think he's returned to his apartment yet."

"Could you possibly find a way of giving him the impression that she hasn't strayed? Buy me some time to find out where she's off to?"

She looked amused.

"And those things you haven't told me. . . ?"

"I'll give you the whole story if you'll do this for me."

She traced my jawline with her index finger.

"All right," she said then. "We have a deal. Don't go away."

She rose, crossed the room, and passed out into the hall, leaving the door a few inches ajar. Why hadn't I had a nice normal affair since Julia? The last woman I'd made love to had actually been under the control of that strange body-shifting entity. Now . . . Now there was the faintest of shadows across the couch, as I realized that I'd rather be holding Coral than her sister. That was ridiculous. I'd only known her for half a day. . . .

There had simply been too much activity since my return. I was getting punchy. That had to be it.

When she returned she seated herself on the couch again, but this time with a couple of feet separating us. She seemed cheerful enough, though she made no move to resume our earlier occupation.

"It's taken care of," she said. "He will be misled, if he asks."

"Thanks," I told her.

"Now it's your turn," she stated. "Tell me things."

"All right," I began, and I launched into the story of Coral and the Pattern.

"No," she interrupted. "Start at the beginning, would you?"

"What do you mean?"

"Give me your whole day, from the time you left the palace together until you parted."

"That's silly," I protested.

"Humor me," she said. "You owe me one, remember?"

"Very well," I agreed, and I started again. I was able to skip over the bit about blasting the table in the cafe, but when I glossed over the business in the sea caves by saying that we'd looked around in them and found them pretty, she interrupted me.

"Stop," she said. "You're leaving something out. What occurred in the caves?"

"What makes you say that?" I asked.

"That is a secret I do not care to share just now," she explained. "Suffice it to say I have a means of spot-checking your veracity."

"It's not relevant," I said. "It will just confuse the issue. That's why I omitted it."

"You said you'd give me the whole afternoon."

"All right, lady," I agreed, and I did.

She bit her lip while I told her about Jurt and the zombies, and she licked idly at the beads of blood that appeared thereafter.

"What are you going to do about him?" she asked suddenly.

"That's my problem," I said then. "I promised you the afternoon, not my memoirs and survival plans."

"It's just that. . . . Remember, I offered to try to help you?"

"What do you mean? Do you think you can nail Jurt for me? I've got news for you: He's practically a candidate for godhood at the moment."

"What do you mean by 'godhood'?" she asked.

I shook my head.

"It would take most of the night to tell you this story properly, and we don't have the time, not if I'm going to start looking for Coral soon. Just let me finish with the business about the Pattern, will you?"

"Go ahead."

I did, and she showed no surprise whatsoever at the matter of her sister's paternity. I was going to question her as to her lack of reaction. Then I said, the hell with it. She's done what I wanted, and I did what I promised. She hasn't had a heart attack. And now it's time to go.

"That's it," I said, and I added, "Thanks."

I began to rise, and she moved quickly and was hugging me again.

I returned her embrace for a moment, then said, "I'd really better be going. Coral could be in danger."

"The hell with her," she said. "Stay with me. We have more important things to talk about."

I was surprised by her callousness, but I tried not to show it.

"I've a duty to her," I said, "and I've got to see to it now."

"All right," she said, sighing. "I'd better come along and give you a hand."

"How?" I asked.

"You'd be surprised," she told me, and she was on her feet and smiling a twisted smile.

I nodded, feeling that she was probably right.

TEN

We hiked back along the hallway to my apartment. When I opened the door and summoned the lights, Nayda did a fast survey of the first room. She froze when she saw my coatrack.

"Queen Jasra!" she said.

"Yep. She had a disagreement with a sorcerer named Mask," I explained. "Guess who won?"

Nayda raised her left hand and moved it in a slow pattern—behind Jasra's neck and down her back, across her chest, then downward again. I did not recognize any of the movements she was performing.

"Don't tell me that you're a sorceress, too," I said. "It seems that everyone I run into these days has had some training in the Art."

"I am not a sorceress," she answered, "and I've had no such training. I have only one trick and it is not sorcery, but I use it for everything."

"And what is that trick?" I asked.

She ignored the question, then said, "My, she's certainly tightly bound. The key lies somewhere in the region of her solar plexus. Did you know that?"

"Yes," I replied. "I understand the spell fully."

"Why is she here?"

"Partly because I promised her son Rinaldo I'd rescue her from Mask, and partly as an assurance against his good behavior."

I pushed the door shut and secured it. When I turned back, she was facing me.

"Have you seen him recently?" she said in a conversational tone.

"Yes. Why?"

"Oh, no special reason."

"I thought we were trying to help each other," I said.

"I thought we were looking for my sister."

"It can wait another minute if you know something special about Rinaldo."

"I was just curious where he might be right now."

I turned away and moved to the chest where I keep art supplies. I removed the necessary items and took them to my drawing board. While I was about it, I said, "I don't know where he is."

I set up the piece of pasteboard, seated myself and closed my eyes, summoning a mental image of Coral, preliminary to beginning her sketch. Again, I half wondered whether the picture in my mind, along with the appropriate magical endorsement, would be sufficient for contact. But now was not the time to mess around being experimental. I opened my eyes and began to draw. I used the techniques I'd learned in the Courts, which are different yet similar to those employed in Amber. I was qualified to execute them in either fashion, but I'm faster with the style I learned first.

Nayda came over and stood near, watching, not asking whether I minded. As it was, I did not.

"When did you see him last?" she asked.

"Who?"

"Luke."

"This evening," I answered.

"Where?"

"He was here earlier."

"Is he here now?"

"No."

"Where did you last see him?"

"In the forest of Arden. Why?"

"It seems a strange place to part."

I was working on Coral's eyebrows.

"We parted under strange circumstances," I said.

A little more work about the eyes, a bit on the hair. . . .

"Strange? In what way?" she asked.

More color to the cheeks. . . .

"Never mind," I told her.

"All right," she said. "It's probably not that important."

I decided against rising to that bait, because I was suddenly getting something. As had occasionally happened in the past, my concentration on the Trump as I put the final touches to it was sufficiently intense to reach through and. . . .

"Coral!" I said, as the features moved, perspectives shifted.

"Merlin . . . ?" she answered. "I . . . I'm in trouble."

Oddly, there was no background whatever. Just blackness. I felt Nayda's hand upon my shoulder.

"Are you all right?" I asked.

"Yes. . . . It's dark here," she said. "Very dark."

Of course. One cannot manipulate Shadow in the absence of light. Or even see to use a Trump.

"That's where the Pattern sent you?" I asked.

"No," she answered.

"Take my hand," I said. "You can tell me about it afterward."

I extended my hand and she reached toward it.

"They—" she began.

And with a stinging flash the contact was broken. I felt Nayda stiffen beside me.

"What happened?" she asked.

"I don't know. We were suddenly blocked. I can't tell what forces were involved."

"What are you going to do?"

"Try again in a little bit," I said. "If it were a reaction thing, resistance will probably be high just now, and it may ease up later. At least she says she's all right."

I withdrew the packet of Trumps I normally carry, shuffled out Luke's. Now seemed as good a time as any to see how he was faring. Nayda glanced at the card and smiled.

"I thought you just saw him a little while ago," she said.

"A lot can happen in a little while."

"I'm certain a lot *has* happened."

"You think you know something about what's going on with him?" I asked.

"Yes. I do."

I raised the Trump.

"What?" I said.

"I'd be willing to wager, you won't get through to him."

"We'll see."

I concentrated and I reached. I reached again. A minute or so later I wiped my brow.

"How'd you know?" I asked.

"Luke's blocking you. I would, too . . . under the circumstances."

"What circumstances?"

She gave me a quirked smile, crossed to a chair, and sat down.

"Now I have something to trade with you again," she said.

"Again?"

I studied her. Something jiggled and fell into place.

"You've been calling him 'Luke' rather than 'Rinaldo,' " I said.

"So I have."

"I'd been wondering when you'd show up again."

She continued to smile.

"I went and shot my eviction-notice spell," I observed. "Can't complain, though. It probably saved my life. Do I owe you that one, in some round-about fashion?"

"I'm not proud. I'll take it."

"I'm going to ask you again what you want, and if you say it's to help me or to protect me, I'm going to turn you into a coatrack."

She laughed.

"I'd have guessed you'd take whatever help you could get right now," she said.

"A lot depends on what you mean by 'help.' "

"If you'll tell me what you have in mind, I'll tell you whether I can be of any assistance."

"All right," I said. "I'm going to change clothes while I talk, though. I don't feel like storming a citadel dressed like this. May I lend you something tougher than a sweat suit?"

"I'm fine. Start at Arbor House, okay?"

"Okay," I said, and I proceeded to fill her in while I garbed myself in tougher fare. She was no longer a pretty lady to me, but rather a nebulous entity in human form. She seated herself while I was talking and stared at the wall, or through it, over steepled fingers. When I was finished, she kept staring, and I went over to my drawing board, took up Coral's Trump, tried again, but couldn't get through. I tried Luke's card, also, with the same results.

As I was about to replace Luke's Trump, square the deck, and case it, I glimpsed the next lower card and a lightning chain of recollections and speculations flashed through my mind. I removed the card and focused on it. I reached. . . .

"Yes, Merlin?" he said moments later, seated at a small table on a terrace—evening skyline of a city behind him—lowering what appeared to be a cup of espresso to a tiny white saucer.

"Right now. Hurry," I said. "Come to me."

Nayda had begun to make a low growling sound just as the contact occurred, and she was on her feet and moving toward me, her eyes fixed upon the Trump, just as Mandor took my hand and stepped through. She halted when the tall, black-garbed figure appeared before her. They regarded each other without expression for a moment, and then she took a long sliding step toward him, her hands beginning to rise. Immediately, from the depth of some inner cloak pocket where his right hand was thrust, there came a single, sharp, metallic click.

Nayda froze.

"Interesting," Mandor said, raising his left hand and passing it in front of her face. Her eyes did not follow it. "This is the one you told me about earlier—Vinta, I believe, you called her?"

"Yes, only now she's Nayda."

He produced a small, dark metal ball from somewhere and held it upon the palm of his left hand, which he extended before her. Slowly, the ball began to move, describing a counterclockwise circle. Nayda emitted a single sound, something halfway between a cry and a gasp, and she dropped forward to her hands and knees, head lowered. From where I stood I could see saliva dripping from her mouth.

He said something very fast, in an archaic form of Thari which I could not follow. She responded in the affirmative.

"I believe I've solved your mystery," he said then. "Do you recall your lessons on Respondances and High Compellings?"

"Sort of," I said. "Academically. I was never exactly swept away by the subject."

"Unfortunate," he stated. "You should report back to Suhuy for a postgraduate course sometime."

"Are you trying to tell me . . . ?"

"The creature you see before you, inhabiting a not unattractive human form, is a *ty'iga*," he explained.

I stared. The *ty'iga* were a normally bodiless race of demons that dwelled in the blackness beyond the Rim. I recalled being told that they were very powerful and very difficult to control.

"Uh . . . can you make this one stop slobbering on my carpet?" I said.

"Of course," he replied, and he released the sphere, which fell to the floor before her. It did not bounce, but began immediately to roll, describing a rapid circuit about her.

"Stand up," he said, "and stop releasing bodily fluids upon the floor."

She did as he ordered, climbing to her feet, her expression vacant.

"Seat yourself in that chair," he directed, indicating the one she had occupied but minutes earlier.

She complied, and the rolling ball adjusted itself to her progress and continued its circle, about the chair now.

"It cannot vacate that body," he said then, "unless I release it. And I can cause it any amount of torment within my sphere of power. I can get you your answers now. Tell me what the questions are."

"Can she hear us right now?"

"Yes, but it cannot speak unless I permit it."

"Well, there's no point to causing unnecessary pain. The threat itself may be sufficient. I want to know why she's been following me about."

"Very well," he said. "That is the question, *ty'iga*. Answer it!"

"I follow him to protect him," she said, her voice flat.

"I've already heard that one," I said. "I want to know why."

"Why?" Mandor repeated.

"I must," she answered.

"Why must you?" he asked.

"I. . . ." Her teeth raked her lower lip and the blood began to flow again. "Why?"

Her face grew flushed and beads of perspiration appeared upon her brow. Her eyes were still unfocused, but they brimmed with tears. A thin line of blood trickled down her chin. Mandor extended a clenched fist and opened it, revealing another metal ball. He held this one about ten inches before her brow, then released it. It hung in the air.

"Let the doors of pain be opened," he said, and he flicked it lightly with a fingertip.

Immediately, the small sphere began to move. It passed about her head in a slow ellipse, coming close to her temples on each orbit. She began to wail.

"Silence!" he said. "Suffer in silence!"

The tears ran down her cheeks, the blood ran down her chin. . . .

"Stop it!" I said.

"Very well." He reached over and squeezed the ball for a moment between the thumb and middle finger of his left hand. When he released it, it remained stationary, a small distance before her right ear. "Now you may answer the question," he said. "That was but the smallest sample of what I can do to you. I can push this to your total destruction."

She opened her mouth but no words came forth. Only a gagging sound.

"I think we may be going about this wrong," I said. "Can you just have her speak normally, rather than this question-and-answer business?"

"You heard him," Mandor said. "It is my will, also."

She gasped, then said, "My hands. . . . Please free them."

"Go ahead," I said.

"They are freed," Mandor stated.

She flexed her fingers.

"A handkerchief, a towel . . . ," she said softly.

I drew open a drawer in a nearby dresser, took out a handkerchief. As I moved to pass it to her, Mandor seized my wrist and took it from me. He tossed it to her and she caught it.

"Don't reach within my sphere," he told me.

"I wouldn't hurt him," she said, as she wiped her eyes, her cheeks, her chin. "I told you, I mean only to protect him."

"We require more information than that," Mandor said, as he reached for the sphere again.

"Wait," I said. Then, to her, "Can you at least tell me why you can't tell me?"

"No," she answered. "It would amount to the same thing."

Suddenly I saw it as a strange sort of programming problem, and I decided to try a different tack.

"You must protect me at all costs?" I said. "That is your primary function?"

"Yes."

"And you are not supposed to tell me who set you this task, or why?"

"Yes."

"Supposing the only way you could protect me would be by telling me these things?"

Her brow furrowed.

"I . . . ," she said. "I don't. . . . The *only* way?"

She closed her eyes and raised her hands to her face.

"I. . . . Then I would have to tell you."

"Now we're getting somewhere," I said. "You would be willing to violate the secondary order in order to carry out the primary one?"

"Yes, but what you have described is not a real situation," she said.

"I see one that is," Mandor said suddenly. "You cannot follow that order if you cease to exist. Therefore, you would be violating it if you permit yourself to be destroyed. I will destroy you unless you answer those questions."

She smiled.

"I don't think so," she said.

"Why not?"

"Ask Merlin what the diplomatic situation would be if a daughter of the Begman prime minister were found dead in his room under mysterious circumstances—especially when he's already responsible for the disappearance of her sister."

Mandor frowned and looked at me.

"I don't understand what that's all about," he said.

"It doesn't matter," I told him. "She's lying. If something happens to her, the real Nayda simply returns. I saw it happen with George Hansen, Meg Devlin, and Vinta Bayle."

"That is what would normally occur," she said, "except for one thing. They were all alive when I took possession of their bodies. But Nayda had just died, following a severe illness. She was exactly what I needed, though, so I took possession and healed the body. She is not here anymore. If I depart, you'll be left either with a corpse or a human vegetable."

"You're bluffing," I said, but I remembered Vialle's saying that Nayda had been ill.

"No," she said. "I'm not."

"It doesn't matter," I told her.

"Mandor," I said, turning to him, "you said you can keep her from vacating that body and following me?"

"Yes," he replied.

"Okay, Nayda," I said. "I am going somewhere and I am going to be in extreme danger there. I am not going to permit you to follow me and carry out your orders."

"Don't," she answered.

"You give me no choice but to keep you pent while I go about my business."

She sighed.

"So you've found a way to get me to violate one order in order to get me to carry out the other. Very clever."

"Then you'll tell me what I want to know?"

She shook her head.

"I am physically unable to tell you," she said. "It is not a matter of will. But . . . I think I've found a way around it."

"What is that?"

"I believe I could confide in a third party who also desires your safety."

"You mean—"

"If you will leave the room for a time, I will try to tell your brother those things I may not explain to you."

My eyes met Mandor's. Then, "I'll step out in the hall for a bit," I said.

And I did. A lot of things bothered me as I studied a tapestry on the wall, not the least being that I had never told her that Mandor was my brother.

When my door opened after a long while, Mandor looked in both directions. He raised his hand when I began to move toward him. I halted, and he stepped outside and came toward me. He continued to glance about as he advanced.

"This is Amber palace?" he inquired.

"Yes. Not the most fashionable wing, perhaps, but I call it home."

"I'd like to see it under more relaxed circumstances," he said.

I nodded. "It's a date. So tell me, what happened in there?"

He looked away, discovered the tapestry, studied it.

"It's very peculiar," he said. "I can't."

"What do you mean?"

"You still trust me, don't you?"

"Of course."

"Then trust me in this. I've a good reason for not telling you what I learned."

"Come on, Mandor! What the hell's going on?"

"The ty'iga is not a danger to you. It really does care about your welfare."

"So what else is new? I want to know why."

"Leave it," he said, "for now. It's better that way."

I shook my head. I made a fist and looked around for something to hit.

"I know how you feel, but I'm asking you to drop it," he said.

"You mean the knowledge would hurt me in some way?"

"I didn't say that."

"Or do you mean that you're afraid to tell me?"

"Drop it!" he said.

I turned away and got control of myself.

"You must have a good reason," I finally decided.

"I do."

"I'm not going to give up on this," I told him. "But I haven't the time to pursue it further against this kind of resistance. Okay, you have your reasons and I have pressing business elsewhere."

"She mentioned Jurt and Mask and the Keep where Brand gained his powers," he said.

"Yes, that's where I'll be heading."

"She expects to accompany you."

"She is wrong."

"I would counsel against taking her, too."

"You'll keep her for me until I've taken care of things?"

"No," he said, "because I'm coming with you. I'll put her into a very deep trance, though, before we depart."

"But you don't know what's been going on since our dinner. A lot has happened, and I just haven't the time to bring you up to date."

"It doesn't matter," he said. "I know that it involves an unfriendly sorcerer, Jurt, and a dangerous place. That's enough. I'll come along and give you a hand."

"But that may not be enough," I countered. "We may not be enough."

"Even so, I think the ty'iga could turn into a hindrance."

"I wasn't referring to her. I was thinking about the stiff lady near the door."

"I'd meant to ask you about her. Some enemy you're punishing?"

"She had been an enemy, yes. And she's nasty, untrustworthy, and has a poisonous bite. She's also a deposed queen. I didn't freeze her, though. The sorcerer who's after me did it. She's the mother of a friend, and I rescued her and brought her back here for safekeeping. I had no reason for releasing her, until now."

"Ah, as an ally against her old enemy."

"Exactly. She's well acquainted with the place I'm going. But she doesn't like me and she's not easy to deal with—and I don't really know whether her son gave me enough ammunition to make her trustworthy."

"Do you feel she'd be a real asset?"

"Yes. I'd like to have all of that animus on my side. And I understand she's an accomplished sorceress."

"If additional persuading is needed, there are only threats and bribes. I've a few private hells I've designed and furnished—for purely esthetic reasons. She might find a quick tour very impressive. On the other hand, I could send for a pot of jewels."

"I don't know," I said. "Her motivations are somewhat complex. Let me handle this, as far as I'm able."

"Of course. Those were only suggestions."

"As I see it, the next order of business is to rouse her, put the proposition to her, and attempt to judge her response."

"There is no one else you might bring along, from among your kinsmen here?"

"I'm afraid to let any of them know I'm going. It could easily result in an order not to, until Random gets back. I haven't the time to wait around."

"I might summon some reinforcement from the Courts."

"Here? To Amber? I'd really be up shit creek if Random ever got wind of that. He might start suspecting subversion."

He smiled.

"This place reminds me a bit of home," he remarked, turning back toward my door.

When we entered, I saw that Nayda was still seated, her hands upon her knees, staring at a metal ball that hovered about a foot before her. The other continued its slow circuit down on the floor.

Seeing the direction of my gaze, Mandor remarked, "Very light trance state. She can hear us. You can rouse her in an instant if you wish."

I nodded and turned away. Now it was Jasra's turn.

I removed all of the garments I'd hung upon her and placed them on a chair across the room. Then I fetched a cloth and the basin and washed the clown makeup off her face.

"Am I forgetting anything?" I said, half to myself.

"A glass of water and a mirror," Mandor stated.

"What for?"

"She may be thirsty," he replied, "and I can just tell she'll want to look at herself."

"You may have a point there," I said, drawing up a small table. I placed a pitcher and a goblet upon it; also, a hand mirror.

"I'd also suggest you support her, in case she collapses when the spell is removed.

"True."

I placed my left arm about her shoulders, thought of her deadly bite, stepped back, and held her at arm's distance with the one hand.

"If she bites me, it will knock me out almost instantly," I said. "Be ready to defend yourself quickly if this occurs."

Mandor tossed another metal ball into the air. It hung there for an unnaturally long moment at the top of its arc, then dropped back to his hand.

"All right," I said, and then I spoke the words that raised the spell.

Nothing as dramatic as I'd feared ensued. She slumped and I supported her. "You're safe," I said, and added, "Rinaldo knows you're here," to invoke the most familiar. "Here's a chair. Do you want some water?"

"Yes," she replied, and I poured some and passed it to her.

Her eyes were darting, taking in everything as she drank. I wondered whether she'd recovered instantly and might not now be stalling for time as she sipped, her mind racing, spells dancing at her fingertips. Her eyes returned more than once to Mandor, appraising, though she gave Nayda a long, hard stare.

Finally, she lowered the goblet and smiled.

"I take it, Merlin, that I am your prisoner," she said, choking slightly. She took another sip.

"Guest," I replied.

"Oh? How did this come about? Accepting the invitation escapes my mind."

"I brought you here from the citadel at the Keep of the Four Worlds in a somewhat cataleptic condition," I said.

"And where might 'here' be?"

"My apartment in the Palace of Amber."

"Prisoner, then," she stated.

"Guest," I repeated.

"In that case, I should be introduced, should I not?"

"Excuse me. Mandor, I introduce Her Highness Jasra, Queen of Kashfa." (I intentionally omitted the "Most Royal" part.) "Your Majesty, I request leave to present my brother, Lord Mandor."

She inclined her head, and Mandor approached, dropped to one knee, and raised her hand to his lips. He's better at such courtly gestures than I am, not even sniffing the back of her hand for the scent of bitter almonds. I could tell that she liked his manner—and she continued to study him afterward.

"I was not aware," she observed, "that the royal house here contained an individual named Mandor."

"Mandor is heir to the dukedom of Sawall in the Courts of Chaos," I replied.

Her eyes widened.

"And you say he is your brother?"

"Indeed."

"You've succeeded in surprising me," she stated. "I had forgotten your double lineage."

I smiled, nodded, stepped aside and gestured.

"And this—" I began.

"I am acquainted with Nayda," she said. "Why is the girl . . . preoccupied?"

"That represents a matter of great complexity," I said, "and there are other things I am certain you will find to be of much greater interest."

She cocked an eyebrow at me.

"Ah! That fragile, perishable item—the truth," she said. "When it surfaces so quickly there is usually a claustrophobia of circumstance. What is it that you want of me?"

I held my smile.

"It is good to appreciate circumstance," I said.

"I appreciate the fact that I am in Amber and alive and not occupying a cell, with two gentlemen behaving in a conciliatory fashion. I also appreciate the fact that I am not in the straits my most recent memories indicate I should occupy. And I have you to thank for my deliverance?"

"Yes."

"Somehow I doubt it was a matter of altruism on your part."

"I did it for Rinaldo. He tried getting you out once and got clobbered. Then I figured a way that might work, and I tried it. It did."

Her facial muscles tightened at the mention of her son's name. I'd decided she'd prefer hearing the one she'd given him, rather than "Luke."

"Is he all right?" she asked.

"Yes," I said, hoping it were so.

"Then why is he not present?"

"He's off somewhere with Dalt. I'm not sure as to his location. But—"

Nayda made a small noise just then, and we glanced her way. But she did not stir. Mandor gave me an inquiring look, but I shook my head slightly. I did not want her roused just then.

"Bad influence, that barbarian," Jasra observed, choking again and taking another drink. "I'd so wanted Rinaldo to acquire more of the courtly graces, rather than doing rude things on horseback much of the time," she continued, glancing at Mandor and granting him a small smile. "In this, I was disappointed. Do you have something stronger than water?"

"Yes," I replied, and I uncorked a bottle of wine and poured some into a goblet for her. I glanced at Mandor and at the bottle then, but he shook his head. "But you have to admit he did well in that track meet against UCLA, in his sophomore year," I said, not to let her put him down completely. "A certain amount of that comes from the more vigorous side of life."

She smiled as she accepted the drink.

"Yes. He broke a world record that day. I can still see him passing over the final hurdle."

"You were there?"

"Oh, yes. I attended all of your meets. I even watched you run," she said. "Not bad."

She sipped the wine.

"Would you like me to send for a meal for you?" I asked.

"No, I'm not really hungry. We were talking about truth a little while ago. . . ."

"So we were. I gather there had been some sorcerous exchange back at the Keep, between you and Mask—"

"Mask?" she said.

"The blue-masked sorcerer who rules there now."

"Oh, yes. Quite."

"I do have the story right, don't I?"

"Yes, but the encounter was more than a little traumatic. Forgive my hesitation. I was surprised and did not get my defenses up in time. That was really all there was to it. It will not happen again."

"I'm sure. But—"

"Did you spirit me away?" she interrupted. "Or did you actually fight with Mask to get me free?"

"We fought," I said.

"In what condition did you leave Mask?"

"Buried under a pile of manure," I said.

She chuckled.

"Wonderful! I like a man with a sense of humor."

"I have to go back," I added.

"Oh? Why is that?"

"Because Mask is now allied with an enemy of mine—a man named Jurt, who desires my death."

She shrugged slightly.

"If Mask is no match for you, I fail to see where Mask and this man should represent a great problem."

Mandor cleared his throat.

"Begging your leave," he said. "But Jurt is a shape shifter and minor sorcerer from the Courts. He also has power over Shadow."

"I suppose that would make something of a difference," she said.

"Not as much as what the two of them apparently plan to accomplish," I told her. "I believe that Mask intends running Jurt through the same ritual your late husband undertook—something involving the Fount of Power."

"No!" she cried, and she was on her feet, the rest of the wine mixing with Nayda's spittle and a few old bloodstains on the Tabriz I'd purchased for its delicately detailed pastoral scene. "It must not happen again!"

A storm came and went behind her eyes. Then, for the first time, she looked vulnerable.

"I lost him because of that . . . ," she said.

Then the moment was gone. The hardness returned.

"I had not finished my wine," she said then, reseating herself.

"I'll get you another glass," I told her.

"And is that a mirror on the table?"

ELEVEN

I waited till she was finished primping, glancing out of the window at the snow and surreptitiously trying again to reach Coral or Luke while my back was turned to her. No luck, though. When she put down the comb and brush she'd borrowed from me and laid the mirror beside them, I gathered she'd finished organizing her thoughts as well as her hair and was ready to talk again. I turned back slowly and strolled over.

We studied each other while practicing expressionlessness, then she asked, "Is anyone else in Amber aware that you have awakened me?"

"No," I replied.

"Good. That means I've a chance of leaving here alive. Presumably, you want my assistance against Mask and this Jurt?"

"Yes."

"Exactly what sort of help do you desire, and what are you prepared to pay for it?"

"I intend to penetrate the Keep and neutralize Mask and Jurt," I said.

" 'Neutralize'? That's one of those little euphemisms for 'kill,' isn't it?"

"I suppose so," I replied.

"Amber has never been noted for its squeamishness," she said. "You have been exposed to too much American journalism. So, you are aware of my familiarity with the Keep, and you want my help in killing the two of them. Correct?"

I nodded.

"Rinaldo has told me that if we were to arrive too late and Jurt had already undergone the transformational ritual, you might know a way to use that same power against him," I explained.

"He'd gotten further into those notes than I'd realized," she said. "I am going to have to be frank with you then, since our lives may depend on it: Yes, there is such a technique. But no, it won't be of any help to us. Some preparations are required to turn the power to such an end. It is not something I could simply reach out and do at a moment's notice."

Mandor cleared his throat.

"I'd rather not see Jurt dead," he stated, "if there's a possibility I could take him back to the Courts as a prisoner. He could be disciplined. There might be a way of neutralizing him without really . . . neutralizing him, as you put it."

"And if there isn't?" I asked.

"Then I'll help you to kill him," he said. "I have no illusions about him, but I feel obliged to try something. I'm afraid that the news of his death could push our father over the edge."

I looked away. He could be right, and even though old Sawall's death would mean his own succession to the title and control of considerable holdings, I was certain he was not anxious to acquire them at that price."

"I understand," I said. "I hadn't thought of that."

"So give me a chance to subdue him. If I fail, I'll join you in whatever must be done."

"Agreed," I said, watching to see how Jasra was taking this.

She was studying us, a curious expression on her face.

" 'Our father'?" she said.

"Yes," I replied. "I wasn't going to mention that, but since it got out, Jurt's our younger brother."

Her eyes were alight now, at the scent of connivance.

"This is a family power struggle, isn't it?" she asked.

"I suppose you could put it that way," I said.

"Not really," Mandor said.

"And yours is an important family in the Courts?"

Mandor shrugged. So did I. I'd a feeling she was trying to figure a way to cash in on that end of it, too, and I decided to stonewall her.

"We were discussing the task at hand," I said. "I want to take us in there and accept Mask's challenge. We stop Jurt if he gets in the way and give him to Mandor. If it is impossible simply to subdue him, we go the rest of the way. Are you with us?"

"We have not yet discussed the price," she said.

"All right," I acknowledged. "I've talked about this with Rinaldo, and he told me to tell you that he's called the vendetta off. He feels things were settled with Amber when Caine died. He asked me to release you if you would go along with this, and he suggested that in return for your help against the new lord of the citadel we restore the Keep of the Four Worlds to your sovereignty. Bottom line, as he put it. What do you say?"

She picked up the goblet and took a long, slow sip. She'd stall, I knew, trying to figure a way to squeeze more out of this deal.

"You've spoken with Rinaldo very recently?" she said.

"Yes."

"I am not clear as to why he is running about with Dalt, rather than being here with us, if he is so much in agreement with this plan."

I sighed.

"Okay, I'll tell you the story," I said. "But if you're with us, I do want to get moving soon."

"Proceed," she said.

So I recounted the evening's adventure in Arden, omitting only the fact that Vialle had placed Luke under her protection. Nayda seemed to grow progressively distressed as I told the tale, uttering small whimpering sounds at odd intervals.

When I was finished, Jasra placed her hand upon Mandor's arm and rose, brushing him lightly with her hip as she passed, and she went to stand before Nayda.

"Now tell me why the daughter of a high Begman official is restrained here," she said.

"She is possessed of a demon that enjoys interfering in my affairs," I explained.

"Really? I've often wondered what hobbies demons might pursue," she observed. "But it seems this particular demon has been trying to say something in which I might be interested. If you would be so good as to free it for a moment's conversation I promise to consider your offer afterward."

"Time is running," I said.

"In that case my answer is no," she told me. "Lock me up someplace and go to the Keep without me."

I glanced at Mandor.

"In that I have not yet agreed to accept your offer," Jasra continued, "Rinaldo would call this an entertainment expense."

"I see no harm in it," Mandor said.

"Then let her speak," I told him.

"You may talk, *ty'iga*," he said.

Her first words were not addressed to Jasra, however, but to me:

"Merlin, you have to let me accompany you."

I moved around to where I could see her face.

"No way," I told her.

"Why not?" she asked.

"Because your penchant for protecting me will actually hinder me in a situation where I will probably have to take some chances."

"That is my nature," she responded.

"And my problem," I said. "I mean you no ill. I'll be glad to talk to you when this is all over, but you're going to have to sit this one out."

Jasra cleared her throat.

"Is that the entire message? Or is there something you wished to tell me, also?" Jasra asked.

There followed a long silence, then, "Will you be accompanying them or not?" Nayda inquired.

Jasra took just as long to respond, obviously weighing her words:

"This is a clandestine, personal operation," she said. "I am not at all certain it would be countenanced by Merlin's seniors here in Amber. While it is true that I stand to gain if I cooperate, I will also undergo considerable risk. Of course, I want my freedom and the restoration of the Keep. It is almost a fair trade. But he also asks a quitclaim on the vendetta. What assurance have I that this means anything here, and that the hierarchy of Amber will not hunt me down as a troublemaker afterward? He cannot speak for the others when he operates on the sly this way."

Somehow, it had become a question addressed to me, and since it was a very good question to which I did not really have an answer, I was glad that the *ty'iga* had something to say:

"I believe that I can persuade you that it would be in your best interest to agree to accompany them and to render every assistance you can," she offered.

"Pray, begin," Jasra told her.

"I would have to speak with you in private on this matter."

Jasra smiled, out of her love for intrigue, I am certain.

"It is agreeable to me," she said.

"Mandor, force her to say it now," I said.

"Wait!" Jasra declared. "I will have this private conversation or you can forget about my help."

I began wondering just how much help Jasra really represented if she couldn't call upon the Fount to dispose of Jurt, should that become our biggest problem. True, she knew the Keep. But I didn't even know for certain how accomplished a sorceress she might be.

On the other hand, I wanted this thing settled now, and one more adept could make the difference.

"Nayda," I said, "are you planning something that could be damaging to Amber?"

"No," she replied.

"Mandor, what do *ty'iga* swear by?" I inquired.

"They don't," he said.

"What the hell," I said. "How much time do you want?"

"Give us ten minutes," she told me.

"Let's take a walk," I said to Mandor.

"Surely," he agreed, tossing another metal ball toward Nayda. It joined the others in orbit about her, a little above waist level.

I fetched a key from my desk drawer before departing. And as soon as we were in the hall I asked him, "Is there any way Jasra could free her?"

"Not with the additional circuit of confinement I established on the way out," he replied. "Not many could figure a way past it, and certainly not in ten minutes."

"She's just full of secrets, that damned *ty'iga*," I said. "Kind of makes me wonder who's really the prisoner here."

"She's only trading some bit of knowledge for Jasra's cooperation," he said. "She wants the lady to accompany us if she can't go herself, since it will mean extra protection for you."

"Then why can't we be present?"

"Nothing that I learned from her sheds any light on this," he said.

"Well, since I have a few minutes, there is a small errand I want to run. Would you keep an eye on things here and take charge if she calls us in before I get back?"

He smiled.

"If one of your relatives strolls by, should I introduce myself as a lord of Chaos?"

"I thought you were also a lord of deception."

"Of course," he said, and he clapped his hands and vanished.

"I'll hurry," I said.

"Cheerio," came his voice, from somewhere.

I hurried off up the hall. It was a little pilgrimage, I suppose—one that I had not made in a long while. On the brink of an enterprise such as this, it seemed somehow appropriate.

When I reached the door, I stood outside it for a moment, my eyes closed, visualizing the interior as last I had seen it. It was my father's apartment. I had wandered through it on many occasions, trying to judge from the furnishings, the layout, his bookshelves, and his curious collections something more than I already knew about the man. There was always some little thing that caught my attention, that answered a question or raised a new one—an inscription on the flyleaf of a book or a note in a margin, a silver hairbrush bearing the wrong set of initials, a daguerreotype of an attractive brunette signed "To Carl, Love, Carolyn," a snapshot of my father shaking hands with General MacArthur. . . .

I unlocked the door and pushed it open.

I did not move for several seconds, however, as a light glowed inside the place. For more long moments I listened, but there were no sounds from within. Slowly then, I entered. A number of candles burned upon the dresser set against the far wall. There was no one in sight.

"Hello?" I called out. "It's me. Merlin."

There came no answer.

I drew the door closed behind me and moved forward. A bud vase stood upon the dresser amid the candles. It contained a single rose, and it appeared to be silver in color. I drew nearer. Yes, it was real, not artificial. And it *was* silver. In what shadow did such flowers grow?

I picked up one of the candles by its holder and moved away with it, shielding its flame with my hand. I crossed to my left and entered the next room. Immediately, on opening the door, I saw that there was no need to have brought the candle. More of them were burning here.

"Hello?" I repeated.

Again, no answer. No sounds of any sort.

I set the candle upon a nearby table and crossed to the bed. I raised a sleeve and let it fall. A silvery shirt was laid out upon the counterpane beside a black pair of trousers—my father's colors. They had not been there when last I had visited.

I seated myself beside them and stared across the room into a shadowy corner. What was going on? Some bizarre household ritual? A haunting? or. . . .

"Corwin?" I said.

In that I'd hardly expected a reply, I was not disappointed. When I rose, however, I bumped against a heavy object hung upon the nearest bedpost. I reached out and raised it for a better view. A belt with a sheathed weapon hung upon it. These had not been present last time either. I gripped the haft and drew the blade.

A portion of the Pattern, contained within the gray metal, danced in the candlelight. This was Grayswandir, sword of my father. What it was doing back here now, I had no idea.

And I realized with a pang that I could not stick around to see what might be going on. I had to get back to my own problems. Yes, timing was definitely against me today.

I resheathed Grayswandir.

"Dad?" I said. "If you can hear me, I want to get together again. But I have to go now. Good luck on whatever you're about."

Then I departed the room, touched the silver rose as I passed and locked the door behind me. As I turned away, I realized that I was shaking.

I passed no one on the walk back, and when I approached my own door I wondered whether I should enter, knock, or wait. Then something touched my shoulder, and I turned around but no one was there. When I turned forward once again Mandor stood before me, his brow slightly creased.

"What's the matter?" he asked. "You appear more troubled than when you left."

"Something totally different," I told him, "I think. Any word from inside yet?"

"I heard a shriek from Jasra while you were gone," he said, "and I hurried to the door and opened it. But she was laughing and she asked me to close it."

"Either *ty'igas* know some good stories or the news is favorable."

"So it would seem."

A little later the door opened and Jasra nodded to us.

"Our conversation is concluded," she said.

I studied her as I entered the room. She looked a lot more cheerful than she had seemed when we'd left. There was a bit more of a crinkling about the outer edges of her eyes, and she seemed almost to be fighting the corners of her mouth down into place.

"I hope it was a fruitful interview," I said.

"Yes. On the whole, I'd say it was that," she answered.

A glance at Nayda showed me that nothing had changed in terms of her position or expression.

"I'll have to be asking you for a decision now," I said. "I can't afford to cut things much closer than this."

"What happens if I say no?" she asked.

"I'll have you conducted to your quarters and inform the others that you're up and about," I said.

"As a guest?"

"As a very well-protected guest."

"I see. Well, I do not really care to inspect those quarters. I have decided to accompany you and assist you under the terms we discussed."

I bowed to her.

"Merlin!" Nayda said.

"No!" I answered, and I looked to Mandor.

He approached and stood before Nayda.

"It is best that you sleep now," he told her, and her eyes closed, her shoulders slumped. "Where is a good place for her to rest deeply?" he asked me.

"Through there," I said, indicating the doorway to the next room.

He took her by the hand and led her away. After a time, I heard him speaking softly, and then there was only silence. He emerged a little later, and I went to the door and glanced inside. She was stretched out on my bed. I did not see any of his metal spheres in the neighborhood.

"She's out of it?" I said.

"For a long time," he replied.

I looked at Jasra, who was glancing down into the mirror.

"Are you ready?" I inquired.

She regarded me through lowered lashes.

"How do you propose transporting us?" she asked.

"Do you have an especially tricky means of getting us in?"

"Not at the moment."

"Then I will be calling upon the Ghostwheel to take us there."

"Are you certain it is safe? I've conversed with that . . . device. I am not sure it is trustworthy."

"It's fine," I said. "Any spells you want to prime first?"

"Not necessary. My . . . resources should be in good order."

"Mandor?"

I heard a clicking sound from somewhere within his cloak.

"Ready," he said.

I withdrew the Ghostwheel Trump and studied it. I began my meditation. Then I reached. Nothing happened. I tried again, recalling, tuning, expanding. I reached again, calling, feeling. . . .

"The door . . . ," Jasra said.

I glanced at the door to the hallway, but there was nothing unusual about it. Then I looked at her and realized the direction of her gaze.

The doorway to the next room, where Nayda slept, had begun to glow. It shone with a yellow light, and even as I watched, it grew in intensity. A spot of greater brightness then occurred at its center. Abruptly, the spot began a slow up-and-down movement.

Then came music, from where I was not certain, and Ghost's voice announced, "Follow the bouncing ball."

"Stop it!" I said. "It's distracting!"

The music went away. The circle of light grew still.

"Sorry," Ghost said. "I thought you'd find a little comic relief relaxing."

"You guessed wrong," I replied. "I just want you to take us to the citadel at the Keep of the Four Worlds."

"Do you want the troops, also? I can't seem to locate Luke."

"Just the three of us," I answered.

"What about the one who sleeps next door? I've met her before. She doesn't scan right."

"I know. She's not human. Let her sleep."

"Very well, then. Pass through the door."

"Come on," I said to the others, picking up my weapons belt and buckling it on, adding my spare dagger, grabbing my cloak off a chair, and drawing it over my shoulders.

I walked toward the portal and Mandor and Jasra followed. I stepped through, but the room was no longer there. Instead, there came a moment of blurring, and when my senses cleared, I was staring down and outward across a great distance beneath a heavily overcast sky, a cold wind whipping at my garments.

I heard an exclamation from Mandor and, a moment later, another from Jasra—behind me and to the left. The great ice field lay bone-white to my right, and in the opposite direction a slate-gray sea tossed whitecaps like serpents in a bucket of milk. Far below, before me, the dark ground simmered and steamed.

"Ghost!" I cried. "Where are you?"

"Here," came a soft response, and I looked down to behold a tiny ring of light near the toe of my left boot.

Directly ahead and below, the Keep stood stark in the distance. There were no signs of life outside its walls. I realized that I must be in the moun-

tains, standing somewhere near the place where I had held my lengthy colloquy with the old hermit named Dave.

"I wanted you to take us into the citadel within the Keep," I explained.
"Why did you bring us up here?"

"I told you I don't like that place," Ghost answered. "I wanted to give
you a chance to look it over and decide exactly where you wished to be sent
within. That way I can move very fast on the delivery, and not expose myself
overlong to forces I find distressing."

I continued to study the Keep. A pair of twisters were again circling the
outer walls. If there had not been a moat, they would probably have done a
good job of creating one. They stayed almost exactly 180 degrees apart, and
they took turns at illumination. The nearest one grew spark-shot with bolts of
lightning, acquiring an eerie incandescence; then, as it began to fade, the
other brightened. They passed through this cycle several times as I watched.

Jasra made a small noise, and I turned and asked her, "What's going on?"

"The ritual," she responded. "Someone is playing with those forces
right now."

"Can you tell how far along they might be?" I asked.

"Not really. They could just be starting, or they could be finished already.
All the poles of fire tell me is that everything is in place."

"You call it then, Jasra," I told her. "Where should we put in our
appearance?"

"There are two long hallways leading to the chamber of the fountain,"
she said. "One is on the same level and the other a floor above it. The
chamber itself is several stories high."

"I recall that," I acknowledged.

"If they are working directly with the forces and we simply appear within
the chamber," she continued, "the advantage of surprise will only be momentary. I can't say for certain what they might hit us with. Better to approach
along one of the two hallways and give me a chance to assess the situation.
Since there is a possibility that they could note our approach along the lower
hallway, the upper one would be best for all our purposes."

"All right," I agreed. "Ghost, can you put us back a distance in that
upper hallway?"

The circle spread, tilted, rose, stood high above us for a moment, then
dropped.

"You are . . . already . . . there," Ghost said, as my vision swam and the
circle of light passed over us, head to toe. "Good-bye."

He was right. We were on target this time. We stood in a long, dim
corridor, its walls of dark, hewn stone. Its one end was lost in darkness. Its
other led into an area of illumination. The ceiling was of rough timbers, the
heavy cross-beams softened by curtains and plumes of spider-webbing. A few
blue wizard globes flickered within wall brackets, shedding a pale light that
indicated they were near the ends of their spells. Others had already gone
dead. Near the brighter end of the hallway some of these had been replaced
by lanterns. From overhead came the sounds of small things scurrying within

the ceiling. The place smelled damp, musty. But the air had an electric quality to it, as though we were breathing ozone, with an edge-of-event jitteriness permeating everything.

I shifted to Logrus Sight, and immediately there was a considerable brightening. Lines of force like glowing yellow cables ran everywhere. They provided the additional illumination I now perceived. And every time my movements intersected one, it heightened the overall tingling effect I experienced. I could see now that Jasra was standing at the intersection of several of these and seemed to be drawing energy from them into her body. She was acquiring a glowing quality I was not certain my normal vision would have detected. When I glanced at Mandor I saw the Sign of the Logrus hovering before him also, which meant that he was aware of everything I was seeing.

Jasra began moving slowly along the corridor toward the lighted end. I fell in behind her and slightly to her left. Mandor followed me, moving so silently I had to glance back occasionally to assure myself he was still with us. As we advanced I became aware of a certain throbbing sensation, as of the beating of a vast pulse. Whether this was being transmitted through the floor or along those vibrating lines we continually encountered, I could not say.

I wondered whether our disturbing this net of forces was betraying our presence, and even our position, to the adept working with the stuff down at the Fount. Or was his concentration on the task at hand sufficiently distracting to permit us to approach undetected?

"It *has* started?" I whispered to Jasra.

"Yes," she replied.

"How far along?"

"The major phase could be completed."

A few paces more, and then she asked me, "What is your plan?"

"If you're right, we attack immediately. Perhaps we should try to take out Jurt first—all of us, I mean—if he's become that high-powered, that dangerous."

She licked her lips.

"I'm probably best equipped to deal with him, because of my connection with the Fount," she said then. "Better you don't get in my way. I'd rather see you dealing with Mask while I'm about it. It might be better to keep Mandor in reserve, to lend his aid to whichever of us might need it."

"I'll go along with your judgment," I said. "Mandor, did you hear all that?"

"Yes," he replied softly. "I'll do as she says."

Then, "What happens if I destroy the Fount itself?" he asked Jasra.

"I don't believe it can be done," she answered.

He snorted, and I could see the dangerous lines along which his thoughts were running.

"Humor me and suppose," he said.

She was silent for a time, then, "If you were able to shut it down, even for a little while," she offered, "the citadel would probably fall. I've been using its emanations to help hold this place up. It's old, and I never got around to buttressing it where it needs it. The amount of energy required to attack the Fount successfully, though, would be much better invested elsewhere."

"Thanks," he said.

She halted, extending a hand into one of the lines of force and closing her eyes as if she were taking a pulse.

"Very strong," she said a little later. "Someone is tapping it at deep levels now."

She began moving again. The light at the end of the hallway grew brighter, then dimmer, brighter, dimmer. The shadows retreated and flowed back repeatedly as this occurred. I became aware of a sound something like the humming of high wires. There was also an intermittent crackling noise coming from that direction. I increased my pace as Jasra began to hurry. At about that time there came a sound of laughter from up ahead. Frakir tightened upon my wrist. Flakes of fire flashed past the corridor's mouth.

"Damn, damn, damn," I heard Jasra saying.

She raised her hand as we came into sight of the landing where Mask had stood at the time of our encounter. I halted as she moved very slowly, approaching the railing. There were stairs both to the right and the left, leading downward to opposite sides of the chamber.

She looked down for only an instant; then she threw herself back and to the right, rolling when she hit the floor. Taking out a piece of railing, a ball of orange flame fled upward like a slow comet, passing through the area she had just quitted. I rushed to her side, slipped an arm beneath her shoulders, began to raise her.

I felt her stiffen, as her head jerked slightly to the left. Somehow, I already knew what I would see when I turned that way.

Jurt stood there, stark naked save for his eye patch, glowing, smiling, a pulse away from substantiality.

"Good of you to drop by, brother," he said. "Sorry you can't stay."

Sparks danced at his fingertips as he swung his arm in my direction. I doubted that shaking hands was foremost in his mind.

The only response I could think of was, "Your shoelace is untied," which of course didn't stop him, but it actually had him looking puzzled for a second or two.

TWELVE

Jurt had never played football. I do not believe he expected me to come up fast and rush him; and when it happened, I don't think he anticipated my coming in as low as I did.

And as for clipping him just above the knees and knocking him back through the opening in the railing, I'm sure he was surprised. At least he

looked surprised as he went over backward and plummeted, sparks still dancing at his fingertips.

I heard Jasra chuckle, even as he faded in mid-fall and vanished before
the floor got to spread him around a bit. Then, from the corner of my eye,
I saw her rise.

"I'll deal with him now," she said, and, "No problem. He's clumsy," even
as he appeared at the head of the stair to her right. "You take care of Mask!"

Mask was on the opposite side of the black stone fountain, staring up at
me through an orange and red geyser of flames. Below, in the basin, the fires
rippled yellow and white. When he scooped up a handful and worked them
together as a child might shape a snowball, they became an incandescent
blue. Then he threw it at me.

I sent it past with a simple parry. This was not Art, it was basic energy
work. But it served as a reminder, even as I saw Jasra perform the preliminary
gestures to a dangerous spell purely as a feint, bringing her near enough to
Jurt to trip him, pushing him backward down the stair.

Not Art. Whoever enjoyed the luxury of living near and utilizing a power
source such as this would doubtless get very sloppy as time went on, only
using the basic frames of spells as guides, running rivers of power through
them. One untutored, or extremely lazy, might possibly even dispense with
that much after a time and play directly with the raw forces, a kind of sha-
manism, as opposed to the Higher Magic's purity—like that of a balanced
equation—producing a maximum effect from a minimum of effort.

Jasra knew this. I could tell she'd received formal training somewhere
along the line. That much was to the good anyway, I decided as I parried
another ball of fire and moved to my left.

I began descending the stair—sideways—never taking my gaze off Mask.
I was ready to defend or to strike in an instant.

The railing began to glow before me, then it burst into flame. I retreated
a pace and continued my descent. Hardly worth wasting a spell to douse it.
It was obviously meant for show rather than damage. . . .

Well. . . .

There was another possibility, I realized then, as I saw that Mask was
simply watching me, was making no move to throw anything else in my
direction.

It could also be a test. Mask might simply be attempting to discover
whether I was limited to whatever spells I had brought with me—or whether
I had learned to tap the power source here directly and would shortly be
slugging things out with him as Jurt and Jasra were now obviously preparing
to do. Good. Let him wonder. A finite number of spells against a near-limitless
source of energy?

Jurt suddenly appeared upon a windowsill, high and to my left. He had
time only for a brief frown before a curtain of fire was rung down upon him.
Both he and the curtain were gone a moment later, and I heard Jasra's
laughter and his curse, followed by a crashing noise off to the other side of
the chamber.

As I moved to descend another step, the stairway faded from view. Suspecting illusion, I continued the slow downward movement of my foot. I encountered nothing, though, and finally extended my stride to pass over the gap and on down to the next stair. It also vanished, however, as I shifted my weight. There came a chuckle from Mask as I turned my movement into a leap to avoid the area. Once I was committed to jumping, the stairs winked out one by one as I passed over them.

I was certain Mask's thinking must be that if I had a handle on the local power, reflex would cause me to betray that connection here. And if I didn't it might still cause me to waste an escape spell.

But I judged the distance to the now-visible floor. If no more stairs vanished I might be able to catch a handhold on the next one, hang a moment, then drop. That would be perfectly safe. And if I missed, or if another stair vanished . . . I still felt I would land reasonably intact. Better to use an entirely different sort of spell on the way down.

I caught the rearward edge of the farthest stair, dangled and dropped, turning my body and speaking the words of a spell I call the Falling Wall. The fountain shuddered. The fires sloshed and splashed, overflowing the basin on the side nearest Mask. And then Mask himself was thrown backward to the floor as my spell continued its course of descent.

Mask's arms rose before him as his body seemed to sop up the swirling glow, his hands to expel it. There was a bright arc between his hands, then a shieldlike dome. He held it above him, warding off the final collapsive force of my spell. I was already moving quickly in his direction. Even as I did so, Jurt appeared before me, standing on the far lip of the fountain just above Mask, glaring at me. Before I could draw my blade, throw Frakir, or utter another spell, however, the fountain welled up, a great wave toppling Jurt from its side, sending him sprawling upon the floor, washing him past Mask and across the chamber toward the foot of the other stair, down which I now saw that Jasra was slowly descending.

"It means nothing to be able to transport yourself anywhere," I heard her say, "if you are a fool in all places."

Jurt snarled and sprang to his feet. Then he looked upward, past Jasra. . . .

"You, too, brother?" he said.

"I am here to preserve your life, if at all possible," I heard Mandor reply. "I would suggest you return with me now—"

Jurt cried out—no recognizable words, just an animal-like bleat. Then, "I do not need your patronage!" he screamed. "And you are the fool, to trust Merlin! You stand between him and a kingdom!"

A series of glowing circles drifted like glowing smoke rings from between Jasra's hands, dropping as if to settle about his body. Jurt immediately vanished, though moments later I heard him shouting to Mandor from a different direction.

I continued to advance upon Mask, who had guarded successfully against my Falling Wall and was now beginning to rise. I spoke the words of the Icy Path, and his feet went out from beneath him. Yes, I was going to throw a finite number of spells against his power source. I call it confidence. Mask had power. I had a plan, and the means to execute it.

A flagstone tore itself loose from the floor, turned into a cloud of gravel amid a grating, crunching noise, then flew toward me like a charge of shot. I spoke the words of the Net and gestured.

All of the fragments were collected before they could reach me. Then I dumped them upon Mask, who was still struggling to rise.

"Do you realize that I still don't know why we're fighting?" I said. "This was your idea. I can still—"

For the moment, Mask had given up on trying to rise. He had placed his left hand in a simmering puddle of light and had extended his right, palm toward me. The puddle vanished, and a shower of fire emerged from the right hand and sped at me, like drops from a lawn sprinkler. I was ready for this, though. If the Fount could contain the fire, then it had to be insulated against it.

I threw myself flat on the other side of the dark structure, using its base as a shield.

"It is likely one of us is going to die," I called out, "since we are not pulling our punches. Either way, I won't have a chance to ask you later: What's your bitch? What am I to you?"

The only reply was a chuckling sound from the other side of the Fount, as the floor began to move beneath me.

From somewhere off to my right, near the foot of the undamaged stair, I heard Jurt say, "A fool in all places? What about close quarters?" and I looked up in time to see him appear before Jasra and seize hold of her.

A moment later he screamed, as Jasra lowered her head and her lips touched his forearm. She pushed him away then, and he fell down the remaining steps, landing stiffly, not moving.

I crept to the right of the Fount, over the sharp edges of the broken flooring, which jiggled and sawed at me within the matrix of Mask's power.

"Jurt is out of it," I commented, "and you stand alone now, Mask, against the three of us. Call it quits, and I'll see that you go on living."

"Three of you," came that flat, distorted voice. "You admit that you cannot beat me without help?"

" 'Beat'?" I said. "Perhaps you consider it a game. I do not. I will not be bound by any rules you choose to recognize. Call it quits or I'll kill you, with or without help, any way I can."

A dark object suddenly appeared overhead, and I rolled back away from the Fount as it came to rest in the basin. It was Jurt. Unable to move normally because of the paralytic effect of Jasra's bite, he had trumped away from the foot of the stair and into the Fount.

"You have your friends, Lord of Chaos, and I have mine," Mask replied, as Jurt moaned softly and began to glow.

Suddenly Mask went spinning into the air, as I heard the flooring shatter. The Fount itself died down, grew weaker, as a flaming tower twisted ceilingward, rising from a new opening in the floor, bearing Mask with it on the crest of its golden plume.

"And enemies," Jasra stated, moving nearer.

Mask spread his arms and legs and wheeled slowly through the middle air, suddenly in control of his trajectory. I got to my feet and backed away from the Fount. I'm seldom at my best at centers of geological catastrophes.

A rushing, rumbling sound now came from the doubled fountain, and a high-pitched, sourceless-seeming note accompanied it. A small wind sighed among the rafters. The tower of fire atop which Mask rode continued its slow spiraling, and the spray in the lowered fountain began a similar movement. Jurt stirred, moaned, raised his right arm.

"And enemies," Mask acknowledged, beginning a series of gestures I recognized immediately because I'd spent a lot of time figuring them out.

"Jasra!" I cried. "Watch out for Sharu!"

Jasra took three quick steps to her left and smiled. Something very much like lightning then fell from the rafters, blackening the area she had just departed.

"He always starts with a lightning stroke," she explained. "He's very predictable."

She spun once and vanished redly, with a sound like breaking glass.

I looked immediately to where the old man had stood, RINALDO carved upon his right leg. He was leaning against the wall now, one hand to his forehead, the other implementing a simple but powerful shielding spell.

I was about to scream for Mandor to take the old boy out, when Mask hit me with a Klaxon spell which temporarily deafened me while bursting blood vessels in my nose.

Dripping, I dove and rolled, interposing the now-rising Jurt between myself and the sorcerer in the air. Jurt actually appeared to be throwing off the effects of Jasra's bite. So I drove my fist into his stomach as I rose and turned him into an even better position to serve as my shield. A mistake. I received a jolt from his body, not unlike a nasty electrical shock, and he even managed a brief laugh as I fell.

"He's all yours," I heard him gasp then.

From the corner of my eye, I saw where Jasra and Sharu Garrul stood, each of them seemingly holding one end of a great long piece of macramé work woven of cables. The lines were pulsing and changing colors, and I knew they represented forces rather than material objects, visible only by virtue of the Logrus Sight, under which I continued to operate. The pulse increased in tempo, and both sank slowly to their knees, arms still extended, faces glistening. A quick word, a gesture, and I could break that balance. Unfortunately, I had problems of my own just then. Mask was swooping toward me like some huge insect—expressionless, shimmering, deadly. A succession of brittle snapping sounds occurred within the front wall of the Keep, where a series of jagged cracks raced downward like black lightning. I was aware of falling dust beyond the spiraling lights, of the growling and the whining sounds—faint now within my ringing ears—of the continuing vibration of the floor beneath my half-numbered legs. But that was all right. I raised my left hand as my right slid within my cloak.

A fiery blade appeared in Mask's right hand. I did not stir, but waited a second longer before speaking the guide words to my Fantasia-for-Six-Acety-lene-Torches spell as I snapped my forearm back to cover my eyes and rolled to the side.

The stroke missed me, passing through broken stone. Mask's left arm fell across my chest, however, elbow connecting with my lower ribs. I did not stop to assess damages, though, as I heard the sword of fire crackle and come free of the stone. And so, turning, I struck with my own more mundane dagger of steel, driving its full length up into Mask's left kidney.

There followed a scream as the sorcerer stiffened and slumped beside me. Almost immediately thereafter I was kicked with considerable force behind my right hip. I twisted away and another blow landed upon my right shoulder. I am sure it was aimed for my head. As I covered my neck and temples and rolled away, I heard Jurt's voice, cursing.

Drawing my longer blade, I rose to my feet, and my gaze met Jurt's. He was rising at the same time, and he held Mask cradled in his arms.

"Later," he said to me, and he vanished, bearing the body away with him. The blue mask remained on the floor, near to a long smear of blood.

Jasra and Sharu were still facing each other from kneeling positions, panting, bodies completely drenched, their life forces twisting about each other like mating serpents.

Then, like a surfacing fish, Jurt appeared within the tower of forces beyond the Fount. Even as Mandor hurled two of his spheres—which seemed to grow in size as they fled down the chamber, to crash into the Fount and reduce it to rubble—I saw what I believed I would never see again.

As the reverberation of the Fount's collapse spread and the groaning and grinding within the walls was replaced by a snapping and swaying, and dust, gravel and timbers fell about me, I was moving forward, skirting the wreckage, sidestepping new geysers and rivulets of glowing forces, cloak raised to protect my face, blade extended.

Jurt cursed me roundly as I came on. Then, "Pleased, brother? Pleased?" he said. "May death be the only peace between us."

But I ignored the predictable sentiment, for I had to get a better look at what I thought I had seen moments before. I leaped over a piece of broken masonry and beheld the fallen sorcerer's face within the flames, head cradled against his shoulder.

"Julia!" I cried.

But they vanished even as I moved forward, and I knew it was time for me to do the same.

Turning, I fled through the fire.

BOOK NINE
KNIGHT OF SHADOWS

This book is for John Douglas

ONE

H er name was Julia, and I'd been damn certain she was dead back on April 30 when it all began. My finding her grisly remains and destroying the doglike creature which I'd thought had killed her were pretty much the way it started. And we had been lovers, which I suppose was how things had really commenced. Long before.

Perhaps I could have trusted her more. Perhaps I should never have taken her on that shadow-walk which led to denials that took her away from me, down dark ways and into the studio of Victor Melman, a nasty occultist I later had to kill—the same Victor Melman who was himself the dupe of Luke and Jasra. But now, perhaps—just barely—I might have been in a position to forgive myself for what I'd thought I'd done, for it seemed that I hadn't really done it after all. Almost.

That is to say, I learned that I hadn't been responsible for it while I was in the act of doing it. It was when I drove my knife into the side of the mysterious sorcerer Mask, who had been on my case for some time, that I discovered that Mask was really Julia. My half brother Jurt, who's been trying to kill me longer than anyone else in the business, snatched her away, and they vanished then, immediately following his transformation into a kind of living Trump.

As I fled the burning, crumbling Keep there at the Citadel of the

975

Four Worlds, a falling timber caused me to dodge to my right, trapping me in a cul-de-sac of crashed masonry and burning beams. A dark metal ball flashed past me then, seeming to grow as it moved. It struck the wall and passed through it, leaving a hole one could dive through—a hint I was not slow in taking. Outside I jumped the moat, using my Logrus extensions to knock aside a section of fence and a score of troops, before I turned back and shouted, "Mandor!"

"Right here," came his soft voice from behind my left shoulder.

I turned in time to see him catch a metal ball, which bounced once before us and dropped into his extended hand.

He brushed ashes from his black vest and ran a hand through his hair. Then he smiled and turned back toward the burning Keep.

"You've kept your promise to the Queen," he remarked, "and I don't believe there's anything more for you here. Shall we go now?"

"Jasra's still inside," I answered, "having it out with Sharu."

"I thought you were done with her."

I shook my head.

"She still knows a lot of things I don't. Things I'll be needing."

A tower of flame began to rear itself above the Keep, halted and hovered a moment, heaved itself higher.

"I didn't realize," he said. "She does seem to want control of that fountain fairly badly. If we were to snatch her away now, that fellow Sharu will claim it. Does that matter?"

"If we don't snatch her away, he may kill her."

Mandor shrugged.

"I've a feeling she'll take him. Would you care to place a small wager?"

"Could be you're right," I said, watching the fountain continue its climb skyward, following another pause. I gestured toward it. "Thing looks like an oil gusher. I hope the winner knows how to cap it—if there is a winner. Neither one of them may last much longer, the way the place is coming apart."

He chuckled.

"You underestimate the forces they've generated to protect themselves," he said. "And you know it isn't all that easy for one sorcerer to do in another by sorcerous means. However, you've a point there when it comes to the inertia of the mundane. With your permission . . . ?"

I nodded.

With a quick underhand toss he cast the metal ball across the ditch toward the burning building. It struck the ground and with each bounce thereafter it seemed to increase in size. It produced a cymbal-like crash each time it hit, entirely out of proportion with its apparent mass and velocity, and this sound increased in volume on each successive bounce. It passed then into the burning, tottering ruin that was the near end of the Keep and for several moments was gone from sight.

I was about to ask him what was going on when I saw the shadow of a large ball pass before the opening through which I had fled. The flames—

save for the central tower from the broken Fount—began to subside, and a deep rumbling sound came from within. Moments later an even larger circular shadow passed, and I began to feel the rumbling through the soles of my boots.

A wall tumbled. Shortly thereafter part of another wall fell. I could see inside fairly clearly. Through the dust and smoke the image of the giant ball passed again. The flames were snuffed. My Logrus vision still granted me glimpses of the shifting lines of power which flowed between Jasra and Sharu.

Mandor extended a hand. A minute or so later a small metal ball came bouncing our way, and he caught it.

"Let's head back," he said. "It would be a shame to miss the end."

We passed through one of the many gaps in the fence, and sufficient rubble filled the ditch at one point for us to walk across on it. I spent a barrier spell then, to keep the re-forming troops off the premises and out of our way for a time.

Entering through the broken wall, I saw that Jasra stood with her back to the tower of fire, her arms upraised. Streaks of sweat lined her face zebra through a mask of soot, and I could feel the pulsing of the forces which passed through her body. About ten feet above her, face purple and head twisted to one side as if his neck were broken, Sharu hung in the middle of the air. To the untutored he might have seemed magically levitated. My Logrus sight gave me view of the line of force from which he hung suspended, however, victim of what might, I suppose, be termed a magical lynching.

"Bravo," Mandor stated, clapping his hands slowly and softly together. "You see, Merlin? I'd have won that bet."

"You always were a better judge of talent than I was," I acknowledged.

". . . and swear to serve me," I overheard Jasra saying.

Sharu's lips moved.

"And swear to serve you," he gasped.

She lowered her arms slowly, and the line of force which held him began to lengthen. As he descended toward the Keep's cracked floor, her left hand executed a gesture similar to one I had once seen an orchestra conductor employ in encouraging the woodwinds, and a great gout of fire came loose from the Fountain, fell upon him, washed over him, and passed on down into the ground. Flashy, though I didn't quite see the point . . .

His slow descent continued, as if someone in the sky were trolling for crocodiles. I discovered myself holding my breath as his feet neared the ground, in sympathetic anticipation of the eased pressure on his neck. This, however, did not come to pass. When his feet reached the ground, they passed on into it, and his descent continued, as if he were an occulted hologram. He sank past his ankles and up to his knees and kept going. I could no longer tell whether he was breathing. A soft litany of commands rolled from Jasra's lips, and sheets of flame periodically separated themselves from the Fountain and splashed over him. He sank past his waist and up to his shoulders and slightly beyond. When only his head remained visible, eyes open but unfocused, she executed another hand movement, and his journey into the earth was halted.

"You are now the guardian of the Fount," she stated, "answerable only to me. Do you acknowledge this?"

The darkened lips writhed.

"Yes," came a whispered reply.

"Go now and bank the fires," she ordered. "Commence your tenure."

The head seemed to nod at the same time it began sinking again. After a moment only a cottony tuft of hair remained, and an instant later the ground swallowed this, too. The line of force vanished.

I cleared my throat. At the sound Jasra let her arms fall and turned toward me. She was smiling faintly.

"Is he alive or dead?" I asked, and then added, "Academic curiosity."

"I'm not really certain," she responded. "But a little of both, I think. Like the rest of us."

" 'Guardian of the Fount,' " I reflected. "Interesting existence."

"Beats being a coatrack," she observed.

"I daresay."

"I suppose you feel I owe you some gratitude now, for my restoration," she stated.

I shrugged.

"To tell you the truth, I've other things to think about," I said.

"You wanted an end to the feud," she said, "and I wanted this place back. I still have no kind thoughts toward Amber, but I am willing to say we're even."

"I'll settle for that," I told her. "And there is a small loyalty I may share with you."

She studied me through narrowed eyes for a moment, then smiled.

"Don't worry about Luke," she said.

"But I must. That son of a bitch Dalt—"

She continued to smile.

"Do you know something I don't?" I asked.

"Many things," she replied.

"Anything you'd care to share?"

"Knowledge is a marketable commodity," she observed, as the ground shook slightly and the fiery tower swayed.

"I'm offering to help your son and you're offering to sell me the information on how to go about it?" I inquired.

She laughed.

"If I thought Rinaldo needed help," she said, "I'd be at his side this moment. I suppose it makes it easier to hate me if you feel I lack even maternal virtues."

"Hey, I thought we were calling things even," I said.

"That doesn't preclude hating each other," she replied.

"Come on, lady! Outside of the fact that you tried to kill me year after year, I've got nothing against you. You happen to be the mother of someone

I like and respect. If he's in trouble, I want to help him, and I'd as soon be on good terms with you."

Mandor cleared his throat as the flames dropped ten feet, shuddered, dropped again.

"I've some fine culinary spells," he remarked, "should recent exertions have roused some appetites."

Jasra smiled almost coquettishly, and I'd swear she batted her eyelashes at him. While he makes a striking appearance with that shock of white hair, I don't know that you'd exactly call Mandor handsome. I've never understood why women are as attracted to him as they usually seem to be. I've even checked him out for spells on that particular count, but he doesn't wear one. It must be some different order of magic entirely.

"A fine idea," she responded. "I'll provide the setting if you'll take care of the rest."

Mandor bowed; the flames collapsed the rest of the way to the ground and were damped therein. Jasra shouted an order to Sharu, the Invisible Guardian, telling him to keep them that way. Then she turned and led us toward the downward stair.

"Underground passage," she explained, "to more civilized shores."

"It occurs to me," I remarked, "that anyone we encounter will probably be loyal to Julia."

Jasra laughed.

"As they were to me before her and to Sharu before me," she replied. "They are professionals. They come with the place. They are paid to defend the winners, not to avenge the losers. I will put in an appearance and make a proclamation after dinner, and I will enjoy their unanimous and heartfelt loyalty until the next usurpation. Mind that third step. There's a loose flagstone."

So she led us on, through a section of fake wall and into a dark tunnel, heading in what I believed to be a northwesterly direction toward the area of the Citadel which I had investigated somewhat on my previous journey this way. That was the day I had rescued her from Mask/Julia and taken her back to Amber to be a coatrack in *our* citadel for a while. The tunnel we entered was totally dark, but she conjured a darting dot, bright in its will-o'-the-wispiness, which preceded us through the gloom and the damp. The air was stale and the walls were cobwebby. The floor was of bare earth, save for an irregular patch of flagstones down its middle; there were occasional fetid puddles at either hand; and small dark creatures flashed past us—both on the ground and in the air—every now and then.

Actually, I did not need the light. Probably none of us did. I held to the Sign of the Logrus, which provided a magical way of seeing, granting a silvery, directionless illumination. I maintained it because it would also give me a warning against magical effects—which might include booby trap spells about the premises or, for that matter, a bit of treachery on Jasra's part. One effect of this seeing was to note that the Sign also hovered before Mandor, who, to my knowledge, has never been much into trust either. Something cloudy and vaguely Pattern-like also occupied a similar position vis-à-vis Jasra, completing the circle of wariness. And the light danced on before us.

We emerged from behind a stack of barrels into what appeared to be a very well-stocked wine cellar. Mandor paused after six paces and carefully removed a dusty bottle from the rack to our left. He drew a corner of his cloak across its label.

"Oh, my!" he observed.

"What is it?" Jasra inquired.

"If this is still good, I can build an unforgettable meal around it."

"Really? Better bring several to be sure then," she said. "These go back before my time—perhaps before Sharu's time even."

"Merlin, you bring these two," he said, passing me a pair. "Carefully, now."

He studied the rest of the rack before selecting two more, which he carried himself.

"I can see why this place is often under siege," he remarked to Jasra. "I'd have been inclined to have a go at it myself had I known about this part."

She reached out and squeezed his shoulder.

"There are easier ways to get what you want," she said, smiling.

"I'll remember that," he replied.

"I hope you'll hold me to it."

I cleared my throat.

She gave me a small frown, then turned away. We followed her out a low doorway and up a creaking flight of wooden stairs. We emerged in a large pantry and passed through it into an immense, deserted kitchen.

"Never a servant around when you need one," she remarked, casting her gaze about the room.

"We won't be needing one," Mandor said. "Find me a congenial dining area and I'll manage."

"Very well," she replied. "This way then."

She led us through the kitchen; then we passed through a series of rooms till we came to a stairway, which we mounted.

"Ice fields?" she asked. "Lava fields? Mountains? Or a storm-tossed sea?"

"If you are referring to a choice of views," Mandor responded, "give me the mountains."

He glanced at me, and I nodded.

She conducted us to a long, narrow room, where we unfastened a series of shutters to behold a dappled range of round-topped peaks. The room was cool and a bit dusty with shelves running the length of the near wall. These held books, writing implements, crystals, magnifying glasses, small pots of paint, a few simple magical instruments, a microscope, and a telescope. There was a trestle table at the room's middle, a bench on either side of it.

"How long will it take to prepare this?" Jasra asked.

"A minute or two," Mandor said.

"In that case," she said, "I would like to repair myself somewhat first. Perhaps you would also."

"Good idea," I said.

"Indeed," Mandor acknowledged.

She led us to what must have been guest quarters, not too far away, and left us with soap, towels, and water. We agreed to meet back in the narrow room in half an hour.

"Think she's planning something nasty?" I asked as I drew off my shirt.

"No," Mandor replied. "I like to flatter myself in thinking that she would not want to miss this meal. Nor, do I feel, would she want us to miss seeing her at her best, having so far seen her at something less than that. And a possibility of gossip, confidences . . ." He shook his head. "You may never have been able to trust her before and may never again. But this meal will be a Time-out if I'm any judge."

"I'll hold you to that," I said as I splashed and lathered.

Mandor gave me a crooked smile, then conjured a corkscrew and opened the bottles—"to let them breathe a little"—before he tended to himself. I trusted his judgment, but I hung on to the Sign of the Logrus in case I had to duel with a demon or avoid a falling wall.

No demons sprang; no masonry toppled. I entered the dining room behind Mandor and watched him transform it with a few words and gestures. The trestle table and the benches were replaced by a round table and comfortable-looking chairs—the chairs so situated as to provide a good view of the mountains from each. Jasra had not yet arrived, and I was carrying the two wine bottles whose respiration Mandor found most appealing. Before I could even set them down, Mandor conjured an embroidered tablecloth and napkins; delicate china, which looked as if it had been hand decorated by Miró; finely wrought silverware. He studied the tableau a moment, banished the silverware, summoned a set with a different pattern. He hummed as he paced and regarded the layout from various angles. Just as I moved forward to place the bottles on the table, he summoned a crystal bowl filled with floating flowers as a centerpiece. I took a step backward then as crystal goblets appeared.

I made a small growling noise, and he seemed to notice me for the first time in a while.

"Oh, set them there. Set them there, Merlin," he said, and an ebony tray appeared on the table to my left.

"We'd better check to see how the wine is holding up, before the lady arrives," he said then, pouring some of the ruby fluid into two of the goblets.

We sampled these, and he nodded. It was better than Bayle's. By far.

"Nothing wrong there," I said.

He rounded the table, went to the window, and looked out. I followed. Somewhere up in those mountains, I supposed, was Dave in his cave.

"I feel almost guilty," I said, "taking a break like this. There are so many things I should be tending to—"

"Possibly even more than you suspect," he said. "Look upon this less as a break than a retrenchment. And you may learn something from the lady."

"True," I replied. "I wonder what, though."

He swirled his wine in his glass, took another small sip, and shrugged.

"She knows a lot. She may let something slip, or she may feel expansive at the attention and grow generous. Take things as they're dealt."

I took a drink, and I could be nasty and say my thumbs began to prickle. But it was actually the Logrus field that warned me of Jasra's approach along the hall outside. I did not remark upon it to Mandor, since I was certain he felt it, too. I simply turned toward the door, and he matched my movement.

She had on a low over-one-shoulder (the left) white dress, fastened at the shoulder with a diamond pin, and she wore a tiara, also of diamonds, which seemed almost to be radiating in the infrared range amidst her bright hair. She was smiling, and she smelled good, too. Involuntarily I felt myself standing straighter, and I glanced at my fingernails to be certain they were clean.

Mandor's bow was more courtly than mine, as usual. And I felt obliged to say something pleasant. So, "You're looking quite . . . elegant," I observed, letting my eyes wander to emphasize the point.

"It is seldom that I dine with two princes," she remarked.

"I'm Duke of the Western Marches," I said, "not a prince."

"I was referring to the House of Sawall," she replied.

"You've been doing homework," Mandor noted, "recently."

"I'd hate to commit a breach of protocol," she said.

"I seldom use my Chaos title at this end of things," I explained.

"A pity," she told me. "I find it more than a little . . . elegant. Aren't you about thirtieth in the line of succession?"

I laughed.

"Even that great a distance is an exaggeration," I said.

"No, Merle, she's about right," Mandor told me. "Give or take the usual few."

"How can that be?" I asked. "The last time I looked—"

He poured a goblet of wine and offered it to Jasra. She accepted it with a smile.

"You haven't looked recently," Mandor said. "There have been more deaths."

"Really? So many?"

"To Chaos," Jasra said, raising her goblet. "Long may she wave."

"To Chaos," Mandor replied, raising his.

"Chaos," I echoed, and we touched the goblets together and drank.

A number of delightful aromas came to me suddenly. Turning, I saw that the table now bore serving dishes. Jasra had turned at the same moment, and Mandor stepped forward and gestured, causing the chairs to slide back to accommodate us.

"Be seated, please, and let me serve you," he said.

We did, and it was more than good. Several minutes passed, and apart from compliments on the soup nothing was said. I did not want to be the first with a conversational gambit, though it had occurred to me that the others might feel the same way.

Finally, Jasra cleared her throat, and we both looked at her. I was surprised that she suddenly seemed slightly nervous.

"So, how are things in Chaos?" she asked.

"At the moment, chaotic," Mandor replied, "not to be facetious." He thought a moment, then sighed and added, "Politics."

She nodded slowly, as if considering asking him for the details he did not seem to care to divulge, then deciding against it. She turned toward me.

"Unfortunately, I'd no opportunity to sight-see while I was in Amber," she said. "From what you told me, though, life seems a bit chaotic there also."

I nodded.

"It's good that Dalt's gone," I said, "if that's what you mean. But he was never a real threat, just a nuisance. Speaking of whom—"

"Let's not," she interrupted, smiling sweetly. "What I really had in mind was anything else."

I smiled back.

"I forgot. You're not a fan of his," I said.

"It's not that," she responded. "The man has his uses. It's just"—she sighed—"politics," she finished.

Mandor laughed, and we joined him. Too bad I hadn't thought to use that line about Amber. Too late now.

"I bought a painting awhile back," I said, "by a lady named Polly Jackson. It's of a red '57 Chevy. I like it a lot. It's in storage in San Francisco right now. Rinaldo liked it, too."

She nodded, stared out the window.

"You two were always stopping in some gallery or other," she said. "Yes, he dragged me to a lot of them, too. I always thought he had good taste. No talent, but good taste."

"What do you mean, 'no talent'?"

"He's a very good draftsman, but his own paintings were never that interesting."

I had raised the subject for a very special reason, and this wasn't it. But I was fascinated by a side of Luke I'd never known, and I decided to pursue the matter.

"Paintings? I never knew he painted."

"He's tried any number of times, but he never shows them to anyone because they're not good enough."

"Then how do you know about them?"

"I'd check out his apartment periodically."

"When he wasn't around?"

"Of course. A mother's privilege."

I shuddered. I thought again of the burning woman down the Rabbit Hole. But I didn't want to say what I felt and spoil the flow now that I had her talking. I decided to return to my original trail.

"Was it in connection with any of this that he met Victor Melman?" I asked.

She studied me for a moment through narrowed eyes, then nodded and finished her soup.

"Yes," she said then, laying her spoon aside. "He took a few lessons from the man. He'd liked some of his paintings and looked him up. Perhaps he bought something of his, too. I don't know. But at some point he mentioned his own work and Victor asked to see it. He told Rinaldo he liked it and said he thought he could teach him a few things that might be of help."

She raised her goblet and sniffed it, sipped her wine, and stared at the mountains.

I was about to prompt her, hoping she'd go on, when she began to laugh. I waited it out.

"A real asshole," she said then. "But talented. Give him that."

"Uh, what do you mean?" I asked.

"After a time he began speaking of the development of personal power, using all those circumlocutions the half-enlightened love to play with. He wanted Rinaldo to know he was an occultist with something pretty strong going for him. Then he began to hint that he might be willing to pass it along to the right person."

She began laughing again. I chuckled myself, at the thought of that trained seal addressing the genuine article in such a fashion.

"It was because he realized Rinaldo was rich, of course," she continued. "Victor was, as usual, broke himself at the time. Rinaldo showed no interest, though, and simply stopped taking painting lessons from him shortly after that—as he felt he'd learned all he could from him. When he told me about it later, however, I realized that the man could be made into a perfect cat's-paw. I was certain such a person would do anything for a taste of real power."

I nodded.

"Then you and Rinaldo began the visitation business? You took turns clouding his mind and teaching him a few real things?"

"Real enough," she said, "though I handled most of his training. Rinaldo was usually too busy studying for exams. His point average was generally a little higher than yours, wasn't it?"

"He usually had pretty good grades," I conceded. "When you talk of empowering Melman and turning him into a tool, I can't help thinking about the reason: You were priming him to kill me, in a particularly colorful fashion."

She smiled.

"Yes," she said, "though probably not as you think. He knew of you, and he had been trained to play a part in your sacrifice. But he acted on his own the day he tried it, the day you killed him. He had been warned against such a solo action, and he paid the price. He was anxious to possess all of the powers he thought would come of it, rather than share them with another. As I said—an asshole."

I wanted to appear nonchalant, to keep her going. Continuing my meal seemed the best measure to indicate such poise. When I glanced down, however, I discovered that my soup bowl had vanished. I picked up a roll, broke it, was about to butter it when I saw that my hand was shaking. A moment later I realized that this was because I wanted to strangle her.

So I took a deep breath and let it go, had another drink of wine. An appetizer plate appeared before me, and a faint aroma of garlic and various tantalizing herbs told me to be calm. I nodded thanks to Mandor, and Jasra did the same. A moment later I buttered the roll.

Several mouthfuls after that, I said, "I confess that I do not understand. You say that Melman was to play a part in my ritual slaying—but only a part?"

She continued eating for a half minute or so, then found another smile.

"It was too appropriate an opportunity to pass up," she told me then, "when you broke up with Julia and she grew interested in the occult. I saw that I would have to get her together with Victor, to have him train her, to teach her a few simple effects, to capitalize on her unhappiness at your parting, to turn it into a full-blown hatred so intense that she would be willing to cut your throat when the time came for the sacrifice."

I choked on something which otherwise tasted wonderful.

A frosty crystal goblet of water appeared beside my right hand. I raised it and washed everything down. I took another sip.

"Ah, that reaction is worth something, anyhow," Jasra remarked. "You must admit that having someone you once loved as executioner adds spice to vengeance."

Out of the corner of my eye I saw that Mandor was nodding. And I, also, had to agree that she was right.

"I must acknowledge it as a well-conceived bit of revenge," I said. "Was Rinaldo in on this part?"

"No, you two had grown too chummy by then. I was afraid he'd warn you."

I thought about it for another minute or so, then, "What went wrong?" I asked.

"The one thing I'd never have guessed," she said. "Julia really had talent. A few lessons from Victor, and she was better than he was at anything he could do—except painting. Hell! Maybe she paints, too. I don't know. I'd dealt myself a wild card, and it played itself."

I shuddered. I thought of my conversation with the ty'iga at Arbor House, back when it was possessing Vinta Bayle. "Did Julia develop the abilities she sought?" it had asked me. I'd told it that I didn't know. I'd said that she'd never shown any signs. . . . And shortly thereafter I'd remembered our meeting in the supermarket parking lot and the dog she told to sit that may never have moved again. . . . I'd recalled this, but—

"And you never noticed any indication of her talent?" Jasra ventured.

"I wouldn't say that," I replied as I began to realize why things were as they were. "No, I wouldn't say that."

. . . Like that time at Baskin-Robbins when she caused a change of flavors 'twixt cone and lip. Or the storm she'd stayed dry in without an umbrella . . .

She frowned a puzzled frown and narrowed her eyes as she stared. "I don't understand," she said. "If you knew, you could have trained her yourself. She was in love with you. You would have been a formidable team."

I writhed internally. She was right, and I *had* suspected, had probably even known, but I'd been suppressing it. I'd possibly even triggered its onset myself, with that shadow walk, with my body energies. . . .

"It's tricky," I said, "and very personal."

"Oh. Matters of the heart are either very simple or totally inscrutable to me," she said. "There doesn't seem to be a middle ground."

"Let's stipulate simple," I told her. "We were already breaking up when I noticed the signs, and I'd no desire to call up the power in an ex-lover who might one day want to practice on me."

"Understandable," Jasra said. "Very. And ironic in the extreme."

"Indeed," Mandor observed, and with a gesture he caused more steaming dishes to appear before us. "Before you get carried away with a narrative of intrigue and the underside of the psyche, I'd like you to try a little breast of quail drowned in Mouton Rothschild, with a bit of wild rice and a few amusing asparagus tips."

I had driven her to her studies by showing her another layer of reality, I realized. And I had driven her away from me because I had not really trusted her enough to tell her the truth about myself. I suppose this said something about my capacity for love as well as trust. But I had felt this all along. There was something else. There was more. . . .

"This is delicious," Jasra announced.

"Thank you." He rose, rounded the table, and refilled her glass manually rather than use a levitation trick. As he did, I noticed that the fingers of his left hand lightly brushed her bare shoulder. He sloshed a little into my glass as an afterthought then and went back and sat down.

"Yes, excellent," I observed as I continued my quick introspect through the dark glass suddenly cleared.

I had felt something, had suspected something from the beginning, I knew now. Our shadow walk was only the most spectacular of a series of small, off-the-cuff tests I had occasionally thrown her way, hoping to catch her off guard, hoping to expose her as—what? Well, a potential sorceress. So?

I set my utensils aside and rubbed my eyes. It was near, though I'd been hiding it from myself for a long while. . . .

"Is something the matter, Merlin?" I heard Jasra asking.

"No. Just realized I was a little tired," I said. "Everything's fine."

A sorceress. Not just a potential sorceress. There had been the buried fear, I now understood, that she was behind the April 30 attempts on my life—and I had suppressed this and kept on caring for her. Why? Because I knew and did not care? Because she was my Nimue? Because I had cherished my possible destroyer and hidden evidence from myself? Because I'd not only loved unwisely but had had one big death wish following me around, grinning, and any time now I might cooperate with it to the utmost?

"I'll be okay," I said. "It's really nothing."

Did it mean that I was, as they say, my own worst enemy? I hoped not. I didn't really have time to go through therapy, not when my life depended on so many external things as well.

"A penny for your thoughts," Jasra said sweetly.

TWO

"They're priceless," I answered. "Like your jokes. I must applaud you. Not only did I know nothing of this at the time, but I didn't make any correct guesses when I did have a few facts to rub together. Is that what you wanted to hear?"

"Yes," she said.

"I'm pleased there came a point where things went wrong for you," I added.

She sighed, nodded, took a drink of wine.

"Yes, it came," she acknowledged. "I was hardly expecting any recoil from such a simple bit of business. I still find it hard to believe that there's that much irony running around loose in the world."

"If you want me to appreciate the whole thing, you're going to have to be a little more explicit," I suggested.

"I know. In a way, I hate trading that vaguely puzzled expression you're wearing for one of delight at my own discomfort. On the other hand, there may still be material able to distress you in some fresh fashion on the other side of it."

"Win a few, lose a few," I said. "I'm willing to bet there are still features of those days that puzzle you."

"Such as?" she asked.

"Such as why none of those April thirtieth attempts on my life succeeded."

"I assume Rinaldo sabotaged me some way, tipped you off."

"Wrong."

"What, then?"

"The ty'iga. She's under a compulsion to protect me. You might recall her from those days, as she resided in the body of Gail Lampron."

"Gail? Rinaldo's girlfriend? My son was dating a demon?"

"Let's not be prejudiced. He'd done a lot worse his freshman year."

She thought a moment, then nodded slowly.

"You've got a point there," she admitted. "I'd forgotten Carol. And you still have no idea—beyond what the thing admitted back in Amber—as to why this was going on?"

"I still don't know," I said.

"It casts that entire period in an even stranger light," she mused, "especially since our paths have crossed again. I wonder . . . ?"

"What?"

"Whether she was there to protect you or to thwart me—your bodyguard or my curse?"

"Hard to say, since the results came to the same thing."

"But she's apparently been hanging around you most recently, which would seem to indicate the former."

"Unless, of course, she knows something we don't."

"Such as?"

"Such as the possibility of a conflict developing between us again."

She smiled.

"You should have gone to law school," she said. "You're as devious as your relatives back in Amber. I can be truthful, though, in saying I have nothing planned that could be taken that way."

I shrugged.

"Just a thought. Please continue with Julia's story."

She proceeded to eat several mouthfuls. I kept her company, then discovered I could not stop eating. I glanced at Mandor, but he remained inscrutable. He'll never admit to magically enhancing a flavor or laying a compulsion on diners to clean their plates. Either way, we did finish the course before she spoke again. And I could hardly complain, considering.

"Julia studied with a variety of teachers after you two broke up," she began. "Once I hit upon my plan, it was a simple matter to cause them to do or say things which would disillusion or discourage her and set her to looking for someone else. It was not long before she came to Victor, who was already under our tutelage. I ordered him to sweeten her stay and to skip many of the usual preliminaries and to proceed to teaching her about an initiation I had chosen for her—"

"That being?" I interrupted. "There are an awful lot of initiations around, with a variety of specialized ends."

She smiled and nodded, breaking a roll and buttering it.

"I led her myself through a version of my own—the Way of the Broken Pattern."

"Sounds like something dangerous from the Amber end of Shadow."

"I can't fault your geography," she said. "But it is not all that dangerous if you know what you're doing."

"It is my understanding," I said, "that those Shadow worlds which contain shadows of the Pattern can only hold imperfect versions and that this always represents a hazard."

"It is a hazard only if one does not know how to deal with it."

"And you had Julia walk this—Broken Pattern?"

"My knowledge of what you refer to as walking the Pattern is restricted to what my late husband and Rinaldo have told me of it. I believe that you follow the lines from a definite external beginning to an interior point where the power comes to you?"

"Yes," I acknowledged.

"In the Way of the Broken Pattern," she explained, "you enter through the imperfection and make your way to the center."

"How can you follow the lines if they are broken or imperfect? The real Pattern would destroy you if you departed the design."

"You don't follow the lines. You follow the interstices," she said.

"And when you emerge . . . wherever?" I asked.

"You bear the image of the Broken Pattern within you."

"And how do you conjure with this?"

"Through the imperfection. You summon the image, and it is like a dark well from which you draw power."

"And how do you travel among shadows?"

"Much as you do—as I understand it," she said. "But the break is always with you."

"The break? I don't understand."

"The flaw in the Pattern. It follows you through Shadow. It is always there beside you as you travel, sometimes as a hair-fine crack, sometimes a great chasm. It shifts about; it may appear suddenly, anywhere—a lapse in reality. This is the hazard for those of the Broken Way. To fall into it is the final death."

"It must lie within all of your spells then also, like a booby trap."

"All occupations have their hazards," she said. "Avoiding them is a part of the art."

"And this is the initiation through which you took Julia?"

"Yes."

"And Victor?"

"Yes."

"I understand what you are saying," I replied, "but you must realize that the broken Patterns are drawing their power from the real one."

"Of course. What of it? The image is almost as good as the real thing, if you're careful."

"For the record, how many useful images are there?"

"Useful?"

"They must degenerate from shadow to shadow. Where do you draw the line and say, 'Beyond this broken image I will not risk breaking my neck'?"

"I see what you mean. You can work with perhaps the first nine. I've never gone farther out. The first three are best. The circle of the next three is still manageable. The next three are a lot riskier."

"A bigger chasm for each?"

"Exactly."

"Why are you giving me all this esoteric information?"

"You're a higher-level initiate, so it doesn't matter. Also, there is nothing you could do to affect the setup. And finally, you need to know this to appreciate the rest of the story."

"All right," I said.

Mandor tapped the table, and small crystal cups of lemon sherbet appeared before us. We took the hint and cleared our palates before resuming the conversation. Outside, the shadows of clouds slid across the mountain slopes. A faint music drifted into the room from somewhere far back along the corridor. Clinking and scraping noises, sounding like distant pick-and-shovel work, came to us from somewhere outside—most likely at the Keep.

"So you initiated Julia," I prompted.

"Yes," Jasra said.

"What happened then?"

"She learned to summon the image of the Broken Pattern and use it for magical sight and the hanging of spells. She learned to draw raw power through the break in it. She learned to find her way through Shadow—"

"While minding the chasm?" I suggested.

"Just so, and she had a definite knack for it. She'd a flair for everything, as a matter of fact."

"I'm amazed that a mortal can traverse even a broken image of the Pattern and live."

"Only a few of them do," Jasra said. "The others step on a line or die mysteriously in the broken area. Ten percent make it, maybe. That isn't bad. Keeps it somewhat exclusive. Of them, only a few can learn the proper mantic skills to amount to anything as an adept."

"And you say that she was actually better than Victor, once she knew what she was about?"

"Yes. I didn't appreciate just how good until it was too late."

I felt her gaze upon me, as if she were checking for a reaction. I glanced up from my food and cocked an eyebrow.

"Yes," she went on, apparently satisfied. "You didn't know that was Julia you were stabbing back at the Fount, did you?"

"No," I admitted. "I'd been puzzled by Mask all along. I couldn't figure any motive for whatever was going on. The flowers were an especially odd touch, and I never really understood whether it was you or Mask behind the bit with the blue stones."

She laughed.

"The blue stones, and the cave they come from, are something of a family secret. The material is a kind of magical insulator, but two pieces—once together—maintain a link, by which a sensitive person can hold one and track the other—"

"Through Shadow?"

"Yes."

"Even if the person doing the tracking otherwise has no special abilities along these lines?"

"Even so," she said. "It's similar to following a shadow shifter while she's shifting. Anyone can do it if she's quick enough, sensitive enough. This just extends the practice a little further. It's following the shifter's trail rather than the shifter herself."

"Herself, herself . . . You trying to tell me it's been pulled on you?"

"That's right."

I looked up in time to see her blush.

"Julia?" I said.

"You begin to understand."

"No," I said. "Well, maybe a little. She was more talented than you'd anticipated. You already told me that. I get the impression she suckered you on something. But I'm not sure where or how."

"I brought her here," Jasra said, "to pick up some equipment I wanted to take along to the first circle of shadows near Amber. She did have a look at my workroom in the Keep at that time. And perhaps I was overly communicative then. But how was I to know she was making mental notes and probably formulating a plan? I'd felt her too cowed to entertain such thoughts. I must admit she was a pretty good actress."

"I read Victor's diary," I said. "I take it you were masked or hooded and possibly using some sort of voice-distorting spell the whole time?"

"Yes, but rather than awe Julia into submission, I think I roused her cupidity for things magical. I believe she picked up one of my tragoliths—the blue stones—at that time. The rest is history."

"Not for me."

A bowl of totally unfamiliar but delicious-smelling vegetables appeared, steaming, before me.

"Think about it."

"You took her to the Broken Pattern and conducted her initiation . . ." I began.

"Yes."

"The first chance she had," I continued, "she used the . . . tragolith to return to the Keep and learn some of your other secrets."

Jasra applauded softly, sampled the veggies, quickly ate more. Mandor smiled.

"Beyond that I draw a blank," I admitted.

"Be a good boy and eat your vegetables," she said.

I obeyed.

"Basing my conclusions concerning this remarkable tale solely upon my experience of human nature," Mandor suddenly observed, "I would say that she wished to test her talons as well as her wings. I'd guess she went back and challenged her former master—this Victor Melman—and fought a sorcerous duel with him."

I heard Jasra's intake of breath.

"Is that truly only a guess?" she asked.

"Truly," he answered, swirling his wine in his goblet. "And I would guess further that you had once done something similar with your own teacher."

"What devil told you that?" she asked.

"It is only a guess that Sharu was your teacher—and perhaps more than that," he said. "But it would explain both your acquisition of this place and your ability to catch its former lord off guard. He might even have had a stray moment before his defeat for a wishful curse that the same fate attend you one day. And even if not, these things do sometimes have a way of running full circle with people in our trade."

She chuckled.

"The devil called Reason, then," she said, a note of admiration in her voice. "Yet you summon him by intuition, which makes it an art."

"It is good to know he still comes when I call. I take it Julia was surprised, however, by Victor's ability to thwart her."

"True. She did not anticipate that we tend to wrap apprentices in a layer or two of protection."

"Yet her own defenses obviously proved adequate—at least."

"True. Though that, of course, was tantamount to defeat. For she knew that I would learn of her rebellion and come soon to discipline her."

"Oh," I observed.

"Yes," she stated. "That is why she faked her death, which I must admit had me completely fooled for a long while."

I recalled the day I had visited Julia's apartment, found the body, been attacked by the beast. The corpse's face had been partly destroyed, the remaining features gory. But the lady had been the right size, and general resemblances had jibed. And she had been in the right place. And then I had become the object of the lurking doglike creature's attention, which had distracted me more than a little from the minutiae of identity. By the time my struggle for my life was concluded, to the accompaniment of approaching sirens, I was more interested in flight than in further investigation. Thereafter, whenever I had returned in memory to that scene, it was Julia dead whom I beheld.

"Incredible," I said. "Then whose body was it that I found?"

"I've no idea," she replied. "It could have been one of her own shadow selves or some stranger off the street. Or a corpse stolen from the morgue. I've no way of knowing."

"It was wearing one of your blue stones."

"Yes. And its mate was on the collar of the beast you slew—and she opened the way for it to come through."

"Why? And why all that business with the Dweller on the Threshold as well?"

"Red herring of the first water. Victor thought I'd killed her, and I thought he had. He assumed I'd opened a way from the Keep and sent the hunting beast after her. I guessed he'd done it, and I was irritated he'd hidden his rapid development from me. Such things seldom bode well."

I nodded.

"You breed those creatures around here?"

"Yes," she replied, "and I show them, too, in several adjacent shadows. I've a number who've taken blue ribbons."

"I'll stick with pit bulls," I said. "They're a lot cuter and better behaved. So, she left a body and a hidden corridor to this place, and you thought Victor had done her in and was setting things up for a raid on your sanctum sanctorum."

"More or less."

"And he thought she'd become sufficiently dangerous to you—as with the corridor—that you'd killed her?"

"I don't really *know* that he ever found the corridor. It was fairly well hidden, as you learned. Either way, neither of us was aware of what she'd really done."

"That being?"

"She'd also planted a piece of tragolith on me. Later, after the initiation, she used its mate to track me through Shadow to Begma."

"Begma? What the hell were you doing there?"

"Nothing important," she said. "I mention it only to show her subtlety. She did not approach me at that time. I know of it, in fact, only because she told me of it later. She trailed me then from the perimeter of the Golden Circle back here to the Citadel. The rest you know."

"I'm not sure that I do."

"She had designs on this place. When she surprised me, I was surprised indeed. It was how I became a coatrack."

"And she took over here, donning a goalie mask for public relations purposes. She dwelled here for a time, building her powers, increasing her skills, hanging umbrellas on you—"

Jasra growled softly, and I remembered that her bite was worse. I hastened into a fresh area of speculation. "I still don't understand why she spied on me on occasion and sometimes threw flowers."

"Men are exasperating," Jasra said, raising her wineglass and draining it. "You've managed to understand everything but her motive."

"She was on a power trip," I said. "What's to understand past that? I even recall a long discussion we once had concerning power."

I heard Mandor chuckle. When I glanced at him, he looked away, shaking his head.

"Obviously," Jasra said, "she still cared about you. Most likely, a great deal. She was playing games with you. She wanted to rouse your curiosity. She wanted you to come after her, to find her, and she probably wanted to try her power against your own. She wanted to show you that she was worthy of all those things you'd denied her when you denied her your confidence."

"So you know about that, too."

"There were times when she spoke freely to me."

"So she cared for me so well that she sent men with tragoliths to track me to Amber and try to slay me. They almost succeeded, too."

Jasra looked away, coughed. Mandor immediately rose, circled the table, and refilled her goblet, interposing himself between us. At that time, while she was wholly blocked from my sight, I heard her say softly, "Well, not exactly. The assassins were . . . mine. Rinaldo wasn't around to warn you, as I'd guessed he was doing, and I thought I'd have one more shot at you."

"Oh," I observed. "Any more wandering around out there?"

"They were the last," she said.

"That's a comfort."

"I'm not apologizing. I'm just explaining, to clear our differences. Are you willing to cancel this account, too? I've got to know."

"I already said I was willing to call things even. It still goes. Where does

Jurt come into all this? I don't understand how they got together and what they are to each other."

Mandor added a touch of wine to my own glass before returning to his seat. Jasra met my eyes.

"I don't know," she said. "She had no allies when we fought. It had to have happened while I was rigid."

"Have you any idea where she and Jurt might have fled?"

"No."

I glanced at Mandor, and he shook his head.

"Neither have I," he said. "However, a peculiar thought has occurred to me."

"Yes?"

"Besides the fact that he has negotiated the Logrus and come into his powers, is it necessary for me to point out that Jurt—apart from his scars and missing pieces—bears you a strong resemblance?"

"Jurt? Me? You've got to be kidding!"

He glanced at Jasra.

"He *is* right," she said. "It's obvious that the two of you are related."

I put down my fork and shook my head.

"Preposterous," I said, more in self-defense than as a matter of certainty. "I never noticed."

Mandor shrugged, very slightly.

"You want a lecture on the psychology of denial?" Jasra asked me.

"No," I said. "I want a little while in which to let this sink in."

"Time for another course anyway," Mandor announced, and he gestured widely and it was delivered.

"Will you be in trouble with your relatives for having released me?" Jasra asked after a while.

"By the time they realize you're gone, I hope to have a good story ready," I answered.

"In other words, you will be," she said.

"Maybe a little."

"I'll see what I can do."

"What do you mean?"

"I don't like to be obligated to anyone," she said, "and you've done more for me than I have for you in this. If I come upon a means of turning their wrath away from you, I'll employ it."

"What could you possibly have in mind?"

"Let it go at that. Sometimes it's better not to know too much."

"I don't like the sound of this at all."

"An excellent reason for changing the subject," she said. "How great an enemy has Jurt become?"

"To me?" I asked. "Or are you wondering whether he'll be returning here for second helpings?"

"Both, when you put it that way."

"I believe he'll kill me if he can," I said, glancing at Mandor, who nodded.

"I fear that is so," he stated.

"As for whether he'll be back here for more of whatever it is that he got," I continued, "you're the best judge. How close did he seem to be to possessing the full powers one might gain from that ritual at the Fountain?"

"It's hard to say exactly," she said, "as he was testing them under very chaotic conditions. Fifty percent, maybe. Just a guess. Will that satisfy him?"

"Perhaps. How dangerous does that make him?"

"Very. When he gets the full hang of things. Still, he must realize that this place will be heavily guarded—even against someone such as himself—should he decide to return. I suspect he'll stay away. Just Sharu—in his present circumstances—would be a formidable obstacle."

I went on eating.

"Julia will probably advise him not to try it," she continued, "familiar as she is with the place."

I nodded my acceptance of the notion. We would meet when we met. Nothing much I could do now to forestall it.

"Now may I ask you a question?" she said.

"Go ahead."

"The *ty'iga* . . ."

"Yes?"

"Even in the body of the duke Orkuz's daughter, I am certain that she did not just walk into the palace and wander on up to your apartments."

"Hardly," I replied. "She's with an official party."

"May I ask when the party arrived?"

"Earlier in the day," I answered. "I'm afraid, though, that I can't go into any detail as to—"

She flipped her well-ringed hand in a gesture of denial.

"I'm not interested in state secrets," she said, "though I know Nayda usually accompanies her father in a secretarial capacity."

"So?"

"Did her sister come along or did she stay home?"

"That would be Coral, wouldn't it?" I asked.

"Yes."

"She did," I replied.

"Thank you," she said, and returned to her food.

Damn. What was that about? Did she know something concerning Coral that I didn't? Something that might bear on her present, indeterminate state? If so, what might it cost me to find out?

"Why?" I said then.

"Just curious," she replied. "I knew the family in . . . happier times."

Jasra sentimental? Never. What then?

"Supposing the family had a problem or two?" I asked.

"Apart from Nayda's possession by the *ty'iga*?"

"Yes," I said.

"I would be sorry to hear that," she said. "What problem?"

"Just a little captivity thing involving Coral."

There came a small clatter as she dropped her fork and it fell upon her plate.

"What *are* you talking about?" she asked.

"A misplacement," I said.

"Of Coral? How? Where?"

"It depends partly on how much you really know about her," I explained.

"I'm fond of the girl. Don't toy with me. What happened?"

More than a little puzzling. But not the answer I was after.

"You knew her mother pretty well?"

"Kinta. I'd met her, at diplomatic functions. Lovely lady."

"Tell me about her father."

"Well, he's a member of the royal house, but of a branch not in the line of succession. Before he was prime minister, Orkuz was the Begman ambassador to Kashfa. His family was in residence with him, so naturally I saw him at any number of affairs—"

She looked up when she realized I was staring at her—through the Sign of the Logrus, across her Broken Pattern. Our eyes met, and she smiled.

"Oh. You did ask about her *father*," she said. Then she paused, and I nodded. "So there's truth in that rumor," she observed at last.

"You didn't really know?"

"There are so many rumors in the world, most of them impossible to check. How am I to know which of them hold truth? And why should I care?"

"You're right, of course," I said. "Nevertheless . . ."

"Another of the old boy's by-blows," she said. "Does anyone keep score? It's a wonder he had any time for affairs of state."

"Anyone's guess," I said.

"To be frank then, in addition to knowing the rumor I'd heard, there was indeed a family resemblance. I couldn't judge on that count, though, not being personally acquainted with most of the family. You're saying there's truth in it?"

"Yes."

"Just because of the resemblance, or is there something more?"

"Something more."

She smiled sweetly and retrieved her fork.

"I've always enjoyed that fairy-tale revelation which sees one rise in the world."

"I also," I said, and I resumed eating.

Mandor cleared his throat.

"It seems hardly fair," he said, "to tell only part of a story."

"You're right," I agreed.

Jasra returned her gaze to me and sighed.

"All right," she said, "I'll ask. How did you know for cer—Oh. Of course. The Pattern."

I nodded.

"Well, well, well. Little Coral, Mistress of the Pattern. This was a fairly recent occurrence?"

"Yes."

"I suppose she is off somewhere in Shadow now—celebrating."

"I wish I knew."

"What do you mean?"

"She's gone, but I don't know where. And it's the Pattern that did it to her."

"How?"

"Good question. I don't know."

Mandor cleared his throat.

"Merlin," he said, "perhaps there are some matters"—he rotated his left hand—"that on reflection you may wish—"

"No," I said. "Ordinarily discretion would rule—perhaps even with you, my brother, as a Lord of Chaos. And certainly in the case of Your Highness"— I nodded to Jasra—"save that you are acquainted and may even have a touch of affection for the lady." I decided against laying it on too thick and quickly added, "Or at least no malice toward her."

"As I said, I'm very fond of the girl," Jasra stated, leaning forward.

"Good," I replied, "for I feel at least partly responsible for what happened, even though I was duped in the matter. So I feel obliged to try to set things right. Only I don't know how."

"What happened?" she asked.

"I was entertaining her when she expressed a desire to see the Pattern. So I obliged her. On the way she asked me questions about it. It seemed harmless conversation, and I satisfied her curiosity. I was not familiar with the rumors concerning her parentage, or I would have suspected something. As it was, when we got there, she set foot upon the Pattern and commenced walking it."

Jasra sucked in her breath.

"It would destroy one not of the blood," she said. "Correct?"

I nodded.

"Or even one of us," I said then, "if any of a number of mistakes be made."

Jasra chuckled.

"Supposing her mother'd really been carrying on with a footman or the cook?" she remarked.

"She's a wise daughter," I said. "At any rate, once one begins the Pattern, one may not turn back. I was obliged to instruct her as she went along. That, or be a very poor host and doubtless damage Begman-Amber relations."

"And spoil all sorts of delicate negotiations?" she asked, half-seriously.

I'd a feeling just then that she'd welcome a digression concerning the exact nature of the Begman visit, but I wasn't biting.

"You might say that," I said. "At any rate, she completed the Pattern, and then it took her away."

"My late husband told me that from its center one can command the Pattern to deliver one anywhere."

"True," I said, "but it was the nature of her command that was a bit unusual. She told the Pattern to send her wherever it wanted."

"I'm afraid I don't understand."

"Neither do I, but she did, and it did."

"You mean she just said, 'Send me wherever you want to send me,' and she was instantly dispatched for points unknown?"

"You've got it."

"That would seem to imply some sort of intelligence on the part of the Pattern."

"Unless, of course, it was responding to an unconscious desire on her part to visit some particular locale."

"True. I suppose there is that possibility. But have you no means of tracing her?"

"I'd a Trump I'd done of her. When I tried it, I reached her. She seemed pent in a dark place. Then we lost touch, and that's it."

"How long ago was this?"

"A matter of hours by my subjective reckoning," I said. "Is this place on anything near Amber time?"

"Close enough, I believe. Why didn't you try again?"

"I've been somewhat occupied ever since. Also, I've been casting about for some alternate way of approaching this."

There came a clinking, rattling sound, and I smelled coffee.

"If you're asking whether I'll help you," Jasra said, "the answer is yes. Only I don't really know how to go about it. Perhaps if you were to try her Trump again—with me backing you—we might reach her."

"All right," I said, lowering my cup and fumbling forth the cards. "Let's give it a try."

"I will assist you also," Mandor stated, rising to his feet and coming to stand to my right.

Jasra came over and stood to my left. I held the Trump so that we all had a clear view.

"Let us begin," I said, and I moved forward with my mind.

THREE

A patch of light I had taken to be a stray sunbeam drifted from its position on the floor to a spot beside my coffee cup. It was ring-shaped, and I decided not to remark upon it since neither of the others seemed to take note of it.

I reached after Coral and found nothing. I felt Jasra and Mandor reaching also, and I tried again, joining forces with them. Harder.

Something?

Something . . . I recalled wondering what Vialle felt when she used the

Trumps. It had to be something other than the visual cues with which the rest of us were familiar. It might be something like this.

Something.

What I felt was a sense of Coral's presence. I regarded her form upon the card, but it would not come alive. The card itself had grown perceptibly cooler, but it was not the same ice-edged chill I normally felt on achieving communication with one of the others. I tried harder. I felt Mandor and Jasra increasing their efforts also.

Then Coral's image on the card faded, but nothing came to replace it. I sensed her presence, however, as I regarded the void. The feeling came closest to that of attempting to make contact with someone who was asleep.

"I cannot tell whether it's simply a difficult place to reach," Mandor began, "or—"

"I believe she is under a spell," Jasra announced.

"That could account for a part of it," Mandor said.

"But only part," came a soft, familiar voice from near at hand. "There are awesome powers holding her, Dad. I've never seen anything like this before."

"The Ghostwheel is right," Mandor said. "I'm beginning to feel it."

"Yes," Jasra began, "there is something. . . ."

And suddenly the veil was pierced, and I beheld the slumped form of Coral, apparently unconscious, lying upon a dark surface in a very dark place, the only illumination coming from what seemed a circle of fire drawn about her. She couldn't have brought me through if she wanted to, and—

"Ghost, can you take me to her?" I asked.

Her image faded before he could reply, and I felt a cold draft. It was several seconds before I realized that it seemed to be blowing upon me from the now-icy card.

"I don't think so, I wouldn't want to, and it may be that there is no need," he answered. "The force that holds her has become aware of your interest and even now is reaching toward you. Is there some way you can turn off that Trump?"

I passed my hand across its face, which is usually sufficient. Nothing happened. The cold breeze even seemed to increase in intensity. I repeated the gesture along with a mental order. I began to feel whatever it was, focusing upon me.

Then the Sign of the Logrus fell upon the Trump, and the card was torn from my hand as I was cast backward, striking my shoulder against the edge of the door. Mandor lurched to his right as this occurred, catching hold of the table to steady himself. In my Logrus vision I had seen wild lines of light flash outward from the card before it fell away.

"Did that do the trick?" I called out.

"It broke the connection," Ghost replied.

"Thanks, Mandor," I said.

"But the power that was reaching for you through the Trump knows where you are now," Ghost said.

"What makes you privy to its awareness?" I inquired.

"It is a surmise, based upon the fact that it's still reaching for you. It is coming the long way round—across space—though. It could take as long as a quarter of a minute before it reaches you."

"Your use of the pronoun is a little indefinite," Jasra said. "Is it just Merlin that it wants? Or is it coming for all of us?"

"Uncertain. Merlin is the focus. I've no idea what it will do to you."

I lurched forward during this exchange and retrieved Coral's Trump.

"Can you protect us?" she asked.

"I've already begun transferring Merlin to a distant place. Shall I do this for you also?"

As I looked up from pocketing the Trump, I noted that the chamber had become something less than substantial—translucent, as if everything were made of colored glass.

"Please," the cathedral-window form of Jasra said softly.

"Yes," came my fading brother's faint echo.

Then I was passed through a fiery hoop into a place of darkness. I stumbled against a stone wall, felt my way along it. A quarter turn, a lighter area before me dotted with bright points . . .

"Ghost?" I asked.

No answer.

"I don't appreciate these interrupted conversations," I continued.

I moved forward until I came to what was obviously a cave mouth. A clear night sky hung before me, and when I stepped outside a cold wind rubbed up against me. I retreated several paces, shivering.

I had no idea where I might be. Not that it really mattered if it brought me a breathing spell. I reached through the Logrus Sign for a great distance before I located a heavy blanket. Wrapping it about myself, I sank to a seated position upon the cave's floor. Then I reached again. It was easier to find a stack of wood and no trick at all to ignite a portion of it. I'd also been looking forward to one more cup of coffee. I wondered. . . .

Why not? I reached again, and the bright circle rolled into view before me.

"Dad! Please stop!" came the offended voice. "I've gone to a lot of trouble to tuck you away in this obscure corner of Shadow. Too many sendings, though, and you'll call attention to yourself."

"Come on!" I said. "All I want is a cup of coffee."

"I'll get one for you. Just don't use your own powers for a while."

"Why won't your action draw just as much attention?"

"I'm using a roundabout route. There!"

A steaming mug of some dark stoneware stood on the floor of the cave near my right hand.

"Thanks," I said, taking it up and sniffing it. "What did you do with Jasra and Mandor?"

"I sent each of you off in a different direction amidst a horde of fake images flitting hither and yon. All you have to do now is lie low for a while. Let its attention subside."

"Whose attention? What's attention?"

"The power that has Coral. We don't want it to find us."

"Why not? I seem to recall your wondering earlier whether you were a god. What's for you to fear?"

"The real thing. It seems to be stronger than I am. On the other hand, I seem to be faster."

"That's something, anyway."

"Get a good night's sleep. I'll let you know in the morning whether it's still hunting you."

"Maybe I'll find out for myself."

"Don't go manifesting unless it's a matter of life or death."

"That wasn't what I meant. Supposing it finds me?"

"Do whatever seems appropriate."

"Why do I have a feeling you're keeping things from me?"

"I guess you're just suspicious by nature, Dad. It seems to run in your family. I've got to go now."

"Where?" I asked.

"Check on the others. Run a few errands. See to my personal development. Check my experiments. Things like that. Bye."

"What about Coral?"

But the circle of light which had hovered before me spun from brightness to dimness and vanished. An unarguable end to the conversation. Ghost was getting more and more like the rest of us—sneaky and misleading.

I sipped the coffee. Not as good as Mandor's, but acceptable. I began wondering where Jasra and Mandor had been sent. I decided against trying to reach them. In fact, it might not be a bad idea, I decided, to fortify my own position against magical intrusion.

I resummoned the Sign of the Logrus, which I had let slip while Ghost was transporting me. I used it to set wards at the cave mouth and about my situation within. Then I released it and took another sip. As I did, I realized that this coffee could not possibly keep me awake. I was coming off a nervous jag, and the weight of all my activities was suddenly heavy upon me. Two more sips, and I could hardly hold the cup. Another, and I noticed that each time I blinked my eyelids were closing a lot more easily than they opened.

I set the cup aside, drew my blanket more tightly about me, and found a relatively comfortable position on the stone floor, having become something of an expert on the activity back in the crystal cave. The flickering flames mustered shadow armies behind my eyelids. The fire popped like a clash of arms; the air smelled of pitch.

I went away. Sleep is perhaps the only among life's great pleasures which need not be of short duration. It filled me, and I drifted. How far and for how long, I cannot say.

Nor can I say what it was that roused me. I know only that I was somewhere else and the next moment I had returned. My position had changed slightly, my toes were cold, and I felt that I was no longer alone. I kept my eyes closed, and did not alter my breathing pattern. It could be that Ghost had simply decided to look in on me. It could also be that something was testing my wards.

I raised my eyelids but the smallest distance, peering outward and upward through a screen of eyelashes. A small misshaped figure stood outside the cave mouth, the fire's remaining glow faintly illuminating his strangely familiar face. There was something of myself in those features and something of my father.

"Merlin," he said softly. "Come awake now. You've places to go and things to do."

I opened my eyes wide and stared. He fitted a certain description. . . . Frakir throbbed, and I stroked her still.

"Dworkin . . . ?" I said.

He chuckled.

"You've named me," he replied.

He paced, from one side of the cave mouth to the other, occasionally pausing to extend a hand partway toward me. Each time he hesitated and drew it back.

"What is it?" I asked. "What's the matter? Why are you here?"

"I've come to fetch you back to the journey you abandoned."

"And what journey might that be?"

"Your search for the lady somewhere astray who walked the Pattern t'other day."

"Coral? You know where she is?"

He raised his hand, lowered it, gnashed his teeth.

"Coral? Is that her name? Let me in. We must discuss her."

"We seem to be talking just fine the way we are."

"Have you no respect for an ancestor?"

"I do. But I also have a shapeshifting brother who'd like to mount my head and hang it on the wall of his den. And he might just be able to do it real quick if I give him half a chance." I sat up and rubbed my eyes, my wits finishing the job of reassembling themselves. "So where's Coral?"

"Come. I will show you the way," he said, reaching forward. This time his hand passed my ward and was immediately outlined in fire. He did not seem to notice. His eyes were a pair of dark stars, drawing me to my feet, pulling me toward him. His hand began to melt. The flesh ran and dripped away like wax. There were no bones within, but rather an odd geometry—as if someone had sketched a hand quickly in a three-dimensional medium, then molded some fleshlike cover for it. "Take my hand."

I found myself raising my hand against my will, reaching toward the fingerlike curves, the swirls of the knuckles. He chuckled again. I could feel the force that drew me. I wondered what would happen if I took hold of that strange hand in a special way.

So I summoned the Sign of the Logrus and sent it on ahead to do my handclasping for me.

This may not have been my best choice of actions. I was momentarily blinded by the brilliant, sizzling flash that followed. When my vision cleared,

I saw that Dworkin was gone. A quick check showed that my wards still held. I perked up the fire with a short, simple spell, noted that my coffee cup was half full, and warmed its tepid contents with an abbreviated version of the same rendering. I reshrouded myself then, settled, and sipped. Analyze as I might, I couldn't figure what had just happened.

I knew of no one who had seen the half-mad demiurge in years, though according to my father's tale, Dworkin's mind should have been largely mended when Oberon repaired the Pattern. If it had really been Jurt, seeking to trick his way into my presence and finish me off, it was an odd choice of form for him to assume. Come to think of it, I wasn't at all certain that Jurt even knew what Dworkin looked like. I debated the wisdom of calling for Ghostwheel to solicit an inhuman opinion on the matter. Before I could decide, however, the stars beyond the cave mouth were occulted by another figure, much larger than Dworkin's—heroically proportioned even.

A single step brought it within range of the firelight, and I spilled coffee when I beheld that face. We had never met, but I had seen his likeness in many places in Castle Amber.

"I understand that Oberon died in redrawing the Pattern," I said.

"Were you present at the time?" he asked.

"No," I replied, "but coming as you do, on the heels of a rather bizarre apparition of Dworkin, you must excuse my suspicions as to your bona fides."

"Oh, that was a fake you encountered. I'm the real thing."

"What was it then that I saw?"

"It was the astral form of a practical joker—a sorcerer named Jolos from the fourth circle of Shadow."

"Oh," I responded. "And how am I to know you're not the projection of someone named Jalas from the fifth?"

"I can recite the entire genealogy of the royal House of Amber."

"So can any good scribe back home."

"I'll throw in the illegitimates."

"How many were there, anyway?"

"Forty-seven, that I know of."

"Aw, come on! How'd you manage?"

"Different time streams," he said, smiling.

"If you survived the reconstruction of the Pattern, how come you didn't return to Amber and continue your reign?" I asked. "Why'd you let Random get crowned and muddy the picture even further?"

He laughed.

"But I didn't survive it," he said. "I was destroyed in the process. I am a ghost, returned to solicit a living champion for Amber against the rising power of the Logrus."

"Granted, *arguendo*, that you are what you say you are," I replied, "you're still in the wrong neighborhood, sir. I am an initiate of the Logrus and a son of Chaos."

"You are also an initiate of the Pattern and a son of Amber," the magnificent figure answered.

"True," I said, "and all the more reason for me not to choose sides."

"There comes a time when a man must choose," he stated, "and that time is now. Which side are you on?"

"Even if I believed that you are what you say, I do not feel obliged to make such a choice," I said. "And there is a tradition in the Courts that Dworkin himself was an initiate of the Logrus. If that is true, I'm only following in the footsteps of a venerable ancestor."

"But he renounced Chaos when he founded Amber."

I shrugged.

"Good thing I haven't founded anything," I said. "If there is something specific that you want of me, tell me what it is, give me a good reason for doing it and maybe I'll cooperate."

He extended his hand.

"Come with me, and I will set your feet upon the new Pattern you must follow, in a game to be played out between the Powers."

"I still don't understand you, but I am certain that the real Oberon would not be stopped by these simple wards. You come to me and clasp my hand, and I will be glad to accompany you and take a look at whatever it is you want me to see."

He drew himself up to an even greater height.

"You would test me?" he asked.

"Yes."

"As a man, it would hardly have troubled me," he stated. "But being formed out of this spiritual crap now, I don't know. I'd rather not take the chance."

"In that case, I must echo your sentiment with respect to your own proposal."

"Grandson," he said levelly, a ruddy light entering his eyes, "even dead, none of my spawn may address me so. I come for thee now in a less than friendly fashion. I come for thee now, and this journey shall I hale thee amid fires."

I took a step backward as he advanced.

"No need to take it personally . . ." I began.

I shaded my eyes as he hit my wards, and the flashbulb effect began. Squinting through it, I saw something of a repetition of the flensing of Dworkin's flesh by fire. Oberon became transparent in places; other places he melted. Within him, through him, as the outward semblance of the kind passed away, I saw the swirls and curves, the straits and channels—black-lined, geometrizing abstractly inside the general outline of a large and noble figure. Unlike Dworkin, however, the image did not fade. Having passed my wards, its movement slowed, it continued toward me nevertheless, reaching. Whatever its true nature, it was one of the most frightening things I had ever encountered. I continued to back away, raising my hands, and I called again upon the Logrus.

The Sign of the Logrus occurred between us. The abstract version of

Oberon continued to reach, scribbled spirit hands encountering the writhing limbs of Chaos.

I was not reaching through the Logrus's image to manipulate it against that apparition. I felt an unusual dread of the thing, even at our distance. What I did was more on the order of thrusting the Sign against the image of the king. Then I dived past them both, out the cave mouth, and I rolled, scrabbling for handholds and toeholds when I struck a slope, coming up hard against a boulder and hugging it as the cave erupted with the noise and flash of an ammo dump that had taken a hit.

I lay there shuddering, my eyes squeezed shut, for perhaps half a minute. Any second, I felt, and something would be on my ass—unless, perhaps, I crouched perfectly still and tried hard to look like another rock. . . .

The silence was profound, and when I opened my eyes, the light had vanished and the shape of the cave mouth was unaltered. I rose slowly to my feet, advanced even more slowly. The Sign of the Logrus had departed, and for reasons I did not understand I was loath to call it back. When I looked within the cave, there were no signs that anything at all had occurred, save for the fact that my wards were blown.

I stepped inside. The blanket still lay where it had fallen. I put out a hand and touched the wall. Cold stone. That blast must have taken place at some other level than the immediate. My small fire was still flickering feebly. I recalled it yet again to life. But the only thing I saw in its glow which I had not seen previously was my coffee cup, broken where it had fallen.

I let my hand remain upon the wall. I leaned. After a time, there came an uncontrollable tightening of my diaphragm. I began laughing. I am not sure why. The weight of everything which had transpired since April 30 was upon me. It just happened that laughter had edged out the alternative of beating my breast and howling.

I thought I knew who all the players were in this complex game. Luke and Jasra seemed to be on my side now, along with my brother Mandor, who'd always looked out for me. My mad brother Jurt wanted me dead, and he was now allied with my old lover Julia, who didn't seem too kindly disposed toward me either. There was the *ty'iga*—an overprotective demon inhabiting the body of Coral's sister, Nayda, whom I'd left sleeping in the midst of a spell back in Amber. There was the mercenary Dalt—who, now I thought of it, was also my uncle—who'd made off with Luke for points and purposes unknown after kicking Luke's ass in Arden with two armies watching. He had nasty designs on Amber but lacked the military muscle to provide more than occasional guerrilla-style annoyance. And then there was Ghostwheel, my cybernetic Trump dealer and minor-league mechanical demigod, who seemed to have evolved from rash and manic to rational and paranoid—and I wasn't at all sure where he was headed from here, but at least he was showing some filial respect mixed in with the current cowardice.

And that had been pretty much it.

But these latest manifestations seemed evidence that there was something else at play here also, something that wanted to drag me off in yet another direction. I had Ghost's testimony that it was strong. I had no idea what it really represented. And I had no desire to trust it. This made for an awkward relationship.

"Hey, kid!" came a familiar voice from down the slope. "You're a hard man to find. You don't stay put."

I turned quickly, moved forward, stared downward.

A lone figure was toiling up the slope. A big man. Something flashed in the vicinity of his throat. It was too dark to make out his features.

I retreated several paces, commencing the spell which would restore my blasted wards.

"Hey! Don't run off!" he called. "I've got to talk to you."

The wards fell into place, and I drew my blade and held it, point lowered, at my right, entirely out of sight from the cave mouth when I turned my body. I ordered Frakir to hang invisible from my left hand also. The second figure had been stronger than the first, to make it past my wards. If this third one should prove stronger than the second, I was going to need everything I could muster.

"Yeah?" I called out. "Who are you and what do you want?"

"Hell!" I heard it say. "I'm no one in particular. Just your old man. I need some help, and I like to keep things in the family."

I had to admit, when it reached the area of firelight, that it was a very good imitation of Prince Corwin of Amber, my father, complete with black cloak, boots, and trousers, gray shirt, silver studs, and buckle—and even a silver rose—and he was smiling that same quirky sort of smile the real Corwin had sometimes worn on telling me his story, long ago. . . . I felt a kind of wrenching in my guts at the sight. I'd wanted to get to know him better, but he'd disappeared, and I'd never been able to find him again. Now, for this thing—whatever it was—to pull this impersonation . . . I was more than a little irritated at such a patent attempt to manipulate my feelings.

"The first fake was Dworkin," I said, "and the second was Oberon. You're climbing right down the family tree, aren't you?"

He squinted and cocked his head in puzzlement as he advanced, another realistic mannerism.

"I don't know what you're talking about, Merlin," he responded. "I—"

Then it entered the warded area and jerked as if touching a hot wire.

"Holy shit!" it said. "You don't trust anybody, do you?"

"Family tradition," I replied, "backed up by recent experience."

I was puzzled, though, that the encounter had not involved more pyrotechnics. Also, I wondered why the thing's transformation into scrollwork had not yet commenced.

With another oath, it swirled its cloak to the left, wrapping it about its arm; its right hand crossed toward an excellent facsimile of my father's scabbard. A silver-chased blade sighed as it arced upward, then fell toward the eye of the ward. When they met, the sparks rose in a foot-high splash and the blade hissed as if it had been heated and were now being quenched in water. The design on the blade flared, and the sparks leaped again—this time as high as a man—and in that instant I felt the ward break.

Then it entered, and I turned my body, swinging my blade. But the blade that looked like Grayswandir fell and rose again, in a tightening circle, drawing my own weapon's point to the right and sliding straight in toward my breast. I did a simple parry in quarte, but he slipped under it and was still coming in from the outside. I parried sixte, but he wasn't there. His movement had been only a feint. He was back inside and coming in low now. I reversed myself and parried again as he slid his entire body into my right, dropping his blade's point, reversing his grip, fanning my face with his left hand.

Too late I saw the right hand rising as the left slid behind my head. Grayswandir's pommel was headed straight for my jaw.

"You're really . . ." I began, and then it connected.

The last thing I remember seeing was the silver rose.

That's life: Trust and you're betrayed; don't trust and you betray yourself. Like most moral paradoxes, it places you in an untenable position. And it was too late for my normal solution. I couldn't walk away from the game.

I woke in a place of darkness. I woke wondering and wary. As usual when wondering and wary, I lay perfectly still and let my breathing continue its natural rhythm. And I listened.

Not a sound.

I opened my eyes slightly.

Disconcerting patterns. I closed them again.

I felt with my body for vibrations within the rocky surface upon which I was sprawled.

No vibes.

I opened my eyes entirely, fought back an impulse to close them. I raised myself onto my elbows, then gathered my knees beneath me, straightened my back, turned my head. Fascinating. I hadn't been this disoriented since I'd gone drinking with Luke and the Cheshire Cat.

There was no color anywhere about me. Everything was black, white, or some shade of gray. It was as if I had entered a photographic negative. What I presumed to be a sun hung like a black hole several diameters above the horizon to my right. The sky was a very dark gray, and ebon clouds moved slowly within it. My skin was the color of ink. The rocky ground beneath me and about me shone an almost translucent bone-white, however. I rose slowly to my feet, turning. Yes. The ground seemed to glow, the sky was dark, and I was a shadow between them. I did not like the feeling at all.

The air was dry, cool. I stood in the foothills to an albino mountain range, so stark in appearance as to rouse comparison with the Antarctic. These stretched off and up to my left. To the right—low and rolling—toward what I guessed to be a morning sun, lay a black plain. Desert? I had to raise my hand and "shade" against its . . . what? Antiglow?

"Shit!" I tried saying, and I noticed two things immediately.

The first was that my word remained unvoiced. The second was that my jaw hurt where my father or his simulacrum had slugged me.

I repeated my silent observation and withdrew my Trumps. All bets were off when it came to messing with sendings. I shuffled out the Trump for the Ghostwheel and focused my attention upon it.

Nothing. It was completely dead to me. But, then, it was Ghost who'd told me to lie low, and maybe he was simply refusing to entertain my call. I thumbed through the others. I paused at Flora's. She was usually willing to help me out of a tight spot. I studied that lovely face, sent out my call to it. . . .

Not a golden curl stirred. Not a degree's drop in temperature. The card remained a card. I tried harder, even muttering an enhancement spell. But there was nobody home.

Mandor, then. I spent several minutes on his card with the same result. I tried Random's. Ditto. Benedict's, Julian's. No and no. I tried for Fiona, Luke, and Bill Roth. Three more negatives. I even pulled a couple of the Trumps of Doom, but I couldn't reach the Sphinx either, or a building of bones atop a green glass mountain.

I squared them, cased them, and put them away. It was the first time I had encountered a phenomenon of this sort since the Crystal Cave. Trumps can be blocked in any of a number of ways, however, and so far as I was concerned, the matter was, at the moment, academic. I was more concerned about removing myself to a more congenial environment. I could save the research for some future bit of leisure.

I began walking. My footsteps were soundless. When I kicked a pebble and it bounced along before me, I could detect nothing of sound to its passage.

White to the left of me, black to the right. Mountains or desert. I turned left, walking. Nothing else in motion that I could see except for the black, black clouds. To the lee side of every outcrop a near-blinding area of enhanced brightness: crazy shadows across a crazy land.

Turn left again. Three paces, then round the boulder. Upward. Over the ridge. Turn downhill. Turn right. Soon a streak of red amid rocks to the left . . .

Nope. Next time then . . .

Brief twinge in the frontal sinus. No red. Move on.

Crevice to the right, next turn . . .

I massaged my temples when they began to ache as no crevice was delivered. My breath came heavy, and I felt moisture upon my brow.

Textures of gray to green and brittle flowers, slate-blue, low on the next talus slope . . .

A small pain in my neck. No flowers. No gray. No green.

Then let the clouds part and the darkness pour down from the sun . . .

Nothing.

. . . and a sound of running water from a small stream, next gully.

I had to halt. My head was throbbing; my hands were shaking. I reached out and touched the rock wall to my left. It felt solid enough. Rampant reality. Why was it treading all over me?

And how had I gotten here?

And where was here?

I relaxed. I slowed my breathing and adjusted my energies. The pains in my head subsided, ebbed, were gone.

Again I began walking.

Birdsong and gentle breeze . . . Flower in a crannied nook.

No. And the first twinge of returning resistance . . .

What sort of spell might I be under, that I had lost my power to walk in Shadow? I had never understood it to be something that could be taken away.

"It's not funny," I tried saying. "Whoever you are, whatever you are, how did you do it? What do you want? Where are you?"

Again I heard nothing; least of all an answer.

"I don't know how you did it. Or why," I mouthed, and thought. "I don't feel as if I'm under a spell. But I must be here for a reason. Get on with your business. Tell me what you want."

Nada.

I walked on, continuing in a halfhearted fashion my attempts to shift away through Shadow. As I did, I pondered my situation. I'd a feeling there was something elementary that I was overlooking in this entire business.

. . . And a small red flower behind a rock, next turn.

I made the turn, and there was the small red flower I had half-consciously conjured. I rushed toward it to touch it, to confirm that the universe was a benign, essentially Merlin-loving place.

I stumbled in my rush, kicking up a cloud of dust. I caught myself, raised myself, looked about. I must have searched for the next ten or fifteen minutes, but I could not locate the flower. Finally, I cursed and turned away. No one likes to be a butt of the universe's jokes.

On a sudden inspiration I sought through all my pockets, should I have even a chip of the blue stones upon my person. Its odd vibrational abilities might just somehow conduct me through Shadow back toward its source. But no. Not even a speck of blue dust remained. They all were in my father's tomb, and that was it. It would have been too easy an out for me, I guess.

What was I missing?

A fake Dworkin, a fake Oberon, and a man who'd claimed to be my father all had wanted to conduct me to some strange place—to compete in some sort of struggle between the Powers, the Oberon figure had indicated, whatever that meant. The Corwin figure had apparently succeeded, I reflected as I rubbed my jaw. Only what sort of game was it? And what were the Powers?

The Oberon thing had said something about my choosing between Amber and Chaos. But, then, it had lied about other things during the same conversation. The devil with both of them! I didn't ask to get involved in their power game. I had enough problems of my own. I didn't even care to learn the rules to whatever was going on.

I kicked a small white stone, watched it roll away. This didn't feel like something of Jurt's or Julia's doing. It seemed either a new factor or an old one which had transformed itself considerably. Where had it first seemed to enter the picture? I guessed it had something to do with the force which had come rushing after me on our attempt to reach Coral. I could only assume that it had located me and this was the result. But what might it be? It would first, I supposed, be necessary that I learn where Coral lay in her circle of fire. Something in that place, I presumed, was behind my current situation. Where then? She had asked the Pattern to send her where she ought to go. . . . I had no way now of asking the Pattern where that might be—and no way at the moment of walking it, to have it send me after her.

It was time, therefore, to resign the game and employ different means to solve the problem. My Trumps having blown a circuit and my ability to traverse Shadow having encountered a mysterious blockage, I decided it was time to up the power factor by an order of magnitude in my favor. I would summon the Sign of the Logrus and continue my shadow walk, backing every step that I took with the power of Chaos.

Frakir cut into my wrist. I sought about quickly after any approaching menaces, but I saw nothing. I remained wary for several minutes longer, exploring the vicinity. Nothing occurred, though, and Frakir grew still.

It was hardly the first time her alarm system had been improperly cued—whether by some stray astral current or some odd thought of my own. But in a place like this, one could not afford to take chances. The highest stand of stone in the vicinity stood at about fifteen to twenty meters, perhaps a hundred paces uphill, to my left. I made my way over to it and commenced climbing.

When I finally reached its chalky peak, I commanded a view over a great distance in every direction. I did not behold another living thing in this strange silent yin-yang universe.

So I decided that it had indeed been a false alarm, and I climbed back down. I reached once again to summon the Logrus and Frakir practically behanded me. Hell. I ignored her, and I sent out my call.

The Sign of the Logrus rose and rushed toward me. It danced like a butterfly, hit like a truck. My newsreel world went away, black and white to black.

FOUR

Recovering.

My head ached, and there was dirt in my mouth. I was sprawled face down. Memory made its way home through the traffic, and I opened my eyes. Still black and white and gray all about. I spit sand, rubbed my eyes, blinked. The Logrus Sign was not present, and I could not account for my recent experience with it.

I sat up and hugged my knees. I seemed to be stranded, all of my extramundane means of travel and communication blocked. I couldn't think of anything to do other than get up, pick a direction, and start walking.

I shuddered. Where would that take me? Just through more of the same—more of this monotonous landscape?

There came a soft sound, as of a throat being gently cleared.

I was on my feet in an instant, having inspected every direction on the way up.

Who's there? I inquired, having given up on articulation.

I seemed to hear it again, very near at hand.

Then, *I've a message for you,* something seemed to say within my head.

What? Where are you? Message? I tried asking.

Excuse me, came the muffled voice, *but I'm new at this business. To take things in order, I am where I've always been—on your wrist—and when the Logrus blasted through here, it enhanced me additionally, so that I could deliver the message.*

Frakir?

Yes. My first enhancement, that day you bore me through the Logrus, involved sensitivity to danger, mobility, combat reflexes, and a limited sentience. This time the Logrus added direct mental communication and expanded my awareness to the point where I could deliver messages.

Why?

It was in a hurry, could stay in this place for only an instant, and this was the only way for it to let you know what is going on.

I didn't realize the Logrus was sentient.

Something like a chuckle followed.

Then, *It is hard to classify an intelligence of that order, and I suppose it doesn't really have much to say most of the time,* came Frakir's reply. *Its energies are mainly expended in other areas.*

Well, why did it come through here and blitz me?

Unintentional. It was a by-product of my enhancement, once it saw that I was the only means of reaching you with more than a few words or images.

Why was its time here so limited? I asked.

It is the nature of this land, which lies between the shadows, that it be mainly inaccessible both to the Pattern and the Logrus.

A sort of demilitarized zone?

No, it is not a matter of truce. It is simply that it is extremely difficult for either of them to manifest here at all. This is why the place is pretty much unchanging.

This is a place they can't reach?

That's about the size of it.

How come I never heard of it before?

Probably because no one else can reach it too readily either.

So what's the message?

Basically, that you not try calling upon the Logrus again while you're here. The place represents such a distorting medium that there's no assurance how any projected energy might manifest outside some convenient vessel. It could be dangerous for you.

I massaged my throbbing temples. At least it got my mind off my sore jaw.

All right, I agreed. *Any hints as to what I'm supposed to be doing here?*

Yes, this is a trial. Of what, I can't say.

Do I have a choice?

What do you mean?

May I refuse to participate?

I suppose. But then I don't know how you get out of here.

So I do get released from this place at the end, if I play?

If you're still living, yes. Even if you're not, I'd imagine.

Then I really have no choice.

There will be a choice.

When?

Somewhere along the way. I don't know where.

Why don't you just repeat all of your instructions to me?

Can't. I don't know what all is here. It will surface only in response to a question or a situation.

Will any of this interfere with your strangling function?

It shouldn't.

That's something, anyway. Very well. Have you any idea what I'm supposed to do next?

Yes. You should begin climbing the highest hill to your left.

Which—Okay, I guess that's the one, I decided, my gaze settling upon a broken fang of blazing white stone.

And so I walked toward it, up a gradually steepening slope. The black sun mounted higher into the grayness. The eerie silence continued.

Uh, do you know exactly what we will find whenever we get to wherever we're going? I tried to say in Frakir's direction.

I am certain that the information is present, came the reply, *but I do not believe that it will be available until we reach the appropriate locale.*

I hope you're right.

Me, too.

The way continued to steepen. While I had no way to measure the time exactly, it seemed that more than an hour passed before I left the foothills and was climbing the white mountain itself. While I observed no footprints nor saw any other sign of life, I did, on several occasions, encounter long stretches of natural-seeming trail, shelflike, leading up that high bleached face. Several more hours must have passed as I negotiated this, the dark sun riding to mid-heaven and beginning its descent toward a west that lay beyond this peak. It was annoying not to be able to curse aloud.

How can I be sure we're on the proper side of the thing? Or heading for the right area? I asked.

You're still going in the proper direction, Frakir answered.

But you don't know how much farther it'll be?

Nope. I'll know when I see it, though.

The sun is going to slip behind the mountain fairly soon. Will you be able to see it to know it then?

I believe the sky actually brightens here when the sun goes away. Negative space is funny that way. Whatever, something is always bright here and something is always dark. There'll be the wherewithal for detection.

Any idea what we're actually doing?

One of those damned quest-things, I think.

Vision? Or practical?

It was my understanding that they all partake of both, though I feel this one is heavily weighted toward the latter. On the other wrist, anything you encounter between shadows is likely to partake of the allegorical, the emblematic—all that crap people bury in the nonconscious parts of their beings.

In other words, you don't know either.

Not for sure, but I make my living as a sensitive guesser.

I reached high, grabbed handholds, drew myself up to another ledge. I followed it for a time, climbed again.

At length the sun went away, and it made no difference in my ability to see. Darkness and light changed places.

I scaled a five- or six-meter irregularity and halted when I finally got a look into the recessed area it rose to. There was an opening in the face of the mountain to its rear. I hesitated to label it a cave because it appeared artificial. It looked as if it had been carved in the form of an arch, and it was big enough to ride through on horseback.

What do you know, Frakir commented, twitching once upon my wrist. *This is it.*

What? I asked.

The first station, she replied. *You stop here and go though a bit of business before moving on.*

That being?

It's easier just to go and look.

I hauled myself up over the edge, got to my feet, and walked forward. The big entranceway was filled with that sourceless light. I hesitated on the threshold, peered within.

It looked to be a generic chapel. There was a small altar, a pair of candles upon it sporting flickering coronas of blackness. There were stone benches carved along the walls. I counted five doorways apart from the one by which I stood: three in the wall across from me; one in that to the right; another to the left. Two piles of battle gear lay in the middle of the room. There were no symbols of whatever religion might be represented.

I entered.

What am I supposed to do here? I asked.

You are supposed to sit vigil, guarding your armor overnight.

Aw, come on, I said, moving forward to inspect the stuff. *What's the point?*

That's not a part of the information I've been given.

I picked up a fancy white breastplate which would have made me look like Sir Galahad. Just my size, it seemed. I shook my head and lowered the piece. I moved over to the next pile and picked up a very odd-looking gray gauntlet. I dropped it immediately and rooted through the rest of the stuff. More of the same. Contoured to fit me, also. Only—

What is the matter, Merlin?

The white stuff, I said, *looks as if it would fit me right now. The other armor appears to be of a sort used in the Courts. It looks as if it would fit me just right when I'm shifted into my Chaos form. So either set would probably do for me, depending on circumstances. I can use only one outfit at a time, though. Which am I supposed to guard?*

I believe that's the crux of the matter. I think you're supposed to choose.

Of course! I snapped my fingers, heard nothing. *How slow of me, that I need to have things explained by my strangling cord!*

I dropped to my knees, swept both sets of armor and weapons together into one nasty-looking heap.

If I have to guard them, I said, *I'll guard both sets. I don't care to take sides.*

I've a feeling something isn' going to like that, Frakir answered.

I stepped back and regarded the pile.

Tell me about this vigil business again, I said. *What all's involved?*

You're supposed to sit up all night and guard it.

Against what?

Against anything that tries to misappropriate it, I guess. The powers of Order—

—or Chaos

Yeah, I see what you mean. Heaped up together that way, anything might come by to grab off a piece.

I seated myself on the bench along the rear wall, between two doorways. It was good to rest for a bit after my long climb. But something in my mind kept grinding away. Then, after a time, *What's in it for me?* I asked.

What do you mean?

Say I sit here all night and watch the stuff. Maybe something even comes along and makes a pass at it. Say I fight it off. Morning comes, the stuff is still here, I'm still here. Then what? What have I gained?

Then you get to don your armor, pick up your weapons, and move on to the next stage of affairs.

I stifled a yawn.

You know, I don't think I really want any of that stuff, I said then. *I don't like armor, and I'm happy with the sword I've got.* I clapped my hand to its hilt. It felt strange, but then so did I. *Why don't we just leave the whole pile where it is and move on to the next stage now? What is the next stage anyway?*

I'm not sure. The way the Logrus threw information at me it just seems to surface at the appropriate time. I didn't even know about this place till I saw the entrance.

I stretched and folded my arms. I leaned my back against the wall. I extended my legs and crossed them at the ankles.

Then we're stuck here till something happens or you get inspired again?

Right.

Wake me when it's over, I said, and I closed my eyes.

The wrist twitch that followed was almost painful.

Hey! You can't do that! Frakir said. *The whole idea is that you sit up all night and watch.*

And a very half-assed idea it is, I said. *I refuse to play such a stupid game. If anything wants the stuff, I'll give it a good price on it.*

Go ahead and sleep if you want. But what if something comes along and decides you had better be taken out of the picture first?

To begin with, I replied, *I don't believe that anything could care about that pile of medieval junk, let alone lust after it—and in closing, it's your job to warn me of danger.*

Aye, aye, Captain. But this is a weird place. What if it limits my sensitivity some way?

You're really reaching now, I said. *I guess you'll just have to improvise.*

I dozed. I dreamed that I stood within a magic circle and various things tried to get at me. When they touched the barrier, though, they were transformed into stick figures, cartoon characters which rapidly faded. Except for Corwin of Amber, who smiled faintly and shook his head.

"Sooner or later you'll have to step outside," he said.

"Then let it be later," I replied.

"And all your problems will still be there, right where you left them."

I nodded.

"But I'll be rested," I answered.

"Then it's a trade-off. Good luck."

"Thanks."

The dream fell apart into random images then. I seem to remember standing outside the circle a little later, trying to figure a way to get back in. . . .

I wasn't certain what woke me. It couldn't have been a noise. But suddenly I was alert and rising, and the first thing I beheld was a dwarf with a mottled complexion, his hands clasped at his throat, lying unmoving in a twisted position near the armor pile.

"What's going on?" I tried saying.

But there was no reply.

I crossed and knelt beside the short big-shouldered guy. With my fingertips, I felt after a carotid pulse but couldn't locate one. At that moment, however, I felt a tickling sensation about my wrist, and Frakir—phasing into and out of visibility—made her way back into touch with me.

You took that guy out? I asked.

There came a soft pulsation then. *Suicides don't strangle themselves,* she replied.

Why didn't you alert me?

You needed your rest, and it wasn't anything I couldn't handle. Our empathy is too strong, though. Sorry I woke you.

I stretched.

How long was I asleep?

Several hours, I'd judge.

I feel kind of sorry about this, I said. *That scrap heap isn't worth somebody's life.*

It is now, Frakir answered.

True. Now that someone's died for the stuff have you gotten the word as to what we do next?

Things are a little clearer, but not enough to act on. We must remain until morning for me to be certain.

Does the information you have include anything on whether there's food or drink available in the neighborhood?

Yes. There's supposed to be a jug of water behind the altar. Also a loaf of bread. But that's for morning. You're supposed to be fasting throughout the night.

That's only if I take this whole business seriously, I said, turning toward the altar.

I took two steps, and the world started to come apart. The floor of the chapel trembled, and I heard my first sounds since my arrival; a deep growling, grating noise came from somewhere far beneath me. A horde of colors flashed through the air of this colorless place, half blinding me with their intensity. Then the colors fled, and the room divided itself. The whiteness grew intense in the vicinity of the archway by which I had entered. I had to raise my hand to shield my eyes against it. Across from this, a profound darkness occurred, masking the three doorways in that wall.

What . . . is it? I asked.

Something terrible, Frakir replied, *beyond my ability to assess.*

I clasped the hilt of the blade I wore and reviewed the spells I still had hanging. Before I could do any more than that, an awful sense of presence pervaded the place. So potent did it seem that I did not feel that drawing my blade or reciting a spell was the most politic action I might take.

Ordinarily I'd have summoned the Sign of the Logrus by then, but that way was barred to me also. I tried clearing my throat, but no sound came forth. Then there came a movement at the heart of the light, a coalescing. . . .

The shape of a Unicorn, like Blake's Tyger, burning bright, took form, so painful to behold that I had to look away.

I shifted my gaze to the deep, cool blackness, but there was no rest for my eyes in that place either. Something stirred within the darkness, and there came another sound—a grating, as of metal being scraped on stone. This was followed by a powerful hissing. The ground trembled again. Curved lines flowed forward. Even before the brightness of the Unicorn etched its lineaments within that mighty gloom, I realized it was the head of a one-eyed serpent which had come partway into the chapel. I shifted my gaze to a point between them, catching each within my peripheral vision. Far better than any attempt to behold either directly. I felt their gazes upon me, the Unicorn of Order and the Serpent of Chaos. It was not a pleasant feeling, and I retreated until the altar was at my back.

Both came slightly farther into the chapel. The Unicorn's head was lowered, horn pointed directly at me. The Serpent's tongue darted in my direction.

"Uh, if either of you want this armor and stuff," I ventured, "I certainly have no object—"

The Serpent hissed and the Unicorn raised a hoof and let it fall, cracking the floor of the chapel, the fracture line racing toward me like a streak of black lightning and halting just at my feet.

"On the other hand," I observed, "no insult is intended by the offer, Your Eminences—"

Wrong thing to say—again, Frakir interjected, weakly.

Tell me what's right, I said, trying for a mental sotto voce.

I don't—Oh!

The Unicorn reared; the Serpent drew itself upward. I dropped to my knees and looked away, their gazes having somehow become physically painful. I was trembling, and all of my muscles had begun to ache.

It is suggested, Frakir recited, *that you play the game the way it is set up.*

What metal entered my backbone I know not. But I raised my head and turned it, looking first to the Serpent, then to the Unicorn. Though my eyes watered and ached as if I were trying to stare down the sun, I managed the gesture.

"You can make me play," I said, "but you cannot make me choose. My will is my own. I will guard this armor all night, as is required of me. In the morning I will go on without it because I do not choose to wear it."

Without it you may die, Frakir stated, as if translating.

I shrugged.

"If it is my choice to make, I choose not to place one of you before the other."

A rush of wind blew hot and cold past me, seemed a cosmic sigh.

You will choose, Frakir relayed, *whether you become aware of it or not. Everyone does. You are simply being asked to formalize your choice.*

"What's so special about my case?" I asked.

Again that wind.

Yours is a dual heritage, combined with great power.

"I never wanted either of you for an enemy," I stated.

Not good enough, came the reply.

"Then destroy me now."

The game is already in progress.

"Then let's get on with it," I answered.

We are not pleased with your attitude.

"Vice versa," I answered.

The thunderclap that followed left me unconscious. The reason I felt I could afford total honesty was a strong hunch that players for this game might be hard to come by.

I woke sprawled across the pile of greaves, cuirasses, gauntlets, helms, and other good things of a similar nature, all of them possessed of corners or protuberances, most of which were jabbing into me. I became aware of this only by degrees, for I had gone numb in lots of important places.

Hi, Merlin.

Frakir, I responded. *Have I been out for long?*

I don't know. I just came around myself.

I didn't know a piece of rope could be knocked out.

Neither did I. It never happened to me before.

Let me amend my question then: Any idea how long we've been out?

Fairly long, I feel. Get me a glimpse out the doorway, and I may be able to give you a better idea.

I pushed myself slowly to my feet, could not remain standing, dropped. I crawled to the entranceway, noting in passing that nothing on the heap seemed to be missing. The floor was indeed cracked. There really was a dead dwarf to the rear of the chamber.

I looked outside, beheld a bright sky, black points disposed within it.

Well? I asked after a time.

If I figure right, it should be morning soon.

Always brightest before the dawn, eh?

Something like that.

My legs burned as their circulation was restored. I pushed myself upright, stood leaning against the wall.

Any new instructions?

Not yet. I've a feeling they're due with the dawn.

I staggered to the nearest bench, collapsed upon it.

If anything comes in now, all I've got to hit it with is an odd assortment of spells. Sleeping on armor leaves a few kinks. Almost as bad as sleeping in it.

Throw me at the enemy and the least I can do is buy you time.

Thanks.

How far back does your memory go?

To when I was a little kid, I guess. Why?

I recall sensations from when I was first enhanced, back in the Logrus. But everything up until we got here is kind of dreamlike. I just sort of used to react to life.

A lot of people are that way, too.

Really? I couldn't think, or communicate this way before.

True.

Do you think it will last?

What do you mean?

Might this just be a temporary condition? Might I just have been enhanced to deal with the special circumstances in this place?

I don't know, Frakir, I answered, massaging my left calf. *I suppose it's possible. Are you getting attached to the state?*

Yes. Silly of me, I guess. How can I care about something I won't miss when it's gone?

Good question, and I don't know the answer. Maybe you would have achieved this state anyway eventually.

I don't think so. But I don't know for certain.

You afraid to regress?

Yes.

Tell you what. When we find a way out of here, you stay behind.

I couldn't do that.

Why not? You've come in handy on occasion, but I can take care of myself. Now you're sentient you should have a life of your own.

But I'm a freak.

Aren't we all? I just want you to know I understand, and it's okay with me.

She pulsed once and shut up.

I wished I weren't afraid to drink the water.

I sat there for perhaps the better part of an hour, going over everything that had happened to me recently, looking for patterns, clues.

I can sort of hear you thinking, Frakir said suddenly, *and I can offer you something in one area.*

Oh? What might that be?

The one who brought you here—

The thing that looked like my father?

Yes.

What of him?

He was different from your other two visitors. He was human. They weren't.

You mean it might actually have been Corwin?

I never met him, so I can't say. He wasn't one of those constructs, though.

Do you know what they were?

No. I only know one peculiar thing about them, and I don't understand it at all.

I leaned forward and rubbed my temples. I took several deep breaths. My throat was very dry, and my muscles ached.

Go ahead. I'm waiting.

I don't quite know how to explain it, Frakir said. *But back in my presentient days you inconsiderately wore me about your wrist when you walked the Pattern.*

I recall. I had a scar for a long time after, from your reaction to it.

Things of Chaos and things of Order do not mix well. But I survived. And the experience is recorded within me. Now the Dworkin and the Oberon figures that visited you back at the cave—

Yes?

Beneath their apparent humanity they were pulsing energy fields within geometrical constructs.

Sounds sort of like computer animation.

Maybe it is something like that. I couldn't say.

And my father wasn't one of these?

Nope. But that wasn't what I was getting at. I recognized the source.

I was suddenly alert.

What do you mean?

The swirls—the geometrical constructs on which the figures were based— they reproduced sections of the Pattern at Amber.

You must be mistaken.

No. What I lacked in sentience I made up in memory. Both figures were three-dimensional twistings of Pattern segments.

Why would the Pattern be creating simulacra to bug me?

I'm just a humble killing aid. Reasoning is not one of my strong points yet.

If the Unicorn and the Serpent are involved, I suppose the Pattern might be also.

We know that the Logrus is.

And it seemed to me that the Pattern demonstrated sentience the day Coral walked it. Say that's true and add on the ability to manufacture constructs— Is this the place it wanted them to bring me? Or did Corwin transport me someplace else? And what does the Pattern want of me? And what does my father want of me?

I envy your ability to shrug, Frakir answered. *Those are what I take it you call rhetorical questions?*

I guess so.

Information of another sort is beginning to come to me, so I assume the night is ending.

I sprang to my feet.

Does that mean I can eat—and drink? I asked.

I believe so.

I moved quickly then.

While I am new to these things, I cannot help wondering whether it might be considered disrespectful to vault over an altar that way, Frakir commented.

The black flames flickered as I passed between them.

Hell, I don't even know what it's an altar to, I answered, *and I've always thought of disrespect as something that had to be identity-specific.*

The ground trembled slightly as I seized the jug and took a deep swallow.

Then, again, perhaps you have a point there, I said, choking.

I carried the jug and the loaf around the altar, past the stiffening dwarf and over to the bench which ran along the back wall. Seating myself, I commenced eating and drinking more slowly.

What comes next? I asked. *You said that the information was flowing again.*

You have kept vigil successfully, she said. *Now you must select what you need from among the armor and weapons you watched, then pass through one of the three doorways in this wall.*

Which one?

One is the door of Chaos, one the door of Order, and I know not the nature of the third.

Uh, how does one make an informed decision in these matters?

I think your way may be barred by all but the one you're supposed to pass.

Then one does not really have a choice, does one?

I believe that the matter of the doorways may be predicated upon the choice one makes in the hardware department.

I finished the bread, washed it down with the rest of the water. I got to my feet then.

Well, I said, *let's see what they'll do if I don't make a choice. Too bad about the dwarf.*

He knew what he was doing, what chances he was taking.

That's more than I can say.

I approached the right-hand door since it was the nearest. It let into a bright corridor which grew brighter and brighter as it receded until sight of it was lost to me beyond a few paces' distance. I kept walking. Damn near broke my nose, too. It was as if I'd encountered a wall of glass. It figures. I couldn't picture myself walking off into the light that way.

You're actually getting more cynical as I watch, Frakir observed. *I caught that thought.*

Good.

I approached the middle one more carefully. It wore gray and seemed to let into a long corridor also. I could see down it perhaps a little farther than the first, though no features other than walls, roof, and floor presented themselves. I extended my arm and discovered that my way was not barred.

Seems to be the one, Frakir observed.

Maybe.

I moved over to the left-hand doorway, its passage black as the inside of God's pocket. Again there was no resistance when I explored for hidden barriers.

Hm. It appears I do have a choice.

Odd. I haven't any instructions to cover this.

I returned to the middle one, took a step forward. Hearing a sound behind me, I turned. The dwarf had sat up. He was holding his sides and laughing. I tried to turn back then, but now something barred my return. Suddenly then the scene dwindled, as if I were accelerating to the rear.

I thought the little guy was dead, I said.

So did I. He gave every indication.

I turned away, back to the direction I'd been headed. There was no feeling of acceleration. Perhaps it was the chapel that was receding while I stood still.

I took a step forward, then another. Not a sound from my footfalls. I began walking. After a few paces I put out my hand to touch the left-hand wall. It encountered nothing. I tried again with the right. Again nothing. I took a step to the right and reached again. Nope. I still seemed approximately equidistant from two shadowy walls. Growling, I ignored them and strode forward.

What's the matter, Merle?

Do you or do you not sense walls to the right and left of us? I asked.

Nope, Frakir replied.

Any idea at all where we are?

We are walking between shadows.

Where are we headed?

Don't know yet. We're following the Way of Chaos, though.

What? How do you know that? I thought we had to pick something Chaosian for the pile to be admitted here.

At this I gave myself a quick search. I found the dagger tucked into my right boot sheath. Even in the dim light I could recognize the workmanship as something from back home.

We were set up somehow, I said. *Now I know why the dwarf was laughing. He planted this on me while we were passed out.*

But you still had a choice—between this and the dark corridor.

True.

So why'd you pick this one?

The light was better.

FIVE

A half dozen steps later even the impression of walls had vanished. Ditto the roof, for that matter. Looking back, I saw no sign of the corridor or its entrance. There was only a vast dismal area. Fortunately the floor or ground remained firm underfoot. The only manner in which I could distinguish the way I traveled from the surrounding gloom had to do with visibility. I walked a pearl-gray trail through a valley of shadow, though, technically, I supposed, I walked between shadows. Picky-picky. Someone or something had grudgingly spilled a minimum of light to mark my way.

I trudged through the eerie silence, wondering how many shadows I passed among, then wondering whether that was too linear a way of considering the phenomenon. Probably.

At that moment, before I could invoke mathematics, I thought I saw something move off to my right. I halted. A tall ebon pillar had come into view, barely, at the edge of vision. But it was not moving. I concluded that it was my own movement which had given it the appearance of motion. Thick, still, smooth—I ran my gaze up that dark shaft until I lost sight of it. There seemed no way of telling how high the thing stood.

I turned away. I took a few more paces. I noted another pillar then— ahead of me, to the left. I gave this one only a glance as I continued. Shortly more came into view at either hand. The darkness into which they ascended held nothing resembling stars, positive or negative; my world's canopy was a simple, uniform blackness. A little later, the pillars occurred in odd groupings, some very near at hand, and their respective sizes no longer seemed uniform.

I halted, reached toward a stand of them to my left which seemed almost within touching range. It wasn't, though. I took a step in that direction.

There came a quick squeeze at my wrist.

I wouldn't do that if I were you, Frakir observed.

Why not? I inquired.

It might be easy to get lost and into a lot of trouble.

Maybe you're right.

I broke into a jog. Whatever was going on, my only real desire concerning it was to have it over with as soon as possible, so that I could get back to matters I considered important—like locating Coral, springing Luke, finding a way to deal with Jurt and Julia, looking for my father. . . .

The pillars, at varying distances, slid by, and items which were not pillars began occurring among them. Some were squat, asymmetrical; others were tall, tapered; some leaned upon neighbors, bridged them, or lay broken at their bases. It was something of a relief to see that monotonous regularity destroyed, in a way that showed that forces played upon forms.

The ground lost its flatness then, though it retained a stylized geometric quality in the stacked, step, and shelflike appearance of its various levels. My own way remained flat and vaguely lighted as I jogged amid the ruins of a thousand Stonehenges.

I increased my pace, and soon I was running past galleries, amphitheaters, forestlike stands of stone. I seemed to glimpse movement within several of these, but again it could easily have been a function of velocity and poor lighting.

Sense anything alive in the neighborhood? I asked Frakir.

No, came the answer.

Thought I saw something move.

Maybe you did. Doesn't mean it's there.

Talking for less than a day, and you've already learned sarcasm.

I hate to say it, boss, but anything I learn I pick up from your vibes. Ain't no one else around to teach me manners and like that.

Touché, I said. *Maybe I'd better warn you if there's trouble.*

Touché, boss. Hey, I like these combat metaphors.

Moments later I slowed my pace. Ahead something was flickering off to the right. There were moments of blue and red within the changing light intensities. I halted. These glimpses lasted only a few moments but were more than sufficient to make me wary. I regarded their apparent source for a long while.

Yes, Frakir said after a time. *Caution is in order. But don't ask me what to expect. It is only a general feeling of menace that I have.*

Perhaps there's some way I could just sneak by whatever it is.

You'd have to leave the trail to do that, Frakir replied, *and since the trail does run through the circle of stones where it's coming from, I'd say no.*

Nobody told me I couldn't leave the trail. Do you have any instructions to that effect?

I know you are supposed to follow the trail. I've nothing specific concerning the consequences of leaving it, though.

Hm.

The way curved to the right, and I followed it. It ran directly into the massive circle of stones, and though I slowed my pace, I did not deviate. I studied it as I drew near, however, and noted that while the trail entered there, it did not emerge again.

You're right, Frakir observed. *Like the den of the dragon.*

But we're supposed to go this way.

Yes.

Then we will.

I'd slowed to a walk by then, and I followed the shining way between two gray plinths.

The lighting was different within the circle from without. There was more of it, though the place was still a study in black and white, with a fairyland sparkle to it. For the first time here I saw something that appeared to be living. There was something like grass underfoot; it was silver and seemed to be studded with dewdrops.

I halted, and Frakir constricted in a very odd fashion—less a warning, it seemed, than a statement of interest. Off to my right was an altar—not at all like the one over which I had vaulted back in the chapel. This one was a rude slab of stone set atop a couple of boulders. No candles, linens, or other ecclesiastical niceties kept company with the lady who lay atop it, her wrists and ankles bound. Because I recalled a similar bothersome situation in which I had once found myself, my sympathies were all with the lady—white-haired, black-skinned, and somehow familiar—my animus with the peculiar individual who stood behind the altar, faced in my direction, blade upraised in his left hand. The right half of his body was totally black; the left, blindingly white. Immediately galvanized by the tableau, I moved forward. My Concerto for Cuisinart and Microwave spell would have minced him and parboiled him in an instant, but it was useless to me when I could not speak the guide words.

I seemed to feel his gaze upon me as I raced toward him, though one side of him was too dark and the other too bright for me to know for certain. And then the knife hand descended and the blade entered her breast beneath the sternum with an arcing movement. At that instant she screamed, and the blood spurted and it was red against all those blacks and whites, and I realized as it covered the man's hand that had I tried, I might have uttered my spell and saved her.

Then the altar collapsed, and a gray whirlwind obliterated my view of the entire tableau. The blood swirled through it to a barber pole-like effect, gradually spreading and attenuating to turn the funnel rosy, then pink, then faded to silver, then gone. When I reached the spot, the grasses sparkled, sans altar, sans priest, sans sacrifice.

I drew up short, staring.

"Are we dreaming?" I asked aloud.

I do not believe I am capable of dreaming, Frakir replied.

"Then tell me what you saw."

I saw a guy stab a lady who was tied up on a stone surface. Then the whole thing collapsed and blew away. The guy was black and white, the blood was red, the lady was Deirdre—

"What? By God, you're right! It did look like her—in negative. But she's already dead—"

I must remind you that I saw whatever you thought you saw. I don't know what the raw data were, just the mixing job your nervous system did on them. My own special perceptions told me that these were not normal people but were beings on the order of the Dworkin and Oberon figures that visited you back in the cave.

An absolutely terrifying thought occurred to me just then. The Dworkin and Oberon figures had had me thinking briefly of three-dimensional computer simulations. And the Ghostwheel's shadow-scanning ability was based on digitized abstractions of portions of the Pattern I believed to be particularly concerned with this quality. And Ghost had been wondering—almost wistfully, it now seemed—concerning the qualifications for godhood.

Could my own creation be playing games with me? Might Ghost have imprisoned me in a stark and distant shadow, blocked all my efforts at communication, and set about playing an elaborate game with me? If he could beat his own creator, for whom he seemed to feel something of awe, might he not feel he had achieved personal elevation—to a level beyond my status in his private cosmos? Maybe. If one keeps encountering computer simulations, *cherchez le deus ex machina*.

It made me wonder just how strong Ghost really was. Though his power was, in part, an analogue of the Pattern, I was certain it did not match that of the Pattern—or the Logrus. I couldn't see him blocking this place off from either.

On the other hand, all that would really be necessary would be to block me. I suppose he could have impersonated the Logrus in our flash encounter on my arrival. But that would have required Ghost's actually enhancing Frakir, and I didn't believe he could do it. And what about the Unicorn and the Serpent?

"Frakir," I asked, "are you sure it was really the Logrus that enhanced you this time and programmed you with all the instructions you're carrying?"

Yes.

"What makes you certain?"

It had the same feeling as our first encounter back within the Logrus, when I was enhanced initially.

"I see. Next question: Could the Unicorn and the Serpent we saw back in the chapel have been the same sort of things as the Oberon or Dworkin figures back at the cave?"

No. I'd have known. They weren't like them at all. They were terrible and powerful and very much what they seemed.

"Good," I said. "I was worried this might be some elaborate charade on the part of the Ghostwheel."

I see that in your mind. Though I fail to see why the reality of the Unicorn and the Serpent defeats the thesis. They could simply have entered the Ghost's construct to tell you to stop horsing around because they want to see this thing played out.

"I hadn't thought of that."

And maybe the Ghost was able to locate and penetrate a place that is pretty much inaccessible to the Pattern and the Logrus.

"I suppose you've a point there. Unfortunately this pretty much puts me back where I started."

No, because this place is not something Ghost put together. It's always been around. I learned that much from the Logrus.

"I suppose there's some small comfort in knowing that, but—"

I never completed the thought because a sudden movement called my attention to the opposite quadrant of the circle. There I beheld an altar I had not noted before, a female figure standing behind it, a man dappled in shadow and light lying, bound, upon it. They looked very similar to the first pair.

"No!" I cried. "Let it end!"

But the blade descended even as I moved in that direction. The ritual was repeated, and the altar collapsed, and everything again swirled away. When I reached the site, there was no indication that anything unusual had occurred upon it.

"What do you make of that one?" I asked Frakir.

Same forces as before, but somehow reversed.

"Why? What's going on?"

It is a gathering of powers. The Pattern and the Logrus are both attempting to force their way into this place, for a little while. Sacrifices, such as those you just witnessed, help provide the openings they need.

"Why do they wish to manifest here?"

Neutral ground. Their ancient tension is shifting in subtle ways. You are expected in some fashion to tip the balance of power one way or another.

"I haven't the faintest idea how to go about such a thing."

When the time comes, you will.

I returned to the trail and walked on.

"Did I pass by just as the sacrifices were due?" I said. "Or were the sacrifices due because I was passing by?"

They were marked to occur in your vicinity. You are a nexus.

"Then do you think I can expect—"

A figure stepped out from behind a stone to my left and chuckled softly. My hand went to my sword, but his hands were empty, and he moved slowly.

"Talking to yourself. Not a good sign," he remarked.

The man was a study in black, white, and gray. In fact, from the cast of the darkness upon his right-hand side and the lay of the light on his left, he might have been the first wielder of the sacrificial dagger. I'd no real way of telling. Whoever or whatever he or it was, I'd no desire to become acquainted.

So I shrugged.

"The only sign I care about here has 'exit' written on it," I told him as I brushed past him.

His hand fell upon my shoulder and turned me back easily in his direction.

Again the chuckle.

"You must be careful what you wish for in this place," he told me in low and measured tones, "for wishes are sometimes granted here, and if the granter be depraved and read 'quietus' for your 'exit'—why, then, poof! You may cease to be. Up in smoke. Downward to the earth. Sideways to hell and gone."

"I've already been there," I answered, "and lots of points along the way."

"What ho! Look! Your wish *has* been granted," he remarked, his left eye catching a flash of light and reflecting it, tapetumlike, in my direction. No matter how I turned or squinted, however, could I find sight of his right eye. "Over there," he finished, pointing.

I turned my head in the direction he indicated, and there upon the top stone of a dolmen shone an exit sign exactly like the one above the emergency door at a theater I used to frequent near campus.

"You're right," I said.

"Will you go through it?"

"Will you?"

"No need," he replied. "I already know what's there."

"What?" I inquired.

"The other side."

"How droll," I answered.

"If one gets one's wish and spurns it, one might piss off the Powers," he said then.

"You have firsthand knowledge of this?"

I heard a grinding, clicking noise then, and it was several moments before I realized he was gnashing his teeth. I walked away then toward the exit sign, wanting to inspect whatever it represented at nearer range.

There were two standing stones with a flat slab across the top. The gateway thus formed was large enough to walk through. It was shadowy, though. . . .

You going through it, boss?

"Why not? This is one of the few times in my life that I feel indispensable to whoever is running the show."

I wouldn't get too cocky . . . Frakir began, but I was already moving.

Three quick paces were all that it took, and I was looking outward across a circle of stones and sparkling grass past a black-and-white man toward another dolmen bearing an exit sign, a shadowy form within it. Halting, I took a step backward and turned. There was a black-and-white man regarding me, a dolmen to his rear, dark Form within it. I raised my right hand above my head. So did the shadowy figure. I turned back in the direction I had initially been headed. The shadowy figure across from me also had his hand upraised. I stepped on through.

"Small world," I observed, "but I'd hate to paint it."

The man laughed.

"Now you are reminded that your every exit is also an entrance," he said.

"Seeing you here, I am reminded even more of a play by Sartre," I responded.

"Unkind," he answered, "but philosophically cogent. I have always found that hell is other people. Only I have done nothing to rouse your distrust, have I?"

"Were you or were you not the person I saw sacrifice a woman in this vicinity?" I asked.

"Even if I were, what is that to you? You were not involved."

"I guess I have peculiar feelings about little things—like the value of life."

"Indignation is cheap. Even Albert Schweitzer's reverence for life didn't include the tapeworm, the tsetse fly, the cancer cell."

"You know what I mean. Did you or did you not sacrifice a woman on a stone altar a little while ago?"

"Show me the altar."

"I can't. It's gone."

"Show me the woman."

"She is, too."

"Then you haven't much of a case."

"This isn't a court, damn it! If you want to converse, answer my question. If you don't, let's stop making noises at each other."

"I have answered you."

I shrugged.

"All right," I said. "I don't know you, and I'm very happy that way. Good day."

I took a step away from him, back in the direction of the trail. As I did, he said, "Deirdre. Her name was Deirdre, and I did indeed kill her," and he stepped into the dolmen from which I had just emerged, and there he disappeared. Immediately I looked across the way, but he did not exit beneath the exit sign. I did an about-face and stepped into the dolmen myself. I did emerge from the other side, across the way, catching sight of myself entering the opposite one as I did so. I did not see the stranger anywhere along the way.

"What do you make of that?" I asked Frakir as I moved back toward the trail.

A spirit of place, perhaps? A nasty spirit for a nasty place? she ventured. *I don't know, but I think he was one of those damned constructs, too—and they're stronger here.*

I headed down to the trail, set foot upon it, and commenced following it once again.

"Your speech patterns have altered enormously since your enhancement," I remarked.

Your nervous system's a good teacher.

"Thanks. If that guy puts in an appearance again and you sense him before I see him, give me the high sign."

Right. Actually, this entire place has the feeling of one of those constructs. Every stone here has a bit of Pattern scribble to it.

"When did you learn this?"

Back when we first tried the exit. I scanned it for dangers then.

As we came to the periphery of the outer circle, I slapped a stone. It felt solid enough.

He's here! Frakir warned suddenly.

"Hey!" came a voice from overhead, and I looked up. The black-and-white stranger was seated atop the stone, smoking a thin cigar. He held a chalice in his left hand. "You interest me, kid," he went on. "What's your name?"

"Merlin," I answered. "What's yours?"

Instead of replying, he pushed himself outward, fell in slow motion, landed on his feet beside me. His left eye squinted as he studied me. The shadows flowed like dark water down his right side. He blew silvery smoke into the air.

"You're a live one," he announced then, "with the mark of the Pattern and the mark of Chaos upon you. You bear the blood of Amber. What is your lineage, Merlin?"

The shadows parted for a moment, and I saw that his right eye was hidden by a patch.

"I am the son of Corwin," I told him, "and you are—somehow—the traitor Brand."

"You have named me," he said, "but I never betrayed what I believed in."

"That being your own ambition," I said. "Your home and your family and the forces of Order never mattered to you, did they?"

He snorted.

"I will not argue with a presumptuous puppy."

"I've no desire to argue with you either. For whatever it's worth, your son Rinaldo is probably my best friend."

I turned away and began walking. His hand fell upon my shoulder.

"Wait!" he said. "What is this talk? Rinaldo is but a lad."

"Wrong," I answered. "He's around my age."

His hand fell away, and I turned. He had dropped his cigar, which lay smoking upon the trail, and he'd transferred the chalice to his shadow-clad hand. He massaged his brow.

"That much time has passed in the mainlines . . ." he remarked.

On a whim, I withdrew my Trumps, shuffled out Luke's, held it up for him to see.

"That's Rinaldo," I said.

He reached for it, and for some obscure reason I let him take it. He stared at it for a long while.

"Trump contact doesn't seem to work from here," I said.

He looked up, shook his head, and handed the card back to me.

"No, it wouldn't," he stated. "How . . . is he?"

"You know that he killed Caine to avenge you?"

"No, I didn't know. But I'd expect no less of him."

"You're not exactly Brand, are you?"

He threw back his head and laughed.

"I am entirely Brand, and I am not Brand as you might have known him. Anything more than that will cost you."

"What will it cost me to learn what you really are?" I inquired as I cased my cards.

He raised the chalice, held it before him with both hands, like a begging bowl.

"Some of your blood," he said.

"You've become a vampire?"

"No, I'm a Pattern-ghost," he replied. "Bleed for me, and I'll explain."

"All right," I said. "It'd better be a good story, though," and I drew my dagger and pricked my wrist, which I'd extended to a position above his cup.

Like a spilled oil lamp, the flames came forth. I don't really have fire flowing around inside me, of course. But the blood of a Chaosite is highly volatile in certain places, and this, apparently, was such a place.

It spewed forth, half into and half past the cup, splashing over his hand, his forearm. He screamed and seemed to collapse in upon himself. I stepped backward as he was transformed into a vortex—not unlike those following the sacrifices I had witnessed, only this one of the fiery variety—which rose into the air with a roar and vanished a moment later, leaving me startled, staring upward and applying direct pressure to my smoking wrist.

Uh, colorful exit, Frakir remarked.

"Family specialty," I responded, "and speaking of exits . . ."

I stepped past the stone, departing the circle. The darkness moved in again, intensified. Reflexively my trail seemed to brighten. I released my wrist, saw that it had stopped smoking.

I broke into a jog then, anxious to be away from that place. When I looked back a little later, I no longer saw the standing stones. There was only a pale, fading vortex, drawing itself upward, upward, then gone.

I jogged on, and the trail began, gradually, to slope until I was running downhill with an easy, loping gait. The trail ran like a bright ribbon downward and off into a great distance before it faded from view. I was puzzled, however, to see that it intersected another glowing line not too far below. These lines quickly faded off to my right and my left.

"Any special instructions pertaining to crossroads?" I inquired.

Not yet, Frakir answered. *Presumably, it's a decision point, with no way of knowing what to base one on till you get there.*

It seemed a vast, shadowy plain that was spread below, with here and there a few isolated dots of light, some of them constant, others appearing, then fading, all of them stationary. There were no other lines, however, than my trail and the one which intersected it. There were no sounds other than my breathing and that of my footfalls. There were no breezes, no peculiar odors, and the temperature was so clement that it claimed no notice. Again there were dark shapes at either hand, but I'd no desire to investigate them. All I wanted was to conclude whatever business was in progress and get the hell out and be about my own affairs as soon as possible.

Hazy patches of light then began occurring at irregular intervals, both sides of the trail, wavery, sourceless, blotchy, popping into and out of existence. These seemed like gauzy, dappled curtains hung beside the trail, and I did not pause to examine them at first, not till the obscure areas grew fewer and fewer, being replaced by shadings of greater and greater distinction. It was almost as if a tuning process were in operation, with increasing clarity of outline indicating familiar objects: chairs; tables; parked cars; store windows. Before long, faded colors began to occur within these tableaus.

I halted beside one and stared. It was a red '57 Chevy with some snow on it, parked in a familiar-looking driveway. I advanced and reached toward it.

My left hand and arm faded as they entered the dim light. I reached to touch the left fin. There followed a vague sensation of contact and a faint coolness. I swept my hand to the right then, brushing away some of the snow. When I withdrew my hand, there was snow upon it. Immediately the prospect faded to black.

"I intentionally used my left hand," I said, "with you on the wrist. What was there?"

Thanks a lot. It seemed a red car with snow on it.

"It was a construct of something picked from my mind. That's my Polly Jackson painting, upscaled to life size."

Then things are getting worse, Merle. I couldn't tell it was a construct.

"Conclusions?"

Whatever's doing it is getting better at it, or stronger. Or both.

"Shit," I observed, and I turned away and jogged on.

Perhaps something wants to show you that it can baffle you completely now.

"Then it's succeeded," I acknowledged. "Hey, Something!" I shouted. "You hear that? You win! You've baffled me completely. Can I go home now? If it's something else you're trying to do, though, you've failed! I'm missing the point completely!"

The dazzling flash which followed cast me down upon the trail and blinded me for several long moments. I lay there tense and twitching, but no thunderclap followed. When my vision cleared and my muscles stopped their spasms, I beheld a giant regal figure posed but a few paces before me: Oberon.

Only it was a statue, a duplicate of one which occupied the far end of the Main Concourse back in Amber, or possibly even the real thing, for on closer inspection I noted what appeared to be bird droppings upon the great man's shoulder.

"Real thing or construct?" I said aloud.

Real, I'd say, Frakir replied.

I rose slowly.

"I understand this to be an answer," I said. "I just don't understand what it means."

I reached out to touch it, and it felt like canvas rather than bronze. In that instant my perspective somehow shifted, and I felt myself touching a larger than life-size painting of the Father of His Country. Then its borders began to waver, it faded, and I saw that it was part of one of those hazy tableaux I had been passing. Then it rippled and was gone.

"I give up," I said, walking through the space it had occupied but moments before. "The answers are more confusing than the situations that cause the questions."

Since we are passing between shadows, could this not be a statement that all things are real—somewhere?

"I suppose. But I already knew that."

And that all things are real in different ways, at different times, in different places?

"Okay, what you are saying could well be the message. I doubt that something is going to these extremes, however, just to make philosophical points that may be new to you but are rather well worn elsewhere. There must be a special reason, one that I still don't grasp."

Up until now the scenes I'd passed had been still lifes. Now, however, a number occurred which contained people; some, other creatures. In these, there was action—some of it violent, some amorous, some simply domestic.

Yes, it seems to be a progression. It may be leading up to something.

"When they leap out and attack me, I'll know I've arrived."

Who knows? I gather that art criticism is a complex area.

But the sequences faded shortly thereafter, and I was left jogging on my bright trail through darkness once again. Down, down the still gentle slope toward the crossroads. Where was the Cheshire Cat when rabbit hole logic was what I really needed?

One moment I was watching the crossroads as I advanced upon it. An eye blink later I was still watching the crossroads, only now the scene was altered. There was now a lamppost on the near right-hand corner. A shadowy figure stood beneath it, smoking.

"Frakir, how'd they pull that one?" I asked.

Very quickly, she replied.

"What do the vibes read?"

Attention focused in your direction. No vicious intent, yet.

I slowed as I drew near. The trail became pavement, curbs at either hand, sidewalks beyond them. I stepped out of the street onto the right-hand walk. As I moved along it, a damp fog blew past me, hung between me and the light. I slowed my pace even more. Shortly I saw that the pavement had grown damp. My footsteps echoed as if I walked between buildings. By then the fog had grown too dense for me to discern whether buildings had actually occurred beside me. It felt as if they had, for there were darker areas here and there within the gloom. A cold wind began to blow against my back, and droplets of moisture fell upon me at random intervals. I halted. I turned up the collar of my cloak. From somewhere entirely out of sight, high overhead, came the faint buzzing sound of an airplane. I began walking again after it had gone by. Tinily then, and muffled, from across the street perhaps, came the sound of a piano playing a half-familiar tune. I drew my cloak about me. The fog swirled and thickened.

Three paces more, and then it cleared, and she was standing before me, back against the lamppost. A head shorter than I was, she had on a trench coat and a black beret, her hair glossy, inky. She dropped her cigarette and slowly ground it out beneath the toe of a high-heeled black patent-leather shoe. I glimpsed something of her leg as she did so, and it was perfectly formed. She removed from within her coat then a flat silver case, the raised outline of a rose upon it, opened it, took out a cigarette, placed it between her lips, closed the case, and put it away. Then, without looking at me, she asked, "Have you a light?"

I hadn't any matches, but I wasn't about to let a little thing like that deter me.

"Of course," I said, extending my hand slowly toward those delicate features. I kept it turned slightly away from her so that she could not see that it was empty. As I whispered the guide word which caused the spark to leap from my fingertip to the tip of the cigarette, she raised her hand and touched my own, as if to steady it. And she raised her eyes—large, deep blue, long-lashed—and met mine as she drew upon it. Then she gasped, and the cigarette fell away.

"Mon Dieu!" she said, and she threw her arms about me, pressed herself against me, and began to sob. "Corwin!" she said. "You've found me! It has been forever!"

I held her tightly, not wanting to speak, not wanting to break her happiness with something as cloddish as truth. The hell with truth. I stroked her hair.

After a long while she pulled away, looked up at me. A moment or so more, and she would realize that it was only a resemblance and that she was seeing but what she wanted to see. So, "What's a girl like you doing in a place like this?" I asked.

She laughed softly.

"Have you found a way?" she said, and then her eyes narrowed. "You're not—"

I shook my head.

"I hadn't the heart," I told her.

"Who are you?" she asked, taking a half step backward.

"My name is Merlin, and I'm on a crazy quest I don't understand."

"Amber," she said softly, her hands still on my shoulders, and I nodded.

"I don't know you," she said then. "I feel that I should, but . . . I . . . don't. . . ."

Then she came to me again and rested her head on my chest. I started to say something, to try to explain, but she placed a finger across my lips.

"Not yet, not now, maybe never," she said. "Don't tell me. Please don't tell me more. But you ought to know whether you're a Pattern-ghost."

"Just what is a Pattern-ghost?" I said.

"An artifact created by the Pattern. It records everyone who walks it. It can call us back whenever it wants, as we were at one of the times we walked it. It can use us as it would, send us where it will with a task laid upon us— a geas, if you like. Destroy us, and it can create us over again."

"Does it do this sort of thing often?"

"I don't know. I'm not familiar with its will, let alone its operations with any other than myself." Then, "You're not a ghost! I can tell!" she announced suddenly, taking hold of my hand. "But there is something different about you—different from others of the blood of Amber. . . ."

"I suppose," I answered. "I trace my lineage to the Courts of Chaos as well as to Amber."

She raised my hand to her mouth as if she were about to kiss it. But her lips moved by, to the place on my wrist where I had cut myself at Brand's request. Then it hit me: Something about the blood of Amber must hold a special attraction for Pattern-ghosts.

I tried to draw my hand away, but the strength of Amber was hers also.

"The fires of Chaos sometimes flow within me," I said. "They may do you harm."

She raised her head slowly and smiled. There was blood on her mouth. I glanced down and saw that my wrist was wet with it, too.

"The blood of Amber has power over the Pattern," she began, and the fog rolled, churned about her ankles. "No!" she cried then, and she bent forward once more.

The vortex rose to her knees, her calves. I felt her teeth upon my wrist, tearing. I knew of no spell to fight this thing, so I laid my arm across her shoulder and stroked her hair. Moments later she dissolved within my embrace, becoming a bloody whirlwind.

"Go right," I heard her wail as she spun away from me, her cigarette still smoldering upon the pavement, my blood dripping beside it.

I turned away. I walked away. Faintly, faintly, through the night and the fog I could still hear the piano playing some tune from before my time.

SIX

I took the road to the right, and everywhere my blood fell reality melted a little. I heal fast, though, and I stopped bleeding soon. Even stopped throbbing before too long.

You got blood all over me, boss.

"Could have been fire," I observed.

I got singed a little, too, back at the stones.

"Sorry about that. Figure out what's going on yet?"

No new instructions, if that's what you mean. But I've been thinking, now I know how to do it, and this place gets more and more fascinating. This whole business of Pattern-ghosts, for instance. If the Pattern can't penetrate here directly, it can at least employ agents. Wouldn't you think the Logrus might have some way of doing the same?

"I suppose it's possible."

I get the impression there's some sort of duel going on between them here, on the underside of reality, between shadows. What if this place came first? Before Shadow, even? What if they've been fighting here since the very beginning, in some strange metaphysical way?

"What if they have?"

That could almost make Shadow an afterthought, a by-product of the tension between the poles.

"I'm afraid you've lost me, Frakir."

What if Amber and the Courts of Chaos were created only to provide agents for this conflict?

"And what if this idea were placed within you by the Logrus during your recent enhancement?"

Why?

"Another way to make me think that the conflict is more important than the people. Another pressure to make me choose a side."

I don't feel manipulated.

"As you pointed out, you're new to this thinking business. And that's a pretty damned abstract line of thought for you to be following this early in the game."

Is it?

"Take my word for it."

What does that leave us with?

"Unwelcome attention from On High."

Better watch your language if this is their war zone.

"A pox on both their houses. For some reason I don't understand, they need me for this game. They'll put up with it."

From somewhere up ahead I heard a roll of thunder.

See what I mean?

"It's a bluff," I replied.

Whose?

"The Pattern's, I believe. Its ghosts seem in charge of reality in this sector."

You know, we could be wrong on all of this. Just shooting in the dark.

"I also feel shot at out of the dark. That's why I refuse to play by anybody else's rules."

Have you got a plan?

"Hang loose. And if I say 'kill,' do it. Let's get to where we're going."

I began to run again, leaving the fog, leaving the ghosts to play at being ghosts in their ghost city. Bright road through dark country, me running, reverse shadow-shifting, as the land tried to change me. And there ahead a flare and more thunder, virtual street scene flashing into and out of existence beside me.

And then it was as if I raced myself, dark figure darting along a bright way—till I realized it was indeed, somehow, a mirror effect. The movements of the figure to my right which paralleled my own mimicked mine; fleeting scenes to my left were imaged to the other's right.

What's going on, Merle?

"Don't know," I said. "But I'm not in the mood for symbolism, allegory, and assorted metaphorical crap. If it's supposed to mean that life is a race with yourself, then it sucks—unless they're real platitudinizing Powers that are running this show. Then I guess it would be in character. What do you think?"

I think you might still be in danger of being struck by lightning.

The lightning did not follow, but my reflection did. The imaging effect continued for much longer than any of the previous beside-the-road sequences I'd witnessed. I was about to dismiss it, to ignore it completely, when my reflection put on a burst of speed and shot ahead of me.

Uh-oh.

"Yeah," I agreed, stepping up my own pace to close the gap with and match the stride of that dark other.

We were parallel for no more than a few meters after I caught up. Then it began to pull ahead again. I stepped up my pace and caught up once more. Then, on an impulse, I sucked air, bore down, and moved ahead.

My double noted it after a time, moved faster, began to gain. I pushed harder, held my lead. What the hell were we racing for anyway?

I looked ahead. In the distance I could see an area where the trail widened. There appeared to be a tape stretched across it at that point. Okay. Whatever the significance, I decided to go for it.

I held my lead for perhaps a hundred meters before my shadow began to gain on me again. I leaned into it and was able to hold that shortened distance for a time. Then it moved again, coming up on me at a pace I suspected might be hard to hold the rest of the way to the tape. Still, it was not the sort of thing one waited around to find out. I poured it on. I ran all out.

The son of a bitch gained on me, kept gaining, caught me, drew ahead, faltered for an instant. I was back beside it in that instant. But the thing did not flag again. It held the terrible pace at which we were now moving, and I had no intention of stopping unless my heart exploded.

We ran on, damn near side by side. I didn't know whether I had a finishing spurt in me or not. I couldn't tell whether I was slightly ahead, just abreast, or slightly to the rear of the other. We pounded our parallel gleaming trails toward the line of brightness when abruptly the sensation of a glass interface vanished. The two narrow-seeming trails became one wide one. The other's arms and legs were moving differently from my own.

We drew closer and closer together as we entered the final stretch—close enough, finally, for recognition. It was not an image of myself that I was running against, for its hair streamed back and I saw that its left ear was missing.

I found a final burst of speed. So did the other. We were awfully close together when we came to the tape. I think that I hit it first, but I could not be certain.

We went on through and collapsed, gasping. I rolled quickly, to keep him under surveillance, but he just lay there, panting. I rested my right hand on the hilt of my weapon and listened to the sound of my blood in my ears.

When I'd caught my breath somewhat, I remarked, "Didn't know you could run a race like that, Jurt."

He gave a brief laugh.

"There're a lot of things you don't know about me, brother."

"I'm sure," I said.

Then he wiped his brow with the back of his hand, and I noted that the finger he'd lost in the caves of Kolvir was back in place. Either this was the Jurt of a different time line or—

"So how's Julia?" I asked him. "Is she going to be all right?"

"Julia?" he said. "Who's that?"

"Sorry," I said. "You're the wrong Jurt."

"Now what else does that mean?" he asked, propping himself on an elbow and glaring at me with his good eye.

"The real Jurt was never anywhere near the Pattern of Amber—"

"I *am* the real Jurt!"

"You've got all your fingers. He lost one very recently. I was there."

He looked away suddenly.

"You must be a Logrus-ghost," I continued. "It must pull the same stunt the Pattern does—recording those who make it through it."

"Is that . . . what happened?" he asked. "I couldn't quite recall . . . why I was here—except to race with you."

"I'll bet your most recent memories before this place involve negotiating the Logrus."

He looked back. He nodded.

"You're right. What does it all mean?" he asked.

"I'm not sure," I said. "But I've got some ideas about it. This place is a kind of eternal underside to Shadow. It's damn near off limits for both the Pattern and the Logrus. But both can apparently penetrate here by means of their ghosts—artificial constructs from the recordings they made of us back when we passed through them—"

"You mean that all I am is some sort of recording?" He looked as if he were about to cry. "Everything seemed so glorious just a little while ago. I'd made it through the Logrus. All of Shadow lay at my feet." He massaged his temples. Then, "You!" he spat. "I was somehow brought here because of you—to compete with you, to show you up in this race."

"You did a pretty good job, too. I didn't know you could run like that."

"I started practicing when I learned you were doing it in college. Wanted to get good enough to take you on."

"You got good," I acknowledged.

"But I wouldn't be in this damned place if it weren't for you. Or—" He gnawed his lip. "That's not exactly right, is it?" he asked. "*I* wouldn't be anywhere. I'm just a recording. . . ." Then he stared directly at me. "How long do we last?" he said. "How long is a Logrus-ghost good for?"

"I've no idea," I said, "what goes into creating one or how it's maintained. But I've met a number of Pattern-ghosts, and they gave me the impression that my blood would somehow sustain them, give them some sort of autonomy, some independence of the Pattern. Only one of them—Brand—got the fire instead of the blood, and it dissolved. Deirdre got the blood but was taken away then. I don't know whether she got enough."

He shook his head.

"I've a feeling—I don't know where it comes from—that something like that would work for me, too, and that it's blood for the pattern, fire for the Logrus."

"I don't know how to tell in what regions my blood is volatile," I said.

"It'd flame here," he answered. "Depends on who's in control. I just seem to know it. I don't know how."

"Then why did Brand show up in Logrus territory?"

He grinned.

"Maybe the Pattern sought to use a traitor for some sort of subversion. Or maybe Brand was trying to pull something on his own—like double-crossing the Pattern."

"That would be in character," I agreed, my breath finally slowing.

I whipped the Chaos blade out of my boot, slashed my left forearm, saw that it spouted fire, and held it toward him.

"Quick! Take it if you can!" I cried. "Before the Logrus calls you back!"

He seized my arm and seemed almost to inhale the fire that fountained from me. Looking down, I saw his feet become transparent, then his legs. The Logrus seemed anxious to reclaim him, just as the Pattern had Deirdre. I saw the fiery swirls begin within the haze that had been his legs. Then, suddenly, they flickered out, and the outline of those limbs became visible once again. He continued to draw my volatile blood from me, though I could no longer see flames as he was drinking now as Deirdre had, directly from the wound. His legs began to solidify.

"You seem to be stabilizing," I said. "Take more."

Something struck me in the right kidney, and I jerked away, turning as I fell. A tall dark man stood beside me, withdrawing his boot from having kicked me. He had on green trousers and a black shirt, a green bandanna tied about his head.

"Now what perverse carrying-on is this?" he asked. "And in a sacred spot?"

I rolled to my knees and continued on up to my feet, my right arm bending, its wrist turning over, coming in to hold the dagger beside my hip. I raised my left arm, extended it before me. Blood rather than fire now fell from my latest wound.

"None of your damn business," I said, then added his name, having grown certain on the way up, "Caine."

He smiled and bowed, and his hands crossed and came apart. They'd been empty going in, but the right one held a dagger coming out. It must have come from a sheath strapped to his left forearm, inside the billowy sleeve. He had to have practiced the move a lot, too, to be that fast at it. I tried to remember things I'd heard about Caine and knives, and then I did and wished I hadn't. He was supposed to have been a master knife fighter. Shit.

"You have the advantage of me," he stated. "You look very familiar, but I do not believe I know you."

"Merlin," I said. "Corwin's son."

He had begun circling me slowly, but he halted.

"Excuse me if I find that difficult to believe."

"Believe as you wish. It is true."

"And this other one—his name is Jurt, isn't it?"

He gestured toward my brother, who had just gotten to his feet.

"How do you know that?" I asked.

He halted, furrowing his brow, narrowing his eyes.

"I—I'm not certain," he said then.

"I am," I told him. "Try to remember where you are and how you got here."

He backed away, two paces. Then he cried, "He's the one!" just as I saw it coming and shouted, "Jurt! Watch out!"

Jurt turned and bolted. I threw the dagger—always a bad thing to do, save that I was wearing a sword with which I could reach Caine before Caine could reach me now.

Jurt's speed was still with him, and he was out of range in an instant. The dagger, surprisingly, struck at the side of Caine's right shoulder point first, penetrating perhaps an inch or so into muscle. Then, even before he could turn back toward me, his body erupted in a dozen directions, emitting a series of vortices which sucked away all semblance of humanity in an instant, producing high-pitched whistling sounds as they orbited one another, two of them merging into a larger entity, which quickly absorbed the others then, its sound falling lower with each such acquisition. Finally there was but the one. For a moment it swayed toward me, then shot skyward and blew apart. The dagger was blown back in my direction, landing a pace to my right. When I recovered it, I found it to be warm, and it hummed faintly for several seconds before I sheathed it in my boot.

"What happened?" Jurt asked, turning back, approaching.

"Apparently Pattern-ghosts react violently to weapons from the Courts," I said.

"Good thing you had it handy. But why did he turn on me like that?"

"I believe that the Pattern sent him to stop you from gaining autonomy— or to destroy you if you already had. I've a feeling it doesn't want agents of the other side gaining strength and stability in this place."

"But I'm no threat. I'm not on anybody's side but my own. I just want to get the hell out of here and be about my own business."

"Perhaps that of itself constitutes a threat."

"How so?" he asked.

"Who knows what your unusual background may fit you for as an independent agent—in light of what's going on? You may disturb the balance of the Powers. You may possess or have access to information which the principals do not wish to see bruited about the streets. You may be like the gypsy moth. Nobody could see what its effect on the environment would be when it escaped from the lab. You may—"

"Enough!" He raised a hand to silence me. "I don't care about any of those things. If they let me go and leave me alone, I'll stay out of their way."

"I'm not the one you have to convince," I told him.

He stared at me for a moment, then turned, describing a full circle.

Darkness was all that I could see beyond the light of the roadway, but he called out in a large voice to anything, I suppose, "Do you hear me? I don't want to be involved in all this. I just want to go away. Live and let live, you know? Is that okay with you?"

I reached forward, caught hold of his wrist, and jerked him toward me. I did this because I had seen a small, ghostly replica of the Sign of the Logrus begin to take form in the air above his head. An instant later it fell, flashing like a lightning stroke, to the accompaniment of a sound like the cracking of a whip, passing through the space he had been occupying, opening a gap in the trail as it vanished.

"I guess it's not that easy to resign," he said. He glanced overhead. "It could be readying another of those right now. It could strike again anytime, when I least expect it."

"Just like real life," I agreed. "But I think you may take it as a warning shot and let it go at that. They have a hard time reaching here. More important, since I was led to believe that this is my quest, do you know offhand whether you're supposed to be helping me or hindering me?"

"Now that you mention it," he said, "I remember suddenly being where I was with a chance to race you and a feeling that we'd fight or something afterward."

"What're your feelings on that now?"

"We've never gotten along all that well. But I don't like the idea of being used like this either."

"You willing to call a truce till I can see my way through this game and out of here?"

"What's in it for me?" he asked.

"I *will* find a way out of this damned place, Jurt. Come along and give me a hand—or at least don't get in the way—and I'll take you with me when I go."

He laughed.

"I'm not sure there is a way out of here," he said, "unless the Powers release us."

"Then you've nothing to lose," I told him, "and you'll probably even get to see me die trying."

"Do you really know both kinds of magic—Pattern and Logrus?" he asked.

"Yeah. But I'm a lot better at Logrus."

"Can you use either against its source?"

"That's a very intriguing metaphysical point, and I don't know the answer," I said, "and I'm not sure I'll find out. It's dangerous to invoke the Powers here. So all I'm left with is a few hung spells. I don't think it's magic that'll get us out of here."

"What, then?"

"I'm not certain. I am sure that I won't see the full picture till I get to the end of this trail, though."

"Well, hell—I don't know. This doesn't seem the healthiest place for me to spend my time. On the other hand, what if it's the only place something like me can have an existence? What if you find me a door and I step through it and melt?"

"If the Pattern-ghosts can manifest in Shadow, I'd guess you can, too. Those of Dworkin and Oberon came to me on the outside before I came to this place."

"That's encouraging. Would you try it if it were you?"

"You bet your life," I said.

He snorted.

"I get the point. I'll go a ways with you and see what happens. I'm not promising to help, but I won't sabotage you."

I held out my hand, and he shook his head.

"Let's not get carried away," he told me. "If my word's no good without a handshake, it's no good with one, is it?"

"I guess not."

"And I've never had a great desire to shake hands with you."

"Sorry I asked," I said. "Would you mind telling me why, though? I've always wondered."

He shrugged.

"Why does there always have to be a reason?" he said.

"The alternative is irrationality," I replied.

"Or privacy," he responded, turning away.

I commenced walking the trail once more. Shortly Jurt fell into step beside me. We walked for a long while in silence. One day I may learn when to keep my mouth shut or to quit when I'm ahead. Same thing.

The trail ran straight for a time but seemed to vanish not too far ahead. When we neared the point of vanishment, I saw why: The trail curved behind a low prominence. We followed this turning and met with another shortly thereafter. Soon we had entered upon a regular series of switchbacks, realizing quickly that they were mitigating a fairly steep descent. As we proceeded down this turning way, I suddenly became aware of a bright squiggle, hanging in the middle distance. Jurt raised his hand, pointing at it, and began, "What . . . ?" just as it became apparent that it was the continuation of our trail, rising. At this, an instant reorientation occurred, and I realized that we were descending into what seemed a massive pit. And the air seemed to have grown somewhat cooler.

We continued our descent, and after a time something cold and moist touched the back of my right hand. I looked down in time to see a snowflake melting in the twilight glow which surrounded us. Moments later several more breezed by. A little after that we became aware of a larger brightness, far below.

I don't know what it is either, Frakir pulsed into my mind.

Thanks, I thought strongly back at her, having decided against advising Jurt of her presence.

Down. Down and around. Back. Back and forth. The temperature continued to decline. Snowflakes flitted. Arrays of rocks in the wall we now descended took on a bit of glitter.

Oddly, I didn't realize what it was until the first time I slipped.

"Ice!" Jurt announced suddenly, half toppling and catching himself up against the stone.

A distant sighing sound occurred, and it grew and grew, nearing us. It was not until it arrived, with a great buffeting gust, that we knew it to be a wind. And cold. It fled past like the breath of an ice age, and I raised my cloak against it. It followed us, softer thereafter, yet persistent, as we continued our descent.

By the time we reached the bottom it was damn cold, and the steps were either fully frosted over or carved of ice. The wind blew a steady, mournful note, and flakes of snow or pellets of ice came and went.

"Miserable climate!" Jurt growled, teeth chattering.

"I didn't think ghosts were susceptible to the mundane," I said.

"Ghost, hell!" he observed. "I feel the same as I always did. You'd think whatever sent me fully dressed to cross your trail might at least have provided for this eventuality.

"And this place isn't that mundane," he added. "They want us somewhere, you'd think they might have provided a shortcut. As it is, we'll be damaged merchandise by the time we get there."

"I don't really believe that either the Pattern or the Logrus has that much power in this place," I told him. "I'd just as soon they stayed out of our way entirely."

Our trail led outward across a gleaming plain—so flat and so gleaming that I feared it to consist entirely of ice. Nor was I incorrect.

"Looks slippery," Jurt said. "I'm going to shapeshift my feet, make them broader."

"It'll destroy your boots and leave you with cold feet," I said. "Why not just shift some of your weight downward, lower your center of gravity?"

"Always got an answer," he began sullenly. Then, "But this time you're right," he finished.

We stood there for several minutes as he grew shorter, more squat.

"Aren't you going to shift yourself?" he asked.

"I'll take my chances holding my center. I can move faster this way," I said.

"You can fall on your ass that way, too."

"We'll see."

We started out. We held our balance. The winds were stronger away from the wall we had descended. The surface of our icy trail, however, was not so slick as it had appeared on distant inspection. There were small ripples and ridges to it, adequate to provide some traction. The air burned its way into my lungs; flakes were beaten into swirling snow devil towers which fled like eccentric tops across our way. It was a bluish glow which emanated from the trail, tinting those flakes which came within its ambit. We hiked for perhaps a quarter mile before a new series of ghostly images began. The first appeared to be myself, sprawled across a heap of armor back at the chapel; the second was Deirdre beneath a lamppost, looking at her watch.

"What?" Jurt asked, as they came and went in a matter of instants.

"I didn't know the first time I saw them, and I still don't know," I answered, "though I thought you might be one of them when we first began our race. They come and go—at random, it would seem—with no special reason that I can figure."

The next was what appeared to be a dining room, a bowl of flowers on the table. There were no people in the room. There and gone—

No. Not entirely. It went away, but the flowers remained, there on the surface of the ice. I halted, then walked out toward them.

Merle, I don't know about leaving the trail. . . .

Oh, shit, I responded, moving toward a slab of ice which reminded me of the Stonehenge-like area back where I'd come aboard, incongruous flashes of color near its base.

There were a number of them—roses of many sorts. I stooped and picked one up. Its color was almost silver. . . .

"What *are* you doing here, dear boy?" I heard a familiar voice say.

I straightened immediately, to see that the tall dark figure which had emerged from behind the block of ice was not addressing me. He was nodding to Jurt, smiling.

"A fool's errand, I'm sure," Jurt replied.

"And this must be the fool," the other responded, "plucking that damnable flower. Silver rose of Amber—Lord Corwin's, I believe. Hello, Merlin. Looking for your father?"

I removed one of the spare clasp pins I keep pinned to the inside of my cloak. I used it to fasten the rose at my left breast. The speaker was Lord Borel, a duke of the royal House of Swayvill and reputedly one of my mother's lovers of long ago. He was also deemed to be one of the deadliest swordsmen in the Courts. Killing my father or Benedict or Eric had been an obsession with him for years. Unfortunately it had been Corwin whom he'd met, at a time when Dad was in a hurry—and they'd never crossed blades. Dad had suckered him instead and killed him in what I supposed was technically a somewhat less than fair fight. Which is okay. I'd never much liked the guy.

"You're dead, Borel. You know that?" I told him. "You're just a ghost of the man you were the day you took the Logrus. Out in the real world there is no Lord Borel anymore. You want to know why? Because Corwin killed you the day of the Patternfall War."

"You lie, you little shit!" he told me.

"Uh, no," Jurt offered. "You're dead all right. Run through, I heard. Didn't know it was Corwin did it, though."

"It was," I said.

He looked away, and I saw his jaw muscles bunching and relaxing, bunching and relaxing.

"And this place is some sort of afterlife?" he asked a little later, still not looking back at us.

"I suppose you could call it that," I said.

"Can we die yet again here?"

"I think so," I told him.

"What is that?"

His gaze had suddenly dropped, and I followed it. Something lay upon the ice nearby, and I took a step toward it.

"An arm," I replied. "It appears to be a human arm."

"What's it doing there?" Jurt asked, walking over and kicking it.

It moved in a fashion which showed us that it was not simply lying there but rather was extended up out of the ice. In fact, it twitched and continued to flex spasmodically for several seconds after Jurt kicked it. Then I noted another, some distance away, and what appeared to be a leg. Farther on, a shoulder, arm attached, a hand . . .

"Some cannibal's deep freeze," I suggested.

Jurt chuckled.

"Then you're dead, too," Borel stated.

"Nope," I replied. "I'm the real thing. Just passing through, on my way to a far, far better place."

"What of Jurt?"

"Jurt's an interesting problem, both physically and theologically," I explained. "He's enjoying a peculiar kind of bilocation."

"I'd hardly say I'm enjoying it," Jurt observed. "But considering the alternative, I suppose I'm glad I'm here."

"That's the sort of positive thinking that's worked so many wonders for the Courts over the years," I said.

Jurt chuckled again.

I heard that metallic sighing sound one does not easily forget. I knew that I could not possibly draw my blade, turn, and parry in time if Borel wished to run me through from the rear. On the other hand, he took great pride in observing every punctilio when it came to killing people. He always played fair because he was so damned good that he never lost anyway. Might as well go for the reputation, too. I immediately raised both hands, to irritate him by acting as if he had just threatened me from the rear.

Stay invisible, Frakir. When I turn and snap my wrist, let go. Stick to him when you hit, find your way to his throat. You know what to do when you get there.

Right, boss, she replied.

"Draw your blade and turn, Merle."

"Doesn't sound too sporting to me, Borel," I replied.

"You dare to accuse me of anything less than propriety?" he said.

"Hard to tell when I can't see what you're up to," I answered.

"Then draw your weapon and turn around."

"I'm turning," I said. "But I'm not touching the thing."

I turned quickly, snapping my left wrist, feeling Frakir depart. As I did, my feet went out from under me. I'd moved too fast on a very smooth patch of ice. Catching myself, I felt a shadow drift into place before me. When I looked up, I beheld the point of Borel's blade, about six inches from my right eye.

"Rise slowly," he said, and I did.

"Draw your weapon now," he ordered.

"And if I refuse?" I inquired, trying to buy time.

"You will prove yourself unworthy to be considered a gentleman, and I will act accordingly."

"By attacking me anyway?" I asked.

"The rules permit this," he said.

"Shove your rules," I replied, crossing my right foot behind my left and springing backward as I drew my blade and let it fall into a guard position.

He was on me in an instant. I continued my retreat, backing past the big slab of ice from behind which he had appeared. I had no desire to stand and trade techniques with him, especially now that I could see the speed of those attacks. Parrying them took a lot less effort while I was backing off. My blade did not feel quite right, however, and as I scanned it quickly I saw why. It was *not* my weapon.

In the glittering light from the trail, bounced off the ice, I saw the swirling inlay along part of the blade. There was only one weapon like this that I knew of, and I had only just seen it recently, in what might have been my father's hand. It was Grayswandir that moved before me. I felt myself smile at the irony. This was the weapon which had slain the real Lord Borel.

"You smile at your own cowardice?" he asked. "Stand and fight, bastard!"

As if in answer to his suggestion, I felt my rearward movement arrested. I was not run through when I ventured a quick downward glance, however, for I realized from his expression that something similar had happened to my attacker.

Our ankles had been seized by several of those hands which extended up through the ice, holding us firmly in place. And this made it Borel's turn to smile, for though he could not lunge, I could no longer retreat. Which meant—

His blade flashed forward, and I parried in quarte, attacked in sixte. He parried and feinted. Then quarte again, and the next attack. Riposte. Parry sixte—No, that was a feint. Catch him in four. Feint. Feint again. Hit—

Something white and hard passed over his shoulder and struck my forehead. I fell back, though the grasping hands kept me from collapsing completely. Good thing I sagged, actually, or his thrust might have punctured my liver. My reflexes or some touch of the magic I've heard may dwell in Grayswandir threw my arm forward as my knees buckled. I felt the blade strike something, though I was not even looking in that direction, and I heard Borel grunt surprisedly, then utter an oath. I heard Jurt mouthing an oath of his own about then, too. He was out of my line of sight.

Then came a bright flash, even as I flexed my legs, stabilizing, parried a head cut, and began rising. I saw then that I had succeeded in cutting Borel's forearm, and fire spurted fountainlike from the wound. His body began to glow, his lower outline to blur.

"It was by no skill you bested me!" he cried.

I shrugged.

"It isn't the Winter Olympics either," I told him.

He changed his grip on his blade, drew back his arm, and hurled the weapon at me—right before he dissolved into a tower of sparks and was drawn upward and vanished above.

I parried the blade, and it passed me to the left, buried itself partway in the ice and stood vibrating there, like something in a Scandinavian's version of Arthurian legend. Jurt rushed toward me, kicked at the hands which held my ankles until they released me, and squinted at my brow.

I felt something fall upon me.

Sorry, boss. I hit around his knee. By the time I reached his throat he was already on fire, Frakir said.

All's well that ends well, I replied. *You weren't singed, were you?*

Didn't even feel the heat.

"Sorry I hit you with that piece of ice," Jurt said. "I was aiming at Borel."

I moved away from the plain of hands, heading back toward the trail.

"Indirectly it helped," I said, but I didn't feel like thanking him. How could I know where he'd really been aiming? I glanced back once, and several of the hands Jurt had kicked were giving us the finger.

Why had I been wearing Grayswandir? Would another weapon have affected a Logrus-ghost as strongly? Had it really been my father, then, who had brought me here? And had he felt I might need the extra edge his weapon could provide? I wanted to think so, to believe that he had been more than a Pattern-ghost. And if he was, I wondered at his part in the entire affair. What might he know about all this? And which side might he be on?

The winds died down as we moved along the trail, and the only arms we saw extended above the ice bore torches which brightened our way for a great distance—to the foot of the far escarpment, actually. Nothing untoward occurred as we crossed that frozen place.

"From what you've told me and what I've seen," Jurt said, "I get the impression it's the Pattern that's sponsoring this trip and the Logrus that's trying to punch your ticket."

Just then the ice cracked in a number of places. Fracture lines rushed toward us from several directions, both sides. They slowed, however, as they neared our trail, causing me to notice for the first time that it had risen above the general level of the plain. We now occupied something of a causeway, and the ice shattered itself harmlessly along its sides.

"Like that," Jurt observed with a gesture. "How'd you get into this mess anyway?"

"It all started on April thirtieth," I began.

SEVEN

Some of the arms seemed to be waving good-bye to us as we commenced our climb after reaching the wall. Jurt thumbed his nose at them.

"Can you blame me for wanting to escape this place?" he asked.

"Not in the least," I replied.

"If that transfusion you gave me really placed me beyond control of the Logrus, then I might dwell here for some indefinite period of time."

"Sounds possible."

"That's why you must realize I threw the ice at Borel, not you. Besides the fact that you're smarter than he was and might be able to find a way out of here, he was a creature of the Logrus, too, and wouldn't have had enough fire if the need arose."

"That had occurred to me also," I said, withholding a possible out I'd guessed at, to keep myself indispensable. "But what are you getting at?"

"I'm trying to say that I'll give you any kind of help you need, just so you don't leave me behind when you go. I know we never got along before, but I'm willing to put that aside if you are."

"I always was," I said. "You were the one who started all our fights and kept me in trouble."

He smiled.

"I never did, and I won't do it again," he said. "Yeah, okay, you're right. I didn't like you, and maybe I still don't. But I won't mess you up when we need each other this way."

"The way I see it, you need me a hell of a lot more than I need you."

"I can't argue with that, and I can't make you trust me," he said. "Wish I could." We climbed a little more before he continued, and I fancied the air had already grown a trifle warmer. Then, "But look at it this way," he finally continued, "I resemble your brother Jurt, and I come close to representing something he once was—close, but not a perfect fit. I began diverging from his model beginning with our race. My circumstances are uniquely my own, and I've been thinking steadily since I gained my autonomy. The real Jurt knows things I do not and has powers I don't possess. But I have his memories up through his taking the Logrus, and I'm the second greatest authority there is on the way he thinks. Now, if he's become such a threat as you've indicated, you might find me more than a little useful when it comes to second-guessing him."

"You have a point," I acknowledged. "Unless, of course, the two of you were to throw in together."

He shook his head.

"He wouldn't trust me," he said, "and I wouldn't trust him. We'd both know better. A matter of introspection. See what I mean?"

"It means neither one of you is trustworthy."

His brow furrowed; then he nodded.

"Yeah, I guess so," he said.

"So why should I trust you?"

"Right now because you've got me by the balls. Later on because I'll be so damn useful."

After several more minutes' ascending, I told him, "The thing that bothers me the most about you is that it was not all that long ago that Jurt took the Logrus. You are not an older, milder version of my least favorite relative. You are a very recent model. As for your divergence from the original, I can't see this short while as making that much difference."

He shrugged.

"What can I say that I haven't said already?" he asked. "Let's just deal in terms of power and self-interest then."

I smiled. We both knew that that was the way it was anyway. The conversation helped pass the time, though.

A thought came to me as we climbed.

"Do you think you could walk through Shadow?" I asked him.

"I don't know," he answered after a time. "My last memory from before I came to this place was of completing the Logrus. I guess the recording was completed at that time, too. So I have no recollection of Suhuy instructing me in shadow-walking, no memory of trying it. I'd guess I could do it, wouldn't you think?"

I paused to catch my breath.

"It's such an arcane matter that I don't even feel qualified to speculate on it. I thought maybe you'd come equipped with ready-made answers for things like that—some sort of preternatural awareness of your limits and abilities."

"Afraid not. Unless you'd call a hunch preternatural."

"I suppose I would if you were right often enough."

"Shit. It's too soon to tell."

"Shit. You're right."

Soon we'd climbed above the line of haze from which the flakes seemed to fall. A little farther, and the winds died to breezes. Farther still, and these subsided to nothing. The rim was in sight by then, and shortly thereafter we achieved it.

I turned and looked back down. All I could see was a bit of glitter through the mist. In the other direction our trail ran on in a zigzag fashion, here and there looking like a series of Morse dashes—regular interruptions, possibly rock formations. We followed it to the right until it turned left.

I reserved some attention for Jurt, looking for signs of recognition at any feature of the terrain. A talk is only words, and he was still some version of the Jurt I'd grown up with. And if he became responsible for my falling into any sort of trap, I was going to pass Grayswandir through his personal space as soon as I became aware of it.

Flicker . . .

Formation to the left, cavelike, as if the hole in the rock opened into another reality. An oddly shaped car driving up a steep city street . . .

"What . . . ?" Jurt began.

"I still don't know their significance. A whole mess of sequences like this were with me earlier, though. In fact, at first I thought you were one of them."

"Looks real enough to walk into."

"Maybe it is."

"It might be our way out of here."

"Somehow that just seems a little too easy."

"Well, let's give it a try."

"Go ahead," I told him.

We departed the trail, advanced upon the reality window, and kept going. In a moment he was on the sidewalk next to the street up which the car was passing. He turned and waved. I saw his mouth working, but no words came to me.

If I could brush snow off the red Chevy, why couldn't I enter entirely into one of these sequences? And if I could do that, mightn't it be possible that I could shadow-walk from there, wending my way to some more congenial spot, leaving this dark world behind? I moved forward.

Suddenly I was there, and the sound had been turned on for me. I looked about at the buildings, at the sharply inclined street. I listened to the traffic sounds, and I sniffed the air. This place could almost be one of San Francisco's shadows. I hurried to catch up with Jurt, who was moving toward the corner.

I reached him quickly, fell into step beside him. We came to the corner. We turned. We froze.

There was nothing there. We faced a wall of blackness. That is, not just darkness but an absolute emptiness, from which we immediately drew back.

I put my hand forth slowly. A tingling began as it neared the blackness, then a chill, followed by a fear. I drew back. Jurt reached for it, did the same. Abruptly he stopped, picked up the bottom of a broken bottle from the gutter, turned, and hurled it through a nearby window. Immediately he began running in that direction.

I followed. I joined him before the broken pane, stared within.

Again the blackness. There was nothing at all on the other side of the window.

"Kind of spooky," I remarked.

"Uh-huh," Jurt said. "It's as if we're being granted extremely limited access to various shadows. What do you make of it?"

"I'm beginning to wonder whether there isn't something we're supposed to be looking for in one of these places," I said.

Suddenly the blackness beyond the window was gone, and a candle flickered on a small table beyond it. I began to reach through the broken glass toward it. Immediately it vanished. Again there was only blackness.

"I'd take that as an affirmative response to your question," Jurt said.

"I believe you're right. But we can't be looking for something in every one of these things we pass."

"I think maybe something's just been trying to get your attention, to get you to realize that you should be watching what appears, that something probably will be presented once you begin noticing."

Brightness. A whole tableful of candles now blazed beyond the window.

"Okay," I hollered. "If that's all you want, I'll do it. Is there anything else I should be looking for here?"

The darkness came. It crept around the corner and moved slowly toward us. The candles vanished, and it flowed from the window. The buildings across the street disappeared behind an ebon wall.

"I take it the answer is no," I cried. Then I turned and beat it back along our narrowing black tunnel toward the trail. Jurt was right behind me.

"Good thinking," I told him when we stood back on the glowing way, watching that rising street get squeezed out of existence beside us. "Do you think it was just pulling these sequences at random till I finally entered one?"

"Yes."

"Why?"

"I think it has more control in those places and could respond to your questions more readily in one of them."

" 'It' being the Pattern?"

"Probably."

"Okay. The next one it opens to me, I'm going in. I'll do whatever it wants there if it means I get out of here sooner."

"We, brother. We."

"Of course," I answered.

We commenced walking again. Nothing new and intriguing appeared beside us, though. The road zigged and zagged, and we walked along it, and I got to wondering whom we might meet next. If I were indeed on the Pattern's turf and on the verge of doing something it wanted, then it seemed that the Logrus might send along someone I knew to attempt to dissuade me. No one appeared at all, though, and we took the final turn, followed a trail suddenly grown straight for some time, then saw it end abruptly within a dark mass far ahead.

Continuing, I saw that it plunged on into a great, dark, mountainous mass. I felt vaguely claustrophobic, just considering the implications, and I heard Jurt mutter an obscenity as we trudged toward it. Before we reached it, there came a flickering to my right. Turning, I beheld Random and Vialle's bedroom, back in Amber. I was looking from the southern side of the room, between the sofa and a bedside table, past a chair, across the rug and the cushions toward the fireplace, the windows which flanked it admitting a soft daylight. No one was present in the bed or occupying any other piece of furniture, and the logs on the grate had burned themselves down to red embers, smoking fitfully.

"What now?" Jurt asked.

"This is it," I replied. "It has to be, don't you see? Once I got the message as to what was going on, it presented the real thing. I've got to act fast, too, I think—as soon as I figure just what—"

One of the stones beside the fireplace began to glow redly. It increased in intensity as I watched. There was no way that those embers could be doing it. Therefore . . .

I rushed forward under the influence of a powerful imperative. I heard Jurt shout something behind me, but his voice was cut off as I entered the room. I caught a whiff of Vialle's favorite perfume as I passed beside the bed. This was really Amber, I was certain, not just some shadowy facsimile thereof. I moved quickly to the right of the fireplace.

Jurt burst into the room behind me.

"Better come out fighting!" he cried.

I whirled to face him, shouted, "Shut up!" then raised a finger to my lips.

He crossed to my side, caught hold of my arm, and whispered hoarsely, "Borel's trying to materialize again! He might be solid and waiting by the time you leave!"

From the sitting room I heard Vialle's voice.

"Is someone there?" she called.

I jerked my arm free of Jurt's grasp, knelt upon the hearth, and seized hold of the glowing stone. It appeared to be mortared in place but came loose easily when I drew upon it.

"How'd you know that one came free?" Jurt whispered.

"The glow," I replied.

"What glow?" he asked.

I did not answer him but thrust my right hand into the opened area, hoping offhandedly there were no booby traps. The opening extended back for a good distance beyond the length of the stone. And there I felt it, suspended from peg or hook: a length of chain. I caught hold of it and drew it forth. I heard Jurt catch his breath beside me.

The last time I had seen it was when Random had worn it at Caine's funeral. It was the Jewel of Judgment that I held in my hand. I raised it quickly and slipped the chain over my head, letting that red stone fall upon my breast, just as the door to the sitting room was opened.

Placing my finger to my lips, once more I reached forward, caught hold of Jurt's shoulders, and turned him back toward the opened wall which let upon our trail. He began to protest, but I propelled him with a sharp push, and he moved off in that direction.

"Who's there?" I heard Vialle ask, and Jurt glanced back at me, looking puzzled.

I did not feel we could afford the time for my explaining by sign language or whisper that she was blind. So I gave him another push. Only this time he stepped to the side, extended his leg, slipped a hand behind my back, and pushed me forward. A brief expletive escaped my lips, and then I was falling. From behind me, I heard Vialle's "Who—" before her voice was cut off.

I tumbled onto the trail, managing to draw the dagger from my right boot as I fell. I rolled and came up with the point extended toward the figure of Borel, which seemed to have found its form once more.

He was smiling, his weapon yet undrawn, as he regarded me.

"There is no field of arms here," he stated, "to provide you with a lucky accident such as you enjoyed when last we met."

"Too bad," I said.

"If I but gain that bauble you wear about your neck and deliver it to the place of the Logrus, I will be granted a normal existence, to replace my living counterpart—he who was treacherously slain by your father, as you pointed out."

The vision of Amber's royal apartments had vanished. Jurt stood off the trail, near what had been its interface with this odd realm. "I knew I couldn't beat him," he called out when he felt my glance, "but you took him once."

I shrugged.

At this Borel turned toward Jurt.

"You would betray the Courts and the Logrus?" he asked him.

"On the contrary," Jurt responded. "I may be saving them from a serious mistake."

"What mistake might that be?"

"Tell him, Merlin. Tell him what you told me while we were climbing out of the deep freeze," he said.

Borel glanced back at me.

"There's something funny about this entire setup," I said. "I've a feeling it's all a duel between the Powers—the Logrus and the Pattern. Amber and the Courts may be secondary to the entire affair. You see—"

"Ridiculous!" he interrupted, drawing his weapon. "This is just made-up nonsense to avoid *our* duel."

I tossed the dagger into my left hand and drew Grayswandir with my right.

"The hell with you then!" I said. "Come and get it!"

A hand fell upon my shoulder. And it kept right on falling with a sort of twist to it, spinning me into a downward spiral which threw me off to the left of the trail. From the corner of my eye, I saw that Borel had taken a step backward.

"You've a resemblance to Eric or to Corwin," came a soft, familiar voice, "though I know you not. But you wear the Jewel, which makes your person too important to risk in a petty squabble."

I came to a stop and turned my head. It was Benedict whom I beheld—a Benedict with two normal hands.

"My name is Merlin and I'm Corwin's son," I said, "and this is a master duelist from the Courts of Chaos."

"You appear to be on a mission, Merlin. Be about it then," Benedict said.

The point of Borel's blade flicked into a position about ten inches from my throat. "You are going nowhere," he stated, "not with that jewel."

There was no sound as Benedict's blade was drawn and moved to beat Borel's off its line.

"As I said, be on your way, Merlin," Benedict told me.

I got to my feet, moved quickly out of range, passed them both cautiously.

"If you kill him," Jurt said, "he can rematerialize after a period of time."

"How interesting," Benedict remarked, flicking off an attack and retreating slightly. "How long a time?"

"Several hours."

"And how much time will you need to complete whatever you're about?" Jurt looked at me.

"I'm not certain," I answered.

Benedict executed an odd little parry, followed by a strange shuffling step and a brief slashing attack. A button flew from Borel's shirt front.

"In that case I'll make this last for a time," Benedict said. "Good luck, lad."

He gave me a quick salute with the weapon, at which moment Borel attacked. Benedict used an Italianate sixte which threw both their points off to the side, advancing as he did so. He reached forward quickly then with his left hand and pulled the other's nose. Then he pushed him away, stepped back a pace, and smiled.

"What do you usually charge for lessons?" I overheard him asking as Jurt and I hurried down the path.

"I wonder how long it does take for one of the Powers to materialize a ghost," Jurt said as we jogged toward the mountainous mass the trail entered.

"Several hours for Borel alone," I said, "and if the Logrus wants the Jewel as badly as I'd guess, I'd think it would have summoned an army of ghosts if it could. I'm certain now that this place is very difficult for both Powers to reach. I get the feeling they can only manifest via the barest trickles of energy. If that weren't the case, I'd never have gotten this far."

Jurt reached out as if to touch the Jewel, apparently thought better of it, withdrew his hand.

"It seems you've definitely aligned yourself with the Pattern now," he observed.

"Looks as if you have, too. Unless you're planning on stabbing me in the back at the last moment," I said.

He chuckled. Then, "Not funny," he said. "I've got to be on your side. I can see that the Logrus just created me as a disposable tool. I'd wind up on the scrap heap when the job's done. I've a feeling I might have dissipated already had it not been for the transfusion. So I'm with you, like it or not, and your back is safe."

We ran on along the now-straight way, its terminus finally grown near. Jurt finally asked, "What is the significance of that pendant? The Logrus seems to want it badly."

"It's called the Jewel of Judgment," I answered. "It is said to be older than the Pattern itself and to have been instrumental in its creation."

"Why do you think you were led to it and obtained it with such ease?"

"I have no idea whatsoever," I said. "If you get one before I do, I'll be glad to hear it."

Soon we reached the place where the trail plunged into the greater darkness. We halted and regarded it.

"No signs posted," I said, checking above and to either side of that entranceway.

Jurt gave me an odd look.

"You've always had a weird sense of humor, Merlin" he said. "Who'd put up a sign in a place like this?"

"Someone else with a weird sense of humor," I replied.

"Might as well go on," he said, turning back toward the entrance.

A bright red exit sign had appeared above the opening. Jurt stared for a moment, then shook his head slowly. We entered.

We took our way down a wandering tunnel—a thing which puzzled me a bit. The artificial quality of most of the rest of this place had led me to expect a ruler-straight trail through a smooth-walled shaft, geometrically precise in all its features. Instead, it seemed as if we were traversing a series of natural caverns—stalactites, stalagmites, pillars, and pools displayed at either hand.

The Jewel cast a baleful light over any features I turned to scrutinize.

"Do you know how to use that stone?" Jurt asked me.

I thought back over my father's story.

"When the time comes, I believe that I will," I said, raising the Jewel and studying it for a moment, then letting it fall again. I was less concerned with it than with the route we were following.

I kept turning my head as we made our way from damp grotto to high cathedral chamber, along narrow passages, down stony waterfalls. There was something familiar here, though I couldn't put my finger on it.

"Anything about this place bring back memories?" I asked him.

"Not for me," Jurt replied.

We kept going, at one point passing a side cave containing three human skeletons. These being, in their fashion, the first real signs of life I had seen since the onset of this journey, I remarked on it.

Jurt nodded slowly.

"I am beginning to wonder whether we are still walking between shadows," he said, "or whether we might actually have departed that place and entered Shadow—perhaps when we came into these caves."

"I could find out by trying to summon the Logrus," I said, causing Frakir immediately to pulse sharply upon my wrist. "But considering the metaphysical politics of the situation, I'd rather not."

"I was just going by the colors of all the minerals in the walls," he said. "The place we left behind kind of favored monochrome. Not that I give a shit about the scenery. What I'm saying is that if we have, it's a kind of victory."

I pointed at the ground.

"So long as that glowing trail is there, we're not off the hook."

"What if we simply walked away from it now?" he asked, turning to the right and taking a single step in that direction.

A stalactite vibrated and crashed to the ground before him. It missed him by about a foot. He was back beside me in an instant.

"Of course, it would be a real shame not to find out where we're headed," he said.

"Quests are that way. It'd be bad form to miss the fun."

We hiked on. Nothing allegorical happened around us. Our voices and our footfalls echoed. Water dripped in some of the danker grots. Minerals flashed. Our way seemed a gradual descent.

For how long we walked I could not tell. After a time stony chambers took on a generic appearance—as if we passed regularly through a teleportation device which rerouted us back through the same caves and corridors. This had the effect of blurring my sense of time. Repetitious actions have a lulling effect and—

Suddenly our trail debouched into a larger passage, turned left. Finally, some variation. Only this way, too, looked familiar. We followed our line of light through the darkness. After a time we went by a side passage to the left. Jurt glanced up it and hurried past.

"Any damned thing might be lurking around here," he observed.

"True," I acknowledged. "But I wouldn't worry about it."

"Why not?"

"I think I'm beginning to understand."

"Mind telling me what's going on?"

"It'd take too long. Just wait. We'll be finding out pretty soon."

We went by another side passage. Similar, yet different. Of course.

I increased my pace, anxious to learn the truth. Another sideway. I broke into a run . . .

Another . . .

Jurt pounded along beside me, the echoes falling about us. Up ahead. Soon.

Another turning.

And then I slowed, for the passage continued ahead but our trail didn't. It curved to the left, vanishing beneath a big metal-bound door. I reached out to my right to where the hook was supposed to be, located it, removed the key that hung there. I inserted it, turned it, withdrew it, rehung it.

I don't like this place, boss, Frakir noted.

I know.

"Seems as if you know what you're doing," Jurt remarked.

"Yep," I said, then added, "up to a point," as I realized that this door opened outward rather than inward.

I caught hold of the large handle to the left and began to pull upon it.

"Mind telling me where we've wound up?" he asked.

The big door creaked, commenced a slow movement as I walked backward.

"These are amazingly like a section of caverns in Kolvir beneath Amber Castle," I replied.

"Great," he said. "And what's behind the door?"

"This is much like the entrance to the chamber which houses the Pattern in Amber."

"Wonderful," he said. "I'll probably go up in a puff of smoke if I set foot inside."

"But it is not quite the same," I continued. "We had Suhuy come and look at the Pattern itself before I walked it. He didn't suffer any ill effects from the proximity."

"Our mother walked the Pattern."

"Yes, that's true."

"Frankly, I think anyone of proper consanguinity in the Courts could walk the Pattern—and vice versa for my relatives in Amber with the Logrus. Tradition has it we're all related from back somewhere in the dim and misty."

"Okay. I'll go in with you. There's room to move around inside without touching the thing, isn't there?"

"Yes."

I drew the door the rest of the way open, braced my shoulder against it, and stared. This was it. I saw that our glowing trail ended a few inches beyond the threshold.

I drew a deep breath and muttered some expletive as I let it go.

"What is it?" Jurt asked, trying to see past me.

"Not what I expected," I told him.

I moved aside and let him have a look.

He stared for several seconds, then said, "I don't understand."

"I am not certain that I do either," I said, "but I intend to find out."

I entered the chamber, and he followed me. This was not the Pattern that I knew. Or rather, it was and it wasn't. It conformed to the same general configuration as the Pattern in Amber, only it was broken. There were several places where the lines had been erased, destroyed, removed in some fashion— or perhaps never properly executed in the first place. The ordinarily dark interlinear areas were bright, blue-white, the lines themselves black. It was as if some essence had drained from the diagram to permeate the field. The lighted area seemed to ripple slowly as I viewed it.

And beyond all of this was the big difference: The Pattern in Amber did not contain a circle of fire at its center, a woman dead, unconscious, or under a spell within it.

And the woman, of course, had to be Coral. I knew that immediately, though I had to wait for more than a minute before I got a glimpse of her face beyond the flames.

The big door shut itself behind us while I stood staring. Jurt stood unmoving for a long time also before he said, "That Jewel is certainly busy at something. You should see your face in its light right now."

I glanced downward and observed its ruddy pulsations. Between the blue-white flux in which the Pattern was grounded and the flickering of that circle of flame I had not noted the sudden activity on the part of the stone.

I moved a step nearer, feeling a wave of coldness similar to that of an activated Trump. This had to be one of the Broken Patterns of which Jasra had been speaking—representative of one of the Ways in which she and Julia were initiates. This placed me in one of the early shadows, near Amber herself. Thoughts began to race through my mind at a ferocious pace.

I had only recently become aware of the possibility that the Pattern might actually be sentient. Its corollary, that the Logrus was sentient, seemed likely also. The notion of its sentiency had been presented to me when Coral had succeeded in negotiating the Pattern and then had asked it to send her where she should go. It had done so, and this was the place to which she had been transported, and her condition was obviously the reason I couldn't reach her by means of her Trump. When I had addressed the Pattern following her disappearance, it had—almost playfully, it seemed at the time—shifted me from one end of its chamber to the other, apparently to satisfy me on the matter of its sentience.

And it wasn't merely sentient, I decided, as I raised the Jewel of Judgment and stared into its depths. It was clever. For the images that I saw within the stone, showing me what it was that was desired of me, represented something I would not have been willing to do under other circumstances. Having come away from that strange realm through which I had been led on this quest, I would have shuffled out a Trump and called someone for a fast exit—or even summoned the image of the Logrus and let the two of them slug it out while I slipped away through Shadow. But Coral slept in a circle of flame at the heart of the Broken Pattern. . . . She was the authentic Pattern's hold over me. It had to have understood something back when she was walking it, laid its plan, and set me up at that time.

It wanted me to repair this particular image of itself, to mend this Broken Pattern, by walking it, bearing the Jewel of Judgment with me. This was how Oberon had repaired the damage to the original. Of course, the act had been sufficiently traumatic to kill him . . .

On the other hand, the King had been dealing with the real thing, and this was only one of its images. Also, my father had survived the creation of his own ersatz Pattern from scratch.

Why me? I wondered then. Was it because I was the son of the man who had succeeded in creating another Pattern? Did it involve the fact that I bore the image of the Logrus within me as well as that of the Pattern? Was it simply because I was handy and coercible? All of the above? None of them?

"How about it?" I called out. "Have you got an answer for me?"

There was a quick pang in my stomach and a wave of dizziness as the chamber spun, faded, stood still, and I regarded Jurt across the expanse of the Pattern, the big door at his back.

"How'd you do that?" he hollered.

"I didn't," I replied.

"Oh."

He edged his way to his right till he came to the wall. Maintaining contact with it, he began moving about the Pattern's periphery, as if afraid to approach any nearer to it than he had to or to remove his gaze from it.

From this side I could see Coral a bit more clearly, within the fiery hedge. Funny. It was not as if there were a large emotional investment here. We were not lovers, not even terrifically close friends. We had become acquainted only the other day, shared a long walk about, around, and under the town and palace, had a meal together, a couple of drinks, a few laughs. If we became better acquainted, perhaps we would discover that we couldn't stand each other. Still, I had enjoyed her company, and I realized that I did want to take the time to get to know her better. And in some ways I felt responsible for her present condition, through a kind of contributory negligence. In other words, the Pattern had me by the balls. If I wanted to free her, I had to repair it.

The flames nodded in my direction.

"It's a dirty trick," I said aloud.

The flames nodded again.

I continued to study the Broken Pattern. Almost everything I knew about the phenomenon had come to me by way of my conversation with Jasra. But I recalled her telling me that initiates of the Broken Pattern walked it in the areas between the lines, whereas the image in the Jewel was instructing me to walk the lines, as one normally would the Pattern itself. Which made sense, as I recalled my father's story. It should serve to inscribe the proper path across the breaks. I wasn't looking for any half-assed between-the-lines initiation.

Jurt made his way about the far end of the Pattern, turned, and began to move toward me. When he came abreast of a break in the outer line, the light flowed from it across the floor. The look on his face was ghastly as it touched his foot. He screamed and began to melt.

"Stop!" I cried. "Or you can find another Pattern repairman! Restore him and leave him alone or I won't do it! I mean it!"

Jurt's collapsing legs lengthened again. The rush of blue-white incandescence which had fled upward through his body was withdrawn as the light retreated from him. The expression of pain left his face.

"I know he's a Logrus-ghost," I said, "and he's patterned on my least favorite relative, but you leave him alone, you son of a bitch, or I won't walk you! You can keep Coral and you can stay broken!"

The light flowed back through the imperfection, and things stood as they had moments before.

"I want a promise," I said.

A gigantic sheet of flame rose from the Broken Pattern to the top of the chamber, then fell again.

"I take it that is an affirmative," I said.

The flames nodded.

"Thanks," I heard Jurt whisper.

EIGHT

And so I commenced my walk. The black line did not have the same feeling to it as the blazing ones back under Amber. My feet came down as if on dead ground, though there was a tug and a crackle when I raised them.

"Merlin!" Jurt called out. "What should I do?"

"What do you mean?" I shouted back.

"How do I get out of here?"

"Go out the door and start shadow-shifting," I said, "or follow me through this Pattern and have it send you wherever you want."

"I don't believe you can shadow-shift this close to Amber, can you?"

"Maybe we are too close. So get away physically and then do it."

I kept moving. There came small crackling sounds whenever I raised my feet now.

"I'd get lost in the caves if I tried that."

"Then follow me."

"The Pattern will destroy me."

"It's promised not to."

He laughed harshly.

"And you believe it?"

"If it wants this job done properly, it has no choice."

I came to the first break in the Pattern. A quick consultation of the Jewel showed me where the line should lie. With some trepidation I took my first step beyond the visible marking. Then another. And another. I wanted to look back when I finally crossed the gap. Instead, I waited until the natural curving of my route granted me that view. I saw then that the entire line I had walked thus far had begun to glow, just like the real thing. The spilled luminescence seemed to have been absorbed within it, darkening the interstitial ground area. Jurt had moved to a position near that beginning.

He caught my gaze.

"I don't know, Merlin," he said. "I just don't know."

"The Jurt I knew wouldn't have had guts enough to try it," I told him.

"Neither do I."

"As you pointed out, our mother did it. Odds are you've got the genes. What the hell. If I'm wrong, it'll be over before you know it."

I took another step. He gave a mirthless laugh.

Then, "What the hell," he said, and he set his foot upon it.

"Hey, I'm still alive," he called out. "What now?"

"Keep coming," I said. "Follow me. Don't stop. And don't leave the line or all bets are off."

There followed another turning of the way, and I followed it and lost sight of him. As I continued along, I became aware of a pain in my right ankle—product of all the hiking and climbing I had done, I supposed. It began increasing with each step. It was hot and soon grew to be quite terrible. Had I somehow torn a ligament? Had I—

Of course. I could smell the burning leather now.

I plunged my hand into the sheath area of my boot and withdrew the Chaos dagger. It was radiating heat. This proximity to the Pattern was affecting it. I couldn't keep it about me any longer.

I drew my arm back and cast the weapon across the Pattern in the direction I was facing, toward the end of the room where the doorway was situated. Automatically my gaze followed its passage. There was a small movement in the shadows toward which it flew. A man was standing there, watching me. The dagger struck the wall and fell to the floor. He leaned over and picked it up. I heard a chuckle. He made a sudden movement, and the dagger came arcing back across the Pattern in my direction.

It landed ahead and to the right of me. As soon as it made contact with the Pattern, a fountain of blue flame engulfed it, rising well above the level of my head, splattering, sizzling. I flinched and I slowed, though I knew it would do me no permanent harm, and I kept walking. I had reached the long frontal arc where the going was slow.

"Stay on the line," I yelled to Jurt. "Don't worry about things like that."

"I understand," he said. "Who's that guy?"

"Damned if I know."

I pushed ahead. I was nearer to the circle of flame now. I wondered what the *ty'iga* would think of my present predicament. I made my way around another turn and was able to see back over a considerable section of my trail. It was glowing evenly, and Jurt was coming on strongly, moving as I had, the flames rising above his ankles now. They were almost up to my knees. From the corner of my eye I saw a movement from that area of the chamber where the stranger stood.

The man moved forth from his shadowy alcove, slowly, carefully, flowing along the far wall. At least he did not seem interested in walking the Pattern. He moved to a point almost directly opposite its beginning.

I had no choice but to continue my course, which took me through curves and turns that removed him from my sight. I came to another break in the Pattern and felt it knit as I crossed it. A barely audible music seemed to occur as I did so. The tempo of the flux within the lighted area seemed to increase also, as it flowed into the lines, etching a sharp, bright trail behind me. I called an occasional piece of advice to Jurt, who was several laps back, though his course sometimes brought him abreast of me and close enough to touch had there been any reason to.

The blue fires were higher now, reaching up to mid-thigh, and my hair was rising. I began a slow series of turns. Above the crackling and the music, I asked, *How're you doing, Frakir?* There was no reply.

I turned, kept moving through an area of high impedance, emerged from it, beholding the fiery wall of Coral's prison there at the Pattern's center. As I took my way around it, the opposite side of the Pattern slowly came into view.

The stranger stood waiting, the collar of his cloak turned high. Within the shadows which lay upon his face, I could see that his teeth were bared in a grin. I was startled by the fact that he stood in the midst of the Pattern itself—watching my advance, apparently waiting for me—until I realized that he had entered by way of a break in the design which I was headed to repair.

"You are going to have to get out of my way," I called out. "I can't stop, and I can't let you stop me!"

He didn't stir, and I recalled my father's telling me of a fight which had occurred on the primal Pattern. I slapped the hilt of Grayswandir.

"I'm coming through," I said.

The blue-white fires came up even higher with my next step, and in their light I saw his face. It was my own.

"No," I said.

"Yes," he said.

"You are the last of the Logrus-ghosts to confront me."

"Indeed," he replied.

I took another step.

"Yet," I observed, "if you are a reconstruction of myself from the time I made it through the Logrus, why should you oppose me here? The self I recall being in those days wouldn't have taken a job like this."

His grin went away.

"I am not you in that sense," he stated. "The only way to make this happen as it must, as I understand it, was to synthesize my personality in some fashion."

"So you're me with a lobotomy and orders to kill."

"Don't say that," he replied. "It makes it sound wrong, and what I'm doing is right. We even have many of the same memories."

"Let me through and I'll talk to you afterward. I think the Logrus may have screwed itself by trying this stunt. You don't want to kill yourself, and neither do I. Together we could win this game, and there's room in Shadow for more than one Merlin."

I'd slowed, but I had to take another step then. I couldn't afford to lose momentum at this point.

His lips tightened to a thin line, and he shook his head.

"Sorry," he said. "I was born to live one hour—unless I kill you. If I do, your life will be given to me."

He drew his blade.

"I know you better than you think I do," I said, "whether you've been restructured or not. I don't think you'll do it. Furthermore, I might be able to lift that death sentence. I've learned some things about how it works for you ghosts."

He extended his blade, which resembled one I'd had years ago, and its point almost reached me.

"Sorry," he repeated.

I drew Grayswandir for purposes of parrying it. I'd have been a fool not to. I didn't know what sort of job the Logrus had done on his head. I racked my memories for fencing techniques I'd studied since I'd become an initiate of the Logrus.

Yes. Benedict's game with Borel had reminded me. I'd taken some lessons in Italian-style fencing since then. It gave one wider, more careless-seeming parries, compensated by greater extension. Grayswandir went forth, beat his blade to the outside, and extended. His wrist bent into a French four, but I was already under it, arm still extended, wrist straight, sliding my right foot forward along the line as the forte of my blade beat heavily against the forte of his from the outside, and I immediately stepped forward with my left foot, driving the weapon across his body till the guards locked and continuing its drop in that direction.

And then my left hand fell upon the inside of his right elbow, in a maneuver a martial artist friend had taught me back in college—*zenponage*, I think he called it. I lowered my hips as I pressed downward. I turned my hips then, counterclockwise. His balance broke, and he fell toward my left. Only I could not permit that. If he landed on the Pattern proper, I'd a funny feeling he'd go off like a fireworks display. So I continued the drop for several more inches, shifted my hand to his shoulder, and pushed him, so that he fell back into the broken area.

Then I heard a scream, and a blazing form passed on my left side.

"No!" I cried, reaching for it.

But I was too late. Jurt had stepped off the line, springing past me, driving his blade into my double even as his own body swirled and blazed. Fire also poured from my double's wound. He tried unsuccessfully to rise and fell back.

"Don't say that I never served you, brother," Jurt stated, before he was transformed into a whirlwind, which rose to the chamber's roof, where it dissipated.

I could not reach far enough to touch my doppelgänger, and moments later I did not wish to, for he was quickly transformed into a human torch.

His gaze was directed upward, following Jurt's spectacular passing. He looked at me then and smiled crookedly.

"He was right, you know," he said, and then he, too, was engulfed.

It took awhile to overcome my inertia, but after a time I did, continuing my ritual dance about the fire. The next time around there was no trace of either of their persons, though their blades remained where they had fallen, crossed, across my path. I kicked them off the Pattern as I went by. The flames were up to my waist by then.

Around, back, over. I glanced into the Jewel periodically, to avoid missteps, and piece by piece I stitched the Pattern together. The light was drawn into the lines, and save for the central blaze, it came more and more to resemble the thing we kept in the basement back home.

The First Veil brought painful memories of the Courts and of Amber. I stayed aloof, shivering, and these things passed. The Second Veil mixed memory and desire in San Francisco. I controlled my breathing and pretended I was only a spectator. The flames danced about my shoulders, and I thought of a series of half-moons as I traversed arc after arc, curve upon reverse curve. The resistance grew till I was drenched with sweat as I struggled against it. But I had been this way before. The Pattern was not just around me but inside me as well.

I moved, and I reached the point of diminishing returns, of less and less distance gained for the effort expended. I kept seeing dissolving Jurt and my own dying face amid flames, and it didn't matter a bit that I knew the memory rush was Pattern-induced. It still bothered me as I drove myself forward.

I swept my gaze around me once as I neared the Grand Curve, and I saw that this Pattern had now been fully repaired. I had bridged all of the breaks with connecting lines, and it burned now like a frozen Catherine wheel against a black and starless sky. Another step . . .

I patted the warm Jewel that I wore. Its ruddy glow came up to me even more strongly now than it had earlier. I wondered whether there was an easy way to get it back where it belonged. Another step . . .

I raised the Jewel and stared into it. There was an image of me completing the walking of the Grand Curve and continuing right on through the wall of flames as if this represented no problem whatsoever. While I took the vision as a piece of advice, I was reminded of a David Steinberg routine which Droppa had once appropriated. I hoped that the Pattern was not into practical jokes.

The flames enveloped me fully as I commenced the Curve. I continued to slow as my efforts mounted. Step after painful step I drew nearer to the Final Veil. I could feel myself being transformed into an expression of pure will, as everything that I was became focused upon a single end. Another step . . . It felt as if I were weighted down with heavy armor. It was the final three steps that pushed one near despair's edge.

Again . . .

Then came the point where even movement became less important than the effort. It was no longer the results but the attempt that mattered. My will was the flame; my body, smoke or shadow. . . .

And again . . .

Seen through my risen blue light, the orange flames which surrounded Coral became silver-gray spikes of incandescence. Within the crackling and the popping I heard something like music once again—low, adagio, a deep, vibrant thing, like Michael Moore playing bass. I tried to accept the rhythm, to move with it. Somehow, then, it seemed that I succeeded—that, or my time sense became distorted—as I moved with a feeling of something like fluidity through the next steps.

Or maybe the Pattern felt it owed me a favor and had eased up for a few beats. I'll never know.

I passed through the Final Veil, faced the wall of flame, suddenly orange again, and kept going. I drew my next breath in the heart of fire.

Coral lay there at the Pattern's center, looking pretty much as she had when last I had seen her—in a copper shirt and dark green breeches—save that she appeared to be sleeping, sprawled there upon her heavy brown cloak. I dropped to my right knee beside her and laid my hand upon her shoulder. She did not stir. I brushed a strand of her reddish hair off her cheek, stroked that cheek a few times.

"Coral?" I said.

No response.

I returned my hand to her shoulder, shook her gently.

"Coral?"

She drew a deep breath and sighed it out, but she did not awaken.

I shook her a bit harder. "Wake up, Coral."

I slipped my arm beneath her shoulders, raised her partway. Her eyes did not open. Obviously she was under some sort of spell. The middle of the Pattern was hardly the place to summon the Sign of the Logrus if one wished to remain unincinerated. So I tried the storybook remedy. I leaned forward and kissed her. She made a small, deep noise, and her eyelids fluttered. But she did not come around. I tried again. Same result.

"Shit!" I remarked. I wanted a little elbowroom for working on a spell like this, a place where I had access to some of the tools of my trade and could call upon the source of my powers with impunity.

I raised her higher and commanded the Pattern to transport us back to my apartment in Amber, where her *ty'iga*-possessed sister lay in a trance of her own—one of my brother's doing, for purposes of protecting me from her.

"Take us home," I said aloud, for emphasis.

Nothing happened.

I employed a strong visualization then and backed it once more with the mental command.

We didn't stir.

I lowered Coral gently, rose, and looked out across the Pattern through the faintest area of the flames.

"Look," I said, "I just did you a big favor, involving a lot of exertion and considerable risk. Now I want to get the hell out of here and take the lady with me. Will you please oblige?"

The flames died down, were gone, for several beats. In the diminished light which followed I became aware that the Jewel was pulsing, like the message light on a hotel phone. I raised it and stared into it.

I hardly expected an X-rated short feature, but that's what was playing.

"I believe I'm receiving the wrong channel," I said. "If you've got a message, let's have it. Otherwise, I just want to go home."

Nothing changed, save that I became aware of a strong resemblance between the two figures in the Jewel and Coral and myself. They were going at it on a cloak at what appeared to be the center of a Pattern, flagrante ad infinitum—rather like a spicier version of the old salt box label, it seemed, if they could be seeing into the Jewel the guy was wearing and watching. . . .

"Enough!" I cried. "This is fucking ridiculous! You want a Tantric ritual I'll send you some professionals! The lady isn't even awake—"

The Jewel pulsed again, with such intensity that it hurt my eyes. I let it fall. I knelt then, scooped Coral up, and stood.

"I don't know whether anyone's ever walked you backwards before," I said, "but I don't see why it shouldn't work."

I took a step in the direction of the Final Veil. Immediately the wall of flame sprang up before me. I stumbled in drawing away from it, fell back upon the outspread cloak. I held Coral to me that she not be cast into the fire. She came down on top of me. She seemed almost awake. . . .

Her arms went around my neck, and she sort of nuzzled my cheek. She seemed more drowsy than comatose now. I held her tightly and thought about it.

"Coral?" I tried again.

"Mm," she said.

"Seems the only way we can get out of here is by making love."

"Thought you'd never ask," she mumbled, eyes still closed.

That made it seem somewhat less like necrophilia, I told myself as I turned us onto our sides so I could get at those coppery buttons. She muttered a little more while I was about things, but it didn't exactly turn into a conversation. Still, her body was not unresponsive to my attentions, and the encounter quickly took on all the usual features, too commonplace to be of much concern to the sophisticated. It seemed an interesting way to break a spell. Maybe the Pattern did have a sense of humor. I don't know.

The fires died down at about the same time that the fires died down, so to speak. Coral's eyes finally opened.

"That seems to have taken care of the circle of flames," I said.

"When did this cease being a dream?" she asked.

"Good question," I replied, "and only you can answer it."

"Did you just rescue me from something?"

"That seems the easiest way to put it," I answered as she drew away somewhat and cast her gaze about the chamber. "See where it got you when you asked the Pattern to send you where you should go?" I said.

"Screwed," she replied.

"Precisely."

We drew apart. We adjusted our apparel.

"It's a good way to get to know each other better . . ." I had begun when the cavern was shaken by a powerful earth tremor.

"The timing is really off here," I observed as we were rocked together and clung to each other for comfort, if not support.

It was over in an instant, and the Pattern was suddenly blazing more brilliantly than I'd ever seen it before. I shook my head. I rubbed my eyes. Something was wrong, even though it felt very right. Then the great metal-bound door opened—inward!—and I realized that we had come back to Amber, the real Amber. My glowing trail still led up to the threshold, though it was fading fast, and a small figure stood upon it. Before I could even squint against the corridor's gloom, I felt a familiar disorientation, and we were in my bedroom.

"Nayda!" Coral exclaimed when she viewed the figure reclined upon my bed.

"Not exactly," I said. "I mean, it's her body. But the spirit that moves it is of a different order."

"I don't understand."

I was busy thinking of the person who had been about to invade the precincts of the Pattern. I was also a mass of aching muscles, screaming nerves, and assorted fatigue poisons. I crossed to the table where the wine bottle I'd opened for Jasra—how long ago?—still stood. I found us two clean glasses. I filled them. I passed one to Coral.

"Your sister was very ill awhile back, wasn't she?"

"Yes," she replied.

I took a big swallow.

"She was near death. At that time her body was possessed by a *ty'iga* spirit—a kind of demon—as Nayda no longer had any use for it."

"What do you mean by that?"

"I understand that she actually died."

Coral stared into my eyes. She didn't find whatever she sought, and she took a drink instead.

"I'd known something was wrong," she said. "She hasn't really been herself since the illness."

"She became nasty? Sneaky?"

"No, a lot nicer. Nayda was always a bitch."

"You didn't get along?"

"Not till recently. She's not in any pain, is she?"

"No, she's just sleeping. She's under a spell."

"Why don't you release her? She doesn't look like much of a danger."

"I don't think she is now. Just the opposite, in fact," I said. "And we will release her, soon. My brother Mandor will have to undo it, though. It's his spell."

"Mandor? I don't really know much about you—or your family—do I?"

"Nope," I said, "and vice versa. Listen, I don't even know what day it is." I crossed the room and peered out the window. There was daylight. It was cloudy, though, and I couldn't guess the time. "There's something you should do right away. Go see your father and let him know you're all right. Tell him you got lost in the caverns or took a wrong turn into the Corridor of Mirrors and wound up on some other plane of existence or something. Anything. To avoid a diplomatic incident. Okay?"

She finished her drink and nodded. Then she looked at me and blushed and looked away.

"We'll get together again before I leave, won't we?"

I reached out and patted her shoulder, not really knowing what my feelings were. Then I realized that wouldn't do, and I stepped forward and embraced her.

"You know it," I said as I stroked her hair.

"Thanks for showing me around town."

"We'll have to do it again," I told her, "as soon as the pace slackens."

"Uh-huh."

We walked to the door.

"I want to see you soon," she said.

"I'm fading fast," I told her, as I opened it. "I've been through hell and back."

She touched my cheek.

"Poor Merlin," she said. "Sleep tight."

I gulped the rest of my wine and withdrew my Trumps. I wanted to do just what she said, but certain unavoidables came first. I riffled my way to the Ghostwheel's card, removed it, and regarded it.

Almost immediately, following the faintest drop in temperature and the barest formation of desire on my part, Ghostwheel appeared before me—a red circle turning in the middle of the air.

"Uh, hello, Dad," it stated. "I was wondering where you'd gotten to. When I checked back at the cave, you were gone, and none of my shadow-indexing procedures could turn you up. It never even occurred to me that you might simply have come home. I—"

"Later," I said. "I'm in a hurry. Get me down to the chamber of the Pattern fast."

"There's something I'd better tell you first."

"What?"

"That force that followed you to the Keep—the one I hid you from in the cave . . . ?"

"Yes?"

"It was the Pattern itself that was seeking you."

"I guessed that," I said, "later. We've had our encounter and sort of come to terms for now. Get me down there right away. It's important."

"Sir, I am afraid of that thing."

"Then take me as close as you dare and step aside. I have to check something out."

"Very well. Come this way."

I took a step forward. Ghost rose into the air, rotated ninety degrees toward me, and dropped quickly, passing my head, shoulders, torso and vanishing beneath my feet. The lights went out as he did so, and I called up my Logrus vision immediately. It showed me that I stood in the passageway outside the big door to the chamber of the Pattern.

"Ghost?" I said softly.

There was no reply.

I moved forward, turned the corner, advanced to the door, and leaned upon it. It was still unlocked, and it yielded to my pushing. Frakir pulsed once upon my wrist.

Frakir? I inquired.

There came no answer from that quarter either.

Lose your voice, lady?

She pulsed twice. I stroked her.

As the door opened before me, I was certain that the Pattern had grown brighter. The observation was quickly pushed aside, however. A dark-haired woman stood at the Pattern's center, her back to me, her arms upraised. I almost shouted the name I thought she might answer to, but she was gone before my vocal mechanism responded. I slumped against the wall.

"I really feel used," I said aloud. "You've run my ass ragged, you placed my life in jeopardy more than once, you got me to perform to satisfy your metaphysical voyeurism, then you kicked me out after you got the last thing you wanted—a slightly brighter glow. I guess that gods or powers or whatever the hell you are don't have to say 'Thank you' or 'I'm sorry' or 'Go to hell' when they've finished using someone. And obviously you feel no need to justify yourself to me. Well, I'm not a baby carriage. I resent being pushed around by you and the Logrus in whatever game you're playing. How'd you like it if I opened a vein and bled all over you?"

Immediately there was a great coalescence of energies at my side of the Pattern. With a heavy whooshing sound a tower of blue flame built itself before me, widened, assumed genderless features of an enormous inhuman beauty. I had to shade my eyes against it.

"You do not understand," came a voice modulated of the roaring of flames.

"I know. That's why I'm here."

"Your efforts are not unappreciated."

"Glad to hear it."

"There was no other way to conduct matters."

"Well, were they conducted to your satisfaction?"

"They were."

"Then you are welcome, I guess."

"You are insolent, Merlin."

"The way I feel right now I've nothing to lose. I'm just too damned tired to care what you do to me. So I came down here to tell you that I think you owe me a big one. That's all."

I turned my back on it then.

"Not even Oberon dared address me so," it said.

I shrugged and took a step toward the door. When I set my foot down, I was back in my apartment.

I shrugged again, then went and splashed water in my face.

"You still okay, Dad?"

There was a ring around the bowl. It rose into the air and followed me about the room."

"I'm all right," I acknowledged. "How about yourself?"

"Fine. It ignored me completely."

"Do you know what it's up to?" I asked.

"It seems to be dueling with the Logrus for control of Shadow. And it just won a round. Whatever happened seems to have strengthened it. You were involved, right?"

"Right."

"Where were you after you left the cave I'd put you in?"

"You know of a land that lies between the shadows?"

"*Between?* No. That doesn't make sense."

"Well, that's where I was."

"How'd you get there?"

"I don't know. With considerable difficulty, I'd guess. Are Mandor and Jasra all right?"

"The last time I looked they were."

"How about Luke?"

"I'd no reason to seek him out. Do you want me to?"

"Not just now. Right now I want you to go upstairs and look in on the royal suite. I want to know whether it is, at the moment, occupied. And if so, by whom. I also want you to check the fireplace in the bedroom. See whether a loose stone which was removed from an area to the right of it has been replaced or is still lying upon the hearth."

He vanished, and I paced. I was afraid to sit down or to lie down. I'd a feeling that I'd go to sleep instantly if I did and that I'd be difficult to awaken. But Ghost spun back into existence before I chalked up much mileage.

"The Queen, Vialle, is present," he said, "in her studio, the loose stone has been replaced, and there is a dwarf in the hall knocking on doors."

"Damn," I said. "Then they know it's missing. A dwarf?"

"A dwarf."

I sighed.

"I guess I'd better walk on upstairs, return the Jewel, and try to explain what happened. If Vialle likes my story, she might just forget to mention it to Random."

"I'll transfer you up there."

"No, that would not be too politic. Or polite either. I'd better go knock on the door and get admitted properly this time."

"How do people know when to knock and when to go on in?"

"In general, if it's closed, you knock on it."

"As the dwarf is doing?"

I heard a faint knocking from somewhere outside.

"He's just going along, indiscriminately banging on doors?" I asked.

"Well, he's trying them in sequence, so I don't know that you could say it's indiscriminate. So far all of the doors he's tried have been to rooms which are empty. He should reach yours in another minute or so."

I crossed to my door, unlocked it, opened it, and stepped out into the hallway.

Sure enough, there was a short guy moving along the hallway. He looked in my direction at the opening of my door, and his teeth showed within his beard as he smiled and headed toward me.

It quickly became apparent that he was a hunchback.

"My God!" I said. "You're Dworkin, aren't you? The real Dworkin!"

"I believe so," he replied in a not unpleasant voice. "And I do hope that you are Corwin's son, Merlin."

"I am," I said. "This is an unusual pleasure, coming at an unusual time."

"It is not a social call," he stated, drawing near and clasping my hand and shoulder. "Ah! These are your quarters!"

"Yes. Won't you come in?"

"Thank you."

I led him in. Ghost did a fly-on-the-wall imitation, became about a half inch in diameter, and took up residence on the armoire as if the result of a stray sunbeam. Dworkin did a quick turn about the sitting room, glanced into the bedroom, stared at Nayda for a time, muttered, "Always let sleeping demons lie," touched the Jewel as he passed me on his return, shook his head forebodingly, and sank into the chair I'd been afraid I'd go to sleep in.

"Would you care for a glass of wine?" I asked him.

He shook his head.

"No, thank you," he replied. "It was you who repaired the nearest Broken Pattern in Shadow, was it not?"

"Yes, it was."

"Why did you do it?"

"I didn't have much choice in the matter."

"You had better tell me all about it," the old man said, tugging at his grisly, irregular beard. His hair was long and could have used a trim also. Still, there seemed nothing of madness in his gaze or his words.

"It is not a simple story, and if I am to stay awake long enough to tell it, I am going to need some coffee," I said.

He spread his hands, and a small, white-clothed table appeared between us, bearing service for two and a steaming silvery carafe set above a squat candle. There was also a tray of biscuits. I couldn't have summoned it all that fast. I wondered whether Mandor could.

"In that case, I will join you," Dworkin said.

I sighed and poured. I raised the Jewel of Judgment.

"Perhaps I'd better return this thing before I start," I told him. "It may save me a lot of trouble later."

He shook his head as I began to rise.

"I think not," he stated. "If you take it off now, you will probably die."

I sat down again.

"Cream and sugar?" I asked him.

NINE

I came around slowly. That familiar blueness was a lake of prebeing in which I drifted. Oh, yes, I was here because . . . I was here, as the song said. I turned over onto my other side within my sleeping bag, drew my knees up to my chest, and went back to sleep.

The next time I came around and gave it a quick glance the world was still a blue place. Fine. There is much to be said for the tried, the true. Then I recalled that Luke might be by at any time to kill me, and my fingers wrapped themselves around the hilt of the weapon beside me, and I strained my hearing after signs of anything's approach.

Would I spend the day chipping at the wall of my crystal cave? I wondered. Or would Jasra come and try again to kill me?

Again?

Something was wrong. There'd been an awful lot of business involving Jurt and Coral and Luke and Mandor, even Julia. Had it all been a dream?

The moment of panic came and went, and then my wandering spirit returned, bringing along the rest of my memories, and I yawned and everything was all right again.

I stretched. I sat up. I knuckled my eyes.

Yes, I was back in the crystal cave. No, everything that had happened since Luke imprisoned me had not been a dream. I had returned here by choice (a) because a good night's sleep in this time line amounted to only a brief span back in Amber, (b) because nobody could bother me here with a Trump contact, and (c) because it was possible that even the Pattern and the Logrus couldn't track me down here.

I brushed my hair out of my eyes, rose, and headed back to the john. It had been a good idea, having Ghost transport me here following my colloquy with Dworkin. I was certain I had slept for something like twelve hours—deep, undisturbed stuff, the best kind. I drained a quart water bottle. I washed my face with more of the stuff.

Later, after I had dressed and stowed the bedclothes in the storeroom, I walked to the entrance chamber and stood in the light beneath the overhead adit. What I could see of the sky through it was clear. I could still hear Luke's words the day he had imprisoned me here and I'd learned we were related.

I drew the Jewel of Judgment up from within my shirt, removed it, held it high so that the light shone from behind it, stared into its depths. No messages this time.

Just as well. I wasn't in the mood for two-way traffic.

I lowered myself into a comfortable cross-legged position, still regarding the stone. Time to do it and be done with it, now that I felt rested and somewhat alert. As Dworkin had suggested, I sought the Pattern within that red pool.

After a time it began to take shape. It did not appear as I had been visualizing it, but this was not an exercise in visualization. I watched the structure come clear. It was not as if it were suddenly coming into existence, however, but rather as if it had been there all along and my eyes were just now adjusting to perceive it properly. Likely this was actually the case, too.

I took a deep breath and released it. I repeated the process. Then I began a careful survey of the design. I couldn't recall everything my father had said about attuning oneself to the Jewel. When I had mentioned this to Dworkin, he had told me not to worry about it, that I needed but to locate the three-dimensional edition of the Pattern within the stone, find its point of entry, and traverse it. When I pressed him for details, he had simply chuckled and told me not to worry.

All right.

Slowly I turned it, drawing it nearer. A small break appeared, high, to the right. As I focused upon it, it seemed to rush toward me.

I went to that place, and I went in there. It was a strange roller coaster of an experience, moving along Pattern-like lines within the gemstone. I went where it drew me, sometimes with a near-eviscerating feeling of vertigo, other times pushing with my will against the ruby barriers till they yielded and I climbed, fell, slid, or pushed my way onward. I lost most of the awareness of my body, hand holding the chain high, save that I knew I was sweating profusely, as it stung my eyes with some regularity.

I've no idea how much time passed in my attunement to the Jewel of Judgment, the higher octave of the Pattern. Dworkin felt that there were reasons other than my having pissed off the Pattern for its wanting me dead immediately following my completion of my bizarre quest and repairing of the nearest of the Broken Patterns. But Dworkin refused to elaborate, feeling that my knowing the reason could influence a possible future choice which should be made freely. All of which sounded like gibberish to me, save that everything else he said struck me as eminently sane, in contrast with the Dworkin I knew of from legend and hearsay.

My mind plunged and reared through the pool of blood that was the Jewel's interior. The Pattern segments I had traversed and those I had yet to travel moved about me, flashing like lightning. I'd a feeling my mind was going to crash against some invisible Veil and shatter. My movement was out of control now, accelerating. There was no way, I knew, for me to withdraw from this thing until I had run its course.

Dworkin felt that I had been protected from the Pattern during our confrontation, when I had gone back to check on the figure I had seen, because

I was wearing the Jewel. I could not keep wearing it for too long, though, because this also had a tendency to prove fatal. He decided that I must become attuned to the Jewel—as were my father and Random—before I let it out of my possession. I would thereafter bear the higher-order image within me, which should function as well as the Jewel in defending me against the Pattern. I could hardly argue with the man who had supposedly created the Pattern, using the Jewel. So I agreed with him. Only I was too tired to do what he suggested. That was why I had had Ghost return me to my crystal cave, my sanctuary, to rest first.

Now, now . . . I flowed. I spun. Occasionally I stalled. The Jewel's equivalents of the Veils were no less formidable because I had left my body behind. Each such passage left me as wrung out as running a mile in Olympic time. Though I knew at one level that I stood holding the Jewel through which I took my initiatory way, at another I could feel my heart pounding, and at another I recalled parts of a guest lecture by Joan Halifax for an anthropology course I was taking, years before. The medium swirled like Geyser Peak Merlot 1985 in a goblet—and whom was I looking across the table at that night? No matter. Onward, down and around. The blood-brightened tide was loosed. A message was being inscribed upon my spirit. In the beginning was a word I cannot spell . . . Brighter, brighter. Faster, faster. Collision with a ruby wall, I a smear upon it. Come now, Schopenhauer, to the final game of will. An age or two came and went; then, suddenly, the way was opened. I was spilled forth into the light of an exploding star. Red, red, red, shifting me onward, away, like my little boat *Starburst*, driven, expanding, coming home . . .

I collapsed. Though I did not lose consciousness, my state of mind was not normal either. There was a hypnagogia I could have passed through at any time I chose, in either direction. But why? I am seldom the recipient of such a delivery of euphoria. I felt I'd earned it, so I drifted, right there, for a long, long time.

When it finally subsided below the level that made indulgence worthwhile, I climbed to my feet, swayed, leaned against the wall, made my way to the storeroom for another drink of water. I was also ravenous, but none of the tinned or freeze-dried foods appealed to me that greatly. Especially when fresher things were not that hard to come by.

I walked back through those familiar chambers. So I had followed Dworkin's advice. It was a pity I'd turned my back before I recalled a long list of questions I wished to ask him. When I turned back again, he was gone.

I climbed. Coming up out of my cave, I stood atop the blue prominence which held the only entranceway I knew of. It was a breezy, balmy, springlike morning with only a few small puffs of cloud to the east. I drew a deep breath for pleasure and expelled it. Then I stooped and moved the blue boulder to block the opening. I'd hate to be surprised by a predator should I come this way again in need of sanctuary.

I took off the Jewel of Judgment and hung it on a spur of the boulder. Then I moved off about ten paces.

"Hi, Dad."

The Ghostwheel was a golden Frisbee, come sailing out of the west.

"Good morning, Ghost."

"Why are you abandoning that device? It's one of the most powerful tools I've ever seen."

"I'm not abandoning it, but I'm about to summon the Sign of the Logrus, and I don't think they'd get on too well. I'm even a little leery over how the Logrus will take to me with this higher-order Pattern attunement I'm wearing."

"Perhaps I'd better move along and check back with you later."

"Stick around," I said. "Maybe you can bail me out if this turns into a problem."

I summoned the Sign of the Logrus then, and it came and hovered before me, and nothing happened. I shifted a part of my awareness into the Jewel, there on the side of the boulder, and through it I was able to perceive the Logrus from another perspective. Eerie. Also painless.

I centered myself within my own skull once again, extended my arms into the Logrus limbs, reached. . . .

In less than a minute I had a plate of buttermilk pancakes, a side order of sausages, a cup of coffee, and a glass of orange juice.

"I could have gotten them for you faster than that," Ghost remarked.

"I'm sure you could have," I said. "I was just testing systems."

As I ate, I tried to sort my priorities. When I finished, I sent the dishes back where they had come from, retrieved the Jewel, hung it about my neck, and stood.

"Okay, Ghost. Time to head back to Amber," I said.

He expanded and opened and sank, so that I stood before a golden arch. I stepped forward—

—and back into my apartment.

"Thanks," I said.

"*De nada*, Dad. Listen, I've a question: When you summoned breakfast, did you notice anything at all unusual in the way the Logrus Sign behaved?"

"How do you mean that?" I asked as I moved to wash my hands.

"Let's start with physical sensations. Did it seem . . . sticky?"

"That's an odd way to put it," I said. "But as a matter of fact, it did seem to take slightly longer than usual to disengage. Why do you ask?"

"A peculiar notion has just occurred to me. Can you do Pattern magic?"

"Yeah, but I'm better at the Logrus variety."

"You might want to try them both and compare them if you get a chance."

"Why?"

"I'm actually starting to get hunches. I'll tell you as soon as I've checked this one out."

Ghostwheel was gone.

"Shit," I said, and I washed my face.

I looked out the window, and a handful of snowflakes blew by. I fetched a key from my desk drawer. There were a couple of things I wanted to get out of the way immediately.

I stepped into the corridor. I had not gone more than a few paces before I heard the sound. I halted and listened. Then I continued, past the stairway, the sound growing steadily in volume as I advanced. By the time I reached the long corridor which ran past the library I knew that Random was back because I didn't know of anyone else around here who could drum like that— or would dare to use the King's drums if he could.

I continued on past the half-opened door to the corner, where I turned right. My first impulse had been to enter, give him back the Jewel of Judgment, and try to explain what had happened. Then I recalled Flora's advice that anything honest, straightforward, and aboveboard would always get you in trouble here. While I hated to give her credit for having enunciated a general rule, I could see that in this particular instance it would certainly tie me up with a lot of explaining when there were other things I wanted to be about—and, for that matter, it might also get me ordered not to do some of them.

I continued to the far entrance to the dining room, where I checked quickly and determined the place to be deserted. Good. Inside and to the right, as I recalled, there was a sliding panel which would get me into a hollow section of wall beside the library, furnished with pegs or a ladder that would take me up to a hidden entrance to the library's balcony. It could also take me down through the spiral stair's shaft and into the caverns below, if memory served. I hoped I never had reason to check that part out, but I was sufficiently into family tradition these days that I wanted to do a little spying, as several muttered exchanges as I'd passed the opened door led me to believe that Random was not alone in there. If knowledge really is power, then I needed all I could get my hands on, as I'd felt especially vulnerable for some time now.

Yes, the panel slid, and I was through it in a trice, sending my spirit-light on ahead. I hand-over-handed my way quickly to the top and opened the panel there slowly and quietly, feeling grateful to whoever had thought to conceal its space with a wide chair. I was able to see around the chair's right arm with comparative safety from detection—a good view of the room's north end.

And there was Random, drumming, and Martin, all chains and leather, was seated before him, listening. Random was doing something I'd never seen done before. He was playing with five sticks. He had one in each hand, one under each arm, and he held one in his teeth. And he was revolving them as he played, moving the one in his mouth to replace the one under his right arm, which replaced the one in his right hand, which he had switched over to his left hand, the left-hand one going up beneath his left arm, the left arm one going to his teeth, all without missing a beat. It was hypnotic. I stared until he wound out the number. His old set of traps was hardly the fusion drummer's dreamworld of translucent plastic with tipped cymbals the size of battle shields set around the snares, a mess of tomtoms, and a couple of basses, all lit up like Coral's circle of fire. Random's set went back to a time before snares grew thin and nervous, basses shrank, and cymbals caught acromegaly and began to hum.

"Never saw that done before," I heard Martin say.

Random shrugged.

"Bit of horsing around," he said. "Learned it from Freddie Moore, in the thirties, either at the Victoria or the Village Vanguard, when he was with Art Hodes and Max Kaminsky. I forget which place. It goes back to vaudeville, when they didn't have any mikes and the lighting was bad. Had to do show-off things like that, or dress funny, he told me, to keep the audience paying attention."

"Shame they had to cater to the crowd that way."

"Yeah, none of you guys would dream of dressing funny or throwing your instruments around."

There followed a silence, and there was no way I could see the expression on Martin's face. Then, "I meant it different from that," Martin said.

"Yeah, me, too," Random replied. Then he tossed three of the sticks down and began to play again.

I leaned back and listened. A moment later I was startled to hear an alto sax come in. When I looked again, Martin was standing, his back still to me, and playing the thing. It must have been on the floor on the other side of his chair. There was a Richie Cole flavor to it that I rather liked, and it kind of surprised me. As much as I enjoyed it, I felt that I did not belong in this room right now, and I edged back, opened the panel, passed through, and closed it. After I'd climbed down and let myself out, I decided to cut through the dining room rather than pass the library entrance again. The music carried for some distance thereafter, and I wished I'd learned a spell of Mandor's for capturing sounds in precious stones, though I'm not sure how the Jewel of Judgment would have taken to containing "Wild Man Blues."

I was planning on walking up the east corridor to the point where it intersected with the north one in the vicinity of my apartment, turning left there, and taking the stairs up to the royal suite, knocking on the door, and returning the Jewel to Vialle, whom I hoped I could get to take a rain check on explanations. And if not, I'd rather explain to her than to Random anyway. I could leave out a lot that she wouldn't know to ask me. Of course, Random would catch up with me with questions eventually. But the later, the better.

But then I was going right past my father's rooms. I'd brought along the key so that I could stop in later, for what I considered obvious reasons. Still, since I was already on the spot, it would be more time-effective. I unlocked the door, opened it, and stepped inside.

The silver rose was gone from the bud vase on the dresser. Odd. I took a step toward it. There came a sound of voices from the other room, too soft for me to distinguish words. I froze. He might well be in there. But you don't just go bursting into someone's bedroom, especially when it's likely there's company present—particularly when it's your father's room and you had to unlock an outer door to get where you were. Suddenly I was extremely self-conscious. I wanted to get out of there, fast. I unbuckled my sword belt, from which Grayswandir depended in its not-quite-perfect fit of a sheath. I did not dare bear it any farther but hung it from one of the garment pegs on the wall near the door next to a short trench coat I hadn't noticed before. I slipped out then and locked the door as quietly as I could.

Awkward. Was he really coming and going with some regularity, somehow managing to avoid notice? Or was some sort of phenomenon of an entirely different order in progress within his quarters? I'd heard an occasional rumor that some of the older chambers had *sub specie spatium* doorways, if one could but figure how to activate them, providing considerable extra closet space as well as private means of entry and egress. Something else I should have asked Dworkin about. Maybe I've got a pocket universe under my bed. I'd never looked.

I turned and walked quickly away. As I neared the corner, I slowed. Dworkin had felt that the presence of the Jewel of Judgment on my person was the thing that had protected me from the Pattern, had it really been tempted to harm me earlier. On the other hand, the Jewel, worn too long, could itself do damage to the wearer. Therefore, he had counseled me to get some rest and then pass my mind through the stone's matrix, in effect creating a recording of a higher power of the Pattern within me along with some measure of immunity to assaults by the Pattern itself. Interesting conjecture. And that's all it was, of course: conjecture.

When I reached the cross corridor where a left would take me to the stairway or a right back to my rooms, I hesitated. There was a sitting room diagonally across the way, to the left, across from Benedict's seldom used rooms. I headed for it, entered, sank into a heavy chair in the corner. All I wanted to do was deal with my enemies, help my friends, get my name off any shit lists it currently occupied, locate my father, and come to some sort of terms with the sleeping *ty'iga*. Then I could see about the continuance of my interrupted *Wanderjahr*. All of which, I realized, required that I now reask myself the now near-rhetorical question, How much of my business did I want Random to know?

I thought of him in the library, playing a duet with his near-estranged son. I understood that he had once been pretty wild and footloose and nasty, that he hadn't really wanted the job of ruling this archetypal world. But parenthood, marriage, and the Unicorn's choice seemed to have laid a lot on him—deepening his character, I suppose, at the price of a lot of the fun things in his life. Right now he seemed to have a lot of problems with this Kashfa-Begma business, possibly having just resorted to an assassination and agreed to a less than favorable treaty to maintain the complex political forces of the Golden Circle at an even level. And who knew what might be going on elsewhere to add to his troubles? Did I really want to draw this man into something I might well be able to handle myself with his never being any the wiser, or ever even bothered, concerning it? Conversely, if I did draw him into my affairs, it seemed likely that he might well lay restrictions on me which could hamper my ability to respond to what seemed the daily exigencies of my life. It could also raise another matter which had been shunted aside years ago.

I had never sworn allegiance to Amber. Nobody had ever asked me to. After all, I was Corwin's son, and I had come to Amber willingly and made my home here for some time before going off to the shadow Earth, where so many of the Amberites had gone to school. I returned often, and I seemed to be on good terms with everyone. I didn't really see why the concept of dual citizenship shouldn't apply.

I'd rather the matter did not come up at all, though. I did not like the thought of being forced to choose between Amber and the Courts. I wouldn't do it for the Unicorn and the Serpent, the Pattern and the Logrus, and I didn't care to do it for the royalty of either court.

All of which indicated that Vialle should not have even a sketchy edition of my story. Any version at all would require an eventual accounting. However, if the Jewel were returned without an explanation of where it had been, then no one would know to come after me on the matter, and things would still be set right. How could I lie if I were not even asked questions?

I mulled that along a little further. What I would actually be doing would be to save a tired, troubled man the burden of additional problems. There was nothing he could or should do about most of my affairs. Whatever was going on between the Pattern and the Logrus seemed mainly important as a metaphysical affair. I couldn't see where much good or bad might come out of it on a practical level. And if I saw something coming, I could always tell Random then.

Okay. That's one nice thing about reasoning abilities. You can use them to make yourself feel virtuous rather than, say, guilty. I stretched and cracked my knuckles.

"Ghost?" I said softly.

No response.

I reached for my Trumps, but even as I touched them, a wheel of light flashed on across the room.

"You did hear me," I said.

"I felt your need," came the reply.

"Whatever," I said, drawing the Jewel's chain up over my head and holding the stone out before me. "Do you think you could return this to its secret compartment beside the fireplace in the royal suite without anyone's being any wiser?" I asked.

"I'm leery about touching that thing," Ghost responded. "I don't know what its structure might do to my structure."

"Okay," I said. "I guess I'll find a way to do it myself then. But the time has come to test a hypothesis. If the Pattern attacks me, try to whisk me to safety, please."

"Very well."

I set the Jewel on a nearby table.

After about a half minute I realized that I had braced myself against the Pattern's death stroke. I relaxed my shoulders. I drew a deep breath. I remained intact. Could be that Dworkin was right and the Pattern would leave me alone. Also, I should be able to summon the Pattern in the Jewel now, he told me, as I do the Sign of the Logrus. There were Pattern-magics which could only be wrought via this route, though Dworkin hadn't taken the time to instruct me in their employment. He'd suggested that a sorcerer should be able to figure the system out. I decided that this could wait. I was in no mood just now for commerce of any sort with the Pattern in any of its incarnations.

"Hey, Pattern," I said. "Want to call it even?"

There came no reply.

"I believe it is aware of you here and what you just did," Ghost said. "I feel its presence. Could be you're off the hook."

"Could be," I responded, taking out my Trumps and sorting through them.

"Whom would you like to get in touch with?" Ghost asked.

"I'm curious about Luke," I said. "I want to see whether he's okay. And I'm wondering about Mandor. I assume you sent him to a safe place."

"Oh, nothing but the best," Ghost replied. "Same for Queen Jasra. Did you want her, too?"

"Not really. In fact, I don't *want* any of them. I just wanted to see—"

Ghost winked out while I was still talking. I wasn't at all certain that his eagerness to please was an improvement over his earlier belligerence.

I withdrew Luke's card and went inside it.

I heard someone passing along the corridor. The footsteps went on by.

I felt Luke's awareness, though no vision of his circumstances reached me.

"Luke, you hear me?" I inquired.

"Yep," he answered. "You okay, Merle?"

"I'm all right," I said. "How about yourself? That was quite a fight you—"

"I'm fine."

"I hear your voice, but I can't see a thing."

"Got a blackout on the Trumps. You don't know how to do that?"

"Never looked into the matter. Have to get you to teach me sometime. Uh, why are they blacked out anyway?"

"Somebody might get in touch and figure what I'm up to."

"If you're about to lead a commando raid on Amber, I'm going to be highly pissed."

"Come on! You know I swore off! This is something entirely different."

"Thought you were a prisoner of Dalt's."

"My status is unchanged."

"Well, he damn near killed you once and he just beat the shit out of you the other day."

"The first time he'd stumbled into an old berserker spell Sharu'd left behind for a trap; the second time was business. I'll be okay. But right now everything I'm up to is hush-hush, and I've got to run. G'bye."

Gone Luke, the presence.

The footsteps had halted, and I'd heard a knocking on a nearby door. After a time I heard a door being opened, then closed. I had not overheard any exchange of words. In that it had been nearby and that the two nearest apartments were Benedict's and my own, I began to wonder. I was fairly certain that Benedict was not in his, and I recalled not having locked my own door when I had stepped out. Therefore . . .

Picking up the Jewel of Judgment, I crossed the room and stepped out into the hall. I checked Benedict's door. Locked. I looked down the north-south hallway and walked back to the stairway and checked around in that area. There was no one in sight. I strode up to my own place then and stood listening for a time outside each of my doors. No sounds from within. The only alternatives I could think of were Gérard's rooms, back down the side corridor, and Brand's, which lay behind my own. I had thought of knocking out a wall—in keeping with the recent spirit of remodeling and redecorating Random had gotten into—adding Brand's rooms to my own, for a very good-size apartment. The rumor that his were haunted, though, and the wailings I sometimes heard through the walls late at night dissuaded me.

I took a quick walk then, knocking on and finally trying both Brand's and Gérard's doors. No response, and both were locked. Odder and odder.

Frakir had given a quick pulse when I'd touched Brand's door, and while I'd gone on alert for several moments, nothing untoward had approached. I was about to dismiss it as a disturbing reaction to the remnants of eldritch spells I had occasionally seen drifting about the vicinity when I noticed that the Jewel of Judgment was pulsing.

I raised the chain and stared into the gem. Yes, an image had taken form. I beheld the hallway around the corner, my two doors, and intervening artwork on the wall in plain view. The doorway to the left—the one that let upon my bedroom—seemed to be outlined in red and pulsing. Did that mean I was supposed to avoid it or rush in there? That's the trouble with mystical advice.

I walked back and turned the corner again. This time the gem—perhaps having felt my query and decided some editing was in order—showed me approaching and opening the door it was indicating. Of course, of the two, that door was locked. . . .

I fumbled for my key, reflecting that I could not even rush in with a drawn blade, having just disposed of Grayswandir. I did have a couple of tricky spells hung, though. Maybe one of them would save me if the going got too rough. Maybe not, too.

I turned the key and flung the door open.

"Merle!" she shrieked, and I saw that it was Coral. She stood beside my bed, where her putative sister the *ty'iga* was reclined. She quickly moved one hand behind her back. "You, uh, surprised me."

"Vice versa," I replied, for which there *is* an equivalent in Thari. "What's up, lady?"

"I came back to tell you that I located my father and gave him a soothing story about that Corridor of Mirrors you told me about. Is there really such a place here?"

"Yes. You won't find it in any guides, though. It comes and goes. So, he's mollified?"

"Uh-huh. But now he's wondering where Nayda is."

"This gets trickier."

"Yes."

She was blushing, and she did not meet my eyes readily. She seemed aware, too, that I was noting her discomfort.

"I told him that perhaps Nayda was exploring, as I'd been," she went on, "and that I'd ask after her."

"Mm-hm."

I shifted my gaze to Nayda. Coral immediately moved forward and brushed against me. She placed a hand on my shoulder, drew me toward her.

"I thought you were going to sleep," she said.

"Yes, I was. Did, too. I was running some errands just now."

"I don't understand," she said.

"Time lines," I explained. "I economized. I'm rested."

"Fascinating," she said, brushing my lips with her own. "I'm glad that you're rested."

"Coral," I said, embracing her briefly, "you don't have to bullshit me. You know I was dead tired when you left. You had no reason to believe that I'd be anything but comatose if you returned this soon."

I caught hold of her left wrist behind her back and drew her hand around to the front, raising it between us. She was surprisingly strong. And I made no effort to pry open her hand, for I could see between the fingers what it was that she held. It was one of the metal balls Mandor often used to create impromptu spells. I released her hand. She did not draw away from me, but rather, "I can explain," she said, finally meeting my gaze and holding it.

"I wish you would," I said. "In fact, I wish you'd done it a bit sooner."

"Maybe the story you heard about her being dead and her body the host for a demon is true," she said. "But she's been good to me recently. She's finally become the sister I'd always wished she'd been. Then you brought me back here and I saw her like that, not knowing what you really planned to do with her—"

"I want you to know that I wouldn't hurt her, Coral," I interrupted. "I owe her—it—for favors past. When I was young and naive on the shadow Earth, she probably saved my neck, several times. You have no reason to fear for her here."

She cocked her head to the right and narrowed one eye.

"I'd no way of knowing that," she said, "from what you told me I came back, hoping to get in, hoping you were deeply asleep, hoping I could break the spell or at least lift it enough to talk with her. I wanted to find out for myself whether she was really my sister—or something else."

I sighed. I reached out to squeeze her shoulder and realized I was still clutching the Jewel of Judgment in my left hand. I squeezed her arm with my right hand instead and said, "Look, I understand. It was boorish of me to show you your sister laid out that way and not to have gone into a little more detail. I can only plead industrial fatigue and apologize. I promise you she's in no pain. But I really don't want to mess with this spell right now because it's not one of mine—"

Just then Nayda moaned softly. I studied her for several minutes, but nothing more followed.

"Did you pluck that metal ball out of the air?" I asked. "I don't recall seeing one for the final spell."

Coral shook her head.

"It was lying on her breast. One of her hands was over it," she said.

"What prompted you to check there?"

"The position looked unnatural, that's all. Here."

She handed me the ball. I took it and weighed it in the palm of my right hand. I had no idea how the things functioned. The metal balls were to Mandor what Frakir was to me—a piece of idiosyncratic personal magic, forged out of his unconscious in the heart of the Logrus.

"Are you going to put it back?" she asked.

"No," I told her. "Like I said, it wasn't one of my spells. I don't know how it works, and I don't want to fool around with it."

"Merlin . . . ?"—whispered, from Nayda, her eyes still closed.

"We'd better go talk in the next room," I said to Coral. "I'll lay a spell of my own on her first, though. Just a simple soporific—"

The air sparkled and spun behind Coral, and she must have guessed from my stare that something was going on, for she turned.

"Merle, what is it?" she asked, retreating toward me as a golden archway took form.

"Ghost?" I said.

"Right," came the reply. "Jasra was not where I left her. But I brought your brother."

Mandor, still clad mainly in black, his hair a great mass of silver-white, appeared suddenly, glancing at Coral and Nayda, focusing on me, beginning to smile, stepping forward. Then his gaze shifted, and he halted. He stared. I had never seen that frightened expression on his face before.

"Bloody Eye of Chaos!" he exclaimed, summoning up a protective screen with a gesture. "How did you come by it?"

He took a step backward. The arch immediately collapsed into a gold-leaf calligraphed letter O, and Ghost slid around the room to hover at my right side.

Suddenly Nayda sat up on my bed, darting wild glances.

"Merlin!" she cried. "Are you all right?"

"So far so good," I answered. "Not to worry. Take it easy. All's well."

"Who's been tampering with my spell?" Mandor asked as Nayda swung her legs over the side of the bed and Coral cringed.

"It was a sort of accident," I said.

I opened my right hand. The metal sphere immediately levitated and shot off in his direction, narrowly missing Coral, whose hands were now extended in a general martial arts defense pattern, though she seemed uncertain what or whom she should be defending against. So she kept turning—Mandor, Nayda, Ghost, repeat. . . .

"Cool it, Coral," I said. "You're in no danger."

"The left eye of the Serpent!" Nayda cried. "Free me, oh, Formless One, and I will pledge with mine!"

Frakir in the meantime was warning me that all was not well, in case I hadn't noticed.

"Just what the hell is going on?" I yelled.

Nayda sprang to her feet, lunged forward, and with that unnatural demon strength snatched the Jewel of Judgment from my hand, pushed me aside, and tore out into the hallway.

I stumbled, recovered.

"Hold that *ty'iga!*" I cried, and the Ghostwheel flashed past me followed by Mandor's balls.

TEN

I was the next thing out into the hallway. I turned left and started running. A *ty'iga* may be fast, but so am I.

"I thought you were supposed to be protecting me!" I shouted after her.

"This takes precedence," she answered, "over your mother's binding."

"What?" I said. "My mother?"

"She placed me under a *geas* to take care of you when you went off to school," she replied. "This breaks it! Free at last!"

"Damn!" I observed.

Then, as she neared the stairway, the Sign of the Logrus appeared before her, larger than any I'd ever summoned, filling the corridor from wall to wall, roiling, sprawling, fire-shot, tentacular, a reddish haze of menace drifting about it. It took a certain measure of chutzpah for it to manifest like that here in Amber on the Pattern's turf, so I knew the stakes were high.

"Receive me, oh, Logrus," she cried, "for I bear the Eye of the Serpent," and the Logrus opened, creating a fiery tunnel at its center. I could somehow tell that its other end was not a place farther along my hallway.

But then Nayda was halted, as if she had suddenly encountered a glass partition, and she stiffened into a position of attention. Three of Mandor's gleaming spheres were suddenly orbiting her cataleptic form.

I was thrown from my feet and pressed back against the wall. I raised my right arm to block whatever might be coming down on me, as I looked backward.

An image of the Pattern itself, as large as the Logrus Sign, had just put in an appearance only a few feet behind me, manifesting about as far in that direction from Nayda as the Logrus was before her, parenthesizing the lady or the *ty'iga* between the poles of existence, so to speak, and incidentally enclosing me along with her. The area about me near the Pattern grew bright as a sunny morning while that at the other end took on the aspect of a baleful twilight. Were they about to reenact the Big Bang/Crunch, I wondered, with me as an unwilling momentary witness?

"Uh, Your Honors," I began, feeling obliged to try talking them out of it and wishing I were Luke, who just might be able to swing such a feat. "This is a perfect time to employ an impartial arbitrator, and I just happen to be uniquely qualified if you will but reflect—"

The golden circlet that I knew to be Ghostwheel suddenly dropped over Nayda's head, lengthening itself downward into a tube. Ghost had fitted himself within the orbits of Mandor's spheres and must somehow have insulated himself against whatever forces they were exerting, for they slowed, wobbled, and finally dropped to the floor, two striking the wall ahead of me and one rolling down the stairway ahead and to the right.

The Signs of the Pattern and the Logrus began to advance then, and I crawled quickly to keep ahead of the Pattern.

"Don't come any closer, fellows," Ghostwheel suddenly announced. "There's no telling what I might do if you make me even more nervous than I already am."

Both Power Signs halted in their advances. From around the corner to the left, up ahead, I heard Droppa's drunken voice, raised in some bawdy ballad, coming this way. Then it grew silent. Several moments passed, and he began singing "Rock of Ages" in a far, far weaker voice. Then this, too, was cut off, followed by a heavy thud and the sound of breaking glass.

It occurred to me that I should be able, from a distance such as this, to extend my awareness into the Jewel. But I was uncertain what effects I might then be able to produce with the thing, considering the fact that none of the four principals involved in the confrontation was human.

I felt the beginnings of a Trump contact.

"Yes?" I whispered.

Dworkin's voice came to me then.

"Whatever control you may have over the thing," he said, "use it to keep the Jewel away from the Logrus."

Just then a crackly voice, shifting in pitch and gender from syllable to syllable, emerged from the red tunnel.

"Return the Eye of Chaos," it said. "The Unicorn took it from the Serpent when they fought, in the beginning. It was stolen. Return it. Return it."

The blue face I had seen above the Pattern did not materialize, but the voice I'd heard at that time responded, "It was paid for with blood and pain. Title passed."

"The Jewel of Judgment and the Eye of Chaos or Eye of the Serpent are different names for the same stone?" I said.

"Yes," Dworkin replied.

"What happens if the Serpent gets its eye back?" I inquired.

"The universe will probably come to an end."

"Oh," I observed.

"What am I bid for the thing?" Ghost asked.

"Impetuous construct," the voice of the Pattern intoned.

"Rash artifact," wailed the Logrus.

"Save the compliments," Ghost said, "and give me something I want."

"I could tear it from you," the Pattern responded.

"I could have you apart and it away in an instant," stated the Logrus.

"But neither of you will do it," Ghost answered, "because such a focusing of your attention and energies would leave either of you vulnerable to the other."

In my mind, I heard Dworkin chuckle.

"Tell me why this confrontation need take place at all," Ghost went on, "after all this time."

"The balance was tipped against me by recent actions of this turncoat," the Logrus replied—a burst of fire occurring above my head, presumably to demonstrate the identity of the turncoat in question.

I smelled burning hair, and I warded the flame.

"Just a minute!" I cried. "I wasn't given much choice in the matter!"

"But there was a choice," wailed the Logrus, "and you made it."

"Indeed, he did," responded the Pattern. "But it served only to redress the balance you'd tipped in your own favor."

"Redress? You overcompensated! Now it's tipped in your favor! Besides, it was accidentally tipped my way, by the traitor's father." Another fireball followed, and I warded again. "It was not my doing."

"You probably inspired it."

"If you can get the Jewel to me," Dworkin said, "I can put it out of reach of both of them until this matter is settled."

"I don't know whether I can get hold of it," I said, "but I'll remember that."

"Give it to me," the Logrus said to Ghost, "and I will take you with me as First Servant."

"You are a processor of data," said the Pattern. "I will give you knowledge such as none in all of Shadow possess."

"I will give you power," said the Logrus.

"Not interested," said Ghost, and the cylinder spun and vanished.

The girl, the Jewel, and everything were gone.

The Logrus wailed, the Pattern growled, and the Signs of both Powers rushed to meet, somewhere near Bleys's nearer room.

I raised every protective spell that I could. Behind me I could feel Mandor doing the same. I covered my head, I drew up my knees, I—

I was falling. Through a bright, soundless concussion. Bits of debris struck me. From several directions. I'd a hunch that I had just bought the farm and that I was about to die without opportunity to reveal my insight into the nature of reality: The Pattern did not care about the children of Amber any more than the Logrus did about those of the Courts of Chaos. The Powers cared, perhaps, about themselves, about each other, about heavy cosmic principles, about the Unicorn and the Serpent, of which they were very probably but geometric manifestations. They did not care about me, about Coral, about

Mandor, probably not even about Oberon or Dworkin himself. We were totally insignificant or at most tools or sometimes annoyances, to be employed or destroyed as the occasion warranted—

"Give me your hand," Dworkin said, and I saw him, as in a Trump contact. I reached and—

—fell hard at his feet upon a colorful rug spread over a stone floor, in a windowless chamber my father had once described to me, filled with books and exotic artifacts, lit by bowls of light which hung without visible means of support high in the air.

"Thanks," I said, rising slowly, brushing myself off massaging a sore spot in my left thigh.

"Caught a whiff of your thoughts," he said. "There's more to it."

"I'm sure. But sometimes I enjoy being bleak-minded. How much of that crap the Powers were arguing about was true?"

"Oh, all of it," Dworkin said, "by their lights. The biggest bar to understanding is the interpretation they put on each other's doings. That, and the fact that everything can always be pushed another step backward—such as the break in the Pattern having strengthened the Logrus and the possibility that the Logrus actively influenced Brand into doing it. But then the Logrus might claim this was in retaliation for the Day of the Broken Branches several centuries ago."

"I haven't heard about that one," I said.

He shrugged.

"I'm not surprised. It wasn't all that important a matter, except to them. What I'm saying is that to argue as they do is to head into an infinite regression—back to first causes, which are always untrustworthy."

"So what's the answer?"

"Answer? This isn't a classroom. There are no answers that would matter, except to a philosopher—that is, none with any practical applications."

He poured a small cup of green liquid from a silver flask and passed it to me.

"Drink this," he said.

"It's a little early in the day for me."

"It's not refreshment. It's medication," he explained. "You're in a state of near shock, whether you've noticed or not."

I tossed the thing off, and it burned like a liquor but didn't seem to be one. I did feel myself beginning to relax during the next few minutes, in places I had not even realized I was tense.

"Coral, Mandor . . ." I said.

He gestured, and a glowing globe descended, drew nearer. He signed the air with a half-familiar gesture, and something like the Logrus Sign without the Logrus came over me. A picture formed within the globe.

That long section of hallway where the encounter had occurred had been destroyed, along with the stairs, Benedict's apartment, and possibly Gérard's as well. Also, Bleys's rooms, portions of my own, the sitting room I had been occupying but a short time before, and the northeast corner of the library were missing, as were the floor and ceiling. Below, I could see that sections of the kitchen and armory had been hit, and possibly more across the way. Looking upward—magic globes being wondrous accommodating—I could see sky, which meant that the blast had gone through the third and fourth floors, possibly damaging the royal suite along with the upper stairways and maybe the laboratory—and who knew what all else.

Standing on the edge of the abyss near what had been a section of Bleys's or Gérard's quarters was Mandor, his right arm apparently broken, hand tucked in behind his wide black belt. Coral leaned heavily upon his left shoulder, and there was blood on her face. I am not sure that she was fully conscious. Mandor held her about the waist with his left arm, and a metal ball circled the two of them. Diagonally across the abyss, Random stood on a heavy crossbeam near the opening to the library. I believe Martin was standing atop a short stack, below and to the rear. He was still holding his sax. Random appeared more than a little agitated and seemed to be shouting.

"Voice! Voice!" I said.

Dworkin waved.

"—ucking Lord of Chaos blowing up my palace!" Random was saying.

"The lady is injured, Your Highness," Mandor said.

Random passed a hand across his face. Then he looked upward.

"If there's an easy way to get her to my quarters, Vialle is very skilled in certain areas of medicine," he said in a softer voice. "So am I, for that matter."

"Just where is that, Your Highness?"

Random leaned to his side and pointed upward.

"Looks as if you won't need the door to get in, but I can't tell whether there's enough stairway left to get up there or where you might cross to it if there is."

"I'll make it," Mandor said, and two more of the balls came rushing to him and set themselves into eccentric orbits about him and Coral. Shortly thereafter they were levitated and drifted slowly toward the opening Random had indicated.

"I'll be along shortly," Random called after them. He looked as if he were about to add something, but then regarded the devastation, lowered his head, and turned away. I did the same thing.

Dworkin was offering me another dose of the green medicine, and I took it. Some sort of trank, it seemed, in addition to whatever else it did.

"I have to go to her," I told him. "I like that lady, and I want to be sure she's all right.

"I can certainly send you there," Dworkin said, "though I cannot think of anything you could do for her which will not be done well by others. Perhaps the time were more profitably spent in pursuit of that errant construct of yours the Ghostwheel. It must be persuaded to return the Jewel of Judgment."

"Very well," I acknowledged. "But I want to see Coral first."

"Your appearance could cause considerable delay," he said, "because of explanations which may be required of you."

"I don't care," I told him.

"All right. A moment then."

He moved away and took down what appeared to be a sheathed wand from the wall, where it had hung suspended from a peg. He hung the sheath upon his belt, then crossed to a small cabinet and removed a flat leather-bound case from one of its drawers. It rattled with a faint metallic sound as he slipped it into a pocket. A small jewelry box vanished up a sleeve without any sound.

"Come this way," he told me, approaching and taking my hand.

He turned me and led me toward the room's darkest corner, where I had not noted that a tall, curiously framed mirror hung. It exhibited an odd reflective capacity in that it showed us and the room behind us with perfect clarity from a distance, but the closer we approached to its surface, the more indistinct all of its images became. I could see what was coming, coming. But I still tensed as Dworkin, a pace in advance of me by then, stepped through its foggy surface and jerked me after him.

I stumbled and regained my footing, coming to myself in the good half of the blasted royal suite in front of a decorative mirror. I reached back quickly and tapped it with my fingertips, but its surface remained solid. The short, stooped figure of Dworkin stood before me, and he still had hold of my right hand. Looking past that profile, which in some ways caricatured my own, I saw that the bed had been moved eastward, away from the broken corner and a large opening formerly occupied by a section of flooring. Random and Vialle stood on the near side of the bed, their backs to us. They were studying Coral, who was stretched out upon the counterpane and appeared to be unconscious. Mandor, seated in a heavy chair at the bed's foot, observing operations, was the first to notice our presence, which he acknowledged with a nod.

"How . . . is she?" I asked.

"Concussion," Mandor replied, "and damage to the right eye."

Random turned. Whatever he was about to say to me died on his lips when he realized who stood beside me.

"Dworkin!" he said. "It's been so long. I didn't know whether you were still alive. Are you . . . all right?"

The dwarf chuckled.

"I read your meaning, and I'm rational," he replied. "I would like to examine the lady now."

"Of course," Random answered, moving aside.

"Merlin," Dworkin said, "see whether you can locate that Ghostwheel device of yours, and ask it to return the artifact it borrowed."

"I understand," I said, reaching for my Trumps.

Moments later I was reaching, reaching . . .

"I felt your intent several moments ago, Dad."

"Well, do you have the Jewel or don't you?"

"Yes, I just finished with it."

" 'Finished'?"

"Finished utilizing it."

"In what fashion did you . . . utilize it?"

"As I understood from you that passing one's awareness through it would give some protection against the Pattern, I wondered whether it might work for an ideally synthesized being such as myself."

"That's a nice term, 'ideally synthesized.' Where'd it come from?"

"I coined it myself when seeking the most appropriate designation."

"I've a hunch it'll reject you."

"It didn't."

"Oh. You actually got all the way through the thing?"

"I did."

"What effect did it have upon you?"

"That's a hard thing to assess. My perceptions are altered. It's difficult to explain. . . . It's subtle, whatever it is."

"Fascinating. Can you move your awareness into the stone from a distance now?"

"Yes."

"When all of our present troubles have passed, I'm going to want to test you again."

"I'm curious myself to know what's changed."

"In the meantime, there is a need for the Jewel here."

"Coming through."

The air shimmered before me.

Ghostwheel appeared as a silver circlet, the Jewel of Judgment at its center. I cupped my hand and collected it. I took it to Dworkin, who did not even glance at me as he received it. I looked down at Coral's face and looked away quickly, wishing I hadn't.

I moved back near Ghost.

"Where's Nayda?" I asked.

"I'm not sure," he replied. "She asked me to leave her—there near the crystal cave—after I took the Jewel away from her."

"What was she doing?"

"Crying."

"Why?"

"I suppose because both of her missions in life have been frustrated. She was charged to guard you unless some wild chance brought her the opportunity of obtaining the Jewel, in which instance she was released from the first directive. This actually occurred; only I deprived her of the stone. Now she is bound to neither course."

"You'd think she'd be happy to be free at last. She wasn't on either job as a matter of choice. She can go back to doing whatever carefree demons do beyond the Rimwall."

"Not exactly, Dad."

"What do you mean?"

"She seems to be stuck in that body. Apparently she can't simply abandon it the way she could others she's used. It has something to do with there being no primary occupant."

"Oh. I suppose she could, uh, terminate and get loose that way."

"I suggested that, but she's not sure it would work that way. It might just kill her along with the body, now that she's bound to it the way she is."

"So she's still somewhere near the cave?"

"No. She retains her *ty'iga* powers, which make her something of a magical being. I believe she must simply have wandered off through Shadow while I was in the cave experimenting with the Jewel."

"Why the cave?"

"That's where you go to do clandestine things, isn't it?"

"Yeah. So how come I could reach you there with the Trump?"

"I'd already finished the experiment and departed. In fact, I was looking for her when you called."

"I think you'd better go and look some more."

"Why?"

"Because I owe her for favors past—even if my mother did sic her on me."

"Certainly. I'm not sure how successful I'll be, though. Magical beings don't track as readily as the more mundane sort."

"Give it a shot anyway. I'd like to know where she's gotten to and whether there's anything I can do for her. Maybe your new orientation will be of help—somehow."

"We'll see," he said, and he winked out.

I sagged. How was Orkus going to take it? I wondered. One daughter injured and the other possessed of a demon and wandering, off in Shadow. I moved to the foot of the bed and leaned against Mandor's chair. He reached up with his left hand and squeezed my arm.

"I don't suppose you learned anything about bonesetting off on that shadow-world, did you?" he inquired.

"Afraid not," I answered.

"Pity," he replied. "I'll just have to wait my turn."

"We can Trump you somewhere and get it taken care of right away," I said, reaching for my cards.

"No," he said. "I want to see things played out here."

While he was speaking, I noticed that Random seemed engaged in an intense Trump communication. Vialle stood nearby, as if shielding him from the opening in the wall and whatever might emerge therefrom. Dworkin continued to work upon Coral's face, his body blocking sight of exactly what he was doing.

"Mandor," I said, "did you know that my mother sent the *ty'iga* to take care of me?"

"Yes," he replied. "It told me that when you stepped out of the room. A part of the spell would not permit it to tell you this."

"Was she just there to protect me, or was she spying on me, too?"

"That I couldn't tell you. The matter didn't come up. But it does seem her fears were warranted. You were in danger."

"You think Dana knew about Jasra and Luke?"

He began to shrug, winced, thought better of it.

"Again, I don't know for certain. If she did, I can't answer the next one either: How did she know? Okay?"

"Okay."

Random completed a conversation, covering a Trump. Then he turned and stared at Vialle for some time. He looked as if he were about to say something, thought better of it, looked away. He looked at me. About then I heard Coral moan, and I looked away, rising.

"A moment, Merlin," Random said, "before you go rushing off."

I met his gaze. Whether it was angry or merely curious, I could not tell. The tightening of the brows, the narrowing of the eyes could indicate either.

"Sir?" I said.

He approached, took me by the elbow, and turned me away from the bed, leading me off toward the doorway to the next room.

"Vialle, I'm borrowing your studio for a few moments," he said.

"Surely," she replied.

He led me inside and closed the door behind us. Across the room a bust of Gérard had fallen and broken. What appeared to be her current project—a multilimbed sea creature of a sort I'd never seen—occupied a work area at the studio's far end.

Random turned on me suddenly and searched my face.

"Have you been following the Begma-Kashfa situation?" he asked.

"More or less," I replied. "Bill briefed me on it the other night. Eregnor and all that."

"Did he tell you that we were going to bring Kashfa into the Golden Circle and solve the Eregnor problem by recognizing Kashfa's right to that piece of real estate?"

I didn't like the way he'd asked that one, and I didn't want to get Bill in trouble. It had seemed that that matter was still under wraps when we'd spoken. So, "I'm afraid I don't recall all the details on this stuff," I said.

"Well, that's what I planned on doing," Random told me. "We don't usually make guarantees like that—the kind that will favor one treaty country at the expense of another—but Arkans, the Duke of Shadburne, kind of had us over a barrel. He was the best possible head of state for our purposes, and I'd paved the way for his taking the throne now that that red-haired bitch is out of the picture. He knew he could lean on me a bit, though—since he'd be taking a chance accepting the throne following a double break in the succession—and he asked for Eregnor, so I gave it to him."

"I see," I said, "everything except how this affects me."

He turned his head and studied me through his left eye.

"The coronation was to be today. In fact, I was going to dress and Trump back for it in a little while. . . ."

"You use the past tense," I observed, to fill the silence he had left before me.

"So I do. So I do," he muttered, turning away, pacing a few steps, resting his foot on a piece of broken statuary, turning back. "The good Duke is now either dead or imprisoned."

"And there will be no coronation?" I said.

"*Au contraire,*" Random replied, still studying my face.

"I give up," I said. "Tell me what's going on."

"There was a coup, at dawn, this morning."

"Palace?"

"Possibly that, too. But it was backed by external military force."

"What was Benedict doing while this was going on?"

"I ordered him to pull the troops out yesterday, right before I came home myself. Things seemed stable, and it wouldn't have looked good to have combat troops from Amber stationed there during the coronation."

"True," I said. "So somebody moved right in, almost as soon as Benedict moved out and did away with the man who would be king, without the local constabulary even suggesting that that was not nice?"

Random nodded slowly.

"That's about the size of it," he said. "Now why do you think that might be?"

"Perhaps they were not totally displeased with the new state of affairs."

Random smiled and snapped his fingers.

"Inspired," he said. "One could almost think you knew what was going on."

"One would be wrong," I said.

"Today your former classmate Lukas Raynard becomes Rinaldo I, King of Kashfa."

"I'll be damned," I said. "I'd no idea he really wanted that job. What are you going to do about it?"

"I think I'll skip the coronation."

"I mean, over a slightly longer term."

Random sighed and turned away, kicking at the rubble.

"You mean, am I going to send Benedict back, to depose him?"

"In a word, yes."

"That would make us look pretty bad. What Luke just did is not above the Graustarkian politics that prevail in the area. We'd moved in and helped straighten out something that was fast becoming a political shambles. We could go back and do it again, too, if it were just some half-assed coup by a crazy general or some noble with delusions of grandeur. But Luke's got a legitimate claim, and it actually is stronger than Shadburne's. Also, he's popular. He's young, and he makes a good appearance. We'd have a lot less justification for going back than we had for going in initially. Even so, I was almost willing to risk being called an aggressor to keep that bitch's homicidal son off the throne. Then my man in Kashfa tells me that he's under Vialle's protection. So I asked her about it. She says that it's true and that you were present when it happened. She said she'd tell me about it after the operation Dworkin's doing now, in case he needs her empathic abilities. But I can't wait. Tell me what happened."

"You tell me one more thing first."

"What is it?"

"What military forces brought Luke to power?"

"Mercenaries."

"Dalt's?"

"Yes."

"Okay. Luke canceled his vendetta against the House of Amber," I said. "He did this freely, following a conversation with Vialle, just the other night. It was then that she gave him the ring. At the time I thought it was to keep Julian from trying to kill him, as we were on our way down to Arden."

"This was in response to Dalt's so-called ultimatum regarding Luke and Jasra?"

"That's right. It never occurred to me that the whole thing might be a setup—to get Luke and Dalt together so they could go off and pull a coup. That would mean that even that fight was staged, and now that I think of it, Luke did have a chance to talk with Dalt before it occurred."

Random raised his hand.

"Wait," he said. "Go back and tell me the thing from the beginning."

"Right."

And so I did. By the time I'd finished we had both paced the length of the studio countless times.

"You know," he said then, "the whole business sounds like something Jasra might have set up before her career as a piece of furniture."

"The thought had occurred to me," I said, hoping he wasn't about to pursue the matter of her present whereabouts. And the more I thought of it, recalling her reaction to the information about Luke following our raid on the Keep, the more I began to feel not only that she had been aware of what was going on but that she'd even been in touch with Luke more recently than I had at that time.

"It was pretty smoothly done," he observed. "Dalt must have been operating under old orders. Not being certain how to collect Luke or locate Jasra for fresh instructions, he took a chance with that feint on Amber. Benedict might well have spitted him again, with equal skill and greater effect."

"True. I guess you have to give the devil his due when it comes to guts. It also means that Luke must have done a lot of fast plotting and laid that fixed fight out during their brief conference in Arden. So he was really in control there, and he conned us into thinking he was a prisoner, which precluded his being the threat to Kashfa that he really was—if you want to look at it that way."

"What other way is there to look at it?"

"Well, as you said yourself, his claim is not exactly without merit. What do you want to do?"

Random massaged his temples.

"Going after him, preventing the coronation, would be a very unpopular move," he said. "First, though, I'm curious. You say this guy's a great bullshitter. You were there. Did he con Vialle into placing him under her protection?"

"No, he didn't," I said. "He seemed as surprised as I was at her gesture. He called off the vendetta because he felt that honor had been satisfied, that he had to an extent been used by his mother, and out of friendship for me. He did it without any strings on it. I still think she gave him the ring so the vendetta would end there, so none of us would go gunning for him."

"That is very like her," Random said. "If I thought he'd taken advantage of her, I was going to go after him myself. The embarrassment for me is unintentional then, and I guess I can live with it. I prime Arkans for the throne, and then he's shunted aside at the last minute by someone under my wife's protection. Almost makes it look as if there's a bit of divisiveness here at the center of things—and I'd hate to give that impression."

"I've got a hunch Luke will be very conciliatory. I know him well enough to know he appreciates all of these nuances. I'd guess he'd be a very easy man for Amber to deal with, on any level."

"I'll bet he will. Why shouldn't he?"

"No reason," I said. "What's going to happen to that treaty now?"

Random smiled.

"I'm off the hook. I never felt right about the Eregnor provisions. Now, if there's to be a treaty at all, we go at it *ab initio*. I'm not even sure we need one, though. The hell with 'em."

"I'll bet Arkans is still alive," I said.

"You think Luke's holding him hostage, against my giving him Golden Circle status?"

I shrugged.

"How close are you to Arkans?"

"Well, I did set him up for this thing, and I feel I owe him. I don't feel I owe him that much, though."

"Understandable."

"There would be loss of face for Amber even to approach a second-rate power like Kashfa directly at a time like this."

"True," I said, "and for that matter, Luke isn't officially head of state yet."

"Arkans would still be enjoying life at his villa if it weren't for me, though, and Luke really does seem to be a friend of yours—a scheming friend, but a friend."

"You would like me to mention this during a forthcoming discussion of Tony Price's atomic sculpture?"

He nodded.

"I feel you should have your art discussion very soon. In fact, it would not be inappropriate for you to attend a friend's coronation—as a private individual. Your dual heritage will serve us well here, and he will still be honored."

"Even so, I'll bet he wants that treaty."

"Even if we were inclined to grant it, we would not guarantee him Eregnor."

"I understand."

"And you are not empowered to commit us to anything."

"I understand that, too."

"Then why don't you clean up a bit and go talk to him about it? Your room is just around the abyss. You can leave through the hole in the wall and shinny down a beam I noticed was intact."

"Okay, I will," I answered, moving in that direction. "But one question first, completely off the subject."

"Yes?"

"Has my father been back recently?"

"Not to my knowledge," he said, shaking his head slowly. "We're all pretty good at hiding our comings and goings if we wish, of course. But I think he'd have let me know if he were around."

"Guess so," I said, and I turned and exited through the wall, skirting the abyss.

ELEVEN

No.

I hung from the beam, swung, and let go. I landed almost gracefully in the middle of the hallway in an area that would have been located approximately midway between my two doors, save that the first door was missing, also the section of wall through which it had provided entrance (or exit, depending on which side you happened to be), not to mention my favorite chair and a display case which had held seashells I'd picked up from beaches around the world. Pity.

I rubbed my eyes and turned away, for even the prospect of my ruined apartment took second place just now. Hell, I'd had apartments ruined in the past. Usually around April 30 . . .

As in "Niagara Falls," slowly I turned . . .

No.

Yes.

Across the hall from my rooms, where I had previously faced a blank wall, there was now a hallway running to the north. I'd gotten a glimpse up its sparkling length as I'd dropped from my rafter. Amazing. The gods had just uptempoed my background music yet again. I'd been in that hallway before, in one of its commoner locations up on the fourth floor, running east-west between a couple of storerooms. One of Castle Amber's intriguing anomalies, the Corridor of Mirrors, in addition to seeming longer in one direction than the other, contained countless mirrors. Literally countless. Try counting them, and you never come up with the same total twice. Tapers flicker in high, standing holders, casting infinities of shadows. There are big mirrors, little mirrors, narrow mirrors, squat mirrors, tinted mirrors, distorting mirrors, mirrors with elaborate frames—cast or carved—plain, simply framed mirrors, and mirrors with no frames at all; there are mirrors in multitudes of sharp-angled geometric shapes, amorphous shapes, curved mirrors.

I had walked the Corridor of Mirrors on several occasions, sniffing the perfumes of scented candles, sometimes feeling subliminal presences among the images, things which faded at an instant's sharp regard. I had felt the mixed enchantments of the place but had somehow never roused its sleeping genii. Just as well perhaps. One never knew what to expect in that place; at least that's what Bleys once told me. He was not certain whether the mirrors propelled one into obscure realms of Shadow, hypnotized one and induced bizarre dream states, cast one into purely symbolic realms decorated with the furniture of the psyche, played malicious or harmless head games with the viewer, none of the above, all of the above, or some of the above. Whatever, it was something less than harmless, though, as thieves, servants, and visitors had occasionally been found dead or stunned and mumbling along that sparkling route, oft-times wearing highly unusual expressions. And generally around the solstices and equinoxes—though it could occur at any season—the corridor moved itself to a new location, sometimes simply departing altogether for a time. Usually it was treated with suspicion, shunned, though it could as often reward as injure one or offer a useful omen or insight as readily as an unnerving experience. It was the uncertainty of it that roused trepidations.

And sometimes, I was told, it was almost as if it came looking for a particular person, bearing its ambiguous gifts. On such occasions it was said to be more dangerous to turn it down than to accept its invitation.

"Aw, come on," I said. "Now?"

The shadows danced along its length, and I caught a whiff of those intoxicating tapers. I moved forward. I extended my left hand past its corner and patted the wall. Frakir didn't stir.

"This is Merlin," I said, "and I'm kind of busy just now. You sure you wouldn't rather reflect someone else?"

The nearest flame seemed, for an instant, a fiery hand, beckoning.

"Shit," I whispered, and I strode forward.

There was no sense of transition as I entered. A long red-patterned runner covered the floor. Dust motes spun in the lights I passed. I was beside myself in many aspects, flickering flamelight harlequinading my garments, transforming my face within a dance of shadows.

Flicker.

For an instant it seemed that the stern visage of Oberon regarded me from a small high metal-framed oval—as easily a trick of the light as the shade of his late highness, of course.

Flicker.

I'd swear an animalistic travesty of my own face had leered at me for a moment, tongue lolling, from a mid-level rectangle of quicksilver to my left, framed in ceramic flowers, face humanizing as I turned, quickly, to mock me.

Walking. Footsteps muffled. Breathing slightly tight. I wondered whether I should summon my Logrus sight or even try that of the Pattern. I was loath to attempt either, though, memories of the nastier aspects of both Powers still too fresh within me for comfort. Something was about to happen to me, I was certain.

I halted and examined the one I thought must have my number—framed in black metal, with various signs from the magical arts inlaid in silver about it. The glass was murky, as if spirits swam just out of sight within its depths. My face looked leaner, its lines more heavily inscribed, the faintest of purple halos, perhaps, flickering about my head within it. There was something cold and vaguely sinister about that image, but though I studied it for a long while, nothing happened. There were no messages, enlightenments, changes. In fact, the longer I stared, the more all of the dramatic little touches seemed but tricks of the lighting.

I walked on, past glimpses of unearthly landscapes, exotic creatures, hints of memory, near subliminals of dead friends and relatives. Something within a pool even waved a rake at me. I waved back. Having so recently survived the traumas of my trek through the land between shadows, I was not as intimidated by these manifestations of strangeness and possible menace as I would likely have been at almost any other time. I thought I had sight of a gibbeted man, swinging as in a strong wind, hands tied behind his back, El Greco sky above him.

"I've had a rough couple of days," I said aloud, "and there's no sign of any letup. I'm sort of in a hurry, if you know what I mean."

Something punched me in the right kidney, and I spun around, but there was no one there. Then I felt a hand upon my shoulder, turning me. I cooperated quickly. No one there either.

"I apologize," I said, "if the truth requires it here."

Invisible hands continued to push and tug at me, moving me past a number of attractive mirrors. I was steered to a cheap-looking mirror in a dark-stained wooden frame. It looked as if it might have come from some discount house. There was a slight imperfection in the glass, in the vicinity of my left eye. Whatever forces had propelled me to this point released me here. It occurred to me that the powers that be here might actually have been attempting to expedite things per my request, rather than simply hustling me in a peevish spirit.

So, "Thanks," I said, just to be safe, and I continued to stare. I moved my head back and forth and from side to side, producing ripple effects across my image. I repeated the movements while waiting for whatever might occur.

My image remained unchanged, but on the third or fourth ripple my background was altered. It was no longer a wall of dimly lit mirrors that stood behind me. It flowed away and did not return with my next movement. In its place was a stand of dark shrubbery beneath an evening sky. I continued to move my head slightly several times more, but the ripple effect had vanished. The bushes seemed very real, though my peripheral vision showed me that the hallway was intact in both directions and still seemed to possess its right-hand wall at both ends.

I continued to search the seemingly reflected shrubbery, looking for portents, omens, signs, or just a little movement. None of these became apparent, though a very real sensation of depth was there. I could almost feel a cool breeze upon my neck. I must have stared for several minutes, waiting for the mirror to produce something new. But it did not. If this was the best the mirror had to offer, it was time to move on, I decided.

Something seemed to stir in the bushes at my back then, causing reflex to take over. I turned quickly, raising my hands before me.

It was only the wind that had rustled them, I saw. And then I realized that I was not in the hallway, and I turned again. The mirror and its wall were gone. I now faced a low hill, a line of broken masonry at its top. Light flickered from behind that shattered wall. Both curiosity and my sense of purpose roused, I began climbing slowly, my wariness yet present.

The sky seemed to grow darker even as I climbed, and it was cloudless, a profusion of stars pulsing in unfamiliar constellations across it. I moved with some stealth amid stones, grasses, shrubs, broken masonry. From beyond the vine-clad wall I now heard the sounds of voices. Though I could not distinguish the words being spoken, it did not seem conversation that I overheard, but rather a cacophony—as if a number of individuals, of both genders and various ages, were delivering simultaneous monologues.

Coming to the hill's top, I extended my hand until it made contact with the wall's irregular surface. I decided against going around it to see what sort of activity was in progress on the other side. It could make me visible to I knew not what. It seemed so much simpler to reach as high as I could, hook my fingers over the top of the nearest depressed area, and draw myself upward—as I did. I even located toeholds as my head neared the top, and I was able to ease some of the strain on my arms by resting part of my weight upon them.

I drew myself carefully up those final few inches, peering past fractured stone and down into the interior of the ruined structure. It appeared to have been some sort of church. The roof was fallen, and the far wall still stood, in much the same condition as the one I clung to. There was an altar in bad repair in a raised area off to my right. Whatever had happened here must have happened long ago, for shrubs and vines grew in the interior as well as without, softening the lines of collapsed pews, fallen pillars, fragments of the roof.

Below me, in a cleared area, a large pentagram was drawn. At each of the star's points stood a figure, facing outward. Inward from them, at the five points where the lines crossed, flared a torch, its butt driven into the earth. This seemed a somewhat peculiar variation on the rituals with which I was familiar, and I wondered at the summoning and why the five were not better protected and why they were not about the work in concert, rather than each seeming off on a personal trip and ignoring the others. The three whom I could see clearly had their backs to me. The two who faced in my direction were barely within my line of sight, their faces covered over with shadows. Some of the voices were male; some, female. One was singing; two were chanting; the other two seemed merely to be speaking, though in stagy, artificial tones.

I drew myself higher, trying for a glimpse of the faces of the nearer two. This because there was something familiar about the entire ensemble, and I felt that if I were to identify one, I might well realize all of their identities.

Another question high on my list was, What was it they were summoning? Was I safe up here on the wall, this close to the operation, if something unusual put in an appearance? It did not seem that the proper constraints were in place below. I drew myself higher still. I felt my center of gravity shifting just as my view of affairs improved yet again. Then I realized that I was moving forward without effort. An instant later I knew that the wall was toppling, carrying me forward and down right into the midst of their oddly choreographed ritual. I tried to push myself away from the wall, hoping to hit the ground rolling and run like hell. But it was already too late. My abrupt push-up raised me into the air but did not really halt my forward momentum.

No one beneath me stirred, though rubble rained about them all, and I finally caught some recognizable words as I fell.

". . . summon thee, Merlin, to fall into my power now!" one of the women was chanting.

A very effective ritual after all, I decided, as I landed on my back upon the pentagram, arms flopping out to my sides at shoulder level, legs spread. I was able to tuck my chin, protecting my head, and the slapping of my arms seemed to produce a break-fall effect so that I was not badly stunned by the impact. The five high towers of fire danced wildly about me for several seconds, then settled once again into steadier blazing. The five figures still faced outward. I attempted to rise and found that I could not. It was as if I were staked out in that position.

Frakir had warned me too late, as I was falling, and now I was uncertain to what employment I might put her. I could send her creeping off to any of the figures with orders to work her way upward and commence choking. But so far I had no way of knowing which one, if any, might deserve such treatment.

"I hate dropping in without notice," I said, "and I can see this is a private party. If someone will be good enough to turn me loose, I'll be on my way—"

The figure in the vicinity of my left foot did an about-face and stood staring down at me. She wore a blue robe, but there was no mask upon her fire-reddened face. There was only a tight smile, which went away when she licked her lips. It was Julia, and there was a knife in her right hand.

"Always the smartass," she said. "Ready with a flippant answer to any situation. It's a cover for your unwillingness to commit yourself to anything or anyone. Even those who love you."

"It could just be a sense of humor, too," I said, "a thing I'm beginning to realize you never possessed."

She shook her head slowly.

"You keep everyone at arms' distance. There is no trust in you."

"Runs in the family," I said. "But prudence does not preclude affection."

She had begun raising the blade, but she faltered for a second.

"Are you saying that you still care about me?" she asked.

"I never stopped," I said. "It's just that you came on too strong all of a sudden. You wanted more of me than I was willing to give just then."

"You lie," she said, "because I hold your life in my hand."

"I could think of a lot worse reasons for lying," I said. "But, unfortunately, I'm telling the truth."

There came another familiar voice then, from off to my right.

"It was too early for us to speak of such things," she said, "but I begrudge her your affection."

Turning my head, I saw that this figure, too, now faced inward, and it was Coral and her right eye was covered by a black patch and she, too, held a knife in her right hand. Then I saw what was in her left hand, and I shot a glance back at Julia. Yes, they both held forks as well as knives.

"*Et tu*," I said.

"I told you I don't speak English," Coral replied.

"Et by two," Julia responded, raising her utensils. "Who says I don't have a sense of humor?"

They spit at each other across me, some of the spittle not quite going the distance.

Luke, it occurred to me, might have tried settling matters by proposing to both of them on the spot. I'd a feeling it wouldn't work for me, so I didn't.

"This is an objectification of marriage neurosis," I said. "It's a projective experience. It's a vivid dream. It's—"

Julia dropped to one knee, and her right hand flashed downward. I felt the blade enter my left thigh.

My scream was interrupted when Coral drove her fork into my right shoulder.

"This is ridiculous!" I cried as the other utensils flashed in their hands and I felt fresh stabs of pain.

Then the figure at the star's point near my right foot turned slowly, gracefully. She was wrapped in a dark brown cloak with a yellow border, her arms crossed before her holding it closed up to her eye level.

"Stop, you bitches!" she ordered, flinging the garment wide and resembling nothing so much as a mourning cloak butterfly. It was, of course, Dara, my mother.

Julia and Coral had already raised their forks to their mouths and were chewing. There was a tiny bead of blood beside Julia's lip. The cloak continued to flow outward from my mother's fingertips as if it were alive, as if it were a part of her. Its wings blocked Julia and Coral completely from my sight, falling upon them as she continued to spread her arms, covering them, bearing them over backward to become body-size lumps upon the ground, growing smaller and smaller until the garment simply hung naturally and they were gone from their points of the star.

There came a slow, delicate clapping sound then, followed by a hoarse laugh from my left.

"Extremely well executed," came that painfully familiar voice, "but then you always liked him best."

"Better," she corrected.

"Isn't poor Despil even in the running?" Jurt said.

"You're being unfair," she told him.

"You liked that mad Prince of Amber more than you ever cared for our father, who was a decent man," he told her. "That's why Merlin was always your pet, isn't it?"

"That's just not true, Jurt, and you know it," she said.

He laughed again.

"We all summoned him because we all want him," he said, "for different reasons. But in the end our desires all come to this, do they not?"

I heard the growl, and I turned my head just in time to see his face slide along the projective curve wolfward, muzzle descending, fangs flashing as he fell to all fours and slashed at my left shoulder, gaining himself a gory taste of my person.

"Stop that!" she cried. "You little beast!"

He threw back his muzzle and howled, and it came out the way a coyote's cry does, as a kind of mad laughter.

A black boot struck his shoulder, knocking him over backward and sending him crashing into the uncollapsed section of wall behind him, which promptly collapsed upon him. He uttered but a brief whimper before being covered over completely by the falling rubble.

"Well, well, well," I heard Dara say, and looking that way, I saw that she also held a knife and fork. "What's a bastard like you doing in a nice place like this?"

"Keeping the last of the predators at bay, it would seem," replied the voice which had once told me a very long story containing multiple versions of an auto accident and a number of genealogical gaffes.

She lunged at me, but he stooped, caught me beneath the shoulders, and snatched me out of her way. Then his great black cloak swirled like a matador's, covering her. As she had done with Coral and Julia, she herself seemed to melt into the earth beneath it. He set me on my feet, stooped then, raised the cloak, and brushed it off. As he refastened it with a silver rose of a clasp, I studied him for fangs or at least cutlery.

"Four out of five," I said, brushing myself off. "No matter how real this seems, I'm sure it's only analogically or anagogically true. So how come you're not cannibalistically inclined in this place?"

"On the other hand," he said, drawing on a silver gauntlet, "I was never a real father to you. It's kind of difficult when you don't even know the kid exists. So I didn't really want anything from you either."

"That sure looks like Grayswandir you're wearing," I said.

He nodded.

"It seems to have served you, too."

"I suppose I should thank you for that. I also suppose you're the wrong . . .

person to ask whether you really bore me from that cave to the land between shadows."

"Oh, it was me all right."

"Of course, you'd say that."

"I don't know why I should if I didn't. Look out! The wall!"

One quick glance showed me that another big section of wall was falling toward us. Then he pushed me, and I sprawled across the pentagram again. I heard the stones crashing behind me, and I half rose and threw myself even farther forward.

Something struck the side of my head.

I woke up in the Corridor of Mirrors. I was lying facedownward, my head resting on my right forearm, a rectangular piece of stone clutched in my hand, the aromas of the candles drifting about me. When I began to rise, I felt pains in both shoulders and in my left thigh. A quick investigation showed me that I bore cuts in all three of those places. Though there wasn't much I could do now to help demonstrate the veracity of my recent adventure beyond this, it wasn't something I felt like shrugging off either.

I got to my feet and limped back to the corridor that ran past my rooms.

"Where'd you go?" Random called down to me.

"Huh? What do you mean?" I responded.

"You walked back up the hall, but there's nothing there."

"How long was I gone?"

"Half a minute maybe," he answered.

I waved the stone I still carried.

"Saw this lying on the floor. Couldn't figure what it was," I said.

"Probably blown there when the Powers met," he said, "from one of the walls. There were a number of arches edged with stones like that at one time. Mostly plastered over on your floor now."

"Oh," I said. "See you in a bit, before I take off."

"Do that," he replied, and I turned and found my way through one of the day's many broken walls and on into my room.

The far wall had also been blasted, I noticed, creating a large opening into Brand's dusty chambers. I paused and studied it. Synchronicity, I decided. It appeared there had once been an archway connecting those rooms with these. I moved forward and examined the exposed curve along its left side. Yes, it had been rendered from stones similar to the one I held. In fact—

I brushed away plaster and slid mine into a broken area. It fitted perfectly. In fact, when I gave it a small tug, it refused to be removed. Had I really brought it back from the sinister father-mother-brother-lovers ritual dream beyond the mirror? Or had I half-consciously picked it up on my return, from wherever it had been blasted during the recent architectural distress?

I turned away, removing my cloak, stripping off my shirt. Yes. There were punctures like fork marks on my right shoulder, something like an animal bite on my left. Also, there was dried blood on my left trouser leg in the area of a tear beyond which my thigh was tender. I washed up and brushed my teeth and combed my hair, and I put a dressing on my leg and left shoulder. The family metabolism would see me healed in a day, but I didn't want some exertion tearing them open and getting fresh garments gory.

Speaking of which . . .

The armoire was undamaged and I thought I'd wear my other colors, to give Luke a happy memory or two for his coronation: the golden shirt and royal blue trousers I'd found which approximated Berkeley's colors almost exactly; a leather vest dyed to match the pants; matching cloak with gold trim; black sword belt, black gloves tucked behind it, reminding me I needed a new blade. Dagger, too, for that matter. I was wondering about a hat when a series of sounds caught my attention. I turned.

Through a fresh screen of dust I now had a symmetrical view into Brand's quarters; rather than a jagged opening in the wall the archway stood perfect and entire, the wall intact at either hand and above. The wall to my right also seemed less damaged than it had been earlier.

I moved forward and ran my hand along the curve of stones. I inspected adjacent plastered areas, looking for cracks. There were none. All right. The stone had borne an enchantment. To what end?

I strode through the archway and looked around. The room was dark, and I summoned the Logrus sight reflexively. It came and served me, as usual. Perhaps the Logrus had decided against holding a grudge.

At this level I could see the residue of many magical experiments as well as a number of standing spells. Most sorcerers leave a certain amount of not normally visible magical clutter about, but Brand seemed to have been a real slob, though of course, he might have been rushed quite a bit near the end there when he was trying to take over control of the universe. It's not the sort of occupation wherein neatness counts the way it might in other endeavors. I passed on along my tour of inspection. There were mysteries here, unfinished bits of business and indications that he had gone farther along some magical routes than I had ever wished to go. Still, there was nothing here that I felt I could not handle and nothing representing grave and immediate danger. It was just possible, now I'd finally had an opportunity to inspect them, that I might want to leave the archway intact and add Brand's quarters to my own.

On the way out I decided to check Brand's armoire to see whether he had a hat to go with what I was wearing. I opened it and discovered a dark three-cornered one with a golden feather, which fitted me perfectly. The color was a little off, but I suddenly recalled a spell which altered it. As I was about to turn away, something to the rear of that top shelf which held the hats glinted for a moment within my Logrus vision. I reached in and withdrew it.

It was a long and lovely gold-chased sheath of dark green, and the hilt of the blade which protruded from it appeared to be goldplated, with an enormous emerald set in its pommel. I took hold of it and drew it partway, half expecting it to wail like a demon on whom one has dropped a balloon filled with holy water. Instead, it merely hissed and smoked a little. And there was a bright design worked into the metal of its blade—almost recognizable. Yes, a section of the Pattern. Only this excerpting was from the Pattern's end, whereas Grayswandir's was from a point near the beginning.

I sheathed it, and on an impulse I hung it from my belt. His old man's sword would make a neat coronation present for Luke, I decided. So I'd take it along for him. I let myself out into the side corridor then, made my way over a small section of collapsed wall from Gérard's quarters and back past Fiona's door to my dad's rooms. There was one thing more I wanted to check, and the sword had reminded me. I fished in my pocket for the key I'd transferred from my bloody trousers. Then I decided I'd better knock. What if . . .

I knocked and waited, knocked again and waited again. In that nothing but silence ensued I unlocked the door and entered. I went no farther than that first place. I'd just wanted to check the rack.

Grayswandir was gone from the peg where I'd hung it.

I backed out, closing and locking the door. The fact that the row of pegs had been empty was an instance of obtaining the knowledge one wanted and still not being certain what one had proved thereby. Yet it had been something I'd wished to know, and it did make me feel that final knowledge was nearer than it had been. . . .

I walked back, past Fiona's rooms. I reentered Brand's rooms through the door I had left ajar. I hunted around till I spotted a key in a nearby ashtray. I locked the door and pocketed the key; that was almost silly because anyone could walk in from my room now and my room was missing a wall. Still . . .

I hesitated before crossing back to my sitting room with its Tabriz stained with ty'iga spit and partly covered by fallen wall. There was something almost restful about Brand's quarters, a kind of peaceful quality I hadn't really noticed before. I wandered a bit, opening drawers and looking inside magic boxes, studying a folder of the man's drawings. The Logrus sight showed me that something small and potent and magical was secreted in a bedpost, radiating lines of force every which way. I unscrewed the knob, found the compartment within it. It contained a small velvet bag which bore a ring. The band was wide, possibly of platinum. It bore a wheel-like device of some reddish metal, with countless tiny spokes, many of them hair-fine. And each of these spokes extended a line of power leading off somewhere, quite possibly into Shadow, where some power cache or spell source lay. Perhaps Luke would rather have the ring than the sword. When I slipped it on, it seemed to extend roots to the very center of my body. I could feel my way back along them to the ring and then out along those connections. I was impressed by the variety of energies it reached and controlled—from simple chthonic forces to sophisticated constructs of High Magic, from elementals to things that seemed like lobotomized gods. I wondered why he hadn't been wearing it on the day of the Patternfall battle. If he had, I'd a feeling he might have been truly invincible. We could all have been living on Brandenberg in Castle Brand. I wondered, too, why Fiona, in the next room over, had not felt its presence and come looking for it. On the other hand, I hadn't. For what it was, it didn't register well at all, beyond a few feet. It was amazing the treasures this place contained. Was it something about the private universe effect said to obtain in some of these rooms? The ring was a beautiful alternative to Pattern Power or Logrus Power, hooked in as it was with so many sources. It must have taken centuries to empower the thing. Whatever Brand had wanted it for, it had not been part of a short-range plan. I decided I could not surrender the thing to Luke—or to anyone with any familiarity with the Arts. I didn't even think I should trust a nonmagician with it. And I certainly didn't feel like returning it to the bedpost. What was that throbbing at my wrist? Oh, yes, Frakir. It had been going on for some small while, and I'd barely noticed.

"Sorry you lost your voice, old girl," I said, stroking her as I explored the room for threats both psychic and physical. "I can't find a damned thing here that I should be worried about."

Immediately she spiraled down from my wrist and tried to remove the ring from my finger.

"Stop!" I ordered. "I know the ring could be dangerous. But only if you use it wrongly. I'm a sorcerer, remember? I'm into these matters. There is nothing special about it for me to fear."

But Frakir disobeyed my order and continued her attack on the ring, which I could now only attribute to some form of magical artifact jealousy. I tied her in a tight knot around the bedpost and left her there, to teach her a lesson.

I began to search the apartment more diligently. If I were to keep the sword *and* the ring, it would be nice to find something else of his father's that I could take to Luke—

"Merlin! Merlin!" I heard bellowed from somewhere beyond my room.

Rising from a tapping of the floor and lower walls, where I had been seeking hollow spots, I returned to my archway and passed through into my own sitting room. I halted then despite another summons in what I now recognized to be Random's voice. The wall which faced upon the side corridor was more than half rebuilt since last I had viewed it—as if an invisible crew of carpenters and plasterers had been silently at work since I had positioned the dreamstone in the gateway to the kingdom of Brand. Amazing. I simply stood and stared, hoping for some betraying bit of business within the damaged area. Then I heard Random mutter, "I guess he's gone," and I called back, "Yeah? What is it?"

"Get your ass up here quick," he said. "I need your advice."

I stepped out into the corridor through the opening which remained in that wall, and I looked upward. Immediately I could feel the capabilities in the ring that I wore, responding like a musical instrument to my most immediate need. The appropriate line was activated as I assented to the suggestion, and I took the gloves from behind my belt and drew them on as I was levitated toward the opening in the ceiling. This, because it had occurred to me that Random might recognize the ring as having once been Brand's, and that could lead to a complicated discussion I'd no desire for at the moment.

I held my cloak close to my side as I came up through the hole into the studio, to keep the blade under wraps also.

"Impressive," Random said. "Glad you're keeping the magical muscle exercised. That's what I called you for."

I gave him a bow. Being dressed up made me feel vaguely courtly.

"How may I be of service?"

"Cut the crap and come on," he said, taking hold of my elbow and steering me back toward the demi-bedroom. Vialle stood at the door, holding it open.

"Merlin?" she said as I brushed by.

"Yes?" I answered.

"I wasn't certain," she said.

"Of what?" I asked.

"That it was you," she responded.

"Oh, it's me, all right," I said.

"It is indeed my brother," Mandor stated, rising from his chair and approaching us. His arm was splinted and slung, his face considerably relaxed. "If anything about him strikes you as strange," he continued, "it is likely because he has had a number of traumatic experiences since he left here."

"Is that true?" Random asked.

"Yes," I replied. "I didn't realize it was all that apparent."

"Are you all right?" Random asked.

"I seem to be intact," I said.

"Good. Then we'll save the particulars of your story for another time. As you can see, Coral is gone and Dworkin is, too. I didn't see them go. I was still in the studio when it happened."

"When what happened?" I asked.

"Dworkin finished his operation," Mandor said, "took the lady by the hand, drew her to her feet, and transported her away from here. It was most elegantly managed. One moment they stood at the bedside; the next their afterimages ran through the spectrum and winked out."

"You say that he transported them. How do you know that they weren't snatched away by Ghostwheel or one of the Powers?" I asked.

"Because I watched his face," he said, "and there was no surprise whatsoever upon it, only a small smile."

"I guess you're right," I admitted. "Then who set your arm, if Random was off in the studio and Dworkin occupied?"

"I did," Vialle said. "I've been trained in it."

"So you were the only eyewitness to their vanishment?" I said to Mandor. He nodded.

"What I want of you," Random said, "is some idea where they flashed off to. Mandor said he couldn't tell. Here!"

He handed me a chain, from which a metal setting hung.

"What's this?" I asked.

"It was the most important of all the Crown Jewels," he said, "the Jewel of Judgment. This is what they left me. The Jewel part is what they took."

"Oh," I said. Then: "It must be secure if it's in Dworkin's care. He'd said

something about putting it in a safe place, and he knows more about it than anyone else—"

"He may also have flipped out again," Random said. "I'm not interested in discussing his merits as its custodian, though. I just want to know where the hell he's gone with the thing."

"I don't believe he left any tracks," Mandor said.

"Where were they standing?" I asked.

"Over there," he said, with a gesture of the good arm, "to the right of the bed."

I moved to that area, feeling through the potencies I ruled after the most appropriate.

"A little nearer the foot."

I nodded, feeling it would not be all that difficult to look back a small distance through time within my personal space.

I felt the rainbow rush and saw their outlines. Freeze.

A power line moved forth from the ring, attached itself, ran rainbow with them, passed through the portal which closed with a mild implosion. Raising the back of my hand to my forehead, I seemed to look down the line—

—into a large hall hung with six shields to my left. To my right hung a multitude of flags and pennons. A fire blazed in an enormous hearth before me. . . .

"I see the place they went to," I said, "but I don't recognize it."

"Is there some way you can share the vision?" Random asked.

"Perhaps," I replied, realizing there was a way even as I said it. "Regard the mirror."

Random turned, moved nearer the looking glass through which Dworkin had brought me—how long ago? "By the blood of the beast on the pole and the shell that is cracked at the center of the world," I said, feeling the need to address two of the powers I controlled, "may the sight be cast!"

The mirror frosted over, and when it cleared, my vision of the hall lay within it.

"I'll be damned," Random said. "He took her to Kashfa. I wonder why."

"One day you'll have to teach me that trick, brother," Mandor commented.

"In that I was about to head for Kashfa," I said, "is there anything special I should do?"

"Do?" Random said. "Just find out what's going on and let me know, will you?"

"Of course," I said, uncasing my Trumps.

Vialle came up and took my hand as if in farewell.

"Gloves," she commented.

"Trying to look a little formal," I explained.

"There is something in Kashfa that Coral seems to fear," she whispered. "She muttered about it in her sleep."

"Thanks," I said. "I'm ready for anything now."

"You may say that for confidence," she said, "but never believe it."

I laughed as I held a Trump before me and pretended to study it while extending the force of my being along the line I had sent to Kashfa. I reopened the route Dworkin had taken and stepped through.

TWELVE

Kashfa.

I stood in the gray stone hall, flags and shields on the walls, rushes strewn about the floors, rude furniture about me, a fire before me which did not completely dispel the dampness of the place, cooking smells heavy on the air. I was the only person in the room, though I could hear voices from many directions; also the sounds of musicians tuning and practicing. So I had to be fairly near the action. The disadvantage of coming in the way I did rather than using a Trump was that there was no one on the spot to show me around and tell me what was going on. The advantage was the same—that is, if there were any spying I wanted to do, now was the time. The ring, a veritable encyclopedia of magics, found me an invisibility spell in which I quickly cloaked myself.

I spent the next hour or so exploring. There were four large buildings and a number of smaller ones within this central walled area. There was another walled sector beyond it and another beyond that—three roughly concentric zones of ivy-covered protection. I couldn't see any signs of heavy damage, and I got the feeling Dalt's troops hadn't met with much resistance. No indications of pillaging or burning, but then they'd been hired to deliver a property, and I'd a feeling Jasra had stipulated that it remain relatively intact. The troops occupied all three rings, and I got the impression from a bit of eavesdropping that they'd be around till after the coronation. There were quite a few in the large plaza in the central area, making fun of the local troops in their fancy livery as they waited for the coronation procession. None of this was in particular bad nature, however, possibly because Luke was popular with both groups, though it did also seem that many individuals on both sides seemed personally acquainted.

The First Unicornian Church of Kashfa, as one might translate its title, was across the plaza from the palace proper. The building in which I'd arrived was an ancillary, all-purpose adjunct, at this time being used to house a number of hastily summoned guests, along with servants, courtiers, and hangers-on.

I'd no idea exactly when the coronation was to take place, but I decided I'd better try to see Luke in a hurry, before he got too swept up into the course of events. He might even have an idea where Coral had been delivered, and why.

So I found me a niche with a blank-walled, neutral background even a native probably couldn't recognize out of context, dropped my invisibility

spell, located Luke's Trump, and gave him a call. I didn't want him to think I was already in town because I didn't want him to know I possessed the power to drop in the way I had. This under the theory that you never tell anybody everything.

"Merlin!" he announced, studying me. "Is the cat out of the sack or what?"

"Yeah, the kittens, too," I said. "Congratulations on your coronation day."

"Hey! You're wearing the school colors!"

"What the hell. Why not? You won something, didn't you?"

"Listen. It's not as festive a thing as all that. In fact, I was about to call you. I need your advice before this goes any further. Can you bring me through?"

"I'm not in Amber, Luke."

"Where are you?"

"Well . . . downstairs," I admitted. "I'm on the side street between your palace and the building next door that's sort of like a hotel at the moment."

"That won't do," he said. "I'd get spotted too quick if you bring me down. Go on over to the Unicorn Temple. If it's relatively empty and there's a dark, quiet corner where we can talk, call me and bring me through. If there isn't, figure something else, okay?"

"Okay."

"Hey, how'd you get here anyway?"

"Advance scout for an invasion," I said. "One more take-over would be a coup-coup, wouldn't it?"

"You're about as funny as a hangover," he said. "Call me."

Break.

So I crossed the plaza, following what seemed marked out as the route of the procession. I thought I might meet some trouble at the House of the Unicorn and need a spell to get in, but no one barred my way.

I entered. It was big and all decked out for the ceremony, with a great variety of pennons on the walls and flowers all over the place. The only other inhabitant was a muffled woman up near the front who appeared to be praying. I moved off to the left into a somewhat darker section.

"Luke," I addressed his Trump. "All clear. Do you read me?"

I felt his presence before I caught the image. "Okay," he said. "Bring me through," and we clasped hands, and he was there.

He clapped me on the shoulders.

"Well, now, let me look at you," he said. "Wonder whatever became of my letter sweater?"

"I think you gave it to Gail."

"I think you may be right."

"Brought you a present," I said, tossing back my cloak and fumbling at the side of my sword belt. "Here. I turned up your father's sword."

"You're kidding."

He took it into his hands, examined the sheath, turned it over many

times. Then he drew it partway, and it hissed again and sparks danced along its tracery and a bit of smoke drifted upward from it.

"It really is!" he said. "Werewindle, the Daysword—brother to the Nightblade, Grayswandir!"

"What's that?" I said. "I didn't know there was any connection."

"I'd have to think hard to remember the full story, but they go back a long way. Thank you."

He turned and took several paces, slapping the weapon against his thigh as he walked. Abruptly he returned.

"I've been had," he said. "That woman has done it again, and I am peeved to the extreme. I don't know how to handle this."

"What? What are you talking about?"

"My mother," he explained. "She's done it again. Just when I thought I'd taken the reins and was riding my own course, she's come along and messed up my life."

"How'd she do that?"

"She hired Dalt and his boys to take over here."

"Yeah, we sort of figured that out. By the way, what happened to Arkans?"

"Oh, he's okay. I've got him under arrest, of course. But he's in good quarters and he can have anything he wants. I wouldn't hurt him. I always kind of liked the guy."

"So what's the problem? You win. You've got your own kingdom now."

"Hell," he said, then glanced furtively toward the sanctum. "I think I was conned, but I'm not exactly sure. See, I never wanted this job. Dalt told me we were taking over for Mom. I was coming in with him to establish order, claim the place for the family again, then welcome her back with a lot of pomp and crap. I figured once she had her throne back, she'd be off my case for good. I'd hit it out of here for more congenial turf, and she'd have a whole kingdom to occupy her attention. Nothing was said about me getting stuck with this lousy job."

I shook my head.

"I don't understand at all," I said. "You got it for her. Why not just turn it over to her and do as you planned?"

He gave a humorless laugh.

"Arkans they liked," he said. "Me they like.. Mom they're not so fond of. Nobody seems that enthusiastic about having her back. In fact, there were strong indications that if she tried it, there would indeed be a coup-coup."

"I suppose you could still step aside and give it to Arkans."

Luke punched the stone wall.

"I don't know whether she'd be madder at me or at herself for having paid Dalt as much as she did to throw Arkans out. But she'd tell me it's my duty to do it, and I don't know—maybe it is. What do you think?"

"That's a hard one to answer, Luke. Who do you think would do a better job, you or Arkans?"

"I honestly don't know. He's had a lot of experience in government, but I did grow up here, and I do know how the place is run and how to get

things done. The only thing I'm sure of is that either of us would be better at it than Mom."

I folded my arms, and I thought hard.

"I can't make this decision for you," I said. "But tell me, what would you most like to do?"

He chuckled.

"You know I've always been a salesman. If I were going to stick around and do something for Kashfa. I'd rather represent her industries abroad, which would be sort of undignified for a monarch. Probably what I'd be best at, though. I don't know."

"It's a problem and a half, Luke. I don't want the responsibility of telling you which way to go."

"If I'd known it was going to come to this, I'd have smeared Dalt back in Arden."

"You really think you could take him?"

"Believe it," he said.

"Well, that doesn't solve your present problem."

"True. I've a strong feeling I may have to go through with this."

The woman up front glanced our way several times. I guess we were talking kind of loud for the surroundings.

"Too bad there are no other good candidates," I said, lowering my voice.

"This must seem like pretty small beer to someone from Amber."

"Hell, it's your home. You've got a right to take it seriously. I'm just sorry it's doing such a job on you."

"Yeah, most problems seem to start at home, don't they? Sometimes I just feel like taking a walk and not coming back."

"What would happen if you did?"

"Either Mom would restore herself to the throne with Dalt's gang to back her up, which would require a mess of executions of people I can think of who'd be against it, or she'd say the game isn't worth the candle and settle for the Keep. If she decided to enjoy her retirement, then the coalition which backed him in the first place would probably spring Arkans and continue things from where they'd had to leave off."

"Which course of action seems most likely to you?" I said.

"She'd go for it and there'd be a civil war. Win or lose, it would mess up the country and doubtless keep us out of the Golden Circle this time around, too. Speaking of which—"

"I don't know," I said quickly. "I'm not empowered to talk Golden Circle Treaty with you."

"I'd kind of guessed that," Luke said, "and that wasn't what I wanted to ask. I was just curious whether anyone back in Amber might have said, 'They just blew it,' or 'Maybe we'll give them another crack at it a little farther down the road,' or 'We'll still deal, but they can forget the Eregnor guarantees.'"

He gave me an artificial grin, and I returned it.

"You can forget Eregnor," I said.

"Figured that," he said. "What about the rest?"

"I get the impression it's 'Let's wait and see what happens.' "

"Guessed that much, too. Give me a good report, even if they don't ask, okay? By the way, I don't suppose your presence here is technically official?"

"Personal," I said, "from a diplomatic standpoint."

The lady up front rose to her feet. Luke sighed.

"Wish I could find my way back to Alice's restaurant. Maybe the Hatter would see something we're missing," he said. Then: "Hey! Where'd he come from? Looks just like you but—"

He was staring past me, and I could already feel the disturbance. I didn't even bother to summon the Logrus, though, because I felt ready for anything.

I turned, smiling.

"Are you ready to die, brother?" Jurt asked. He had either managed to regrow his eye or was wearing an artificial one, and he now had sufficient hair that I could no longer tell about the ear. His little finger was partly regrown also.

"No, but I'm ready to kill," I said. "I'm glad you happened by."

He bowed, mockingly. There was a faint glow about him. I could feel the power that flowed through and around his person.

"Have you been back to the Keep for your final treatment?" I inquired.

"I don't believe that will be necessary," he said. "I am more than adequate for any task I've set myself, now I've control of these forces."

"This is Jurt?" Luke asked.

"Yes," I replied. "This is Jurt."

Jurt cast a quick glance Luke's way. I could feel him focusing on the blade.

"Is that a power object you bear?" he inquired. "Let me see it!"

He extended his hand, and the weapon jerked within Luke's grip but did not come loose.

"No, thanks," Luke said, and Jurt vanished. A moment later he appeared behind Luke, and his arm went around Luke's neck in a choke. Luke gripped it with one hand, bowed, and turned and threw him over his shoulder.

Jurt landed on his back before him, and Luke made no move to follow up on his action.

"Draw that blade," Jurt said, "and let me see it." Then he shook himself like a dog and rose to his feet. "Well?" he said.

"I see no need for a weapon in dealing with the likes of you," Luke told him.

Jurt raised both hands above his head and formed them into fists. They met, remained in contact for a moment. Then he drew them apart, his right hand somehow drawing a long blade out of his left.

"You ought to take that show on the road," Luke said, "now."

"Draw it!" Jurt said.

"I don't like the idea of fighting in a church," Luke told him. "You want to step outside?"

"Very funny," Jurt replied. "I know you've got an army out there. No thanks. I'll even take a certain pleasure in bloodying a Unicorn shrine."

"You ought to talk to Dalt," Luke said. "He gets his kicks in weird ways, too. Can I get you a horse—or a chicken? Maybe some white mice and aluminum foil?"

Jurt lunged. Luke stepped backward and drew his father's blade. It hissed and crackled and smoked as he parried lightly and drove it forward. There was a sudden fear on Jurt's face as he threw himself backward, batting at it, stumbling. As he fell, Luke kicked him in the stomach and Jurt's blade went flying.

"That's Werewindle!" Jurt gasped. "How did you come by the sword of Brand?"

"Brand was my father," Luke said.

A momentary look of respect passed over Jurt's face.

"I didn't know . . ." he muttered, and then he vanished.

I waited. I extended magical feelers all over the place. But there was just Luke, myself and the lady, who had halted some distance from us, watching, as if afraid to come any nearer on her way out.

Then Luke collapsed. Jurt was standing behind him, having just struck him on the back of the neck with his elbow. He reached then for Luke's wrist, as if to seize it and wrench the blade from his hand.

"It must be mine!" he said as I reached through the ring and struck him with a bolt of pure energy which I thought would rupture most of his organs and leave him a bleeding mass of jelly. Only for an instant had I considered using anything less than lethal force. I could see that sooner or later one of us was going to kill the other, and I'd decided to get it over with before he got lucky.

But he was already lucky. His bath in the Fount must have toughened him even more than I'd thought. He spun around three times, as if he'd been clipped by a truck, and was slammed up against the wall. He sagged. He slipped to the floor. Blood came out of his mouth. He looked as if he were about to pass out. Then his eyes focused and his hands extended.

A force similar to the one I'd just thrown at him struck at me. I was surprised by his ability to regroup and retaliate at that level with that speed. Not so surprised that I wasn't able to parry it, though. I took a step forward then and tried to set him afire with a beautiful spell the ring suggested. Rising, he was able to shield against it within moments of his clothes' beginning to smolder. I kept coming, and he created a vacuum around me. I pierced it and kept breathing. Then I tried a battering ram spell which the ring showed me, even more forceful than the first working with which I'd hit him.

He vanished before it hit, and a crack ran up three feet of the stone wall which had been behind him. I sent sense-tendrils all over and spotted him seconds later, crouched on a cornice high overhead. He launched himself at me just as I looked up.

I didn't know whether it would break my hand or not, but I felt it would be worth it, even so, as I levitated. I contrived to pass him at about the midway point, and I hit him with a left, which I hoped broke his neck as well as his

jaw. Unfortunately it also broke my levitation spell, and I tumbled to the floor along with him.

I heard the lady cry out as we fell, and she came rushing toward us. We lay stunned for several heartbeats. Then he rolled over onto his stomach, reached, hunched and fell, reached again.

His hand fell upon the haft of Werewindle. He must have felt my gaze as his fingers tightened about it, for he glanced at me and smiled. I heard Luke mutter a curse and stir. I threw a deep freeze spell at Jurt, but he trumped out before the cold front hit.

Then the lady screamed again, and even before I turned, I knew that the voice had been Coral's.

Reappearing, Jurt half collapsed against her from the rear, finding her throat with the edge of that bright, smoldering blade.

"Nobody," he gasped, "move . . . or I'll carve her . . . an extra smile."

I sought after a quick spell that would finish him without endangering her.

"Don't try it, Merle," he said. "I'll feel it . . . coming. Just leave me . . . alone . . . for half a minute . . . and you'll get to live . . . a little longer. I don't know where you picked up . . . those extra tricks . . . but they won't save you—"

He was panting and covered with sweat. The blood still dripped from his mouth.

"Let go of my wife," Luke said, rising, "or there'll never be anyplace you'll be able to hide."

"I don't want you for an enemy, son of Brand," Jurt said.

"Then do as I say, fella. I've taken out better men than you."

And then Jurt screamed as if his soul were on fire. Werewindle moved away from Coral's throat, and Jurt backed off and began jerking, like a puppet whose joints have seized up but whose strings are still being yanked. Coral turned toward him, her back to Luke and me. Her right hand rose to her face. After a time Jurt fell to the floor and curled into a fetal position. A red light seemed to be playing upon him. He was shaking steadily, and I could even hear his teeth chattering.

Abruptly, then, he was gone, trailing rainbows, leaving blood and spittle, bearing Werewindle with him. I sent a parting bolt after, but I knew that it did not reach him. I'd felt Julia's presence at the other end of the spectrum, and despite everything else, I was pleased to know that I had not slain her yet. But Jurt—Jurt was very dangerous now, I realized. For this was the first time we'd fought that he hadn't left a piece of himself behind, had even taken something away with him. Something deadly. He was learning, and that did not bode well.

When I turned my head, I caught sight of the red glow before Coral lowered her eyepatch, and I realized what had become of the Jewel of Judgment, though not, of course, why.

"Wife?" I said.

"Well, sort of . . . Yes," she replied.

"Just one of those things," Luke said. "Do you two know each other?"

PRINCE OF CHAOS

To Jane Lindskold—

Gramercy, lady, for your help.
This one was yours from the start.

ONE

See one coronation and you've seen them all. Sounds cynical and probably is, especially when the principal is your best friend and his queen's your inadvertent lover. But there's generally a procession, with a lot of slow music, and uncomfortable, colorful garb, incense, speeches, prayers, the ringing of bells. They are tedious, generally hot, and requiring of one an insincere attention, as at weddings, commencements, and secret initiations.

And so Luke and Coral became the sovereigns of Kashfa, in the same church where we'd fought almost—but, unfortunately, not quite—to the death with my mad brother Jurt but a few hours before. As Amber's only representative at the event—albeit of, technically, unofficial status—I was accorded a ringside standing-place, and eyes were often drifting my way. So I had to keep alert and mouth appropriate responses. While Random would not permit formal status to my presence at the ceremony, I knew he'd be irritated if he heard that my behavior was less than diplomatically sound.

So I wound up with hurting feet, a stiff neck, and colorful garments soaked with sweat. That's show biz. Still, I wouldn't have had it any other way. Luke and I go back through some of the damnedest times, and I couldn't help but think of them—from sword's point to track

1115

meets, from art galleries and into Shadow—as I stood there sweltering and wondering what would become of him now that he wore a crown. Such an occurrence had changed my uncle Random from a happy-go-lucky musician, footloose and degenerate, into a sage and responsible monarch—though I've only my relatives' reports when it comes to knowing about the first. I found myself hoping it wouldn't mellow Luke out all that much. Still—again—Luke was a very different person than Random, not to mention ages younger. Amazing what years can do, though—or is it just the nature of events? I realized myself to be a lot different than I had been not so very long ago, from all that had happened to me recently. A lot different than I'd been yesterday, come to think of it.

During the recessional Coral managed to pass me a note, saying that she had to see me, giving a time and a place, even including a small map. It proved to be an apartment to the rear of the palace. We met there that evening and wound up spending the night. She and Luke had been married as kids, by proxy, I learned then, part of the diplomatic arrangement between Jasra and the Begmans. It didn't work out, though—the diplomatic part, that is—and the rest kind of fell by the wayside. The principals had sort of forgotten about the marriage, too, till recent events served as a reminder. Neither had seen the other in years. Still, the record showed that the prince had been married. While it was an annullable thing, she could also be crowned with him. If there were anything in it for Kashfa.

And there was: Eregnor. A Begman queen on the Kashfan throne might help smooth over that particular real estate grab. At least, that had been Jasra's thinking, Coral told me. And Luke had been swayed by this, particularly in the absence of the guarantees from Amber and the now-defunct Golden Circle Treaty.

I held her. She was not well, despite what seemed an amazing postoperative recovery. She wore a black patch over her right eye and was more than a little reactive should my hand stray near it—or even if I looked at it for too long. What might have led Dworkin to replace the damaged eye with the Jewel of Judgment, I could not even guess. Unless he somehow considered her proof against the forces of the Pattern and the Logrus in their attempts to recover it. My expertise in this area, though, was nonexistent. Having finally met the diminutive mage, I had become convinced of his sanity—though this feeling in no way served to penetrate those enigmatic qualities that ancient wise men tend to possess.

"How does it feel?" I asked her.

"Very strange," she replied. "Not pain—exactly. More like the way a Trump contact feels. Only it's with me all the time, and I'm not going anywhere or talking to anyone. It's as if I'm standing in some sort of gateway. Forces are moving about me, through me."

In an instant I was at the center that was the gray ring with its wheel of many-spoked reddish metal. From the inside, here, it was like a great web. A bright strand pulsed for my attention. Yes, it was a line to a very potent force

in distant Shadow, one that might be used for probing. Carefully, I extended it toward the covered jewel she wore in her eye socket.

There was no immediate resistance. In fact, I felt nothing as I extended the line of power. An image came to me of a curtain of flame, however. Pushing through the fiery veil, I felt my extension of inquiry slowing, slowing, halted. And there I hovered, as it were, at the edge of a void. This was not the way of attunement, as I understood it, and I was loath to invoke the Pattern, which I understood to be a part of it, when employing other forces. I pushed forward and felt a terrible coldness, draining the energies I had called upon.

Still, it was not draining the energy directly from me, only from one of the forces I commanded. I pushed it farther, and I beheld a faint patch of light like some distant nebula. It hung against a background the deep red of port wine. Closer still, and it resolved itself into a form—a complex, three dimensional construct, half-familiar—which must be the pathway one takes in attuning oneself to the Jewel, from my father's description. All right, I was inside the Jewel. Should I essay the initiation?

"Go no further," came an unfamiliar voice, though I realized it to be Coral who was making the sounds. She seemed to have slipped into a trance state. "You are denied the higher initiation."

I drew back on my probe, not eager for any demonstrations that might come my way along it. My Logrus sight, which had remained with me constantly since recent events in Amber, gave me a vision of Coral now fully enfolded and penetrated by the higher version of the Pattern.

"Why?" I asked it.

But I was not vouchsafed a reply. Coral gave a little jerk, shook herself, and stared at me.

"What happened?" she asked.

"You dozed off," I replied. "No wonder. Whatever Dworkin did, plus the day's stress . . ."

She yawned and collapsed back on the bed.

"Yes," she breathed, and then she was really asleep.

I pulled off my boots and discarded my heavier garments. I stretched out beside her and drew a quilt over us. I was tired, too, and I just wanted someone to hold.

How long I slept I do not know. I was troubled by dark, swirling dreams. Faces—human, animal, demonic, moved about me, none of them bearing particularly cheerful expressions. Forests fell and burst into flame, the ground shook and split, the waters of the sea rose in gigantic waves and assailed the land, the moon dripped blood and there came up a great wailing. Something called my name. . . .

A great wind rattled the shutters till they burst inward, flapping and banging. In my dream, a creature entered then and came to crouch at the foot of the bed, calling softly to me, over and over. The room seemed to be shaking, and my mind went back to California. It seemed that an earthquake was in

progress. The wind rose from a shriek to a roar, and I heard crashing sounds from without, as of trees falling, towers toppling. . . .

"Merlin, Prince of the House of Sawall, Prince of Chaos, rise up," it seemed to say. Then it gnashed its fangs and began again.

At the fourth or fifth repetition it struck me that I might not be dreaming. There were screams from somewhere outside, and steady pulses of lightning came and went against almost musical rolls of thunder.

I raised a protective shell before I moved, before I opened my eyes. The sounds were real, as was the broken shutter. So was the creature at the foot of the bed.

"Merlin, Merlin. Rise up, Merlin," it said to me—it being a long-snouted, pointed-eared individual, well-fanged and clawed, of a greenish-silver cast of complexion, eyes large and shining, damp leathery wings folded against its lean sides. From its expression, I couldn't tell whether it was smiling or in pain. "Awaken, Lord of Chaos."

"Gryll," I said, naming an old family servant from the Courts.

"Aye, Lord," it replied. "The same as taught you the bonedance game."

"I'll be damned."

"Business before pleasure, Lord. I've followed the black thread a long and horrid way to come calling."

"The threads didn't reach this far," I said, "without an awful lot of push. Maybe even not then. Do they now?"

"It's easier now," he replied.

"How so?"

"His Majesty Swayvill, King of Chaos, sleeps this night with the ancestors of darkness. I was sent to fetch you back for the ceremonies."

"Now?"

"Now."

"Yeah. Well, okay. Sure. Just let me get my stuff together. How'd it happen, anyhow?"

I pulled on my boots, donned the rest of my garments, buckled on my blade.

"I am not privy to any details. Of course, it is common knowledge that his health was poor."

"I want to leave a note," I said.

He nodded.

"A brief one, I trust."

"Yes."

I scrawled on a piece of parchment from the writing table, *Coral, Called away on family business. I'll be in touch*, and I laid it beside her hand.

"All right," I said. "How do we do this?"

"I will bear you upon my back, Prince Merlin, as I did long ago."

I nodded as a flood of childhood memories returned to me. Gryll was immensely strong, as are most demons. But I recalled our games, at Pit's-edge and out over the darkness, in burial chambers, caves, still-smoking battlefields, ruined temples, chambers of dead sorcerers, private hells. I always seemed to

have more fun playing with demons than with my mother's relatives by blood or marriage. I even based my main Chaos form upon one of their kind.

He absorbed a chair from the room's corner for extra mass, changing shape to accommodate my adult size. As I climbed upon his elongated torso, catching a firm hold, he exclaimed, "Ah, Merlin! What magics do you bear these days?"

"I've their control, but not full knowledge of their essence," I answered. "They're a very recent acquisition. What is it that you feel?"

"Heat, cold, strange music," he replied. "From all directions. You have changed."

"Everyone changes," I said as he moved toward the window. "That's life."

A dark thread lay upon the wide sill. He reached out and touched it as he launched himself.

There came a great rushing of wind as we fell downward, moved forward, rose. Towers flashed past, wavering. The stars were bright, a quarter moon just risen, illuminating the bellies of a low line of clouds. We soared, the castle and the town dwindling in an eyeblink. The stars danced, became streaks of light. A band of sheer, rippling blackness spread about us, widening. The Black Road, I suddenly thought. It is like a temporary version of the Black Road, in the sky. I glanced back. It was not there. It was as if it were somehow reeling in as we rode. Or was it reeling us in?

The countryside passed beneath us like a film played at triple speed. Forest, hill, and mountain peak fled by. Our black way was a great ribbon heaving before us, patches of light and dark like daytime cloud shadows sliding past. And then the tempo increased, staccato. I noted of a sudden that there was no longer any wind. Abruptly, the moon was high overhead, and a crooked mountain range snaked beneath us. The stillness had a dreamlike quality to it, and in an instant the moon had fallen lower. A line of light cracked the world to my right and stars began to go out. There was no feeling of exertion in Gryll's body as we plunged along that black way; and the moon vanished and light grew buttery yellow along a line of clouds, acquiring a pink cast even as I watched.

"The power of Chaos rises," I remarked.

"The energy of disorder," he replied.

"There is more to this than you've told me," I said.

"I am but a servant," Gryll responded, "and not privy to the councils of the mighty."

The world continued to brighten, and for as far ahead as I could see our black ribbon rippled. We were passing high over mountainous terrain. And clouds blew apart and new ones formed at a rapid rate. We had obviously begun our passage through Shadow. After a time, the mountains wore down and rolling plains slid by. Suddenly the sun was in the middle of the sky. We seemed to be passing just above our black way, Gryll's toes barely grazing it as we moved. At times his wings hardly fluttered before me, at other times they thrummed like those of a hummingbird, into invisibility.

The sun grew cherry-red far to my left. A pink desert spread beneath us.. . . .

Then it was dark again and the stars turned like a great wheel.

Then we were low, barely passing above the tops of the trees. . . .

We burst into the air over a busy downtown street, lights on poles and the fronts of vehicles, neon in windows. The warm, stuffy, dusty, gassy smell of city rose up about us. A few pedestrians glanced upward, barely seeming to note our passage.

Even as we flashed across a river, cresting the housetops of suburbia, the prospect wavered and we passed over a primordial landscape of rock, lava, avalanche, and shuddering ground, two active volcanoes—one near, one far— spewing smoke against a blue-green sky.

"This, I take it, is a shortcut?" I said.

"It is the shortest cut," Gryll replied.

We entered a long night, and at some point it seemed that our way took us beneath deep waters, bright sea creatures hovering and darting both near at hand and in the middle distance. Dry and uncrushed, the black way protected us.

"It is as major an upheaval as the death of Oberon," Gryll volunteered. "Its effects are rippling across Shadow."

"But Oberon's death coincided with the re-creation of the Pattern," I said. "There was more to it than the death of a monarch of one of the extremes."

"True," Gryll replied, "but now is a time of imbalance among the forces. This adds to it. It will be even more severe."

We plunged into an opening in a dark mass of stone. Lines of light streaked past us. Irregularities were limned in a pale blue. Later—how long, I do not know—we were in a purple sky, with no transition that I can recall from the dark sea bottom. A single star gleamed far ahead. We sped toward it.

"Why?" I asked.

"Because the Pattern has grown stronger than the Logrus," he replied.

"How did that happen?"

"Prince Corwin drew a second Pattern at the time of the confrontation between the Courts and Amber."

"Yes, he told me about it. I've even seen it. He feared Oberon might not be able to repair the original."

"But he did, and so now there are two."

"Yes?"

"Your father's Pattern is also an artifact of order. It served to tip the ancient balance in the favor of Amber."

"How is it you are aware of this, Gryll, when no one back in Amber seems to know it or saw fit to tell me?"

"Your brother Prince Mandor and the Princess Fiona suspected this and sought evidence. They presented their findings to your uncle, Lord Suhuy. He made several journeys into Shadow and became persuaded that this is the case. He was preparing his findings for presentation to the king when Swayvill

suffered his final illness. I know these things because it was Suhuy who sent me for you, and he charged me to tell them to you."

"I just assumed it was my mother who'd sent for me."

"Suhuy was certain she would—which is why he wanted to reach you first. What I have told you concerning your father's Pattern is not yet common knowledge."

"What am I supposed to do about it?"

"He did not entrust me with that information."

The star grew brighter. The sky was filled with splashes of orange and pink. Shortly, lines of green light joined them, and they swirled like streamers about us.

We raced on, and the configurations came to dominate the sky fully, like a psychedelic parasol rotating slowly. The landscape became a total blur. I felt as if a part of me dozed, though I am certain I did not lose consciousness. Time seemed to be playing games with my metabolism. I grew enormously hungry and my eyes ached.

The star brightened. Gryll's wings took on a prismatic shimmer. We seemed to be moving at an incredible pace now.

Our strand curved upward at its outer edges. The process continued as we advanced until it seemed we were moving in a trough. Then they met overhead, and it was as if we sped down a gun barrel, aimed at the blue-white star.

"Anything else you're supposed to tell me?"

"Not so far as I know."

I rubbed my left wrist, feeling as if something should have been pulsing there. Oh, yes. Frakir. Where was Frakir, anyway? Then I recalled leaving her behind in Brand's apartment. Why had I done that? I—my mind felt cloudy, the memory dreamlike.

This was the first time since the event that I had examined that memory. Had I looked earlier I would have known sooner what it meant. It was the clouding effect of glamor. I had walked into a spell back in Brand's apartment. I'd no way of knowing whether it had been specific to me or merely something I'd activated in poking about. It could, I supposed, even have been something more general, enlivened by the disaster—possibly even an unintentional side effect of something that had been disturbed. Somehow I doubted the latter, however.

For that matter, I doubted any generality about the business. It was just too *right* to have been a booby-trap Brand had left lying about. It had confounded a trained sorcerer, me. Perhaps it was only my present distancing from the vicinity of its occurrence that had helped to clear my mind. As I reviewed my actions from the time of exposure I could see that I had been moving in something of a haze since then. And the more I reviewed the more I felt the spell to have been specifically tailored to enfold me. Not understanding it, I could not consider myself free of it with this knowledge either.

Whatever it was, it had caused me to abandon Frakir without thinking twice about it, and it had caused me to feel—well—strange. I could not tell

exactly how it might have influenced, might still be influencing, my thoughts and my feelings, the usual problem when one is caught up inside a spell. But I didn't see how it could possibly have been the late Brand himself who had set the thing up against such an unpredictable occurrence as my having rooms next to his old ones years after his death, from which I would be prompted to enter his quarters in the disastrous aftermath of an improbable confrontation between the Logrus and the Pattern in an upper hall of Amber Castle. No, it seemed that someone else had to be behind it. Jurt? Julia? It didn't seem too likely that they'd be able to operate undetected in the heart of Amber Castle. Who then? And could it have had anything to do with that episode in the Hall of Mirrors? I drew blanks. Were I back there now I might be able to come up with a spell of my own to ferret out the one responsible. But I wasn't, and any investigation at that end of things would have to wait.

The light ahead flashed more brightly now, winking from heavenly blue to baleful red.

"Gryll," I said. "Do you detect a spell upon me?"

"Aye, m'lord," he replied.

"Why didn't you mention it?"

"I thought it one of your own—for defense, perhaps."

"Can you lift it? I'm at a disadvantage, here on the inside."

" 'Tis too tangled in your person. I wouldn't know where to begin."

"Can you tell me anything about it?"

"Only that it's there, m'lord. Does seem rather heavy about the head, though."

"Could be coloring my thoughts a certain way, then?"

"Aye, a pale blue."

"I wasn't referring to your manner of perceiving it. Only to the possibility that it could be influencing my thinking."

His wings flashed blue, then red. Our tunnel expanded suddenly and the sky grew bright with the crazy colors of Chaos. The star we followed now took on the proportions of a small light—magically enhanced, of course— within a high tower of a sepulchral castle, all gray and olive, atop a mountain the bottom and middle of which had been removed. The island of stone floated above a petrified forest. The trees burned with opal fires—orange, purple, green.

"I'd imagine it could be disentangled," Gryll observed. "But its unraveling be a bafflement to this poor demon."

I grunted. I watched the streaking scenery for a few moments. Then, "Speaking of demons . . ." I said.

"Yes?"

"What can you tell me about the sort known as a *ty'iga?*" I asked.

"They dwell far out beyond the Rim," he replied, "and may be the closest of all creatures to the primal Chaos. I do not believe they even possess true bodies of the material sort. They have little to do with other demons, let alone anyone else."

"Ever know any of them—uh—personally?"

"I have encountered a few—now and then," he replied.

We rose higher. The castle had been doing the same. A fall of meteors burned its way, brightly, silently, behind it.

"They can inhabit a human body, take it over."

"That doesn't surprise me."

"I know of one who has done this thing, several times. But an unusual problem has come up. It apparently took control of one on the human's deathbed. The passing of the human seemed to lock the *ty'iga* in place. It cannot vacate the body now. Do you know of any way it might escape?"

Gryll chuckled.

"Jump off a cliff, I suppose. Or fall on a sword."

"But what if it's tied to its host so closely now that this doesn't free it?"

He chuckled again.

"That's the breaks of the game, in the body-stealing business."

"I owe this one something," I said. "I'd like to help her—it."

He was silent for a time, then replied, "An older, wiser *ty'iga* might know something about these matters. And you know where they are."

"Yeah."

"Sorry I can't be more help. They're an old breed, *ty'iga.*"

And now we bore down upon that tower. Our roadway under the shifting kaleidoscope that was the sky dwindled before us to but the tiniest of streaks. Gryll beat his way toward the light in the window and I peered past him.

I glanced downward. The prospect was dizzying. From some distant place a growling sound came up, as if portions of the earth itself were moving slowly against each other—a common enough occurrence in this vicinity. The winds beat at my garments. A strand of tangerine clouds beaded the sky to my left. I could make out detail work in the castle walls. I caught sight of a figure within the room of the light.

Then we were very near, and then through the window and inside. A large, stooped, gray and red demonic form, horned and half-scaled, regarded me with elliptically pupiled yellow eyes. Its fangs were bared in a smile.

"Uncle!" I cried as I dismounted. "Greetings!"

Gryll stretched and shook himself as Suhuy rushed forward and embraced me—carefully.

"Merlin," he said at last, "welcome home. I regret the occasion but rejoice in your presence. Gryll has told you. . . ?"

"Of the passing of His Highness? Yes. I'm sorry."

He released me and stepped back a pace.

"It is not as if it were unanticipated," he said. "Just the opposite. Too much so, in fact. Yet there is no proper time for such an event."

"True," I replied, massaging a certain stiffness out of my left shoulder and groping in my hip pocket after a comb.

"And he had been ailing for so long that I had grown used to it," I said. "It was almost as if he'd come to terms with the weakness."

Suhuy nodded. Then, "Are you going to transform?" he asked.

"It's been a rough day," I told him. "I'd as soon save my energy, unless there's some demand of protocol."

"None at all, just now," he replied. "Have you eaten?"

"Not recently."

"Come then," he said. "Let's find you some nourishment."

He turned and walked toward the far wall. I followed him. There were no doors in the room, and he had to know all the local Shadow stress points, the Courts being opposite to Amber in this regard. While it's awfully hard to pass through Shadow in Amber, the shadows are like frayed curtains in the Courts—often, you can look right through into another reality without even trying. And, sometimes, something in the other reality may be looking at you. Care must be taken, too, not to step through into a place where you will find yourself in the middle of the air, underwater, or in the path of a raging torrent. The Courts were never big on tourism.

Fortunately, the stuff of Shadow is so docile at this end of reality that it can be easily manipulated by a shadowmaster—who can stitch together their fabrics to create a way. Shadowmasters are technicians of locally potent skill, whose ability derives from the Logrus, though they need not be initiates. Very few are, although all initiates are automatically members of the Shadowmaster Guild. They're like plumbers or electricians about the Courts, and their skills vary as much as their counterparts on the Shadow Earth—a combination of aptitude and experience. While I'm a guild member I'd much rather follow someone who knows the ways than feel them out for myself. I suppose I should say more about this matter. Maybe I will sometime.

When we reached the wall, of course, it wasn't there. It just sort of grew misty and faded away; and we passed through the space where it had been— or, rather, a different analogous space—and we were passing down a green stairway. Well, it wasn't exactly a stairway. It was a series of unconnected green discs, descending in spiral fashion, proper riser and tread distance apart, sort of floating there in the night air. They passed about the exterior of the castle, finally stopping before a blank wall. Before we reached that wall we passed through several moments of bright daylight, a brief flurry of blue snow, and the apse of something like a cathedral without an altar, skeletons occupying pews at either hand. When we finally came to the wall we passed through it, emerging in a large kitchen. Suhuy led me to the larder and indicated I should help myself. I found some cold meat and bread and made myself a sandwich, washing it down with tepid beer. He nibbled at a piece of bread himself and sipped at a flagon of the same brew. A bird appeared overhead in full flight, cawing raucously, vanishing again before it had passed the entire length of the room.

"When are the services?" I asked.

"Redsky next, almost a whole turning off," he replied. "So you've a chance to sleep and collect yourself before then—perhaps."

"What do you mean, 'perhaps'?"

"As one of the three, you're under black watch. That's why I summoned you here, to one of my places of solitude." He turned and walked through

the wall. I followed him, still bearing my flagon, and we seated ourselves beside a still, green pool beneath a rocky overhang, umber sky above. His castle contained places from all over Chaos and Shadow, stitched together into a crazy-quilt pattern of ways within ways. "And since you wear the spikard you've added resources for safety," he observed.

He reached out and touched the many-spoked wheel of my ring. A faint tingling followed in my finger, hand, and arm.

"Uncle, you were often given to cryptic utterances when you were my teacher," I said. "But I've graduated now, and I guess that gives me the right to say I don't know what the hell you're talking about."

He chuckled and sipped his beer.

"On reflection, it always became clear," he said.

"Reflection . . ." I said, and I looked into the pool.

Images swam amid the black ribbons beneath its surface—Swayvill lying in state, yellow and black robes muffling his shrunken form, my mother, my father, demonic forms, all passing and fading, Jurt, myself, Jasra and Julia, Random and Fiona, Mandor and Dworkin, Bill Roth and many faces I did not know. . . .

I shook my head.

"Reflection does not clarify," I said.

"It is not the function of an instant," he replied.

So I returned my attention to the chaos of faces and forms. Jurt returned and remained for a long time. He was dressing himself, in very good taste, and he appeared to be relatively intact. When he finally faded there returned one of the half-familiar faces I had seen earlier. I knew he was a noble of the Courts, and I searched my memory. Of course. It had been a long while, but now I recognized him. It was Tmer, of the House of Jesby, eldest son of the late Prince Rolovians, and now lord himself of the Ways of Jesby—spade beard, heavy brow, sturdily built, not unhandsome, in a rugged sort of way; by all report a brave and possibly even sensitive fellow.

Then there was Prince Tubble of the Ways of Chanicut, phasing back and forth between human and swirling demonic forms. Placid, heavy, subtle; centuries old and very shrewd; he wore a fringed beard, had wide, innocent, pale eyes, was master of many games.

I waited, and Tmer followed Jurt followed Tubble into vanishment amid the coiling ribbons. I waited longer, and nothing new occurred.

"End of reflection," I announced at last. "But I still don't know what it means."

"What did you see?"

"My brother Jurt," I replied, "and Prince Tmer of Jesby. And Tubble of Chanicut, among other attractions."

"Most appropriate," he responded. "Entirely appropriate."

"And so?"

"Like you, Tmer and Tubble are both under black watch. I understand Tmer is at Jesby, though I believe Jurt has gone to earth somewhere other than Dalgarry."

"Jurt's come back?"

He nodded.

"He could be at my mother's Fortress Gantu," I mused. "Or, Sawall did have a second stead—the Ways of Anch, at the very Rim."

Suhuy shrugged.

"I do not know," he said.

"But why the black watch—for any of us?"

"You went off into Shadow to a fine university," he said, "and you have dwelled in the Court of Amber, which I would deem highly educational. Therefore, I bid you take thought. Surely, a mind so well honed—"

"I realize the black watch means we face some sort of danger. . . ."

"Of course."

". . . But its nature eludes me. Unless . . ."

"Yes."

"It has to do with Swayvill's death. So it must involve some sort of political settlement. But I've been away. I don't know what matters are hot just now."

He showed me row upon row of worn but still nasty fangs.

"Try the matter of the succession," he said.

"Okay. Say the Ways of Sawall are supporting one possible successor, Jesby another, Chanicut another. Say we're at each other's throats over the matter. Say I've come back into the middle of a vendetta. So whoever's giving the orders right now has declared us under watch as a matter of keeping things from getting messy. I appreciate it."

"Close," he said, "but it's already gone further than that."

I shook my head.

"I give up," I said.

From somewhere there came up a wailing sound.

"Think about it," he replied, "while I welcome a guest."

He rose and stepped into the pool, vanishing immediately.

I finished my beer.

TWO

It seemed but moments later that a rock to my left shimmered and emitted a bell-like tone. Without conscious intent my attention gathered itself at my ring, which Suhuy had referred to as a spikard. I realized in that instant that I was preparing to use it to defend myself. Interesting, how familiar I felt with it now, how adapted I seemed to have become to it in so short a time. I was on my feet, facing the stone, left hand extended in its direction when Suhuy stepped through the shining place, a taller, darker figure at his rear. A moment later and that figure followed him, emerging into substantiality and shifting from an octopal ape form to that of my brother Mandor, humanized, wearing black as when last I had seen him, though the garments were fresh and of a

slightly different cut, his white hair less tousled. He quickly scanned the area about us and gave me a smile.

"I see that all is well," he stated.

I chuckled as I nodded toward his arm in its sling.

"As well as might be expected," I replied. "What happened in Amber after I left?"

"No fresh disasters," he answered. "I stayed only long enough to see whether there was anything I could do to be of assistance. This amounted to a little magical clearing of the vicinity and the summoning of a few planks to lay over holes. Then I begged leave of Random to depart, he granted it, and I came home."

"A disaster? At Amber?" Suhuy asked.

I nodded.

"There was a confrontation between the Unicorn and the Serpent in the halls of Amber Palace, resulting in considerable damage."

"What could have occasioned the Serpent's venturing that far into the realm of Order?"

"It involved what Amber refers to as the Jewel of Judgment, which the Serpent considers its missing eye."

"I must hear the entire tale."

I proceeded to tell him of the complicated encounter, leaving out my own later experiences in the Corridor of Mirrors and Brand's apartments. While I spoke, Mandor's gaze drifted to the spikard, to Suhuy, and back. When he saw that I noted this he smiled.

"So Dworkin is himself once more . . . ?" Suhuy said.

"I didn't know him before," I replied. "But he seemed to know what he was about."

". . . And the Queen of Kashfa sees with the Eye of the Serpent."

"I don't know that she sees with it," I said. "She's still recovering from the operation. But that's an interesting thought. If she could see with it, what might she behold?"

"The clear, cold lines of eternity, I daresay. Beneath all Shadow. No mortal could bear it for too long."

"She is of the blood of Amber," I said.

"Really? Oberon's?"

I nodded.

"Your late liege was a very active man," he observed. "Still, it would be quite a burden of seeing, though I speak only from guesswork—and a certain knowledge of principles. I've no idea what may come of this. Only Dworkin could say. Be he sane, there is a reason for it. I acknowledge his mastery, though I've never been able to anticipate him."

"You know him, personally?" I asked.

"I knew him," he said, "long ago, before his troubles. And I do not know whether to rejoice or despair in this. Recovered, he may be working for the greater good. Then again, his interests may be totally partisan."

"Sorry I can't enlighten you," I said. "I find his actions cryptic, too."

"I'm baffled also," Mandor said, "by the disposition of the Eye. But it still sounds pretty much a local matter, involving Amber's relations with Kashfa and Begma. I don't see that there is anything to be gained at this point by speculation. It's better keeping most of our attention for more pressing local matters."

I felt myself sigh.

"Such as the succession?" I suggested.

Mandor quirked an eyebrow.

"Oh, Lord Suhuy has briefed you already?"

"No," I replied. "No, but I heard so much from my father of the succession in Amber, with all its cabals, intrigues, and double crosses, that I almost feel an authority on the subject. I imagine it could be that way here, too, among the Houses of Swayvill's descendants, there being many more generations involved."

"You have the right idea," he said, "though I think the picture might be a bit more orderly here than it was there."

"That's something, anyway," I said. "For me, I intend to pay my respects and get the hell out. Send me a postcard telling me how it gets settled."

He laughed. He seldom laughs. I felt my wrist prickle where Frakir usually rides.

"He really doesn't know," he said, glancing at Suhuy.

"He's just arrived," Suhuy answered. "I hadn't the time to tell him anything."

I groped in my pocket, located a coin, withdrew it, and flipped it.

"Heads," I announced, on inspection. "You tell me, Mandor. What's going on?"

"You're not next in line for the throne," he said.

It being my turn to laugh, I did.

"I already knew that," I said. "You told me not that long ago, over dinner, how long the line was before me—if someone of my mixed blood could be considered at all."

"Two," he said. "Two stand before you."

"I don't understand," I said. "What happened to all the others?"

"Dead," he replied.

"Bad year for the flu?"

He gave me a nasty smile.

"There has been an unprecedented number of fatal duels and political assassinations recently."

"Which sort dominated the field?"

"The assassinations."

"Fascinating."

". . . And so you three are under black watch protection of the Crown, and were given into the care of your respective Houses' security."

"You're serious."

"Indeed."

"Was this sudden thinning of the ranks a matter of many people simulta-

neously seeking advancement? Or was it a smaller number, removing roadblocks?"

"The Crown is uncertain."

"When you say 'the Crown,' who, exactly, are you referring to, right now? Who's making decisions in the interim?"

"Lord Bances of Amblerash," he replied, "a distant relative and longtime friend of our late monarch."

"I sort of recall him. Could he have an eye on the throne himself, and be behind any of the—removals?"

"The man's a priest of the Serpent. Their vows bar them from reigning anywhere."

"There are usually ways around vows."

"True, but the man seems genuinely uninterested in such a thing."

"That needn't preclude his having a favorite, and maybe helping him along a bit. Is anybody near the throne particularly fond of his Order?"

"To my knowledge, no."

"Which doesn't mean someone mightn't have cut a deal."

"No, though Bances isn't the sort of man one would approach easily with a proposition."

"In other words, you believe he's above whatever's going on?"

"In the absence of evidence to the contrary."

"Who is next in line?"

"Tubble of Chanicut."

"Who's second?"

"Tmer of Jesby."

"Top of the line, your pool," I said to Suhuy.

He showed me his teeth again. They seemed to rotate.

"Are we at vendetta with either Chanicut or Jesby?" I asked.

"Not really."

"We're all just taking care then, huh?"

"Yes."

"How did it all come to this? I mean, there were a lot of people involved, as I recall. Was it a night of the long knives, or what?"

"No, the deaths have been occurring steadily for some time. There wasn't a sudden bloodbath when Swayvill took his turn for the worse—though a few did occur just recently."

"Well, there must have been some investigation. Do we have any of the perps in custody?"

"No, they either escaped or were killed."

"What of those who were killed? Their identities might indicate their political affiliations."

"Not really. Several were professionals. A couple of others were general malcontents, arguably among the mentally ill."

"You're saying there are no clues as to who might be behind it all?"

"That's right."

"What about suspicions then?"

"Tubble himself is of course suspect, though it is not a good idea to say it aloud. He stood to benefit the most, and now he's in a position to do so. Also, there is much in his career of political connivance, double-dealing, assassination. But that was long ago. Everyone has a few skeletons in the cellar. He has been a quiet and conservative man for many years."

"Tmer, then—He's close enough to generate suspicion. Is there anything to connect him with the bloody business?"

"Not really. His affairs are hardly open. He's a very private man. But he was never associated with such extremes in the past. I do not know him all that well, but he has always struck me as a simpler, more direct person than Tubble. He seems the sort who'd simply attempt a coup if he wanted the throne badly enough, rather than spend a lot of time intriguing."

"There could, of course, be a number of people involved, each acting in his own interest—"

"And now that the matter is imminent they'll have to surface soon?"

"It would seem so, wouldn't it?"

A smile. A shrug.

"No reason for a coronation to end it all," he said. "A crown does not automatically make a person dagger-proof."

"But the successor would come to power with a lot of bad baggage."

"It wouldn't be the first time in history. And if you stop to think about it, some very good monarchs have come to power under such a cloud. By the way, has it occurred to you that the others might be speculating along these lines about you?"

"Yes, and it makes me uncomfortable. My father wanted the throne of Amber for a long time, and it really messed up his life. He was only happy when he said the hell with it. If I learned anything from his story, that's it. I have no such ambition."

But for a moment, I wondered. What would it feel like to control a massive state? Every time I complained about politics, here, in Amber, back in the States on the Shadow Earth, there was the automatic corollary of considering the way I'd manage situations if I were in charge.

"I wonder?" Mandor repeated.

I glanced downward.

"Perhaps the others are looking into their own scrying pools just now," I said, "hoping for clues."

"Doubtless," he responded. "What if Tubble and Tmer did meet untimely ends? What would you do?"

"Don't even think about it," I said. "It won't happen."

"Suppose."

"I don't know."

"You really should make some sort of decision, just to have it out of the way. You're never at a loss for words when you know your own mind."

"Thanks. I'll remember that."

"Tell me more of your story, since last we met."

And so I did, Pattern ghosts and all.

Somewhere near the end the wailing sound began again. Suhuy moved toward the rock.

"Excuse me," he said, and the rock parted and he passed within.

Immediately, I felt Mandor's gaze heavy upon me.

"We probably only have a moment," he said. "Not enough time, really, to go into everything I wanted to cover with you."

"Very private, huh?"

"Yes. So you must arrange to dine with me before the funeral. Say, a quarter-turning hence, bluesky."

"All right. Your place, or the Ways of Sawall?"

"Come to me at Mandorways."

The rock phased again as I nodded, and a lithe demonic figure entered, shimmering bluely within a veil of cloud. I was on my feet in an instant, then bowing to kiss the hand she extended.

"Mother," I said. "I hadn't anticipated the pleasure—this soon."

She smiled, and then it went away in a swirl. The scales faded, the contours of her face and form flowed. The blue went away into a normal though pale flesh color. Her hips and shoulders widened as she lost something of height, though still remained tall. Her brown eyes grew more attractive as the heavy brow ridges receded. A few freckles became visible across her now-human, slightly upturned nose. Her brown hair was longer than when last I had seen her in this form. And she was still smiling. Her red tunic became her, simply belted; a rapier hung at her left hip.

"My dear Merlin," she said, taking my head between her hands and kissing me upon the lips. "I am pleased to see you looking so well. It has been quite a while since last you visited."

"I've had a very active existence of late."

"To be sure," she said. "I've heard some report of your various misadventures."

"I'd imagine you would have. It's not everyone has a *ty'iga* following him about, periodically seducing him in various forms, and making life, in general, very complicated with unwanted efforts at protection."

"It shows that I care, dear."

"It also shows that you have no respect for my privacy nor trust in my judgment."

Mandor cleared his throat.

"Hello, Dara," he said then.

"I suppose it must seem that way to you," she stated. Then, "Hello, Mandor," she went on. "What happened to your arm?"

"A misunderstanding involving some architecture," he replied. "You've been out of sight, though hardly out of mind, for some time."

"Thank you, if that's a compliment," she said. "Yes, I go a bit reclusive every now and then, when the weight of society becomes troublesome. Though you're hardly the one to talk, sir, vanishing for long stretches as you do in the labyrinths of Mandorways—if that be indeed where you take yourself."

He bowed.

"As you say, lady, we appear to be creatures of a kind."

Her eyes narrowed, though her voice was unchanged, as she said, "I wonder. Yes, I can sometimes see us as kindred spirits, perhaps even more than in our simplest cycles of activity. We've both been out and about a lot of late, though, haven't we?"

"But I've been careless," said Mandor, indicating his injured arm. "You, obviously, have not."

"I never argue with architecture," she said.

"Or other imponderables?" he asked.

"I try to work with what is in place," she told him.

"Generally, I do, too."

"And if you cannot?" she asked.

He shrugged.

"Sometimes there are collisions."

"You've survived many in your time, haven't you?"

"I can't deny it, but then it has been a long while. You seem made of very survivable stuff yourself."

"So far," she responded. "We really must compare notes on imponderables and collisions one day. Wouldn't it be strange if we were similar in all respects?"

"I should be very much surprised," he answered.

I was fascinated and slightly frightened by the exchange, though I could go only by feeling and had no notion of specifics. They were somehow similar, and I'd never heard generalities delivered with quite that precision and emphasis outside of Amber, where they often make a game of talking that way.

"Forgive me," Mandor said then, to the company in general, "but I must absent myself to recuperation. Thank you for your hospitality, sir." He bowed to Suhuy. "And for the pleasure of crossing—paths with you"—this to Dara.

"You've barely arrived," Suhuy said, "and you've taken no refreshment. You make me a poor host."

"Rest assured, old friend, there is none could perform such a transformation," he stated. He looked at me as he backed toward the opening way. "Till later," he said, and I nodded.

He passed into the way, and the rock solidified with his vanishment.

"One wonders at his deliveries," my mother said, "without apparent rehearsal."

"Grace," Suhuy commented. "He was born with an abundance."

"I wonder who will die today?" she said.

"I am not certain the implication is warranted," Suhuy replied.

She laughed.

"And if it is," she said, "they will certainly expire in good taste."

"Do you speak in condemnation or envy?" he asked.

"Neither," she said. "For I, too, am an admirer of grace—and a good jest."

"Mother," I said, "just what's going on?"

"Whatever do you mean, Merlin?" she replied.

"I left this place a long time ago. You sent a demon to find me and take

care of me. Presumably, it could detect someone of the blood of Amber. So there was some confusion between myself and Luke. So it settled by taking care of both of us—until Luke began his periodic attempts to kill me. Then it protected me from Luke and tried to determine which of us was the proper party. It even lived with Luke for a time, and later pursued me. I should have guessed at something of this because it was so eager to learn my mother's name. Apparently, Luke was just as closemouthed about his parentage."

She laughed.

"It makes a beautiful picture," she began. "Little Jasra and the Prince of Darkness—"

"Don't try to change the subject. Think how embarrassing that is for a grown man—his mother sending demons to look after him."

"The singular. It was just one demon, dear."

"Who cares? The principle's the same. Where do you get off with this protective business? I resent—"

"The ty'iga probably saved your life on more than one occasion, Merlin."

"Well, yes. But—"

"You'd rather be dead than protected? Just because it was coming from me?"

"That's not the point!"

"Then what is the point?"

"It seems you just assumed I couldn't take care of myself, and—"

"Well, you couldn't."

"But you had no way of knowing that. I resented your starting with the assumption that I needed chaperoning in Shadow, that I was naive, gullible, careless—"

"I suppose it would hurt your feelings if I said that you were, going to a place as different from the Courts as that Shadow is."

"Yes, I can take care of myself!"

"You weren't doing that great a job of it. But you are making a number of unwarranted assumptions yourself. What makes you think that the reasons you gave are the only possible ones for my taking such an action?"

"Okay. Tell me that you knew that Luke was going to try to kill me every April thirtieth. And if the answer is yes, why didn't you just tell me?"

"I did not know that Luke was going to try to kill you every April thirtieth."

I turned away. I clenched my fists and relaxed them.

"So you just did it for the hell of it?"

"Merlin, why do you find it so difficult to admit that other people might sometimes know things you don't?"

"Start with their unwillingness to tell me these things."

She was silent a long moment. Then, "I'm afraid there is something to what you say," she replied. "But there were strong reasons for not talking of such matters."

"Then start with the inability to tell me. Tell me now why you didn't trust me then."

"It wasn't a matter of trust."

"Is it okay to tell me now what it was?"

Another, longer silence followed.

"No," she finally said. "Not yet."

I turned toward her, keeping my features composed and my voice level.

"Then nothing has changed," I said, "nor ever shall. You still do not trust me."

"That is not true," she answered, glancing at Suhuy. "It is just that this is not the proper time or the proper place to go into these matters."

"Might I fetch you a drink or something to eat, Dara?" Suhuy said immediately.

"Thank you no," she replied. "I cannot stay much longer."

"Mother, tell me, then, something about the *ty'iga.*"

"What do you wish to know?"

"You conjured it from someplace beyond the Rim."

"That is correct."

"Such beings are bodiless themselves, but capable of taking over a living host for their own purposes."

"Yes."

"Supposing such a being took over the body of a person at or near the moment of death, making it the sole animating spirit and controlling intelligence?"

"Interesting. Is this a hypothetical question?"

"No. It's really happened with the one you sent after me. It doesn't seem able to quit that body now. Why not?"

"I am not really certain," she said.

"It is trapped now," Suhuy offered. "It can only come and go by reacting with a resident intelligence."

"The body, with the *ty'iga* in control, recovered from the illness that killed its consciousness," I said. "You mean it's stuck there now for life?"

"Yes. So far as I know."

"Then tell me this: Will it be released when that body dies, or will it die with it?"

"It could go either way," he replied. "But the longer it remains in the body, the more likely it is that it will perish along with it."

I looked back at my mother.

"There you have the end of its story," I stated.

She shrugged.

"I've done with this one and released it," she said, "and one can always conjure another should the need arise."

"Don't do it," I told her.

"I shan't," she said. "There is no need to, now."

"But if you thought there were, you would?"

"A mother tends to value her son's safety, whether the son likes it or not."

I raised my left hand, extending the forefinger in an angry gesture, when I noticed that I was wearing a bright bracelet—it seemed an almost-holograma-

tic representation of a woven cord. I lowered my hand, bit back my first response, and said, "You know my feelings now."

"I knew them a long time ago," she said. "Let us dine at the Ways of Sawall, half a turning hence, purplesky. Agreed?"

"Agreed," I said.

"Till then. Good turning, Suhuy."

"Good turning, Dara."

She took three paces and was gone, as etiquette prescribed, out the same way by which she had entered.

I turned and strode to the pool's edge, stared into its depths, felt the muscles in my shoulders slowly unknot. Jasra and Julia were down there now, back in the citadel of the Keep, doing something arcane in the lab. And then the strands were flowing over them, some cruel truth beyond all order and beauty, beginning to form themselves into a mask of fascinating, frightening proportion.

I felt a hand on my shoulder.

"Family," Suhuy said, "intrigues and maddens. You are feeling the tyranny of affection at the moment, are you not?"

I nodded.

"Something Mark Twain said about being able to choose your friends but not your relatives," I answered.

"I do not know what they are up to, though I have my suspicions," he said. "There is nothing to do now but rest and wait. I would like to hear more of your story."

"Thanks, Uncle. Yeah," I said. "Why not?"

So I gave him all the rest of my tale. Partway through it, we adjourned to the kitchen for further sustenance, then took another way to a floating balcony above a lime-colored ocean breaking upon pink rocks and beaches under a twilit or otherwise indigo sky without stars. There, I finished my telling.

"This is more than a little interesting," he said, at last.

"Oh? Do you see something in it all that I don't?" I asked.

"You've given me too much to consider for me to give you a hasty judgment," he said. "Let us leave it at that for now."

"Very well."

I leaned on the rail, looked down at the waters.

"You need rest," he said after a time.

"I guess I do."

"Come, I'll show you to your room."

He extended a hand and I took hold of it. Together, we sank through the floor.

And so I slept, surrounded by tapestries and heavy drapes, in a doorless chamber in the Ways of Suhuy. It might have been in a tower, as I could hear the winds passing beyond the walls. Sleeping, I dreamt. . . .

I was back in the castle Amber, walking the sparkling length of the Corri-

dor of Mirrors. Tapers flickered in tall holders. My footsteps made no sound. The mirrors came in all manner of shapes. They covered the walls at either hand, big ones, little ones. I passed myself within their depths, reflected, distorted, sometimes re-reflected. . . .

I was halted before a tall, cracked mirror to my left, framed in tin. Even as I turned toward it I knew that it would not be me whom I regarded this time.

Nor was I mistaken. Coral was looking at me from out of the mirror. She had on a peach-colored blouse and was not wearing her eyepatch. The crack in the mirror divided her face down the middle. Her left eye was the green I remembered, her right was the Jewel of Judgment. Both seemed to be focused upon me.

"Merlin," she said. "Help me. This is too strange. Give me back my eye."

"I don't know how," I said. "I don't understand what was done."

"My eye," she went on, as if she had not heard. "The world is all swarming forces in the Eye of Judgment, cold—so cold!—and not a friendly place. Help me!"

"I'll find a way," I said.

"My eye . . ." she continued.

I hurried by.

From a rectangular mirror in a wooden frame carved at its base in the form of a phoenix, Luke regarded me.

"Hey, old buddy," he said, looking slightly forlorn, "I'd sure like to have my dad's sword back. You haven't come across it again, have you?"

" 'Fraid not," I muttered.

"It's a shame to get to hold your present for such a short period of time. Watch for it, will you? I've a feeling it might come in handy."

"I'll do that," I said.

"After all, you're kind of responsible for what happened," he continued.

"Right," I agreed.

". . . And I'd sure like to have it back."

"Yeah," I said, moving away.

A nasty chuckle emerged from a maroon-framed ellipse to my right. Turning, I beheld the face of Victor Melman, the shadow Earth sorcerer I had confronted back when my troubles were beginning.

"Son of perdition!" he hissed. " 'Tis good to see you wander lost in Limbo. May my blood lie burning on your hands."

"Your blood is on your own hands," I said. "I count you as a suicide."

"Not so!" he snapped back. "You slew me most unfairly."

"Bullshit," I answered. "I may be guilty of a lot of things, but your death is not one of them."

I began to walk away, and his hand emerged from the mirror and clutched at my shoulder.

"Murderer!" he cried.

I brushed his hand away.

"Bugger off!" I said, and I kept going.

Then, from a wide, green-framed mirror with a greenish haze to the glass, Random hailed me from my left, shaking his head.

"Merlin! Merlin! What are you up to, anyway?" he asked. "I've known for some time that you haven't been keeping me abreast of everything that's afoot."

"Well," I replied, regarding him in an orange T-shirt and Levi's, "that's true, sir. Some things I just haven't had time to go into."

"Things that involve the safety of the realm—and you haven't had time?"

"Well, I guess there's something of a judgmental factor involved."

"If it involves our safety, I am the one to do the judging."

"Yes, sir. I realize that—"

"We have to have a talk, Merlin. Is it that your personal life is mixed with this in some way?"

"I guess that's true—"

"It doesn't matter. The kingdom is more important. We must talk."

"Yes, sir. We will as soon as—"

" 'As soon as,' hell! Now! Stop screwing around at whatever you're up to and get your ass back here! We have to talk!"

"I will, as soon as—"

"Don't give me that! It verges on the traitorous if you're withholding important information! I need to see you now! Come home!"

"I will," I said, and I hurried away, his voice joining a continuing chorus of the others, repeating their demands, their pleas, their accusations.

Out of the next one—circular, with a blue braided frame—Julia regarded me.

"And there you go," she said, almost wistfully. "You knew I loved you."

"I loved you, too," I admitted. "It took me a long time to realize it. I guess I messed up, though."

"You didn't love me enough," she said. "Not enough to trust me. And so you lost my trust."

I looked away.

"I'm sorry," I said.

"Not good enough," she responded. "Thus, we have become enemies."

"It doesn't have to be that way."

"Too late," she said. "Too late."

"I'm sorry," I repeated, and I hurried away.

Thus, I came to Jasra, in a red, diamond frame. Her bright-nailed hand reached out and caressed my cheek.

"Going somewhere, dear boy?" she asked.

"I hope so," I said.

She smiled crookedly and pursed her lips.

"I've decided you were a bad influence on my son," she said. "He lost his edge when he became friends with you."

"Sorry about that," I said.

". . . Which may make him unfit to rule."

"Unfit or unwilling?" I asked.

"Whichever, it will be your fault."

"He's a big boy now, Jasra. He makes his own decisions."

"I fear you've taught him to make the wrong ones."

"He's his own man, lady. Don't blame me if he does things you don't like."

"And if Kashfa crumbles because you've softened him?"

"I decline the nomination," I said, taking a step forward. It was good that I was moving, for her hand shot out, nails raking at my face, barely missing. She threw expletives after me as I walked away. Fortunately, they were drowned amid the cries of the others.

"Merlin?"

Turning to my right again I beheld the face of Nayda within a silver mirror, its surface and curled frame of a single piece.

"Nayda! What are *you* down on me for?"

"Nothing," the *ty'iga* lady replied. "I'm just passing through, and I need directions."

"You don't hate me? How refreshing!"

"Hate you? Don't be silly. I could never do that."

"Everyone else in this gallery seems irritated with me."

"It's only a dream, Merlin. You're real, I'm real, and I don't know about the others."

"I'm sorry my mother put you under that spell to protect me—all those years ago. Are you really free of it now? If you're not, perhaps I can—"

"I'm free of it."

"I'm sorry you had so much trouble fulfilling its terms—not knowing whether it was Luke or me you were supposed to be guarding. Who'd have known there'd be two Amberites in the same neighborhood in Berkeley?"

"I'm not sorry."

"What do you mean?"

"I came for directions. I want to know how I can find Luke."

"Why, in Kashfa. He was just crowned king the other day. What do you need him for?"

"Hadn't you guessed?"

"No."

"I'm in love with him. Always was. Now that I'm free of the *geas* and have a body of my own, I want him to know that I was Gail—and how I feel. Thanks, Merlin. Good-bye."

"Wait!"

"Yes?"

"I never said thanks for your protecting me all those years—even if it was only a compulsion for you, even if it got to be a big bother for me. Thanks, and good luck."

She smiled and faded away. I reached out and touched the mirror.

"Luck," I thought I heard her say.

Strange. It was a dream. Still—I couldn't awaken, and it felt real. I—

"You made it back to the Courts in time for all the scheming, I see"—this from a mirror three paces ahead, black-bound and narrow.

I moved to it. My brother Jurt glared out at me.

"What do you want?" I asked.

His face was an angry parody of my own.

"I want you never to have been," he said. "Failing that, I'd like to see you dead."

"What's your third choice?" I asked.

"Your confinement to a private hell, I guess."

"Why?"

"You stand between me and everything I want."

"I'll be glad to step aside. Tell me how."

"There's no way you can or will, on your own."

"So you hate me?"

"Yes."

"I thought your bath in the Fountain destroyed your emotions."

"I didn't get the full treatment, and it only made them stronger."

"Any way we can forget the whole thing and start over again, be friends?"

"Never."

"Didn't think so."

"She always cared more about you than me, and now you're going to have the throne."

"Don't be ridiculous. I don't want it."

"Your desires have nothing to do with the matter."

"I won't have it."

"Yes, you will—unless I kill you first."

"Don't be stupid. It's not worth this."

"One day soon, when you least expect it, you will turn and see me. It will be too late."

The mirror grew entirely black.

"Jurt!"

Nothing. Aggravating, having to put up with him in dream as well as waking.

I turned my head toward a fire-framed mirror several paces ahead and to my left, knowing—somehow—it was next on my route. I moved toward it.

She was smiling.

"And there you have it," she said.

"Aunty, what's going on?"

"It seems to be the sort of conflict generally referred to as 'irreducible,' " Fiona replied.

"That's not the sort of answer I need."

"Too much is afoot to give you a better one."

"And you're a part of it?"

"A very small one. Not one who can do you much good just now."

"What am I to do?"

"Learn your options and choose the best one."

"Best for whom? Best for what?"

"Only you can say."

"Can you give me a hint?"

"Could you have walked Corwin's Pattern that day I took you to it?"

"Yes."

"I thought so. It was drawn under unusual circumstances. It can never be duplicated. Our Pattern would never have permitted its construction had it not been damaged itself and too weak to prevent its coming into being."

"So?"

"Our Pattern is trying to absorb it, incorporate it. If it succeeds, it will be as disastrous as it would have been were the Pattern of Amber destroyed at the time of the war. The balance with Chaos will be totally upset."

"Isn't Chaos strong enough to prevent this? I'd thought they were equally potent."

"They were until you repaired the Shadow Pattern and Amber's was able to absorb it. This increased its strength beyond that of Chaos. Now it is able to reach for your father's against the power of the Logrus."

"I don't understand what is to be done."

"Neither do I, yet. But I charge you to remember what I have said. When the time comes you must make a decision. I've no idea what it will involve, but it will be very important."

"She's right," came a voice from behind my back.

Turning, I saw my father within a shining black frame, a silver rose set at its top.

"Corwin!" I heard Fiona say. "Where are you?"

"In a place where there is no light," he said.

"I thought you somehow in Amber, Father, with Deirdre," I said.

"The ghosts play at being ghosts," he answered. "I have not much time, for my strength is low. I can tell you only this: Trust not the Pattern, nor the Logrus either, nor any of their spawn, till this matter be settled."

He began to fade.

"How can I help you?" I asked.

The words ". . . in the Courts" came to me before he vanished.

I turned again.

"Fi, what did he mean by that?" I asked her.

She was frowning.

"I get the impression that the answer lies somewhere in the Courts," she replied slowly.

"Where? Where should I look?"

She shook her head and began to turn away.

"Who would know best?" she said.

Then she, too, was gone.

Voices were still calling to me, from behind, from ahead. There was weeping and laughter, and my name being repeated. I rushed ahead.

"Whatever happens," Bill Roth said, "if you need a good lawyer, I'll handle it—even in Chaos."

And then there was Dworkin, squinting at me from out of a tiny mirror with a twisted frame.

"Nothing to be alarmed about," he remarked, "but all sorts of imponderables are hovering about you."

"What am I to do?" I cried.

"You must become something greater than yourself."

"I don't understand."

"Escape the cage that is your life."

"What cage?"

He was gone.

I ran, and their words rang around me.

Near the end of the hall was a mirror like a piece of yellow silk stretched upon a frame. The Cheshire Cat grinned at me from within.

"It's not worth it. The hell with them all," he said. "Come to the cabaret, old chum. We'll tip a few brews and watch the man paint."

"No!" I cried. "No!"

And then there was only a grin. This time I faded, too. Merciful, black oblivion and the sound of the wind, somewhere, passing.

THREE

How long I slept, I do not know. I was awakened by Suhuy's repeating my name.

"Merlin, Merlin," he said. "The sky is white."

"And I've a busy day," I answered. "I know. I'd a busy night, too."

"It reached you, then."

"What?"

"A small spell I sent, to open your mind to some enlightenment. I hoped to lead you to answers from within, rather than burden you with my guesswork and suspicions."

"I was back in the Corridor of Mirrors."

"I knew not what form it might take."

"Was it real?"

"As such things go, it should have been."

"Well, thanks—I guess. It reminds me that Gryll said something about your wanting to see me before my mother did."

"I wanted to see how much you knew before you faced her. I wanted to protect your freedom of choice."

"What are you saying?"

"I'm sure she wants to see you on the throne."

I sat up and rubbed my eyes.

"I suppose that's possible," I said.

"I don't know how far she's willing to go to effect this. I wanted to give you a chance to know your own mind before you're exposed to her plans. Would you care for a cup of tea?"

"Yes, thanks."

I accepted a mug he proffered and raised it to my lips.

"What are you saying about her beyond a guess at her wishes?" I asked. He shook his head.

"I don't know how active her program might be," he said, "if that is what you mean. And whether she was connected with it or another, the spell you came wearing has faded now."

"Your doing?"

He nodded.

I took another swallow.

"I never realized how close I'd gotten to the head of the line," I added. "Jurt *is* number four or five in the succession, isn't he?"

He nodded.

"I've a feeling it's going to be a very busy day," I said.

"Finish your tea," he told me, "and follow me when you would."

He walked away through a dragon tapestry on the far wall.

As I raised the mug again, the bright bracelet on my left wrist came free and drifted before me, losing its braided outline, becoming a circle of pure light. It hovered above the steaming brew, as if enjoying its cinnamony aroma.

"Hi, Ghost," I said. "Why'd you weave yourself about my wrist that way?"

"To look like that piece of rope you usually wear," came the reply. "I thought you must be fond of the effect."

"I mean, what were you up to the whole time?"

"Just listening, Dad. Seeing how I might be of help. These people are all your relatives, too?"

"The ones we've met so far, yes."

"Is it necessary to go back to Amber to speak ill of them?"

"No, it works here in the Courts, too." I took another sip of tea. "Any special ill you have in mind? Or was that a general question?"

"I don't trust your mother or your brother Mandor, even if they are my grandmother and uncle. I think they're setting you up for something."

"Mandor's always been good to me."

". . . And your uncle Suhuy—he seems eminently stable, but he reminds me a lot of Dworkin. Might he be sitting on all sorts of internal turmoils and ready to flip out anytime?"

"I hope not," I said. "He never has."

"Oh-oh, it's been building, and this is a time of stress."

"Where are you getting all this pop psychology, anyway?"

"I've been studying the great psychologists of the Shadow Earth. It's part of my ongoing attempt to understand the human condition. I realized it was time I learned more about the irrational parts."

"What brought all this on?"

"The higher order edition of the Pattern I encountered in the Jewel, actually. There were aspects of it I simply could not understand. This led to considerations of chaos theory, then to Menninger and all the others for its manifestations in consciousness."

"Any conclusions?"

"I am wiser therefor."

"I mean, concerning the Pattern."

"Yes. Either it possesses an element of irrationality itself, like living things, or it is an intelligence of such an order that some of its processes only seem irrational to lesser beings. Either explanation amounts to the same thing from a practical standpoint."

"I never had the opportunity to apply some of the tests I'd designed, but can you say from self-knowledge whether you fall into such a category yourself?"

"Me? Irrational? The notion never occurred to me. I can't see how it could be."

I finished my tea and swung my legs over the side of the bed.

"Too bad," I said. "I think some measure of it is what makes us truly human—that, and recognizing it in ourselves, of course."

"Really?"

I rose and began dressing myself.

"Yes, and controlling it within oneself may have something to do with intelligence and creativity."

"I'm going to have to study this very closely."

"Do that," I said, pulling on my boots, "and let me know your findings."

As I continued dressing, he asked, "When the sky turns blue you will breakfast with your brother Mandor?"

"Yes," I said.

"And later you will take lunch with your mother?"

"That's right."

"Later still, you will attend the late monarch's funeral?"

"I will."

"Will you need me to protect you?"

"I'll be safe with my relatives, Ghost. Even if you don't trust them."

"The last funeral you attended got bombed."

"That's true. But it was Luke, and he's sworn off. I'll be okay. You want to sightsee, go ahead."

"All right," he said. "I do."

I rose and crossed the chamber, to stand before the dragon.

"Can you tell me the way to the Logrus?" Ghost asked.

"Are you joking?"

"No," he stated. "I've seen the Pattern, but I've never seen the place of the Logrus. Where do they keep it?"

"I thought I gave you better memory functions than that. In your last encounter with the thing, you pissed it off in the max."

"I suppose I did. Do you think it would hold a grudge?"

"Offhand, yes. Upon consideration, yes. Stay away from it."

"You just advised me to study the chaos factor, the irrational."

"I didn't advise you to commit suicide. I put a lot of work into you."

"I value myself, too. And you know I have a survival imperative, the same as organic beings."

"It's your judgment I wonder about."

"You know a lot about my abilities."

"It's true you're good at getting the hell out of places."

"And you owe me a decent education."

"Let me think about it."

"That's just stalling. I suppose I can find it myself."

"Fine. Go ahead."

"It's that hard to locate?"

"You gave up on omniscience, remember?"

"Dad, I think I need to see it."

"I haven't the time to take you there."

"Just show me the way. I'm good at concealing myself."

"I'll give you that. All right. Suhuy is Keeper of the Logrus. It lies in a cavern—somewhere. The only way I know to it begins in this place."

"Where?"

"There are something like nine turnings involved. I'll lay a seeing upon you, to lead you."

"I don't know whether your spells would work on something like me—"

I reached out through the ring—pardon me, spikard—superimposed a series of black asterisks upon a map of the ways he must follow, hung it in the space of my Logrus vision before him, and I said, "I designed you, and I designed this spell."

"Uh, yes," Ghost replied. "I feel as if I suddenly possess data that I can't access."

"It will be presented to you at the appropriate times. Form yourself into the likeness of a ring upon my left index finger. We will quit this room in a moment and pass through others. When we are near the proper way I will indicate it by pointing. Proceed in that direction and you will pass through something along your route which will conduct you into another place. Somewhere in that vicinity you will find a black star indicating the next direction you must take—to another place and another star and so on. Eventually, you will emerge in a cavern that houses the Logrus. Conceal yourself as completely as you can and make your observations. When you wish to retreat, reverse the process."

He shrank himself and flew to my finger.

"Look me up later and let me know your experiences."

"I was planning to," came his tiny voice. "I would not wish to add to your probable present paranoia."

"Keep it up," I said.

I crossed the room and entered the dragon.

I emerged in a small sitting room, one window looking out over mountains; the other, a desert. There was no one about, and I stepped out into a long hallway. Yes, just as I recalled.

I moved along it, passing a number of other rooms, till I came to a door on my left, which I opened to discover a collection of mops, brooms, buckets,

brushes, a heap of cleaning cloths, a basin. Yes, as I remembered. I pointed to the shelves on my right.

"Find the black star," I said.

"You're serious?" came the small voice.

"Go and see."

A streak of light proceeded from my index finger, grew distorted as it neared the shelves, folded itself into a line so thin it was no longer present.

"Good luck," I breathed, and then I turned away.

I closed the door, wondering whether I had done the right thing, consoling myself with the thought that he would have gone looking and doubtless located the Logrus eventually, anyway. Whatever was to be on this front, would be. And I was curious as to what he might learn.

I turned and took myself back up the hallway to the little sitting room. It might be my last opportunity at being alone for a time, and I was determined to take advantage of it. I seated myself on a pile of cushions and withdrew my Trumps. A quick run through the deck turned up the one I had hastily sketched of Coral on that recent hectic day back in Amber. I studied her features till the card grew cold.

The image became three-dimensional, and then she slipped away and I saw myself, walking the streets of Amber on a bright afternoon, holding her hand as I led her around a knot of merchants. Then we were descending the face of Kolvir, sea bright before us, gulls passing. Then back in the cafe, table flying against the wall. . . .

I covered the card with my hand. She was asleep, dreaming. Odd, to enter another's dreams that way. Odder, to find myself there—unless, of course, the touch of my mind had prompted unconscious reminiscence. . . . One of life's smaller puzzles. No need to awaken the poor lady, just to ask her how she was feeling. I supposed I could call Luke and ask him how she was doing. I began searching for his card, then hesitated. He must be pretty busy, his first few days on the job as monarch. And I already knew she was resting. As I toyed with Luke's card, though, finally pushing it aside, the one beneath it was revealed.

Gray and silver and black. . . . His face was an older, somewhat harder version of my own. Corwin, my father, looked back at me. How many times had I sweated over that card, trying to reach him, till my mind tied itself into aching knots, with no result? The others had told me that it could mean he was dead, or that he was blocking the contact. And then a funny feeling came over me. I recalled his own story, in particular when he'd spoken of the times they had tried to reach Brand through his Trump, being at first unable to because he had been imprisoned in such a distant shadow. Then I remembered his own attempts to reach through to the Courts, and the difficulty imposed by the great distance. Supposing that, rather than being dead or blocking me, he was greatly removed from the places I had been when I had made the efforts?

But then, who was it had come to my aid that night in Shadow, bearing me to that peculiar place between shadows and the bizarre adventures that

befell me there? And though I was totally uncertain as to the nature of his appearance to me in the Corridor of Mirrors, I had later encountered indications of his presence in Amber Castle itself. If he'd been in any of those places, it would seem he hadn't really been too far off. And that would mean he'd simply been blocking me, and another attempt to reach him would probably prove equally fruitless. Still, what if there were some other explanation for all these occurrences and . . .

The card seemed to grow cold beneath my touch. Was it just my imagination, or was the strength of my regard beginning to activate it? I moved forward in my mind, focusing. It seemed to grow even colder as I did so.

"Dad?" I said. "Corwin?"

Colder still, and a tingling feeling in my fingertips that touched it. It seemed the beginning of a Trump contact. It could be that he was much nearer to the Courts than to Amber, within a more reachable range now. . . .

"Corwin," I repeated. "It's me, Merlin. Hello."

His image shifted, seemed to move. And then the card went totally black.

Yet, it remained cold, and a sensation like a silent version of contact was present, like a telephone connection during a long pause.

"Dad? Are you there?"

The blackness of the card took on the aspect of depth. And deep within it, something seemed to be stirring.

"Merlin?" The word was faint, yet I was certain it was his voice, speaking my name. "Merlin?"

The movement within the depth was real. Something was rushing toward me.

It erupted from the card into my face, with a beating of black wings, cawing, crow or raven, black, black.

"Forbidden!" it cried. "Forbidden! Go back! Withdraw!"

It flapped about my head as the cards spilled from my hand.

"Stay away!" it screeched, circling the room. "Forbidden place!"

It passed out the doorway and I pursued it. It seemed to have vanished, though, in the moments it was lost to my sight.

"Bird!" I cried. "Come back!"

But there was no reply, no further sounds of beating wings. I peered into the other rooms and there was no sign of the creature in any of them.

"Bird . . . ?"

"Merlin! What's the matter?"—this from high overhead.

I looked up to behold Suhuy, descending a crystal stair behind a quivering veil of light, a sky full of stars at his back.

"Just looking for a bird," I replied.

"Oh," he said, reaching the landing and stepping through the veil which then shook itself out of existence, taking the stair along with it. "Any particular bird?"

"A big black one," I said. "Of the talking sort."

He shook his head.

"I can send for one," he said.

"This was a special bird," I said.

"Sorry you lost it."

We walked out into the hallway and I turned left and headed back to the sitting room.

"Trumps all over the place," my uncle remarked.

"I was attempting to use one and it went black and the bird flew out of it, shouting, 'Forbidden'! I dropped them at that point."

"Sounds as if your correspondent is a practical joker," he said, "or under a spell."

We knelt and he helped me to gather them.

"The latter seems more likely," I said. "It was my father's card. I've been trying to locate him for a long while now, and this was the closest I've come. I actually heard his voice, within the blackout, before the bird interrupted and cut us off."

"Sounds as if he is confined to a dark place, perhaps magically guarded as well."

"Of course!" I said, squaring up the edges of my deck and recasing it.

One cannot shift the stuff of Shadow in a place of absolute darkness. It is as effective as blindness in stopping one of our blood from escaping confinement. It added an element of rationality to my recent experience. Someone wanting Corwin out of commission *would* have to keep him in a very dark place.

"Did you ever meet my father?" I asked.

"No," Suhuy replied. "I understand that he did visit the Courts briefly, at the end of the war. But I never had the pleasure."

"Did you hear anything of his doings here?"

"I believe he attended a meeting with Swayvill and his counselors, along with Random and the other Amberites, preliminary to the peace treaty. After that, I understand he went his own ways, and I never heard where they might have led him."

"I'd heard as much in Amber," I said. "I wonder. . . . He'd killed a noble—a Lord Borel—near the end of the final battle. Any chance Borel's relatives might have gone after him?"

He clicked his fangs twice, then pursed his lips.

"The House of Hendrake . . ." he mused. "I think not. Your grandmother was Hendrake. . . ."

"I know," I said. "But I didn't have much to do with them. Some disagreement with Helgram. . . ."

"Hendrake Ways is very much of the military sort," he went on. "Glory of battle. Martial honor, you know. I can't see them as holding a peacetime grudge for a wartime happening."

Recalling my father's story, I said, "Even if they considered the killing less than honorable?"

"I don't know," he said to that. "It's hard to guess attitudes on specific questions."

"Who is head of the House of Hendrake now?"

"The Duchess Belissa Minobee."

"The duke, her husband—Larsus. . . . What happened to him?"

"He died at Patternfall. I believe Prince Julian of Amber slew him."

"And Borel was their son?"

"Yes."

"Ouch. Two of them. I didn't realize."

"Borel had two brothers, a half brother and a half sister, many uncles, aunts, cousins. Yes, it's a big House. And the women of Hendrake are as doughty as the men."

"Yes, of course. There are songs, such as 'Never Wed a Hendrake Lass.' Any way of finding out whether Corwin had any doings with Hendrake while he was here?"

"One could ask about a bit, though it's been a long while. Memories fade, trails grow cold. Not easy."

He shook his head.

"How long till bluesky?" I asked him.

"Fairly soon," he said.

"I'd better be heading for Mandorways then. I promised my brother I'd breakfast with him."

"I'll see you later," he said. "At the funeral, if not before."

"Yes," I said. "I guess I'd better clean up and change clothes."

I headed back through the way to my room, where I summoned a basin of water, soap, toothbrush, razor; also, gray trousers, black boots and belt, purple shirt and gloves, charcoal cloak, fresh blade and scabbard. When I had made myself presentable, I took a way through a forested glade to the receiving room. From there, I exited onto a thruway. A quarter mile of mountain trail later, ending abruptly at a chasm, I summoned a filmy and crossed upon it. Then I bore right to Mandorways, traveling a blue beach beneath a double sun for perhaps a hundred yards. I turned right, passing through a remembered archway of stone, moving briefly past a bubbling lava field and through a black obsidian wall, which took me to a pleasant cavern, over a small bridge, through a corner of a graveyard, a few steps along the Rim and into the receiving area of his Ways.

The entire wall to my left was composed of slow flame; that to my right, a non-returnable way, save for light, giving sight of some sea-bottom trench where bright things moved about and ate one another. Mandor was seated humanformed before a bookcase directly ahead, wearing black and white, feet propped on a black ottoman, a copy of Robert Hass's *Praise*, which I had given him, in his hand.

He smiled as he looked up.

" 'Death's hounds feared me,' " he said. "Nice line, that. How are you this cycle?"

"Rested, finally," I said. "Yourself?"

He placed the book upon a small, legless table that floated near just then, and rose to his feet. The fact that he had obviously been reading it because

I was coming in no way detracted from the compliment. He had always been that way.

"Quite well, thank you," he replied. "Come, let me feed you."

He took my arm and steered me toward the wall of fire. It fell away as we drew near and our footsteps sounded in a place of momentary darkness, succeeded almost immediately by a small lane, sunlight filtered through arching branches overhead, violets blooming at either hand. The lane took us to a flagged patio, a green and white gazebo at its farther end. We mounted a few stairs to a well-set table within, frosted pitchers of juice and baskets of warm rolls near at hand. He gestured and I seated myself. At his gesture a carafe of coffee appeared beside my setting.

"I see you recall my morning predeliction," I said, "from the Shadow Earth. Thank you."

He smiled faintly as he nodded, seating himself across from me. Birdsongs I could not identify sounded from the trees. A gentle breeze caused leaves to rustle.

"What are you up to these days?" I asked him as I poured a cup of coffee and broke a roll.

"Observing the scene, mainly," he replied.

"Political scene?"

"As always. Though my recent experience in Amber has led me to regard it as part of an even larger picture."

I nodded.

"And your investigations with Fiona?"

"Those, too," he answered. "These are shaping up into very unusual times."

"I've noticed."

"It seems almost as if the Pattern-Logrus conflict were making itself manifest in mundane affairs, as well as on the cosmic scale."

"I feel that way, too. But then I'm prejudiced. I got caught up in the cosmic part early, and without a scorecard. I've been run all over the place and manipulated every which way recently—to the point where all of my affairs seemed part of their bigger picture. I don't like it a bit, and if I had some way to make them back off I'd use it."

"Hm," he said. "And what if your whole life were a study in manipulation?"

"I wouldn't feel good about it," I said. "I guess I'd feel just the way I do now, only perhaps more intensely."

He gestured and an amazing omelet appeared before me, followed, moments later, by a side dish of fried potatoes, mixed with what appeared to be green chilies and onions.

"All of this is hypothetical," I said as I began eating, "isn't it?"

There followed a long pause as he took his first mouthful, then, "I think not," he said.

"I think the Powers have been moving madly for a long while now," he went on, "and we're finally nearing endgame."

"What makes you privy to these matters?"

"It began with a careful consideration of events," he said. "Then followed the formulation and testing of hypotheses."

"Spare me a lecture on the use of the scientific method in theology and human politics," I said.

"You asked."

"True. Go ahead."

"Do you not feel it somewhat odd that Swayvill expired just when he did, when so many things are coming to fruition simultaneously, after having hung on for so long?"

"He had to go sometime," I said, "and all the recent stresses probably proved too much."

"Timing," Mandor said. "Strategic placement. Timing."

"For what?"

"To place you on the throne of Chaos, of course," he replied.

FOUR

Sometimes you hear an unlikely thing and that's all it is. Other times, you hear something improbable and it strikes an echo. There is an immediate feeling of having known it, or known something very like it, all along, and just not having bothered to pick it up and examine it. By rights, I should have choked at Mandor's pronouncement, then snorted something such as "Preposterous!" Yet, I'd a peculiar feeling about this business—whether his conclusion was right or wrong—as if there were something more than conjecture involved, as if there just might be some overall plan moving me toward the circle of power in the Courts.

I took a long, slow drink of coffee. Then, "Really?" I said.

I felt myself smiling as he sought my eyes, studied my face.

"Are you consciously party to the effort?"

I raised my coffee cup again. I had been about to say, "No, of course not. This is the first I've heard of the notion." Then I recalled my father's telling me how he had duped Aunt Flora into giving him vital information his amnesia had washed away. It was not the cleverness with which he had done it that had impressed me so much as the fact that his mistrust of relatives transcended consciousness, existed as a pure existential reflex. Not having been through all the family rivalries Corwin had, I lacked responses of such intensity. And Mandor and I had always gotten along particularly well, even though he was a few centuries older and had very different tastes in some areas. But, suddenly, discussing such a high-stakes matter as we were, that small voice Corwin referred to as his worse-if-wiser self suggested, "Why not? You could use the practice, kid," and as I lowered the cup again I decided to try it out, just to see how it felt, for a few minutes.

"I don't know whether we both have the same thing in mind," I said.

"Why don't you tell me about the middle game—or perhaps even the opening—for what you see rushing to conclusion now."

"Both the Pattern and the Logrus are sentient," he said. "We've both seen evidence of that. Whether they are manifestations of the Unicorn and the Serpent or the other way around makes no real difference. Either way, we are talking about a pair of greater-than-human intelligences with vast powers at their disposal. Whichever came first is also one of those useless theological points. We need only concern ourselves with the present situation, as it affects us."

I nodded.

"A fair assessment," I agreed.

"The forces they represent have been opposed but fairly evenly matched for ages," he went on, "and thus a kind of balance has been maintained. They have constantly sought small victories over each other, each attempting to add to its own domain at the expense of the other. It appears to be a zero-sum game. Both Oberon and Swayvill were their agents for a long while, with Dworkin and Suhuy as their intermediaries with the powers themselves."

"So?" I said as he took a sip of juice.

"I believe that Dworkin had touched the Pattern too closely," he continued, "and so became subject to manipulation. He was sufficiently sophisticated, however, that he realized this and resisted. This resulted in his madness, with a reciprocal damaging effect on the Pattern itself because of their close connection. This, in turn, caused the Pattern to leave him alone, rather than risk further trauma. The damage was done, though, and the Logrus gained a small edge. This allowed it to act in the realm of order when Prince Brand began his experiments to increase his personal abilities. I believe he laid himself open to control and became an unwitting agent of the Logrus."

"That's a lot of supposition," I said.

"Consider," he responded, "that his aims seemingly became those of a madman. They make much more sense when seen as the goal of something wanting to destroy all order, to restore the universe to chaos."

"Continue," I said.

"At some point, the Pattern discovered—or perhaps possessed all along—the ability to create 'ghosts,' short-lived simulacra of those who had negotiated it. Fascinating concept, that. I was very interested to learn of it. It provided a major mechanism, supporting my thesis of the Pattern's and possibly the Logrus's, direct action in the promotion of physical events. Might they have figured in the setting up of your father as the Pattern's champion against Brand? I wonder."

"I don't follow," I said. "Setting him up, you say?"

"I've a feeling he was really the Pattern's choice as the next King of Amber, easy to promote, too, as it seemed to coincide with his own wishes. I've wondered about his sudden recovery in that Shadow Earth clinic, and particularly about the circumstances surrounding the accident that put him there, when even with differing time streams it seemed possible that Brand might have had to be in two places at the same time—imprisoned and looking

down the sights of a rifle. Of course, Brand is no longer available to clarify the matter."

"More supposition," I said, finishing my omelet. "But not uninteresting. Please continue."

"Your father had second thoughts about the throne, however. Still, he *was* Amber's champion. Amber *did* win the war. The Pattern *was* repaired. The balance *was* restored. Random was the second choice as monarch—a good maintainer of the status quo—and that choice *was* made by the Unicorn, not by the Amberites following any of their versions of the Rules of Succession."

"I never looked at it all that way," I said.

"And your father—inadvertently, I believe—provided a bonus. Afraid that the Pattern had not been repaired, he drew another. Only, it *had* been repaired. Thus, there were two artifacts of order, rather than one. Though, as a separate entity, it probably did not add to the Pattern's strength, it added to order, as such, diminishing the effects of the Logrus. So your father set the balance right, then proceeded to tip it again—in the other direction."

"This is your conclusion from the investigations you and Fiona made of the new Pattern?"

He nodded slowly, took a sip of juice.

"Hence, more Shadow storms than usual, as a mundane effect," he said, "bringing us up to present times."

"Yes, present times," I said, pouring more coffee. "We've noted they've grown interesting."

"Indeed. Your story of the girl Coral, asking the Pattern to send her to an appropriate place, is a case in point. What did it immediately do? It sent her to a Shadow Pattern and turned out the lights. Then it sent you to rescue her, repairing that edition of itself in the process. Once it was repaired it was no longer a Shadow Pattern, but another version of itself that it was then able to absorb. It probably absorbed that entire shadow as well, adding considerably to its own energies. Its edge over the Logrus increased even more. The Logrus would need a big gain to restore the balance after that. So it risked an incursion into the Pattern's domain, in a desperate effort to obtain the Eye of Chaos. That ended in a stalemate, though, because of the intervention of that bizarre entity you call Ghostwheel. So the balance remains tipped in the Pattern's favor, an unhealthy state of affairs."

"For the Logrus."

"For everybody, I'd say. The Powers will be at odds, the shadows in turmoil and disorder in both realms till things have been righted."

"So something should be done to benefit the Logrus?"

"You already know that."

"I suppose I do."

"It communicated with you directly, didn't it?"

I recalled my night in the chapel in the place between shadows, where I had been faced with a choice between the Serpent and the Unicorn, the

Logrus and the Pattern. Resenting the bullying in such a forced format, I had refused to choose either.

"Yes, it did," I answered.

"It wanted you for its champion, didn't it?"

"I suppose it did," I said.

"And . . . ?"

". . . And here we are," I replied.

"Did it indicate anything that might support my thesis?"

I thought about that trek through the Undershadow, mixing menace with ghosts—Pattern, Logrus, or both.

"I suppose it did," I repeated.

But, ultimately, it had been the Pattern I had served at the end of that journey, albeit unwittingly.

"You are prepared to execute its design for the good of the Courts?"

"I'm prepared to seek resolution of this matter, for everybody's peace of mind."

He smiled.

"Is that a qualification or an agreement?"

"It's a statement of intent," I said.

"If the Logrus has chosen you, it has its reasons."

"I daresay."

"It almost goes without saying that having you on the throne would strengthen the House of Sawall immensely."

"The thought had occurred to me, now that you mention it."

"For one with your background, of course, it would become necessary to determine where your ultimate loyalty lies—with Amber or with the Courts."

"Do you foresee another war?"

"No, of course not. But anything you do to strengthen the Logrus will arouse the Pattern and provoke some response from Amber. Hardly to the point of war, but possibly to that of retaliation."

"Could you be more specific as to what you have in mind?"

"I'm only dealing in generalities at the moment, to give you opportunity to assess your reactions."

I nodded.

"Since we're talking generalities I'll just repeat my statement: I'm prepared to seek a resolution—"

"All right," he said. "We understand each other to this extent. In the event you make it to the throne, you want the same thing we do—"

" 'We'?" I interrupted.

"The House of Sawall, of course. But you don't want anyone dictating specifics to you."

"That says it nicely," I replied.

"But of course we're speaking hypothetically, there being a couple of others about with stronger claims."

"So why argue contingencies?"

"If the House were able to see you crowned, however, do you acknowledge you would owe consideration for this?"

"Brother," I said, "you *are* the House, for all major purposes. If you're asking for a commitment before taking out Tmer and Tubble, forget it, I'm not all that eager to sit on a throne."

"Your wishes are not paramount in this," he said. "There is no reason for squeamishness when you consider that we've long been at odds with Jesby, and Chanicut's always been a troublemaker."

"Squeamishness has nothing to do with it," I said. "I never said I wanted the throne. And, frankly, I think either Tmer or Tubble would probably do a better job."

"They are not designates of the Logrus."

"And if I am, I should make it without any help."

"Brother, there is a big gap between its world of principles and ours of flesh, stone, and steel."

"And supposing I have my own agenda and it does not include your plan?"

"What is it, then?"

"We're speaking hypothetically, remember?"

"Merlin, you're being obstinate. You've a duty in this, to the House as well as to the Courts and the Logrus."

"I can assess my own duties, Mandor, and I have — so far."

"If you've a plan to set things right, and it's a good one, we'll help you to effectuate it. What have you in mind?"

"I do not require help at this point," I said, "but I'll remember that."

"What do you require right now?"

"Information," I said.

"Ask me. I have a lot."

"All right. What can you tell me about my mother's maternal side, the House of Hendrake?"

He pursed his lips.

"They're into soldiering, professionally," he said. "You know they're always off fighting in Shadow wars. They love it. Belissa Minobee's been in charge since General Larsus's death. Hm." He paused. Then, "Do you ask because of their rather odd fixation involving Amber?"

"Amber?" I said. "What do you mean?"

"I recall a social visit to the Ways of Hendrake one time," he said, "when I wandered into a small, chapel-like room. In a niche in one wall there hung a portrait of General Benedict, in full battle regalia. There was an altarlike shelf below it bearing several weapons, and upon which a number of candles were burning. Your mother's picture was there, too."

"Really?" I said. "I wonder whether Benedict knows? Dara once told my father she was descended from Benedict. Later, he figured this an out-and-out lie. . . . Do you think people like that would hold a grudge against my father?"

"For what?"

"Corwin slew Borel of Hendrake at the time of the Patternfall War."

"They tend to take such things philosophically."

"Still, I gather it was a somewhat less than kosher engagement from the way he described it—though I don't believe there were any witnesses."

"So let sleeping wyverns lie."

"I've no intention of rousing them. But what I was wondering was that if they had somehow heard details they might have been out to clear some debt of honor on his behalf. Do you think they could have been behind his disappearance?"

"I just don't know," he replied, "how that would fit in with their code. I suppose you could ask them."

"Just come out and say, 'Hey, are you responsible for whatever happened to my dad?' "

"There are more subtle ways of learning a person's attitudes," he responded. "As I recall, you had a few lessons in them in your youth."

"But I don't even know these people. I mean, I might have met one of the sisters at a party, now I think of it—and I recall having seen Larsus and his wife in the distance a few times—but that's it."

"Hendrake will have a representative at the funeral," he said. "If I were to introduce you, perhaps you could apply a little glamour to obtain an informal audience."

"You know, that may be the way to go," I told him. "Probably the only way. Yes, do that, please."

"Very well."

He cleared the table with a gesture, filled it with another. This time, paper-thin crepes with a variety of fillings and toppings appeared before us; and fresh rolls, variously spiced. We ate for a time in silence, appreciating the balminess and the birds, the breezes.

"I wish I could have seen something of Amber," he said at length, "under less restricted circumstances."

"I'm sure that can be arranged," I replied. "I'd like to show you around. I know a great restaurant in Death Alley."

"That wouldn't be Bloody Eddie's, would it?"

"It would, though the name gets changed periodically."

"I've heard of it, and long been curious."

"We'll do that one day."

"Excellent."

He clapped his hands and bowls of fruit appeared. I freshened my coffee and swirled a Kadota fig in a bowl of whipped cream.

"I'll be dining with my mother later," I remarked.

"Yes. I overheard."

"Have you seen much of her recently? How's she been?"

"As she said, rather reclusive," he replied.

"Do you think she's up to something?"

"Probably," he said. "I can't recall a time when she hasn't been."

"Any idea what?"

"Why should I guess when she'll probably tell you outright?"

"You really think she will?"

"You have an advantage over everyone else, in being her son."

"Also a drawback, for the same reason."

"Still, she's more likely to tell you things than she would anyone else."

"Except, perhaps, Jurt."

"Why do you say that?"

"She always liked him better."

"Funny, I've heard him say the same thing about you."

"You see him often?"

"Often? No."

"When was the last time?"

"About two cycles ago."

"Where is he?"

"Here, in the Courts."

"At Sawall?" I had visions of him joining us for lunch. I wouldn't put something like that past Dara either.

"One of its byways, I think. He's rather reticent concerning his comings and goings—and stayings."

There being something like eight byway residences to Sawall that I knew of, it would be difficult to run him down through byways that could lead well into Shadow. Not that I'd any desire to, at the moment.

"What brings him home?" I asked.

"The same thing as yourself, the funeral," he said, "and all that goes with it."

All that goes with it, indeed! If there were a genuine plot to put me on the throne, I could never forget that—willing or unwilling, successful or unsuccessful—Jurt would be a step or two behind me all the way.

"I may have to kill him," I said. "I don't want to. But he's not giving me a whole lot of choice. Sooner or later, he's going to force us into a position where it has to be one or the other."

"Why do you tell me this?"

"So you'll know how I feel about it, and so that you might use whatever influence you may still have to persuade him to find a different hobby."

He shook his head.

"Jurt moved beyond my influence a long time ago," he said. "Dara's about the only one he'll listen to—though I suspect he's still afraid of Suhuy. You might speak to her concerning this matter, soon."

"It's the one thing neither of us can discuss with her—the other."

"Why not?"

"It's just the way it is. She always misunderstands."

"I'm certain she's not going to want her sons killing each other."

"Of course not, but I don't know how to put the matter to her."

"I suggest you make an effort to find a way. In the meantime, I would contrive not to be alone with Jurt, should your paths cross. And if it were me,

in the presence of witnesses, I would make certain that the first blow was not mine."

"Well taken, Mandor," I said.

We sat for a time in silence. Then, "You will think about my proposal," he said.

"As I understand it," I replied.

He frowned.

"If you have any questions. . . ."

"No. I'll be thinking."

He rose. I got to my feet, also. With a gesture, he cleared the table. Then he turned away and I followed him out of the gazebo and across its yard to the trail.

We emerged after a stroll in his external study cum receiving room. He squeezed my shoulder as we headed for the exit.

"I'll see you at the funeral then," he remarked.

"Yes," I said. "Thanks for the breakfast."

"By the way, how well do you like that lady, Coral?" he asked.

"Oh, pretty well," I said. "She's quite—nice. Why?"

He shrugged.

"Just curious. I was concerned about her, having been present at the time of her misadventure, and I wondered how much she meant to you."

"Enough that it bothers me a lot," I said.

"I see. Well, give her my good wishes if you should talk to her."

"Thanks, I will."

"We'll talk again later."

"Yes."

I strode into the way, making no haste. I still had considerable time before I was due by the Ways of Sawall.

I paused when I came to a gibbet-shaped tree. A moment's reflection and I turned left, following an ascending trail among dark rocks. Near its top, I walked directly into a mossy boulder, emerging from a sandbank into a light rain. I ran across the field before me, till I came to the fairy circle beneath the ancient tree. I stepped to its middle, made up a couplet with my name for the rhyme, and sank into the ground. When I was halted and the moment's darkness went away, I found myself beside a damp stone wall, looking downhill across a prospect of headstones and monuments. The sky was fully overcast and a cool breeze wandered by. It felt to be one of the ends of a day, but whether morning or twilight lay near, I could not tell. The place looked exactly as I remembered it—cracked mausoleums hung with ivy, falling stone fences, wandering paths beneath high, dark trees. I moved down familiar trails.

As a child, this had been a favored playground of mine, for a time. I met here almost daily, for dozens of cycles, with a little shadow girl named Rhanda. Kicking through boneheaps, brushing by damp shrubbery, I came at length to the damaged mausoleum where we had played house. Pushing aside the sagging gate, I entered.

Nothing had changed, and I found myself chuckling. The cracked cups

and saucers, tarnished utensils, were still stacked in the corner, heavy with dust, stained with seepage. I brushed off the catafalque we'd used as a table, seated myself upon it. One day Rhanda had simply stopped coming, and after a time I had, too. I'd often wondered what sort of woman she had become. I'd left her a note in our hiding place, beneath a loose floor stone, I recalled. I wondered whether she'd ever found it.

I raised the stone. My filthy envelope still lay there, unsealed. I took it out, shook it off, slid out my folded sheet.

I unfolded it, read my faded childish scrawl: *What happened Rhanda? I waited and you didn't come.* Beneath it, in a far neater hand, was written: *I can't come anymore because my folks say you are a demon or a vampire. I'm sorry because you are the nicest demon or vampire I know.* I'd never thought of that possibility. Amazing, the ways one can be misunderstood.

I sat there for a time, remembering growing up. I'd taught Rhanda the bonedance game in here. I snapped my fingers then, and our old ensorcelled heap of them across the way made a sound like stirring leaves. My juvenile spell was still in place; the bones rolled forward, arranged themselves into a pair of manikins, began their small, awkward dance. They circled each other, barely holding their shapes, pieces flaking away, cobwebs trailing; loose ones— spares—began to bounce about them. They made tiny clicking sounds as they touched. I moved them faster.

A shadow crossed the doorway, and I heard a chuckle.

"I'll be damned! All you need's a tin roof. So this is how they spend their time in Chaos."

"Luke!" I exclaimed as he stepped inside, my manikins collapsing as my attention left them, into little gray, sticklike heaps. "What are you doing here?"

"Could say I was selling cemetery lots," he observed. "You interested in one?"

He had on a red shirt and brown khakis tucked into his brown suede boots. A tan cloak hung about his shoulders. He was grinning.

"Why aren't you off ruling?"

His smile went away, to be replaced by a moment of puzzlement, returned almost instantly.

"Oh, felt I needed a break. What about you? There's a funeral soon, isn't there?"

I nodded.

"Later on," I said. "I'm just taking a break myself. How'd you get here, anyway?"

"Followed my nose," he said. "Needed some intelligent conversation."

"Be serious. Nobody knew I was coming here. I didn't even know it till the last minute. I—"

I groped about in my pockets.

"You didn't plant another of those blue stones on me, did you?"

"No, nothing that simple," he replied. "I seem to have some sort of message for you."

I got to my feet, approached him, studying his face.

"Are you okay, Luke?"

"Sure. As okay as I ever am, that is."

"It's no mean stunt, finding your way this near to the Courts. Especially if you've never been here before. How'd you manage it?"

"Well, the Courts and I go back a long ways, old buddy. You might say it's in my—blood."

He moved aside from the doorway and I stepped outside. Almost automatically, we began walking.

"I don't understand what you're saying," I told him.

"Well, my dad spent some time here, back in his plotting days," he said. "It's where he met my mother."

"I didn't know that."

"It never came up. We never talked family, remember?"

"Yeah," I said, "and no one I asked seemed to know where Jasra came from. Still, the Courts. . . . She's a long way from home."

"Actually, she was recruited from a nearby shadow," he explained, "like this one."

"Recruited?"

"Yes, she worked as a servant for a number of years—I think she was fairly young when she started—at the Ways of Helgram."

"Helgram? That's my mother's House!"

"Right. She was a maid-companion to the lady Dara. That's where she learned the Arts."

"Jasra got her instruction in sorcery from my mother? And she met Brand at Helgram? That would make it seem Helgram had something to do with Brand's plot, the Black Road, the war—"

"—and the Lady Dara going looking for your father? I guess so."

"Because she wanted to be a Pattern initiate as well as one of the Logrus?"

"Maybe," he said. "I wasn't present."

We moved down a gravelly trail, turned at a huge cluster of dark shrubbery, passing through a forest of stone and over a bridge that crossed a slow black stream that reflected high branches and sky, monochrome. A few leaves rustled in a stray breeze.

"How come you never mentioned any of this later?" I asked.

"I intended to, but it never seemed urgent," he said, "whereas a lot of other things did."

"True," I said. "The pace did seem to keep picking up each time our trails crossed. But now—Are you saying it's urgent now, that I suddenly need to know this?"

"Oh, not exactly." He halted. He reached out and leaned upon a headstone. His hand began to grip it, growing white about the knuckles, across the back. The stone at his fingertips was ground to powder, fell snowlike to the earth. "Not exactly," he repeated. "That part was my idea, just because I wanted you to know. Maybe it'll do you some good, maybe it won't. Information is like that. You never know." With a crunching, cracking sound, the top of the headstone suddenly gave way. Luke hardly seemed to notice this,

and his hand kept on squeezing. Small pieces fell from the larger one he now held.

"So you came all this way to tell me that?"

"No," he answered, as we turned and began walking back the way we had come. "I was sent to tell you something else, and it's been pretty hard holding off. But I figured if I talked about this first, it couldn't let me go, would keep feeding me till I got around to the message."

There came a huge crunch, and the stone he held turned to gravel, falling to mix with that on the trail.

"Let me see your hand."

He brushed it off and held it out. A tiny flame flickered near the base of his index finger. He ran his thumb over it and it went out. I increased my pace, and he matched it.

"Luke, you know what you are?"

"Something in me seems to, but I don't, man. I just feel—I'm not right. I'd probably better tell you what I feel I should pretty quick now."

"No. Hold off," I said, hurrying even more.

Something dark passed overhead, too quick for me to make out its shape, vanishing among the trees. We were buffeted by a sudden gust of wind.

"You know what's going on, Merle?" he asked.

"I think so," I said, "and I want you to do exactly what I tell you, no matter how weird it might seem. Okay?"

"Sure thing. If I can't trust a Lord of Chaos, who can I trust, eh?"

We hurried past the clump of shrubs. My mausoleum was just up ahead.

"You know, there really is something I feel obliged to tell you right now, though," he said.

"Hold it. Please."

"It is important, though."

I ran on ahead of him. He began running, too, to keep up.

"It's about your being here at the Courts, just now."

I extended my hands, used them to brake myself when I came up against the wall of the stone building. I swung myself through the doorway and inside. Three big steps, and I was kneeling in the corner, snatching up an old cup, using the corner of my cloak to wipe it out.

"Merle, what the hell are you doing?" Luke asked, entering behind me.

"Just a minute and I'll show you," I told him, drawing my dagger.

Placing the cup upon the stone where I had been seated earlier, I held my hand above it and used the dagger to cut my wrist.

Instead of blood, flame came forth from the incision.

"No! Damn it!" I cried.

And I reached into the spikard, located the proper line, and found the flowing channel of a cooling spell that I laid upon the wound. Immediately, the flames died and it was blood that flowed from me. However, as it fell into the cup it began to smoke. Cursing, I extended the spell to control its liquidity there, also.

"Yeah, it's weird, Merle. I'll give you that," Luke observed.

I laid the dagger aside and used my right hand to squeeze my arm above the wound. The blood flowed faster. The spikard throbbed. I glanced at Luke. There was a look of strain upon his face. I pumped my fist. The cup was more than half-full.

"You said you trust me," I stated.

"Afraid so," he answered.

Three-quarters. . . .

"You've got to drink this, Luke," I said. "I mean it."

"Somehow, I suspected you were leading up to this," he said, "and, really, it doesn't sound like such a bad idea. I've a feeling I need a lot of help just now."

He reached out and took the cup, raised it to his lips. I pressed the palm of my hand against the wound. Outside, the winds were gusting regularly.

"When you've finished, put it back," I said. "You're going to need more."

I could hear the sounds of his swallowing.

"Better than a slug of Jameson," he said then. "Don't know why." He replaced the cup on the stone. "A little salty, though," he added.

I removed my hand from the incision, held the wrist above it again, pumped my fist.

"Hey, man. You're losing a lot of blood there. I feel okay now. Was just a little dizzy, that's all. I don't need any more."

"Yes, you do," I said. "Believe me. I gave a lot more than this in a blood drive once and ran in a meet the next day. It's okay."

The wind rose to a gale, moaning past us now.

"Mind telling me what's going on?" he asked.

"Luke, you're a Pattern ghost," I told him.

"What do you mean?"

"The Pattern can duplicate anybody who ever walked it. You've got all the signs. I know them."

"Hey, I feel real. I didn't even do the Pattern in Amber. I did it in Tir-na Nog'th."

"Apparently, it controls the two images as well, since they're true copies. Do you remember your coronation in Kashfa?"

"Coronation? Hell no! You mean I made it to the throne?"

"Yep. Rinaldo the First."

"God damn! Bet Mom's happy."

"I'm sure."

"This is kind of awkward then, there being two of me. You seem familiar with the phenomenon. How does the Pattern handle it?"

"You guys tend not to last very long. It seems the closer you are to the Pattern itself the stronger you are, too. It must have taken a lot of juice to project you this far. Here, drink this."

"Sure."

He tossed off a half cupful and handed the cup back.

"So what's with the precious bodily fluids?" he asked.

"The blood of Amber seems to have a sustaining effect on Pattern ghosts."

"You mean I'm some kind of vampire?"

"I suppose you could put it that way, in a sort of technical sense."

"I'm not sure I like that—especially such a specialized one."

"It does seem to have certain drawbacks. But one thing at a time. Let's get you stabilized before we start looking for angles."

"All right. You've got a captive audience."

There came a rattle, as of a rolled stone, from outside, followed by a small clanking noise.

Luke turned his head.

"I don't think that's just the wind," he stated.

"Take the last sip," I said, moving away from the cup and groping after my handkerchief. "It'll have to hold you."

He tossed it off as I wrapped my wrist. He knotted it in place for me.

"Let's get out of here," I said. "The vibes are getting bad."

"Fine with me," he replied as a figure appeared at the doorway. It was backlighted, its features lost in shadow.

"You're not going anywhere, Pattern ghost," came an almost-familiar voice.

I willed the spikard to about 150 watts illumination.

It was Borel, showing his teeth in an unfriendly fashion.

"You are about to become a very large candle, Patterner," he said to Luke.

"You're wrong, Borel," I said, raising the spikard.

Suddenly, the Sign of the Logrus swam between us.

"Borel? The master swordsman?" Luke inquired.

"The same," I answered.

"Oh, shit!" Luke said.

FIVE

As I probed forward with two of the more lethal energies of the spikard the Logrus image intercepted them and turned them off.

"I didn't save him for you to take him out this easily," I said, and just then something like the image of the Pattern but not really the same flashed into existence nearby.

The Sign of the Logrus slid to my left. The new thing—whatever it was—kept pace with it, both of them passing silently through the wall. Almost immediately, there followed a thunderclap that shook the building. Even Borel, who was reaching for his blade, paused in mid-gesture, then moved his hand to catch hold of the doorway. As he did this, another figure appeared at his back and a familiar voice addressed him: "Please excuse me. You're blocking my way."

"Corwin!" I cried. "Dad!"

Borel turned his head.

"Corwin, Prince of Amber?" he said.

"Indeed," came the reply, "though I'm afraid I haven't had the pleasure."

"I am Borel, Duke of Hendrake, Master of Arms of the Ways of Hendrake."

"You speak with a lot of capitals, sir, and I'm pleased to make your acquaintance," Corwin said. "Now, if you don't mind, I'd like to get through here to see my son."

Borel's hand moved to the hilt of his blade as he turned. I was already moving forward by then, and so was Luke. But there was a movement beyond Borel—a kick, it seemed, low—causing him to expel a lot of air and double forward. Then a fist descended upon the back of his neck and he fell.

"Come on," Corwin called, gesturing. "I think we'd better get out of here."

Luke and I emerged, stepping over the fallen Master of Arms of the Ways of Hendrake. The ground off to the left was blackened, as if from a recent brushfire, and a light rain had begun to fall. There were other human figures in the distance now, moving toward us.

"I don't know whether the force that brought me here can get me out again," Corwin said, looking about. "It may be otherwise occupied." Several moments passed, then, "I guess it is," he said. "Okay, it's up to you. How do we flee?"

"This way," I told him, turning and breaking into a run.

They followed me up the trails that had brought me to this place. I looked back and saw that six dark figures pursued us.

I headed uphill, past the markers and monuments, coming at last to the place beside the old stone wall. By then, there were shouts from behind us. Ignoring them, I drew my companions to me and came up with an impromptu couplet that described the situation and my desire in somewhat less than perfect meter. Still, the charm held, and a hurled cobble only missed me because we were already sinking into the earth.

We emerged from the fairy ring, coming up like mushrooms, and I led my companions across the field, jogging, to the sandbank. As we entered there I heard another shout. We exited the boulder and descended the rocky trail to the gibbet tree. Turning left on the trail, I began to run.

"Hold up!" Corwin called. "I feel it around here somewhere. There!"

He left the trail to the right and began running toward the base of a small hill. Luke and I followed. From behind us came the sounds of our pursuers' emergence from the way at the boulder.

Ahead, I saw something flickering between two trees. We seemed to be heading toward it. As we drew nearer, its outline became clearer, and I realized that it possessed the contours of that Pattern-like image I had beheld back in the mausoleum.

Dad did not break stride as he approached, but charged right into the thing. And vanished. Another cry rose up behind us. Luke was next through the shimmering screen, and I was close on his heels.

We were running through a straight, glowing, pearly tunnel now, and when I glanced back I saw that it seemed to be closing in behind me.

"They can't follow," Corwin shouted. "That end's already closed."

"Then why are we running?" I asked.

"We're still not safe," he replied. "We're cutting through the Logrus's domain. If we're spotted there could still be trouble."

We raced on through that strange tunnel, and, "We're running through Shadow?" I asked.

"Yes."

"Then it would seem that the farther we go, the better—"

The whole thing shook, and I had to put out a hand to keep from being thrown down.

"Oh-oh," Luke said.

"Yes," I agreed as the tunnel began to come apart. Big chunks seemed to be torn out of the walls, the floor. There was only murk behind these rents. We kept going, leaping the openings. Then something struck again, soundlessly, completely shattering the entire passage—around us, behind us, before us.

We fell.

Well, we didn't exactly fall. We sort of drifted in a twilit fog. There didn't seem to be anything underfoot, or in any other direction either. It was a free-fall sensation, with nothing to measure possible movement against.

"Damn!" I heard Corwin say.

We hovered, fell, drifted—whatever—for a time, and, "So close," I heard him mutter.

"Something that way," Luke suddenly announced, gesturing to his right.

A big shape loomed grayly. I moved my mind into the spikard and probed in that direction. Whatever it was, it was inanimate, and I commanded the spike that had touched it to guide us to it.

I did not feel myself moving, but the thing loomed larger, took on familiar outlines, began to show a reddish complexion. When the fins became apparent, I knew for certain.

"Looks like that Polly Jackson you have," Luke remarked. "Even has the snow on it."

Yes, it was my red and white '57 Chevy that we were approaching, there in Limbo.

"It's a construct. It's been pulled from my mind before," I told him. "Probably because it's vivid, I've studied it so often. Also, it seems very appropriate just now."

I reached toward the door handle. We were coming up on the driver's side. I caught hold and pushed the button. It was, of course, unlocked. The others touched the vehicle in various places and drew themselves along to the other side. I opened the door, slid in behind the wheel, closed the door. Luke and Corwin were entering by then. The keys were in the ignition, as I'd expected.

When everyone was aboard I tried starting it. The engine caught immediately. I stared out across the bright hood into nothingness. I switched on the headlights and that didn't help.

"What now?" Luke asked.

I shifted into first, released the emergency brake, and let out the clutch. As I gave it the gas, it seemed the wheels were turning. After a few moments I shifted into second. A bit later I put it into third.

Was there the tiniest feeling of traction, or was it only the power of suggestion?

I fed it more gas. The foggy prospect seemed to brighten slightly, far ahead, though I supposed this could simply be some effect of my staring in that direction. There was no particular feedback from the steering wheel. I pushed harder on the accelerator.

Luke reached out suddenly and turned on the radio.

"—hazardous driving conditions," came an announcer's voice. "So keep your speed to a minimum." There immediately followed Wynton Marsalis playing "Caravan."

Taking it as a personal message, I eased up on the gas. This produced a definite feeling of light traction, as if, perhaps, we were gliding on ice.

A sensation of forward movement followed, and there did seem a brightening in the distance. Also, it seemed as if I had acquired some weight, was settling more deeply into the seat. Moments later the sensation of a real surface beneath the car became more pronounced. I wondered what would happen if I turned the wheel. I decided not to try it.

The sound from beneath the tires became more gritty. Dim outlines occurred at either hand, increasing the feeling of movement and direction as we passed them. Far ahead, the world was indeed brighter now.

I slowed even more because it began feeling as if I were negotiating a real road, with very poor visibility. Shortly thereafter, the headlights did seem to be operating with some effect, as they struck a few of the passing shapes, giving them the momentary appearance of trees and embankments, shrub clusters, rocks. The rearview mirror continued to reflect nothingness, however.

"Just like old times," Luke said. "Goin' out for pizza on a bad evening."

"Yeah," I agreed.

"I hope the other me has someone open a pizza parlor in Kashfa. Could use one there, you know?"

"I'll come by and try it, if he does."

"Where do you think this whole business is going to leave me, anyway?"

"I don't know, Luke."

"I mean, I can't keep drinking your blood. And what about the other me?"

"I think I can offer you a job that will take care of the problem," Corwin said to him. "For a while, anyway."

The trees were definitely trees now, the fog real fog—moving about a bit. Beads of moisture began to form on the windshield.

"What do you mean?" Luke asked.

"In a minute."

There were breaks in the fog now, real landscape visible through them. Abruptly, I became aware that it was not a real road surface on which I was

driving, but rather a fairly level piece of ground. I slowed even more to accommodate this.

A big section of haze dissolved or blew away then, revealing the presence of an enormous tree. Also, a section of the ground seemed to be glowing. There was a familiar feeling to this partial tableau. . . .

"This is the place of *your* Pattern, isn't it?" I asked, as our way grew even clearer. "Fiona brought me here once."

"Yes," came the reply.

"And its image—That's the thing I saw confronting the Sign of the Logrus back in the graveyard—the same thing that led us into the tunnel."

"Yes."

"Then—It's sentient, too. Like Amber's, like the Logrus—"

"True. Park it over there, in that clear area by the tree."

I turned the wheel and headed toward the level spot he had indicated. Fog still hung about the place, but nowhere near as heavy and all-encompassing as on the trail we had taken. It might have been twilight, from the shading of the mist, but the glow from that eccentric Pattern brightened our cup-shaped world beyond a day's end dimness.

As we climbed out Corwin said to Luke, "Pattern ghosts tend not to last long."

"So I understand," Luke replied. "You know any tricks for someone in this position?"

"I know them all, sir. It takes one to know, as they say."

"Oh?"

"Dad . . . ?" I said. "You mean . . ."

"Yes," he replied. "I do not know where the first version of myself might be."

"You are the one I encountered a while back? The one who might have been present in Amber recently, also?"

"Yes."

"I—see. Yet, you don't seem exactly like others I've encountered."

He reached out and clasped my shoulder.

"I'm not," he said, and he glanced toward the Pattern. "I drew that thing," he went on, a little later, "and I'm the only person ever to have walked it. Consequently, I'm the only ghost it can summon. Also, it seems to regard me with something other than utilitarian attention. We can communicate, in a way, and it seems to have been willing to devote the energy needed to keep me stable—for a long while now. We have our own plans, and our relationship seems almost symbiotic. I gather that those of Amber's Pattern and those of the Logrus are more in the nature of ephemera."

"That's been my experience," I said.

"—except for one, to whom you ministered, for which I am grateful. She is under my protection now, for so long as it shall last."

He released my shoulder.

"I haven't been properly introduced to your friend yet," he said then.

"Excuse me. A bit of extenuation there," I said. "Luke, I'd like you to

meet my father, Corwin of Amber. Sir, Luke is properly known as Rinaldo, son of your brother Brand."

Corwin's eyes widened for an instant, then narrowed as he extended his hand, studying Luke's face.

"Good to meet a friend of my son's, as well as a relative," he said.

"Glad to know you, too, sir."

"I'd wondered what it was that seemed so familiar about you."

"It kind of slows down with appearances, if that's what you're getting at. Maybe even stops there."

Dad laughed.

"Where'd you two meet?"

"In school," Luke replied. "Berkeley."

"Where else might a pair of us come together? Not in Amber, of course," he said, turning away then to face his Pattern fully. "I'll get your story yet. But come with me now. I want to do an introduction myself."

He headed off toward the shining design and we followed him, a few wisps of fog drifting past us. Save for our short footfalls, the place was silent.

When we came up to the edge of his Pattern we halted and stared out across it. It was a graceful design, too big to take in at a glance; and a feeling of power seemed to pulse outward from it.

"Hi," he said. "I want you to meet my son and my nephew, Merlin and Rinaldo—though I believe you met Merlin once before. Rinaldo has a problem." There followed a long silence. Then he said, "Yes, that's right," and after a time, "You really think so?" and, "Okay. Sure, I'll tell them."

He stretched and sighed and took a few paces away from the Pattern's edge. Then he extended his arms and put them around both our shoulders.

"Men," he said then, "I've got an answer of sorts. But it means we're all going to have to walk this Pattern, for different reasons."

"I'm game," Luke said. "But what's the reason?"

"It's going to adopt you," Corwin said, "and sustain you as it does me. There's a price, though. The time's getting nearer when it will want to be guarded full-time. We can spell each other."

"Sounds fine," Luke said. "This place is kind of peaceful. And I didn't really want to go back to Kashfa and try to depose myself."

"Okay. I'll lead, and you hold on to my shoulder in case there are any funny vibes to deal with. Merlin, you come last and maintain contact with Luke, for the same reason. All right?"

"Sure," I said. "Let's go."

He released us and moved to the place where the line of the design began. We followed, and Luke's hand was on his shoulder as he took the first step. Soon we were all of us on the Pattern, struggling the familiar struggle. Even when the sparks began to rise, though, this one seemed a little easier than I recalled from Pattern walks in the past, possibly because someone else was leading the way.

Images of avenues lined with ancient chestnut trees filled my mind as we trudged along and fought our way through the First Veil. By then, the

sparks came higher about us and I felt the forces of the Pattern beating about me, penetrating me, body and mind. I recalled my days in school, remembered my greatest efforts on the athletic field. The resistance continued to rise, and we leaned into it. Moving my feet became a great effort, and I realized that—somehow—the effort was more important than the movement. I felt my hair beginning to rise as a current passed entirely through my body. Still, this had not to it the maddening quality of the Logrus the time I had negotiated it, nor the adversarial feeling I had felt upon Amber's Pattern. It was almost as if I traversed the interior of a mind, one not unkindly disposed toward me. There was a feeling—of encouragement, almost—as I struggled along a curve, executed a turn. The resistance was as strong, the sparks came as high as on the other at about this point, yet I somehow knew that this Pattern held me in a different fashion. We pushed our way along the lines. We turned, we burned. . . . Penetrating the Second Veil was a slow-motion exercise in stamina and will. Our way eased for a time after that, and images from all over my life came to frighten and console me.

Walking. One, two. . . . Three. I felt that if I were able to take ten more steps I would have a chance to win through. Four. . . . I was drenched with perspiration. Five. The resistance was awful. It took all the effort of running a hundred meters just to inch my foot ahead. My lungs were working like a bellows. Six. The sparks reached my face, passed my eyes, enveloped me completely. I felt as if I had been transformed into an immortal blue flame and that I must, somehow, burn my way through a block of marble. I burned and I burned and the stone remained unchanged. I could spend all of eternity this way. Perhaps I already had. Seven. And the images were gone. All of memory had fled. Even my identity was on vacation. I was stripped to a thing of pure will. I was an act, an act of striving against resistance. Eight. . . . I no longer felt my body. Time was an alien concept. The striving was no longer striving, but a form of elemental movement now, beside which glaciers rushed. Nine. Now I was only movement—infinitesimal, constant. . . .

Ten.

There came an easing. It would become difficult again at the center end, but I knew that the rest of the walk was anticlimax. Something like a slow, low music buoyed me as I trudged ahead, turned, trudged. It was with me through the Final Veil, and as I passed the midpoint of that final stride, it became something like "Caravan."

We stood there at the center, silent for a long while, breathing deeply. Exactly what I had achieved, I was uncertain. I did feel, though, that, in some way, I knew my father better as a result. Strands of mist still drifted, across the Pattern, across the valley.

"I feel—stronger," Luke announced later. "Yes, I'll help guard this place. It seems a good way to spend some time."

"By the way, Luke, what *was* your message for me?" I asked.

"Oh, to tell you to clear out of the Courts," he replied, "that things were getting dangerous."

"I already knew the danger part," I said. "But there are still things I must do."

He shrugged. "Well, that's the message," he said. "No place really seems safe just now."

"There won't be any problems here yet," Corwin said. "Neither Power knows exactly how to approach this place or what to do with it. It's too strong for Amber's Pattern to absorb, and the Logrus doesn't know how to destroy it."

"Sounds pretty easy, then."

"There will probably come a time later, though, when they will try to move against it."

"Until then, we wait and watch. Okay. If some things do come, what might they be?"

"Probably ghosts—like ourselves—seeking to learn more about it, to test. You any good with that blade?"

"In all modesty, yes. If that's not good enough, I've studied the Arts, as well."

"They'll fall to steel, though it's fire they'll bleed—not blood. You can have the Pattern transport you outside now, if you wish. I'll join you in a few moments to show you where the weapons are cached, and the other supplies. I'd like to take a little trip and leave you in charge for a while."

"Sure thing," Luke said. "What about you, Merle?"

"I've got to get back to the Courts. I've a luncheon engagement with my mother, and then Swayvill's funeral to attend."

"It may not be able to send you all the way to the Courts," Corwin said. "That's getting awfully near the Logrus. But you'll work something out with it, or vice versa. How *is* Dara?"

"It's been a long time since I've seen her for more than a few moments," I answered. "She is still peremptory, arrogant, and over-solicitous when it comes to me. I get the impression, too, that she may be involved in local political scheming as well as aspects of the larger relationship between the Courts and Amber."

Luke closed his eyes for a moment and vanished. Shortly afterward, I saw him beside the Polly Jackson car. He opened the door, slid onto the passenger seat, leaned and fiddled with something inside. A little later I could hear the radio playing music across the distance.

"It's likely," Corwin said. "I never understood her, you know. She came to me out of nowhere at a strange time in my life, she lied to me, we became lovers, she walked the Pattern in Amber, and she vanished. It was like a bizarre dream. It was obvious that she used me. For years I thought that it was only to get knowledge of the Pattern and access to it. But I've had a lot of time for reflection recently, and I'm no longer certain that that was the case."

"Oh?" I said. "What, then?"

"You," he replied. "More and more I'm coming to think, what she really wanted was to bear a son or daughter of Amber."

I felt myself grow cold. Could the reason for my own existence have been

such a calculated thing? Had there been no affection there at all? Had I been intentionally conceived to serve some special purpose? I did not at all like the notion. It made me feel the way Ghostwheel must, carefully structured product of my imagination and intellect, built to test design ideas only an Amberite could have come up with. Yet he called me "Dad." He actually seemed to care about me. Oddly, I had begun feeling an irrational affection for him myself. Was it partly because we were even more alike than I had consciously realized?

"Why?" I asked. "Why would it have been so important to her that I be born?"

"I can only remember her final words when she had completed the Pattern, turning into a demon in the process. 'Amber,' she said, 'will be destroyed.' Then she was gone."

I was shaking now. The implications were so unsettling that I wanted to cry, sleep, or get drunk. Anything, for a moment's respite.

"You think that my existence might be part of a long-term plan for the destruction of Amber?" I asked.

" 'Might,' " he said. "I could be wrong, kid. I could be very wrong, and if that's the case I apologize for troubling you this much. On the other hand, it would also be wrong of me not to let you know what the possibility is."

I massaged my temples, my brow, my eyes.

"What should I do?" I said then. "I don't want to help destroy Amber."

He clasped me to his breast for a moment and said, "No matter what you are and no matter what's been done to you, there will have to be some element of choice for you, sooner or later. You are greater than the sum of your parts, Merlin. No matter what went into your birth and your life up to now, you've got eyes and a brain and a set of values. Don't let anybody bullshit you, not even me. And when the time comes, if it comes, make damn sure the choice is your own. Nothing that's gone before will matter then."

His words, general as they had to be, drew me back from the place in my spirit where I had retreated.

"Thanks," I said.

He nodded. Then, "While your first impulse may be to force a confrontation on this matter," he said, "I would advise against it. It would achieve nothing other than making her aware of your suspicions. It would be prudent to play a more careful game and see what you can learn."

I sighed.

"You're right, of course," I said. "You came after me as much to tell me this as to help me escape, didn't you?"

He smiled.

"Only worry about important things," he said. "We'll meet again." And then he was gone.

I saw him, suddenly, over near the car, talking to Luke. I watched as he showed him where the caches were located. I wondered what time it was back in the Courts. After a while, they both waved to me. Then Corwin shook

hands with Luke and turned and walked off into the fog. I could hear the radio playing "Lili Marlene."

I focused my mind on the Pattern's transporting me to the Ways of Sawall. There was a momentary swirling of blackness. When it cleared I was still standing at the center of the Pattern. I tried again, this time for Suhuy's castle. Again, it refused to punch my ticket.

"How close can you send me?" I finally asked.

There was another swirling, but this one was bright. It delivered me to a high promontory of white stone beneath a black sky, beside a black sea. Two semicircles of pale flame parenthesized my position. Okay, I could live with that. I was at Fire Gate, a way-exchange in Shadow near to the Courts. I faced the sea and counted. When I'd located the fourteenth flickering tower on my left, I walked toward it.

I emerged before a fallen tower beneath a pink sky. Walking toward it, I was transported to a glassy cavern through which a green river flowed. I paced beside the river till I found the stepping-stones that took me to a trail through an autumn wood. I followed this for almost a mile till I felt the presence of a way near the base of an evergreen. This took me to the side of a mountain, whence three more ways and two filmies had me on the trail to lunch with my mother. According to the sky, I had no time to change clothes.

I halted near a crossroads to dust myself off, straighten my apparel, comb my hair. I wondered, as I was about the business, who might receive my calling were I to try to reach Luke via his Trump—Luke himself, his ghost, both? Could the ghosts receive Trump calls? I found myself wondering what was going on back in Amber, too. And I thought of Coral, and Nayda. . . .

Hell.

I wanted to be somewhere else. I wanted to be far away. The Pattern's warning, via Luke, was well taken. Corwin had given me too much to think about, and I hadn't had time to sort it through properly. I did not want to be involved in whatever was going on here in the Courts. I did not like all of the implications involving my mother. I did not feel like attending a funeral. I felt somehow, also, uninformed. You'd think that if somebody wanted something from me—something very important—they'd at least take the time to explain the situation and ask for my cooperation. If it were a relative, there was a strong possibility I'd go along with it. Getting my cooperation would seem a lot less dicey than any trickery intended to control my actions. I wanted to be away from those who would control me, as well as the games they were playing.

I could turn and head back into Shadow, probably lose myself there. I could head back to Amber, tell Random everything I knew, everything I suspected, and he would protect me against the Courts. I could go back to the Shadow Earth, come up with a new identity, get back into computer design. . . .

Then, of course, I would never know what was going on and what had gone before. As for my father's real whereabouts—I'd been able to reach him

from the Courts, never from anywhere else. In this sense, he was nearby. And there was no one else around here likely to help him.

I walked ahead and turned right. I made my way toward a purpling sky. I would be on time.

And so I came, again, into the Ways of Sawall. I had emerged from the red and yellow starburst design painted high upon the gateside wall of the front courtyard, descended the Invisible Stair, and peered for long moments down into the great central pit, with its view of black turbulence beyond the Rim. A falling star burned its way down the purple sky as I turned away, headed for the copper-chased door and the low Maze of Art beyond it.

Within, I recalled the many times I had been lost in that maze as a child. The House of Sawall had been a serious collector of art for ages, and the collection was so vast that there were several ways into which one was cast within the maze itself, leading one through tunnels, a huge spiral, and what seemed an old train station before being shunted back to miss the next turn. I had been lost in it for days on one occasion, and was finally found crying before an assemblage of blue shoes nailed to a board. I walked it now, slowly, looking at old monstrosities, and some newer ones. There were also strikingly lovely pieces mixed in, such as the huge vase that looked as if it had been carved from a single fire opal, and a set of odd enameled tablets from a distant shadow whose meaning and function no one in the family could be found to recall. I had to stop and see both again, rather than shortcutting the gallery, the tablets being a particular favorite of mine.

I was humming an old tune Gryll had taught me as I came up to the fiery vase and regarded it. I seemed to hear a small chafing noise, but glances up and down the corridor revealed no one else in the vicinity. The almost sensual curves of the vase begged to be touched. I could remember all of the times I had been forbidden to do so as a child. I put my left hand forward slowly, rested it upon it. It was warmer than I'd thought it might be. I slid my hand along its side. It was like a frozen flame.

"Hello," I muttered, remembering an adventure we'd shared. "It's been a long time. . . ."

"Merlin?" came a small voice.

I withdrew my hand immediately. It was as if the vase had spoken.

"Yes," I said then. "Yes."

Again, the chafing sound, and a bit of shadow stirred within the creamy opening, above the fire.

"Ss," said the shadow, rising.

"Glait?" I asked.

"Yess."

"It can't be. You've been dead for years."

"Not dead. Ssleeping."

"I haven't seen you since I was a kid. You were injured. You disappeared. I thought you'd died."

"I ssleep. I ssleep to heal. I ssleep to forget. I ssleep to renew mysself."

I extended my arm. The shaggy snake head rose higher, extended itself, fell upon my forearm, climbed, wrapped itself.

"You certainly chose elegant sleeping quarters."

"I knew the jug to be a favorite of yourss. If I waited long enough I knew you would come by again, sstop to admire it. And I would know and rise up in my ssplendor to greet you. My, you have grown!"

"You look pretty much the same. A little thin, perhaps. . . ."

I stroked her head gently.

"It is good to know you are with us still, like some honored family spirit. You and Gryll and Kergma made my childhood a better thing than it might have been."

She raised her head high, stroked my cheek with her nose.

"It warmss my cold blood to ssee you again, dear boy. You've traveled far?"

"I have. Very."

"One night we shall eat mice and lie besside a fire. You will warm me a ssaucer of milk and tell me of your adventuress ssince you left the Wayss of Ssawall. We will find ssome marrow boness for Gryll, if he be sstill about—"

"He seems to serve my uncle Suhuy these days. What of Kergma?"

"I do not know. It hass been sso long."

I held her close to warm her.

"Thank you for waiting here for me in your great drowse, to greet me—"

"Iss more than friendliess, helloss."

"More? What then, Glait? What is it?"

"A thing to show. Walk that way."

She gestured with her head. I moved in the direction she indicated—the way I had been heading anyhow, to where the corridors widened. I could feel her vibrating against my arm with the barely audible purring sound she sometimes made.

Suddenly, she stiffened and her head rose, swaying slightly.

"What is it?" I asked.

"Mi-ice," she said. "Mi-ice nearby. I musst go hunting—after I show you—the thing. Breakfasst. . . ."

"If you would dine first, I will wait."

"No, Merlin. You musst not be late for whatever—brought you here. There is importance in the air. Later—feasst—vermin. . . ."

We came into a wide, high, skylighted section of the gallery. Four large pieces of metal statuary—bronze and copper, mostly—stood in an asymmetrical arrangement about us.

"Onward," Glait said. "Not here."

I turned right at the next corner and plunged ahead. Shortly, we came to another display—this one resembling a metal forcst.

"Sslow now. Sslow, dear demon child."

I halted and studied the trees, bright, dark, shiny, dull. Iron, aluminum, brass, it was most impressive. It was also a display that had not been present the last time I had passed this way, years before. Nothing odd about that, of course. There had also been changes in other areas I had passed through.

"Now. Here. Turn in. Go back."

I moved on into the forest.

"Bear right. The tall one."

I halted when I came to the curved trunk of the tallest tree to my right.

"This one?"

"Yess. Negotiate it—upward—pleasse."

"You mean climb it?"

"Yess."

"Right."

One nice thing about a stylized tree—or, at least, *this* stylized tree—was that it spiraled, swelled, and twisted in such a fashion as to provide better handholds and footholds than at first seemed apparent. I caught hold, drew myself up, found a place for my foot, pulled again, pushed.

Higher. Higher, still. When I was perhaps ten feet above the floor I halted.

"Uh, what do I do now that I'm here?" I asked.

"Climb higher."

"Why?"

"Ssoon. Ssoon. You'll know."

I drew myself about a foot higher, and then I felt it. It is not so much a tingling as it is a kind of pressure. I only feel a tingling, too, sometimes, if they lead someplace risky.

"There's a way up there," I said.

"Yess. I wass coiled about a branch of the blue tree when a shadowmasster opened it. They sslew him afterwardss."

"It must lead to something very important."

"I ssuppose. I am not a good judge—of people thingss."

"You have been through?"

"Yess."

"Then it *is* safe?"

"Yess."

"All right."

I climbed higher, resisting the force of the way until I'd brought both feet to the same level. Then I relaxed into the tugging and let it take me through.

I extended both hands, too, in case the surface was uneven. But it wasn't. The floor was beautifully tiled in black, silver, gray, and white. To the right was a geometric design, to the left a representation of the Pit of Chaos.

My eyes were directed downward for only a few moments, though.

"Good Lord!" I said.

"Wass I right? It iss important?" Glait said.

"It is important," I replied.

SIX

There were candles all about the chapel, many of them as tall as I am, and nearly as big around. Some were silver, some were gray; a few were white, a few black. They stood at various heights, in artful disposition, on banks, ledges, pattern points on the floor. They did not provide the main illumination, however. This obtained from overhead, and I first assumed it to proceed from a skylight. When I glanced upward to gauge the height of the vault, though, I saw that the light emanated from a large blue-white globe confined behind a dark metal grate.

I took a step forward. The nearest candle flame flickered.

I faced a stone altar that filled a niche across the way. Black candles burned at either hand before it, smaller silver ones upon it. For a moment, I simply regarded it.

"Lookss like you," Glait remarked.

"I thought your eyes didn't register two-dimensional representations."

"I've lived a long time in a musseum. Why hide your picture up a ssecret way?"

I moved forward, my gaze on the painting.

"It's not me," I said. "It's my father, Corwin of Amber."

A silver rose stood within a bud vase before the portrait. Whether it was a real rose or the product of art or magic, I could not tell.

And Grayswandir lay there before it, drawn a few inches from the scabbard. I'd a feeling this was the real thing, that the version worn by the Pattern ghost of my father was itself a reconstruction.

I reached forward, raised it, drew it.

There was a feeling of power as I held it, swung it, struck an *en garde*, lunged, advanced. The spikard came alive, center of a web of forces. I looked down, suddenly self-conscious.

". . . And this is my father's blade," I said, returning to the altar, where I sheathed it. Reluctantly, I left it there.

As I backed away, Glait asked, "Thiss iss important?"

"Very," I said as the way caught hold of me and sent me back to the treetop.

"What now, Masster Merlin?"

"I must get on to lunch with my mother."

"In that case, you'd besst drop me here."

1175

"I could return you to the vase."

"No. I haven't lurked in a tree for a time. Thiss will be fine."

I extended my arm. She unwound herself and flowed away across gleaming branches.

"Good luck, Merlin. Vissit me."

And I was down the tree, snagging my trousers only once, and off up the corridor at a quick pace.

Two turns later I came to a way to the main hall and decided I'd better take it. I popped through beside the massive fireplace—high flames braiding themselves within it—and turned slowly to survey the huge chamber, trying to seem as if I had been there a long while, waiting.

I seemed the only person present. Which, on reflection, struck me as a bit odd, with the fire roaring that way. I adjusted my shirtfront, brushed myself off, ran my comb through my hair. I was inspecting my fingernails when I became aware of a flash of movement at the head of the great staircase to my left.

She was a blizzard within a ten-foot tower. Lightnings danced at its center, crackling; particles of ice clicked and rattled upon the stair; the banister grew frosted where she passed. My mother. She seemed to see me at about the same time I saw her, for she halted. Then she made the turn onto the stair and began her descent.

As she descended, she shifted smoothly, her appearance changing almost from step to step. As soon as I realized what was occurring I relaxed my own efforts and reversed their small effects. I had commenced changing the moment I had seen her, and presumably she had done the same on viewing me. I hadn't thought she'd go to that extent to humor me, a second time, here on her own turf.

The shift was completed just as she reached the bottommost stair, becoming a lovely woman in black trousers and red shirt with flared sleeves. She looked at me again and smiled, moved toward me, embraced me.

It would have been gauche to say that I'd intended shifting but had forgotten. Or any other remark on the matter.

She pushed me out to arm's distance, lowered her gaze and raised it, shook her head.

"Do you sleep in your clothes before or after violent exercise?" she asked me.

"That's unkind," I said. "I stopped to sightsee on the way over and ran into a few problems."

"That is why you are late?"

"No. I'm late because I stopped in our gallery and took longer than I'd intended. And I'm not very late."

She took hold of my arm and turned me.

"I will forgive you," she said, steering me toward the rose and green and gold-flecked pillar of ways, set in the mirrored alcove across the room to the right.

I didn't feel that called for a response, so I didn't make one. I watched

with interest as we entered the alcove, to see whether she would conduct me in a clockwise direction or its opposite about the pillar.

The opposite, it turned out. Interesting.

We were reflected and re-reflected from the three sides. So was the room we had quitted. And with each circuit we made of the pillar it became a different room. I watched it change, kaleidoscopically, until she halted me before the crystal grotto beside the underground sea.

"It's been a long time since I thought of this place," I said, stepping forth upon the pure white sand into the crystal-cast light, variously reminiscent of bonfires, solar reflections, candelabra, and LED displays, functions of size and distancing perhaps, laying occasional pieces of rainbow upon the shore, the walls, the black water.

She took my hand and led me toward a raised and railed platform some small distance off to the right. A table stood full set upon it. A collection of covered trays occupied a larger serving table inland of it. We mounted a small stair, and I seated her and moved to check out the goodies next door.

"Do sit down, Merlin," she said. "I'll serve you."

"That's all right," I answered, raising a lid. "I'm already here. I'll do the first round."

She was on her feet.

"Buffet style then," she said.

"Sure."

We filled our plates and moved to the table. Seconds after we had seated ourselves a brilliant flash of light came to us across the water, illuminating the arching dome of the cavern vault like the ribbed interior of some massive beast that was digesting us.

"You needn't look so apprehensive. You know they can't come in this far."

"Waiting for a thunderclap puts my appetite on hold," I said.

She laughed just as a distant roll of thunder reached us.

"And that makes everything all right?" she asked.

"Yes," I replied, raising my fork.

"Strange, the relatives life gives us," she said.

I looked at her, tried to read her expression, couldn't. So, "Yes," I said.

She studied me for a moment, but I wasn't giving anything away either. So, "When you were a child you went monosyllabic as a sign of petulance," she said.

"Yes," I said.

We began eating. There were more flashes out over the still, dark sea. By light of the last one I thought I caught sight of a distant ship, black sails full-rigged and bellied.

"You kept your engagement with Mandor earlier?"

"Yes."

"How is he?"

"Fine."

"Something bothering you, Merlin?"

"Many things."

"Tell Mother?"

"What if she's a part of it?"

"I would be disappointed if I were not. Still, how long will you hold the business of the *ty'iga* against me? I did what I thought was right. I still think it was."

I nodded and continued chewing. After a time, "You made that clear last cycle," I said.

The waters gave a small sloshing sound. A spectrum drifted across our table, her face.

"Is there something else?" she asked.

"Why don't *you* tell *me*?" I said.

I felt her gaze. I met it.

"I don't know what you mean," she answered.

"Are you aware that the Logrus is sentient? And the Pattern?" I said.

"Did Mandor tell you that?" she asked.

"Yes. But I already knew it before he did."

"How?"

"We've been in touch."

"You and the Pattern? You and the Logrus?"

"Both."

"To what end?"

"Manipulation, I'd say. They're engaged in a power struggle. They were asking me to choose sides."

"Which did you choose?"

"Neither. Why?"

"You should have told me."

"Why?"

"For counsel. Possibly for assistance."

"Against the Powers of the universe? How well connected are you, Mother?"

She smiled.

"It is possible that one such as myself may possess special knowledge of their workings."

"One such as yourself. . . ?"

"A sorceress of my skills."

"Just how good are you, Mother?"

"I don't think they come much better, Merlin."

"Family is always the last to know, I guess. So why didn't you train me yourself, instead of sending me off to Suhuy?"

"I'm not a good teacher. I dislike training people."

"You trained Jasra."

She tilted her head to the right and narrowed her eyes.

"Did Mandor tell you that, also?" she asked.

"No."

"Who, then?"

"What difference does it make?"

"Considerable," she replied. "Because I don't believe you knew it the last time we met."

I recalled suddenly that she had said something about Jasra back at Su-huy's, something implying her familiarity with her, something to which I would ordinarily have risen save that I was driving a load of animus in a different direction at the time and heading downhill in a thunderstorm with the brakes making funny noises. I was about to ask her why it mattered *when* I learned it, when I realized that she was really asking from whom I'd learned it, because she was concerned with whom I might have been speaking on such matters since last we'd met. Mentioning Luke's Pattern ghost did not seem politic, so, "Okay, Mandor let it slip," I said, "and then asked me to forget it."

"In other words," she said, "he expected it to get back to me. Why did he do it just that way? I wonder. The man is damnably subtle."

"Maybe he did just let it slip."

"Mandor lets nothing slip. Never make him an enemy, son."

"Are we talking about the same person?"

She snapped her fingers.

"Of course," she said. "It was only as a child that you knew him. You went away after that. You have seen him but a few times since. Yes, he is subtle, insidious, dangerous."

"We've always gotten along well."

"Of course. He never antagonizes without a good reason."

I shrugged and went on eating.

After a time she said, "I daresay he has made similar comments about me."

"I am unable to recall any," I answered.

"Has he been giving you lessons in circumspection, too?"

"No, though I've felt a need to teach myself, of late."

"Surely, you obtained a few in Amber."

"If I did, they were so subtle I didn't notice."

"Well, well. Can it be I need despair of you no more?"

"I doubt it."

"So, what might the Pattern or the Logrus want of you?"

"I already told you—a choice of sides."

"It is that difficult to decide which you prefer?"

"It is that difficult to decide which I dislike less."

"Because they are, as you say, manipulative of people in their struggle for power?"

"Just so."

She laughed. Then, "While it shows the gods as no better than the rest of us," she said, "at least, it shows them as no worse. See here the sources of human morality. It is still better than none at all. If these grounds be insufficient for the choosing of sides, then let other considerations rule. You are, after all, a son of Chaos."

"And Amber," I said.

"You grew up in the Courts."

"And I have dwelled in Amber. My relatives are as numerous there as they are here."

"It is really that close, then?"

"If it were not, it might have simplified matters."

"In that case," she said, "you must turn it around."

"What do you mean?"

"Ask not which appeals the most to you, but which can do the most for you."

I sipped a fine green tea as the storm rolled nearer. Something splashed within the waters of our inlet.

"All right," I said, "I'm asking."

She leaned forward and smiled and her eyes darkened. She has always had perfect control of her face and form, shifting them to suit her moods. She is obviously the same person, but at times she may choose to appear as little more than a girl, at other times becoming a mature and handsome woman. Generally, she seems somewhere in between. But now, a certain timeless quality came into her features—not age so much as the essence of Time—and I realized suddenly that I had never known her true age. I watched as something like a veil of ancient power came across it.

"The Logrus," she said, "will lead you to greatness."

I continued to stare.

"What sort of greatness?" I asked.

"What sort do you desire?"

"I don't know that I ever wanted greatness, on its own. It seems rather like wanting to be an engineer, rather than wanting to design something—or wanting to be a writer, rather than wanting to write. It should be a by-product, not a thing in itself. Otherwise, it's just an ego trip."

"But if you earn it—if you deserve it—shouldn't you have it?"

"I suppose. But so far I've done nothing"—my eyes fell to a bright circle of light beneath the dark waters, moving as if running before a storm—"except perhaps for an odd piece of equipment, which might fall into that category."

"You are young, of course," she said, "and the times for which you were meant to be uniquely qualified have come sooner than I'd anticipated."

If I were to use magic to summon a cup of coffee, would she resent that? Yes, I believed. She would. So I decided on a glass of wine. As I poured it and took a sip, I said, "I'm afraid I don't understand what you're talking about." She nodded.

"It is hardly something you could learn from introspection," she said slowly, "and no one would be so rash as to mention the possibility to you."

"What are you talking about, Mother?"

"The throne. To reign in the Courts of Chaos."

"Mandor had sort of suggested I think about it," I said.

"All right. No one, excepting Mandor, would be so rash as to mention it."

"I gather mothers get a certain kick out of seeing their sons do well, but

unfortunately you've named a job for which I lack not only skill, aptitude, and training but also any desire."

She steepled her fingers and regarded me from just above them.

"You are better qualified than you think, and your desires have nothing to do with the matter."

"As an interested party, I must beg to differ with you."

"Even if it were the only way to protect friends and relatives both here and in Amber?"

I took another sip of wine.

"Protect them? Against what?"

"The Pattern is about to try redefining the middle regions of Shadow in its own image. It is probably strong enough to do it now."

"You were talking of Amber and the Courts, not of Shadow."

"The Logrus will have to resist this incursion. Since it would probably lose in a direct confrontation with its opposite, it will be forced to employ agents strategically, in a strike against Amber. The most effective agents would, of course, be champions of the Courts—"

"This is mad!" I said. "There must be a better way!"

"Possibly," she replied. "Accept the throne and you'll be giving the orders."

"I don't know enough."

"You will be briefed, of course."

"What about the proper order of succession?"

"That's not your problem."

"I rather think I'd have an interest in how it's achieved—say, whether I'd owe you or Mandor for the majority of deaths."

"In that we're both Sawall, the question becomes academic."

"You mean you're cooperating on this?"

"We have our differences," she said, "and I draw the line at any discussion of methods."

I sighed and took another drink. The storm had grown worse over the dark waters. If that strange light effect beneath their surface were indeed Ghostwheel, I wondered what he was up to. The lightnings were becoming a steady backdrop, the thunder a continuing soundtrack.

"What did you mean," I said, "when you spoke of the times for which I was meant to be uniquely qualified?"

"The present and the immediate future," she said, "with the conflict that will come."

"No," I responded. "I was referring to the business about my being 'meant to be uniquely qualified.' How so?"

It must have been the lightning, for I had never seen her blush before.

"You combine two great bloodlines," she said. "Technically, your father was King of Amber—briefly—between the reign of Oberon and that of Eric."

"Since Oberon was still alive at the time and had not abdicated, neither reign should be considered valid," I responded. "Random is Oberon's proper successor."

"A case can be made for an implied abdication," she said.

"You prefer that reading, don't you?"

"Of course."

I watched the storm. I swallowed some wine.

"That is why you wished to bear Corwin's child?" I asked.

"The Logrus assured me that such a child would be uniquely qualified to reign here."

"But Dad never really meant that much to you, did he?"

She looked away, out to where the circle of light was now racing toward us, lightnings falling behind it.

"You have no right to ask that question," she said.

"I know that. But it's true, isn't it?"

"You are mistaken. He meant a great deal to me."

"But not in any conventional sense."

"I am not a conventional person."

"I was the result of a breeding experiment. The Logrus selected the mate who would give you—what?"

The circle of light swam nearer. The storm followed it, coming closer in to the shore than I'd ever seen one reach here before.

"An ideal Lord of Chaos," she said, "fit to rule."

"Somehow I feel there's more to it than that," I said.

Dodging lightning bolts, the bright circle came up out of the water and flashed across the sand toward us. If she responded to my last remark, I couldn't hear it. The ensuing thunders were deafening.

The light came onto the decking, paused near to my foot.

"Dad, can you protect me?" Ghost asked in a lull between thunderclaps.

"Rise to my left wrist," I bade.

Dara stared as he found his place, taking on the appearance of Frakir. In the meantime, the final flash of lightning did not depart, but stood for a time like a sizzling stalk at the water's edge. Then it collapsed into a ball that hovered in the middle air for several moments before drifting in our direction. As it came on, its structure began to change.

When it drifted to a position beside our table it had become a bright, pulsing Sign of the Logrus.

"Princess Dara, Prince Merlin," came that awful voice I had last heard on the day of the confrontation at Amber Castle, "I did not wish to disturb your repast, but that thing you harbor makes it necessary." A jagged branch of the image was flipped in the direction of my left wrist.

"It's blocking my ability to shift away," Ghost said.

"Give it to me!"

"Why?" I asked.

"That thing has traversed the Logrus," came the words, differing at seeming random in pitch, volume, accent.

It occurred to me that I might defy it now if I were really as valuable to the Logrus as Dara had indicated. So, "It's theoretically open to all comers," I responded.

"I am my own law, Merlin, and your Ghostwheel has crossed me before. I'll have it now."

"No," I said, moving my awareness into the spikard, seeking and locating a means of instant transport to an area where the Pattern ruled. "I'll not surrender my creation so readily."

The brightness of the Sign increased.

At this, Dara was on her feet, moving to interpose herself between it and myself.

"Stay," she said. "We've more important matters to deal with than vengeance upon a toy. I have dispatched my cousins Hendrake for the bride of Chaos. If you wish this plan to succeed, I suggest you assist them."

"I recall your plan for Prince Brand, setting the lady Jasra to snare him. It could not fail, you told me."

"It brought you closer than you ever came, old Serpent, to the power you desire."

"That is true," it acknowledged.

"And the bearer of the Eye is a simpler being than Jasra."

The Sign slid past her, a tiny sun turning itself into a succession of ideograms.

"Merlin, you will take the throne and serve me when the time comes?"

"I will do what is necessary to redress the balance of power," I replied.

"That is not what I asked! Will you take the throne under the terms I set?"

"If that is what is needed to set things right," I answered.

"This pleases me," it said. "Keep your toy."

Dara moved aside, and it passed near to her before fading.

"Ask him of Luke and Corwin and the new Pattern," it said, and then it was gone.

She turned toward me and stared.

"Pour me a glass of wine," she said.

I did this. She raised it and took a swallow.

"So tell me of Luke and Corwin and the new Pattern," she said.

"Tell me of Jasra and Brand," I countered.

"No. You will go first in this," she said.

"Very well," I said. "It neglected to mention that they were Pattern ghosts. Luke's appeared to me on the way over here, sent by the Pattern to persuade me to depart this realm. The Logrus sent Lord Borel's to dispose of Luke."

"Luke being Rinaldo, the son of Jasra and Brand, husband of Coral and King of Kashfa?"

"Very good. Now tell me of all that business at the end. You set Jasra to snare Brand, to guide him down the path he took?"

"He would have taken it anyhow. He came to the Courts seeking power to further his ends. She merely made things a little easier for him."

"That's not how it sounded to me. But does that mean my father's curse was not really a factor?"

"No, it helped—in a metaphysical way—making it easier to extend the

Black Road to Amber. Why is it you are still here, when King Rinaldo bade you depart? Is it loyalty to the Courts?"

"I had a date with you for lunch, and it's been a while. Hated to miss it."

She smiled, very slightly, and took a small sip of wine.

"You change the subject well," she stated. "Let us return to it now. The ghost of Borel dispatched that of Rinaldo, I take it?"

"Not exactly."

"What do you mean?"

"My father's ghost showed up about then and dealt with Borel, permitting us to depart."

"Again? Corwin bested Borel again?"

I nodded.

"Neither remembered their first encounter, of course. Their memories only go back to the time of their recording, and—"

"I understand the principle. Then what happened?"

"We fled," I answered, "and I subsequently came here."

"What did the Logrus mean in referring to the new Pattern?"

"My father's ghost was apparently generated there, rather than by the old one."

She sat upright, eyes suddenly wide.

"How do you know this?" she demanded.

"He told me," I answered.

She stared past me then at the now-silent sea. "So the third power is actually taking a part in things," she mused. "This is fascinating, as well as disconcerting. Damn the man for having drawn it!"

"You really hate him, don't you?" I said.

Her eyes focused again upon my own.

"Let that subject be!" she ordered. "Save for this," she amended a moment later. "Did he give you any indication as to the new Pattern's allegiance—or its plans? The fact that it sent him to protect Luke might be seen as a seconding of the old Pattern's action. On the other hand—either because it was created by your father, or because it has its own uses for you—I can see it simply as an effort at your protection. What did he say?"

"That he wanted to get me away from where I was."

She nodded.

"Which he obviously did," she said. "Did he say anything else? Did anything else happen that might be important?"

"He asked after you."

"Really? And that was all?"

"He had no special message, if that's what you mean."

"I see."

She looked away, was silent for a time. Then, "Those ghosts don't last very long, do they?" she said.

"No," I replied.

"It's infuriating," she said at last, "to think that, despite everything, he is still able to play a hand in this."

"He's alive, isn't he, Mother?" I said. "And you know where he is."

"I'm not his keeper, Merlin."

"I think you are."

"It is impertinent to contradict me this way."

"Yet I must," I responded. "I saw him off on his way to the Courts. Certainly, he wanted to be here with the others for the peace settlement. Even more, though, he must have wanted to see you. There were so many unanswered questions in his mind—where you came from, why you came to him, why you parted as you did—"

"Enough!" she cried. "Let it be!"

I ignored her.

"And I know he was here in the Courts. He was seen here. He must have looked you up. What happened then? What sort of answers did you give him?"

She rose to her feet, glaring at me now.

"That will be all, Merlin," she said. "It seems impossible to conduct a civilized conversation with you."

"Is he your prisoner, Mother? Do you have him locked away somewhere, someplace where he can't bother you, can't interfere with your plans?"

She stepped quickly away from the table, almost stumbling.

"Wretched child!" she said. "You're just like him! Why did you have to resemble him so?"

"You're afraid of him, aren't you?" I said, suddenly realizing this could well be the case. "You're afraid to kill a Prince of Amber, even with the Logrus on your side. You've got him locked away somewhere, and you're afraid he'll come loose and blow your latest plans. You've been scared for a long time now because of what you've had to do to keep him out of action."

"Preposterous!" she said, backing away as I rounded the table. There was a look of genuine fear on her face now. "You're just guessing!" she went on. "He's dead, Merlin! Give up! Leave me alone! Never mention his name in my presence again! Yes, I hate him! He would have destroyed us all! He still would, if he could!"

"He is not dead," I stated.

"How can you say that?"

I bit down on the desire to tell her I'd spoken with him, held it back.

"Only the guilty protest so strongly," I said. "He's alive. Where is he?"

She raised her hands, palms inward, and crossed them upon her breast, elbows low. The fear was gone, the anger was gone. When she spoke again, something like mockery seemed her main humor: "Then seek him, Merlin. By all means, seek him."

"Where?" I demanded.

"Look for him in the Pit of Chaos."

A flame appeared near her left foot and began orbiting her body in a counterclockwise direction, spiraling upward, leaving a line of fire to blaze redly behind it. By the time it reached the crown of her head she was entirely

concealed. It went out with a faint whooshing sound then, taking her along with it.

I moved forward and knelt, feeling the area on which she'd stood. It was a little warm, that's all. Nice spell. Nobody'd ever taught me that one. Thinking back on it then, I realized that Mom had always had a flair when it came to entrances and exits.

"Ghost?"

He danced away from my wrist to hover in the air before me.

"Yes?"

"Are you still barred from transporting yourself through Shadow?"

"No," he replied. "That was lifted when the Sign of the Logrus departed. I can travel—in or out of Shadow. I can provide transportation for you. Would you like me to?"

"Yes. Take me into the gallery upstairs."

"Gallery? I plunged directly from the place of the Logrus into the dark sea, Dad. I'm not quite sure as to the lay of the land here."

"Never mind," I said. "I'll manage it myself."

I activated the spikard. Energies spiraled from six of its tines, encaging Ghost and myself, swirling us upward to the place of my desire in the Maze of Art. I tried for a flash of fire as we went, but had no way of knowing whether I'd achieved it. Makes you wonder how the really good ones get their practice.

SEVEN

I delivered us into that eerie hall that had always been old Sawall's chief delight in the maze. It was a sculpture garden, with no outside light sources and small base lighting only about the huge pieces, making it several times darker than my favorite lounge. The floor was uneven—concave, convex, stepped, ridged—with concavity being the dominant curve. It was difficult to guess at its dimensions, for it seemed of different size and contour depending upon where one stood. Gramble, Lord Sawall, had caused it to be constructed without any plane surfaces—and I believe the job involved some unique shadowmastery.

I stood beside what appeared to be a complicated rigging in the absence of its ship—that, or an elaborate musical instrument fit to be strummed by Titans—and the light turned the lines to silver, running like life from darkness to darkness within some half-seen frame. Other pieces jutted from walls and hung like stalactites. As I strolled, what had seemed walls became floor to me. The pieces that had seemed floored now jutted or depended. The room changed shape as I went, and a breeze blew through it, causing sighs, hums, buzzes, chimes. Gramble, my stepfather, had taken a certain delight in this hall, whereas for me it had long represented an exercise in intrepidity to venture beyond its threshold. As I grew older, however, I, too, came to enjoy

it, partly for the occasional *frisson* it provided my adolescence. Now, though —
Now I just wanted to wander it a few moments, for old times' sake, as I sorted
through my thoughts. There were so damned many of them. Things that had
tantalized me for much of my adult life seemed near to explanation now. I
was not happy with all of the possibilities that tumbled through my mind.
Still, no matter which ones came out on top, it would beat ignorance.

"Dad?"

"Yes?"

"What is this place, anyway?" Ghost asked.

"It's a part of the big art collection here at the Ways of Sawall," I explained. "People come from all over the Courts and nearby Shadow to see
it. It was a passion with my stepfather. I spent a lot of time wandering these
halls when I was a kid. There are many hidden ways in this place."

"And this particular room? There's something wrong with it."

"Yes and no," I said. "I guess it depends on what you mean by 'wrong.' "

"My perceptions are strangely affected just now."

"That is because the space itself is folded in here, like some odd origami
figure. The hall is much larger than it seems. You can wander through many
times and witness a different array of displays on each occasion. There may
even be some internal movement involved. I was never sure. Only Sawall
knew for certain."

"I was right. Something's wrong with it."

"I rather like it this way."

I seated myself on a silver stump beside a sprawled silver tree.

"I want to see how it folds," he said at last.

"Go ahead."

As he drifted off, I thought of my recent interview with my mother. I was
reminded of everything Mandor had said or implied, of the conflict between
the Pattern and the Logrus, of my father as the champion of the Pattern and
intended king in Amber. Had she known this, known it as fact rather than
speculation? I imagined she could have, for she seemed to enjoy a special
relationship with the Logrus, and it would surely have been aware of its
adversary's more prominent decisions. She'd admitted that she did not love
the man. It seemed as if she had sought him for whatever genetic material
had so impressed the Pattern. Had she really been trying to breed a champion
for the Logrus?

I chuckled as I considered the result. She had seen me trained well in
arms, but I was nowhere near Dad's league. I'd preferred sorcery, but sorcerers
were a dime a dozen in the Courts. Finally, she'd shipped me off to college
on that Shadow Earth the Amberites favor. But a degree in Computer Science
from Berkeley didn't much qualify me to uphold the banner of Chaos against
the forces of Order either. I must have been a disappointment to her.

I thought back to my childhood, to some of the strange adventures for
which this place had served as a point of departure. Gryll and I would come
here, Glait slithering at our feet, coiled about a limb or riding somewhere
amid my garments. I would give that odd ululant cry I had learned in a

dream, and sometimes Kergma would join us, come skittering down the folds of darkness, out some frayed area of twisted space. I was never sure exactly what Kergma was, or even of what gender, for Kergma was a shapeshifter and flew, crawled, hopped, or ran in a succession of interesting forms.

On an impulse, I voiced that ancient call. Nothing, of course, happened, and I saw it moments later for what it was: a cry after a vanished childhood, when I had at least felt wanted. Now, now I was nothing—neither Amberite nor Chaosite, and certainly a disappointment to my relatives on both sides. I was a failed experiment. I'd never been wanted for myself, but as something that might come to pass. Suddenly my eyes were moist, and I held back a sob. And I'll never know what sort of mood I might have worked myself into because I was distracted then.

There came a flare of red light from a point high on the wall to my left. It was in the form of a small circle about the feet of a human figure.

"Merlin!" called a voice from that direction, and the flames leapt higher. By their light, I saw that familiar face, reminding me a bit of my own, and I was pleased with the meaning it had just given to my life, even if that meaning was death.

I raised my left hand above my head and willed a flash of blue light from the spikard.

"Over here, Jurt!" I called, rising to my feet. I began forming the ball of light that was to be his distraction while I readied the strike that would electrocute him. On reflection, it had seemed the surest way of taking him out. I'd lost count of the number of attempts he'd made on my life, and I'd resolved to take the initiative the next time he came calling. Frying his nervous system seemed the surest way to ice him, despite what the Fountain had done for him. "Over here, Jurt!"

"Merlin! I want to talk!"

"I don't. I've tried it too often, and I've nothing left to say. Come on over and let's get this done—weapons, hands, magic. I don't care."

He raised both hands, palms outward.

"Truce!" he cried. "It wouldn't be right to do it here in Sawall."

"Don't give me that scruples shit, brother!" I cried, but even as I said it I realized there might be something to it. I could remember how much the old man's approval had meant to him, and I realized that he'd hate to do anything to antagonize Dara here on the premises. "What do you want, anyway?"

"To talk. I mean it," he said. "What do I have to do?"

"Meet me over there," I said, casting my ball of light to shine above a familiar object that looked like a giant house of cards made of glass and aluminum, bouncing light from hundreds of planes.

"All right," came the reply.

I began walking in that direction. I saw him approaching from his, and I angled my course so that our paths would not intersect. Also, I increased my pace so as to arrive ahead of him.

"No tricks," he called out. "And if we do decide we can only take it to the end, let's go outside."

"Okay."

I entered the structure at a point around the corner from his approach. Immediately, I encountered six images of myself.

"Why here?" came his voice from somewhere near at hand.

"I don't suppose you ever saw a movie called *Lady from Shanghai?*"

"No."

"It occurred to me that we could wander around in here and talk, and the place would do a lot to keep us from hurting each other."

I turned a corner. There were more of me in different places. A few moments later, I heard a sharp intake of breath from somewhere near at hand. It was followed almost immediately by a chuckle.

"I begin to understand," I heard him say.

Three steps and another turn. I halted. There were two of him and two of me. He was not looking at me, though. I reached out slowly toward one of the images. He turned, he saw me. His mouth opened as he stepped back and vanished.

"What did you want to talk about?" I asked, halting.

"It's hard to know where to begin."

"That's life."

"You upset Dara quite a bit. . . ."

"That was quick. I only left her ten, fifteen minutes ago. You're staying here at Sawall?"

"Yes. And I knew she was having lunch with you. I just saw her briefly a little while ago."

"Well, she didn't make me feel too good either."

I turned another corner and passed through a doorway in time to see him smile faintly.

"She's that way sometimes. I know," he said. "She tells me the Logrus came by for dessert."

"Yes."

"She said it seems to have chosen you for the throne."

I hoped he saw my shrug.

"It seemed that way. I don't want it, though."

"But you said you'd do it."

"Only if there's no other way to restore a certain balance of forces. It's a last resort sort of thing. It won't come to that, I'm sure."

"But it chose you."

Another shrug.

"Tmer and Tubble precede me."

"That doesn't matter. I'd wanted it, you know."

"I know. Seems a pretty dumb career choice."

Suddenly, he surrounded me.

"It does now," he admitted. "It was getting that way for some time,

though, before you got designated. I thought I had the edge each time we met, and each time you came a little closer to killing me."

"It did keep getting messier."

"That last time—in the church—in Kashfa, I was certain I could finally take you out. Instead, you damn near did me in."

"Say that Dara or Mandor removed Tmer and Tubble. You knew you'd have to take care of me yourself, but what about Despil?"

"He'd step aside for me."

"You asked him?"

"No. But I'm sure."

I moved on.

"You always assumed too much, Jurt."

"Maybe you're right," he said, appearing and vanishing again. "Either way, it doesn't matter."

"Why not?"

"I quit. I'm out of the running. The hell with it."

"How come?"

"Even if the Logrus hadn't made its intentions clear, I was beginning to feel nervous. It was not just that I was afraid you'd kill me either. I got to thinking about myself, and the succession. What if I made it to the throne? I'm not so sure as I once was that I'm competent to hold it." I turned again, caught a glimpse of him licking his lips, brows knotted. "I could mess up the realm severely," he went on, "unless I had good advice. And you know that, ultimately, it would come from Mandor or Dara. I'd wind up a puppet, wouldn't I?"

"Probably. But you've gotten me very curious. When did you start thinking this way? Might it coincide with your treatment in the Fountain? What if my interruption made yours closer to the correct course there?"

"It's possible there's something to that," he said. "I'm glad now I didn't go the full route. I suspect it might have driven me mad, as it did Brand. But it may not have been that at all. Or—I don't know."

There was silence as I sidled along a passageway, my puzzled images keeping pace in the mirrors at either hand.

"She didn't want me to kill you," he finally blurted from somewhere off to my right.

"Julia?"

"Yes."

"How is she?"

"Recovering. Pretty rapidly, actually."

"Is she here at Sawall?"

"Yes."

"Look, I'd like to see her. But if she doesn't want to, I understand. I didn't know it was her when I stabbed Mask, and I'm sorry."

"She never really wanted to hurt you. Her quarrel was with Jasra. With you, it was an elaborate game. She wanted to prove she was as good as—maybe better than—you. She wanted to show you what you'd thrown away."

"Sorry," I muttered.

"Tell me one thing, please," he said. "Did you love her? Did you ever really love her?"

I didn't answer him immediately. After all, I'd asked myself that question many times, and I'd had to wait for the answer, too.

"Yes," I finally said. "I didn't realize it till it was too late, though. Bad timing on my part."

A little later I asked, "What about you?"

"I'm not going to make the same mistake you did," he replied. "She's what got me to thinking about all these things. . . ."

"I understand. If she won't see me, tell her that I said I'm sorry—about everything."

There was no reply. I stood still for a time, hoping he'd catch up with me, but he didn't.

Then, "Okay," I called out. "Our duel's ended, so far as I'm concerned."

I began moving again. After a time, I came to an exit and I stepped through it.

He was standing outside, looking up at a massive porcelain face.

"Good," he said.

I drew near.

"There's more," he said, still not looking at me.

"Oh?"

"I think they're stacking the deck," he stated.

"Who? How? What for?"

"Mom and the Logrus," he told me. "To put you on the throne. Who's the bride of the Jewel?"

"I guess that would be Coral. It seems I did hear Dara use that term at some point. Why?"

"I overheard her giving orders last cycle, to some of her Hendrake kin. She's sending a special team to kidnap this woman and bring her here. I got the impression she's intended as your queen."

"That's ridiculous," I said. "She's married to my friend Luke. She's Queen of Kashfa—"

He shrugged.

"Just telling you what I heard," he said. "It had to do with this balancing of forces thing."

Indeed. I hadn't thought of that possibility, but it made perfect sense. With Coral, the Courts would automatically obtain the Jewel of Judgment, or the Eye of the Serpent as it was known hereabout, and that balance would certainly be affected. A loss for Amber, a gain for the Courts. It could be sufficient to achieve what I wanted, the harmony that might postpone catastrophe indefinitely.

Too bad I couldn't let it occur. The poor girl had been jerked around too much, because she happened to be in Amber at the wrong time, because she happened to take a liking to me. I can recall once feeling philosophical in the abstract and deciding, yes, it would be okay to sacrifice one innocent

for the good of the many. That was back in college, and had something to do with principles. But Coral was my friend, my cousin, and technically my lover—though under a set of circumstances that should hardly count; and a quick check of my feelings, so as not to be caught up short again, indicated that I could fall in love with her. All of which meant that philosophy had lost yet another round in the real world.

"How long ago did she send these people off, Jurt?"

"I don't know when they left—or even *if* they've left yet," he replied. "And with the time differential, they could be gone and back already for that matter."

"True," I said, and, "Shit!"

He turned and looked at me.

"It's important in all sorts of other ways, too, I suppose?" he said.

"It is to her, and she is to me," I answered.

His expression changed to one of puzzlement.

"In that case," he said, "why don't you just let them bring her to you? If you have to take the throne, it will sweeten things. If you don't, you'll have her with you, anyhow."

"Feelings are hard enough to keep secret, even around non-sorcerers," I said. "She could be used as a hostage against my behavior."

"Oh. I hate to say this pleases me. What I mean is . . . I'm pleased you care about someone else."

I lowered my head. I wanted to reach out and touch him, but I didn't.

Jurt made a little humming noise, as he sometimes had when pondering things as a kid. Then, "We've got to get her before they do, and move her to someplace safe," he said. "Or take her away from them if they've already got her."

" 'We'?"

He smiled, a rare event.

"You know what I've become. I'm tough."

"I hope so," I said. "But you know what'll happen if there are any witnesses to say it was a couple of the Sawall brothers behind this? Most likely a vendetta with Hendrake."

"Even if Dara talked them into it?"

"It'll look like she set them up."

"Okay," he said. "No witnesses."

I could have said that averting vendetta would save a lot of other lives, but that would have sounded hypocritical even if I didn't mean it that way. Instead, "That power you gained in the Fountain," I said, "gives you something I've heard referred to as a 'living Trump' effect. Seems to me you were able to transport Julia as well as yourself with it."

He nodded.

"Can it get us from here to Kashfa in a hurry?"

The distant sound of an enormous gong filled the air.

"I can do anything the cards can do," he said, "and I can take someone

along with me. The only problem is that the Trumps themselves don't have that range. I'd have to take us there in a series of jumps."

The gong sounded again.

"What's going on?" I asked.

"The noise?" he said. "That's notice that the funeral is about to begin. It can be heard throughout the Courts."

"Bad timing."

"Maybe, maybe not. It's giving me an idea."

"Tell me about it."

"It's our alibi if we have to take out some Hendrakes."

"How so?"

"The time differential. We go to the funeral and get seen. We slip out, run our errand, come back, and attend the rest of the service."

"You think the flow will allow that?"

"I think there's a good chance, yes. I've done a lot of jumping around. I'm starting to get a real feel for flows."

"Then we'll give it a try. The more confusion the better."

Again, the gong.

Red, the color of the fire of life that fills us, is the color of mourning garments in the Courts. I used the spikard rather than the Sign of the Logrus to summon suitable clothing for myself. I'd a desire to avoid any commerce, even the most mundane, with that Power, for now.

Jurt then trumped us to his quarters, where he had suitable garments of his own from the last funeral he'd attended. I'd a small desire to see my old room, too. Sometime, perhaps, when I wasn't rushed. . . .

We washed up, combed, trimmed, dressed quickly. I took on a changed form then, as did Jurt, and we went through the ritual again at this level, before garbing ourselves for the occasion. Shirt, breeches, jacket, cloak, anklets, bracelets, scarf, and bandanna—we looked incendiary. Weapons had to be left behind. We planned to return for them on the way out.

"Ready?" Jurt asked me.

"Yes."

He caught hold of my arm and we were transported, arriving at the inward edge of the Plaza at the End of the World, where a blue sky darkened above a conflagration of mourners milling along the route the procession would take. We passed among them, in hope of being seen by as many as possible. I was greeted by a few old acquaintances. Unfortunately, most wanted to stop and talk, not having seen me for some time. Jurt had similar problems. Most also wondered why we were here, rather than back at the Thelbane, the massive, glassy needle of Chaos far to our rear. Periodically, the air would vibrate as the gong continued its slow sounding. I felt it in the ground, also, as we were very near to its home. We made our way slowly across the Plaza, toward the massive pile of black stone at the very edge of the Pit, its gate an archway of frozen flame, as was its downward stair, each tread and riser time-barred fire, each railing the same. The rough amphitheater below us was also fire-furnished, self-illumed, facing the black block at the end of everything,

no wall behind it, but the open emptiness of the Pit and its singularity whence all things came.

No one was entering it yet, and we stood near the gates of fire and looked back along the route the procession would follow. We nodded to friendly demonic faces, quivered to the note of the gong, watched the sky darken a little further. Suddenly, my head was filled with a powerful presence.

"Merlin!"

I immediately had an image of Mandor in a changed form, looking down his red-clothed arm, hand invisible, presumably regarding me through my Trump, wearing the closest thing I'd seen in a long while to an irritated expression.

"Yes?" I said.

His gaze moved past me. His expression suddenly changed, eyebrows rising, lips parting.

"That's Jurt you're with?" he asked.

"That's right."

"I'd thought you not on the best of terms," he said slowly, "as of our last conversation."

"We agreed to put aside our differences for the funeral."

"While it seems very civilized, I'm not certain how wise it is," he said.

I smiled.

"I know what I'm doing," I told him.

"Really?" he said. "Then why are you at the cathedral rather than here at Thelbane?"

"Nobody told me I was supposed to be at Thelbane."

"Odd," he responded. "Your mother was supposed to have informed both you and Jurt that you were to be part of the procession."

I shook my head and turned away.

"Jurt, did you know we were to be in the procession?" I asked.

"No," he said. "On the one hand, it makes sense. On the other, there's the black watch, which might recommend we maintain a low profile. Who's telling you this?"

"Mandor. He says Dara was supposed to let us know."

"She didn't tell me."

"You catch that?" I said to Mandor.

"Yes. It doesn't matter now. Come on through, both of you."

He extended his other hand.

"He wants us now," I said to Jurt.

"Damn!" Jurt mouthed, and came forward.

I reached out and clasped Mandor's hand just as Jurt came up and caught hold of my shoulder. We both moved forward then—

—into the slick and gleaming interior of Thelbane's main hall at ground level, a study in black, gray, mossy green, deep red, chandeliers like stalactites, fire sculptures about the walls, scaly hides hung behind them, drifting globes of water in the middle air, creatures swimming within them. The place was filled with nobles, relatives, courtiers, stirring like a field of flame about the

catafalque at the hall's center. The gong sounded again just as Mandor said something to us.

He waited till the vibrations subsided, then spoke again: "I said Dara hasn't arrived yet. Go pay your respects, and let Bances assign you places in the procession."

Glancing toward the catafalque, I caught sight of both Tmer and Tubble in the vicinity. Tmer was talking to Bances, Tubble to someone who had his back turned this way. A horrible thought suddenly struck me.

"What," I asked, "is the security situation for the procession?"

Mandor smiled.

"There are quite a few guardsmen mixed in with the group here," he said, "and more spotted along the way. Someone will be watching you every second."

I glanced at Jurt to see whether he'd heard that. He nodded.

"Thanks."

Keeping my litany of obscenities subvocal, I moved toward the casket, Jurt at my back. The only way I could think to produce a double would be to talk the Pattern into sending in a ghost of myself to take my place. But the Logrus would detect the ringer's projected energies in no time. And if I just left, not only would my absence be noticed, but I'd probably be tracked— possibly by the Logrus itself once Dara called a conference. Then it would be learned that I'd gone off to thwart the Logrus's attempt to rebalance order, and the headwaters of Shit Creek are a cruel and treacherous expanse. I would not make the mistake of fancying myself indispensable.

"How are we going to do this, Merlin?" Jurt said softly as we found our way to the end of the slow-moving line.

The gong sounded again, causing the chandeliers to vibrate.

"I don't see how we can," I answered. "I think the best I can hope for is to try getting a message through as I walk along."

"It can't be done by Trump from here," he answered. "Well, maybe under perfect conditions," he amended, "but not with all these distractions."

I tried to think of some spell, some sending, some agent to serve me in this. Ghost would have been ideal. Of course, he'd drifted off to explore the spatial asymmetries of the Sculpture Hall. That could keep him occupied for a long while.

"I could get there pretty quickly," Jurt volunteered, "and with the time differential I might make it back before anyone noticed."

"And you know exactly two people in Kashfa you might tell," I said. "Luke and Coral. They both met you in church, when we were trying to kill each other—and you stole Luke's father's sword. Offhand, I'd say he'd try to kill you on sight and she'd scream for help."

The line advanced somewhat.

"So I don't ask for help," he said.

"Un-uh," I told him. "I know you're tough, but Hendrakes are pros. Also, you'd be faced with a very uncooperative rescuee in Coral."

"You're a sorcerer," Jurt said. "If we find out who the guards are, couldn't

you lay a spell on them so that they *think* they see us for this whole affair? Then we disappear and no one's the wiser."

"I've a hunch either Mom or our big brother has laid protective spells on the guards. At such an ideal time for an assassination, I would. I wouldn't want anyone able to mess with my people's heads if I were running security here."

We shuffled a little farther along. By leaning to one side and stretching my neck I was able to get a few glimpses of the wasted demonic form of old Swayvill, resplendently garbed, serpent of red-gold laid upon his breast, there in the flame-formed coffin, Oberon's ancient nemesis, going to join him at last.

As I moved nearer, it occurred to me that there was more than one approach to the problem. Perhaps I'd dwelled too long among the magically naive. I'd gotten out of the habit of thinking of magic against magic, of multiple mixed spells. So what if the guards were protected from any fiddling with their perceptions? Let it be. Find a way to work around it.

The gong sounded again. When the echoes died, Jurt leaned near.

"There's more to it than everything I said," he whispered.

"What do you mean?" I asked.

"Another reason I came to you back at Sawall was because I was scared," he replied.

"Of what?"

"At least one of them—Mandor or Dara—wants more than a balance, wants a total victory for the Logrus, for Chaos. I really believe that. It's not just that I don't want to be party to it. I don't want it to happen. Now that I can visit Shadow I don't want to see it destroyed. I don't want a victory for either side. Total control by the Pattern would probably be just as bad."

"How can you be sure one of them really wants this?"

"They tried it before with Brand, didn't they? He was out to destroy all order."

"No," I said. "He planned to destroy the old order, then replace it with his own. He was a revolutionary, not an anarchist. He was going to create a new Pattern within the Chaos he brought forth—his own, but still the real thing."

"He was duped. He couldn't have managed a thing like that."

"No way of knowing till he tried, and he didn't get the chance."

"Either way, I'm afraid someone's going to pull the plug on reality. If this kidnapping takes place, it'll be a big step in that direction. If you can't manage something to cover our absence, I think we should just go anyway and take our chances."

"Not yet," I said. "Hang on. I'm working something out. How's this sound? I don't locate the guards and hallucinate them. Instead, I do a transformation. I cause a couple of other people to look like us. You trump us out as soon as I do. That won't be a hallucination for anyone. Everyone will see them as us; we can go about our business—and check back if we have to."

"You do it and I'll get us out of here."

"Okay, I'll do it to the two guys in front of us. As soon as I've finished I'll gesture like this," I said, lowering my left hand from shoulder-height to waist-level, "and we both stoop as if one of us had dropped something. Then you take us away."

"I'll be ready."

The spikard made it easier than working out a transform spell. It was like a spell processor. I fed it the two end products, and it ran thousands of variations in a trice and handed me the finished products—a pair of spells it would have taken me a long while to work out along classical lines. I raised my hand as I hung them and accessed one of the many power sources the thing commanded off in Shadow. I fed juice into the constructs, watched the change commence, dropped my hand, and leaned forward.

There followed a moment's vertigo, and when I straightened we were back in Jurt's apartment. I laughed and he slapped my shoulder.

Immediately then, we were changing back into our human forms and garments. As soon as that was done, he caught hold of my arm again and trumped us to Fire Gate. A moment later, and he'd jumped us again, this time to a mountaintop overlooking a blue valley beneath a green sky. Then again, to the middle of a high bridge above a deep gorge, the sky putting away stars or taking them on.

"Okay, now," he said, and we stood atop a gray stone wall damp with dew, possibly even the remains of a storm. Clouds were taking fire in the east. There was a light breeze out of the south.

This was the wall that surrounded the innermost zone of Jidrash, Luke's capital in Kashfa. There were four huge buildings below us—including the palace and the Temple of the Unicorn directly across the Plaza from it—as well as a number of smaller buildings. Diagonally across the way from where we stood was the wing of the palace from which Gryll had fetched me (how long ago?) from my rendezvous with the queen. I could even make out the broken shutter of our window amid an expanse of ivy.

"Over there," I said, gesturing. "That's where I last saw her."

An eyeblink later we stood within the chamber, its only inhabitants. The place had been straightened, the bed made up. I withdrew my Trumps and shuffled out Coral's. Staring then till it grew cold, I felt her presence and reached for it.

She was there yet she wasn't. It was the disjointed sense of presence one encounters in dream or stupor. I passed my hand over the card and ended our tenuous contact.

"What happened?" Jurt asked.

"I think she's drugged," I replied.

"Then it would seem they've already got her," he said. "Any way you can trace her in that state?"

"She could also be in the next building, on medication," I said. "She wasn't well when I left."

"What now?"

"Either way, we've got to talk to Luke," I said, searching for his card.

I reached him in an instant on uncovering it.

"Merlin! Where the hell are you?" he asked.

"If you're in the palace, I'm next door," I said.

He rose to his feet from what I now realized to be the edge of a bedstead, and he picked up a long-sleeved green shirt and drew it on, covering his collection of scars. I thought that I glimpsed someone in the bed behind him. He muttered something in that direction, but I could not overhear it.

"We've got to talk," he said, running his hand through his rusty hair. "Bring me through."

"Okay," I said. "But first, you'd better know that my brother Jurt is here."

"Has he got my dad's sword?"

"Uh—No."

"Guess I won't kill him right now," he said, tucking his shirt into his waistband.

Abruptly, he extended his hand. I clasped it. He stepped forward and joined us.

EIGHT

Luke grinned at me, scowled at Jurt.

"Where've you been, anyway?" he asked.

"The Courts of Chaos," I replied. "I was summoned from here at the death of Swayvill. The funeral's in progress right now. We sneaked away when I learned that Coral was in danger."

"I know that—now," Luke said. "She's gone. Kidnapped, I think."

"When did it happen?"

"Night before last, I'd judge. What do you know of it?"

I glanced at Jurt. "Time differential," he said.

"She represented a chance to pick up a few points," I explained, "in the ongoing game between the Pattern and the Logrus. So agents of Chaos were sent for her. They wanted her intact, though. She should be okay."

"What do they want her for?"

"Seems they feel she's specially suited to be queen in Thelbane, what with the Jewel of Judgment as a piece of her anatomy and all."

"Who's going to be the new king?"

My face felt warm of a sudden.

"Well, the people who came for her had me in mind for the job," I replied.

"Hey, congratulations!" he said. "Now I don't have to be the only one having all this fun."

"What do you mean?"

"This king business ain't worth shit, man. I wish I'd never gotten sucked into the deal in the first place. Everybody's got a piece of your time, and when they don't someone still has to know where you are."

"Hell, you were just crowned. Give it a chance to shake down."

" 'Just'? It's been over a month!"

"Time differential," Jurt repeated.

"Come on. I'll buy you a cup of coffee," Luke said.

"You've got coffee here?"

"I require it, man. This way." He led us out the door, turned left, headed down a stair.

"I had a funny thought," he said, "while you were talking back there— about you reigning, and Coral a desirable queen. I could get the marriage annulled pretty damn quick, since I'm in charge here. Now, you want her for your queen and I want that Golden Circle Treaty with Amber. I think I see a way to make everybody happy."

"It's a lot more complicated than that, Luke. I don't want the job, and it would be very bad for us if my kinsmen back in the Courts got custody of Coral. I've learned a lot of things recently."

"Such as?" Luke said, opening a postern that let upon a walkway to the rear of the palace.

I glanced back at Jurt.

"He's scared, too," I said. "That's why we're a little more cordial these days."

Jurt nodded.

"It's possible Brand could have been partly victim of a plan originated in the Courts," he said, "part of an idea that's still alive there."

"We'd better go for the whole breakfast," Luke said. "Let's swing around back and take it in the kitchen."

We followed him down a garden path.

And so we ate and talked as the day brightened about us. Luke insisted I try Coral's Trump again, which I did with the same result. Then he cursed, nodded, and said, "Your timing's actually pretty good. The guys who grabbed her were reported to have taken off along a black trail into the west."

"It figures," I said.

"I've reason to believe they didn't make it back to the Courts with her."

"Oh?"

"I understand these black thoroughfares you guys use are dangerous to outsiders," he observed. "But I can show you what's left of this one—it's a black pathway now, actually. I'd like to follow it, but I don't know that I can get away for long. Also, is there a way to protect me from the trail itself?"

"Just being in our company would keep you from harm as we traveled it," Jurt said.

I stood. The cook and two dishwashers glanced in our direction.

"There is somebody you have to meet, Luke," I told him. "Right now."

"Why not?" he said, rising. "Where is he?"

"Let's take a walk," I said.

"Sure."

We got to our feet, headed back to the servants' door.

"So, whether she was a willing accomplice or a magical time bomb, Mom might have conned Dad into his efforts to take over in Amber—and, ultimately, to change the world," Luke said.

"Well, I gather he didn't exactly come to her with clean hands," I said.

"True, but I wonder how elaborate his plans really were, to begin with," Luke mused. "This is the most cheerful thing I've heard all month."

We exited into the little covered walkway that ran along the side of the palace. Luke halted and looked around.

"Where is he?" he asked.

"Not here," I said. "I just needed a point of departure with no witnesses to say I'd kidnapped the king."

"Where *are* we going, Merlin?" Jurt asked, as I swirled a spiral from the center of the spikard, drawing upon sixteen different power sources.

"Good idea. Kidnap away," Luke was saying as he was caught up along with Jurt.

I used it as I had when I'd transported myself from Amber to Kashfa, forming the target from memory rather than discovered vision. Only this time there were three of us and a long, long way to go.

"Have I got a deal for you," I said.

It was like stepping into a kaleidoscope, and passing through about 120 degrees of cubist fragmentation and reassembly, before emerging on the other side beneath a towering tree, its top lost in the fog, in the vicinity of a red and white '57 Chevy, its radio playing Renbourn's "Nine Maidens."

Luke's ghost emerged from the front seat and stared at the original. Luke stared back.

"Hi," I said. "Meet each other. You hardly need an introduction, though. You have so much in common."

Jurt stared at the Pattern.

"That's my dad's edition," I said.

"I could have guessed that," Jurt told me. "But what are we doing here?"

"An idea I had. But I thought Corwin would be here, and I might discuss it with him."

"He came back, and he left again," said the resident Luke, overhearing me.

"Did he leave a forwarding address, or say when he might return?"

"Nope."

"Damn! Look, something that got said just a little while ago gave me the idea that you Lukes might want to change places for a time—if this Pattern could be persuaded to approve some leave."

Luke, whom I decided to continue calling Luke when his ghost was around, brightened suddenly. I resolved to think of his double as Rinaldo, to keep things sorted.

"It's an experience no man should do without," he said.

"Then why are you so anxious to get away from it?" Rinaldo replied.

"To help Merle find Coral," Luke said. "She's been kidnapped."

"Really? By whom?"

"Agents of Chaos."

"Hm." Rinaldo began to pace. "Okay, you know more about it than I do," he finally said. "If Corwin gets back soon and the Pattern excuses me, I'll help you any way I can."

"The trail will be getting colder while we wait," Luke observed.

"You don't understand," Rinaldo said. "I've got a job to do here, and I can't just take off—even if it's to go and be a king somewhere. What I do is more important."

Luke glanced at me.

"He's right," I said. "He's a guardian of the Pattern. On the other hand, nobody's about to hurt Coral. Why don't Jurt and I pop on back to the Courts for a few minutes, to check on the progress of the funeral? Corwin might show up while we're about it. I'm sure you two will find something to talk about."

"Go ahead," Luke told me.

"Yeah," said Rinaldo. "I'd like to know what we've been doing."

I looked at Jurt, who nodded. I went and stood beside him.

"Your turn to drive," I said.

"Back soon," I remarked as we faded into the first jump.

. . . And so again to the Ways of Sawall, and back into our ruddy garb over demonform. I also changed our facial appearance to the nondescript before Jurt returned us to the funeral party, not wanting a matching set marching along.

The Thelbane proved deserted. A quick check outside, however, showed us the procession, perhaps a quarter way across the Plaza, halted and in a state of confusion.

"Uh-oh," Jurt remarked. "What should I do?"

"Take us down there," I told him.

Moments later, we were at the outer edge of the crowd. Swayvill's blazing casket had been lowered to the ground, a guard posted about it. My attention was immediately attracted to a knot of figures perhaps twenty feet off to the right of it. There was some shouting going on, something lay upon the ground, and two demonic forms were being held tightly by several others. My stomach tightened as I saw that the two were the pair I had ensorcelled to resemble Jurt and myself. Both were protesting something.

As I pushed my way forward, I withdrew my spells, causing the two to revert to their own appearance. There were more shouts as this occurred, including an "I told you!" from the nearest. The response to this was a "Yes, they are!" from someone I suddenly realized to be Mandor. He stood between them and the thing on the ground.

"It was a trick!" Mandor said. "A distraction! Release them!"

I decided the moment was propitious for dropping the spells that masked Jurt and myself. Glorious confusion!

Moments later, Mandor saw me and signaled for me to approach. Jurt, I saw, off to my right, had stopped to talk to someone he knew.

"Merlin!" he said as soon as I was near. "What do you know of this?"

"Nothing," I said. "I was way to the rear, with Jurt. I don't even know what happened."

"Someone gave two of the security guards your appearance and Jurt's. This was obviously intended to create confusion when the assassin struck. They rushed forward insisting they were guards. Obviously, they weren't. Clever—especially with you and Jurt on their black watch list."

"I see," I agreed, wondering whether I had helped an assassin to escape. "Who got hit?"

"Tmer, with a very professional dagger stroke," he explained, left eyelid twitching. A faint wink? Meaning? "And he was gone in an instant."

Four mourners, having made a stretcher of cloaks, raised the fallen body. After they'd moved only a few paces with it, I saw another knot of people beyond them.

Seeing my puzzled expression, Mandor glanced back.

"More security," he said. "They're surrounding Tubble. I think I'll order him out of here for now. You and Jurt, too. You can come to the temple later. I'll see that security's even heavier there."

"Okay," I said. "Is Dara here?"

He glanced about.

"I haven't seen her. Don't now, either. You'd better go."

I nodded. As I turned away, I saw a half-familiar face off to my right. She was tall and dark-eyed, shifting from a swirl of multicolored jewels to a swaying flowerlike form, and she had been staring at me. I had been trying to recall her name earlier, and had failed. Seeing her brought it back, though. I approached her.

"I have to leave for a time," I said. "But I wanted to say hello, Gilva."

"You do remember. I was wondering."

"Of course."

"How are you, Merlin?"

I sighed. She smiled her way into furry, half-human solidity.

"Me, too," she said. "I'll be so glad when this is all settled."

"Yes. Listen, I want to see you—for several reasons. When would be a good time?"

"Why, anytime after the funeral, I guess. What about?"

"No time now. Mandor's giving me angry looks. See you later."

"Yes. Later, Merlin."

I hurried back to Jurt and caught him by the elbow.

"We're ordered to leave," I said. "Security reasons."

"All right." He turned to the man he'd been talking with. "Thanks. I'll see you later," he told him.

The world slipped away. A new one dawned: Jurt's apartment, our clothes strewn about it.

"Good timing for us. Bad for Tmer," he remarked.

"True."

"How's it feel to be number two?" he asked as we changed again—both clothing and form.

"It advances your case, too," I said.

"I've a feeling he died on your account, brother, not mine."

"I hope not," I said.

He laughed.

"It's between Tubble and you."

"If it were, I'd be dead already," I said. "If you're right, it's really between Sawall and Chanicut."

"Wouldn't it be funny, Merlin, if I were sticking with you because it's the safest place to be just now?" he asked. "I'm sure our guards and assassins are better than Chanicut's. Supposing I'm just waiting, saving my final effort till Tubble's out of the way? Then, trusting me and all, you turn your back—Coronation!"

I looked at him. He was smiling, but he also seemed to be studying me.

I was about to say, "You can have it, without the trouble," in a joking way. But I wondered just then: Even in jest, if it were a choice between the two of us . . . It occurred to me that if we were the only options, this was a circumstance under which I'd agree to take the throne. I'd resolved to give him the benefit of the doubt, to meet him more than halfway. But I couldn't help it. For all his conciliatory talk and apparent cooperation, a lifelong habit is a hard thing to break. I couldn't bring myself to trust him anymore than I had to.

"Tell it to the Logrus," I said.

A look of fear—the widening of the eyes, the shifting of the gaze downward, a small forward tightening of the shoulders—then, "You really do have an understanding with it, don't you?" he asked.

"There seems to be an understanding, but it only works one way," I said.

"What do you mean?"

"I'm not about to help either side wreck our world."

"Sounds like you're prepared to double-cross the Logrus."

I raised a finger to my lips.

"It must be your Amber blood," he said then. "I've been told they're all a little crazy."

"Maybe so," I said.

"Sounds like something your father would do."

"What do you know of him?"

"You know, everybody has a favorite Amber story."

"Nobody around here ever told any to me."

"Of course not—considering."

"Me being a half-breed and all?" I said.

He shrugged. Then, "Well, yes."

I pulled on my boots.

"Whatever you're doing with that new Pattern," he said, "it probably won't make the old one too happy."

"Doubtless you're right," I agreed.

"So you won't be able to run to it for protection if the Logrus is after you."

"I guess not."

". . . And if they're both after you, the new one won't be able to stand against them."

"You think they'd really get together on anything?"

"Hard to say. You're playing a wild game. I hope you know what you're doing."

"Me, too," I said, rising. "My turn."

I unwound the spikard at a level I'd never attempted before, and I got us there in a single jump.

Luke and Rinaldo were still talking. I could tell them apart by their garments. Corwin was nowhere in sight.

Both waved as we made our appearance.

"How's everything in the Courts?" Luke asked.

"Chaotic," Jurt replied. "How long have we been away?"

"Six hours, I'd guess," Rinaldo replied.

"No sign of Corwin?" I asked.

"No," Luke said. "But in the meantime, we've worked out a deal with each other—and Rinaldo's been in touch with the Pattern here. It will release him and continue his maintenance as soon as Corwin returns."

"Regarding that . . ." Jurt said.

"Yes?" Rinaldo asked.

"I'll stay here and cover for Rinaldo while you go find the lady with the glass eye."

"Why?" Rinaldo asked.

"Because you'll do a better job together and I'll feel a lot safer here than I would most other places."

"I'd have to see whether that's acceptable," Rinaldo said.

"Do it," said Jurt.

He moved off toward the Pattern. I searched the fog in all directions, hoping to see my father returning. Jurt studied the car, its radio now playing a Bruce Dunlap number from "Los Animales."

"If your father comes back and relieves me," Jurt said, "I'll return to the funeral and make excuses for you if you're not there. If you get back and I'm not there, you do the same. All right?"

"Yes," I said, wisps of mist rising like smoke between us. "And whichever of us is free first and has something worth saying . . ."

"Yes," he agreed. "I'll come looking if you don't get to me."

"Didn't happen to pick up my sword while you were back in the Courts, did you?" Luke asked.

"Didn't have time," Jurt replied.

"Next time you're back, I wish you'd make time."

"I will, I will," Jurt said.

Rinaldo moved away from the Pattern, returned to us.

"You're hired," he said to Jurt. "Come with me. There's a spring I want to show you, and a store of food, some weapons."

Luke turned and watched them move off to our left.

"I'm sorry," he said softly, "but I still don't trust him."

"Don't be sorry. I don't either. I've known him too long. But we have better reasons for trusting each other now than we've had for a long time."

"I'm wondering whether it was wise to let him know where this Pattern is, and now to leave him alone with it."

"I'm pretty sure the Pattern knows what it's doing, and that it can take care of itself."

He raised a pair of crossed fingers.

"I'd've argued against it," he said, "save that I need my double."

When they returned, a deejay's baritone suddenly rolled forth, saying, "It all goes to show, timing is everything. Road conditions are fine. It is a good day for travel." Immediately, there followed a drum solo I'd have sworn was something I once heard Random play.

"You're on duty as of now," Rinaldo said to Jurt. To us, he nodded. "Anytime."

I caught us up with the spikard and spun us back to Kashfa, bringing us into Jidrash near twilight, to the same walltop vantage I had enjoyed earlier with my brother.

"And so at last," Rinaldo said, looking out over the town.

"Yes," Luke replied. "It's all yours—for a time." Then, "Merle, how's about jumping us to my apartment?"

I turned to the west where clouds had gone orange, glanced upward to where several hung purple.

"Before we do that, Luke," I said, "I'd like to use what daylight's left for a look at that black trail."

He nodded.

"Good idea. Okay, take us over there."

His gesture indicated a hilly area to the southwest. I caught us up and spikarded us to it, creating a verb for which I felt a need in the same act. Such is the power of Chaos.

Arriving on a small hilltop, we followed Luke down its far side.

"Over this way," he said.

Long shadows lay all about us, but there is a difference between their dimness and the blackness of a travel-thread from the Courts.

"It was right here," Luke finally said when we came to a place between a pair of boulders.

I moved forward into the area but I felt nothing special.

"You sure this is the place?" I asked.

"Yes."

I advanced another ten paces, twenty.

"If this is really where it was, it's gone now," I told him. "Of course . . . I wonder how long we've been away?"

Luke snapped his fingers.

"Timing," he observed. "Take us back to my apartments."

We kissed the day good-bye as I sent forth a lead and opened our way through the wall of dark. We stepped through into the room I had occupied earlier with Coral.

"Close enough?" I asked. "I'm not sure where your rooms are."

"Come on," he said, taking us out, to the left and down the stair. "Time to consult the resident expert. Merle, do something about this guy's appearance. Too much of a good thing might cause comment."

It was easy, and the first time I'd made anyone look like the big portrait of Oberon back home.

Luke knocked on a door before entering. Somewhere beyond it, a familiar voice spoke his name.

"I have some friends with me," he said.

"Bring them in," came her reply.

He opened the door and did so.

"Both of you know Nayda," Luke announced. "Nayda, this is my double. Let's call him Rinaldo and me Luke while we're together. He's going to run things for me here while Merle and I are off looking for your sister."

I changed Rinaldo back then, in response to her puzzled look.

She had on black trousers and an emerald blouse, her hair bound back by a matching green scarf. She smiled as she greeted us, and when she regarded me she touched her lips lightly, almost casually, with a fingertip. I nodded immediately.

"I trust you are recovered from any misadventures in Amber," I said. "You were, of course, there at a bad time."

"Of course," she responded. "Fully recovered, thank you. Kind of you to ask. Thanks, too, for the recent directions. It was you, I take it, who spirited Luke away these two days past?"

"It's really been that long?" I said.

"It has, sir."

"Sorry about that, my dear," Luke said, squeezing her hand and looking long into her eyes.

"That explains why the trail's faded," I said.

Rinaldo seized her hand and kissed it, while executing an elaborate bow.

"Amazing how much you've changed from the girl I knew," he stated.

"Oh?"

"I share Luke's memories as well as his appearance," he explained.

"I could tell there was something not quite human about you," she remarked. "I see you as a man whose very blood is fire."

"And how might you see that?" he inquired.

"She has her means," Luke said, "though I thought it only a psychic bond with her sister. Apparently it goes somewhat further."

She nodded.

"Speaking of which, I hope you can use it to help us track her," he continued. "With the trail gone and a drug or a spell barring a Trump call, we'll be needing assistance."

"Yes," she answered, "though she is in no danger at the moment."

"Good," he said. "In that case, I'll order us all food and set to briefing this good-looking fellow on what's going on in Kashfa these days."

"Luke," I said. "It sounds like an ideal time for me to head back to the Courts for the rest of the funeral."

"How long would you be gone, Merle?"

"I don't know," I replied.

"Back by morning, I trust?"

"Me, too. What if I'm not, though?"

"I've a feeling I should go looking without you."

"Try reaching me first, though."

"Sure. See you later."

I drew my cloak of space about me, shrugging Kashfa away. When I opened it again I was back in Jurt's quarters at Sawall.

I stretched, I yawned. I did a quick turn about the room, making certain I was alone. I unfastened my cloak and tossed it upon the bed. I paced as I unbuttoned my shirt.

Halt. What was it? Also, where?

I retraced a few paces. I had never spent a great deal of time in my younger brother's rooms, but I would have recalled what I was feeling.

There was a chair and table in the corner formed by the wall and an armoire of dark, almost black wood. Kneeling on the chair and reaching over the table, I could feel it—the presence of a way, not quite strong enough for transport, though. Ergo. . . .

I moved off to my right, opened the armoire. It had to be inside, of course. I wondered how recently he had installed it. I also felt slightly funny about poking about in his quarters this way. Still, he owed me for a lot of misery and inconvenience. A few confidences and a little cooperation hardly cleaned the slate. I hadn't learned to trust him yet, and it was possible he was setting me up for something. Good manners, I decided, would have to be sacrificed to prudence.

I pushed garments aside, making a way clear to the back of the thing. I could feel it strongly. A final shove at the garments, a quick shuffle to the rear, and I was at the focus. I let it take me away.

Once there was a forward yielding, the pressure of the garments at my back gave me a small push. That, plus the fact that someone (Jurt, himself?) had done a sloppy shadowmastering job resulting in mismatched floor levels, sent me sprawling as I achieved destination.

At least, I didn't land in a pit full of sharpened stakes or acid. Or the lair of some half-starved beast. No, it was a green-tiled floor, and I caught myself as I fell. And from the flickering light all about me I guessed there was a mess of candles burning.

Even before I looked up I was sure they'd all be green.

Nor was I incorrect. About that or anything else.

The setup was similar to that of my father, with a groined vault containing a light source superior to the candles. Only there was no painting above this altar. This one featured a stained-glass window, lots of green in it, and a little red.

Its principal was Brand.

I rose and crossed to it. Lying upon it, drawn a few inches from its sheath, was Werewindle.

I reached out and took hold of it, my first impulse being to bear it away with me for eventual restoration to Luke. Then I hesitated. It wasn't something I could wear to a funeral. If I took it now I'd have to hide it somewhere, and it was already well-hidden right here. I let my hand rest upon it, though, as I thought. It contained a similar feeling of power to that which Grayswandir bore, only somehow brighter, less tragedy-touched and brooding. Ironic. It seemed an ideal blade for a hero.

I looked about. There was a book on a reading stand off to my left, a pentagram upon the floor behind me, worked in different shades of green, a smell—as of a recent wood fire—hung in the air. Idly, I wondered what I might find if I were to knock a hole in the wall. Was this chapel located upon a mountaintop? Beneath a lake? Underground? Was it drifting somewhere in the heavens?

What did it represent? It looked to be religious in nature. And Benedict, Corwin, and Brand were the three I knew about. Were they admired, respected—venerated—by certain of my countrymen and relatives? Or were these hidden chapels somehow more sinister?

I removed my hand from Werewindle, stepped to the vicinity of the pentagram.

My Logrus vision revealed nothing untoward, but an intense scan with the spikard detected the residue of a long-removed magical operation. The traces were too faint to tell me anything of its nature, however. While it seemed possible I might probe further after this and come up with a clearer picture, I also realized I hadn't the time such an operation would require.

Reluctantly, I retreated to the vicinity of the way. Could these places have been used to try to influence the individuals involved?

I shook my head. This was something I would have to save for another day. I located the way and gave myself to it.

I stumbled on my return, also.

Catching hold of the frame with one hand, I seized a garment with another, kept myself upright, straightened, and stepped out. Then I shifted the clothing back into place and shut the doors.

I stripped quickly, altering my form as I was about it, and I donned my mourning garb once again. I felt some activity in the vicinity of the spikard, and for the first time I caught it drawing upon one of the many sources it commanded to alter its shape, accommodating the changing size of my finger. It had obviously done this several times before, though this was the first time I had noted the process. This was interesting, in that it showed the device capable of acting independent of my will.

I didn't really know what the thing was, what its origin might have been. I kept it because it represented a considerable source of power, an acceptable substitute for the use of the Logrus, which I now feared. But as I watched it change shape to remain snug upon my changing finger, I wondered. What if it were somehow booby-trapped to turn upon me at exactly the wrong moment?

I turned it a couple of times upon my finger. I moved into it with my mind, knowing this to be an exercise in futility. It would take ages for me to run down each line to its source, to check out hidden spells along the way. It was like taking a trip through a Swiss watch—custom-made. I was impressed both with the beauty of its design, and with the enormous amount of work that had gone into its creation. It could easily possess hidden imperatives that would only respond to special sets of circumstances. Yet—

It had done nothing untoward, yet. And the alternative was the Logrus. It struck me as a genuine instance of the preferability of the devil one didn't know.

Growling, I adjusted my apparel, focused my attention on the Temple of the Serpent, and bade the spikard deliver me near its entrance. It performed as smoothly and gently as if I had never doubted it, as if I had not discovered in it yet another cause for paranoia.

And for a time, I simply stood outside the doors of frozen flame, there at the great Cathedral of the Serpent at the outer edge of the Plaza at the End of the World, situated exactly at the Rim, opened to the Pit itself—where, on a good day, one can view the creation of the universe, or its ending—and I watched the stars swarm through space that folded and unfolded like the petals of flowers; and as if my life were about to change, my thoughts returned to California and school, of sailing the *Sunburst* with Luke and Gail and Julia, of sitting with my father near the end of the war, of riding with Vinta Bayle through the wine country to the east of Amber, of a long, brisk afternoon spent showing Coral about the town, of the strange encounters of that day; and I turned and raised my scaly hand, stared past it at the spire of Thelbane, and "they cease not fighting, east and west, on the marches of my breast," I thought. How long, how long . . . ?—irony, as usual, a three-to-one favorite whenever sentimentality makes its move.

Turning again, I went in to see the last of the King of Chaos.

NINE

Down, down into the pile, into the great slag heap, window onto the ends of time and space, where nothing is to be seen at the end, I went, between walls forever afire, never burnt down, walking in one of my bodies toward the sound of a voice reading from the Book of the Serpent Hung upon the Tree of Matter, and at length came into the grotto that backed upon blackness, widening semicircles of red-clad mourners facing the reader and the grand catafalque beside which he stood, Swayvill clearly in view within it, half-covered with red flowers dropped by mourners, red tapers flickering against the Pit, but a few paces behind them; across the rear of the chamber then, listening to Bances of Amblerash, High Priest of the Serpent, his words sounding as if spoken beside me, for the acoustics of Chaos are good; finding a seat in an otherwise empty arc, where anyone looking back

would be certain to notice me; seeking familiar faces, finding Dara, Tubble, and Mandor seated in frontal positions that indicated they were to assist Bances in sliding the casket past the edge into forever when the time came; and in my divided heart I recalled the last funeral I had attended before this: Caine's, back in Amber, beside the sea, and I thought again of Bloom and the way the mind wanders on these occasions.

I sought about me. Jurt was nowhere in sight. Gilva of Hendrake was only a couple of rows below me. I shifted my gaze to the deep blackness beyond the Rim. It was almost as if I were looking down, rather than out— if such terms had any real meaning in that place. Occasionally, I would perceive darting points of light or rolling masses. It served me as a kind of Rorschach for a time, and I half-dozed before the prospect of dark butterflies, clouds, pairs of faces—

I sat upright with a small start, wondering what had broken my reverie. The silence, it was. Bances had stopped reading.

I was about to lean forward and whisper something to Gilva when Bances began the Consignment. I was startled to discover that I recalled all of the appropriate responses.

As the chanting swelled and focused, I saw Mandor get to his feet, and Dara, and Tubble. They moved forward, joining Bances about the casket— Dara and Mandor at its foot, Tubble and Bances at its head. Service assistants rose from their section and began snuffing candles, until only the large one, at the Rim, behind Bances, still flickered. At this point we all stood.

The ever-eerie light of flame mosaics, worked into the walls at either hand, granted additional illumination to the extent that I could detect the movement below when the chanting ceased.

The four figures stooped slightly, presumably taking hold of the casket's handles. They straightened then and moved toward the Rim. An assistant advanced and stood beside the candle just as they passed it, ready to snuff the final flame as Swayvill's remains were consigned to Chaos.

A half-dozen paces remained. . . . Three. Two. . . .

Bances and Tubble knelt at the verge, positioning the casket within a groove in the stone floor, Bances intoning a final bit of ritual the while, Dara and Mandor remaining standing.

The prayer finished, I heard a curse. Mandor seemed jerked forward. Dara stumbled away to the side. I heard a *clunk* as the casket hit the floor. The assistant's hand had already been moving, and the candle went out at that moment. There followed a skidding sound as the casket moved forward, more curses, a shadowy figure retreating from the Rim. . . .

Then came a wail. A bulky outline fell and was gone. The wail diminished, diminished, diminished. . . .

I raised my left fist, caused the spikard to create a globe of white light as a bubble pipe does a bubble. It was about three feet in diameter when I released it to drift overhead. Suddenly, the place was filled with babbling. Others of sorcerous background having exercised their favorite illumination

spells at about the same time I had, the temple was now over-illuminated from dozens of point-sources.

Squinting, I saw Bances, Mandor, and Dara in converse near the Rim. Tubble and the remains of Swayvill were no longer with us.

My fellow mourners were already moving. I did, too, realizing that my time here was now extremely limited.

I stepped down over the empty row, moved to the right, touched Gilva's still humanized shoulder.

"Merlin!" she said, turning quickly. "Tubble—went over—didn't he?"

"Sure looked that way," I said.

"What will happen now?"

"I've got to leave," I said, "fast!"

"Why?"

"Somebody's going to start thinking about the succession in a few moments, and I'm going to be smothered with protection," I told her. "I can't have that, not just now."

"Why not?"

"No time to go into that. But I'd wanted to talk to you. May I borrow you now?"

There were milling bodies all about us.

"Of course—sir," she said, apparently having just thought about the succession.

"Cut that out," I said, spikard spiraling the energies that caught us and took us away.

I brought us to the forest of metal trees, and Gilva kept hold of my arm and looked about her.

"Lord, what is this place?" she asked.

"I'd rather not say," I replied, "for reasons that will become apparent in a moment. I only had one question for you the last time I spoke with you. But now I have two, and this place figures in one of them, in a way, besides being fairly deserted most of the time."

"Ask," she said, moving to face me. "I'll try to help. If it's important, though, I may not be the best person—"

"Yes, it's important. But I haven't time to make an appointment with Belissa. It concerns my father, Corwin."

"Yes?"

"It was he who slew Borel of Hendrake in the war at Patternfall."

"So I understand," she said.

"After the war, he joined the royal party that came here to the Courts to work out the Treaty."

"Yes," she said. "I know that."

"He disappeared shortly thereafter, and no one seemed to know where he'd gotten off to. For a time, I thought he might be dead. Later, however, I received indications that he was not, but rather was imprisoned somewhere. Can you tell me anything about this?"

She turned away suddenly.

"I am offended," she said, "by what I believe you imply."

"I'm sorry," I said, "but I had to ask."

"Ours is an honorable House," she said. "We accept the fortunes of war. When the fighting is ended, we put it all behind us."

"I apologize," I said. "We're even related, you know, on my mother's side."

"Yes, I know," she said, turning away. "Will that be all, Prince Merlin?"

"Yes," I answered. "Where shall I send you?"

She was silent for a moment, then, "You said there were two questions," she stated.

"Forget it. I changed my mind about the second one."

She turned back.

"Why? Why should I forget it? Because I maintain my family's honor?"

"No, because I believe you."

"And?"

"I'll trouble someone else for an opinion."

"Do you mean it's dangerous, and you've decided against asking me?"

"I don't understand it, so it could be dangerous."

"Do you want to offend me again?"

"Heaven forbid!"

"Ask me your question."

"I'll have to show you."

"Do it."

"Even if it means climbing a tree?"

"Whatever it means."

"Follow me."

So I led her to the tree and climbed it, an enormously simple feat in my present form. She was right behind me.

"There's a way up here," I said. "I'm about to let it take me. Give me a few seconds to move aside."

I moved a little farther upward and was transported. Stepping aside, I surveyed the chapel quickly. Nothing seemed changed.

Then Gilva was at my side. I heard a sharp intake of breath.

"Oh, my!" she said.

"I know what I'm looking at," I said, "but I don't know what I'm seeing, if you follow me."

"It is a shrine," she said, "dedicated to the spirit of a member of the royal house of Amber."

"Yes, it's my father Corwin," I agreed. "That's what I'm looking at. But what am I seeing? Why should there be such a thing here in the Courts, anyway?"

She moved forward slowly, studying Dad's altar.

"I might as well tell you," I added, "that this is not the only such shrine I've seen since my return."

She reached out and touched the hilt of Grayswandir. Searching beneath

the altar, she found a supply of candles. Removing a silver one and screwing it into the socket of one of a number of holders, she lit it from one of the others and placed it near Grayswandir. She muttered something while she was about it, but I did not make out the words.

When she turned back to me again she was smiling.

"We both grew up here," I said. "How is it that you seem to know all about this when I don't?"

"The answer is fairly simple, Lord," she told me. "You departed right after the war, to seek an education in other lands. This is a sign of something that came to pass in your absence."

She reached out, took hold of my arm, led me to a bench.

"Nobody thought we would actually lose that war," she said, "though it had long been argued that Amber would be a formidable adversary." We seated ourselves. "Afterward, there was considerable unrest," she continued, "over the policies that had led to it and the treaty that followed it. No single house or grouping could hope for a deposition against the royal coalition, though. You know the conservatism of the Rim Lords. It would take much, much more to unite a majority against the Crown. Instead, their discontent took another form. There grew up a brisk trade in Amber memorabilia from the war. People became fascinated by our conquerors. Biographical studies of Amber's royal family sold very well. Something like a cult began to take shape. Private chapels such as this began to appear, dedicated to a particular Amberite whose virtues appealed to someone."

She paused, studying my face.

"It smacked too much of a religion," she went on then, "and for time out of mind the Way of the Serpent had been the only significant religion in the Courts. So Swayvill outlawed the Amber cult as heretical, for obvious political reasons. That proved a mistake. Had he done nothing it might have passed quickly. I don't really know, of course. But outlawing it drove it underground, made people take it more seriously as a rebellious thing. I've no idea how many cult chapels there are among the Houses, but that's obviously what this is."

"Fascinating sociological phenomenon," I said, "and your cult figure is Benedict."

She laughed.

"That wouldn't have been hard to guess," she said.

"Actually, I had the chapel described to me by my brother Mandor. He claimed to have wandered into it at a party at Hendrake, not knowing what it was."

She chuckled.

"He must have been testing you," she said. "The practice has been common knowledge for a long while. And I happen to know he's a cultist himself."

"Really? How do you know this?"

"He made no secret of it in the old days, before the general proscription."

"And who might his personal patron be?" I said.

"The Princess Fiona," she replied.

Curiouser and curiouser. . . .

"You've actually seen his chapel to her?" I asked.

"Yes. Before the ban it was not uncommon to have your friends over for a service whenever you were feeling particularly disgruntled with royal policy."

"And after the ban?"

"Everyone claimed publicly that their shrines had been destroyed. Many were simply relocated, I think, up hidden ways."

"And the business of having friends over for services?"

"I'd guess it would depend on how good a friend you're talking about. I don't really know how organized the Amber cult is." She gestured widely. "A place like this is illegal, though. Good thing I don't know where we are."

"I guess so," I said. "What about the relationship between the cult figure and the real thing? I'd say that Mandor really does have a thing about Fiona. He's met her, you know, and I've been present and seen it. Someone else I know stole something belonging to his—patron?—and keeps it in his shrine. And that"—I rose, crossed the altar, and picked up Corwin's sword—"is the real thing. I'd seen Grayswandir close-up, touched it, held it. This is it. But what I'm getting at is that my father is missing, and the last time I saw him he was wearing that blade. Would it be in keeping with the tenets of this cult to keep your patron prisoner?"

"I never heard of such a thing," she said. "But I don't see why not. It is really the spirit of the person that is being venerated. There is no reason the person could not be imprisoned."

"Or dead?"

"Or dead," she agreed.

"Then fascinating as all this is," I said, turning away from the altar, "it doesn't really help me to find my father."

I moved back to her, across what must have been a representation of Amber, stylized as the pattern on a Caucasian rug, there in the dark and light tile, the Chaotic one far off to my right.

"You would have to ask the person responsible for his blade's being there," she said, rising.

"I already asked the person I believed responsible. The response was not satisfactory."

I took her arm to steer her back toward the way to the tree, and she was suddenly standing very close.

"I would like to serve our next king any way I might," she said. "Though I may not normally speak for our House, I am certain Hendrake would agree to help you bring pressure upon the person responsible."

"Thanks," I said as we embraced. Her scales were cool. Her fangs would have shredded my human ear, but it was only a nibble in demonform. "I will talk to you again if I need help along those lines."

"Talk to me again, anyway."

It was good to hold and be held for a time, and that is what we did, till I saw a shadow move in the vicinity of the way.

"Masster Merlin."

"Glait!"

"Yess. I ssaw you come thiss way. Manform, demonform, grown or ssmall, I know you."

"Merlin, what is it?" Gilva asked.

"An old friend," I told her. "Glait, meet Gilva. And vice versa."

"Pleassed. I came to warn you that ssomeone approachess."

"Who?"

"Princess Dara."

"Oh, dear!" Gilva remarked.

"You suspect where we are," I said to her. "Keep it to yourself."

"I value my head, Lord. What do we do now?"

"Glait, to me," I said, kneeling and extending an arm.

She flowed up it and made herself comfortable. I rose and caught hold of Gilva with the other. I sent my will into the spikard.

Then I hesitated.

I didn't know where the hell we were—really, physically, in terms of geography. A way can deliver you next door, or somewhere thousands of miles distant from its point of origin, or somewhere off in Shadow. It would take a while to have the spikard figure where we were and then work out the way back, if we were going to bypass the way. Too long, I was certain.

I could simply use it to render us invisible. But I feared my mother's sorcerous sensitivity would be sufficient to detect our presence at levels beyond the visual.

I faced the nearest wall and extended my senses past it on a line of the spikard's force. We were not underwater or drifting on a sea of lava or quicksand. We seemed to be in a wooded spot.

So I walked toward the wall and passed us through it when we got there.

Several paces later, in the midst of a shaded glade, I looked back and beheld a grassy hillside, with no singing coming from beneath it. We stood under a blue sky, orange sun nearing its top. There were bird and insect sounds about us.

"Marrow!" Glait exclaimed, unwound herself from my arm and vanished into the grasses.

"Don't stay away long!" I hissed, trying to keep my voice low; and I led Gilva away from the hill.

"Merlin," she said, "I'm frightened at what I've learned."

"I won't tell anyone if you won't," I said. "If you'd like, I can even remove these memories before I send you back to the funeral."

"No, let me keep them. I can even wish there were more."

"I'll figure our location and get you back before you're missed."

"I'll wait with you while your friend hunts."

I half expected her to continue, ". . . in case I never see you again," what with the near skateboarding of Tmer and Tubble off this ever-mortal helix. But no, she was a demure and well-bred battle-maid—with over thirty notches on the haft of her broadsword, I later learned—and she was above stating the distasteful obvious in the presence of her possible future liege.

When Glait returned after an appropriate time, I said, "Thanks, Gilva. I'm going to send you back to the funeral now. If anyone saw us together and wants to know where I am, tell them I said I was going into hiding."

"If you do need a place to hide . . ."

"Talk to you sometime later perhaps," I said, and I sent her back to the temple at the edge of everything.

"Good vermin," Glait remarked, as I commenced my shift humanward. (It's always easier that way for me than the demon-shift.)

"I'd like to send you back to Sawall's sculpture garden," I said.

"Why there, Masster Merlin?"

"To wait for a time, to see whether you behold a sentient circle of light. And if you do, to address it as Ghostwheel and tell it to come to me."

"Where shall I tell it to sseek you?"

"That I do not know, but it is good at that sort of thing."

"Then ssend me. And if you are not eaten by ssomething bigger, come tell me your sstory one night."

"I shall."

It was the work of but a moment to hang the serpent back in her tree. I've never been sure when she's joking, reptilian humor being more than a little strange.

I summoned fresh garments and garbed myself in gray and purple Fetched me blades long and short then, also.

I wondered what my mother might have been up to in her chapel, but decided against trying to spy on her. I raised the spikard and regarded it for a moment, then lowered it. It seemed possibly counterproductive to transport myself to Kashfa when I was uncertain how much time had passed and whether Luke was actually still there. I took out my Trumps, which I had had along in my mourning garb, uncased them.

I located Luke's, focused upon it. Before too long it went cold and I felt Luke's presence.

"Yes?" he said. "That you, Merle?" at about the same time as his image swam and altered, causing me to see him mounted and riding through a part-blasted, part-normal countryside.

"Yeah," I answered. "I gather you're no longer in Kashfa."

"Right," he said. "Where're you?"

"Somewhere in Shadow. How's about yourself?"

"Damned if I know for sure," he responded. "We've been following this black path for days—and I can only say 'somewhere in Shadow,' too."

"Oh, you located it?"

"Nayda did. I didn't see anything, but she just led me on. Eventually, the trail got clear to me. Hell of a tracker, that gal."

"She's with you now?"

"That's right. She says we're gaining on them, too."

"Better bring me through then."

"Come ahead."

He extended a hand. I reached forward, clasped it, took a step, released his hand, began walking beside him, a pack horse to the rear.

"Hi, Nayda!" I called, to where she rode at his other side. A grim figure was mounted upon a black horse ahead and to her right.

She smiled.

"Merlin," she said. "Hello."

"How about Merle?" I said.

"If you wish."

The figure on the dark horse turned and regarded me. I halted a death strike that ran from reflex to the spikard so fast that it scared me. The air between us was smudged and filled with a screeching note, as of a car grabbing pavement to avert collision.

He was a big, blond-haired son of a bitch, and he had on a yellow shirt and black trousers, black boots, lots of cutlery. The medallion of the Lion rending the Unicorn bounced upon his broad chest. Every time I'd seen or heard of the man, he'd been about something nasty, damn near killing Luke on one occasion. He was a mercenary, a Robin Hood figure out of Eregnor, and a sworn enemy of Amber—illegitimate son of her late liege Oberon. I believed there was a price on his head within the Golden Circle. On the other hand, he and Luke had been buddies for years, and Luke swore he wasn't all that bad. He was my uncle Dalt, and I'd a feeling that if he moved too quickly the flexing of his muscles would shred his shirt.

". . . And you remember my military adviser, Dalt," Luke said.

"I remember," I stated.

Dalt stared at the black lines in the air that faded, smokelike, between us. He actually smiled then, a little.

"Merlin," he said, "son of Amber, Prince of Chaos, the man who dug my grave."

"What's this?" Luke asked.

"A little conversational gambit," I replied. "You've a good memory, Dalt—for faces."

He chuckled.

"Hard to forget something like a grave opening itself," he said. "But I've no quarrel with you, Merlin."

"Nor I you—now," I said.

He grunted then and I grunted back and considered us introduced. I turned back toward Luke.

"Is the path itself giving you any trouble?" I asked.

"No," he replied. "It's nothing at all like those stories I'd heard about the Black Road. It looks a little bleak at times, but nothing's really threatened us." He glanced downward and chuckled. "Of course it's only a few yards wide," he added, "and this is the broadest it's been, so far."

"Still," I said, opening my senses and studying its emanations with my Logrus sight, "I'd think something might have threatened."

"I guess we've been lucky," he said.

Again, Nayda laughed, and I felt foolish. The presence of a *ty'iga* would

count as surely as my own in offsetting the dire effects of a Chaos roadway in the realm of Order.

"Guess you had a little luck coming," I said.

"You're going to need a horse, Merle," he said then.

"I suppose you're right," I agreed.

I was afraid to use Logrus magic and call attention to my location. Still, I had already learned that the spikard could be used in a similar fashion, and I entered it with my will, extended, extended, made contact, summoned. . . .

"It'll be along any minute," I said. "Did you say something about our gaining on them?"

"That's what Nayda tells me," he explained. "She has an amazing rapport with her sister—not to mention a high sensitivity to this pathway itself."

"Knows a lot about demons, too," he added.

"Oh, are we likely to encounter any?" I asked her.

"It was demonformed warriors from the Courts who abducted Coral," she said. "They seem headed toward a tower up ahead."

"How far ahead?" I asked.

"Hard to say, since we're cutting through Shadow," she answered.

The trail, which consisted of blackened grasses and which produced the same effect on any tree or shrub that so much as overhung it, wound its way through a hilly area now; and as I stepped onto and off of it I noted that it seemed brighter and warmer each time I departed. It had reached this point now after having been virtually undetectable in the vicinity of Kashfa—an index of how far we were into the realm of the Logrus.

A little past the next bending of the trail, I heard a whinny from off to the right.

"Excuse me," I said. "Delivery time," and I departed the trail and entered a grove of oval-leafed trees.

Snorting and stamping sounds reached me from ahead, and I followed them down shaded ways.

"Wait up!" Luke called. "We shouldn't separate."

But the wood was fairly dense, not at all easy going for someone on horseback, so I hollered back, "Don't worry!" and plunged ahead.

. . . And that, of course, was why he was there.

Fully saddled and bridled, his reins tangled in the dense foliage, he was cursing in horse-talk, shaking his head from side to side, pawing at the earth. I halted, stared.

I may have given the impression that I would rather pull on a pair of Adidas and jog through Shadow than plunge through on the back of a beast driven half-mad by the changes going on about it. Or ride a bicycle. Or hop through on a pogo stick.

Nor would this impression be incorrect. It is not that I don't know how to drive the things. It is just that I'd never been particularly fond of them. Admitted, I never had the use of one of those wonder horses, such as Julian's Morgenstern, Dad's Star, or Benedict's Glemdenning, which stood to mortal

horses in terms of life span, strength, and endurance as did Amberites to the inhabitants of most shadows.

I looked all about, but could detect no injured rider. . . .

"Merlin!" I heard Luke call, but my attention was nearer at hand. I advanced slowly, not wanting to upset him further. "Are you all right?"

I had simply put in an order for a horse. Any old hay burner would have served, for purposes of keeping up with my companions.

I found myself looking at an absolutely lovely animal—black and orange-striped like a tiger. In this, he resembled Glemdenning with his red and black striping. In that I didn't know where Benedict's mount came from either, I was glad to let it be the place of magic.

I advanced slowly.

"Merle! Anything wrong?"

I didn't want to shout back a reply and frighten the poor beast. I placed my hand gently upon his neck.

"It's okay," I said. "I like you. I'll undo it and we'll be friends, all right?"

I took my time untangling the reins, using my other hand to massage his neck and shoulders. When he was free he did not pull away, but seemed to study me.

"Come on," I said, taking up the reins, "this way."

I led him back the way I had come, talking the while. I realized by the time we emerged that I actually liked him. I met Luke about then, a blade in his hand.

"My God!" he said. "No wonder it took you so long! You stopped to paint it!"

"You like, huh?"

"You ever want to get rid of that one, I'll make you a good offer."

"I don't think I'll be getting rid of him," I said.

"What's his name?"

"Tiger," I said without premeditation, and then I mounted.

We headed back to the trail, where even Dalt eyed my mount with something like pleasure. Nayda reached out and stroked the black and orange mane.

"Now we may be able to make it in time," she said, "if we hurry."

I mounted, and I guided Tiger over onto the trail. I anticipated all manner of reactions to the trail, as I recalled from my father's story the possibly intimidating effects of the thing upon animals. It didn't seem to bother him, though, and I released the breath I hadn't realized I was holding.

"In time for what?" I asked as we found a formation—Luke in the lead, Dalt behind him and to the right, Nayda to the left of the trail, rear, me to her right and somewhat back.

"I cannot tell for certain," she said, "because she is still sedated. However, I do know that she is no longer being moved; and I have the impression that her abductors have taken refuge in the tower, where the trail is much wider."

"Hm," I said. "You wouldn't have happened to notice the rate of change in width per unit of distance traveled on this trail, would you?"

"I was in liberal arts," she said, smiling. "Remember?"

She turned suddenly then, glancing in Luke's direction. He was still an entire horse's length ahead, eyes front—though he had looked back moments before.

"Damn you!" she said softly. "Being with you both this way gets me to thinking about school. Then I start talking that way—"

"In English," I said.

"Did I say that in English?"

"Yes."

"Shit! Help me if you catch me at it, will you?"

"Of course," I said. "It seems to show you'd enjoyed it somewhat, despite its being a job Dara'd laid on you. And you're probably the only *ty'iga* with a degree from Berkeley."

"Yes, I enjoyed it—confused as I was over which of you was which. Those were the happiest days in my life, with you and Luke, back in school. For years I tried to learn your mothers' names so I'd know who I was supposed to be protecting. You were both so cagey, though."

"It's in the genes, I guess," I observed. "I enjoyed your company as Vinta Bayle—appreciated your protection as others, too."

"I suffered," she said, "when Luke began his yearly attempts on your life. If he were the son of Dara I was supposed to protect, it shouldn't have mattered. But it did. I was already very fond of both of you. All I could tell was that you were both of the blood of Amber. I didn't want either of you harmed. The hardest thing was when you went away, and I was sure Luke had lured you into the mountains of New Mexico to kill you. By then, I suspected very strongly that you were the one, but I was not certain. I was in love with Luke, I had taken over the body of Dan Martinez, and I was carrying a pistol. I followed you everywhere I could, knowing that if he tried to harm you the *geas* I was under would force me to shoot the man I loved."

"You shot first, though. We were just standing talking, by the side of the road. He shot back in self-defense."

"I know. But everything seemed to indicate that you were in peril. He'd taken you to a perfect spot for an execution, at an ideal time—"

"No," I said. "Your shot went wide, and you left yourself open for what followed."

"I don't understand what you're saying."

"You solved the problem of possibly having to shoot Luke by setting up a situation where he shot you."

"I couldn't do that, under a *geas*."

"Maybe not consciously," I said. "So something stronger than the *geas* found a way."

"You really believe that?"

"Yes, and it's all right for you to admit it now. You're released from the *geas*. My mother told me. You told me—I think."

She nodded. "I don't know exactly when it came undone, or how," she

said. "But it's gone—though I'd still try to protect you if something threatened. It's good that you and Luke are really friends, and—"

"So why the secret?" I interrupted. "Why not just tell him you were Gail? Surprise the hell out of him—pleasantly."

"You don't understand," she said. "He broke up with me, remember? Now I've another chance. It's like it was, all over again. He—likes me a lot. I'm afraid to say, 'I'm really the girl you once broke up with.' It might get him to thinking of all the reasons why, and make him decide he was right the first time."

"That's silly," I said. "I don't know what reasons he gave. He never told me about it. Just said there'd been an argument. But I'm sure they were specious. I know he liked you. I'm sure he really broke up with you because he was a son of Amber about to come home on some very nasty business, and there was no room for what he thought was a normal shadow girl in the picture. You'd played your part too well."

"Is that why you broke up with Julia?" she asked.

"No," I said.

"Sorry."

I noticed the black trail had widened about a foot since we'd begun talking. I was in the market for a mathematical problem just then.

TEN

And so we rode—six paces along a city street, amid the blare of horns, our black way edged by skid marks; a quarter mile along a black sand beach, beside a soft green sea, stirring palms to our left; across a tarnished snowfield; beneath a bridge of stone, our way a dead and blackened streambed; then to prairie; back to wooded way—and Tiger never flinched, even when Dalt put a booted foot through a windshield and broke off an antenna.

The way continued to widen, to perhaps twice its width when I had first come upon it. Stark trees were more common within it now, standing like photographic negatives of their bright mates but a few feet off the trail. While the leaves and branches of these latter were regularly stirred, we felt no wind at all. The sounds—of our voices, of our mounts' hooves—came somehow muted now, also. Our entire course had a constant, wavery twilight atmosphere to it, no matter that a few paces away—which brief excursion we essayed many times—it might be high noon or midnight. Dead-looking birds were perched within the blackened trees, though they seemed on occasion to move, and the raspy, croaking sounds that sometimes came to us may well have been theirs.

At one time, a fire raged to our right; at another, we seemed to be passing near the foot of a glacier on the left. Our trail continued to widen—nothing like the great Black Road Corwin had described to me from the days of the war, but big enough now for us all to ride abreast.

"Luke," I said, after a time.

"Yeah?" he answered, from my left. Nayda rode to my right now, and Dalt to her right. "What's up?"

"I don't want to be king."

"Me neither," he said. "How hard they pushing you?"

"I'm afraid they're going to grab me and crown me if I go back. Everybody in my way died suddenly. They really plan to stick me on the throne, to marry me to Coral—"

"Uh-huh," he said, "and I've two questions about it. First, will it work?"

"The Logrus seems to think it will, at least for a time—which is all politics is about, anyhow."

"Second," he said, "if you feel about the place the way I feel about Kashfa, you're not going to let it go to hell if you can help it—even if it means some personal misery. You don't want to take the throne, though, so you must have worked out some alternative remedy. What is it?"

I nodded as the trail turned sharply to the left and headed uphill. Something small and dark scuttled across our path.

"I've a notion—not even a full idea," I said, "which I want to discuss with my father."

"Tall order," he said. "You know for sure that he's even alive?"

"I talked to him not all that long ago—very briefly. He's a prisoner, somewhere. All I know for sure is that it's somewhere in the vicinity of the Courts—because I can reach him by Trump from there, but nowhere else."

"Tell me about this communication," he said.

And so I did, black bird and all.

"Sounds like busting him out's going to be tricky," he said. "And you think your mom's behind it?"

"Yep."

"I thought I was the only one with these maternal problems. But it figures, seeing as yours trained mine."

"How come we turned out so normal?" I said.

He just stared at me for several seconds. Then he started to laugh.

"Well, I *feel* normal," I said.

"Of course," he said quickly then, "and that's what counts. Tell me, if it came to an out-and-out crossing of powers, do you think you could beat Dara?"

"Hard to say," I told him. "I'm stronger now than I ever was before, because of the spikard. But I'm beginning to believe she's very good."

"What the hell's a spikard?"

So I told him that story, too.

"That's why you were so flashy back in the church when you were fighting with Jurt?" he said.

"That's right."

"Let's see it."

I tried to pull it off, but it wouldn't pass the knuckle. So I simply extended my hand. Luke reached for it. His fingers halted a couple of inches above it.

"It's holding me off, Merle. Protective little devil."

"Hell," I said, "I'm not a shapeshifter for nothing." I took hold of it then, slimmed my finger suddenly, and slid it off. "Here."

He held it in the palm of his left hand as we bounced along, regarding it through narrowed eyes. Suddenly, I felt dizzy. Withdrawal symptoms from the thing? I forced myself upright, reversed my breathing, refused to let it show.

"Heavy," Luke said at last. "I can feel the power there. Other things, too. It won't let me in, though."

I reached for it and he drew his hand away.

"I can feel it in the air all around us," he said. "Merle, this thing lays a spell on anybody who wears it."

I shrugged.

"Yes," I said. "A benign one, though. It's done nothing to harm me, and it's helped me a number of times."

"But can you trust anything that came to you in such an odd way— almost by trickery, caused you to abandon Frakir when she tried to warn you about it, and for all you know has been influencing your behavior ever since you put it on?"

"I admit to a kind of disorientation at first," I said, "but I think that was just in the way of accommodation to the levels of voltage it draws. I've been back to normal for some time now."

"How can you tell for sure? Maybe it's brainwashed you."

"Do I seem brainwashed to you?"

"No. I was just trying to say that I wouldn't completely trust anything with such questionable credentials."

"Well taken," I agreed, holding forth my hand. "But so far the benefits have outweighed any hypothetical dangers. Consider me warned, and I'll take my chances."

He handed it back.

"If I think it's making you act weird I'm going to hit you over the head and pull it off, though."

"Fair enough," I said, slipping it back on. Immediately, I felt a rush of energy throughout my system as the lines of control were reestablished.

"If you're not sure you can force the information out of your mother," he said, "how do you propose finding Corwin and freeing him?"

"Several things suggest themselves," I said. "The simplest way may be a foot in the door technique. That is, I'd open all of the channels on the spikard and go for another Trump contact. As soon as there's any sort of opening I'd just push ahead with full force, jamming any spells that try to stop me and burning them out."

"Sounds as if it could be dangerous."

"I can't think of any way to go about this that wouldn't be."

"Then why haven't you tried it?"

"It only occurred to me recently, and I haven't had the time since then."

"However you go about it, you're going to need some help," he said. "So count me in."

"Thanks, Luke. I—"

"Now, about the king business," he said. "What happens if you simply refuse to take the throne? Who's next in line?"

"It's a bit tangled when you come to Sawall," I said. "By rights, Mandor should be first in line of succession from our House. He'd removed himself from the line years ago, though."

"Why?"

"I believe he claimed he was unfit to rule."

"No offense, Merle. But he seems like the only one of you who *is* fit for the job."

"Oh, without a doubt," I responded. "Most of the Houses have someone like him, though. There's usually a nominal head and a de facto one, someone for show and someone for scheming. Mandor likes the climate behind the scenes."

"Sounds as if your House has two," he said.

"I'm not really clear on it," I said. "I don't know Dara's status right now in her father's House—Helgram—or her mother's—Hendrake. But it might be worth a power struggle within Sawall if that's where the next king is coming from. Still, the more I learn of Mandor the more intimidating such a struggle would seem. I'd guess they're cooperating."

"I take it you're next in line, and then Jurt?"

"Actually, our brother Despil is next after me. Jurt said that Despil would probably step aside for him, but I think that was wishful thinking. I'm not at all sure he would. Anyhow, Jurt says now that he isn't interested."

"Ha! I think he's just taking a different approach. You whipped him too many times, and he's trying to get in good with you. Hope that spikard can protect your back."

"I don't know," I said. "I'd like to believe him. He spent a lot of time making sure that it wouldn't be easy, though."

"Supposing you all decline. Who's next?"

"I'm not certain," I said, "but I think it would go to Hendrake then."

"Damn," Luke said. "It's as twisted a place as Amber, isn't it?"

"Neither one's twisted, exactly. Just a little complicated, till you've learned the ropes."

"What say I just listen, and you fill me in on everything that you haven't so far?"

"Good idea."

So I talked for a long while, breaking to summon food and water. We halted twice during that time, causing me to realize just how tired I had become. And briefing Luke reminded me yet again that I should be telling all of this to Random. But if I got in touch and tried it I was certain he would order me back to Amber. And I couldn't disobey a direct order from the king, even if I was almost his opposite number.

"We're getting nearer," Nayda announced somewhat later, and I noted

that our roadway had widened even more, almost to the point she'd described. I drew a jolt of energy into my system, digested it, and kept going.

Shortly thereafter, she remarked, "Much nearer."

"Like just around the corner?" Luke asked.

"Could be," she answered. "I can't be more precise, the condition she's in."

But a little later, we heard distant shouts.

Luke drew rein.

"Something about a tower," he said.

She nodded.

"Were they heading for it, holing up in it, or defending themselves there?"

"All of the above," she said. "I understand now. Her captors were pursued, headed for a place of refuge, reached it, are there now."

"How come you're suddenly that precise?"

She gave me a quick look that I took as a request for an explanation other than *ty'iga* powers.

"I was using the spikard," I offered, "trying to see whether I could give her a clearer vision."

"Good," Luke said. "Can you boost it even more, so we can see what we're up against?"

"I can try," I said, narrowing my eyes at her in inquiry. She responded with a very slight nod.

I wasn't certain how to go about it, so I just fed her energy in the way of that jolt I'd given myself a while back.

"Yes," she said after a few moments, "Coral and her captors—six of them, I believe—have taken refuge in a tower near here. They are under attack."

"How large is the party of attackers?" Luke asked.

"Small," she said. "Quite small. I can't give you a number."

"Let's go and see," Luke said, and he led the way, Dalt behind him.

"Three or four," Nayda whispered to me, "but they're Pattern ghosts. That's probably all it can maintain this far from home, on a Black Road."

"Ouch," I said. "This makes it tricky."

"How so?"

"It means I have relatives on both sides."

"It also looks as if Amber's ghosts and the Court's demons are only agents, and that it's really a confrontation between the Logrus and the Pattern."

"Damn! Of course!" I said. "It could easily escalate into another of those. I'm going to have to warn Luke what we're riding into."

"You can't! Not without telling him what I am!"

"I'll tell him I learned it myself—that I had a sudden insight into a new spell."

"But what then? Which side are you on? What do we do?"

"Neither," I said. "We're on our own, and against both of them."

"You're crazy! There's no place you can hide, Merle! The Powers divide the universe between them!"

"Luke!" I cried. "I just probed ahead, learned the attackers are Pattern ghosts!"

"You don't say?" he called back. "Think we should be taking their side? It's probably better for the Pattern to take her back than for the Courts to get her, wouldn't you think?"

"She shouldn't be used that way," I said. "Let's take her away from both of them."

"I agree with your feelings," he stated. "But what if we succeed? I don't really care to be struck by a meteor or transported to the bottom of the nearest ocean."

"As near as I can tell, the spikard doesn't draw its power from the Pattern or the Logrus. Its sources are scattered through Shadow."

"So? I'm sure it's not a match for either one, let alone both."

"No, but I can use it to start an evasion course. They'll be getting in each other's way if they decide to pursue us."

"But eventually they'd find us, wouldn't they?"

"Maybe, maybe not," I said. "I have some ideas, but we're running out of time."

"Dalt, did you hear all that?" Luke asked.

"I did," Dalt replied.

"If you want out, now's your chance."

"And miss an opportunity to twist the Unicorn's tail?" he said. "Keep riding!"

We did, and the shouts grew louder as we raced ahead. There was a certain timeless feeling to it, though—with the muffled sounds and the dimness—as if we had always been riding here and always would be. . . .

Then we rounded a bend and I saw the top of the tower in the distance, heard more shouts. We slowed as we came to the next turn, advancing more cautiously, working our way through a small stand of black saplings.

Finally, we halted, dismounted, worked our way forward on foot. We pushed aside the final screening branches and looked down a slight slope to a blackened, sandy plain beside a three-story gray tower with slit windows and a narrow entranceway. It took a while to sort out the tableau at its base.

There were two demonformed individuals standing to either side of the tower's entrance. They were armed and their attention seemed focused upon the contest taking place on the sands before them. Familiar figures stood at the far end of this impromptu arena and at either side: Benedict stroked his chin, expressionless; Eric hunkered and smiled; Caine juggled, flipped, palmed, and passed a dagger, reflexively, through some private routine, an expression of amused fascination on his face. From the tower's top, I suddenly noted, two horned demons leaned forward, their gazes as intent as those of Amber's Pattern ghosts.

At the circle's center Gérard faced a demonformed son of Hendrake, of his own height and greater girth. It looked to be Chinaway himself, who was said to have a collection of over two hundred skulls of those he'd dispatched. I preferred Gérard's collection of a thousand or so mugs, steins, and drinking horns, but your ghost will walk, you lover of trees, in an English lane, if you know what I mean.

Both were stripped to the waist, and from the scuffed-up condition of the

sands about them I guessed they had been at it for some time. Chinaway tried to trip Gérard just then, who caught his arm and head as he stepped behind him, and sent him cartwheeling away. The demon lord came up on his feet, however, and immediately advanced once again, arms extended, hands weaving a sinuous pattern before him. Gérard simply waited in a ready position. Chinaway stabbed taloned fingers toward Gérard's eyes and hooked a blow against his rib cage. Gérard caught hold of his shoulder, however, as Chinaway dropped and caught him about the thigh.

"Let's wait," Dalt said softly. "I want to watch."

Luke and I both nodded as Gérard locked Chinaway's head and Chinaway wrapped his other arm about Gérard's waist. Then they simply stood there, muscles bulging beneath two hides, one pale and smooth, the other red and scaly. Their lungs worked like bellows.

"I assume the thing's been dragging out," Luke whispered, "and they decided to settle it champion against champion."

"Looks that way," I said.

"Coral must be inside then, wouldn't you think?"

"Wait a minute."

I ran a quick probe into the structure, locating two people within. I nodded then.

"Her and a single guard, I'd say."

Gérard and Chinaway still stood like statues.

"Now might be the best time to grab Coral," Luke said, "while everybody's watching the fight."

"You're probably right," I told him. "Let me see whether I can make myself invisible. That might simplify matters."

"Okay," he said about a quarter minute later. "Whatever you did just then worked. You're gone."

"Indeed I am," I said. "Back in a bit."

"How will you get her out?"

"I'll decide after I've reached her. Just be ready."

I moved slowly, careful not to scuff the sand. I skirted the circle, passing behind Caine. I approached the door to the tower, soundless, checking about me constantly. Gérard and Chinaway still stood exactly as they had been, locked, and applying enormous pressures to each other.

I passed between the guards, entering the dim interior of the tower. It consisted of a single round room with a bare earth floor, stone pedestals beneath each slit window. A ladder led up to the second floor through a hole in the ceiling. Coral lay upon a blanket to my left; the individual who was ostensibly guarding her stood upon a pedestal, watching the fight through the nearest window.

I moved nearer, knelt, caught up her left wrist and felt her pulse. It was strong and steady. I decided against trying to awaken her, though. Instead, I wrapped the blanket around her, raised her in my arms, and stood.

I was about to try extending the invisibility spell to include her when the watcher at the window turned. I must have made some noise in moving her.

For a moment, the guard stared at the sight of his prisoner drifting below him. Then he opened his mouth, as if to give alarm—leaving me with small choice but to shock his nervous system into insensibility with a charge from my ring.

Unfortunately, there was a rattle of arms as he fell from his pedestal to the floor. Almost immediately, I heard a cry from overhead, followed by sounds of rapid movement.

Turning, I hurried to the door. I had to slow and turn because of its narrowness. I wasn't certain what the guards outside would think when a comatose Coral drifted by, but I didn't want to be trapped inside. Peering ahead, I saw that Gérard and Chinaway seemed in the same position as before. Seconds later, however, as I turned my body and took my first sidling step, there came a sudden, sharp twisting movement from Gérard, followed immediately by a sound like that of a snapping stick.

Gérard let his arms fall and stood erect. The body of Chinaway hit the ground at his side, neck at an unnatural angle. Eric and Caine applauded. The two guards beside the door moved forward. Behind me, within, the ladder rattled at the other side of the room. I heard a cry from that direction.

Two more steps and I turned, headed left. The outside guards were rushing toward their fallen champion. A half-dozen paces, and there were more cries at my back, as my pursuers exited the tower; and there were human cries as well, from the killing circle.

I knew that I couldn't outrun any of them, carrying my burden; and all that motor activity interfered with my concentration to the point where I was incapable of performing magical operations.

So I dropped to my knees, lowering Coral to the ground before me, turned without even rising, and extended my left fist, plunging my mind deep within the ring, calling for extreme measures to halt the pair of Hendrake commandos who were only a few paces away now, edged weapons ready to pierce and to slash.

. . . And then they were caught up in the midst of flames. I think they screamed, but there was a lot of noise just then. Two paces more, perhaps, and they fell, blackened and twitching, before me. My hand was shaking, from its proximity to the powers that caused this; and I hadn't time, even, to think or to feel as I swung toward the sandy place of the recent contest and whatever might be coming at me from that direction.

One of the two guards who had rushed forward lay smoldering on the ground at Eric's feet. Another—who had apparently attacked Caine—clutched at the knife in his gullet, fires spreading outward, downward, upward, from his throat, as he sank slowly, then toppled to the rear.

Immediately, Caine, Eric, and Benedict turned to stare at me. Gérard, having just drawn on a blue shirt, was buckling his swordbelt in place. He turned, too, just as Caine said, "And who, sir, are you?"

"Merlin," I replied, "son of Corwin."

Caine actually looked startled.

"Does Corwin have a son?" he asked the others.

Eric shrugged and Gérard said, "I don't know." But Benedict studied me. "There is a resemblance," he said.

"True," Caine agreed. "All right, boy. Even if you are Corwin's son, that woman you're making off with belongs to us. We just won her fair and square off these well-done Chaosites."

With that, he began walking toward me. A moment later, Eric joined him. Then Gérard fell into step behind them. I didn't want to harm them, even if they were only ghosts, so I gestured and a line was drawn in the sand before them. Immediately, it caught fire.

They halted.

Suddenly, a huge figure appeared at my left. It was Dalt, a naked blade in his hand. A moment later, Luke was there. Then Nayda. The four of us faced the four of them, across the fire.

"She's ours now," Dalt said, and he took a single step forward.

"You are mistaken," came the reply, and Eric crossed the line, drawing his weapon.

Dalt was a couple of inches taller than Eric, and he had a longer reach. He moved forward immediately. I expected some kind of cut from that big blade he carried, but he went in for a point-attack. Eric, using a lighter weapon, sidestepped and came in under his arm. Dalt dropped the point of his blade, moved to his left, and parried it. The two weapons were suited for very different styles—Eric's being at the heaviest end of the rapier class, Dalt's at the lighter end of broadsword. Dalt's could be a single-handed weapon for a big-enough, strong-enough guy. I'd have had to use it two-handed myself. Dalt tried an upward cut just then, of the sort a Japanese swordsman would refer to as *kiriage*. Eric simply stepped back and tried for a wrist cut as it passed him. Dalt suddenly moved his left hand to the haft and executed a blinding two-handed cut of the sort known as *naname giri*. Eric continued to circle, trying for the wrist yet again.

Suddenly, Dalt opened his right hand and let it drift back, as his right foot performed a huge semicircular step to his rear and his left arm moved forward, leaving him in a left-handed European *en garde* position, from which that massive arm and matching blade immediately extended, performing an inside beat upon Eric's blade followed by a lunge. Eric parried as his right foot crossed behind his left and he sprang backward. Even so, I saw a spark as his guard was creased. He feinted in *sixte*, however, dropped his point beneath the parry that followed, extended his arm in *quatre*, raised himself and his blade into something resembling a stop-thrust targeting the left shoulder as the parry crossed, turned his wrist, and slashed Dalt across the left forearm.

Caine applauded, but Dalt simply brought his hands together and separated them again, executing a little hop-step as he did so, leaving him in a right *en garde* position. Eric drew circles in the air with the point of his weapon and smiled.

"Cute little dance routine you have there," he said.

Then Eric lunged, was parried, retreated, sidestepped, threw a front kick at Dalt's kneecap, missed, then moved with perfect timing as Dalt attempted

a head cut. Switching to the Japanese himself, he spun in to the larger man's right, a maneuver I'd seen in a *kumatchi* exercise, his own blade rising and falling as Dalt's cut swept past. Dalt's right forearm went suddenly wet, a thing I did not really notice until after Eric had rotated his weapon, blade pointing outward and upward, and, the guard covering his knuckles, had driven his fist against the right side of Dalt's jaw. He kicked him then behind the knee and struck him with his left shoulder. Dalt stumbled and fell. Eric immediately kicked him, kidney, elbow, thigh—the latter only because he missed the knee—set his boot upon Dalt's weapon and swung his own about to bring its point in line with the man's heart.

I had been hoping all along, I suddenly realized, that Dalt would kick Eric's ass—not just because he was on my side and Eric wasn't, but because of the rough time Eric had given my dad. On the other hand, I doubted there were too many people of such ass-kicking prowess about. Unfortunately, two of them stood on the other side of the line I had drawn. Gérard could have outwrestled him. Benedict, Master of Arms at Amber, could have beaten him with any weapon. I just didn't see us as having much of a chance against them all, with Caine thrown in for good measure—not even with a *ty'iga* on our side. And if I were suddenly to tell Eric that Dalt was his half brother, it wouldn't slow his thrust by an instant, even if he believed me.

So I made the only decision I could make. They were, after all, only Pattern ghosts. The real Benedict and Gérard were somewhere else at this moment and would in no way be harmed by anything I did to their doubles here. Eric and Caine were, of course, long dead, Caine being the fratricidal hero of the Patternfall war and subject of a recent statue on the Grand Concourse, on the occasion of Luke's assassinating him for killing his father. And Eric, of course, had found a hero's death on the slopes of Kolvir, saving him, I suppose, from dying at the hands of my father. The bloody history of my family swam through my head as I raised the spikard to add a footnote to it, calling again for the wave of incineration that had taken out two of my Hendrake kin.

My arm felt as if someone had struck it with a baseball bat. A wisp of smoke rose from the spikard. For a moment, my four upright uncles stood unmoving. And my fifth remained supine.

Then, slowly, Eric raised his weapon. And he continued to raise it, as Benedict, Caine, and Gérard drew theirs. He straightened as he held it before his face. The others did the same. It looked strangely like a salute; and Eric's eyes met mine.

"I know you," he said.

Then they all completed the gesture, and faded, faded, turned to smoke, and blew away.

Dalt bled, my arm ached, and I figured out what was going on just moments before Luke gasped and said, "Over there."

My line of fire had gone out some time ago, but beyond the mark it had left, where my faded kinsmen had just been standing, the air began to shimmer.

"That will be the Pattern," I said to Luke, "come calling."

A moment later the Sign of the Pattern hovered before us.

"Merlin," it said, "you certainly move around a lot."

"My life has become very busy of late," I said.

"You took my advice and left the Courts."

"Yes, that seemed prudent."

"But I do not understand your purposes here."

"What's to understand?"

"You took the lady Coral away from the agents of the Logrus."

"That's right."

"But then you attempted to keep her from my agents as well."

"That, too, is correct."

"You must realize by now that she bears something that contributes to our balance of power."

"Yes."

"So one of us must have her. Yet you would deny us both."

"Yes."

"Why?"

"It's her whom I care about. She has rights and feelings. You're treating her like a game piece."

"True. I recognize her personhood, but unfortunately she is become both."

"Then I would deny her to both of you. Nothing would be changed, in that neither of you has her now, anyway. But I would take her out of the game."

"Merlin, you are a more important piece than she is, but you are still only a piece and you may not dictate to me. Do you understand?"

"I understand my value to you," I said.

"I think not," it responded.

I was wondering just then how strong it really was in this place. It seemed obvious that in terms of energy expenditure, it had been necessary for it to release its four ghosts to be able to manifest itself here. Dared I oppose it with every channel on the spikard opened? I had never tried accessing every Shadow source it controlled simultaneously. If I did this, and if I were to move very quickly, could I get us all out of here before the Pattern reacted? If I couldn't, could I punch through whatever it raised up to stop us? And if I succeeded—either way—to what place should we flee?

Finally, how might this affect the Pattern's attitude toward me?

(. . . if you are not eaten by something bigger, come tell me your story one night.)

What the hell, I decided. It is a good day to be listed à la carte.

I opened all the channels.

It felt as if I had been jogging along at a good clip and a brick wall had suddenly appeared six inches before me.

I felt the smash and I went away.

* * *

I lay upon a smooth, cool stone surface. There was a terrible rushing of energies in my mind and body. I reached into their source and took control of them, dampening them to something that didn't threaten to take the top of my head off. Then I opened one eye, slightly.

The sky was very blue. I saw a pair of boots, standing a few feet off, faced away from me. I recognized them as Nayda's, and turning my head slightly, I saw that she wore them. I also saw then that Dalt lay sprawled several yards off to my left.

Nayda was breathing heavily, and my Logrus vision showed a pale red light about her vibrating hands, menacing.

Propping myself upon my left elbow and peering about her, I saw that she stood between me and the Sign of the Pattern that hovered in the air perhaps ten feet away.

When it spoke again it was the first time I'd heard it express anything like amusement: "You would protect him, against me?"

"Yes," she replied.

"Why?"

"I did it for so long that it would be a shame to fail him when he really needs it."

"Creature of the Pit, do you know where you stand?" it asked.

"No," she said.

I looked beyond them both at a perfectly clear blue sky. The surface upon which I lay was a level area of rock, perhaps oval in shape, opening onto nothing. A quick turning of my head showed that it seemed bitten out of a mountainside, however, several dark recesses to the rear indicating the possibility of caves. I saw, too, that Coral lay behind me. Our stony shelf was several hundred meters wide. And there was movement beyond Nayda and the Sign of the Pattern. Luke had just hauled himself up into a kneeling position.

I could have answered the question put to Nayda, but there was no percentage in my doing so. Not when she was doing such a fine job of holding our captor's attention and providing a crucial respite.

To my left, I saw gold-pink swirls within the stone, and though I had never been here I recalled the description from my father's story and knew this to be the place of the primal Pattern, the deeper level of reality that underlay Amber itself.

I rolled onto all fours then, and crawled a few steps, seaward, Patternward.

"You are at the other end of the universe, ty'iga, in the place of my greatest power."

Dalt groaned and rolled over, sat up, massaged his eyes with the palms of his hands.

I could feel something like a vibration just at the edge of hearing coming from Nayda now, and her entire form had taken on that reddish glow. I knew that she would die if she attacked the Sign, and I realized that I would attack it myself if it killed her.

I heard a moan from Coral.

"You will not hurt my friends," Nayda said.

I wondered then at its slapping me down before I could use the spikard, and transporting us immediately to its stronghold. Did this mean I might actually have had a chance against it, out there in Logrus territory where it was weakened?

"Creature of the Pit," it told her, "such a doomed, pathetic gesture as yours verges on the heroic. I feel a certain fondness for you. Would that I had such a friend. No, I will not harm your companions. But I must detain Coral and Merlin here as power counters, and the rest of you for political reasons, until this dispute with my adversary is settled."

"Detain?" she said. "Here?"

"There are comfortable quarters within the rock," it said.

I rose carefully to my feet, fumbling at my belt for my dagger.

Luke got up and walked over to Coral, knelt beside her.

"Are you awake?" he asked.

"Sort of," she answered.

"Can you stand?"

"Maybe."

"Let me help you."

Dalt rose while Luke was assisting her. I continued to sidle toward the design. Where was Dworkin when I really needed him?

"You may enter the caves behind you and inspect your quarters," the Sign said. "But first you must remove that ring, Merlin."

"No, now's hardly a time to be unpacking and getting comfortable," I answered, slashing my left palm with the dagger and taking a final step. "We won't be staying long."

A sound like a small thunderclap emerged from the Sign of the Pattern, but there was no lightning, nor did I think there would be. Not when it realized what I was holding in my hand, and where I was holding it.

"A thing I learned from Luke's father," I explained. "Let's talk."

"Yes," said the Sign of the Pattern, "like the reasonable beings that we are. Would you care for some cushions?"

Immediately, three such objects appeared nearby.

"Thanks," I said, drawing up a green one. "I could sure use an iced tea."

"Do you take sugar?"

ELEVEN

Seated upon a cushion, dagger at my side, I held my left hand out over the Pattern, cupped palm filled with my blood. The Sign of the Pattern hovered in the air before me, seeming, of a sudden, to have forgotten Coral, Nayda, Dalt, and Luke. I sipped from the frosted glass in my right hand, a sprig of fresh mint visible amid the ice.

"Prince Merlin," inquired the Sign, "tell me what it is that you desire, and let us resolve this matter quickly. Are you sure I mightn't fetch you a

napkin to place at the danger point? It would not minimize your bargaining ability, if you stop to think of it. But it would serve to prevent accidents."

"No, that's okay," I said, half-gesturing with the blood-filled hand, so that its contents were stirred, a small line of red trickling up my wrist. "Thanks, anyhow."

The Sign of the Pattern vibrated, grew still.

"Prince Merlin, you have made your point," it said. "But I do not think you realize the full implications of your threat. A few drops of your blood upon my physical design could disturb the functioning of the universe."

I nodded.

"I know," I said.

"Very well," it answered. "State your demands."

"Our freedom," I said. "Let us go, and you remain intact."

"You give me small choice, but the same applies to your friends."

"What do you mean?"

"You may send Dalt whenever you wish," it said. "As for the demon lady, I relinquish her with regret, as I feel she would have provided good company—"

Luke regarded Nayda.

"What is this 'creature of the Pit,' 'demon lady' business, anyway?" he asked.

"Well, there are a few things you don't know about me . . ." she responded.

"Is it a long story?" he asked.

"Yes."

"Am I an assignment? Or do you really like me?"

"You're not an assignment, and I really like you."

"Then we'll hear the story later," he said.

"As I said, send her," it went on. "And Dalt. And Luke. I will be happy to send the three of them wherever you wish. But does it occur to you that you and Coral are probably safer here than anywhere else?"

"Maybe. Maybe not," I answered. "Coral, how do you feel about it?"

"Get me out of here," she said.

"So much for that notion," I told it. "Now—"

"Wait. You want to be fair to your friends, don't you?"

"Sure I do."

"Then let me point some things out to them which they may not have considered."

"Go ahead."

"Lady," it said, "they want your eye in the Courts of Chaos. Your feelings on the matter are immaterial. If this can only be achieved by making you a prisoner, then it will be done."

Coral laughed softly.

"The alternative being to remain your prisoner?" she asked.

"Think of yourself as a guest. I will provide for your every comfort. Of course, there is a positive gain for me in this state of affairs—apart from

denying the adversary your presence. I acknowledge this. But you must choose one of us, else the other will grab you off."

I looked at Coral, who shook her head slightly.

"So what'll it be?" I asked.

Coral came over and placed her hand upon my shoulder.

"Get me out of here," she said.

"You heard 'em," I told it. "Everybody goes."

"I crave your indulgence a moment more," it said.

"For what?" I asked.

"Consider. Choosing between the Logrus and myself is not a mere matter of politics—of selecting this person or that to do a particular job. My adversary and I represent two fundamental principles by means of which the universe is organized. You may tag us with nouns and adjectives from most languages and dozens of disciplines, but we represent, basically, Order and Chaos—Apollonian and Dionysiac, if you like; reason and feeling, if you prefer; madness and sanity; light and dark; signal and noise. As much as this may seem to indicate it, however, neither of us seeks the other's extinction. Heat death or fireball, classicism or anarchy, each of us proceeds along a single track, and without the other it would lead to a dead end. Both of us know this, and the game we have played since the beginning is a far more subtle thing—ultimately, perhaps, to be judged only esthetically.

"Now, I have gained a significant edge over my ancient adversary, for the first time in ages. I am in a position now to produce a historian's dream throughout Shadow—an age of high civilization and culture such as shall never be forgotten. If the balance were tipped the other way we would be contemplating a period of upheaval at least on par with that of an ice age. When I spoke of you as game pieces it was not to minimize your roles in this. For this is a time of great fluidity, when the Jewel and the man who would be king will make a difference. Stay with me, and I will guarantee the Golden Age of which I spoke, and you a part in it. Leave, and you will be snatched away by the other. Darkness and disorder will follow. Which would you have?"

Luke smiled.

"I know a good sales pitch when I hear it," he said. "Narrow it down to a simple choice. Make them think it's their own."

Coral squeezed my shoulder.

"We're going," I said.

"Very well," said the Sign. "Tell me where you want to go, and I'll send you all there."

"Not all," Luke said suddenly. "Just them."

"I do not understand. What about you?"

He drew a dagger and slashed his palm. He advanced and stood beside me, extending his hand out over the Pattern, also.

"If we go, only three of us may arrive," he said, "if that. I'll stay here and keep you company while you deliver my friends."

"How will you know I've done it in a satisfactory fashion?"

"Good question," he said. "Merle, you got a set of Trumps on you?"

"Yes."

I removed them and showed them to him.

"Still got one of me in there?"

"Last time I looked I did."

"Then get it out and have it ready. Figure your next move before you take off. Stay in touch with me till you make it."

"What about yourself, Luke? You can't sit there forever as a bloody threat to Order. It's only a temporary stalemate. You have to surrender your position sooner or later, and when you do—"

"Do you still have some odd cards in that deck?"

"What do you mean?"

"The ones you once referred to as the Trumps of Doom."

I riffled through. They were mostly near the bottom.

"Yes," I said. "Beautifully executed. I wouldn't have tossed them."

"You really think so?"

"Yeah. Get together a bunch of stuff this good, and I'll get you an exhibit back in Amber."

"You serious? You're not just saying that because—"

The Sign of the Pattern emitted a growling sound.

"Everybody's a critic," Luke observed. "Okay. Pull all the Trumps of Doom."

I did this.

"Mix 'em up a little. Keep 'em face down, please."

"All right."

"Fan 'em."

He leaned forward, took a card.

"Okay," he said. "I'm in business. Whenever you're ready, tell it where to take you. Stay in touch. Hey, Pattern, I want an iced tea of my own."

A frosty glass appeared near his right foot. He stooped and took it up, sipped from it.

"Thanks."

"Luke," Nayda said, "I don't understand what's going on. What will happen to you?"

"Nothing much," he replied. "Don't cry for me, demon lady. I'll see you later."

He looked at me and quirked an eyebrow.

"Send us to Jidrash," I said, "in Kashfa—to the open area between the palace and the church."

I held Luke's Trump in my moist left hand, near to a humming spikard. I felt the card grow cold just as Luke said, "You heard him."

And the world swirled and unswirled, and it was a brisk, windy morning in Jidrash. I regarded Luke through his Trump. I opened channel after channel of the ring.

"Dalt, I might as well leave you here," I said. "You, too, Nayda."

"No," the big man said, just as Nayda said, "Hold on a minute."

"You're both out of the picture now," I explained. "Neither side wants you for anything. But I've got to get Coral someplace safe. Me, too."

"You're a focus of the action," Nayda said, "and I can help Luke by helping you. Take me along."

"I feel the same way about it," Dalt said. "I still owe Luke a big one."

"Okay," I said. "Hey, Luke! You hear all that?"

"Yeah," he said. "Better be about your business then. Shit! I spilled it—"

His Trump went black.

I didn't wait for avenging angels, tongues of fire, lightning bolts, or an opening of the earth. I got us out of jurisdiction real quick.

I sprawled on the green grass beneath the big tree. Wisps of fog drifted by. Dad's Pattern sparkled below me. Jurt was seated cross-legged on the hood of the car, blade across his knees. He hit the ground when we made our appearance. Corwin was nowhere in sight.

"What's going on?" Jurt asked me.

"I am beat, bushed, and whacked-out. I am going to lie here and stare at the fog till my mind goes away," I said. "Meet Coral, Nayda, and Dalt. Hear their story and tell them yours, Jurt. Don't wake me for the end of the world unless it has very good special effects."

I proceeded to do as I had promised, to the tune of a fading guitar and the distant voice of Sara K. The grass was wondrous soft. The fog swirled through my brain. Fade to black.

And then, and then. . . . And then, sir. . . .

Walking. I was walking, almost drifting, through a California shopping mall I used to frequent. Knots of kids, couples with infants, women with parcels, passed, words smothered by sounds from a music store speaker. Potted oases sheltered, deli smells drifted, sale signs promised.

Walking. Past the drugstore. Past the shoe store. Past the candy store. . . .

Narrow corridor to the left. I'd never noticed it. Must turn. . . .

Odd there should be a carpet—and candles in high holders, and sconces, and candelabra atop narrow chests. The walls glittered with their re—

I turned back.

There was no back. The mall was gone. The corridor ended in that direction at a wall. A small tapestry hung upon it, depicting nine figures who looked back at me. I shrugged and turned again.

"Still something left to your spell, Uncle," I remarked. "Let's be about it then."

Walking. In silence now. Ahead. To the place where the mirrors glittered. I had seen this place long ago, I recalled, though its disposition—I suddenly realized—was not peculiar to Amber Castle. It was right there, on the tip of memory—my younger self passing this way, not unaccompanied—but the price of that recollection would be loss of control here, I knew. Reluctantly, I released the image and turned my attention to the small oval mirror to my left.

I smiled. So did my image. I stuck out my tongue and was so saluted in return.

I moved on. Only after several paces did I realize that the image had been my demonformed self, while my person had not.

A soft throat-clearing sound occurred to my right. Turning in that direction, I beheld my brother Mandor within a black-framed lozenge.

"Dear boy," he stated, "the king is dead. Long live your august personage as soon as you have assumed the throne. You had best make haste to return for a crowning at the End of the World, with or without the bride of the Jewel."

"We ran into a few small problems," I said.

"Nothing worth resolving just now. Your presence in the Courts is far more important."

"No, my friends are," I said.

A momentary smile touched his lips.

"You will be in an ideal position to protect your friends," he said, "and to do as you would with your enemies."

"I will be back," I said, "soon. But not to be crowned."

"As you would, Merlin. It is your presence that is desired."

"I promise nothing," I said.

He chuckled, and the mirror was emptied.

I turned away. I walked on.

More laughter. From the left. My mother's.

From within a red frame of carved flowers, she stared at me, a look of vast amusement upon her features.

"Seek him in the Pit!" she said. "Seek him in the Pit!"

I passed, and her laughter continued at my back for a time.

"Hsst!"

To my right, a long, narrow mirror bordered in green.

"Masster Merlin," she said. "I have ssought, but the ghosst-light hass not passsed my way."

"Thanks, Glait. Keep looking, please."

"Yess. We musst ssit together in a warm place by night once again and drink milk and talk of the old dayss."

"That would be nice. Yes, we must. If we are not eaten by something bigger."

"S-s-s-s-s!"

Could that be laughter?

"Good hunting, Glait."

"Yess. S-s-s!"

. . . And on. Walking.

"Son of Amber. Wearer of the spikard"—this from within a shadowy niche to my left.

I halted and stared. The frame was white, the glass was gray. Within was a man I had never met. His shirt was black and opened at the neck. He wore a brown leather vest, his hair dark blond, eyes perhaps green.

"Yes?"

"A spikard was hidden in Amber," he stated, "for you to find. It conveys great powers. It also bears a series of spells that will cause its wearer to act in certain ways under certain circumstances."

"I suspected this," I said. "What is it set to do?"

"Formerly worn by Swayvill, King of Chaos, it will force the chosen successor to take the throne, behave in a certain fashion, and be amenable to the suggestions of certain persons."

"These being?"

"The woman who laughed and cried, 'Seek him in the Pit.' The man in black, who desires your return."

"Dara and Mandor. They laid these spells upon it?"

"Just so. And the man left it for you to find."

"I hate to surrender the thing just now," I said, "when it's proving so useful. Is there a way to lift these spells?"

"Of course. But it should not matter to you."

"Why not?"

"The ring you wear is not the one of which I speak."

"I do not understand."

"But you will. Never fear."

"Who are you, sir?"

"My name is Delwin, and we may never actually meet—unless certain ancient powers come loose."

He raised his hand, and I saw that he, too, wore a spikard. He moved it toward me.

"Touch your ring to mine," he commanded. "Then it can be ordered to bring you to me."

I raised mine and moved it toward the glass. At the moment they seemed to touch, there was a flash of light and Delwin was gone.

I let my arm fall. I walked on. On an impulse, I stopped before a chest and opened its drawer.

I stared. There was no way to one-up this place, it seemed. The drawer contained a miniature, scaled-down representation of my father's chapel—tiny colored tiles, diminutive burning tapers, even a doll-sized Grayswandir upon the altar.

"The answer lies before you, dear friend," came a throaty voice I knew yet did not know.

I raised my gaze to a lavender-bordered mirror I had not realized hung above the chest. The lady within had long, coal-black hair and eyes so dark I could not tell where the pupils left off and the irises began. Her complexion was very pale, emphasized perhaps by her pink eye shadow and lip coloring. Those eyes. . . .

"Rhanda!" I said.

"You remember! You do remember me!"

". . . And the days of our bonedance games," I said. "Grown and lovely. I thought of you but recently."

"And I felt the touch of your regard as I slept, my Merlin. I am sorry we parted so, but my parents—"

"I understand," I said. "They thought me demon or vampire."

"Yes." She extended her pale hand through the mirror, took hold of my own, drew it toward her. Within the looking glass, she pressed it to her lips. They were cold. "They would rather I cultivated the acquaintance of the sons and daughters of men and women, than of our own kind."

When she smiled, I beheld her fangs. They had not been apparent in her childhood.

"Gods! You look human!" she said. "Come visit me in Wildwood one day!"

Impulsively, I leaned forward. Our lips met within the mirror. Whatever she was, we had been friends.

"The answer," she repeated, "lies before you. Come see me!"

The mirror turned red and she was gone. The chapel stood unchanged within the drawer. I closed it and turned away.

Walking. Mirrors to the left. Mirrors to the right. Only myself within them.

Then—

"Well, well, nephew. Confused?"

"As usual."

"Can't say as I blame you."

His eyes were mocking and wise, his hair red as his sister Fiona's or his late brother Brand's. Or Luke's, for that matter.

"Bleys," I said, "what the hell is going on?"

"I've the rest of Delwin's message," he said, reaching into his pocket and extending his hand. "Here."

I reached into the mirror and accepted it. It was yet another spikard, like the one I wore.

"It is the one of which Delwin spoke," he said. "You must never wear it."

I studied it for several moments.

"What am I to do with it?" I asked.

"Put it in your pocket. A use may suggest itself at some point."

"How did you come by it?"

"I switched it after Mandor left it, for the one you wear now."

"How many are there, anyway?"

"Nine," he replied.

"I suppose you know all about them."

"More than most."

"That wouldn't be hard. I don't suppose you know where my father is?"

"No. But you do. Your lady friend with the sanguinary tastes told you."

"Riddles," I said.

"Always preferable to no answer at all," he responded.

Then he was gone and I walked again. After a while, this was gone, too. Drifting. Black. Good. So good. . . .

* * *

A bit of light found its way through my eyelashes. I shut it out again. But the thunder rolled, and after a time the light leaked in once again.

Dark lines in brown, great horny ridges, ferny forests. . . .

A little later the faculty that evaluates perceptions awoke and pointed out that I was lying on my side staring at the cracked earth between a pair of roots from the tree, clumps of grass dotted here and there across the prospect.

. . . And I continued to stare, and there was a sudden brightness as of a lightning flash followed almost immediately by a crack of thunder. The earth seemed to shudder with it. I heard the pattering of drops upon the leaves of a tree, the hood of a car. I continued to stare at the largest crack that traversed the valley of my regard.

. . . And I realized that I knew.

It was the numb knowledge of awakening. The sources of emotion still dozed. In the distance, I could hear familiar voices in soft converse. I could also hear the sounds of cutlery against china. My stomach would awaken in a bit, I knew, and I would join them. For now, it was so very pleasant to lie here wrapped in my cloak, hearing the gentle rain and knowing. . . .

I returned to my micro-world and its dark canyon. . . .

The ground shook again, this time without benefit of lightning or thunder. And it kept on shaking. This irritated me, for it disturbed my friends and relatives, causing them to raise their voices in something like alarm. Also, it stirred a dormant California reflex at a time when I just wanted to loll and savor my fresh-acquired knowledge.

"Merlin, are you awake?"

"Yes," I said, sitting up suddenly, giving my eyes a quick rub, and running my hands through my hair.

It was the ghost of my father that knelt beside me, having just shaken my shoulder. "We seem to have a problem," he said, "with rather extreme ramifications."

Jurt, standing behind him, nodded several times. The ground shook once again, twigs and leaves fell about us, pebbles bounced, dust rose, the fogs were agitated. I heard a dish break in the vicinity of the heavy red and white cloth about which Luke, Dalt, Coral, and Nayda sat eating.

I untangled my cloak and rose to my feet, realizing then that someone had removed my boots while I slept. I drew them back on. There came another tremor, and I leaned against the tree for support.

"This is the problem?" I said. "Or is something bigger about to eat it?"

He gave me a puzzled look. Then, "Back when I drew the Pattern," he said, "I'd no way of knowing that this area was faulted, or that something like this would one day occur. If these shocks should crack the Pattern, we've had it—in more ways than one. As I understand it, that spikard you wear can draw upon enormous sources of energy. Is there some way you could use it to defuse this thing?"

"I don't know," I told him. "I never tried anything like it."

"Find out fast, okay?" he said.

But I was already spinning my mind about the circle of tines, touching

each one to life. Then I seized upon the one possessed of the most juice, drew hard upon it, filled myself, body and mind, with its energy. Ignition completed and engine idling, with me in the driver's seat, I shifted into gear then, extending a line of force from the spikard down into the ground.

I reached for a long while, seeking a conversion metaphor to the subjective for anything I might discover.

. . . Wading out from the beach into the ocean—waves tickling my stomach, my chest—feeling with my toes the rocks, the strands of seaweed. . . . Sometimes a rock would turn, slip, bump against another, slide. . . . I couldn't see to the bottom with my eyes. But I saw the rocks, the wrack, in their disposition and movement, just the same, beheld them as clearly as if the bottom were fully illuminated.

Feeling, feeling my way now, down through the strata, single toe soft as a flashlight's beam running along rocky surfaces, testing the pressures of one upon another, isostatic kisses of mountains beneath the earth, orogenic erogenies of slow movement, flesh caressing mineral in the darkest of secret places—

Slip! The rock slides off. My body follows. . . .

I dive for it, following the sliding passage. I race ahead, pouring forth heat, cracking rock, splintering new pathways, outward, outward. . . . It was coming this way. I broke through a wall of stone, another. Another. I was not certain this was the way to divert it, but it was the only one I knew to try. Go that way! Damn it! That way! I accessed two more channels, a third, a fourth—

There was a slight vibration within the ground. I opened another channel. Within my metaphor the rocks grew stable beneath the waters. Shortly thereafter, the ground ceased its vibration.

I returned to the place where I had first felt the slide begin, stable now, yet still stressed. Feel it, feel it carefully. Describe a vector. Follow. Follow it to the point of original pressure. But no. This point is but a confluence of vectors. Trace them.

Yet again. More junctions. Trace them. Access more channels. The entire pressure structure, intricate as a nervous system, must be described. I must hold its tree within my mind.

Another layer. It may not be possible. I may be courting infinity in my topographic branchings. Freeze frame. Simplify the problem. Ignore everything beyond the tertiary. Trace to the next junction. There are some loops. Good. And a plate is now involved. Better.

Try another jump. No good. Too big a picture to contain. Discard tertiaries.

Yes.

Thus general lines sketched. Vectors of transmission simply drawn—back to plate, almost. Pressure exerted less than full pressure extended. Why? Additional point of input along second vector, redirecting shear forces this valley.

"Merlin? Are you all right?"

"Let me be," I hear my voice respond.

Extend then, input source, into, feeling, transmission signature. . . .

Is this a Logrus that I see before me?

I opened three more channels, focused on the area, began heating it.

Soon rocks were cracking, but a little later they melted. My newly created magma flowed down fault lines. A hollowed-out area occurred at the point whence the precipitating force had originated.

Back.

I withdrew my probes, shut down the spikard.

"What did you do?" he asked me.

"I found the place where the Logrus was messing with underground stresses," I said, "and I removed the place. There's a small grotto there now. If it collapses it may ease the pressure even more."

"So you've stabilized it?"

"At least for now. I don't know the limits of the Logrus, but it's going to have to figure a new route to reach this place. Then it's going to have to test it out. And if it's doing a lot of Pattern watching just now, that may slow it."

"So you've bought some time," he said. "Of course, the Pattern may move against us next."

"It could," I said. "I've brought everyone here because I thought they'd be safe from both Powers."

"Apparently you made the payoff worth the risk."

"Okay," I said. "I guess it's time to give them some other things to worry about."

"Such as?"

I looked at him, Pattern ghost of my father, guardian of this place.

"I know where your flesh-and-blood counterpart is," I said, "and I'm about to set him free."

There came a flash of lightning. A sudden gust of wind lofted the fallen leaves, stirred the fogs.

"I must accompany you," he said.

"Why?"

"I've a personal interest in him, of course."

"All right."

Thunder crashed about us, and the fogs were torn apart by a fresh onslaught of wind.

Jurt came up to us then.

"I think it's begun," he said.

"What?" I asked.

"The duel of Powers," he said. "For a long time the Pattern had an edge. But when Luke damaged it and you snatched away the bride of the Jewel, it must have weakened it more, relative to the Logrus, than it's been in ages. So the Logrus decided to attack, pausing only for a quick attempt to damage this Pattern."

"Unless the Logrus was just testing us," I said, "and this is simply a storm."

A light rain had begun while he was speaking.

"I came here because I thought it was the one place neither of them would touch in the event of a contest," he went on. "I'd assumed neither

would care to divert energy from its own attack or defense for a swipe in this direction."

"That reasoning may still hold," I said.

"Just for once I'd like to be on the winning side," he stated. "I'm not sure I care about right or wrong. They're very arguable quantities. I'd just like to be in with the guys who win for a change. What do you think, Merle? What are you going to do?"

"Corwin here and I are going to head for the Courts, and we're going to free my father," I said. "Then we're going to resolve whatever needs resolving and live happily ever after. You know how it goes."

He shook his head.

"I can never decide whether you're a fool or whether your confidence is warranted. Every time I decided you were a fool, though, it cost me." He looked up at the dark sky, wiped rain from his brow. "I'm really torn," he said, "but you could still be King of Chaos."

"No," I said.

". . . And you enjoy some special relationship with the Powers."

"If I do, I don't understand it myself."

"No matter," he said. "I'm still with you."

I crossed to the others, hugged Coral.

"I must return to the Courts," I said. "Guard the Pattern. We'll be back."

The sky was illuminated by three brilliant flashes. The wind shook the tree.

I turned away and created a door in the middle of the air. Corwin's ghost and I stepped through it.

TWELVE

Thus did I return to the Courts of Chaos, coming through into Sawall's space-warped sculpture garden.

"Where are we?" my ghost-father asked.

"A museum of sorts," I replied, "in the house of my stepfather. I chose it because the lighting is tricky and there are many places to hide."

He studied some of the pieces, as well as their disposition upon the walls and ceiling.

"This would be a hell of a place to fight a skirmish," he observed.

"I suppose it would."

"You grew up hereabout, huh?"

"Yes."

"What was it like?"

"Oh, I don't know. I don't have anything to compare it to. I had some good times, alone, and with friends—and a few bad times. All a part of being a kid."

"This place . . . ?"

"The Ways of Sawall. I wish I had time to show you the whole thing, take you through all of the ways."

"One day, perhaps."

"Yes."

I began walking, hoping for the Ghostwheel or Kergma to appear. Neither did, however.

We finally passed into a corridor that took us to a hall of tapestries, whence there was a way to a room that I desired—for the room let upon the hallway that passed the gallery of metal trees. Before we could depart, however, I heard voices from that hallway. So we waited in the room—which contained the skeleton of a Jabberwock painted in orange, blue, and yellow, Early Psychedelic—as the speakers approached. One of them I recognized immediately as my brother Mandor; the other I could not identify by voice alone, but managing a glimpse as they passed, I saw it to be Lord Bances of Amblerash, High Priest of the Serpent Which Manifests the Logrus (to cite a full title just once). In a badly plotted story they'd have paused outside the doorway, and I'd have overheard a conversation telling me everything I needed to know about anything.

They slowed as they passed.

"That's the way it will be then?" Bances said.

"Yes," Mandor replied. "Soon."

And they were by, and I couldn't make out another word. I listened to their receding footsteps till they were gone. Then I waited a little longer. I would have sworn I heard a small voice saying, "Follow. Follow."

"Hear anything just then?" I whispered.

"Nope."

So we stepped out into the hallway and turned right, moving in the opposite direction from that which Mandor and Bances had taken. As we did, I felt a sensation of heat at a point somewhat below my left hip.

"You think he is somewhere near here?" the Corwin ghost asked. "Prisoner to Dara?"

"Yes and no," I said. "Ow!"

It felt like a hot coal pressed against my upper leg. I jammed my hand into my pocket as I slid into the nearest display niche, which I shared with a mummified lady in an amber casket.

Even as my hand closed about it, I knew what it was, raising all manner of philosophical speculations I had neither time nor desire to address at the moment and so treated in the time-honored fashion of dealing with such things: I shelved them.

It was a spikard that I withdrew, that lay warmly upon my palm. Almost immediately a small spark leapt between it and the one that I wore upon my finger.

There followed a wordless communication, a sequence of images, ideas, feelings, urging me to find Mandor and place myself in his hands for the preparations for my crowning as the next King of the Courts. I could see why Bleys had told me not to put the thing on. Unmediated by my own spikard,

its injunctions would probably have been overpowering. I used mine to shut it off, to build a tiny insulating wall about it.

"You have *two* of the damned things!" Corwin's ghost observed.

I nodded.

"Know anything about them that I don't?" I asked. "That would include almost anything."

He shook his head.

"Only that they were said to be very early power objects, from the days when the universe was still a murky place and the Shadow realms less clearly defined. When the time came, their wielders slept or dissolved or whatever such figures do, and the spikards were withdrawn or stashed or transformed, or whatever becomes of such things when the story's over. There are many versions, of course. There always are. But bringing two of them to the Courts could conceivably draw a lot of attention to yourself, not to mention adding to the general power of Chaos just by virtue of their presence at this pole of existence."

"Oh, my," I said. "I'll order the one I'm wearing to conceal itself, also."

"I don't think that'll work," he said, "though I'm not certain. I'd think they must maintain a constant flux-pin with each source of power, and that would give some indication of the thing's presence because of its broadcast nature."

"I'll tell it to tune itself as low as it can then."

He nodded.

"It can't hurt to make it specific," he said, "though I'd guess it probably does that anyhow, automatically."

I placed the other ring back in my pocket, departed the niche, and hurried on up the hallway.

I slowed when we neared what I thought to be the area. But I seemed mistaken. The metal forest was not there. We passed that section. Shortly, we came to a familiar display—the one that had preceded the metal forest, on approaching it from that direction.

Even as I turned back, I knew. I knew what had happened. When we reached what had been the area, I stopped and studied it.

"What is it?" my ghostly father asked.

"It seems a display of every conceivable variety of edged weapon and tool that Chaos has ever spewed forth," I said, "all of them exhibited point up, you'll note."

"So?" he asked.

"This is the place," I answered, "the place where we were going to climb a metal tree."

"Merle," he said, "maybe this place does something to my thought processes, or yours. I just don't understand."

"It's up near the ceiling," I explained, gesturing. "I know the approximate area—I think. Looks a little different now. . . ."

"What's there, son?"

"A way—a transport area, like the one we passed through to the place of the Jabberwock skeleton. Only this one would take us to your chapel."

"And that's where we're headed?"

"Right."

He rubbed his chin.

"Well, there were some fairly tall items in some of the displays we passed," he observed, "and not all of them were metal or stone. We could wrestle over that totem pole or whatever the hell it is, from back up the hall, clear away some of the sharp displays below that place, set the thing up—"

"No," I said. "Dara obviously caught on to the fact that someone had visited it—probably this last time around, when she almost surprised me. The display was changed because of this. There are only two obvious ways to get up there—transport something unwieldy, as you suggest, and clear away a lot of cutlery before we climb. Or rev up the spikard and levitate ourselves to the spot. The first would take too long and probably get us discovered. The second would employ so much power that it would doubtless set off any magical wards she's installed about the area."

He took hold of my arm and drew me on past the display.

"We've got to talk," he said, leading me into an alcove containing a small bench.

He seated himself and folded his arms.

"I've got to know what the hell's going on," he said. "I can't help properly unless I'm briefed. What's the connection between the man and the chapel?"

"I figured out something I think my mother really meant when she told me, 'Seek him in the Pit,' " I explained. "The floor of the chapel bears stylized representations of the Courts and of Amber worked out in tiles. At the extreme of the Courts' end is a representation of the Pit. I never set foot in that area when I visited the chapel. I'm willing to bet there's a way located there, and at the other end is the place of his imprisonment."

He'd begun nodding as I spoke, then, "So you were going to pass through and free him?" he asked.

"Right."

"Tell me, do these ways have to work both ways?" he said.

"Well, no. . . . Oh, I see what you're getting at."

"Give me a more complete description of the chapel," he said.

I proceeded to do so.

"That magic circle on the floor intrigues me," he said. "It might be a means of communicating with him without risking the dangers of presence. Some sort of image-exchange, perhaps."

"I might have to fool with it a long while to figure it out," I said, "unless I got lucky. What I propose doing is to levitate, enter, use the way at the Pit to reach him, free him, and get the hell out. No subtlety. No finesse. If anything fails to do what we expect, we force our way through it with the spikard. We'll have to move fast because they'll be after us once we start."

He stared past me for a long while, as if thinking hard.

At length, he asked, "Is there any way her wards might be set off accidentally?"

"Hm. The passage of a stray magical current from the real Pit, I suppose. It sometimes spews them forth."

"What would characterize its passage?"

"A magical deposit or transformation," I said.

"Could you fake such a phenomenon?"

"I suppose. But what would be the point? They'd still investigate, and with Corwin gone they'd realize it was just a trick. The effort would be wasted."

He chuckled.

"But he won't be missing," he said. "I'm going to take his place."

"I can't let you do that!"

"My choice," he said. "But he's going to need the time if he's going to help stop Dara and Mandor from advancing the conflict between the Powers beyond anything at Patternfall."

I sighed.

"It's the only way," he said.

"I guess you're right."

He unfolded his arms, stretched, and rose to his feet.

"Let's go do it," he said.

I had to work out a spell, a thing I hadn't done recently—well, half of a spell, the effects half, as I had the spikard to juice it. Then I lay it in a swathe across the display, turning portions of blades into flowers, joined at the molecular level. As I did, I felt a tingling I was certain was the psychic alarm taking note of the enterprise and reporting it to central.

Then I summoned a lot of juice and lofted us. I felt the tug of the way as we neared it. I had been almost dead-on. I let it take us through.

He whistled softly on regarding the chapel.

"Enjoy," I said. "It's the treatment a god gets."

"Yeah. Prisoner in his own church."

He stalked across the room, unbuckling his belt as he went. He substituted it for the one upon the altar.

"Good copy," he said, "but not even the Pattern can duplicate Grayswandir."

"I thought a section of the Pattern was reproduced on the blade."

"Maybe it's the other way around," he said.

"What do you mean?"

"Ask the other Corwin sometime," he said. "It has to do with something we were talking about recently."

He approached and passed the lethal package to me—weapon, sheath, belt.

"Be nice if you take it to him," he said.

I buckled it and hung it over my head and shoulder.

"Okay," I told him. "We'd better move."

I headed toward the far corner of the chapel. As I neared the area where the Pit was represented I felt the unmistakable tug of a way.

"Eureka!" I said, activating channels on the spikard. "Follow me."

I stepped forward and it took me away.

We arrived in a chamber of perhaps fifteen feet square. There was a wooden post at its center and the floor was of stone with some straw strewn upon it. Several of the big candles, as from the chapel, were spotted about. The walls were of stone on two sides, wood on the others. The wooden walls contained unlatched wooden doors. One of the stone walls contained a windowless metal door, a keyhole at its left side. A key, which looked about the right size, hung from a nail in the post.

I took down the key and checked quickly beyond the wooden door to my right, discovering a large barrel of water, a dipper, and a variety of dishes, cups, utensils. Behind the other door were a few blankets and stacks of what were probably toilet tissues.

I crossed to the metal door then and knocked upon it with the key. There was no response. I inserted the key in the lock and felt my companion take hold of my arm.

"Better let me do that," he said. "I think like him, and I think I'll be safer."

I had to agree with the wisdom of this, and I stepped aside.

"Corwin!" he called out. "We're springing you! It's your son Merlin and me, your double. Don't jump me when I open the door, okay? We'll stand still and you can take a look."

"Open it," came a voice from within.

So he did, and we stood there.

"What do you know?" came the voice I remembered, finally. "You guys look for real."

"We are," said his ghost, "and as usual, at times such as this, you'd better hurry."

"Yeah." There came a slow tread from within, and when he emerged he was shielding his eyes with his left hand. "Either of you got a pair of shades? The light hurts."

"Damn!" I said, wishing I'd thought of it. "No, and if I send for them the Logrus might spot me."

"Later, later. I'll squint and stumble. Let's get the hell out."

His ghost entered the cell.

"Now make me bearded, thin, and grimy. Lengthen the hair and tatter the clothes," he said. "Then lock me in."

"What's going on?" my father asked.

"Your ghost will be impersonating you in your cell for a while."

"It's your plan," Corwin stated. "Do what the ghost says." And so I did. He turned and extended his hand back into the cell then. "Thanks, buddy."

"My pleasure," the other replied, clasping his hand and shaking it. "Good luck."

"So long."

I closed and locked the cell door. I hung the key on its nail and steered him to the way. It took us through.

He lowered his hand as we came into the chapel. The dimness must have been sufficient for him to handle now. He drew away from me and crossed to the altar.

"We'd better go, Dad."

He chuckled as he reached across the altar, raised a burning taper, and used it to light one of the others that had apparently gone out in some draft.

"I've pissed on my own grave," he announced. "Can't pass up the pleasure of lighting a candle to myself in my own church."

He extended his left hand in my direction without looking at me.

"Give me Grayswandir," he said.

I slipped it off and passed it to him. He unfastened it and buckled it about his waist, loosened it in its sheath.

"All right. What now?" he asked.

I thought fast. If Dara was aware that I had exited through the wall last time—a distinct possibility, considering—then the walls might well be booby-trapped in some fashion. On the other hand, if we went out the way I had come in we might encounter someone rushing this way in answer to the alarm.

Hell.

"Come on," I said, activating the spikard, ready to whisk us away at the glimpse of an intruder. "It's going to be tricky because it involves levitation on the way out."

I caught hold of him again and we approached the way. I wrapped us in energies as it took us, and I lofted us above the field of blades and flowers as we departed.

There were footfalls from up the corridor. I swirled us away to another place.

I took us to Jurt's apartment, which didn't seem a place anyone was likely to come looking for a man who was still in his cell; and I knew that Jurt had no need of it just then.

Corwin sprawled on the bed and squinted at me.

"By the way," he said, "thanks."

"Anytime," I told him.

"You know your way around this place pretty well?" he said.

"It doesn't seem to have changed that much," I told him.

"Then how's about raiding an icebox for me while I borrow your brother's scissors and razor for a quick shave and haircut."

"What would you like?"

"Meat, bread, cheese, wine, maybe a piece of pie," he said. "Just so it's fresh and there's lots of it. Then you're going to have a lot of story to tell me."

"I guess I am," I said.

And so I made my way to the kitchen, down familiar halls and ways I

had traversed as a boy. The place was lit by just a few tapers, the fires banked. No one was about.

I proceeded to raid the larder, heaping a tray with the various viands requested, adding a few pieces of fruit I came across. I almost dropped the wine bottle when I heard a sharp intake of breath near the doorway I had entered.

It was Julia, in a blue silk wrap.

"Merlin!"

I crossed to her.

"I owe you several apologies," I said. "I'm ready to make them."

"I'd heard you were back. I heard you were to be king."

"Funny, I heard that, too."

"Then it would be unpatriotic of me to stay mad, wouldn't it?"

"I never meant to hurt you," I said. "Physically, or any other way."

Suddenly, we were holding each other. It lasted a long time before she told me, "Jurt says you're friends now."

"I guess we sort of are."

I kissed her.

"If we got back together again," she said, "he'd probably try to kill you again."

"I know. This time the consequences could really be cataclysmic, too."

"Where are you going right now?"

"I'm on an errand, and it's going to take me several hours."

"Why don't you stop by when you're finished? We've got a lot to talk about. I'm staying in a place called the Wisteria Room for now. Know where that is?"

"Yes," I said. "This is crazy."

"See you later?"

"Maybe."

The next day I traveled to the Rim, for I'd heard a report that the Pit-divers—those who seek after artifacts of creation beyond the Rim—had suspended operations for the first time in a generation. When I questioned them they told me of dangerous activities in the depths—whirlwinds, wings of fire, blasts of new-minted matter.

Sitting in a secluded place and looking down, I used the spikard I wore to question the one I didn't. When I removed the shield in which I'd encased it, it commenced a steady litany, "Go to Mandor. Get crowned. See your brother. See your mother. Begin preparations." I wrapped it again and put it away. If I didn't do something soon he was going to suspect that I was beyond its control. Did I care?

I could just absent myself, perhaps going away with my father, helping him at whatever showdown might finally develop over his Pattern. I could even ditch both spikards there, enhancing the forces in that place. I could still rely on my own magic in a pinch. But—

My problem was right here. I had been bred and conditioned to be a

perfect royal flunky, under the control of my mother, and possibly my brother Mandor. I loved Amber, but I loved the Courts as well. Fleeing to Amber, while assuring my safety, would no more solve my personal problem than running off with my dad—or returning to the Shadow Earth I also cared for, with or without Coral. No. The problem was here—and inside me.

I summoned a filmy to bear me to an elevated way to take me back to Sawall. As I traveled, I thought of what I must do, and I realized that I was afraid. If things got pushed as far as they well might, there was a strong possibility that I would die. Alternatively, I might have to kill someone I didn't really want to.

Either way, though, there had to be some resolution or I'd never know peace at this pole of my existence.

I walked beside a purple stream beneath a green sun atop a pearly sky. I summoned a purple and gray bird, which came and sat upon my wrist. I had thought to dispatch it to Amber with a message for Random. Try as I might, however, I could phrase no simple note. Too many things depended on other things. Laughing, I released it and leapt from the bank, where I struck another way above the water.

Returned to Sawall, I made my way to the sculpture hall. By then, I knew what I must try to do and how I must go about it. I stood where I had stood— how long ago?—regarding massive structures, simple figures, intricate ones.

"Ghost?" I said. "You in the neighborhood?"

There was no response.

"Ghost!" I repeated more loudly. "Can you hear me?"

Nothing.

I dug out my Trumps, located the one I had done for Ghostwheel, bright circle.

I regarded it with some intensity, but it was slow to grow cool. This was understandable, considering some of the odd areas of space to which this hall gave access. Also, it was irritating.

I raised the spikard. Using it here at the level I intended would be like setting off a burglar alarm. Amen.

I touched the Tarot with a line of subtle force, attempting to enhance the instrument's sensitivity. I maintained my concentration.

Again, nothing.

I backed it with more force. There followed a perceptible cooling. But there was no contact.

"Ghost," I said through clenched teeth. "This is important. Come to me."

No reply. So I sent power into the thing. The card began to glow and frost crystals formed upon it. Small crackling sounds occurred in its vicinity.

"Ghost," I repeated.

A weak sense of his presence occurred then, and I poured more juice into the card. It shattered in my hand, and I caught it in a web of forces and held all of the pieces together, looking like a small stained-glass window. I continued to reach through it.

"Dad! I'm in trouble!" came to me then.

"Where are you? What's the matter?" I asked.

"I followed this entity I met. Pursued her—it. Almost a mathematical abstraction. Called Kergma. Got caught here at an odd-even dimensional interface, where I'm spiraling. Was having a good time up until then—"

"I know Kergma well. Kergma is a trickster. I can feel your spatial situation. I am about to send bursts of energy to counter the rotation. Let me know if there are problems. As soon as you're able to Trump through, tell me and come ahead."

I pulsed it through the spikard and the braking effect began. Moments later, he informed me, "I think I can escape now."

"Come on, then."

Suddenly, Ghost was there, spinning about me like a magic circle.

"Thanks, Dad. I really appreciate this. Let me know if there's ever anything—"

"There is," I said.

"What?"

"Shrink yourself down and hide somewhere about my person."

"Wrist okay again?"

"Sure."

He did that thing. Then, "Why?" he asked.

"I may need a sudden ally," I replied.

"Against what?"

"Anything," I said. "It's showdown time."

"I don't like the sound of that."

"Then leave me now. I won't hold it against you."

"I couldn't do that."

"Listen, Ghost. This thing has escalated, and a line must be drawn now. I—"

The air began to shimmer, off to my right. I knew what it meant.

"Later," I said. "Be still."

. . . And there was a doorway, and it opened to admit a tower of green light: eyes, ears, nose, mouth, limbs cycling about its sea-like range—one of the more inspired demonic forms I'd beheld of late. And, of course, I knew the features.

"Merlin," he said. "I felt you ply the spikard here."

"I thought you might," I replied, "and I am at your service, Mandor."

"Really?"

"In all respects, brother."

"Including a certain matter of succession?"

"That in particular."

"Excellent! And what business were you about here?"

"I was but seeking something I had lost."

"That can wait upon another day, Merlin. We have much to do just now."

"Yes, that is true."

"So assume a more pleasing form and come with me. We must discuss

the measures you are to take upon assuming the throne—which Houses are to be suppressed, who outlawed—"

"I must speak with Dara immediately."

"I would rather lay some groundwork first. Come! Shift, and let us be away!"

"Would you know where she is just now?"

"Gantu, I believe. But we will confer with her later."

"You wouldn't happen to have her Trump handy, would you?"

"I fear not. I thought you carried a deck of your own?"

"I do. But hers was inadvertently destroyed one night when I was drinking."

"No matter," he said. "We will see her later, as I explained."

I had been opening channels on the spikard as we spoke. I caught him at the center of a whirlwind of forces. I could see the transformation procedure within him, and it was a simple matter to reverse it, collapsing the green and spinning tower into the form of a white-haired man clad in black and white and looking very irritated.

"Merlin!" he cried. "Why have you changed me?"

"This thing fascinates me," I said, waving the spikard. "I just wanted to see whether I could do it."

"Now you've seen it," he said. "Kindly release me to turn back, and find a more fitting form for yourself."

"A moment," I said, as he attempted to melt and flow. "I require you just as you are."

I held him against his effort, and I drew a fiery rectangle in the air. A series of quick movements filled it with a rough likeness of my mother.

"Merlin! What are you doing?" he cried.

I suppressed his effort to extricate himself by means of a transport spell.

"Conference time," I announced. "Bear with me."

I didn't just meditate upon the impromptu Trump I had hung in the air before me, but practically attacked it with a charge of the energies I was cycling through my body and the space about me.

Suddenly, Dara stood within the frame I had created—tall, coal-black, eyes of green flame.

"Merlin! What's happening?" she cried.

I'd never heard of it being done quite this way before, but I held the contact, willed her presence, and blew away the frame. She stood before me then, perhaps seven feet tall, pulsing with indignation.

"What is the meaning of this?" she asked.

I caught her as I had Mandor and collapsed her down to human scale.

"Democracy," I said. "Let's all look alike for a minute."

"This is not amusing," she responded, and she began to change back.

I canceled her effort.

"No, it isn't," I answered. "But I called this meeting, and it will be run on my terms."

"Very well," she said, shrugging. "What has become so terribly urgent?"

"The succession."

"The matter is settled. The throne is yours."

"And whose creature am I to be?" I raised my left hand, hoping they had no way of telling one spikard from another. "This thing confers great powers. It also charges for their use. It bore a spell for control of its wearer."

"It was Swayvill's," Mandor said. "I got it to you when I did to accustom you to the force of its presence. And yes, there is a price. Its wearer must come to terms with it."

"I have wrestled with it," I lied, "and I am its master. But the main problems were not cosmic. They were compulsions of your own installation."

"I do not deny it," he said. "But there was a very good reason for their presence. You were reluctant to take the throne. I felt it necessary to add an element of compulsion."

I shook my head.

"Not good enough," I said. "There was more to it than that. It was a thing designed to make me subservient to you."

"Necessary," he responded. "You've been away. You lack intimate knowledge of the local political scene. We could not simply let you take the reins and go off in your own direction—not in times such as these, when blunders could be very costly. The House needed some means to control you. But this was only to be until your education was complete."

"Permit me to doubt you, brother," I said.

He glanced at Dara, who nodded slightly.

"He is right," she said, "and I see nothing wrong with such temporary control until you learn the business. Too much is at stake to permit otherwise."

"It was a slave-spell," I said. "It would force me to take the throne, to follow orders."

Mandor licked his lips. It was the first time I'd ever seen him betray a sign of nervousness. It instantly made me wary—though I realized moments later that it may have been a calculated distraction. It caused me to guard against him immediately; and, of course, the attack came from Dara.

A wave of heat swept over me. I shifted my attention at once, attempting to raise a barrier. It was not an attack against my person. It was something soothing, coercive. I bared my teeth as I fought to hold it off.

"Mother—" I growled.

"We must restore the imperatives," she said flatly, more to Mandor than to me.

"Why?" I asked. "You're getting what you want."

"The throne is not enough," she answered. "I do not trust you in this, and reliance will be necessary."

"You never trusted me," I said, pushing away the remains of her spell.

"That is not true," she told me, "and this is a technical matter, not a personal one."

"Whatever the matter," I said, "I'm not buying."

Mandor tossed a paralysis spell at me, and I pushed it away, ready for anything now. As I was doing this, Dara hit me with an elaborate working I

recognized as a Confusion Storm. I was not about to try matching them both, spell for spell. A good sorcerer may have a half dozen major spells hung. Their judicious employment is generally enough for dealing with most situations. In a sorcerous duel the strategy involved in their employment is a major part of the game. If both parties are still standing when the spells have been exhausted, then they are reduced to fighting with raw energies. Whoever controls a greater quantity usually has the edge then.

I raised an umbrella against the Confusion Storm, parried Mandor's Astral Club, held myself together through Mom's Spirit Split, maintained my senses through Mandor's Well of Blackness. My major spells had all gone stale, and I had hung no new ones since I'd begun relying on the spikard. I was already reduced to reliance on raw power. Fortunately, the spikard gave me control of more of it than I'd ever held before. All I had to do was force them to use up their spells, then all trickiness would be removed from the situation. I would wear them down, drain them.

Mandor sneaked one partway through, hurting me in a brush with an Electric Porcupine. I battered him with a wall of force, however, slamming him into a system of revolving discs that flashed off in all directions. Dara turned into a liquid flame, coiling, waving, flowing through circles and figure-eights, as she advanced and retreated, tossing bubbles of euphoria and pain to orbit me. I tried to blow them away, hurricane-wise, shattering the great porcelain face, uprooting towers, family groups with holes in them, glowing geometries. Mandor turned to sand, which filtered downward through the structure upon which he sprawled, became a yellow carpet, crept toward me.

I ignored the effects and continued to beat at them with energies. I hurled the carpet through the flame and dumped a floating fountain upon them. Brushing out small fires in my clothing and hair, I forced my consciousness through numbed areas in my left shoulder and leg. I fell apart and drew myself back together again as I mastered Dara's spell of Unweaving. I shattered Mandor's Diamond Bubble and digested the Chains of Deliverance. On three occasions, I dropped my human form for things more suitable, but always I returned to it. I hadn't had a workout like this since my final exams with Suhuy.

But the ultimate advantage was obviously mine. Their only real chance had lain in surprise, and that was gone now. I opened all channels on the spikard, a thing which might have intimidated even the Pattern—though, now I thought on it, it had gotten me knocked senseless. I caught Mandor in a cone of force that stripped him down to a skeleton and built him back up again in an instant. Dara was harder to nail, but when I blasted her with all of the channels, she hit me with a Dazzlement spell she'd been holding in reserve, the only thing that saved her from turning into a statue as I'd intended. Instead, it left her in mortal form and restricted to slow motion.

I shook my head and rubbed my eyes. Lights danced before me.

"Congratulations," she said, over a span of perhaps ten seconds. "You're better than I'd thought."

"And I'm not even finished," I replied, breathing deeply. "It's time to do unto you as you'd have done unto me."

I began to craft the working which would place them under my control. It was then that I noticed her small slow smile.

"I'd thought—we might—deal with—you—ourselves," she said as the air began to shimmer before her. "I was—wrong."

The Sign of the Logrus took form before her. Immediately, her features grew more animated.

Then I felt its terrible regard. When it addressed me, that pastiche-voice tore at my nervous system.

"I have been summoned," it said, "to deal with your recalcitrance, oh man who would be king."

There came a crash from downhill as the house of mirrors collapsed. I looked in that direction. So did Dara. Mandor, just now struggling to his feet, did also.

The reflective panels rose into the air and drifted toward us. They were quickly deployed all about us, reflecting and re-reflecting our confrontation from countless angles. The prospect was bewildering, for space itself seemed somehow bent, twisted now in our vicinity. And in each image we were surrounded by a circle of light, though I could not detect its absolute source.

"I stand with Merlin," Ghost said, from somewhere.

"Construct!" the Logrus Sign stated. "You thwarted me in Amber!"

"And a short thwart for the Pattern, too," Ghost observed. "It sort of balances out."

"What are your wishes now?"

"Hands off Merlin," Ghost said. "He'll rule here as well as reign. No strings on him."

Ghost's lights began cycling.

I pulsed the spikard, open on all channels, hoping to locate Ghost, give him access to its energies. I couldn't seem to make contact, though.

"I don't need that, Dad," Ghost stated. "I access sources in Shadow myself."

"What is it that you want for yourself, construct?" the Sign inquired.

"To protect one who cares for me."

"I can offer you cosmic greatness."

"You already did. I turned you down then, too. Remember?"

"I remember. And I will remember." A jagged tentacle of the constantly shifting figure moved toward one of the circles of light. There was a blinding rush of flame when they met. When my vision cleared, however, nothing had changed. "Very well," the Sign acknowledged. "You came prepared. It is not yet time to weaken myself in your destruction. Not when another waits for me to falter.

"Lady of Chaos," it stated, "you must honor Merlin's wishes. If his reign be a foolish thing, he will destroy himself by his own actions. If it be prudent, you will have gained what you sought without interference."

The expression on her face was one of disbelief.

"You would back down before a son of Amber and his toy?" she asked.

"We must give him what he wants," it acknowledged, "for now. For now . . ."

The air squealed about its vanishment. Mandor smiled the smallest of smiles, reflected to infinity.

"I can't believe this," she said, becoming a flower-faced cat and then a tree of green flame.

"Believe as you would," Mandor told her. "He's won."

The tree flared through its autumn and was gone.

Mandor nodded to me.

"I just hope you know what you're doing," he said.

"I know what I'm doing."

"Take it however you would," he said, "but if you need advice I'll try to help you."

"Thanks."

"Care to discuss it over lunch?"

"Not just now."

He shrugged and became a blue whirlwind.

"Till later then," came the voice out of the whirlwind, before it blew away.

"Thanks, Ghost," I said. "Your timing's gotten a lot better."

"Chaos has a weak left," he replied.

I located fresh garments of silver, black, gray, and white. I took them back to Jurt's apartments with me. I had a long story to tell.

We walked little-used ways, passing through Shadow, coming at length to the final battlefield of the Patternfall War. The place had healed itself over the years, leaving no indication of all that had transpired there. Corwin regarded it for a long while in silence.

Then he turned to me and said, "It'll take some doing to sort everything out, to achieve a more permanent balance, to assure its stability."

"Yes."

"You think you can keep things peaceful on this end for a while?"

"That's the idea," I said. "I'll give it my best shot."

"That's all any of us can do," he said. "Okay, Random has to know what's happened, of course. I'm not sure how he's going to take having you as an opposite number, but that's the breaks."

"Give him my regards, and Bill Roth, too."

He nodded.

"And good luck," I said.

"There are still mysteries within mysteries," he told me. "I'll let you know what I find out, as soon as I have something."

He moved forward and embraced me.

Then, "Rev up that ring and send me back to Amber."

"It's already revved," I said. "Good-bye."

". . . And hello," he answered, from the tail end of a rainbow.

I turned away then, for the long walk back to Chaos.